PAUL GOLDING

THE ABOMINATION

Paul Golding lives in London. This is his first novel.

The Abomination

THE
ABOMINATION

PAUL GOLDING

VINTAGE CONTEMPORARIES

VINTAGE BOOKS

A DIVISION OF RANDOM HOUSE, INC.

NEW YORK

FIRST VINTAGE CONTEMPORARIES EDITION, MAY 2002

Copyright © 2000 by Paul Golding

All rights reserved under International and Pan-American Copyright
Conventions. Published in the United States by Vintage Books, a division
of Random House, Inc., New York. Originally published in Great Britain
by Picador, an imprint of Macmillan Publishers, Ltd., London, and subsequently published in hardcover in the United States by Alfred A.
Knopf, a division of Random House, Inc., New York, in 2000.

Vintage is a registered trademark and Vintage Contemporaries and
colophon are trademarks of Random House, Inc.

The Library of Congress has cataloged the Knopf edition as follows:
Golding, Paul, 1959–
The abomination / Paul Golding.—1st American ed.
p. cm.
ISBN 0-375-41055-4
1. Gay men—Fiction. 2. Autobiographical memory—Fiction.
3. Boarding schools—Fiction. 4. Parent and child—Fiction.
5. London (England)—Fiction. 6. Spain—Fiction. I. Title.
PR6057.O42 A64 2000
823'.92—dc21   00026166

Vintage ISBN: 0-375-72439-7

Book design by Robert C. Olsson

www.vintagebooks.com

Printed in the United States of America
10 9 8 7 6 5 4 3 2 1

This book is dedicated to Richard Fowler.

ACKNOWLEDGEMENTS

The author would like to thank Cara Denman,
Nigella Lawson, Susan Moncur, Jane Reid, Sarah Spankie
and, especially, Meredith Daneman.

THE ABOMINATION

PART ONE

HIGH SUMMER in a sweltering London club, and I'm getting into my drunken stride after midnight, rubbing sweat with the shoulders that pass by, and thinking vaguely about another drink, or about cruising the pissoirs, or about peeling off my vest and closing my eyes and drifting through the dry ice into the dancing multitude, which is a great safe wave to me, when suddenly the lights blast on, white, as on a stage, and the music goes dead, a bang of silence, and it seems that the air-conditioning's packed up and they can't get anyone to fix it this late at night, and the management regrets that for reasons of safety our club has to close, so could we finish our drinks up and remember to collect our coats on the way out, and no dawdling on the street, lads, and don't make a racket out there; and get yourselves safely home; hurry up please, it's time.

I wander away, disconcerted by this sudden sense of having been cut short, frozen in mid-flow. Timing is crucial in this business and you have to pace yourself to a tee if you want a decent score. Have you trapped?, they used to ask in the old days, before the troubles, and mostly you had. But tonight, well, who could have known? And besides, who cares in the end? Perhaps I do, a bit, and so, perhaps, does he: a young boy in an old suit, still clutching his pint-glass to his chest, weaving like a maniac through the traffic, flirting with death to reach me and he is smiling as if at a memory. And his hair is drenched, and he has a face that could shatter your calm, and he just follows me back to my flat, five paces behind, past the garden gate, up the entrance steps, through the front door, which I've left slightly ajar, and into the lift, which is the beginning of every one of my many nameless one night stands.

He wants a drink. He wants a smoke. Do I have a joint? He wants to go to Australia to work with handicapped kids. Drops his jacket, and the dregs of his beer, around the corridor. Lurches into the bedroom, staggers towards the bed. Sits down, then slumps. Tries to pull off his trousers; can't. Kicks away his shoes, which bang against the wall. Falls back against the pillows and stares up at the ceiling-light, which is dimmed and shaped like the moon. Half-opens his mouth; seems to give up. But now he looks down, as if puzzled, and pulls from his heart-patterned boxer shorts a half-hearted hard-on. Tugs absently at the foreskin, forgets to air his balls, fiddles about briefly, calmly, humming to himself as if already he were in Australia; and before I can prove a thing to him, or please myself, he has blessed the patch of sheet between his thighs with a glutinous emission, like a weak stream of snot, devoid of colour or fervour or sense. And then he tells me to get him a towel. And he tells me to fetch him his clothes. And he tells me that he hates my fucking guts, you fucking bender. Which is enough; and I am suddenly enraged and awake and strong; and I yank him by the knot of his tie and hoist him back onto the floor and pull him staggering behind me; and I pick up his shoes as I go along, and I drag him all the way to the hall and grab hold of his jacket and push him like a bag of filthy garbage onto the communal landing and I hurl his junk out with him, telling him, as secretly I tell myself, to get some fucking dignity. And all that I'm left with is the small sight of him assembling himself through my spyhole, then skulking off. And as I turn back into my life, shaking slightly, I let out a sigh of the sort that you don't, not unless you really are alone.

I begin to turn off the lights; but as I approach the bedroom, I notice, on the floor, fallen from that poor pathetic boy's dark coat, a lurid, flimsy, men's contact magazine, hardly even pornography. But I take it to my bed. And backwards I open it. And desultorily I scan the personal ads. And then I come to the escorts, the models, the whores. And my eye flickers about, jumping over words such as young, and new, and anytime. And then my eye drops like a stone into a lonely printed pool, which reads, like a message from the depths: Big Uncut Man. Handsome, lean, muscular, mature, trustworthy. 0370 566 909. And I dial. But the voice of some unpromising female tells me that the mobile which I have called may be switched off, please try later—

which I don't. Instead, I extinguish the lamp by my bed and think of that drunken boy and tell myself a different, better story about us as I masturbate myself to sleep, over his patch, still in my clothes. Good night, sweet ladies, good night.

LATE IN THE MORNING, near noon, I dial again—only to hear the woman once more. He'll be at it already, I suppose, servicing some punter, or some female, come to that, or out shopping with his wife, or posing in a porno flick, or recovering from an arduous night, or worse, worse still, and probably there, right next to the disconnected telephone, asleep in his lover's arms. I replace my ivory receiver, affronted, offended, red. His penis, I hear myself think, may well be uncut, but I bet and I hope that his heart has been cut a thousand times. My reaction takes me aback; why should I feel even the hint of a rising jealousy over some printed fragment, over a mere string of syllables at the end of an absurd mag, a figment who fails even as a character, who lacks face and voice and name, and is probably dull, and whose face and voice and name and very dullness I could have at a whim, done, for less than the price of a decent dinner or an elementary leather mask? I'm getting angry. And yet I cut him gently out of his page and tuck him into my wallet, and I place the wallet inside the jacket on my chair, the chair where one day he will sit; and the wallet slides with treacherous ease into the very place where he should not be, which is close to my breast, poised to bang into my heart.

I rise and stretch and shower and shave and pace about, and smoke about him once or twice. And God knows what I do all day but, at dusk, I dial again—for the third and surely final time. Click. (A pause.) Hullo, he goes, so low and loud it's almost risible. And then, again but softer, he goes: hullo. I am breathtaken, thumping inwards, lost in my own time, at my great leisure, in my own home. My mouth is dry; I am unvoiced; but I persevere and, somehow, manage to admit about the ad, the mag. That, I say, is pretty well it. How can he help me, he asks with the seductive innuendo of a shrink or priest. First, I reply, he can help me by explaining whether, were I to, erm, engage his services (what can I sound like, like my father?), we'd be dealing with a big man who happens not to be circumcised, or with someone possessed of a large uncircumcised penis, or what exactly. He chortles profoundly. I loathe him already. And he savours his retort for a few smug moments before conceding that yes, people do often ask him that. Well?, I snap. Well, he explains, his entry is (momentous silence) deliberately ambiguous. Deliberately Ambiguous. Catch that mouthful? Hope it promises good head. Anything else I'd like to ask? Yes: what he looks like. And now the (metric) statistics begin to roll, like credits one can never quite catch, and the meaningless self-description ends with the news that Mr. Big Uncut Man elects to sport his hair close-cropped—Number Two, to be precise—because he's thirty-nine. Articulate perhaps, but no slave to logic, this guy. Any other questions? Well, inevitably, I suppose, his fee. Sixty, in cash, he says. And to come out, I ask, to come to my flat? Seventy. (My silence now.) Pricey, I meanly remark. He's worth it, he assures me. But I cannot resist assuring him that he'll have to allow me to be the judge of that. Still, the bargain is effectively struck. So, when can we meet? He's afraid he only works nights (the vampirical harlot—how's that for a mouthful?), and I'm afraid I have no nights to spare this week, but I should like, if I may, to ring again when I'm less tied up, as it were, so to speak, and, when I do, so as to spare us both a reprise of this introductory chat, he may as well know, and I tell him, my name. His name is Steve. Yes, well, goodbye Steve, and thanks. No problem, he replies: he looks forward. As do I. And I hang up, first. And then I go out for supper, sickened but starved.

IN THE MORNING, early, after a choppy night of unrecordable dreams, I drive south, too fast, to Hampshire, to my friends R and E and their doll-sized daughters, D and W and J, who make me melt and make me laugh and at times make me envy the lot of that other, greater half. Bowl of soup, glass of wine, and, with E, the mother, the young wife, a stroll along the beach beyond the pines, sidelit today by a hesitant sun that teeters on the brink of the Isle of Wight; then back to the house. She treats me timidly, retreatingly, as if I were a prince with woes, in need of rest, and she suggests a siesta in the room with the best view. As I draw the ivy curtains closed, I see R, the father, the poet, mowing the high grass out there, and the girls, further out still, white bobs flying in their faces, taking turns on the swing which hangs from the tree that shields and secludes them from the world, and I turn and collapse on the bed and am gone.

I awake, exhausted, after sundown. The girls, in old linen night-gowns of Chekhovian white, have already been fed and bathed, and are running about barefoot, clambering into cots of wrought iron in the small room where, a summer ago, their mother painted the walls with flowers. On my way down I meet their father, my old friend, older now of course, but glowing in a way that he never did as he climbs the wooden steps to double-check nappies and read a tale to his girls, whom he calls ladies, his Ladies, before kissing them good night and laying them to sleep, which they do by candlelight, and this is the sort of scene I mean when I speak of envy.

Supper is such an easy affair, with heaps of plain food, and plentiful drink, and candles all about, and home-made medleys of recorded songs from remembered (and imagined) times, and teasing, and laughter, and waves of silent calm, broken occasionally by pensive smiles, or unconscious hums, and, as always in this house, flowing, flowing effortlessness. I leave the table earlier than I politely should; earlier than I should have liked, but I feel washed-out and these are my friends and nobody minds, and on my way to bed I think of them intimately, the perfect pair in their perfect life and, although I know that nothing ever can be perfectly perfect, I think: If this is imperfection, I wouldn't mind a slice. And as I go under the blankets in the dark, I turn to my side and press a pillow to my gut and then I hear, piping up from the ground, the sound of one of the Waterboys singing out, asking himself how long he will love, and want, and hold a beloved whom I don't know but dream I could become. And then comes his answer, his theory, his own dream, which is the eternal beautiful lie, as he claims and believes and belts out in his innocent Irish voice that he will love as long as the seasons need to follow their plan and as long as the sea is bound to wash up on the sands. And I'm left with no hope of sleep. Yet I don't hear my friends retire, nor chatter into the night, much less make love, which I'm certain they do the whole time. And the next thing that I know is a hardened sun pushing through the curtains, and my watch pointing to the fact that the dawn is still unthinkably young. Yet I know that I must rise and not rest, and go, and hope to be forgiven, which by such friends I always am. And I brush my teeth and wet my face and comb my hair and, like a disappointed thief, I light a cigarette and creep out into the frost, past a congregation of moronic partridge—probably on their unsuspected last day out—and I get into my car. And then I race back to town with the thrill of a sinner returning to hell.

I walk into my flat with the guilty pleasure of one who has taken an extended holiday at the cost of neglecting the things that he loves. I shower and dress afresh, in colours of stone, and make myself a fiddly, spinstery breakfast; and while I pick at it, I also pick through the bones of the newspaper delivered to my mat. Nothing strikes me, nothing save a shoddy piece in a Saturday magazine about escaped criminals living in the community, a piece redeemed and lent life by a good hard shot in black and white of a man's hands with grimy nails, held behind a hairy arse, and manacled by a pair of gleaming chromium cuffs. And when I fold away the paper and slide it along the table to open the mail with a kitchen knife, I find, malingering near the telephone, that small, excised, oblong, hooker's ad. And I scrunch it into a tight ball and flick it into the dustbin and forget entirely about him. And on my way out, I ring the house in the country—not to explain, since I don't myself quite understand, but to try to apologize. And I am told by my friend's adorable wife, who has become equally my friend and doesn't even listen to my discomfited mumbles, that I must return soon, at no notice at all, whenever I want.

DAYS PASS. The worst part of a week, in fact. The middle part. Dull, drizzling, pewter days in an autumn without charm. And the following Friday, it must be—yes, Friday—I go for supper to the flat of a girl whom I like, whose good-looking boyfriend is away for the night, and who says she can do with a laugh, which I attempt to provide, along with two bottles of wine, one red, one white, both drunk. Then, a couple of Armagnacs and we go on to dance at my vapid local club, where I presume that the air-conditioning vents, if not the odds of success, have been fixed by now, and on our way we swallow some drug, Ecstasy probably, the drug of the times, and after a long, sweaty spin with the people who grin and touch and contort beneath the strobing ultraviolet stars and lipsync to hits about making it to the top and putting your loving arms around me in the full knowledge that none of it means a thing and never did, we stagger out, my friend and I, back into the vaporous street, grinning and touching and unable to care very much. And I deliver her to her door, safe and dishevelled and seemingly sated, in a dodgy man's battered minicab with a fluorescent rosary and a keyring of miniature boxing-gloves dangling under his eastern eyes on the rear-view mirror at the front.

Then something happens to me, snaps inside, because, instead of telling him the obvious—my clear-cut home address—my voice seems to switch slightly, to deepen, darken, and I tell him to take me to a subterranean club I've heard of, in a distant and more dissolute part of town. Name?, he asks. You mean of the club? Yeah, he replies. Fist, or Shit, something like that, for queers and stuff, stays open till six, ring a bell? Jumping a red light on a tame Chelsea street, he swerves acutely to the right and speeds like a poisoned arrow, poisoned by the horror of his snap commission, which is to ferry filth to further filth, in the direction of a rough borough on the south side, over the river, which looks perfect for suicides at this hour, so calm, and he turns and cuts and hurtles through flickering backstreets towards my foul, underlit destination, which lurks beneath a disused railway bridge and, like so many of my adventures, starts with a lift, but not like the lift to my flat. This one is vast, industrial, wooden, empty, doorless, piss-drenched, and only going down.

I alight at a neon lobby which pumps music that I cannot recognize but only guess at, and at the ticket booth, a fat, half-naked dole-queen, pierced through the dugs, loaded with delusions of importance and munching a soggy cigar, takes my jacket with disdain, and informs me—in no uncertain and, in retrospect, quite funny, finger-jabbing terms—that if I want to pass the portals of this place, which is specialist, Specialist in case you didn't understand, not for naff bloody Sloanes, I can start by taking off my shirt, mate, and the body'd better be worth it, and lucky I'm wearing jeans, otherwise: Forget It. And next time, he adds, wear leather or rubber or combat or (give us a tenner) you're Out. And don't flick your filthy ash all over my tip-plate-like. And take that smirk off your fucking face, girl. Thanks so much, I reply (and thank God I'm still stoned).

I VENTURE WITHIN. Beyond the metal swing-door, which opens onto a scene less like a nightclub than a busy screen inside a hard-core cinema, I have no recollection of steps or ramps or other forces of physical descent; yet my impression, instant and cold, is of being lowered morally, and medically, into a threatening pool, made pestilent by the seepage of sexual incontinency, fetid with the fumes of decomposing amyl nitrite, heavy with fungal sweat, rank and virile and truffled and glandular and muddled and strong with emanations of putrescent cheese and rotten eggs and cabbage and trenches and plagues. And though my impulse is to flee, my compulsion is to stay—to taste and imbibe and partake of these rites. So I wade, half-blind and half-stunned, through the miasma, towards a distant light which I take to be a bar; and there I order a bottle of mineral water, which I drink in a frenzy and chase down with a tumbler of vodka, no rocks. And then I start to look around.

The place is heaving, but no one utters: the music, the noise, is too loud, like bombs coming down. Heads droop and loll inanely. Everyone seems to be drugged and, as far as I can tell, more efficiently, more resolutely drugged than I. I can see a spectral teenager wilting in a corner, sobbing, claimed by some mournful trance, gazing away, possessed of a strange sombre beauty. For I don't deny that a strange loveliness lurks in this place at this late hour, a doleful slowness, a stateliness almost, a certain elegance—among those who are resting, among dancers beginning to flag, even among the hardened cruisers, the scavengers.

When a man passes by you, which, on account of the crowd, is closely, he generally moves unaccompanied, and is courtly of demeanour, and he lowers his eyes even as he sizes you up from the ground on which you stand to your crotch and back down, and he only raises an eyebrow (appreciative or otherwise) if he's a fool, or if he's very sure—and that type of man, to my mind, tends to be both; but a serious man, one worth his salt, say this one, him now, will move on past you, smoothly beyond you, and only turn to look when he thinks that you think that he's gone, is lost to you. And then he scans the next stage of you, the stage that you cannot see: your arse, your back, your nape, your ears, whatever he wants; or the parts of you which of course you can see but might at this moment have forgotten: your tattoo, if you have one, or your brand, if you've gone that far, or your smoking hand, if you still smoke, or a vein down your arm, or the line of your shoulder, or the texture of your skin, or its colour, or some godforsaken spot. But he is polite about it, this man, discreet, regardless of his impression, whatever his predilection. That is my point. After all, as he well knows (and he looks to me like he's been round enough blocks to do so) the boot of appraisal may yet find itself on the other foot—yours—in which case he'll be grateful if it turns out not to kick or stamp or crush.

Now let us imagine that he wishes to take matters one step further, that he wants, having sized you up and liked the size, to give you a try, to try to spark a story which, even if it turns out not to need a formal ending, even if it dwindles halfway, which sometimes can be way enough, nonetheless warrants, in his opinion, the benefit of the doubt, the chance of a start. Well, then, he's going to have to catch your eye—however falsely bright the lens may be upon your iris, however dilated the pupil at its crux, however retracted, however shot your deadened white may be with blood—he's going to have to catch it; he must. For it is with the eyeball that all stories of this order, since forever in our history, have started, and, despite all the setbacks, continue to start.

Whatever scrutiny may have led up to this moment has been but preparation, research, vague hypothetical wanky musings akin to scanning the contact mag that I described. Incidental; largely irrelevant. Because here, not over there where he stands and peers, is where he needs to be. He can't hope to engage you from afar. We're not at the spacious Savoy Grill now, nor at the empty crush bar during boring acts at the Opera House, much less flying to Sydney, First Class, for Mardi Gras, with time and space and lots of champagne to hand. No. We're in the very underworld, and the place is packed. So he's going to have to come out for the thrill, in for the kill, and he'd be wise not to hang about.

I know that no one likes to sin of over-eagerness, but nor should he, the man, prolong his game too much: for if he takes what seems like undue time to you, and makes you begin to fear that you're being messed about, or not wanted enough, and it all begins to rattle you, you might feel forced to pull yourself together and start to epitomize the only useful word in the French language; and you'll perform that word to perfection, like a star-among-stars, which you are, because you, after all, and after all the hard practice, can act it up and act it out and act it all the way to bloody oblivion. And the word, the word is this: *In-sou-ciance*. And such is yours, so subtle and chilled and acquired, like an oyster, that by the time that he, the miracle of miracles, deigns to materialize, he may find himself forced, retching very slightly, to swallow his pride. For by then, which is sorry-too-late, he may find that your eye, your vital historical eye, is otherwise occupied, or pretending so to be, or closed (which is just about allowed), or so close to the eye of some other man that it can no longer focus, never mind bequeath upon the former Mr. Sexual Salt the favour of a sideward glance. Because you, my dear, are not cross-eyed but cross. And he, less fucked than fucked right over. But let's not be petulant at this late hour, three-thirty, four, can't make it out; and who cares anyhow: you know it backwards—the hour when you must score even if it kills you, when you would trade for the germ of triumph, which is greedier and deadlier than the germ of lust, every racing corpuscle in your power. Admit: who wants to go on and on and on and on, living endless, unsuspected, undetected, unrequited, single-handed love affairs alone, night after night after night? Not you, you swear, no longer, no more. In which case, look at the whole thing another way, more dreamily, more bravely now, and put your precious untouchable dignity on the line for once. Reel back, rewind to the point where the target of your desire deserves, even as he stands apart from you, to know where he stands; for he has seen you and, as you have seen, passed by you and then observed you from a distance and liked you—yes, liked you—and he's decided, for richer, for poorer, for better, for worse, in sickness and in health, to come to you, and he has not a thing to lose and whole firmaments to gain and he's going to catch your eye, which darts like a comet, and he's going to entrap it and hold on to it, and devote to it the total, undivided best of all his stuff, till death or daylight do you part. And as far as he's concerned, which concerns you utterly, the rest of the club can die. And this is the point at which you have to banish all defensive foreign tongues and concentrate upon another word—trickily English this time, and murderous to enact—a word which yields and tugs and yields and tugs like the very valve that drives you, and the word is: Compromise. So do it. Now. And smile. And don't look sarcastic. And remember that just possibly, remotely, maybe, if you could see yourself from where, and as, you are now, you too might want to love you. And relax.

Which, of course, you don't. You can't. It may be late and you may be drunk and you may still, marginally, be drugged, but as for smiling, well, you'd rather swill down a long glass of saliva. Yet you do manage, and without edge for once, to look at him as he advances: hotly, directly you look, and long enough to verify that although he doesn't smile either, he hugely stares back, as if ravenous. And you think to yourself that this is a man who could stand on a cliff and place his open palm beneath the small of your back and raise you like the feather of a gull and send you flying. And you see, as he draws away his can of beer and his Adam's apple gulps, you see the outline of the shadow of the orb of the back of his head, which in your mind's eye you have already sculpted a thousand times, tilt back, as if in agony. But you cannot help or redeem him. You have expired. And then, as you begin to turn your neck minutely away, by two degrees, in sheer black terrified panic, he does that thing which strong, modern, hopeful lovers do with their mouth, and he does it pointedly, unmistakably and without question at you, aiming at the outer ridge of your right, bared, clavicle. He blows. Like a god bringing you to life, he blows. And then he blows again. And that's when you know that you've won. Which is the very instant of your loss. Again and again.

THIS IS HOW IT LOOKS to you: as if you were standing impassive on the hillock of a battle where, though you had not greatly advanced, you had at least managed to hold your ground. And this is how it feels: as if you were staring over a fog of gunshot and puncturing lights into the theatre of a war which, unbeknown to you, had already been declared lost; and it feels, too, as if, too late for apology or a gesture of surrender, you had, bewilderingly, been bayoneted below the neck by one of your own men; and as if, in the split seconds before your fall, you couldn't recall a final prayer or summon the sign of a cross. For this, for you, is how it always is: your triumph as defeat; your victory as death, time after time. And this, it seems, is how it must always be: an image, a false memory of yourself as some other, as a frightened, witless soldierboy, picking yourself a bunch of valedictory excuses on your way home, like thistles—fresh, but actually old, and randomly chosen, and messily gathered, and dated long before their prime. And you desert the battleground of your own making without the head of the enemy that you lost, without the heart for which you hungered, telling yourself Oh Christ, who cares: that was no leading man, and this, this morbid bloody set, no production to write home about. A mere nocturnal obsession exhumed within the safe confines of a catacomb. That's all.

So forget it, and spare yourself a gutful of regrets. View the man properly, with clarity: sure, you like the quick allure of his tricked-up musculature, but go beneath the sheen of his skin, and, in your bones, you will know that when he turns to you and opens his mouth, which is the true horn of his plenty, bound to have sucked on every cock in Christendom and spat into every arsehole in the pagan world, you will be struck not by some sacred introduction to a lifetime of romance, but by the collective stench of all the men who pump up and stuff themselves with tuna fish and steak tartare before venturing into clubs in the dark, men whose pores and pits and groins, though coated with the musk of soap *pour homme,* cannot suppress the festering reek of carrion, like the belches of street dogs fed on the droppings of passing garbage trucks. And remind yourself, while you can, that his voice, when it comes, is likely to be high and crass and pitched in a minor key, and could never in a million years engulf you in the moaning groaning rumbling waves of abandon, only irk you with its piercing coital squeaks, like the spirited yelps of some skipping majorette. And think beyond the veneer of his front teeth, think of the rasping surface of his reptilian tongue, and of the abscesses hidden along his gums, and of the tang of his suppurating dental blood, like a slow warm sea, flowing down his gullet, carrying in its stream gobs of soft mucus and the undigested fishy remnants of his supper. Come on, get out. You've had enough.

Yet far from getting out, you find that with the inadvertent ease which sometimes is ascribed to fate, you've gone right in, and that far from having followed any guiding light to any bar, you've in fact crossed an imperceptible black arch and drifted through the final boundary-line and gone beyond the pale. And what you have entered is the pulsing heart, the very sanctum of this club: the flower of its evil, which is the back room, the dark room, the dungeon, the tabernacle, the underbelly of the mire. And you are blinded for a while. But you can smell rising fumes of flatulence and spent rivers of urine and wafts of rotting poppers and the bitter discharge of loss. And you can hear gasps and sighs and slurps and gobs and the creak of heavy chains being adjusted, and thudded blows being delivered, hard, by gauntlets onto rumps, and you can hear cries being sent up from a valley of rapture and pain and proof and surprise and wonder and hunger and terror which is the valley of this haunting, unspeakable variant of love; and now you begin to believe your eyes, which seem to sting; and through a foggy cloud of dope, the first thing that you discern, in the unfathomable distance, is a fat joint, or a cigar, its tip aglow, circling the shadows like a red halo—quickly described; then, sunk behind a horizon of amorphous mounds.

You decide to lurch towards a wall, avoiding as best you can a couple of pairs of interlocked army boots and, above them, kissing leather masks. And you reach out for the backdrop, and you touch it at last, and it is a sheet of black rubber, weeping but cold, and you turn your back to it and stand there, not quite leaning. And as you linger thus, not even thinking, an unknown hand from nowhere strokes you, with disarming gentleness, where it presumes that you wish to be stroked; and you find, to your surprise, to your slight relief, that already you are hardening, approaching hardness. And the hand which by now has earned itself a wan, emaciated arm, begins to fiddle, a little frantically, as if it were pilfering from a cash-till, with the buttons of your flies. And you try, calmly, to remove the hand, to move it away, but it latches onto your own sweaty unsteady one, your right—no watch to worry about—and it grabs you, bites at your wrist, as if for comfort, as if for more; but you think to yourself Fuck-off-you-bore-why-don't-you; and now you push the hand away more harshly down, making it drop. And this is the sort of moment when, whether you like it or not, whether it's openly admitted or not, you must move on: because you might get hurt, punched in the dark. And so you wade away, vaguely in search of an exit but uncertain of your route; and what you thought was a way out turns out to be a secret grove within a grove, a hidden arbour, wrought of scaffolding and oily ropes and sagging nets of camouflage and, like dead birds, leaves of grimy cloth. And as you turn to quit this corner that is forever Sodom, you find yourself entangled: you find that you are caught, caught by the wrist once more. And as you try to pull away, you look down to the source of your trouble and discover that this time the trouble does lie with your watch, which has become entrapped in the glinting nipple-ring of a downturned, genuflecting, shaven-headed, all but naked, leather-harnessed clone, whose weakling face has, against all the rules of his role, swung up to meet yours, eyes wide, mouth closed. And as you release him from his torture and his shock, you catch yourself, absurdly, and in equal contravention of the rules, apologizing, for God's sake, blurting out how you're So Sorry, and forgetting, in the process, even to deepen your voice. Just like the naff bloody Sloane for which you were taken, unable to pass muster even as a voyeur. Like some pitiful bumpkin, staring at guests at a Vatican ball.

You must move, preferably towards a different arch—that one, for instance, which, viewed from within this darkened maze, glows with the outside promise of an amber sky, and a storm of flashing tropical lights, and the hope of escape onto some bark near the dance-floor. And so you decide to head for it, keeping your eyes firmly upon it, like a captive nearing his goal. But first, before you reach it, you must, as if by way of final forfeit, steer your course round a many-headed heaving beast, a core of vultures set about a carcass, a team of attendant midwives at a critical birth—though in the place of muslin draped from the beak of some unseen stork, what you see (for your vision has swerved towards the action, admit it) is a black leather sling, suspended by chains from a blackened vault. And slumped on the sling, bare as a monstrous baby except for his studded collar, which is fit for a mastiff, lies the self-appointed, self-evident victim, the sacrificial beast, his wrists manacled behind him to chains which act as head-columns on his fourposter cot. And he is moaning from a place of high pleasure, his own mid-heaven. And leaning into him, between his parted knees, between his splayed legs, which dangle lifelessly, stands the master of the ceremony, the expert, the surgeon, the high priest—inserting, slowly, and slowly sliding into the protagonist's distended anus, which is a cathedral of mysteries, a considerate, considerately lubricated (but ungloved) fist. And in, *in* it all goes, the whole worshipful offering: the wrist, the base of the forearm, its widest part, masterfully flexed all; and just as the fist-fucker seems on the point of introducing his elbow, which is when matters are stretched to their optimum without risk of what medics call trauma, the arm begins, almost ruefully, its retreat, like a great slug, slowly releasing itself, and releasing along with it an unearthly stench of sewage which men who say that they know, men who claim that they have lived, however ignorantly, swear is no stench at all, no, but the ultimate perfect exchange of elemental manly everything, a sort of life-force, communion. And out, and down, comes the arm, which the assemblage admires and exalts in tones of reverence, yessing and hissing with envious wonderment. Down all the way to the knuckles it slips, and round a bit, an extra twist, then back, back in once more, but easy, easy man, that's it, and further, and up, and over and further still and, eventually, sadly, down again; then up, all the way, and once more out, and in, and on and on it goes. And you, of course, of course you can believe what you're witnessing. In your time, after all, you've seen this ceremony performed not just with saving hands, but with penitential feet. And also in your time, which is the old days really, before the troubles, such scenes, such spectacles, were routine, even mandatory, at least among those who liked to be considered worldly. But to watch it now, in the aftermath, well, it practically gives you goose pimples. Because it feels nostalgic. Like fan-dancing in discos.

So, what do you do next? It's so predictable: you topple, you fall from your voyeuristic podium and throw your hand in, literally, placing it on the hairy breast of the victim, over his heart, which has been touched from within but seems to beat slower than you have ever known a heart to beat. And you slide your hand down that soft hairy belly, which is strewn with other hands, and a whole assortment, you suppose, of amalgamated substances; and you proceed to move your fingers over the man's shaven pubic mound and onto his penis, which is withered, half-asleep; and then, as you remove your hand to leave, you bring the fingers that you have driven down his person up, up to your face, and you press them into yourself, inhaling for traces of faecal grease or semen or spittle or piss. But the cream which you smear onto yourself smells, puzzlingly, of nothing. Nought. And then you drift away from the feast, and out, into the brightness once more.

As YOU EMERGE, you find yourself frozen by the glare of a hard beam, which bleaches your jeans to a whorish pallid hue, a sleazy half-white. And your torso, drenched with the sweat of the back room, is turning cold. And your nipples, chilled by some draft, have stiffened suddenly. And your eyes, though shielded by your hand, the hand that smelt of nothing, tell you that out here, beneath the brilliant lights, is where the true victors can be found, the sinister beauties of tonight. Strange and distracted and almost too well-angled sometimes. Heavily shadowed and sinuous and raw. Impossibly lovely. Impossible ever to love. And you can tell me to grow up, to realize, Christ Almighty, that they're only spotlit, oily, anabolic, ordinary boys; but I am here to tell you that in their way they're gods, gods parading in pouches of chainmail, pouches worn under black leather chaps that proffer ideal naked buttocks up, as if to dare you, as if for grabs; gods strutting in black Lycra jockstraps, visibly engorged, and proud: catch their bodies in profile, in motion, and you will see their swollen bollocks straining to get out; gods glinting with metal studs: studded belts and studded cuffs and studded armbands gripping muscles into which you would sink your teeth, for which you would become a cannibal; gods with perfect gleaming flesh—shaven, front and back and scalp and all around, this very night. Even their mouths, for the present, are perfect: slim-lipped but wide of cast, and glossy, and fractionally opened, as if set for a photograph, yet free of vanity, devoid of curl, and soundless. And sometimes these mouths are all that you can see below the visor of a leather cap. And at other times they are accented by a close-cropped beard, or by the circumflex of a moustache. But always, these beautiful mouths, whatever their raging inner thirst, seem to be warning: No: Back Off. Because the trouble for these rare, preternatural creatures, you see, is that their very electedness is a sort of bane, heavy to endure. Can you not understand? They have more to protect; must take greater care. How can they hope to make headway when burdened with the contraband of their present incredible bloom? They must be patient; must save themselves; ride out the storm; wait until the clouds of youth have passed and simplified the sky. And they dance while they wait. And they dance like a dream. Like dreamers. Eyes closed. Souls shuttered off. But where, tell me, where, for any of them, for any of us, is the victory in that?

Nor is fate kinder to their admirers, to those who, faithfully as they harbour secret hopes of miracles, and gladly as they would have, oh, any one of these unbelievable young men, and gratefully as they might take from them, and give to them, and trade with them, and hold them and hold onto them, and perhaps, who knows, even teach them the distinction between saving and salvation, are, for their very believable pains, repeatedly, more repeatedly than can be good for any man, punished, thwarted, denied the chance of a chance of a chance. Because all that they, these hopers without a hope, are ever granted by way of consolation is a jumble of false images, snatches, like the trailer of a film too sublime and risky ever seriously to have been meant to be coming to a cinema near them soon. And as a consequence, all that these pitiful crestfallen idolaters ever do, ever can do—and you can spot them a mile off, trudging away, slightly stooped, before the final lights of the club come on, before the merciless truth can dawn—is make their solitary way back to their flatlets, to steal into their moistening beds and roll about the seas of their synthetic quilts and float on their flabby backs and frott themselves to kingdom come about some golden argosy that could, but would hardly, have set sail for such an unpromising shore. Inventing, as best they can, as they go along, a groaning dialogue that never was.

I must get out, go home; for though the music thunders on, the scene looks quieter, emptier now, grown morbid. I catch quick sight of an unsung hero, a tall youth, wandering like a star without a sky, unattached, his eyes scintillating with exasperation. And not far from him, I see a pair of ageing skinny men in rubber, lizards of liquorice, clinging yet entwined without harmony: one stands pinned to a metal pole, bent at the hip like some travesty of St. Sebastian; his partner slithers about in an attempt to engage, to immerse himself, almost slipping at one point, but then he lunges forward, only to miss the other one's mouth. They smile like débutantes. I walk morosely down a passageway which has a shiny black floor and glistens like a stream through a darkened cavern; and halfway through this stream, which widens, I have to veer round some lone rock of a man whose chest is bare as an undiscovered coast, but whose firmly crossed great arms seem to proclaim: Into These Waters You Will Not Go. His leathered legs, thick as a henchman's, are wide of stance and, frankly, too rigidly parted either for his comfort or my conviction. His very ruggedly handsome face—more handsome now than in its youth, I would suppose—is so determinedly fixed on the opposite wall that he must be stoned, or hell bent on not seeing me. Trying to fend me off. But as I, less a golden argosy than a cautious dinghy, steer round his promontory, I catch him breathing in, sucking from the belly, which strikes a chord in me, of two clashing notes: high admiration for his indefatigable self-absorption, underscored by a pity that borders on scorn.

And at last I make it to the coat-check, where the freak with the perforated tits, still munching a cheroot and still enthroned, is busy, by the look of things, extracting grot from the underside of an elongated fingernail with the assistance of a car-key. The platter for the tips seems to be gone. I place my numbered ticket, 19, or 61—who gives a toss—on the beer-slopped counter, and I watch it gradually turn to a liver shade of pink as I wait a reverential, needless length of time for his bovine holiness to arise from his great arse and fetch my contentious jacket, which, when restored to me, is held out at arm's length, extended with the sneering sort of spite that some people affect when dealing with furs. I quickly snatch it back, and turn, as if to escape. But a few steps on, I hear a reprimanding, under-parlour-maidy whine pursue me: 'Ere gel, 'ere, don't forget yer T-shirt now; ooh dear, someone seems've trod on it. Sorray—followed by a stage guffaw. So back I go, and while I'm at it, grab another, and another of those useless pick-up magazines from piles placed on two stools beside a counter where choice regulars of this discerning venue (Specialist; beg your pardon) like to perch, earlier in the evening, cross-leggèd and all neat. And I lurk, getting dressed, by the grill to the lift, until I twig, of all the final straws, that the lift doesn't go up. And actually, I think, why the fuck not? But I'm just too tired to find a reply. And I trail behind a few dilapidated queens, the last of whom, like some dumbfounding angel of redemption, holds open the fire-door for me; and I climb the concrete stairs, only just avoiding a strategic gob of bloodied phlegm on the first landing, and I go round the second, and the third, until, after a couple more, I'm returned to the real world without end. And eventually I get back to my flat. Don't ask me how. Feeling like shit.

(I suppose that, if only for the sake of accuracy, I should here include a recollection snatched from the interval between swallowing thirty milligrams of soporific and succumbing to its eventual drowse; a recollection of lighting candles all about the sitting room—on the gilt sconces and along the mantelshelf and on the marble console—and of playing, inconsiderately loudly for my neighbours, who've just had a baby, one of those ancient gorgeous stupid sentimental pop songs that form a part of everybody's secret repertoire, its title both too precious and too crass to be divulged. Yet what I can divulge is that in this recollection I'm shown kicking off my shoes and ripping off my clothes and flinging the whole bundle in the direction of the door; and then, dancing, dancing can you believe, naked, and alone—or almost. And I say almost because, in this shaming, swaying recollection, I can hear myself, despite the noise, and oblivious to the lyrics of the song, mumbling as if into the ear of no one in particular, no one that I know: Oh my great love it's been so long. And, more shaming still, I fail to pay this camp vignette the usual tribute of a good sob. Because, as you know, I'm bad at going the whole hog.)

I CANNOT TELL YOU to what sort of day I come around, but I seem to be walking about the flat a little too jauntily to be, as yet, properly sober; and as I go to boil water for strong coffee, I notice my distended image spreading itself on the kettle's mirror; and then I gaze vaguely down and, as the water gathers steam, my gaze seems to drift over the Mandalay tiles of the kitchen floor, which are all a different shade of tawny slate, like unlikely relatives, and prone, even on clear-headed days, to distract: you keep wanting to bend down and pore over them singly, over each one's individual mottles and contours and tones, as if every one of these tiles were a map of some elusive place to which you might, at some point, wish to go. And when the kettle clicks off, I open the cupboard for a cup, and I look, above it, at the clock, and discover that already it's past half-past-four in the afternoon. I plonk the cup down on its saucer, unload some coffee into the small cafetière for two, for one, then chase the grounds with boiling water and, before pushing down the plunger, I cross the hall and go to the front door for the paper, which I scoop up, along with the post: a few buff envelopes, which can wait; a computer catalogue for the flat's previous owner, now deceased, I'm told; a promising, festively stamped letter from an American friend in Paris, which I stash, for suspense, in the drawer of the table at which I now sit, staring at a postcard from a trick who recently tried, hunched over my lavatory bowl, to impress me by vomiting and ejaculating in unison—some unrepeatable mistake of a man to whom I recall having given a fictitious, or maybe just erroneous, telephone number, but who, on taking leave of me, has obviously also taken stock of my address. Because his postcard, which was funny fifteen years ago, bears an overvivid colour portrait of a dog, with its back turned to the viewer, defecating by a picturesque canal. And the caption, which oozes below the beast in fuchsia toothpaste script, laments, or asserts: "Amsterdam . . . Shit City," a sentiment with which I could not agree more. But to what I cannot quite as easily agree is the message from its sender, who, plainly unwise to my telephonic ruse and to the disenchantment which, if learnt, such a ruse would teach, barks, imperatively, as if in an attempt to dominate his own submissiveness: Next time Beat me for this!! And, underneath, he inscribes the more revealing and pathetic symbol of a puppy's paw, tiny claws and all, and, beside it, in cobalt blue, the initial T (Trevor? Terry? Tony?), toppling backwards—the entire tacky missive addressed, simply, wrongly, and naturally without a surname, to Jim. When I never lie about my name.

I slide the postcard under the telephone, pour myself some coffee, light a cigarette and, pushing my sleeves up try to figure out how I come to be wearing a nightshirt after a night like the last; but my attention shifts to the newspaper, or rather, to its magazine, for my feet seem to have become embroiled in some rustling supplement which must have fallen to the floor and which I rescue without looking. But picking it up, I realize that what I'm holding, far from being some Business section, or Sport (the sort of rubbish whose prompt disposal makes the chore of keeping up with the world so much less onerous), is, in fact, the head of a cover-boy on one of the contact pamphlets that I dragged home—his lubricious, touched-up face smirking out defiantly at me. Or at you. Or at his mum. Or even, I suppose, at the woman within him.

I push aside the weekend papers, which have lost any hope of a hold on my curiosity, and instead, I move on to the trashy contact mag, backwards of course. And next, guess what? Bull's eye: you've got it: here, and gracing, I note, a different publication, he appears once more. Big Uncut Man, swelling beyond the print. And so? Go on, give him a ring, why not. Enough time has passed, after all. For what? For your interval to seem decent. Are you completely insane? Controlled then, controlled. And if, after this interval, he's forgotten our original talk, well, so what? Big deal. Call it an omen; take it as a sign—to abstain, leave off, dump the whole nonsense. Dear God, it's so simple:

you dial, you speak, you see; and if you catch him at a loss, or pretending so to be, you just hang up, quietly. Done it before. Come on. Look: just go and have a bath, and a good think.

I have never found it easy to obey myself, so instead I take a shower. And as I stand beneath the scalding torrent, scrubbing my back with a long-handled brush, and trying to find a word that describes the indolent play of sunlight against the pale mosaic tiles, a strange inkling crosses me, and stops my senses, will not pass. And what I see, though I have closed my eyes and am lathering shampoo onto my scalp, is a vision from last night, a brightened memory of the surly behemoth in the dark corridor, the lone rock-of-a-man, still staring vacantly over his rebuffing arms, chest still pushed out, head still borne high. But his lingering presence seems—with the incredible certainty at which bearable fiction scoffs, but which flashing intuition insists its bearer must not ignore—to connect in some way with the words at the back of the contact mag. And out of nowhere, everything seems to fall, neatly, sinisterly, into place. And, for an instant, I bet myself anything that my premonition will be proved right, and an instant later I tell myself to pull myself together and drop the whole absurdity. And I turn off the shower, and towel myself dry; but in the steamed shaving-mirror I catch sight of my face, blotchy with anticipation, flushed, and curious beyond care now.

I dial. His phone rings once and twice and again and then a fourth time and, on the fifth ring, his unmistakable voice, fractionally more sullen perhaps, replies. I start to talk. My words echo round a hollow. I reach the end of my opening circular line, and wait, and, at last, Yeah, he replies, he thinks he remembers me, how's it going? Fine. (Silence.) I thought we might meet up. Sure, he brightens up; if I like. How's he fixed? Actually, pretty quiet, can fit me in, well, sort of more or less whenever. Like? Like, howsabout tonight? Tonight why not what time? Eightish suit you? Eight'll be fine. So I surrender my address, and spell out my street, which he reads back, mispronounced. My whereabouts sound dreamy in his mouth. Anything special I'd like him to wear?, he wonders. My mind groans at the thought of the word Specialist, the prospect of combat gear and gas mask, or rubber vest and waders, or wellingtons and fireman's helmet, or brown acrylic three-piece suit with cowboy hat, or overgrown boy-scout uniform, or zip-mouthed balaclava, or muzzle and collar, or diapers and outsize bonnet, or riding boots and jodhpurs plus equestrian crop; and I hear myself reply, though less decisively than I should have liked, that he should wear whatever feels comfortable. He wonders whether he should give me another buzz before he sets off. I think, Whatever for?, but I say: Why? And this time it is he who spells it out: In case you've changed your mind. Which is when I grasp that this is a game with fluctuating rules, where the hottest man is allowed to get cold feet and still pass Go—wallet intact. But I say: No, just come at eight. And he says: Anyway, if you need to, you can always access me on my mobile. And talking of Access I reiterate the holy sum of seventy pounds. And he reiterates the words In Cash. And I conclude with Sure, of course. And then he hangs up with a stroking See You. And God knows why, but I'm smiling inside, profusely.

He arrives bang on time. I know because as the voice of the telephone-clock gets to Precisely, I hear my front door buzzer go. But on the entry screen, all I can discern is a blurred ear, uttering my name with the close conspiratorial charm of an old friend who has not visited me for years, or perhaps hasn't been here before. I direct my caller, too dryly for comfort, up to the third floor, on the right. I hear his ear say Thanks. And during the suspense of his ascent, I torment myself with all the dimmers in the flat, turning down each switch a further minuscule notch. I close the bedroom door for no reason at all. My sweating palm slithers round the knob. I suddenly find myself fearing the impending scene with the same fear as, in the past, used to grip me during examinations, round the throat. Morning, boys. Welcome to the world of impossible multiple choice. Subject: Global Economics—General Knowledge Paper One. You will be given thirty seconds to formulate your answers. No dictionaries; no calculators; no slide-rules; no help of any description. Understood? On your marks, get set, ding.

I hide my notes, three twenties and two fivers, inside a silver cigarette-case which, like a mocking relic of my past, lies, these days, on the table in the hall, but which, in its prime, sat snugly in the linen pocket of the waistcoat of an ancestor of mine who boasted the finest hands around, and a nose like a knife, and the narrowest trews in town, and philandered his way through the coastal estates of his much younger wife, but ended his days slumped like a cur on a boat bound for nowhere, biting at the spikes of his lavender-waxed moustache and railing at the shameful ravages of syphilis and God, and growling, on occasion, at the pet names of low women whom no one had ever heard of. And I snap closed the sapphire clasp and replace the silver case, and gaze around, and try to wonder whatever next, and turn, of a sudden, pale with the shock of two knocks at the door, strong knuckle-raps, delivered high, nearer to the spyhole than the letter-box. Odd that I shouldn't have heard the lift creak ajar and clatter closed. My guest must have come up the stairs. And I find myself retreating, tip-toeing back from the entrance, as if the event ahead were a high-jump which, for success, required preparation, needed gathered momentum. Yet when I do set off to open, it is too slowly, too loudly, over-deliberately; it is with the saunter of a gentleman whom I could never be; it is at the leisured pace of that disgraced forefather before he fell from grace; it is a ghost of a spatted walk from another story. Nothing to do with me. And yet—oh for Christ's sake, he's only a bloody whore, not some mighty conqueror demanding an audience. Open up, and have done with it. And since, ladies and gentlemen, my hand is on the key, and my fingers are now turning it, and the door is already starting to swing open, allow me to present to you: Steve, the lean, the handsome, the muscular, mature and trustworthy: Big Uncut Man, aka BUM.

No feet on the mat. They stand, army-booted and at ease, far back against the remotest wall of the landing, which has never seemed so wide or bright before. He wears the same gladiatorial stance as last night at the club, but his head is now tilted down. And as I flick a look at him, I see his thighs flinch with surprise, then soften out; and from his gut I hear the sound of my name rumbling to the ground and rolling incredulously towards me. I swing the door wide open, as if I had nothing to hide and he were welcome to verify as much, but only once my back has been safely turned to him do I tell him to come in, Steve. He closes the door with noiseless calm, as if he'd been to this place a thousand times, almost as if he were home at last; and he follows me to the kitchen. But he prefers to stand outside in the corridor, out of the lights, posturing very slightly, just enough to convey that even though he's a nice uncomplicated regular kinda guy, he can also play the host and the hero and the heart of any elaborate creepy fantasy that I might happen to espouse. Good at his job, remember. Worth it.

I pour myself some whisky, attack the freezer for ice, stroke my soggy palm on my thigh, return the cap to its glassy spiral. Would he like a drink?, I ask. In a soft husky whisper he replies that water would be nice. I don't bother asking whether fizzy or still, because a man who doesn't use a lift is bound to want it straight from the tap. But for the nervous hell of it, just to be certain, I repeat to myself, low as I can: Water. And he nods and goes—not Yeah, not Yup, but—Yuss, before claiming that he's afraid he's driving. I think: Oldest trick in the book, and I try to restrain my eyebrow as I pour his libation into the most delicate, fanciful, feminine, devotedly cut glass that I can find, while the rocks of my drink rattle round a beaker crafted from a horn of buffalo. But when I hand him his water, which glints for a shaky instant between us, he proves to be possessed of agile, competent hands, for, despite their hairy enormity, and the girlish fragility of the glass, and the whole horrible embarrassing exchange, he manages to make his knuckles gently stroke mine. What a tosser, I tell myself; hookers shouldn't pretend to be in the business of romance. And by the time I've clicked off the kitchen light, he's walked ahead, away from me without a word, into the room where, not so long ago, I was dancing alone in a blaze of candlelight, and it now feels, oddly, as if I'd abdicated all charge of the proceedings and it were he who was in charge, as if I'd been summoned by this stranger to this flat. He moves along on the balls of his feet, like a child that's been pushed to walk before time; but before I can tell him that he can sit down, he already has, widely and squarely at the centre of the dark velvet sofa, knees far apart, toecaps turned out. And he puts down his glass and shrugs off his leather jacket and lays it on the floor; and then he waits on the edge of his seat, hesitating at last. But I'm still drifting about, observing him through the mirror as I light a cigarette and inhale, keeping my head down. Would he like one, does he smoke? No thanks, not tobacco. Mind if I do? Your life, he replies. Most people's are, I retaliate, like an idiot. But cigarettes can kill you, he pipes up. And I smile, and say that so can lots of things, including love. And he smiles too, but hardly back; no, he smiles past the curtains of bronze taffeta, out of the window and abroad, as if trying to picture the features of some other man. I settle in the end for the wings of a chair across the room, diagonally distant, diametrically opposed, in a quarter of my own making. I do not recall ever before having sat with such awkwardness, with such gaucheness or discomfort—for all of the fine feathers that upholster my flanks. I find myself having to fight every fibre of my being not to cross my legs, as if I were my mother, but I can't bear the tension, so once more I stand up, pretend to stomp around. I think: the fact of the matter is this: if a third and neutral party were to see us now; to witness us thus—he, Steve, with his pale unhappy handsome face, dressed in a loose brown T-shirt and baggy, blue-black 501s, and looking, for all the world, content, even smug, and I, by contrast, glossily tanned and care-fully toned and trashily vested and trussed into strategically frayed and fitted jeans and utterly lacking in composure or class, like a soubrette who's fluffing all her lines, well—the conclusion would be foregone, wouldn't it: Steve, inevitably, would be cast as the lucky punter, while the rôle of the whore would be perfectly mine. None of this fits any bill. And another thing: I look younger than he does by far too far. Because Steve here, let me tell you, is Big all right; Uncut, I have little doubt; most of the other things that he claims to be, perhaps; but as for the business of age, about his being thirty-nine, well, even in the soft embrace of my charitable light, and I happen to be feeling polite, I'm dealing with a liar who was probably already twenty-five and most likely getting Coca-Cola bottles shoved up his arse during the Stonewall riots of '69. This man could be my sire. And the ludicrous irony, though he will never know the cost of his lie, the sheer waste of it, is that, had he only volunteered the truth of his years from the start, and not pre-sumed that I was hoping for some imbecilic Tom of Finland cut-out, I would gladly have tripled his price. But he shocks me back to my senses with one dreary word: Relax. I want to say Fuck off, get out. But I say, revoltingly: I am; just a bit shy. And then I sit down.

I STARE AT HIM with the lengthy impudence of a newly rich collector mulling over the actual worth of an inflated piece of art, and while I'm trying to formulate the proper words for this-shit-is-a-rip-off-man-come-on-you-must-be-mad, he asks whether I had a good time last night. I answer back: Last night? Yes, he persists, You know, at that club. (Christ.) No more than usual, I reply; why, was he there? Mm, he grins, wincing around the eyes. Oh, I lie, I didn't see him. And I put on some distracting music, crap that I think he might like, banalities from adolescent chartland that I habitually play for the sake of pick-ups. Nothing like the songs which, secretly, I might have elected to support us, chosen as our perfect background. And then I start to fire my questions at him, like a vengeful examiner at a viva, determined to wear him down, resolved to see him out.

I refer to myself as the Punter. He prefers the term Client. And what, I continue (not imagining Big Uncut Man really to be admissible), does he reckon that we should call him? Steve will be fine. Oh will it? I take it that Steve is a pseudonym. I'm correct, he says (not right). He also has Another Name. And might we know what that other name happens to be, or would such a disclosure seem sort of unprofessional? He's afraid that it would, seem sort of. Well, I must say—and I do—that he strikes me as a likely Keith. He ignores my snotty quip and moves on to The Point, which is that he needs to protect his identity because he has a job, a proper job, you see. Only does This for the money, short-term-basis type of thing, in the evenings; needs to supplement his income for a bit. I see. His life during the day is, he says, altogether different. Oh-my-God-don't-tell-me-Steve: you're a writer, right? Not exactly; but writing does, he concedes, have something to do with it. Journalist, maybe? Look, he asks, could we just leave this? Please not quite yet, Steve; it was just starting to get interesting, honestly. All right, he yields, but only for another couple of minutes, then we drop it, agreed? Agreed it is. And then, Yes, he admits, his job does have something to do with the written word; and yes, it is creative to a degree; and yes (yet again), writing does happen to be something which, though he says so himself, he can in fact do pretty—er competently. And then, as if to round off the clues, he explains that this accounts for the surprising success of his advert. Because it's designed to intrigue the consumer, you see, to attract a wide spectrum of interest. How, specifically? By being deliberately ambiguous, of course. Of course: Deliberately Ambiguous. I'd almost forgotten. But so it is, so it was. And so, back to square one.

Stalemate. Tell you what (I'm suddenly finding it tricky to say Steve, his other, other name): let's start again. If I like, he goes. Good: we're going to play this game another way, would he mind? He claims that he wouldn't (not yet, at any rate). Given which, I begin: Right, let's say that you're the Punter, and I, the Whore. No, no, he blurts, he must stop me right there; he insists that I be the Client; and he, his name, as I know, is Steve. I give up, give in. First round to him. We proceed.

Round Two, question one: Is the stopwatch still busy ticking? He half-smiles and removes some overflashy contraption from his diver's wrist and deposits it rather preciously in an inner pocket of the bomber-jacket at his feet. No need to worry about the time, he assures me. Whereupon he starts to look around as if hoping to discover a clock.

Question two: What, realistically, should be the extent of a punter's—sorry—client's expectations? Silence. He's thinking. He imbibes his first, and only, sip. Gulp. Wipes his mouth with the side of a finger. I elaborate: For instance, is a client justified in expecting a full erection from the hooker—escort I mean? Steve feels, a little sniffily, that yes, a client is in principle entitled to a hard-on from a guy who's Working. What principle? Well, come On, he says, everything is relative. Relative to what, exactly, Steve: to the efficacy of one's genital jewellery, the tightness of one's energy-ring? Or to a drug-induced upswing in the pervading mood? Steve laughs at this point, but not altogether freely. I'm becoming flushed. No, he explains, with great slow labour: It doesn't work that way. Oh really? Well how then would he, in his wisdom and experience and incredible desirability, propose that It, whatever It may be, did work? His face grows sombre suddenly; his knees spread absolutely, shamelessly; his arms reach forward and flex as if to welcome me; and then, baring a set of American teeth, and purring profoundly, as if he were some naughty-naughty daddy-oh, and I, a sensationally dumb blonde, suggests: Hey, c'mover here. He doesn't, I regret to say, add the endearment Baby; but after a pregnant pause, he does propose: Let me show you.

I do not think so, Steve-whatever-your-real-name-is, but thanks for the offer anyway. Try to relax, he suggests again; you're very hyped-up, he diagnoses, and prescribes, this self-appointed doctor-prostitute, that I help myself to another whisky. D'you know, I say, I think I will; top-up for you? If he replies to this inanity—and I wouldn't have put it past him—I'm no longer around to hear him. Already I'm in the kitchen, downing a great swig from the bottle-neck and guzzling it quickly, like a mutinous servant-girl, then pouring myself a liberal, trembling, triple. When I return to him, he is standing by the window, presumably still vainly searching for a clock, but platitudinizing now, if only for expediency, about the favourable nocturnal panoramic out yonder, and the surprising quiet within, and the miracle of decent—by which he means expensive—insulation, and the admirable reduction of the disturbance rising from the bustling—by which he means sordid—street below blar blar blar. I turn the tape over, and sneak a look at my watch (wrong watch to've worn—too chi-chi, too small) and I see, unbelievably, that we're only half an hour into this misery. I swing round, and resume: Won't he sit down? He'd rather not. Please, he's making me anxious. Why? Well, I mean, he's just so Big. All right, he weakens; if I insist. Oh I do, Steve; I really do.

We progress, or rather descend, to Round Three, which is our Special Subject section. My treat. A single question of many parts, otherwise known as the thousand-dollar mother-fucker and devised, since Steve is the sole candidate entered for this heat, especially and all for him. And I do cross my legs now; it seems almost befitting: because I have become, not just literally and figuratively, but also self-gratifyingly, Chairperson of the Evening. And though I may be growing a little agitated from within, I'm still managing to smile at him—a trifle coquettishly, I will admit; because, shame of low-down secret shames, I'm hardening slightly, I do believe.

He looks as ready as he will ever look, legs stuck out defiantly at me; but one of his knees is beginning to twitch. So enough suspense, I privately decree. The question, let's just sock it to him. Here goes: Given that Steve (he nods encouragingly) saw me at that club last night, which patently he did (nods again), and given that he elected not to make any contact with me then—am I not right to deduce a fundamental lack of interest from him in me, to infer that I failed to attract him? Already he looks eager to interject, but I can't allow it. Instead, I repeat what I've said, word for bumptious word, with the precise recall and fluid articulacy that a sharp intake of alcohol can sometimes bequeath. After which, I proceed: And given his indifference, can I now seriously be expected to imagine that he could suddenly, as if miraculously, find me to be pleasing? (Poor man's frantic to butt in, so I soften.) Look, he splutters, he doesn't know where any of this is leading, quite, but last night, if I really must know (my turn to nod vigorously), he had a really-really busy time and, after his appointments, just went to that club because it's near where he lives—Battersea actually—and because it stays open till late, and he needed to chill out for a bit. Get it? Just happened to be there. Just as I happened to be. He wasn't on the look-out for anyone or anything, though I may've been. And anyway, where's this all leading? He thinks I'm getting heavy.

Hear that? Catch it? Steve thinks I'm getting heavy—which comes as a surprise to me, because, my dear, *I* feel as if I could be waltzing around the place in a crinoline, or bombing about on pink-diamond amphetamines. I mean to say, it's hardly as if we're talking the third-degree here, Steve. Be realistic. Heavy? This? What, for a great Big Uncut Man like you? (Needless to say, I don't risk voicing any such thing, much less what I mean, which is: Heavy, Stevie Babe, is the shit I'm about to sock to you. And if you're half the hulk you proclaim to be, you'll manage to shift it. Because I, don't forget, can bring you good business; and you, if you're to be believed, have quite a name to keep.) Instead of which, my eyes glaze over a painting of a naked woman above him as I try to gather back the threads of where I was headed, before the Heavy bit, and then I continue: Let me tell you where I fear that this is leading, Steve: to nowhere that I can think of. Because it all went wrong almost as soon as you walked in. No fault of yours, of course, unless we choose to regard your revelation about having spot-ted me at that club last night as foolhardy, which perhaps we ought to do, since that one snippet alone has, in my opinion, exposed you more than any amount of nudity or disclosed pseudonyms or flights of heartfelt writing. In normal circumstances, or should I say general, I suspect that parties involved in exchanges such as ours, transactions such as this, would not have clapped eyes on one another before the initial tryst, which we might call exploratory. And in the extraordinary instance that their paths *had* crossed previously, I suppose that both would feel at liberty, and have the sense, to just say Hot Potato, let's call the whole thing off. Because my belief, but do correct me—once I've said my piece—is that so long as both sides come together as strangers, which is half the point, and in a climate of secrecy, which probably constitutes the other, the whole question of satisfactory congress remains open; there still exists a world of possibilities, not least since it's in everybody's interest to make the bloody thing (Calm Down) succeed. Repeat jobs, of course, are another matter entirely, dependent, ultimately, on whether the punter has found the whore to have been, how can I put this, worth it, and worth further bookings. The whore's opinion, I have to be candid, scarcely impinges, since the objective for an accomplished prostitute, as for any gifted professional, is not so much to notch up an infinity of one-off commissions as to secure a steady commercial stream, to earn a flow of dependable regulars: in short, to win a following. And a whore will countenance most things, will brave almost any indignity, in the hope that a performance be judged a bravura, and that he, or she, be rewarded with a string of contractual encores. But it remains, in the final analysis, the punter who decides whether a rendition has, or has not, been pleasing. Which, strangely enough, brings us back to us, to here and now, doesn't it?

STEVE STANDS UP ABRUPTLY, and stares, and does at this moment look enormous. His face glowers down at me, and sags as if he were fucking me from the front. His mouth begins to open, but it's just too bad: I have to go on. He has come to me, I claim, from nowhere, from a tatty page torn out of some tatty publication. I have never clapped eyes on him before. (I can hardly believe my gall. It inflames my loins.) Yet it would appear that he, by contrast, has most certainly seen *me*—clocked me, so to speak—and, for all that I know, already scrutinized me. He cannot, I go on, have volunteered the snippet about the club out of stupidity, for even I know that in these competitive times, the epithet Rent Boy is not synonymous with the words pretty moron. A great many prostitutes, I understand, are as bright as they are personable, tip-top post-graduates in some instances, champions not just of the bed chamber but also of the boardroom. And Steve, who's clearly been around rather longer than such boys, and doubtless, in his time, learnt more than they could possibly yet know, must have been prompted to divulge his information for some reason subtler than mere shortage of conversation. Could the reason have been a desire in him to impose, with the bombshell of his foreknowledge, some sort of control; or could it even have been a suspicion that what I seek is a figure of authority? Because the facts, as I see them, are that Steve (out there on the open market, in the great dark open) was prepared to throw me, and whatever I may have had to offer, overboard. And did. And I'm sorry, Steve, because, strange as it might seem, I do not fuck with men who would not fuck with me. Just isn't stuff I get off on. Correction: stuff on which I get off.

He huffs around, then stops; and hammering a fist against the marble, protests that he just happened to see me, that's all—adding, for inexplicable measure, that when he saw me he remembers thinking: Dishy (which dates him). Yes, he continues, he's not too proud to admit it; why should he be? Reckons I might fare quite well on the game myself if I chose to—assuming, and don't get him wrong, that I'm not already on it. Steve has often paid for sex, he says. An interesting scene, he explains. Hotter, very often. Hotter than what? You know what I mean, he replies; don't try to get clever with me; and as for this stuff about reasons and control, well, it's way out of hand man. Kind of neurotic. Neurotic, says Steve, who feels that I have some weird agenda simmering, as if I bore the world some sinister grudge, as if I needed to settle some bizarre earlier score, nothing to do with him. All of my shit, he concludes, lies way outside the realm of his (considered pause) obligations—no, responsibilities. And he wonders whether I've ever thought of getting help, like therapy. I ignore him. So he rounds off his monologue with the revelation that although it takes two to Get It On (the man is sickening), I seem determined not to give him the opportunity. I suddenly feel lonely, as if I needed a friend to partake of my ridicule.

I say OK, wait there. And now he does do as he's told. And I go back to the hall and pick up the cigarette case, and slip the wages into one of my back pockets; and I return, and I address him, and I ask whether a chance is really what he needs. And he replies that it rather looks like it, doesn't it? So I tell him that I'll offer him two. First: here's his money: he's free to leave. And I pause enquiringly. He looks, to my confusion, shattered, as if he'd been delivered a sudden, hefty blow; seems to be deflating on the spot; I wouldn't be surprised if he began to sob. Because I do understand, with just a tinge of guilt now, that the part of Major Reject doesn't figure in his work description; it lies out of his bounds. Let's face it: this is someone who's accustomed to flirtation, adulation, salivation, masturbation, fornication, gratification—things that can be played with seasoned panache—handsome remuneration even. But to be relegated to the shadows thus, thus unceremoniously? Must be a first for him. *My* first. *Cum Laude.* Ding. And yet the man will not be moved, will not be shown the door, not quite so easily, oh no. So instead, I show him the Roman face of my prissy watch, and offer him Chance Two, telling him that as he can see there still remain thirteen minutes, or just under, left to go. And I challenge him with my proposal that, if I'm to be persuaded that he amounts to anything more than a disappointing piece of print, he'll manage the seemingly impossible, which is to fix the damage of his conversational blunder by getting into top gear, fast, and redirecting this whole trip—skewed, I fear, so regrettably off-course. And I add, to taunt us both, that should he prove able to find a way to do so, to turn this awkward corner, I would like to think that we might even continue, the exchange of money becoming incidental, the sum of his prowess and my pleasure becoming all.

I'm standing with my back against the wall next to the corridor. He approaches me with astounding new calm and stops one step away from me. He spreads his legs, and lowers his hips, and stretches out his arms and brings them round to place the palms of his hands on the wall behind me, in line with my jaw. I can feel the heat of him. My back is frozen. I want to close my eyes. But he starts to twist his face into a contortion which, though it looks deranged, I recognize as meant to seem turned-on, and he puffs out his chest and tells me to go on, to relax, that I can touch him, not to be inhibited, that we should have done all this last night, at the club, when he first saw me. But suddenly I push away his arm, and stagger beyond his resistance, and I can hear myself cackling in response and, through the convulsions of my sickening laughter, my voice says: Forget It, Steve, really don't worry, thanks, but I think that it's better if you go.

Next thing is incredible: like some spurned and mortified great love of mine he murmurs that he'll only go if I'm quite sure it's what I want. And I confirm, seriously now, though smiling with aborted hope, that I'm certain that it is. Yet still he stalls, and wonders now, if you don't mind, whether he could borrow, Borrow he says, my john. My john; like some laid-back old New Yorker. The idiot. And in he goes, and closes the door; and while he's in there in the dark (I know because the switch is on the outside wall), I hear absolutely no noise. And a pang of loneliness chimes inside me as I try to envisage him. No rising lid, no gurgling flush, no gushing tap being turned off. He might be counting the lucre, I suppose; but I conclude, more realistically, more resignedly, that he must have gone To The John to remove some winching-contraption from his big, uncut, and unrequited cock. And when he emerges, which he does almost stealthily, as if expecting to be told off, he gathers his bomber-jacket from the floor and resurrects his sinister charm in order to touch me once more, somewhere vaguely around my shoulder. And I confess that as I lead him out I do feel slightly victori-ous, as if I'd vanquished temptation, beaten down some common dog. And at the door he leans towards me strangely, and strangely we kiss; but it is with the formal, chilled hypocrisy of concelebrating priests. And then he pats me on the buttock, routinely. And then I draw back. And once he is out of my darkened sphere, and safely on the bright landing to the world, he looks round, sees no one, and remarks, for the third and final time, that I should learn to relax. And just to finish me off, he adds, sneering rather than smiling, that he thinks I think too much.

I LOCK THE DOOR so silently that you might have thought that I'd left it open, but my head which thinks too much is yelling so hard inside that you could drown in the noise. And I go to the bog, where there is no sign of him, not one, and I apply a winching-strap of my own. And in the bedroom I open the wardrobe and fling myself into a black leather jacket which makes me feel squashed but has, in the past, proved a reliable draw. And on my way out, I ignore the great Venetian mirror in the hall, and the framed photographs of friends whom I love, or whom I've loved (for some of them I have lost), and I just walk out, out of the flat, ignoring the reasons, but ashamed to find myself alone. I creep down the stairs very slowly, to be sure that he has properly gone; and he has; and I step into a stinking urban night of the most dispiriting sort, full of belching louts and their clattering molls, and hooligans chanting retarded football songs and munching fish-'n-chips, or puking up, or pissing against the trees on the road; and I set off in the direction of my nearest faggot pub, which is famous for being rough—though it's decades since I've found it to be so—and famous, too, for being the oldest of its type in town, which I can well believe, because it is so historically sad.

And walking along, disengaged from the world, as if jet-lagged, or lost in some foreign town, I realize, from the liveliness of the traffic and the eagerness on the faces that pass by and the glow of the street-lights and the vigour of the wind in my eyes, that—for all of my detachment—I'm slap in the middle of the rush to a new night out. And as I approach a zebra crossing, I hear, through the open window of a car that I cannot make out, a recording of some unknown adoles-cent's voice, singing a laughable song of the sort which, you know, dissolves me. Because this unknown voice, which is the voice of a starry-eyed loner like the frightened witless soldierboy of whom I spoke, is chanting in a wild, hypnotic monotone that his corny quest, his, is to fight the unbeatable foe, and to bear the unbearable sorrow, and to run where the brave dare not go, and to right the unrightable wrong. And then, the lights go red. And I begin to cross. And I seem to be engulfed by a rowdy, rolling crowd which prevents me from hearing any more; which, in fact, is just as well, because my idiot face is cours-ing with filthy tears that I have to wipe with a black leather cuff. But later, what seems like ages later, and from a growing distance, as the car speeds away behind me, I hear the boy's voice once more, telling me, warning me to be willing to march into hell for a heavenly cause. And I think, fleetingly, of Steve, who by now will be racing back home; and I wish, absurdly, that the voice of that boy had been streaming like a ban-ner out of Steve's own car-window; and more absurdly still I wish, in my waking, walking dream, that the voice had not been the anonymous issue of some recording, but that it could have been mine, my own voice, and that I were still myself as hopeful, as willing, as young as that boy, and travelling away with Steve, being carried along. And then somebody bashes into me, which is what always happens at such moments, and a voice says Sorry Mate, and I go back to thinking of Steve, though in a more credible realm now, in a more realistic mental film where he can be pictured approaching his home and drawing up to the kerb, probably parking at this very moment, then grabbing his keys, and fumbling about for his mobile to check whether anyone's tried to get hold of him, and deciding that, if not, he'll just go indoors and make himself a cupper, right out of beer but too knackered to go to the shops; and he'll take off his boots and put up his feet and roll him-self a joint with the last of the grass that he keeps on a tray in the airing-cupboard; and he'll switch on the Box, in case there's a chat-show or some old sitcom to take his mind off things; and if not, he can always watch a dirty video, get him horny. But first he's going to put away the dosh from this really fucked-up guy he's just been to, totally, up on the shelf which is stacked with mags he used to pose for, plus some paperbacks that he's enjoyed, thrillers and what have you. And at the very top—you can just see the lid—there's a box labelled Hollidays, which come-to-think-of-it reminds him that he'd better give a bell to this bisexual mate of his called Nige who's also on the game (potty about his kids, mind you), used to be on the rigs, still has a brilliant bod, goes to the gym four times a week—when he's not on a bender, that is—and all-being-well-touch-wood, plans to go with Steve to the States to visit friends of his—of Steve's, he means—friends from the old days, who they can stay with, but probably for the last time: not too good, apparently, the pair of them. Oh well, no good moping and OK, so San Francisco's not what it was in the Seventies, but Christ bloody knows they could do with a break and the weather's always great out there, and you can get these really cheap return flights now-days; and anyway, word is the scene in the U.S. of A.'s starting to look up again with loads of hunky boys and brilliant bars and nobody gives a toss whether you're a hustler or whatever and, hey, Steve reckons he might decide to just say Sod It, and stay on for a while, rent a nice place, noth-ing too flash, put himself about, meet some new blokes, ring his mum in Grimsby once a fortnight, keep things ticking, turn a few tricks, pays for the blow, can't be bad.

I PUSH AGAINST THE DOOR of the pub and walk into a hot, tenebrous fog. I should be able to describe the place to you, on this of all nights, but I can't, because, two steps in, two breaths on, I practically collide, of all pathetic jokes, with Steve, Big Uncut Man. Standing alone. Look-ing, to grant him his due, not unembarrassed; and I, though I might well be shocked, seeming merely surprised, I hope; ironically struck. Yet I feel, for reasons which I cannot fathom, secretly pleased, half-comforted, as if I'd run into someone I liked in a place where generally I don't. Does he offer me a drink? Does he buggery. Do I offer him one? Of course, like an automatic Sloane—which, speedily, he de-clines, frowning and smiling at the same time, as if my gesture were preposterous. And I, using the din and the dark and the crush as my alibis, lean up to him, into him, and I mouth to his ear, which is cold, that after this evening I should like, if we should meet by accident, to think that he might afford me the passing courtesy, however slight, of an acknowledgement. And he has the front to suggest, this sombre sullen god of a man, that he would never not, that blanking isn't his style. And I look at him with flat neutrality, and make no excuses as I push my way to the bar and order myself a drink and dawdle about for the change. And only once a golden coin has plopped like a discarded talisman into my quaking, outstretched hand, do I dare turn my head—to see the back of the head of this stranger who corrodes me walking away, out of the pub. I swallow my double in one, grimacing as if it were linctus; and then I, too, get out.

Next stop is ten yards down the road: the club where the air-conditioning broke down what seems like yesterday, but must, in fact, be the best part of a month ago. Doesn't time fly? Isn't it fun? This is the place which gave me the boy who left me the mag which carried the ad that led me all the way to Big Uncut Man. I don't know who to thank. I walk in, past a leather-gloved bouncer who calls me Love, but this time I come warned—as well I might—and no sooner have I dumped my jacket at the coat-check and disappeared through the haze to yet another bar for yet another ineffectual vodka than I catch sight of him, Steve, over there, looking out from the wings, as if in wait for someone. Only a beam of lilac light catches his thighs. The rest of him is dark—holding, I think, a can of mineral water. And I begin to reel with strange pique, to move beside myself, to fly toward my shadow as I turn into my own best enemy, my own worst shining example.

I work the bogs quite fast. I flash my cock around, manipulate it, and bare the top-slice of my buttocks for the benefit of the queue behind. I certainly don't piss, but I wear my blossoming sleaziness like a prize, and I belt up noisily and walk out before I'm ready, like a slattern, flies still half-undone. I stagger onto the couple-stricken dance-floor and move around for a while, trying to make sense of the nonsensical phonetics that issue from some vocalizing robot, and I try to have a quick one-man romance, a romance with no body. Then I grow bored; walk off, mid-song; trip on a step, and get offered a drink by some dickhead from the urinals. Another vodka. My suitor orders me a large one, in sign language. He already possesses a beer, untouched. Attacks the froth. Grins straight at me. Starts to talk: German; married; wife understands; children grown up and gone; lives in Cologne; here on a convention. London, he assures me, is *goot* for him. And I, for him (what shall I be?)—a croupier, that's it. Club in Mayfair; members only. Do I enjoy this? Quite, I reply discouragingly. And Tonight? Night Off. *Quelle chance,* he exclaims, bewilderingly. And so, as if this were the logical course of action, I invite him home. To spite Steve, who doesn't warrant the spiting; Steve, who, on my way out, throws me a look that is hard to define, a look less of acknowledgement than of enlightenment, yet tinged with complicity—as if he were the Deus, and I, the mere machina, as if, at last, he understood me to be some prowling domestic feline who had dragged a mangled rodent to the feet of its master and, for its pains, expected, if not actual recompense, at least some attention, or a good slap.

Of the incidental German, needless to say, I recall not very much: that he fumbled down the back of my jeans for a while; that, using both his hands to conceal a soft-on, he tossed himself off; that he came, desultorily, over the kitchen floor; that he went to the bathroom for a posthumous leak, which splashed onto the seat and also hit the floor; and that following a quick wash of hands (no soap) he consigned himself, with dull ease, to history. Every queen has had one of those.

I wipe up the spunk in the kitchen, which is too clear and runny to be flattering; and, with private embarrassment, I go to the bathroom and crouch to wipe the drops of piss around the lavatory bowl. And then, though now with no shame at all, I find myself, against all wisdom or sense or best interest, ringing Steve's number once more. And the recorded message clicks on, then drones along, finally halting for me to talk, and I just say, without thought, like the machine that I've become, that I'm sorry if the evening went wrong, could he call me at midday. Which he does—at ten minutes past.

THE 'PHONE AWAKES ME. I can hear the rasp of my voice; I cough; I try to clear my throat. I summon what meagre spittle I can, phlegmy gunk. Hang on, I croak, and put down the receiver while I fumble for the bedside lamp. I grab a bottle of water from the floor, and swill down the dregs, straight from the neck. That's better. But I can hear Steve's diminished voice, still drifting unawares towards me from the handset, which lies abandoned on a pillow, asking whether this is double seven double six, and whether I'm all right, or is this a bad time. I pick up the 'phone. No, it's fine. Did he wake me?, he wonders. Yes, but I ought to be getting up anyhow: going out for lunch. Ah, he goes. Makes no mention of last night, thus banishing all awkwardness, and adds without the slightest tremor that perhaps we should consider giving this whole Thing another go. Makes me fetch my diary. I light a cigarette during my search for it, and then I sneak into the bathroom for a piss, and I squeeze a gob of toothpaste into my mouth, which is ridiculous. I lick it around as I climb back into bed. I shake the blankets about. Right, I tell him, and we discuss our respective availabilities for the coming week, sparing ourselves undue details about other commitments. In the end we settle for Wednesday, eight-thirty, here. But no, on second thoughts (of his), could we make that eight o'clock? Sure, if he wants. He'd prefer, he says; would make life easier. Doesn't elaborate. And so: eight o'clock it is. And I ask him whether perhaps, this time round, he might dispense with his car: he can always use my cab account. Good idea, he replies, though his tone sounds unpersuaded. Fine, I begin to end, See you then; yet before I can repeat our financial reality, or thank him for having rung, he has again engulfed me in one of those great, sonorous goodbyes. Instantly I replace the receiver, sweating. Almost as fast, I grab it back and dial Directory Enquiries. I ring the restaurant where I'm supposed to be lunching, to check whether the friend I'm meant to be meeting has booked, expects me; and he has, he does, dependable to the last. Two people; table nine; reservation for one-forty-five. Thanks very much.

I get up. Strange chorus of birds in my heart. I unbutton my nightshirt. I open the wings of the wardrobe. I glance inside. This time next year, one year from now, I promise myself, I shall be redefined, shot of all this stuff. I shall wear myself like a man, and like a gentleman at that: in single-breasted suits of faultless cut; in pure white shirts of various weights but one plain style. No rings; no links; no pins. No giddy breast-pocket handkerchieves. No dapper braces. Sober socks only, devoid of pattern. Trousers and cuffs without turn-ups. Shoes without accent: lace-ups. And briefly I picture myself on the crest of this forth-coming prime, grown faintly grey at the temple, dressed in Prince-of-Wales at springtime, or blue-black linen on summer nights, walking, walking without a conscience down some corso or rambla or boulevard towards a waterfront full of departing boats and flags and lights and—

God give me new horizons.

PART TWO

No BEGINNING: just an ingrained sense of embarrassment, of ancient, premature sadness, of displacement, of too much knowledge too early on, of wishing that all were otherwise, that I were adult, elsewhere, of having missed some crucial joke; yet no formal beginning. Press me (as you do) to recall it, and watch me redden, stumped by my inability to reward your interest with a single, clear, determining first truth. But yes, there was a general flavour to my infancy: rich and slightly sickly and tending to warm, like *marrons glacés* eaten in the sun.

When sounds from that first era return to me, faint and diffuse, they seem to filter through the summer curtains of my earliest siestas—starched white poplin, polka-dotted—from an unknown middle distance. I hear the plopping of tennis balls, an occasional clap, idle laughter . . . but then these sounds become muddled in my turning head (No pillows, darling, not for little boys) with the echo and the fall of a fairy-tale picturebook closing, sliding, dropping to the waffled bedside rug, which is laundered daily.

In my dreams of childhood I still hear, while my parents lunch on the terrace, splashes like cymbals from neighbouring swimming pools, and the hush of tropical afternoon breezes soothing the hot red feathers of a dozen flamboyants, planted in a great circle, like a botanical bandstand, at the front of our house when I was born. Sometimes I hear the slow creaking of giraffe-bamboos, tall and tougher than drought, scratching their necks against my shutters. Their leaves seem, from the harbour, to fringe our high wall from the world but, within my world, they shed a cool, lime light on the blank wall behind me—blank but for a wrought old Spanish crucifix of silver, a relic from my christening which, though hammered into the brick with a large black

47

nail, appears suspended in mid-air by a flawlessly arranged, arrow-tailed, aquamarine satin bow.

Ahead of me, when I lie sideways, folded into that state of woozy dormancy which continental children remember as enforced repose, I glimpse, at the outermost edge of my domain, like a blur beyond the hillock of my knees, those long white poplin curtains of my first few summers: full enough to evoke presences, silhouettes, postures, yet short enough to prevent any unseemly tumbling to the ground, the curtains rise, then withdraw like spectral, absurdly balletic messengers from the nearby sea—now filling out like intrepid twin sails set for unimaginable realms, or slimming down, brushing, overlapping, soft and oblivious as the skirts of novice missionary nuns, then stretching out once more, and tautening into the flanks of deserted tents from the Old Testament, but finally fluttering, and lingering in space for a moment, rueful, reluctant, lost in a landscape which, from the inclination of my sombre young eyes, already suggests flags of surrender, leaving forever, waving goodbye. Life has changed since the day when my Mam'zelle packed her bag, was quiet, went away.

THE NANNY WHO REPLACED her comes into my room with such slyness that I do not hear the turn of the green-glass four-leaf clover which acts as doorknob. But her appearance heralds the second half of my day and follows directly upon her lunch, taken in solitary silent splendour in the breakfast room, that socially indeterminate region which, tucked between the kitchen and the dining room, is papered in blue china teacups and whiffs, on account of its closeness to the swimming pool, faintly of chlorine. My parents will be drifting calmly through their own lunch still, the tempo of which, in summer, on the terrace as I said, is orchestrated by my mother with the assistance of a small, jewelled bell, a wedding present I seem to recall, whose frivolous tinkle, in my memory, is invariably accompanied by the jingle of her charm-bracelet, which glints with keepsakes and talismans and whose most recent addition is my first, gold-mounted milk tooth.

From autumn until spring, however, the tempo, which runs more legato, is conducted by means of an electrical contraption concealed beneath the carpet in the dining room, which, when my mother elects to extend her slim foot and press, manages, by some act of inexplicable wizardry, to buzz in the pantry in a variety of coded signals, thus alerting the servants as to what precisely is required: more iced water, more white wine, more red, more bread, second helpings, or the next course, or the next.

Nanny now rushes in to me, filling the air with her personal rendition of whatever hit happens, this week, to have taken her fancy—Winchester Cathedral (You're Bringing Me Down), I'm tempted to imagine—as she trots over the mottled granite tiles towards me. She sports—though of course I can't yet see them, for I'm still pretending to be asleep—her freshly painted, white leather lace-ups, and her signature stockings of seamed white lisle. All of a chirrup she heads for the room's centrepiece, a circular rug of thick-cut moquette, festooned along its sandy border with a miscellany of prancing circus beasts, at the heart of which there presides a bewildering mutant—turned, at my insistence, to face away from me—whose lower half may suggest a clown with pointy pumps and pom-poms, astride a penny-farthing, but whose upper body unquestionably belongs to some muscular ringleader with a handlebar moustache and a flying whip. Over the rug Nanny proceeds, in the determined direction of the curtains which, once reached, she always attacks with simultaneous outward armswings, like a conductor launching into a symphony, and then ties back—invariably, and with blithe indifference, parting them at the summit with a carelessness that both offends my precocious sense of order and elicits a deafening ring-against-pole squeal.

Within seconds, she is cantering back to my white iron bed with such gusto that her presence can no longer be ignored, not politely. I open one eye. Her straining thighs, striped in blue and white, are the first sight to confront me, swiftly followed, as she bends down, by the top of her pin-stabbed head. She stoops and reaches down for my favourite sandals, which are cherry-red and have been standing on the floor, waiting at the foot of the bed, patiently and slightly pigeon-toed, like friends. She carries them away, across the room, to the rocking chair where my clothes sit folded, and she lets them drop, like dead weights, to the ground. Then she returns to where I am and, tearing my top sheet away from me, exhorts me, far too loudly, as if trying to earn the attention of an adjoining room, Wakey Wakey Now. As if anyone could possibly not have done.

So down I clamber in my underpants, which are all that I'm allowed to wear during my siesta, and I tip-toe over the chilly tiles to the furthest edge of the rug, from where, avoiding the floor and stretching across, I manage, just, to grab my piqué shorts, the ones with crossover straps; yet no sooner have I found the balance to insert a foot into them than I am told, No No, to start again, Properly, which means in Nanny's particular order. Off with the shorts, on with my shirt—short-sleeved, tiny-holed, abrasive—and at last into my sandals, though even this part is spoiled, for socks aren't allowed in summer, despite the grate of toes against the petal cut-outs on the leather. I crouch down, resigned, and, in a posture of sulky genuflection, deal with the buckles, but as I finish tucking away the second strap, I feel myself being lifted by the elbow and directed, with a vigour that practically levitates me, towards the dressing-table, which has recently been glossed, like the bed, with a coat of white.

With the possible exception of the wardrobe, under which I'm the only person small enough to crawl, the dressing-table is my favourite piece of furniture here, with its collection of small, intricate drawers, and its vast, swivelling mirror, which lends a mysterious underwater floatiness to the ceiling and its hanging lamp—this, fashioned as a dovecote and complete with feathered doves along the parapet. But much as I might favour it, I have often been reminded that the dressing-table, which saw my mother through her fragrant youth, is mine on temporary loan only, which means until such time as we're blessed with a Sister, in whose honour pink tassels will swing from the dainty keys, and the drawers be lined with hand-printed seraphim, and the contents be laced with pomanders and sachets and frills. And the girl's array of silver brushes and frames and porcelain figurines, and her pearl and coral beads and half-eternity rings, and candy-striped enamel eggs on jade and amber stands, and tortoiseshell haircombs and hairbands of grosgrain, and goblets of powder with ivory-handled puffs, and crystalline phials from the great perfumerers, and velvet ranunculi, and daily-delivered posies, and fans of billets-doux, stashed with flirty insouciance beneath the faceted edge of the table's sheet of glass, which, by then, will surely have been tinted to the perfect shade of oyster-pink, will, at long last, restore the poor dejected dressing-table to its former glory. Which my mummy calls much more Appropriate.

Before the mirror we now stand, Nanny and I, a ludicrous coupling: she, panting and decapitated by the frame; I, stuck in front of her, and, although up on tip-toe, deprived of a visible body, like a head-and-shoulders putto by Murillo fluttering about the aura of some obscure Virgin. But with greater spirit than grace, Nanny now sets to work on the final phase of my grooming: taking a small white brush in her left hand and, in her other, a bee-embossed bottle of eau de cologne, which she nearly drops, she pours a torrent of lemony liquid onto my scalp, narrowly missing my eyes; then, noisily, she puts the bottle back down, and stoppers it. Gripping the brush while ruffling my dark hair with her unencumbered hand, she suddenly takes off, still Winchester Cathedralling, but much faster now: down, down, down and across, she brushes, then over, hard; and she delivers one last stroke to the back of my head, which, after biting into my nape, stumbles onto my collar. Which means that I'm ready. The time has come.

As on every afternoon except Sunday, when the servants are given their day off and I must go to Church and stay awake, Nanny and I rush out of my room and scurry along a landing which, in my memory, will forever be suffused with the immoderate scent of the tuberose. We run past my parents' rooms and, once beyond, Nanny hurries me down the top flight of stairs, which I tackle by grabbing the banisters one at a time—climbing them is easier, for some reason, and I can manage without props. And assuming, which generally we can, that I haven't skidded, or tumbled onto a polished board, or tripped on the end of a brass rod, soon we arrive at the landing below, on the first floor, which (unless there are luncheon guests—in which case, this is where we halt, outside the double doors to the drawing room) we go round, and down to the level of the ground, to the lily-pond courtyard and quickly past the front door, which is often left ajar to encourage a breeze, and along the shaded edge of the entrance, under the palm tree where once a blood-red macaw which had escaped from the municipal gardens trailing the chain of its captivity to the skies became entangled and was shot, until we reach the musty room which my father calls his study, where he likes to smoke his (medium-sized) cigars. This, too, is where he and my mother choose to sit after lunch, to drink the tiniest cup of coffee—Black for me, my dear; no, no sugar, thank you, is what he says, always; or, if she is tired, camomile tea for my mother—a preferred, if less proper, prelude to her siesta, which is later and longer than mine. And at the study we stop. Nanny has suddenly vanished, and I, gripped to the post and blinded by the light that comes crashing through the french windows, am grimacing rather than smiling, and alone. There he is, my parents proclaim in weary unison.

But when I recall this tableau, it seems at once to reel me back to an earlier occasion. I must be in my second year and fresh to the trauma of walking. Same room, same cast, same time, same time of year. As if jolted from some nocturnal terror, I find myself struggling from my father's flannel knee, scrambling as if for my life, appalled by his smooth, veined hand, which holds me round the ribcage as he laughs, a little nervously. I see his great fingernails curled monstrously about me and I'm fighting with all the passion I can summon to divorce myself from his grasp, from his ghastly contact, until, finally, after a suicidal leap, I'm down on the rug and, though paralysed in mid-intake of breath, raising myself to my bare feet; and after a suffocating eternity, as if I'd been held below water for perilously long but in the end let go, my long-awaited howl breaks out, a howl of such outrage as, since, I have only heard rise from the hearts of our beautiful expiring men; and I am rocking, bent double, swaying on the spot with such rhythmic violence as, since, I have only seen madmen sway; and I'm holding my arms up, though they rise no higher than the suede arm of my father's chair; and then I fall; and no amount of sugar-crystals will appease me; and then, through the tears that course from my nose, I see my mother rise with a long regretful sigh from her brocaded chaise, and I watch her pale slippers move gracefully to the door, and as I turn my neck towards her heartbreaking head, I see her lacquered nail press the bell by the lightswitch once, twice, and a third time; and, in no time at all, my nurse, the nurse that I lost, my Mam'zelle, appears; and after a quick exchange of busy mumbles I am raised like a runt saved from drowning, and taken in those strong womanly arms out of the room, back upstairs, disgraced but released.

To the nursery. Mam'zelle doesn't talk: she holds me on the nursing chair, hot and close to her large, low breast; and when I look up, I see her looking out into an impossible distance, and then, from the far corner of her upturned eye, like a sacred answer to a despairing prayer, one slow, heavy tear bursts forth and demurs, then slides down and down her beloved face to my mouth. And then I fall asleep.

I AWAKE TO THE EARLY evening light, swaying, floating in space. Mam'zelle, still silent, is smiling down. She kisses my brow and rises, like a goddess from the seas, my limp body ever in her arms, and paces proudly about the nursery, which is shaped like a horseshoe, with barred gable windows at the extremities, and suffused with shafts of dust; and she parades me about as if I were a princeling, bears me aloft before my vassals, my entertainers, my playthings; and I, restored, revived, as if after a mutinous battle, survey the exotic wasteland of toys in this barren kingdom of mine.

Now that it no longer exists, and that I've grown to appreciate the distinction between fantasy and falsehood, I view the nursery which my mother conceived as a victory of good taste over good will: consciously arranged in that Anglophilic, puritanical fashion which we associate with English suburban life between the wars (a punishing decorative manner which corresponds more precisely to the period of my mother's own infancy than to mine), this arid paradise, which demanded the use of electric light at all times, must, then, have struck the innocent observer as a reflection of the domestic propriety which underpinned my parents' style of life. I do not recall ever having seen this room in the state of jagged disarray which customarily denotes a child at play: I recollect it as a place of stasis. My memory even tricks me to picture it in sepia, as a meticulously appointed, sparse but discerningly styled variation on a softly focused photograph, carefully excised from some half-forgotten *Country Life,* already dated yet emblematic of young discipline *chez les hauts-bourgeois.* I happen not to be left-handed (let's leave left-footery for later) but I was born to that last high wave of well-intentioned people who considered it their duty to knock this sinistral aberrance, along with thumb-sucking and bed-wetting, out of the systems of their testing, if adorable, progeny.

All around me then, and round the corners of the horseshoe, lie poised, as one might expect exhibits in a museum of toys to lie, such specimens as my begetters, and legion other begetters of their generation and class, felt best fomented the wholesome (gender) development of their suggestible—dare one suggest malleable—offspring.

Thus, at the entrance to the nursery and to the left, on the floor, we see a miniature railway, already antique and embellished with tiny telegraph poles and sponges of shrubbery and station-masters and diminutive flags, which, on account of the monotonous circularity of the track and the engine's irritating chug, I don't think that I ever once, of my own volition, cared to activate. But I daresay that, on occasion, I may have been instructed so to do, probably as a courtesy to whichever of my parents' (male) minions happened to amuse himself some overcast autumnal afternoon assembling the contraption, or possibly for the sake of guests. For I do distinctly envisage myself, at various intervals in this early phase of my life, sitting sullen and cross-legged at the centre of the action, feigning rapt fascination for the benefit of those adults—cooing, upstanding ladies, ruby talons on short-skirted knees; and closer still, their crouching husbands, knees swung apart—but fancying myself, the while, some Arabian mountain, or Apache chieftain, or lumpen great Buddha, mildly riled by the hypnotic locomotion of this mechanized, wingless, overgrown fly.

Further along the flank of whitewashed wall, and neatly fitted into the first corner of the room, directly beneath a large framed engraving of a pond under a prison that is called my father's Alma Martyr, sits, again on the floor, a downscaled model of a garage, some two feet wide by three feet long by, let us say, twelve inches high—crafted of balsa wood, with a vaulted roof, and painted charcoal. In front of this building, someone has parked a whole gleaming fleet of primary-coloured Dinky toys, along with a mystifying contraption, a Noddy car, and a bulbous black one, a Cab; then there's a Red Cross ambulance, and an army lorry in camouflage, and, oddest of all, a crimson double-decker bus. I've had it explained to me, though I cannot think whom by—the family chauffeur? some clever-dick cousin who's occasionally foisted on me? I certainly don't think of my father as a visitor to my recreational quarters; still—it has been explained to me that the object of this garage-versus-vehicle exercise is to drive all four-wheelers into the depot and park them, not prang them, then drive them all out again and reposition them, perhaps in a new line.

Well, I can't speak for grown-ups or cousins or anyone very much, but nor can I see the point in crawling around on splintery planks of floor, so the game which I've devised for myself is this: leave all the cars exactly where they are (perhaps move the ambulance as a mitigating formality); then, with extreme care, crawl into the garage and curl up, like a snail into its shell, as tightly as you possibly can, knees hitched to your chin because the space can hardly accommodate you but feet sticking out is cheating; and remember to keep your head twisted to the right, turned into the room, so that once you're installed in your new habitat, you can gaze through the midget windows and imagine the world as a snail might, or an ant. In reality, however, with my overscaled face squashed and steaming against the panes of celluloid, I must more closely resemble the monstrous tabby in the *Tailor of Gloucester* at that ghastly moment when he glares into the workshop to menace the embroidering mice; for, on the occasions when, to my mortification, I've been caught in the throes of this covert ritual, the expression which has instantly attached itself to Nanny's face has been one of sudden frozen gaping horror, revulsion almost, which, following the arching of an eyebrow, has gradually settled into a look of relieved perplexity.

AGAINST THE FIRST of the two nursery windows, too low for me to be able to install myself and simultaneously watch the shaking, angry heads of the tallest trees outside, though I can sometimes hear them, languishes a dark, old desk for a child, which, to judge by the deep compass-graffito on the side nearest to my elasticated belt with a snake-clasp, was once the property of my maternal grandfather, who died in the year of my birth and everyone says I look like. This is incredible to me, for I have seen his picture peering down from the top of the tall-boy in my mother's dressing room, where she wears her petticoat, and he is old with shiny hair and a wonky bow with spots, none of which I've ever been or had, and very dark eyes, which I do, I suppose. But anyway: Juan Zamora Gonzaga, the inscription on the desk goes (I'm told), and then continues: Santa Cruz 1906, which is long ago and how I know that this desk belonged to him one time.

But the whole artefact seems a mystery to me, for the seat is attached to the writing part by means of parallel metal bars, rather like train tracks, which run along the uneven wooden floor and make the whole thing wobble. Where you sit is too far back from the writing part for you ever to get comfortable, and, even if you slouch forward (the way that you're not supposed to at lunch), the lid slopes so hard that you must hold your book, or block, or the leaves which you might want to press with blotting paper, down, or rather up, otherwise everything will slide and slip and tumble to the ground. And the white porcelain ink-well is all very fine, as is the rusty dip-pen, which you're not allowed to touch, not ever, because it's sharp and you could spike yourself blind; but as I'm only just beginning now to write my first name, which is long, in pencil not in pen, I can only surmise that this strange departed grandfather of mine, when he was young, must have been very clever, very fat, and very bored.

Deeper down the nursery hangs a pair of ornamental shelves, white as the dressing-table, and set too high for me. But I can see that the upstairs level carries a collection of lead soldiers in fancy Waterloo dress belonging to my father, who is confident that I shall learn to enjoy them once I'm sent to England to his school or Alma Martyr where he was once Head Boy, although it seems to me that, well, by then, if I am bigger, surely these small soldiers will have grown too small; I do not know. But the lower of the shelves holds a pageant of pieces in wood of black and red for a game that is slow and Mam'zelle calls *échecs* and my father calls chess my mummy, who knows best, says that here, which is Spain, it is called *ajedrez*. And she promises to teach me very soon how it goes, as already I can almost play a thing called draughts, which is a start, and I keep the board, which is also Appropriate for this chess, in the desk of my grandfather who died.

In the middle of the horseshoe attic, behind the nursing chair and facing a sprawling sofa of loose-covered cretonne, ablossom with verdigris hydrangeas, stands the bookcase: tall as a temple, important, its lower half perpetually locked, the section above encased by doors of harlequin glass. Reaching the contents is a perilous enterprise, for it entails dragging a chair up to the bookcase and kneeling on its seat, and then, drawing myself, despite its rickety legs, up to my full height, in order to open the outer of the two doors, taking care not to let anything fly back and topple me before I can pluck out a book, maximum two, which I tuck under one arm while, with the other, I slowly close the case, until at last, like a one-armed mountaineer, I climb down, backwards, to the swaying floor and, once returned to terra firma, I run over to the sofa, hurl myself onto the hydrangeas and position myself to start. And inserting the chilly spine of some chosen book between my thighs, I part the covers and explore the pictures and the colours, not the words.

WHEN I RETURN to that earliest indigestible reading matter, I am filled with a sense of no wonder. Savour the cream of my first library: a small accordion of Beatrix Potter books with pastel yarns of dolled-up persecution; upper-case tales from the Holy Bible, with muted pictures of a basketed baby posted downstream in a nappy, and of a denuded old man being hurled to the lions, and of a bearded head swimming in a lagoon of aubergine blood on a silver platter; the illustrated lives of the Saints, blinded but smiling, or ravaged by leprosy, or aflame with stigmata, or bucked to the ground in the night, or traversed by quivering arrows of gold, or immobilized into eternity by rusty ropes and rusty chains, or simply stoned to death; a synopsis of *A Midsummer Night's Dream,* in Spanish, with its appurtenant visual freak-show; enough crusty volumes of Dickens to fill the whole toy garage, one monochrome sketch to every fistful of unreadable pages; the adventures of William, Just William—or was it Poile de Carotte?—whose freckled face resembles a saffron-spattered tambourine; a Tintin book—extraordinarily, for cartoons were normally taboo, and in French (so presumably a smuggled present from Mam'zelle)—in which our intrepid young Belgian, bizarrely attired in a kilt, is accosted by a grunting great gorilla, object of my first remembered erection at five years of age; an *ABC of Names* (X is for Xavier); an *ABC of Musical Instruments* (X is for Xylophone); an *ABC of Ancient Cities* (X is for Xanthus, or sometimes Xanadú); an *ABC of Rivers* (X is for Xingú); an *ABC of Anatomy* (X is for Xiphisternum); an *ABC of Minerals* (X is for Xenocryst); an *ABC of Plants* (X is for Xerophyte); mercifully summarized biographies of Thérèse of Lisieux and Teresa of Avila and Joan of Lorraine and Bernadette of Lourdes and Francis of Assisi and John of the Cross and Jesus of Nazareth. Spoilt for choice.

But my real choice propels me away from the books and the saints and the cars and the train and, rather, round to the far, forbidden end of the horseshoe nursery, which lies virtually concealed from view and briefly basks in the dusty, roseate warmth of the late-afternoon light—that remotest region of my kingdom which I shall never legitimately conquer, that most delicate wing of the toy museum which, as if set apart by an invisible cordon, I can never honourably visit, only trespass upon. My mother's former province. My future sister's province. Not mine.

It seems strange to me now that the fondest fragments of my earliest remembrance should simultaneously suggest themselves as the stillest, stealthiest, saddest you could say. For on the rare occasions when I do, despite the risks of rebuke and ridicule, dare to venture over that unseen but hotly felt boundary line into the outlawed section of the nursery, which draws me like a shaming fetish to its bosom, my spirits lurk at half mast, the tide of my restraint has dropped treacherously low. I seem always to be wearing my tartan velvet slippers, and a creamy Viyella dressing-gown which skirts to the ground, and I'm generally convalescing from some demoralizing ailment: measles, or mumps, or chicken pox, or croup, or newly excised tonsils, or (rare this) infant haemorrhoids, or (rarer still) the myxomatotic bloating of an eye, occasioned by a well-aimed hornet's sting.

I find myself confined, as for days past, to the nursery, consigned to my own devices. And almost involuntarily, as if directed by a trance, I seem suddenly to have turned that beckoning corner and entered the sanctum, to have disappeared from the world, and I am moving with consummate care about the tabernacle of my mother's childhood treasures, avoiding certain critical floorboards yet scarcely raising my feet from the hallowed ground, as if floating, or walking on waves. I come to rest before a colossal rocking-unicorn, a former incumbent, I imagine, of some fairground carousel, for I can see the tonsure at its neck through which a lance of brass would once have been driven, and I look at its painted lashes and astonished eyes, and then I hitch up a knee and insert my slipper in a gilded stirrup and strain to lift myself, and swivel slightly as I mount, and at last I lower myself, softly, sideways, onto the animal's buttoned-velvet saddle, which is profoundly pink—upholstered, as it once was, for my young mother's pleasure. Poised like a Highness set for uncharted lands, my excellent robe tumbling over the muscular flank of my valiant borrowed stallion, I stroke its flaming, windswept, wooden mane, and its spiralling silver horn, and the braid of its bridle, and its inhaling cheek and neck and gently pulsing shoulder and I've begun to sway forward, am moving, moving with elegant gathering speed, galloping toward the high realm through the window, beyond the bars, heading for the distant palms, and the mossy roofs, and the violet hills and, further still, the glittering colour-less sea, and the descending sky-without-a-cloud, and on and on until evening begins to fall and the first halo of a moon smokes into view, but my horse must not grow weary; he must rest; we must wait; so I slide off and drift over to a low platform like an altar, on which stands my mother's doll's-house, built for her in honour of her First Holy Communion, with visible, lasting devotion, by a former family carpen-ter, Cook's father, in fact.

THE DOLL'S-HOUSE: behold it, marvel: three paces wide and three storeys high, white-white and august it stands, with a pink-gravelled entrance and crescent-shaped benches like the ones that we have in the garden outside, and a front colonnade with a diadem pediment, shaped like a Russian crown whose central wreath of ivy-leaves looks out, like the eye of God, from the face of my mother's first house. And look, there are marbled lateral terraces, and a tradesman's entrance discreetly to the back, and a miniature topiary, and a kitchen garden with a per-gola of tiny lilies-of-the-valley, like dots; and still, a generation on, that old carpenter's surviving gift of love presides intact, grand as an embassy, bright as a bride. And if you walk your fingers round the cir-cular drive and step them up, one at a time, as if they had alighted from a long, long-touring motorcar, smartly but exhausted, up the steps to the front, and if you help them to push the front door ajar, it will not creak, and you will see, though you should not climb, the principal staircase, which is shaped like a lyre, and if you listen hard, you may just hear the forgotten tinkles of the ear-ring chandelier, and all but inhale the smoke of the birthday candles that lit it once, and you will know, without a doubt, that magic has happened in this great, miniature house.

And next to it, in the ottoman of calico, is where my mother's dolls lie, have lain for twenty years: a wool-plaited Poupée which she made at her convent, with a circular mouth and appliquéd cheeks and limp long legs and plaits; and then there is Celia, who sometimes smiles and opens her eyes if you lift her head of china, and never worries if you hold her, and is patient. And she has many dresses, Celia does have, made for her, an age ago, by my mummy's mummy in the days when everyone was young. Of course, the red gingham one with matching bloomers and white smocking is the one that she prefers, and is my favourite also, and my mummy when she was a girl who liked to play with Celia had a dress the same exact, and my father keeps a picture on his desk and, though the photograph is dark, you can see Celia being cradled by my small mummy, and they're identically dressed, the two of them, smiling out from the past. And Celia's other clothes, which are also hidden in the ottoman, are many: see: a tartan Viyella one; an organdie party dress with a sash; a velvet coat with a matching winter bonnet; her First Holy Communion gown, with gloves and veil and tiny missal; and every time that Celia had a dress, my mummy, who was little then (but not so little as Celia) did also have one.

When I'm in the nursery for a length of time, I sometimes go to visit the ottoman which is a best place to play. I lift the lid and take Celia by the arms and pick her up and hold her while I close the lid back down, and I sit upon the ottoman and talk to her, and I change her clothes if she asks. But always I must not forget to put her back in the red gingham dress with matching bloomers because no one is allowed to know that Celia is my friend, apart, that is, from Mam'zelle, who went away, for once upon a time while I was giving Celia one pretendy-bath on the hydrangeas, Nanny, who came after my Mam'zelle, crept up without making her noise and saw us both and laughed, and how she did laugh, and then, in a sudden whispering fury that made her face go white, No No she said, and then there was a noise that burnt the back of her hand across my face and made me cry, and she threw Celia harshly to the ottoman and Celia also cried. I remember. But it was never so with Mam'zelle, who did like Celia, and said that she could be my friend, but friend in secret, don't forget, for grown-ups do not always understand these things of friendship, which I do not think they always do—understand.

AND ALSO MAM'ZELLE did say that she would help me soon to send a note to Papá Noel, which she, my Secritty, would write but I shall be in charge and I'm allowed to sign with my own thumb in purple; and what I wish to say is this to him: that this year, when he comes, what I would like, and Please, is not more books or cars or engine-trains with which the nursery is replete, but: a turquoise trampoline to help me leap and summersault like a blue dolphin from the Cape of Good Hope to some very farawayness; and a retinue of sea-green seahorses, and terrapins with flaming cheeks, to escort me through the night on my voyage to the honey-coloured coastline of Hawaii, perhaps; and an iridescent sherbet-lemon hoolahoop to dance around my waist as I circulate along the lilac beach when I arrive; and a garland of hibiscuses to blossom round my neck for when I meet the wide-eyed faces of the ladies of that land; and a rainbow-speckled ray-fish with wings wider than a carpet, on which to sit like an Aladdin and escape if the ladies are not friendly, or the men; but if they are, which my Mam'zelle is sure they very are, then I shall need a dressing-up box with a shirt of tiger-lilies to protect me from the sun which in Hawaii is Huge; and a loincloth of Sicilian leopard with a tail down to the sand, and a waist-length wig of mermaid-hair for my Mam'zelle, who says you never know, she may yet come, and a skirt of finest grass, which I believe she will be needing if she does; and I would like a picnic-hamper with a checkered cloth in black and white to lay politely upon the ground and teach them, using gold and silver coins of chocolate, which nobody is allowed to eat, how to play draughts, and I hope that in exchange the ladies of Hawaii might teach me how to pluck and strum their caramel guitar, and teach Mam'zelle to do their dance; and in the hamper I do think that we should have a never-ending set of saucers and of cups, and a pot, shaped like a dragon, to spout refreshing tea (they should have sugar in Hawaii), and teaspoons, don't forget; and a coffer full of treasures from the bottom of the sea (pearl and coral beads and half-eternity rings and candy-striped enamel eggs on jade and amber stands and tortoiseshell, like the treasures for my sister) with which to buy, and bring, when Mam'zelle and I come back eventually to our island, a young orang-u-tang to play with me when I get bored at home, and a magician's cape and a top hat, and glasses for the sun, and one cigarette (a trick one), and a ball of bubbly gum—but Mam'zelle says that she's afraid that, even in Hawaii, bubbly gum is not allowed and anyway, she thinks that I've already asked for far too much, it's high time for my bath.

WHEN I THINK of my first nurse, even now, all this time later, a strange soft weakness wells within me, a stillness, a pang which almost comforts me. I think of her rescuing me from my father's study, and parading me about the old nursery; I think of her awaking me in the morning, fresh and strong and ready to do battle all day long on my behalf; I think of her dear face, astonished each and every time that I pick lowly flowers from the kitchen garden for her delight; but above all, even today, when I think of her, I think of her when I take a bath.

My Mam'zelle is full of grace, blessed among women as she leans at the edge of my eau-de-nile porcelain. I stand beside her on the sunny mosaic floor, my ankles kissing, purely naked, while she ties the ribbons of her apron. And once the waves have been stilled, she takes me into her warm wet hands and raises me reverently and with love towards the heavens, as if I were an innocent being returned to celestial flight; and she holds me above her open, upturned face for an instant, frozen in time, like a host, like a chalice, then lowers me in slowest gentlest motion through the mystical steam, through my personal cloud, down into the uterine waters of my scented bath. My Mam'zelle.

While she soaps my ribs and panting chest with a sponge of softest ocean-plant, she holds my nape, which tends to loll, in the cradle of her other arm. I raise a leg into the scented mist of evaporating bath-salts and gaze at the receding motions of the tropical fish that swim about her apron. The blossoming sponge dips between the cleavages of my toes, strokes the rigid arch of my foot, which slithers on the palm of her hand; and then, I feel the sponge lather my calf and slide to the back of my knee and roll onto my kneecap and float up, like a whisper, up my left thigh. I close my eyes. I breathe through my mouth. I arc my back. Through the song of the cicadas and the retiring tropical birds and the occasional sound of a passing gull, I hear Mam'zelle, as she assumes my other leg, suggest, then glide into our regular chant, last year's winner of the Eurovision, which, through the slow velvet monotone of her rendition, I have come to learn and learnt to love:

> *Un premier amour* (she begins), *premier amour, premier amour,*
> *Ne s'oublie jamais, s'oublie jamais, s'oublie jamais,*
> *Un premier amour, on le cherche toujours dans*
> *D'autres amours; toute sa vie on court après.*
> *Il nous a troublé, et fait rêver, et fait trembler,*
> *Ce premier amour, premier amour, premier amour;*

Mais, l'enfant qu'on est, l'enfant qu'on est resté,
Frémira toujours au souvenir de cet amour.

The sponge swims around my front, circles my navel like a wreath, then dies, sinking very slowly to the bloom between my thighs, separates my legs, navigates the gulf, charms the crevice of my buttocks up from the bed of the bath and reaches, as I straddle her forearm, the hollow of my back. And then she turns me. My chin now rests on the ledge of her elbow, as if I were a fish that couldn't swim, though my feet are beginning to paddle and froth about, and I feel the sponge on my back, on my neck, around the secrets of my underarms. And Mam'zelle, who has sailed to the brink of her verse, now pauses and waits for me to take over, and my reply flies out, cuts into the air like an injured swordfish, glittering and shrill and far too fast and stupid and doomed:

Et toi, et toi qui j'aimais, Qu'as-tu fait de toi? Qu'as-tu fait sans moi?
Et moi, moi qui t'ai perdu, Qu'as-tu fait de plus? Qu'ai-je fait de tant
de bonheur?

I'm back on the fringed bath-mat and about to start to shiver, but Mam'zelle wraps me in an enormous peppermint towel, which cowls about my shoulders and trails about my feet, and she hugs me to her kneeling warmth and dries me with the vigour of her arms. She withdraws the towel, as if to inspect me one last time, and peppers my person with talcum, front and back; and then she enfolds me once more, pausing only to blow a few random specks of powder from my fat cheeks. Rising, she guides me into the sleeves of my nightshirt, white, and combs my hair, and helps me brush my teeth; but realizing that she's forgotten my slippers, she lifts me to dangle about her; and as we leave the bathroom and set off to the bedroom where she will kiss my brow and lay me down, I hear the heavy sound of soap falling into the frantic escaping water with a great splash.

THEN THERE ARE SMALLER SPLASHES, choppier, harsher, stuck in the faded Kodacolour album of my childhood scraps: I must be four, certainly no more, because I'm wearing the primrose towelling swimming-trunks that I wore on the day that Kennedy died and everyone went home looking glum—the trunks with that impossible metal clasp which I can never undo alone and is a source of agony to me if I need to go to the Lav; the belt-clasp which, a magnet to the sun, scorches my tummy every time that I bend down for seashells in the sand. But I'm not at the beach villa now; no, I can see myself from high above, as if from our town house at the top of the cliff, a seagull's view. My head is a dot like an aspirin far below, blinding-white in the noonday sun, white and almost wider than my shoulders, and crowned, I realize as I zoom down, with my sailor-hat—ghastly: the elastic cuts into my chin, and the brim just won't stay down. Endless tantrums.

I'm at the Nautical Club, where Nanny and I have been driven and, from eleven until one, deposited for my one-to-one beginner's swimming class, which lasts half an hour. This will be our weekday routine for the whole of the month. And what month might that be, dear? June is the month. June did you say, dear? Are we quite sure about that? Don't mumble now. (I'm Positive.) This Nanny thinks that she's so funny, always trying to catch you out, but my last Nanny, Mam'zelle, who was much more *gentille,* which means nicer in another country, and smelt of oranges not lavender, and did not wear white gloves and had no Exima, taught me all of the months, in English and in French as well as Spanish, which I have not forgotten, though I miss my Mam'zelle when the time comes for my bath. And do you know how *this* Nanny says Junio, which is June in Spanish? Like so, with her mouth all wrinkled up: Joo-Knee-Oh. *Joo-Knee-Oh! Imaginez-toi!* And just because I don't repeat the months out loud to her a lot, this English Nanny thinks that I'm a bit not very clever, which I am Not not. I shall show you: I shall tell you how I know that June, which is now, is June: because May comes before June and now cannot be May because my birth-*anniversaire* does always fall in May, near to its end, which was too long ago; and now is not July, which comes straight after June, because in July (but Nanny doesn't know because she hasn't been my Nanny long enough), in July is when our chauffeur Pepe throws his cap into the air, which Mummy says is naughty, and then goes off into his Hols, and so do we. We all jump into our motorcar, my mummy and daddy and nanny and me, or I; and our motorcar is long, long as a bus but black, and white on the inside but not in the boot which is dark and scary with a light that comes on when you open it up.

But in July the boot is not scary one bit, for it is chock-oh-block of suitcases and a big round box with stripes of pink and white, which is where my mummy hides her summer hats; and also in the boot is where we put my net for catching butterflies, and my kite of lilac, which on my own I cannot fly, but Daddy helped me once when the kite flew up and up and far-far away and too high from the beach because of the wind and the clouds, or so my daddy said, and then it dropped down, and still more down, and it fell to the waves and very nearly drowned; it did; and also in the boot we put another net, the one with smaller holes for fishes, which I do not like to catch as they are wet. And anyway in June, I mean July, the car that is our motorcar is also huge and high with trunks which get strapped to the roof: *two* huge trunks which Mummy hugely packs with the help of Mam'zelle (but this year it is Nanny) and Mummy says that I'm allowed to help as well if I do learn to swim before July without my yellow rubber ring or armbands at the club (but not to dive), which I very want to do because in July, in *July* is when we get into the car and drive past the cathedral and out of the city and up to the forest and over the mountains and stop for a minute so I can do weewees and put on a pully, then round the volcano which often is snowing and down to the town where we park to have lunch that is always in fiesta and then we go on past banana plantations with baby bananas and fields of tomatoes that belong to my aunts and, further along, we turn left onto a track that goes bumpitty bump and is not straight at all but now that I'm bigger I never get sick and we sing "Frère Jacques" until I go wrong which is sometimes quite early but we all have such . . . *fun;* then we cross a small bridge with plants that are cactuses over a ditch that floods in the winter and sends all the lizards all dead to the sea but not in July which is when we go down at the end of the day to the house in the south which is christened La Villa and my grandfather built for his wife my abuela before he was dead, but she died as well so it's Mummy's house now though Daddy's invited and I am allowed and it's white with round windows like moons, though there isn't a garden or trees or a pool which we do have in town, but the Villa which sits overlooking the ocean you reach from the door at the back of the house, which is really the front, because there are steps made of wood that is blue and go down to the sand, which is sandy, and the sea, which in summer is warm, and the sky, which does shine all day long, but of course not at night when you look at the stars from your bed and then sleep with the sound of the waves in your dreams with the sound of the waves in your dreams.

NO DREAM. I'm back at the Nautical Club, that sprawling Deco gem which, designed to mimic a great liner, dominates the city's splendid maritime avenue and welcomes strangers from the seas. I am four or five. The sun is near to noon. I'm wearing my uncomfortable sailor hat. I've already given Nanny my small, square Omega (whose time, in truth, I can't yet tell). Nanny has zipped the watch into the inner pocket of her soft, pink-lined basket, a hand-me-down from my mother, and extracted her wing-tipped sunglasses, which she now applies, along with a gob of lotion, to her long nose. Humming out to the horizon she hands me my beach towel, which is vast and in one corner bears the tangled monogram of my initials, floating in ornamental symmetry within a life-saver's ring:

She deposits herself with a book and a sigh on a bench and waves me away, past the awnings along the terrace and the tennis courts of clay and the poolside bar and the boat-huts and still further, beyond the sheds for water-skis and the stand that sells ice-cream, to which I hope to return, and along the edge of the Olympic pool, which has diving planks to the sun, and round the salt-water one, all the way to the glinting square beneath the cliff, which is the pool for beginners. I turn and wave to Nanny, who could not see me. I think that her specs are too dark.

I am sitting on my towel, perched like a question mark at the shallow end of the pool, the paddling end, where there are no steps and my coach, who's just finishing with some other boy, older than I, has exhorted me, with the vigorous use of his stiff forefinger, to wait, *esperar*. I can see my grey feet, distorted, dangling like jellyfish in the water, netted by my detestable transparent plastic sandals.

The other boy is being hoisted like a jubilant monkey, knees swinging in the air, onto the pool's far pumice shore. Beneath his dark glossy waist, where his wet trunks have fractionally dropped, a line of pallor flashes across his upper buttocks. His flat, unbladed back is turned to me as he wipes his eyes; and his thick dark hair now rises in spikes, like a black sun, or a sunflower by night. His mother (I presume—because she's not wearing a uniform) threads his head through the eyelet of a towelling poncho, flattens the rebel hair with her palm, kisses the wet crown of her small victor and leads him away, and both are smiling and thanking and gone.

The swimming coach now turns, his hand still waving, round towards me. He wades slowly in my direction, vastly, like Poseidon rising from the waves. His opalescent teeth emerge through his dark beard, flashing as he speaks to me; but I can hear nothing. I see his tongue dart across his lips. My innards are thumping at me. I drop my face into the shadow of my lap and remove my hat, and fumble about, and push the hat into the wrinkled folds of the towel beneath me; and then I look out. His shoulders are wider than the very pool now; his strides are monstrous. The water froths about his hairy thighs, teases at his indigo trunks as he comes towards me, hands outstretched, water falling like great wings from his colossal arms. I think of my mother momentarily; then his fingers are upon me, freezing the breath out of me; but he is kneeling at my feet.

We begin gently, like dear friends, or lovers. As he lowers me gradually into the font of my induction, I clamp my puny frame to his gleaming shield of a chest; I cling to his power like a blind orphan limpet. I panic. I dig my fingers into the muscles round his neck. He says that everything's all right and tells me to relax, to calm down, which I can't, and he orders me to let go, commands me, and again he commands, and then, it happens: he just wrenches me up and throws me like a sponge to the clouds, up and up and I am spinning and my legs are thrashing and my mouth, though agape and howling, is soundless; I must be dying; and then I come crashing down on the volcanic edge of the pool, splat, and my head is thrown back into the water, splash, and the sky is suddenly below me, then vanishes in an explosion of loud, deep bubbles; but my foot, I realize as I swallow and choke and splutter below the world, is still stuck, ripping, to the border of stone. I must be dead, or divided. And then he fishes me out, and he is laughing, laughing; but at last I find my voice and it is murderous and rages out, shouting: Don't push me! Don't push me! Don't! *Nanny!* Tell him to *stop*! *Nanny!* But she is nowhere about.

When, in the fullness of time, my nanny does materialize, it is with a mien of genteel weariness, as if she'd been caught in the sun carelessly long without a hat. She bundles me into my towel without a murmur, and raises her dark-spectacled visage to the heavens as if for sustenance. She wrinkles her desiccated features into a prettily puckered grimace of distaste and lugs me under one arm—my mother's old basket swinging about the other—through the bronzed, brow-raising multitude, up the reverberating white steps of iron to the cocktail terrace, past the archipelago of clubhouse stalwarts, through the hollow vestibule, and fast across the cloakroom as I bawl and bawl without further care or restraint. But discovering, as she reaches the high front portico of the club, that our driver has not yet arrived, she nods, commendably unflustered, to the doorman, who nods to a lingering taxi, whose driver opens a door for her to step inside as she issues instructions in atrocious Spanish and, simultaneously, dumps me on the sweaty beige leatherette beside her. And as I drop and slump against the open, full-to-bursting ashtray, my head collapses like the head of my mother's forgotten rag-doll, and I see the blood from my ankle leak and blossom through the paleness of my towel like a dark flower of foreboding.

(The event above, I was later to learn, did in fact occur during the month of June, and not July; for our family's summer vacation that year was, exceptionally, relegated to August on account of three factors: one, a miscarriage suffered by my mother in the sixth month of her second pregnancy; two, the quiet posthumous baptism of the baby girl, named Constancia after my mother's own dead mother; and three, ensuing gynaecological complications for the patient, who underwent an expedient, if, as it transpired, unnecessary hysterectomy in her thirty-third year—my age now.)

MY NAME IS Santiago Moore Zamora, but my mummy, who is Spanish, calls me Iago when she likes. My father is English. I am six years old. Today is my birthday. I was born on 28th May, the feast of Corpus Christi. And today, though not a holy holiday, is the last such day that I shall spend at the house of my birth: future ones will pass at boarding school abroad and, I suppose, beyond. But now I'm sitting in the breakfast room for the first time. My mummy has her breakfast later, poised high on her high bed, with a posy on her tray. My father has gone to his office long ago. Still, Nanny is here, and Cook's about, and the sun is shiny, and the sprinklers are chugging on the grass. Happy Birthday to me.

Ever since I was a little boy, my birthday chair has always been a special one, decked and adorned with flowers and leaves like a throne; and today, though I am sitting on a proper grown-up chair known as a carver, today is no exception: for this, my latest (final) birthday throne is of a beauty full: its legs and arms and back are planted with palm leaves like spears or high fans, arranged for me by Cook, I think, or her husband who's called Gardener. And the back of the chair, which when undressed is heavily carved in wood, is today laced and over-laced with tendrils of ivy in many waxy greens; and on the seat, one upon the other, sits a pair of cushions that I have never seen before in a colour called vermilion and a cloth of damask silk, plumpy cushions with tassels like golden grapes at the corners, and fringing, and, at the soft centre, a garland, shaped like the heart of a lady, with African violets embroidered, and miniature daisies, and ivory strawberries, and occasional tufts of moss. And spread about the palm leaves of my birthday throne, are, like a painting or a dream, real roses of red, and dahlias, which are flowers of jollity, and sweet-peas in pale blue and pinky white, which do not really smell or last but my mummy calls divine, and yellow carnations, like sponges, where I rest my arms; and behind me, looking startled above my head, twin purple-and-orange strelitzias, which means, for they do resemble, birds of paradise.

This my anniversary tablecloth, which smells of soap or summer fruits, of something imprecise but strong, falls to the floor like a vestment, and appears, at the corners, to be pushed out by ghostly linen knees, paler than vanilla milk. And this cloth, though starched to fresh rigidity, is older, richer in birthdays than I; for every faultless stitch along the border of its broad and oscillating hem was rendered hollow, one by one and perfectly, by my mother in the afternoons of the days of the months when she sat, not thinking, garnering her trousseau.

My parents were married on Christmas Eve, two years before my birth, at the chapel of the convent which my mother attended; but it was not a grand affair, their wedding, for her father, my abuelo, is said to have contracted such a virulent exception to the match that the event was restricted to what Spaniards of a certain swagger term *petit comité*. And yet, despite the pursed discretion of the occasion, insular folklore relates that my mother, the loveliest ice-organza bride of her day, wept disconsolately, and without maids in attendance, throughout the religious ceremony; and further, that no sooner returned from the honeymoon, which conveyed the newlyweds to Palermo by night, thence to Portofino and on to Venice, where she first became homesick in her waterlogged hotel, and via the Vatican to Fommentor and Barcelona, then back, at last, to the embrace of their hesperidian isle, my mother dragged her melted, wilted wedding dress up the servants' stairs to the sewing room, where she instructed the sempstress to unpick each seam and stow away the diaphanous great skirts of her miserable matrimony: skirts which were, in due course, to be released from their paper tissue pupa and chrysalized into the gossamer wings of my first crib.

SIX YEARS ON, I'm trying to smooth down the hardened breakfast cloth, which threatens to engulf my legs in its folds as I survey the festive promontory on the long table before me. Nanny secures the corner of a napkin to my neck with a safety pin of gold, which pierces, then emerges from the Peter Pan collar of my primary-school pinafore. The napkin reaches down to my knees. My feet, buttoned into sandals, swing about as if I were perched on a branch of hope. I think I'm smiling at the array which, like a great necklace of jewelled stones, or islands, or planets, grows outwards from my sides and sweeps in a lavish curve as far as the opalescent glass comport, a legacy of my mother's unhappy honeymoon, which, these days, bears honeycombs of butter and crystal jars of syrup and plum-tomato jam and, like a neutral principality, divides Nanny's dull end of the table from mine.

Some of the presents before me are large, some not, but all, with one diminutive exception near the centre, look covetable, wrapped in brilliant sheets of tissue, and cellophane like stained glass, and decked in dancing patterns of dice and air-balloons and dominoes, and candy stripes and tangerine tartan, and frigates and sailors and pirates, and embellished with watery bands of moiré and ribbons of wired taffeta. Yet I cannot reach half these birthday fruits alone. Nanny's going to have to help me. Nanny? Please? She looks across and—First, she announces, we breakfast like grown-ups, birthday or no, *then* we can open our (our?) prizes, which she calls Gifts. I cannot think that I'm still smiling.

Nanny is spooning up her cornflakes and sipping, slurping really—Mam'zelle would have died—her cup of special particular tea which is posted to her from a London street called Pecadillo or Piccaninny or some such thing; and Nanny says it is a special street and very special tea indeed and grey, though, from where I sit, it looks like a perfectly normal tea to me, the colour of sweet consommé. And my mummy told me in a whisper once that no lady, or gentleman come to that, should even think of drinking El Grey tea before the proper time for scented tea which is at four in the afternoon and not at breakfast; but never, she said, mind.

So, breakfast. Mine unfolds in careful stages, like a play, and opens with the juice of three carrots, freshly uprooted from the kitchen garden, and scrubbed and peeled and shredded and pulped and liquefied by Cook, who's just made her entrance in the breakfast room. She winks in my direction and, swinging her huge, hilarious hips to the rhythms of a soundless folk *Isa,* which, for fear of puncturing Nanny's seemly English air, she dare not hum, much less whistle, which is what she does while washing up, she slow-waltzes her espadrilled way to my throne. Bowing with comical reverence over my left side, she strokes my back with her free hand and now drums it with her great fingers, as if mine were the back of a battered, but unbroken, old guitar—which nearly makes me burst out laughing; but Nanny, engrossed in the final shovellings of her cereal, doesn't catch us. With a theatrical swing of her other arm, Cook now presents me with my juice, in its usual Russian tea-glass, with its matching frosted saucer, on which, to one side, to the left as always, lie two bright carrot-leaves and the crescent of a lime. And I take the crescent between my middle-finger and thumb and, without squinting, without flinching, squeeze it over the mouth of the tall glass into the carrot juice, which is more intensely orange than the juice of any orange, or any blossoming sun. I stir my drink with a spindly silver spoon, and I remember Mam'zelle who went away. And then I raise the liquid to my lips, and drink it in one smooth motion, silent, my gullet open as that of a mute, resentful bird which, starved of sound, can only swallow its imaginary song. And as the empty glass lands back on its saucer, Cook returns to the room.

She moves more purposefully this time, bearing aloft, as befits a proud feat or trophy, and on a silver salver with three lions' claws which, far from clawing, seem tamely to paddle in the rippling morning light, my egg, medium-boiled, which I prefer, and pinkly-pied, and poised, as if in an open carriage, on its ivory cup, ivory with a tinily-engraved band like a fine belt for a young girl—the egg-cup which my abuela won when she was young and a girl at a tennis championship before the Nautical Club existed, before even my mummy and her dolls existed, at the (I can't make out the spidery inscription) in the days when they say that this volcanic, mid-Atlantic isle of ours was, truly, paradisal.

Cook shadows over me, interrupting my shoulder to remove the emptied glass; and after a couple of slow seconds have elapsed behind me, introduces, with a slight rattle, the next installment of my breakfast, the egg. I take up a small knife that is almost a butter one, with a mother of pearl handle but a serrated blade, and, forgetting briefly that the egg is but an egg, supposing instead that it's the head of someone not exactly far away, I deal it one good blow. The crown gapes open, creaks almost, and then, to my very glee, it plonks pathetically onto the plate below—plain white, a boring plate, really.

I pick up a small spoon of gold that does not tarnish or taste tangy, and start to investigate the veinless yolk which, even if unveined, I dread to pierce. When I was less than six, and took my meals in the alcove beside the kitchen where Cook does sometimes sneak to make her pastry, I was allowed to dunk a toasty soldier in the crater of my egg and dunking always did the trick in those straightforward days; but now that I have moved into the breakfast room for grown-ups, Nanny says that soldiers will no longer do, and I suspect that she is looking at me now, in wait, so I must act, and lance the yolk without a toast or soldier, lance it with my spoon, like so, and done it is; and out, after a spurt, the yellow smoothly oozes, threatening to overflow. Quick-quickly I dig the spoon into the jelly-white and excavate the lump to allow the liquid of the egg to curl into the scoop and form a pool and stop a more disgusting mess, which I have done, but only just, and just in time, and I am starting not to like this everyday boiled egg; but if I eat and eat without a breath or thought, soon breakfast will be done and over with. Nanny turns a wing of her newspaper and pretends to be behind it. But do not think that I am fooled: she could still catch me.

COOK IS BACK, thank God, and though my head is down and I am putting down my spoon, I'm looking at her hard, and harder still I pray that, though I haven't finished by a long chalk, she will pick up my egg and take away its ugliness and straighten out my birthday morning— which, yes, is what she mercifully does. Next: a prickly pear of amber-green complexion, which Cook, with Gardener's gloves, in case, has from our spiralled cactus tree pulled down; and she has snapped away the painful spikes and scrubbed, under a tap of brass, the fruit; and she has lain it on a wooden slab and taken up a kitchen knife and brought the knife down sharply, thus, and thus again, truncating both the ends, which are like elbows of a bogeyman; and she has sent the severed elbows in a wide arc like a rainbow through a shaft of morning light into the furthest of the noisy metal bins, which is reserved for dumping pods and bones and rinds and skins and apple-cores for the wild boars which she keeps captured in a dry reservoir near her home on a hill called the country. And though I have not ever met these boars, Cook has made their scary noise for me and laughed out loud, predicting that her Gardener soon will slaughter one in honour of his brother's bride-to-be when she becomes a bride which means a wedding belle. For boars, Cook says, and Gardener agrees, can be, when roasted out of doors, beasts of special succulence. And the prickly pear, also a thing of succulence, though not a beast, is, once plucked, soft and warm and regularly bumped, like the peel of the belly of an ostrich. And the belly of the pear before me is neatly cut from side to side. And I'm allowed to use my hands.

I tease at the gash, struggle with it till the pinkish innards of the cactus slide out of their sweating yellowing husk, and plop, exhausted and stillborn, onto the porcelain. But slicing is easy: the knife works mechanically, like a toy saw, through the skinless body, which falls away in neat wheels, collapsing to the side. The bony pips squirm, like maggots, as I push the posthumous flesh into my face, which begins to bloat; I cannot swallow; can scarcely breathe; am about to retch, when Nanny lowers a corner of her newspaper and declares across: Eat up now, slice at a time, no need to be greedy. I am munching like a cow; can hear myself. I look down, then lift the napkin fast, and hurriedly void the contents of my foul mouth into it, pretending to be calm, but I think of Mam'zelle again, and return the lumpy cloth, crumpled and warming, to the shame of my thigh. On my birthday.

I sink back into the floral throne, defeated, deflated, to think. I don't know where to look. I look to the shadows. Nanny comes into gradual focus as she forces her napkin into its ring and consults her watch and clicks her specs and vanishes her paper away; and then I hear her loudly proclaim, as if triumphantly, to the kingdom of my prizes, which is lost: Oh dear, we have taken far too long, have we not, yes indeed, and look, not even properly finished our especially delicious breakfast which Cook took trouble to prepare; hardly what one would expect of grown-up boys of six who've been allowed into the breakfast room for the first time, is it? More like the behaviour of a silly baby, very silly indeed because as a result we haven't left ourselves sufficient time to open all these glorious-looking gifts, not if our Birthday Boy's to get to school in time. Driver Pepe must be waiting by the car, doubtless wilting in this heat, poor man.

Everything, says Nanny, must be left untouched for later, lunchtime at the earliest, when Mummy and Daddy are here, and they can decide. I am dumbfounded, blank; but Nanny, like some darkening great queen, now turns to leave the room and, as she strides towards the hall, booms back: And you can get down from that ridiculous throne. Now. And then, she's gone.

I HAVE TO MOVE FAST: dump the sodden napkin on the table cloth, scramble over the embroidered cushions, crouch onto the table, crawl in a meanderline towards the centre, stretch out and grab the tiny, most ordinary-looking prize, which no one will notice has gone, and I stuff it into the pocket of my school pinafore. And now, over the arm of the carver I go, and back down to the floor; and next I'm sprinting over the dark Persian flowers of the carpet, and across the parquet, and past my distorted reflection on the samovar between the windows, and through the pair of lacquer screens that lead back to the hall, which smells of lilies, and sounds of a clock. Nanny is opening the front door. I snatch my satchel from the console and, for the first time that I recall, I race out into the light, down those long steps of stone.

I stop to look. Beyond the visor of my hand, I see, stationed by the flamboyants, which this year are late to blossom, my father's gleaming black motor, waiting to take me to school. As Pepe turns towards me, a yawn of cigarette smoke spins out of his shaded face, spirals beside him briefly, then dissolves into the morning. I reach the passenger door ahead of him, but cannot open it. He does it for me. I step into the creamy interior and, before I've managed to position myself properly, the door, with a padded thud, has closed. We set off without a word. He sucks the final breath out of his cigarette, then flicks it reeling through his open window to the blistered tarmac of the drive. He switches on the wireless. A foreign song from England, or perhaps America. I rummage in my pocket and extract the little package lifted from the breakfast table. It is wrapped in brown paper, and tightly strung, and stamped from a land that begins with a B, with the face of a king, and my heart is everywhere. I bite at the knot and wrench the string round a hard corner, and pull away the paper, and am filled without warning with the scent of oranges from the past. Within the paper folds, there sits a small, domed, purple leather box, and, inside the box, which is lined with purple velvet, a thwarted dream, look, from my departed Mam'zelle who went away but never did forget the thing I wanted most in all the world for this my sixth anniversaire, which once I did to her confess, and here it is: a grown-up ring, with a setting like a crown, and, in the crown, a huge, cut-glassy oval stone known as an Esmerald, which is greener than a thousand 7-Ups lined on a wall against the setting sun.

When I take the ring with care out of its cushioned bed and put it on the palm of my hand, it does not feel too heavy, which is good. And though, when I come to try it on, it flips right over because the golden hoop must be too large, I need not worry. This ring is so well-thought that you can squeeze the hoop and make it quite more small. Which I do. But my fingers still seem loose and slidy, until, at last, the esmerald from my Mam'zelle who went away glides onto the fore of my fingers, which is your index and never for pointing, and the ring is perfect, fit for a pontiff.

Pepe rounds a corner and I'm suddenly aware of loud squawks from the school yard, the screeches of many children in flight, and I find myself secretly longing for the quietness of my nursery, and for days gone by, and for the scented stillness of my vanished Mam'zelle. There is pain around my throat. There is damp around my eyes. We have stopped. The passenger door opens. I get out. Pepe has no cap and does not speak to me. I tell him, as I step onto the pavement, that today is my *anniversaire*. And Pepe peers far down until his stare meets my right hand. And That, he says, pointing hard, is a Sissy Ring; now get to class. I do not even bother to look back, for Pepe does not know a thing and he is smelly.

MY SCHOOL LOOKS over a square with a floor of Andalusian tiles, and a central fountain of china swans spouting watery rhymes to the sky. My school looks like a castle in a book from olden times, with pointy turrets of fish-scales, and tall granitty stairs, and railings painted in silver, and an everlasting palm tree at the front. And children are everywhere, huge and wild and flapping and screaming about. The bell has rung. I must go up, three flights, to the infant class. I clench my fist. But at least I can feel the heat of the ring in my hand.

This is how my class goes: twenty low desks in a circle with a high desk at the front, which belongs to our teacher, Don Jesús, who has a face with cheeks that flush, and a dark moustache. His suit is always of a stripy grey, and the tips of his collar are pinned down under his tie. His shoes are large and black with little holes, and his hands are fat and puffed, with many great hairs from the knuckles to the cuffs. He is not a priest, which often teachers are, for he does not wear a skirt of any kind. But what he does wear, in the pocket of his jacket, is a hankie, bright with flowers.

The day begins with a prayer, standing up. Then we sit down. The lesson is a drawing one and we must draw a happy house to fill with colour. And while we draw, Don Jesús returns our homework to us, one by one. My mind is in blank. Is it Spelling that he's handing back? But anyway, my turn won't come till near the end, because although my

English surname, Moore, falls near the middle of the Spanish alphabet, there are lots of B and C boys in this class, not really friends of mine. Yet by the time I hear myself called out, I feel the butterflies. I do not think they show, although my pinafore gets caught on a corner of the desk as I get up. The class is in hush. I hear traffic outside as I walk over the tiles to the teacher. I stand by his side. He smiles and always breathes too loud somehow. And I see him see my ring. He sees everything. He winks, and whisperingly asks about it. So I explain, not loud and looking down, that today is my birthday, and the ring, a present from my Mam'zelle who went away and calls my birthday my *anniversaire*. And the butterflies do start to rise but I must not, not cry. Which I do not, for I am six now. And as I watch his pencil-hand hover over my words, which were correctly spelt—for it says B for *Bien* in red at the bottom of the page—I feel his other, big, warm hand moving down the back of my thigh, then up, and upper to my shorts, and down. And I say nothing. And although there is a sort of shame, it does feel nice. And then he gives me back my spelling-book and I return to my place and the rest of the morning melts away until, somewhere in the midst of chanted multiplications, the bell rings out, and I wake up, and Pepe must be back with the car. But I wait for the stampede to pass before I go down.

AT HOME ALL IS CHANGED, gone dark, grown cool. Shutters drawn against the midday sun. Beeswax and flowers. Gleaming floors. But in the breakfast room, look: presents all gone. Table: covered in trays that are covered with tea-cloths, damp. Sandwiches in shadow. Row upon dewy row; serried ranks of cheese and cucumber, and watercressed egg, and mustardy ham. My throne: also vanished. I turn about, and walk. Dump satchel in the hall. Think of school and Don Jesús as I march towards the kitchen and push open the swing-door and am struck without warning by the heat and the disorder. A wild commotion. Cook is leaning over her sink, which is a battleship of pans, issuing instructions through the window, telling someone outside in the garden to hurry, hurry up, that's fine, yes, back a bit, fine, there, stop, for heaven's sake, just leave it there.

I ask if anybody's going to help me undo my pinafore. Cook tells me to come over here and promise to be good because we're busy getting ready for the—there, take the pinafore—the party. Her word smacks me across the forehead. What party? Yours, you silly boy, like last year, remember, when you were given the swing and the slide and all those other children came along and the magician did a . . . Cook is cut short, because now Nanny strides into the steam and all goes quiet. She's wearing her going-out uniform with starchy hat and cuffs and her bright badge, but I have my ring on my hand. Where have all my presents gone?, I ask. Nanny takes my hand without answering, squeezing the esmerald without meaning to, and leads me away into the still rooms of the house.

No sooner out of earshot than her prattle starts: First, young man, we're going to the hall to pick up the satchel which, as we very well know, we've been told a thousand times, belongs not—and don't drag that pinafore—anywhere that happens to take our fancy, but, quite so, in the nur-se-ry, where we'll find a tray with a light lunch. The breakfast room is full of preparations for the party. And your presents, which are upstairs, you can open after lunch.

And my mummy, will she be there when I open my prizes?

Your parents are both busy at the minute, but you're to join them over coffee in the study before you wash and change for the party. Now come along and hurry. Of course you're not tired. Ridiculous notion.

LOOKING BACK, I seem to muddle the presents from that particular birthday with presents of other early years—always stylishly wrapped, yet their substance somehow disheartening, richly dull, which I presume is why, all this time on, as I struggle in search of a truth for you, the general inappropriateness of those objects seems to eclipse more specific details, harder facts. If, for clues, I attempt to rummage through an imaginary catalogue of toys likely to have been given to a child in Spain in the mid-Sixties, my visual memory blurs instantly, fails me, and merges with another, more nebulous but more pervasive faculty: emotional recall. And what I recall is a sense of abasement akin to receiving a trick chocolate and having to smile at the joke, of having to pretend to appreciate a thing which fundamentally one does not. And coupled with this discomfort comes an instant need for its conceal-ment, in order not to cause offence, not at any cost, even if the cost be dishonesty, and even if I am alone, for no amount of privacy can dispel disappointment, or diminish feelings that might seem out of joint.

What little I can tell you about this birthday party I owe, in fact, to a photograph which, over a decade later, while clearing out, I was to find lodged at the back of a bureau in my old bedroom. The date is written faintly in pencil on the back. The shot, taken in the garden, is aimed vaguely at a tree—an avocado, I think—much of which is missed: only the trunk and a segment of a branch can be seen. The bottom of the picture, which is the only section in true focus, is crowded with the backs of heads, swung up, of children whom I suspect I knew as scarcely then as, now, they are recognizable. But something about those soft napes, untouched as yet by barbers' clippers, and those gleaming ponytails, tied back with the pastel velvet ribbons which were then in fashion, feels, to me, typical of the period. Hovering over the image of those children, you can almost smell the cologne that would have been sprinkled onto their heads, almost feel the hot pudginess of those greedy little hands, wanting more sweets forever.

Around the blurred edges of the discoloured image are some nannies, variously uniformed, holding the odd small cardigan and smiling a little sardonically, almost competitively, past one another. But at the centre of the scene, which presumably explains why the shot ever came into my property, you can see me, aged six, knock-kneed, fat-arsed, caught turning awkwardly away from the camera, my mouth twisted into a tentative grin. I am stuffed into the classic party clothes of the era—white poplin shirt, with pleated front and short sleeves; pale shorts, of a yellowish cream, which seem to button at the sides; white ankle-socks, turned down, and, improbably, white lace-up shoes. My eyes are covered by some dark sort of blindfold, and I seem to be trying to hold up what looks like a broomstick. Above me, from the branch, hangs the *piñata,* a staple effigy at children's parties in those days; perhaps, for all I know, a staple still. Fashioned of *papier maché,* embellished with fringes of crêpe paper, and loaded with streamers and trumpets and treats, this particular one, which is almost bigger than I am, is intended, I suspect, to resemble Charlie Chaplin.

The point of the *piñata* game, which has always struck me as self-defeating, is that each child, in dreary turn, be blindfold and armed with a stick and given three tries at cracking open the effigy, so that eventually its colourful entrails spill forth and cascade onto the children. And I say it's self-defeating because, by the time the supposed victor, the child who has brought about this torrent of wonderful things, manages to remove the blindfold and to put down the stick, the rest of the company has grabbed all the goodies. And try telling the empty-handed winner to cheer up and not to be spoilt because the last shall be first in the kingdom of heaven.

Observing the photograph slightly more closely, I notice that on my white-knuckled fingers, which are gripping the broomstick, there's no sign of the treasured green ring which Mam'zelle had sent and I had with such pride put on to go to school that morning. And now, as if it were then, the whole incident floods back—not so much the memory of being shoved blind into the centre of the clearing under the tree; nor my three pathetic failed attempts at hitting the effigy (or was I just pretending to miss?); nor even the jeers of derision from older cousins and their nannies, whom I could tell had joined in, along with assorted other creeps, my beautiful treacherous mother included; no: what floods back still is the grief, for, inflated as it sounds, I do think grief is what sank me when I discovered the loss of that precious ring, which Nanny would doubtless have deemed a common, nasty, unsuitable thing, and spirited away while I was changing, that's when she would have done it. And next I recall standing by the garden gates at the start of the party, and being told to greet other strange infants, and being nagged, over and over, to thank them for the presents that they were carrying, probably their own repackaged rejects; and then, bang, I realize, and panicking, suddenly need to rush upstairs, desperately to look for my missing trophy, and I even ask permission to do so, which of course is denied me, until at last, like a fool, I grasp Nanny's trickery. To this day I can picture that visage of hers, arched with simulated ignorance as she offers me—Silly boy, what a fuss about nothing—her snide assurance that tomorrow she will help me find the ring, when in my bones I know with a terminal, adult certainty that my most prized possession is gone, and gone for good; and I can still see, as if they were being exchanged at this instant, covert winks being trafficked by grown-ups above me; and I can practically summon still the tears which my rage could ill contain but my pride could not permit to be seen. And yet, oddly—such is the resilience of memory, or its selective fickleness—I now seem, in mid-reminiscence, to break off, as if bored, and my party seems to lead into, merge with, indeed become, some further party, later that day perhaps, or perhaps on some other evening. For what now enters my head is a much larger, lusher affair, nothing to do with children.

Up in my bedroom, although my light has been turned out, I'm wide awake, not so much because of the lingering evening heat and the pink sun which splashes onto my shutters, as on account of the bustle downstairs, and the mysterious sound of adult laughter, and the noise of high shoes, clicketty-clacking on the parquet, and the air of flirtatious excitement. I creep out of bed and, not daring to open the door to spy through the banisters, I go, instead, to the window and, from there, watch the activity unfolding in the garden. Much later, at boarding school in England, where I imagine that, as respite from the misery of cross-country runs during hailing winter afternoons, other boys perhaps sought comfort in fantasies of being at home, sitting cosily by a fire, toasting crumpets with long forks, or playing Monopoly with their siblings while the family spaniel lay snoring about, I would seek escape from the gloom and the splattering mud and the stench of pig manure which, for me, was to become integral to that whole landscape, by remembering snatches of scenes from the parties which my parents used to give for the beautiful people of their small island all those summers ago under the ocean stars.

Envisage the women of my childhood, alighting at our house from their highly polished, slightly old-fashioned motorcars and being led with studied casualness through the courtyard, round the high palm tree, by their husbands, who, for the most part, wore tuxedos during the hot months, and whose bronze heads, slicked back, would incline to meet and almost kiss the satin hands extended to them by other men's wives. Savour the rising American tobacco, and the Parisian fragrances which filtered through that house; and picture the smoke of chiffon stoles floating back from the necks of those powdered women and fluttering, as if whispering, behind them; listen to the swish of their shantung shifts as they head for oval silver platters, borne high, from which, expertly, scarcely glancing, they pluck a glass of something chilled and strong and tropical. And you can hear the clinking and the surprising, and greetings in various colonial languages and, once in an occasional while, a trill of delight as some young girl, recently married and new to the art of hosting parties, steps out onto the terrace and marvels at the set where, soon, dinner will be served on white-skirted tables round the swimming pool, which tonight, on my mother's instructions, has been covered with a glistening floor of parquet so that guests may, in due course, dance.

I'm peering down through the slats. The falling night is decked with paper lanterns—rust, green, amber, occasionally ivory—which glow suspended from the high bamboo trees lining the walls of the garden. As people begin to drift through the terrace into the cool stillness outside, onto the darkening grass, they break off in small groups, or couples, or, every so often, into pairs of young women walking arm in arm and laughing superbly, their pearlescent lips casually parted, their gigantic lashes blackened, their elaborate hairpieces tilted back. From up here, high, I see an elderly accordionist appear at the edge of the scene and start to wander about, weaving old Spanish melodies into the gathering, shrugging his shoulders this way and that, half-bowing as he advances. But the women, hearing themselves serenaded with old tangos and *fandangos,* tunes from way back, from the romances unknown of their own mothers, seem, after inadvertently striding in time for a few bars, to grow nostalgic and pause, and to turn to one another, trying to recall the words of some particular, particularly saccharine line, which now they chant out, half-embarrassed, half-convulsed, like the convent-girls that they were not so far into the past; and then they amble on, smiling separately, a little distractedly, slowly to return to their earlier subject—their own unflavoured marriages, perhaps—and as they stroll under the lanterns, which highlight them momentarily, ethereally, they seem to become ghosts of themselves, then pass. Starched servant-girls, with aprons that cross at the back, tied into stiff bows of excessive size, pursue such wayward guests, with the pretext of canapés, out of the shadows and back to the heart of the party, where my mother, whom I can distinguish only by the ostrich hem of her tunic of sand gazaar, is darting about with a zest unknown to me, at once kissing cheeks and holding out her high hand and trying to steer people towards their respective tables, which flicker with long candles planted into bowls of bloodshot camellias.

As guests begin to take their seats, gilt chairs with backs like fans, I hear, then see tuning up, a small band, discreetly lit on a low podium at a slight distance from the furthest diners. The accordionist is up there now, next to a guitarist, and behind them, a drummer; and seated cross-legged, some other character plucking a mandolin, while, at the front of the platform, standing by a microphone, a fifth performer, with a head of black gelatine and a shirt of frilly icing, wields a gaudy electric guitar. But the sound, when the group first strikes up, is so subdued that you're hardly aware of it, and to begin with rises only in gentle waves above the drone of the diners, deferring to the racket of cutlery and to shrill outbursts of laughter; yet, as the merriment grows, so, gradually, does the prominence of these performers, who, around coffee time, begin to play in earnest. And now the accordion, which is like a full heart, begins to swell and contract in that childish, enquiring way that it has; and the electric guitar properly to slide; and the plectrum of the mandolin to pluck; and the metal brush to stroke and tease at the snare-drum as the voices of the band mingle and chant, in the syrupy, high-pitched harmony that was then the style, hopeless lyrics about hopeless, shipwrecked love. But the effect, for all of the hopelessness, is so sublime that you could be in Hawaii tonight, I swear to you, hoola-hooping on its honey-coloured coastline with hibiscuses garlanded about you. And next, unable to resist the lure of the musicians, some couple unknown to me, not my parents, a younger pair, smiling, rise and, as if this were their own party, take to the floor and open the dance; and the people from their table start to cheer and to clap at the sheer enchanting audacity; and the growing applause spreads out to embrace the members of the band, who beam back delightedly. I can see that the dancing man has an arm wrapped around the woman's low-cut back, while his other holds her right hand up, to the moon; and as they turn and turn again and again, her glittering bracelet catches the light. But now she signals excitedly, and exhorts her dinner compan-ions to join her—Come-on-you-lot-you-promised, she shouts, as if caught-out—and by the time that I've fetched a cushion to make myself comfortable, a whole crowd has leapt up to dance; and you should see the sudden burst of colour, like a float at carnival-time; and now the band is in full swing, no holds barred, and the beat is growing more frantic, and people are spinning and whirling, and some of them are even dancing apart, and changing partners over and over, and suddenly, at last, I see my mummy down there among them, arm in arm with some man whom I can't quite make out, my father most likely, and every time her head turns towards the house I hope that she will glance up to my shutters, and I hope it for a patient while. But she doesn't—which doesn't really matter, because as I climb, yawning, back into bed, I can still pretend to myself that I'm saying good night to her, and that I'm telling her that she's the most beautiful of all the mummies and that her party's been an absolute—what's that word which she likes?—triumph. And I remember, vividly, awaking the morning after, and finding, floating about the granite tiles, like kisses blown, like promises forgotten, wisps of feather, warm as sand.

MY MOTHER STANDS in ballerina slippers in the linen room upstairs, ironing an evening dress which makes you think of an enormous gaping flower. She says you cannot trust the servants with organza. Layer after layer of skirt she lifts and turns inside out, with gestures rhythmic as nocturnal waves unfolding onto a coastline. The dew of her spray-starch clings to the heavy air in tiny pearly bubbles which, when you peer at the window that frames her profile, you can see refusing to burst, struggling to survive, but in the end floating down the peachy light, to drown. I am sitting on a stool by the door; my back, warm against the wall of papered violets; my head, conscious of the ivory lightswitch next to it with its twin buzzer. Her slowered motions fascinate me—the way she steers her iron, the way it sails heavily along the scalloped shores of her ball-gown, the fizzing sound it makes as it navigates the frothy patches of starch, the clouds of scented vapour, like incense, which result, the mounting mounds of pale diaphanous stuff, like chalky cliffs, behind her arm, which, in a rolled-up shirtsleeve, now removes the iron and parks it on its rack. Her bracelet jingles with charms as the painted tips of her fingers raise a further layer of underskirt—the seventh that I've counted—delicately up and over, to make way for the next, paler than dust, which she now smoothes out along the calico-quilted board before starting to iron. Sometimes she sighs;

and yet, if you ask why, she seems not to notice you, hardly answers. Occasionally, if pressed, she might momentarily gaze at the wall in front of her and say, half-absently, that she doesn't really know (which is a lie), that having me watch her makes her uncomfortable (which is more like it); and then she will resume her ironing, even humming sometimes; and then I will pretend to swivel my attention, because, although she mesmerizes me, I feel embarrassed, impolite; and instead I peer into the open cupboard behind her, with its shelves of faded gingham boxes brimming with treasures from, I don't know, before she was married: creamy flowers of faille that may once have sprouted from her hip, or shoulder, or from beneath the brim of some picture-hat; glittering buttons that I vaguely recognize from photographs around the house; a sewing-basket that plays a waltz when its lid is lifted; secret bits of history and haberdashery and stifled passion. But I do not think that turning my attention to such objects can improve matters, because, sooner or later, she always seems to say: Aren't you getting a bit old to be dawdling about doing nothing, what on earth's become of Nanny? And with that final word, she lands the iron on its backside, walks to where I am, aims her hand somewhere close to my head and, exhaling resignedly, presses the buzzer three times, which— give or take the minute it takes Nanny to arrive—means, as it always did, Off you go now.

My mother kneels on the circus-rug at the foot of my bed, arched over an open wooden box with corners studded like a trunk, but smaller, into which you can tuck secrets if you want to, which is why it's called a Tuck-Box. One of her slippers is slipping off but I don't suppose that she can have noticed, because she's busy flustering over a roll of shiny, papery plastic with a sticky back that makes a squishing noise and is causing her aggravation. And collapsed about her lie her tape measure from the waltzing basket, and a pencil with a crimson tassel, and an India rubber, pink and blue, and huge scissors which must weigh a ton; and everywhere about are curls of shaven scraps in chaos. The paper that she's trying to cut has brightly coloured shapes with heavy outlines, called cartoons—a dog and a boat and a tree and a clown—and although she's too occupied to explain things to me, I think that she wants to stick the sticky paper in the box, inside, to line it.

In the afternoon we're going to the photographer's, my mummy and I, for me to have my picture taken for a book not meant for reading, called a passport. And I must wear, she says, a tie for the first time for this, which she knows how to do up because she used to wear one in her day, when she was younger and went riding at gymkhanas; and she tells me to keep still for just one second, would I, and to stand in front of her, and face the mirror on the dressing-table, and to stop, for once, bombarding her with questions over and over; I'm giving her a migraine. She says she's sure I'll learn to do my own tie soon enough, but her voice sounds wobbly to me, like when you know you're not to cry. This tie is Scots, which means a type of tartan—grey and blue and bottle-green with now-and-then a tiny yellow stripe—but it is not a happy one, which I think would be red as a ladybird with dots dancing the polka. My hair she combs to the side, and makes a parting—boys to the left, girls to the right. My coat is flannel, double-breasted, and the collar, which is green as the ring that was lost from me, is upholstered in velvet. But she says I may not wear, although it is my favourite, my velvet beret with the petersham rosette. Not for a passport photograph; please don't be tedious.

A MATTER OF DAYS LATER, we're all on our way to the airport and squashed up in the back, me in the middle and my mummy dressed in tweed and Pepe wearing his cap and driving with a pile of luggage stacked beside him, plus in the boot, plus on the roof-rack, plus he's talking to my father through the mirror about a problem known as Franco, with the car even more loaded than the car is when we go down to the beach house in July. I have kissed goodbye to Cook and Gardener, who say that I must write to them from England in my neatest fountain-hand but not in English, or they will not understand, and then they laugh and say that they will miss me double-much. This is a joke, because the truth is that although I have an English Nanny at our house, I do not yet speak English rightly, nor escribe its spelling which can trick you up, other than my name, which is Santiago; but in English you write James; and to learn my father's language is a reason why we're going to England now, my mummy says, and to make the Friends Who Last Your Lifetime. (I think that I may miss my Cook and Gardener.)

Today is the first time that I do climb upon a plane, which is exciting 'cos an aeroplane does fly as high as any kite and faster than a train, but you must promise not to be sea-sick in the sky, which sometimes people are, which is not brave nor, Nanny says, considerate. Nanny has to stay behind upon our island, but the sight of us, readied and packed and on our way out, gives her, she says she must confess, a nostalgia for Blighty, and you could easily call this feeling a homesickness, but not if you're Nanny who must be brave and considerate as she waves a hand and wishes us Bon Voyage, which means au revoir in the language of my Mam'zelle who went away—but none of this will make it easier for Nanny or her homesickness one jot, or even an iota small as an ant. Because I did not forget about the vanished esmerald.

In the plane I'm allowed to have a window seat, which has a view, and my mummy's going to sit beside me, and on her other side will sit my father, who calls a corridor an Isle—if ever, he says, he's given a chance. She straps my safety belt as tight as it will go but still it feels loose around me. She says to never mind. She hands her camel coat up to my father. She removes her gloves and her sunglasses and puts them in various pockets of her handbag. She undoes her silken headscarf, which ripples with reins and stirrups and bridles, and knots it round the handle of her crocodile bag. Now she closes her eyes, as if she had one of those headaches that she says are confounded; and when the plane at last kicks off with a great rumbling Vroom down in the deep of your tummy, she makes a sign of the cross, which means, she says, asking God to grant us safe passage. This does not mean an Isle.

We have landed now, but it is dark. Through the rain we're driven in a high black cab, like the one in the toy garage, and I'm going backwards on a seat that flips down, captivated by the sight of receding rows of identical houses, unpainted but beamed and bricked and stained-glassed, moving away round long distant bends and vanishing; and there's the constant intermittent glow of Catseyes on the carriage-way, blinks in the night; and splashes like tiny fishes hitting the approaching headlights; and, inside the car, there's the exhausting lullaby of windscreen wipers, and I suppose I must have drifted off into some sleep, because, next thing, there is a jolt; and I can hear voices announcing that we've arrived; and now we're driving up to a white hotel with flags from many countries waving in the middle of a town that must be London, and the taxi-doors are opened from outside, and open hands in gloves assist us to the ground after our travels, and lead us up the front steps, as if we were smart but exhausted fingers going into my mother's doll's-house, into the hall inside, and we're swept into a lift that goes many floors up. My room is pallid green, like water when you get out of the bath, and the lamp-light by the bed is fuzzy-dull. The candlewick bedspread, like a garden scattered with ashes, is grey and embossed with grey flowers; and, if you stand very still in my room, you can't hear a sound, but you can smell the strong smell of ashtrays and of steamed suppers floating up from the dining room. And if you peer beyond the curtains, which are sticky to the touch, you will see a park even paler than ash, like sand after dusk, spread out before you and planted with a lake, and clouded with a mist that looks like the mist that you make when you suck a strong mint and breathe out.

I AM UP, and dressed already without Nanny, and with my parents I have been to breakfast in the dining room, which was fullish with ladies both elderly and smiling, and whispering waitresses, and a few sorts of grandfathers, and a very beardy man wearing a monocle, which doesn't mean my uncle, stuck to his eye. And also we have been to a shop with many floors like an hotel but with a staircase made of iron that rises as you climb and is an Eskilator, and you must keep your wits about you the whole time because if you mislay your wits about you for one second even and forget to jump at the last second Off, you could get swallowed by the metal teeth and gobbled up.

And we have carried many shopping bags downstairs and back away with us, of uniforms of clothes like jumpers with a stripe to wear for when I meet the friends who last your lifetime, and shorts that look too long for me, I think, and shirts both grey and white; no nightshirts: striped pyjamas; and ties to wear on weekdays, green and white, and one plain dark one, almost black, for Holy Days and Sundays, and a suit of worsted charcoal, and elastic garters to make sure your socks stay up, and, in one bulging bag, three burgundy rugger shirts and three pairs of football shorts, and different socks for games called sports I have not played, and plus, at the bottom of this biggest bag which my father carries, a cricketing blazer the colour of an esmerald which is a colour that reminds you but you're not allowed to wear until the summer term comes round after the autumn and the winter which is not yet now, for patience is a virtue.

Back in my parents' room at the hotel, I'm dazed by the sight of their beds, which are heaped with folded stacks of my new clothes, regulation items that couldn't be purchased earlier, at home, abroad. My mother is sitting in a quilted chair shaped like a shell, her legs crossed tight and held together as if bound, angled in a prim posture sharply to the right, her ankles rigid, her feet locked out in the manner of a decorous stocking advert. I, meanwhile, am hovering over a desk with stationery racks, complimentary Biros and a folded street-map, which lurks under the window at the far side. My father has just opened the door—to go out to a nearby pub in Kensington to meet old friends of his, who're called The Chaps and he claims not to've seen since he was a bachelor. He looms on the threshold, puffed up. My mother, immobile, looks small to me by contrast, reduced in stature, as if vanquished in this foreign land where, stripped of her native vassals and the riches of her language, she seems to have lost the power to conjure. Possibly she feels humiliated. Certainly she won't be humbled. I know my mother. I flow with her blood. Rage has frozen her over, paralysed her in her shell of quilted satin—but only momentarily. Suddenly she leaps to her feet and flies to the adjoining bathroom. My father stops in his tracks, closes the door, steps back inside. I hear the sound of her enamel pill-box being rattled; then, prized ajar. I recognize the snap of its clasp, which can be obstinate; there follows a respite of water, gluggelling into a toothmug. She must be swallowing her pill down. Silence. Keep quiet. And now she returns to the bedroom, a little sloppily, sulkily, dragging her body behind her like some exiled empress who, without warning, has found herself embroiled in a conspiracy that is beneath her. She makes for a cracked china vase that is propped on the mantel, a vessel conceived along classical lines which, at some stage, has been dropped and glued together in a hurry, so that arteries of dark adhesive run down it, but which, since, as if to camouflage the damage, has been bunged up with dried flowers, stiff and miserably coloured, beige and peach and lilac. And this is where my pathetic impoverished mother now runs, to fiddle with those tawdry stems, to tease at their desiccated petals—her back, though hunched, resolutely turned against my father. But from where I stand, a little anxious, I can observe her figure in profile: her breathing is consternated, her ribcage has grown frantic; her fine hands, so full of composure once, are apprehensive now; her lacquered fingers peck at the foliage erratically; the stars in her rings glint angrily; and although her bracelet jingles as it always does, its peal seems less carefree, more measured, somehow.

There ensues the first open quarrel that my parents ever held before my eyes; and even if my memory has admittedly repressed the most part, or perhaps because my shock at the time prevented me from absorbing the scene with any degree of accuracy, nevertheless there remains, ingrained in me, the image, the sight of them turned animal, like hounds baying at their shadows; he, aiming his growl at the door leading out; she, directing her howling diatribe toward the fire. I feel seized by a fear that she might shatter the vase, yet part of me wants her to do so, to prove to me her courage; and though I am shamed and disgusted by the revelation of my mother's latent violence, yet my sympathies somehow lie ensnared with her unhappiness. Neither she nor her husband is listening to the other, nor properly answering; rather, they are yelling simultaneously, though not in unison, and often in discordant languages. My mother is babbling in Spanish as she staggers over to her low cheap throne of quilted satin and dumps herself onto the sheen of its padding. Her legs do not cross now: they're stuck out, heels dug hard into the carpet. My father doesn't look at her, but keeps imploring, over and over, as if she were a fool, or in the clutches of hysteria: For goodness' sake my dear calm down—over and over. And she, the while, is shouting, over and over too, *Lo siento, lo siento muchísimo,* I'm sorry, I'm frightfully sorry—meaning not that she feels regret, but that she refuses, that she won't do whatever it is that he wants. And then, like the solution to some absurd enigma, comes, I remember, the fated mention of Nametapes, which I think is what must have ignited the flare-up. And although my mother's strength is beginning to flag, I surmise from my far corner that she's referring to all the things that need to be marked in time for my departure tomorrow: those mounds of dull clothes which lie heaped, like remnants gathered from some skirmish, upon the battlefield of their twin beds. And she's frightfully sorry, she says yet again, she can't be expected to manage without help, he should have thought of this whole problem earlier, she hasn't come to London to play the seamstress, the trip has all been of his making anyway, if he likes he can talk to the chamber-maids, they're bound to do the job if he pays, or he can ask the nuns at the Assumption if he prefers, not that she could care, not less, does she make herself plain? After which, switching tack minutely, she modulates from the problem of the clothes to the true heart of her problem, and she mumbles something about the boy being given a bit of attention and his last day with her, would a trip to Madame Tussaud's be too much to ask? And God, she exclaims, what a spectacle he's had to witness, it's a disgrace. Lamentable, she calls it, and suggests, in a burst of sanctimonious outrage, that her husband go to confession, and then, to my horror, she drops her beautiful head in her beautiful hands and wails as if this were her end. Which leaves me winded.

THE FIRST WORDS that he utters the next day, pacing about my room but facing out, as if addressing a crowd in the frosted park, are that we're running late thanks to my mother. Typical, he says. Never mind that there's a train to catch. Nothing to be done; woman simply will not hurry up, not for anything, nor anyone. (I like my mother's slow calm, her elegance.) Doesn't *know* the meaning of the words On Time—never did, matter of fact, practically drove your grandfather to drink, poor man. I explain, in case he doesn't understand, this frothing un-bridled father of mine, that my mother needs her length of time in order to become—and then I can't think of the word, and I say: Beau-tified. *Beautified?,* he splutters, What kind of pansy word is that? Be-a-ti-fied more like, which is what I deserve to be when I'm six foot under. I ask why. Why?, he shouts at the quaking window; Good God Man, for putting up with her ruddy nonsense every day of my life, hang it all. Beyond a joke. Drive one to drink. Wouldn't say no to a shot of brandy, matter of fact. I mean, it's not as if I mind how bally long she takes to get herself togged up; all I've ever asked is that we be Punctual. Punctual, that too much to ask? I tell you, he tells me, Though for heaven's sake don't tell your mother: number of Masses we've been to which, strictly speaking, haven't been valid because we've walked into church bang in the middle of the blasted Consecration (my father can be vulgar), well, it's beyond count. And is she ever embarrassed, one might be forgiven for wondering? Is she my arse (he really can). And has she ever, once in her life, so much as apologized? Oh no, not she. Woman couldn't care a damn, floats about with her head in the clouds like some blessed film star. Too blimming much. And, while we're on the subject, I'll have you know the same goes for dinner invitations, same exactly: never mind the fact that other guests might be famished, or that the soufflé might have gone phut, or that the hostess might be cursing us, swearing never to have us back. Why should any of that worry your mother? What's the big hurry? Oblivious, the woman; always was. You realize that even when we were courting I used to be made to wait outside in the car for at least half an hour? Well I was, m'boy, without fail, every confounded time. Almost put me off the wretched gal, truth be told. Miracle, quite frankly, she ever made it to her own wedding: 'parently your grandfather had to put a stop to her silly carry-on: great last-minute drama to do with the veil, too thick to see through, or too transparent, or was it the train, hardly matters: old man, end of his tether, just stormed into her room and dragged her out of the house. And then, few weeks later, what d'you think she does? Gets this barmy notion into her head, sneaks up to see the sewing-woman, has the whole bally thing cut up. Arm and a leg it had cost, I gather, silk or what-have-you from Brussels, orgranzy. Can you credit such a thing? Stark raving mad. For your crib, you say? Don't recall to be honest, wouldn't put it past her. Take my advice, m'lad: steer clear of women long as you can. Nothing but trouble. I'm not saying—don't misunderstand me: she does always look marvellous, your mother, prettiest woman on the island, no doubt about it—which is actually, actually, my point precisely: why must she fuss so, fuss-fuss-fuss, every single time we go out?

And now, as if enlightened, he threatens: Anyway, time gets too tight, I'll just have to take you to Euston m'self and see you onto the train without her, what? Simple as that. Only herself to blame, m'afraid. Oh do stop snivelling, for God's sake; try to act like a man. And then, what the hell, he knocks back a brandy.

I stand pinned to the wall, next to the tuck-box that my mother tucked, which is secured with a combination known only to the pair of us, a duffel coat with clumsy wooden toggles, folded roughly, a chest-nut satchel with my new monogram, punched in black onto the flap—

all these piled like a pyramid onto my padlocked trunk, the key to which is buried in a pocket of my shorts. Wedged between these strange belongings and the door-frame to the bathroom, I'm beginning to squirm sideways because I need to go to the lavatory: I've been holding and holding as hard as I can, but I don't think I can last much longer. I'm going to have to ask him for permission. What?, he barks, Speak up, laddy. I confess the question a second time, but to me it sounds no louder, half-strangled. Well, *go* then, for God's sake. And as I escape, he mutters that the boy's got the bladder of a puppy-dog, which I take be a compliment. I sequester myself, but I do not dare to lock, and I sit to pee so that no one can hear me outside. I wash my hands and smell the soap. There's a face in the mirror that I hardly recognize. A foreign boy in foreign uniform. I ignore him and open the door.

MY BEDROOM has suddenly grown loud with a pair of bell-boys wheeling a trolley and lugging my luggage onto it; and a chambermaid being told to come back later, but would she thank the ladies who marked the boy's clothes—by my father of course. And when my mother enters, knocking hesitantly, she seems not so much late, as lost. To me, she looks like never before—disguised, remote, hounded almost. Her head does not swoon about the clouds that my father had thought, but is held together, bandaged, in a turban dark as ebony. Her unfed body, camouflaged in spotted fur which has been dragged out of cold storage, rattles in a swing-coat of ocelot. Her eyes convalesce behind black lenses. A dark foulard, tight as a snake, throttles her neck with a knot, flips over, then slithers inside her collar. Her hand grips a limp pair of gloves, suede the colour of mole, and flicks them about as if swatting flies in the servants' quarters. She wears no charms this morning. There is no jingle. As she moves towards me, I catch sight, instead, of a slim band of diamonds simmering on her wristbone, mute and cold. One ring upon her finger only, an eternity. She comes to rest directly in front of me, breathing shakily, and lowers herself slightly from the knees. She inspects, then adjusts my tie, but only cursorily, a formality. Her powdered earlobes quiver with small brilliants. Her lips are hard and bloodied. Her jaw pulses wildly. The scent of her gardenias devours me. I look down to her feet, in high brown lace-ups, like hooves for treading concrete, or stampeding. Not a murmur from her, but she pats my cheek in benediction. She rises, straightens up, and turns to survey the emptying room, retrieves her moribund handbag from a stool, and hooks it hard round the pelt of her sleeve. She exits. I follow suit. My father lingers on, probably to leave a tip. And this time, as my mother and I proceed ahead, as we start to begin to take our leave, she elects the stairs rather than the lift, and as we descend and descend soundlessly, almost floating, my hand feels the grip of her fingers, icy, twitching involuntarily.

Once our taxi has been loaded by a disgruntled cabbie and one of the hotel minions, and the partition glass inside been shut with due asperity, we are ferried across to Euston—in solid silence, its weight almost palpable. My parents, whose legs are crossed pointedly away from each other, direct their heads to opposite sides of the wide city roads, as if engrossed in disconnected, or conflicting, versions of heavy traffic. Despite the chasm of leathered upholstery throbbing between them, I, again, am travelling backwards: it has become our custom. From where I sit, I feel tempted to stare at them, to scrutinize their every action, for, faced at such proximity, they seem magnified, like characters towering in the foreground of some film that I were watching from the front row at our local cinema. And yet, just in case, not to provoke matters, I keep my sights low, allowing my eyes to wander no higher than the region around their feet, which wiggle sporadically. I notice now, above my line of vision, the silhouette of my mother's sleeve moving very slowly, like the sleeve of a dowager, to raise a tiny hanky from her tiny bag toward her cheek. She sniffs embarrassingly, then sighs extendedly; and just when I think that she's run out of breath, she states, in Spanish, with spirit, that she wants him to remember that she never wanted this whole boarding thing, which sounds like a secret between them. He clears his throat, pulls down the pane of his window, and proceeds, with some ceremony—cuff-shooting, that sort of flourish—to ignite one of his medium-sized cigars, at which he puffs repeatedly. He inspects its glowing tip and seems to grant himself approval, and, wriggling about his patch of seat, stretches a trouser-leg of herringbone towards where I sit, diagonally; then, carefully avoiding my mother's acutely elbowed sleeve, he insinuates his glistering lighter into the entrails of his pocket and lets it drop, and down it goes, clinking against the loose pieces of his silver.

My mother wonders if I could possibly open her window, which is my privilege. The great noise of the street now invades our echoing interior and claims it, and I turn around in the cab to stare through the front windscreen, I can't resist, and I watch us being driven towards a vast building beginning with an E. And next thing, we are hurtling down into a tunnel, full of taxis, braking and screeching.

THE SLOPING PLATFORM swarms with boys identical to me—identical, that is, till we draw near: all of us are uniformly dressed, of course, but there are bigger boys, blonder boys, more animated, stronger boys shouting to others like them whom they've known since before the summer holidays and who shout back as if repeating some coded joke, meaningless to me. Their mothers, none of whom seems to be wearing a fur coat, much less a turban, are trotting about in A-line skirts, or kilts, and patterned cardigans, and dragging, at their stout heels, the odd fat Corgi. My mother reclaims my hand; her soft glove, now assumed, possesses me. I think that she and I must be walking too slowly, because my father seems suddenly to be surging ahead, forward beyond us, separately. He is waving at something in the distance, and laughing aloud for no reason that I can think of—as you might from the terrace at the Nautical Club wave and laugh at strangers on a passing liner. He turns abruptly to the porter beside him, tells him to deposit my trunk and tuck-box in the guards' van, along with that of other boys who've missed Luggage In Advance, jiggles in his pocket, pays the man off, and then hands me my satchel, and my mother my coat, which she unfolds and hangs over her arm with distaste, I can tell, as if it were the cloak of a vagrant. He tells my mother to go and find a seat for me, anywhere on coaches A, B, or C, and tries to explain to her, in urgent panting blurts, that he's just caught sight of Such-And-Such, some great old long-lost chum from school, Deputy Head when he was Head Boy, triffickly brave in the war, we'll forgive him if he dashes over, must just say Hullo, train won't be leaving for a few minutes, no need to worry, back in a jiffy-what. And rejuvenated by the sudden prospect of this reunion, he canters off—knees knocking, thighs rubbing, Old Boy tie flapping proudly over his shoulder.

My mother seems depleted, too sedated to be annoyed. She inclines her head towards me, and attempts, with her narrow painted mouth, to summon the ghost of a smile. I grin back forcedly, as if for a camera. She links my arm around hers, but it must feel wrong to her, not comfortable, because now she swaps us round, laces her arm through mine as befits a proper couple, weak woman leaning on stronger man, and I do try to support her, and I'm flattered by the compliment, even if it raises the level of my elbow to the level of my jaw. Yet in truth, as we advance down the ramp, I don't suppose that we could look more foreign, more preposterous, the two of us: she, garbed in the anachronism of her finery—her robes and furred gowns; and I, despite the banality of my uniform, tarred by the hot brush of our tropical sun. And I remember pacing down the concrete, which unrolls before us like a sombre sprawling great road to nowhere, and humming, without a scrap of irony, a few bars from a laconic old *milonga*—conceived, no doubt, in Buenos Aires, but inspired, I have since learnt, by the futile chants, centuries old, of slaves who, manacled in Africa, used, after a brief stop on our beauteous island, to be commended to the high seas and sold at the harbour of Havana—a song which my mother had hummed to me by way of lullaby, long before I knew it by heart and its dreadful lyrics could impress me with their mawkish loveliness:

No me llames extranjero porque baya nacido lejos,
O porque tenga otro nombre la tierra de donde vengo . . .
No me llames extranjero porque fue distinto el seno,
O porque acudió a mi infancia otro idioma de los cuentos . . .
No me llames extranjero, ni pienses de donde vengo,
Mejor saber donde vamos, adonde nos lleva el tiempo.
Y me llamas extranjero porque me trajo un camino,
Porque nací en otro pueblo, porque conozco otros mares
Y un día salté de otro puerto. Si siempre quedan iguales en el adiós
Los pañuelos y las pupilas borrosas de los que dejamos lejos.
No, no me llames Extranjero: traemos el mismo grito,
Y el mismo cansancio viejo que viene arrastrando el hombre
Desde el fondo de los tempos, cuando no exitían fronteras,
Antes de que vinieran ellos, los que dividen y matan,
Los que roban, los que mienten, los que venden nuestros sueños,
Ellos son, ellos son los que inventaron esta palabra: Extranjero.

Don't call me foreigner just because my birth was far away,
Or because the land whence I come goes by another name . . .
Don't call me foreigner just because I knew a different breast,
Or because my childhood tales were told with other words . . .
Don't call me foreigner, or wonder whence I hail:
Better to know whither we go, whither time takes us.
And yet you call me foreigner simply because a path conveyed
　me,
Because I began in another place, because I know other waves
And once from another port I sailed. Farewells do not
　discriminate
Between the handkerchieves or misted pupils of those left in
　our wake.
No, don't call me foreigner: for we carry the same wail
And the same ancient weariness that man has been dragging
Since the beginning of time, when there were no frontiers,
Before they came: those who divide and kill,
Who steal, who lie, who sell our dreams.
It is they, they who invented this word: foreigner.

OF THE THREE COACHES, C is the furthest from the gate. It requires the longest journey, but A and B were taken. My mother, imperious as a warring queen, leads our small procession down the passageway, and ignores, with the bristle of her coat, the insignificance of other parents and their braying offspring. Some sticky teenage daughter, someone's lumpy sister, is rushing back against the flow, is headed towards us, and pushes past with an unconvincing Sorry. My mother's neck turns round briefly, high above me, astonished. I seem to be shaky, churning for some reason—as if I were in trouble. I clutch my satchel to my stomach. My mother halts, having found, to her right, a carriage with an empty seat for me, next to the sliding door, which she now slides, her glove gripping the handle heavily and pulling open the partition. My seat is furthest from the window, next to the corridor. The boys already boarded are screaming—unintelligibly to me, in an unheard other idiom—and shoving and horsing-about and cheering. I catch occasional words only. All look several years older than me, apart from one, quietly opposite where I'm to be seated, who could conceivably be my contemporary. His mousy head, with ginger spectacles attached, and freckles, is buried in an action comic. I notice, in passing, soft flecks of dandruff around his dark collar. No one stops, or lowers the noise when we come in; but my mother, undeterred, inspects the luggage-rack directly above the empty seat—only to find it stuffed with other people's belongings. She tells me to sit down, ensconces me. And now she swings round to the boys in here, and tells them, in her execrable continental embarrassing English, to remove the offending articles—which one of them does, ashen with terror. And then she tells him to learn to stand up when a lady comes in, and would he be so good, since I cannot reach, as to put my duffel coat up on the rack for me. Flabber-gasted, he obliges. Most kind, thank you. The compartment is deadly stilled. Yet my mother, to my utter horror, now begins to prattle at me in Spanish with a voice that is not hers—it's absolutely bewildering, squeaky and quick and almost silly—about being a good boy, and say-ing my prayers last thing, and writing to her very soon indeed and—she breaks off paralysed by the sound of a whistle. She must go and find my father, she says, fetch him back immediately. She is vanished in an instant.

I must be blushing: my face is scorching. Everyone is staring at me, and I can tell that it isn't just with interest. Theirs is a different sort of stare: at once slimy and superior. I try to fix my sights directly ahead of me, over the head of the boy with the comic, because I lack, for now, the courage to look out of the window. My mind is charging back to my origins, crashing down to my beginnings. I can't think what I'm think-ing, but a voice in my innards finds itself suddenly rattling off bits of the Hail Holy Queen mother of mercy hail our life our sweetness and our hope to you do we cry poor banished children of Eve to you do we send up our sighs mourning and weeping in this vale of . . . And then, the sudden black moon of my mother's turban appears to me from the platform. Another whistle goes, lengthier. My father is not with her. He must be on his way, or perhaps she cannot find him. She peers, worried and frowning slightly towards the place where I must be, but I don't know whether she can see me through the resurrected antics within. My own view is obstructed by the bobbing heads of these wretched older people, as if, today of all days, it were I who were stuck at the back of our local cinema while they, from their front-row seats, were lapping up the best scene. As the train begins to pull away—and for once I'm moving forward, face to the future—the glass that freezes my mother from me seems to grow like a great screen. And to me, despite her face of absolute shock, which stares aghast at the inevitability, she looks every inch the famous film star now—glamorous, beautiful, stricken. And yet, as if condemned to the melodramatic mime of a silent picture, she can only mop her brow with her glove, and wave a little languidly. But at the desperate last, her mouth opens wide, in a cavernous rictus, and seems to groan like the mouth of a battered ocelot, going, very slowly, from a great Oh, to a deep Ah, and from that, back to an incredulous Oh, and, as she stands there, abandoned, unescorted, I can't properly tell whether her dying vowels are meant to mean Iago, or *Adiós*.

PART THREE

MY NEW NAME is James Moore, and my number 293, which I must not forget, but if my memory should fail me, my mother says that I will find these details written on my handkerchief. After hours of chugging drudgery through increasingly unpromising territories, relieved only by spells of simulated sleep and quick visits to the lavatory, where I could not reach the mirror to check that my tie looked decent, we have finally come to a juddering halt, and trooped off the train with the others ahead of me; but when I had a panic on the platform about my suddenly remembered trunk and tuck-box, which I fear may have gone missing, and which, if she finds out, will make my mother not pleased, a man with a hat and a coat and a whiteness at the collar hurry-hurried me *this* way, boy, pointing and shouting over the confusion: To the bus. He slaps me on the back as I lag behind the rush of pupils, struggling to get into my duffel coat, which is too large and cumbersome and impossible to toggle closed. I feel frozen. I can't seem to find one of my gloves. No time to search for it. Later. I pretend to trot along, as if my body were in sympathy with the general urgency, but my insides have ground to slow motion.

Our bus is double-decker like the one in my toy garage, and even though the ride is bumpy here above and full of swerves, you can see a good deal around you, or could, if it weren't already getting dark. I have a window seat, which is a luck, and the boy by my side looks new like me, which means that we don't have to talk, another luck. The roads wind with the convoy of our many buses through the muddied countryside, and my bus, which is for Juniors, is the last in line, so it's not much use trying to look out of the front.

It is night and quite dull. Nothing to call special that I can notice, just ordinary houses and a village with a tavern called a Swan and some cottages with gnomes smirking like gargoyles, and fields of something ploughed, and trees and hedges and roads, but not a single windmill in sight as round more roads, getting smaller, we go. There is much noisiness here inside, as well as on the floor below, which must mean that some of the boys have been on this bus before, and some of the new ones, I think, may have older brothers who do not want to know them any more because it's soft. But when we come to a cross in the middle of a minor roundabout, everything seems to stop. There is a general quietening, and now we go through a rusty gate along a shady, still more narrow road.

I sense that things are changing. I feel our final approach. The buses hurtle onwards, gathering speed perhaps. But the way is growing darker, seems to be bound for some distant forest. I don't know. Headlights cast mad circling beams across a sea of black fields beneath us, like introductory spots wanting to prove that the next act of the circus will take place without nets for protection. Fields seem neither to rise nor to fall, but gently to slope like an arena for miles around, until, ahead of me, as we grow closer, I catch sight of a vast great statue of stone, a frozen ghost of Our Lady, balanced on a crescent-shaped trapeze and presiding over a black uncharted globe. One arm she holds out, as if wishing to direct you to another school; but her head is coyly tilted away from view, and her other arm lingers about her breast in an attitude of beatific insouciance, so that the language of her posture is rendered unfathomable.

And almost quicker than I realize, the bus now veers with such violence to the right that the boy sitting next to me topples into the aisle, then gathers himself back up, blushing—to a sudden angry burst of public cackles. But rubbing the steam on my patch of window and staring out, I now witness the thing that is my father's Alma Mater. And it is an eternal concrete road, much longer than any station platform, flanked on both sides by enormous carpets of dirty grass and, further down, huge sheets of corrugated water, and there are fields all around, and trees so distant that they look tiny under the brown sky, and, at the end of where you look, there are small lights, to show you a building quite enormous which for centuries has lain in wait for you, like a massive tarantula. I do not flinch: I am not sunk. But my chest tightens so hard that I have to let myself breathe out. The bus rushes on regardless, without apparent caution, as if there really were no danger, as if the spider were held fast, or were stuffed; but as it draws closer, it seems to grow very much larger, which means it can't be stuffed because then it would stay the same size. And here all goes quieter and quieter, and the merriment is starting to die, and some of the buses ahead seem already to have parked in the drive, in the middle of the night, and to be disgorging onto the glistening tarmac bigger boys, who are shouting but no longer really laughing. And yet, just as our turn comes, my turn, the bus for Juniors sweeps in a great miracle to the left and ferries us away to an escape somewhere beyond, as yet out of sight—which, a few hundred metres down some curving lane, I discover leads to another building, not so fearful-looking now, more like a great block of boredom—in fact a former seminary, even if its glumness does suggest a sanatorium, or asylum—which is the place known as Preparatory.

I still don't know what has become of my trunk and tuck-box. Perhaps they were stolen by my father's porter, which I may have to report, as I have no pyjamas to put on. When I climb down, my nose instantly begins to run, like a tap, and I have to blow it at least twice with the handkerchief of which my mother spoke. My hands are numb. I still can't find that other glove. Perhaps it's in the satchel after all. But the pressure to my chest exerts such force upon my ribcage that my skin somehow seems loose for me now, too large, baggy, and my movements accordingly awkward, gormless as I lollop on the ground, stunned by the lamps on the school façade and the glare of headlights. I see some cases being pulled from the boot of the bus, then plonked down at random. I turn around disoriented, but can see no sign of a horizon, only hedges and fences and goalposts for some game or other. And now I see my tuck-box appear, like a mercy, like a prize; but the driver dumps it without care, without the care with which it was packed. I go and pick it up and put it by the entrance. By the time my trunk emerges, and it seems to be the only one about, most of the boys have already gone inside, but I can't lug this weight alone, and I'll never be helped by that driver; and then, at the final hour, a teacher comes, the teacher, my saviour, and he smiles into my eyes more warmly than any parent ever smiled; more warmly, too, than any friend who might ever last your lifetime. Because although I do not even know his name, and though you'll scoff because I'm childish, I know with absolute certitude that this redeemer, this most handsome smiler-among-smilers, who from this juncture onwards makes my life just about sufferable, will one day be mine.

OF THAT FIRST NIGHT at boarding school, which so many children, right through their lives, recall with an intensity that verges on the bridal, I remember nothing save collapsing into bed, shattered, and, just before falling over the cliff into sleep, being seized by a quaking, chilling inner rage, a rancour so profound and unforgetting that although I've managed to tame it, I don't think, puerile as it may seem, that I've ever quite managed to exorcize it.

But I do remember, with a searing lucidity, escaping after breakfast to the passage where tuck-boxes were kept at that place, stacked on slatted shelves which ascended according to seniority. And I remember kneeling reverentially on the painted concrete, the level for new boys, and my hand shaking for the secret combination, and I remember feeling that sacred click, and then, as if I were opening a tabernacle, gradually raising the humble wooden lid, and being assailed without warning by a wave of such sadness as nearly deranged me. I went dizzy. Nobody must see, I remember thinking, not for anything, because the contents of this box, the fruits of my mother's labour, which a matter of days earlier I'd observed with such spoilt indifference, were suddenly splashing with tears.

I wipe my face with my sleeve before proceeding. Then, momentarily robbed of courage, I close the lid once more and blow my nose for relief. When I resume my inspection, I see, first of all, the inside of the lid, papered with the clowns and the boats of my mother's vinyl, and this alone transports me to a time which, morosely as I spent it, now strikes me as idyllic. Lost children of Eve. But next, as I hunch on the floor and crane my neck in, just as she had done while I sat back at a distance, I'm assaulted by the mass effusion of her scent, which is communion to me. I inhale as you would inhale after being strangulated, bestially. And again. I can hardly control it. Then I decide to stop and be quick, to save it, to keep the genie of my mother's loveliness trapped within.

The contents of this box, which was to become like an altar to me, a place of worship which I would visit with dogged regularity, were, in fact, largely treasures of redundancy. At the top of the trove lay a small mohair travelling rug, of the sort which a lady might spread over her knees on a car ride up to the hills. This rug, of softest aquamarine, was to grow, for me, into a sort of security blanket, and I used, when nobody was looking, to rub it against my face as if the mohair were my mother's cheek. And though this ritual felt like a sin, and regressive, like a betrayal of all the prayers for progress which my parents had offered up for me, yet it felt irresistible. And I went on doing it, compulsively, for week after week, until the memory of my mother was all but extinguished.

Beneath the rug was a collection of beautiful obsolete things: my old silver crucifix, which nobody, so far as I could see, hung over beds in dormitories; a hot water bottle in quilted satin, which Matron, spying it on my pillow before I'd decided what to do with it, confiscated for safe-keeping and would, at the end of that first term, return to me— one corner blemished with the frotted remnants of some pinky lipstick. There was also a box of *turrón,* packed among these things because it would survive the journey without perishing, and because it was typical of my homeland, sweet and rich. Then there was an oval silver frame like a large pendant, with a hanging-loop through which my mother had laced a long sad ribbon of green petersham, like the ribbon which had rosetted the beret of my last spring of liberty; and into this locket she had inserted a formal, sensual, softly focused portrait of herself, draped in a shawl from Manila—an image which, like the silent-film star that she appeared, she had dated and dedicated to me. And so, although with the exception of the *turrón*—which I learnt to nibble meanly, calculating as I did so, as if it were an advent calendar, the remaining days of my imprisonment—all the contents of my tuckbox were useless, yet they were, paradoxically, life-saving. But then, in the little side compartment, which had a further lid, I found, tucked between a cartoon dog and a cartoon tree, the first letter which my mother ever wrote to me.

THIS, THOUGH UNSTAMPED, was the model on which all her subsequent letters would be based, its airmail envelope flowing with penstrokes of deep turquoise—an apt reflection, you might say, of her mildly exotic femininity—and addressed (as if I were a teacher, I remember thinking at the beginning) to Master James Moore. But she, unable, after writing my surname, to resist the force of her own blood-line (just as she was to prove unable, throughout the years that we held a correspondence—though correspondence does seem too fine a word for the vapid bulletins which I, week after week, before Mass on Sundays, was compelled to invent and surrender, unsealed, for franking), she now attaches to my surname, as is customary among her people, her own, her maiden one, Zamora—its capital dealt a spectacular flourish. And though this very flourish would instantly mark me out as an object of peculiarity in the eyes of those who huddled, every lunchtime, over a table reserved for incoming mail and tightly rolled comics, I cannot claim that even then I minded this conspicuousness, for the lineage to which my mother drew such exaggerated emphasis is, for all of its heated arrogance, what has, I sometimes believe, saved me from drowning.

But she didn't merely write, my mother: to say that she Wrought comes closer to the fact, for hers, unlike that of her spouse, whose scribblings scuttled along his company stationery as if scratched by the Osmiroid of some pent-up secretary with aspirations to librarianship, hers was a patrician hand, bold and angular and elegantly inclined and identical in style, if not in colour, to that of all girls of her background during that era. And although her words were frequently illegible to me, and later merely uninteresting, for they told of a world which had relinquished me, or which I was myself relinquishing, the fine tissues of her pages, which used to be known as onion-skin, and which traversed the heavens headed with a cross of her own making, were always infused (even if she was later to deny such an absurdity) with the enduring scent of her white gardenias. And it was for that, for her scent, more than her news, that I then lived.

Queridísimo Iago, Dearest Iago, she begins, adopting the diminutive that she was to favour, oh, for terms and terms to come—until the chill set in, when she chose to dilute the intimacy to a more correct, more cool *Querido Hijo,* Dear Son. She addresses me in the slightly archaic Spanish which I would come to associate with her, and tells me, without further ado, that she misses me greatly—a thing which, in this first letter, I find tricky to believe, since her thoughts must have been concocted while I still hovered in her company. She tells me that the house feels empty without me, which again I find puzzling, since, at the time of her writing, I did little but dwell in her vicinity. She hopes that I approve of the items included in the tuck-box, and trusts that I won't eat all the *turrón* at one sitting. I must try to make it last, but I may share with other boys if this seems suitable. She's sure that I'm enjoying my new life and making friends aplenty. She reminds me to be courteous at all times, for in this way, I shall see, I shall make myself popular among my peers. She encourages me to pay attention in class, and not to be frightened to say when I don't understand things. She has no doubt that before I realize it, I shall have become a fluent Englishman, and how that will please my father. She thinks that she may have to accompany him on a cruise to Sicily, stopping off at Madeira on the homeward lap, but, if the plan goes ahead, she promises to write from her cabin, and to send me postcards numerous. Nanny, alas, has had to leave us, and has gone to look after a large family. Anyway, I'm a big boy now, aren't I? She reminds me to say my prayers without fail every night—¡even if it's in Spanish!—and then, after declaring that she is my mother who loves me, she signs off with great old-fashioned ceremony, her name trailing away like a plume claimed by the wind from a magnificent hat.

LOOKING BACK, I think of my earliest days at that establishment as a time not of anything so obvious as crisis, for, despite my outward manner, which was more sedate, more self-possessed than that of most of my contemporaries (and, for that matter, than that of some of the staff, who, soon enough, I began to overhear referring to me as supercilious—an observation which, rather like my father's bladder-of-a-puppy-dog, I took to be a plaudit), inwardly I felt too fraught with the business of keeping up with the changes which were flying at me, like pigeons in a bathroom, to register what beneath the smoothness of my surface was really happening. I would find myself walking down endless galleries, close, wherever possible, to the radiators and heating-pipes, and alone most of the time, as if where others went I knew not to venture, for my sense of difference from them could only aggravate my sense of loneliness in their company. I think that even the poor teachers regarded me with bewilderment at the beginning—later they would do so with a prurient disgust, for rumour, by then, would whisper that I held the key to some unspeakable vice, some monumental sin which both repelled and engorged them. But for now, they merely extended to me the semblances of smiles, sidelong and suspicious, sly as the smiles which my parents might have proffered to some deaf-mute servant, preferably a black one. But that these teachers should, by allowing me to wander unsupervised in my spare time, fancy that they were granting me a chance to dispel my foreign anxieties, to adapt to my new environment, to settle down, did not, even then, cut ice: to the young, such ruses are transparent. I entertained no doubt that these pedagogues-apparent were, in reality, summarily washing their hands of my irksome linguistic handicaps. Yet ironically, this very negligence was to prove vital to me, for it enabled me not so much to recover from the alteration in my external life, which couldn't have been drabber, but, more pressingly, to come to terms with my false reality. Because although I may have appeared to be a pretty child, and assured, and refined—not that such attributes are of advantage at places that peddle holy dogma—I knew that I'd become, and dramatically, something quite other, which is what I needed to learn to manage. And my air of confident precocity, which resulted, I suppose, from that congenital bravado filtered down to me through my mother's line, served to mask the fact that I was trying, much more than to adapt to my surroundings, to contain the rage that now belched like a beacon inside me, and which at times, such as during indoor games, or sports, or runs—none of whose rules or objectives I could fathom—surged to murderous fantasies incorporating my detestable father. So that whereas, in their absence of didactic nous, those foolish guardians of my welfare believed that by leaving me to my own devices they might at least seem to be granting me indulgence, showing me compassion, such a notion could not have been further from the mark. For the real transformation, the sudden conversion, had already happened, like a crack, on that first night. And the result had been a fissure in my being so pronounced that any possible further claim to the realm of childhood had been swept away; and I, at once neglected and indulged, found myself suddenly landed at that bleaker place, perilous and more dark than any satanic mill, which is the inarticulable province of the premature adult, of the lover before time. I had learnt, with a bolt, the meaning of corrosive anger, and it struck me with a force that was as good as biblical. Not once had I felt abandoned, for my emotions then were still entangled, like weeds, in the waters of my mother, but I did feel made over to danger, thrown to the lions. And my task, more crucial than any education, English or otherwise, became, from that first day, to discover a means of survival. Guile, manipulation, call it what you like. Art. Slime. But I needed an accomplice, and I wasn't going to find him in class.

I MUST WRITE in Quink of royal blue and not in black, which my mother says is the best colour for a man, though not with my own fountain pen which glows like lunar opal, but with a dip-one handed out from the cupboard. And exercise books no longer come with squared paper, to help you make your letters round, but lined with line after line after line. Orthography they call spelling; Calligraphy, writing. Even punctuation is different: colons are no longer to open the way like headlights: they're out of bounds. And semi-ones are no longer like long commas, to give you respite, but sloppy foreign excuses for a perfectly decent full-stop. And words may no longer be broken by means of a hyphen at the end of a line; no, you have to pace yourself, pause, then move on to the next level down. And if for some reason, the teacher said, you make a mistake, don't use that expensive rubber of yours and make a great mess, much less tear a page out, which isn't allowed: simply (and he explains this at a snail's pace, as if I were deaf) put-a-sin-gle-stroke-through-the-off-end-ing-sy-lla-bles—like so, denoting an error—and use your brain next time, that's what it's there for. And my Sevens can no longer be crossed, nor can my Zeds, nor the figure One be given a hat—continental habits, to be discouraged. When your parents have sent you all this way, boy, it isn't for nothing, it's for an Education—by which he means a Proper One. For which, the teacher says, I shall one day be grateful.

And in the margin at the top of your essay, you have to insert AMDG, an acronym for Latin words which I don't yet know, meaning To the Greater Glory of God. But in order to remember I just say to myself: *Alas Me Den Gloria,* let wings give me glory, which seems to do the trick. And then, at the end of your Prep, which stands for homework not done at home, you write the letters BVM, for Blessed Virgin Mary, though some boys, to be funny, squash their Vs at the bottom, so that it reads more like BUM.

No more pesetas, of course, but pennies which, when small, are hate-pennies, and, when bigger, grow into pences. They come in dozens, called shillings, not *decenas,* which are tens. And finished are litres and grammes: it's gallons and ounces now, and different pounds, though these aren't for spending, and anyway, spending a penny is another matter. And kilos have become stones, but not as in throwing. And insects of metres, like millis and centis, are inches—twelve of which make up a foot which is twice the length of your shoe on a ruler. And three such rulers equal a yard, which has nothing to do with patios. And miles is more than kilometres, and can also mean a lot, and afar, like your home and your homeland.

Of all the boys in my class this morning, I'm the only one who knew the meaning of a Diphthong, which I guessed from the *diptongos* taught by Don Jesús. But my guess did not, I do not think, impress this teacher here, because he looked put-out, as if I'd ruined his joke, as did the other boys, who call me a Dago, which is one sort of foreigner, but different from a Wop or a Frog, though any foreigner is, I think, known as a Wog.

I suspect that people in this language must be colour-blind, because so many shades turn out to be not what they seem: a lilac flower, for instance, they call a Bluebell; and a dog which is fawn, a yellow Labrador; and a red coat for the foxes is described as pink, when pink, deep and true, is what you get on the cape of a toreador. And when they say that a horse is grey, they don't mean like our horses in Vienna: they mean it's white as snow must, I suppose, be driven.

And there's a new page in the Atlas to be learnt, full of green and pleasant lands and mountains running up the middle like a spine. But when I was asked about this, I went into a confusion and heard myself reply Pyrenees, when I meant Pennines, which everyone did find Hilarious (new word). And after my mistake, the teacher, who has spearhead sideburns such as I have only seen on peasants in the mountains of our island, told me not to look so constipated, boy—which seemed to me like his mistake, because, in Spain, when you're *constipado,* it means you've caught a cold, a thing which I have not, as yet. But everyone laughed anyway.

I WALK INTO the communal lavatories, which are empty and tranquil with the sound of trickling waters. I head straight for the middle cubicle. As I go in, I notice, washing his hands behind the door, the school carpenter, who makes fences and teaches woodwork and is called Mr. Brown. Quite a fat man. Not young. He does not even say Good Morning. I go into the cubicle and lock the door, which needs a shove. You would think he might repair it—Carpenter would, in no time. As I barricade myself in, I hear the steps of older-sounding boys, with deeper voices, approaching, and now using the stand-ups—without partitions, which I think is Ancestral (another new word). I begin to pull down my shorts but, as I turn to face the lavatory, I suddenly see, sunk in the water, and surrounded by a yellow glow, like a revolting seamonster in the depths of the bowl, a massive turd, so fat and solid that it has failed to flush and swim into the sewage. Logged. I am appalled. This has been done by him. I could never have produced such a monstrosity. I have never witnessed the like. I can hardly believe it. And now I have a problem: I can't walk straight back into some other cubicle because I'll be seen by those boys outside. I can't flush and then flush again because I'd be stuck here for hours, which would look peculiar, and even if I did, it might not go away, and then what? Yet I can't conceivably Go while this Thing lurks below me. And even if I went, just supposing that I did, over a whole lot of paper, how do I know that it won't make things worse? Someone could think I was responsible.

I pull up my shorts and close the lid. I flush in the hope that the monster will go, and I leave quickly—tricky because of the stiff door—and I pretend to wash my hands, flick them about, don't bother to dry, and go off, press ahead and escape to the yard behind the kitchens, near the shed for carpentry, and then, as I begin to relax, just then, I hear myself, half-sick with the tension, half-dead with the shock, having an Accident. Blessed is the fruit of Thy womb. I think of my mother. It feels like her fault. I walk, trying to be invisible, unsmellable, up to my dormitory, which is empty, thank God. I stand by the far side of the bed, facing out, and in a flash I have my shorts off, and with them, their repulsive contents, which I'd happily throw out of the window, except that they have my nametape on, and anyway, I don't have fresh undies. The rest of your uniform they lock in the linen room.

I roll the pants as carefully as my squeamishness allows, get into my shorts once more, and hide the soiled rag in my pocket. I go off, fleeing from my own stench, half-closing the door behind me in an attempt to stifle it, and I walk, much faster now, scampering along the top corridor; and when I come to the stairs, which are adorned with cases of stuffed pheasants and partridges and pelicans, I race down to the washroom, where I rush to a remote basin of cracked porcelain, without a doubt ancestral also. I run my filth under a scalding gush of water, and my sins flee down the plug-hole. I leave the mess for a second, and go to fetch my nail-brush and soap. I try to scrub in a manner that approximates the motions of the maids at home. I pound the pants against the side of the basin, trying to keep down the noise, and mercifully the stains do seem to lose their colour, gradually begin to look as if they might go. I squeeze with fury, rinsing over and over. And then I hang the pants, to dry, on the hook which bears my number, and I hide them under my towel, which is yellow and long, but I'm frightened that someone might come in and notice strange drops plopping to the floor. I take the risk. I have no option. And then I quickly unzip my shorts, and using my sponge, which was plucked from the bed of the ocean, I wipe myself between my thighs all the way to my bottom. And I feel the damp and fetid patch inside my shorts grow cold. And then I have to throw away the sponge. And, half-relieved, half-revolted, I spend the rest of the day worrying. But when later I return like a robber to the washroom, my pants, though stiff and wrinkled, have dried, alleluya, and look vaguely white once more. My heart recites the (Spanish) Gloria. And I creep upstairs to put the pants back on, and I pray that tomorrow may come soon, which means clean bundles of clothes.

A THING THAT IS PECULIAR: nobody here puts on clean clothes in the morning, only on the days known as Laundry. Nor do they have baths every evening. Not allowed. You have your bath in a room full of other baths, ranged like boats in a harbour, after games one afternoon a week; otherwise, communal showers, which I find difficult. And when you have a bath, using a tiny towel called a flannel which is fit for a dolly not a boy, you have it under the beady eye of Matron, whose other title is Miss Hogan, and I find that sometimes she smells a bit like the brandy to which my father wouldn't say no. And she twitters in a trilly voice at bathtime, and when she gets to where I am she always tells me not to wash sitting down, to stand up, which is embarrassing; and then she sings to me as she goes by: Calypso, Calypso, Calypso My Own— which of course I'm not her own, because I belong to my Mam'zelle who went away, and because none of these boys did ever have an esmerald, which once upon my finger I did sport. And while I'm sploshing about, thinking of the seagulls and the bathsalts of my past, and wondering whatever happened to the Eurovision, the others scream and laugh and throw nail-brushes behind Matron's back and sometimes they sing some hymn about a golden chalice or a cup, and a saint or hero by the name of Bobby Moore, though he can be no relative of mine. Time's up, she shouts; Everyone get dried. We step out. And to me she says, Buck Up Now, and clatters away like a lady-pig on trotters, still singing about her Calypso.

They often tell you to Buck Up here, which doesn't mean that your shoes need buckling. Except that mine, which are loafers from the Americas, turn out to be non-regulation, according to a teacher of older boys, not a Mister but a Kernel. My mother bought them for my uniform, I reply, somewhat affronted. Bully for you, he barks, your mother should learn to read instructions, doesn't she understand English? You're to report to the linen room and knock on the door and ask one of the ladies to order you a proper pair of slip-ons from the village cobbler, same as other boys. Tell her that I said so. (But I do not know his name, apart from Kernel, and the slip-ons that he means are *elasticated,* very hideous.) I nearly say *Muy Bien,* but luckily I remember to switch over, and reply: Very Well. *Very Well?,* he yells, infuriated. What you mean, boy, is Yes *Sir.* I pause to consider this, which sounds more like the answer you'd expect from a waiter . . . but in the end I just want to get away from all the staring, so I parrot back: Yes Sir. That's better, he reckons. Now go and do as you're told.

And this linen room which is warm and full of ladies' cigarette-smoke is at the other end of the school, upstairs but far from my dormitory, which is where I sleep without the sound of the waves in my dreams. And although I try to rest in peace, this is not always simple.

For I have a voice in my head that always wants to translate, and though I try to tell it to stop and let me learn the English which my mother, for my father's sake, does hope, it will not stop, not even after lights out. And sometimes in the night, the others wake me up, shouting Shut Up, which means Keep Quiet, because this voice of mine, they say, bursts out from my mouth and starts jabbering rubbish in Spanish. Which must be lies.

I REMEMBER, in the mornings, being awoken by the sound of a bell which, as if Rise-'n-Shine were not enough, the master on duty would clang from dormitory to dormitory. And as it drew nearer to yours, its gloomy knell would make you feel that you were being returned from the coma of purgatory to an insipid version of hell. That's how it felt. And then he would switch on a measly frosted bulb. It made me rabid. I would want to scream, not just groan, which is what the others did, good sports that they were; yet for all my stifled rage, my inherent petulance would incline me to ignore the bearer of these dreary matutinal tidings, to play dead. However, my show of indifference must, if anything, have proved too effective—to have spoken, rather than stifled, the silent volumes of my derision—for I recall, on several occasions, having had my sheets torn off me by a teacher—a Liverpudlian with a streaky page-boy cut and elongated nails on his right hand, who, aside from his penchant for the popular guitar, though his lack of aptitude would have inspired the ridicule even of schoolchildren in my country, was partial, I could sense, to natural blonds who were also natural athletes. And the impertinence of his assault provoked in me, such was my rising bile, a much keener resentment than ever I had felt when similarly accosted by my former Nanny after the siestas that I have recounted. Now, I would fantasize about leaping, as his hand dragged my bedclothes up, onto it and biting. Drawing blood. Licking the blood from my canines. And I did leap up whenever he thus affronted me, but predictably in a manner that was less mordacious than cowed, for although I may have been imaginative, I was also a coward. And so, shivering on my threadbare bedside-rug, I would strip off in prudent stages, to protect my pudor, and pull on my long socks and underclothes and shorts and, as I did so, I would catch the outlines of other boys standing about without shame and stretching like barn animals, which at my house would never have been countenanced, and I would hear them burping and farting and laughing, which, in my prissy former Eden, would have been *inaudito,* unheard of.

After breakfast, which first acquainted me with school porridge, I would return to my dormitory to fret about my bed, which nobody had ever taught me to make, and which, particularly when stripped to its foundations, to its stained mattress, I could never properly redress. And I would rue the beautiful crispness of my former beds, and the gentle care which my mother's maids had taken, and the pristine comfort of my daily laundered, waffled bedside rugs. But as often, I would rail in silence at my defective father, who—just as he had failed to inform me of the various rules pertaining to various games, or about the apparently proper way to eat at this place, which seemed to involve leaving one hand limply on your lap—so, similarly, he had never troubled, along with how to polish my shoes and knot my tie, to prepare me for this trivial task which others had already refined to the pitch of hospital-corners and apple-pies. And then, by extension, I would hate my mother for ever having married the man.

But the final straw of my disabusement came with my eau de cologne. This was the fracas that really caused the scales to fall from my smarting eyes. For, in my folly, in my blindness to the peril which, as predictably as day follows night, my actions would give rise, I would use a splash of toilet-water to flatten my hair in the morning, as I had done throughout my recollected life. This went unnoticed for a brief while, because people were still keeping their distance, sounding me out. But when the aroma of those few paltry limes was eventually retraced to me, and accusatory fingers duly pointed at my blushing outline, there rose from my peers, in the break between two periods, such an avalanche of (largely incomprehensible) spite that I grasped in a flash what is meant by wanting the earth to open up and swallow you. And next I recall plucking from the great babble, and hoping against hope for relief from the insults, which stung like stars, one word alone, and it was Woman. I thought of my mother. But then I understood that even those two short syllables were aimed derisively. And in that split second, the crowd, as one, realized that whereas the gamut of their other names had left me looking nonplussed, here at last was a something that I did understand, and wounded me. And Woman, You Woman, they would constantly chant, preferably when a teacher was about. And I swore to myself then that one day, even if it killed me, I'd get my own back. On each and every one of them.

The bell for the next lesson goes, but the disruption drags on regardless. The teacher walks in, and smiles routinely, then tells them to quieten down. I'm sitting, as I was to sit for the remainder of those early years, at the back of the class, next to a window, which, for now, is set too high to see out of, to fly through. The teacher wants, inevitably, to know what's been going on, what all the rumpus is about. And then one of them, Steel (a boy of skewering intelligence who will dog me in years to come), gets up, cool as a dozen cucumbers, and tells him. And I don't need to understand the details of the disclosure, for the accuser's tone is jubilant. All heads, uncontaminated by cologne, are turned to me. Open up earth. But now everything alters, backfires. I can tell that the teacher, the one who helped me with my trunk on that first night, is telling them off, and I hear from his lips words that delight me, like Stupid and Silly and Childish. And though his comments incite a steam of hissing and, by way of grudging compromise, an audible shift from Woman to Dago, basically the room has returned to order. But now I know where, in this order, he, Mr. Wolfe, stands, which is as if above, apart from the scum. And once the storm of the majority has been calmed, and as books are finally being opened up, he looks over to my corner, where the sun is suddenly shining, and smiles directly at me, and he embellishes the smile with a well-aimed wink, which shoots out. And it flies straight as an arrow. And it must have pierced my side. Because I think, looking back, that I may, at that instant, have fallen in love.

NONE OF THIS, naturally, does a thing to improve my standing in the class hierarchy, of which, in any case, I wasn't ever really a part—I was viewed, which indeed I felt, as a separate object, like a mule among cart-horses, or a blade of grass sprouted in spiked mud; but the incident did inspire in me the intuition that the closer I could bring myself to the man who had already saved my skin twice, the further I would be placed from danger. And though during Prep I would pore over my mother's letters, only to discover with what ease her Iago could, by means of a few treacherous curlicues, be embellished into a Dago, and although, when I defaced the backs of her envelopes with dagodago-dagodago and then, a second later, looked again and the line seemed to insist that there was agodagodagod, I knew that the only god who could help me now was not floating around vaguely up there, but correcting essays two doors down.

At lights out, when he was on duty, I felt able to endure anything, even the day to come, in the knowledge that this Mr. Wolfe would soon be coming along to say good night. And after reaching our door and telling us all to be quiet, and just before the light went out, he would wink at me, which no one ever seemed to notice; and although, to begin with, I would just smile at him lopsidedly, in time I gained the confidence to wink back. And this happened often: he was often on duty, for he was our supervisor. And when the winking grew dull, I noticed that he had added a further motion to his repertoire, and this gesture was a sort of sulking mouth which I think was meant to mimic mine, but which I now recognize as a pout—a thing that my mother had sometimes done and which I must have contracted through her blood. And so, as the weeks passed, and the lights went out, Mr. Wolfe and I, this foreign Moore, would exchange the briefest of winks and the slightest of pouts, like kisses in the making, and when the lights went out, I would sleep as if under the stars, praying for the sound of waves in my dreams.

WHEN HALF TERM STRUCK, a strange thing happened: it suddenly transpired that since my parents were still on their cruise, there was nowhere for me to be parked, and although I imagined that some correspondence on the subject would have passed between my father and the headmaster—a lip-smacking advocate of corporal punishment who worried his fingernails, sweltered profusely, and liked to tuck his tie inside his shirt during lunch—I was, until the last minute, kept in ignorance of my status as a Problem. In the event, some kindly couple offered to put me up, local publicans whose poor son, a day-boy two years my senior, and therefore a complete stranger, dragged me on foot, one dark afternoon, to the nearby village—even offering (I remember because it left me flabbergasted) to carry my bag. I would have accepted, of course, for I then found such attentions to my liking, but the suspicion that his courtesy, which was delivered in the guise of a mumble, resulted less from spontaneous good manners than from his mother's instructions, made me think twice. If it were secretly to embarrass him, I judged, my acceptance could ultimately prove detrimental. At any rate, I know that I declined. And we spent our half term thus: he, wearing his mufti; I, trapped in my uniform, though it was decided that I might dispense with my tie; he, playing with trains and electric cars of unremitting dreariness; I, pretending to read bad children's books on a bad sofa. At night, the plan was that we would share a bed—which, despite my new fear of waking others up, I rather welcomed, for such a sophistication was new to me. Yet on the first night, just as I was getting into my pyjamas, it was suddenly sprung on me that the arrangement did not stop there: it came with a codicil, namely the accommodation of his magisterial tabby. This prospect paralysed me, and I recall that we argued about it—I may even have tried to bribe him—but he won out. This was his bed, his room, his house. And I did see his point, little as the point pacified me. To me, that creature was hair-raising, for, on my island, cats had been wild marauders of the mountains; and sometimes you would hear them scrapping and yowling and up to Lord-knew-what in the night. So that when this beast eventually ensconced itself between the two of us, emitting purrs which I found repugnant, I recited my prayers with a fresh degree of fervour, but took care to leave my parents out. And at the end of that break, I complained to them about the whole arrangement as strenuously as the limitation of unsealed envelopes allowed, but while it is true that never again was I farmed out to strangers, it is also true to say that the alternative did not exactly improve matters. Because, for years to come, I found myself foisted upon distant relatives of my father's, fusty people who, far from feeling like relatives of mine, habitually voiced their contempt for anyone who elected to live under that Generalissimo chap and, in their demeanour, differed scantly from the teachers who disliked me. I think that just as I dreaded being inflicted upon these assorted couples, most of whom were dotted about London, they too regretted my appearances on their doorsteps. All were far too tied up ever to meet me off any train, and besides, there was no need, I should just jump in a taxi, there's a good fellow, and when I arrived, or so they claimed, they would pay the cabbie. In the event, none of them ever did, not until I plucked up the nerve to ask for my taxi fare. But their repeated oversights had bitten hard into my funds, as if to aggravate the fact that my father (I would invariably discover at the Bureau de Change in London) made a habit of short-changing me on my pocket money. Without exception, those disparate relatives seemed to view me, particularly as I grew more contorted and rarefied, with an edgy discomfort, and were at certain stages to inform my parents, I later learnt, that I struck them not as other boys of my age, but as withdrawn, peculiar. They should keep close tabs.

THE SECOND HALF of that first term is less memorable for the ritual indignities which I brought upon myself on the playing field, where it seemed to be permissible for members of staff to flex the muscle of their tongues (You're meant to be a Full Back, Moore, not a bloody Goalie, you great Woman), nor for the minor ailments which I suffered—chapped hands, chilblains, colds, the usual trivia—nor even for my growing awareness of the nauseous smells which, as the weeks passed, seemed to filter with increasing pungency through the establishment—rotting fruit in the locker rooms, exudations of recycled lard in the refectory, manure from outside creeping into the galleries—as for the alterations which, without conscious planning, had begun to suggest themselves to my behaviour. It seems to me now that I grew, in her absence, more like my mother—by which I don't mean effeminate so much as romantic, sentimental, taciturn.

In the afternoons when I wasn't at games, I would make a habit of knocking on Mr. Wolfe's door, not even armed with a decent pretext half the time, and he would smile over his music and beckon me in, as if for my succour, to look after me. I would stand by his window, taking care to remain out of sight, brushing myself on the curtain and thanking my lucky stars that I wasn't stuck outside in all that filthy mud. Sometimes he would offer me an apple from a bright bowl which he kept on a shelf, and I would accept, charmed, despite the fact that I was nervous to chomp at it, to eat it without a knife. But I would never have admitted this reluctance: I just tried to keep the noise down, because the juice that sprang from the pulp of his crushed fruit was sharper, lovelier to me than nectar. As I grew bolder, I took to standing by the chair where he sat working at his desk, and sometimes he would stroke my thigh, as my former teacher at primary school had done, but my grateful pleasure now must have been apparent, for my knee would often be heard to crack. While one of his hands wrote on, the other was warm with protection. This gentle bond between us seemed to me to compensate for my general sense of exclusion, my loud unpopularity, and to reduce my fears, to grant me reassurance, if only for a brief while. It nourished me. And in time, I grew hungrier—and more guileful.

Despite my absolute lack of comprehension, my complete inability to figure out any plot in English, never mind the intricacies of some raffish wartime cine-drama (though I found myself perfectly able to understand *Lord of the Flies*), I would attend the films which were shown on Sunday evenings, and I would ensure that I sat right at the back, for I knew that as soon as the lights went out, Mr. Wolfe, who showed the films, would emerge from the projection room and sit beside me. Thus placed, we would both, as if by tacit agreement, cross our arms, and this combination enabled me to smuggle my hand into his cuff and stroke his palm, and his wrist, and even the stem of his forearm. Sometimes he would stroke me back, but despite the darkness, it was never with the same ease as in his room, which was marked Private. Without ever needing, at that time, to verbalize matters, I think that we both understood that although what we were doing was in some way extraordinary, almost beautiful, it also lay beyond the horizon of what was admissible. In chapel, during prayers, he would stand in a small loft to supervise the congregation; but no matter where I stood or knelt, and though I resisted the temptation to turn round, I knew that his eyes were burning into my back.

THEN CAME the Christmas holidays, marking my first of countless trips in the unenviable capacity of Unaccompanied Minor, which, in my experience, simply involved needing to be supervised for longer than necessary, having to ask permission even to go to the lavatory, being pestered to join some club for peripatetic pre-pubescents from all over the globe, and being smothered by the condescending sympathies of uniformed women who resembled my snappy former Nanny. Contrary to what one might have supposed, I do not think that when the moment came I was ever as exhilarated by the prospect of returning home as were other boys, for the complicated journey back filled me with trepidation. I would have to navigate my way through the stormy spirits of my peers, which would grow less bridled, more venomous, on the train as we approached London; next, I would have to pretend to be indebted to some uncle and aunt in Kensington, who were in due course to be appointed my official guardians; and after being dumped the next morning at an airline terminal in town (assuming that this was when the plane took off, which sometimes it was not, thus furthering the protraction), came a bus trip to the airport, a possible plane-stop halfway through the haul—sometimes at Madrid, Málaga more usually—and at last, at night, I would walk down those metal steps, back onto the tarmac of the island of my mother's ancestors.

My first return was odd, for though she came to meet me at the airport, and demonstrated every sign of effusion, and kissed me repeatedly, and still, to me, looked captivating, yet something about my mother wounded me. Even if her gardenias had not altered, her tone was unquestionably more animated, more frothy than I remembered, as if my absence, far from having depleted her, had rather served to effect a revival. And to me, even if I couldn't rationalize it, this felt, though venial, like a betrayal. She found me pale; my tan had waned. She found me skinny, but perhaps I had grown. She'd organized children's parties for me to attend. In addition, of course, though I could hardly even admit this to myself, there was a corner of my soul which now yearned for, missed, the uniqueness of that teacher's attention. The power of his protection seemed to me, in my confusion, of greater worth than that of my parents, for it was only towards him that I felt grateful. My bedroom at home—and this had been trumped up as a Surprise, so as to exonerate my mother from the need to consult me—had been redecorated in a manner that I disliked on sight and never thereafter ceased to dislike. And for the first time that I recall, I risked earning her disapproval by telling her what I thought; but she replied that I was young, that my taste was not yet formed. There was something autumnal about the paper—leaves, I suppose, or bracken, possibly; and the floor, in line with the new insular vogue, had, from wall to wall, been carpeted darkly as pounded olives, which must have been intended to convey manliness. My circus-rug was gone. I took to snoozing in the nursery, on the sofa with hydrangeas of cretonne, because, now that Nanny was no more, there was less general bossiness. And I used my bedroom as little as possible, for although the nursery was short on secret drawers, there was, in any case, nowhere for me to hide my secrets now other than in my chest, which was locked.

Nothing about that holiday was special, memorable. But a month later, to the day, just after the feast of the Epiphany, which at home was not observed because my father, being English, saw fit not to, I was returned to the airport and waved off. I did not feel that my mother liked me so much any more. She had such a multitude of other things to like now, you see, she who, disguised as an ocelot, had struck me as so desolate only a brief while back, whose sadness had half-slain me when I left her stranded on the platform at Euston; she who, since that time, had penned me at least a dozen epistles of turquoise longing. But she appeared to have grown frivolous, skittish, lightweight, and to be absorbed by flitting trends and forthcoming balls and glossy magazines and her couturier in Barcelona and, how can I forget, the heated argument of whether her lustrous chestnut mane should, or should not, be cropped. She seemed forever to be attached, laughing, to the telephone in her bedroom; and though, even outside it, she had become less reserved, yet she had become, somehow, less accessible. Her siestas were briefer now, she was less tired, but the issues which excited her were no longer of concern to boys.

THE WINTER TERM that they call spring cannot, by contrast, be forgotten, for it was punctured by a pair of shocks. The first concerned Mr. Wolfe. I had dared to wonder whether he had thought of me. I had thought of nothing but him on that long journey north. And when the bus dropped us off, I witnessed, to my stupefaction, that he was transformed. He still smiled. He was still handsome. But he had grown a beard, and I'd been given no warning. It was full, and dark, and belonged to that complex tone of brown which coppers in the sun. I found myself bristling with the same resentment as I had felt over the alteration to my bedroom. Why had my feelings been ignored, I to whom it mattered so crucially? But unlike the bedroom, to which I was never to warm, I did, despite my initial stabs at sarcasm, soon warm to his new mask, which at once seemed to conceal my passion from the public and to render me lustful, for the child is capable of lust. Gradually, and almost without realizing, I grew consumed. My visits to his room in the afternoons became more frequent; my conduct, less demure. Now, as he stroked my leg, I dared to stroke his beard, and as he smiled, I hardened in my shorts. It was, from then on, only a matter of time. The road was paved; I did not plan it; but it glittered before me.

I wake up in the middle of the night, and put on my slippers and my dressing-gown. I go to the lavatory, squinting. There's a soft votive light in the corridor, to guide me O thou great Redeemer. And on my return, like a sleep-walker, I choose to lose my way back to the dormitory and find myself, instead, at his door. I'm nine years old. Don't look so shocked. I knock. He says: Come in—as if he'd been expecting me all along. My eyes, now, are like orbs. I am in orbit. I say: I cannot sleep. He tells me to close the door. I lock it. And I walk, as always, to the window. His curtains are not drawn.

IN THE SEDUCTIVE GLOW, which, two storeys beneath the radiator where I stand, facing out, spreads across the purple grass beyond the school portico, I see, I saw, like a sombre revelation from the darkened English heavens, brown-paper leaves, fluttering down, long after autumn, fluttering in pairs from the birches beyond the window, swooning for a moment in the sky-without-stars, being sidetracked briefly by a misleading gust, and shifted, but ultimately abandoned and falling, falling first not so much furious, as disenchanted after the event, like spiralling butterflies resigned to die.

I TURN INTO THE ROOM, which seems pungent suddenly, acrid, and deathly quiet despite the soft whirr of his gramophone. I stare blind into the glare of his anglepoised light for what feels like a lifetime; and now, though I can neither breathe nor give credence, he brings me over to where he sits and I find myself within his crouching, trembling hold. His great knees, like quaking horses, are about my thighs. He levitates my heavy dressing-gown from my shoulders, and it rises to reveal my buttoned-up front, then drops, with the posthumous thud of a tassel, to the forgotten ground. And now he takes me up, and I, at last, am suspended in the heights, caught up but safe, and out of the spot, and in the embrace of his arms, which are thicker than my thighs, and held, like a swing, behind my rump. My slippered feet have flung out and crossed idly round his lower back. His glorious head, like the head of an unhappy conqueror, or an accursed emperor, now bows forward to meet mine; and his soft clean hair tumbles over his eyes and I can no longer see out, for his lips are sealed to my brow; and I am blessed at last. Do not be mistaken: this first gentle bearded kiss was perfectly, sacredly right.

My lover takes me up fully now, gathers me like a word of honour to his breast, which feels stronger and broader than the bed of my early siestas. I am cautiously calm, as if I'd come unharmed through some perilous crossing yet were not quite landed. His heart, which I can feel thumping against my side, must be anxious, fearful; and for a split second only, and only for him, I am filled with a sharp, inexplicable sorrow, like some lost mother wailing out from another country.

Together we seem to rise, he and I, into the clouds of this unknown land, to drift about like joined but uncertain spirits, to turn and turn like slow dancers about the edges of our floor, softly knocking into an occasional table, brushing past some unexpected frame and fumbling for safety—but together, held in unison. One of his arms has moved away from me, like the arm of God, and with a muffled click extinguished the light. We are awash in moon, flooded.

I tighten the grip of my thighs and kick off, one-two, my slippers. As they hit the wooden planks, he flinches with surprise, recoils a fraction; but now he relaxes from the mounds of his shoulders, down his veined arms, to his hands. And though I can hardly make him out, I can tell that his outline has smiled in the dark, for the creases round his eyes have cracked and burst like rays of silent laughter. The comfort of his lips is returned to my brow. And now my arms shoot out without thinking, enraptured, up to the skies, like parallel fireworks, bursting at my fingers, which stretch like starbursts. My sleeves are sliding back, gathering in warm wrinkles about my shoulders; and my hands now join and twist around, holding tight behind the neck of this new god of mine, then dropping like a lament over the vale of tears which is his muscular back.

Clasped head-to-head, as if inseparably, he steers us round the desk of our unspoken courtship, and past the shelf with the bowl of shining apples, to the far wall by the fireside. My head tilts back as he leans forward, over me, to replace with his uncommitted hand the needle which has been hovering at the end of a record—some Nocturne—back on the outer groove of its vinyl, on its soundless introduction. He closes the lid as if impatiently, a little roughly, and by the time that the music has once again struck up, we're moving toward his bed, which is single and open and white. He brings me down to his sheets, which smell of him, more delicately that I recall ever having been brought down, until I'm placed, most gently, on my back; and then I let go; and we separate for a brief while, are in limbo.

He exhales, or sighs, and stretches out before me, twisting up like the trunk of an ancient Roman tree, some great laurel. And next I witness the terrifying miracle, for which I have longed, for which I have lusted, which is the absolute fullness of his nakedness. But I feel diminished by it, as if reduced by some mysterious shame, probably my ignorance. I close my eyes. I suppress the urge to cover myself. I wish I knew how to pass out. The retch of a match strikes out from nowhere, and I hear the fizz of a wick bring alive a candle, vaguely behind the pillow, somewhere near a pile of exercise books above the bed, essays unmarked. One of mine festers among them. I blush in my shadow. The room must be catching fire. I cannot believe the heat. Only my feet are frozen.

He starts with my pyjama top, which he undoes almost desultorily, as if already I represented a let-down, some small (but irrevocable) error—button by button, sleeve at a time, nothing that I couldn't myself have done; and he discards the jacket in the murky direction of the radiator, where it drops. I hear, aghast, a button clank against the iron, and it sounds like a coin of little value clanking into a begging-bowl. And to me, the merciless echo of this brittle sound, as it races along the trembling labyrinth of school pipes, seems to announce to the slumbering world that although I'm not personally accountable for the mishap, yet I have transgressed, passed over. Treachery is in the air. I tell him to check that my nametaped handkerchief hasn't escaped from the breast-pocket. It had.

The unveiling of my pyjama trousers, their shedding, I cannot relate on account of the blinding embarrassment which invades me as he tugs at the bow of my cord, which seems to have squirmed down towards my hip-bone. I turn for respite onto my front and try to escape into thoughts of those indolent days spent, pretending to be dead, on the beaches of the summers of my past. My mouth is salty, dry; but as I swivel further round, to face the wall, to face the waves, I hear my breath rasping loud and too fast, like the breath of a lecherous mongrel. Yet he, as if to dispel any spectres that may be hovering about my head, as if to show to me that he can read me like a testament, slowly and with devotion now approaches the soles of my feet with his beard, like a faithful animal.

I am rigid. His eyelashes, like insects, teeter over the backs of my heels; the hair of his head brushes the hollows of my knees; and then I sense the mattress beginning to move, shifting heavily, like a sand dune. He is crawling like a predator over me, but he does me no harm. He merely breathes, pants vaguely above the line between my utterly clenched buttocks. With his tongue, which flicks, he licks at the globes behind me, one of which, I have a sudden memory, bears a small birthmark, like an island. Then he moves up, along the length of my back, pausing on every knuckle of my spine until he comes to rest at the clearing between my shoulder blades, my wings which give me glory, my AMDG.

But now he must have risen slightly, for his head is inclined, and his mouth rests, clasps, half-bites the back of my neck with a kiss of life, hot into it. He is upon me, yet he does not weigh me down. His elbows are like brackets beside me, scaffolding. All I can feel is the tremor of his fur, and the assumption of his beard. Hovering over me, over my ear, too closely in fact, and audibly demurring but ultimately finding the courage, he now whispers to me those words which have been whispered since time immemorial, the fatal line that this is, must be, cannot but be, and I must never, ever forget, our Special Secret. I do not flinch. I could not for the life of me. And then he goes and shows me, proves it all to me. Bequeaths me the very world. Undoes me. I have never cared less. Take this, all of you, and eat it: this is my body which will be given up for you.

He turns me round onto my back, to face him, to face the ceiling; but his enormity now covers my nudity entirely, conceals me from view. His head, collapsed, rests on the bed much higher than my own head does; his feet lie far beyond mine. Yet his chest and his thighs and his mound and all of the hair that is stifled between us, all of these things are precisely poised as he slides himself, slowly but not entirely surely, between my upturned thighs, which are reluctant, and under my horribly white parts, which have yet to ripen.

He withdraws unexpectedly and, in a faint huff, seems to kneel up; and though my eyes-without-scales are closed, I hear him spitting like a tramp; and though I cannot tell at what, nor why, my instinct feels insulted. But yet again, I must be mistaken; for now, with greater ease and a little less calm, and after coaxing the banks of my thighs slightly apart, he introduces himself like the wetted neck of a swan, or a serpent, or a dragon. And there begins a motion, a rhythm of such balminess as I have never before experienced; and gradually a progress is established, and my knees, of their own volition, seem to rise with his rising thighs, and to fall with them and rise and fall and rise, and our breathing is absolutely one—though his, of course, is much louder than mine, louder still and louder, and then I hear, after his latest fall and rise, a sudden gasp or grunt, and then another, and then I sense some vague diminished writhing, a cooling rallentando. And returned to life, I now grow conscious of a smell exuded by some warm creamy substance, like a disease of slime which, smeared along the insides of my thighs, is starting to slither backwards.

Ours is an understated unwinding, unremarkable even, and the curtain which comes down on this first act, a slightly abrasive stripy towel of many colours—introduced between my loins, inserted to allay my repulsion. And it is left there to rest a while, quietly. But there is loud applause in my heart.

As I put my clothes back on, I look out of the window once more, but now from the perspective of somebody other, older somehow. And the tiny lights that wink from afar, motorways or rail-tracks racing over some viaduct, and the hoots which I can hear in the distance, or perhaps can only imagine, all seem to point to a world of freedom beyond, into which I would like to run, to the circus, to the Russian ballet: I would learn to do the splits, to dance on wires, to tame great tigers, to swallow tongues of fire. I could do anything. And yet, as I gather myself up and unlock the door and creep back into the world of linoleum corridors and extinguished chapels, a part of me wishes to turn back, to rewind, that I were once again a child, and that just as he had lowered me to his sheets by candlelight, he would now raise me in his arms and carry me, like an ailing infant, back to the feathers of my eiderdown. But, of course, such thoughts are futile: the cage that entraps me allows for no such devoted licence. My job is to reach my bed undetected; and while the others snore and grunt about pitches where they score every run and every goal and every try, and where the roars of approval are theirs entirely, I sneak into bed and slide back into a coma.

ON THE MORNING after that first night, I remember stealing into Mr. Wolfe's room while everyone was on the way to breakfast and, whether out of shame, or jealousy, or perhaps out of straightforward love, approaching his sheets and removing a few pubic hairs which horrified me, for I did not possess such things, and proceeding, I who could hardly make my own, to make his bed, to cover our tracks. I felt as if propelled, however prematurely, into the role of lady-of-the-house, or perhaps I was just the valet. In any event, my days now became lengths of enforced patience, like stretches of unrelieved cloud, perpetually overcast: Being your slave, what should I do but tend upon the hours and times of your desire? I have no precious time at all to spend, nor services to do, till you require. And while I waited for the world-without-end hour, to which I would awake like clockwork, like some mechanical cuckoo, at eleven o'clock every night, I delivered myself to a life which I now see was upside down. I longed for nothing but the dark. It was like existing in reverse. Like dwelling inside a negative. But I was, in fact, never tired. That, I suppose, is what love does: it adds, not subtracts. And those hours of nocturnal rapture, which meant more to me than any number of runs or goals or tries, were my soaring score, my constant prize. I felt revived by them as my mother had been revived by my absence.

Towards the end of that term, leading up to Easter, I think that my patience must have snapped, or my sense of power suddenly risen, for I remember going to the wall outside the changing-rooms, which was covered with notice boards for all the various matches—elevens or fifteens or whatever-it-was-a-sides. Anyway, these boards were cluttered with names on movable wooden pegs, each peg denoting a given player's position in a game, as allocated by whichever master happened to be the referee for that particular match. I viewed these boards, which were arranged on a daily basis, with abhorrence, for to me they spelt only one thing: humiliation: they reminded me of my father . . . until one day I realized how easy it would be simply to remove my peg, to disappear from sight. I'd been an idiot not to think of it earlier. So I stole my surname from its hole—goalie, full back, whatever—and threw it with some gusto into a dustbin, pushing it hard to the bottom. I told no one, nobody noticed, and for a while I just lurked, basking in the glow of my own ingenuity, behind the door of my dormitory. If anyone happened to step onto the corridor and threaten to approach, I would slide under a bed and hide. It was not difficult. But eventually, predictably, I was found out, and the teacher in question, the geographer with the sideburns, sentenced me to four strokes.

This needs explaining. Although the standard instrument for the infliction of pain at that school was a thick rubber object, known as a ferula, which was shaped like an ox-tongue, and which, depending on the culprit's status, was administered either to his buttocks, or later, when he was older, on his open palms, younger boys such as I were beaten across the bottom with a table-tennis bat, of all silly contrivances. (My father, needless to say, later boasted that in his virile day the birch had been the crowning glory of punishment, but by the time that softies such as I were sent along, the latter had been rendered obsolete.) I now recognize the custom of penalizing pupils' misconduct by means of a wallop less as barbaric, or retarded, than as laden with sado-masochistic undertones. I can only compare the punitive measures of those days with antics which, in the fullness of time, as you know, I was to witness at heavy orgies, or in night-club dungeons. For without exception, and whatever the weapon or number of strokes, which could, if necessary, escalate to a dozen (I think that this was the maximum, but I couldn't swear to it), the pupil was obliged, under penalty of a repeat dose, to thank the teacher for the pleasure. Thank you, Sir. Amazing, no? And although, until the peg fiasco, I had never myself been beaten, it was the concept of verbal acknowledgement, more than the agony, which made me baulk. My brain could not digest the idea of being coerced, within this context, into a semblance of gratitude. And, as if such a semblance were not sufficient, the custom regarding the bat for Juniors was that following its infliction the boy must sign his name along the instrument, both to prove his wordliness, and to symbolize that no grudges were harboured against the aggressor. It made my Spanish blood boil. And when the hour for my first beating loomed, I discovered (which was my next shock) that the master on duty, was, of course, Mr. Wolfe.

There is a jumpy queue outside his door. Just gone seven o'clock. I'm third in a line of four. First boy's already in there. Whack, whack, whack, the bat goes; then, brief pause, presumably for the autograph, and—hey presto, here comes the hero, hopping about, face flushed like a tomato. In goes the next transgressor, who, like me, is up for four. It passes surprisingly slowly. But when I walk in, to say that Mr. Wolfe is staggered would be to sell him short. He is panic-stricken, frozen; and I, by contrast, am suddenly struck with a wily notion. It doesn't need to be spelt out—it's better than eloquent—for I have narrowed my eyes and locked my jaw. I cannot now recall the details, but either I wouldn't bend over, or he couldn't bring himself to exact the punishment. Either way, a frantic wordless compromise is reached: he places a cushion over my rump and thrashes it dramatically. But he looks both shameful and furious. Not a whisker of a smile now: he's biting his own mouth. He loathes me. And then, with consummate smugness, I stuff my hands in my pockets and leave him no option but to inscribe his weapon with the daft irony of my surname, Moore—which he does in capitals. But when I walk out, I do, if only for the sake of fair play, manage to simulate a passable, agonized hop. God only knows how the fourth boy got on. Yet this was the start of my trouble, the real one, which was my sudden discovery that, in my grasp, I held a great pot of molten gold.

AT LIGHTS OUT HE BLANKS ME, and instead, can you believe, beams at the creep in the bed next door. And in the night, though as always I wake up with a jolt, I dare do nothing. I feel too nervous. This is my true penance. I fear that if go to him he might ignore my knock, or turn me away, or worse, take me to task for the whole fiasco. What happened, he will say, was all my fault. Only myself to blame. I mean, removing one's peg, how stupid can one be? And how dared I undermine his authority as I did? I've behaved disgracefully. He's ashamed of me. Never again, he'll claim. He means it, he'll say. Couldn't I just steer clear of trouble, for God's sake? And what if it happened again, what then? (Silence.) He wouldn't hesitate to beat me, he insists. Same as anyone else. And I tell myself that I'd answer back, counter him, refuse point blank. In which case, he'd reply, I'd come off the worse: he'd hand me over to some other member of staff. Oh really? And what would his reason for not beating me be? A meeting, something, mind my own business. Sure, sure thing. And as I lie awake in bed, with all this conjectured hogwash tumbling around my skull, I feel the force of my split: yes, of course I've won out, got off scot-free, and two fingers to the yob with the sideburns who calls me Woman; but, deep in my darkness, my conscience gnaws at me, for secretly I feel guilty, unworthy of the privilege of Mr. Wolfe, unfit for his intimacy, which is vital to me; and so, in a sense which is more real, I conclude that I'm defeated. And, though I skip my prayers after all this worry, I do resolve, before drifting off to sleep, not to give up. To bide my time, wait for a sign, be prudent, muster an apology if need be.

Yet in the morning, I rise feeling stronger, more invigorated, and I bypass his pubic bed, condemn it to its own making. Perhaps, after all, I can survive without his services. Who can tell? I go about my business as if there'd been no mishap. I don't clap eyes on him at breakfast, much less do I seek him out. Instead, I back my resolution to reform, to quash my sinful love, with an elaborate internal analysis of his basic wickedness. How can a man keep, just along from those apples, which are the fruit of Paradise, a figure of some devil called Beelzebub and not be at least a Heretic? Explain that to me. He pretends that his small ogre is the original Lord of the Flies, but I've heard that, actually, which sounds more likely, it's the prince of devils who presides in hell alongside Satan. And what's more, the little bronze idol is so especially treasured by its owner, who calls it his Mascot, that one boy who wouldn't listen, and carried on playing until he dropped it and it broke, was given three Detentions in a row, plus three thousand lines—which he had to do all over again because he couldn't spell Beelzebub. No question about it, Mr. Wolfe must be a Heretic, which, as sins go, I'm afraid is a whopper; and besides, the demon is horrible to look at, reminds me of the gnomes which I caught smirking at the bus when I was first sent to this dump.

I compound my inner diatribe with reminders about how, when you stop to consider, his room is stuffed with creepy things: the skin of a sheep, a blackish kaftan, joss-sticks; and what about that picture called the Tree of Misery and Death? Who, in their right mind, other than a Heretic or secret worshipper of Satan, would want such a thing near them, advertising Misery and Bad Habits and Torment and Derangement and Guilt and, biggest of all, running proudly up the trunk, which is coiled with the snake of Eden, Drunkenness? See what I mean?

And then I tell myself that anyway, his desert boots are hideous, and I hate their squeak, and his patchwork ties are ghastly, as is the fact that, though I detest it, he insists on liking rugger and dragging mud into his room and leaving dirty kit strewn about. And those films he shows are boring anyhow. I should just revert to being good while I can. So I try to summarize my predicament with the fact that whatever the perks of his company, which can't be that great because next time, he says, he'll beat me regardless, he's basically using me to do that thing, that secret, which, sooner or later, I might have to admit at confession, though at the moment I couldn't begin to describe it.

I make myself scarce. Today he doesn't teach my class, and I get through my other lessons without particular trouble. In the afternoon, which for those in my year is recreational, I don't bother going to basketwork or leatherwork or pottery or carpentry. I walk out into the wilds. This valley, like a shallow bowl which, abandoned in a damp courtyard, has begun to rust, is dotted with a few stone houses, like dead flies. It makes you yearn for the red flame of a brick cottage, which, if ever you spot one, always turns out to belong to some master, and brings you back to bleak reality. The wind around these parts blows not as the wind on my beach had done, whose sound was like the salty music of a shell brought to your ear by seas from sunny lands. This wind engulfs you, races through your head, renders you deaf to your own mind. It claims you. And though it brings water to your eyes—which, even if such tears are unfounded, you feel you should disguise—yet there is a peace despite the howl, for, with luck, you will cross the path of no one, pupil or master. And you can stop at the Post Office on your way back, and buy a bag of pear-drops and a bottle of pop with your pocket money. And when you walk into school, at least you can remove the weight of your duffel coat, which is heavier than a camel, and forget the problem of your missing glove, and, despite the smell of sprouts, the warmth of the school feels almost comforting.

I DECIDE TO GO to the library. I do not read the notice on the door, for I have read it once, which is enough. Because it threatens, in letters like those of an old Bible:

> **For him that stealeth a Book from this Library, let it change into a serpent in his hand and rend him. Let him be struck with Palsy, and all his Members blasted. Let him languish in Pain crying aloud for Mercy and let there be no surcease to his Agony till he sink in Dissolution. Let Bookworms gnaw his Entrails in token of the Worm that dieth not, and when at last he goeth to his final Punishment, let the flames of hell consume him for ever and aye.**

Talking is not allowed, though you can look at the *National Geographic*s if you want, and, if no one's got there before you, you can go to the shelf marked Records and play, say, the *Carnival of the Animals*. But never loud, boys.

This was not, however, always easy, owing to a pudgy mythomane by the name of Hardy, whose soft great head was attached to the rest of him by means of a much-vaunted spastic neck, which, whenever he pleased to raise it in the infirmary, exempted him from games. Hardy boasted an impressive line in faking teachers' signatures, and I now suspect that he may have been my (thwarted) rival in the affections of Mr. Wolfe. He further claimed to be in direct descent of the Marlboroughs, and did, to grant him his due, succeed in hoodwinking lots of us, including the more gullible domestics. But perhaps as a consequence of his high claim, he would, in much the same way as a certain class of tourist insists on monopolizing the best deck chair, insist on monopolizing the library gramophone, only ever to play the rousing strains of "Land of Hope and Glory," which projected him into visible raptures. It made you want to strangle not just the smitten devotee, but also both the Sirs whom, in their different ways, I held accountable: Winston Churchill and Edward Elgar.

This strange fantastical creature was older than I, and more eager of body, so that when his number was finally up—because someone with a conflicting passion for Purcell's Trumpet Voluntary clobbered and nearly properly crippled him—he resolved, instead, to become Grand in a manner which, to me, was far more intriguing. And his party trick became, for the benefit of anyone who cared to request a viewing (I don't think that he charged a fee), the leisurely retraction of his advanced foreskin. A specific facial attitude accompanied this action, but I'm sure that you can envisage it. And yet his grandeur did not stop there, for when he gained access to that realm which, to us, was far more fabulous than any Blenheim, namely the realm of the honest-to-goodness Ejaculator, he would, by way of confirmation, trap the jisms of his seed in the glassy confines of an old ink-bottle, which he carried about his person—you never knew who might require proof positive.

I suppose that in his keenness to earn the popularity of which my mother spoke so highly, he could conceivably have concocted his magical goo with a pinch of sherbet and splosh of milk, or by rummaging around in the chemistry laboratory, but such ruses then eluded me, for I wasn't so much devious as deviant. And later, when I learnt about the whole mystery of cavaliers, a clan of which, it turned out, I was a member, I did obliquely badger my mother for an explanation about the phenomenon that was roundheads—among whom, once I grew more inquisitive, I discovered Mr. Wolfe to figure—but she simply blanched with pure ignorance. And when, one day on the terrace at lunch, she was inspired to invoke my father's assistance, the latter replied that circumcision was a thing that happened to Jews. Which, since the school was so rampantly Catholic, somewhat baffled me.

MY RESOLVE TO AVOID Mr. Wolfe was to prove, needless to say, short-lived, not so much because I feared myself incapable of surviving without his favours—after all, insults and bullying didn't kill you, they just made your life a misery—but for other, more delicate reasons. What I found myself in, where I was steeped, little though I then realized it, was a place infinitely more risky, which is, I'm ashamed to admit, (or was), the pit of idolatry. To me he mattered more than a mountain of Beelzebubs. And aside from all his other attributes—his strength, his touching humour, his gentleness, his kindness—the man was just so beautiful. My mother had declared that men could not be such a thing; it was not possible: a man could only at best be handsome, and a handsome man (by which, I suspect, she automatically meant a gentle-man) should play his looks down, carry himself with modesty, not like some flashy word in italics. But Mr. Wolfe (for even in my recollection that is what he would always be—his Christian name having somehow felt inadmissible, unutterable) really was beautiful. Oh Mother he was, though you were never to see it. You were too busy seeing to your own exquisiteness.

His (how could it not have been?) was a shifty kind of beauty: large but twitchy, strong yet uneasy, almost criminal, or political, or wounded. Certainly there was, to me, a magnetic danger about it. His head may, I think, have been too small for his frame, or perhaps his body was too massive, or perhaps it's simply that I became accustomed to admiring him upwards. He was the tallest member of the staff, and, though hugely adult to my mind, among the youngest. I now surmise that he must have been in his mid-twenties, but the great age-gap between us felt more miraculous than mad, like a stormy sea that had been crossed against all wisdom, but crossed without (apparent) mishap. When I did observe him, and astonish myself at the sight, he was always fully clothed, for his nakedness, to me, was simply a fluores-cence in a dream, otherworldly, flickering and shadowed and amor-phous as a wilderness, to do with everything but my eyes, which, during our nights, preferred to be closed. No, it was in the day that I absorbed my good fortune. But after hours, it was he who feasted on me and my young prettiness, which, then, was the most that I can have provided. Yet our appreciation, if not simultaneous, was mutual. Of that, to this day, I remain certain.

There was something athletic about him. You could imagine him throwing a discus high over my father's Alma Mater, and then smiling at his triumph, but coyly. And it was really this mix of strength and unlikely demureness that I found so striking, of vastness and vulnera-bility. Perhaps others weren't aware of it—which suited me: I had no need of eagle-eyed creeps like Hardy (not yet, at any rate). My lover's trousers were always, in my opinion, a fraction tight. When he sat at his desk marking essays, the seams of his inside legs puckered like scars, and these emphasized his thighs, which, conflictingly, I never thought could be tight enough. I tried never to look at his crotch. He had no hips; he was built like a man. But when he stood in the refectory during grace, he sometimes fidgeted with his buckle, or with the metal tongue of his zip, which drove me to hunger. Because he was my sole appetite, you see, my only nourishment.

His eyes were Irish, or American, beyond England. They were grey and dappled and heavy-lidded, a little sinister, with very long straight lashes, immensely dark. His skin was, by contrast, most fair, and fine, and might even have veered towards a pale sort of freckledness. And then there was, of course, that savage beard, clipped but thick and coppered, both redder and coarser than the hair on his head, which was soft, and which often flopped, and which, in another life, he might have let grow like the hair of a Christ. But the beard, you just wanted to stroke it, to rub it, as if, by doing so, you might tame a wild animal, the one inside you. The thrill of it was audible.

He wasn't really a talker, as I recall, other than in class, but there, in any case, everything was the wrong way round. He taught me English for a while, but the language that he really taught me was far richer and sweeter and more complex than any language ever to issue from my father. Mr. Wolfe had a weakness for poetry; but when he read it out, he sometimes bit his lip between stanzas, as if he were harbouring a distraction. And those poems, well, you have to believe me, they were principally recited for my benefit. Who else in the room, other than the two, the two, the two of us could possibly know how the world, which seemed to lie before us like a land of dreams, so various, so beautiful, so new, hath really neither joy, nor love, nor light, nor certitude, nor peace, nor help for pain? As I say, there was something wounded about him—but beautifully so, heartbreakingly.

Once I began to nurse my own half-broken heart, the remembrance of gardenias seemed no longer to suffice. I had too much lonely blood inside me, too much of it to pump around, and I needed help to keep myself alive. Ultimately I believe that it was my emotional hunger, my craving for survival on this front, more than any precocious desire for control or wish for exemption from those activities which I considered unpalatable, that accounted for my susceptibility in the face of this new surrogate love. Its physical dimension felt, at the start, but incidental, part of the life-saving package, and I think that the satisfaction which I derived, the replenishment, lay closer to solace than to anything approaching sated lust: I was too prudish, too mental. Too childish. I sometimes suspect that my pleasure then was akin to the pleasure felt by many grown women, which flows without a need of climax. My ungrown body, smooth and fresh and tanned, may have provided him with incentive, provocation even, but in retrospect, from my perspective, I would say that it gave me away, betrayed me, for its awkward incompleteness manifested outwardly the unformed state of my character. Still, I was grateful to have been perceived by him, and adopted, and salvaged; and besides, there was more to our union than mere reciprocal charity.

At evening prayers, I sit carefully towards the rear of the chapel but, on my way out, I catch sudden sight of his bearded mouth beaming from the loft above, baring its teeth at me; and though I instantly avert my eyes, as if I'd noticed him before he'd clapped eyes on my back, my entrails are going mad, leaping and jolting and banging. Singing praises; giving thanks. And when he goes round the dormitories later that night, his composure is such that never in a million years would you have dreamt that any obstacle, least of all a Ping-Pong bat, had ever separated us. You would have assumed that I'd genuinely been thrashed. His smile, now, as if to verify this fact, is broader than ever, loaded with indulgence, persuading me that we must let bygones be precisely that. And it is followed, this shameless subtle smile, by the wink and the pout of better times, which makes me melt, and close my eyes, and start to choke up.

There follows the inevitable resumption of our romance, its first reunion having felt perhaps a fraction rough. I remember him biting me, quite hard, but I also remember feeling so exhilarated, so grateful that he should have chosen to rise above, to leave unmentioned the original subject of our discord, which stemmed less from any inherent fear of violence on my part than, ironically, from an abhorrence of sports involving contact, that frankly, I would have let him, had this been the price of his generous silence, take a chunk out of my calf. For just as one might recognize an old flame on a busy street even after decades have passed, I recognized, however briefly, however confusedly, what it was to be Back. And I was unwilling to go without my twilight happiness. My difficulty, if any, became less the business of offering myself up than the thought of tearing myself apart from the making of our inexplicable love; and returning to my bed is what began to feel like the real, cold lie. And thus we met, in this enchanted, repetitive ritual, which sometimes lasted until the sky diluted to violet, night after night. And my person was never once harmed. And as term grew to a close, what began to fill me with dread was not so much the return to the land of my forefathers as another severance from the source of my love.

DURING THE EASTER HOLIDAYS, because I was growing more obviously disagreeable about my (public) school life, and also, she had remarked, because I seemed "introverted" around the house, my mother gave me, to mollify me, a tiny battery-operated record player which was, then, the last word in technical gadgetry. This, when I returned to school, I locked among my other tuck-box secrets and, when I was free, I would (though always clandestinely) play my Spanish forty-fives. Those banal renderings, which unlike their English counterparts seemed always to tell stories rooted in regret and duplicity and rotten love, were like hymns to me, anthems, chants of disembodiment. I knew every lyric; I learnt every harmony. There was an imaginary nostalgia attached to the whole experience, as if truly, at that moment, I were the long-suffering secretary, or the neglected wife, or the Love of Man (Amor de Hombre), or the woman singing Eres Tú (You are), whose words, swollen into hysterical orchestrations, sobbed along with lengthy eulogies versed in abstracted similes—like a dagger when it cuts, or a cloud which raises me from the ground and nails me to the sky like a word, or like a game of chance which seeks neither to lose nor to triumph, or like a guitar in the night. And just as later I was to identify with the hero and the victim and the mongrel and the woman and the close-up in the pornographic pastimes which were to crowd the years of my maturing, so, here, I became every voice, every mood, every wretched figure in the songs, for they appealed to my sentimental hollows, and taught me, if not as yet to lie persuasively to others, to do so, and soundly, to my own innards. Yet there was to my activity, which felt risky as well as thrilling, a basic honesty, a pure suspension, such as is recommended when receiving the sacrament of Communion.

To begin with, I played my records covertly, in places where I knew that I wouldn't be seen: behind the gymnasium, or in the woods if it wasn't raining. The showers, too, when empty, provided me briefly with an indoor venue—at least until, one careless afternoon, I found myself being bawled asunder by the Kernel and his band of mountaineers. Drenched in the torrent of their collective ridicule, I was thereafter to find sanctuary in Mr. Wolfe's room, where our arrangement became that if he went out he would lock me in, and, on his return, after protractedly fiddling with his noisy keys, would kick the door as though it were jammed (like the door in the lavatories) three times before walking in. As the plot thickened, of course, we were to devise more sophisticated codes, to denote hide-in-the-cupboard-I've-got-people-with-me, or blow-out-the-joss-sticks, or stop-smoking-and-open-the-window, or get-off-the-phone, that sort of thing; I can't recall the exact details. But for now, this small trinity of kicks did me nicely.

IT WAS AROUND THAT PERIOD that a nebulously sacred show was set to hit the West End scene, the libretto of which, with canny commercial prescience, had already been scored, recorded, and widely distributed. The songs of this musical (which luckily remained, as yet, unseen, for it turned out to be a trifle racy) provided the archaic religious sector with the means to doff a biretta vaguely in the direction of modernity, which I suppose encompassed contemporary Christianity. This music became popular both among staff and pupils at my school, and although Mr. Wolfe had not exactly struck me on account of his spiritual leanings, nowhere was this double album more prized than in his room, for he was devoted to theatre-going generally and to musical theatre in particular. For my own part, I disliked the majority of those numbers, which, one after another, seemed to scream and shout towards the genre of rock-'n'-roll—an anathema to me still—but there was one ballad in particular which did manage to bewitch me horribly, and I use that adverb advisedly: for, while I was magnetized by its melody and the visceral soprano of Mary Magdalene (who'd been no saint, that much I knew), her lyrics about not knowing how to love him, or what to do, or how to move him, and about being changed and seeing herself and seeming like someone else—all of these things discomfited me. And then she would ask the whole world whether she should bring him down, whether she should scream and shout, whether she should speak of love, let her feelings out. But the woman was a tease: much as I listened to her moaning and her fretting, she offered me no solutions, she came without answers. But anyway, Mr. Wolfe—and perhaps this was my doing—contracted an equal fascination with the song, so that the Nocturnes of our earlier congress now gave way to the first of those LPs. And though bizarre as an accompaniment, it felt almost mandatory. But because I was only really obsessed with that one minor hit, which was to become weirdly ours, and ours forever, long after it was all history, I would get up with greater frequency than the Land of Hope and Glory boy could, even in his most outlandish imaginings, have dreamed conceivable, ever to return the needle to its place of origin, which, as the nights grew longer, grew scratchy. And I remember how, in my idiocy, every time I crossed that candle-lit room to fulfil my self-inflicted duty, I would hide my corrupted but unfinished body in my dressing-gown, which itched.

Sometimes, though, I'd let the record run to its natural end, particularly if Mr. Wolfe had risen to a second apex, which, though heavier for me, and more arduous, somehow felt more flattering, more amorous: it must have been for my benefit, I imagined, that he was putting himself through this additional exertion. It was as if, unable to believe the experience, he were forcing himself to return to the top of a beautiful mountain to show me the view. And after his descent we would both, briefly, feel more tired, so that the needle of the record, left to go round and round, would suggest the dreamy sound of a small wave lapping against a harbour. And occasionally the candle would go out. And we might even snooze for a while, my body saved from the cold of the wall by the wall of his warm arms. But I would never allow myself to drift off entirely, for I sensed danger in that extravagance, and furthermore, the flexing floorboards in the corridor never properly let up.

TODAY, HOWEVER, the most natural thing happens. I awake in his bed to the initial clangs of the early-morning bell. Obviously Mr. Wolfe isn't on duty, which for him is just as well, but for me this feels like my certain funeral. I must, without detection, get myself back to the dormitory, and sharpish. I leap into my pyjamas. Mr. Wolfe, in his stupor,

doesn't seem to grasp the catastrophe. I ignore him for now, and, paralyzed, stand inside the doorway. Then, once the duty master has gone
by, and his bell died down, which means he's busy ripping someone
else's blankets up, I unlock the door and creep out; but I feel so hot that
it's far worse than blushing. More as if a raging fever had suddenly
claimed me, as if I were starting to die. I'll have to pretend to the rest of
the dorm that I was feeling sick and went to the night-lav.

But when I reach my dormitory, I know that I've had it. The master
on duty, who, though he looks Indian, claims to be a Scot of Italianate
extraction—Mr. Bonifacio was, I think, the name under which he travelled until dismissed for playing strip-poker *tête-à-tête* with some older
pupil—is engrossed over my bed, and patting my bottom sheet, which
must be incriminatingly frosty, with the palm of his dusky hand. For a
man rarely without either a cigarette or jibe to mouth (and usually it is
both), today seems like a miracle, a nightmare: he is absolutely silent . . .
until at last, and rather quietly, he asks me to account for my absence. (I
can't say the chapel because it's locked at night. I can't say the lavatory
because you can't be there for hours. I can't say my classroom because
the lights have been dark.) So in the end—and fast thinking is required—I produce a clever fabrication of what's really happened. I say
that I've just been with Mr. Wolfe. Oh *really*? (He seems not quite to
believe me, which feels unjust.) Yes, I reply, I went to see Sir because I
couldn't sleep, but he said I wasn't allowed a sleeping pill, and told me to
watch TV for a while, and then I must have gone to sleep, because he
didn't wake me up until I woke up on his sofa. Mr. Bonifacio grins as if
he's suddenly got the gist, and I think that I may have fooled him,
because now he's walking very slowly out, looking pleased with himself,
or with me, relieved that I haven't done anything really serious like stealing, or setting the place on fire. And then he starts to swing his bell
again and, nodding to left and right, he resumes his early-morning
round. And although all these oafs with gunky eyes stand about gawp-
ing at me, no one quite dares to mention the subject. Peace in our time.

After the drama with the missing rugger peg, and the unspoken difficulties to which it gave rise, I decide, sensibly enough, not to scuttle
off like some sneak to tell Mr. Wolfe what has happened; instead, since
Mr. Bonifacio fell hook-line-and-sinker for my version, I resolve to

keep this new matter, which seems trivial by comparison, quiet. On second thoughts, I might just tell Mr. Wolfe tonight, for a laugh.

I AWAKE WITH THE GLARE of a torch pointed hard at my eyes. I turn to my side, try to identify the clever prankster. But it's Mr. Bonifacio, prodding my shoulder and whispering to me in his frantic Scottish voice to get up fast and not disturb the others. He tip-toes back to the corridor and dawdles on a creaky floorboard. I fumble around in the dark, belt my dressing-gown tightly, and follow him outside. In the gloom of the tunnel he shines the torch along the floor, like a stream of yellow brightness, like a river running away from India; and about his face I glimpse a smile that looks a bit nervy, sort of servile, as if he needed to request some favour from me, help with a translation or something. I feel quite flattered, grown-uppish. This might spell the start of my mother's keenly commended popularity. And I'm almost excited when he lets me accompany him down the principal staircase, which is thickly carpeted and reserved for the use of staff and prefects, although one of the latter once toppled over the banister and fell to the feet of Our Lady, crashing against the stone floor and fracturing his skull. This was before my time, but people still spoke, with expressions of recollected horror, of the tragedy. Because all the school's doctors and all the school's prayers couldn't put Prefect together again.

Mr. Bonifacio cedes me the way into his room, a courtesy which slightly surprises me, but still, I thank him, go in ahead, and wait in the middle of his shag-pile. He closes the door behind him—thereby suggesting to me that the matter under discussion is to be adult, confidential. He goes over to his desk, sits down with a cough, and offers me the opposite chair, which must be for parents because it feels high and rather comfortable. The room is dimmed. Only an anglepoise lamp stands, like a stork, on the oxblood leather of his desk, and now he directs the light straight into my eyes, like a spot in a circus. My sudden exposure blinds me. I can no longer even imagine his outline. I ask whether the beam could be shifted slightly. He says it's fine like that, which irks rather than frightens me, for his behaviour strikes me, particularly after the entrance ceremonial, less as menacing than as ill-mannered. I know that I could move my chair back a fraction, but something tells me not to push my luck. I put my hands in my lap. I look down. I resign. I hear him opening a drawer and plonking a paper pad in front of him. He plucks a Biro from his jacket and clicks it ready for action.

He begins: Now, I want you to tell me all about last night. What exactly were you up to, you and Mr. Wolfe? Goes without saying you can rest a hundred per cent assured nothing you say will go further than these four walls. Strictly private and confidential. (I was right.) He offers me his word of honour. His Biro now seems to be on its marks, and set . . . and yet it cannot go, for though my shrivelled heart is racing like the clappers, my mouth just will not start, is cramped at the gullet. We remain in our respective attitudes for what seems like an embarrassment, until he sighs and pretends to reassure me: Take your time; it's all right; I understand this can't be easy for you . . . —But the oils of his charm cannot assuage the turbulence of my muddy waters.

Next, he tries another tack: he's going to make things less difficult, he says, and provides a few simple questions. He asks whether I like Mr. Wolfe. Yes, Sir. Glad to hear it, he replies, and does Mr. Wolfe like you? I rein myself in and reply that I think so. Quite right too, you strike me as a nice chap, though we don't really know one another all that well, do we? I suppose not. Now tell me, why was it that you couldn't sleep? Don't know. Don't know *Sir.* Yessir. Does this happen to you often? Sometimes it does. And when it happens do you go to Mr. Wolfe? Not always. But sometimes you do, right? Yes, Sir. And then, what happens? Nothing, Sir. Are you sure? Positive. (Doubtful silence.) Listen, he smarms, you know you can trust me, don't you? I've given you my word of honour, haven't I? Yes, Sir, I know; you have. So tell me, what went on? (Eternal almost blissful nocturnal pause.) Nothing, I reply.

I can tell that I'm beginning to get up Mr. Bonifacio's nose. He extracts a packet of fags. Offers me one—his little joke. Would I like to light his cigarette for him? If he likes, Sir. He puts a shiny lighter on the desk, and slides it across to my side. I stand up and, at long last, am out of the beam, which has been scorching me like the white sun from the cliff above my childhood. He hoicks the bulge in his trousers, leans forward in his seat, and approaches me. As my flame trepidates toward the tip of his cigarette, his hand, like the hand of Judas, embraces mine; it kisses my fingers. My loyalties screech with sudden outrage, but I don't let on. Not a flinch; not a hint. For I begin to see more clearly now the place to which we're headed; yet though I glimpse the signpost of our dealings, it seems to point, like a two-headed eagle, in opposite directions. I decide that whichever road he hopes to take, whether it's to fetch me into his life or to slay Mr. Wolfe, both routes must be blocked. And I yearn very fleetingly for the softness of my lover's lips upon me. Mr. Bonifacio inhales superlatively, like an elderly maharani reliving her story, and when his smoke is in due course expelled, pearl-grey ringlets seem to hang about the shiny edges of his face. I want to go.

But this is not going to happen yet, I can tell you. Indeed, the interrogation drags on and on and on and on. He's trying to wear me down, to run me out, and he's not doing the job half badly. I stifle a yawn. I reply in monosyllables to what my mother would call his impertinences. He manages to ascertain, and to record, the facts that on That Night I couldn't sleep, that I went to Mr. Wolfe's room, that we sat on the sofa, that we watched TV, though I can't remember exactly what (*Colditz*?)—a lapse of memory which strikes him as unlikely, no? I do not admit whether Mr. Wolfe did or did not touch me during the proceedings. There are limits. Three times I refuse. The room is so still that you could have heard a cock crow.

Mr. Bonifacio is not too pleased with me. He thinks I'm not being co-operative. I think that he's being nosy. He says that I'm not to mention our little chat to anyone, understood? I allege that I won't. He tells me to go straight back to bed now; and as he pats my creeping back, he adds that he hopes there won't be a repetition of this unfortunate incident, by which I don't think he means our interview. Good night, Sir. Good night, Moore. And once he has closed his door, I make my leaden way all the way to the end of the corridor, lit only, and only at occasional intervals, by misty forms which, like oblongs of grey gauze, seem to steal in through the classroom windows. And I climb, exhausted, up the back stairs—for servants and common-or-garden boys. I do not, though I long for his embraces more fervently than ever before, dare to knock on Mr. Wolfe's door, and I drift like a diminished ghost back to my dormitory. And although, once in bed, I tell myself that I've acquitted myself passably, nor do I imagine that I'm yet out of the woods: for my intuition fears that I may yet find myself hurtling, like the rapids of a river, towards a forest without clear exit. And were it not for the fact that my stomach is still in spasms, you could have thought that I was already dead, dead meat, a corpse.

IN THE MORNING, my former caution now thrown to the rising winds of panic, I scour the place in search of Mr. Wolfe: dormitories, washrooms, dining room, chapel loft. I put my ear to the masters' lavatory: not a murmur. I even stick my head round the door of the staff common room: nothing. But, just before assembly, I find him at last, coming, drained of blood, out of the headmaster's study. He yanks me aside and orders me, with a lack of caution equal to mine, his eyes wilder than fury, to meet him in his room at once, to skip assembly, get up there fast.

He closes his door. Seems already to know what's gone on. Doesn't appear annoyed so much as fretful, and now begins to shake with sinister force, like a man in the late throes of Parkinson's. Even the legs of his dark trousers seem to be quivering, which I find alarming. Shouldn't he go to the infirmary? As he tries to talk to me, his mouth sounds drained of saliva. He clears his throat several times. He stays well away from me, as if he feared me suddenly, as if I were a Danger sign. Doesn't bother to berate me—no time—nor even to ask me why I didn't warn him I'd been caught by Bonifacio. Appreciates how, after the interview last night, I didn't dare to come to him. It's all right. He'd actually suspected something might be up.

It turns out that Mr. Bonifacio has recorded the entire interrogation, and taken the tape to the headmaster, who's already played it back to Mr. Wolfe, who says that they're determined to get to the bottom of the matter. Mr. Wolfe tells me, with sudden gravity, as if everything depended on my grasping this fact, that he is not, repeat not, a Homosection, but Bi, which sounds confusingly mathematical. I nod moronically. He tells me that we're in serious trouble, both of us, but stresses that his plight is more critical than I may realize. His entire career, he says, hangs in the balance. They're out for his blood, even though yes, the whole thing's a set-up, it's obvious: Bonifacio just wants to stab him in the back and go for the job of supervisor. More responsibility; better money. For both our sakes I must call the headmaster's bluff, which sounds like he wants me to insult him. I must deny-deny-deny. Nothing went on, remember. Not a word on that tape that I need to retract. Mustn't give in to the pressure. Stick to my story, volunteer nothing. My age, my innocence, my lack of experience all count in my favour. But Mr. Wolfe says I have an old head on my young shoulders, and that he knows he can rely on me. He's proud of me. If I play my cards right, the whole thing might just blow over, storm in a teacup stuff. Headmaster says he wants to see me straight after assembly, but is eager that the business be kept under wraps, so I'm not to stand outside his study: his orders are just to go in without knocking, and wait for him to arrive. Mr. Wolfe's trembles have abated marginally, but I, by contrast, now find myself steeped back in the waters of my turbulence, and being dragged alone downstream, flailing, as I had feared, towards the forest of disaster. I can go now, he says, sitting down. And good luck.

I FOLLOW MY INSTRUCTIONS. The headmaster's study, to which I have never before been granted access, is identical in shape to the room of my nocturnal travels, but more busily decorated, in shades of chestnut and almond and raisin and walnut, like breakfast cereal, or feed for a hamster. The overall effect of his walls, which are flocked with papers of clashing pattern, as if slapped up with unrelated ends-of-lines, brings to mind a struggling provincial restaurant, too genteel to stoop to white, too poncy quite to fool the punter. The drapes, tied back with cords better suited to a dressing-gown, are Georgian-striped in treacle and milk-chocolate. The pelmet droops lopsidedly. Next to a foam-filled sofa, covered with a stretchy homage to autumnal foliage and circular cushions of fake tapestry, is a three-legged side-table bearing an onyx ashtray with a dainty brass plaque, and a lamp in the shape of a Taiwanese pagoda, its ruched shade swooping in creases of caramel nylon, and festooned, in café-au-lait, with dolly tassels. I suspect that implicated in these arrangements has been the proud plebeian hand of the headmaster's wife, a pockmarked lump of a woman with puffy ankles, a frantic tic about her piggy eyes, and a propensity for perfume such as is to be found at funfairs, who ekes her own stipend by helping at Reception part-time—courtesy not of her husband but of Mr. Pitman, she'll have you know, can touch-type good as the next one. Along from the desk stands a teak-effect filing cabinet, its top drawer, half-opened and labelled Juniors, set too high for me to peer inside. A vast, engraved and crested cup of silver plate, lid dented, worn to copper round the handles, and set upon a flaking pedestal of simulated ebony, presides over alphabetical folders of cardboard. On the radiator sits a soggy tea-towel with a harvest scene, shepherdesses on haystacks, stained with patches of unattributable gunge; and, propped next to the pipes, directly below where my pyjama-button once struck, a folded shooting stick with a seat of pigskin, in plastic. On the other side, a muddy bag of golf irons, no putt. A cracked-veneer bookcase, gleaming with leatherette volumes amassed by mail-order from Sunday supplements—some laid horizontally, for the style—displays, on a dusty Bible, a pale wooden crucifix with a basic stand, its resinous Christ glued into agony and designed to be luminous. Flung into the wastepaper basket there huddles a small mound of teabags, like a drowned litter of newborn mice. And on the desk itself, peeping from beneath a mess of timetables and files stacked over a virginal dictionary, I detect, for the first time, the black oxtongue of a ferula. I have no desire to touch it. I perch on one end of the sofa, avoiding its clammy arm, and let my eyes glaze over the fitted carpet which, needless to say, is richly patterned with lozenges and goldy medallions. But my body leaps to its feet as soon as I hear him arriving.

As HE ENTERS in sharp profile, led by his paunch and followed by a tweedy hump, the headmaster resembles a pompous great hamster, like a puffy rodent from a children's book, but sweatier, and exudes the powdery stench of that class of man who, a stranger by birth to pomade and essence of vetiver and sandalwood and extract of lime, has lately broadened the coal-tar of his toilet to encompass, as well as unisex hair-lacquer and an electric dryer (handy for the reduction of moisture from unwashed underarms), musky products which, found at the local supermarket and designed to deodorize, he employs, less complicatedly, simply to mask. Fabergé, if I'm not mistaken, was the misleading brand.

He sees me, of course, but pretends to find himself in private. He goes to the window and looks out absently, in an unconscious approximation of my motions by candlelight one floor above; then, he turns abruptly to face me, his coat-pockets flapping. He smacks his lips. Beads on his upper lip jump. Long, gingery hairs creep up from the

slack collar of his paisley shirt, which he wears with a natty corresponding tie. I cannot, even for the sake of Mr. Wolfe, to whom I owe
my courage, muster the travesty of a smile. Sit down, Moore, says the
headmaster, and I return myself to the stretchy sofa, trying not to look
too disgusted, like a society woman at the lodgings of her wet nurse, as
if this were the kind of motion I underwent every day of my life.

A matter of some gravity has, he announces, been brought to his
attention; and although the circumstances, he adds, may not be my
responsibility entirely, he would, notwithstanding, like to be availed of
my version of the facts. (Deny-deny-deny: this is my mantra.) His
questions are dull, identical to those of Mr. Bonifacio, and I answer
them just as dully; but I pretend, for the sake of authenticity, for the
sake of my lover, to be more thrown than I am: I have a bash at melodrama: I fidget with my hands, jiggle my ankle, yank an earlobe once or
twice. And, when chance allows it, I sneak a look out of the window
and think of the viaduct, of the circus, of Russia.

The headmaster makes one error only—though, to me, it is of significant advantage: by failing to disclose Mr. Bonifacio's recording of
our séance, which is the sole source of his (somewhat restricted) information, and instead pretending that we're starting from scratch, he cannot even fast-forward me to a more detailed confession. His feigned
ignorance empowers me, feels like a second try at the same demeaning
part—and now, furthermore, performed in easy broad daylight and
before a less ambiguous auditioner. He encourages me to blab, not
least by sliding out, from beneath the mound of administrative paper-
work, his pet ferula, and by tapping it against his podgy hand. Wafts of
his onion-odour pass me. I disregard them, but long to wrinkle my
snout, and wish that I were upstanding, for my mother's haughty blood
is pricking at my snobbish arteries. I don't look down, I don't look up. I
look straight ahead, and from where I sit, all that I can see, as he struts
about like a fat fool in a pantomime, is his low-slung wobbly rear and,
when he paces back, the compression of his tautened little crotch—
which I keep dodging. To stare seems inadvisable.

Behind the sweaty blubber of my inquisitor hangs a large monochrome photograph, like an advert for invisible hearing aids, depicting
the side of a corvine head in a pose of burning concentration. The sitter, the 28th General of our Society, otherwise known as the Black

Pope, who, to my sudden shock, I now read to be a Spaniard, bestows, in a looping but disjointed hand, his holy blessing, to which the head-master is welcome. And next to the crow, in gaudily contrasting colour, hangs the face of an ancient nurse or nun, with gums grinning out through a burnished landscape of wrinkles, and whose veil, though less pastoral than the article on the radiator, closely resembles a tea-towel.

We're not doing very well, the headmaster fears. I fear we could be going round forever, ring-a-roses. He keeps repeating, with dogged cir-cularity, the impoverished repertoire of his enquiries—bed, Wolfe, sofa; TV, sleep, Bonifacio—as if in the hope of boring me into bleating some titillating new snippet, but of course he comes too late, poor man. For, overnight, I have become the sort of liar blessed with the gift genuinely to believe his own lies, to merge with his fiction. Yet there is no confusion about me: I could recite my replies in my dreams, or under oath, or back to front if needed be—at least in Spanish. Yet he does hold one, great, trump surprise up his sleeve; and, after a colour-ful bunch of what sound like clichés about chickens and eggs and rights and wrongs and sanctity and marriage and smoke and fire and rhyme and reason and method and madness—plus, obviously, about old heads upon young shoulders—he unearths a poisoned fork from within the fronds of his verbal shrubbery, to inform me that my father has been apprised of my activities, and is, even as we speak, winging his way over. Won't be long before we get to the bottom of this whole mat-ter. And then, with one last triumphant smack of lips, he alludes to pipers and to tunes.

THE WEATHER, when my father came, could not have been more fair to him: I remember it as one of those rare idyllic days when the English countryside seems to be sanctified by radiance. Seas of green velvet, hills of magenta rhododendrons, cornflower skies unblemished by a single worrisome cloud. Sunshine fit for Alma Maters, worthy of fathers and sons.

I had been instructed, by means of a scrappy telephone message, to meet him at the front of the school tomorrow, Saturday, straight after class; and as I stood there on the entrance steps while the others trooped off to lunch, I remember that I didn't know quite how to be, whether apprehensive about his visit or relieved by it, but I had

dressed as sprucely as I could, not so much to present a neat picture—
a front of impregnability—as in the hope of pleasing him. He might
even tell my mother that I was looking smart. Meanwhile, I reviewed
the question of my innocence from every conceivable angle: my mind
was clear: nothing at all had happened: couldn't have done: I couldn't
let anyone down: deny-deny-deny. But I *was* frightened, I can't claim
otherwise. For my father, even if no shrewder a man than the teachers
to whom he had entrusted me, was a better placed examiner, had
stronger access to my insides—and not because he understood me
any better than the headmaster or Mr. Bonifacio, never mind my lover
(he certainly didn't), but because, unlike them, he did enjoy a claim
upon my history. And perhaps because I associated him with my beautiful fragile mother, or perhaps because I had not yet properly crossed
the border of the Commandments and learnt (though I did already
dishonour him) to despise him, I knew that my work with him would
be more arduous. And this knowledge seemed to accelerate my pulse,
for, now, as well as concealing my activities, I would have to preserve
the tenuous fabric of my emotions from unravelling. I think that I
wanted my father to love me. I don't think I knew that he didn't know
how to.

He rolls up at the wheel of a rented car, maroon of all colours. I try
to quash my embarrassment, and tell myself that it doesn't matter. I
notice, as he steps out, that he's wearing the same tweed suit as he wore
when he dropped me off at Euston, along with his Old Boy tie, and
something about the repetition of this costume briefly calms me. But
now, as if to symbolize the victory of his pride in the school over my
failure to do it justice, his gold-and-navy stripes defy the balmy wind-
lessness and flap over his shoulder, which is strong as any burden, I am
sure, resilient as the shoulder of St. Christopher.

When he climbs out of the car, he seems a kingdom away, closer to
my motherland, and the gravel that divides us feels like an ocean. As he
proceeds in my direction, although his steps never shorten, his pace
seems to diminish. His chestnut brogues grind into the gravel. His face
is briefly shaded, but as it emerges, I see, I fear, how badly he wishes
that the reason for his descent were otherwise, that he were come to
visit some other pupil, a properly English one, a promising sportsman,
a future prefect, a mathematician if you must. And now, as he looms

over me, he confirms my suspicion by withholding from my cheek the kiss of Latin custom and, instead, sticking out his right hand.

I shake it credibly, convincingly, as my mother might have shaken the hand of officialdom. He brings his tie back down, and strokes it nostalgically, which makes me oddly sad, almost sorry for him. Together we turn our backs to the building, but he leads the way, walking markedly faster now. I half-trot to keep up. Inside the motorcar, I notice the prong of a loose spring under my seat, but I tell myself that he can't have known this; it's not his fault; stop it. And then I'm struck by the smell of his cigars. I think about asking for permission, decide not to disturb him, and unwind my window—which is reluctant. I struggle. He switches on the radio . . . only to be rewarded by an irreparable wartime crackle. He flicks off the contraption and tuts, fed up. We drive along in silence, through the fields and lakes and past the insouciant Madonna, and I pray that no one will recognize me in this hideous car. But then I tell myself that I don't care: I'm travelling with my father, and what's good enough for him is good enough for both of us.

He stops at the next village, not far from my half-term pub, and we go into some kind of inn, where I suspect that he may be staying, though I don't attempt to enquire. None of my business. He goes straight past the bar, walks into an underpopulated dining room which smells of sprouts, and settles for a corner table by a window overlooking a meagre lawn with a hillock of mown grass. Our waitress would like to offer me choices, but he orders on both of our behalfs. Simpler.

Though I'm learning my father's English in leaps and bounds, I haven't opened my mouth—which is just as well, because it would appear that he, bafflingly, has all but forgotten my mother's Spanish. Still, I can understand him—perhaps because, to start with, he restricts his talk to the weather and the bore of driving on the left-hand side. He is being chatty, I can tell, as if I were a car enthusiast. Our food arrives: pure cuisine Alma Mater. Trouble with the vegetables. He says he hopes I'm not going to play up. (Biafra.) I pretend, as I munch, to find myself suddenly and inordinately captivated by the sight of that great lump of mown grass outside. His reflection in the glass tells me that his interest, conversely, is turned inwards, has fixed itself on other diners, on the heartening sight of ordinary English life in progress. He decides that we'll skip pudding if that's all right. He lights one of his smallish cigars, puff, puff. No coffee for the boy, thank you; just for him, yes, black; no sugar, thank you; and I say, he adds, might he have a brandy?

WE RETURN TO THE CAR and trundle back over humps of pocked asphalt in the unmistakable direction of the school, as if the place and the man should not be parted, as if their proximity lent him sustenance. Halfway down the length of the drive, he grips the troublesome gear-stick and forces it down, and down again, and then, as we pass a damaged, spindly railing which, despite its mangled metal, has recently been glossed in white, he brings us to a halt, shudderingly. He turns off the ignition, but allows the hired key to linger in its crevice, as if our stop were only a stop-gap. We could not be more prominently, or uncomfortably, parked. We are tilted into a ditch of grassy mud. Surveyed from the building thus, this fine Old Boy and his unequal son, we must look like a couple of soggy dolls abandoned in a rusted pram by some careless child. I think of my mother and her forgotten doll's-house.

He lights another cigar, which in church is not allowed, but he thinks that we should be joined, he says, in prayer. Luckily he suggests the Our Father, which I now know by heart, and perhaps that's why he's chosen it, to help me out, to make it easier. It can't be easy for him either, all this travelling. Full of grace, he begins, surprisingly loudly. He's a grown-up, that must be why. Then: hallowed be Thy name (I seem to be lagging behind a fraction; I can't hear myself quite; but he doesn't seem to mind, perhaps he isn't angry). And forgive us our trespasses . . . and lead us not into temptation. His Amen, which vibrates upwards, is of fervour, meant—even as it echoes and dwindles around the dank upholstery of the car. His cigar has gone out.

I stare out of the windscreen to free my eyes, and I let them gambol about a hill in front of us, which is bordered by a leafy lane favoured by local sweethearts. I can't think of anything intelligent to ask, or even funny, such as whether in his day wolves ever marauded about these parts, but just as I'm starting to rack my brain for the start of that thing which is the art of conversation, he begins on my behalf. He lets me off the hook, kindly. I listen hard, as if this were an oral exam, but so baroque and intricately strung are the pearls of his investigative wisdom that, by the end of his soliloquy, I'm afraid I've lost any hope of a grip on their unifying clasp. Befuddled silence. I think of my mother's letter last autumn: Don't be frightened to say when you don't understand. And I do just that. Could he please repeat the question? His brow shoots up to his hair-line, which is scraped back, and his eyeballs turn, I think, briefly to white. But I couldn't swear to it, because his head, like mine, seems to be glued to the countryside. Perhaps he was just invoking Our Father for patience, because he doesn't lash out. He understands. He is a clever man.

So he repeats his complicated words and, for my benefit, does so in slightly baby language. He tells me everything that he has heard from the headmaster, which the headmaster heard from Mr. Bonifacio, and of course there are words like Untoward and Irregular and Peculiar and Suspect, but then, as if he were swerving round some awkward question-mark, he adds that he knows how I can be imaginative (which I can), and how this is all very well, but not, you see, always wise, because sometimes stories can be construed (which I think means constructed) as fibs. What is fibs, I mean what are? Lies, boy, bloody lies. (I hope this swearing doesn't mean he's cross like when we went to Euston.) No, it's all right, I don't need to worry, because now he's talking slowly down, so that I can understand and see what he thinks, which is this: that I was probably nosing around, or up to some minor Mischief (which means naughty, not an important young lady) and that I just panicked when I thought I might be punished. But now, uh-uh, I'm starting to follow him without any difficulty at all, because although his pace is speeding up and his volume rising as in prayer, the sense, the sense of his words could not be clearer—my nonsense, he calls it.

My father is quite sure that nothing Untoward (again) can have happened, least of all with my supervisor—who's an Old Boy, he gathers, though I had no idea—nothing at all, not possibly, let's be realistic; so really he has no option but to dismiss the whole rumpus as some childish fabrication on my part (which means a sort of construction, as in building-blocks and castles in the sand and dreams and sounds and waves and sea). Making up. Inventing. Fibs, or lies, whatever. Sins even. But it doesn't feel fair, not really.

To my relief he says that it's all right. I can profit by this incident. I can treat it as a lesson for the future, to do with self-control or something, and now he talks about Truth. And next we're back to prayer. Because at difficult times prayer can help you, help you out, you see. Prayer can provide comfort (like a mohair blanket?). He recommends it, and he also recommends—though it sounds more like an order to me—that I do the decent thing, which, though he sees it won't be easy, will certainly be honourable (this sounds important). And the important thing is that after confessions tonight, I go and apologize for the embarrassment which I have caused to Mr. Wolfe and Mr. Bonifacio, not forgetting the headmaster. My father is confident that they'll be understanding (which means more than translating, it's more like forgiving our trespasses)—kind men all, as well as good Catholics. He reassures me, even though I cannot feel it, that in no time this whole fuss will die down and become a thing of the past. The sooner I get back to a normal school life, the better, he says, for everyone.

But something happens now. It feels as if I'm stuck, unable to wind back the clock of love, yet unable, too, to go forward and do what he wants. I want to please my father, but I cannot tell more lies. They are too much, too heavy to carry, and I do not have the shoulder of St. Christopher. Stuck. I feel myself flushing. I sink in a pause. I must not blub. I think of my mother. And then I stop thinking and tell him that I've made up none of the things which he calls Inventions. What happened, I insist (feeling a little stronger because he's keeping quiet), happened. We remain dug in this silence for a small while, but then he starts to argue in a telly-offy sort of way, and he tells me not to Contradicked him, and I tell him that I'm not, that I'm just sticking up, not being a liar. Not-not-not (Deny-deny-deny).

He never knew, he says, that I could be so Tarsome. And now the question marks, despite his earlier avoidance of the first awkward one, do, like sudden gunfire, begin to fly. And you could understand them in any language, even in Biafran, because there is something enormous about them. What in God's name, he wants to know, is it that I propose be done about this whole preposterous matter? Do I think he's come all this way just to have me waste his bally time? Can I honestly suppose that he's prepared to go to the headmaster to corroborate my stupid lies? How can I conceivably imagine that anyone believes I spent the night on the supervisor's sofa? Isn't it more likely that I was up to—

does he have to spell it out—no good, so to speak, rifling about, pinching something for instance? (My face is scarlet now.) And why, he adds, am I blushing if he's so white-of-the-mark? Am I some kind of idiot? Do I think he never went to school himself, that he doesn't have a clue what he's talking about, that he's entirely devoid of experience, that he was born yesterday? And what, pray, *what* is he meant to tell my poor mother?

Which is when I crack. Like an hysteric and without warning I just begin to howl. He gazes back towards the school flag, relieved finally to have been blessed with a reaction. And I go on howling, as I once did at the Nautical Club, spluttering with anger and longing and misery and injustice. He tells me to cut out the blubbing and pull myself together. At once. Got a good mind to smack me. I stop as abruptly as I began. Right, he decides, that's more like it, perhaps now we can get down to business. Wiping my tears from my chin and my lap (using my nametaped handkerchief) I nod that we can. I've had enough.

But I still need to protect my lover, so I decide to leave out the bits that might get him into trouble. Yet I do tell the (tyrannous) father (who has dared to lash me with the memory of the lost mother) that I'm tired, that I'm not popular, that I can't understand half the time, that I'm no good at anything, that the other boys are ghastly, that nobody washes here, that you can't even use cologne, can you imagine, that the teachers despise me—yes, they despise me—that some of them call me Woman, that I sometimes despair, that I give up. I also tell him, warming to my defence, that Mr. Wolfe is the only kind person among all these Catholics, the only one who likes me, and gives me apples, and cares when I have nightmares, and sometimes, when I feel sad, gives me kisses and hugs because he says affection matters. And although I feel more trapped than any endangered David, I now find the courage to tell the truth to my Goliath, which is that I'm sorry to be such a letdown. But again my tears burst forth in a second rush.

HE FLIES, NAUSEATED, out of the car, plods about the grass, and punches the boot a few times. We're going for a Walk! he orders. (Oh no.) He heads up Lovers' Lane. I take my time. He reaches a stile, and hitches his knee to the first step, as if posing for a hearty snap. He shouts: For God's sake hurry up! And: For God's sake, I think to myself, he's dragging me into that swamp of cow-pat. I stop at the top of the stile before jumping down, not just because the leap worries me, but because now I can peer at him from above, as if I were a high-diver for a moment, and he, still floundering in the beginners' class. Predictably enough, the thought of a helping hand doesn't occur to him. What kind of a sissy am I? Jump.

He forges ahead towards the horizon, less as if he sought to face the future than as if he were in search of his schoolboy past, trying to relive that moment of all moments when he was crowned Victor Ludorum— which, to me, had always sounded like some matinée idol, related to Rodolfo Valentino perhaps, whom my father scarcely resembled, though my mother's own father had done. (I think that even a whole silver jubilee down the line, my father still kept, in one of the drawers of his study, a commemorative medal of the cruel honour—cruel to me, for, in time, that small tarnished coin would come to reflect the sheer magnitude of my failure in his eyes. But I'm sure that whenever he took a peep at that medal, his eyes would have grown sentimental, and the strings of his gold-and-navy heart would have struck up, as the strings of mine, which was livid, had done when I'd floated in my belovèd nurse's arms, or later, as I'd watched my beautiful mother dance, or more lately still, as I'd brought my lover over to the land of rapture.)

I saunter along beside him like a dim-witted beagle, and try to ease matters by kicking a solitary tuft of grass, but, so pitiful is my attempt to be more boyish than I am, I trip, stumble, and nearly go flying. He must have noticed, of course, but, presumably out of pity for me, he refrains from rubbing my nose in the bungle—or so I imagine, until I discover, to my shock and dismay, that now the floods of self-pity are pouring from *his* eyes, not mine, as if *he* were the little boy lost in the middle of nowhere. I pretend to tie my laces while he mops his sorrow with a starched handkerchief—no nametape; white monogram—but I realize, as soon as I reach the ground and genuflect, that my shoes are held together with elastic. Now, he says, with an air of regained composure, let's remain calm about all this, shall we.

Things have to be sorted out, and he's sure that they can; but nobody needs a scandal—wouldn't help anyone. Naturally, he adds, he will make no decision until he's sought guidance tomorrow at Mass. Nothing rash. My welfare is, it goes without saying, of concern to him, but we can't allow that single issue to cloud our judgement. My personal circumstances are—how can he put it?—let's just call them Specific; don't affect other pupils; he doesn't see why the rest should suffer. One can't hold a whole community to ransom, you know. So let him make one thing absolutely crystal clear: the standing of the school is what he considers Paramount (as in a film?). We can't allow the reputation of the place to suffer. I had better understand that. So whatever I'm insisting has gone on Must Not, he says, Get Out.

This last imperative makes my position sound like a cul-de-sac, and yet he forges ahead regardless. He's not saying what's my fault and what isn't; he's just saying that we can do without negative press from provincial hacks, never mind the national papers—field day, they'd have, the school's detractors, all those chippy Protestants; he can practically read the headlines. So—am I listening?—this whole thing Must Not Get Out (Deny-deny-deny). Anyhow, he concludes, he's sure I've had a tiring afternoon, so I'm to run along for tea or what have you now (what have I?) and he'll see me in the morning after Mass.

I SLEEP LIKE A LOG. Not a wave, not a sound, though by the time we convene outside the chapel, it transpires that a good deal of confabulation has gone on during my slumbers. But now that matters seem to be settled, my father is in a sudden hurry, would like to be off straight after lunch. He suggests a quick bite and a chat, and he'll be on his way, long trip back. He claims to have been satisfied by his three sets of drinks with the three relevant members of staff. Mr. Bonifacio my father found a most affable fellow, solely keen, you understand, to pre-empt unwanted trouble—you know how in small communities tongues can wag. And Mr. Wolfe also struck him as most pleasant, perhaps a trifle shy, but clearly a gent: turns out that my father was at school with one of the Wolfe uncles, isn't that a coincidence. Mr. Wolfe's principal concern, or so my father reckons, revolves around my problems adapting to English boarding-school life, and my apparent unhappiness; but my father has explained to my supervisor—as if the latter were ignorant of such platitudes—that it's only natural that boarding school should prove tricky at the start, tricky for anyone, particularly an only child, but next year everything will seem routine to me and my spirits are bound to improve dramatically, he's certain, especially after a summer in the sun. As for the headmaster, well, my father does agree that the man seems rather to err on the plebby side—a convert, he suspects—filthy booze and most peculiar newfangled views on education. (Later, when it was all beyond repair, I discovered that there'd been talk of sending me to a child psychiatrist, which must, as my father swilled his filthy booze, have contributed to his splutters.) Still, he tells me that I'm simply to stick to the rules, and that if things get tricky—say I'm being picked on or whatever—I can write home and tell him about it: he has a couple of chums who sit on the board of Governors. I remind my father that letters are censored on the way out. He reminds me not to be such a ninny: write in Spanish.

I reiterate that I'm miserable. Couldn't I just be moved to some other school, where at least they taught Spanish, so that I could be good at Some Thing? He nods and smiles at the same time. No, no, he explains: I don't seem to quite follow him; there's no need for drastic measures. All public schools are much on a par, none is more or less fun than any other, and furthermore, very few of them are Catholic. He's adamant that a sound religious education is vital, and from that vital point he won't be budged. But he does offer me two pairs of alternatives. First, either I stay where I am and lump it, or I go back to day school at home, thereby squandering any chance of a decent education. Well? he demands. Make up your mind. Which would you rather? It doesn't feel like a choice to me, but: To stay, I reply. Good, so that settles that. And second, he says, if I'm absolutely certain that my plight (and I should examine my conscience carefully on the matter) would be improved in the absence of Mr. Wolfe, he's prepared, just this once, to approach the Governors and moot the possibility of his removal. And something about my father's machination, its confidentiality, its cool corruption, alerts me to the sudden vastness of my power, to the fact that I could wreak havoc—should I bring him down, should I scream and shout, should I speak of love—but of course, it's futile: how could my existence be rendered anything but unendurable in the absence of my saviour? And so, with a look of mock-maturity, I wave this last option aside: No; no need, things aren't that bad. (But I shall never again play rugby.)

Last he reverts to the subject of my mother, with whom he can't possibly be expected to discuss the less savoury aspects of this regrettable saga: wouldn't be fair on her; she wouldn't understand; would just upset her; no point in that. So what he's resolved (again), to help me out, is that he'll pretend I was involved in a theft, some internal enquiry, nothing to worry about, schoolboy stuff, all sorted out. With which, he slaps down his napkin, stands up, tells me that I'll be home in a month, so to look forward to that, and then he suggests that it's probably best, while he settles his account, if I see myself back, he's got to get going. And remember, he adds: no more trouble, get on with your studies, write home when you're told to, and not a word about this to anyone, least of all your mother. He (too) counts on me. I stand back far enough to avoid his hand, and as I lead myself out, backwards, I ask him, in Spanish—which seems to disgruntle him—to give her my love. And I notice, as I scarper, a slight dent on the boot of the maroon car.

BUT MY FATHER'S determination to spread a coat of whitewash over the mess of my misconduct did not succeed in halting the rot of the walls which have ears, for within a matter of days, they began oozing waxy tell-tale stains of my corruption. To begin with, I perceived an alteration in the attitude of teachers, whose formerly indifferent glances gave way to glances of (supercilious) aversion, and, soon there-after, in the attitude of other boys, now grown fearful as well as hostile. No one went so far as actually to confront me with the reports which, like a racing tumour, must have been spreading through the body of the school, but wherever I went, I sensed the unmistakable vacuum of a wide berth. In class, you could not but notice that the desks to either side of mine had been shifted away, shunned it; and even in the chapel people went to pains not to sit beside me. Those who happened to find themselves on my bench (and they varied every time) had to be told to move up, to close ranks; but as they did so, they positioned themselves at an emphatic outward skew, their neighbouring shoulder turned away from my pestilence. It was as if a great sea of repulsion had parted around me, and although I understood the meaning of this new long solitary road ahead, which, even if open-ended, was a sort of prison, and although I could hear the echoes of my hollow search for a way out, I found that I had nowhere to walk, nowhere to run, and no means of filling the chasm of this new life which I had, in my manner, but thanks to my father, chosen. A similar reserve is, I know, traditionally afforded to boys who've recently suffered a bereavement in the family, or who find themselves stricken with eczema, or to persistent bed-wetters, or to those who face expulsion, but this distance of mine somehow felt more marked, icier, more akin to the distance which, at his departure, I had kept from my father's hand; and though the width of the road before me was later to alter, and to surprise me with unforeseen turns of direction, and though its climate was to brighten with odd patches of sun, as a feature, as a state, it was to remain permanent.

THAT FIRST SUMMER back on the island, part of which was spent by the sea, marked, I now realize, a turning-point of sorts for me, for I became properly cut off, deaf to my surroundings. A variety of factors probably contributed to this, but the most obvious (though its cause was so deep a secret that I can scarcely, then, have considered it) was my need to uncrush, as if such a thing were possible, my spirit. I had no real quibble with my mother, who disported herself much in the manner that I had come to expect of her—stylish, languorous, comfortably superficial—but I felt that her obdurate refusal to allude to those events which, but a few weeks earlier, had summoned her husband to England, betrayed a new seed of mistrust between us. This seed had, of course, been sown and fomented by the man who, whatever his claims to my welfare, had plainly, I now see, not only reneged on me but further dared to insult his wife with the patronage of his protection. It amazes me to realize, now that he's dead and well-buried, with what terminal efficiency that despicable great Catholic, who was a disgrace to his religion, succeeded in stunting any future possibility of growth in his wife, whom he cultivated at a temperature of such beautiful static ignorance that, though she flowered by the fashion season, she was never to know maturity, and became, as a consequence of his artificial limits, severed from the development of my being—a being which, though certainly twisted, he, at least, was never quite able to cripple. But that small, deft, tactical switch of his, that invented theft which in truth was but the purchase-price of my survival, for which I was to pay dearly, turned out to be a stroke of vicious genius. For by thus dividing his wife from her son, he managed to create a mutual suspicion between my mother and myself which, like some venomous prehistoric cactus, grew and grew and was to prove, in emotional terms, catastrophic. I suspect that neither she nor I was ever fully to recover from the damage of his interference, and even if my mother suppressed the desire to dwell on such intimate deficiencies, I can safely speak for her now. It ruined her; it left her a midget. And next to that brittle, pristine, frozen, covetable figurine of a woman, I felt, as I grew more embittered and unruly, nearly desperate. I no longer knew what she knew, nor what she can have imagined, nor what she feared. Indeed, the mystery was never to be solved; the topic, not once discussed in all the time that I knew her. And though I also remained in ignorance of my father's activities, largely because I had no interest in those subjects which appeared to engross him, I did find that whereas once the man had merely bored me, now, after this ill-quashed scandal, he struck me as more than a mere occupational stranger, for he had already proved to me his mettle as an enemy—as, indeed, he would continue to do. I learnt to view his presence as hazardous: I feared him more than any overactive fantasy of the sort that he called fibs. And from the refuge of my distance, I grew to recognize in him the simpler traits of the bully: for when he lied, it was not, as was the case with me, out of a frantic need for safety, but simply in order to get his way, to impose his will, to be more spoilt than me. I had not yet made the connection between tediousness and tyranny, not yet realized with what pathetic ease one can be both a bore and a bully, but, despite my blindness, I could, even then, recognize one thing: that my father's was a strong sort of weakness.

I WAS RELIEVED, of course, no longer to be under the control of a governess, yet the freedom which her riddance afforded me felt more like a burden than anything approaching luxury. Luxury to me meant emeralds. Now, I had to drag myself about the hidden gloom which, despite all the apparent blessings of my gilded domestic privilege, was henceforth to blight all of my school holidays. I would read when my concentration allowed it; rise as late as I wished; choose my own daily breakfast; play my records at will; swim in the pool without supervision, sunbathe occasionally, feed my bones with heat.

I also tried to write to my old Mam'zelle, though taking care (in order not to upset her) to circumvent the shame that had befallen her birthday jewel. I strove, in a muddle of languages—but without

entirely omitting to hint at my condition, which, though more pronounced of late, remained what it had been from the moment of her
leaving, which was a state of isolation—to imbue my words with biographical embellishments, hoping to make her earlier devotions to me
appear rewarded by some semblance of fruition; but I realized, as I did
so, that the task which I had set myself lay beyond my infantile capabil-
ities. I could not please everybody. I could hardly please myself. For
while the chronology of my recent life was easy enough to relate, the
events comprising it, like the dark beads of my mother's rosary, which
she kept in a drawer by her bed, I found harder to tell. Yet even if I
hadn't, at that stage, mastered the skill of writing between the lines, and
though doubtless my letter glinted with transparent fantasies, my childish tales were never really designed to inspire wonderment: they merely
longed to earn your smile.

In the event, however, my efforts to reach my former nurse were to
be dashed, for, once I'd drafted a neat copy of my letter to her, and the
moment came to enquire after Mam'zelle's address, which I had never
known, my mother claimed to be no wiser on the subject than I, and
suggested that, if I must, I try my father—assuming, of course, that
the woman's details still held good after all this time—and assuming,
too, which she rather doubted, that his pigskin address book still concerned itself with such forgettable redundancies. *(Un premier amour ne
s'oublie jamais . . . Et toi qui j'aimais, qu'as-tu fait de toi? Qu'as-tu fait sans moi?
Et moi qui t'ai perdu, qu'ai-je fait de tant de bonheur?)* As one grew up, my
mother had added, one should look forwards, not backwards.
Mam'zelle's job was done; she had moved on; that was the way of the
universe. I had another life now. The world would soon be her Iago's
oyster. But the truth is that I, my father's James, lived in dread of the
future, and had already begun to think in retrospect—not so much
because I rued the calendar of my history, strewn though it was with
leaves of disenchantment, but because some frustrated part of me
would have liked for my story to have been granted a second chance,
the chance to start afresh, to rewrite itself in a new garden, to recover
lost ground. But as I hoped, so I lost hope. The letter was never posted.
And Mam'zelle, though she was never forgotten, was never, even with
lies, to be thanked for her devotion.

·   ·   ·

My MOTHER, in an attempt to lend respectability to my passage from childhood into puberty, further complicated matters by orchestrating a subtle (and awkward) modulation in the manner which her servants were now meant to regard me, for, in advance of this first long holiday, they had been instructed no longer to call me what they'd called me ever since I'd been in nappies, which was Santiago, but instead, from now on—which, to be fair, was the ridiculous convention in all the households of my parents' acquaintance—to address me as Señorito. Later, in my late teens, this prissy courtesy would alter once more, to a more honourable, more authoritative Don, which, in the event, I didn't have to endure for long, since neither honour nor authority were to prove my strong points. But for now, this Señorito stuff killed me, and robbed me, in addition to the loss of Mam'zelle, of the affections of Cook and Gardener, both of whom, though I daresay they didn't blame me personally, must nevertheless have understood the meaning of the switch: I was being groomed away from their friendship and primed for a chilly superior distance. All very well, my mother had declared, to be familiar in infancy, but after a point you couldn't con- tinue to fraternize with these people, not in the same way, there'd be hell to pay, they'd walk all over one, anarchy. For we're all, *all* of us (she would remind me gravely), slaves to someone.

At meal times, I noticed that with the pretext of encouraging my English, conversation was increasingly turned away from my mother- tongue toward my father's language, yet this occurred most noticeably between courses, so as to ensure—as if the demands of balancing all those pitchers and trays and tureens were not sufficiently demanding— that whoever was waiting at table couldn't enjoy the illicit added thrill of eavesdropping on my parents' spoutings. Never did this device prove more convenient than on the occasion when I, returning from some errand, pressed the entryphone at the front gate (for such mea- sures had, of late, become security must-haves, like baubles from some desirable *bijoutier*) and the buzzer duly went off, as it was wired to do, in the kitchen; but finding myself alone on the street and forced publicly to volunteer my poncy, false identity to Cook, who had answered the ring, I side-stepped the mess of my mother's protocol and simply stated that it was Santiago, to let me in. Inevitably, the Lady of the House happened at that moment to find herself in the kitchen (peeling sticky price-tags from her delivered groceries, to spare the servants the shock of the cost of living), and managed, just as inevitably, to over-hear my voice blaring down the receiver. But she chose to make no mention to her staff of the liberty which I had taken, and which, I was soon enough to discover, she interpreted as impertinent, undermining of me, a barefaced betrayal of everything in which she and my father believed. Instead, she decided to wait until the three of us had sat down to lunch, so that her consort could support her in my verbal lynching—which, when delivered, after the soup, proved, though rife with his-panicisms, to be strategically versed in English.

EVEN AS I PACKED my trunk, a month in advance of the beginning of term, so that it could be shipped across the Atlantic, it hadn't occurred to me, such was my short-sightedness, that despite the changes which had taken place at home—the broken trust, the barriers of formality—I would nonetheless miss the peace, and I would miss the sun, and above all I would miss the spell of the sea. But by the time that my parents took me to the airport (and my father was driving, for some reason), I remember sitting alone on the back seat, queasy with fore-boding. For I had a habit, resulting perhaps from my mother's capri-cious influence, but, more likely, from plain insecurity, which my father found maddening; and although as a trait of ill-discipline it has dimin-ished, I do not think that, to this day, I've altogether conquered it. Because whenever I take a trip, and wherever this may be, however near, however briefly, I feel compelled to pack far more than I could ever need—the Just-In-Case syndrome, the What-If disease. So my father, determined to set an early precedent, had, in tones of heavy authority, cautioned me to pack into my trunk as much junk as I pleased, but to remember to restrict the weight of the suitcase which was to accompany me on the plane, to the regulation limit of twenty kilogrammes. And yet, regardless of the trunk, which had long since disappeared, my spiralling dread of the hell to which I was returning propelled me at the last minute to cram my case with all manner of things, to do with comfort and identity, which I would never be able to find in England—a giant bottle of avocado hair-conditioner, a great sausage of heavy chorizo, extra shoes to wear outside the bounds of school, wooden shoe-trees—all in the belief that such extras would render less daunting my progress through the minefield of the next twelve weeks. And although my father had been perfectly firm, perfectly fair about my need to observe the official weight restriction, I, as the porter lugged my case onto the scales by the desk where I was to be checked in, and as my mother rummaged in her handbag for a scented handkerchief, and as her husband tapped the spine of my passport against the counter, witnessed the gleaming silver arrow of my latest atrocity swing round, right past twenty, which was doomsday, to twenty-three, thereby formalizing the start of my association with Excess Baggage—which was to remain something of a love/hate relationship, for while baggage makes me groan, excess has never displeased me. But my father simply stood there and glowered down at me, not even needing to tell me that he had told me so, that I'd been given ample warning, and forced me, through the pressure of his silence, to pay for my indulgence with what meagre funds I'd managed to save during the holidays. I think that my mother must secretly have disputed the timing of such exemplary severity, for while her husband, in an interlude between two brandies, stalked off to use his urethra, she turned to me and slipped into the pocket at my breast a large fresh banknote, which smelt of gardenias. And just as my father had counted on me not to divulge to his wife my regrettable little incident at school, so she now counted on me not to divulge to him her kind act of treachery.

MY SECOND YEAR at prep school did not, despite my father's forecast, see any improvement, let alone a dramatic one, in the temperature of my spirits: mere scholastic drudgery had never been a factor in my difficulties. I remember noticing the occasional new boy, looking as demolished by the shock of this bleak environment as I had been at my start, but after the complications which had later arisen for me, and all the ensuing skulduggery, I still felt too wary and, frankly, too lacking in conviction to muster a tenor of reassurance for the sake of anybody. I recall, in particular, a diminutive Belgian boy, hair cut *en brosse,* eyes of a screaming electric green, forehead stricken with the furrows of a frown which seemed never to spare his forsaken countenance, and feeling for him a pang of sympathy—perhaps because he hailed from that same elusive place as had given me my Mam'zelle, my stolen emerald; but perhaps, more simply, because, like me, he was nationally alien, a proper exile. Du Castel was his surname; and I remember noticing that when he went to bed he wore over his pyjamas a *matelot* jumper of the type which buttoned at the shoulder and instantly spelt a Continental; and some part of me recognized that beyond the cold in the dormitories, which was considerable, his striped pullover was meant, like my mother's mohair blanket, to alleviate a greater coldness, which was inner. And I did briefly consider exchanging with him, in what meagre remnants of French might still be squatting about the corners of my cluttered memory, a few vague words of friendliness; but, almost as swiftly, I realized that any association between us, even one of those hilariously formal handshakes at which young Gauls seemed then to excel, could only have worsened his predicament, have spelt trouble for him: because the other pupils, despite whom, amazingly, I had managed to survive a year, seemed, rather than to have been civilized by a period spent among their families, merely to have returned fatter-faced and fortified, and this fortification had done nothing to diminish their enduring derision for me. Not only had they grown physically, but also in the breadth of their worldly wisdom, and they seemed, along the way, to have gleaned a clearer, more vivid and censorious picture of my supposed wantonness, my whispered iniquities; so that whereas earlier they had straightforwardly avoided me, now, since they publicly voiced their suspicions, I knew that they were properly on the look-out, spying, longing to catch and report me—if not actually to the authorities, which might have been construed as Sneaking, at least to their parents, which, from my point of view, amounted to the same thing. Yet as targets went, I, second time around, cannot have presented much of a challenge, or offered any great novelty, but better the devil you know, a bird in the hand, that kind of cliché. And, of course, I still exuded a certain blue-tinged mystique, which they, armed with their brave new knowledge, wanted further to investigate. The bottom of it.

BUM-CHUM, SUCKER-UPPER, arse-licker, such were the terms which now flavoured their references to me, for the conspiracy was, as I say, no longer tacit; and though I had, in all probability, sailed close to the foul rocks of which I stood accused, I couldn't yet fathom the literal meaning of those pejoratives. But one insult which I did understand— in part because, like the word Woman, it was so simple, but partly, too, because it fell so pathetically short of the truth—was the tag Daddy's Boy, a misnomer which was unmistakably intended to relate me to Mr. Wolfe, who, for all of his childlessness (then), had been dubbed Daddy by some previous wave of schoolboy geniuses. I must admit that, as nicknames went, Daddy's Boy didn't strike me as impressive, but then this was a place where impressiveness was not encouraged. Excellence was—and not, it goes without saying, when applied to the exertions of adults and minors in their shady privacy, but to the exertions displayed on the playing fields by strict contemporaries.

It is almost superfluous to relate how, once delivered back to the mire, I discovered what little solace was to be found in non-regulation shoes, or bottles of hair-conditioner, or the bloodied chunks of pig which, like a ravenous savage, I devoured, skin and all, from the arm of chorizo that lay entombed in my tuck-box, and which, once I was embarked upon the gorge, did not survive beyond the first measly novena. Its loss enraged me, for, even as I tore my way through the fiery flesh, I saw, clear as any writing on any wall, that no amount of school sausages, which tasted more of rancid dishcloths than ever they did of pork, never mind humbugs and gobstoppers, which were but suckers' fodder, would ever sate the mournful hunger that corroded my soul. It was like devouring the contents of some great love story, only to be punished for one's gluttony by the discovery that, whereas the unlikely protagonists had, after all their tribulations, ascended to the plane of happiness-ever-after, you, greedy reader, were left at a loss, dumped back in the very place of your starving lovelessness.

Throughout this time, Mr. Wolfe resembled a flag at half-mast, seemed out of sorts; but his discolour didn't only become manifest, like some sudden debilitating virus, when he happened to drift into my vicinity; for though, causally, I may have been contributory, the symptoms were there for all to witness. Now, when he smiled, stars no longer burst from his eyes, which bore crescents of gloom beneath them. Only seldom did you hear his laugh, and when you did, it sounded dry, closer to a cough provoked by nicotine. His walk no longer squealed with its former brio: it had grown spongy, stodgy, like the walk of the sickly—for the heart, I knew, had gone out my former lover; his flame, now, only flickered. He moved like a drab shadow of his earlier charisma, paler, drabber; and as we trudged over the linoleum and the rugs of our designated wastelands, he treated me not so much with distance as with polite neutrality, like an excellent footman, and even took care, I suspect, not to upset me, not to ignite my volcanic ill-humour, which, in this confined inferno, he must have feared to be simmering just beneath the cool sourness of my surface—because the repercussions of my father's visit had never been discussed between us: the meeting held by them while I was sleeping; the narrowness of our respective escapes; the burdens thrust upon me since the whole upheaval, and, of course, the heavy debt which, little though Mr. Wolfe could as yet suspect it, his imperilled career now owed to me. But any possible way forward, any possible stab at reparation, seemed, after the summer hiatus, blurry to me, open to question; and our former nocturnal congress, if not quite consigned to history, did become relegated to the back burner of our dealings. He still winked at me occasionally, and occasionally, at lights out, a nostalgic pout might return to my lips, but it all felt tepid, unconvincing—and with good reason, for he had resolved, I was subsequently to learn, that our safest course of action lay with the transfer, from him to me, of the burden of initiative. And once I'd run out of hot Spanish food to nurse my inner freeze, and my hair had drunk up all its conditioner and gone dry, and my tasselled loafers, stylish as they seemed to me, found themselves buried without apparent hope of an airing, I found my feet, slippered in sheepskin at eleven o'clock, set once again upon the long and winding road that led to his door.

I KNOCK. His reply sounds too vigorous, too sudden for him to be expecting a visitor, never mind this one. I go in: it is not difficult: it feels, in fact, like the most natural thing, like the rightest progression. He's already in bed. His lights are off. He says nothing. I close the door behind me, less out of discretion than because I don't want the dirty light of the corridor to filter in, to pollute me. He doesn't ask what's wrong, which previously, between us, had been the pretextual form. Instead, he now tells me not to lock the door, not to make a noise, just to slide the latch which he's installed—and which I treat as the sign that I've been waiting for. I do as I'm told. Plain sailing from now on. I go to the window and draw the curtains wide open, as if to reveal to the world the next episode, as if we'd run away to the circus and no longer cared a tinker's toss. I move to the gramophone and flick through a few records, skipping the Nocturnes, because to me this feels like a positive dawning, and skipping Mary Magdalene, since, now, I do know how to love him, and I settle for an album which provides us, at a gentle and low volume, with a bridge over our troubled waters. He lights, as if it had been reserved for this moment, a virgin candle, bigger than his earlier ones, and taller and, instead of churchy white, green as grapes, and veined like marble, and boasting, at its plateau, not one but two small wicks, like pilgrims on a darkling plain, carrying flambeaux in the wind.

If the first night after the rumpus of the vanished rugger peg had been rough, this one couldn't have proved more tranquil or, in its way, more poignant. I remember clambering into his bed in my pyjamas and, on this occasion only, keeping them on. And just as he'd trembled after the Bonifacio episode, so, now, he began to tremble once more. But there was nothing wrong, he claimed, no problem other than a rush of emotion, and instead of telling me that he was bisexual, he now held me close and told me how he had missed me, how sorry he was, and how relieved that I hadn't given up on him. He would make it up to me, he said; he would show me. We must, of course, be more cautious than ever, but we weren't going to let anyone or anything stand between us from this moment on, no more separations, it was a promise. Our time was precious, he explained: for all we had left (and he seemed to have counted, because when I said Two years, he replied Not even) was a mere eighteen months. Before we knew it, he said, I would be gone and it would all be over; but to me, regardless of his love, the thought of another eighteen months buried in this catacomb felt like murder.

He had said that we must be more cautious, and we were. Apart from the bolt on the door, he also mentioned the importance of using his alarm clock, and we agreed to split the job. From now on, on those nights when I came to see him, which would be most, he undertook to set the alarm for six-thirty in the morning, so that, even if we fell asleep, I could get back to my dormitory without fear of being caught. And my task, on leaving his warmth, was to press the bell to Off, so that once I was safely gone, he could sleep without interruption. As for his duty mornings, no need to worry: he would just order an alarm-call the night before. And thus it was settled, and, as a scheme, it was never to go wrong.

I could tell, as he held me immobile to his chest on that first night after the storm which nearly broke us, that his eyes were streaming with relief, but I was neither frightened nor revolted—this man was not my father. Instead, I felt a niggle of responsibility for his silent sobs, and faint guilt that I couldn't return the compliment. And after dismissing from my thoughts the business about never again playing rugger (which would have to wait), and wondering how precisely he intended to make it up to me, I did let myself drop off . . . and when, hours later, I awoke, he was still alert as a sentinel, with his arms still wrapped about me like ribbons round a present; and after saying good night and turning off the clock, I put on my dressing-gown, my daggerless cloak, and went to slide back the bolt and, just as I opened the door, I heard him whisper: Hey, Pssst, Thanks (which I ignored), followed by God Bless, which for a second made me wonky.

JUST AS THE RESUMPTION of our activities made them feel twice as precarious, so must the doubled charge of our reunion have made itself, in some unspoken way, felt to the outside world. For not long after we'd reverted to the abnormality which we considered normal, I remember rushing into class just before a lesson, skirting round the oaf with the sideburns who liked to call me Woman, who was already limbering up at the door, and finding, chalked huge upon the blackboard, though far too late for possible erasure, the following annunciation: Moore ♂ Mr. Wolfe. And although the teacher chortled like a well-chuffed punter as he rubbed out the graffito (scrawled, I suspect, by the boy of skewering intelligence who was later to dog me), and although the rest of the class just hooted at the brilliance of their ploy, I confess to having felt, even if exposed, unashamed, for what was being proclaimed, and despite its intention, which was simply to humiliate, was nothing less than true. I did. I loved. I could deny it till the cows came home, but I couldn't fool my own soul.

Beyond my return to the embraces of the man who had become my life-source, and beyond the fact that I never did again play rugger (he saw to it that I became a "musician"—yippee), the main event of that year took place, for me, during the middle term, leading up to Easter. I remember, one lunchtime, sitting in the refectory and finding myself worryingly close to the top of my table, a position which, since it invariably entailed having to speak to somebody senior—on occasion even a teacher, God help you—I avoided keenly. But I must have walked in at the tail end of the surge, because this was the only space that I could see left available. And the gap was hardly surprising, for, at the head of that table, there presided a rabbit-faced creep who, for all of his pride at recently having been appointed Prefect (which status entitled him to his hallowed *emplacement*—yippee for him) was, I can honestly affirm, no more popular than I was, and, at the risk of sounding conceited, somewhat less prepossessing: because this creature, who was known to regard washing with an even greater antipathy than I did sporting activities, not only gnawed his grubby fingernails but, despite already being stricken with adolescent acne and a few grimy hairs on his upper lip, was still into thumb-sucking—a combination which no doubt accounted for the revolting state of his buck teeth. He wasn't a charm to be near.

Although, of course, I hope that he no longer does, should he, by some misfortune, happen still to lurk among the living, I would hazard that he's a vegetarian now, and keen as ever on kagools, and probably knife-collecting in the lowlier ranks of the Territorial Army. He will probably be addicted to solitary television, though he will pay no attention to programmes on corrective dental surgery; and he will reside somewhere glamorous, such as Purley. Thumb-sucking will, surely, still figure among his pursuits. But sadly we lost touch, so I cannot be precise about him. Yet what I can be precise about is the fact that, in the lesson leading up to lunch, which had been Latin, this imbecile had come in for a spectacular bollocking from the relevant teacher, who (extraordinarily, now that I think of it) had been the headmaster. Yet only I, unlike the others at our table, was aware of the rabbit's recent academic humbling, because, though he was senior to me, I used to go up a year for Latin: languages being, as my father never tired of telling me, my unfair advantage. So, as you can imagine, I was not exactly the disgraced prefect's most desirable luncheon companion.

I can't recall how we warmed to the argument, which had to do with names, but perhaps it was a letter from my mother, which I would just have collected, because my foreignness was, of course, brought up by him, and I remember that in defence—it was too irresistible—I alluded to the hysterical unsuitability for someone of his density to be lumbered with a surname such as his, which was Newton. My handling of English, I remember thinking, must be improving, because he's gone quiet, I've managed to silence him . . . But not, as it turns out, into defeat. What ensues is almost a blur to me: all that I recall is being struck suddenly, with the summary force of a sideways arm-swing, somewhere about the face, then bitten on my retaliating hand by those enormous teeth, and next thing, though I'm not yet in pain, there's blood all over my food, and all over my clothes—pouring, I realize, from my nostrils—and there's nothing to be done, I cannot stem the haemorrhage, and, with my napkin clamped to my face, I have to ask permission to go to the infirmary.

Matron, who's been enjoying a little nap, and emerges rubbing gunk from her eyes, looks not best pleased. She wants to know what in the name of Jesus-Mary-and-Joseph has happened. I tell her I got hit. Hit by what? Hit by a fist. Whose fist? I volunteer the identity of the culprit: Newton. She takes me into her surgery and sits me down. She takes a squeamish look, as if my face were contagious, and sounds a bit bewildered: a nose-bleed is one thing, she decrees, but this looks more serious. It's all swollen, she says, and the bridge could, she supposes, be broken. But she cannot, even for Calypso, judge the position with any greater certitude, so, for confirmation, she bundles me into a taxi and sends me off to the school doctor, who, this afternoon, is doing his rounds at the local hospital.

My father only ever taught me one thing—well, three really, let's not be churlish: three identical letters which (unlike languages—for languages, notwithstanding his disclaimers, were to prove my gift) did now earn me an advantage that might legitimately be called unfair. Because when a quick set of X-rays revealed that my nose was indeed fractured, and that as a result I'd have to be admitted without delay for its correction (not that this prospect displeased me: freaky as rhinology sounded, I could do with a reprieve from school), I was able to volunteer, proudly as any motto, in a tone probably so defensive that it sounded vindictive, the code-letters PPP, thereby asserting my claim to private medical insurance, a privilege which spared me the gruesome collective palliness of a public ward and entitled me, in addition to a separate room, to my own adjoining bathroom and television. The view from my private window, however, did not exactly offer a prospect: a high black wall of Dickensian brick. But again, let's not quibble.

HERE I AM, sitting on the hospital bed, still in my bloodied uniform, which has grown scabrous down the front of my pullover. I can hear myself clogged up, forced to breathe through my mouth as I stare out of the window at the black wall facing me. Another wall, of silence, now descends: no one explains a thing: I wait; I wait and wait. Footsteps on the corridor blithely pass by. I lie down, but not for long, don't want to nod off. I get to my feet, decide to nose around: Bible in chest of drawers; switch for bedside lamp; telephone, inoperable; bathroom, glossed in sputum-green and reeking of antiseptic. But even though, in one corner of the painted concrete floor, there grows—like a reminder of Nature's supremacy over mere medicine—an incipient tuft of fungus, to me, compared with the school washroom, this feels like luxury. If only I had a clean change of clothes, or pyjamas, I would gladly take a bath in peace, unsupervised and relieved of football hymns. I attempt, instead, to distract myself with the television, yet, much as I fiddle, I cannot seem to fix its reception, which blights all three channels to an homogeneous foreground blizzard. Here comes a film called *Coronation Street,* which I suppose might be regal. Sudden knock on the door. Click off, quick. A nurse appears, bearing a tray which she claims to be my tea, though it looks more like an institutional attempt at supper, unsavoury down to the biscuit of mint-flavoured chocolate which comes sealed in foil of lurid green. I couldn't be less hungry, but I can always dispose of the food down the lavatory, so, to dissimulate my plan, I thank her. That's all right, dear, she says, and pats me. She tells me to eat up now, there's a good lad, and not to forget, when I've finished, to take that little tablet in the plastic beaker, a painkiller; then adds, almost as an afterthought, that by the way, there's someone coming over to see me. Me? Yes, from your school, dear. Who from school? She couldn't say, dear, but not to worry—they'll be here presently. And presently she leaves.

Although unnerved by her message, at least I'm prepared for this forthcoming visit (please let it not be from Matron), but when the door opens, which it does very smoothly and very quietly, as if apologetically, all that I can see, wide as the doorway, is a massive great bunch of yellow tulips, their cellophane aquiver, their stems tied together with an enormous ribbon the colour of leaf; and at first, of course, I suspect a mistake, they've got the wrong room—*I* haven't had a baby—but when I see the commiserating smile behind the tribute, I realize that it's all right, that this is for me, the first bunch of flowers that I've ever been given. (Whereas, unlike most people, I cannot pinpoint when, technically, I lost my virginity, I do recall, with the same blinding clarity as my first experience of snow, which came so late in my infancy, the first time that flowers were brought to me, because they came so prematurely.) I remember feeling, all of a sudden, confusingly grown-up, girlish but flattered, embarrassed but thrilled, as if I were my mother yet were still me. And although the hand that holds the tulips belongs, of course, to Mr. Wolfe, it strikes me as bizarre to see him outside the context of school and rules and subterfuge and sin, so that when he leans down to kiss me—on the forehead, in order not to hurt me—it is I who, flinching, must have hurt him, hurt his feelings by bristling like some prim old spinster who regarded such gestures as forward, a liberty.

He brings me lots of things: dark chocolates from Brussels, which briefly make me pine for Mam'zelle; a couple of books: one, a Brontë paperback indebted to the morbidity of the region—I still have the copy, tattered and yellowed by history—and then, some fat biography with lots of depressing Victorian pictures, which I decide to relinquish to the ward upon release; my slippers; my washbag (inside which, I note with relief, he has not been), plus a small transistor—the latter, he's afraid, only on loan while I'm here. But rather than bother with the linen room he has also brought me—purchased, I presume, en route to the florist—a new pair of what he calls Jim-Jams. (Later, like other presents from him, those innocuous pyjamas were to land me in a quandary, for though I knew that he liked to see me striped in their soft pink and cream, and though I was not, in this regard, averse to obliging him, I realized, as the year drew towards its finish that, were I to take them back home with me, I'd have to provide my mother with some explanation as to their origin; and so, when the moment came and I found myself trapped in the dilemma between indulging him and arousing her suspicion, I panicked and threw them into a bin.)

. . .

BECAUSE THE DRAMA of my broken nose had unfolded with such unforeseen speed, and because administration at my school was not exactly what it might have been, my guardians were only informed about the "accident" after I'd been wheeled back out of the operating theatre—minus my underpants, which had scandalized me—by which stage my condition, though concealed from view, had been declared to be tickety-boo. The doctors' satisfaction, combined with the fact that, in those days, to have rung my parents would have involved liaising with a lengthy sequence of half-witted operators (not to mention, I suppose, that the idea of making a transatlantic call merely in order to relay details of a *fait accompli* would have struck those sensible guardians of mine as utter profligacy), prompted them to adopt a stance of restraint over one of responsibility, so that, when they were telephoned by the school secretary, their reaction was to suggest that she, or I, if she preferred, apprise my parents of my circumstances in writing—no need for a telegram, what a fuss about nothing. Look here, they said, were matters happily resolved or weren't they? Could the secretary see any point of causing my parents needless worry? Precisely. Thank you. (Models of sobriety, those people.)

Once I had recovered from the phantom removal of my underpants, and regained sufficient balance to stagger to the lavatory, I examined my face, which I discovered to be muzzled in plaster, with stripes of white tape across my eyebrows and cheeks, like the markings of an Apache, and the effect, its mix of exoticism and pugnacity, did not, I confess, distress me. But my notion of allure was destined to be short-lived; for soon after Mr. Wolfe had ferried me back to school in his zippy white convertible—a Vitesse, I think, was the model that he steered—I realized that what I'd interpreted as a glamorous emblem of my revenge upon Newton was in fact taken by the general public visibly to confirm my assailant's supremacy, for, apart from a mild dressing down from the headmaster, he had come away unscathed—with the further bonus that, very soon, he would also be laughing. The day after my return, I was myself summoned to the hamster's study, which did not come as a surprise; but what did stagger me was finding myself, once in the cage of that stinking rodent, robbed of the benefit of self-account, and instead, as if there existed no room for doubt, being apportioned full blame for the fracas, and accused of being a bilious, mealy-mouthed troublemaker, and of having needled Newton—who, being a Prefect, knew more about mature conduct than I did—to such a point that he'd been left no option but to take corrective action. My fault entirely. (No mention of Latin.) And now, just to drive the point home, as if the fracture had been insufficient penalty, the headmaster orders me to hold out my hands. And out comes the ferula and, after a couple of swishes in the musky air, he brings it whacking down, once, twice, three times on my right hand; and then, he tells me to put that hand down, grabs my left, and, such is his excitement after two further strokes that, on the sixth and last, he misses my palm entirely and comes crashing down on my wrist, managing to smash the glass of my watch into a thousand smithereens. I have often been as shocked, but rarely so angry; and the further effort of having to control myself enough to thank the man for his disciplinary trouble nearly rips off my Apache plaster.

By the time of my unveiling six days later, bruises had blossomed like dark pansies round my eyes, but the watch, thanks to Mr. Wolfe, had been to the mender and back. I didn't write to my parents for the remainder of that term, because, apart from the exhausting prospect of relating the whole convoluted incident, any hope of sympathy from my mother's quarter was outweighed by the certainty that my father would greet the news of my thrashing with covert delight. In any case, just to complicate matters, I now proceeded to develop, as a suspected reaction to the general anaesthetic (though, with hindsight, I'd suggest that, more likely, it was simply an eruption of nervous tension), an outbreak of shingles, like a belt of weeping lesions around my abdomen and lower back. Matron's milky ointments weren't up to much, and, for the first time since my arrival at that establishment, I genuinely could not get to sleep at night. Compared to the pain of this new mishap, the agony of the ferula had indeed been a laughing matter.

Mr. Wolfe proved, throughout these brief weeks, to be made of solid platinum. I would go to his darkened room with my midriff in bandages, and he wouldn't even bother to comment on the fact. I don't suppose that the friction of his lovemaking can much have aided my condition, for I still bear small residual markings, but whatever harm his ardour might have caused my skin was easily outstripped by the great good which it did me to feel his loyalty wrapped about me. And he would slip me painkillers on the sly, for Matron had decided that I was just being theatrical about a slightly nasty rash. All that was required was a bit of time for it to dry. And on those painkillers I somehow lasted until my flight back to the island.

My mother was aghast. She blamed my father, who in turn blamed me, suggesting that I'd probably aggravated matters by scratching, when my vanity alone would have prevented such foolhardiness. So now I felt obliged to tell the story from the start. He, while still defending the system, and defending my guardians, and even defending the boy Newton, nonetheless attempted, in his absurd repetitive way, to calm my mother. I did nothing of the sort: I told her that I was on fire. The family practitioner was summoned, and initially he took her side. Those English doctors, he ranted, with their snooty aversion to injections and suppositories and a good strong course of antibiotics, as had so blatantly been required, were a pack of savages. Look at me: I was crawling with bacteria, doubtless in severe discomfort, and infectious at that. My mother recoiled, horrified. But he, perhaps in an attempt to shame her for having drawn back from her own son, boldly stepped forward and asserted that if my physical state was any reflection of the wonders of English public schools, well, she was welcome to them; rather the flesh of *her* flesh, he threw in as a final stab, than any of his young sons. My mother, I must say, took it like an amazon; but at lunch that day, and oblivious (for once) to the servants, and in her most spectacularly rhetorical Spanish, she let my father have it. And bugger the pain: now it was my pleasure at his verbal laceration which felt unutterable.

THE EASTER BREAK was largely sacrificed to my convalescence, which laid me low, and prevented me from swimming or sunbathing, and more or less kept me confined to the house. But since my mother was as reluctant to have the fact of my contagion publicized as I was to attend children's parties, my isolation was treated not as some aberration on my part but as a sensible compromise. The swellings on my face began to subside; my bruises, to wither into pallor and depart, and the girdle of scabs, at last to shrivel and die. But meanwhile, in this climate of self-scrutiny, I could not help but notice that the hideous ogre of puberty now held me in its clutches. Those hairs, so sparse yet so dark, repelled me, they frightened me: for while I'd known about looking like a child, and knew what a man looked like, I now found myself thrown into a ludicrous uncharted hinterland which could only undermine me; and just as, at the start with Mr. Wolfe, I'd regretted the incompleteness of my body, its immaturity, the fact that it was too young, now I began to fear that the changes which slowly but relentlessly were set to corrupt me, would render me too old for his love, would reduce my appeal in his eyes. What we had shared until then I judged to have been a marriage of contrasts, a perfect difference; but now that I saw myself delivered to this state of self-sabotage, with nothing left to conquer other than my embarrassment, I knew that every microscopic alteration which I suffered, even if left unspoken, was bound to be detected by him, and measured with regret, and held against me like a disappointing black star. My body was losing the innocence which, now that it was too late, I realized had glittered like a hallmark in our alliance. I was growing tarnished. I was fast falling in value.

Although I was never to experience the messy privilege of a wet dream, for I had learnt about dry orgasms long before my sperm would oblige, I hid such covert pleasures from Mr. Wolfe: I regarded my personal gratification, like thoughts of sinfulness, as deserving no place in the congress between us. My coarse biological drive was extraneous to our love, whereas his sacred satisfaction was his prize. Like our songs, and the dark open sky, and the smoothness between my buttocks, it, his satisfaction, had been a vital ingredient from the start; but this new growing roughness along my gulf, and my growing genitals, and the growths under my arms, and the growing cracks that broke my vowels, these I viewed as handicaps of nature which I could not allow to upset the stability of our nights. And so, threatened by my diminishing appeal, and by my fears of superannuation, I opted for corrective camouflage: I trimmed, and later plucked, and pretended, even to myself, that nothing at all was happening.

THAT YEAR, as I recall, though activities at school groaned on regardless, there was no summer—but at least Sports Day proved a washout. The sight of all those fat-gutted fathers tripping up as they hopped in sodden sacks filled me with delight; and the mothers, trying not to panic while slithering in stockinged feet over the mud, and struggling to balance a boiled egg on a spoon of aluminum, struck me as laughable. I only regretted that my own parents, despite the shame of my non-existent sporting acumen, could not, on this occasion, have been present, for I would have relished seeing my mother, who would never have participated in such inanities, trying to suppress her derision for my father, who most certainly would have done, her Victor Ludorum. But while I fantasized about them, the general clapping became muffled by the rumble of encroaching thunder; rain-soaked speeches grew increasingly snappy; trophies were handed over hurriedly and half-dropped occasionally, and all that there remained in the aftermath of this thwarted marvellousness was a sodden network of silly, coloured flags flapping beneath a stormy sky, like a boat headed for disaster, and a mountain of soggy strawberries with sweetened cream that no one in their right mind would have wanted.

Everything from that point on became, for me, penultimate: my second last set of exams before the big ones, my second last dormitory, my second last classroom, my second last birthday before departure. In fact, birthdays were to prove my own personal washouts—invariably devoid of a single flower, never mind the garlanded thrones of my childhood, and invariably graced by not so much as a card, for every year I was doomed, instead, to receive a telegram, tickertaped with the garbled message MANY HAPY RETRUNS LOVE FRM MOTER FATHR STOP—which always, in any case, reached me at least a day after the event, and came without the consolation of a cake at tea. For, by the time I'd managed to discover that you could order one of these through the local Post Office and your parents would stump up, I'd decided to waive the privilege of the sponge-filled football-pitches and icing-sugared tennis-rackets and Battenberg warships which were habitually provided, in part because I shied from the pressure of being watched blowing out candles, but largely because, gluttonous as schoolboys are, I doubted that any of those in the refectory liked me enough to stomach a slice of any cake of mine. In any case, a much more popular boy than I shared my date of birth, so the resulting connection would have dismayed him as much as it would have stolen my piddling thunder. And I therefore resolved, before the event and from then on, to ignore a day which, let's face it, was hardly more auspicious than any other.

By my third and final birthday at that place, however, my dealings with Mr. Wolfe were hurtling towards a climax. Hard as I tried, I could no longer conceal from him the alterations in my body, and he, for his part, could no longer conceal his panic at what would happen to us beyond July. But his attitude was ambivalent, almost contradictory: on the one hand he would try, night after night, to persuade me to reach orgasm, to ejaculate in his company, imagining perhaps that this activity, which, to me, was so utterly private, so separate, would in some mysterious way confirm something that our love had not yet done, as if such a love could not now be complete until we had emitted in unison. It would seal our mutual trust as adults, like a game of blood-brotherhood for grown-ups. Ludicrous: how could I, I who was seized up with inhibition, suddenly do as he asked? And the more he went on imploring, the remoter became the likelihood that I could ever oblige. For my real fix was mental, and my head and body had already become divided.

His second line of argument was more ominous, and related not to the present but to the future, to the business of priming me before my time at prep school had expired. Those remaining eighteen months of which, only a brief while back, he had spoken, now seemed, like an accordion at one of my mother's parties, to have deflated and become reduced to one; and I think that as much as fearing what, beyond that last month, I would do about him, or to him, he feared how he would cope without me—because, by the beginning of the end, our dependence, even if contrasting, had become mutual. Teachers tend, as a rule, to be resigned: they must resign themselves at artificially brisk intervals to the notion of pupils' departure, which they interpret more as relinquishing their charges than ever as being outgrown by them, never mind supplanted. But Mr. Wolfe was, by that final month, far from resigned: he was frantic: I do not think that he quite trusted me. Yet to me, questions of trust aside, and on top of the academic pressures which had lately begun to burden me, it felt as if he were wanting secretly to tutor me for some further exam, the ultimate extra-curricular one, whose subject was, of course, Life. Life, he would say, was a strange thing, not always easy to understand, and though all manner of experiences lay before me—great ones, he had every (false) hope, for after the constraints of school I deserved to flourish—he now implored me, as he had once implored me to believe that he was bisexual, to believe that everything that had gone on between us had been conceived in love. He begged me never to forget that fact. He warned me how, in years to come, people who understood nothing of these matters would condemn as wicked relationships such as ours, and wish, invariably, to drive the hatchet of blame into the neck of the adult; but I must know as well as he did, for I (as ever) had an old head on my young shoulders, that between us there had been no fear, no pain, no coercion, nothing bad. We had no cause for reproach, either of us. We should be thankful for the chance that we'd been granted, for this great affair of the heart. And I must promise—it was vital for his peace of mind—that I understand this fact, that I say as much, that I agree that his influence had never been corruptive. We must never, whatever the pressures, whatever happened, betray one another. (It Must Not Get Out.) He would always, he claimed, be there for me; I would always be able to count on him. He yearned for us to remain life-long friends, for friends, as I well knew, were thin on the ground. We must be strong and fight not to let destiny, which was soon to wrench us asunder and force us under separate houses, oppose us, make ene-mies of us. There could never be a question of an Adieu between us; only, at most, an Au Revoir. And then, he'd go ahead, help himself, and come. But I liked this: there was a freedom about it.

THAT LAST BIRTHDAY, my thirteenth, we celebrated at midnight. He had bought me a tiny heart-shaped cake with a single candle, which I proceeded, as he took my picture—flash—to blow out. I remember sitting half-unbuttoned on the desk where, in the early days, he had stroked my leg with his erring hand, and where later I had forced him to write my name along his table-tennis bat. But now he handed me a tiny box which I recognized as coming from a jeweller's shop, and which, after Mam'zelle's ring, filled me with apprehension, like a pre-monition of loss. In this dark little box there lay, together with a long slim chain of gold, a glinting medal, slightly too large for a child, which, on the reverse side, had been engraved with the letters HWB (Hot Water Bottle, a euphemistic endearment of his), while, on the front, there glittered my sign of the Zodiac. And although, naturally, I smiled with cosmetic gratitude, as my mother might have done, the object itself discomfited me, for it struck me as pagan, slightly distasteful; but, of course, he was so right, it was so apt: Gemini: Twins: separate yet forever intertwined. I was just too young to be appreciative, too woolly with my own ignorance.

That medal became a problem: I needed to conceal it from other boys; I needed to reveal it to him at night; but I needed, most importantly, to decide what should be done about it before I went back to the island, for, like the hospital pyjamas, it mustn't be allowed to fall into my mother's hands. Otherwise, over lunch on the terrace, she would pounce: HWB? Who *was* that? And where did I get this thing? And how? Either she would not believe my fabricated answer, or she would worry, or she might even, if she were anywhere near my father, think that I had stolen it. But, for now, I let it live in the pocket of my dressing-gown, and I would put it on at night, and rub it warm against my chest as I made my way to Mr. Wolfe's side, and then I'd take it off once we'd begun, and back into the pocket it would slide until next time. He had never intended such a thing, I know, but to me that medal felt like pressure, it weighed me down. And at the end of term, after my exams, as I began to plan my packing, I decided that it must go, the moment had come. Yet some small romantic part of me just couldn't bring itself to discard it irrevocably, so, very early one morning, in a secret lonely ritual, I buried my trophy—which, unlike my father's, was not of dulled silver but of screaming gold, and commemorated my many victories in the much more arduous games which I had brought about—under one of the trees in the woods, near the mouth of a priest's hole, telling myself that one day I'd go back to reclaim my property.

BUT THE END was not the end. He couldn't give me up, couldn't bring himself to bury his own prize, not yet, not quite; and in order to defer our separation (as much as, let's be fair, to delay my return to the island, for by that stage I'd begun to regard the proximity of my parents as a trial), a plan was hatched: namely to attach ourselves to half a dozen pupils from my year who were obsessed with lead soldiers and war games and history—in which, needless to say, I had no interest what-

ever—and who had planned a jaunt to bits of Belgium with the ultimate goal of visiting the battlefield of Waterloo. Good old Wellington.
And so, at the final hour, I telephoned home (with remarkable ease, as
it happens, the operators couldn't have been more helpful) and
explained about this trip which had been organized by a group of my
contemporaries, whom I made sound deeply serious (scholarship
material, prefects, captains of various teams, head of the school, future
generals—you name it, I said it), and then, of course, I pretended to
have contracted a throbbing fixation with the Napoleonic campaigns
and soldiers like the very ones which my father had displayed from high
in my old nursery. And I suppose that it must all have sounded wholesome and appropriate and desirably social, because my father (perhaps
also swayed by the fact that I'd done well in my exams, winning some
trivial sum of money which enabled me, since he would never have
done so, to buy my first fiddle—which turned out to be a poisoned
chalice, but that came later), my father agreed to postpone my homeward flight and allowed me to join the expedition. Mr. Wolfe, whose
identity I omitted to divulge, jumped, as planned, on the bandwagon;
and suddenly, one crisp morning, there we all were, crammed into the
school minibus and off—the original six; Mr. Wolfe, of course; me . . .
plus, at the head of the gang, a deranged Nazi casualty who'd staggered
for safety to the priesthood, spent some years in Kenya pounding the
faith into the blackies, and in due course, after a rumoured dalliance
with the bottle, been appointed our school Chaplain. Fr. Bridgefall he
was called: I remember because mention of his name is what clinched
the deal with my father. That dog-collared old trooper was mad keen
on mortal sin, especially of the fleshy sort, and Onanism, as you would
expect, was a favourite topic with him: but you should have seen with
what labour his oral sphincter would pucker in its effort to expel the
word. Anyway, it was he who drove us down to Dover; and from Dover
we sailed across to Ostend—with me (for I was later given a photograph) doubled over the railings, puking my guts out.

I'm sure we did lots of things Cultural, but, though our first stop
was Bruges, my memory selects only the stench of the canals in the
midday heat and the sight of bonnetted women crafting doilies along
the cobbled walkways, for my attention was so heavily claimed by the

dual tasks of appearing, on the one hand, to interact with a group for whom, in truth, I felt no amity, while simultaneously trying to cope with Mr. Wolfe, who, now that he was no longer, strictly speaking, in charge of us, was growing, I felt, too pally by half with the others, as if having forgotten that, only recently, they'd been tormenting me in letters the size of goalposts about him. But worse still, and doubtless as a consequence of the fact that I was on the brink of leaving prep school, was his attitude towards me specifically, which had grown tactile and unguarded to the point of folly, as if he were struggling to salvage a floundering marriage when, in my hardened heart, we had already parted—for fate (I then believed) had already divorced us. I was still alive; his career had survived intact; it seemed to me that I was free to go now. But he, with a lack of ingenuity which I found irksome, would make sure, despite the fact that our sunlit minibus was hardly the darkened prep-school cinema, that he sat next to me when the priest was driving; and when his own turn came to take the wheel, he would order me, in a parody of authority, pretending that I needed strict handling, to take the passenger-seat at the front beside him. And when I did as he commanded, though it disproved my recalcitrance, it also proved to me my position among the company, for, as we trudged along those flattened lowlands, I remember hearing giggles and wolf whistles at my back. It was hideous. I should have gone home at the proper time. I could be lying by the sea by now.

Most of the stops along our route escape me. It was just driving and driving and the relentless English radio playing some atrocious song of the moment to do with Puppy Love. But then we did a quick detour through Brussels, where everyone had a good hoot at the Mannequin Pis and Mr. Wolfe bought me more chocolates, and I just drifted along behind the soldiering historians, slightly detached—like someone who has lost a lover but longs for them with such ardour that their brain tricks them into attaching the face in their mind's eye to the face of strangers—longing, in my stupidity, to fall in this way upon the face of my long lost Mam'zelle.

As we approached Waterloo, everything changed: the boys grew more excitable, but Fr. Bridgefall grew more grave, and, on his instructions, Mr. Wolfe now halted the minibus at a roadside. First, and with a ceremony worthy of the sacraments, we were introduced to the delights of crawling Camembert and cheap red wine. And then, the good padre delivered us a snappy sermon, making plain to me that he was as addicted to snobbery as I was to the sin of Onan: we were all, his finger wagged, to be on our very best behaviour for the next couple of days, and if there was any trouble from any of us (quick glance at my dark aura) we could forget about visiting any historic battlesite; that much he promised. We were going to stay with the parents of du Castel—the small foreign boy who, through my feebleness, I had never dared to befriend—whose father, a Count (which title Fr. Bridgefall had no difficulty whatever in enunciating, its aplomb was sonorous), owned a château nearby, where the family spent their summers, and where the boy, probably dreading our descent, would already be waiting. And it was to here that we would be driving after lunch.

THE CHÂTEAU HAD TO BE the loveliest house that I had ever seen. It made me conjure the birthday cake of my fantasies, of apricot and marzipan and almonds. You approached it through a sprawling woodland, like a dark bottle, which funnelled into a narrow avenue of what I now surmise must have been pleached limes. To left and right as you drove in, peering through the intervals between gnarled trunks, you could see expanses of brilliant grass, bordered by modest orchards, and fields, and a low sky. As you emerged from the tree-lined drive and felt the minibus dip fractionally onto scrunching pebbled ground, the house now rose into view and, though moderate in scale, and simple in structure, it stood there proudly, smiled. It dazzled you. I remember hearing myself gasp, then shrinking back with embarrassment; but the building, decked in the verdant swags of these pastoral surroundings and faced with brick the colour of fading sunsets, seemed, to me, perfectly to match a child's image of a castle from a fable.

The first feature that you noticed were four pointed turrets tapering up like medieval hats; and once your eye had hopped about the small windows which, randomly inserted, seemed to wink with panes of leaded glass, your gaze suddenly swooped down and plunged into the moat which swam around the fortress, whose pewter waters, as you drew closer, reflected flashes of cloud; then, once returned to your senses, with your sights fixed back on solid ground, you realized how, echoing the spires, great box-cones stood impaled at the far corners of the castle, and that at its entrance an ancient drawbridge lay lowered to welcome you. You could have topped the picture with a great heraldic banner, fluttering from the past.

Du Castel's mother, whom, on my arrival, I discovered to be Spanish (and whom the boy had told about me), hailed, it transpired, from Jerez de la Frontera and, in one of those bizarre coincidences that defy credibility, had met my own mother years back at some Feria, indeed recalled her, she said, for her beauty and for the eagerness with which—the Countess laughed nostalgically—the Andalusian beaux of the time had swarmed around her at parties. How was my mother?, she asked; I was to give her the Countess's regards—at which point she mentioned her maiden name—always assuming, she added, that my mother still remembered her. And in truth, the Countess, who wore thick, tinted spectacles, was as unremarkable to the eye as she was blessed with charm; yet, though she was never to know it, not even by virtue of my careful subsequent letter of thanks, that woman managed, after the three years of my undiluted misery, to dumbfound me by proving through her gentle attentions that, against all my expectations, it was actually possible to claim links with my school and not be a monster.

WE WERE LED to our respective quarters. Four of the boys had been put into double rooms with adjoining showers, at the top of the main stairs; two were given, further down that corridor, single rooms with an interconnecting bathroom; and only I, to the others' befuddlement, was graced with a room to myself—a merciful flight below theirs, leading off a tapestried landing with a monumental vase of aromatic foliage on a gilded console, and a couple of ancestral children's portraits to either side of it, small girls. Mr. Wolfe was to sleep on the same floor as I, though at the opposite end of the gallery; and as for Fr. Bridgefall, God knew, you didn't ask such things, he probably lurked somewhere between Mr. Wolfe's bed and mine.

To begin with, there was among the boys a good deal of rushing about and inspecting and, of course, comparison. Even though all of our rooms were characterized by a pristine, retrospective smartness, mine, it has to be said, outstripped the rest: decorated in red *toile-de-Jouy,* with ivory curtains tumbling from gesso rails, it boasted the first fourposter on which I'd ever slept, with pilasters of carved wood, a covered canopy, and built so high that you had to jump to get onto it. Its cotton drapes were hung with narrow stripes of red and *blanc cassé,* and lined in good plain linen; but the ceiling of the canopy had been covered with a panel of the pastoral design, as if to ease you into your slumbers. On both the bedside tables, in silver jugs, were identical posies of mixed roses, stripped of thorns and leaves. And between the windows, which overlooked the garden, there blossomed a dressing-table—I remember because it was so feminine—clothed in white-frilled skirts of voile with threaded ribbons of red velvet, and, on its surface, a silver set of hair-brushes and hand mirrors, engraved with the name Amélie—whoever she was, or might have been—and, on a shelf above, which formed part of the main mirror, various jars of crystal and a pair of figurines—a shepherd and shepherdess of porcelain so fine that sunlight seemed to steal through their skin.

The others' showers and bathroom were, I noted, tiled in cream, with sets of primary coloured towels and curtains, but I, like Mr. Wolfe, whose bedroom was papered in grey and upholstered in blue ging-ham, enjoyed a vast bathroom clad in pale alabaster, with a separate shower, a wardrobe full of extra towels, an armchair and, at the cen-tre of the room, between bath and basin, a luxury which I'd never before come across in such a setting, a Persian rug—of silk, you could tell: the sensation was of treading velvet rather than felt. My good for-tune, however, did not prevent the others, who broke in as I was unpacking, from shrieking with laughter at the sight of a bidet. Yet I, for once, felt bolstered by my foreignness.

I locked the door and took a siesta; for (even if geographically this was not the case) I felt further from the imprisoning rules of school than I did from home. That other incarceration, which of course yet loomed, I tried to banish from my thoughts; I remained, for now, quite happy. I suspect, looking back, that this trip, and this stop particularly, betrayed, in the narrowed eyes of my contemporaries, my first retarded steps towards assertion: it must have galled them to discover that whereas, up to this point, they had regarded me as an outcast, and a ludicrous one at that, now it was I who seemed the most integrated, for although my parents had never lived at the pitch of the du Castels, I recognized the signals of these people, and appreciated the finery of their details as I surrendered to the crisp cool linen of their coronetted sheets.

DINNER THAT EVENING WAS, in several senses, a spectacle. We wore, as we'd been told to do, the charcoal worsted suits that at school were reserved for Sundays and holy days of obligation; and, once herded by the priest, we followed him down to the drawing room for aperitifs. I remember that du Castel, the boy, was already there to greet us, looking at first relieved that we, like him, were dressed more or less formally—which his father, whom we had not yet met, apparently expected—but then I noticed his expression turn to a wince as he realized that while we, who were older, were stuck in shorts, he, by glaring contrast, was wearing a long-trousered suit of very fine dark gabardine, and that (to aggravate matters) his tie was not, like ours, regulation, but tartan. He blushed fleetingly, not knowing where to look, until the smooth natural mechanism of his breeding surfaced to assist him. Addressing Fr. Bridgefall with spectacular aloofness, he explained that his parents would be down presently, that we were to help ourselves to drinks, and directed us to the less showy end of the room, which was brocaded rather than tapestried, away from the great fireplace with its ornate clock of gilt and candlesticks of ormolu. There was, in fact, no helping ourselves to be done, for no sooner had we sunk into the lavish silks of our collective awkwardness than a footman and two maids came in, followed by Mr. Wolfe, who, though panting, nonetheless lent, by dint of his laity, a certain welcome casualness to the proceedings. But he was got-up in a blazer, the crassness of which I found vicariously embarrassing: already he was becoming a disappointment to me. The priest, in his hallowed dog-collar, was, of course, forgiven anything.

The manservant carried, and expertly—not a rattle, not a clink—a platter crowded with flutes of champagne deliberately exceeding the dozen that was strictly needed, as if observation of numbers were a vulgarity. The first of the maids bore a large tray of *amuse-bouches*—tiny mushroom vol-au-vents, bits of foie gras *truffé*, asparagus tips *en gelée*—neat little canapés of the type which, then, were considered stylish; and the second girl, who was younger, followed her leaders' trajectory along the plum and green Aubusson with a small silver salver of impeccably starched cocktail napkins, the first of which the priest plucked and flicked open, like some handkerchief, while the last, du Castel—perhaps in a bolsh at being served after the rest of us—refused. I couldn't help but note that apart from myself and Mr. Wolfe and one other boy whose parents were at some embassy, the remainder were starting to look decidedly tetchy, as if these inexplicable napkins, which were not mentioned but simply left to rot on side-tables, spelt the prelude to some disappointing TV supper.

And then our hosts appeared, arms linked. We rose in unison, only to hover about for what felt like an absurdity. The Countess walked across the room in a superbly plain, superbly cut little cocktail dress—a short-sleeved trapeze, entirely of that period—fashioned, I suspect, of matt black crêpe. Pinned to the left, she wore a modest diamond-and-enamel brooch which looked, to me, more like some papal decoration than hereditary. Her hair had been tied back with a black velvet ribbon; she no longer wore spectacles; her lips were painted pink; her heels were lowish. Though androgynous despite her tailored femininity, she looked tentatively pretty as she guided her husband—whose arm she now released—first towards our Chaplain, as protocol, I suppose, decreed. The Count turned out to be considerably taller, and older, than his wife, and almost entirely bald; his frame was gaunt; his carriage, ponderous; his mien, pallid but gleaming. He wore an old-fashioned dinner jacket, double-breasted, which I thought was pushing it a bit, but perhaps this was the custom among gentlemen of his generation, or perhaps with the Belgian aristocracy, or perhaps he just felt safer clad in such armoury. For it transpired that his command of English was minimal, so that his wife, whose accent reminded me of my mother's, was reduced to interpreting for him. Once or twice, however, our Chaplain took it upon himself to come to the rescue by dredging from the horror of his war decomposing fragments of French, a move less courteous than witless. Our hosts then ambled round the remainder of the semicircle, so that the Count could, a bit stiffly, shake hands with his young guests, and, when my turn came, the Countess explained to him that I was the one from Spain, which earned me a slow Ah Bon. And at last we sat down again, and were left to mutter among ourselves, like extras on a stage, while the two members of staff chatted to our hosts, along with poor du Castel, whom they had inveigled and, anyone could see, was finding it all hellish.

THE MANSERVANT now entered to advise the Countess that dinner was served, at which point we all sighed with relief and leapt up, too eagerly. The dining room, which was approached through two pairs of double doors on either side of the fireplace, looked dark until you reached it, for it was panelled in sombre wood and lit solely by means of candles. The damask curtains, in a shade which, then, was known as *tête-de-nègre,* were heavily drawn to. There were no pictures on the *boiserie.* The floor was herringboned in slippery parquet the colour of molasses; no carpets; and, perhaps on account of the candles, or because of the polishing wax, the air was infused with a scent of honey. The number of servants, meanwhile, had doubled: to two men and four women, attendants in the shadows.

Next, the Countess began to gesticulate an *emplacement,* but only vaguely, because, to her, most of the boys must have seemed interchangeable, and besides, she was the only woman in our midst. One of our group, not thinking, sat down—only to be ordered to get to his feet at once by our mortified Chaplain, to whom our hostess now accorded the honour of her right. I was put to her left, with my back to the window and facing a massively carved *buffet.* Mr. Wolfe was directed to the Count's right, which meant, mercifully, that I couldn't see him or his blazer, and du Castel was told to sit opposite him, presumably in order to lend support to his beleaguered father. The interchangeable half-dozen was left to arrange itself as it saw fit, and once the commotion had died down, Fr. Bridgefall was requested to say grace—which he elected to do in French, if you please, naturally bungling the whole thing and concluding, in preference to a common Amen, with an obsolete *Ainsi soit-il.* Then, with a footman helping each of our hosts to their carvers, and the maids assisting those of us who'd been placed alongside them, we were finally able—though to the accompaniment of appalling scraping, worse than the benches in our refectory—to sit and breathe with greater ease. But there followed a sudden deathly hush, inspired, I suspect, by the sight of our first course, which was artichokes.

The priest must have been preoccupied with indicating to his charges, by dint of meaningful grimaces, that they were not to be daunted by this confounding vegetable, but simply to follow his urbane suit and pluck the leaves, because I remember finding myself compelled to converse with the Countess, who, as soon as it seemed permissible, lapsed into a whispery Spanish, spoken with greater warmth than either of her other languages. I remember complimenting her on the table's centrepiece, which resembled a seventeenth-century *bodegón,* for though its splendour betrayed a corruptive Flemish influence, the style of its arrangement reminded me of certain old Spanish paintings—by Meléndez, and the early Velázquez, that sort of thing. I don't suppose that any of the components of the display had been chosen for their symbolic worth, but for their plain beauty, which was unquestionable, and yet the decorative tone of the tableau tended less towards the quotidian than the ecclesiastical. I suspect that the Countess, who'd apparently turned the former stables of the château into a private chapel, where the local priest came daily, at dawn, to offer communion to her, sought to drown the sobs of her melancholy in the greater waters of religion—quite a Latin thing to do in that era. At any rate, when I asked about the cloth upon which her set had been created, which, though fashioned of worn velvet, like an ancient altar frontal, possessed, at the extremities, mysterious pockets, closer to an *alforja,* she explained that—yes, wasn't it curious—the piece had originally been designed for Catholic priests during the Reformation, but though indeed cut, in order to invest it with the semblance of a secular use, along the lines of a saddle-bag, its secret function had been to enable former members of our clergy, when threatened with sudden persecution, to bung their sacred paraphernalia into the pockets, roll up the whole business, and flee.

The still life was at once ascetic and luxuriant, suggestive both of a low Mass and a bacchanal. The objects which, arranged with feigned informality around a swanlike jug of tarnished silver, graced that long table, owed as much to the early Eucharist as to a tale of sensual indulgence. There were, of course, numerous candles, haphazardly inserted into clashing sticks, of bronze and pewter and dull brass, their heights varying considerably; and yet the ensemble, at least from my position, looked well balanced, felicitous. There were also great standing goblets, like chalices, and others laid on their side, as if drained of their contents and abandoned; and from some of these, which seemed to gleam with gilded insides, there poured torrents of grapes darker than Málaga wine, mingled, as they reached the velvet surface, which had mellowed to the colour of mud, with bunches of alabaster ones. And there was dark bread, like Testamental loaves, with severed chunks; and occasional shells of mother-of-pearl, presumably to shoot the light; and black cherries of glass, their stems made of metal, and walnuts, and scattered almonds, and figs, incised with a cross into segments that curled out like tongues. And here and there, as if stolen from a Sevillian shrine at Eastertime, deep purple carnations, like secrets, or offerings of penance.

As I was about to express my surprise that carnations could be cultivated in Belgium, I saw the Countess look across, round from the priest towards her husband; and at that critical instant, there was a distracting flash, like a mirror hit by sun, along one side of the company; and as, in a joint reflex, we turned, she and I, to the source of this light, we saw that one of the boys, the one who had laughed about the bidet in my bathroom, had picked up his silver finger-bowl and taken a glug. This gaffe did not escape the Count, who, unlike the apocryphal seigneur, did not seek to put his guest at ease by similarly imbibing, but looked back to his wife, smiled, and left the perpetrator to be publicly admonished by the Chaplain, and die. The whole vignette, perversely, made me think of my father: I should have loved him to have witnessed it, for he was fond of boasting to the people of our island about how, in his day, the priests at his old school had even taught one to carve. Young Gentlemen, and all that.

The next course came with a great flourish, but augured no better as straightforward nourishment, for what we were served, along with a warm purée of salsify, was roast quail. The sensibilities of my English peers were visibly strained by the sight, on a steaming great platter, of all those dead little birdies, requiring, after a few initial cuts, dismemberment by squeamish adolescent fingers; but I suppose that they managed the unsavoury task, for after the artichokes they must have been starving. I asked about carnations in Belgium. The Countess, who'd been discussing with our Chaplain the faults and merits of the Tridentine Mass (not the most gripping of subjects, but I don't suppose that this was exactly the place to raise the topic of the Vatican's intransigence on contraceptive matters), now turned to me, looking, at first, glad of the chance of conversational distraction, and then embarrassed, as if my enquiry had, in some way that I couldn't fathom, caught her off guard, exposed her. We reverted, at her initiative, to Spanish, but her words were accompanied by a look of such fixity as to suggest not that she was engrossed in me particularly but that she didn't quite dare to look elsewhere, or let her comments be broadcast. Her tone became actively conspiratorial now, and I was soon to glean the reason behind her reticence: you could, she said, indeed grow such flowers here, if necessary in hothouses, though carnations were resilient—hers flourished in the cottage garden on the kitchen side of the château. She held an affection for them, she admitted, along with geraniums and jasmine and plumbagos, for they reminded her of her Andalusian background; but the Count, you see, preferred the conventional botanical refinements, such as lilies and roses and ornamentals, with the result, she confessed, that a truce had needed to be drawn not long after their marriage, when she had felt at her most, how could she put it, nostalgic—and most stubborn, she admitted with a smile; and thus it was agreed that she was at liberty to grow her floral banalities within the walled discretion of the kitchen garden, and welcome, if she so desired, to place them in her private apartments, so long as the Count could, if she didn't mind, be entrusted, as he'd been entrusted ever since inheriting the house, with the supervision of his ancestors' formal landscape. I began to see how, despite the advantages of her match, the Countess had suffered by her removal from her homeland, must feel a sense of foreignness akin to mine; and, conversing with her in our shared native tongue, I was struck by the irony that, just as I had failed to develop into my father's proper English son, so, in some illogical way, I must have reminded this woman, whose firstborn was being primed with a specific view to assuming his Belgian title, of the Spanish son whom she had never had.

TODAY IS WATERLOO, our Mecca. After breakfast, during which Mr. Wolfe keeps trying to catch my eye, we're given a quarter of an hour to get ourselves together, fetch our coats—bound to be cold—and collect whatever we might want: cameras, notepads—not that I have either. I go upstairs and lie on my bed, and wish that I could be forgotten, stay behind; but, all too soon, I hear the dread commotion start, so I resign myself, exhale, get up.

Details regarding that defunct battleground seem to elude me. I can't recall a single feature of interest about it. Was there a strategic hillock? Was there a herd of grazing cattle? Was there some commemorative statue? Whatever there was, all that I can picture in the dreary aftermath is a blur of driving rain and sombre skies and soggy grass, indistinguishable from the sludgy panoramic of the northern English wilds; and boys jotting copiously on sodden paper pads, and taking pictures which require a flash, and reliving an unlived past with the help of phrases such as Rearguard Action. Then, at last, back into the minibus we climb, resuming our earlier positions, to trundle over a monotony of empty roads in search of some tavern where we might be served a fortifying country lunch. The Chaplain finds just such a place, deserted and in the nick of time, and falls, on his way to the lavatory, not merely upon some postcards, but, to quote him, upon *quelques* jolly *cartes postales*. Hurrah, Father.

By evening, it was plain that certain changes had been effected at the house, perhaps as a result of the trials of dinner the previous night. Certainly the Count had chosen to absent himself, pleading an engagement in town, where he was to stay overnight; and though we were treated to drinks in the drawing room, we didn't have to don our suits, and the Countess, who joined us wearing a powdery cashmere cardigan draped over her shoulders, hoped that we didn't mind if tonight was a little less formal: she had arranged, she explained, that a buffet be prepared for us in the parlour where we'd had breakfast. And when we went through, though I forget the food, I observed that in the absence of the Count the room had been decked with bowls of flowers taken from her cottage garden; and that although we were served *sangría,* which we boys guzzled down, the padre spluttered and coughed until he'd been brought a restorative bottle of burgundy, which he graciously offered to share with his hostess, who thanked him but declined. I grudgingly took part in a game of after-supper cards, but, with the announcement of Fr. Bridgefall's next inspired idea, namely a cheery round of French charades, I excused myself, feigning exhaustion, and took myself to bed, having, as was clearly required (for she had inclined her profile), kissed the cheek of the Countess. Sod the others, I thought. But, deep down, I was starting to grow panicky.

WHEN I DREW my curtains closed, I knew that I was doing so for the last time: tomorrow we would be starting our long journey back, our objective fulfilled, my pretext done. Yet I was to be proved wrong on all fronts; for, in the deep of the night, as I darted fitfully in and out of dreams of drowning in fire, I heard my door being opened slowly, slyly, and my instinctive first terror was of a burglar; then, of some last-ditch schoolboy prank. I lay there paralysed. But as my eyes began to focus in the dark, I saw Mr. Wolfe's bearded outline move towards the curtains and open them, just as I had opened his during the course of the last three years. And then he removed his dressing-gown in an echo of what I myself had so often done, and he stole into my bed without permission. But there was no music to be heard, and there were no candles to be lit—none, at any rate, that I would allow; forget it. I recall that I felt enraged: aside from the effrontery of his intrusion, the gauntlet that he was running seemed to me far riskier than all the risks which, in my former desperation, I had run. I wished that I'd remembered to lock my door, had kept him out. This visit seemed maniacal, frightening. I feared our discovery in this house far more powerfully than I had ever done at school in England. It seemed to me that for the truth of my iniquities to be relayed by the appalled Countess to my appalled mother would have proved an exposure infinitely more shaming than the half-baked revelations of my former headmaster. I don't know what I would have done, there would have been no telling. I told Mr. Wolfe to get out, and to be quiet about it.

But, of course, he would have none of this. He, too, had earned his rights. This was our closing night. He couldn't believe that I was being so hard-hearted: What had happened to me? Couldn't I see that it was he, not I, who was putting his neck on the line? And hadn't he always covered for me? And did I really value what we shared at nothing? And thus, with his frantic whispered pleas, he gradually wore me down. I would just, I remember thinking, have to go through with it, endure it like some prostitute. Yet if there was a price to be paid, the price was to be mine, for as he ripped off his pyjamas and heaved himself upon me, he asked me, told me, threatened that this story of great love could not be complete unless I met his supplication, for the final time, that we come in unison. And so it was to be, so we were to come; but what he never knew was that as we did, I was thinking of some other, imaginary man, some perfect stranger. And then, I helped myself to his pyjama top and used it to mop up.

BY MORNING, I had put it all behind me; though as I stood, packed and poised on the threshold of the next phase of my life, I felt undermined by a chill of residual discomfort, not just about my treatment of Mr. Wolfe but regarding the broader change which had affected my feelings towards him. I could hardly believe that I no longer cared a toss, literally, for the man who, until recently, had meant so much to me, without whose love I'd feared that I might flounder. It made me feel cheap, this lack of consistency, this ingratitude, and yet I couldn't allow mere fickleness to belittle me. I had to get on, you see, gather my strength for the next ordeal—for that is how, then, I viewed my existence: as a relentless assault course, like hurdle after treacherous hurdle rushing at me from a hostile future. So I appeased myself with the argument that he and I had struck a deal, and that the deal, mutually beneficial as it had been, was simply complete. We were both, even if on the verge of severance, in one piece. Surely the honour was implicit? But as I took one last look at the crimson *toile-de-Jouy,* at that moment, just as I was turning to leave, I found myself, as if I were my mother, steeped into a crisis of superstition by the monstrous sight of a peacock—its back turned to me; its train raised into a full, iridescent fan of doom.

Leavetaking was easy: just the Countess, back from Mass. Du Castel had gone out riding. I was last in the departing queue. She reminded me to convey her regards to my mother, wished me luck at the Big School, hoped to see me next time she was in England, said that I was welcome to return whenever I liked, or to visit their house in Brussels in winter. *Adiós,* Santiago, she added; and after I had mumbled my thanks, we kissed. And as she stood on the gravel, waving, the minibus, with my redundant lover at the wheel, drove off through flashes of lime, and a strange sorrow welled within me, like a phantom homesickness, for I knew that I should never return to this place which I regretted leaving more than, when the moment came, I would regret leaving Mr. Wolfe.

I HAD FORGOTTEN that we were to return to Brussels for one night, to sleep at some seminary, which was empty during the summer but where Fr. Bridgefall had some business to attend to, some meeting. We arrived early, for Mr. Wolfe had driven like a demon, and were given the afternoon to amuse ourselves, walk around, see the shops, buy presents for our families. Mr. Wolfe latched on to me, inevitably, and we broke off from the rest of the group, leaving the building through a back door. I found that I had nothing to say now; it felt odd; it was as if last night had been the culmination of one chapter and we were now embarked upon a connection of a further sort, more healthy, more grown-up, but duller. Letting go. Moving on. He wanted to buy things for me—not quite gifts of propitiation, tokens of endurance—for which I had no wish. But nor did I wish to offend him, for he, though guileless, and ignorant of my rotten core, had not been Wrong. So in the end I found myself pointing towards fripperies of no interest to me—a porcelain bowl, a vase, yet another box of chocolates—things which, bizarrely, I chose with my mother in mind, as if I needed to earn her forgiveness for transgressions which she didn't know that I'd committed, as if the single blessing of her love could wipe away the mess of my serial sins, which was mortal.

After the hollow spree, and as the gloom began to feel engulfing, we stopped at some great square to drink milky coffee; and suddenly the prospect of prolonging this ill-considered journey seemed to me unendurable—the drive all the way to Ostend, the sea-crossing to Dover, the trip back to London, the inevitable night with my vile guardians, the train journey to Heathrow, the flight, which included a midway stop . . . I just lacked the stamina, could no longer cope; and in a burst of inspired lachrymosity, I now begged Mr. Wolfe, as he had begged for simultaneous ejaculation, to grant me one parting gesture, one last proof of his loyalty: to help me change my flight, so that directly from Brussels I could flame it to my island, first thing in the morning. Miraculously, he acceded to my request, and though compelled to pay some supplement, managed to effect the transfer. From the travel agency, I telephoned home and, since my parents were out, I told Cook to send the chauffeur to collect me from the airport *tomorrow*, at two in the afternoon; yes, I'd be arriving a day early; never mind if she hadn't had time to prepare my favourite food. I wasn't exactly hungry.

My taxi came before the rest of the group had awoken. I crept out of my seminarian cubicle, and only Mr. Wolfe was up to see me off, his eyes puffy, suddenly grown old. I thanked him for having made my flight back possible. He thanked me for Everything. We did not kiss; nor were hands shaken: we compromised on a mutual wink and pout, concealed from the driver's view, and the rest of the business was left unspoken in mid-air, to loll, like a doubt, in the lap of the gods.

And when I returned home, burdened by my superfluous trophies, my mother, though pleased enough to receive the chocolates, suggested that I rewrap the vase and bowl and give them to the servants, who would be so grateful. And at dinner that evening, when my father demanded an explanation for the change in my travel arrangements, my answer was simple: it seemed more efficient, and Mr. Wolfe (Yes, he came too, didn't I tell you?) had been in full accord. But when I regaled my mother with the anecdote about my hostess at the château and their coincidental meeting at the Feria years before, she jingled her great bracelet and denied any recollection of any girl from Jerez having married any Belgian count, then or ever.

IN THOSE EARLY DAYS—though later she would grudgingly concede surrender—my mother focused her efforts for me on her special subject, which was Society. No sooner had I ripped off my uniform than she would begin to cajole me into attending children's parties, whole litanies of them, and simply would not take any kind of No for an answer. Out of the question. What was I, for heaven's sake, some peasant down from the mountains? What was wrong with me? Could I not see how essential it was for me to maintain links with my motherland?—to which, I think, she secretly hoped I would return to settle in time, armed with international qualifications and prospects to earn me the easy pick of the best girls in town, as if the marriage game were a fan of canasta cards, as if she had learnt nothing from her own miserable mismatch. The links which she espoused on my behalf were obviously restricted to links of a good class—as words went, *élite* and *échelon* didn't strike her as such bad ones—and to parties given for the off-spring of women who, even if they hadn't boasted great dowries (and always provided that their spouses passed muster), had at least attended the Assumption. She was familiar with all such women on the island, not just from their shared past but because she would run into them at every turn of the circuit at cocktail parties; at charity-benefit fashion shows; at the Nautical Club regatta; at the Casino when the latest garland of virgins came out; at the Golf Club on carnival night; at the airport—flying off, flying back, or meeting someone; at music recitals, though no *Lieder* for her, thank you; in church and afterwards, outside; at funerals, which, even in the elegant days of mantillas, my mother tried to avoid, though mourning and commiseration did appeal to my father; at art openings (if you could call them that); in chic boutiques; at the embroidery woman's house; at the theatre, whose rear elevation once had to be demolished in order to accommodate a touring production of *Aïda;* at occasional discothèques, which used to be called *boîtes;* at the one and only decent hairdresser's, whither all such women flocked to have their pieces buttressed to their scalps; every 15th August, at tombolas hosted by the Old Girls of the Assumption . . . and in this way, through these repetitive encounters, my poor foolish mother ensured that wherever there was a desirable children's party, I was not forgotten, that hostesses, even in my absence, rather than risk her displeasure, invited me. She would sometimes mention these events to me—the magicians and the prizes and the hideous piñatas and the mouth-watering birthday cakes and the treasure hunts—describing them, with breathless superlatives and a suspect preponderance of exclamation marks, in her letters of deep turquoise.

NOW THAT I'D OUTGROWN a governess, my mother would sometimes take me to these fledgling parties, but would, on our eventual departure, and oblivious to the driver, launch into me, berate me for my bad manners, my sulky, stand-offish attitude, my refusal not just to involve myself in any of the entertainments, but to feign what even a mere yokel would regard as basic friendliness. I had plenty of charm when I wanted to deploy it, she was all too aware of that, so what on earth was wrong with me? Why couldn't I make more of an effort? And why did I object to the other children anyway, all perfectly well brought up, and all, so far as she could tell (apart from me), having a marvellous time: you could hear their laughter from the pergola where mothers were taking tea at the far end of the garden. So why, she would implore, must I always embarrass her?

But she did not understand (how could she have done?) the extent to which I felt estranged from such celebrations, the fact that, beyond the more obvious oddity of being schooled in another country, which increasingly made me feel foreign here in Spain as well as over in England, I also felt oppressed by the weight of my other problem—my strange, sinful love—which, irrespective of its secrecy, distanced me yet further from the wide-eyed children at those parties, conspired to make me feel like a much older alien. And the result was that I simply found myself with nothing to talk about, in any language.

WHERE I WENT to drown my silence, particularly in the summers to come, became nobody's business. Up to my twelfth year, in view of my reluctance to socialize, I found myself more or less restricted to the bamboo fringes of our house, and only exceptionally did I go out unchaperoned; but thereafter I began to be sent on errands by my mother, to the watchmaker's, to the stationer's, to buy buttons for the sewing-woman, and I was allowed to walk to the Nautical Club, and, after my siesta, to go to the cinema. And this new licence led to an abundance of opportunities for me. I felt oddly nervous when I first ventured beyond the bandstand of flamboyants, as if, at any moment, some excruciating acquaintance of my parents' might pounce on me, or as if, absent-mindedly crossing the Rambla, I might collide with some speeding car, for when I'd walked the moors and fells and woods of the English countryside, I never ran into anything or anyone. This new environment was too crowded, too noisy for my liking. But soon enough I grew accustomed to it, and simply looked to the ground— both in order to avoid detection and to check where my feet were guiding me. Often it would be, though briefly, to the Nautical Club, where I would swim a few lengths in a great hurry and walk out before being accosted by someone's flip-floppy mother or, just as bad, some relic of a boy from my discarded childhood, and I would set off clutching my rolled towel by way of alibi. Because my feet would no longer lead me, as instructed by my mother, into a taxi and back up to the house.

Instead they would stray, directed by some odd desire for transgression, by some incomprehensible need for corruption, into the exotic womb of the Municipal Park. I would stroll, pretending to be entranced, past the aviary with all its spectacular parrots, like the one shot down from our palm tree, and the great sheet of water with its fascist sculptures and its fountain, and the concrete course for mini-golfers, and sometimes I would stop at the ice-cream stand. But once I had effected this round, which became customary, I would sit on a stone bench along one of the paths in some more secluded section of the park, not far from the public lavatories. These alleyways were, in fact, more like tunnels, for the sky was almost entirely obscured from view by jungles of green foliage, trained from arch to arch to arch for great stretches at a time. And once you entered the hollows of these giant caterpillars, it was as if you had entered a world divorced from reality, where all life was different and your heart pounded with anticipation.

To begin with, the men just smiled at me. Later, when they began to recognize me, they would beckon me—first, with their heads, soon thereafter, hand on crotch—to follow them. In time, I grew bold enough to do so, and would find myself going down the steps to the place called *Caballeros,* and approaching the urinals, and standing next to these beckoners, and I would voluntarily enter into congress with these creatures who, for the most part, were like tramps. And either because my extreme youth spelt extreme danger, or because the danger was itself a source of frenetic excitement, they would ejaculate against the wall of the urinals in a matter of seconds. They would frot my buttocks, or stroke my front, or guide my fingers to their hardened phalluses, or use me to squeeze their hairy testicles. And the sight of them, turned more salacious than the apes that were caged outside, and the access which they granted me to all their variations on the theme of grown-up genitals, made me feel desired as well as educated, more so than at any local First Night. My lessons were quick, uncomplicated, and never unpleasant. Those men were too wary of the risk which they were running, of their brush with crime: for homosexual acts, never mind such acts performed in a public place with a blatant minor, were, at least then, instantly imprisonable. No remand. Bang. Whether I'd fully entered the mire of puberty by this time, I cannot say, but my voice certainly hadn't yet broken, which was one reason why I always kept my mouth shut. The other was that I couldn't bear to be kissed by those strangers.

ONCE, HOWEVER, a man did talk to me, and he seemed more assured, more poised than the usual marauders. I remember that he was dark as a gypsy, and that he wore white trousers, tight and slightly transparent. For once, I talked back. It didn't take me long to suss from his harsh sibilants that he came from the mainland, and that, like me in a way, he was an outsider. I said that I was English. He couldn't believe the fluency of my Spanish. I pooh-poohed his compliment as my mother might have done, with flirtatious bashfulness. I even lowered my lashes. He managed to light a cigarette with his second waxy match. He thought the park was a bit grubby, that I was special. He had nowhere to take me, but he did have a car. We could go for a drive. Did I have time? I had an hour before lunch. My fear was not palpable: I was too het-up, and too hot, to decline. He seemed trustworthy enough. What could be the harm? He was parked round the corner, which provided me with my first obstacle, namely avoiding the detection of anyone who might know my family, and there were plenty of candidates. But I passed with flying colours. I got into that car, also white, also tight, quick as a flash; in fact, so set was I on my illicit ride that, frankly, I could have done it in a pencil-skirt and spikes. And off we went into the adventure. I slid down my seat to the level of the dashboard. He turned on the wireless. I remember a drivelling religious programme, which he quickly switched over, visibly embarrassed, to local folk music, tambourines and guitars in triple-time. Smoky laugh, followed by a phlegmy yok, expelled through his open window.

He puts my hand on his crotch, which is hard, as is mine. Tells me to stroke him, but not to take it out. That feels lovely. Looks into my eyes. I look at him like an enquiring harlot. I need to be sophisticated. We're going to a beach on the edge of town, not far from the Nautical Club. Great, I say, but I slide further down. He doesn't seem to notice. He's happy so long as I don't let up. Purrs like a tiger, is beginning to leak through his pants. Once we're out of danger, by which I mean beyond the entrance to the Nautical Club and on our way, I relax a fraction, and he relaxes almost entirely into a mood of slow pleasure. He can't wait, he says, to get his hands on me. His hands, on the wheel, are like sausages. Cheap-looking ring, taxi-driverish. Round his neck dangles a crucifix of gold, no cadaver, just the symbol, which, with the bumps of the road, jumps in and out of his tangles of dark fur. He strokes my working hand. Changes gear now. Looks out of the rear-view mirror. And again. But something's up. Seems fractionally worried. Sighs. Sucks at his saliva. Flicks his cigarette out of the window. Moves my hand off his trousers, makes me feel rebuffed. He says there's a bit of a problem: he's being tailed by a police car. No, he tells me, don't turn round. My head is suddenly pounding. We're in the middle of nowhere and I've got no money, blown it all at the ice-cream stand. If he dumps me now, I'll never get back in time for lunch. I'll have to hitch-hike. But I might get recognized. He suddenly swerves like a television robber into a side-street and races round the block and, before I know it, we seem to be headed back to town. Perhaps he knows of some other place somewhere. But as he checks the mirror once again, it becomes plain that the law is still cruising behind him. He's getting agitated now, turns off the wireless. He explains, very precisely, as if he were bisexual, that he hopes this won't get unpleasant. If it does, I must pretend to be his nephew. But I don't care, because with every one of his sibilants we're getting closer to home, speeding up the Rambla now: yet as we approach a set of traffic lights, which are turning from green to amber, I suddenly hear, directly behind us, the appalling demented wail of a police siren. Before I can think twice, and before he gets the chance to speed away, and before the pigs behind can grab me, I just open the door and jump out and don't even look back. And the lights must have gone green, because all the traffic races off as I stagger— Christ Almighty, I've lost my towel—up the hill to lunch on the terrace. But it was better and scarier than any orgasm.

AND THEN THERE WAS THE SEA. The sea turned me sexually amphibian. I think that my love of bathing *à deux* must date from that time. For when we went to the idyllic house with wooden steps that led down to the honeyed sand and my mother seemed, for a few miraculous weeks, to forget the rounds which, in town, at once excited and exhausted her, I would spend hour upon careless hour darting in and out of the navy waves. I was also allowed to swim after supper, while the tide went out in the dark—though, even if the beach was deserted, naked never. My father, when not playing golf in the mountains, or attending a funeral—*someone* had to represent the family—and despite my point-blank refusals to join him in any volley game of anything upon the sand, or his to help me fly my kite—do it yourself, you're perfectly capable—seemed nonetheless delighted by my growing aquatics. Who knows, he would say to my mother, the boy might yet turn out to be a Swimmer—as if this were a vocation. And I would recall how, back at school, I had surveyed him from my high plank on the stile.

My mother had for years retained a couple, an old fisherman and his wife, who lived just behind our beach house, to guard it when it was empty, for local hooligans enjoyed looting and setting fire to villas such as ours. The old lady would, in her fishy way, cook for us, and make our beds, and clean the bathroom which, to my mother's annual irritation, had to be shared by all three of us, like Goldilocks' bears—though there were, doubtless to her proportional relief, enough bedrooms to go round. Actually, I preferred the divan in the alcove off the dining room and, as a treat, would occasionally be permitted to sleep there. But never on the hammock outside, not at night—stars, moon, or the very firmament. Open your window.

Meanwhile, the old fisherman, who had no teeth but smoked like a furnace, acted as handyman: would go to market when required, would wash the car, water plants, replace lightbulbs, mend shutters, sweep outside. His were chores of this nature. But his principal function was, every morning at ten-thirty, and please no earlier, to position my mother's white-slatted lounger, angled to face the sun and decked with a buttoned mattress, on the beach, directly beneath the steps that led down. A few minutes later, she would emerge, ready to face the day, clad in one of that year's patterned towelling robes, which were more like gowns—they practically had trains—her eyes shielded by a pair of the latest sunglasses, which varied according to fashion but tended to be large and very dark; and, if the wind wasn't up, a vast, straw wheel of a sun-hat. Just as a cardigan, in Spain, was known as a Rebecca—for, before that film, the populace had never beheld such an article—hats of the type which my mother favoured were known as Pamelas, presumably in homage to some now forgotten Hollywood diva. I presume this because, when my mother emerged thus covered, she would hold her hand up towards her crown with such choreographed *élan* that you would have thought she was balancing an invisible platter of mangoes and foliage and clouds. The side of her wide brim would curl up against her risen arm, and though I know I sound sardonic and campy, the sight of her descent was, in fact, sublime. And in this sublime attitude, which included a flat basket hung about her other arm, her bare feet, with toes lacquered crimson, would lead her very slowly to partake, for an hour or two, of the summer sun.

THEN SHE WOULD DISROBE; and this ritual, too, entranced me. Her swimming costume—for never in her life would my mother (this wasn't Hollywood, that was her line) have sunk to the lowness of a two-piece—invariably corresponded to the robe that engulfed it. It was a rule with her, stringent as a commandment. And the towel which, like a beach in itself, she would spread out over her lounger was always of burnt gold, like the sand, like her skin, which I worshipped. She was never to veer from this tone, and bought it by the half-dozen before having it monogrammed to the precise matching shade of ochre. One year alone, for a change, she had her towels initialled in red, to go with her toes, but later she claimed to have made the greatest mistake, said that she reminded herself of the national flag: blood and sand; ketchup and mustard.

Now she would recline on her back, one knee always up, and close her shaded eyes, and let out a sigh which was not of complaint but of gratitude, of sacred hedonism, for, at heart, at least until my father got her, I think that she carried the latent flame of the sensualist. And when he was away from the beach, and she and I were left in peace, I would come and go and do as I pleased, and nothing in those days pleased me more than to build lavish sandcastles for her, with courtyards and moats and starfish and shells and the whole paraphernalia, which—Later, later, she would beg—she would christen with my bucket, full of water from the sea, for these castles which I made were hers to reign in. And she, humming in paradise, would apply rarefied unguents to her legs, which, though she would not let me feel them, were smooth as polished stone; or she would turn on her front, and leaf through her magazines, which, once through, she would let me attempt to read; or when at last the heat overwhelmed her, she would send me back to the house bearing her hat while she slipped on her bathing cap, her crowning glory, which, like the varying swimsuits and robes, altered on a daily basis—until some eventual vogue decreed such contrivances passé. And when she swam, her neck held to the heights, it was in a regal breaststroke, timeless, biblical. And although soon enough my paddle would be left in her smooth wake, smooth because her feet never frothed, I would linger in the shallows and await her return, to reclaim her. And I would have to say that in those early days, at the beginning, with her to myself, I, at least, was perfectly content.

OF COURSE, the idyll was not to last. With the passage of those summers, I outgrew the thrill of sandcastles, discarded the disappointment of my kites, gave up chasing butterflies, and sought, instead, amusements that were more challenging. My mother, for so many possible reasons—her encroaching middle years, her reptilian husband, her frustration that I wasn't turning into her plan, to mention but the more obvious likelihoods—became firmer with me, forbad me to browse through her magazines, which were for women; forbad me from wearing those colours which I favoured, such as primrose, and which, overnight, she condemned, with a venom that I have never heard rivalled, as Effeminate; forbad me from having my tight jeans further tightened; forbad me from riding a moped; forbad me from staying behind in town. So that in this new state of tension, in this small house by the beach, I felt entrapped. It was like the sea which at school had parted around me—nowhere to walk, nowhere to run—until, in the end, my sole escape became, of all the ironies, the very sea: I went to the waves for release. And soon thereafter, I went to them for revenge, for satisfaction.

It was a horrible time. My mother would lie on the sand, her shape perhaps less waisted now, swathed in pareos of printed muslin. There was something sad about them. But I would ignore the sadness and get up late, long after she had taken to the sand. I would breakfast on my own, and sunbathe nowhere near the house, slink off as far as the tide and narrow limits of the beach allowed. My black swimming-trunks— or white, once I was tanned—were so brief that my father commanded me to wear those obscenities nowhere near him, banished them from his sight. But he must have seen them hanging on the clothesline (inside out, which is how I pegged them up, to annoy him), for we argued about them frequently: about their cut, about their commonness, particularly that of the white ones, about their vulgar sheen, about the way that they clung: you could see Everything: it was disgusting. I would reply with a recusant smirk that they couldn't be *that* ghastly since they came from London—as indeed they did, though they were actually manufactured in Paris, which I found miles more fabulous. He would say that London had become a city of trash. He would rant about those grubby, long-haired hippies, would lament the demise of capital punishment, bemoan the day they did away with conscription. But then, one day, rather than simply criticize me, he changed tack and—his pallid paunch pointed to the sun, the sog of his baggy cotton shorts moulding upon him—enquired *why* I wore those minuscule briefs, why it was that I liked them. And I remember replying that soon my body wouldn't be young enough to carry them. And this is the only occasion when I properly succeeded in leaving my mother's consort at a loss for a contradiction. But it didn't feel like victory.

Victory for me lay in the water, in the sting of the salt, and the pull of the people—for by now the beach had become more popular. Later, its appeal would become so endemic, and so sexy, that my outraged parents, not once stopping to wonder whether I, their sole heir, might have liked, in the fullness of time, to own the property which my mother had herself been bequeathed by her family, sold off the Villa, at a phenomenal profit—only to see it demolished within minutes of settling the deal—never replaced it, and just travelled from then on: to Madeira; to Capri, when the place was still bearable; to Ibiza, ditto; to Crete, Malta, and Cyprus before the explosion of package tourists . . . you get the general idea, safe and prosaic. But for now our beach was merely more popular, had not as yet been turned into what my parents were later to judge a cheap resort for servants, who these days owned Cars, if you pleased, and for shopgirls who were no better than prostitutes, and for the worst kind of air-steward, unspeakable.

I HAD OVERHEARD that nearby, round the Red Mountain, nudists had colonized a further beach, smaller and more savage than ours, and the license of their lifestyle riveted me—their drugs and their guitars, their naked bathing in broad daylight, the wafts of their patchouli, their joss-sticks when the sun went down, their barbecues, which my parents thought despicable, their improvised canopies of psychedelic paisley, their loving and peacing on the dunes, where wild flowers grew, and the first resulting generation, in tiny T-shirts of tie-dye, of out-of-wedlock babies deemed just about *sortable,* for even my parents knew the maiden names which had committed these Slip-ups—but I felt too young to wander there alone, too tentative, and, in my perverse way I preferred to break the rules of propriety within striking distance of my own people. I would throw my sinful summer stones at the glasshouse of my parents' making, and dump my shit on the hereditary steps which led down to the beach. But my parents were never to see this, for the pair of them lived resolutely in oblivion.

I would go into the sea when it wasn't too busy, just after lunch, when the sun was scorching and even the local padre took his siesta, when the waves were at their roughest and the surf at its most conceal-ing. My mother, tired of warning that if I didn't complete my digestion before going back to swim I'd be seized by stomach cramps and perish on the instant, now modulated her exaggerations to lamer entreaties about walking into the sea very gradually—to which I was willing to agree, for, while not specially worried about my stomach, I was aware of the threat of jellyfish, which surfaced occasionally. And so, there-after, I would wait until my parents had finished their coffee and retired to rest, or digest, or whatever it was that they did, and then I'd set off alone, racing over the blazing sand until I reached that cool tawny car-pet of wetness which led up to the water's edge, the shore, the end of the earth, the beginning of freedom.

Anyone who swam at this time of day, when the sun was fiercest and the sea at its most treacherous, was considered to be going against the grain of the place: either they didn't own a seaside property, so were intruders, or they were too broke to take their lunchtime custom to the shade of the local café, so were useless, or else they were Nordics and Germans, dubbed eccentric but dismissed as libertines from the hotel which, though discreetly built at the opposite end of the golden sickle, had sparked off the disgruntlement that was, in due course, to rev into disgust and drive my parents away. But I loved that beach, and after lunch, I loved it particularly.

It was as if, when you went into the roar and delivered yourself to the devouring embrace of that bluest of oceans, you were entering a realm which, like the tunnel of green in the city, bore no connection to normality or the strictures which, in my parents' society, attached to it. In this liquid kingdom, you could spit and piss and nobody minded; you could be a dolphin, a mermaid, a net full of fish, a boat from the Bible, St. Peter before he earned his flashy keys. This was your life, and no one gave a damn for lost emotions, but the freedom of those waves, their recklessness, did enable you to witness miracles which, out of water, wouldn't have been conceivable. Sometimes, when you dived down and held your breath and swam about with your eyes opened, you would see the luminous rippling shapes of men whom you had never seen (women seemed to stick to the prudence of the beach), and the feet of those men would kick and shimmer like flippers, while their arms rose and sank like the arms of dancers in the sea, and their hands would sometimes stroke their own bodies with disbelief and play with them, play without censure. And I would sometimes see those men, who, to me, from the watery silence of the deep, seemed to glow like visions, strip naked below the glassy surface of the sea, stepping in slow motion out of their trunks, which were far briefer than mine had ever been; and then, in order not to lose them, one leg of the trunks would be pushed over the heads of these beautiful creatures, and left to blossom about their necks, like wreaths of seaweed.

It was all so different in here. Men who couldn't tell what you were, whether seed-pearl or swordfish, would on occasion smile, and signal a little guardedly, and though the great sound of the waves made talking, in any language and from any distance, an impossibility, these signallers were sometimes willing to entertain you. I remember how, seeing me plunge into the depths, and snake around like an eel beneath them, they would part their legs and let me pass between. And if you did this enough (and, on emerging, didn't grin, but just looked natural, as if the game were your mutual right—you didn't want to give a false impression of childishness or innocence) you would find that sooner or later, when you flipped back down and swam about again, they would let your oily body slither past their inner thighs and rub against them, and this was the cue for them to grab you, which always felt fantastic. And if the man had a wreath around his neck and was prepared to proceed, you knew for sure that you weren't up against some avuncular retard who thought you wanted to play at pirates and frigates. You knew you'd hit the jackpot, that neither you, nor he, would sail away without treasure of some description.

THE MAN FIRST holds you by the wrists, as if to capture you, but this does not prevent you from slipping away, from escaping, so his next move is to get you by the waist and draw you nearer, and now you're allowed to soften slightly; and he might even let you put your arms, as if for safety, round him, but you must remember to continue paddling, otherwise you'll both be sunk and have to start from the beginning. Despite the difference in your statures, which, on land, would be conspicuous, out here, in the equalizing water, there seems to be no distinction between you. Sometimes he will position himself behind you, seat you upon himself as if he were your throne and you his prince, or—if the sea is tranquil enough to allow such a thing—have you treat him like an inflatable mattress: you place your back upon his front, and lie, limp as a body, on top of him, and the sky is all that you can see, but you can close your eyes if you desire because he will be working his feet for both of you, will be keeping you going. His arms, when he wraps them round your ribs, feel safer than any rubber-ring or any life-saver. But I never remove my trunks: I lack the courage. I do, however, let him peel me down enough to release me, and I let him rub himself against the whiteness that reveals itself behind me, and sometimes against my front, a trickier position, for even as he holds me there, I feel too high to be practical. But he will always ultimately want to slide himself into the smoothness between my thighs, between me, which is the true source of his relish and my delicacy, my one great contribution to this feast on the high seas, where, in contrast to the park, I do let the man kiss me, not just because the water makes him clean, but because I like the taste of salt upon his lips and, on his tongue, his contrasting sweetness. And by this stage, it will often be over for him, but the spurts of his result will be nowhere to be seen, you don't have to wipe anything, all gone, forgiven. And generally (and now that it's safe, a smile *is* permissible) I swim back to shore ahead of him—just as, when I later graduated from urinals to cubicles, I always tried to be the first to leave—not because I was ashamed, not because I was afraid, not even because I was unrelieved, but because I was in the greater hurry to resume my search for the dream which oppressed me.

PART FOUR

THE BIG SCHOOL, as the Countess had quaintly referred to it, boasted a turbulent history dating back to the reign of the first Elizabeth, who, in the textbooks of my Spanish infancy, had been portrayed not just as the daughter of some fat murderous polygamist, but, more pointedly, as the harridan responsible for the committal of our mighty Armada to its aquatic sepulchre. Bald as a coot, partial to pelicans, and, as if that weren't enough, barren (for the Lord, we had been told, will not be mocked), we regarded that Protestant Queen as altogether most peculiar. Still, I suppose that, if nothing else, the Countess owed to her the cloth of antique velvet which now impressed her guests at dinner.

During the Elizabethan period, English Catholics (or at least those with the means) who strove to have their offspring tutored in accordance with their religious allegiance were reduced, owing to the perils of the Reformation, to shipping their progeny overseas in order to see this wish fulfilled; and initially, when the school amounted to little more than a handful of pupils, I think that it was to France, or perhaps to Belgium, that they were ferried. But after a quick couple of centuries, during which the augmenting community appears to have been shunted hither and thither, England at last seemed—on account of the Catholic Relief Act, or some similar edict—a safer place in which to learn Popish. And so, back they all came, itinerant boys and priests, to settle on the site where my father's Alma Mater was, in architectural dribs and drabs, and in a hotchpotch of styles, eventually to be built.

By the time of my arrival, the school, regardless of its messy past and messy appearance, had grown bloated both physically and in prestige; and despite the fact that, so far as I was aware, no former alumnus had ever achieved any great degree of notability—for this tentacle of the Faith seemed not to encourage worldly ambition, regarding it as tantamount to vanity, or perhaps it was greed—the establishment nonetheless vaunted its spiritual laurels like a drag queen might vaunt her great wig. The weight of its history weighed upon you.

At last we were allowed to wear long trousers, which I greeted with relief, but we were also expected to don detachable collars—ostensibly, I suppose, in deference to sartorial antiquity, or perhaps it was in order to reduce the workload at the laundry, or just to encourage thrift. Whichever: this apparent resistance to progress, when ordinary shirts were just as accessible as the increasingly technological rugger boots and running spikes which were decreed mandatory, appeared perverse to me: it seemed to encourage people to cultivate sweaty shirts beneath the studded deception of a starched neckline just at the time when schoolboys are known to be at their most unappetizing—lazy and clammy and stinky. And to support my suspicion, I now discovered that after games on the playing fields, and runs across country, the custom at this time-honoured institution was to wear swimming trunks in the showers, as if wetting your ears were of greater import than washing your privates. Deodorant, just as cologne had earlier been, was needless to say reviled, viewed as a violation of nature—womanish, queer. But I daresay that, these days, my successors wallow in whole ranges of designer unguents, and are permitted ornaments such as earrings and tongue-studs and tattoos and genital piercings, for I gather that public school coffers ain't looking too good.

During the calm of the previous summer, I had lulled myself into imagining that since Mr. Wolfe and all that business now lay safely behind me, I'd be able, with my transfer to the senior school, to make a fresh start, to wipe my slate clean; but I could not, as it transpired, have been more deluded, for although the boys who accompanied me from prep school accounted only for a negligible proportion of the newcomers, I'd failed to reckon with two other factors: namely that, ahead of me in the hierarchy, there swaggered dozens of people who still recognized the gaseous whiff of my former notoriety; and that those who had never before laid eyes on me, recruits from various other left-footed bastions around the country, plus the occasional foreigner, including a singularly handsome Nigerian, were readier to be apprised of my earlier infamy than to keep an open mind and draw their own conclusions. And within a matter of hours, as I took my first steps into the new refectory, I realized that already I was more known-against than knowing; and I sensed, furthermore, that if this information didn't already extend to the staff, it wouldn't take long to do so, for my mere presence seemed to tax their eyebrows.

The staff itself comprised, to my unease, far more clergy than I had ever before encountered, and came, despite the (relative) uniformity of its habit, in a whole spectrum of ages and guises. There were doddery priests, methuselahs who'd taught some of our own fathers, and who, at some point since, had been retired from their didactic offices (in which this order took particular pride) and put out to grass. You could see them shuffling about the gardens in massacred lace-ups, or down the galleries—their half-mooned beaks stooped over breviaries, a grubby hankie dribbling from a coatsleeve, their waxy shoulders rife with dandruff, their shiny heads bisected by centre partings which, older than their ordinations, had, with the passage of the decades and the thinning of their scalps, grown wide as tracks. But there was a charm to these old buffers: you felt that their ancient hairstyles belied another life—as if, had Poverty, Chastity and Obedience never impinged, they might still be doing the tango at some *thé dansant*. And (if you avoided the deaf ones, who tended to shout) it was they, the oldies, who, at confession, gave you the easiest ride.

Not so with the younger clergy. These were the ones who, despite the sobriety of their preponderant black, allowed themselves an occasional Disobedient touch—coloured socks, for instance, blue or brown—and whose cuffs, in defiance of Poverty, could be seen to glint with flashy links, or a valuable wristwatch on an alligator strap. Quite how they chose to break the deadlock of Chastity was, of course, their own concern; but what I knew was that in the confessional they behaved less like agents of mercy than as procurers: How many times? In what way? Where? Could you explain that? Was it pleasurable? Their questions would come at you half-strangled, excited, in little grunts. And you—even as you admitted to but a fraction of the smut which they were after—presumed that in the darkness behind the screen they'd be holding a gummy handkerchief, clutching at it. Sporadic scrunching of rosary beads fooled no one. And now for your penance:

Three Hail Marys and three Our Fathers, and remember to pray for me, my son. (You bet, Father.) God be with you. (Ditto.) But once I'd charged through my soul-saving shopping list, I would throw in, by way of insurance, the Memorare, whose tone of underhand defiance appealed to my spirit: Remember, O most loving Virgin Mary, that it is a thing unheard of that anyone ever had recourse to your protection, implored your help, or sought your intercession, and was left forsaken. So there.

CHAPELS, they were scattered all about. Some were more intimate and creepy; others, wider and more public; but all were modelled, with a glut of Gothic arches, along the lines of some greater original. There were unrelenting rows of classrooms: E, D, C, B, A—streamed, in my case, according to our Common Entrance results, which luckily pushed me up; a great Tudor hall, rank with the school's past and decked with portraits of former incumbents: stuffed shirts, puffed into khaki uniforms and loaded with medals; a dusty theatre to which we stomped for morning assembly and the occasional play or recital; a museum of sorts, chocker with canonical memorabilia—scraps of old vestments, jewelled crucifixes, decomposing books of hours; a vast library, where graffito, as always in such places, flourished; a neglected little art room, with a broken skylight; a tatty music basement, with glass cubicles in which, beneath the glare of neon lights, you could practise; plus, of course, a thousand places for the furtherance of sportsmanship: gymnasium, squash courts, shooting range, swimming pool (conveniently tiled in yellow), tennis courts (of indoor clay and outdoor grass); endless pitches for football and rugger, grudgingly made over to cricket in the summer; an athletics track, of terracotta gravel; only half a golf course, I regret to say; but still, as hearty packages went, my father's Alma Mater didn't do badly. Fencing, hockey, basketball, archery: you name it, these chaps were up for it. And then, of course, there was the Cadet Corps—compulsory in the second year—which my father thought top-hole, a splendid idea.

But compulsory in the first year was music. Everyone was obliged to take up (no electric guitars, thank you) an orchestral instrument, even if this was the triangle, and to undergo, even if tone-deaf, an audition for the school choir, which, let's face it, wasn't as bad as the test in which they made you Cough to double-check your testicles. My singing voice, although a little shrill, still clung rather desperately to the range of treble (my time as an alto was to prove more satisfactory, because I could hide in the second row and relax, and sometimes, to be jazzy, harmonize a semitone flat, which drove the worthies mad); but my musical ear, combined with my instrumental scratchings, which sounded less intolerable on my own violin than on a school fiddle, earned me an advantage, and led me to hope that I might be off to a more promising start: I was in the top stream of my year; I had a place in the orchestra; I was wanted in the choir. Perhaps, now, I might be able to contribute to school life.

THE FIRST-YEAR DORMITORIES, reminiscent of the empty seminary in Brussels, were not, as mine had been at prep school, rooms of six beds apiece, but vast cold spaces with punitive wooden cubicles ranged along the walls—each with a bed, a shelf, a chair, and a brown curtain for privacy, like the skirt of a monk. You might, if you were lucky, have a window which, though set well above you, was a bonus in the summer, for your awakening became natural. And so, while on the one hand you enjoyed autonomy within the confines which, by means of a sticky label, had been alphabetically designated to you, and which, within reason, you could decorate as you pleased, now you were under danger of siege, not just by the few who might have shared your earlier dormitory, but by the forty who populated this one. As balances went, it felt touch and go, dodgy.

The other cubicles which, in their way, also afforded privacy were to be found in the music basement, three flights below the first-year sleeping quarters, at the sunken base of a stone staircase—more lumpen than imposing. Halfway down, screwed to the wall, there was a charcoal drawing of some dapper Old Boy in infantry officer's uniform, dated 1915, to which I never paid much attention; but when my mother, some time later, came to visit me, she was prompted, almost despite herself, to remark upon it, for the sitter, she confided, was the spitting image of a former suitor of her mother's, who, while on a posting to our island, had been shot dead in a (whispered) duel. This incident had left my grandmother, who was never again to mention the name of her lost lover, desolate, with the result that she declined proposals of marriage for years thereafter, until her bloom was gone and the spectre of spinsterhood began to loom on the societal horizon. Yet my mother's grandmother (that is to say, my great-grandmother, who had died decades before my birth, but had relayed the tale to my mother in the latter's girlhood) had apparently kept a framed photograph of the hapless swain propped on her piano throughout her life, seemingly indifferent to the nature of his demise, which, as well as illegal, was, in our Catholic country, regarded as opposite to ecclesiastical dictates. And it was the sudden recollection of that long-vanished photograph which had prompted my mother, in a burst of morbid romanticism, to pass on to me the anecdote. Later, I was to think, insanely, that this might have been the man who might have danced with the girl who was to become the grandmother whom I was never to know. But for now, I paid no notice to the drawing, and just went down.

Like the caterpillar in the Municipal Park, and the thalassic embrace of the beach, the music basement was a place that didn't correspond to ordinary life, life as it was supposed to be lived, for it offered promise, and the spectrum of fantasy, and the opportunity for respite from the stranglehold of routine. One of the many oddities of our educational system was its refusal to run along the usual (vertical) lines of school houses, but instead to be organized by the year (horizontally). Those canny priests did their damnedest to prevent boys who were not exact contemporaries from ever enjoying contact: you slept among your peers, you studied in their midst, you ate and washed alongside them and, even in church (unless you were in the choir), you sat in their cramping vicinity—a policy which I believe was intended to foment camaraderie while discouraging precocity and other odd habits. But in the music basement, all such artifice went out of the Gothic windows. No one cared in what year you happened to be vegetating: the sole question in this underworld was what you could bring to the feast.

Those who filled the glassy cages in the practice rooms were like exotic fish in an aquarium. (No-hopers, forced at the start to learn an instrument, didn't trouble, other than for music lessons, which they couldn't really circumvent, to make an appearance: they were far too busy with rugger.) No, only the school's most phantasmagorical oddballs regularly ventured down here—those who set off fire alarms during High Mass, when the ensuing chaos could be trusted to surge to fever pitch; who played pranks on village shopkeepers and never owned up to it; who harboured illicit terrapins; who mimicked teachers and performed elaborate vignettes of ridicule; who smuggled oysters back from exeats; who stole from the kitchens; who adopted fancy dress, smoked cocktail cigarettes and photographed each other exhaling; who drank champagne through straws; who played Scott Joplin; who refused to have their hair butchered by the school barber and preferred, instead, to cut one another's; who sang falsetto; who tap-danced; who could walk on point. Of course, in order to justify their presence in the depths of the school, all had to be musically proficient, but nothing as dreary as gifted, for true musicians were a little serious for our liking, and there was quite enough seriousness upstairs, in the main part of the school, to be going on with. Some of the serious types, whom you could spot at a glance, were priests in the making, bony-fingered mutterers who practically crossed themselves before surrendering to the seduction of ivories. I think that they regarded the rest of us, though charitably—for, in their fashion, they were just as peculiar, and part of a still smaller minority—as not quite the thing. But though we, self-styled exotics, cultivated glamour in the face of adversity, yet there was, I now think, an innocence to our antics. Certainly we exchanged no prurient sexual banter, for we considered ourselves, you see, far too sophisticated for it, were meant already to know Everything.

BUT ONE EVENING in the second term, when I was down in the basement, practising dreary studies for the violin—by Pleyel, very probably—and the rest of the place was all but empty, and most of the lights were out, I heard a tap on the glass at my door; and I turned round, shocked out of some tricky sequence and nearly dropping my bow, to be confronted by the sight of the director of music, who looked like an old Kaiser. Would I step into his office a minute?

His name was Dr. Fox; and just as my former headmaster had resembled a well-fed hamster, so, too, as animals went, this one made a stout one. The orbicularly tailored waistcoats that he wore, which even his watch chain was stretched to navigate, alone paid credence to his portliness. Everyone was terrified of him, for he used to condemn boys to be beaten at the drop of a quaver, and he slapped the backs of heads with alacrity. His temper was often challenged; he was not patient; and because he wore spectacles thicker than tumblers, his icy blue eyes seemed to project a magnified leer, involuntarily to glare down. He had the lashes of a cow, but he was not placid. If, in my childhood, Mr. Wolfe's beard had resembled a gentle field of autumn bracken, Dr. Fox's facial landscape, now that I was adolescent, seemed to me like a spikier site, a thornier promontory, for he sported a billy-goat the colour of ash, and lush Edwardian moustaches which he frequently twirled and tugged, a tail at a time, thereby distorting his fleshy little mouth, which was like a rosebud, too pink for my liking. Something about the contrast of those nubile lips against their surrounding shrubbery disgusted me. But it didn't frighten me: for, at least as regarded beards, I felt like an explorer on the way back, a veteran.

He deplored loutish conduct, and scruffy dress, and inky paws, and sloppy diction (yeah); but, most of all, he deplored the disproportionate status accorded by the school to sporting antics, which seemed always to clash with, and overrule, his musical endeavours. These, before he lost heart and sank into apathy, had been ambitious, enthusiastic, for as an organist he'd enjoyed a glittering start (truncated, I seem to recall, by financial difficulties in his family) and later, despite the impoverishment, an equally brilliant academic career, which accounted for his professorial title; yet this rare combination of practical and theoretical excellence which, thanks to him, had been brought to the school, appeared, now that he was established, no longer to be valued. And the slight therein implicit seemed to have soured him. He had, at some earlier point, converted to Catholicism, but, on account of the Second Vatican Council, subsequently felt reason to regret his transfer of spiritual allegiance, which probably aggravated his spleen. Certainly he considered our resident priests, especially the happy-clappy younger ones, to be both foolish and provincial—in which appraisal he was, to a great extent, right. As a breed, they were tawdry little specimens, whereas Dr. Fox, by contrast, was nothing if not refined: to him, only two things mattered: whether people were clever, and whether they amused him. Well, there was a third thing, but this wasn't really discussed: Favourites—small pets, as it were. I think that he was lonely.

THOUGH HE KEEPS his office darkened—for hard sunlight, I have noticed, pains his eyes—it is furnished with a richness which, at least in this establishment, is unknown to me, and which, though evocative of my past, paradoxically feels singular, peculiar to him. As you go in, looking down at the flagstones, the first thing that impresses you is a sprawling Persian rug, its background bluer than his eyes, and upon it, toward the far side, a concert grand, lid up. Along the length of the wall opposite to the fire, which is stoked throughout the winter months, and overhung—courtesy of the authorities, I have a feeling—with an olden portrait of an heavily gowned Honourable Jane Something-or-other, whose lips are as pink as his, though her moustache is milder, there runs a massive bookcase of ebony, detailed with gilded fluting and stacked with musical scores whose spines I can't make out. There's a vast desk, presidential, behind which lurks his throne, its rotating leather back turned to the external world, while over here, where I stand, there's a pair of wing chairs, ball and claw, one of which, of worn green velvet, grown olive with time, he now directs me into. Next to a hefty coal box behind me, lidded to provide a bench when the need arises, the door, which has been covered in felt so as to contain the sound of his piano, appears, of its own accord, to click shut.

I sit where I'm told. He goes round to his side. He smiles. I hardly know this man. (Be on your guard.) I half-smile back. He cuts, then smells, then lights a cigar, not like the half-sized inanities favoured by my father, but a proper, long, cool, portly Montecristo, whose box lies on the armchair beside mine. He removes the decorative paper-ring, twirls the cigar in mid-air and admires it; leans back. His chair creaks out. He crosses his legs now: I can see his shins swapping in the gap between the drawers of the desk that hides him. He shifts his weight onto one thigh. One foot alone swings out, almost slippered, so narrow and fine is his pump. I sense an unpleasant delicacy about the man.

It's all most civilized. He smiles a second time, and I do likewise. He wonders, as he puffs, whether, since I already play the violin and am part of the choir, I've ever considered taking up the piano. He says that it would help with my sight-reading, which—good as my ear is—he's noticed tends to let me down at orchestra practice: weak counting. I won't find it so easy to bluff my way through harder parts as I move up the ranks, you know—and down the choir, for that matter, which will involve more complicated harmonies, trickier tempi and so forth. You can't expect to carry the tune forever, he laughs, a little clumsily . . .

Well, yes, he grants me, on the violin perhaps; but come-come, the Piarno-four-*tay*, he rhapsodizes, marv'llous instrument, no comparison, the only truly self-sufficient one, fundamental, far and away the richest repertoire. He agrees that you can't exactly travel round the world with one, but try travelling with an organ, my dear chap, he chuckles; anyway, he thinks I should consider his suggestion. Don't we have a piano at home? Well then, there you *are;* what could be simpler? You can keep up your playing during the holidays, hmm? Makes perfect sense. But still; he says that I can take my time mulling it over, no rash decisions, it isn't a trivial matter, requires commitment, et cetera, et cetera, et cetera. I'm just to let him know when I feel ready, say in forty-eight hours, would that seem reasonable? And then he removes his heavy spectacles, which he lets swing in one hand, while, with the thumb and forefinger of the other, he massages the bridge of his nose, which is purple and ridged by the burden of his poor sight, and I notice, as he rubs them, that his enormous glassy eyes have recoiled and diminished and sunk and all but disappeared into his skull. And, far from a great ogre, he now looks like a pathetic blind baby, and the switch comes as a shock to me; but after a few seconds he returns his specs to their proper function, mercifully to restore his former countenance. As he rises to his weary dainty feet, and comes round to where I'm sitting, I now realize that his nose, though finely set despite the hump, is shot with veins the colour of claret, and that his forehead is flaky. Yes, he concludes, he'd be delighted for me to have piano lessons—from him, naturally—and looks forward to hearing my decision. He can't imagine, after all, that I'm too enamoured of the alternatives—football, rugger, mountaineering. I roll my eyes dramatically and, as I do so, realize my first blunder with this man: my roll is flirty. And then I fly up the stone steps to supper.

OF COURSE, I'm madly flattered. Who needs irreligious worldly ambition to succumb to vanity? Dr. Fox is known only to bother with the most promising pupils, and he makes me feel as if I could become one. Besides, how can I really decline his offer, and risk his displeasure, when I see the man twice a week in the orchestra and a further twice at choir practice? Then, as if further to sway me to his side, a thought of my father, like a moth, flutters into my mind, hovers briefly, then scorches me with pleasure: *two* musical instruments would feel like a double victory. But I must be calm about it. Best not to seem impetuous.

Later, sauntering down the gallery, I decide to treat myself at the tuck shop, to celebrate my stroke of luck. There's a disheartening queue, lengthy, unruly, constantly increased by sixth formers who keep pushing in, yet no one dares to confront. But you see, they've just started selling hot dogs, and the smell is irresistible—the smoky lure of frankfurters drifts and curls towards you like the promise of a holiday. I remember my mother's towels, and her toes, and the Spanish flag: mustard and ketchup. Yum. Dinner was disgusting; there's masses of time before lights out; and I'm sure I've got enough money; so, no problem, I'll join the back of the line and be patient. While I wait, I rewind to the cameo with Dr. Fox, and sense a certain oddity about it, a tiny niggling doubt; but I'm sure that I'm just being stupid. Why should he have bothered to approach me unless he were serious? For fun, for God's sake? You're being idiotic. Be thankful that he's singled you out: it exempts you from rugger and, what's more, stuffs your father. And gradually, gradually, lost in this rumination, and with my gut starting to rumble, I edge my way to the front.

When I reach the hatch, I see that I'm going to be served by a prefect called Payne, elder brother of someone from the music basement, and himself, now that I think of it, not exactly a he-man; but just after I've cleared my throat and asked for a hot dog, I hear (though he avoids meeting my eye) his reply, which he seems to want to broadcast for the sake of the general public, and particularly for the benefit of his fellow servers, who, like him, get paid for their trouble: Bugger Off!, he shouts, We Don't Serve Pouffters Here. And I am aghast; but not as aghast as I am next, when the entire surrounding crowd bursts into rapturous clapping. (I don't think that I returned to the tuck shop, not alone, at any rate, for the next three years, by which time I was in the fifth form and inured to such affronts; and in the intervening time, either I asked some brave, rare friend to buy sweets on my behalf, or I simply went without. Because soon enough, in any case, I was to find other means of acquiring them.)

Reeling from the hot dog fracas, I now head for the lavatories, ostensibly for a piss, but, if it's quiet, for a restorative smoke in the sit-downs. Needless to say, since it's after supper, the place turns out to be packed, and in order to get to the cubicles at the back, you have to sneak past a fog of older boys who like to pretend to be older than they are. One of these, who played Toad in *Toad Hall,* and whose father, each time that he descends, brings a different doxy in a different sports car, catches sight of me and shouts: Oy, you, hand 'em over! Hand what?, I reply. Your *fags,* you dirty little queer. But after the tuck shop incident, I'm not quite in the mood for this casual banter—my angry blood is running too high, coursing too fast; so I just peer at him and tell him to bugger off and buy his own. Stunned reaction from the whole pally gang, a collective intake of breath, a scuffle, and next—it's so sudden—my head is down on the pissoir, my snout in the rivulet of frothy yellow water, my jacket slithering on the sodden tiles, the people who've been using the trough leaping back, flies still undone. There are hands all over my pockets, and there's a knee against my back, and then, through the deafening silence, I hear a punch crack against my spine, and then I'm left alone.

With hindsight, I wonder whether, had the tables been turned, and the cards of power been stacked in my hand, I wouldn't have acted as the toad had done. It's possible, I might have done, particularly if the victim was someone as fearsome and loathsome as I was generally found. I was, after all, myself the son of a bully. Only one thing, I suppose, might have deterred me (just), namely the tacky brand of those louts' tobacco, which I think was Embassy (Mild, not even Regal). I myself preferred to inhale the fumes of Winston, which, to me, tasted of grown-up American summers, and I would buy my supplies after I'd got rid of my parents, on the flight back to England. Only once did some nit-picking air-hostess hesitate to oblige with my request, claiming, the silly cow, that I was under-age for such purchases—to which I remember replying that it was on my parents' instructions that I had to buy those cigarettes, as a present for my guardians. Luckily, she swallowed my lie, and, though still looking dubious, surrendered the carton. But I didn't, on the plane, have the gall to light up.

Still, back to the school lavatory. I gather myself up from the pissoir, sluggishly, dopily, like someone who'd blacked out. As on the occasion when I fouled my underpants, I now think of my mother, but this time, bizarrely, she seems to be laughing in a strange garden, detached, happy. My cigarettes are gone, as is my lighter; and then, in a final humiliation, I have to crouch to recover one of her letters, fallen to the ground during the débâcle, and I see that her turquoise ink is weeping down the face of the envelope. Which, added to the hot dog incident, settles the matter.

I GO TO MY CLASSROOM and open my desk. I don't know what propels me next (further vanity, perhaps, or some desire to single myself out), but the sheet which I select is not of headed school paper: it is a leaf of my own personal stationery, cream, thick as card, and engraved at the top with my Spanish coat of arms, for (even if by the time that I reached my majority, and became properly entitled, I was no longer to do so) I still, then, considered such vulgarities to be smart. I close the desk. I date the letter for tomorrow—less impulsive—and then I write, as evenly as my shaky, cigaretteless hand allows: Dear Sir. (Mistake. I tear up the sheet and go back to square one.) Dear Dr. Fox, I have thought about your kind offer and think that it's a good idea. I can start whenever you like. Yours (I dither over sincerely, decide to leave it out, append a comma, and sign), James Moore. I lick the envelope closed, since its stubborn flap is too large to be tucked; I turn it over and write his name on the front, underline it; and now, the whole missive is burning in my hand, and I doubt that I can wait suspended a whole night; so I put it in my pocket and creep down to the basement, where all is dark, and with my eyes wide as an owl's I slide my fate into the stillness of his lair, which is my trap. And on my way to bed, I try to weigh up which is preferable: whether to impress Dr. Fox or to depress my father—until I realize that I can achieve both objectives in one.

Next day, although I've got no musical commitments, I still escape, during Break, downstairs—to mess around, see who's there, practise for a while. Such calls have become habitual. Dr. Fox is not in evidence—still busy teaching, or perhaps having coffee in the staff common room. I trudge back to class. I float through the next two periods, double maths, and I get through lunch, which these days is self-service, and then I climb to my dormitory to fetch a clean handkerchief (or was it to rummage in my padlocked trunk for a fresh packet of gaspers?). The cause evaporates into irrelevance, because, when I reach my bed, I find, half-tucked under the pillow, as if intended for no eyes but mine, a sealed note, addressed in an illegible squiggly hand, like the hand of an elderly optician: Dear Moore, I am delighted by your prompt decision. Please present yourself at my office for your first lesson at two o'clock this afternoon. And he signs it A. Fox. I look at my watch: three minutes to the hour. On my way out of the dormitory, my steps precise as a metronome, I glance in the mirror to comb my hair and yank up my tie. But I can't sustain the controlled rhythm. I rush to the washroom, give my nails a scrub. Adrenaline is pumping round me. I turn off the tap and sprint across the main quadrangle and through the Tudor hall, trying not to slip on the floor of harlequin marble; I run down a waxen gallery, bang into someone, race on regardless to a darkened corridor which yawns into a vaulted landing. As I approach the narrowing stairs to the basement, the clock on the tower begins to strike (One), and I tackle my downward flight like a frantic scale, *molto vivace,* but one at a time, because the stony surface of the steps is worn, untrue, not to be trusted. And as I skid to a halt before the mahogany door marked Director of Music, the clock sounds its second post-meridian hour (Two)—its chime fractionally flat. I knock hard, high up; then, a further time. My chest is going mad. But next, like an electric shock, the school bell wails out, wild as a siren . . . and only once its echo has ebbed away entirely does the punctilious Dr. Fox care to shout: *Avanti!*

I GO IN. He lowers his newspaper, peers across, then greets me with one of those magnified smiles of his. He stands up. The lid of the piano has been lowered. He leads me to the shuttered keyboard as if he were introducing me to a coffin; opens it, bares its grinning teeth at me. He spins the leather stool clockwise, raising it to accommodate me. He sits me down, pats my back on the precise spot where it was punched last night, and positions me with care, exactitude: good posture from the outset being, he says, primordial. He outlaws, for the present, the use of pedals. Nor is there any need, as yet, for sheet music. I may remove my jacket if I wish. I don't of course: I couldn't have borne the embarrassment. His reaction—As you like—sounds faintly rebuffed; but next, almost without warning, we're off, we have begun.

That-there was Middle C; the rest would follow automatically. My right hand went up; my left trickled down. First they scaled separately; later, in unison; and in due course he made them cross, over and under, then continue. It was all, compared to the violin, so rudimentary that it looked stupid, yet my fingers turned out to be bad stretchers, latent enemies; and while I possessed basic aptitude, I also recognized myself to be devoid of the talent, or the promise, or the brilliance, or any of the other attributes which hallmarked the fine body of his private pupils; and I sensed that as a consequence—and sooner rather than later—he was bound to despair, to give up on me, and that I would find myself fed, once again, to the jaws of rugger. And yet, looking back, I think that at the start—for all the quickness of his temper—his patience, not mine, was the greater. He would sit, as an old-fashioned analyst might have done, behind me—out of danger, out of sight—musing from a wing chair and stroking his watch chain, which grated against his signet-ring of cornelian; or sucking on a sugared violet, which I could smell as I struggled with my fingering. The swirls of his saliva made my stomach churn. And his fire, always crackling, seemed, as I sweated through my initiation, to mock me at my back.

The bulk of his pupils was upward of Grade 7, proper pianists—some, indeed, of such a calibre as to have been encouraged to forgo university in favour of a conservatory. Those students, who to me were like adults—daily shavers, licensed drivers—would even be sent, as a favour to Dr. Fox, up to London several times a term for additional coaching by one of his erstwhile professors, and I envied both their musical escapades and their musical prowess. Now that they are men, I sometimes hear those former boys tinkling over the airwaves, though not frequently—for our school, remember, was bigger on the spiritual life than on worldly ambition; but back then, the simple, glaring chasm between my preliminary struggles and their sheer panache, which could be witnessed most afternoons in the practice cubicles and stun you, rendered my mediocrity the more crushing, and, in a sense, robbed my piano lessons of pleasure. For I feared that in the long run, once I'd been dispatched, my father would have won.

And yet, when I made mistakes, which drove me frantic with frustration, Dr. Fox would try to soothe me with dark sounds of appeasement, velvet murmurs from his low octaves. And when I became so flustered that I was forced to halt, he would never allow me properly to stop, but would urge me to continue, to struggle on, to show perseverance, however hard this might seem: for all things, he would claim, even bad ones, must eventually come to an end. I now suspect that he derived a perverse enjoyment from those errors of mine; for as I, with each of them, drew further away from his standard of excellence, so he was drawing inexorably closer to the fruits of his determination, which were not, in the strictest sense, musical.

One morning, I remember going through the motions of some piece for him, some young person's sonata, and enjoying a run of good luck through its introductory passage, but playing, probably due to the anxiety which underscored my bluff, too fast for my fortune to last. I suddenly lost my place, my fingering came unstuck, everything fell apart, and my charade just ground to a standstill. Although I felt like hammering my fists against those fucking ivories, I remember keeping absolutely still, seized by the certainty that his patience had finally snapped and that he was about to shout at me . . . so I just sat on that stool, resigned, like the dead loss that I felt, frozen despite the burning silence.

I heard him get up and approach my back with ominous calm. I wanted to protect my head, to shield it from his inevitable slap, yet when his palm did land upon me, it wasn't with the expected bang, but with the equivalent of a whimper, for he placed it, almost apologetically, upon my shoulder. And then he pressed it down, curving his fingers towards my clavicle, beyond the lapel of my jacket. His voice was so soft that I could hardly hear it: You *can* do this, old chap, he whispered, it's so nearly there, coming together very nicely, just try to go slower, but you mustn't give up, you're more than capable. I wanted to cry with gratitude, and yet, hardened by my sense of failure, I replied that he was just being kind: I knew that I was useless. No you're not. Yes I am. You're not. I am. Not. Am. Not. Am. And thus, thus confusedly, began our pantomime.

I practised like a fiend for my next lesson and, emulating those serious types upon whom the princes of the basement looked down, I managed to get the sonata up to scratch. Yet when the actual lesson came to pass, all my application—which resulted less from wounded pride than from an urge to avoid danger—proved to be futile, and my rendition, if you could call it that, turned out to be more deficient still than the previous one. Where, for God's sake, was the justice? I should just bite the bullet and give up. But there was, of course, no real question of my doing so: Dr. Fox would never have countenanced such weakness in my character—for he, you see, was only just warming to his theme, assuming his dominance in our counterpoint. And the real progress, as we both knew, was proving to be his, not mine.

HE COMES UP behind me and leans into my spine. I sit up, straight as a fiddle, but feel, hard against my backbone, the pressure of his lower gut, and the cold rub of his watch chain, like a necklace, purring against my collar. He places, this time round, not one but both of his hands upon my shoulders, and then he brings them forward past me, together to the front, landing them, like fat pigeons, over mine, his fluttering pudginess all but covering my skinny fingers. He suggests that we go back to such-and-such a bar, and then, in the most testing of harmonies, he guides me over the keyboard. I try to resume the sonata. To my surprise, he does not weigh me down: there is a lightness about him, a nimble strength about his motion, and for a decent while our hands dance together in partnership, together yet decorously apart, never quite touching. But there is so much apprehension in my head, such throbbing at my temple, that my concentration, inevitably, shuts down, and yet again I foul up, and his fingers do, now, pounce, and properly mount mine, and writhe upon them momentarily. His flesh is hotter than the flesh of a faith healer, and as clammy. I long to wipe my hands against my trousers. Though he directs us back to the same merciless bar, he seems somehow to be adjusting his position behind me, to be lowering himself, removing his belly from my back in order to set his myopic face in line with the score in front of us, the better to read his pencilled markings—which surely he knows back to front, but anyway—his head, next, moves next to mine, and his beard brushes my neck, and the sticky arm of his spectacles keeps touching my profile. Faint moans issue from him, dreamy moans of abandon, but his breath seems to have quickened, as if a baton were cutting through it, staccato, and the hot steam of his smoky violets makes me want to twist askance. But before I can, he reverses us, and tells me to place my palms over the backs of *his* hands now, like twins on twin lilos but without the blessing of water; and though we surf over the keyboard, it is pointless, senseless, nonsensical, for my numb, dumb fingers have given up, given up the ghost, and can only float along with his tide. But no mistakes this time, not one, a bravura performance. See? You *can* do it. Dr. Fox must think that I'm a fool, and, in part, he's right, but my folly lies not so much in having fallen for his lies as in having flung myself into his trap, from which, now that I'm steeped, I can see no way of flying out. And though he smothers me with blandishments, I entertain no doubt that I'll never make his grade of pianist; and yet, what I, from my hardened linguist's heart, have interpreted with pinpoint accuracy is the significance that throbs like poisoned stars between the music of his lines.

THERE ARE MELODIES that I cannot hear without thinking of the man. No sooner, say, has the second chord of that half-buried sonata been plucked from its score and struck and released into space by the wireless, than I become deaf to the present. All that I can hear, then, is his sound; all that I can see, now, are his puffy hands at the piano. He has asked me to get up. He has taken my position. He has parted his jacket and leaned back and, after a brief pause, begun to play the piece in earnest, slowly, lushly, but it doesn't feel as if he wished, by it, to highlight my crassness, nor as if he intended, though he employs the pedals, to depress me with his musicality. We are beyond music or humiliation now: we are drifting towards a greater swamp, a place of ugly beauty. He seems transformed in the manner which sometimes can transfigure performers, who, though weary and taciturn in ordinary life, shambolic even, become energized from the moment that they take to the platform. He doesn't regard the score, but gazes, half-entranced, out of the room, up towards the gardens, as if they held the promise of Babylon—or I, that of its whore. Only occasionally does he turn to stare at me, to burn into his captive audience; and I am stepping backwards now, for I feel as if I'd broken into some secrecy of which I should better have been kept in ignorance. I reel right back, as far I can go, all the way to the shadowy coal box by the door, but I remain on my feet: I keep on my toes: I no longer feel sure of my position—subject, object, target, voyeur. The waters of our connection seem to have been warmed, like mud in the shoals. There is a strangeness to his expression, of sadness stirred with ardour. His mouth, motionless but slightly open, is like the mouth of the drowned; and it is as if he wished, by playing on my behalf, to court me, to persuade me of intentions which, though harboured hard, he dare not verbalize.

And I recognize that just as my earlier life had flowed with the strains of Nocturnes, there will, from now on, forever be the echo of this sonata to haunt me, over and over. But after all my failures at his instrument, all the pointless steps which he has forced me to take in order to reach this stage, I cannot be receptive to the charm of his music, nor grateful. He, not I, should have played it from the start, and young musicianship be damned. And yet, when his fingers come to a halt, and rise like frozen claws in the late morning, I don't know which way to burst, into tears or applause.

He stands large as a monarch, pale as a ghost, at once imposing and forlorn, and he advances towards me as if revisiting some painful history, a territory more often lost than conquered. Yet this time, he comes furnished not just with the shield of his authority, nor driven merely by the power of his determination, but, uniquely, availed of certified information guaranteed to topple his new adversary, whom I suddenly recognize to be James Moore. His leer, projected through that glassy visor, announces to me, louder than a bugle call, the obvious, which is, of course, what I've suspected since my first visit to the refectory, namely that he comes armoured with knowledge, knowledge aforethought. And now, as our eyes gallop into a lock, I realize that he knows that I know that he knows—what?—that I've already surrendered my innocence, sold away the very weapon which, in the young, constitutes their great invincible sword.

His vitreous glare seems to imply that, since I've already played, and reputedly of my own volition, hostage to fortune, I cannot now, merely because of his attentions, claim to be worse off. And although what I do possess, against the pressure of his despoiling, is, ironically, the very wealth of my former corruption—my share from the original sale of my soul—I glean that the value of currencies such as mine can fluctuate wildly, depending on the place of the deal and the nature of the contest. Out there in the real world (where you are now, in parks and open beds and oceans), my relinquished innocence would, in fact, have sent my worth soaring, rendered me, as a commodity, covetable, collectable almost—for I, in addition to exuding an outward semblance of being young, a presumed virginity which I could lavish ad infinitum, and infinitely lose, also reduced for my shareholders the risk of perdition in a criminal court. I was no judge, that was for sure: I was an inveterate accomplice; so that to enter into congress with me, to assume my purchase, was, in reality, to reach a consensual truce, not to venture onto some battleground fraught with pitfalls. And this, you see, is why, to him, I must have felt like a simpler, safer bet than some sweet but unpredictable novice.

My rate of exchange, like that of a whore in prison, seemed to have plummeted into free fall, to have crashed into deficit. For in places of incarceration, even when the nonces do possess the means to purchase favours from some manacled prostitute, few feel a moral compunction to do so. There exists a different law. And it was this other law that was to kill my heel, to prove my downfall, for what earlier had guaranteed my conquests now became my one critical flaw. I was no longer like a precious multi-faceted (green) stone, but sullied goods, beyond the hope even of hock, and I could see no means, without provoking retribution, of saying No. Dishonour Among Thieves, that was the unspoken motto. But still, let's not moan, for though Dr. Fox was never to welcome me like a windfall into his impoverished, embittered life, nor yet did he ever quite treat me like a final reduction, as if I were being robbed.

HE COMES SO close that, as his gut prods my chest, I fall back onto the coal box, and am left sitting on this pew like a disgraced chorister. He takes no notice. My lowering has been his aim all along. He leans down towards me, clutching at my neck with both his claws, and assaults my face with a flock of dry pecks, to my forehead and the sides of my face and my nose. He avoids my mouth, keeps it in reserve, though his beard, like a bird's nest, brushes over it. My lips are pursed to avoid the tickling abrasion. My eyes are closed. My wings are folded. I put up no resistance, for I conclude that he may as well go on, just do it, get it over with; I can worry later. He removes one of his claws and it sounds as if he's fiddling up there, perhaps loosening his stiff collar, or the buttons of his waistcoat, as he continues with this kissing-of-sorts, this pecking at my eyelids, designed to ensure, I suppose, that they remain closed—blind to the score.

But as he begins to stroke my nape, he pulls me slightly forward towards him, inclines my head; and now his own head seems to have risen high above me, as if in preparation; and when I open my eyes, which, believe me, no longer roll with inexplicable flirtation—they have frozen, agog—I see that I'm up against his flies, which are unbuttoned, and that through the diagonal slit in his baggy undershorts he has extracted his sweating cock, which protrudes without reference to pubic hair or balls. Dr. Fox turns out to be a stocky Cavalier, pale and loose-skinned and thick-veined and topped by a shiny purple helmet, like a bishop on a chessboard. The stench which emanates from him, his cheesing grot, so repulses me that I block my nose and breathe through my throat—but only for a few seconds, because next, he shoves himself between my lips, forcing his fat retracted cock against my teeth, which have been clenched, but which, now, I must part philosophically. What am I supposed to do, bite him? I retch; and then I feel ashamed, as if, again, I were failing. Can I do nothing respectably? But he could no longer care. I think he farts. And now he begins to pump, thrusting himself in and out and in and out and it is I who feel like the bird, my beak wrenched ajar. But while I try, despite my straining gullet, to meet his desires, I distract myself with the thought that the thing which I'm being force-fed is, oddly enough, itself known as a pecker, and I wonder, in a further foreign twist to my ornithological conceit, whether this might explain why Italians sometimes call a pecker an *uccello,* or bird.

Suddenly, the bell screams out for lunch. I think: Time to fend for myself, to get out and seek my own nourishment. But he grabs my neck in an instant, restrains it, then grips at my ears and gathers speed. I recognize the mounting *accelerando* from my previous trysts, though these have never involved such oral insistence, and next, without warning, his bird begins to spit and spit, and it spurts its bile onto the roof of my mouth and against the back of it; and when he, once done, extracts a handkerchief to minister to the dregs of his issue, I extract my own small square of linen, which my mother said would help with my identity, and though I feign merely to dab, I disgorge his spillage into it. The tang of his residual semen bounces around the amalgam of my fillings, but I dare not lick about—which, even with the communion host, is just about allowed.

.   .   .

IT ALL LED to complications. Whereas (except for that final night in Belgium) it had always been I who'd sought out the company of Mr. Wolfe, always I who'd assumed the initiative, the current in the case of the cunning Dr. Fox was contrary, flowed against me; and when he began to call for my services, sending envoys to hunt me down, I found myself unable to ignore his orders, because to do so would be to land some unwitting go-between in trouble, and myself in further jeopardy. Sometimes, however, Dr. Fox would try to confuse me: would have me cross the length of the school merely in order to offer me a sweet that led to nothing, or to ask me to remind him of some question to which he well knew the answer; or he would make me stand, for all to see, outside his office while he took his time disposing of some other pupil, only to pretend, once I'd been inveigled into his darkness, possession of some small enlightenment regarding whatever piece of music I happened to be struggling with, or to ask me to polish up some descant for his next choir practice, always last-minute and always pitched too high for my beak to master. These were his little tricks, outward stabs at officialdom, as if by exposing me before my peers he could place himself above suspicion.

But then, when I least expected it, I'd be back on that coal box, proffering my jaw for him, rounding my mouth into a receptacle for his shuddering disseminations. As he grew more assured of my compliance, he dispensed with the nicety of his jockey slit, which, technically, must have hampered him, and instead, he would ruck his underpants down to his pimply thighs, revealing, above his tumescent penis, a pale, fluffy gut, and beneath it, darkish testicles, already shrivelled, crinkled with thrill, and spiked with the occasional white pubic sprout. He would help himself to my hand and plonk it on his sac, gripping me to grip at him, committing our fingers to a brief marriage of ghastly intimacy. But I learnt fast, not least in order to speed him to satisfaction; I learnt how to tug, how to frot him with my other hand, how to lubricate him with my—rather than his—saliva; and yet my lessons covered more than merely the ground of his quick fulfilment, for I now see that they taught me, more lastingly, about feeling cheap: what this involved, how to rise above it, what else to imagine. But when he, on occasion, bent down to grope at me, I seemed always myself to be hard, and this conspired to add to my confusion: my body was betraying me: my mother's blood kept rushing to all the wrong parts. It was, as I say, complicated.

BY THE SUMMER TERM, his mounting hunger had outgrown the feasts on offer in the music basement. What must earlier have been like banquets to him seemed to have dwindled into a semblance of snatched apéritifs and, by June, it was as if he could no longer be sated within the limits of that shaded chamber. The more voracious became his gluttony, his shameless desire for fuller helpings, the greater his need to loosen his garb, a procedure positively Edwardian in its complexity: what with the unthreading of his watch chain, and the removal of his waistcoat in order to slip off his braces, which, no sooner unlooped, gave way to other obstacles, such as billowing shirttails which, in order to be placed out of harm's way, as it were, required knotting behind his buttocks, a move itself demanding additional unbuttoning at the front, to unveil, between the pendulums of his necktie, creamy bosoms with flattened teats the colour of sausage meat—not to mention the collapse of his trousers, and the ensuing peril of tripping over his own tailored crotch as he hobbled to encroach upon me, plus, of course, the ordeal, in the aftermath, of burrowing for a handkerchief . . . It all made him irritable, steamed up, as if the sight of himself in partial undress, a state more belittling than total obese nakedness, somehow pricked at his identity, undermined his sense of authority—a porous notion in any case, which, even when he was formally suited, I suspect to have been concocted artificially, built without wisdom, too fast, too high, and too treacherously close to the brink of ruin.

I myself always remained primly uniformed at these meetings, for only my head was then of apparent import to him; but had anyone, particularly some other member of staff, chanced to knock at the door while he was hunched over me in this farcical dishabille, Dr. Fox would have had, if not an actual seizure, certainly his work cut out accounting for the ensuing delay in answering, never mind explaining my puzzling proximity to his fluster, which none of the cupboards could hide. Only once, in fact, did footsteps happen to saunter up to the felted door of his directorship while he was privately occupied; and though, miraculously, no knuckles went so far as to rap against the mahogany, I remember with what sudden brutal force he clamped his hand over my mouth. But I also remember how his spectacles fell with a sad thud from his burning ears to the wrinkles of gabardine about his ankles. And I knew then that this arrangement could not last, that a further stage would have to be found, and that even as he trussed himself back into masterfulness, he was donning his thinking-cap.

HE WAS NOT long about it. Within days, I was summoned to his bedroom, which lurked at the end of a creaking corridor, high in the oldest wing of the building, and out of bounds to all but those who slept there, fifth formers who, so far as I could tell, spent their recreation oafing away the hours, since no exams threatened them for another year. As you sneaked by, trying not to look too junior, you could hear the racket of clashing rock bands blasting out of various rooms, and punches of boorish laughter, and, sometimes, through a carelessly open door, you caught flashes of posters—bleachy starlets; Hollywood fishnets in strappy stilettos; the smuttier Dalís; some popular lovely with a cone of ice-cream wedged between her tits. The whole place stank: burnt toast, Pot Noodles, illicit ash. I think that pupils were allowed to cook up there, or to boil.

The wooden floor seemed to sway beneath you; the scuffed walls, to curve and wobble and funnel. It was like visiting a slum in a forgotten industrial town. I remember losing my way the first few times, and having to ask directions, and blushing to a colourblend that combined many red emotions. Looking for Dr. Fox's room, are we?, they would reply, always too loud. Say *no more.* (Great slow winks of salacious innuendo; downward cackles.) Those boys were men of the world. They wore platforms.

You had to climb two steps onto a linoleum landing of marbleized slime in order to reach his private quarters: a bed-sitting room to the left, and, opposite it, to the right as you arrived, an ancient bathroom, spacious, gloomy, and lit by a bare bulb. Over the sink, above a mirrored cabinet, there was a candle propped in a glass, along with a soggy-looking box of matches—presumably meant for power cuts. His actual room, across the way, possessed two doors to keep the world at bay, but was smaller than his office, and felt more stuffy. Its insides heaved with acrylic brocaderie: measly repeats of some curlified motif in corresponding tones of Camembert and burgundy. His bed, most single, was tucked behind an alcove which he curtained away when its contents were not made, but which, once the cleaner had been, was revealed as overspread with the paler, less alluring shade of runny cheese.

At some unwise earlier juncture (before he'd taken up residence, I presume) the floorboards had been laid, wall to wall, with a swirling carpet that made you think of seaside B & B's after the war; and over this mistake, as if to obfuscate it, Dr. Fox had unrolled an inferior Persian rug, comfortingly frayed, and bald in patches, but rather too small for the task, with the result that far from it dissimulating the decorative gaffe, lurid margins of fitted greeny-purple-orange pile tended to jump out at you—but perhaps this oversight escaped his faulty eyes. When he lumbered about without glasses, he would always park them, with finicky precision, for easy access, on exactly the same spot of his Victorian fireplace, which was wooden, coarsely grained, and sealed with a slapdash coat of varnish.

The mantel was afflicted with an outbreak of bric-à-brac: dead rose-heads in a dusty vase; ancient (Greek) postcards; defunct wedding invitations (declined); a mutilated teddy bear with a missing eye; a brass carriage clock (operated by batteries) and, just off-centre, in half-profile, a bronzette bust of Beethoven—for which, I was later to learn, he had saved up as a child. I found it hard to envisage Dr. Fox in such an incarnation, unwhiskered. And at the edge of the shelf closest to the alcove, next to a face-mirror nailed at head height, there was, permanently wired up, an electric shaver, its tawny cable trailing away to some elusive socket behind the curtain. Dr. Fox's problematic vision had, ever since puberty—his premature pretence to adulthood—made the task of shaving between those ornate facial growths of his a daily trial, at least until the advent of this timely modern contraption, which, reducing as it did the danger of razor cuts, he had adopted with uncharacteristic newfangled gusto.

The grate, laid daily by some manservant whom I was fortunately never to meet, Dr. Fox would light in the afternoons, and shovel with coal right up to the crest of the evening, when the national anthem was played on television. His hours of heated darkness were long ones: he was insomniac. He never wore nightclothes; and yet, notwithstanding this immodesty, it astonished me that a man so enormously fat should be able to stand the swelter. Placed at a diagonal to the flames, and upholstered in yet more burgundy, there was a genteel little sofa with sides of crackling basketweave, low to ground and fit for the parlour of a maid; and this is where you, the guest, in principle sat, squirming perhaps: for facing you, but turned, as ever, away from the window, there was a preposterously high great wing chair, a chesterfield which could rock and swivel about, and which boasted a mechanical footrest where, puffy ankles crossed, Dr. Fox usually presided in velvet smoking slippers embroidered with treble clefs, and lined in red—for he would sometimes allow one to dangle half-casually. His pictures, too, struck me as a let-down: a couple of unremarkable little prints in the vicinity of the light-switch, probably cathedrals possessed of famous organs; and then, hung over the fire, a gilt-framed watercolour, girlishly pastoral—pinky, frilly, lakey, lilac. I know he was a musical man—not visual; yet I couldn't but be struck by the chasm between his public and private personae. Dr. Fox looked fifty-nine. He was, in fact, thirty-five.

ON THE FIRST OCCASION that I was invited to his eyrie, I noticed but few of the things which I describe; yet I do, by contrast, recall marvelling at the view of the avenue away from the school, for I had never witnessed the lethargic Lady's statue so pleasingly diminished from such a height. Also, under his window, I remember being impressed by a great stack of records ranged along the ground—the longest collection which, up till then, I had encountered: entirely classical, as one would expect, and entirely amassed, it later transpired, courtesy of the funds of the music department: Research Material was the heading under which such perks were routinely entered in the accounts. But on this particular occasion, which was mid-afternoon, teatime, I wasn't able to absorb a great deal: only vague colours, graven shadows, the ghosts of lavender and bachelor cigars. It seemed ill-mannered to nose about, and ill-advised besides, for even as he fiddled within the cosy confines of his trouser-pocket, and uncrossed his ankles to stand up on my arrival, I could tell that his beady, spectacled eye was famished.

Dr. Fox was partial to fine jams—greengage, cherry, damson—but since the shops at the local village carried only basic produce, he was compelled to purchase his select preserves, by the tinload, further afield, from a superior purveyor with whom he enjoyed a healthy rapport and a still healthier tab. Often donning a narrow dicky-bow for these forays, and snapping, if it was sunny, tinted shades onto his glasses, he would set off in his classic two-tone Bentley, gunmetal and black, and roll away over the hills, puffing and humming and salivating, and occasionally turning his head towards the roadside, as if this were bordered by flag-waving crowds, until he came cruising, like some landed earl calling on third-generation tenants, up to his destination, whereupon, with blind unconcern for parking restrictions, he would bring his motor to a soft, whirring halt at the old-fashioned shopfront of his choice—the grocer's, of course—where he was invariably accorded a rapturous morning by the hand-rubbing staff, who doubled as welcoming committee. Dr. Fox played up to their fawning attitudes and approved of their pristine overalls. It gave him faith in tradition. Anything else for Dr. Fox, at all?, they would wonder with great monotony. And he would reply, as if this were a refrain: I think there *might* just be; now, let me think: anchovy paste, grained mustard, quails' eggs, aromatic pepper, coffee beans, castor sugar, double cream. It was always a drawn-out procedure, a ritual, reminded him of what he construed as The Old Days.

Much later, circumstances were to push us into an approximation of friendship, and even though, by then, his finances had suffered a conspicuous dent—with the result that he was constrained not just to sell his concert grand, but also to exchange his beloved Bentley for a humbling Morris Minor (which I secretly felt better suited his shape, and in which, almost as secretly, he would eventually teach me to drive)—yet he remained, despite the reduction of his income, a dogged sybarite. I remember how, during the half term in which I came of age—an occasion which my parents saw greater cause to regret than celebrate—he took me, in an exceptional flight of extravagance which I suppose he could justify as largesse, for my first dinner at Claridge's, even going to the trouble, as if I were his ward, or he my great-uncle, of introducing me to the Maitre d', who'd known him for aeons—a futile formality, as it happened, for I wasn't to venture back into that gourmandizing sanctum for two decades to come, by when, frankly, who cared? He was boring about food, boring in the sense that he would veto conversation while the culinary marvels laid before his great napkin, which he tucked under his jowels, threatened to lose heat; yet he could be perversely imaginative, and did attempt, in the final instance, to imbue me with confidence despite my prissiness.

I have not forgotten how, when the pudding trolley was wheeled up to us and I asked to have wild strawberries, white (which appealed to my prissy side), he took the bottle of vintage claret to which he'd been initiating me, some stupendous Latour—'45 seems to come to mind— and with spectacular (some would say sacrilegious) audacity, bloodied my fruit with the last flourish of his priceless wine, muttering, a little formally, a little sadly: Now, my dear chap: you've tried the finest food in the land, and wine from one of the greatest vineyards, separately as well as together. Best of both worlds, one could say. Too late for me, of course, but let nobody tell you that you can't have your cake and eat it. You can. You will. Happy eighteenth birthday. And then he encouraged me to eat the best of both worlds with my fingers, not to be bourgeois about it. But such tokens of goodwill, such toasts, lay, as yet, hidden in the future: I was still at the stage of toasted bread, and he needed jam to sweeten it.

THE INITIAL LURES to his privacy, the first half-dozen or so, felt, despite the informality of his backless waistcoats and his stripy shirt-sleeves, uptight to me, twitchy. I would try to act politely and, even if famished, would limit my rations to a demure minimum—as if these meetings of ours were really interviews, and as if, though my application for the job had been foisted on me rather than prompted by personal initiative, the slightest sign of hunger could rob me of the offered position. One single slice of toast, lavishly buttered and jammed for me by him, and relieved of its hoary crust and cut into four segments, triangles, and delivered to my clenched lap on a brittle plate of flowery porcelain, is all that I permitted myself—against his easy five: it was difficult not to count. Earl Grey tea, poured from a pot with little feet, which took me back to the genteel English nanny of my early days. I pretended to eschew milk, and declined his offer of sugar, however refined—not because I lacked a sweet tooth, but in order to minimize the fuss of stirring, and the risk of spilling, and the predictable charade of mopping me clean.

I did not feel at ease; nor, very possibly, did he; and yet despite the heavily scored bass line of our dealings, which, though unperformed in this new venue, still resounded inside me with the echoes of his office far beneath, we did, in a fashion, manage to converse here, went through the higher trills of civility. I suppose that, encouraged by my oral acquiescence on the coal box, he now felt encouraged to pursue a fuller acquaintanceship, the route to which appeared to lie in sounding me out socially, verbally, encouraging me to make admissions. Only once, however, did we skirt round the wide subject of my sexual delinquency, which represented his trump card in the gamble for me; for, though he, as adults in his position mostly do, enjoyed the upper hand in the proceedings, I was determined to pretend to be keener to learn from him than to discuss the closed subject of my former teacher.

I needed to save my skin—that much I knew—so I proceeded cautiously, slow prudence being, though dull of me, at least not punishable. (Later, I was to learn that while he toyed with the prospect of my suitability as his ganymede, he'd taken himself to the office of the rector's secretary and rifled through some file relating to me, in order to check, as if this were a qualification, the supposed quotient of my intelligence.) And thus, with his every forward step into prurience, I found myself taking another of retreat, back into a resistance that masqueraded as timidity. I remember attempting chatty detours—my teasing equivalents of his sweets that led to nothing—and, for instance, lampooning the school's sporting absurdities as viewed from the cynical place where I then lived, and I would find myself, in return, rewarded for my attempts at a deferral (which both of us probably knew could not last indefinitely) by collusive little hoots from him. I might even, in order to avert his intentions, have (further) flirted—for this, if only in theory, committed me to nothing. It was a respectable skill; even my mother deployed it; but I remember sweating with the great heavy effort of distracting him.

Those early teas seemed to me to stretch into dispiriting eternities, for, despite my apprehension, I never quite dared to take my unsolicited leave—in case he should block me, and draw close, which might swell into anything; and so, instead, I would wait and wait and wait until he, rendered as hesitant by his new attempts at friendship as earlier he had been bold to abuse his authority—and unable, in consequence of the switch, to cross the boundary from trivial antics to bodily, finally gave up, accepted defeat, and allowed me to return, a little frayed but almost free, to wherever I should have been. Until the next time, obviously. And as the pace of his invitations escalated, and the slices of his toast blossomed into scones and crumpets and sandwiches of cucumber dipped in vinegar, and sometimes even syllabub, it did not escape me that, despite the treats which seemed so coolly to raise me above the young multitude, he was quietly turning up the heat.

Now comes the day, a Friday. When I go in, I do not—which has been the routine—find him rising wearily from his wingèd chesterfield: he's already upstanding, and lurking a little too close to the door for my ease. The fire is blazing. In order to circumvent him, I have to squeeze between the back of the low sofa and the bed in the alcove behind it— not a straightforward procedure, for the ground is strewn with programmes and reviews and books—historical biographies, mainly: Richelieu, the Sun King, Mazarin. Dr. Fox is keen on stories of magnificent skulduggery. While I try to steer myself towards my usual position, he pretends, with a friendly tut of admonition, that I haven't closed the door properly, and goes to secure it; but though he coughs elaborately, I catch the sound of a turning key, its clandestine squeal.

As I round the far side of the sofa, I notice his reflection in the shaving-mirror: he's moving with an eager sort of speed, as if racing me to my seat. He wins: I don't make it to safety. I stop in my tracks. His waistcoat, I now see, is already undone, and breathing heavily. His shirted gut comes on to me, the dimple of his navel straining against its fabric. The curtains beyond his shoulders are practically drawn to: only a narrow shaft of light cuts across the ceiling. I take a half-step back from him—so he takes a whole one forward, into me. His whiskers are curling into a sort of grin, revealing a fissure between his front teeth. His eyes wince for me to follow his lead. Follow how? Like this: he places a velvet slipper between my feet, thereby forcing me to stumble against some mystery behind me. I fall onto the bed awaiting. It feels much the same as sitting on the coal box did, save that the surface beneath me now lacks solidity, is less supportive still. Not a word has passed between us. There seems not to be a need.

I know what is required of me, but what I cannot gauge are the new parameters of his bedroom greed, quite where, or how far, he intends to take me. The bulk of his divestiture occurs with Dr. Fox already plugged into me, between my lips, his penis held more or less still while my gullet labours on it. Words like diligence and application and industry race through my head, words of the type that you like to read on reports from teachers. And then I think of promise and of interest, and of that other non-curricular word, popularity, and fleetingly I think of my mother, and of the sun, which I suddenly miss, and of seaweed wreaths. I notice fragments of clothing being slung about behind him—a salvaged flash of tie; a rib of white collar, stiff; buttons of shell on a waistcoat; a glint from a cufflink. The braces have already been released; the trousers, left to slither and wilt on the embroidered slippers.

These, the slippers, he removes stealthily, and while one of them sneaks off behind the valance, its partner seems to become wedged between my feet, for I recognize the dry rubbing of velvet against my heels. He now steps out of his trouser legs, thus enabling him to sway more confidently, almost to swagger with relief. As he kicks away the mound of gabardine, I notice, below my line of vision, a greyish blur of baggy underpants about his knees, and below, in a stunted perspective, elasticated garters attached to a pair of stockinged feet, which stand turned out, pointing to the corners of the room behind me. He leans down without releasing me, and unclicks the elastics on his shins, but I cannot see what happens beyond this point, not without losing my purchase on his penis. He seems to raise one foot to his rear, and to wobble one-legged in an effort to pull a sock free. I envisage a fat flamingo. He swaps unsteadily to the other foot. Now there follows a disharmony between us: I must thrust out my mouth if I'm to keep him in, but, if I push my face any further into his groin, he will lose his balance and keel. He shoves me back onto the bedsprings. Out of my mouth he pops, a model of rigidity; his glistening knob, purple as a two-day bruise.

I sit uncertainly. Yet he stands firm, pointing himself back at me, so closely that he blurs my vision. He begins to tug at my neck, half-throttles me in his haste to remove the tie which contains it, which he first attempts to slide the wrong way round, as if I were a mirror, and which, once off, he seems not to know what to do with. He tries to crouch to kiss me with his fleshy rosebud lips and, meanwhile, slings the noose of my father's Alma Mater, like a skipping rope, over his head, leaving it there to hang. His spectacles bash into my cheek, but he, with a quick hard independent middle finger, pushes them back onto their greasy bridge.

The pallor of his blubber in this light is tinged with underwater green. His shins, I see, are varicose, riddled with worms, diseased eely ribbons of aquamarine. I try to swim away, to immerse myself in adjectives about the sea, to vanish. He begins to shed my jacket for me, but my body appears not to be co-operating, so he shoves at the collar, yanks at the lapels as if I were thick-skinned, or just thick. I look up at him, blankly, without possible meaning, but suddenly he's smiling back, creepily cheered. He raises me by my underarms to my feet. In one deft heave. Dr. Fox is stronger than you might think, like most musicians. The clothes of my upper half—jacket, jumper, collar, shirt—come off briskly, roughly, inside out and back to front, as in a locker room. My torso looks so burnt in the hot gloom, and so skinny next to the white mountain of him, that you would think I'd spent my life starving in the tropics, and he his, stuffing himself with cheese in cold countries. The hair under my arms feels regrettable to me, unfitting and implicating. I hunch my shoulders in, to hide this defect. He sits me on the bed, more delicately now, and sets me down on my back as if I were a baby whose nappy needed changing. I grow more feeble by the minute. I cannot make this easier.

Like some governess, he takes my clothes across the room and places them tidily over the arm of his chair, folding each garment in half, down the middle. The back of his head is flat, like the butt of a bullet. He flies back to me now, soundlessly, as if to check that I'm still alive, still breathing. I lie slumped across the bed, half-denuded yet belted, eyes closed for simplicity. But even without peering, I can tell that now, in his private domain as opposed to his public office, he wants more than just the head of me. Here we inhabit a different kingdom, differently crayoned, broader and wilder than the controlled territory of music. I do not blame him. I once yearned for Mr. Wolfe entirely, for the whole vast savage continent of him. But that was before I grew thick, or thick-skinned.

Kneeling on the edge of his bed, and pushing a curtain which might hamper him, he places an arm behind my neck, and another behind my knees, as if I were feverish, delirious. He tries to swivel me into position, to carry my head onto his brocaded pillow. I can feel him straining to lift me, his stubborn penis prodding my right kidney. I help him to heave me; I raise my legs of my own volition, but I do so as if I were moribund, or moving in my dreams, turning in a womb. He removes my shoes, and slowly peels my socks away from me, like a pedicurist. My feet are freezing, but it could be worse, I tell myself: at least my toe-nails are trimmed. I hear him patter across the room to place the shoes with the rest of my property, and I'm left to hope that he hasn't stuffed my socks inside them.

He tip-toes back, as if not wishing to disturb me, and begins to pull at my trousers, from my feet—pull, pull, harder pull still; but my arms, as if predicting this initiative, have crossed and clamped against my middle. I cannot let the man strip me, not completely. I think of Mr. Wolfe, of my squandering of him. I realize that I have earned this. I own up to my deficit, decide to pay the penalty: unbuckle, unclip, unzip automatically. Dr. Fox is free to proceed. Dr. Fox is rich. I arc my spine, and raise my buttocks an embarrassed minimum, just the fraction nec-essary for him to effect his transaction smoothly, and he rewards me with a calculated interim during which he conveys the trousers of my undoing, taking care to preserve their crease, over to the resting-place of my other belongings. I think that he lets me hang on to my under-pants; but I have to peer down the length of myself to be certain. For I feel, despite the swaddle of whiteness across my hips, naked anyway.

A PAIR OF PANTS. That much—that little—he has permitted. But now, this great blancmange of a man is clambering onto the bed, trying to keep his heavy spectacles in place as he draws one foot upwards, and then, with a great gasp, the other. He staggers over my flatness, his pale fleshiness overhanging. The mattress makes waves. He wobbles, throws an open palm against the wall, regains a balance of sorts, and begins gradually to lower himself upon me, crouching by cautious degrees until he's straddling my middle. He wriggles to make himself comfortable. I gaze at the ceiling, float around it. He slides upwards, northwards, along me a fraction, and rests his crevice, which he pulls asunder with the rough use of his hands, precisely upon the front of my underpants. These have hardened within, but against my wish: it is my mere body betraying me, mocking me. Typical, I remember thinking—the whole untimely ambivalence. My loins are an open book: interpret it, I tell you, as you see fit, but remember, when you come to draw conclusions, that when you're young, when *you* were young, horns such as mine are not, were not, summoned: such things reared up, they rear for no good reason, fuelled as easily by boredom, or fear, as ever by a sense of thrill.

Nothing seems clear-cut as I squirm beneath him. I feel weighed down by contradictions. It amazes me to discover that I can endure his great bulk without expiring, but I daresay that there's a perfectly good reason for this, relating to springs and momentum and body weight and mass, tucked between the pages of my physics file. His knees stick out on either side of me, toward me, like ancillary sharks. He starts to push them down, one at a time; and now they have dropped out of sight, returned to the ocean, though his varicose veins, his eels, must be slithering about my thighs. A smell of perished seafood—rising, I suspect, from the unplumbed depths of his umbilical cavern—invades the curtained alcove, spreads its putrefaction around the confines, like the rotting innards of dead fish thrown in a monger's bucket. My nostrils flare with repugnance. The distended rolls of his flab seem, from where I lie, to be piled onto me in circular rings of flaccid rubber. My gaze ventures upward from his undergut and belly to his dugs, and past his bearded jowls and chin and cheeks, which are whiskery and flushed, all the way to his teeny, disappearing eyes. He has removed his spectacles, clicked them shut—click-clack—and next, he's trying to lurch forward, seems to be tugging at a corner of counterpane near the bedhead of Formica, in order to place his glasses beneath the pillow, to bury them safely. I wonder what he can look like from behind, with his fluffy, sweaty hindquarters splayed thus, and whether he has ever caught, clambering out of the bath perhaps, a glimpse of his own sight.

But as he bathes upon me despite my dryness, he is blind, can hardly pick me out, is reduced to touching me—and from my point of view this feels almost like a comfort, a small mercy. I am A. N. Other now, anonymously slumped for his enriching, or his wastage, a mere faceless return on some high-risk investment. But he, by contrast, remains very much himself, utterly his own speculator, enormously naked—naked, that is, except for the pinky-ring of pale cornelian, the last vestige of his gravitas, which gleams near my face as he guides his cock up, up to my death mask. But no, he changes his mind. Instead he plunges me with his dark tongue. I try to curl my own, right back, as if to hide it; but I can't, so I flatten it against the parched base of my mouth. He stifles me with his grunting breath of warmish truffles. I try to inhale from my nose and directly through my windpipe, but when I can no longer hold out against the mounting slime of his saliva, I wrench my lips away from his ardour, and turn my sweating head in profile.

He will not have this. He returns my effigy to face him, to lick around the edges of its mouth, which, as far as I'm concerned, he can lick to his heart's desire, for now I am flying around the ceiling above. He slurps over my nostrils, scratching the edge of my nose with his pulsing nasal brushes, and at last he attends to my eyes with his tongue, in order to help them shut. And given, I suppose, my unreasonable reluctance even to feign desire, my refusal to provide him, after all that he has done, with so much as a simulacrum of passion, but to reward him for his pains only with abstraction, he rams himself where I deserve, where I have come to expect, which is inside my mealy mouth. He chokes me less when I am supine: my neck can be thrown back. He traps my arms, my wings of flight, under his knees, and pins me down. And now that I'm immobile, he takes his claws behind his back and begins to tug at my waistband, gripping and wrenching my underpants as far as they will go, which is down to my calves.

He withdraws from my face once more, and shifts his weight from my chest to my crotch, which is my great embarrassment. He must have grown either angered or elated now, because he has begun to sway about, to rock and moan and grind his sticky parted arse against my genitals, which are turning raw with the rub of his lust. And after pumping himself for a few fraught moments, and churning the contents of his shrivelled sac, he scatters his musical seed over my face and forehead and hair, spurting as far as the headstone of Formica; and I am left with a taste of indifference mixed with sadness, as if I'd attended the funeral of someone unknown to me, some vague acquaintance of the family. We dress in a quiet hurry, and then we settle down to tea, as if nothing had happened. And this, over and over, becomes the pattern; and I oblige with my company frequently, disaffectedly, as if there were no tomorrow, or as if tomorrow would be no different.

.   .   .

IN MY SECOND YEAR, a most unlikely thing happened: I managed to make a friend—not necessarily of the type that my parents would have encouraged, such as someone descended from a noble line of English Catholics, but still; to me, the whole surprise alliance felt like a miracle, and my new ally, like a harbinger of bravado. When this olive-skinned stranger with jutting cheeks and narrowed eyes turned to me at assembly on the first morning of the new term, and whispered some well-crafted barb concerning the rector (of whom I, not having been granted a dog-collared glance, hadn't troubled to form an opinion, but whom my neighbour had obviously decided to despise on sight, for the sheer glorious hell of it), I found myself bowled over, smitten by this newcomer's venomous charm. He was the most disrespectful and sarcastic boy that I had ever met, and entirely without fear, or so it seemed to me. Certainly he was the first whom I had ever known to kick against the rule of compulsory confessions, which he described as an affront to one's integrity and an abuse of civil liberty. He was a born winner, you could just tell—not brilliant academically, for he was far too self-possessed to bother with industry—but he exuded flamboyance and anarchy, and bristled, wherever he ventured, with angry energy. Plus, we were soon to discover, we had common interests, not least the shared acidity of our humour, our burgeoning style of waspishness.

Cross was his surname, but like me, he held dual nationality thanks to his mother, who was South American. He insisted on carrying two passports, not only in case a sudden war erupted and he needed to get out of England, which he said that he absolutely would do, but also (and I suspected this to be the more alluring reason) for the pleasure of confusing airport authorities. Though—also like me—he was bilingual, his English was more Hispanic than Yankee, reminiscent of my mother's in intonation, while his Spanish, which was slower and more melodic than mine, was infused with wavier cadences. When he spoke, it sounded almost as if he were chanting. I adored some of the words that he used, which, strictly, were not so much Castillian as flourishes of onomatopœic slang derived from the oral tradition of Peruvian troubadours. Those syllables of his were like species of new butterflies to me, constant surprises, small blessings. Both of us claimed to detest, and without exception, every single other inmate in this pit, and we always spoke in Spanish—nice and loud, to irritate our peers—switching back to English only when bothered by some dreary priest or teacher, for the staff viewed our bond as unhealthy, schoolgirlish. But we became, as far as we could (even though we sat in different streams), inseparable. Dr. Fox detested him—considered him *nouveau riche*, and wouldn't even give him a voice audition. My friend was a latecomer. That was the excuse. Sorry.

His parents were on the brink of divorce, a circumstance of which, in that period, honest-to-goodness Catholics would have taken a dim view. I found it glamorous, racy. His father, Mr. Cross, whom I was given to believe had lent his name to a line of slick executive Biros which then glittered with status all over the shop, had, since his conjugal upheaval a couple of years before, removed to Chicago, to be near a ravishing young heiress—one of those incredibly refined American society blondes, all cashmere and overblown smiles and jodhpurs—whom he had met playing polo in Newport, I think it was, and whom he planned to marry as soon as the papers of his matrimonial severance came through. In the meantime, while he waited for the moment to place a band upon the beauty's finger, he entertained her from some high-rise *garçonnière* in the vicinity of her family home—the latter being, the boy later told me, one of the oldest houses in the city, a whopping great mansion, set in equally whopping grounds, and full of black servants in full livery, apparently.

MY FRIEND HAD PINNED a photograph of the contentious extramarital pair onto the wooden partition of his cubicle, and I remember thinking that his burnished father, raffish and black-eyed and brilliantined, looked sexy as all get out, but I never dared to admit this. It was to remain among my secrets. And my friend's secret, though he seemed to be at less pains to conceal it, was that he obviously preferred his father's new concubine (whom, against his mother's pleas, he had met on a number of occasions while weekending in Chicago) to either of his parents, for she was younger than they, more like an older sibling, and hip as hell to boot. Plus, of course, she spoiled him—it was in her emotional interest—and was forever giving him expensive attempts at friendship: a pocket-sized television, utterly up-to-the-minute; a cut-velvet jacket with curvy lapels; silky polo-necks; metallic suitcases. I don't know how the boy's mother took all this, but I was fascinated.

Next to the photograph of the soon-to-be-weds, who, snapped from a balcony overlooking some sunny midday swimming pool, almost glowed with reflected romantic azure, there was another picture, in black and white, which, though larger in format, had been doctored at some point since its development. This had been intended to portray a formal family group, until, that is, my friend decided to excise two of the heads from the gathering—his own, and his father's. The resulting oval holes looked, against the wooden surface of the cubicle, like hollowed eye-sockets to me, sinister. I would have filled them in, tried my hand at collage of some description, had a bash at reparation. No matter; what remained on view was centrally, essentially, an exotic dusky female with lilies planted in her upswept hair, and enormous silver hoops circling down from her lobes to her shoulders, which were swathed in a flurry of white frills. This woman, I discovered, had been my friend's mother in days of greater matrimonial harmony. She was flanked by four girls of varying ages, from fifteen to about three, also frilled in whiteness, though not so seductively, and all with sulky dark mouths. Eyes like angry moons: the Cross sisters. But why had my friend removed his father from the scene? Ohhh, he replied in the manner of a languorous adult, because his father had another life now, obviously. And then he waved a hand, forefinger extended like a dancer's in fifth position, towards the colour picture. And why himself? Because his mother had forced him to wear a bow tie to the studio. I saw his point, I admit.

Señora Cross and her girls had remained at the family home in Ecuador, but fond of them as my friend doubtless was, for he spoke of them in tones of affection, as if they belonged to a sentimental film, it was also apparent that he was looking forward to spending, after the decree absolute, long chunks of holiday in the centre of Chicago, which, unlike the stultifying outskirts of Guayaquil, was, he told me, a really groovy place to be. And he also told me that once his father and the society beauty had found a new place and settled in, and he himself had a chance to check out the decent shops and clubs and naughty cinemas, then, he said, I too could visit: there was bound to be masses of room. I returned this compliment, and invited him to visit me, though I dreaded inflicting my ghastly father upon him, and exposing myself to the fact that I had no friends of our age to amuse him.

HIS FIRST NAME was Louis, which his family apparently pronounced Lewis, not even Luis. It sounded peculiar to me. So instead, when we were alone, I would call him by his second name, which I thought just screamed of Hollywood. It was Clifford. Clifford Cross: wasn't that fabulous? He, in turn, never bothered to call me James, because, as names went, we both found it pathetic. So instead, he adopted my mother's diminutive, and was always to call me Iago during the heady period of our friendship. Clifford turned out to be the sole boy with whom, in those eight long years of education, I was to share such an intimacy.

Like his father (I suspected), he was a born cheat, and, what is more, always managed to get away with his misdemeanours. If there existed a rule, he simply had to bend it—not actually break it, you understand: it would never have done for his exploits to backfire on him. That would have spelt what he termed Gratuitous Humiliation, *humillación gratuita*. I revelled in that phrase: its very sound, its rolling sophistication, made me tingle. But anyway, the point is that the lure of insurrection was beyond his resistance. Take our school uniform: half the time he wore the jacket slung over his shoulders, letting it swank about like the cape of some Latin seducer—a departure which, though frequently criticized by teachers, and openly scorned by other pupils, was not, in itself, against the rules. Or his jumpers: Clifford had been taught to sew by his older sister, presumably to help relieve the Ecuadorian tedium—so that confronted with the horror of our lanky regulation pullies, he simply grabbed his needlework kit and set to work, somehow managing to take in the sides of his jumper without the entire mess unravelling. I have a suspicion that he reinforced the seams with the use of a stapler (though he would never have admitted this, not even to me), but anyway, next he raised the waistband to the level of his ribs and, as if by magic, he suddenly owned a passable approximation of a fashion item, good and skinny, about which there wasn't a goddamn thing that anyone could do. When interrogated by fuddy-duddy members of the staff about his irregular appearance, he just claimed that his jumper had been shrunk by the school's lamentable dry-cleaning people, and that, if anything, the authorities should be thinking in terms of reimbursing him. His nerve in the teeth of authority was unflinching, and filled me with a vicarious sense of bravery, as if, though I wasn't even instrumental, I had been an active partner in his mischief. It strengthened me. The way he customized his ties, too, was extraordinary: he would make, with the wide end, the broadest knot imaginable; then, dock the excess of narrow dribble; and finally, hand-roll the raw edge to prevent fraying. He made everything easy, Clifford.

AT THE HATED TUCK SHOP, he calmly stepped into the breach for me and set about avenging my earlier indignity. I'd told him the story about Payne Senior, and he replied that Payne Senior made him sick. While I stood back and soaked up the scene, he would join the queue and squint and start counting, planning his moment carefully, holding back, giving way to people behind him if necessary, until he was certain of being dealt with by that one specific prefect. Payne alone would do. And after having purchased a wild excess of sweets both for himself and for me, but before having paid for these, he would suddenly, at the last instant, demand to buy, for instance, lipstick. He would, of course, be told not to be so bloody stupid, but the voice admonishing would have grown jittery. And Clifford, pretending to be outraged, would, every time, begin to bang a noisy coin against the ledge of the hatch and simply insist. Come on!, he would scream, surely Payne had *lipstick* to sell, under-the-counter sort of thing, or was money not the right currency? Clifford could be a spectacular nuisance, fantastically impudent; drove his victims, even older ones, to distraction; and was able, despite his lowly position in the hierarchy, to prove to our seniors, and to me, how bullying had nothing to do with winning. Bullying didn't worry him: it was the prospect of winning that appealed.

His style was brasher than mine, showy by comparison to my congenital chi-chi, but there was an undeniable glamour to his flashiness, which, even if I didn't emulate, enthralled me: he was, in a way, my alter-ego. He didn't smoke, which I emphatically did, but he drank superbly, preferably duty-free tequila, decanted into a hip flask and secreted about his person, for he swore that tequila helped him concentrate on prayers at benediction, and improved his sacred incantations beyond belief. He also possessed a stash of his mother's amphetamines, and claimed that given the execrable standards of nutrition in this prison, no sensible person could afford the risk of an appetite, which was a recipe for food poisoning. He even sported jewellery: not the cheap, ethnicky beads that aspiring hippies in the sixth form liked to conceal, along with grandad vests, beneath their uniforms, but an adjustable bracelet, fashioned like the bangles of coiled elephant-hair which were then considered trendy—though his, typically, was made of gold, the real thing, no shit for him. He wore it on the same wrist as his watch, which was the last word in chronometric desirability: you could have dived, without it coming to grief, the whole thousand leagues down to the bottom of the sea—were it not for the fact that he purposely left its chain to dangle loosely, with the result that, submerged other than in bath water, he probably would have risked losing it.

He gave himself manicures—again, a trick learnt from his sister—most often, I gathered, during prep in the evenings; Clifford couldn't have objected less to people staring at him while he performed this procedure, for he considered his cuticles to be magnificent, and exhorted me to regard with special suspicion those priests whose fingernails were bitten. He wore contact lenses, of all amazing tricks, and wielded dental floss, like spun silk, which I had never seen. He even went to a hygienist to bleach his teeth (which in Europe, at that time, was an unheard-of thing, revolutionary). And when back in Guayaquil, he would take his regulation slip-ons to some local cobbler, have him stack the soles an imperceptible but effective centimetre, and further instruct him to replace the heels with something a little more... Cuban. ¡*Viva La Vida!* You have to live. I loved his spirit.

BECAUSE HE LENT me strength, and shared my isolation with me, I grew to trust him. First we exchanged mild confidences about friendship generally and loyalty being everything; then, we moved on to crushes and pashes and things that happened at girls' schools, a sort of madness which afflicted virgins when they became women, as if the two conditions, madness and virginity, were mutually exclusive, which in turn led us to the heavier stuff that apparently went on in convents, and made us shriek with disbelief, because, well, we just could not fathom what the hell girls did get up to when there was nothing to *get* up? He said they rubbed. I told him not to talk rubbish. To me, girls seemed like creatures from another galaxy (less so to him, because he had sisters, but still): all those periods and tampons, month after month for the rest of their lives, and no swimming when there was blood, and the whole revolting business of pregnancy, and the thought of parents doing it, which I said didn't even bear imagining. He replied that he could envisage his father french-kissing his fiancée, which meant spitting in her mouth. I told him that he was disgusting.

And then we'd grow thoughtful for a while, ruminative, until one of us eventually erupted with laughter and put us back on track, which was really the track of love—love, that is, between humans (pets weren't allowed), and reciprocal love in particular, which I didn't think could ever really work, not if it got tangled up with biology and, more pointedly, with lustfulness, which was a sin, because fornication (which he, in his worldly way, insisted on calling erotic union) just wrecked everything in my opinion, though he didn't think that it did, not necessarily: look at Tristram and Iseult, he said, or Romeo and Juliet. What utter crap, I countered: those were just figures in fables that someone had made up, and besides, the people in those stories never actually, you know, well *you know*. I argued that when people did—did what?, he asked; Did Intercourse, I snapped: look it up in the dictionary. Fuck off, he retaliated, in Spanish—one person was always the loser, and the other, the taker; and anyway, that was between women and men; and men who wanted women were only ever really after *that* (and then I pointed to my flies, which must have confused matters), but still, I bet him that any girl who played the truth game would admit that sexual stuff had nothing to do with friendship or love, not really, not like friendship between males, sort of like us. Take the Greeks, I pronounced (we were starting the Symposium, so I felt entitled), and then I droned on, feeling important, until, in the manner of these things, we eventually got round to boys, and how relations between boys didn't always have to be Platonic, though I considered it prudent if they, well, stopped short, short of groping. But for the moment, I steered clear of dealings between adults and children; I didn't want to muddle us. All in good time.

In the event, neither Clifford nor I was so reckless as to discuss specifics, but both of us did on occasion hint at past experiences, small histories. Although my views on sexual morality were undermined by religion, handicapped, his turned out to be strong, heretical, and surprisingly well backed. He knew, for instance, about African initiation rites, and about the Aztecs, and about people called Yoruba, who practised sexual voodoo and were magicians, and all about the stars. My Catholic mumbo-jumbo regarding mortal sin, he said, was total guff. I mean, he explained, take the Chinese, whose culture and philosophy were far more ancient than our poxy Christianity (a tradition which, by comparison, was just a jumped-up cult of superstition, more tied up with political greed and the propagation of fear than any quest for fulfilment): Where, he challenged me, *where* in all of their learned writings about ying and yang (who, even symbolically, were masculine—they were shaped like sperms, for God's sake) did the Chinese condemn homosexuals, whom we called Queries? Well? Hmm? I was, of course, dumbfounded—but also strangely encouraged, as if I might yet find a remedy to salve my wretched conscience.

He must have felt that the printed word might, if not actually restore me to inner health, at least remedy my stupefied silence, because next he dragged me to the library and pushed me up a spiral staircase onto a balcony and, from the depths of a dusty shelf, yanked out some fat book about Hinduism, riffling (not for the first time, I imagined) through the index at the back, until he came to some obscure law about Queries like us, a law which he now looked up in the main part, quite near the front. I remember his manicured finger skating triumphantly down the page, then skidding to a halt just before the passage that he was after. But to make doubly sure that there wasn't any possible room for confusion (since I was being so moronic—which I denied: I called it sceptical), he drew forth one of his eponymous Biros and, his back turned to the room in case the librarian happened to be staring up, he underlined the relevant sentence twice, which declared that: "A twice-born man who commits an unnatural offence with a male shall bathe, dressed in his clothes." I scanned it, and scanned it again, then stared at him in utter befuddlement. He raised his eyebrows in exasperation, slammed the book shut, dumped it where it didn't belong, and led us back out.

Well?, he said. Well *what*?, I answered. He began to look pissed off now. Bathing with your clothes on, he hissed, is hardly a scary punishment; and anyway, that's only for people who believe in second time round, which doesn't include us. Look, he went on, it's all a load of cack, don't you see? We're only on this planet once, so make hay while the sun shuns. Shines, I corrected him, ever the pedant. You know what I mean, he countered, so don't try to be a clever dick. I had no wish to. I was desperate to agree: I needed him to show me the light, the way beyond the mangle of my scruples. Clifford would be my beacon.

THROUGHOUT THE MONTHS of our increasing closeness—good months for the most part, carefree and irreverent, sunny despite the winter—a couple of subjects had nevertheless been niggling at me, the most obvious being whether the muck of my former infamy had yet been raked up for Clifford's benefit by some blabbing prat, which I felt sure must have happened, and, if so, why Clifford hadn't yet asked me to come clean about the gossip. The second was the darker topic of Dr. Fox, who continued to summon me to his bedroom with undiminished frequency. I had even, by this stage in my career, graduated to the luxury of home-made sherry trifle, for I had learnt, despite my unappetizing partner, to ejaculate in his company and simulate satisfaction.

Although Clifford was perhaps the more vociferous party, he and Dr. Fox held each other in mutually low regard, and the clash between them did little to simplify my life, for, at base, I felt culpable. My friend had battled for me at the tuck shop, I worried; the least I could do now was intercede on his behalf, attempt to negotiate a diplomatic solution to the impasse. But Dr. Fox remained adamant: he had plenty of altos, thank you; wouldn't hear another word on the subject. Not once did Clifford blame me for having failed him on the music front, but what, by the same token, he was never to forgive (and we were equally rancorous, so I understood his stance) was the injustice of having been barred from joining forces with me in the second line of the choir.

He was, as it happened, perfectly musical: when we were bored, and ambling about outside, we would sometimes resurrect two-part childhood songs, lullabies and madrigals which, despite the difference of our origins, were rooted in a folklore common to both our motherlands. Clifford sang like a grown woman, with warbling adult passion. But what seemed really to inflame his emotions (his fury at being denied what he claimed to be his basic educational right), was that I, his best friend, should, as if to rub salt into the wound of injustice, be a favourite with Dr. Fox. For despite the latter's continuing efforts to camouflage his weakness for my company by belittling me in public, the truth of my status was clear as a diamond: it sparkled with exposure. I told Clifford that I hated the whole set-up, but that my hands were tied. He looked unpersuaded by my argument, for he was aware that I returned to those teas on a regular basis, which he presumed to be a privilege, the chance to be civilized. I tried to convince him that it was all hellish, nerve-wracking to get there, and boring once you'd arrived. You never knew what to talk about; it was excruciating; I wouldn't wish it on my worst enemy. But I begged him not to discuss those dreadful teas with anyone, not even the worst enemy on whom I wouldn't have wished them, because if the superficial details were ever to get out—about the scones and jams and clotted cream and sherry trifles—these would only serve to exacerbate my unpopularity. I made him promise. And promise he did. He protected me.

Eventually, needless to say, the subject of Mr. Wolfe, whom Clifford had never met but only heard about, did surface, but it was all mooted softly, without pressure or sarcasm; and because, by now, I knew enough about Clifford's liberal stance, I felt able to reciprocate the loyalty which we agreed was vital between friends such as us, friends who meant to be friends for life. So I told him, somewhat sketchily, about what had happened to me at prep school—not from my angry muddled heart, but as if from someone else's memory, as if relating some documentary, vaguely described to me way back in the past, third hand. I found myself concentrating on the bit about being found out, skipping all the boring interrogations, jumping to the episode with my repellent father. This, as we sat in Clifford's cubicle, gossiping in Spanish just before lights out, I made the blinding focus of my account: the ghastly maroon car, the Old Boy tie, the disgusting pub, the stench of his cigars, the preparatory prayer (which sent Clifford into paroxysms), the punching of the boot (which made him punch the wooden slats of his partition), the stroll in the cowpat, the horrible sight of my father blubbing, the confabs which had gone on behind my back, and last, how, in a manner which I'd never quite managed to work out, I'd got away with the whole fandango. The scandal had died down, and— apart from the whispering campaign, the endurance of which scarcely needed spelling out—I'd been left to get on with my life. He took it all on board, and in good spirit; he laughed at the right moments, and, once he knew the truth, he simply knew the truth, that was that. Let's face it, he said, now that we were older, it sounded like pretty tame stuff. And I recall how, straight after my half-baked confession, Clifford mumbled (by way, I suppose, of trading trust) something about having been interfered-with by some garage mechanic once; but he was forced to tell his tale in a rush, because the monitor on duty was chucking him out, and besides, I wasn't wildly interested: I had, as it was, enough of my own baggage. I felt laden enough. Nor had I yet stopped travelling.

It can't have been long after this exchange that I arrived at the next milestone, for I remember still basking in the relief of having managed, however guardedly, to unburden myself to somebody. I'd been bottled up for years, fermenting under cover, and though I wasn't to recognize this fact until the pressure had actually been alleviated, the tension within me had, I realize now, grown all but uncontainable, come close to nervous catastrophe. But at last, as agreed with my new confidant, Mr. Wolfe became prehistory, and was consigned to my puerile beginnings, never again to warrant allusion. I felt grateful.

My teas with Dr. Fox endured, of course, but they remained my private business, not fodder for intrigue; and though Clifford must have found it all a trial (torn as he doubtless was between loyalty to me and loyalty to his injured musical pride), he nevertheless proved true to his word. My friend was a brick; my luck was looking up. I felt, in every way, better equipped to handle my new life—lighter, stronger, saner, older, steadier without the clutter of those dirty secrets which had for so long clogged up, and weighed down, one side of my brain, the side where my spirit was housed. I found that having banished the constant interruptions with which the malevolent voice of my conscience had earlier tormented me, I could now concentrate for longer intervals, study more determinedly. And I also found that since I spent all my free time with my constant companion, my former sense of loneliness had been swept away, and with it, too, my converse dread of the public: before the godsend of Clifford, I had found the threat of crowds—marauding gangs and swaggering teams of sportsmen—just as daunting as the hollows of Coventry; but now that I was supported, now that we were a united front, everything felt different, almost exciting.

We were, by and large, disinclined to provoke others, although, admittedly, there figured exceptions to this tendency (such as spotty old Newton, whose relentless baiting, now that he'd shrivelled into scholastic insignificance, we obviously regarded a matter of principle; or Hardy, whose retractions and emissions now seemed less like a cause for wonderment than a pretext for loud hilarity); but we tended, in the main, to derive a tarter relish from bitching among ourselves in our own lingo. And I say lingo because, with the growth of our friendship, so, too, our communication was to grow into a florid idiomatic hybrid—blooming with Spanish expletives pronounced in English, and trailing with unfathomable non-sequiturs which were code for other things—nurtured and refined, in part, to frustrate the eavesdropping band of Gibraltarians who hung around our fragrant double-headed shadow.

These simian louts, whom we had dubbed The Curse of Barbary, were thick as bricks, and filthy, and claimed, furthermore, to possess a smattering of Spanglish, an assertion which, much as we might have liked to, we couldn't entirely refute. Their sole contribution to the school, so far as we could see, apart from their fondness for wearing sunshades inside the building (in an attempt, presumably, to disguise their dilated pupils), was to peddle stinking hashish, which Clifford deemed both pricy and impure compared to the beautiful marijuana leaves of Brazil. But their personal drugginess tended, in any case, to earn its traffickers expulsion more swiftly than ever it did profit, for the reek that clung to their rags exceeded even the high fug of their patchouli, purchased in some Moroccan souk.

Still, though Clifford and I rarely bothered to assume the offensive, we could, as a pair under siege, prove daunting, provide our aggressors with a good run for their cheap money, especially if such aggressors came in the guise of guffawing rugger jocks, or as the united offspring of local industrialists—ugly bastards with spiky hair-dos and a penchant for slatterns at the village fish-'n-chip shop—or even, come to that, as latent (to us, blatant) other Queries. For by now, after all our verbal industry, our tongues had surpassed the merely dextrous, and grown toxic—especially Clifford's: mine certainly spat its poison with accuracy, but his managed also to cackle while delivering its sting, which was doled out more lavishly.

Knowing, in the dormitory, that he lay but a few cubicles away from me, within safe reach, I was, for once in my life, able to sleep, and did so soundly. And even if it were true that I still yabbered in the night, and that I yabbered in Spanish, and that I continued to jolt others out of their precious English dreams, which they insisted that I did, I told myself that should Clifford happen to figure among the awoken, and were he to overhear my (perhaps incriminating) outpourings, and to grasp their meaning, well, big deal. My involuntary revelations were safe with him: he was, oh, he was better than a brother to me. He was, I now see, my best sister.

WE WERE IN the final term of that most character-building of bodies, the Cadet Corps, which, as I said earlier, was compulsory for all in the second year: no exemptions. The CCF, as it was called, sought to instil in us boys, as well as the qualities of self-reliance and perseverance (with which we didn't really take issue) those of self-discipline and leadership, which we somehow doubted we'd be requiring in the future. Anyway, despite our fear that some official busybody might have attempted to frustrate our scheme, both Clifford and I managed, by some amazing fluke, to inveigle ourselves into the same platoon, which was the shooting contingent. Clifford should, on account of his imperfect vision, have been disqualified outright, but since the knowledge of his contact lenses was safely restricted to him and me, his deception went unnoticed; and thus the pair of us had swung into the armoury, pleased as punch at our good fortune. He was always lucky, and I, lucky with him.

We'd chosen this particular branch of the corps not just because—compared, say, to orienteering, or canoeing—it demanded minimal exertion, but also because, in wider terms, in terms of the world, we thought it likelier that we might, one day, find ourselves needing to watch our backsides in trigger-happy American cities than exploring the Amazon, or white-water rafting down the Grand Canyon. And we concluded that after becoming familiar with rifles (which, according to the commander in charge, we were not to call guns, because a gun is what he had between his legs, and if you didn't watch your step he'd damn well show it you) wielding a pistol should prove a cinch. I rather fancied the idea of a nifty muff gun with a mother-of-pearl handle, which I could secrete about my person in much the same way as Clifford secreted his hip flask; I might even, since my army beret passed muster, don one for the part—more viciously slanted, of course, in the manner of a gangster's bit of fluff. But Clifford claimed that, as regarded weapons, he'd be looking for something more on the butch side, closer to a revolver—to complement the fedora on which, in those days, he had set his heart. He'd recently seen *The Godfather* and, as a consequence, I imagine, been inspired by thoughts of the Mafia; but when I expressed doubts about his chances, and suggested that Queries might not be welcomed by Cosa Nostra, he said why did I always have to go and wreck everything. I didn't, I argued; but why couldn't we just run off somewhere like Chicago, and open a glamorous Forties-style cocktail bar? Couldn't we just do that, without the danger of shoot-outs? Well, he softened, even if we did, he'd still be wanting his fedora.

THE CCF USED to convene—perhaps still does—on Thursday afternoons. However well or direly we might later happen to fare at the indoor shooting range (lying bum up on a sandbag—a posture which, though Clifford didn't seem to mind, struck me as undignified), the proceedings always kicked off with a parade—an excuse, in effect, for grown men to bark like retards, and for schoolboy corporals to admire themselves in our toecaps. Clifford and I had, by that summer, resigned ourselves to two minor tragedies: not being able to swing our hips as we marched, and being placed, week in, week out, on a charge. A charge was an enfeebled relative of a court martial—a lesser sanction, akin to being dealt penalty points for speeding rather than losing your licence entirely. And the reason for our regular punishment was that neither of us could bear the itchy roughness of the regulation shirts which cadets were prescribed, items thick as blankets dating back to World War I, and which, for all that we knew, had been dragged off the backs of corpses in the pestilent trenches of France.

To combat what, beyond obvious revulsion, amounted to an allergy (for without corrective underclothing we both flared up in a rash), he and I—with Matron's permission, which, in the event, turned out to hold no sway whatever—would slip white cotton T-shirts beneath our rebarbative khakis. But this forbidden measure of protection was detected, with early efficiency, by one of the corporals, the son of an Old Boy (the latter, a contemporary of my father's, as ill-luck would have it), who called us a couple of weedy pansies. He was, notwithstanding this observation, friendly with Payne Senior.

Although in the sixth form—and so, one would have thought, less preoccupied with the pleasures of kicking juniors about than with the imminence of end-of-school exams—this corporal was, as well as a smug little moron (geography, geology, religious studies), a virtual midget. Though Clifford and I were only of average—as yet nowhere near full—height, he was obliged to stand on tippy-toe in order to peer inside our collars. And he would carry his shiny leather baton like a woman clutching her evening bag, hard under the elbow—unless, that is, he happened to be raising it, in which case, the baton became a sceptre, the better to prod around our crudely woven ties. He was nominally a Scot, for his surname came afflicted with a Mc, or perhaps it was a Mac, but his family (though relegated by now to some unremarkable suburb of London alas) had, for centuries past, lived in Argentina. I don't think that Clifford's South American passport exactly aided our plight.

The midget corporal's colonial ancestors had been In Cattle. I knew this from my father, who, despite my complaints, found even the unintentional mention of one of his old pals heartwarming. Whenever I spat out that surname, the Mc or Mac, my father's eyes would glaze and gloss over, swim with nostalgia. But it puzzled me to think how this hallowed family, despite the limitless quantities of beef which it must, for all those generations, have been shovelling down, could continue to produce descendants so conspicuously undersized. I said as much. My father told me not to talk balderdash: diet bore no relation to genetic make-up: had I learnt nothing in biology class? And anyway, he added, I was hardly myself Johnny Weissmuller. Thank God for that, my mother piped up. She thought the actor a fright. Man shaved his legs and chest, I ask you.

Although there had followed, from the moment that our T-shirts were discovered, the bore of a weekly penalty, we didn't care. We were prepared to suffer for our epidermis, never mind our principles; and besides, we were always punished together, and unimaginatively, so that, if anything, the act of polishing boots or brass buckles or buttons for some fat-arsed army man, while pretending to be a couple of maids in a Genet drama, increased our sense of solidarity. Charges didn't daunt us. What was, however, to land me in trouble, was the fact that, on one particular Thursday, after we'd completed our regular penance (sweeping the armoury had, I think, been the chore on that occasion), and just as we were dusting ourselves down to flounce out—Clifford to tea, assuming he still had time; I, to Dr. Fox, who'd summoned me— the Major, for reasons unknown, was moved to wolf-whistle at us. Nor do I know what possessed me next, but I remember that before I could stopper my gob, I was laughing back across the room, and shouting: I shouldn't whistle like that, Sir, or we might have to tell your wife. Which did it: Clifford was dispatched (promising me, in a burst of whispered loyalty, to get word to Dr. Fox, notifying him of my plight), while I was forced to stay behind for the infliction of some further irrelevant penalty—which must have lasted hours, because by the time I'd bathed and changed, the bell for evening prep had already rung, so it was only after it, at suppertime, that I was able to reach Dr. Fox and all the treats he had in store for me: a casual tumble in the alcove, naturally; a light supper of salad and pâté, smuggled up from the staff dining room; and then, as a consolation prize for my altercation with the commander, a film on television, the viewing of which, said Dr. Fox, was prescribed; for when the picture, as he called it, had first been screened at the cinema, the reviews had, he recalled, been staggering. What's more, he added, the subject matter was bound to be, well, of interest to me. And thus we sat down: he, on the wingèd chesterfield; I, on the burgundy sofa—both of which had been swung round the room for the occasion.

IT CAME IN WAVES, the film—slow ones, laden with intensity—cerebral, quietly hysterical, and largely devoid of dialogue; just softly focused glances over bowls of hydrangeas, and glints, and little shivers of repugnance. Great open spaces. Dead sea, not a ripple.

The prescribed viewing was based on a novella, written early in the century—a couple of years, I surmised, before our cadet clothes were being salvaged from the trenches—and turned out to be a sumptuous, morbid tale about some fidgety middle-aged German, a writer, who, laid low by neurasthenia, is advised by his physician to travel for the purposes of recovery to Venice in late May, but who, far from being restored to health, contracts, as well as a feverish obsession (a crush or pash) for a pubertal male at his hotel near the Lido, Asiatic cholera, for God's sake; with the result that by the time you get to the end, well, it's all a bit of a swizz really, because you can't tell why the Querie, slumped on a deckchair, stuffed into a suit of rumpled linen, and with rivulets of hair-dye streaming down his face, has actually collapsed: whether from a properly broken heart, or from the plague—malaise or malady.

Swathed in great repeating segments of dismal minor-key movements from the (then) little-known symphonies of a Moravian composer who went over to Rome, both the film and its lugubrious soundtrack were soon thereafter to be elevated to the status of a cult, and adopted with messianic fervour by melancholy inverts everywhere, men quite old enough to know worse, plus the odd like-minded woman—or rather, intelligent lady. The film assumed, at the time of my youth, a hefty cultural import, even if people like my father were never to be brought round. But I knew none of these things as I sat, knees clamped, on my seat at the end of that testing day, waiting, if not actually to be entertained (for I had a feeling that entertainment didn't figure in the equation) at least to be educated.

I seem to be staring at all the wrong things, like the women. The boy is bizarre, almost freakish: outsize head, stunted legs, amateur make-up, highlights like the shopgirls in the village. I mean to say: how many Poles of fourteen do you know with streaks of ash-blonde whooshing through their hair? But the mother, look at her, she sends shivers down the spine. Beyond a register of whispers that suggests less Polish than Italian, she appears to possess only the strength to utter one sad, single word, something like Tadjú—Tadjú!, Tadjú!, she calls, in an attempt to earn her son's attention. She reminds me—oddly, given that she drifts about in period costume—of my own forgetful mother. The eagle nose, the gliding walk, the throwaway vanity, the whole otherworldly consummate over-weening foreignness of the woman: these things they have in common, the mother of Tadjú and mine. And despite the fact that mine glimmers with sultry gloss in my recollection, the powdered pallor of the mother on screen is no more, no less than the pallor favoured by the people of our island in the days when my grandparents were alive, so that the throwback, the fictive suspension, feels simple: since my mother could, once, have been, so she becomes the woman in the film: too lovely to be true, too miserable, as good as husbandless, perfectly cast for whimpering tragedy. Her son, the wretched boy, will, to be sure, one day provide it. But I am elsewhere for a while, overtaken by asides. The film drones on and on. Sailor collar, swimsuit, indigo doublet; pearls, heavy with teardrops, chokers of diamonds; dabby-dabby napkins; knives, clinking and flashing; an (upset) glass: a spilt lagoon of wine; grey sand, grey sky, grey water. Who the hell, in their right mind, would wish to visit such a place? Venice is moribund, or a morgue.

The sound of drowning; the sense of sinking in cold music; monstrous, strangulated chords sailing out, forever and ever. Now the Querie wants to vanquish his affliction, takes himself to be restored. He minces off to a posh *barbiere* who behaves like a complete smoothie-chops and would make a brilliant madam in a Spaghetti Western, and lets him pour a bottle of ink over his head—*arrivederci* to all that *grigio*—and trim his bushy moustache into a joke, like that of the grease-pot in *Cabaret*—*Willkommen, Bienvenue,* Welcome—and daub his pinched little mouth with crimson lippy, like Payne Senior, and smear his cheeks with too much rouge, and, look, behold, the Tragic Fairie beams at last, quite recovered, and gets up, patting his bosom with his puffy hand, which wears a cornelian that reminds me of Dr. Fox.

And then I turn to glance at him, but the vision chills me, for the imperturbable countenance of our director of music is, can you believe, stricken with tears: not like those of Mr. Wolfe, which were the tears of a secret love, nor those of my father, which were the tears of a lost boy, but with the tears of the girl with fleshy rosebud lips whom I suspected from the first moment; and I have to look elsewhere. Back in the film, the boy, the boy, the boy is running and laughing along the drabness of the ocean, and rolling on the sand and cavorting and falling until Bang: I grasp the irony—which is that I too have fallen, though not in a film. I have fallen for a heavy deception. His, the boy's, is another story, full of ignorance and wile and false hope. But I am educated now, apprised, committed suddenly to my own memory—in one deft go, at a stroke. For the youth on the boring beach is identical to, therefore becomes, someone further up the school, a streaky-haired confident blond with a ramrod walk and a smile that could charm the very gods, called Albany; and in some manner that I cannot comprehend, though I feel it absolutely—I know it despite not knowing—it becomes clearer to me than any translucent Venetian sky that Albany, who hasn't needed to twitch a muscle for the distinction, much less toil on my mentor's bishop, has nonetheless conquered and made off with (but ignored) the sobbing heart of pathetic Dr. Fox. Mine, I now see, has all along been another purpose; mine, duties ancillary. Outlet patients are my cause. The nature of my care is palliative; my function, merely to assist with the cooling of blood—even if, in the glassy opinion of my host, I lack the vintage. Neither blond nor strong-limbed am I, still less a ramrod walker. But my head, notwithstanding such flaws, is fixed at last. No love lost. Not one iota. And I decide, there and then, thanks to the borrowed strength of my belovèd Clifford, thanks to the lightness which he has brought to my soul, thanks, even, to the shock of my role in this brocaded hell-hole—my part in the whole absurdity, which can only be the part of the absurd cheated prostitute—that never again shall I bed with Dr. Fox. Not ever. Never more. Keep your creamy cakes and yummy scones: not even for a bursting sack of ancient gold. And I rise as the credits begin to float; I rise more slowly and assuredly than the reputedly staggering notices. And I notice, in my departing, that the boy is not called Tadjú after all, but Tadzio, and I think that it must have been Iago that my mother meant, and not *Adiós,* and I leave without a word of explanation, unlocking the door as if it were my own, and I see myself out for myself, and find myself released into the throbbing fifth-year corridor without a hint of shame any more, without a care in the underworld, because from this dark day, from this night on, no, there will be no further secrets, nor sessions, nor foul exudations. I have turned a great heavy leaf, not just a corner, and Dr. Fox had better start auditioning for my successor. And besides, in two weeks we go home.

ACTUALLY, WE DIDN'T. First we went to army camp—though not, of course, Clifford: he, the child of fortune, managed to get himself let off—because his flight back to Ecuador, booked months in advance (his mother had written), ruled out any question of extra-curricular activities for my friend beyond the date when term, as decreed by the school calendar, came to an official close. Greatest apologies. Sincerely yours, Amaranta Rodríguez de Cross. Clifford had shown me the photocopy. That, and not the niceties of small-bore, is, I remember thinking, what I call proper ammunition. My father, by tough contrast, said he'd never heard such piffle, and would on no account (or so he claimed) be a party to collusion. My pal, as he called him, was a spoilt brat, and obviously able to twist his mother round his little finger; but in the long run, my father banged on, Clifford's parents were doing the boy no favours by indulging his every whim. Rules were rules, and camp was for one's own good—it would make a man of me—so I was to get a grip, did I hear, and stop pestering him. Plenty of time to laze about in the summer. He was, by his own admission, a lost cause.

I shall ignore, needless to say, details of those army manoeuvres in Wales, performed on a site still drearier, if such a thing can be conceived, than the moors of northern England, or, indeed, the battlefield of Waterloo—ignore, that is, all save the fact that I was unable to play my violin in the run-up to a charity concert due to be given the day after camp by the school orchestra at Westminster Cathedral. My inability to practise worried me, not just out of musical vanity (for I had a slightly exposed, hurtling solo to engineer), but also because I didn't want to give vent, by performing below par, to the spleen of Dr. Fox, who was to be conducting—clad in a frock-coat from Savile Row, naturally. I couldn't afford, after my recent recoil from his charms, further to upset the delicate imbalance: he'd come down on me with a vengeance, with his full weight from his great directorial height.

Just as earlier in the year I'd felt trapped between Clifford and the director of music, now, at its end, I felt trapped between the director of music and, surprisingly enough, my father, for Dr. Fox's opinion was that by forcing me to go to camp, the Old Boy was showing himself to be both a philistine and a fool. All the wrong priorities. Who cared about the blasted army? What did the man expect me to become, some brigadier? Much as, inwardly, I might have agreed with these comments, I nonetheless found them irksome, perhaps because I felt, in some ludicrous way, that the criticism filtered down to me through my bad blood, which was thick. That my father (my mentor persisted) should be a dullard was only to be expected—most former pupils were—but what Dr. Fox could not comprehend was why I hadn't managed to persuade my mother to do something to prevent the inanity of army camp when I had a concert for which to prepare, and when, judging from my comments, she was a woman of discernment. And I suppose it was this last elaboration which, even if supportive, even if well-intended, needled me the most—his meddlesome criticism of my mother—for I felt that Dr. Fox was no more entitled to bitch about her than I was in a position, then, to bitch about him.

The sole mitigation of camp proved to be the phoney camaraderie of sitting among real-life squaddies in the Formica canteen, which reeked of fry-ups and beer—sulking, and, for the first time, smoking overtly, and drinking (without tequila to comfort me) gin, like some deserted sweetheart in a wartime movie. The song of the moment, which was played on the jukebox constantly, and which, despite conflicting with the period of the film in which I visualized myself appearing, became a sort of anthem for that futile week, was a heavy great number by some new glam-rock band, in which a stubborn long-haired youth, a curly-haired angel of the pop charts, insists, in a ragged, deadpan voice, that, no matter if fools say we can't win, he knows he's gonna fall in love again, but seeing as we've still got a chance, maybe, of love and sweet romance, won't I Roll Away The Stone. I felt so gloomy without Clifford, so bored with my own company, that I became perversely addicted to that raucous melody; and the upshot was that by my final day in the bosom of the British army, I felt readier to roll away the stone than the three Marys in the gospels.

A COUPLE OF SUMMERS LATER, I was to be confronted—in circumstances which, since I hadn't been given a word of warning, were to leave me all but winded—with the possibility of a second taste of the military: for it transpired that, on account of my dual nationality, I was about to be called up for conscription into the Spanish army, a fact which my father must have regarded as some sort of emancipation, for he insisted on calling it Becoming Legally Eligible. Preliminary papers and dates had already been delivered to our address, and yet the spectre of a second CCF (though ten times worse, for it involved—just as I was poised to apply for a place at university—further truncating my life by two years) struck me as so ludicrous that I could scarcely make it register. I remember clamming up when the subject was first raised, setting my jaw into a truculent clench similar to the one I'd adopted when I refused to be beaten by Mr. Wolfe, getting up from the lunch table, and taking myself off to sunbathe, to quake in silence beneath the blistering rays. My parents were starting to make me feel old. And to make matters worse, the swimming pool at home had been covered up, buried, to allow for terracotta tiles and a pergola.

I had discussed the problem of Spanish conscription with the careers tutor at school, who, though a stuttering, wimpy man, turned out to hold surprisingly spunky convictions. He described himself, for instance, as a devotee of García Lorca, whom I was studying at the time, and this devotion probably explained his eagerness to impress on me, first and foremost (over and above his hispanophilia, which was palpable), his disapproval of Franco; for he thought that even ignoring the horrors of civil war, the cultural damage wreaked by that dreadful dictator, that Nazi sympathizer, upon the nation of my birth was a scandal and a crime, and that no English person with a conscience should countenance living in that country. He also suggested that if my father was seeking, in view of my personality and general b-b-bent, to hamper my further education for fear of where knowledge might lead me, he was probably deranged—though this was strictly off the record. Never mind degree courses and choices of university: how could a man so besotted with the English system even think of allowing, let alone pressuring, his son to surrender to the laws of a fascist régime? Just didn't make sense to him. Incidentally, he threw in with an insurrective grin, he didn't suppose I'd considered drama school, had I?

The truth of the matter is that my father, incensed, I imagine, by his great school's correspondingly great failure to inculcate in me the virtues for which he had so fervently prayed, and in which he had so lavishly invested (sportsmanship, manliness, popularity, rectitude—the mere mention of which made me retch), determined, in despair, to subject me to corrective, as opposed to merely basic, discipline. Later, at the end of his tether, he would investigate the possibilities of electroconvulsive therapy, but in the meantime he merely sought a snare without psychological cachet, so as to teach me a good hard lesson. He threatened that if I refused to observe the laws of my native country—my *mother's* country, he couldn't resist stressing—the repercussions for me would be severe: I'd be unable, for fear of having my British passport confiscated, to set foot on Spanish soil between the ages of eigh-teen and twenty-five. Seven whole years, he pointed out. (Actually, it would have been six, but never mind.) Did I understand? No: I couldn't even conceive of the man. And my mother, the while, said nothing—not having been, she later claimed, in a position to comment. Her lip-stick was darker than blood.

That evening, I reiterated my intention to go to university. What!, he bellowed, To read *Lyan*guiges! He didn't call *that* going to university, called it an excuse to twiddle your thumbs for four years. And don't imagine that he didn't know what undergraduates got up to these days: he'd read all about it in the English papers (by which he meant his *Tele-graph*, always two days late). The varsities, he pronounced, were dens of iniquity, full of druggies and hippies, dropouts with delusions of bril-liance. And why, if I was so determined to continue studying, couldn't I read a serious subject anyway, like the law, or med'cine? Or, better still, scrap this whole further education lark and just Get-A-Pro-Per-Job when the time came, join an influential City firm, learn about f'nance sort of thing, stocks and shares, mmh? What was the bally use of a degree in modern languages, for heaven's sake? So that I could become a teacher? A secretary? Or perhaps I harboured hopes of becoming an air-steward. He despaired, he said. *He* despaired. And then he reiter-ated the word: Army. And then he added: my lad.

Although the careers tutor had primed me for this next scene, no amount of rehearsing could have prepared me for the terror which, when the moment to perform befell me, battered my chest. This, I sud-denly realized, was more momentous than any play, because trapped on my parents' real-life stage, without prompt or curtain or distance to protect me, I couldn't forget myself. And the reality of that first con-frontation with my owners—my puny desperation pitted against their front of armoured union, felt entirely other than the reality which I'd been expecting: colder despite the blazing summer, slower despite my unbridled nerves. My intention (my instruction) had been to seem con-ciliatory, to appear reasonable in an attempt to show them sense. I had been warned, above all things, to be adult, not petulant. Firm, and full of wisdom. I must suppress all rage, and hate, and the other toxins which infected my veins—even indifference. There was nothing to fear, I had been told: for, just as they had faith on their side, so I had justice. But in the event, because I knew that my countenance must remain that of an assured grown-up, even while my innards wanted to wail like an infant, all confidence seemed to desert me, and I found, to begin with, that all I could muster were the motions of an argument, not the words. I remember setting my napkin down with great deliberateness, as if this action settled something, then smuggling my shaking hand beneath the table. Next, I remember how my head seemed to sway moronically, to swivel this way and that in an attempt to decide which of them to address, my father whom I could hardly bear to look at, or my mother whom I couldn't bear to hurt. And in the end, I think that I must have spoken into thin air, for I recall neither of their faces in the cameo. My speech, when it leaked out, must have had the charm of skidmarks on the pants of a cadet, a dead one. My syllables were cold and colourless, and what I said, even if right in content, was wrong in tone: priggish and foolish and harsh. I cannot speak, I began, to either of you on this subject, but I want you to understand that unless you resolve this preposterous state of affairs by whatever means you consider necessary you should give up any notion of my returning to your house until I'm twenty-five. (And then, after a new intake of breath, I added:) If ever. And then I stood up and left the dining room. I had finished my pudding.

My mother and I did not revert to the subject of conscription during the remainder of that holiday, but the following autumn, at half term, my father duly flew to London and took me—his face like thunder—to the Spanish Consulate, where he did his damnedest to disown me in the waiting room. An empty chair was left to preside between us, like the invisible mausoleum of some other family. And when we were finally summoned to the consular office, he strode in without a word, and, of course, without me—so that he could present the more sensitive points of his case, the shaming unnatural reason why I wasn't really cut out for the military—Spanish or otherwise—in private: gent to gent, man to man, father to red-faced father. I had a good flick through the latest *Vogue,* browsed through a not very exciting *Harper's,* and then, at last, the pair of them emerged, my father and the good Consul— puffing cigars and practically slapping each other's backs—to inform me, after the Consul's pointedly virile handshake, that an indefinite deferment of my enlistment had, in the circumstances, been granted. I could have curtsied. We left together, my pater and I, but I declined to have lunch with him at his club. His job was done. I tore off my school tie. (But all of this happened later, two summers after English army camp.)

IT MUST HAVE been the film about the Polish blondyboy with the short-arse, and the Querie who fell ill in Venice, and their combined truckloads of make-up, because, after CCF camp, I went to my guardians' house and, while preparing to go to the cathedral—to play in the concert for which I'd been unable to practise—I treated myself to a good rummage in the bathroom cabinet, found a pile of slap, and set to work on my face, trying to transform it into a symphony of melancholy. I needed to look worn out, so as to mitigate my lack of preparation and elicit a droplet of indulgence from our volatile conductor. I'm sure that if I were shown a snap of the result now, I would dismiss my first attempt at cosmetic artifice as the daubings of a pitiful novice; but at the time, I was amazed by the rings of darkness which, simply by means of the wrong foundation and flecks of somebody else's liner, all smudged up, could be engendered under one's eyes. Then I dealt myself an emaciated set of cheekbones, by smearing charcoal shadow along the line that ran from my nose to the hinge of my mandible, and rubbing it in hard; and finally, I powdered lightly above the edge where I had sucked, so that by the time that was done, I looked like I'd come out of a concentration camp. The effect must have worked like a charm in the gloomy light of the sacred site, for no one in the orchestra addressed a single word to me, and Dr. Fox (despite my rusty playing) smiled with a fond indulgence, as if trying, after my ordeal in the land of the dragon, to lend me sustenance, to revive me. And I understood then that having walked out of his bedroom was the wisest thing I'd ever done, for the tables of power had suddenly been turned, and turned forever, and now I was sitting in a chair far more elevated than any wingèd chesterfield, on a throne closer to the floral carvers of my first birthdays. Because, from this point on, it would be he who needed to keep *me* happy. His responsibility had suddenly become not his pleasures, but preserving me from danger, from the danger of blabbing in his aftermath. I felt triumphant, as if I'd performed better than a virtuoso; and yet, regardless, it all came to an end in silence, for, given that we were in a cathedral, there was no chance of a good clap. Much grander, Dr. Fox would have said. More eloquent, more dignified. *Avanti!*

CONTRARY TO WHAT my father had led me to imagine, I was not, in the summer straight after CCF camp, to be granted much time to laze about, because by then, he and my mother wanted me kept thoroughly occupied—devil, work, idle hands. To this end they had organized, in advance of my return to their island, that I give English tuition, one-to-one, to various of their friends (perhaps in the hope of impressing them), and to some of their friends' daughters (in the hope, presumably, of impressing me). It didn't do the trick; it was all dead dreary; but I did earn a bit of grace at home, and some decent pocket money, for I pitched my fees good and high: that, I told my mother, was my proviso for submitting to the whole plan. She, when she first heard the sum which I had in mind, had been scandalized by my cupidity: I couldn't possibly charge such amounts; but in the end we managed to arrive at a compromise, and it was this: that whatever I earned from my pupils (and she suggested half of what I was threatening to demand, which would have embarrassed her), she would double, on condition—her proviso now—that I not tell my father. I thought I might manage that.

Apart from a girl with a harelip and a great constellation of acne, who contracted a crush or pash for me but was doomed to flounder, less in my regard (for she was sweet-natured enough) than before her board of re-examiners (who couldn't have cared less about natures), the only other pupil worth mentioning was a middle-aged notary, verging on handsome, rolling in money, and eager to master English for professional purposes: he hoped, he said, to expand his practice within Europe. He was a bachelor—a predicament which, according to my mother, simply meant that he hadn't found the right girl to marry, because, you see (she explained to me before I met him), poor chap had spent his whole youth studying—to the detriment of his sociability, she emphasized—so that now, successful as he was, and he was hugely so, he was also withdrawn, and shy in the company of women, fearing that every potential wife was a potential gold-digger. Pity, really, but there you were. Charming man.

I, however, was to discover otherwise: my parents, inadvertently, almost hilariously, had set me up. But by now, aged fifteen, I felt like a dab hand at unwelcome advances, and managed to sail through those hours of tuition smoothly as a gondola. Wherever the notary sat, I always sat opposite, ensuring that I kept the oars that were my legs tucked beneath my chair, that kind of stuff. And in this spiteful way of mine, he found himself relegated to the rôle of distant observer, like the drooling Querie who got cholera, while I held back, like the captivating Polish short-arse. Still, at least I was getting paid for my distance—and, by the notary specially, for, on the back of my initial hunch, I was prompted, when we came to discuss the horny subject of my rate per hour, to charge him extra. Services unrendered. My mother was never to find out.

I received two postcards, about a month apart, from Clifford that summer. The first came stamped from Guayaquil, which, he said, he was finding boring. He was off to visit his father. The second, in early September, told me, hastily, that he was adoring Chicago and dreaded having to return to school in England. Meanwhile, I presumed that my own letters, posted to Ecuador, were piling up at his mother's house, because I somehow doubted that the bereft Amaranta would feel inclined to forward her son's mail to her errant husband's new whereabouts. It hardly mattered: because suddenly, October was upon me.

I DIDN'T BOTHER, on the train back north, to bag a seat for Clifford: I knew that he was catching a connecting flight from Gatwick up to Manchester, from where he'd be driven to school by taxi—typical Clifford, lucky to the last. But my own trip, for once, passed in a flash: I had so many things to tell him (about the Querie notary and the girl with the harelip and my immoral earnings; about my new gadgets—though not a moped, worst luck—and the recent songs that I'd discovered; about the tedium of army camp; about the miracle of make-up; about my minuscule white swimming trunks; about my arguments with my father; about rolling away the stone and the dream of love . . .) that I spent the journey trying to juggle my news into some sort of order, and wondering whether to regale him chronologically or in a more considered jumble, so as to elicit greater laughs. And thus it was that, only once the bus had dumped us at the school's front quadrangle and I'd staggered up a spiral stair of stone to the third-year sleeping quarters—spread over two floors of an overbearing Victorian wing which had been abutted to a flank of the original Elizabethan house—I began to look for Clifford in earnest.

The new academic year heralded, along with other supposed privileges, an end to cubicles. To me, however, this felt like a distinct reversal, a return to enforced exposure, but communal sleeping arrangements were regarded by the powers that be as character-forming: one had to learn to get along with people, to be mature about it. Clifford and I—to limit the perils of group habitation—had requested (which was allowed, lots of people did it) to be kept in the same hutch; but when I scoured the noticeboard on the first landing, though I discovered my own name fast enough, and the name of my dorm (Leviticus), Clifford didn't seem to figure among its occupants. God those priests were spiteful. And because I suddenly found myself ambushed by a scrum of louts, shoving and jostling for a look-in, and telling me to get lost, I decided not to persist with the search for my friend's whereabouts, but instead, to try to beat the rush and grab myself a decent bed by a window. I'd get hold of Clifford later, I reasoned, after I'd sorted myself out and unpacked enough junk to stake a claim on my new territory. And once I'd tracked him down, we could put our heads together and hatch a plan: decide which of our respective dorms we preferred, bribe someone in there to volunteer to swap with whichever of us was wanting to shift, and drag our victim with us to the new year master (a complete madman, as sinister as he was violent—Clifford and I would probably need a preparatory glug of tequila) in order to request the transfer. But with Clifford beside me, it would all be sorted out. Bound to be some administrative oversight, I was certain.

The oversight, as always, was mine. After I'd unpacked (but nowhere near a window, for all the best beds had been snapped up by people who'd come by car, early arrivals), I headed out of the dormitory, back towards the noticeboard, and caught a glimpse in the distance of the rector (whom Clifford had so memorably ridiculed at our first meeting, exactly a year earlier). The priest was busy exchanging greetings with a bunch of sporting paragons, but as I drew closer, he suddenly cut short his banter, dug his hands into his pockets, and made a bee-line towards me—not to welcome me back, but to say, in a slightly unnerving tone—absolutely flat—that he'd like to see me in his office straight after evening prayers. I remember his hairy Adam's apple bouncing up and down. It made me want to swallow.

Dry hot needles began to shoot down my arteries. I could tell that I was blushing, yet I couldn't fathom why. Had somebody died? Had I done something at CCF camp? Had my make-up been noticed in the Cathedral? I pretended that nothing was happening and went on looking for Clifford on the board, but I couldn't concentrate on the lists that were staring back at me; my eyes, instead of scouring the print, just swam about. My head was clogged up. I would call on Dr. Fox. No, I'd go down to the music basement. No, I'd go back to the dorm in case, by now, Clifford was searching for me. I finished my unpacking in a trance, disconnected from my actions. Still no sign of Clifford. Plane must have been delayed. Perfect.

MY BED WAS behind the door, but placed along a wall, like a divan, so that it felt slightly sheltered. I was nearest to the basin, which was a bonus: I would colonize it. The rest of the boys in Leviticus were bearable, nobody too gruesome: a couple of harmless weirdos—second-rate scientists; a couple of Mr. Populars (one, a cricketing star and regular chess champion; the other, a burgeoning dropout—the son of a very young admiral—grubbily handsome, and handsomely endowed, I seem to remember); me, of course, against the back wall; and then, to my right, was Marcus Steel—Steel, as he was simply known.

Even though, ever since prep school, we'd been in the same class, I knew him only slightly. I'd tended to avoid him in the past—perhaps because all those years back, when I could scarcely speak English, he'd been the one to tell Mr. Wolfe that people called me Woman. Kind of boy who enjoyed embarrassing you, bit of a sneak, bit of a loudmouth; but I'd almost forgotten those things about him. Slightly later, he'd figured among the clique of war-gaming fanatics with whom I'd travelled on the minibus to Waterloo and, during that trip, he'd seemed both to resent and be riveted by my exchanges with the Countess, because, although he was blessed with a skewering intelligence, his professed contempt for all things foreign (instilled, I suspect, by his parents—provincial doctors both) had dissuaded him from stooping to speak any foreign language. This seemed odd to me, given that he was an aspiring historian, and academically thorough; but he would have argued that he was on the side of good old Wellington, remember, not of Napoleon; and anyway, everyone spoke English, old chap: British Empire and all that. Yet his sudden nervous glimpse, first-hand, of a world beyond the Union Jack and Rule Britannia, and of my apparent ease in that other realm which he called Wogland, had made him sit up. He had seemed to eavesdrop, then, even on conversations which he could not hope to understand, to be taking note, to be wanting to learn fast, as if hoping to make up for wasted chances. He was, as I say, exceedingly bright, and, like all bright historians, a strategist at heart: eyes like a hawk, didn't miss a trick, always up to something. And yet, for all his brilliance in the classroom, he was (to his annoyance, I think) tone-deaf, without musical hope—which is why, of late, between my stints in the basement and the great garlands of time which I had spent in Clifford's company, Steel and I hadn't had very much contact.

By the third year, as I watched him unpack, he seemed altered almost beyond recognition. Though he'd always veered towards the lanky, Steel had, during the last months, and more markedly over the summer, suddenly sprouted to a shrill height, way over six foot, which I think embarrassed him, because, as if to counter this conspicuousness, he had grown subdued, toned himself down, and learnt to walk with a slight stoop, torso hunched like a saluki on the point of voiding its bowels. His clever head appeared, as a result of this sudden rise, now shrunken, to nestle like some forgotten collector's piece above the sloping shelf of his shoulder-line. His legs, meanwhile, went on for miles—you could only encompass them by means of a wide-angled glance—but they were brittle at the ankle, and clumsy. He was forever tripping up, and bumping into things, and going blast and buggeration. It was as if, in the throes of such a dramatic physical alteration, he were having to retrain himself to inhabit his new, stretched carapace. But then, we were all changing, having to adjust.

How was I?, he suddenly asked. Fine, I replied (a bit taken aback). Enjoy your summer? Sort of, I s'pose. Oh well, he went on, Mine was great; went to Scotland; lousy to be back, but I say, a relief to be in the same dorm as somebody civilized, we're thin on the ground, us chaps. I was so cheaply heartened in those days, so desperately grateful, that it shames me now to recollect the pleasure brought to me by that remark.

And I also remember thinking, as a result of it, that, if worst came to worst, and Clifford and I were doomed to be kept apart, Steel, though I doubted that he'd ever be my friend, might, at least, become an ally. We could respect one another.

If Clifford was my alter-ego, Steel was really my antithesis. Apart from his stature, which far exceeded mine, he was the palest creature imaginable. Grey veins, like winter boughs, branched out along his temples, and he had very fair hair—straight, and on the greasy side, cut almost in a bob, then swept back like a curtain—which often fell in a deep, diagonal fringe over his eyes. These, his eyes, were like pale blue marbles, heavily lidded and narrow, virtually feline, and would become shot with blood if he went anywhere near water. His nose, though fine, turned purple at the nostrils if he caught the slightest suggestion of a cold—a frequent occurrence, for there was a skinny unhealthiness about him. Perhaps he was anaemic: certainly his parents, the general practitioners, were forever plying him with fizzy vitamins. His ears protruded somewhat, and were transparent in the light, rife with tiny red vessels, like the egg yolks of my childhood. Long, abnormally long lobes, like those of an old woman.

I had often, in the past, sat at a desk behind him in class. His hands, as he wrote, were skeletal, with salient joints and knuckles, and when he answered questions, he spoke with his fingers splayed out, for emphasis. He treated our teachers like retards, and was not always mistaken in doing so. Steel's fingernails were square and soft and moonless; they looked almost gelatinous. You felt that you could have peeled them back and blown into their quicks without causing discomfort. But his most pronounced feature was, without a doubt, his mouth: this eclipsed all else about him, for his lips were vast and wide and shapeless, less sensual than anatomically curious, as if they'd been rolled over and stitched down, raw red lengths of blubber. They were grotesque, and had earned him, around the time when I was a Woman, the sobriquet Rubber Lips; but you tended to avert your eyes from the sight, not just because he was sensitive on the subject, and liable to lash out, but because there was something embarrassing, abhorrent, about that mouth. It made him look naked, worse than naked; more as if, were you to continue staring, the rest of his body might be pulled through the ever-expanding orifice and turned inside out.

He was the youngest in a triumvirate of brothers—all three, by accounts, fantastically clever, and all (doubtless as a result of medical prudence, rather than God-trusting *que será*) conceived at organized five year intervals. The eldest, a reputed prodigy, had already come down with a congratulated First from Oxford, where he had read history at New College. The second was up there currently, reading the same subject at the same place. But Steel, my one, though also destined to study history, planned to go (as indeed he would) to Magdalen— being, he said, above such trifles as nepotism. He would, in point of fact, eventually win a top scholarship to the college of his choice, though already, three years in advance of those entrance exams, our school had his academic laurels in mind. Steel was good news for my father's Alma Mater.

Despite his avowed contempt for inherited privilege, he, or his parents perhaps, had requested that he be furnished with the same school number as his eldest brother, which, astonishingly for a religious hothouse—but perhaps not, perhaps it added fuel to the sacred fire—was 666. Steel seemed to be proud of this numerical sequence, and not merely because it represented the sum-total of the roulette table. But I was myself too ignorant then of the Book of Revelation to see beyond the sexy catchiness of that trio, or to understand the demonic significance at the root of six hundred threescore and six, the Number of the Beast. Yet I suppose that, in a sense, he was suited to it, because, in the showers, I had observed (as you couldn't fail to do) that he was singled out, marked, by a concave thorax. You could have inserted your fist, firmly clenched and without difficulty, into the central cavity that hovered above his sternum, between his ribs and clavicle; and although this deformity used to make people grimace with squeamishness, they, he said, were stupid idiots, because his brother, the former owner of the significant number, had told him that in Greek mythology the feature of a hollowed breast spelt heartlessness, for which my future ally chose to read mental strength, courage. But anyway, just as Steel was above nepotism, so I tried to be above superstition. You had to be grown up about things. I mean, take another boy in our year, Curzon, who'd been born with webbed toes, but took—declaring that they attested to the purity of his lineage—an heraldic pride in them. We were all, I reminded myself, different, even though, whenever I saw the owner of those funny feet, I couldn't but think of the purity of the diced turtle-meat that went into my mother's Lady Curzon soup. It made me hungry just to think of it.

AFTER SUPPER THAT EVENING, I go to the rector's office. I knock on the door, hard and slowly, deliberately. He's expecting me, of course, and calls for me to come in. Blended wafts of incense and stale sweat envelop the room. He doesn't tell me to sit down, tells me instead that he'll come straight to the point, Moore, won't beat about the bush: Clifford (whom he calls Cross) has, he claims, been taken away by his parents to continue his studies in the States, has left. You're kidding, I blurt out. He corrects: I beg your pardon? I correct myself: Sorry, Father, I mean, I find that incredible. As, indeed, does he, he says, because the reason for my friend's abrupt departure, apart from his chronic home-sickness (which comes as news to me), seems to be that according to his parents (which means according to Clifford), certain pupils at our school are known to, to be . . . *involved,* as it were, with certain teachers. (Thumping silence.) Do I understand what he means? Slowly I say that I think that I might do. (I must be puce.) Can I shed any light on my friend's extraordinary allegation? I'm afraid that I can't, Father, sorry. He says that somehow he didn't imagine that I would. (I want to murder Clifford.) Look here, the rector continues, his Adam's apple prodding at his dog-collar, I happen to be perfectly aware of your reputation at prep school, but I prefer to treat all that, your chequered history, as lying in the past. (You said it, Father: Lying in the past, that's me all over.) He continues: I do not know precisely what Cross meant when he told his parents of Involvements between boys and teachers, but I want you to understand, and categorically, that you have caused the school, and caused me personally, the greatest embarrassment, and should even the faintest wind confirming your friend's claim happen to reach me, you will, you have my word, be out on your ear. Do I make myself plain? Yes, Father. You'll be asked to leave. Yes, Father.

The rector says that he intends to investigate the matter further, fully, and that I'd be well advised, from this point on, to watch my step and tread exceedingly carefully. My academic potential, he snorts, is insignificant next to the school's Repute (re-*pute,* a double whore, I muse). And warming to his homily he adds that I'm starting to display, he regrets to say, all the hallmarks of degeneracy, that he suspects me of being a congenital invert, that I seem to lack any conception of the meaning of sin, like some squalid libertine. Morals of an alley cat, he throws in. He extracts a plastic pouch of workman's tobacco, along with a roll-up gadget (like those employed by The Curse of Barbary to enjoy hashish), and plonks his props in front of him; but, as he fumbles in search of cigarette papers, he looks away, wincing with disdain out of the window. And then, as if encouraging me, the amoral alley cat, to leap through some invisible pet flap into the garden, he quietly tells me to get out, vamoose.

CLOSE SHAVE, you might think, but leaving that room only increased my panic. I went over the interview, time and again, reliving it and perishing. I could scarcely bear to think of Clifford beyond the turmoil into which his defection now threw me. Never in my life had I encountered such perfidy. It defied belief, defied speech. Of course I understood his desire to break free—God knows I shared it. Of course I saw that he was entitled to remain in Chicago with his father and the society beauty—in the process besmirching, if he so pleased, his poor abandoned mother's white frills, and his sisters as they scowled in the torpid heat—the better to explore shops and naughty cinemas in his adopted new city, and to patronize glamorous cocktail bars, even without me, and hang all our plans and all my dreams. That was his own business, private. But *Why*, I howled inwardly, had he decided to drag my secrets into the open, to threaten my safety for the sake of his grubby scheme? Why had he chosen to take me hostage, to stab our friendship, to trample on our confidences as if they'd been mere dead leaves? He had turned what I most valued, the only strength that I possessed, and just as I was starting to flourish, squarely against me, without a thought for the consequences, for the mess in which his traducement would land me. Was Clifford really that selfish, that callous, that deceitful? How could it be? How could I've let myself be taken in? My spirit was in torment, and further taunted by the ever-turning wheel of the rector's generalities: what had he meant by those creepy plurals—teachers, pupils? Were there others apart from me? Had Clifford mentioned more than just Mr. Wolfe? Had he guessed about Dr. Fox's teas, or had he made up stories just to get himself removed? Was my sabotage really the price of my lost friend's liberty? And now, I asked myself, now what was I supposed to do? Wilt from the fear? Wither in solitude? Thank you, Clifford. I never got over it.

My reaction was, to begin with, muddled, for while my instinct cursed the very name of Clifford, and wished him dead—preferably shot through the mouth by a silver bullet from his own precious pistol, snatched from his treacherous hand during a gangster brawl at a cocktail bar in Chicago—yet my stubborn heart could not but grieve for the loss of him, bemoan his heavy absence, ache with the palpable amputation which he had inflicted on me. Whenever I found myself alone, reduced to time which was optimistically described as free, I felt not so much free as sentenced to busying myself without him, forced to seek distraction, distraction, distraction. I remember even being driven to scour the fat book upstairs in the library, and resorting to the underlined bit about the twice-born man bathing in his own garments, as if those musty words were some mantra, and the book which contained them, a treasured talisman, as if this whole twist of fate had been some misunderstanding, some innocent prank gone hideously awry. And stroking the page where his finger had once skated with such life, I would fantasize that Clifford might yet prove to be the exception to the Christian rule and be restored to me from some mystical Hindu cloud. But then, when I stepped back, fed up, and slammed the hard covers shut, shoving the book into any old shelf, as he had done, I sometimes feared that the turn of my thoughts echoed the beginnings of what the French writers whom I was reading (in lazy translation) meant when they referred to the process of quietly going mad.

Nor did it take long for others to cotton on to the alteration which I had undergone—my reversal to insipid oneness—for, aside from the glaring evidence that my friend no longer swaggered beside me, his jacket billowing about his shoulders like the cape of some Cuban-heeled dandy, his manicured index jabbing the high air in front of anyone who dared to confront us, I myself drifted about, not as if halved by the severance, but as if evaporated entirely, like a phantom, like the very air at which he had once so vigorously jabbed. It wasn't that I'd lost one half of my identity: I seemed to have lost it entirely; and, just to exacerbate my reduction to my own colourless company, the consensus regarding Clifford's evanescence proved to be a blunt Good Riddance. In many ways, I was worse off than earlier, because whereas, before his luminous advent in my life, I'd striven to circumvent altercations with other pupils, later, after we'd become an established duo and been welded into inseparability, we'd almost welcomed the chance of locking horns with our enemies, had thought nothing of fanning grievances, had revelled in felling our aggressors with our lightning tongues. But now, as well as being deprived of his friendship, I was left to bear the brunt of those collaborative hostilities single-handedly, maimed, the strength gone out of me.

OF THE PUPILS in our year, only Steel, really, was sympathetic to my plight; and, just as he had changed physically, so, I began to realize, he had matured mentally. Ignoring his irksome jingoistic attitudes (which I suspected to be puerile affectation, soon to be discarded, like a pair of outgrown trousers), he otherwise strove to be liberal, broad of mind. In fact, a couple of times, as I mooched about Leviticus, or sat on my bed playing Patience before lights out, he did express, and carefully, his regret at what he understood must, for me, amount to a small mourning. He even advised that perhaps, in order to diminish my melancholy, I should write to my old best friend, my former BF, and endeavour to sustain our bond in the afterlife, as it were, beyond the petty world of school and all its confines; but though I simulated gratitude for his noises of concern, inwardly I scoffed at the uselessness of such a suggestion. He didn't know what he was talking about, didn't have a clue about my (broken) pacts and (shattered) fantasies with Clifford, which, if anything had ever done, had indeed soared beyond the confines of the petty world to which Steel was now alluding. Almost by definition, our dreams had been cast in grown-up, otherworldly venues—hot American cinemas, glamorous cocktail bars, great mansions bursting with black servants in full livery. And yet, though Steel couldn't possibly have been aware of these things, it was as if he possessed a six-six-sixth sense, suspected his own ignorance, and simply sought more facts, more details before he could properly prove himself to be of help to me, become my confidant—because, undaunted by my silence, he went on to enquire why it was that Cross, who'd seemed so integrated here, and so comfortable in my company, had suddenly gone off without so much as a by-your-leave to study in America, of all rum places. Everyone knew that the British educational system far surpassed that of the Yanks, who couldn't even spell, and weren't taught Latin, and had no sense of culture, and no history to speak of. So why the sudden change of plan? I told Steel that he'd have to ask Clifford's parents that (I left the rector well out of it), because I, at any rate, didn't have the foggiest. And then, as if lent confidence by my pretence at bewilderment, as if propelled by some looming hunch, he proposed that Clifford and I had been so, you know, so well matched, that . . . Cross hadn't been expelled by any chance, had he? We hadn't been caught out or something? Caught out how?, I replied, genuinely mystified. Come on, he persisted: kind of boys' stuff. (To me, boys' stuff sounded like games of conkers and swapping annuals and going rat-a-tat the whole time.) What the hell did he mean? He raised his eyes, just like Clifford after the twice-born man. Did he have, he hissed, to spell it out? He looked around, a little flustered, and then just repeated: boys' stuff—as in yours with Mr. Wolfe.

I let my eyes drift out of focus, avoiding his mouth. Look, he insisted, I'm not like all those other bigots, you know; each to his own, that's my attitude. I don't believe in being censorious. I don't cast stones. His blurred raw lips rounded into ominous vastness. I'm not some shockable prig, he reassured me; surely you realize that; after all, we've known each other for yonks, haven't we? I nodded that I supposed that we had. Exactly. And then he went on to confess that he'd presumed, though perhaps he'd been wrong to've jumped the gun—I didn't have to say either way, *he* wasn't prurient (one of his pet new adjectives, more recent than Censorious)—but he'd presumed that Clifford and I had been best friends in the proper sense of the word, the full sense, like in the Symposium, sort of bosom chums. And suddenly I felt as if I couldn't stand it a moment longer.

To be accused, in however liberal a guise, of having performed with Clifford the very acts which he, in order to effect his own removal, had claimed that I'd performed with someone else, seemed to spear me into a childish crisis. My corner felt too tight; I was choking up. So I took a deep breath and betrayed the betrayer, explaining to Steel, whom—it was true—*had* known me all those years, that far from Cross and I having been what he called bosom chums, we hadn't, as it turned out, been friends at all—full or otherwise—couldn't have been, because my supposed great pal (ha ha) had engineered his escape from school by telling his hypocrite of a father, who didn't live with his wife but was shacked up with some trollop in Chicago, of the rumour about me and Mr. Wolfe dating back to prep school. That creep had proved doubly true to his name, had double-crossed me through and through. And the rector, if you please, had already dragged me into his study and given me a bollocking about the whole thing; and now I felt as if I was living under a microscope, that my every tiny move was being monitored and analysed and ticked every two minutes. Cross was a complete judas.

Steel, who liked to boast that he'd heard it all before, admitted that he'd never heard anything like it. He called it beastly. His feline eyes spread far with disbelief; his fleshy great lips drooped to his chin. He didn't blame me for being browned off, not a bit, not now that he knew what he knew. Absolutely livid he'd be. Took back all his advice about Cross; filthy sneak; of course I mustn't write to him. Shocking, such a betrayal of friendship. And while I gathered up the cards of my unfinished game, and prepared to crawl into bed, he patted my shoulder and said never mind, I was probably better off without him, always best to know the truth about such people sooner rather than later. I'd make new friends, I'd see, stronger ones, stauncher. And then he told me not to worry, I could trust him implicitly, the story was safe with him, as houses. But it was, he agreed, unbelievable. Anyway, good night, and try to get some sleep. And in the morning, I felt that yes, a new bond had indeed been forged between myself and Steel, and I sensed that in some unspoken way, he would look over me, after me, that he would ensure that I was allowed the requisite peace, the necessary time to lick my wounds.

I WAS TO NEED IT. Because, only a further morning into that term, a letter, sent to me through the internal mail, was delivered to my desk during morning studies, before assembly, which was when the post monitor came round. The missive seemed to come from Mr. Wolfe, for

its envelope, though typed, displayed on its flap the emblem of my former prep school. Its contents, however, were less easily identifiable: A
single sheet of paper, unheaded, undated, and, furthermore, unsigned,
simply bore along its middle crease, precisely where it had been folded
into two, one single question, also typed—in loud, recriminatory capitals: WHAT HAVE YOU BEEN SAYING? The rector, I reasoned,
had obviously hauled him in and given him a grilling. I felt as if we were
back at the beginning, returned to the old climate of subterfuge and
sin. Well, I concluded: this time Mr. Wolfe could take care of his own
hide. I'd already saved his skin once, and he, at least, had suffered no
damage that I was aware of, for, not long after his time with me, he'd
been elevated to deputy head of the junior school. His precious bisexual career plainly remained on track, destined for didactic glitteriness.
He was no longer my responsibility. I no longer loved him; I had no
love to give, nor loyalty beyond indifference. And so, taking out a sheet
of my own inflated stationery—like the first fated sheet to Dr. Fox—I
wrote, in steady lower case script, the true word: n o t h i n g. And
unlike his tawdry single crease, I folded my sheet twice, into three sections, and licked the envelope securely, and even stretched, again unlike
him, to a postage stamp—newly decimal, first class, and blue as a bad
blazer. I printed his address in the most unrecognizable hand that I
could muster, and consigned my reply to Her Majesty's gracious mail.
And stuff him. Steel agreed that I'd done the right thing.

Dr. Fox, meanwhile, had been made aware of Clifford's departure,
and could scarcely conceal his relief. He became the most condoling of
creatures, claimed to be extremely sorry to hear about all this—for my
sake, naturally—yet his warm show of sympathy made me uneasy. We
had reverted to scones and tea (though, of course, without the cheesy
extras—which, like Clifford, were finished). But I didn't quite dare, as I
sat on the burgundy brocaderie, to discuss the nature of the whole
betrayal, the shock that it had given me, because I remained unsure as
to whether Dr. Fox himself might not have been dragged into Clifford's story—pupils, teachers, plurals. And this, in turn, made me wonder whether the rector might not already, just as he'd presumably done
Mr. Wolfe, have approached Dr. Fox, and whether the latter might not
now be putting up, to sound me out, a pretence of ignorance, or

whether he had braved the ostensible interview with his customary ease: a blink, perhaps; a sneer; and then: What utter piffle, Rector, really; that Cross boy seemed like bad news from the moment he got here: peculiar background, yes? Parents divorced, am I right in thinking? And that would have been it. Albany, Albany, you never knew it; but you, like Tadzio, had it easy.

In answer to my earlier question about the departed Clifford, I, like the Querie by the Lido, did wilt; I did wither; I don't deny it. And yet it was as if, the deeper I withdrew, the more singled out I became among my peers. With my self-inflicted isolation, the others must have sniffed the renewed tenuousness of my position. And though I stood, very still, in the middle of my small clearing, which was the clearing of lone silent misery, and though they could not properly see me, yet they were, I could tell, on the trail of me, on to my scented shadow and rendered high-blooded by it, like hunting dogs which, in advance of the season, have been starved for weeks. I could sense them steadily drawing nearer, not quite baying for my gizzards, yet growling and panting as they ran across the fields around me, the fields of ordinary activity. And they seemed, furthermore, to grow fiercer and louder and wilder as they raced into the forest immediately surrounding me—the thick forest of our collective puberty—bent on tracking me down and ultimately getting me. Not to finish me off. That was never their objective. Just for the sport of it.

Did I give in? Of course I did, repeatedly, serially, and mainly—since they represented my most pressing anxiety—to the others in Leviticus. One by one by one, I relieved them: the middling scientist; the admiral's son (frequently); even, between games of chess, Mr. Popularity. And once, though it was all passed off as horseplay, or wrestling, or war games or something, Steel. I'd become like my own hostage, there for the taking—in the night lavatory, over the basin in the dormitory, in the deserted locker room, out in the fields. Wherever those boys thought it safe and convenient, I brought their hectic zips to glutinous fruition. And though it was hardly a case of notching up conquests, those acquiescences of mine did provide me with an effective means of gagging my fellow criminals, of ensuring that they could no longer be out-and-out enemies, not overtly, for into my ready hands and mouth they had, they knew, fed me warm shots of ammunition.

Yet as they tucked their shirt-tails back in, and flicked the dollops of slime from their sticky guilty fingers, or rubbed these dry, without a word—even helping themselves, sometimes, to my handkerchief—I did reflect on what a difference Clifford had made to me, of how none of this would be happening if he had stayed beside me. And then I also thought, as if for exoneration from my cheapness, as if in search of absolution, of the beautiful men whom I'd encountered at high noon in the sea. Those watery gods of my youth, decked about with wreaths of seaweed, those miraculous lifesaving kissers—while my parents slept their untroubled siestas in separate bedrooms.

In separate bedrooms along the way from Leviticus, there were twin brothers, named Nye—Thomas and Timothy. Because their parents hadn't thought of simplifying their lives by furnishing the pair with different first initials, nor bothered with second names at all, which I thought stylish, the Nye boys were, so far as I was aware, the only pupils, who, in order to be distinguished, were granted the privilege, when it came to roll-calls or rotas or lists, of having their first names included: Nye, Tom; Nye, Tim. It made them sound nocturnal, like night owls. Yet for all the system's attempts at telling them apart in theory, they couldn't, in practice, have been more different, less identical.

Tom was tall and dark, and, though currently pimply, it was obvious that he enjoyed, both in the school and out of it, the benefit of greater popularity. He was athletic, lean, and headed for handsomeness. Tim, by contrast, was at least six inches smaller, at least six inches rounder, dull-haired, and outwardly uninteresting. You sensed that he was the runt of the meagre litter, and that having been robbed in the womb of his fair share of nutrition, he now fed himself like a fiend in response to some vestigial struggle to live. He always carried a packet of something incredibly sweet about him, like the half-melted corpses of white chocolate mice, or lumps of Kendal mint, or chunky dice of coffee fudge or, rattling about in a tin, shards, like blades, of Harrogate toffee. Probably in order to compensate for his brother's more favourable position in the galaxy, he was, of the two, the louder—zany, wry, larky to me. If Tom was the straight-guy, Tim was the funny-man, the clown of the family. When he cackled, it was like unleashing a loony. How close they were emotionally, I do not know; but if some bond did exist between those twins, it must have been telepathic, because, during the time that I knew them, I never once saw them exchange a single syllable. They existed almost too separately. Tom had lots of chums, sporty establishment types, while Tim appeared to have fewer, and weirder ones, among whose number, I, peripherally, figured.

I suppose that, in the wake of Clifford's desertion, I must have seen more of Tim Nye than in previous years, made a more concerted effort to be sociable in my quest for renewal. He owned a vast collection of tapes by seedy-looking vocalists who mystified me; I remember because he made a crusade of trying to correct my ignorance on what he regarded as serious popular music—music which, he said, required committed listening. He would lend me fantastically depressing songs by some gravel-voiced balladeer who had driven his guitar teacher to top himself, songs about being fed tea and oranges (*awe-ringes,* the singer called them, which is probably what Clifford would *waaand-up doin'* if he didn't watch that slackened gob of his), and about having no love to give, and about Jesus knowing for certain that only drowning men could see him. It made me, for all of Nye's goodwill, want to fall asleep, get away from it. But there was one particular number which I did have difficulty ignoring, because, in it, Mr. Gravel Voice, who sounds like he's shattered after too many amphetamines, goes: Father, change my name; the one I'm using now, it's covered up with fear and filth and cowardice and shame. And that, for some reason, seemed to ring a bell.

Whenever Nye, helmeted by his ear-phones, heard some new lyric which he considered to be of significance, but which generally I found to be impenetrable, he would scrawl it on a scrap of paper and, if I wasn't in Leviticus, leave it on my bed, or sometimes tuck it for safety under my pillow, which irritated me. It felt invasive. Recently, over a dozen years later, I discovered one such cryptic message in a folder from that murky period. Written along an oblong, in green adolescent felt-tip, are the following words: And another pretty woman, she was leaning in her Darkened door, she cried to me, hey, why not ask for more.

I still can't make out why Nye decided to darken that door with a capital D, nor why he omitted the question mark which belonged at the end of the line; but I also wonder whether he wasn't trying to suggest, rather than request, something. And yet, at the time, any such subtlety would have eluded me: I wouldn't have heard it: there was too loud a wind in my head, for I was myself too wrapped up in the waves of a French song that brought Clifford to mind, a fantasy woven into my reality, delivered by a man who, like Mr. Gravel Voice, talked his way through the music, but whose rendition—flooded by strings and wailing trumpets and back-up girls going da-da-da—seemed to hold me in thrall to its repetitive banality. I suppose that it must have been the European hit of the previous August, my unwitting anthem to the unimaginable loss of Clifford. A bad prose poem, really:

> *Tu sais, je n'ai jamais été aussi heureux que ce matin-là. Nous marchions sur une plage un peu comme celle-ci. C'était l'automne, un automne où il faisait beau, une saison qui n'existe que dans le nord de l'Amérique. Là-bas on l'appelle l'Eté Indien—mais c'était tout simplement le nôtre . . . Et je me souviens très bien de ce que je t'ai dit ce matin-là, il y a un an, il y a un siècle: On ira où tu voudras quand tu voudras, et l'on s'aimera encore lorsque l'amour sera mort . . . Aujourd'hui . . . je pense à toi: Où es-tu? Que fais-tu? Est-ce que j'existe encore pour toi? Je regarde cette vague qui n'atteindra jamais la dune. Tu vois: comme elle, je reviens en arrière; comme elle, je me couche sur le sable et je me souviens des marées hautes, et du soleil, et du bonheur qui passait sur la mer, il y a une éternité, il y a un siècle, il y a un an. On ira où tu voudras quand tu voudras . . .*

Except, of course, that we didn't. He went off without me. And those questions—*Où es-tu? Que fais-tu? Est-ce que j'existe encore pour toi?*—seemed to take me back, of all peculiar things, to my time with Mam'zelle, to our Eurovision chant, to that final couplet which had been mine to yell out, ten years earlier, in the bath: *Et toi, et toi qui j'aimais, Qu'as-tu fait de toi? Qu'as-tu fait sans moi? / Et moi, moi qui t'ai perdu, Qu'ai-je fait de plus? Qu'ai-je fait de tant de bonheur?* To which there was no possible answer other than to lie on my bed in Leviticus, and turn to my side, and face the wall which had been the waves and the beaches and the summers of my childhood, when I first delivered myself to

Mr. Wolfe's inexplicable love. And then, I would try not to cry. Try to grow up.

OUR YEAR MASTER, though he looked like a man of the cloth, was a mongrel. The church should have muzzled him. His temper, even concealed beneath the limp black wings of a clerical habit, was rabid. I took pains never to look at him directly, not just because he was unattractive—which he irredeemably was, being afflicted with colourless moles on his sallow cheeks, a snout for a nose, pointed ears, and perpetually grimy hair (often scraped across, in public, with a broken plastic comb which festered in a pocket at his backside)—but also because he seemed resentful of the unsolicited eyeball. You feared that even a sidelong glance from the wrong quarter might ignite his ferocity. He was intellectually pretentious, intellectually inadequate, and sexually (you sensed) hampered. I pictured his penis as salamanderish.

He liked to suggest, in the wry, roundabout way that priests sometimes have, that once upon a time he'd been a man of the world, oh yes, a *bon viveur,* and that there existed no beverage, or narcotic, or position in the (unexpurgated) *Kamasutra* which he hadn't, at some point in his agnostic history, sampled. There was a whiff of Damascus about him; certainly he was a convert, a late one. He strutted about in scuffed old winkle-pickers, no longer black, closer to dusty charcoal now, with natty laces to the side—less, you suspected, as an act of sartorial penance than as if those pointed embarrassments, which wouldn't have tempted even the lowlier among our domestics, attested to his spivvy past, to his days spent scooting through la dolce vita. He would, you felt, have known hookers biblically; but nor could you help feeling that those very hookers would have sniggered as he sauntered back into the cobbled penumbra. Getting it up wouldn't have been his forte: his forte was lager; or, if he was lucky, brandy. He referred to his charges as lads, and was keener on the discussion of rugby tackles and skirt, as he called women, than ever on matters of doctrine, or conscience, never mind the business of loving. His (infrequent) addresses from the pulpit were rife with sporting analogies, and he celebrated the snappiest of Masses, as if the sacrament of the Eucharist were a steeplechase, and the rite of consecration a hurdle to be cleared. His legs were bowed.

On the subject of discipline, you suspected that he, like my father, rued the demise of the birch; but, as if to make up for this sadness, he was an undisputed wow with the ferula. He shredded the flesh from people's palms: a mere few strokes into his discipline, and he had drawn your blood. He didn't so much breathe as simmer; there was broiling fire in his gut; you could smell its fumes rising to the light of his dry gullet, ulcerous and acrid. So you will understand why, even though he treated me like a snotty, very silly shopgirl, selling Joy to her friends in the hiatus before baring her shoulders to society, I didn't think it wise to attempt to disabuse him of his assumption. He was everything that I reviled. But for the duration of that year, we were stuck with one another. And I was the stucker.

Whatever subject it was that he attempted to teach, and my memory murmurs elementary Mathematics, this was never to the top stream, so, at least on my academic timetable, I was spared the benefit of his snarling mediocrity. When he herded us together for impassioned little pep-talks on adolescent mores and matters of manly propriety (such as not wenching out of bounds, and not getting sozzled in the village), I would always sit as far back as decency allowed, or my position seemed to require—like one of the kitchen minions—while he paid tribute to our latest sporting victors and tried to humiliate boys whom he suspected not to be living up to the school's high principles. My father's Alma Mater didn't take kindly to being let down, not one bit, my lad. He spoke with his thumbs hooked into his belt loops, like a hoodlum, and swayed on the spot as he did so, rocking back and forth from his heels to the curled tips of his winkled toes. The whole motion made you slightly queasy, like a black-and-white film about the warring British navy. The hem of his cassock was torn at the rear, as if lashed by a storm at sea, and splattered with mud from the shores of the rugger pitch. His shiny trousers were too short, and overly tight at the ankle, as if they sought to hark back to the period of his younger antics; and peeping from the past, above his shrunken socks of patterned nylon, you could glimpse gaps of waxy calf. But I tended to be spared his lower details at such gatherings, for, even as he stood on the podium, which was his preference—otherwise a table would suffice— the stems of his worsted legs were invariably decorated by the budding, bobbing, variegated heads of those who preferred to have their characters developed closer to his wisdom.

ONE EVENING LEADING up to Christmas, the year master caught me coming out of Nye's dormitory, where I'd gone to return one of those tapes of important popular music. My friend hadn't been in—probably off for his after-supper ciggy—so I left the cassette (which had its owner's name safely stuck onto it in plasticized tape—its letters, like bullets, shot out by one of those little pistols which were then considered cool gadgets of stationery) on his bedside chair. And I scrawled a brief covering message on a pad, which, along with a small torch, lived there. I think that Nye had begun to annotate his dreams around that time, and to dredge obscure poems from his lyrical subconscious stream. Anyway, my note just said: Thanks, enjoyed it—any more? But my handwriting, which in those days felt like my sole permissible licence to detach myself from the italicized rabble, was easily recognizable, provocatively florid and too large, too strident, too full of false confidence. And although the year master had feigned not to see me as I returned to Leviticus, I, on the other hand, did notice him creeping into Nye's empty dormitory, which was called Exodus. The tosser in the winkle-pickers was probably on the look-out for some sweaty jock to share a can of lager with him in his room.

This room, I now discover (for it is I, not the sweaty jock, whom, it appears, he wants to see), is enormous and lugubrious, large as a dormitory for six of us, with a double-aspect corner view, beheld through grimy Gothic windows, of the school church (a Catholic pauper's imitation of one of the finest Anglican chapels in Cambridge) and, to the other side, of the gardens into which, at the start of term, the rector had seemed to wish me to vamoose. The year master tells me to sit on a grubby club-chair of moth-eaten moquette with balding deco patterns and obnoxious springs. Thank you, Father.

But oh dear me, how to sit? Do so hate to make decisions. I could pose like the jock of his dreams, my chest thrust out and proudly, my hands alluding to my priapic genitals, my knees spread to the far edges of his corner view; or like the pretty lady, grown too weary to continue leaning on the darkened door of Nye's fantasies; or as if, swathed in

Joy, my shoulders had already been bared for the benefit of society; or like the psychiatric patient whom my father would never have countenanced; or like some teasing young tutor of English, muse to a salivating notary. But, of course: none of these comes naturally. Instead, I sit like my mother. Imagine: I dare to cross my legs; I rest one of my elbows on the arm of the chair, letting my hand flourish in mid-air as if it were entertaining a scented handkerchief. I wish I were bedecked in Clifford's glistering jewels. I allow my wrist to wilt, to flop, as if the bone had been extracted from me in childhood, or as if Yahweh had never furnished me with one, not even for the glory of Onan. I gaze at my interlocutor like a fluttering *ingénue,* charmed by the surprising privilege of his attention, as if half-expecting him, at any moment, to thrill me with a proposal of marriage, as if he were seeking to declare something so precious and so vital that it required subtle coaxing, the wiles of a chic young woman. But inwardly, I do feel slightly insulted; for the year master, already wedded to his vows of poverty, couldn't possibly afford me.

Poor man is being timid, I can tell, because, to start with, he says nothing: just picks up a piece of paper from his desk, as if it were inscribed with his forthcoming speech (the climax to our courtship, which has been nothing if not whirlwind), and glances at it—trying to memorize it, I rather think. But as he turns the paper to face me, and holds it up to the light, I recognize my own recognizable hand, swirling and curling with the green of Nye's adolescent felt-tip; and now I realize precisely what this memo is, and where the priest has found it. He wants me to explain its contents, which he describes as thoroughly incriminating. I would have thought that they were self-explanatory, but he thinks: far from it, what exactly *is* this stuff about enjoying it meant to mean? It means that I enjoyed the tape which Nye had lent me (obviously). Oh really? Yes, really. (I may be sounding too familiar: The year master, let's not forget, is not, as yet, affianced to me.) Well, he doesn't believe me, not for an instant. His voice, as he leans against his desk—not, I regret to say, like some self-effacing suitor, but like a greasy spiv, pressing his plastic comb into his bony rear—is deepening, growing harsher and more bestial. As they say in America, and doubtless as Clifford will soon be saying: here is the thing: the year master reckons that I'm pestering Nye, that I have designs on him, that I'm a dirty little pervert seeking to debauch another pupil. He calls me a piece of shit. (Clifford, can you believe this? Can't you help me?) On and on, round and round, over and over goes Christ's ordained minister, fulminating as if from his pulpit, and rising to his pointed feet; and yet I, notwithstanding his mounting fury, can feel myself swelling from within, swelling with the strength and unholy impudence of Clifford, as if his fearless spirit were suddenly being poured into the vessel of my fear, like an agent of alchemy; and the moment that I hear a pause in the year master's diatribe, and even though I've only caught random syllables of his lunacy, I find myself replying (as I did to the commander) without hesitation, being hoist with my own petard. And what I say to this great frothing imbecile is: Actually, Father, I prefer the attentions (I may even have said favours) of adults. And then, to drive the knife right in, I add: grown men, *mature* ones. Whereupon, the priest (as they say in America, but as they properly do in Hades) freaks right out. He loses his mind.

It can be a challenge to view the familiar with new eyes, to try to reappraise it as its creator, or first purchaser, might have done, to invest it with new value, new life. Yet, faced as I am by the year master, I now find no difficulty in rising to such a challenge; indeed, I lack an alternative, for though he doesn't directly confront me, the man is suddenly beside himself, transmogrified, howling like a common mongrel. And I, with a self-protective jolt, have backed into my chair; and my ringless fingers are gripping at its moquette arms; and my legs have uncrossed, and sharpish, and are ready to run for cover, less like the silken legs of some desirable maiden than those of a great unsung sprinter, some wasted champion from my father's glory days at the Alma Mater.

The year master, the while, is haranguing God knows what, yelling at some repulsive mystery. He makes no sense whatever, but I bet that his reverberating roars can be heard outside. He just seems to rail in the abstract, at the apparent putrefaction around him, as if he, not I, had suddenly seen it with new eyes, smelt it with a new snout, the stench of his engulfing yeast and damp, had awoken as if to the ghost of some old provincial public house after hours. Just as the woman crying out for Tadzio could so easily have been my mother, so, now, the year master could, within the mental scheme of things, be my erstwhile suitor, thrashing about in the face of my refusal, wailing at his discovery that my heart belongs to some other daddy, baying for a duel even, like my grandmother's hapless young infantry officer. In Clifford's cocktail bar, I would, at this point, have had to request another tequila slammer, but here, there isn't so much as a measly sip of lager to be had, not even to quench the worthy thirst of a frustrated Olympic decathlete. If I had the means, or my father's Catholic contacts, I would commission the year master's exorcism—for his own good, you understand, like army camp—and instanter. I would see to it that the raging tyke were dowsed with holy water and slung into one of the school's holy hides. But I can't; and nor is the battle yet over.

IT ENDED WITH *The Battleship Potemkin* and five thousand words on the œuvre of Eisenstein. I told you that the mongrel was pretentious. And as I left his kennel—only to bang into the approaching sweaty jock for whom he had really been hankering—my first task became trying to memorize the incomprehensible subject of my chastisement. Back in Leviticus, Steel, who was as astonished as I about this whole rumpus over unlikely Nye, and who, with his skewering intelligence, knew about most matters, said that it wasn't Einstein at all, but Ei-*sen*-stein—was I thick or something?—and that the essay which I'd been told to write had nothing whatever to do with the theory of relativity, nor with any real-life battle, but with a film, Moore, a film from *ages* back, before the bloody talkies, a classic of the genre, in black and white—which I, needless to say, had never seen, not even in the days when Mr. Wolfe, with such great care, had manned the dark projections of my past. I was up a gum tree, or was it Shit Creek without a paddle?

I resorted to the library. I rummaged through all the books on which I could lay my hands. There wasn't a paragraph, never mind five thousand words, to be had on the elusive great moviemaker. I wandered away from the meagre shelf devoted to film and theatre; and then, by the grace of Shiva (third god of the Hindu trimurti, the destroyer and reproducer), I came across a snippet, in some dictionary of Russian biography, which said that Sergei Eisenstein had described his life as intense, joyous and tormented. Born to a wealthy family, his secure childhood was darkened by a tyrannical father. Rejecting the "almost hysterical" religion and comfortable expectations of his class, he became an atheist, a thinker, and an artist whose ironic wit and style matched the substance of his ideas—a summary which, like the lyrics of Mr. Gravel Voice, when he had asked to change his name, seemed to ring with truthful resonance. It inspired me.

I went over to Exodus, and, though concealing from Nye the real reason why I found myself in trouble (an admission which would have proved just too excruciating for both of us), I invoked his help with my punishment, which had to be completed, and delivered back to the kennel, within forty-eight hours, before lights out. Just as Nye was keen on important popular music, it turned out that he fancied himself a bit of a movie buff, and was fond of racing through the vowels of that most daunting of hexasyllabic nouns: Cinematography. He confirmed that the subject of my essay was indeed a crummy old film, obscure and silent, and that the task wasn't going to be easy, but he seemed to have a sounder grasp of the topic than—even after a whole year of swotting—I could ever have had.

He knew, for instance, and from the top of his madcap head, that *The Battleship Potemkin* had, not once, but twice, been voted best film of all time, though he added that this accolade meant absolutely nothing, and that it was unlikely to assist my plight; that it had been made in 1925 (not long after my grandmother's infantry officer had died); that it lasted some 69 minutes (the length of a respectable Mass, unlike the mongrel's full-pelt religious travesties) and that its soundtrack had been composed by Eisenstein's friend and frequent collaborator, Prokofiev, whose Orthodox name, like that of the director, was also (he paused—for the glamour of it) . . . *Sergei*. Nye was being a show-off now. Sergeis, I said, were two a penny, or rouble, or whatever they had in St. Petersburg. Which, the expert snapped back, was a complete irrelevance, and the place, anyway, was called Leningrad: did I want his help or didn't I? Christ, I groaned, trying to avoid an argument. A film about a mutiny on a battleship. No wonder the year master swayed and rocked about, the great seafaring prat. But I only had two days in which to acquit myself; otherwise, I may as well be drowned.

Like Dr. Fox when he sought to raise the finer points of our acquaintanceship from the music basement up to his private quarters, I now donned my thinking-cap. I thought of Clifford. Clifford would never have buckled under this pressure. He, the child of fortune, would always, somehow, have won out. And in the night, at lonely last, it came to me: the solution. I would *buy* my way to victory, not fight it, and decided to this end that I'd invest the remainder of my spoils from the notary and the girl with the harelip—my ill-gotten tutorial gains. Because words, I told myself, were merely words, and talk, God knew, was cheap; but money—money sings out like a great aria. Therein lay the route to my salvation, in lyrical pieces of silver.

It all took a bit of haggling and cajoling, of course, but in the end, after breakfast, Nye finally consented to my proposal and agreed that for the equivalent of four weeks' pocket money he, not I, would write the deadly essay for the mongrel; though he did, like a whore without so much as a darkened door now, demand half of the payment upfront—as a token of my goodwill, he argued. He got it, no problem. But once this first small deal had been clinched, I seemed to become ambitious, hungry for further glory, and decided that after Nye had done his bit for my cause I wouldn't even deign to transcribe his five thousand dreary words on the *oeuvre* of bloody Eisenstein. Clifford would never, on principle, have done so—if only to spite the mongrel.

And thus it was that I, like Pythagoras, that demigod of basic Mathematics, suddenly thought of good old Hardy, the prodigious foreskin retractor, devotee of Elgar and self-styled nobleman who, in our early days, had proved my (thwarted) rival in the affections of Mr. Wolfe, but who, more pertinently, in view of my current predicament, happened also to be, you may recall, a forger of some renown. Since our time at prep school, Hardy had, in point of fact, defected from the camp of cavaliers (like Dr. Fox) to that of roundheads (like Mr. Wolfe), having pressed and pestered his family doctor so relentlessly that, once the befuddled medic had been ground down, the imaginary patient succeeded (and on the National Health, would you believe) in having himself circumcised—not *ritually,* he had grandiloquently apprised me—purely for cosmetic reasons, which, he felt, were more legitimate. Because, despite his exhibitions of yesteryear, he had, in maturity, come to the realization that foreskins were Ectually, he said, ugly superfluous anatomical extras, and, therefore, best excised. I don't, however, think that his wobbly neck could as yet have received much in the way of surgical attention, because, when he spoke, he still tilted his head a fraction, like a slightly deaf (or was it insouciant) madonna.

Hardy turned out to be exorbitant, though in a sense I couldn't blame him, for Clifford and I had given him a bit of a rough ride in the recent past; and vengeance, I could see, was not exclusively mine to exact. But first I had to make him swear, on his (ugly) mother's life, never to reveal to *anyone,* least of all to Nye, his fee for imitating my handwriting—a calligraphy which he evinced the smirking insolence to describe as problematic. His price (the grasping pig) was in excess of a full term's pocket money, too disgraceful to divulge, a rip-off if ever there was one; but, by this stage, I was beyond thoughts of beating him down or striking bargains, because although I was the undisputed mastermind, boss, bankroller and godfather of the whole scheme, I also had to acknowledge to myself that decent forgers in this dump were at a bit of a premium. So I availed him of one of my old exercise books—English compositions, I imagine, which contained the neatest samples of my writing—and instructed him to meet Nye-Tim during break in the library, where the two of them would, throughout the next two days' snatches of free time, work in conjunction—Hardy replicating, in his artful approximation of my hand, whatever resulted, page by stultifying page, from Nye's polysyllabic cinematographic studies. In the event, though all turned out without mishap, the great faker didn't prove himself to be quite as fabulous as he liked to make out, for he'd been sloppy, I discovered, about my e's, having elected to emulate only one single style, whereas I liked to lay claim to at least three such, adopted or rejected depending on which I felt looked best at whichever point in a given word the need for that letter happened to arise.

Once the commission was complete, and submitted to me for approval, I insisted on crossing all the zeds myself, which naughty Hardy had not done; and then, I paid off my accomplices, placing their wages in separate envelopes, as my mother paid her servants—although Hardy was vulgar enough to count his earnings on the spot, with his stooping, spastic neck turned away from his collaborator. Still, despite the offence implicit in this gesture, and even though I remained entirely ignorant about the contents of those seventeen pages of drudgery, the challenge was met and duly delivered to the kennel (slipped under the door without a sound, to avoid the danger of growling) doubtless to merit not so much as a glance. But my dignity emerged, at least in my own eyes, intact from the fiasco, and the year master, thanks be to Shiva, wasn't to address another word to me, not one, not even with an uncrossed z, ever again in my school career. Yet his madness had cost me a small fortune, the squandering of which I was soon enough to rue—and to rue far more sorely than anyone ever rued the demise of any bloodied birch.

THE LIFE TO which I returned after this punitive interlude was quiet, spectral, like the life of a room which, though host in the past to colour and hilarity, has since, for protection during a long absence, been submerged beneath a sea of dustsheets. I retained, of course, the vague contours of my past, the vestiges of my inverted attitudes, yet I suppressed the character which had once animated them, such character as had been moulded and warmed and nourished during my sunny season with Clifford, my Indian summer. I needed time to adjust now, in order to release him from my consciousness and learn to survive, alone, through the old landscape of shadows, in order to manage through the drought, or frost, or ashes—the moribund state into which, more than his quick-fire betrayal, his eternal absence had cast me.

I also began to avoid Nye, not because I no longer had time for him (how could I not, when all that he had ever shown me had been his eccentric and, in retrospect, edifying brand of fellowship?) but because I feared a repetition of my altercation with the mongrel. Hardy, however, I didn't avoid: he I cut dead without a qualm, both because (other than genitally) he remained what he had always been, which was a leering oleaginous creep, and because, regardless of what further punishments fate might have yet tucked up its sleeve for me, the one thing which I knew with certainty was this: that I should never again be able to afford the pomp and circumstance of that prohibitive scrivener's underhand criminality. Occasionally I saw Steel, and spoke to him, in class or in Leviticus, but while the place of my dashed hopes and dreams, that region of my brain which housed my spirit, continued to float in limbo, waiting one day to be roused from its state of gloomy abeyance, to be relieved of its dustsheets, I mostly took myself to neutral spaces, to safe but hazy areas which bore as little connection to school life as, indeed, they did to my derelict existence during the holidays, places like the music basement. I still escaped for meals to Dr.

Fox's room, for I'd grown to dread the ordeal, on my own, of the refectory; and he, Dr. Fox, despite my surly refusal ever again to feast on his naked obesity, did continue—with remarkable forbearance, when you think of it—to lavish upon me the privilege of his superior groceries. It is possible that his care was prompted by a lingering sense of wariness, but I somehow doubt it, because, as I explained earlier, circumstances, whatever our original positions, had by now drawn us into a semblance of friendship—which was to survive, if not forever, at least beyond the conclusion of my dreadful education. I think that on balance his loneliness probably outweighed his lust. I know that mine did; of that, I have no doubt.

But there *were* occasional snatches of respite, privileges extended to us as the year assumed a lull (in the middle term, when most of the days were dark, almost Scandinavian), nocturnal chances to venture beyond the system and broaden our dimming horizons. We were allowed, for instance, to sign up for extra-curricular evening classes at some neighbouring industrial town, and most people opted, predictably enough, for car maintenance, or mechanical engineering (subjects held up as manly, and all held in the same building, a former warehouse)—followed by a quick pint at a nearby pub, which provided pupils with the opportunity to bump into strange women on the lounge side. I would certainly, had Clifford still been with me, have opted for flower arranging, and brought my trophies back to Leviticus, and debated with the teacher—more likely, in these parts, to be a woman than a Querie, but still—what constituted good floral taste and what didn't; and yet, on my own, and without the chance of a cocktail bar to deck in my arid future, the prospect didn't seem so enticing.

So instead, I enrolled on a course of shorthand and typing, and, just as predictably, turned out to be the only pupil to do so, which disgruntled the bus driver, who, as a consequence of my poofy pretensions to become some kind of girl Friday, used to have to ferry me to a quite different part of town, nowhere near a pub, and hang about for me until I was done. There was, in fact, an irony about my secretarial penchant, since those weekly classes brought me, unlike the rest of my contemporaries, into a place of exclusively female company—though this was admittedly of a more serious disposition than the bosomy lovelies who nightly tottered for a quick one at the local. *My* women wore sensible spectacles, and very hard hair indeed, and their pencils were sharp as intravenous needles. They would never, you sensed, have stepped into a public house, not even for the pleasure of a genteel crème de menthe—vigorously frappé, and served in a lady-sized brandy glass—much less for a tequila slammer. They seemed, if anything, sick of places where faithless husbands guzzled the week's wages in one evening, and you suspected that behind their aspirations to office life lay not so much a vague quest for distraction as clear plans for a safer existence, beyond the vagaries of matrimony. Those women, my father would have said—as if they'd been cave dwellers, or gypsies—were quite misguided, obviously not Catholic; their marriages lacked proper religious grounding; that was the problem: no real staying power; no gumption. Divorce was too easy a sin. (Was it, Clifford?)

There were also trips further afield, to theatres in the cities—Sheffield, Manchester, Liverpool—and to concerts of classical music. I would sign up, and blindly, to join any such expedition, regardless of whether the play or programme advertised was of interest to me, and irrespective of whether later, during the actual performance, I fell asleep, which sometimes I did. Because those forays seemed to me—at very long last—like flights beyond the teasing, glinting viaduct of my earlier imprisonment, like chances to sample a new, third universe—not school, not home, but real living. I wouldn't claim (because of the handicap of travelling *en troupe*) that it was actually civilized, but it did provide me with a foretaste of freedom: of liberated women, contracepted, unbrassièred and flashing with embroidered glints of mirror; of men with thick manes, in tapestry hipsters; of couples kissing under flickering chandeliers; of obvious, unembarrassed Queries, dressed in devoré, wound about in foulards, and eyed with liner—touches, then, of hope to me.

If you wore a decent coat, and turned up the revers to hide your uniform, waiters at the crush bar, rushed off their feet, didn't have time to tell that you were underage for the purchase of liquor; and if you stood on your toes and lowered your voice a bit, and could afford it, you could immerse yourself in a glass of wine, wander off, and disown your peers. When you went into the Gents, you sometimes met with elongated looks of approval, of embraces that might have been; and, despite the backdrop of crackled Victorian porcelain, and despite the offence of bleach, it felt more romantic than seedy. But the journeys back to school were, in my view, the loveliest part of the experience—balmy, dreamy—for with the swell of symphonies still ringing in your ears and the lights of the bus switched off within and half of the boys already asleep, you, you could just gaze into the luminous night and fantasize that you were on your way somewhere quite else, that you were set on some fantastical journey, full of promise and stars—to Chicago, to the healing waters of Buthanatha, to the land of milk and honey.

THE FIRST TIME that it happened was after one such outing. I'd come back from a concert feeling mildly resuscitated, optimistic even. I remember half-humming some lingering passage from that night's closing encore, a sweeping minor-key rhapsody. Our return to our respective dormitories—it being long after lights out—had, always and by very strict order, to be both speedy and mute. Absolutely no talking; even to whisper was a risk. Any trouble, or official complaint from some sneak to the effect that you'd disturbed him, and you were barred from all further trips—a fate which earlier in the term had befallen Nye, when he became embroiled, incautiously close to where the mongrel happened to be prowling, in a disagreement about some absurd production of Ionesco which we had been to see that evening. But Nye had, in fact, been only the first in a line of casualties; half a dozen others had, since, fallen; so that the rest of us, and I very particularly, took this rule about silence seriously, stopped humming. My routine, to avoid the possibility of being shopped by anyone in my dormitory, was to get into my pyjamas in the dark, turn down my bed, and then head off to the night lavatory for a last-minute pee, and to brush my teeth over the small, rather grubby, basin in there.

I was still groping about the shadows of Leviticus, changing out of my uniform, when, as I fumbled for my pyjamas under my pillow, I felt what at first I took to be one of those invasive cassettes which Nye sometimes left hidden—but which, once picked up, felt too light somehow, and its shape not quite right, and made of cardboard rather than plastic, more like a packet of cigarettes than a tape, but empty. Some prank, no doubt; someone treating my bed as a bin—how funny. The remainder of the dormitory were all out for the count. Nothing to be done; no one to confront. So I finished changing, put on my dressing-gown and slippers, grabbed my towel, and went off to wash, with the mystery package shoved inside my sponge-bag. The corridor was already dark, darker than the night of my inquisition at the hands of Bonifacio; all I had to guide me now was a faint uneven distant glimmer, signalling, like a faraway lighthouse, the night lavatory.

It was all so odd that it might have been comical, absurd in the manner of Ionesco, for the small box proved, as I'd suspected, to be an empty packet of cigarettes (of once-stunted ones, like the legs of Tadzio), and of a tawdry brand which took me back to the fracas when my head had been dunked in the school pissoir—not Nye's class of cigarette at all: he, in matters of nicotine, I knew to be a strict existentialist, to favour aromatic French tobacco with a philosophical blue tinge. No, this packet had once housed a cheaper breed of gasper altogether, popular among the car-maintenance louts, who, like truckers pretending to be Teddy boys, or husbands merrily squandering the housekeeping, would pride themselves in opening their cool mouths wide, like fish, and expelling smoke rings—slowly to spin and float and disperse in the dense umber fogginess which hung about the pub lounge after evening class.

But I was wrong to imagine that the packet might have been empty: it was, as it happened, loaded. And what I found inside, meticulously folded, like a collapsible ladder, was a long thin strip of paper with lines like rungs, torn from a distinctive style of jotting pad which was then popular. You probably remember the type: exceedingly oblong, with a flashy picture on the cover, generally of an elongated figure to suit the format: a decadent former theatre-heroine with hair like a brainstorm and slippers like nibs, or a soft illustration of some cereal goddess called Eté, because she came from Montparnasse, some gangly lady with braids and bad sandals, draped in a diaphanous toga and waving something natural, such as a burnished sheaf of barley. The pads had a hole through the top, near the garlands and tendrils and diadems of these assorted dramatic damsels, so that you could hang them.

·   ·   ·

THE MESSAGE WAS written in crayon, dark red and blunted, and delivered in wonky capitals by someone pretending to be using the wrong hand, or to be a retarded car mechanic. Such a coarse approach ruled out Hardy, whose skills in this department had always aspired towards refinement, but anyway: the substance of the neatly folded length of paper, signed by someone claiming to be Al Capone (which, fleetingly, foolishly, made me imagine that Clifford might be back, posing as a full-fledged gangster to effect my phoney abduction) was as baffling as it was violent. To this day I recall, with the slow-motion clarity of a car crash, verbatim and graphically, like an epitaph, the venomous snake of red words which slithered down that ladder of faint lines:

> WE KNOW ABOUT
> YOU DIRTY FUCKING
> QUEER HAND OVER
> FIFTEEN QUID IN THIS
> BOX AND PUT IT UNDER
> THE LEFT GAZEBO BY
> MIDNIGHT TOMORROW
> ELSE WE GO TO THE RECTOR
> WERE WATCHING YOU
>   SIGNED
>   AL CAPONE
>   BYE BYE

And at that instant I knew precisely what, even in translation, those French authors meant when they described the process of going mad.

IN BED, I told myself to calm down. I told myself to grow up. I told myself not to be that word which had lately come into pop-parlance—paranoid. Yet I couldn't get to sleep—neither for love, nor for the money which I no longer had. Fifteen quid. How the hell was I supposed to lay my hands on that, when I'd already squandered my tutorial stash—never mind within twenty-four hours? If, in the recent past, I had worried about what Clifford's parents might have said to the rector, and about the latter's creepy plurals, and about what his hairy, bobbing Adam's apple might have said to Mr. Wolfe, or, indeed, about what Dr. Fox might have been—and might still be—concealing from me, now I worried on a scale far beyond the scope of basic Mathematics. The upsurge of my panic defied quantifying.

After Clifford's betrayal, I had felt as if I were slowly dying; now I felt that I actually wanted to die, wished that I'd drowned in the treacherous arctic waters of Eisenstein, wished that I'd never laid eyes on Nye. Suddenly, insanely, I became convinced beyond a red-crayoned shadow of a doubt that the blunt left-handed deception scrawled down the faint rungs of that neatly folded paper ladder was, in fact, of course, just a further, more rapacious twist of Hardy's calligraphic lies. Yet how could my blackmailer only be Hardy? The message, remember, said We, not I. Could it be a case of both Hardy *and* Nye? Maybe they'd ganged up against me. Come on, I told myself, be realistic: those two weren't even friends, never mind likely partners in crime, fellow gangsters. And besides, they had no ammunition against me, couldn't have had, since neither of them knew about the Clifford fiasco, nor about the real cause behind my run-in with the rabid year master. But then: Don't bank on it, I cautioned myself, because perhaps the mongrel, behind my back, had got hold of Nye and told him to watch out for my degeneracy, turned him against the shit which I'd been dubbed. Christ, perhaps the phantom scribbler was actually the mongrel, hungry to sink his ravenous fangs into my shoulders before they were bared for the benefit of society. After all, the empty packet of stunted cigarettes certainly matched *his* spivvy smoking style. And the gazebo, which lay beyond the gardens into which the rector had seemed to wish me exiled, was out of bounds to all but the top year of the school and members of staff. But then again—surely not—yes it could, could even be the rector, putting me to the test, lying in wait for the faintest wind of what he had called confirmation, trying to give me rope with which to hang myself, like a damsel from a pad, for the sake of the repute of my father's Alma Mater. Father, change my name. Clifford, shed your light upon my darkened door; because it could also be some shady sixth former—Payne Senior, for instance, or his pal, the midget corporal, or even the slimy toad from the bogs, or, God, all three aligned, with military precision, like a trinity of evil-fearing monkeys. For they, unlike me, were at liberty to wander around the maze of those grounds where legend claims that centuries ago the last heir of the house, in his infancy, lost his bearings, ate some berries—succulent with poison—and died. Yet how could those boys, at the top of the school, have managed to get the mystery package sneaked beneath my pillow? Might they have commissioned someone, like rabbit-faced Newton, or even the burgeoning dropout in my dorm, he of the handsome endowment? Or might Payne Senior, the midget, and the toad not be in cahoots with the mongrel? I was sweating. My thoughts leapt, like an alley cat, from my bed to the left gazebo.

There was, in fact, a pair of small pavilions, identical in design—unlike the Nyes—at the back of the gardens, but I'd only ever seen these from a distance, from the viewpoint of a minion, through the mist of the high windows in Leviticus. The twin gazebos stood, topped by a couple of stone eagles, at the corners of the far wall. Viewed from the dormitory, there could be no doubting Al Capone's instructions. But more carefully considered, all became confusion, because, since the eagles were turned, their wings outstretched, to face the school and not away from it, that which, to unobservant eyes, might have seemed like the left gazebo, was, in fact, the right, and vice versa; and it was while I lay there trying to predict Steel's opinion, which was always learnèd, and his advice, without which I could scarcely manage, that I must have sunk into heavy slumber. Because, next thing, the wake-up bell had rung, and whereas, in the altercation with the mongrel, the strong unholy spirit of Clifford had suddenly welled within me, now, as soon as I stirred, all strength seemed to flow out of me—only to be replaced, in a blink, by the previous night's incalculable panic. I rummaged under my pillow. The empty packet of once-stunted cigarettes, and the crimson snake slithering down its ladder, had been no nightmare. Morning, boys; rise and shine.

AFTER BREAKFAST with Dr. Fox (during which he, while shaving with the electric razor, shouted to me across the room that I seemed a bit off-colour), I returned to make my bed in Leviticus. Next stop was morning prayers, followed by assembly. No time to waste: the clock in my chest was ticking, relentless as a taxi-meter. I found Steel hovering in the dormitory, vaguely in the vicinity of the windows. This was my chance to consult him. But I must have looked shell-shocked, because, before I'd even got started, he interrupted to enquire what was up. I needed his help, I said—well, his advice more like. What with?, he asked most slowly, his glare narrowing with curious suspicion, as if I were about to beg for his history notes, or maths, at which I habitually cheated. But then I found that I couldn't bring myself to explain the problem, it just seemed too complicated, like an insoluble formula; so, to simplify matters and speed them up, I pulled the cigarette packet out of my pocket and placed it without a word upon his hand. Thanks but no thanks, he said, repelled by the sight of the exhibit: I don't smoke; all medical opinion runs counter to it. (Medical parents; vitamins; anaemia.) Just *open* it, I insisted. And out came the retractable ladder, which he pulled from its case rather too roughly (for I wanted it, so far as was possible, preserved in good order, like a letter from officialdom, or evidence to be brought before a jury). But I kept my trap shut while I watched his feline eyes race down-and-up, and up-and-down the steps of hard red crayon, over and over. He, too, saved his breath while he continued with these exertions, until, at last, he quietly read out, as if posing himself a question: Al Capone?

I, of course, had secretly hoped that he might have dismissed the whole message as some pathetic joke, that he might have encouraged me to ignore such nonsense, but he did not: he was bright enough to see that though expressed in red, the whole black tone of the thing was serious—blood-curdling in fact, that's how he put it—one didn't mess with this kind of stuff; you couldn't underestimate the brains behind it. And then he led me out, in pensive silence, to the corridor, where he reckoned that, in my position, which he admitted he didn't envy, he'd probably be tempted to cough up and have done with it. That, in his opinion, seemed like the most sensible strategy. He said that there was just too much riding on it for me: I couldn't afford to get myself slung out before the end of the year, which is when we sat our first lot of external exams. I told him that I couldn't afford to cough up, didn't have the moolah. He took me back into Leviticus, and rummaged in his wallet, pondering the whole problem at what felt like unkind leisure, as if gloating very slightly, but then he volunteered that he could probably lend me, if it helped, let's see, seven quid, but only for a couple of weeks, all right? I didn't have time to answer, because my fingers, like the jaws of an alligator, had already snapped at his palm and captured the money, three crisp notes—a fiver, blue; two singles, green—underwater colours from the Ganges. And yet, now that he'd become not just my ally and confidant but properly implicated, an active accomplice in my bid to escape from hot water, he wanted to know more, more than he'd ever wanted to know about Clifford: suddenly he wanted to know from where this note had come, exactly when and where I'd found it, who I thought might be responsible, on and on he wanted to know. But now that I had half the money, it was too late for such enquiries; I just needed the other half, plus a pound, and fast. Sorry, Steel; thanks a million; and off I rushed, forgetting to ask my second question. Yet I remember how, as I ran out, he shouted (over the milling heads of the other boys whom, at various times, I had serviced in silence, but whom, at that same instant, in an epiphany, I swore never again to service): Don't forget, Moore, I need it back within the fortnight. All *right,* I replied with gritted teeth, in case the mongrel were around—Keep your hair on. He turned away, flicking his pale bob aside.

AT BREAK, elevenish, I returned to Dr. Fox for toast. What on earth was eating me?, he asked. Nothing, I made out. Don't be stupid, he persisted, something's obviously wrong; this is *I* to whom you're talking. And so, again, I produced the packet of fags—slamming it on the mantel, and telling him: Well, since you're so determined to find out, just take a look at *that.* Dr. Fox seemed taken aback by my reaction: emotional outbursts being, as far as he knew, untypical of my repertoire; but he appeared to compose himself speedily—if only to adopt a sluggish motion. He slid his glasses up, and then took hold of the mystery package (slightly warily, as if it were some party-joke, childishly explosive), and once he'd made himself very gradually comfortable upon the leather quilt of his wingèd chesterfield, as Sherlock Holmes might have done, the myopic private eye claimed to be baffled. So, one more maddening time, I had to tell him to inspect the contents. And as he did so, the box fell to his lap; and as he read the poisoned diatribe, my mentor blushed. But as soon as he began to implore me to be sensible, to keep my wits about me, I realized that I was on my witless own, floundering in my personal quagmire—to do with which he would have nothing.

Look, I said, forgetting our differing positions in the official hierarchy, I've thought about it good and hard, didn't get a wink of sleep all night, and I've decided that I've just got to pay up. That, he advised, would be madness. *Why?,* I yelled back. Be-*cause*—and keep your voice down—one should never, on principle, give in to blackmail: it's a pernicious practice, underhand and criminal. Deaf to his moralizing, I reminded him that I could get expelled for this, did he realize. Nonsense, he said, You're too promising for the school to want to kick you out. And yet, to me (whom the rector had already threatened with expulsion), Dr. Fox did not seem any calmer than I. I told him that I didn't have the money. He said absolutely nothing, as if he, now, were the deaf one; but, as he folded away the message and returned it to its package, I noticed that his puffy pianistic fingers were trembling very slightly . . . *How,* he suddenly asked, can you not have the money— what, none whatever? I claimed that I had half, pretending that Steel's seven pounds were properly mine. In which case, he suggested, perhaps—though I don't at all approve of this sort of thing, you understand—perhaps you should offer your Al Capone (*my* Al Capone, he said) those seven pounds, and explain in a note of reply that at present it's all you have. Take a chance.

Dr. Fox must be denser than I'd realized. I inhaled profoundly, like my mother on the brink of dismissing a servant. Couldn't he see that I was involved not in some minor transaction which offered room for manoeuvre, but in a crisis which—to quote Steel—was blood-curdling? Negotiation just didn't come into it. Dr. Fox admitted that yes, it was all somewhat unpleasant, and potentially embarrassing, but really no worse than that. And then he added that, since I'd already had my fair share of embarrassment in life, I should be inured to it by now—a cynical nugget which I found more offensive than constructive. I said as much. He apologized. I told him that what I needed was not some lofty lecture, but the other half of the money. Couldn't he lend it to me? Out of the question, he replied—less like an ethical detective than a tight-fisted banker. I feared that he was going to force me to blub, to crank up an act, but, as I looked down, I caught sight of my watch and realized that break was practically over. No time for theatricals. Sod him, I thought; and then I stood up and took the cigarette-packet; but as I moved away from his lumpen great uselessness, he surprised me by saying that just as he objected to blackmail, so he disapproved of lending money: if one was reduced to the indignity of borrowing, the last thing that one needed was the additional pressure of having to repay debts, and, after a further, suspended hiatus, he said that—on condition that it be the end of the matter and that I never allude to it in the future—he would let me have (*have*, he made clear, not borrow) the remaining eight pounds, though not as a means for me to submit to criminality. As a quite unconnected present. I could've sucked him off on the spot, but the bell had already gone. I had to get back to class. I thanked him, said I'd be back at lunchtime, and fled down the fifth-year corridor.

BETWEEN THE NEXT two periods, just before Latin, which was taught by a mousy closet-baronet who used to wince if you called him *Sir* with feeling, I got hold of Steel again and whispered to him my second question: whether, on account of the stone eagles pointing in our direction, he thought that the gazebo to the left was indeed the left, or, more likely, the right. Probably as a result of his knowledge of history and war campaigns and battle standards, he knew the answer almost without thinking: left, he said, was always left as viewed by us. The enemy's perspective was of no relevance. Remember Waterloo, he added. (How could I not?) According to Steel-the-budding-general, we were the ones in charge, and only our direction mattered; forget that vital piece of strategy, and you may as well surrender, start waving the white flag. So now at least I knew where to go, knew which of the gazebos was my target, my command. And then he said—with feeling, which now made *me* wince: Don't forget my seven quid; pay me back within the fortnight or you're history. *Annale,* in Latin. Amen in Catholic.

BACK TO DR. FOX, ostensibly for lunch, but really to collect the rest of the money, which he, as if wishing to divorce himself from my shaming weakness in the teeth of hoodlums, had deposited under the electric shaver on the (dusty) mantel. I swept up the notes and married them to the contents of my wallet (an article which I'd once told Clifford was wrought from the foreskins of pelicans. *God* how exotic, he had exclaimed. Well, Clifford, maybe your father's mistress would like one now.) But then, as Dr. Fox presented me with a plate, piled high with farmhouse paté purchased from his superior grocer, and no doubt on account (the *indignity* of borrowing), I had a sudden brainwave, which did, next, require a good authentic blub. With remarkable facility, I discovered, I began to sob like a war-torn widow. What's the matter *now*?, he groaned, prevented in mid-crouch from settling to attack his grub. (The matter was the gazebo itself, of course, in the gardens which were out of bounds to all but sixth formers and members of staff.) I was scared, I said, to be seen venturing into enemy territory by the rector. In which case, Dr. Fox suggested, jump over the wall round the back. What?, I gasped, and get myself lynched by some local farmhand? Was he completely mad? Dr. Fox was starting to look a teensy bit narked, beady-eyed: he could tell, I could tell, where I was heading, could guess at the request which was coming. Look, I said—again forgetting the polarity of our positions—had I ever, *ever* asked him for any favour? (The favours which, by contrast, had once been granted to his sweaty crotch hung in mid-air like threatening clouds, like the Venetian clouds which once had overhung the Lido.) His glacial spectacles made plain to me that he could see precisely where I was leading him, which was neither to redemptive water nor in the direction of his obliging grocer, but inexorably towards grass. And again, like this morning, he blushed, though no longer quite so innocently, for he must, in his gut, have felt a rumble of discomfort, the feeling that he did, indeed, owe me one. And even if it took, because he could be stubborn, a lavish dollop of my most persuasive smarm, in the end, he did consent, poor man, to oblige.

He undertook, on my behalf, to take a stroll to the left gazebo (which I had to insist was the one to his left As He Walked Out), and he agreed to tuck Al Capone's blood-money under one of the corners of that *specific* stone pavilion; and then, he said, he would return for tea, by which time he sincerely hoped that I'd have put the whole business behind me; but the situation was, he said, frankly ridiculous. And I, conceding to his frankly ridiculous hypocrisy only by virtue of my newfound gratitude, nodded that I knew that it was, and that I was sorry to put him in this awkward position. And although, following my extraction of his commitment, I found myself with ample leisure to kneel at his feet and gratify his cheesy penis, I'm sorry to say that instead I conceived an urgent need to go to the basement and prepare for his next orchestral meeting. I'd be back for tea.

Dr. Fox was a greedy man; but not, in the final instance, wicked; and when I dragged my apprehension back to his room, he confirmed, to my spiralling relief, that the deed was done, as he put it. He also told me, by way of proof of his obedience, that he'd found a very obvious crevice under one of the corners of the relevant gazebo, which meant that the criminal element, as he now called Al Capone, must have known exactly what it was up to. Still, Dr. Fox had proved true to his word, had deposited the money—and Yes, he reassured me, carefully out of sight of anyone. And next, as if this were *his* cut of the deal, he insisted that I now forget the whole thing and get on with some proper revision. Only six weeks to go before you start your O levels, he nagged, no time to phootle about, old chap. I said that I would buckle down without further demurring; yet, in the event, I found myself unequipped to honour such a promise, for, in truth, it had only been a far-fetched intention (not a pact, Clifford, still less a marriage vow).

NEXT MORNING, I needed to know the state of play. My deadline had been met, and Al Capone's instructions, against all the odds and despite my hysteria, been fulfilled, like an exam completed within the requisite time limit. Yet whether the blackmailer had actually taken possession of the loot remained to be seen. Dr. Fox nearly lost his rag when I tried to suggest that perhaps he could go back and take a peep. He reminded me of my agreement never again to refer to this unpalatable (his word) subject. So during break, I took myself, affecting a look of tedium but practically succumbing—as if terror-stricken at prep school—to an attack of the shits, to the back side of the rear wall of the gardens, above which the left gazebo could be seen at a weird perspective, like the dovecote in the bedroom of my infancy, swaying slightly. I looked up from the field of filthy grass. I could hear a tractor in the distance, or a combine harvester, threatening sounds of farming. To be quite frank (and not just prissy), you really needed a ladder to get up there. But then I saw a succession of scuff marks leading vaguely vertically, the tracks of shoes which had struggled to climb, and this encouraged me—for as well as suggesting that my blackmailer, having avoided the gardens, was unlikely to be a sixth former or a member of the staff, those tracks pointed to the likelihood that the money had been collected, and, therefore, that my torment was over at last. I just needed to verify the fact, for my own peace of mind.

My ascent can't have been dignified. I fancied myself an aesthete, not an athlete, and this concluding ordeal felt like Gratuitous Humiliation. But, as I climbed, I tried to imagine wartime escapades, and spotlit Nazi interrogations, and Colditz in real life, and even Mr. Bonifacio, and somehow, assisted by these thoughts, I managed to heave myself onto the level of the gardens. I crept round the gazebo, found the corner which Dr. Fox had described, and, to my puzzlement, then horror, discovered that the packet of cigarettes was still there, soggy-looking but intact. A surging, boiling quandary now beset me: should I leave the money in place, or take it back? I decided to reclaim my ransom, lest it should fall into the hands of some overefficient gardener. But next, just to make sure before embarking on the downward climb, I took a look inside the packet. The money was gone. In its place, I found another paper ladder, effectively identical to the first, again scrawled in red crayon, and again demanding fifteen pounds, though this time granting me—how kind—a whole week's grace in which to comply with the demand. I leapt over the wall and somehow landed alive.

As I sloped back to class, squelching over the sludge, I dusted myself down, restyled myself, and tried to review the position. First I needed seven quid to get Steel, the loan-shark, off my back; then, a further fifteen quid to keep Al Capone gagged, which totalled twenty-two. Actually, I still had two in my PO account, so call it twenty. And thus, resigning myself to a stultifying dose of double Mathematics, I began to wonder on whom, next, I could rely for help, rely with confidence. On whom could I bring pressure to bear, as Al Capone had brought his own unbearable pressure onto my old head on young shoulders? And then, once more: Eureka. Because, just along from my circular mental sum of twenty pounds, the vital little parallels which now suggested themselves to my nonfinancial mind, the = sign, pointed, and unequivocally, like the sudden, accurately copied answer to a formerly open-ended equation, to one unmistakable quantity, one sole known word, one man, one name alone: Wolfe, of course. But I knew better than to howl with euphoria. Instead, while pretending to rack my brain of a stupid joyless shopgirl over some baffling set of exercises, I scribbled him a note, on cheap school stationery, which I later sent through the internal mail—I wasn't Rockefeller—informing my erstwhile supervisor that there was s o m e t h i n g that I needed to discuss with him, and that the matter was of urgency. And I ended the missive with love: what did I have to lose by that? Zero. A great big nought, absolutely round, like a hollow pie chart—nothing like the shape of an old heart, or a pair of interwoven zodiacal symbols, Gemini.

HIS REPLY REACHED ME within forty-eight hours, and, in accordance with his suggestion (but without official permission, least of all from Dr. Fox), I went, the following afternoon, to meet him in his room at my old prep school. It all turned out to be oddly familiar, by which I mean familiar in odd ways. From reception, I was ushered up by some young secretary, cropped and trousered and sexy, perhaps even bi-sexy—who could tell? I wouldn't have put Sappho past her, nor her past Sappho, for there was a butch *quelque chose* about her, a chic aggressiveness, as if, beneath her wide black trousers, she might have been concealing high boots with spurs attached. Her face, new since my day, wore, I remember thinking, too much make-up; her eyes were spiked with mascara, like man-eating spiders; and she exuded as she went up, two steps at a time, a strong musky scent, almost unpleasant—not Joy, that was for sure, much less gardenias. With the amazon in charge, we climbed past the holy statue to whose feet some poor boy had, before either of our times, crashed—never to be fixed again, not even by the miraculous adhesive of communal prayer. Eventually we reached the level of the junior dormitories, and then, Mr. Wolfe's door, the door of my former covert entrances and exits, the idolatrous portal of my childhood tabernacle, on which Bisexy Amazon now knocked—too hard—before stalking off on some other business. My former lover didn't answer. He came out.

I discovered that the setting of my early nocturnal abandon had undergone an overhaul, been revamped—presumably to reflect Mr. Wolfe's raised position in the establishment; but the result, when compared to the period when I'd known those four walls, and known them intimately, appeared, to me, visually inferior. There was a plain, self-patterned bedspread now, crushed velveteen, I think, the colour of cold curry. Next to the bed, which otherwise looked unaltered, there was a new (but already grubby) sheepskin rug—for Mr. Wolfe had, it transpired, lately become the beaming owner of a pallid Labrador, for which sloppy breed I felt as good as nothing. Borzois and salukis, then, were more my style, elegant hounds from enormous paintings and great Russian palaces. Flicky, I think the dog was called, so perhaps it was a bitch who wouldn't answer to Felicity. I told him to get the slobbering creature off me, even if it *was* young, which, ironically, is how he tried to excuse his obvious failure to control it. He did as I instructed. And the animal, a picture of sycophancy, curled itself beneath his desk, not so far from where my short-trousered legs had once, when I myself had been a dark-eyed sycophant, been stroked. No mention of the rector, nor of Clifford, nor of n o t h i n g. Let sleeping dogs lie. I remember little else about those premises, for I was in a hurry, and out of my own bounds, and in a blinding Latin fury. My mother's blood, Lord love it.

He tried, as my father had tried during the storm in my preparatory teacup, to shake my hand. I ignored the inanity. Next he encouraged me to sit, like a Labrador; but I remained standing, digging my hands into my pockets as I'd done when I refused to let him beat me with a table-tennis bat. (See? Familiar but different.) He sat at his desk, near the window, near the dog's foul basket. Did I want some music? No, I replied; silence was fine. He can't have agreed, because, almost immediately, he stood up, and went round, no longer towards the pick-up gramophone of my past, but towards a cassette-recorder, like a bulky vanity-bag, portable. He had the sense to play nothing which harked back to the two, the two, the two of us; left Mary Magdalene's musical sobs safely out of his modernized environment; kept his hands off my Nocturnes (it was four o'clock, not midnight); made no attempt to build a nostalgic bridge over our moribund waters. I recall that instead of music with an emotive charge, he, as if trendified, chose a turgid pop song by some gang of tone-deaf yobs going on and on about not needing no *edgy-cation*.

Yet as I observed him, this altered Mr. Wolfe, I still recognized traces of what once upon a time had drawn me to his arms, and drawn me so badly, traces of why I'd loved him with such fraught childish passion, of why I couldn't have resisted doing what I had done, night after night. But I was also able to see why, three years after our valedictory pout outside that seminary in Brussels, I no longer felt much more for him than I did for his snoring Labrador, why my innards had grown cold, and my spirit chilled in his regard. He felt untrustworthy now, or reputable perhaps—either way, uncomfortable. From my sullen, mercenary point of view, all that remained, despite his never-setting sunburst smile, was a buried bond, an impoverished connection which would take years to assume proper shape and surface and be acknowledged—though, even then, never openly. Our great secret, remember; Special. But as I stood there, under the hideous fringes of some recently installed ceiling-light, I realized that the task which awaited me was steeply uphill, steep as my struggle to climb the wall to the gazebo.

WHAT CAN HE do for me?, he asks, less like a former lover than a put-upon employer. I need some money, I reply in the tone usually employed for the review of one's salary—falsely cool, impassive. But he looks at me oddly, as if I were speaking the wrong language—I on whom, at the end of our romance, no amount of money squandered had seemed excessive, no number of useless fripperies too great a profligacy. How much?, he wonders, as if I were a hooker trying to haggle with a punter, or the other way round. Twenty, I say, more flatly than Shrove Tuesday. Twenty, he repeats, ashen as a Wednesday; then, nothing. But after a protracted rumination, Gosh, he goes, That seems a bit hefty, doesn't it?—as if my request were a holy cow. Still, he does at least manage to smile about it, even if a trifle meanly—meanly as I, much later, would, as you know, smile over my own negotiations. Yet, for now, I remain utterly serious, deadly; desperate. Twenty, he forces me to say a second time. He shudders—to think. Why so much?, he asks. I don't bother to reply. Instead, I peer at the dull, diminished viaduct over which now I *can* properly fly—not to the circus, I grant you, nor to Russia, but at least to concerts and to plays in which my head can escape to the few naughty cinemas and cocktail bars that Clifford hasn't managed to monopolize.

Mr. Wolfe now dares to enquire how come I need such a sum, don't my parents give me enough? I claim that it's none of his affair (the affair of teachers and pupils about which Clifford had blabbed). Will he simply part with the lucre, or will he deny it? (Will he be a deputy head, or will he be a paedophile?) He looks telepathically insulted. Am I in trouble? Sort of, I half-answer. With whom, the authorities? (Still no actual mention of the rector.) I don't know with whom exactly. (I bet he thinks I'm lying—after all, if you're in trouble, surely you know the quarter from which you're running. But I was running back to the left gazebo, you see, and getting breathless while I was at it.) Again I say that I'm in trouble, that I just need the money, that it's all too boring to explain in detail, so either to let me have (not borrow) twenty pounds—in fivers, I specify, larger notes are not convenient—or to turn me down, but to stop messing me around. He asks if I'm taking drugs. I say that I'm not (and nor, then, was I). He asks how my revision is going. I tell him to stuff it up his jumper. He smiles more widely still, seems to approve of my shopgirly defiance, as if it were a sign that I'd finally grown into myself, into my precocious shoulders, into my eventual genitals. And then, at long bloody last, he surrenders to the injustice of my power, like a cropped and trousered, hard but gentle, bisexual secretary.

The dosh, unlocked from a drawer, he places in an envelope, as my mother does, as I myself have done. There's a certain circularity, like the rounded sum of twenty pounds, to the whole demeaning enterprise. It just happens to be my own turn now, my personal moment of reckoning, as ironically logical as the infinity implicit in parallel lines, lines unable ever to meet and entwine like zodiac symbols on the golden surface of a medal buried long ago beneath the ground. He slides the envelope smoothly along the desk, as Bonifacio, once, had slid his golden lighter for me to ignite him—even though I, in obliging that first of my interrogators (precursor to the hamster, father, fox, rector, and mongrel—quite a little album), had only managed to fire him closer to anger than carnality. I leave Mr. Wolfe's envelope behind, like a disposable afterthought, and place his (considerate) quartet of banknotes in my wallet, which has grown glossy with the tears of pelicans. I have a bash at thanking him, but in my depth I resent being back in this dump, which, however redecorated, feels no better for it. Even my father's pub-lunch, followed by his sobs, would have been preferable.

I'm about to pocket the lucre and run, but Mr. Wolfe, now that our minor unpleasantness is over, rises to warm humour and decides to approach me with sentiment, like That. I can interpret the undeveloped language of his body better than my own—which, being a dialect, can give rise to confusion. And as he draws towards a hopeful proximity, he begins to say how pleased he is to see me, and how marvellously well I look—and in the manner of these things, well, let's just say that he gets me. And do I oblige? Of course I do: as with the members of Leviticus, I provide him with the semblance of a service, for which Mr. Wolfe is at least, let's face it, paying—my first honest-to-goodness punter. Nursery slope stuff, really, hardly going to kill me. Because killing isn't Mr. Wolfe's speciality: killing is Al Capone's.

ALL THAT I MAY have told you about our first night six years earlier, and about the rapture at the start of that foremost beginning, and about our million subsequent hours of love made beneath the northern stars, and about the second wave of our great songs, and the flaring beauty of our votive torches, you may now wipe out, erase from memory, extinguish, subtract like a gift of great value taken back, the gift of an Indian giver. Because, on this singular afternoon, and even before he's got started, Mr. Wolfe, well, just goes and wrecks it. Instead of leaving me alone and letting bygones be gone by, he now wants to know what I like, now that I've grown—hmm, Let me look at you (let him look at me)—yes, into quite a young man, we're almost the same height. And for the only time in our connection—a word which I select advisedly, since our love affair is more than done—the sexual act does not take place upon the bed of my many childish makings, which perhaps, in my wake, has become the province of some hairless successor. Instead, it takes place standing up, and fully clothed, as if this refurbished tabernacle were a public lavatory. His beard has grown shabby, like the beard of a vagrant, and begun to blotch to a dirty mushroom, and his kisses no longer feel like the answers to the prayers of anyone (other than a dog, perhaps), but kisses to be avoided, first smelling, then almost tasting of gravy and onions, of steak and kidney pie. Our congress proves more tawdry than the tawdriest grope in the municipal cottage, because here, now, I can't even try to pretend, I just mime very badly, far worse than any amateur. His penis, that sovereign roundhead of my infantile wonderment, now makes me squirm on his account, disgusts me, for it looks half the length and half the girth that I remember—miserable, miserly, diminished even in its hardness. It slides about my mouth, like a red crayon, blunted. In order to suck, I must, of all the memories, pout—although, now that I'm grown into quite the young man of his false flattery, I do not suck like a girlish child; certainly not: I suck like a prat in an Old Boy tie puffing at his medium-sized cigar.

And yet the shame, it can't all have been mine; for surely Mr. Wolfe, that former apple of my young eye, that core of my rotten deuteronomy, must have realized, as he burnt the back of my jacket with tortuous Japanese circles, stroking me round and round and round and round ad infinitum, that he'd forgotten how to love and love forever, like an eternally indebted supervisor, grateful everlastingly. But suddenly, for no good reason, his deputy head relieves itself inside my pouting mouth; and I reel across the room to the very radiator against which the button of my pyjamas had once, like a treacherous coin, clanked, and I spit him out onto his own towel—the latter, plain, no longer striped, yet reminiscent still of the towel whose theatrical falls had once filled my heart with loud applause. And then, slamming the door—which had not been locked—I get the hell out; I get out of hell. We were never to meet again, he and I, nor to make contact; but later, you know, by when, of course, it was all no good, I came to regret the severance. Perhaps he was owed an explanation. And I, perhaps, a better rate of exchange than twenty pounds.

MUCH LATER, as I say, while searching for a direction, or even a style of life, I lived in a small hotel on the borders of Chelsea, near the river. Here, over breakfast one winter day, Decemberish, I accidentally fell upon a notice at the back of some newspaper, a notice placed by a firm of Mancunian solicitors acting on behalf of Mr. Wolfe's estate, the executrix of which appeared to be his widow—a surprise to me, rather like Clifford's once-surprising claims to home-sickness. I pictured the former Ms. Bisexy Amazon as the woman bereaved, poised at the side of some wuthering grave in a black silk topper with a half-veil of mesh, the very image of dressage, and racking her (retired) secretarial brain as to how in heaven's name someone of whom she'd never heard came to figure in her departed husband's last will and testament. I also surmised that Mr. Wolfe must have died of heart failure; it seemed fitting, merited. Gone but not forgiven, sort of thing. Yet the tiny, reconciling print before my eyes sought to trace me by any means, under any of my several names—Spanish, English, or the one which, since, I've elected by deed-poll—though not, to my relief, under the alias Woman, nor under the initials HWB. For secrets, like secretaries, should be kept concealed, interred intact, never betrayed, never released to the skies with the levity of cremated ashes. Whether I was bequeathed propitiatory coins, to add to the blue quartet of banknotes made over to me in his life, or whether I'd been left some small but significant memento (an early edition of Lewis Carroll seemed likely), I could not say; for I affected, in that era, never to read the papers, and my affectation mattered more to me than his departure from this world. His wishes, like his bisexual antics and the mounting rhythms of his career, were as little my business as they felt of interest. Besides, by then, I was financially free, no longer strapped for posthumous interest, and too old for propitiation anyway. Too senile for forgiveness. I couldn't even remember the words of the Creed.

(EVEN IF, in time, I was to feel that an explanation might have been due to Mr. Wolfe,) when I returned, after that last inglorious congress which had cost him twenty crumpled quid, to what the Countess had described as the Big School, but which, like Mr. Wolfe's penis, appeared to have diminished, I explained nothing to anyone. I just shelled out. Steel I reimbursed in a crested envelope, which, though it may have pricked his historical interest, he scarcely acknowledged, as if its contents were an insignificance between friends, which in a sense they were, trivial; but Al Capone I paid more handsomely, with greater ceremony: not in his grubby sodden packet of fags, the squalor of which, for all of my own squalor, I could not bear to keep about me. Instead, I chose an empty box of cocktail cigarettes, which the colourful inhabitants of the music basement sometimes liked to bring to their illicit feasts on Sunday afternoons. I must have decided, after one of those sessions in the glassy cubicles, to keep this particular packet, which was black and slim and shiny, in order to store stamps and air mail stickers; but since I had no one to whom to write and, consequently, scant need for the stamps within, the container felt like a redundancy, desk clutter. And so I reasoned that if I was going to have to submit to Al Capone's villainy one final time, I may as well, while I was at it, rather than further comply with his nasty notions of packaging, assert my superior stylishness, like the stoical last Empress of Russia (who would have detested Eisenstein), or a proud borzoi, come to that. Al Capone, I told myself, might indeed be an expert criminal, but I would teach him, if it was the last thing that I did, the meaning of the word *aesthete*. And thus I folded the triptych of blood money, which was blue as the blood of murdered monarchs, inside the gilded inner wrapper, closed the small casket, and braced myself for the committal.

I STOLE OUT to the wall behind the gardens. I could have done with Clifford to lend me a leg-up—like a groom helping a pearl-encrusted tsarina onto her side-saddle, or raising a dressing-gowned child to the profoundly pink velvet of its mother's rocking unicorn. But these were impoverished times, fearful ones, and the only hand that you could trust was your own shaking ringless one, to tug at your own reins lest you bolt into the distance. I clamber up the wall, wearing gloves on this occasion. All is stiller than a graveyard. I lay the black box in the stone niche, stooping as you must stoop to place a wreath upon the tomb of someone you have loved. No time for a prayer. (No, Clifford, not a thought of one.) I leap back down. I land. I stumble. I return to the building hobbling slightly.

At tea, Dr. Fox finds me peculiar. I tell him that it's just all this revision. He understands, he says, but I mustn't let it get me down. If I'm organized, there won't be any need for last-minute heebie-jeebies. I nod like a nodding Indian cow, or like the head of an ornamental dog plonked on the back of a gangster's car. Have some toast, he says. I couldn't, I reply. Or some cake, perhaps? Look, I blurt, I'm really not hungry. Surely a cup of tea?, he persists. OK, I surrender. (In dainty china it comes, rattling sofawards.) Thank you. But he ignores me now, for his eyes are busy rolling at the mirror, as if he were making signs to someone behind my back, suggesting that I'd lost my marbles, that the time had finally come to call for my straitjacket.

WHAT EVER HAPPENED to the rest of that term? Where can it have gone? Nowhere much: I did nothing; I grew numb; I gave up; I don't even recall the songs of the time. Tweeting birds on a transistor left out on the grass? Someone squeaking about Loving You (is easy 'cos you're beautiful)? I couldn't say for sure. All that I know is that I didn't dare to return to the gazebo to check whether Al Capone's money had flown, because I couldn't have coped with a further demand. Instead, I glided through boring exam after boring exam, as if I were drugged, drugged like my mother, as if the papers and questions and time-bells were figments of someone else's unimaginative reality, my father's perhaps. And whereas in recent terms I'd grown to dread the days before returning to my parents' house, now I found that I couldn't stop counting. And when the end did come, the foul weather was fine; and my dismal flight, blessedly bland. At the airport on the island, I felt too tired to muster a filial smile. I needed to convalesce in silence. But first, before I could concentrate on recovery, I loudly refused to teach English to anyone, salivating notary or harelipped girl with acne. My mother acceded, for she could see, she said, that those exams had wiped me out—poor Iago. I sunbathed naked on her terrace, trying to bring my skin back to life, to save it with a concoction of cooking oil and lemon juice and iodine. I locked myself into privacy, from the outside. I didn't go to a single party for The Young. I looked up depression in an old encyclopedia. I put myself out of my mind.

My exam results, addressed to me, arrived some morning in mid-August, but it was my father who, before I came down for breakfast, saw fit to slice open the envelope—a liberty which he concealed until we were safely seated on the terrace, late into lunch, as the fruit was being brought round. He said that if I managed to hang on to a place at school, it would be by the skin of my teeth, or on the wings of a prayer, or some such inanity, and that he'd probably have to ring his friends-in-high-places to get them to persuade the rector to keep me on in the senior school. My Adam's apple wobbled slightly. My father continued: certainly I'd have to re-sit Mathematics, whether I went to university or elsewhere—somewhere sensible. And as for the rest of my grades, well, a pretty poor show, if he might say so (he already had), nothing to be proud of. Nothing, I replied with spiky pedantry, of which to be proud.

Oblivious to my correction, he turned his attention to the passing platter and took, with a grunt, a mango, a fruit which he invariably chose, and invariably ate (even my mother agreed with me on this) like a savage, peeling it with his fingers and tearing at the stringy flesh, letting the sticky juice dribble down his jowls and gnawing at the stone, slurping at the rancid sweetness and munching at the pulp. While I averted my eyes from the spectacle of the man, and did my best not to hear him, I tried to weigh up what would happen if I were to find myself flung out: whether his victor's wreath would wilt with misery at my failure to bring credit to his Alma Mater, or whether, on the contrary, he might not quietly be thrilled, because, just as I knew myself to be vindictive, so I knew from which side of my faulty gene-pool the trait of vengefulness had been rained down—or, at least, its greater (mathematical) percentage. I gauged that his reaction would be a mixture of the two, a blend, in equal (mathematical) measures, of thrill and misery, the proportions befitting a bullying masochist. And his reaction now, merely about my results (rather than expulsion, which was altogether a grander matter), proved me right, proved to be that very mix in miniature—a perfectly balanced little confusion.

He handed me the official sheet, forcing me to stretch further towards him than he was prepared to exert the length of his sleeve. I suspected that my mother had already surveyed the impersonal print, as if it had contained the foregone results of some blood test for shingles, because she demonstrated no surprise at all, still less curiosity. She was beautifully impassive, or on pills, and wearing—of all the tragi-comedies—dark glasses. I couldn't look at her. I resisted stating the obvious, namely that this letter had been mine to open, not his, and that its contents, at least in the first instance, had been none of anyone else's sodding business. Instead, guided by wary prudence, I scanned the document down-and-up and up-and-down, in the manner of Steel. And what I learnt, inevitably, was that I'd indeed performed beyond my wildest imaginings, acquitted myself laughably. Like a dunce on sedatives.

Maths, Physics, Biology, Chemistry: all failed, and outright—with U's (unclassified). History, Latin, Greek: passed, but miserably, with C's. Spanish, English, French: top grades, but this, as my father knew oh, better than anyone, was the least that could be expected. And somewhere in the middle of it all, in the insipid realm of the B's, I managed to bluff my way to a grade in Religious Studies.

Yet much as my father cared for the practice of sanctity, I don't think that he exactly warmed to its theory, its room for uncertainty, the splitting of spiritual hairs, what he dismissed as my silly doctrinal nit-picking. Perhaps I should tell him to get me to a monastery. I wondered how such an exhortation might affect him. Would he, just as he had prayed for the collapse of my obstinacy regarding Mr. Wolfe—my lies, my overly coloured fancy—fall to his knees and implore Our Father to strike down this imbecile, or would he punch a dent into the boot of his own motor? My musings were cut short, because Bright, he now went on, bright as I considered myself to be, the proof of the pudding, laddy, was in the eating. And then he trotted out a further couple of clichés—just desserts, mighty fallen—which he crowned with a piece of sublime wit, to the effect that the ego had landed. Briefly he chortled with satisfaction, chortled as Al Capone had probably done on collecting his winnings; and then, my venerable pater resumed his dressing down.

He was bound to point out, he claimed, that he'd experienced no academic difficulty in his day, when one had sat the school certificate—much harder exams than these newfangled O levels, which, according to him, were just an excuse to lower the standards for the sake of comprehensive thickos. How, he went on, I could even pretend to be a linguist simply defeated him. Pretend how?, I bristled. For a start, he explained, I hadn't even studied German (unlike his majesty). So what? I retorted. So a very great deal; romance languages were a doddle, let's face it; it was Teutonic ones that told the men from the boys. Well, I replied, at least I'd studied Greek. Glad you call a C-grade studying, you piffling squit; and anyway, Greek's just a lazy excuse for dons and other like-minded pansies. And German, I countered, is the language of the Nazis. Which is when he went ballistic: German, I'll have you know, is the language of the Future! Of modern Industry!—a subject about which you, to judge by your performance, you insolent brat, appear to be spectacularly ignorant, so kindly get out of my sight this instant before I wring your weedy neck. (I thought of Hardy and his tilted head, the head of a deaf madonna.) My mother, in profile, closed her shaded eyes and vanished into her personal darkness. And I, feeling as if I were hovering on the brink of some court martial, rolled, as if calmly, my napkin into its silver noose, and rose with a brow so arched that it was worthy, if not of Johnny Weissmuller, certainly of Hollywood before the talkies; but then I decided, at the last minute, to mind my hips as I performed my exit.

I walked back into a landscape of taunting shadows. If any calls were made to his cronies by my father, I was not apprised, but left to stew in the juices of my own jittery ignorance. So, a couple of weeks before my return to England, while my father was at his office, and my mother (for a change) out at a fitting, I decided to 'phone Dr. Fox, who must, I surmised, by now be back at school. I had trouble with the secretary because I didn't want to volunteer my identity in case she laughed about my ego having landed, but the bitch drove a hard bargain and, in the end, did manage to prize my surname out of me. With maddening protraction, she now put me through to the basement. When Dr. Fox eventually answered, his Yes? . . . sounded glum. And yet, hearing my voice, he seemed to perk up, as if his whiskers were smiling at the end of the line, which crackled with distance, and then he said that he was fine, splendid thank you, just back from Salzburg; what about me, where had I been? Nowhere, I replied. Well, what had I been up to? (Up to what had I been?) Nothing much. Why ever not? I ignored this fatuous line of enquiry, and got straight to the point, and confessed, as if I were confessing to a shameful breakdown, that my exam results had been atrocious. He said that he was perfectly aware of the fact, but added that it didn't really matter. I said that it was all the fault of Al Capone. He said that he didn't want to discuss any of *that,* the subject was closed. Well anyway, I struggled on, had I forfeited my place at school or hadn't I? Why on earth? Because of my lousy grades, of course. (Fatty was about to make me lose my temper.) But then he went and almost lost his own; yet his impatience, as it began to flow, seemed to bathe me in sustenance. Because what he said was: Look, just get on the train with all the others, and I'll pick you up from the station—you may as well skip the bus ride. All you need do once you're back is *not* rise to the bait, keep out of trouble, and work like a demon. You'll re-sit Mathematics in a couple of months, which I've already squared with the rector; and I shall be your moral tutor, as was always the plan. You'll concentrate on languages, which are your speciality (Speciality, Father), and if you do exactly as I say, you'll see that everything will turn out fine. I know this system inside out. Your results are a bore, admittedly, but not an impediment to your future, and certainly not grounds for not returning. So: see you in a fortnight, and don't forget that I'll be at the station to collect you. I'll be waiting in the car park. Now kindly stop fretting, and don't annoy your parents, do you understand? And for God's sake *do* something. Goodbye.

I don't recall uttering another word during the remainder of that fortnight, other than at a tobacconist's where I went to buy Dr. Fox some Montecristos, which I could get for a fraction of what you had to pay for them in England. And when the holiday slithered to its conclusion, I borrowed my mother's bathroom scales, to ensure that, if nothing else, I had no excess baggage. No chances; no fear. Bad odour; bad blood. The driver took me to the airport.

FROM THE START of my time in the senior school, the flow of my life became separate from the main tide, satisfactorily estranged. Now, not far from Dr. Fox's brocaded alcove, I had a room of my own, which I decorated to suit me, with framed pictures of the sea, and old wooden boxes which you could lock—conveyed in my trunk all the way from my island—along with cushions whose covers had been made by the seamstress at home, but whose stuffing was provided by Dr. Fox, and a heavy counterpane of woven cloth which took me back to my time by the beach before it all went wrong. At last I could play my own music— not droning lyrics about pretty ladies leaning on Darkened doors, but my tangos about Cádiz and Havana and the sentimental foreign pop songs of my earlier summers—and I could do this without the need of ear-phones or the risk of ridicule, though I would instantly click Off if anyone knocked. I had a basin in there too, which meant that apart from showering when I knew that the showers were empty, I was self-sufficient. I'd begun to shave by this point, a development which I loathed, for bristle felt less like maturity to me than it did like irreversible loss, but at least I was spared the need to perform the whole indignity shirtless in some public washroom. I kept an illicit kettle in my wardrobe, to avoid the boiler in the corridor; I laced my coffee with cocoa, and, at night, sharpened it with a glug of whisky from a bottle which I kept locked in one of my boxes. Either I ate in my room, or I ate with Dr. Fox, but I was never to return to that filthy canteen which stank of bleach and soggy dishcloths—yet was grandiloquently termed the refectory.

My tutor, though not unkindly, treated me like a patient, for we both knew that in order for me to succeed in my own terms—in terms that excluded my parents from my rainbow—two years of hard academic slog lay ahead of me, like my long view of the uphill drive towards the statue of the insouciant Madonna, who was now, miraculously, shielded from my sight by a tangle of branches. Dr. Fox, being insomniac, would prod me awake at dawn, so that I could shower, dress, breakfast in his company, and still be back at my desk before the bulk of the school had risen. He supervised my daily routine with military precision, but I was grateful for this discipline, which, to me, from him, felt like protection. I no longer bothered with morning assembly, and scarcely troubled to glance at noticeboards.

On the sly, to spare me the patronage of some in-house teacher, Dr. Fox found me a private coach, an undergraduate at some nearby university whom he paid out of his own pocket, and who came to the office in the basement three evenings a week in an attempt to cram into my skull the requisite numerical sense for me to be able to re-sit Mathematics. I began to type my A-level notes; I learnt to be organized; and I also learnt that whereas, earlier, it had been I who'd been reduced to craven borrowing, now, it was others who kept creeping up to beg access to my translations and compositions. Although, as ever, I sat at the back of the class, I no longer felt as if I were hiding, or wanting to fly out, but rather, biding my time, waiting in the wings of patience. During lessons, I contributed a meagre minimum. My Spanish teacher, for instance, was a Methodist yokel from the locality, keen on nylon slacks and keener still on football, so you will understand why there wasn't, in reality, awfully much to be contributed by someone in my position. He would attempt, with irksome regularity, to correct my pronunciation, which felt as if he were daring to correct my mother. Quite why he did this still remains a mystery; perhaps it was to teach me Methodist humility, to puncture my snobbish arteries; yet there was never any mystery about the fact that his own pronunciation of my native tongue was purest package tourist. He'd probably done a stint as a waiter in some plastic hotel in Torremolinos, though I'm certain that he wouldn't ever have been tempted by the local vino. When once I asked whether he thought that Lorca's work might have been inspired by a homosexual sensibility, he yanked me out of class, accused me of being disruptive, and told me to cut out my sickening irrelevancies if I wished to continue to be taught by him. You get the gist.

A FEW WEEKS into the term, as I was beginning to find my feet, I walked into my room (after orchestra practice, it must have been) and picked up an envelope—unaddressed, like a charity circular—which had been slipped under my door. I opened it absent-mindedly while I moved towards the window to dump my violin. When I reached my desk, I looked down, glanced at the contents and . . . there was scarcely a need to read. Yet another paper ladder, again scrawled in red crayon, and again inflamed with threats and expletives, but demanding, this time, a more rounded twenty pounds to be delivered by the end of the week to the left gazebo, you dirty queer. And yet now, for some indefinable reason, the abuse struck a different, weaker chord within me. Perhaps it was the repetitiveness of the formula, its dreary predictability, or perhaps it was my growing hopes for my own future; because, even though I knew that I couldn't resort to Dr. Fox for help on this issue, much less to Mr. Wolfe, never mind my parents, who were worse than useless—they were proper enemies—I also knew that the joke was in some way at an end, that I could never again go through with it. Beyond the fact that I'd taught no one during the previous summer, and that, since I'd earned no extra money, I wasn't in a position even to contemplate acceding to Al Capone's escalating greed, some profounder, darker part of me had toughened up, grown obstinate—refused even to seek a financial solution. What, instead, it sought, once and for all, was exposure of the blackmailer's identity, confrontation, the horrible truth. If I couldn't go to the authorities for assistance, well, big deal, I'd go elsewhere, for neither authority nor assistance was solely the preserve of school. I was coming up to my retake, and the last thing that I could risk was another failure, for, once I had Maths under my belt, I could, if necessary, do my A levels elsewhere, or independently. What I needed was to settle this problem urgently, but no longer for Al Capone's benefit. For my own. It was my wish. My last will and testament.

It didn't take me long to reach a decision. I had learnt, God knows how, perhaps from some thriller on Dr. Fox's television, about an invisible solution which, once touched by the unsuspecting criminal, turned his fingers to an ecclesiastical, but indelible, purpurine, instantly betraying his culpability. This substance, which was known as Smart Water, would, at long last, provide me with the means of outsmarting my foe, priest or boy. I could don a pair of gloves, paint the invisible liquid onto a message of financial refusal, and soon enough Al Capone would be revealed. All I needed was to avail myself of this magical juice, which was the property of private detectives, of whom I knew none, and of the police, whom I didn't need to know, because the police were supposedly there to help you. And so, the following afternoon, I walked up to the local village and waited for a bus to ferry me to a police station a couple of miles down the road, where, in my naïveté, I imagined that I'd be able, without imparting my reason, to learn how I might obtain this vital solution. But as I lurked beneath the shelter, I noticed a few of my peers meandering back from the pub, among them Steel, and as they passed, he, waving the others on, stopped to chat to me, probably a bit pissed.

I noticed that his bob was gone. His hair had been cut short, not chopped but layered expensively, which, at that point in our lives, generally spelt parental coercion, a conciliatory bribe to the stroppy teenage son. At any rate: up he strolled, hands in pockets, to where I (legs crossed, I have a horrible feeling) was sitting, and then—did I mind?—he plonked himself down beside me. Why should I?, I replied with surly indifference. Our shoulders were almost level, almost touching, not so much because I'd suddenly grown over the summer, which I don't think that I had, as because he, if not actually physically, seemed to have shrunk emotionally or morally or something. His erstwhile braggadocio, his former gleaming suit of armour, appeared to have suffered, to have been dented—somewhere about his chest, or, perhaps, his helmet. Apparently his O-level results hadn't matched those of his brilliant older brothers, but this was not discussed between us. It was hardly as if my own grades filled me with pride. Instead, we remained silent, mulling over our separate problems, delivered to the sort of brooding into which adolescents often wander. I tried to envisage him at home during the holidays, ever the sickly baby of the family, being stuffed with vitamins by his parents, and being sneered at by his know-all, musqueteering brothers, who must have seemed, to him, like unfair rivals. I felt glad, for once, to be an only child. No feuds between siblings; no squabbles over inheritance.

How were my hols?, he began. Total washout. Why was that? Because my parents made me want to vomit. So did his, he admitted, though not half as much as his bloody brothers. I had never known him so overt, so trusting. Got a girlfriend? I asked, as if I were his aunt. Hardly, he laughed, somewhat sourly. What d'you mean? Too much effing work to do, for Christ's sake; I'm expected to get a scholarship to Awksford, he said sarcastically. Ah, I replied, as if what I were expected to get were a husband. I don't think that he liked my fragrant air of distance, my mother's vacant superiority. It seemed to make him edgy. I sensed that he wanted me either to (for Christ's sake) sympathize with the pressures that had been piled upon him, or to give him a piece of whatever it was that had lately fortified me. Perhaps he envied me slightly. It had never occurred to me, before that memorable afternoon, that I was capable of inspiring such a sentiment, for, despite my privileges, which were manifold, and despite my mental aptitude, which, though not remarkable, was nevertheless of value, and despite my physical attributes, which, though these hardly catapulted me to the stratosphere of the raving exotic beauty, neither did they condemn me to the cess-pit of the downright ugly, despite all these things, I had been bred, or grown over the years, to consider myself unsatisfactory.

I produced a packet of fags. He stared at it, as if taken aback. Cigarette?, I offered. He recoiled, but only minimally, perhaps in order to suggest that, though he remained a nonsmoker, such enduring rectitude bore no connection to his parents' medical sermons. I understood. But I lit up. He looked oddly troubled, trapped, as if life had dealt him a hand which made it impossible for him, at least at home, ever to draw on a trump. What was the good of a skewering intelligence if it was doomed never to skewer enough? The injustice made you resentful, vengeful, sort of bad. That was the inference. A strange, perverse closeness seemed to blur us. He turned to scrutinize me, did so almost pruriently, as if to explore my stupid, joyless, but paradoxically enviable interior. The blueness of his eyes assumed a shade of intimacy, which warmed towards lilac. One of his eyelids quivered. It was very nearly embarrassing. I hoped that he wasn't after a repetition of our (one and only) forgettable fumble. Who knows, I remember thinking, maybe that's why he hasn't got a girlfriend.

So how were things?, he asked, with a tone of genuine interest, as if my welfare, now that we were in the senior school, were really of import. I exhaled. I thought about it. And then I told him that I'd received yet another of those ruddy blackmail notes. He looked startled, shocked on my behalf. I supposed that, once I'd paid him back his seven pounds, he'd forgotten all about my dramas. Couldn't say I blamed him. Anyway, I explained that I'd received another demand, but added that, this time, the game was up: I was through with the whole racket. I pretended, for some reason, that I had pots of cash about me, as if I needed the fantasy of money to lend me courage in my principled resolve to unmask the culprit. What was I going to do about it?, he wondered. Oh, I said—then paused, and had another gasp before going on to tell him that I was waiting for a bus to take me into town. I was on my way to the police about the matter—which, in unconscious homage to Dr. Fox, I described as frankly ridiculous. I'd had enough. Was sick of it. He looked down at the ground seriously, to consider my problem with the gravity that it warranted. He remained in that position for a good long while. The suspense made me impatient, jumpy. And then he looked up and looked out beyond the road toward the moors which blighted any hope of a horizon, and said, quite quietly: sorry. (Sorry?) Yes, that's what he said. Because, you see, it turned out that Steel and Al Capone had been one and the same person.

I REACTED with a confusion reminiscent of my father, reminiscent of his misery-and-thrill about my results; for, as I surveyed the face of Lucifer, I found myself filled with a conflicting blend of rage and gratitude. Perhaps I should have told the demon—to whom I never again spoke—how sorry I, for my own part, was that, although he'd been clever to write like a retard, and clever to choose such an improbable drop for the money, he would never be as clever as either of his brothers. But the sorry truth is that I, no less than he, was a coward; and so instead, in a travesty of forgiveness (prompted perhaps by the fact that neither of us fancied the long way back), we strolled towards the building as if together, side by side yet absolutely separate. However, the silence that ensued, oh yes, the silence of that walk was gloriously mine, deliriously and entirely. And when I marched into tea with Dr. Fox—guess what?—he no longer found me peculiar. And now I regaled him with my version of the tale of Al Capone, excluding Mr. Wolfe but climaxing, in a manic flurry, with Steel. And when my tutor began to calculate the funds which had been extorted from me, and to think of how best they might be recovered, it fell on me to insist that the matter was closed. Unpalatable. *Finito.* And then I stuffed myself with cakes. To bursting.

My life was back on track. I re-sat Mathematics, and, within hours of that exam (thanks to the coach whom Dr. Fox had enlisted, who performed a post-mortem on my answers, a post-mortem which, unlike the open-ended ones which are the best that one can ever perform on love, could be taken as conclusive, for maths are nothing if not exact), I knew that I had passed—not with any glamour, let's be honest, but with the certainty than I would never again have to keep a slide-rule, nor be married to a protractor. When, in dull due course, the official announcement was delivered to my parents' house—only to be left, this time, slumped a little warily, and unopened, on the silver salver at the entrance—it was I who treated the flimsy envelope as if it bore the foregone conclusion to some blood test for shingles—without interest, surprise, or sunglasses. And besides, I'd already left word that I was out for lunch, which I was—wearing a yellow hat.

Instead of subjecting myself to one of my parents' deadly repasts, which increasingly seemed to involve strangers (often the very strangers who once had squatted to gawp at my monotonous miniature chug-chug), I would slink off to the Nautical Club, to bronze myself in the Christmas sunshine; but I use that verb, that tone—bronze—loosely, liberally, like too much oil of coconut. Because although I could have assumed a perfectly respectable suntan locked out on my mother's terrace, or, indeed, practically anywhere else on the island, the Nautical Club of my childhood seemed no longer to spell public humiliation for me, nor terror, nor anxiety. Quite the reverse. It thrilled me now, thrilled me with its indecency, which simmered beneath the ripples. You could practically smell it. Briny.

I would lie around, with one knee up (which boys just didn't), wearing what the French, by then, had christened a *cache-sexe,* though mine was barely even that, it was really just an excuse to stretch a few scales of acrylic snakeskin over my absolutest basics: half my buttocks were out (yes, Father, out—out and succulent): because, by that stage, I felt it incumbent on me not merely to teeter on the most *risqué* precipice of fashion and define myself, for all to witness, as the very epitome of *le dernier cri,* but also to distance myself from those smug small-islanders, those privileged lovers of Franco whose respectable, reproductive lifestyles were as interesting and varied as is striped canvas, navy and white, a conventional cover against undesirable hotness.

Children went off to paddle and splash with their nannies, while their mothers sat by the bar, drinking papaya juice and, even if expected home for lunch, tucking into calamari and Russian salad. Meanwhile, those who lounged around the grown-up pool, smoking and rubbing lotion into one another, and shrieking at in-jokes more opaque than sunglasses, and turning mahogany but never—God forbid such a catastrophe—ever peeling, tended to be the girls, who, at that age, were stupidish but lovely, long-haired nymphs in pink bikinis, with diamond ear-studs and sparkling smiles, hanging about for that one Big catch while pretending to be expecting their brothers, who were no less stupid but far less lovely, for there was a whiff of Barbary about them, a loutishness. Yet their fathers, and their uncles, and the hosts of their older male cousins, removed once and twice and thrice, those gentlemen of Spain, they were another matter. They, the guys with the masses of chest hair and sweaty great cocks and low-slung hangers, those sinners of good caste were Alive, and sizzling with frustration, and they excited the hell out of me. And gradually-gradually I began to realize that if some of them, from beneath the brim of my hat, looked familiar, it wasn't because their offspring had once attended nursery school with me, nor because I'd seen those men strutting their stuff, and scratching it hard about the changing rooms of the club, nor even because they sometimes shot me odd glances (as if there were something intriguingly not quite right about me, like blond dreadlocks), but because I recognized them from my forays into the Municipal Park. Naughty. Still, no one ever addressed me directly, which was gratifying, because just as my Methodist teacher of Spanish liked to imagine that he was conversant with my mother-tongue, so I, by now, had become determined to convey by my demeanour not merely that I was you know, *comme ça,* but that I'd become exotically de-hispanicized, like the Duchess of Carnaby.

ON THE OCCASIONS when I was forced to be at my parents' house while they were entertaining (and my mother would even pretend that her guests were desperate to see me, rather than admit how desperately my repeated absences embarrassed her in the face of company), I would capitulate to her entreaties, but on my own terms, my tail twitching with sting. The unspoken custom at home was that my father would greet guests as they came in, kissing the women's hands, slapping the men on the back, and guffawing like a good Old Boy as he led them through rooms arrayed with standards of white gladioli, or out into the garden if the weather inspired it. Then, ages later, when everyone was comfortably ensconced and well into their drinkies, and marvelling at the bits of deliciousness borne along from the kitchen, my mother would come swirling down the stairs, light on her dancing feet, and fragrant, and pretending to apologize to all and sundry but always being flattered despite it, and always, to be truthful, looking heavenly, the best, for she wouldn't have had it any other way, not even in her own house, the house of an insular beauty without a care in the universe.

My trick was to stay—sometimes even switching off the light—in my bedroom, and hang back until I'd heard her make her descent; and only once the resulting commotion downstairs had died down, would I condescend to follow suit and glide into the assemblage. It thrilled me to note how the men stood up on my arrival, while my parents—awkwardly natural, naturally awkward—exclaimed in unison, as they'd exclaimed ever since the beginning: There he is. And then everyone would laugh, though not quite comfortably—for by my high teens, I had perfected a look of uneasy (girlish) bashfulness to enhance those late entrances of mine. As I did the murderous rounds, I would kiss the women twice, which in Spain, in those days, wasn't really done; it somehow seemed too much; but too much, you see, was exactly what I then encouraged, perhaps because I'd had too little of what counted.

At any rate, when my parents coerced me into mingling with their public, I paid close attention to my outfits, taking pains to ensure that my colours corresponded with those worn by my mother (which I would have seen in advance, hanging in her ironing room)—so that once we were both immersed in the social morass, we presented the suggestion of a united front against my father, who was never really happier than in the hackneyed trappings of the clubhouse ex-pat. And once I'd arranged myself among these strangers, always placing myself close to my mother, on whom I blamed the whole nightmare, she would do most of my talking on my behalf, as if I were a retard (as opposed to ill-mannered, which I think was considered to be a more grievous handicap), while I began to sip at vodka through a straw, like tonic, and too fast, so that far from unwinding I would soon find myself wound into coiling postures that spoke of unspeakable feminine tension. The most frequent such posture, which I also deployed when I knelt at communion, involved crossing my legs and wrapping my shins around each other (hosed in long socks of silk), until my feet, thus interlocked, felt less like actual feet than like the fishtail of a mermaid. Everyone would notice my nellie contortions: it was obvious, not least because they took such blatant pains to appear not to, as if their gazes were carefully skirting round the sight of a thalidomide victim. I think that they pitied my parents, those people, and I could picture them chortling, on their drives back home, about the merits of an expensive English education.

Dinner itself was easier. Since my mother, just as she was meticulous about her menus, was insistent that her *emplacements* be tailored to suit properly mixed company, by which, predictably, she meant alternating genders, and since I amounted to a male of sorts, and since the ladies of my parents' society didn't seem to think that it was required of them to make efforts at conversation, but, rather, that their role was simply to react to the fascinating insights of their masculine companions, who always pretended to be suitors, the result was that I could be as spoilt as both of the spoilt women at my sides, who would turn outwards for social survival, like flowers desperate for sunlight. Instead, I would practise sign-language with the servants, and grew fantastically irksome about it, disrupting the proceedings by asking them to fetch me some extra little queenery, such as ice, or (after deliberately dropping and trampling on mine) another napkin could you, or even, between courses, an ashtray, like a Hollywood slut; and while my mother fulminated in her knife-pleated chiffon, her guests did their outward damnedest to have a wonderful time, since the last thing that anyone ever wanted was a fracas, you see, least of all on account of the insufferable brat. Because life, to them, was all about harmony—whereas harmony, I'm afraid to say, to me meant hairspray.

My favourite wheeze, however, I would reserve for later, for when dinner was over and people had either removed to the drawing room, or, in the warmer months, sauntered a little squiffily back out to the garden, where sometimes, despite a sea of flickering candles, they managed, as they navigated their way over the grass, to—whoops—bang into low tables, which, though happily now cleared of earlier débris, made not a jot's worth of difference when it came to the annoyance of laddering one's tights, until, exhausted, everyone eventually collapsed, laughing and laughing, onto the painted wicker chairs, whose cushions, in their absence, would have been plumped up. This was the time when, as my mother poured coffee and tempted her friends to sample the novelty that was saccharine, and everyone began to implore my father *please* for home-made liqueurs (or, if you were a proper chap, to bark for brandy and cigars), I produced my cigarette packet, which I would wield not warily—not like a souvenir from some former black-mailer, nor with false nostalgia, the false memory of all the colourful cocktails which I never got to have with Clifford—but with a refined certitude, *élan,* as if the dainty box in my slim fingers were something infinitely more sinister than a mere vessel for coffin nails.

I can't think where I can have learnt this conjuring fantasy, but it must have been back in England, because here, on this parochial little planet, it caused (especially among the women, who, even in the shadows, recognized exactly what I was up to) a sensation, speechless consternation. No clapping, sadly. At any event, as I manipulated the cardboard packet this way and that, and tilted it backwards ever so slightly, well, don't you know, it just seemed to assume a life of its own, and turn into a sort of mirrored powder-compact, and I, as a result, to become quite another character, a coquette or soubrette or courtesan. I would always, for the sake of propriety, first make a point of extracting a cigarette, which, rather than beg to be lit, seemed to prefer to dangle about my hand like a slim pencil of eye-liner while I peered inside the lid of the packet, as if a tiny looking-glass were secreted in there. I would slowly swivel my head from left to right, and begin—the horror of it—to pretend to be checking my *eyebrows,* and to shape them with a middle finger, which I sometimes licked in advance, for the method; and now I would rub my lips together, mmm, which luckily passed muster, didn't need touching up; and my nose, what a relief, was not too shiny under the moonlit sky. And at last I could quietly snap the compact shut, and lean back, and light up without a care in the universe, as my mother, had she smoked, might have done, and admire the constellation of stars above.

But I suppose that it *was* a little much for someone of my tender age to be performing such seasoned vanities in public: I should really have slipped away to the powder room—an oversight which presumably explains why certain of the ladies looked so discomfited by my actions. But perhaps they feared that I was flirting with their husbands; and perhaps they were right to do so, for it is not impossible for a perfectly good husband to be susceptible to the charms of the young invert. Only on occasion, after everyone had departed, did my mother draw my attention to my cosmetic illusion, and demand, in seething whispers (because of the servants, who were clearing up), an explanation for what she called my quite extraordinary conduct. But I just rolled my eyes with mimed *étonnement,* as if to suggest that her medication was finally getting the better of her mind; and Mother, I replied, I have simply no idea what you're talking about. But she must have known very well the answer to what she had been asking, because, from that night on, she banned me from smoking when guests came to her house—it reflected badly, that was her argument. But it didn't reflect as badly as the fact that, once she'd got wise to my retarded entrances, she always made a point of fishing me out of my room and forcing me, like bait, to go down before her, while she, my rival actress, held back for a good while, ostensibly to attend to her last-minute touches—though, in reality, the better to choreograph that long-anticipated moment when she finally managed to flutter to the ground, as ever to enchant the gathered company.

THE COMPANY WHICH I, meanwhile, kept was odd: occasional men without names, occasional prescribed texts, melancholy pop songs, and, most of all, fashion magazines. By this stage, my mother had begun to criticize my clothes, not just in pale shades of objection, such as primrose, but in earnest, and to claim that if I went about, wearing, for instance, such wide, or high-waisted, or tapered, or loudly patterned trousers—whatever that season dictated—people on the streets would laugh at me. I told her that nobody laughed in London, quite the opposite, and that anyway, I hoped *her* acquaintances were not so superficial as to judge by appearances. She, of course, concurred on this last particular, but added that she wasn't concerned by her friends as such, so much as by the general masses. The *masses*?, I spluttered; why on earth, since one didn't know them, should one care about the opinions of the masses? She said that being my mother, she felt embarrassed on my behalf, and then she stung me with the claim that she no longer felt comfortable to be seen out in my company, for she had noticed people doing double takes as I advanced and passed—an elaboration which, from my point of view, went some small way towards mitigating her insult, because nothing, then, would have upset me more than the disgrace of not being noticed. But I told her that there was no need, in the future, for us to venture forth together, that I was perfectly able to find my own way around (and how), and that if she didn't deem me a suitable companion for her gracious promenades, well, that was her prerogative—just as it was mine to refuse to wear her silly sports shirts emblazoned with grinning alligators.

She said that the problem didn't lie with suitability: it lay with *extremes*. Couldn't I see that gentlemen should always, by definition, be attired discreetly? Since when?, I demanded. Since man became civilized, was her ignorant, and equally uncivil, reply. What about the Incroyables at Versailles, I countered, and the great English Dandies? Did the name Beau Brummel mean nothing to her? When would she get it into her skull that I belonged to a long and noble tradition of sartorial peacocks? She told me not to speak to my mother like that, as if she were a separate entity, and then went on to state that she couldn't care less about peacocks, which were just harbingers of ill-omen, nor about the history of costume, still less for my apparent fascination with effeminate fops—in-bred undesirables, she called them, look at all those Habsburgs. No, what worried her, she insisted, and for my sake rather than her own, was the fact that I seemed unable to differentiate between modernity, which was just vulgar and ephemeral and commercial and nothing to do with taste (her *sine qua non,* her *non plus ultra, mea* most *maxima culpa*), and elegance, which was eternal, the hallmark of true class.

Such edicts struck me as rich coming from a woman who'd never even heard of *L'Uomo Vogue,* which at that time was my absolute bible, a source of information infinitely more directional that any encyclical from the Vatican, so I told her that she ought to make a point (in the unlikely instance that it should ever consent to be screened on her precious island) of going to see a film called *Roma,* and that she might pay particular attention to the scene of the ecclesiastical fashion show, which was my idea both of modernity *and* of elegance (not to mention fantabularity, but she wouldn't have understood such a refined hybrid); yet she, to my sudden surprise, and quicker than I could say Fellini, rounded on me with the name Pasolini, which, though wrong, was nevertheless impressive for an uneducated beauty. I raised an appreciative eyebrow, like Tadzio's mother.

Next, however, she reversed into the name of the director whom she had cited with a snort of disgust, followed by some piece of wisdom, muttered as a half-aside (because, yet again, servants were lurking about), to the effect that if the Italian cinematographer had been murdered, it wasn't because of his subversive talents, which, like his absurd Communist posturings, were a secondary issue, but because—as the whole world knew, she said—he was a pervert, a degenerate, and a criminal. And then she went racing into some diatribe about never minding if the Mafia had been implicated in the whole business, and would I kindly not try to sidetrack her about the irony of Ostia (the town where Pasolini had met his maker) being named after the sacred host, because her point was that having his head cracked open by a rock, hurled at him by a street urchin, before being run over by the wheels of his own car, had been, in her considered (Catholic) opinion, a right and fitting end for such an . . . *Amoralista*—which, to me, sounded paradoxically amorous. But I think that this was the first time my mother managed really to shock me, profoundly, properly to scandalize me; and I began, after this altercation (which, incredibly, had kicked off with a contentious pair of trousers), to fear that the woman, as well as being addicted to socially accepted barbiturates, was actively sinister, wicked, in the clutches of some evil—like Steel. And whatever shame she might earlier have claimed to feel on my behalf now dwindled into insignificance next to what I felt on hers, which was stark gaping horror, like the creature in *The Scream*. And back in the safety of my own room, I was forced to conclude that, as holidays went, this one had proved still less productive than the unproductive rule.

WHEN I REACHED the sixth form, the first thing that I did was to decline to wear a prefect's tie, for even if this (unearned) privilege was my entitlement, and even if the tie itself, ruby as Dorothy's slippers, was more fetching than the dreary common-or-garden one, which was forgettable, I was as unfit to impose authority as I felt prepared to knot it round my neck and sport it. And yet, despite the fact that younger boys couldn't tell that I was a senior, my movements at the top of the school felt smoother somehow, less careful: I could walk with Clifford's swagger, outswagger him even, and flaunt the lissom hips which God had fitted on me, and pout like Lolita, and perform my powder-compact trick at whim, and suck the end of my fat pen in class, and suck it, of course, that trifle too provocatively, and flutter my eyes like a preparatory secretary, safe in the knowledge that, whichever of these things I did, I couldn't be taken to task by the banes of my early days here, twerps like Payne Senior, and the toad, and the midget corporal—consigned long since to oblivion, all three of them, and reduced, no doubt, to ignominious polytechnics in the provinces, or the military. Good luck, boys, see you. *See you?* Bollocks to that: what I meant was: not bloody likely, you bunch of creeps, not if I can help it.

Helping it, however, did present me with a bit of a problem as I neared the end of my eight-year imprisonment, for what I lacked in accumulated gravitas, I'd grown to amass in subversiveness. Sometimes I felt as if I were bursting from frustration, like a permanently boiling kettle with too tight a lid, or like the men who scratched their swelter-ing genitals round the Nautical Club changing-rooms. And so, in order to let off steam, I was sometimes driven to capers which, though insur-rective in the tradition of Fellini's fashion scene, didn't actually consti-tute breaking the rules: my iniquities were too girlie for my father's Alma Mater ever to have envisaged a need to forbid them. And besides, had his school taken into account the existence of misfits such as I, its book of regulations, like that of Revelations, would have grown as lengthy as it would have been rendered ludicrous.

I'LL GIVE YOU a self-ridiculing instance of my adolescent misdemeanours, if only to convey the flavour of my cheek, which was overblown in spirit—more Genet than Ionesco, really. The choir at school was sometimes required to perform for extra-curricular inconveniences, such as the boring nuptials of former alumni, and one such imposition befell us early in my final summer, on a Saturday afternoon leading up to A' levels, when I could have been getting on with revision. But no, like it or lump it, the entire choir had to sing. Dr. Fox, can you believe, just wouldn't exempt me from this dismal ceremony. So this is what I did to avenge the infliction.

On the morning of the wedding, I sneaked out, earlier than breakfast, to the gardens behind the observatory, which, now that I was a senior, I was legitimately permitted to visit. What was less legitimate, however, was that I should scuttle, as I did, under the rose bushes, pilfering petals from the ground and stuffing them into a plastic bag—emblazoned with the name of one of my mother's smart boutiques—which I'd employed, when my trunk had sailed back to England, to wrap a giant bottle of avocado conditioner, in case it leaked. But once the dewy grass had been raked clear of fallen botany, as if a scrupulous gardener had attended to it, I found my bag still to be half-empty, and its supply of proper confetti—as opposed to paper (the barbaric notion of rice didn't even bear thinking about)—to be measly, unsatisfying. Confetti was like scent, I reminded myself: a mere sprinkling was worse than nothing: what you needed was abundance, profusion—which is when I found myself forced to make a decision, and quickly.

I took a chance and, hoping that no one was spying on me from the building, I turned my back on the Gothic windows, and began, like a born-again shepherdess decked with panniers, to sway along the flowerbeds, surreptitiously tugging and wrenching at the actual roseheads, as if their petals were nasty embellishments on swimming-helmets, and as if I, far from denuding them, were in fact doing them an aesthetic favour. But I tried, even in my haste, to exercise discretion, and selected to pluck only the palest, most pastel shades. Anyway, by the time that my task was complete and the poppers on the bulging bag were safely secured and I'd resumed a semblance of composure despite the fact that my nerves were going demented, you might have presumed that I'd merely been out to collect a cushion, forgotten after a siesta in the Left Gazebo.

Following lunch, which I ate in my room, I crept up to the loft in advance of the choir, while Dr. Fox was warming up—twiddling around with stops and keys and repositioning his anglepoise, which the cleaners, to his regular annoyance, seemed always to shift. I shoved the plastic bag under my seat in the back row, where, these days, I hardly bothered to join in, for the sound of my grown voice was like somebody else's, grating and unreal; and then I went over to my uncooperative mentor, who, improvising some Gregorian ditty, sat barricaded behind his organ, which looked more like a witness-box than a musical instrument. When he saw me appear at his side and beam, he briefly flashed his spectacles at me, and grinned like an unholy innocent before returning his glare to the rigours of musicianship. So far, I thought, so good.

The entrance procession, when it began, did sound quite grandiose, for Dr. Fox was giving it his organistic everything, although, to be quite frank, he might have cooled it a bit on the tempo: this wasn't a barndance, for God's sake. But I had more pressing concerns, you see, because I hadn't yet managed to get a glimpse of the bride—couldn't until she was up at the altar—and when I did, well, let's say she wasn't exactly stately: outfit too folksy by half, with a strong stylistic whiff of prairieland and an ill-advised assortment of appliquéd flowers around a wobbly hemline. No train; cropped little veil; what a waste of a one-and-only Catholic chance. The drip of a girl, instead of carrying a sumptuous great bunch of gardenias, was probably clutching some crummy little posy of freesias, as if being joined in matrimony were tantamount to undergoing surgery. As for her bridesmaids—best be brief: four of them, frizzy-haired, forced into printed pinafores, and burly to a woman, like milkmaids off-duty. Despite the fact that their heads had been ribbonned to suggest a rural girlishness, the gang looked not so much pastorally nubile as seasoned consumers of the

Pill. Far better to have been corseted like eighteenth-century shepherdesses gone out to gather roses, with voluptuous panniers to disguise the width of their beams. A lamentable spectacle, as my mother would have said. But ours is not to reason. Sure thing.

Once the marriage had survived some dreary homily by one of the shuffling centre-parted priests, and an everlasting signing of the register in the sacristy, and a glut of concelebrated prayers in Latin, and a queue to communion by only half of the congregation (thus betraying the appliquéd prairie-girl as a Prot), the leader of the clerical pack performed a ludicrous sequence of crosses which led you to fear that he might never stop, but suddenly, Dr. Fox, in a strop, had attacked the keyboard. His concluding number, one of those corny old toccatas, he took at a hurtle-and-a-half—presumably to show off. I could see, from where I stood, the top of his head bobbing with technical proficiency and swelling with the glory of his own volume. Meanwhile, the bride, whose mimsy veil was now up, was trying to grin at everyone, but seemed able to focus on no one while she progressed in a daze through the fug of incense, as if, too late to turn back, she had gleaned the Catholic hell to which she had committed herself, and to which she had vowed to surrender the blessing of future progeny. Her bloated groom, the father-to-be, had a dearth of hair on his head, straight and gingery, but what little remained was scraped defiantly across, in the style of some air force. And beneath his straining tails, he was buttoned into a noisy waistcoat, striped in blue-and-gold, the colours of the proud Old Boy.

I didn't have long. As the couple began their procession back down the central aisle, with the organ booming forth, all systems go, I grabbed my bag and crept to the front of the choir loft, the middle of which was next to the organ. I needed to be symmetrical. Dr. Fox, whose back was turned to the altar, was absorbed by the demands of his score, flicking musical pages and hurtling over the keys and pedalling his little feet like billy-o, and probably humming along; but I was too busy to tell, because, by this stage, I was frantically wedging the bag between my stomach and the edge of the balcony, as if now *I* were the pregnant milkmaid, far too late for contraception; and from my great bulge I next began, as if claimed by a Grande Polonaise Brillante of my own making, to extract an Abundance, a Profusion of pastel petals of rose, which I hurled into the air, to left and to right and to heaven, like an explosion of benison, like omens of hope—not for the future of those newly-weds, but for my own. To begin with, however, the bride seemed not to notice, and since the groom looked mesmerized by the flagstones, I grabbed more and more of my mythical confetti, grabbed it by the fistful, until, at long last, the Protestant bride did look up, and smiled with gratitude, and suddenly I could envisage her as a child down there, and she didn't look unpretty in this picture. And at the point when she was about to vanish under the balcony and walk out into the marital gloom, I, in desperation, turned the whole bag upside down, and just let the rest of my rebellion against Dr. Fox—who must have noticed some blurry commotion at his side, but couldn't do a thing to stop it—shower down onto the non-existent train of the bride, and, instead, fall onto the ribbonny heads of her pinafored retinue, who, though not obviously pregnant, did look ravished. And then, before my mentor could have a chance to finish his bravura performance, for which he, unlike us, was paid—and not in groceries—I returned to my place, looked around at the other choristers, who appeared to be shell-shocked, and told everyone that we could go. And for once in my life, the crowd did as I ordered.

ON MY WAY back to my room, not quite patting my own back, as my father liked to pat the backs of all his chums, but certainly feeling what used to be called chuffed, which I don't think that my father ever really stopped feeling, a treble came up to tell me that I was wanted in the Great Hall, which is where wedding receptions and other such celebrations were hosted. Blood raced to my face: some freeloading priest, guzzling without regard either to chastity or poverty, but clearly with an eye still keenly fixed upon obedience, was obviously warming up to give me a piece of his wisdom. Who wanted me?, I asked the boy. He didn't know. A priest? Nope. Teacher? Couldn't tell, he said, some woman. Which calmed me enough to stuff the empty bag in a bin near the kitchens, before bracing myself for the onslaught.

But when I reached the Great Hall, which was already swelling to boisterousness, I was confronted at the door by one of the bridesmaids, a huge specimen of womanhood who, for all of her size, couldn't make herself heard through the din; so she grabbed my arm and frog-marched me across the gathering, past wafts of noxious perfume and hearty bursts of male commotion, and led me up to the Protestant Bride, whom she prodded, and who turned her bouncing ringlets to me for a couple of seconds, thanked me for that wonderful surprise, how kind, and told me to stay and have a drink and meet everyone. Which, needless to say, I didn't—not just because of the marauding evidence of the rector and the mongrel in the distance, but because I thought that any woman who married an Old Boy must be bonkers.

NOT LONG AFTER this incident (about which Dr. Fox, however incensed, was rendered powerless to rebuke me, for the wedding party made a point of congratulating him on his marvellous idea of getting one of the boys to throw petals over the choir loft), my parents graced me with a visit, carefully planned to coincide with a jamboree known as Victors' Weekend—the supposed highlight of the year, which, depending on which way you looked at it (say downwards, as I did), could also be regarded as the lowest point in the school diary. If Dr. Fox and I ever concurred on anything, it was on the dismal prospect of such festivities, which boiled down, year in, year out, to a mass assault on the community by more overaged children than one imagined conceivable, and children whose regressive high spirits were not restricted to Old Boys, for their wives invariably proved themselves to be similarly vociferous participants: I remember hearing piercing female screeches from the sports fields as mothers forgot all composure in order to spur their cherished offspring to Go-Go-Go-Julian, Nicky, Simon, Peter, Andrew, Tim. (Why was there never an Arthur, for crying out loud, or a Peregrine, or an Aubrey, or even an Evelyn?)

Beyond an epidemic of sporting events through the weekend, its apex being an Old Boys' cricket match which fortunately drew the crowds outdoors for a few hours, those three days of collective hijinks also incorporated an hilarious display of army manoeuvres, an interminable prize-giving ceremony, a school play (which invariably bore a cautionary note, even when that note was jollied into a musical), and, on the closing evening—by which time, half the parents had already vanished (some, it should be said, with *caravans* in tow)—there was a classical concert: always, by tradition, ill-attended, and always characterized by clapping between movements.

During these celebrations, there hung in the library what passed for an art exhibition—enough pinned-up watercolours of pockmarked oranges to sink a battleship. Meanwhile, all over the science laboratories, to which I only once went during such festivities (to mess around with Clifford and indulge in a spot of creative graffito) there were baffling displays of experimental projects which never seemed to arrive at any convincing conclusion. Clifford and I would have liked to have seen, not charts and senseless grafts, but a show of half-dissected frogs, or axolotls, pinned down and disembowelled, or foetuses suspended in formaldehyde—yet this was not to be. Instead, by way of more seemly entertainment, there were endless drinks parties for parents and teachers (warm wine, or beer—never a cocktail, no chance of such a thing), so that grown-ups could hobnob and mingle and charm each other rigid.

On Saturday night, a great dinner-dance was always held in a vast nylon tent, pitched in a field, with wobbly trestle-tables and plastic cutlery, and paper plates, and a platform at one end, where some army band attempted to provide music in the gaps between speeches made by various of our Reverends, hip-hip-hooray. This is when the wilder of the boys' sisters (who all seemed to attend the same convent in Essex) liked to sneak away, to neck or worse (heavy petting, I think that they called it) with their brothers' friends in the thickets of rhododendron. And the following morning, everyone would troop back for a very High (hung-over) Mass, followed by a barrage of rattling collections in aid of the most farfetched of causes—rosaries for maimed Liberians, baptismal fonts for Bangladeshis, Catechisms for blind orphans, that kind of genius. There were also shameful tombolas, with prizes so pitiful that no one in their right mind could ever have meant to win one—a year's supply of cat-litter; a teapot cosy (rheumatically knitted); a transparent-plastic Virgin, filled with water from Lourdes and rife with bacteria: Clifford once got saddled with one of these ladies, whose contents, later, desperate for distraction, we drank with tequila—not, in fact, as bad as you might think, uplifting. To your very good health, Father.

.   .   .

BUT BACK TO WHEN my parents came. They motored north in their own car—shipped over in advance of their flight. Having booked into a nearby guesthouse, the one reputed to be smartest, which my mother nevertheless dismissed as frightful, they arrived—presumably due to my father's mounting anticipation—in advance of the hour when I'd been told to keep an eye out. The weather was the balmiest that we'd enjoyed all summer, yet my mother still claimed to be absolutely frozen, and to have brought all the wrong clothes from their hotel in London. She would catch a chill, she felt certain. But she was wrong; she was fine. My mother, let me say one final time, did look beautiful, and would, as the pace of the weekend mounted, be carried along on a tide of admiring glances—a tide on which I, in my possessive childish way, also felt, for that brief period, entitled to ride.

When I first saw her, she was standing on a lawn, patiently nodding while one of my teachers struggled to ingratiate himself, probably with assurances that I was doing well in his subject. Her hair, now, was cropped shorter than mine had been cropped when she'd first waved me off as a child, but was flicked up at the back, and arranged with a slim ribbon of satin, ice blue, tied in a small bow at one side. She wore a shirt-waister. I remember this because her upper body hinted at a strange boyishness, seemed to draw attention to the facial resemblance that existed between us—once, a source of mutual pride; of late, a growing source of discomfort for her. Her dress, I realize with hindsight, was regardless of its time, rose above popular fashion. Perhaps that is how my mother was—coutured to the last unseen stitch, yet influenced by a style which glanced over its own shoulder, back to her youth, which had blossomed twenty years earlier, and was bleakly romantic.

At any rate, among the staff in their greasy suits and greasy gowns, and husbands in nostalgic panamas and the occasional stripy blazer, and wives whose pleated skirts and patterned cardigans had, by this stage, given way to cheesecloth sacks, and clogs on corky platforms, and clanky beads and gypsy hoops and—squeezed over the odd unfortunate posterior—a pair of ill-advised bell-bottoms, my mother stood in profile, slim and tanned, and holding a glass of white wine—a little away from her, as if it were a malodorous flower. Part of my fascination lay in the fact that I was observing her as if afresh now that she'd been transplanted to this new land. I recall, for instance, being surprised to discover that she was not, after all, a tall woman, but rather, of average stature; and yet she was possessed of that quality which I think is nowadays discredited slightly (in favour of attributes such as informality and casualness of manner), which is the gift of poise. My mother had poise in abundance, and charm when she wanted it, and a certain ignorant intelligence. And these three qualities combined, even when she could hardly comprehend a language, conspired to render her alluring, to make her stand out.

She remained stranded in the middle of the gathering, saddled with the oleaginous teacher until, eventually, a little later, when I snapped out of my reverie, I went to her rescue. She had already been abandoned by her husband, who (though I could hear the forced reverberations of his English laughter) had strutted off to consort with more congenial company—a discourtesy which, throughout their visit, would remain the pattern. No matter, her unruffled poise seemed to imply. For there she stood, as if unaware, in pale blue ballerina pumps, gloriously impractical, which reminded me of the pumps that she had worn during those slow, entrancing afternoons in her ironing room. Yet the skirt of her dress, I realized as my gaze moved up from the ground, was neither slow nor entrancing. It was violent. For all the neat rigour of her bodice, and its matching belt and covered buckle, and the discretion of its printed cotton-satin, which gave sheen but did not shine, the skirt was full and unbridled, like the sea around Java. Its sudden explosion of pattern suggested the result, not of a mere rock hurled onto a homosexual head by a street urchin in an Italian town named Ostia, but of that moment when a whole eruption of lava goes crashing through the waves to collide with the bed of the ocean. The cloth seemed to froth and whirl about her waist, to spin around her, blue and blue and blue and white, like gigantic bubbles of marbling. And this stormy skirt of hers, as well as voluminous, was long, almost reached her ankle; and down its front, there glimmered buttons of mother-of-pearl—the last few, left undone. But after the shocking thrill of all that rushing pattern, I was returned to a feeling of calm; and perhaps because of the neutrality of my uniform, which was beyond objection, all our recent disagreements seemed to be washed away, to be forgotten. And now, at last, I did walk up, like a jealous lover, to claim her from the importunate advances of that didactic prat. We kissed (twice). She embraced me with the power of her gardenias. And then we walked away from the crowd, arm in arm, hers laced through mine—as I, long ago, had been taught that this should be done.

I TOOK HER ON a brief guided tour of my past, to dormitories and classrooms at which she neither marvelled nor gasped, but nodded, as if relieved to note that I had left such places behind, and survived. I showed her the theatre, which, since its walls were painted burgundy while the stage-curtain was turquoise, seemed not to do much for her; and I took her to the Gothic chapel (the main one, whose sides were carved with confessionals), which was, she whispered, cold as a sepulchre, let's get out. It must have been during one of those walks, up or down the staircase to the music basement (of which she did approve, because, she said, she could envisage me there, which struck me as an irony), that she was halted in her tracks by the resemblance between the sketch of a young man with a moustache and my grandmother's poor dead infantry officer. I remember feeling grateful for that anecdote about love and death and sadness, feeling flattered by her maudlin confidence, which had been withheld so long, like her warmth, like my trust.

My father seemed altered, not so much outwardly, for he sported the same old tweeds and the same flapping Old Boy tie, as in his attitude: he had grown restless, boisterous, like a child at holiday camp. I felt this bursting enthusiasm to be coarse, unseemly, and I suspect that my mother felt likewise; but since in this northern wilderness she was not so much the queen of an exotic island as a foreign consort in unconquered territory, reduced to the role of a powerless formality, she probably considered it wiser to ignore his juvenile conduct than to reprimand him on the subject—at least for now. Still, the ancillary benefit of his apparent eagerness to glue himself to the non-entities of his youth, and to stand on the sidelines of matches played by their equally irrelevant sons, was that for much of that time my mother and I were left to our own devices, as we had been, oh, ages before, in another life, in the days of the flight of wooden steps that led from the beach house down to the summersands of my childhood.

On their first afternoon with me, my mother said that she was completely exhausted from the car journey up, six hours of unutterable tedium, the time it took to whip round the coastline of our island, and she pleaded that if she was expected to accompany my father to some crummy Drinks for parents and teachers that evening, she must, whatever else, be permitted to take her customary siesta. Grudgingly, her husband drove us, her and me, to the guesthouse where they were staying, dumped us at the door, and then flew, like a bird let out of a cage, back to the healthy open air of his Alma Mater. Strange how one man's imprisonment can, to another, seem like liberation.

IT TURNED OUT that they were sharing a bed, a circumstance which appeared to embarrass my mother, as if a certain obscenity attached to it, but her (unsolicited) explanation was that since this tavern, as she called the place, was heaving with other parents (a word which she uttered as if to mean lice), there had been no alternative but acceptance on her part (by which she meant resignation—a sort of facing the music–cum–biting the bullet). While she explained these things, she turned the central heating up, up to the utmost; and then she lit a scented candle which she'd included in her luggage—thereby evincing a canny presence of mind, for the room stank of damp. My father, she moaned, hadn't properly unpacked, but she was damned if she was going to do so on his behalf; yet the truth of the matter, I soon discovered, was that she'd already monopolized the wardrobe, which she now opened—to reveal . . . *wire* coat-hangers, can you imagine.

From a drawer, she extracted and handed to me a box of chocolates, secured with a wide taffeta ribbon in stripes of aubergine and rust, and fashioned into a flower on top, like a picture-hat from the Edwardian period. The chocolates themselves, though purchased in London, were actually Belgian, and the irony did not escape me that, just as once she had given away the presents which I had chosen for her in Brussels, now it was I who had been cast in the rôle of ingrate, who would play Pass The Parcel—most likely to Dr. Fox—for, by this late stage in my contortions, I had learnt, if not to resist carnality, certainly to resist the temptation of fattening substances—with the notable exception of my binge to celebrate the unmasking of Al Capone.

But next, from some other recess, she conjured a shoe box with a label from Jermyn Street, I think that it was—containing, it transpired, a surprise far greater than mere chocolate; but I steeled myself before lifting the lid, because even if, then, I still considered my mother's dress sense to be above reproach, she and I, you will recall, no longer saw eye to eye on the mercurial subjects of modernity and elegance in menswear. But she suggested, as she vanished into the bathroom to change into a travelling dressing-gown (pink lightweight satin, pale as the petals which had once flown down from the choir), that I try the shoes for size, in case they were too small or too tight or whatever, and yet she appeared—which struck me as optimistic on her part—not to be concerned that, beyond the question of fit, the articles themselves might not appeal to me. Rather she seemed to be suggesting that the mystery stowed within that box (which I envisaged as some ghastly pair of clumpy brogues) was a sartorial wonder, one of her *non plus ultras*. As I rustled with the tissue, I heard her, next door, turning off a tap, and spraying herself with atomized gardenias, and then, well, I have to admit that I was just bowled over. Because, for once—perhaps even for ever—our differences of taste were annulled.

It was a pair of patent leather dress-pumps in honour of my first formal dance—not nasty, pointy lace-ups like my father's, which were fit for a turf accountant, but almond-toed slippers with flat bows of grosgrain, reminiscent of the years of elegance leading up to the Great War, and evocative of the balls attended by my grandmother with her poor dead infantry officer—and yet, simultaneously, those pumps were absolutely modern, perfectly attuned to the latest pages of *L'Uomo Vogue*. My mother had, at least on this occasion, hit the cobbler's nail on the head—spot on, old girl, as my father would have said. Cinderella, I thought, move over; and then, I yelped like a bare-shouldered débutante dazzled by the sight of a jewel to commemorate her launch into society. Rubbing beauty cream onto her face, my mother now emerged from the bathroom to volunteer the fact that she had told the shop assistant to include, along with the pumps, a pair of black silk socks, in case mine were all at home, which, in the event, they were. But I did not, in fact, bother to try on my new trophies, not here; instead, I merely held their soles against those of the loafers which I had on— both because the prospect of donning virgin silk hose over my unwashed feet was more obscene to me than any double bed, and because I knew that, whatever happened and without question, I would, tomorrow night, squeeze my stockinged feet, like an ugly sister, into those gleaming slippers—even if agony were the price of my ecstasy.

I could happily have stayed in my mother's room and, like the flame of her scented candle, kept vigil during her rest, but she, doubtless unaccustomed to being admired while she slept, suggested that I get back to school now, and earned the pleasure of her privacy by packing me off in a taxi. I didn't see her again that day, and although, during the drinks party in the evening, Dr. Fox made a point of introducing himself to her, he irritated the hell out of me next morning, when—after I'd given him the Belgian chocolates, on condition that he save me the ribbon—he proved incapable of describing exactly (be fair, he said, I *knew* he lacked a visual memory) *exactly* what my mother had been wearing, or how she had seemed, beyond the obvious fact (which, frankly, I could have told him) that she was the most beautiful woman in the room. But he did, by contrast, horrify me with the detailed revelation that, at the makeshift bar, my father had buttonholed him, and droned on and on and loud, within full earshot of the assembled public, about how dreadfully he lamented the fact that I cared so obviously less for him than I did for my mother, whom he described as his wife. Dr. Fox thought my father a deathly dullard, and suggested that I flee his soulless nest at the first possible opportunity; and although, in that illogical paradox of thick blood and thin water, a part of me bristled at my mentor's opinions, yet I made a grateful mental note of the support implicit in his comments.

NEXT DAY, while my father took himself off for a spot of puerile nonsense, my mother and I lunched alone at a restaurant, not worthy of mention—though she took pains to mention how flatteringly, during the previous evening, Dr. Fox had spoken of me, and how much she had enjoyed meeting my moral tutor. (I wondered if she would have enjoyed the experience quite so much had she known what she could not possibly know.) But then we drifted towards my nearing exams, about which, even if I wasn't worried, she worried that I sounded too confident—one couldn't, she reminded us both, ignore my catastrophic O levels. But since I'd never told her about Al Capone, nor could I now bless her with the relief of his unmasking, his consignment to insignificance; so instead I moved on to my immediate future, explaining that before taking my A's, I was due to go up for an interview, arranged by Dr. Fox, at an Oxford college—a decent one, I pointed out, meaning: without connection to my father's Alma Mater. She rebuked me for being ungrateful. I told her that I was merely being truthful. She rattled off some Spanish adage about progeny being like crows—bring them into the world and they'll peck your very eyes from you. I bettered her mawkish little simile with a lamentation from one of my texts about how sharper than a serpent's tooth it is to have a thankless child, but I was only quoting for effect, not because I found the words themselves personally applicable. All that I owed to my father (though I didn't have the nerve to inform her of this) was a kick in the goolies. Anyway, I continued: in the instance of the forthcoming interview not going my way, meaning if I wasn't offered a place conditional on my A-level grades, I could always sit the official entrance papers in the autumn, and take the rest of next year off. One way or another, I vowed (just as I had vowed not to join the Spanish army), I would go to university, because even a red-brick had to be preferable to some stony job in the City. But she deftly now changed tack, probably to avert the mounting danger of a quarrel, and resurrected the safer topic of her undying exhaustedness.

In the afternoon was the prize-giving ceremony, but since, even if I deserved an award, I was too unpopular (and, frankly, too unpleasant) to be a likely recipient, I saw my mother off in a cab back to her tavern, so that she could repose in preparation for that night's Victory dance. God knows where my father might be, probably in a pub knocking back the marvellous English beer and rolling out the barrel, and cockling and musseling with some lively band of equally jolly good fellows; but since I knew that, regardless of his present whereabouts, he was bound, sooner or later, to change into black tie, and would therefore be joining my mother, I didn't bother to worry. She and I simply agreed that all three of us would convene at eight p.m. at the school gates—on the *dot,* I specified, not ages before, as was his tendency, nor, as was hers, long past the hour.

·   ·   ·

IN THE END, I do go to the prize-giving (though I sit at the back, up in the gods, looking forward to my pumps, which fit to perfection)—the reason being that Dr. Fox has suddenly gone all mysterious on me, as if to suggest that there might, after all, be some award in the offing, and since the whole ceremony is meant to be compulsory, I can't risk detection of my absence. Despite the odds of honour being stacked, by dint of my unpopularity, against me, I do, in the event, win some prizes—four in total: senior French, rapidly followed by senior Spanish, both of which (bugger my unpleasantness, never mind my father and his unfair advantages) are fully merited. Everybody claps; fair's fair-enough. But deeper into the proceedings, I hear my name called out for a prize in religion, an accolade not merely less deserved but little short of unthinkable, since of late I have refined myself into a most obnoxious agnostic; yet I suppose that the book which I win, *The Four Loves,* and which I quickly lose (though I wouldn't have misplaced a money order), is my reward for having scrutinized the small print of Catholic doctrine, as opposed to merely doodling, which is the norm in that subject. This time round, however, there's a noticeable drop in the warmth of applause, and as I return to my seat I catch the odd, audible snort, which tempts me to sneak away through the fire door—though on second thoughts, since the proceedings are nearly over, I may as well sit out the hell of the remainder.

But when, practically at the end, I hear myself announced yet again, and this time for a special music prize, which means Dr. Fox, the least suspected thing occurs: the crowd, parents included, begins to tut with disapproval, then openly to boo at the whiff of favouritism. I freeze, of course, and heads seem to turn to gloat at my frozenness, yet I can't stay here forever, have to go through with the performance, must collect the award, which I suspect to be a record—Bach most likely, given the donor. And so, Fuck them, I think, fuck the lot of them; and as I make my way down the steps of this revolting burgundy theatre with sticky carpeting and curtains of turquoise, down towards the stage where the rector awaits (looking, to be fair, pretty uncomfortable, bobbing his famous Adam's apple), I just envisage the scene in black and white and slightly blurrily, and concentrate on carrying myself with hair-flicking indifference to the world, like Rita Hayworth. But you will understand why, for once, I feel relieved that my parents aren't present to witness the shame of their one-and-only. And when, at last, I barge my way out of the place, all that I can do is hope that no well-meaning prat of an Old Boy proves crass enough to commiserate with my father over the fracas.

AT EIGHT—and on the dot—I go down to the gates at the front quadrangle, but my parents, like angry spears, are already in evidence; and, as soon as I appear, they join forces to accuse *me* of being late now. I ignore their childishness, don't even pretend to hear it: they've probably been bickering and want an easy scapegoat. Well, forget it, darlings, I've had enough aggravation to last me the night. Through the annoyance of the half-light, I try as best I can to distract myself by peering at the appearance of my mother, and I peer with such a concentration that, to begin with, I fail to notice what my father is wearing: not a proper bow, conventionally black, but instead, would you believe, the ass has knotted round his scraggy neck an absolute sartorial nightmare: a dicky-bow striped in blue-and-gold. What the hell is *that*?, I blurt out, unable to conceal my horror, and further unable to restrain myself from pointing. My mother, as she does on my behalf at her infernal dinner parties, now answers for her husband—though not to spare herself, or him, embarrassment. Not at all: boast is what she does. Because, with some ingenuity, she opines, she's taken a pair of Old Boy ties from my father's considerable collection, and instructed the sempstress at home to unpick them both, follow some pattern, and concoct—wouldn't you know—the Original Alma Mater Bow. I cannot believe either her catastrophic error of judgement, which is twenty thousand times more catastrophic than my O-level results, nor the sight of my father's countenance, which has never looked more chuffed than it does at this moment. And as we amble towards the nylon tent where the night's revelry is doomed to unfold, I understand that the earlier marriage of my mother's taste to mine at the altar of my dancing-pumps has been but a mirage, or worse, a preparatory bribe; for this, this miserable lapse in style is the real, true gauge of my parents' aesthetic, an aesthetic which I can no longer fool myself that they do not share, for they share it wholeheartedly, matrimonially. The two of them are steeped in this shit together, and no mistake.

My mother is cloudy, shadowed, overcast; I cannot make her out. But once we've stepped inside the tent, which reeks of paraffin, I'm able to verify that her reduced visibility has, in part, been caused by the fact that she's wearing black, a colour which, on our island (probably on account of the heat), is largely reserved for semblances of mourning, from which the bereaved like to shift, as soon as seems seemly, to the grieving half-shades of grey and lilac. But black, that great supposèd flatterer, is not, I now discover, a shade that flatters my mother, and this discovery disappoints me as much as it lets her down; it ages and diminishes her. For, no matter how fabulously fashioned on her behalf, black conspires to undermine the glow of her tan, which seems to have shifted from luminous amber to an uglier, more chalky umber—slightly goose pimpled tonight.

My father ferries us towards the table at which we're to be seated—next to God knows whom. My mother has already specified that she doesn't want to be put near some deafening band, because, as it is (she claims), she has her work cut out trying to converse in English, thanks very much—*muchísimas gracias*—but nor can she have imagined that her husband has reserved for us about the most unappetizing table to be had: marooned on the outer edges of the action, sloping downwards, placed suspiciously close to the bar and lurking in the region of some secondary entrance. If you sit with your back to the tent, you're assailed by a constant racing draft, and any hope of a view is dashed by the ranks of tables in front; and if, to avoid the draft, you should turn your back to the crowd, your view will be reduced to a wrinkled canvas of pistachio nylon, relieved only by a gap, like a hungry mouth, through which the serving staff will soon be rushing in and out screaming and cursing and dropping things on their way to and from the mobile kitchens, very attractive.

When we reach our trestled travesty, which has been covered in paper of a festive character, and decked with occasional tufts of shrivelled carnation embedded on skeletons of asparagus plant, I feel relieved to see, if nothing else, that we're the first to arrive, which means that we can grab whatever places we like; but my mother, unaccustomed to making entrances without a clutch of admirers in ready attendance, now complains—she who a few minutes ago had complained that I was late—that we're far too early. And yet, undaunted, like a disappointed but utterly composed hostess, she makes directly for one end of the table, while my father saunters off in search of what (for the first time in my recollection) he describes as libations. Before she sits—which she will eventually do by means of a slow half-curtsey—she requests a glass of champagne, and I, for the sake of simplicity, follow her lead and do the same: I doubt that my father can be trusted to produce tequila. Nor can he; because, when the Original Alma Mater Beau does eventually come lurching back, with spillage down his pleated shirtfront, he brings us a couple of tumblers of warm Pomagne—oh do stop whining. I, in his absence, have already beseeched my mother, before it's all too late, not to choose the top of the table, please not, but to sit along one of the sides instead, so that I can plonk myself between her and her husband and not have to talk to strangers; but she treats my plea with the derision which, perhaps, it deserves, and tells me not to be so anti-social, I'm not a peasant, and kindly to draw out the chair which she has selected. And then, moaning in our mother-tongue about how regrettable it is that I've forgotten even the most rudimentary courtesies due to a lady, she takes pride of place at the head—with the grace and weightlessness of a star falling from the firmament. Others begin to arrive now, parents of no one I've ever noticed, flanked by their unnoticeable offspring; so I raise the volume of my Spanish in an attempt to deter them from venturing near us.

While I still have the chance, in advance of the crowds, I drink my mother in, hurry to absorb her. Her scent seems to have grown, like gardenias opening for the moon, from eau-de-toilette to concentrated perfume. Her make-up has sharpened, darkened, grown more sensual. I suspect that she has painted slightly beyond the natural contour of her lips, but I can't tell for sure: I don't dare to gawp like the peasant whom I'm not supposed to be, least of all when I feel more like a burgeoning model-girl, new to the business and ravenous not for food but beauty tips. Her stole, of indigo mink, is, by now, slung over the back of her chair, against which she seems determined not to lean; and while she perches erect, craning slightly and swivelling her visage and pouting just a smidgeon, I notice, near the ground, which is a carpet of soggy grass, her monogram embroidered in oyster pink on the fur's oyster satin lining. Her dress is of black chantilly, with a very fitted bodice and long narrow sleeves, which end, near her knuckles, in delicate scallops, dainty with lashes, as do the shores around her neck, through which her clavicle juts fractionally—but you can only glimpse this from the side, or if, like me, you're a complete cow. Her head-of-a-gamine is glossy, as if she'd recently come, running, out of the sea; and on her ears she wears a pair of plain but socking great brilliants, painfully screwed, absolutely no quivering.

The skirt, at the hem, is fuller than full, but, at the waist, teeny, so you can almost picture it being planned, blocked out, and cut to a pattern of perfect circularity. Perhaps to relieve the overall bleakness of her blackness, which might have been thought to veer towards the grotesque, the Goyaesque, there's a satin slither, the colour of a cherub's skin, loosely slung around her upper hip and tied in a small bow behind her. Beneath the skirt, you can see, when she sits cross-kneed, smoky underskirts of organdie, as if the wings of my first crib had been dipped in squid's ink; and her stockinged ankle, hanging limp and bony-thin, is sheer as dark transparency (crystalline brown, the colour of sugar-crystals—one of her low-denier tricks). And her evening shoes, which are fantastically steep and slim-heeled, have, insanely, superbly, been covered in matching chantilly, so that given the context, and my father's dancing skills, they stand little chance of surviving what I suspect to be their first night out.

On the table, along from her paper plate and not far from my glass of fizzy piss, lie a black grosgrain evening purse, dead plain, like a small envelope, and, upon it, asleep, a still life of my mother's lovely fingers. Her nails are painted paler than in my childhood; and although I recognize the rose-cut solitaire which rings her second finger, the massive diamond gauntlet attached to her left wrist, dazzling over a cuff of chantilly, is unknown to me. I enquire after its history. She tells me to desist from such common enquiries—what *is* this, the Inquisition? I persist that the bracelet is beautiful (I might even have dared to say heavenly, although—to her doubtless relief—I would have exuded the word in Spanish). She replies that gentlemen don't remark on ladies' jewels; and that if other ladies ever do, it's only because they're consumed with envy, which is a sin. By which stage, our table is complete.

Over dinner—if dinner isn't too tasteful a term for a crusty slab of salmon and a lump of mayonnaise—faintly *gorne-orf,* as you'd expect—

my father sits regrettably opposite me, savouring accolades about his fancily dressed neck, and replying to all and creepy sundry: So glad you think so, rather pleased with it m'self-what; and into his riveting story he draws the fine complicitous hand of his clever wife-here, great style, marvellous ideas—while she, the turncoat, smiles along, not quite smacking her lips, but obviously thrilled and nodding-and-nodding in an attempt to convey that absolutely, why not, if the school pleases to follow her Victor Ludorum's sartorial lead and mass-produce his humble contribution to its honourable tradition, it is, well, more than welcome to do so, how very flattering. And as the nosh begins (between munches of ancient leaving-dates, and soundbites from the Battle of Britain) to get shovelled down, and as the fruity but tepid Alsatian wine is clinked and cheered and swilled and gulped (though some of our chaps prefer to stick with the beer, if you don't mind—grape and grain and all that), assorted elbows seem to crawl up, and then, to slump over the creased paper cloth and slide around; and tissued serviettes, smeared with remnants of lipstick and the inconvenience of an untimely sneeze—I *do* beg your pardon—find themselves crushed by hot fists and left, half-groaning, to rot on the moistening scene like soiled evidence of female joviality. And now, at last, the spirits of the assemblage can be felt to be rising, to spin away like a Victorious boomerang in the clear direction of jollity, of happy history, of future reminiscence—hopefully to be returned, one fine eventual day, back to this very company, and shared with the male children of our male children, all of whom will have been put down at birth—not literally, you fool—enlisted in their turn to join the privileged ranks of my father's Alma Mater.

During the first few speeches, my mother, who plainly cannot understand a thing, nevertheless looks most amused, taken in, while her husband, the better to enjoy the oratory, turns his folding chair to face the speakers, and seems to be rendered so mirthful by the whole retrospective priestly hoot, that, watching him, you begin to pray that he topples backwards and collapses onto the table with a good thud, his head slumped like the head of the Baptist upon the flanny gelatinous mess of his pudding, his gob ajar, his striped propeller of a tie, inactive, unactivated, unable to revolve and soar like an old Spitfire into the nylon galaxies; his furry ears unplugged but garnished by the odd chunk of tinned pineapple. Yet in boring reality, he just rummages about his pockets, and then he lights a medium-sized cigar. Anyone care for one?

Nobody, thank God, does; but, to my disbelief, my mother, who has always reviled tobacco, now accepts the offer of a stunted cigarette (blithely unaware of the ghastliness of its brand) from some nearby drudge—a School Governor, I gather; and when she begins to puff, desperately trying not to blink despite the sting in her eyes, which serves her right, I don't know whether to be more gratified by the fact that she can't inhale, but only act the part, or by my realization that she's squandering the drudge's last revolting gasper, which, when he finally cottons on, he will regret having wasted on that woman who, now that everyone's feeling much more up-tempo, seems to be speaking English like there's no tomorrow and no stopping her, and broadly smiling into the bargain, like an old-style ambassadress from a backward country. Is my father as surprised as I am by my mother's conduct? Not a bit of it: he looks, if anything, delighted by the larkiness of his wife, her ability to join in the spirit of things, to share in the fun. Wink-wink, darling. I catch him. And anyway, now the band is trying to tie a yellow ribbon with the help of a regimental trumpet, and everyone is delighted, oh yes, especially the ladies, who, as they heave themselves up, trilling snatches of song and dum-dee-dahing, stomp about in sturdy heels and the same moth-eaten dress-skirts as their mothers must have worn in Burma. But my own mother, who has thought it all out, says that it's the thought that counts, the whole mood of the thing, the celebration, not the latest fashion or questions of extravagance, why must I be so superficial. What's that? my father asks. So the bitch goes and blabs. *Abserlootly,* he concurs—always bally criticizing, the wretched pip-squeak; just ignore him, darling; care to dance? *Enchantée,* she replies in the diplomatic language, sounding as grateful as if she'd been offered the chance of another life; then rises. She tells me to keep an eye on her bag, and next thing, having (purposely?) trodden on one of my pumps, she leads the way onto the boards, weaving herself between a clutter of tables and an absurdity of chairs worthy of Ionesco, until, inevitably, the lilt of her slim hips is obscured from view by the screen of my father's thick back, which jigs about without concern for rhythm and nonsense. It's been eight long years, do you still want me, I'll stay on the bus, forget about us, put the blame on me, tie a yellow ribbon round the ole oak tree.

Dancy-dancy-dance. The youngsters at our table all vanish, presumably to cross-fertilize and make deals regarding rhododendrons. And I, for my sins, for my refusal to join in, get lumbered with some boring woman wearing a moustache and hair like the Queen Mother who does something or other good in Somerset and is Thingummy's ma and wants to know, as she colonizes the creaking chair beside me, what sports I like. (Water-sports, my dear, and big-game hunting when I get the chance.) But, with typical cowardice, I just say: None—to which she replies: I see, swivels her arse, and that's that. I try not to look as if I've noticed. I try, instead, to look towards my mother. I try not to remember with what shaming adoration I had looked at her once, peered down at her between the slats of the shutters of my infancy. For she is unrecognizable now. She has become my dreadful father's dreadful wife. We have all gone to pieces. We are all beyond repair. It isn't, any longer, even sad. Just dreary, unnecessary.

When my mother asks me to dance, it's only because my father wants to spend a penny—presumably at the bar—but I think that she fears that I might turn her down, which would never do; so she sits for a moment, again half-curtseying, in order to sound me out, to butter me up. She asks how I am. Fine, I reply. (Fucking awful, you stupid woman.) In which case, she exclaims: Come on, Iago: *¡A bailar!* She seems younger again, and lighter of touch, but once we're up there, her hand in mine, her diamond gauntlet resting on my rigid shoulder, she tells me, through a rictus smile, not to look down while we're moving around. (I'm actually trying to check how her priceless shoes are surviving.) I apologize, then play dumb. She tells me that I should be talking to her. I tell her that I'm trying to keep up. She tells me, still smiling, that I shouldn't need to, that I'm in charge, I'm the man. And to be fair to my father's wife, she does follow like a dream, goes where she's taken—backwards, round, and to the side—always stepping out of trouble, never banging into anyone, and I begin to understand how this marriage of theirs has been managed: gingerly, cautiously, as if beautifully, till a painful death do them part. Now she asks me who This boy is, and That one, and That—creeps who (can you believe the nerve of it) keep flirting with my mother as they whizz past; and without exception I tell her that I don't know, that I haven't got the foggiest. Come on, she enquires, still ever-smilingly, have I *no* friends to introduce to her? And now I do treat her to the truth, which is: Not likely. And suddenly we have ground to a bewildering standstill, but instantly she is rescued from the awkwardness by some oafish admirer, somebody's fleshy ruddy father, wearing an eye-patch, and she's perfectly obliging, and offers her hand, and as I mooch back to the table, wiping my sweating brow, I hear her distinctive voice admonishing me, telling me (in Spanish, to my own relief now) not to use my hand, for heaven's sake, to use a *handkerchief*.

The rest is brief. I go to the bar, avoiding the section where my father, holding court, has surrounded himself with a scrum of similar sots, and I order myself a whopping vodka, but have to make a fuss about ice—what am I (the barman seems to imply), a Yank? I return to our table, where my mother's bag remains intact. I wonder whether there's any dosh to be had from it, but other pupils keep tripping past, so I dare not look inside, and instead I notice how some of the girls that giggle round these boys also throw snide glances in my direction, and how then, like strumpets consulting procurers, they consult their brothers, only to be told that they're entirely mistaken, *no* chance; and next, they all go on their way, laughing their dizzy heads off, and occasionally turning round and shouting: hello ducks. My mother, meanwhile, moves seamlessly from partner to partner, inexhaustible now, being quite the best value, having quite the best of times. I clutch her bag as if it were a memory, can feel, within it, the relic of her silver compact, can smell the ghost of her lost gardenias, but none of these seems to sustain me any longer. I give up. I grab a paper napkin, place it like a shroud over her bag, and scribble a note, telling her that I'm tired and will see her tomorrow.

In fact, I hardly do so, because during Mass, I'm upstairs in the choir loft. When I join them afterwards, she's wearing a cream linen suit and a black straw hat, its brim curled severely down, so that anyone who looks at her will see not her shifting eyes, but only her expertly painted mouth. We do not kiss; she makes sure of that—by standing safely back: facial contact could disarrange her. We lunch at the dump where they've been slumming it, because her hung-over husband hasn't thought of booking anywhere more appetizing, and while I sit in their company, sweltering in fumes of gravy, they exchange anecdotes about last night, and ask and tell each other who was whom, and who did what, and what year such and such left the Alma Mater; and I just stare at the couple of them, trying to remain impassive, indifferent, calm; yet inwardly, there's no real other option left for me: I resign, resign on the spot and without notice. That was the moment. And by the time of my concert in the evening, they must already have been charging back, racing through the darkening outskirts of London, triumphant, victorious in their conjugal chariot.

IN A WAY, from that day on, my life began; my own. When I went, by train, to Oxford, I wore, instead of my uniform, a navy suit with very faint stripes—bit dreary for my liking, but when I'd had it made, my father and his tailor-chappy, who was a consummate arse-kisser, had already joined forces in advance of my first fitting, and put the cloth aside on my behalf. Still, I got my own back by insisting on a short, boxy jacket and very baggy trousers. The interviews weren't as hard as I had feared, but they did, I remember, surprise me. For a start, all the people who interrogated me were courteous, almost courtly, and didn't seem to want to catch me out—unlike the slimeball inquisitors of my past. Some of the dons seemed even (by means of dry snorts—intended, I think, to irritate the more pious among their colleagues) to sympathize with me for having suffered the misfortune of a Catholic boarding school. I detected more than the odd Querie at these various gatherings designed to judge my potential as an undergraduate: a youngish German academic in particular, with a pince-nez, floppy wrists, and an Alsatian at his feet—a tableau which seemed to put me in mind of J. R. Ackerley, who developed an erotic penchant for that breed, went on to write about it and, when awarded a literary prize, readers thought the world of him.

It was the German don who, once the formal tests were done and everyone pretended to let me relax, fired me the one single question on which, at that instant, I somehow recognized my whole future to be balanced. And the shot wasn't about my linguistic ability, nor about my grasp of current affairs (which amounted to nil), still less to do with my general knowledge (same thing), nor about the history of European literature, nor to do with the rudiments of philology, nor even about specifics such as Lorca's women, or Ionesco's chairs, or Genet's maids, or the Bard and his serpent's teeth and thankless children, but about the oddest thing: whistling.

It turned out that the German could see, not just from my appearance (which, in retrospect, *was* perhaps a bit overslick), but from the details on my CV, that, despite my father's surname, I was not straightforwardly English; and it was the place of my birth, my mother's once-exotic island, that prompted him—not to test me, I don't think, but—to hope that I might enlighten him on an obscurity, that's how he put it. And then he asked about a curious code of whistling which was of vague folkloric interest, and which, centuries back, before the island's first indigenes, called Guanches, were colonized, had been devised and refined by them as a means, from mountain to mountain, of alerting other natives to impending invasions. Later, this code would be employed merely to convey trivia—such as (I suppose) Bring us some goat's milk, or Come and kill a pig—but vestiges of the idiom survived even into my infancy, when on the eves of feast days you could hear, as I had done when Mam'zelle gave me my bath, descendants of those early whistles flying like arrows through the sunset, which was lit (I could see through the window when she lifted me) with great fires along the jagged purple hills. Cook and Gardener and all their relatives, whose lives were closer to the soil and to the origins of that volcanic landscape, could, I recall, discern scraps of significance in those piercing whistles, of which women were the finest exponents.

And then, the interview moved on to the relationship between music and meaning, and sound and emotion, and sense and communication and all of that pseudy drivel, and although I squirmed about as if I had worms, and dredged up words like phonetic and dissonance and onomatopœic, I felt myself to be, after the whistling bit, if not home and dry, hopefully on the way to my own type of victory. And two days later, back at school, I received a letter confirming this, offering me a place conditional on my A-level results, but demanding such easy grades as to make my acceptance a foregone gift; and for once in my life, the cheapness of that offer made me feel not insulted, but wanted. I remember nothing about actually sitting those papers, except that I dragged into the exams, which were held in the gymnasium, a vast Indian cushion on which to park my rump, armloads of bangles whose rattle was intended to distract other candidates, and a can of air-freshener to quell the stench of humanity. Invigilators turned a blind eye to me, of course, because, by now, it was in the Alma Mater's interest to collude with my campery. Oxbridge, let us not forget, was Oxbridge.

AFTER THOSE EXAMS, I suddenly found myself loaded not just with bangles but with an extravagance of spare time, because there was still a concert coming up, from which, like the wedding of the thousand petals, Dr. Fox wouldn't exempt me; but I can't claim to have minded the imposition this time round: there were jobs to be done, scores to be settled, slates to be wiped clean. First I went to the bursar's office and demanded that, since I had no desire to be kept in touch with the school's activities, or remain in any way connected to it, the money which, throughout my time at the institution, had yearly been tagged onto my bills (by way of eventual membership to the Old Boys' Association) kindly be refunded. The bursar, an affable bumpkin, scratched his thatch and knitted his brow into a quandary, for—never mind the Original Alma Mater Bow—active refusal of an Old Boy tie seemed to be without precedent. He didn't, he confessed, quite know *what* ought to be done. I said that the money should obviously be returned—no, not to me, I wasn't suggesting that, but to its source, to my father (whom I knew would be mortally stung).

My only regret was that I wouldn't be there, like a hornet hovering over the salver in the hall, to witness the delivery of his agony, because the next thing I did was to write home and inform my parents about my offer from Oxford, and further inform them—since permission, now that I was of age, didn't strike me as a requisite—that I wouldn't be going home for the summer, but getting a job in London (a pouffy little boutique, I thought, might be quite fun, but I withheld details of such a plan: I didn't want Interpol on my back, not now that my back was bare at last, and firmly turned away from the benefit of my parents' society). And then there was the matter of the school photograph, taken once every five years, and due to be taken now.

I know I could have opted out and hidden, but somehow that felt unsatisfactory, too passive. I know I could have pulled stupid faces at the camera, but that didn't strike me as either funny or flattering. Nor could I be bothered to sprint round the back row of boys and beat the slow exposure merely in order to be immortalized twice, because, as japes went, that one was both unoriginal and, if detected, punishable. No, what I decided to do, quite simply, was to drop my head, like a penitent, at just the right moment—so that where my face should have been, there would, I hoped, figure a conspicuous but anonymous circle of black, an eclipse, a numberless number. And when the first print (so that worthies could order lots of extra copies for their parents as well as themselves, and for their future sons and grandsons) duly appeared—crested and dated and all hoolied up—on the main noticeboard, a smug little smirk rose to my eyes, for anyone could see that my trick had worked like a charm. I'd become the ultimate blot on the beaming horizon, circular as my mother's dark turban eight years back, when she had stood on my first railway platform, waving her scented gloves and washing her moral hands; circular as her dark, concealing hat when, recently, she had vanished into oblivion, carried off in the conjugal chariot.

Dr. Fox seemed perplexed as he reclined on his wingèd chesterfield, scanning the horizontal scroll of photograph from left to right and back, and slower and slower, and holding it ever closer to his glassy eyes and muttering the while, yet unable, for all of his exertions, to find me. Was I *in* the picture? Of course I was. Well *where,* for God's sake? I advised him to look harder: I was obvious. But nothing doing. Eventually, starting to feel unkind, I did put him out of his misery, and pointed myself out, thereby apprising him both of my presence and of my absence; but he, far from sharing in the laugh, instantly rounded on me, saying that I'd been childish, stupid, brattish—an outburst which struck me as disproportionate to the crime. He seemed actively aggrieved, for some reason, as if I'd insulted not so much the school, about which neither of us cared in the slightest, but him personally, as if I'd struck against my mentor at the final hour. The whole episode baffled me at the time; but now, looking back, I realize that simply by having lowered my head I'd inadvertently managed to deprive Dr. Fox of any evidence of a past which, however contentious, and however cluttered by irrelevant other heads, had, in a sense, been shared by us. And given the imminence of my departure, this last-minute refusal of mine to allow him to remember me even by one-six-hundredth of a dreary institutional photograph must have felt, to him, hurtful; but you see, my urgent determination to separate myself, insofar as I could, from the plague of my father's Alma Mater outweighed, by then, any concerns about whatever documentary consideration might have been due a man who, even if he had taken me to Claridge's, and even if he had taken my side against my father, had also taken more than his fair share of advantage. Because although his task regarding my education was all but complete now, his coercions both on the coal box and in the brocaded alcove (even as he dreamt of pumping his cheesiness into the fair but unavailable mouth of Albany) could never be undone.

Dr. Fox took out his pocketwatch and suddenly realized that he was running late for some meeting in the basement. He told me, while he washed up our teacups (a chore which I never offered to do, not so much from inherent queenliness as from fear of detection in the masters' bathroom), to fetch him his academic gown from the wardrobe. So while he busied himself across the way, I complied with this request; but as I unhooked the limp crow of cloth from its hanger, a shimmer, far behind, in the musty depths of the mahogany, caught my eye. It was a woman's dress, which had once, I seem to recall, belonged to his mother, and which he retained for the same incomprehensible reasons of sentiment that most of us keep incomprehensible mementos, such as a child's mohair blanket. And while he was next door, sloshing about—it's so odd to tell—I went and stole the dress; borrowed it, at any rate; slung it in its transparent plastic cover over my arm, shouted at him that I had to go, and raced to my room. I would return it when I was done.

THAT LITTLE black number was fit for a Charleston. It was the perfect flapper's dress, cut like a chiffon vest, loose-hipped and low-waisted, covered with tiny jet beads, and finished by a fringe of crystal bugles which swished over the edge of its hem. Like the school itself, it seemed to weigh with its own history, but unlike my father's Alma Mater, it glittered with thrill, shimmered with stories of parties and kisses and drink; and even if its initial wearer no longer lived, the surviving dress seemed to retain a life, a vivacity about it; for despite the acrid smell of lavender which hung from a sachet at its neck and clung to it, you could sense, still, that the original girl would have worn with it some essence of greater freshness, orange-blossom or primrose, or jasmine even, which was the flappers' favourite. You could picture it all in its heyday, that youthful dress bobbing about on parquet, and twirling and kicking, and skipping energetically along the galleries of great country mansions, demolished long since.

The scene, from my perspective, had almost less to do with Dr. Fox, who rarely referred to his parentage, than it did with me, for it reminded me of the time when my young grandmother, head over heels in love, must have danced with her infantry officer before he was killed. (I was later to learn, while clearing my mother's effects, that the diamond gauntlet which she had worn to the Victors' Dance, but of whose history she had so peevishly deprived me, had been meant as an engagement present from the hopeful officer to his sweetheart— delivered, after that fatal duel, by the boy's distraught mother to the daughter-in-law who, following the tragedy, my grandmother was never to become.) But this dress felt, as it lay on my bed, like an heirloom, a great gift—for me to do with as I pleased. And, for reasons that still remain unclear, what I pleased to do with it was this: get into it. And it fitted me as perfectly as, a few weeks earlier, my mother had been fitted into her couture chantilly—even if, as in her case, black proved not to be a colour that especially flattered me. No matter: I would flatter my self, and not just in private: I would flatter myself at quite another dance, and flaunt my flattery.

Since the local village was as ill-equipped as it was risky for that which I had in mind, I took a bus into town and went into one of those shops that sell everything for next to nothing. I bought a cassette, to distract the gaggle of shopgirls, and then lifted, in very quick succession, an elasticated diamanté bracelet, a lipstick (which fortunately turned out to be dark, accurate) plus some nail polish, about which I did suffer a dilemma on the trip back, because I couldn't be sure of the date when such enamels first became popular in Europe. But when I placed the spoils upon my desk, which, by now, had obviously become a dressing-table, I realized that I'd forgotten to filch a pair of tights. Tough. I'd manage somehow. Necessity is the mother of subversion.

That night, a leaving party was to be held in honour of the sixth form, who, by this stage in the year, were all through their exams. It was due to take place in the senior common room, where, exceptionally, people would be allowed to drink and smoke without the hassle of supervision, and where, less exceptionally, slags from a couple of local convents were to be herded in, presumably to provide incentive for experimental mating rituals. The planned jamboree was to kick off at eight p.m., but must, by official dictate, end at the midnight hour. Still, people seemed, despite the infliction of a deadline, animated enough, listless and a little reckless in their preparations, like prisoners thinking of birds with big jugs, because now, our boys could contemplate activities which, if discovered before the exams, might not have been viewed as too prudent. It was their first taste of freedom, really. As, in a weird way, it was mine.

I TAKE A SHOWER. I return to my room, draw the curtains, jam a chair against the door. I switch on my music, though not as loud as I might have liked. I beam my anglepoise into the mirror and I deliver myself to my task, vaguely aware, in the breaks between my songs, of mechanical thuds, of party action drifting from the other end of the corridor; and, every so often, I hear the squeals and shrieks of heavy-soled lasses as they stomp along in a total antithesis of the sylph who first wore my dress and skipped her slippered way along the marble terraces of those now-forgotten mansions.

It won't be a breeze, I realize, but it feels bloody exciting, like guzzling sweet wine in the sacristy, or wanking into the mongrel's chalice. I slip into a pair of underpants, then step into the long silk socks donated to me by my mother, which I stretch like stockings over my knees, but which keep slipping down. Ignore them for now. I don a dressing-gown, my negligée, like an actress preparing to grease up, and I smear my face with moisturiser, which feels in character. No hairband required. Next I sit down—cross-leggèd, naturally. The manicure, given my shaking fingers, proves pretty dicey, but I know not to take it all too seriously: I'm after effect, not exactitude; this is theatre, not fashion; and besides, the lights at the disco will be dark—not just to encourage uninhibited dancing, but to enable the boys who like to sprawl on the banquettes to explore the undergrowth of pencil-skirts without embarrassment; and, I suppose, for the girls to reciprocate with a juggle.

But can you believe that until this moment I hadn't given a thought to mascara? What to do? *Mon Dieu, quoi faire?* Improvise, you idiot. What, I wonder, did all those dramatic chorus-women do in ancient Athens? Not a clue; but I decide to burn a few matches and employ the soot to emphasize my eyes; and I apply a couple of hyphens of lipstick to my eyelids, which lends them ardour; and then I run a pencil along my brows, comb them, pluck out the odd spike (because already I own tweezers, my dear, oh yes) and the result looks almost passable. To finish off, I touch up, with a black felt-tip now, the end of every single one of my lashes, which I regret to admit do err a trifle on the short side. This latest procedure doesn't, in cosmetic terms, seem to make much difference, but the feeling of rightness, of actressiness, more than makes up for it. And as I toil, I think of my mother's dainty lace scallops, their lashes.

The music down the corridor seems to be growing louder, or perhaps the rest of our quarters are emptier, hollowed out. Anyway, time for a bit more lipstick, rubbed into the cheeks by way of blusher, but don't go overboard, I tell myself, you don't want to look like that slattern in Berlin, Elsie from Chelsea or whatever her name was, the one who had the gory abortion and kept saying divinely decadent darling. Right; done; that's enough. I grease my hair into a sort of Eton crop, with the strictest of side-partings, but, unable to resist the influence of the great Marcel, I sculpt a rolling ornamental wave which I allow to kink over one eye. Lips are easy, not just because I've been watching my mother paint her beautiful, venomous own for years, but because I'm myself a mistress of lip-salve: chaps, as you know, are the bane of this climate. But suddenly, to my horror, I realize that, on this night of all first-nights, I have no earrings to wear to the party . . . and well, I'll just have to hope that Dr. Fox, or his departed mother, will forgive me if they should ever find out, because, in creative desperation, I snip a couple of shimmery beads from the back of the dress and glue them onto my lobes. And although it's tricky without wrecking my lacquered fingers, the outcome again passes muster. Yes, I look tastefully accessorized, chic even (assuming that chic meant anything to a flapper), because God is on my side. And then I slip into the dress, which luckily has no rusty zips or hooks-and-eyes. I tug at my socks and garter them up, tourniquet-tight, and step into my patent leather dancing-pumps (thank you, Mother, how clever of you). And last, I place the elasticated diamonds round my wrist: gorgeous, the whole thing, if a little grippy—I should have preferred their dazzlement to dangle more casually, like a relaxed engagement, not some hasty gun-shot. Never mind. I turn up my music further, turn off the merciless anglepoise, and then, turn to take a fresh and final look at myself in the soft light of the boudoir. I could do with a cocktail, sure, but even in sobriety, let me tell you: if I had the nous, I would pre-set my camera at this moment, pose (hand on hip would seem suitable), and take my own photograph—obviously in black and white. Say *Fromage*.

My boyish bosom is going like the clappers; but I can't hang about to lose heart; I have to get moving, like an ever-onward soldier marching as to war, terrified but ecstatic, unequipped for the future yet too late for turnabouts and cowardice. Hold on, you've forgotten your Baccy: cigar*ettes,* for God's sake, I'm not some bloody *cadet,* dear; I'm a warrior-maiden. So I grab a cigarette packet, slip a lighter inside it and, seeing as I have no evening bag, tuck the lot into my knickers. (What would you have done?) And then I spray myself with atomizer—honeysuckle and amber, perfect scent-notes for the occasion. And I step into the night without a chaperon.

The lights in the corridor are dark. The stench of beer isn't encouraging, but I'm beyond such trivia now, nothing can hold me back. And anyway, I tell myself, backstage was never meant to be Versailles. And as I emerge from the shadows, I see a few people leaning about in shockingly bad outfits and smooching outside the common room, couples-of-sorts, too absorbed and far-gone to spare me a thought, plus a smattering of young bachelors, spotty lonesomes-tonight, whose bleary eyes, when they clap sight of me, seem to proclaim Wow, what a gal (when I wish to be a vamp, actually, but still): flattery's flattery, even if my admirers are too sozzled to recognize me. And at least they have the decency, as I proceed with a very controlled sashay towards the public, to clear a path for my entrance. Make way: Head Girl.

FLASHES-AND-STARS and kisses-of-fire and flashes-and-stars and kisses-of-fire, and well, here we are at last. Good evening one-and-all, and welcome. It's going to be fine. One of your favourite songs is coming on now. You recognize the intro. You could do with a shot of something, but you don't really think you've got time. And bugger the introductions, frankly, because you're just so glamorous in your own right, and charismatic, and covered in class, and back in the roaring twenties—even if the song is of the moment—and isn't it all just a fabulous confusion, everyone? Divinely decadent darling. You should have worn gloves.

But: You Can Dance, the song starts up, so you move sideways towards the floor, which is packed, and you weave your slip of girlishness towards its centre. Again the singers say that You Can Dance, as if repeating their permission, which is nice; and then they remind you that you're Having The Time Of Your Life—which, already, you sort of are, for you're immersed and sublime and bang in the spotlight and regretting none of this for a moment. And now the song is telling the rest to See That Girl, to Watch That Scene, because, of course, you have become, therefore you are: The Dancing Queen. And now you do take off; transvested and transformed and transfigured, but, to begin with, you swivel your hips quite slowly, because you don't want to seem too keen any more than you wish your socks to be seen. Yet you can act this whole thing to perfection, like the utter natural that you are, because in a way you've spent your life preparing for this instant, swaying in your own space, turning and waving and smiling and hoping and longing despite the suffocating flood of your guilty secrets and the drowning uterine waters of your misconceived, miscarried past.

Friday Night And The Lights Are Low, the song continues, and aptly: for today is indeed Friday, and the lights are low all right. The vocalists begin to harmonize about Looking Out For A Place To Go Where They Play The Right Music, which, of course, is precisely here and now; and here and now, though you look at no one in particular, but simply stare into the light of heaven that blinds you, you can tell that the dancers around you, your mismanaged troupe, your chorus of bad Greek women, are heeding the warning to See That Girl, to Watch That Scene, and some of the bitches have already wised up to your strange magic, and are nudging their partners to wake up and realize it, some of them even shrieking that you're no less than You, while others just stare aghast at the vision, tragic and wide-eyed and nauseous like your mother. But you, you're way beyond mothering now, for you have become your absolute best at last, an emancipated, independent, liberated flapper. So you just think of the words, which are your anthem, but you hardly part your painted lips about it, for these have become more perfect than (from this day on) those of your mother will ever be. And you're telling yourself that You're In The Mood For A Dance, which you certainly are, and that When You Get The Chance, which is right now (so you give yourself a spin while you can), You-Are-You-Are-You-Are The Dancing Queen. And you're congratulating yourself for the victory, and even pretending that you're still Young and Sweet, even if you haven't been for aeons, and you make out that you're Only Seventeen—which you no longer are, but that's nobody else's business—because, from this your new majority, you can Feel The Beat From The Tambourine, so you rattle your priceless diamonds accordingly. But don't get too carried away by the whole thrill, because you've forgotten to shave your armpits.

Something odd begins to happen next: a greater space seems to have been cleared, a wider firmament made over to your stellar beauty, to your feminine grace and unassailable elegance, which, unlike your mother's falling star, are finally in the ascendant, and you, you couldn't care an eclipse whether these people are giving you a wide, horrified berth, or admiring your incredible chic, or both, or neither of these things, because you are, again and again, as you shall remain, for years to come, the Alma Mater's one and only Dancing Queen. But now the song runs away, a little indiscreetly, to reveal that really You're A Teaser, that You Turn 'Em On—and, as if to confirm this, some drunken imbecile comes up to meet you, to face you, chewing a cigarette like some scummy hero, and thinking that he's writhing and being sexy, when Mr. Funk can't dance to save his poxy skin, doesn't know the *meaning* of the word *rhythm;* but you don't want to appear too supercilious (ever), so you remain, absorbed and contained and delicious, poised like a doll on your own precious pinnacle, which peaks at the epicentre of this dream. And the lyrics admit that You Leave Them Burning, which you're sure that you could, and further reveal that Then, You're Gone, Looking Out For Another, which very soon you will be, and that Anyone Will Do, which is practically the truth, and next, as if to confirm those very lyrics, another boy, in a reconstruction of the success which your mother enjoyed with all her ruddy victors, comes up to you, and it seems to be—indeed it is—the grinning son of the admiral, whose big endowment you can glimpse, though you can't quite tell whether this is thanks to you or to the hooker slithering up to him; and who cares, really, because it's all been heavenly, Mother, hasn't it. And anyway, the song, as so many good things must, is inevitably approaching its end, which is climactic; so sweaty brows and laundered handkerchieves and all the rest of the decorum be damned, because couldn't you just kill for a drink? Make mine a triple, darling, with ice.

So I step off the floor, and my public is, look, amazed by me, especially the country girls, who're my greatest fans, see: I bet they want to learn everything, but really I think that deodorant is all that need concern them for the minute; and as I begin to head for the bar in order to point my painted index at some exotic beverage (sorry, libation), I suddenly find myself interrupted by the idiot who first came up to dance with me, the scummy hero whom I jilted in favour of the boy with the admirable endowment, and although another song is starting up—quite the wrong one, as it happens, some moronic rock-track—and although I'm out of my natural light, the cuckold, undaunted, swaggers up to me and, can you believe the cheek of it, makes as if to kiss me; but I retreat with utmost smoothness, like my mother in her black straw hat trying to avoid the peril of disarrangement, so he returns his smouldering cigarette to his dry mouth in order to disguise his floundering manhood; yet still, like a man, he will not take the hint, because next, he tries to touch me somewhere near my slinky hip, as if to toy, to mess with me, and I can tell that people are watching now, and I can hear them behind me; jeering Go on, show the dirty queer, and other similar endearments; but I just stare at my challenger, because, oddly enough, I've rarely felt braver or more virile than I do at this instant, and I stare him out of his pathetic wits, as if he were a bully like my father yet my name were really David, though my flattened chest, again, is racing, for none of this feels quite as safe as it did when I was the undisputed Dancing Queen, and it's hardly surprising—since, almost before I click, he dares to raise his filthy impudent hand to me, and attempts (when my visage has been crafted to the last impeccable millimetre)—just credit the nerve of this—to slap me; but luckily, I duck; and he, the drunken scummy hero, misses. And despite the holy fluke, let me assure you: I'm not about to make a run for it and allow my dignity to be poured like a pint of bitter down the tubes, for, endangered as I am, I remain a strong young woman, so I snatch his grimy ciggy from his lower lip, swivel it adroitly, and stub it out, hard and with providential symmetry, in the middle of his stunned forehead, that at least he may learn the true meaning of the word Smouldering. I hear him fizzle. I smell his sizzling skin. But really he ought to be grateful for the cauterizing, because, at a stroke, I seem to have transformed him from a nothing into an Indian deity—though, admittedly, without an Indian summer, or the luxury of an Indian cushion on which to nurse the wound of my beneficence. And then, very composedly, I swish out of the room—thank you, ladies, thank you, hope you've enjoyed the evening, personally I've loved a good deal of it—and my bugle-beads are still dancing and kicking and swishing historically about my (shaky) knees.

NEXT MORNING—before any gossip could reach him—I returned the victory dress, miraculously unscathed, and without detection, to Dr. Fox's wardrobe; and after he'd completed what he called his ablutions, we had breakfast as if nothing. My make-up had come off like a dream. My nails, after a scrape with a pair of scissors, looked dodgier, but Dr. Fox wouldn't have noticed such details. And yet I felt uneasy, for, much as I might have welcomed the chance of a debate with the school authorities on the contentious—and to the best of my knowledge, also unpunishable—subject of transvestism, which Catholics liked to fob off as a filthy perversion favoured by Protestant inverts (to which I would have replied that it was a tradition rich with history, as favoured by the Vatican—remember Fellini—as by European grandees and heterosexual English kings), I certainly didn't want to get called in by the rector at the last minute, and given a thrashing for having scorched some prat who deserved it, when, with the exception of Dr. Fox's concert, I was effectively free to leave.

On my return to my room, I found my cushion slashed to ribbons, I wonder by whom, but this gesture of contempt just spurred me to more contemptuous gestures of my own. The first, which later, briefly, for a couple of minutes, I did regret a bit, was to hurl all my books into the incinerator. The second was dutifully to unpick, as my mother's sempstress had once unpicked the many skirts of her bridal organdie, every stitch sewn round the nametapes of my uniform and linen. I tried to count the threaded stabs, in an attempt to discover how their total sum compared with the number of days spent in this nightmare: but it didn't, not by a long chalk: I was owed, oh terms' worth. Then I packed my trunk meticulously, locked it, chucked the key out of the window, and poured the reminder of my bottle of nail polish on the lid, over my English initials. While the blood was drying, I put the rest of my belongings—my tapes, my pumps, a couple of small pictures, odds and ends of normal clothing—into a suitcase. I closed the cover of my violin. I plonked my plants in the common room, which could do with a bit of cheering, and then I went downstairs in search of a couple of juniors. I bribed them to drag my trunk to the place where trunks were supposed to be deposited—next to the tuck shop, once the fortress of Payne Senior, but closed now, out of season—before being boarded onto lorries and trains and ships. I gave those children clear instructions to cover my trunk with the trunk of some other pupil, and only then to come back to me for payment. In the end it took four of the blighters to carry my chattels, which weighed heavier than a corpse, so my extravagance proved quite costly, but the cause justified it.

I took a final shower, and dressed, in my own clothes. I scrawled a note to Dr. Fox, apologizing for the haste of my departure, explaining that sudden bad news from the family necessitated my missing his concert, and telling him that I would let him know where I could be reached as soon as I myself knew this. And then I went to the coin box, and ordered a taxi, for which I waited near the gates where my parents had once stood like angry spears, and as I saw my own blessed chariot speed round the insouciant Madonna and approach, I grabbed my suitcase and my violin and ran to meet my freedom, but my race against myself must have looked less like an act of vindication than like the early scene from *The Sound of Music* when the singing novice is put back on the streets to find a more suitable calling. And then, as I was about to step inside the car and flee, one of those juniors ran out to hand me a letter, addressed by my father, which I might otherwise have missed, and which I read on the train. And from it I learnt one last thing, which is that the course of spite, more than the course of love, is what never runs smooth:

Dear Iago (not James), the letter begins—instantly betraying the collaboration of his wife.

We returned without mishap after a few very pleasant days in London. Since then, your mother and I have been talking and feel concerned about you. Both your attitude at school, which seems to be one of non-involvement in any wholesome activity and your conduct at home, which we find socially quite unacceptable, there's no need to expound on this, you know exactly what we mean, has led us to take a hard but unavoidable decision. Since you do not wish to come here for the summer, we suggest that you remain in England for the moment.

You should contact my bank manager Mr. Palmer, who I haven't met (I've spoken to him on the telephone) at Lloyd's in St. James's. Make an appointment to see him, and we beg of you, try to look respectable. He has instructions about your finances, regarding both the immediate future and the longer term. Once he's opened an account for you, he will be advancing you by direct debit a monthly allowance as well as your termly fees for Oxford, since you appear to be headed there after all, because even though you're English, I gather from the school that you're not eligible for a grant. This deals with current matters.

As you know, the bulk of your money from your grandfather's trust will be made over to you when you reach the age of 25 by when we sincerely hope that even if you have to learn the hard way you will have matured. Think about it, James (aha!), and ask yourself whether you have shown your mother and I sufficient signs of appreciation for the tremendous sacrifices that we have undergone on your account. And in the meantime, try to understand that this necessary distancing, though harsh, is the right decision both for you and us.

Since you seem determined to ignore social decency, I feel bound as your father to add (though your mother naturally knows nothing of this) a verse from the Holy Bible which I hope will make plain to you, while you have the time to correct it, your moral position in the eyes of the Lord: "If a man lies with a male as with a woman, both of them have committed an abomination; they shall be put to death, their blood is upon them." This comes from the book of Leviticus, and you would do well to read it in its entirety.

In the hope that you will see the light of reason, your mother joins me in prayer on your behalf.

Yours aye,

HJM

P.S. And for goodness sakes before you go to the bank get your hair cut.

PART FIVE

G OD GIVE ME NEW HORIZONS. While my bath runs, I make some coffee and throw the news of the day, unread, into the bin. As I open the drawer of the kitchen table, I find, after all this time, that half-forgotten missive from my friend in France, a woman of birdlike beauty, and I open it with the care that I owe to her, using an agate letter-knife. Inside the tissued envelope, behind a picture of a bronze-and-naked dancer leaping in mid-air, frozen in mid-life, her message, which has lain in wait, now flies out to me like a stab, and reads, in black: I think of you more often than you hear from me. You are important to my well-being, but I don't mean to sound like a burden, or a responsibility—it's my pleasure. Much love. And as I step into the bath, which is slippery with oils of frankincense and lavender, ironic oils, said to help you to relax, I wonder what is becoming of my life, why I neglect my friends; and I reflect on how I abuse the blessings that I've been granted, how I drink too much, how I fritter away my time. And I resolve to set all these wrongs to right, to return to church one of these days, to make myself over to another land. Then I sit down.

I'M SITTING at the table in the restaurant and trying, less out of concern than simulated courtesy, to keep my eyes involved in the open, glossy hopeful features of my friend, my host, my sometime confidant, who seems impatient to regale me with every twitch and tweak about some glorious youth just down from university, encountered in a classic *coup de foudre* on the way out of an acclaimed recent production of a (naturally) baroque opera. And they've been, since, out to dinner twice, talked about everything under the sun: first, in Arlington Street, no less; then, somewhere quieter, more *intime*. But of course, there's been, as yet, none of That Stuff—why must I always be so tacky? Although there has, he gulps, there has, as a matter of fact, been a kiss, just one, since I ask, on the hand. On the hand? God almighty, what is *wrong* with queers these days? My friend regards me piteously. He's not ashamed, he says. He's prepared to wait. To wait for what? There's no big rush, he replies with impatience: love is not a train. And then he adds that he, unlike others he could mention (though there scarcely seems a need), knows when a thing warrants . . . considered investment, when it deserves to be taken—oh, how can he put it? I put it for him: *doucement-doucement*—and the fool agrees. But it transpires, as my companion begins to confide, which he now does with a vengeance, his hand grabbing at my recoiling cuff with a force that betrays panic, that, for all of his cool collectedness, he's gone and booked ten days for two at some fabulously manicured Moroccan snazz-hole with cascades of bougain-villaea and oh, sand-dunes of gazelles and palm trees of green parrots and the thing is, well, here comes the rub: he can't figure out a way to tell the boy, doesn't know how to invite him. Should he send a note, a note with flowers, or would that seem too campy? (What, campier than opera, *mio caro*?) For heaven's sake, he spits, swiftly retracting his grip from my sleeve. What's wrong with me these days? Don't I know any-thing any more?

All I know is this, and I'm not about to tell him: first, that he'd do well to give up those natty cravats of his; and second—more worry-ingly, from my point of view—that earlier today, as I stepped out of the bath and began to towel myself dry and thought not about what I should wear for lunch, which was obvious, but what I would wear next time that Steve came round, comes round, I discovered, like a mockery from above, bang slap at the epicentre of my left buttock, a developing pimple, a lesion, a bloody volcano. I can feel it now, pulsing against the wicker of my chair.

BACK IN MY FLAT I decide to face facts: Steve will have to be put off, postponed for a few nights, and I must travel, travel as far as he's con-cerned. Not a crisis, exactly, nothing so grand; just some unforeseen but unavoidable circumstance. And where, pray, shall I be bound on this trip that I plan? Nowhere so remote that I risk flying out of his mind, nor yet to a place so near as to render my pretext banal. And catching a providential glimpse of the card from my friend in Paris, I realize that yes, it's obvious, that's where I shall go, where I must pretend to be gone. Well, not to Paris exactly—too *bonjour mesdames* for comfort—rather somewhere flatter and duller and buried without need of a mention vaguely in France. So I leave a message on his Ansaphone saying that it turns out that I have to be out of the country on Wednesday and that although I'm due back in the evening, late afternoon in fact, I'm a bit worried that my flight might be delayed or something, and I may not manage to get home in time for our (I nearly say date) appointment; anyway, could he let me know whether he'd prefer to reschedule or whatever, thanks, 'bye. And I head off for a siesta and take off my trousers and suddenly realize—guess what?—that the spot on my bum no longer feels nor—hang on—looks nearly so bad. And I unplug the 'phone beside me.

When it rings a while later, though I pick it up mechanically, the receiver is dead at my end; so I just lie back and listen to the pump of my startled breast as the machine clicks on in another room; and I hear, after waiting an eternity for my irksome outgoing voice to reach its suspension, the voice of Steve acknowledging my call and saying no problem, he's doing nothing else that night, just to ring him when I get in, or from the airport if I like, might be an idea, so long as it's, say, before eleven, later might be pushing it, I might be tired, but either way, not to worry, speak on Wednesday, 'bye for now. And hey, he adds, by way of salacious afterthought, have a good time. Then, a chuckle, and he's gone. I hurl myself out of bed, as if I'd overslept. I can hardly think— I, who think too much.

BUT BY WEDNESDAY, feast of the Transfiguration, I believe that I have thought of most things—prepared for the future, if not quite with the fervour of a novice on the verge of the veil, certainly with the rigour of a patient bound for an intervention so delicate, so critical that he must face the possibility of never returning from that dreaded sacred place, the operating theatre. I have, of course, long hence written my will, but I've double-checked the contents just to ensure that no small thing has carelessly been left to persons who, since its composition, may happen to have disappointed me, or kicked the bucket. And all is serene: no thing has. I have tidied every tape and book and disc and plate and glass and knife and fork and spoon and thing in my possession. A denim apron which has always been a source of shame to me I have finally thrown away, along with the tattier of my tea-towels, which bear the frayed initials of my mother as a maiden. I have defrosted the fridge and, with the exception of a bottle of poppers, rid it of all perishables. On the occasions when I've felt a need for reflection, I have waxed the kitchen floor-tiles, on my knees, a servant to myself. They gleam. The window cleaner has been. The linen spread upon my bed is fresh and crisp and fine as a shroud which a palliative sister might long to retrieve before a patient's refrigeration. The flowers that I have placed in a tall vase of uncut crystal, flowers known as black roses, would do credit to most shrines. My small dark car has been scrupulously cleaned, and polished by hand, and parked directly outside the gates of the building where I am. All notes and cards and letters and telegrams and invitations ever received have been catalogued in files and shelved: some alphabetically, some chronologically; the rest, by theme. Personal papers which I regret having written, testaments to juvenile imprudences, have obviously been binned, as have unguarded photographs, images that might mislead. In the early hours of today, I dumped two family-sized bags, stuffed full of biographical redundancies, in a nearby skip outside a grotty local hotel, and was caught in the act by a marauding rubber queen who scowled, then rubbed her constricted packet at me. All of my clothes, except for those on my back, which I plan to chuck at the last opportunity, are clean. My seventy-eight pairs of shoes, which, let me tell you, have strutted and trampled and danced in their time, are in full sheen—with the exception of a half-forgotten pair of fifties lamé party-spikes which I thought it wiser to discard. My coats hang in a cupboard in the hall, ranged by the season and by colour and by cut, like a catalogue of moods. I have dusted my umbrellas, out on the landing, and returned them to their stand—furled but not clasped. I own no hats.

And so, as you can see, at least the place where I reside is orderly, fit to receive, in readiness. Were I to die today, which, given a choice, I should prefer to do other than on these premises, somewhere less sightly, such as a backroom, I cannot imagine that my spiralling ghost would have reason to fret over any posthumous domestic scrutiny. And my executor, who most likely has forgotten how years ago, in the throes of a passionate if overpatternly acid trip, he offered to execute on my behalf, will, when called upon to effect the mixed privilege of his duties, exhale with relief that my affairs lie not in the surrealistic state of disarray which he might have feared. I mean, given the accounts which you hear about untimely departed members of the sorority—the dildos, the dick-pumps, the sticky mounds of pornography, the incriminating Polaroids, the medical pamphlets on how to reconstruct a foreskin, the (I'm sorry to be prissy, but frankly) lamentable state of those duvets—well, my own demise, were it to strike me now, would surely strike my jittery intimates as a blessedly neat piece of, not quite justice, of mercy. Like a funeral without a family. Or a kiss without false teeth.

I'VE TAKEN a look at myself and taken myself in hand and, after numerous recent lapses, returned to the gym: on Monday, and on Tuesday, and, like some frenzied client attending a last-minute fitting, very early this morning. You know how a certain type of rich, undignified woman, generally divorced and pushing fifty, will commend herself to her couturier with the Brief, disguised as a plea, that—whatever the cost of the creation (which is immaterial to her), and whatever its cut and cloth and strategic padding—the marriage of her money to his skill must recompense her, at a predetermined party, with the advances of a man on whom she has designs; well, I, similarly, have engaged a personal trainer—a female, predictably, for females tend best to understand these things, these urgent dreams. And I have asked her, without actually divulging the grubby nature of my need, to invest in me, for this brief time, every detail of her body-sculpting expertise. But I must sound too breathless, too frantic, like a neglected actor suddenly called up for a part demanding nudity. And I suspect that she can hear the beat of my anxiety, because, before we begin, she pulls me into a corner and tries to appease me by claiming that there's no need to get into a state about things. After all, she explains, you're slim, can't weigh more than what, eleven, eleven and a half stone—exactly. And she has the elegance to describe me as lean, which is the polite word for scrawny; and then, pointing at the mirror, she tells my reflection to look at itself. See? Whereas (she whispers) just *get* the other desperados in this gym—as if their pasty flabbiness could bring solace to me. This, she goes on, is what we're going to do: tighten up my rump a bit; pump out my shoulders a little; burn off some fat on the exercise bike; and we can do some cardiovascular moves on the step-machine. But, she warns, suddenly looking serious, You're not to expect miracles. Oh I don't, I reply: in three days I only expect to be resurrected, not reincarnated. And she laughs aloud, beefily, and her mirth disrupts the surrounding, panting gravity. A few heads turn, and glare disapprovingly, as if we were gossiping in church, or yakking at a cinema; and for a chilling instant I imagine that one of those sweaty faces belongs to Steve. Stop it. She trains me with such fierce concentration, as if I were her chosen candidate for some vital competition, that I could almost describe her attention as devoted. Her eyes seem never to leave me. She hardly speaks. Very occasionally, as I move onto a higher weight or some harder machine, she encourages me. I find that I have grown, in this short, frenetic period, disconcertingly fond of a woman whom I scarcely know, whose personal story is a mystery to me. But already my time is up; her job is done; I'm ready to leave. And although, of course, I look nothing like a vision, I've half been turned into what some, if suitably starved and drunk, might regard as a passing object of interest. But she stresses that what we have done, what she has done for me, is only a cheat, won't last beyond a week. And as I hand back my locker key, she asks what this whole thing is about anyway, some love job? Her guess flushes me violently, but I tell her not to be silly, just off on holiday. Oh yeah, she grins, where to, the moon? Most probably, I admit. And then I feel the kindness of her hand patting the troubles in my old kit-bag, as if for luck; so I, in turn, lean across and, not exactly professionally, kiss her cheek.

LEAVING THE GYM, since I still have most of the day to kill, I decide to stop at a local coffee bar which, today, seems to be packed with animated foreign kids, chaperoned by a knitworn older man. But the edges of the place are planted with a typical smattering of queens, hardy perennials, inserted singly along the walls, into the shade, dug down and drooping slightly from the graftings of the previous evening. One of these I recognize from God knows when, way back: a forgettable fuck, bleary-eyed from skunk, who spares me the hassle of a glance. At the counter, I order a large espresso and an orange juice; no, no ice, thanks. Toast?, he goes, Danish? Croissant? Bap? No, nothing;

this'll be fine. Two fifty-nine, he announces, as if I'd asked for the time in Cape Town; and he returns my change, along with an unconvincing smile and the exhortation: There you go now. Pisses me off when they say that. Go where, and when, precisely?

Go towards the window at the front, away from the crowd. Sit down. Light up. Look out. Notice, across the street, beyond a row of parked cars, a (closed) shop of gay paraphernalia, inside which you will find poppers, cock-rings, cock-straps, ball-weights, tit-clamps, harnesses, douche-bags, soft-core videos, specialist literature, coffee-table books of homographic art, greetings cards (both funny and funereal), T-shirts with slogans ("I Can't Even Think Straight"; "Stuff A Chicken Tonight"; "Trouble," and, for Trouble's little friend, "Strife"); pump-action lubricant, in various flavours and sizes; double-strength condoms, extra-length condoms (designed to accommodate both larger Prince Alberts and udder-loads of urine); a fancy range of underwear (thong, pouch, brief, mesh, stud-front, zip-back), plus, of course, a spectrumful of colour-coded back-pocket handkerchieves, displayed as a rainbowed flower.

My head is still loitering around the dark interior of the shop when, for no apparent reason, it seems to flutter out onto the street and gaze at the display of running-vests and latex shorts and vinyl caps and combat boots and leather waistcoats and a solitary cat-o'-nine tails lying unconscious on the floor, which I can see between two cars; and then my mind returns to me, bearing, like a vulture or a hawk, the question which I suppose I've been trying to avoid: Tonight, what do I put on? And instantly, here I go: you could, of course, simply repeat the previous lot of clothes, for safety, but that might suggest a desire for repetition, when a reprise of events is the least of your hopes. Or you could, alternatively, just dress as if for comfort, as if this second meeting were less sexual than social, in chinos, with a rolled-up shirt of Oxford cotton, and brogues. Or you could try to test his erotic know-how by donning an armour, something rebarbative, like a flannel suit and stiff collar and cufflinks with pearls and a handmade tie from Rome. Or you could even open the door wearing nothing at all, starkers, which is the ultimate challenge and the ultimate turn-off (you've had it done to you; you know). And finally it occurs to you, the secret, the solution, the perfect formula. You will model yourself on the very

man whom you want to get to know, disguise yourself as an unde-
tectable whore, dress as an irony.

Decided, then. Tonight, when he walks in, assuming that he does,
and assuming that he's remotely perceptive, Steve will spot my emula-
tion of that earlier him, will recognize a darker, younger, slighter version of the way he looked at our first meeting. He will find me wearing
a brown T-shirt (though mine, of lycra from Los Angeles, is more
poncy), and baggy blue-jeans (though mine, underworn, aren't as convincing as his), and heavy black boots (though mine don't stop at the
ankle: they rise to mid-calf under my jeans, to pad out my legs, which
are weedy). I suddenly envisage him appearing in the identical, original
outfit, and instantly turning me into his puny mimic, his idiot twin, and
the prospect tries to finish me. I dismiss it by dwelling on the veins up
his arms and the veins on his neck and the strong vein at his temple,
and I think of his head and then I think of mine and I think bloody hell
and practically sprint to an old-fashioned barber's down the road (the
sort of butchy place, I bet you, to which Steve himself would go), and
the shop is empty; and on the window, in red, it says seven quid—lucky
number to begin with, but also a perfect fraction of that other, greater
figure, seventy, in cash: a sort of replica, a fated miniature. So I walk in,
and Sweeney Todd turns out, to my relief, to be a jokey little Greek. No
need to talk. I signal Short; he signals Shorter? I signal No; he nods No
Problem, and now we're off. He stands on a linoleum step to carry out
my yob-crop, and kicks the platform around me at irregular intervals,
pushing my ears down, forcing my neck forward; occasionally, snort-
ing. And a matter of minutes later, during which I've been vacant, in a
sort of limbo, absorbed by the mystique of scissors and clippers and
cut-throats, and wondering how certain people can claim such things as
fetishes, how they can regard the process of being shorn as a turn-on,
I'm done, done-for: he swirls his sheet away from my chest with the
panache of a triumphant matador, and I'm left resembling the mug-
shot of some mugger. My regular hairdresser, an impossibly sophisticated lesbian who dismisses clients who cannot discuss the latest
novels, and who, for years, has refused my impetuous visits to her salon
(Go home, give it some thought, then telephone and make an appointment), would knock my block off. And I return to my flat still preoccu-

pied by the subject of hair: no longer, however, that on my head; rather the stuff that sprouts about my body.

I FIND THAT often people are reluctant to discuss the issue of body hair outside the homosexual ghetto, as if it, the hair, didn't exist, or didn't warrant attention. By contrast, at the time of which I write, which falls late into the century, this whole dialectic has, among gays, become something of an obsession. I cannot claim to be a conversant inhabitant of the queer nation, much less an arbiter of what is, and what is not, homopolitically appropriate. Nor can I pretend to be an aficionado of parlours that promise painless, or, come to that, excruciating depilation. So, before you start to ask from where I derive my peculiar notions on the topic, let me admit that what scant experience I possess has been garnered in private, at close quarters—not thanks to the wonder of Dutch video pornography, which, incidentally, is the only one of its type worth watching; nor, indeed, thanks to American skinny-pics, which tend to be less arousing than comical; but through sly observation and, still more systematically, through tactile perception. I have literally felt my way around the subject, perfected for myself a secret sort of body Braille; but this has nothing to do with discernment, for, in the case of others, I run into trouble when trying to distinguish between what is a feature and what is a fault: to me, it's all information. And yet, in my personal instance, my attitude swings with such frequency between acceptance and resignation that, for the sake of my sanity, I have had to adopt a stance of moderation, to steer a cowardly middle course, that of weaklings and prevaricators, details of which can wait. But let's get one thing straight: I have been described as a bitch, and regularly; as a cunt, most certainly; as a motherfucker too, and mostly by women; but never (that I know of) have I been described as hirsute. Not that the subject doesn't interest me. It fascinates me. Because, from my antics, which in my recent aimless life have practically amounted to academic investigation, both distant and committed, detached yet riveted, I have been led to surmise that, these days, the manner in which men, gay men, choose to groom or, conversely, elect to preserve their personal fur has become as telling an indication of how they perceive themselves and, by extension, of how they would wish to be perceived, as previously, say fifteen years back, around the time when I came out, were such issues as patter, profession, purported income, apparent intelligence, brand of car, colour of same, musical preferences, linguistic fluency, favourite restaurants, number (where applicable) of dependants, criminal convictions (ditto), religious pretensions, shoe size, star sign, approximate age and (admit it) taste in decoration.

You see: I sometimes wonder whether the root of this whole corporal hair mania might not lie with domestic interiors, specifically with black leather and chrome, those traditional emblems of the aspirational queer's living quarters: half-classy, half-coarse; smelly but clean; sensuous but butch, and suitable for all occasions. I mean, earlier in the annals of furnishing history, say just after the Stonewall fandango, do you seriously imagine that men were going to clip and trim and pluck and prune their skins down to the texture of the petal of a camellia simply to copulate against splintery planks of pine, cushions of kilim, and walls of filthy hessian? Hardly. In those days, unbelievable as it may now seem, they did it in their open cheesecloth shirts and peeling, unbuttoned loons. And really, if I'm ever to explain my theory about the connection between body hair and décor, I have to revert to 1969, a year which, even if not exactly an aesthetic zenith, nonetheless figures in our mythology as a year for which we should be grateful. And the reason is a story.

One afternoon on Christopher Street, while the drag queens of New York were being hounded for the millionth time by that city's constabulary, news was relayed to them from London announcing that Judy Garland, whom they divinized, not least because she had sung that the dreams that you dare to dream really do come true, had, after multiple bodged attempts, finally managed to do herself in with the help of barbiturates. Such tragic intelligence naturally put the queens in a black passion; and it probably seems absurd to relate—absurd because, had they only known, then, how many more, other, sadder mournings were to follow, they might not have shed so many tears so fast—but anyway, they were stricken at the time, rendered incoherent, inconsolable and, after one too many ugly confrontations between some anonymous pig and some nameless transvestite close to the Hudson, they snapped: the Stonewall riots were sparked, and by then, as far as the drag queens were concerned, the battle could have been unfolding on the banks of the Nile. And together they let rip in their trashy finery, and they hollered and kicked and fought until they'd beaten the shit out of the fuzz. And although some queens did, inevitably, sustain injuries, and pretty nasty ones, the point is that because, for once in his finite mercy, the Lord happened to be on their side, our side, they won, we won. Victory actually came to pass. And they rose tall, these unholy amazons, and then they brushed themselves down, and then, graciously waving and smiling at the crowd, which was aghast, they pissed in the eyes of the law. And although I do not doubt that most of those fabulous creatures will since have died, and died in misery, I sometimes tell myself, when I despair at the misfortunes that plague us now, that, no matter how unfairly the current cards may appear to be stacked, there runs, somewhere on the grimacing face of Justice, an eroded rivulet of moral urine which I consider nominally to be mine. Bless you, girls; and thank you.

But back to those riots. No sooner had our drag queens resumed their composure and been legally counted, though caring less than less because they still couldn't get over the shock of Judy Garland, than, hot on their high heels, and eager to give them a light, came the truckers and professors and the butchers and the bell-boys—not many politicians, but that's no great surprise—and before anyone could say Mea Maxima, out-out-out, like exploding beads of quicksilver in the night, or a boil that had been waiting to burst since bloody biblical times, came the whole bang shoot of waiters and skaters and hookers and florists and nurses and dancers and sculptors and models and sample machinists and décorateurs and coiffeurs and masseurs and textile designers and theatre designers and fashion designers and even more drag queens, but much better dressed, and vicars with houseboys and lawyers and molesters and beautiful trannies with big-time regrets and bell-boys and jewellers and dollies, no trolleys, and, after a milliner, quite a few drunkards and ashen librarians and ancient historians and, standing behind an artistic director . . . a fat sobbing mum with her perfect ovation of twelve gorgeous sons, no twins, all gay.

And the principal upshot of this rebellion, which of course culminated in a huge celebration, was that it opened the way for what we now describe as Gay Liberation. But I don't want to bother whining about whether it was all a false start, or a bad joke, or even a mistake, because that's all dreary conjecture, whereas facts, subject though facts can be to touches of colour and fantastical interpretation, remain by their very nature incontestable. And the facts, let me give them to you: as the movement which earned us our emancipation, that baptism of fiery transvestites which cynics have since dismissed as a great puffball without direction, and ingrates within our force as a strategic embarrassment, rolled forward and gathered momentum, our men, who were strong, went out and built, for themselves and their successors, bathhouses of such splendour and debauchery as have not been recorded since the days of Classical Rome; and they hosted orgies and bacchanals more unbridled even than those held during the pagan festivals of Athens before the days of Plato. And they abandoned their false friends and families, not for a measly forty days in any wilderness, but for a lifetime of fast metropolitan splendour. And in the summertime they colonized savage beaches on every continent, and, on the way to such beaches, for instance, they stopped along motorways and some secondary roads to call in to public conveniences, which they rechristened Cottages, and here they consorted with other men from nowhere. And while they hung about for further communicants, they perfected the art of graffito, and employed their keys as tools for carving out the screens between cubicles, and they carved with such determined industry that in the fullness of time they created openings in the partitions which became known as Glory Holes, because occasionally you could find glory there—through them, through their auspices: between the thighs, or in the mouths, or with the hands of utter strangers. They were like confessionals, those cubicles, I sometimes think, because they fostered anonymity, and anonymity, to my mind, helps when you want to tell the truth. And it wasn't unheard of for these glory holes to be approached, like oracles, by men whose motorcars, though safely parked in the shade, and locked for further safety, were laden, not with luggage and valuables, but with their owners' wives and families. Respite, relief, relaxation or some similar thing, is, I believe, what those men, whom we call Breeders, called their covert activities. But I have never heard it said that they regarded, much less referred to, such extra-curricular congresses as remotely—Lord forbid—homosexual. The very notion.

And then our men, our pioneers, those unsung messiahs who have with such dull frequency been dismissed as the end of a bad line, as fruitless, futile and unreproductive, created the god that was Disco (*genitum, non factum,* begotten, not made) which resulted in the fusion between a rushing breathless tempo and slow romantic irony, an irony borne upon its lyrics, lyrics which now that I recall them, now that I repeat them, now that I try to sing them, strike me as dark and sad and faintly bitter. Almost predictive. They choke me slightly. Because we remember those men, you see, our pioneers, who, though technically vanished, survive brightly and wisely and so bloody funnily in heads such as mine; we remember them, I swear to you, not being wheeled around consulting rooms for injections into their eyeballs, nor vomiting into the laps of their horrified mothers, who came running at the last, nor pushed into incontinency pants for their final European flights, nor planning their valedictory performances—their songs of departure, their readings, their flowers—nor ravaged by pustules and lesions and scabs, nor emaciated beyond recognition, staring out, staring down, to sign papers of authorization for the poisoned chalice that is morphine, nor, a matter of days later, wrapped in magnificently monogrammed shrouds, or slipped into pathetically large burial outfits, or boxed into nasty little urns which had been languishing in wait beneath the hospital beds of their demented Significant Others until such time as their ashes could, in accordance with their joint instructions, be mingled and married by their friends, and cast to the high winds of Caledonia, or smuggled onto transatlantic planes and hurled down the highways of California. No, not us: we remember them walking with their heads held high against the winds of catastrophe, walking with that special nonchalant grace that so characterized them; or, their heads thrown up for drama, telling tales of a luminous blue about themselves, about people like us, about the outcast children of Sodom and Gomorrah. Bless you, darling boys; and thank you.

In reality they didn't worry overmuch, those boys, about shrouds and suits and cloth and ash, for, in their prime, they'd already invented a new meaning for clothes, had redefined the boundaries between regular garb and uniforms and costume, had translated what they wore and what it meant into a language that only they, and later we, could understand. Sometimes, of course, especially on the boardwalks, or in moonlit parks, they took off what they wore, or had it taken off; but on other occasions, such as their carnivals, which have grown to be momentous, Fantabulosa Galas for those among us still familiar with Polari, they displayed a penchant for chiffon, which, just as sequins are their stars, is the gossamer of the gods. And against the odds, but in keeping with all that is noble, it came about that some of these men fell in love with one another—they fell and they fell, further and further, over and over. And some were moved to relinquish their flat-shares and to leave their studios and walk into new premises and set up home. High windows. High hopes. Sometimes, on Saturdays, you saw such lovers shopping. And when their affairs, as these always must, it seems to me, went wrong, both the heartbreakers and the broken were received back in the Scene as if they'd never been gone. And all of this time, remember, these men, who for centuries had been written off as good-for-nothing-pooftah-faggot-fairy-nancy-friends-of-Dorothy, worked like buggery for their treacherous futures, which then seemed to beckon with promise. And they earned quite a lot of handbag, as they called it; and what they earned went not, as is popularly presumed, up each other's rears, nor into their veins, nor, indeed, up their nostrils, but smartly into the folds of their hot wallets, thus giving rise—once the entrepreneurial sector had cottoned on—to what has since come to be called the pink pound and the pink mark and the pink franc and the pink rand and even, I suppose, the pink yen. But, most powerfully, the pink dollar—not that it's pink any more: gay money has become the colour of the rainbow. And the trouble, all these years on, is that the coffers are running low. Because there is no lullaby left for us, and because troubles do not melt like lemon drops, and because the clouds are never so far behind us, and because birds, as it happens, cannot fly over any rainbow. I'm getting lost.

Back to black leather and chrome. That's where I was. Smooth interiors and smoothened bodies. Right. The ethnic decorative trends of the Seventies gave way to the slick and seductive, democratic but impersonal furniture that I've mentioned, and queers were overcome. The hardened gleam of metal and the raw hides of animals seemed to strike a chord in us, probably because they echoed our night-clubs and our pleasures and our dark dungeons. And the connection between our homes and our haunts encouraged an illusion whereby our sitting rooms were no longer just our sitting rooms, but could also become our favourite hell-holes. We grew less concerned about safeguarding our privacy than about winning, half-naked in our stark settings, the approval of some insatiable, invisible onlooker, some tall, dark, mythical stranger who was bound to materialize, or so we thought. Our former sociability, or mine, turned inwards, into a clandestine routine created round a constant and mysterious personal video. Future fact and actual fantasy combined to create a style that was Life as Pornography. Furniture seemed both to grow and to recede in dominance, veering between status object and stage property. And we, its ostensibly proud owners, veered, in our shameless capsules, between the parts of self-auditioned actors, self-centred directors, and, sometimes, even walk-on beasts of sexual burden, or faceless dirty voices, or grunts.

Me, for instance. I could cease to be myself. I could become another, any other, many others, all at once, or in sections. Up here could be my head and my sense of my eyes and my dry, open mouth, breathing hard; below, and separate from me, could be my tumescent cock and tightened balls and perhaps one of my hands. Yet right across the room, miles away, and enlarged, and up in lights, I could watch, to the sound of some foreign track, my dripping and distended arse getting fucked, by me if I so pleased, or, if I so pleased, by the fist of my free hand, or the fist of anyone else whose cock I liked, and on which I might have liked to suck. It was so easy, so broad and free, the landscape of my intimate sordidness. I could be both the pompous judge of all this unfolding smut and, equally, by association, by simple reflection, the hero of the stinking pit, or the victim, or his employer, or the guy in the garage, or the dog that might have stuck it to the mechanic's wife. I could even fake my own orgasm. Whatever I chose. Whomever I liked. Whenever. And so, day after day, night after night, I, and plenty of others like me, learnt to watch, and came to emulate those ever-engorged rôle models, those repeatedly desirable paragons who were stoned out of their minds and who, by now, are also most likely all gone, poor sods.

Compulsive observation of this sort made us, to begin with, self-conscious, because, though you could fool yourself, you couldn't fool others. You were merely you, but a porn star is a porn star; which is why we all scuttled off in search of the local gymnasium. And gymnasia became basilicas. And slowly we were transformed into approximations of our prayers: our bodies blossomed, and with them, our sense of confidence. And once immersed in this new religion, it didn't take an ordination to discover that a smoothened skin can only enhance the shadows and the ripples and the contours of a sculpted torso. And besides, remember, there were suddenly so Many of us, so many new converts, that, even if we no longer felt the need to fight so hard for recognition or tolerance, we were having to struggle as never before to get to communion, to score. That, at least, was my experience, was to become my problem. But it wasn't everyone's. I mustn't discount fat men, or bald men, or, for that matter, monorchids, or men in toupées, or devotees of the handlebar-moustache and other facial adornments, or men in rubber waders, or weirdos into diapers and bonnets. For although such hybrids never exerted more than a minor influence on our burgeoning scene, they were, nevertheless, active participants and, believe it or not, picky ones. Strange, fussy creatures, easily subject to caricature perhaps, but crawling without inhibition around the colder recesses of our sexual morass. Yet, because they were so specifically defined, so exact, these men tended, in the pursuit of whatever one pursues, to restrict themselves to others of that exact type, who were in sympathy, or sympathized. But sometimes they mystified: what did they get up to, and how? I would envisage a pair of obese fags, like a couple of soft boiled eggs, rolling and rolling and farting once in a while, but never managing to get to grips with one another, forever prevented from making proper contact. I just couldn't understand. Perhaps they liked to be tantalized. Perhaps they simply admired, stood back and gazed, up and down, and drooled, mmm, at those mutual rolls of flab, at those spreading thighs, those dugs, those soft great arms, those pudgy wrists, those tiny feet, so miraculously light. Who knows. Marriages are made in heaven. Maybe it was all to do with sumo wrestlers, or mountainous opera divas, or even directors of music. Either way, these people counted. As indeed did hairy men, by which I mean Really hairy ones, freaks who described themselves as Bears but in reality resembled gorillas, whose body-covering suggested some monstrous secret persona, whose sprouting jungles round collar and cuffs, like hints of bestiality to come, could, at times, turn you into a gibbering Jane. It used to concern me, the sense of some unresolved primal urge creeping up on me, as if to threaten my sense. But I've

been spared undue shame in this department, for my researches confirm that, whatever he may like to pretend, Tarzan's gorilla will, for
choice, select the embraces of gorillas of his own. Which in a way is
just as well: for were such gorillas, in captivity, to turn their affections
away from their identical inmates and towards the keepers of their
cages, life, for gullible suckers such as I, would long hence have become
one neverending, agonizing rash. Don't laugh. Have a banana.

I remember being approached by one such gorilla once, whom, I
suppose, looking back, must have been an anthropological exception, a
departure from type. For I should explain that this particular departure
of a man happened, despite his massive eyebrows and walrus moustache, to be utterly bald, and, as if to complicate matters, to come
equipped with impenetrable sunglasses, heavy nipple-rings, and waders
up to the latter; so that I was (be fair) being served an embarrassment
of signals, a bit of a fruit salad. Within a brief time of our encounter at
some pub, it became apparent that whatever his interest in me might
be, this lay nowhere near the obvious—my face, my body, the lacerated
denim which I recall that I was wearing—much less my conversation,
which tended, in those days, towards the curt, was surly. Now that I'm
older I try to pretend to be friendly, but no matter. The point is that this
man's interest, sole interest in fact, seemed to rest, can you believe (it
was so bizarre) with . . . my hands. I could see them in the mirror of his
glasses. His own hands, to me, were perfect: colossal and hairy, with a
silver skull-ring stuck somewhere. But mine? He picked one up as if he
were proposing, in order to check its relative slimness, the precise
length of my middle finger, the maximum width of my knuckles,
which he squeezed a little absently. I felt like a glove, or a puppet. And
then, very specifically and without making any bones about it, he
focused on my nails: their overall condition, their shape, their moons,
their growth to the last millimetre, any underlying muck, the state of
my cuticles and so on. No warts; no cuts; no calluses; no eczema; could
be cleaner, he supposed, but basically he was satisfied. What the fuck
could all this be about? I remember leaning against the bar, imagining
in my drunken idiocy that, perhaps—which for me would have been a
first, and a freebie with any luck—I had met a Palmist. And then, dis-
carding this possibility, which seemed just too unlikely, I began to suspect that I had landed myself, which nobody could have predicted, with

a manicurist. But in the end, the elusively obvious was brought home to me—by then, almost defiantly. It was so simple, you see: the dude merely happened to be looking, quick before the bell went ding-ding-ding, for a cosy hand to fist him. Humiliation, like gloves, can come in many shapes and sizes, which is why I like to get out.

I GET OUT MY KEY and, back in my flat, am struck by a sense of dislocation. The place no longer feels mine. I prowl about like a visitant at the wrong address, or a forensic expert on an unlit stage between cancelled performances. But the show? Must go on. Make a mess. Break a leg. Oh fuck off. I go into the bathroom. Switch on the spots. The alarm clock on the window-sill warns that, since leaving the gym, I've managed to waste one and a half measly hours. I open the window, wide. I hear a train chortle by. In theory I could still go to France and be back in time.

I place my tools along the basin surround. They glisten like surgical cutlery against the pallid marble slab. The face that I catch in the shaving-mirror, magnified, seems to belong to some other, some sweaty practitioner. I look down. I pick up the tweezers. I run them under the hot tap. I wipe them on a towel. I wash my hands. I strip. I sit upon the lavatory, bare as a thinker; lean down. I start to pluck the hairs along my toes. Down between my parted thighs into the bog they drop, small corpses downstream. I flush, but stay where I am, squatted over a waterfall, which trickles for a while, the quiet waters by. I attend to a couple of thick recurring hairs on my upper arms, one on each side, awkwardly to the back. Viewed at close quarters, as such hairs always are, they resemble stakes of burnt wood impaled on arid land. No freckles. No markings to brighten the site. The hairs slide and curl to start with, then yield at the last. Snap, and out they come. They wriggle like the severed tails of young lizards. I wrap them in a square of lavatory paper, which I fold closed and shove down. No sound. Paper must have stuck to the side. I stand, affronted. Flush for a second time.

I turn towards the shaving-mirror and flip the circular glass, so that it no longer magnifies. I yank it closer towards me. I take hold of my nose and focus on it, twist it to this side and that, distort it, as if it were part of a Bacon canvas. My nostrils: I stare straight up them: they breathe with independent life, bristle like terrified animals. I approach these burrows with caution at first, as if wishing to take their contents by surprise; then, I act fast, attacking the undergrowth round the edges of the disfigured orifices, wrenching the bristles out. Flesh creeps. I work my way inwards. Some of the traumatized hairs that emerge have turned white, and are coarse, stubborn, like stitches. I continue to pluck and pull and tug until beads of irritating pain begin to dilute my vision. The mirror is steaming up. I wipe it, and blink, and continue. My nose twitches, begins to itch. I pause to rub it with the side of my hand. The crevices look cleaner now, shinier. A few more plucks, hard, and finally my snout feels smooth, restored, fit to be investigated by another man's tongue. I snort, snort up and swallow. Then I rip out a couple of pubes from my eyebrows. And again I wash my hands.

I move on to my tits. I crick my neck as I stare down. My nipples look foolish, like the nipples of a skinny child—perter perhaps, perhaps a bit darker, but infantile. Now and then some freaky hair will sprout on one of the surrounds. I spy a couple of such hairs right now, both on the same side. I hoick my left breast up and, with tweezers in my opposite hand, I pluck at the longer of the two, which seems to lengthen as it emerges yet gives way without a struggle. But now its follicle rises in fury, swells out, whitens. Before it can subside, I seize the other hair, which is softer and fairer, too new, too fresh as yet to have darkened, a sapling; and I pluck. But it snaps, halfway along the stem, so that I have to go further down this time, closer to the root, to avoid further mishap. Done. The rest of my chest is smooth, thank Christ.

I return the tweezers to the slab, and deposit them between nail-clippers and file. I raise my feet, by turns, onto the cool enamelled edge of the white bath. Sprawled out thus, they appear grotesquely broad and flat, skeletal, like claws gripping at a glacier. I trim all nails except for those on my big toes, which I cut with scissors made for infants—blunted ends and pale blue handles. Then I smoothen the edge of each nail with a virgin file, using the grey side, which, though softer than the pink, still burns my flesh numb. Powdered skin floats to the tips of my fingers, like dust. From the floor of the bath I scoop up fallen crescents of nail and, doubting that the cistern will countenance a further flush in such a hurry, I condemn them to the basin, turning on the taps and

standing back and watching the remnants of my ministrations slithering towards the plug-hole and rushing away like dismembered bits of
ancient insects, ivoried by time.

Now I need a comb with medium teeth, not too fine, which I pick
up and run through the hair under my arms. I put the comb back down.
I let my arms hang dead, in line with my sides, and peer into the glass
on the wall over the basin. I spy tendrils creeping out from each pit. I
take a pair of hairdressing scissors, with that vital extra metal comma
designed to steady unsteady fingers, and I slide them onto my weaker
hand. (Forget to attend first to the trickier arm and you'll never manage
to equalize both sides.) I turn my body in profile to the glass and hold
my right hand up, uncomfortably high, behind my head. The underarm
is thrown into relief; its hair, against the backlight, looks like a doll's lace
fan. I begin to trim along its edge, crunching my way up the scallop.
Now I swap round, which feels more manageable. Compare sides. No
one would know. Have a rest. Take an interval.

THIS LINE, like a false trail, of hairs leading from my navel to my
pubes, makes you think of crusty spunk. Deal with it, but ensure that
your tamperings remain above detection, that they look like a proper
(venial) lie. Take no measures that are radical: no razors; no wax. Work
outwards from the central axis, which is like a backbone, and thin out,
hair by hair if necessary: the result must look natural. (Blonds can
afford to go shorter.) Next bit is tricky. Stand up. Lean into the basin
surround. Pubic mound meets marble. My genitals drop beneath the
parapet. I press in, to achieve a decent horizontal. I am a spirit-level. I
comb through the furred mound, severally; and then, I trim the
growth—not like some minor medic attending to a pre-operative patient, more like a gardener attending to his prized topiary—and the cut-
tings drop away, paler, softer than you would imagine. I gather the fluff
into a wiry ball and blow it out of the window, checking that it doesn't
float back inside. I inspect myself down. Just need to cut a few curls
from my inner thighs, mostly on the left side; is nothing ever balanced.
I remember, all of a sudden, the nails on my hands, which I haven't yet
shortened. I clip at them, quite fast; and, on a reflex, give them a scrub.
I tidy up, put away the hardware, cover my tracks. I step into the bath
and draw the see-through plastic curtain round me. I turn the lever for

the shower clockwise to Max, and within seconds the water is scalding. And I move in at last, and vanish in the vapour.

Next I concentrate on my cock and balls, wielding a razor which I purposely reserve for those parts. Fresh blade always. Shaving cream tends to sting, or provoke a rash: use soap of glycerine to lather up. First I work on the underside of my penis, flipping it up to face me, and I rasp with downstrokes, grating against the grain until the skin, which I feel with my free thumb, is smooth, smooth as it warrants. I let my cock flop down, and shave off the hairs at its base, which are like weeds grown round the stem of a drooping plant. I scoop up my testicles and squeeze their sac away from me, so that it grows taught, waxen, lined with sharp vessels of dark blood. Lovers do this for each other. My shavings mingle with the froth as twigs and seaweed mingle with the shallows of a scummy tide. I flick the razor as you might flick a fountain pen, brusquely down. Then, I proceed. I bend over myself to probe beneath myself, between my thighs, inspecting the crevice that leads from my testicles to my anus. I work backwards towards the rear of me, watching out for that central ridge of embossed skin which appears like a neat surgical seam, a scar, a vestige of the time when the two lost halves of man were first united. Blood floods down into my head. I straighten up. I rinse my genitals using a sponge. I turn off the shower, push the curtain ajar, grab a towel, and start to rub myself dry. But I stay inside the bath.

Not yet done. I sit on one edge, spreading my knees out wide, like a harlot or Big Uncut Man, and I put my feet up, on the opposite side. Once I feel securely wedged between the two banks of bath, I slide down fractionally and press against the base of my spine, as if I had a tail to crush. My arsehole becomes freed thus, innocent, vulnerable; and it gapes yet puckers, as if displayed for the benefit a medical consultant. Avoiding my genitals, which, at this point, always obstruct, I grab the prescribed paddle for the next procedure, and anoint my circumanal region with depilatory cream, effective in five minutes. I now have to heave myself up and get out of the bath and walk into the longest five minutes imaginable. I pretend to busy myself around the flat, ambulating like a parody of some swaggering he-man, the only time that I ever get to act like John Wayne. I strut from kitchen clock to video clock to alarm clock to lingering wristwatch and, by minute number four, I'm loitering back near the bath. I wipe a flesh-coloured smear off the enamel. It reeks; the whole place does; and so must I. I get back in the bath and kneel like an Anglican, bum out; I turn on the taps and cup the water in my hands while it grows warmish, warm. I begin, with trepidation, to rinse away the gunk around my arse and inner buttocks, which feel raw. I pat myself with caution, to test my way around, to check the extent of my damage. The cream, like softish icing on a rancid cake of sponge, clings to me briefly, then drops off, in gobs— which I push down the plug-hole with my forefingers, encouraging them. And next I take a proper shower, a thorough one now, as if my hide hadn't seen running water in months.

Finally it feels as if I can start, as if I'm past the ugly stuff. I apply moisturizer to myself entirely, and rub it in with great swirls of pattern, Indian paisleys and African stripes and waves of Italian psychedelia. I take unusual trouble over my elusive regions, such as the shorn expanse above my neck, the gaps between my toes, the backs of my thighs. I stop at nothing. And in case of microscopic cuts, I rub some antiseptic cream around my anus and my genitals. You never know, can't be too careful. Sign of the times. And I resist applying deodorant to my underarms—which feels incomplete, but there you are: that's what lovers like.

I move up to the face. Different razor; different blade, but fresh once again for the occasion, closer, finer. And as I coat my chin and jowls and the margins where others grow sideburns and the break for a moustache with cream that smells of almonds, using a badger brush, fat and fitter for bristle heavier than mine, I view my face as if in a new light—retrospective yet critical—and I reflect on the men who have liked it entirely; and on those who have preferred to pick out disconnected features of it—my ears, small fossils; my classical mouth, evenly sculpted; my eyes, my obvious eyes—and then I think of those who've despised it all, the lot of it, and said as much—Get Your Fucking Face Away From Me—like that; and I see that my nose has grown with the passage of time, grown pronounced and petulant, like the nose of my ancestors, knifelike; and I see that the tops of my ears are no longer aligned to my temples, which throb in the glass; and I see that a second chin lurks just below the horizon, and that my eyebrows are now thick, the thick unmistakable eyebrows of a middle-aged man, which I can scarcely believe, because I sometimes feel so puerile; and I see that the skin about my eyes is about to crack. I peer. Crack. There you are. And I smile at that face. But the smile can fool no one, for even though my lips are crimson in the snow, the teeth that grin back are far from white. Shouldn't smoke so much. Stop nagging. Let me wipe away the clots of shaving cream behind my ears, and wash my face, and cleanse, and moisturize. And you would think, would you not, that after all this, I would start to relax. Very funny.

FRANCE IS WHERE I'm meant to be. I shove myself into a threadbare pair of jeans, torn at the knee, worn at the crotch; I ram my unsocked feet into a pair of penny loafers; and cover my undressed upper-half with a baggy navy winter coat which swings about me as I set off for the local newsagent. Late afternoon now, freezing. My flat must be sweltering, like the flat of an old woman. I buy a cartonload of cigarettes, and a packet of pellets of sugarfree gum, and, from the back of the Foreign rack, I yank—in the irritating absence of *Le Monde,* which would have been more suitable—a copy of this morning's *Figaro.* I walk back faster than I should walk, like a shoplifter clutching his spoils, and, hardly through the door, I tear off my clothes. Then, on impulse, I bundle both the shoes and jeans into the bin. But not the coat: it, I drape with studied elegant languor over a chair in the hall. I smack the paper against my bare thigh, as if I needed housebreaking, but still it looks too crisp to pass muster, so I give it another thwack, and dump it on the seat of the chair, next to the revers of the coat. I climb up a ladder, which squeals for want of oil and, from an overhead cupboard, grab the smaller, plainer of my holdalls—no buckles or straps or interlocking logos—and I stuff it with a jumper and some books, plus a couple of afterthoughts, forgettables—such as the carton, presumably. And then I park the gaping bag at the foot of the chair, like an obedient dog left to guard its master's topcoat and his folded journal: FIG is all that shows. And from a drawer I take my passport, along with an obsolete air ticket which I find inside it, and I place them, in a careful balancing act, on the sleeve of the coat on the arm of the chair at the edge of this fabricated still-life for a traveller. I wonder whether I might not (and then dismiss the urge to) add an umbrella to the tableau. Instead, I slide a glove into one of the pockets, ensuring that the leather cuff shows; and the other glove, in an inauspicious gesture of defiance to no one, I let drop to the floor, and it lands open-palmed. But then I think better of the ruse with the passport, and take it back and plant it on the table near the entrance, by the silver frames, in the shade of the black roses, which is where, in my proper life, it would have gone. And for good measure, I rattle round a tin of foreign money that I keep in a locked drawer, and I also pick a few French notes, together with a clutch of dulled coins which I slowly sprinkle onto the mahogany. And they fall as clods of earth fall onto a coffin. But the scene looks alive. Professional.

Two hours to go. Already I feel exhausted, but: back to the bathroom. A sudden pathetic quandary: should I clean the bath and basin now, while I have time, or after my last ablution; should I aim to produce impeccable gleaming tiles and enamel and porcelain, or, when Steve arrives, present myself dripping with cool freshness, and bugger the splashes on the shower-curtain and up the wall, and the puddle on that small but invariable patch of floor? Do both, of course: bulk of the job now; details later, last-minute. And so I enter a new frenzy, and rub and buff and scrub until my toiling face appears reflected in the pupil of a bleary eye that swims about the nickel of the taps. And then a drop of sweat goes splosh onto the metal. Get that off. Which I do. And don't forget to wipe the handle for the flush, plus the lavatory pedestal. I don't. And clean the stem of the bog-brush, would you. Stand up now. I was about to. Deal with that window. I have. And what about those specks of toothpaste on the bevel of the mirror?

I replace one of the spherical bulbs which has just blown—isn't that typical—on the track of lights above the basin. And when the room has been reduced to a mess of soggy paper towels and empty disinfectant bottles and redundant cleaning sponges, I pick them all up and go to the bin and watch them tumble inwards and fall; and then I extract the gunmetal liner, and throttle it with a good knot. I sneak into my white towelling robe, and next, rather than upset the order outside my own front door, I creep up a couple of flights and dump the bag by the flat of some old queen who gets his meals on wheels—unlikely to notice. Porter takes away the rubbish in the morning. But supposing someone goes and looks inside the plastic liner? What on earth for? To identify the culprit, of course. Oh for God's sake, come on, I hardly think some jeans and a pair of loafers among a pile of cleaning stuff amounts to what you'd call incriminating evidence. Stop it, you two, and get back downstairs before somebody catches you acting oddly. And lock that door.

ALTHOUGH MY GUT is aching, it still feels like too soon to make the dreaded call to Steve, announcing my return, pretending to be back, wondering whether he's still, well, On—his kinda word. It could be five o'clock in the morning. Got to sleep, just a few minutes. Don't mess with your hospital corners, which are impeccable, surgical. OK: I'll go to the bathroom and spread a towel on the tiles on the floor. Look, like so. And with my head under the lavatory bowl and my feet pointed at the door, I make me down to lie. And I cross my hands over my chest, left over right, and although I know that the blood will run down, and my fingers will go numb, any position now would be wrong. I close my eyes, try to exclude all noise; but it is hopeless. Juggernauts trundling north-north-north, traffic bound for home, people headed for evenings of muted pleasures and the comfort of—and then it hits me like a collision: the horrible irony that this story, in which I no longer even recognize my character, or my direction, might already be over; because Steve might, of course, never pitch up. And I'm quaking with sudden fury, and up so fast that I feel almost faint as I grab that bloody 'phone and punch out his number, and his machine comes on. Wouldn't you know. Slam. I get back down, lie on my back. Try to forget; breathe in hard. Hard to breathe at all. No good. Flip round. Do fifty press-ups at breakneck speed. The head of my cock bobs against the floor. Then I get up again, but this time, yes, I do leave a message, and breathlessly, as if I'd come running up the stairs, eager and excited, and I divulge my name and the time and the date, and I ask him to ring me at my flat, and next, for safe measure, I append my number. Again my stomach groans. I must be famished. I wonder about the silence that now stretches out before me, further than perhaps I can endure, and the uncertainty, and the disappointment, and the hidden pang of ridicule. I'll give it an hour, one only, no more. And if by then he hasn't returned my call, it'll be too bad: I'll just unplug the 'phone and take a triple dose of sleeping pills, which is all that you need to drift through half a day without incident, the length of a flight from here to Los Angeles—

after which, think of the surprise of waking not in that desolate dreary place but in the relief of your own safe confines. The 'phone is ringing. Answer it, for God's sake. Forget it. His voice begins: (no name): Got your message, see you at eight. Click. I feel such a sudden surge of elation that I could happily disintegrate—or, conversely, stand him up and swallow the sulphurous fumes of victory.

Everything happens fast. I pour myself a mug of coffee, so bitterly strong that it tastes like undiluted chicory, and by the time that I've drunk down the contents, and rinsed and dried the mug and returned it to its cupboard and, remembering suddenly, gobbled a handful of vitamins, I find myself doubled up on the lavatory—at once constipated to the point of nausea and propelled towards a fevered urge to evacuate. I catch myself belching; my head swelters; my elbows dig into my thighs; my sweaty hands support my purpled face. My faeces feel so packed, so black, that my sphincter, forced to perform without notice, baulks at the exertion, throbs at the veins, contracts but resists, won't obey. I feel stuck. I hunch down, and further. I have to inhale, hold tight, and then, I push beyond what is bearable. My lower body starts to yield, but no— not yet in earnest. Try again. I grit my teeth. My ribs ache out, groaning for respite. My head drops to my chest like the head of a simpleton. I grip my knees. And then: it's done, in one. Water splashes back against my buttocks. I force my anal muscles out, to double-check, but nothing. Fine. I can get up. And so I stand, unsteadily, and my hands are shaking so insanely and my teeth chattering so uncontrollably that I decide to take the risk, and, like a rodent, gnaw at the sweetish, chalky edge of a sedative. And now, for the last shower. Forget the leisurely ritual: I attack myself with the vigour of an athlete, ransacking myself, practically fucking myself with the soap, which is ovoid, and scrubbing my scalp, and scouring every evasive revolting embarrassing part of me. And then I wash the soap. Naturally.

I'VE ALREADY PLANNED, as you know, what to wear tonight; and my choices lie at the foot of the bed, pathetic as exhibits, deflated, and dimly lit by the veined alabaster lamp that hangs from above. A thin line of shadow, thin but strong, like a Japanese inkstroke, describes one side of the clothes—a sleeve of brown T-shirt, an edge of its hollowed rib-cage, the tail of a belt, a darkening denim leg which breaks at the knee and drops over the edge—while the other side of the clothes seems to fade away, vanishes into the obscurity of the blurring counter-pane. A brighter beam, from the corridor behind me, catches the caps of a pair of bulbous boots, which stand with their heels abutted to the fringes that graze the floor and point at me intimidatingly, as if they belonged to some great lumbering oaf in authority.

The business of dressing should prove a doddle: all I need to do is go through the motions, as if, for the umpteen-hundredth time, I were donning a uniform. It's like signing a cheque: once you've named your payee, and filled in the sum, and matched the numbers to the words, and settled the date, you just scrawl along that line, automatically, no longer considering whether you might be endorsing a mistake, an over-draw. Children, before they've even learnt to read their name, never mind sign it, are told how to get dressed, and in precisely what order, and the first thing on which adults insist is always underclothes; but, much as I've aged, and much as I've dressed—up, down, and across—I still don't seem to have outgrown the urge to disobey what I've been taught. Which is why I go straight for my socks. What, no pants? Nope. Why not? Because: Swiss cotton briefs, he'll think I'm just pissy; silk boxer shorts, he'll think I'm a ponce; funky black jockstrap, he'll think I'm an arsehole; so: why bother at all? Well, don't wear pants and he'll think you're a whore. Not once I've paid him he won't. Anyway: socks: I've picked out a pair of thickish ones, dove-grey, which should look pale enough in a dark light to help my dwindling tan, yet dark enough in a bright spot to make it clear that they're not white, which, I regret to say—for such is the snobby language of clothes—has become the pre-serve of the snappy provincial British homo.

The T-shirt proves, as I had feared, too close-fitting not to risk appearing common, and only avoids the charge thanks to its dark redemptive tone—most bitter chocolate, Othello. And since I haven't got time to start doubting, just let me straighten the seams on the shoulders and, come on, admit, it does make my tits look passable, doesn't it? I know there are plenty of tits like mine in town, and plenty better, got the point, but I can at least, if nothing else, claim that since the T-shirt is a custom-made one-off by a dead designer in New York, it, if not I, is equal to none. Next come the jeans, which feel so baggy that I'd better get the belt done up before they drop. I walk my fingers around the rotunda of the waistband, to check that I haven't missed any loops, and then I buckle up, though not so hard as to risk marking flesh, which is just bad styling, sloppy. I distribute the denim unevenly, strategically, spreading it tightest across my backside, looser at the sides, and almost bulkily, greedily, around my flies. As I begin to fiddle with a metal button, I think of cockrings and cockstraps and bollock-dividers and thongs, and from a box full of such props, which I keep hidden (too tidily, if truth be told) in one of my bedside drawers, along with tubes of water-soluble lubricant and condoms (devoid of nipples—which are the only style of latex sheath to avoid turning a hard-on into an eyesore), I take the tamest of my appliances, a black leather strap with pressure studs at regular one-inch intervals—designed to accommodate the entire gamut of cocks, from prawns to monsterschlongs—and I put the strap on, though not so stringently as to hinder eventual Engorgement—what a word. Because given the likelihood that Steve, wishing to impress me with his own marvellous form, will already have attired himself with a genital enhancer of some sort, I may as well reciprocate with one of my own. And if, by any chance, it should turn out that Big Uncut Man is so cocksure as to present himself unadorned, it'll be easier for me to whip off my own accessory (fumbling over the kitchen sink, I daresay, as I pour myself another drink; or crashing around the freezer in search of a bottle of poppers, to help the proceedings along) than ever it could be to snap on some gadget without giving rise to his suspicion, or worse, his scorn. And so, snap-snap, on it goes, and I push it down under my balls, and up round the base of my cock, and it merges with what remains of my black pubic froth. And then I shove my dispirited genitals into the jeans, going going gone, and I dress to the left, as right-handers tend to do, and I leave no eyelet unclosed, because even if some people find the convention of flies left half-open arousing, I find it slovenly, not to say cold; and I try, once I'm done, not to think about the need to summon an erection.

And last of all, the chunky boots—a stage which, for all of its intended butchiness, always strikes me as ironically camp. First I gather my trouserleg up, almost to the knee, and straighten out my sock in the process; next, I raise my knee into the air until my thigh is parallel with the floor; and then I point my foot down, arching it like some ballerina on tip-toe, all so that finally I may enter the high stumps of these gul-lumping clodhoppers—of uncertain Teutonic origin, heavily rubber-soled and purchased second-hand, for credibility, from a shop which claims to purvey the Art of Control, tells you never to polish, and rec-ommends a generous fit for that hunkier proportion. And once I have, with the pull-loops provided, managed to force my way into their damp interiors, like the wandering soldierboy at the Somme, I drape the jeans back down over my leathered shins in extravagant folds of ruched *serge de Nimes*. And then, of course, I practise my deportment, strutting about like some lout on patrol, which isn't always that easy: I'm not jok-ing: on more than one occasion I have seen some hapless queer forget to affect the proper walk and, forgetting, stagger stupefied and pigeon-toed across a pub to the cottage—in search of a fresh piece of meat for the evening, or perhaps driven by the urge to void his takeaway kebab—and, in his haste, I have seen him bash one foot against its hefty regulation partner and trip as a result, and spill his pint near the disgusted company, which always turns its back, and then the poor bas-tard has collapsed to the stinking sodden linoleum like a war-bride swooning at the news of the demise of her heroic young husband in action. Face down.

NEARLY THERE. (No kidding.) Inspect yourself in the full-length mir-ror, and this time, don't wear a watch: those pathetic wrists of yours hardly need emphasis; let yourself be led by the kitchen clock. Now pull down those jeans, bit more, to your hip, like that; and pull the T-shirt up just fractionally, that's right; let it ruck around your waist, looks less precious. Stand back for a cursory glance. And then my vision blurs, reminding me, thank God, of contacts (lenses, not mags). In the bathroom, and practically beside myself now, I unscrew their cylindri-cal Perspex case and fiddle with the bottle of saline and try to govern my shaking fingers as the small quivering satellites approach their ocu-lar globes; and I push the lenses in, push, and then I push a second time, until both have adhered, and in the process my mouth opens wide, like the mouth of a woman applying mascara, like the astonished face of my own mother. And with a stick of brown eye-liner, slightly blunted, I fill in a zig of my left brow which recent bouts of nervous picking have balded, made absent. I rub unflavoured lipsalve along my mouth to grout any surface cracks. And then (a thing I never divulge to anyone) I trace lightly with the pencil round the outline of my upper lip, to enhance its bow, to hint at a younger pout, as if my mouth belonged to an insipid sketch in need of sharper contrasts. I draw my lips together. They slide about, purse as the lips of a woman purse when she comes to close her compact. And much of the artifice comes off, recedes into the past, leaving only the slightest of impressions, a faint darker gleam, virtually matt—so expertly sly that it wouldn't give me away, not even if I were to put my lips to the lip of a cocktail glass. I conceal my materials in the unit beneath the basin—not in the mirrored wall-cabinet, which is the first place that people look if they want to learn your secrets, such as the tablets you've been prescribed. And at the base of my shaven neck, just above the nape, where men so seldom seem to kiss, much less be kissed, I dab the ghost of a fragrance, a memory practically, and I sour my flesh with a hint of essence distilled from sodden leaves of tobacco.

As I pace about the kitchen now, all these years later, during breaks between writing, I can summon still the panic of that night, summon it almost without trying. The blood just rushes up. I recall my right arm stopping in mid-air, caught in the act of reaching for a whisky bottle, caught in the hope of an illicit first glug—which never makes it to my mouth because the entryphone to the flat has just buzzed. He's arrived. No turning back. My walk becomes leaden, resigned. No need to talk; just press the buzzer; let him up. Unlock the door. Return the bottle to its cupboard, fast; and no, no time to wash your hands; straighten the base of that lamp; and don't start tweaking the bloody flowers: he's bound to catch you. Skirt round the traveller's still-life—carefully. And yet still, still he hasn't arrived. What's the fucker on, Valium?

I GET TO THE DOOR and Christ knows what possesses me, but I try to sneak a look through the spy-hole and just as my eyelash meets the halo of the glass, a hard sudden knock sends the door smack into my face, and I reel against the wall behind, and bash my head and freeze, stunned, as he swings in, his great bloody lordship, smiling and turning and all but waving as he locks the door with an ease that dumbfounds me and leaves the keys dancing on their ring. Once he has entrapped me in my own space, he just stands there, in front of me, and lends me one of those significant stares which, from performances of my own, I recognize as lies. But the trouble is, you see, that my thinking has become so wishful, it's an embarrassment. And so, when he cradles my elbows in the palms of his hands and waits for me to make the first proper pass, I cannot, unlike the first time, bring myself to think You-silly-wanker-what-is-this-travesty-of-romance? Oh no: I think: This man could throw me to the stars; he could feed me to the sharks, could devour me, drown me, fall for me. And I would do anything he wanted, at all. And then I draw back, ashamed at myself, away from him.

He follows me towards the kitchen, whistling faintly, like a nervy plumber. Drink?, I ask. Whisky-water, he replies; Tap's fine, half-'n-half, thanks. And I decide to have the same, less out of courtesy than to avoid the awkwardness of having to bend for ice in front of him. But do you remember how, last time, he just loitered around the corridor, hung about the shadows, posing? Well, tonight, as I close the cupboard and turn to the fridge (not the tap) for water, I discover him already in here, leaning against the oven and watching me intently, as if wanting to get to grips with me, and smiling. And if you had seen that smile of his, you would know what it means to watch out, to be on your guard. I notice that his face is clean-shaven tonight, which makes him look politer somehow, gentler, more benign. Disappoints me fractionally. But now, as if he were attuned to my mind and wanted to redeem himself, he clears his throat and compliments me on my own appearance. Tells me I'm looking good. My reaction is leaden; I may even have grunted; I'm too wrapped up in whether he's sussed my sartorial replica, or clocked my inverted haircut, or whether he's just being banal, flattering to the punter, mindless. He steps without warning past me and walks across the kitchen to the bin and lifts the lid, all of which embarrasses me, don't quite know why. He turns his back and seems to inspect the contents of my (non-existent) rubbish, until at last I hear a light muffled thud and realize that he's only disposing of a ball of chewed gum which, if you really want to know, he could just as well have spat into my mouth. And then, he simply explains: gum, and replaces the lid, and picks up his glass, and seems to start moving. I turn off the light and lead him out, eager to stay ahead and guide him into a different room this time, determined to furnish us with a fresh start. And so we go into the study, which is smaller and less formal, more suitable for tonight. And I steer him towards the very chair on which, God, before this whole thing had even begun—you've probably forgotten—when the story amounted to a folded scrap of newsprint, shoved into the wallet of some sad pathetic faggot, a scrap tucked into the breast pocket of his jacket, I told you that Steve, who, at that stage, was merely Big Uncut Man, would one day sit. And he lowers himself into the chair by degrees, as if he didn't quite trust it, but just watching him fulfil my prediction, however tentatively, swells me with a dreamy, irrational pride akin to the pride of a mother who, marvelling at her child's first small triumph, begins to build whole empires of unfounded hopes and ambitions upon it. And now that he's safely installed, well, be fair, be fair to me: see how fantastically he sits enthroned, this great monster of mine; mark his huge frame supported by the curve of pale sycamore at his back, and his solid arms rested lightly on those lightly carved ones, and his strong whitening knuckles locked to form a bracket beneath his jaw, as if to support his massive handsome head, which tilts forward slightly, almost mournfully. Come on, admit to the beauty of the man. Grant me the soundness of my judgement.

I VANISH NEXT DOOR in search of music and, shit, can hardly believe my stupidity: none planned. I ask him, out loud, what we should have, and he replies, in a voice that seems to echo round the flat, nothing too dancy, whatever you feel like. And to me it feels like much later at night, as if we'd just got back from some club and were headed for bed in the manner of lovers, which is hardly the fact. I tell myself to cut out the crap and make up my mind. I pick the first tape that comes to hand, and take it from its cassette, and commend myself to fate as I drop it, label unread, into the stereo deck, the transparent door of which I now click shut; and I depress the Play button and wait for it to oblige. And I have to wait the length of a Bible, while the spools of the tape turn wearily, silently, before deigning at last to free into the atmosphere, like a cloud of incarnadine incense, or a slow swarm of cinnamon butterflies, the drawn-out, doleful, almost sulky sound of an Urdu *ghazal,* a wailing Indian incantation which, despite the beguiling rhythms of the sitar and the lulling taps of the tabla and the accompanying bells and violins and delicately delivered hand-claps, is, I happen to remember from the blurb inside the cover, an unremitting dirge about deserts of longing and veils of deception and moribund gardens and unfulfilled promises and tapering hands, like flames of painted henna, rising and joining and begging some stony deity for release from this terrible tortured love, and on and on she goes, the chanting maiden from the missing cover, who, with her huge eyes and hairy arms, and all got up in her grandmother's sari, lilac, and laden with bracelets and a blanket of hair grown down to her arse, looks, frankly, more like a eunuch than a damsel, like a eunuch whining for the chance of a good fuck. But no matter: something about the music—its slowened swaying, I suppose, its wilting and rising, its whole mystery—makes it feel right, worth trusting. So I turn up the volume and, encouraged, return to the study, where I find Steve hunched over my desk, engrossed, like a practitioner of origami, in a small piece of card which he seems to be coiling, and thin folded tissues for smoking cigarettes of marijuana, a weed whose female flowers alone can inspire euphoria. And as he licks the edge of the skin with the side of his tongue, I see the tongue flick muscularly, pinky-grey and mucous as the flesh of a premature infant. And he looks up now, as if he, the child put to walk before time, were himself a small boy in a parlour, assembling a model aircraft before his doting, aproned mother; and he looks up and says to me, with the use of that smile: Hope you don't mind if I roll us a spliff, got to unwind: godawful day I've had; how was France? I blush but don't reply, and he taps the crafted joint, and feeds it to his lips, and offers it a blazing light, and draws hard and slowly upon it, and then he just holds it there while he tilts his head back to open his throat wide, and he moulds himself into his chair, which creaks very slightly, and when at last he starts to inhale, I watch his back rear up and I see that it arcs like the back of a woman in rapture. And after a pause more sacred than the pause before a climax, I see that to exhale, he closes his eyes. And next, he hands the joint across to me; but I feel so bizarrely moved, so grateful, so nervous, that I want to laugh. To distract myself, I turn away and take my measly drag. I mustn't wetten the end from which I suck, which they call the roach-end, nor splutter. Stop getting flustered. Let out the smoke calmly. And when I return the joint to him, which I do backwards, as if I were returning a borrowed pen or knife, the thought occurs to me, to diminish me, that such courtly gestures are but a fanciful preamble to a squalid transaction. And this sudden realization so disheartens me that I opt, there and then, here and now, while he's busy with his next toke, to cough up in advance; and I slip the money into his idle hand. He doesn't trouble even to glance at the notes which line his palm, let alone to count them: he slides them into his jacket discreetly, almost with elegance, like an old-time diplomat tucking away a freshly used handkerchief. But then he winks at me, like a slut. I pull up a chair to face his own, and arrange myself so that we are perfectly aligned, legs squared, opposite and parallel; and yet, though I know our seats to be at identical heights, somehow I feel the lower of the two of us, undermined. Our toe-caps bump by accident. I pretend that no such accident has happened. He moves his boots outwards and around, so that his shins enclose mine, seem to hug them, and now he begins to push his knees inwards and harder. I yield to the pressure reluctantly, less out of ardour than politeness, and once my thighs have been clamped together so tightly that they bring to mind the thighs of a girl protecting her virtue, or just desperate to escape to the lavatory, he lays down the joint on an ashtray beside him and stretches out his hands and grips at the sides of my chair and begins to raise the bulk of his torso until his head hovers like a planet above me, over mine, and then he begins his journey down and approaches my face—until, in the fullness of time, his lips land on my mouth, and they strike me as surprisingly smooth, and cool, and innocent, like the lips of a young girl at her first dance. But just as I resolve to corrupt this gentle contact by insinuating my tongue into his mouth, he claims a stronger purchase on the kiss, and first, he sucks, and now, he sends into my unsuspecting gullet a spiral of fragrant smoke from the burnt flowers of marijuana, some of which, stupidly, I swallow, the rest of which I manage to blow back. And as I do, just at that moment, my eyes find themselves so locked into his sapphire stare, so affianced, that I remember telling myself to break it off, to step back from the lie. It's like when, for no reason at all, a kindled match, brought close to your face to offer you a light, suddenly fizzes into a second efflorescence, at once more spectacular and more treacherous than the first: you instinctively pull away, recoil out of caution. And yet to this day I know that even as I listened to myself and acted on my own advice and drew back from the whole nonsense and decided to be sensible, some small unfinished part of me, at that instant, just cracked, and succumbed, almost audibly.

I GO ACROSS the room and park myself against the ledge of the book-case. It digs into the crease above my thigh. My buttocks flinch, then tighten. He turns his chair towards me, fully to face me, so that the sight of him arrests me. I watch him suck at the joint one final time, then terminate it. He takes a gulp of whisky next. His other hand, the one that earlier took the wages, now sets to work, but his eyes remain so firmly affixed to me that you would think that the fumbling was for my benefit, not his; and yet my superlative prissiness prevents me from looking down at his crotch, from gloating as he promotes a hard-on, so that what I perceive, what I tell you, comes from a region far below my line of vision, feels secondary. The heel of his palm seems to be tread-ing over and over a place which I take to be his bulge; his fingers—whether cupped or extended I cannot surmise—are labouring at his scrotal mound. I wonder whether he shaves his bollocks, but do so only fleetingly, half-heartedly, for my main attention is concentrated on his face, at once brave and dejected, wise but weary, open yet weather-beaten, commonplace in many ways, like the rugged face of a me-chanic newly chosen to promote some classic brand of lager or tobacco, slapped onto billboards everywhere. It shames me to confess that I think Steve is the most handsome man I've ever seen. It further shames me that I care what he thinks of me; and that, like some clammy con-vent girl, I want dear God to make him fall in love with me. But look how he slips off his jacket, with what graceful ease, and how, without so much as a glance, he hangs it. And what he wears is so ingeniously non-committal, so bloody navy, that you'd never guess that he was, you know, working; rather you'd imagine that here was some regular guy relaxing at a friend's pad. He peels off his sweater, and lets it drop to the ground beside him, and now he rises to his feet, to his full height, almost stretching, almost yawning, and starts coming towards me so enormously that I tell myself (and I believe it) that everything else must have been bullshit, that this has to be the beginning of everything, the true beginning. And I tell myself that I shall prove it to him. And then his shadow, which precedes him, looms over and drowns me in the calmest of darknesses before yielding, as it passes beyond me, to a glare of sudden brilliant light, and next, at last, a kiss, purely dry, is granted to me, and my eyes, can you believe the stupidity of it, the sheer cringing amateurism, just close.

He holds me, bizarrely, by the hips, as if I were a stolen statue that needed shifting, and he presses his own hips, which stand higher than mine, against me, digging himself vaguely into my pelvis. His mouth is also pressed to me, and he suddenly surrounds my own with his, captures it, but when I try to move my lower lip, to free it, he prevents me—by biting. My eyes are open wide now, but his own remain half-shut, his sandy lashes flickering fast. His hands seem to have moved up to my wrists, which they grip to the point of bruising in an effort to force behind me. I do not resist. I pretend to be up to this. Nor do I resist his tongue, which, instead of hinting at dope or whisky, tastes, more insultingly, distinctly of peppermint, and is now jabbing at, and rasping round, the soft gutter of wet flesh above my upper teeth, like some strange fish flicking about in search of scraps of dental detritus. He is forcing my head back, and I go along with the scheme, less out of curiosity than in order not to incite him, for I suspect that he'd like me to struggle against him, thereby giving him a reason to slap me, and slap me again, for my impudence. My neck seems to have tilted back as far as it can tilt, and to be leaning, slumped uselessly, like the neck of a handicapped baby, on one of the shelves, the second one up. My head is shoved into some books, fits into them, wears them like a pathetic bonnet. And I can tell you precisely what those books are, because they're still there in evidence, untouched, frozen in a semicircular memento of the evening: books by people beginning with P: Paglia, Pakula, Parker, Peck, Pickles, Plath, Pontalis, Priest—and there the concavity ends, narrowly and tactfully avoiding Proust. And then I realize that Steve is now holding both of my wrists with one of his hands alone, but in a ferocious grip, and I sense that the toes of his boots are hovering over mine so as to pin me, should there be a need, and then I hear him say, quite loud, and slowly, but entirely without emphasis, the peculiarest thing: You're so . . . jaded. And then? He slaps me anyway, on the left side of the face, too near to the eye, altogether too high for the act to seem professional, and I am filled not with rage, not with pain, but with a queasy disillusion at the poverty of the scene. I don't let on. Some perverse instinct halts me—my well-earned shame, you will doubtless say, or my weakness; but you would, this once, be mistaken—for what I actually feel is a sniffy loftiness: if it were a scent, it would carry a note of myrrh in it. My response to the blow is in fact perfectly seemly, well-bred even: as if, in London on a rainy evening in spring, I had chanced upon a flower stall in, say, Bloomsbury—deserted, evocative, no longer popular—and though filled with a desire for tuberoses to take home, I could see before me only an array of disappointment—chrysanthemums, irises, daffodils, garish blossoms without fragrance—and yet, it's as if, despite my regret, I had elected not to turn on my heel and vanish, but to linger awhile, feigning interest, perhaps even purchasing some small unwanted bunch of something rather than offend the pride of the old vendor, mittened and whistling beneath his torn awning. That's how it seems to me. Or, more bluntly put, it's as if you were casting hunks for a porno film and, presented with some pumped-up idiot with a button-nose, you had decided, out of piteous courtesy, to go through the motions of a second lot of test shots—without actually letting the film roll, obviously.

BUT NOW IT FEELS as if he's trying to hold me down in earnest, properly to restrain me, with one of his legs wedged between my knees, as if to remind me who's really in charge here. My wrists remain immobilized behind me. My head is still stuck on the shelf that I showed you. My eyes have closed again. I want to guess, to imagine. He smells of suntan cream. The scene, I tell myself, could be unfolding on an empty beach. His hand is frisking one of his front pockets—please not in search of a black handkerchief with which to blindfold me. Handcuffs? Unlikely: I would have clocked them earlier, when he was shoving himself into me. Bit early for condoms, surely? Wait and see. And he now appears to have found whatever it was that he was looking for, because a rugger-shirted arm is roughly moving round my ribcage and heading for my buttocks, no, my wrists, and, of course, how dense of me, it's a leather thong with which to bind these, which he now does, panting a little, as if he could be fitter, or less excited. I hear myself asking myself to tell me now: payer or payee, which is the greater whore in this? I do not bother answering; and next, I admit, I cheat: I offer up the bones of my wrists, not stuck together in a Siamese hold but more ritually positioned, as a cross, so that after he's secured them behind me, and he's just about finished, it won't be too tricky for me, with one abrupt movement, to wriggle free. Besides, leather knots always slide— they have, as they say, give; but had this been a length of twine, of cable, or a chain that ended with a padlock click, well, I wouldn't be sounding so relaxed (*relaxed?*) about it. But let's face facts: he's a bit of a dilettante, this so-called Steve; I mean, he hasn't even volunteered a code-word to use in the event of crisis. He can't be taking me seriously. Or thinks that I lack experience. Or that I'm a wimp. Or that I just want to play at pupils and prefects. Or all of these things. Shut up and get on with it, would you, for his pleasure and your dignity. Other way round, don't you mean? I open my eyes. He has moved away, abandoned me.

NEAR THE ENTRANCE to the room, in front of the light-switch, which he now presses with his back, but only manages to dim, so that we plunge into virtual darkness, he stands and looks, I'm afraid, irre- sistible. He starts to take off his rugger shirt, which fits him slightly too tightly and presents him with some difficulty, to reveal, underneath, a T-shirt the colour of midnight, through which I can make out the ridge of a vest running along his cleavage. And instantly I begin to predict that he's going to give me the layering routine, the slow striptease, to piss away the minutes. But he doesn't. His hands drift down to his jeans, and his cock, he shows me, is hard under the dark denim. You can see it, jutting from his thigh, plainly outlined. Maybe it does have to do with me. Maybe I do arouse him. Look, stop getting your stupid hopes up and start worrying about your wrists.

He leans over the chair and darts a couple of fingers into his jacket, and out, predictable as a magician's rabbit, comes a small bottle of amyl—which he plonks on the table with a loud, brash flourish, less as if to ask whether I mind, whether we might, as to impress upon me his assumption that I like the stuff, because poppers are part of his act and he doesn't perform without them. But if my expression is blank, it isn't because I feel indifferent—as a matter of fact I'm relieved—it's just that I'm trying to release my hands, hands which, in my own small con- juring trick, I now bring round and produce, and they plop onto my lap like a surprise, like a childish miracle. I don't expect to be compli- mented for this gesture, which could be regarded as unco-operative, but nor could anything have prepared me for the succession of looks which now parades past Steve's dark countenance: needless to say, there is no trace of a smile—big as Steve is, I don't think he's big in the humour department—no, rather there's an initial bewilderment, akin to that of an unjustly beaten bloodhound, which rapidly gives way to a mien of stroppiness, supposed, I suspect, to indicate that he can see that I'm going to be trouble; but in the end his features settle for a face of great overweening boredom, meaning that if I'm going to be so bloody puerile, I shouldn't have called him, should I.

I DO NOT KNOW how to take us beyond this pass, but he, with providential timing, now starts to swagger up to me. Something about his elbow, its rising angle, makes me think: not again, he's going to slap me. But his hand, instead, aims for my waist, and is followed by his other hand, and together they pull at my T-shirt, pull outwards, and then they begin to peel it up, off my chest, over my chin, and past me. I watch his thuggish arm send it, with surprising slow elegance, to the background. And now he runs one finger, which, though I dare not look, I take to be his index, from my navel to my clavicle, and the nail is fractionally too long, so that it scratches as it travels back down; and then it trips over my waistband; and now his entire hand seems to be covering my genitals, perhaps to gauge my cock-size, or perhaps the level of my arousal. I let him verify that I'm already getting hard, but then, panicked by his incipient rubbing, I move his help away, as calmly as I can, hoping to convey that he doesn't have to worry about me, I'm fine; but he takes the meaning of my body language either amiss or to heart, because, next thing, Big Uncut Man is again sitting down.

He helps himself to another blast of amyl, but is this time disinclined to share and share alike, has grown sulky, like the bloodhound. I go to the kitchen for my own supply. I can hear him behind me, alone in the study, inhaling through his second nostril, and the sheer ungenerosity of his action strikes me as sad. I am in darkness, blushing. I grope around the depths of the freezer, and hold my breath, as if this could reduce the noise of my search for that vital little bottle on which my pride now seems to hinge; and at last I find it and, unlike his, mine is still sealed, virginal. I bite off its plastic wrapper, which is white and drops to the ground. A small, menial part of me would like to crouch down and search for it and grab it and dispose of it in a fashion that is orderly; but a larger, weaker, more insidious part, which lives in fear of ridicule, leaves the wrapper on the tiles, as if overlooked, or forgotten. And then, on my way back to him, to my duties as paying host, I appease myself with the thought that if my snortings are fated to be solitary, at least I shall be spared the insult of having shared the fumes of Steve's unstable, volatile yellowish aroma with his other, more favoured clients, or even, who can tell, some possible secret lover. Imagine.

By the time I've turned the tape over, and then changed my mind, and swapped the *ghazals* for something louder, and faster, and closer to home, still foreign but occidental, I find Steve slumped in the study, puce thanks to his poppers, and in a brief world apart. His eyes are blearily downturned, and aimed at his crotch, which he seems to be surveying with lazy wonder, as if his groin were a banquet. His mouth hangs half-open, like the mouth of someone not bright. His knees, as usual, are flung apart. And next, he affects a snarl, more contemptuous than rabid, as he begins to maul his hard-packed cock-and-balls, to which, as part of his performance, he now gives a slow swipe. It is a muffled sound. His breathing has modulated into a humid rasp, wet and irrelevant and laden with unintelligible monosyllables, and at last I realize, recognize, that he's aping the antics of all those thick-haired American porn-stars from way back, from the days when you could only catch their performances in backstreet cinemas; where your seat, if you sat down, was likely as not to be smeared with slugs of cooling spunk; where, if you walked about, which seemed more practical, your buttocks were patted by gnarled, arthritic hands; and where, if you progressed to fresher pastures, towards some other wall, or closer to the exit light, you had to wade through the reek of leaky crap. Steve, I now see, has modelled himself on the pin-ups from that time, when he himself was young, before things got ugly for us, but his act seems to have frozen at the stage of boys with swirling sideburns and corduroy flares and Californian tans. And for a moment he strikes me as an old actor from another vintage, charismatic in his way, but wrong for our moment, miscast; and the effect is faintly pitiful; and my recognition of this, and of how he misjudges me, and of the injustice of our positions, the mutual disadvantage, all makes me a little melancholy.

· · ·

IT'S CRETINOUS OF ME, I know, but it makes me want to say: look, never mind, you don't have to pursue this nightmare on my account. It makes me want to suggest: we could just go to bed if you liked. And he? He would think that I was touched, mental, out of my tiny mind. To bed? With a fucking man-whore? Am I thick, or just from out of town? Beds aren't for sex, mate, he would say. Because beds have become private places, don't you see, where the queers of today like to think, and sometimes eat, and even smoke—though, unless it's hash, they will rarely admit to doing so—and it's where they pop the occasional pill, both prescribed and recreational, and it's where they sip their peppermint tea, remembering Taroudant, or drink Japanese beer, longing for Kyoto, and it's where they plan tomorrow's outfit, which, too often, is for a funeral; and bed is also where they dream of escaping, and dream of rewinding, and, once in a while, it's where they let themselves drift into a light, filmy siesta, set in the deep South, but skipping out the bits about disgust and mendacity, and starting, every time, with a shot of the back of the hero, his Achilles heel in plaster, hobbling in your direction. My, this sticky heat. Steve is standing up.

But it has nothing to do with me, his rising, because, back on his feet, he begins to inflate his chest and to extravert his knees and to curve out his elbows and to project his chin much in the manner of a bodybuilder, and I realize, with faint humiliation, that he has to puff himself up before proceeding, that his routine depends more on fuelling his own vanity than on gleaning, much less meeting, my own erotic (erotic?) needs. Maybe he reckons that, sexually, he's got me sussed, that I'm your typical twinky queen, gagging, despite my snottiness, for a dose of passive agony, which, of course, is nothing he can't deal with, nothing that a bit of rough-handling can't meet. All logic deserts me; confusion besets me—my undeniable attraction, my mental revulsion, my longing, my loathing, my pitiful little dreams. I can feel my throat tightening up: *Globus histericus*. I pretend not to be watching when his unveiling starts, which it does at this instant, yet the truth is that as I unscrew my bottle of poppers, and dig my snout into its neck by way of pretext, and involve myself in grotty inhalations, I can see him, obliquely but clearly, from the corner of my eye, which stretches like the eye of a lizard. Steve begins to unbutton his jeans, his pinkie ludicrously cricked, as if his flies were a suburban cup of tea; but, paradoxically, I find this reflex of genteelness, which in any other circumstance would have struck me as a scream, here touching, almost endearing, and the thought distracts me, must have done, because by the time I've stoppered the poppers back, his cock has been lobbed forth, let out. His belt, however, remains as securely fastened as when he first walked in, so that the display seems less an integral part of the man than a neutral, good-looking piece of meat hung for effect against a backdrop of denim. In my experience, cocks, unlike dogs, rarely grow to resemble their owners, but in Steve's case, well, let's just say that even if he'd ordered it from a reputable breeder he couldn't have been supplied with an appendage more suitable: it's spot-on, symbolic, epitomic even: big, as advertised, handsomely proportioned—not artificially pumped—and, as promised, uncut—faultlessly, to my eyes: no sign of strain on the retracting foreskin, which he now strokes as if to warm, nor excess gristle dribbling beyond the helmet. It's perfect. He inserts his hand in his flies once more, but deeper inside this time, as if he were burrowing into a pocket, and, after an awkward twist of the wrist and a slight grimace, he produces a good pair of bollocks, pendulous and leathery—and shaved, I note—and swollen by the throttle of a glinting metal ring, which he now forces back, as if adjusting a tightened collar, back to the base of his cock. No sign of underwear, which reassures me. He rubs his thumb over the head of his leaking knob, over the hole, and licks at the seepage, as if testing a subtle sauce or trying to tell his own sexual temperature. And then he allows his cock to drop, and it bounces against his balls, which hang almost as heavily and as low. And next, he just stands there, proffering himself with such assuredness that you begin to understand why it is that he does this job: he hooks his thumbs into his pockets and keeps his fingers off the action and just watches his utterly befitting cock grow hard and, after a couple of involuntary bobs, swell out, like its proprietor, into a handsome, lean, muscular, mature and trustworthy hard-on—which rises, not to meet his abdomen like some frantic adolescent ramrod, but at a calm, and expert, and unwavering horizontal.

HE NOW TAKES a fresh blast of poppers and, with the veins at his temples still throbbing, comes over to where I am. Not even bothering to check what he's doing, he unloops the tail of my belt and flicks it back and, with one deft tug, unbuckles me—a manoeuvre which, instead of seeming attentive, strikes me as so perfunctory, so patronizing, that I prickle with affront and halt his confident hand, which stops and moves away like a pendulum rising. I think: I'd like to take my own cock out, if you don't mind. And I do precisely that; plus my balls while I'm at it. And yet, for all of my intended brazenness, I find myself looking away like some apathetic model at a life-drawing class, gazing at a distant ceiling of non-existent clouds, as if to suggest that whatever the state of my arousal, which, in fact, approaches murder, Steve would be wise not to imagine that my hard-on is in any way connected to his proximity. The presumption. What we have before us, I seem to be trying to imply, is but an incidental occurrence, a common physiological reflex, a thing of absolutely no significance. Not even a coincidence. But Steve is patently not buying any of my act, not one single scrap of it, because next he raises a sceptical eye and downturns his head to survey my open groin from his great height and then he brings his face to my neck, and slides his mouth about it, and around, and, to my horrified surprise, to my chilled elation, he kisses me like a boyfriend, kisses me like a bride, fucks my gob with his enormous tongue and it feels like being invaded by some docile great animal. And without thinking, I, who think too much, whack his hard rump. But he doesn't flinch: makes out that he's immovable. So I whack him a second time. And now, *now* I hear him grunt from the depths of his open gullet, up through his nose, into my ear, round the inside of my head and back down. And when I grab my poppers for desperate urgent courage I discover that I needn't press a finger against my non-inhaling nostril, because it's already been plugged-up—by the pulsing wet flesh of Steve's tongue. And as I squeeze the muscles behind my eyes and swoon for a moment like the sentimental faggot that I am, I see that this, at long last, feels more like an affair than it does a contract.

WHEN I WAS YOUNG and avid in my dreams, I used to tell myself that there would come a time when, like the answer to some ancient riddle, my one true love would be revealed to me. And I believed that he, this fated counterpart, could, once delivered, transform my whole existence, miraculize it. Doubts, dreads, inhibitions—such hindrances, I reassured myself, would recede and slip away with the liquid ease of falling satin; and words which formerly had been without meaning for me, like rapture and devotion and commitment, would now ignite with significance. Nothing, I fancied, no matter how trite to others, or dull, or risky, or plain illegal, would seem too small, or great, for the rich realm of our possibilities. It was only, I knew from within, a matter of faith, of resoluteness. Because, in the end, when I took off, when I became complete, oh, there would be nothing that I would not do for him, nothing at all, whatever you may like to think. And when that day came, when it comes, you would not, will not, recognize me.

You could not imagine. I would bend down to tie the laces of his shoes when we went out, and it would be my job to lock the door after he passed. At plays and at recitals, I would sit with his strong hand held publicly in my grasp; and if afterwards, as so often seems to happen, it happened to be raining outside, I would open, like a canopy, an umbrella for us. And when I hailed a cab and it drove up, again it would be I who, even if my lover were the older and the stronger and the wiser of the two of us, opened the door and waited for him to climb inside, for I would surely be the prouder, the more honoured party. I would watch his sacred profile flickering through the night as we drove by—now amber, now emerald—and I would run my open hand along the red-lit leg of his dark trouser. At the restaurant, which I would have booked in advance, we would find that, if we spoke at all, it was in a language that no one else could fathom: I can envisage us fucking with our eyes across the candlelight. In fact, I picture candles all over our love: alight on that table between us, alight on his side of the bed late at night, alight by the bath as we loll in the steaming water, drinking and smoking and swallowing drugs; and, of course, I see candles lit before the altars of the churches from which some would have us cast out, churches where we would kneel to give thanks, and where we would cross ourselves with holy water. We would swim in many seas, my lover and I, naked at high noon and naked beneath the blinking stars; and after midnight, at black-tie parties, brilliantined and starched and diamond-studded we would dance, chest to chest and arm in arm, and as we moved about the patent floor, the only couple of our sort in sight, the matrons would stare aghast, and mutter, scandalized, to one another while I murmured deep profanities in the ear of my lover, who would smile, or just grunt back, but never flinch, even if I painted his soft eyelids with my tongue. And after it was all over, after these boring parties, we would go home, he and I, and undress at once, and we would lie together, and breathe in unison, even in our slumbers; and only our lashes, kissing, would flutter.

I would grow up and flourish in this love; I would become reliable; I'd learn to cook, for instance; I'd serve him seven-course repasts without a hitch, and single-handedly; and never once would I feel the tremor of servility. Because, for all of my dependability, I would bask in my own dependence, wallow in it. I'd take my food directly from his mouth, like a fledgling, and such would be my confidence that I would now find myself flying over the walls of propriety, soaring beyond what the world might consider to be right. This man: I would eat his very body-waste if he so desired, and, rather than have him rise in the night, I would drink the pungent streams of his hot urine; and if, during the course of the day, a sense of bloatedness should overcome him, he could seek relief by belching into my gullet, or by clamping my face to his arse, for I would absorb his wind, and do so gladly, as if it were the issue of the cheeks of the clouds. I would wash him with the warm devoted waters of my mouth, and rub him dry with my enfolding arms; and yet, should he forbid it, I would myself abstain from bathing—for weeks, for months, for however long he demanded. For even if I reeked to high heaven, high heaven, thanks to him, is where I would be.

And for a fleeting, honey-coloured instant, it's as if Steve could read my unholy dreams of allegiance, almost as if he agreed with them, for his whole body seems unexpectedly to have softened, to have warmed to me. He curves out his back, so as to lower himself for my comfort, and then, holding me still, he dips a little further down, and wordlessly introduces his genitals into my unbuttoned jeans. And down into my underworld I feel his cock slide, between my thighs, and wedge itself hard almost behind me, in the grip of my clenched buttocks. He pulls me to his chest as if he'd nearly lost, or finally found me, and while he embraces me, he kisses the crown of my head and the side of my brow, which is scorching, and frankly, say what you like, laugh if you want, but to me this feels like It, The Big One. I begin to stroke him, not in the manner that you might expect, not with the mauling motions of the hard-boiled bitch, but in the way which, for all of my pretences, I actually wish to stroke him, which is most tenderly, as if I were lulling him.

His shoulders are so smoothly curved that they defy belief, and my astonished palms just slide down the sinews of his arms, down to his wrists, which are too thick for my fingers to surround; and he takes up my hands and, with grave virility, now draws my knuckles to his face and kisses them. And then he stares at me, over my puny bones, with such intensity that, in anybody else, I would have described it as a stare of hatred. But not in Steve; you just wouldn't. And with sudden impact I think back to similar scenes which friends have described to me, sacred stories of their own kissed hands, and I recall the scorn which such confidences elicited from me once, my tawdry quips; and at this moment, although they cannot hear me, I hear myself asking those friends for forgiveness. Because now I understand that when your beloved kisses you thus, it can be enough to reduce you to tears.

I LOOK DOWN: he has pulled himself out of my jeans, and backing away very slightly, is returning himself to his full height, which leaves my eyelids level with his jaw-line. He releases both of my hands at once, but exceedingly slowly, which gives me time to catch them, and now he returns his attention to his cock, which he stretches out and tugs, leaving brief white thumbprints where pressure has been applied; and he turns it this way and that, as if it were some special piece of merchandise which I might like to sample, and he slaps it hard against his open palm, a couple of times, just to prove how well it works, how hard it can become. And next he lets a slow gob of spittle slide out of his mouth and fall, gathering speed, all the way down, and it lands with an audible splodge somewhere on the surface of his cock-head, which now he polishes up. He takes hold of his bollocks with his other hand and yanks the scrotum down, starts to churn the spunk, and as his body-weight shifts from one heavy foot to the other and back, I feel my inhibitions growing light, rising and evaporating; and suddenly I seem to be conducting myself like the whore that parades inside me. Already I have his balls in my grasp, and they are cold to the touch; I flick a finger hard against them, as if trying to find a good vein, but he doesn't react. I squeeze the sac slowly to start with, then harder, but I keep my attention stubbornly raised to his eyes, and now, rewardingly, I catch his lids drooping to half-mast, and the whites of his eyeballs rolling as if upwards, and the lashes flickering like the flickering lashes of a madman. His lips separate fractionally, so that he can rasp through his mouth, and then his jaw just droops ajar as he delivers himself to what, from my own past, I know to be an intake of pleasure, and just remembering this moment makes me blush. I slap his cock down, to check quite where we stand, to see what he does, and his hands swing rapidly, mechanically, to his back, as if cuffed. And this gesture of willing enslavement incites me to a blur of actions where I lose all sense of pride and just crouch down, like that, and tilt my jawbone up and let his rigid cock enter my mouth; and I detect, as I suck on it, as I rummage around the skirt of his foreskin with my tongue, that its taste is slightly sweaty, rancid, as if he'd been made anxious in my company; and the smell of this anxiety, far from disgusting me, makes me feel that I've caught him out, empowers me. His balls have swollen and hardened and tightened up, like the balls of a young man; but the eyelet of his grown-up cock is oozing salty tears of pre-seminal slime onto the roof of my mouth, and I lick them eagerly, vulgarly, as if I were parched. His arms, which seem to be hugging him, now begin to pull at his vest, over his head, but they take care not to remove it entirely, so that folds of dark cloth remain stretched, like a halter, around his neck and the pits of his arms. I sense Steve's elbows jutting out like spiky wings above me, and his hands hovering briefly about his chest before swapping sides, left moving over to right breast and vice-versa, and while I service his groin with my mouth, he begins to taunt his own nipples, which are large, and he rolls them like fat pearls of flesh between his indices and thumbs, tweaking them, and digging, occasionally, the edge of a nail into one of the craters. My own hands, as I crouch, are on my genitals, but their motion feels subsidiary to me now that the focus of my interest has shifted to Steve's arse—which I can't quite get at. I hear him grunting up there, and pausing for a frantic extra snort of poppers, only to resume his grunts, which he prolongs almost mournfully, privately—as if I were absent. And I take advantage of his distraction in order to unbuckle his belt and quickly unbutton his waistband, and he appears to let me do these things, appears prepared to indulge me, and further permits me to slide his jeans down, though only as far as his hip-line, but all the same this is enough to enable me to feel the shaven skin beneath his balls, which is taut and finer than any kid glove, and so, spitting on my palm, I return my hand between his legs and coat his underside with my saliva, and I also smear the top of his rump, which spasms at my touch, then expands. I lick around his front, up and down the ornamental scrolls of muscle which link his pelvis to his inner thigh, and he hisses and shudders at my tongue, as if the feeling were unbearable, as if such pleasures were not allowed. And now he allows my face to travel round his waist and approach the region of his buttocks, which are absolutely smooth, probably waxed, and full-blown, and suntanned. I taste them, of course; I cannot but. And, as if to help me, to provide easier access, Steve begins, I can hardly believe it, to bend forward very slightly, and I encourage him as carefully as I can, and as gently; and it's suddenly as if the whole game were up, because, next, he's bent right over the chair where he was seated earlier, and he's leaning forward for support against the wooden arms; and I draw back for a split second to catch my breath and, frankly, to worship the sight, which is of obscene beauty. And I try to freeze it for ever in my mind, to commit it to memory, because, at this moment, I have no trouble at all in believing that the sun could shine out of Steve's arse. And I spread his cheeks flat outwards with my hands, and press my face to the warm wetness inside, and I smother his hole with my open tongue. I recognize, in the tasting, a faint trace of antiseptic cream, which, though an irony, strikes me as a welcome one, as a sign despite itself, of care, of caution. And then I spit into his crack, and instantly his cheeks contract; but I try to soothe matters with still more saliva and return my mouth to that perfect arse, which is my trophy, and my tongue moves in circles round-and-round the crown of muscle, until at last I feel him dilating, relenting, surrendering to the rapture, which, in such circumstances, I suspect that everybody truthful ultimately must—man, woman, child.

Yet, just as Steve is starting properly to succumb, before I've had the chance to feel confidently embarked upon my own voyage, he—Christ—he suddenly and inexplicably wriggles away from my mouth, and then, abruptly, takes one step to the side, and pulls himself together, literally, yanking the back of his jeans back up. I stand. My face must be scarlet. His, disconcertingly, is drained of blood and rigid and bristling with professional affront, as if to tell me to watch it, man, not to push my bloody luck, as if to say—now of all times—that I've had my fun, and better value for money than most of his punters, who're lucky if they even get to wank him, and everything for me is beginning to tumble, to tumble and fall apart. My chest is throbbing with shock. My cock feels pathetic now. It is my head, not his, that resembles the head of some dog that's been robbed of a bone only to be struck with it across the snout, and though I'm fucking shattered by it all, I'm also nevertheless enraged, as enraged as when that boy in the old suit at the start of all this called me a fucking bender, remember, and said that he hated my guts; and I am seized with the same rabid impulse, and I just say, and I can hear the dryness in my false neutrality, Steve, Get The Fuck Out, and this time he doesn't look surprised, not for an instant, and, of course, now you understand why he's remained half-dressed, to simplify his passage out, and I, oh fucking Christ, I am, after all this, and despite all the signs, well, it's so absurd, so shaming to recount, I'm stunned, stunned and dismayed and broken, broken-hearted you could say; but believe me: I'll get over it, I promise you that much, I swear to it. And I am left, left to observe this poor ridiculous beautiful man, strapping his watch back on, and patting his jacket for his money, which is no real currency, and slithering like a guilty secret out of my life, this time for good and ever. And as he departs, stooping slightly, I notice that my music has come to an end.

PENGUIN BOOKS

SELECTED STORIES

Alice Munro was born and grew up in Wingham, Ontario. After high school she spent two years at the University of Western Ontario, married, and moved to Vancouver and Victoria, where she had three daughters. She returned to southwestern Ontario in 1972. She and her second husband now divide their time between Clinton and Comox on Vancouver Island.

Every year her writing continues to reach a wider audience, with magazines such as *The New Yorker*, *The Paris Review* and *Atlantic Monthly* all clamouring for her stories.

Her fame abroad is matched by the admiration she enjoys in Canada where she has won the Governor General's Award three times, for *Dance of the Happy Shades* (1968), *Who Do You Think You Are?* (1978) and *The Progress of Love* (1986), which was also selected as one of the best books of the year by the *New York Times*. Her other works, *Lives of Girls and Women* (1971), *Something I've Been Meaning to Tell You* (1976), *The Moons of Jupiter* (1982), *Friend of My Youth* (1990), *Open Secrets* (1994), and *Selected Stories* (1996), continue to attract discriminating readers.

ALSO BY ALICE MUNRO

❧ *Selected Stories* ❧

ALICE MUNRO

Penguin Books

PENGUIN BOOKS

Published by the Penguin Group

Penguin Books Canada Ltd, 10 Alcorn Avenue, Toronto, Ontario, Canada M4V 3B2

Penguin Books Ltd, 27 Wrights Lane, London W8 5TZ, England

Penguin Books USA Inc., 375 Hudson Street, New York, New York 10014, U.S.A.

Penguin Books Australia Ltd, Ringwood, Victoria, Australia

Penguin Books (NZ) Ltd, cnr Rosedale and Airborne Roads, Albany, Auckland 1310, New Zealand

Penguin Books Ltd, Registered Offices: Harmondsworth, Middlesex, England

First published as a Douglas Gibson Book by McClelland & Stewart, 1996

Published in Penguin Books, 1998

10 9 8 7 6 5 4 3 2 1

Manufactured in Canada.

CANADIAN CATALOGUING IN PUBLICATION DATA

Munro, Alice, 1931–
    Selected stories

ISBN 0-14-026775-1

I. Title.

PS8576.U57A6 1998   C813'.54   C97-932386-X   PR9199.3.M86A6 1998

The stories in this collection were originally published in the following: *Dance of the Happy Shades:* "Walker Brothers Cowboy," "Dance of the Happy Shades," "Postcard," "Images." *Something I've Been Meaning to Tell You:* "Something I've Been Meaning to Tell You," "The Ottawa Valley," "Material." *Who Do You Think You Are?:* "Royal Beating," "Wild Swans," "The Beggar Maid," "Simon's Luck." *The Moons of Jupiter:* "Chaddeleys and Flemings," "Dulse," "The Turkey Season," "Labor Day Dinner," "The Moons of Jupiter." *The Progress of Love:* "The Progress of Love," "Lichen," "Miles City, Montana," "White Dump," "Fits." *Friend of My Youth:* "Friend of My Youth," "Meneseteung," "Differently." *Open Secrets:* "Carried Away," "The Albanian Virgin," "A Wilderness Station," "Vandals."

Stories from *Who Do You Think You Are?* (1978) and *The Moons of Jupiter* (1982) by Alice Munro are reprinted by permission of Macmillan Canada. Stories from *Dance of the Happy Shades* (1968) by Alice Munro are reprinted by permission of McGraw-Hill Ryerson Limited.

Some parts of the Journal section in "A Wilderness Station" are copied from the accounts written by Robert B. Laidlaw in 1907. With that exception, all of the characters in this book are fictitious and any resemblance to actual persons living or dead is purely coincidental.

Visit Penguin Canada's web site at www.penguin.ca

for
Virginia Barber

My essential support and friend
for twenty years

Contents

❧ *Introduction* ❧

LIKE MANY WRITERS, I get letters from people who would like some brass-tacks information. Should I consider writing as my career? some ask. How much yearly income can I expect as a writer? How much education should a writer have? Is it necessary to work on a computer? Have an agent? Associate with other writers?

Some clarifying statements about my work are requested by others. What do you consider to be your basic themes? Your major strengths/weaknesses? Why do you choose to write short stories instead of novels? Do you write from a feminist perspective, and if not, why not? How do you feel that you contribute to the view of Canada held by a reader inside/outside the country? Do you prefer to write about relationships between people rather than important events, and if so, why? Do you prefer to write about rural and small-town people rather than sophisticated people, and if so, why? Are you a regional writer?

All this is rather flattering because it assumes that I am a person of brisk intelligence, exercising steady control on a number of fronts. I make advantageous judgments concerning computers and themes, I chart a course which is called a career and expect to make progress in it. I know what I am up to. Short stories, yes. Novels, no. I accept that rural folk are never sophisticated and sophisticates are never rural, and I make my choice. Also I keep an eye on feminism and Canada and try to figure out my duty to both.

This isn't exactly the kind of writer I'd like to be, but I wouldn't mind being a little more that way. In control, and pretty certain about what is going on, when I sit down with a pen and scribbler to do a first draft. Of course, if I was that kind of writer I might not know what a scribbler was, and I would pick up a pen only to write checks and autographs.

I am forced, in writing this introduction, to give the whole matter some thought, and I might as well start by answering a question.

I did not "choose" to write short stories. I hoped to write novels. When you are responsible for running a house and taking care of small children, particularly in the days before disposable diapers or ubiquitous automatic washing machines, it's hard to arrange for large chunks of time. A child's illness, relatives coming to stay, a pile-up of unavoidable household jobs, can swallow a work-in-progress as surely as a power failure used to destroy a piece of work in the computer. You're better to stick with something you can keep in mind and hope to do in a few weeks, or a couple of months at most. I know that there are lots of women who have written novels in the midst of domestic challenges, just as there are men (and women) who have written them after coming home at night from exhausting jobs. That's why I thought I could do it too, but I couldn't. I took to writing in frantic spurts, juggling my life around until I could get a story done, then catching up on other responsibilities. So I got into the habit of writing short stories.

In later years my short stories haven't been so short. They've grown longer, and in a way more disjointed and demanding and peculiar. I didn't choose for that to happen, either. The only choice I make is to write about what interests me in a way that interests me, that gives me pleasure. It may not look like pleasure, because the difficulties can make me morose and distracted, but that's what it is—the pleasure of telling the story I mean to tell as wholly as I can tell it, of finding out in fact what that story is, by working around the different ways of telling it.

Generally speaking, these don't seem to be very straightforward ways. But I think they're necessary.

The reason I write so often about the country to the east of Lake Huron is just that I love it. It means something to me that no other country can—no matter how important historically that other country may be, how "beautiful," how lively and interesting. I am intoxicated by this particular landscape, by the almost flat fields, the swamps, the hardwood bush lots, by the continental climate with its extravagant winters. I am at home with the brick houses, the falling-down barns, the occasional farms that have swimming pools and airplanes, the trailer parks, burdensome old churches, Wal-Mart, and Canadian Tire. I speak the language.

When I write about something happening in this setting, I don't think that I'm choosing to be confined. Quite the opposite. I don't think I'm writing just *about* this life. I hope to be writing about and *through* it.

When I first thought about what I would write, I set my stories—they were novels then—in special countries derived from fiction and then obsessively organized and colored by my imagination. When I was eleven or twelve I had worked out—mostly in my walks to and from school—an adventure-narrative inspired mostly by *The Last of the Mohicans,* and by the true story of the fourteen-year-old heroine Madeleine de Verchères, who held her family farm against the Iroquois near Montreal in 1692. The devouring woods, the bears, and the Indians, the perilous fields outside the palisades. All to be pushed aside, obliterated—so that I've only now retrieved it—when a couple of years later I came across *Wuthering Heights.* Its long shadow fell over all the remaining years of my adolescence, and I carried in my head a whole demonic tragedy in which people were riven by love, blasted by curses, and died young, all in a landscape of windy moors inserted into Huron County. I didn't give up on this novel until I went to college. But during the time I carried it, there was a disturbance—something happened that had to do with writing, but in a way I could not understand.

I was standing at a window in the library in the Town Hall. (Our town was the only one in the county that had refused a Carnegie Library, not wishing to have to maintain such a building and forgo the taxes on the property.) I was around fifteen years old. I had finished picking out my books. I was just at the window, waiting. Perhaps I was waiting for a friend, or for a ride home—I lived a mile or so west of town.

Snow was falling straight down, in the gentle meditative way that it often seemed to fall in town, between the buildings. That didn't mean that once I left the shelter of town, on my westward walk home, I would not be facing into a whirlwind of snow whipped off the tops of the drifts, or a primal blast, coming across Lake Huron and Lake Michigan right out of the freezing heart of the continent.

Snow falling straight down. The window looked out on the town weigh-scales and a high board fence beyond. A corner of the Town Armouries came into view. Like all armouries, it was a thick-walled, scowling building of red brick.

A team of horses, pulling a sleigh, was moving onto the scales. The sleigh was piled high with sacks of grain. The man who was driving the team had a winter cap pulled down on his head, fur-lined flaps over his ears. The horses were heavy work-horses, still used then on some farms. In a few years such horses would have vanished. The farmer would be taking the grain to the chopping mill. He would get a slip from the scales operator stating the total weight. The net weight would be arrived at by subtracting the weight of the empty sleigh. There was some mud tracked onto the snow around the scales, a scattering of hay and grain from other loads, and a fresh mound of horse manure on which the snow immediately melted.

This description makes the scene seem as if it was waiting to be painted and hung on the wall to be admired by somebody who has probably never bagged grain. The patient horses with their nobly rounded rumps, the humped figure of the driver, the coarse fabric of the sacks. The snow conferring dignity and peace. I didn't see it framed and removed in that way. I saw it alive and potent, and it gave me something like a blow to the chest. What does this mean, what can be discovered about it, what is the rest of the story? The man and the horses are not symbolic or picturesque, they are moving through a story which is hidden, and now, for a moment, carelessly revealed.

How can you get your finger on it, feel that life beating?

It was more a torment than a comfort to think about this, because I couldn't get hold of it at all. I went back to stringing out my secret and gradually less satisfying novel.

I never wrote a story about the man and the horses. It doesn't work like that anyway. The scene which is the secret of the story may not seem to be close to what it's "about." For instance, the story "Open Secrets" is "about" a girl who disappears on an overnight camping trip, and the ripples set up in the community by her disappearance. There you have the central incident, the "what happens" of the story. But the scene that I could not do without, the scene that seems to hold the most essential key to the story (but not necessarily to the plot), is the one in the back yard, with the dog. The woman, the dog, the deranged man, the pump, the heat, the pain of the boil. I don't mean that these are things put into the story and that they seem to work well, I mean that they were there from the beginning and it was to an extent because of them that I was able to discover or invent the rest of the story.

"Open Secrets" is a story not included in this book. And perhaps this is a good time to mention that the decision about which stories were to be put in, and which left out, was not always based on preference, but on length and adequate representation of different periods in the writing.

The story I am working on now owes its existence mostly to a long, straight path, a hard-beaten dirt path running between a double row of spruce trees. I know now who walked that path and where they were going, but in the beginning there was just the path.

I don't talk about these beginnings or essentials very much, because they are hard to explain and tend to fade anyway after the story has been put out in the world and become a stranger to me. But I can tell you that in "Walker Brothers Cowboy" it's the father speaking to the tramp, and in "Simon's Luck" it's the girl in her costume dress bending over the kittens, and in "A Wilderness Station" it's the splendid silent voyage of the Stanley Steamer—about which I now know a host of details that the story's architecture wouldn't support. In "Labor Day Dinner" it's the car without its headlights on, shooting through the intersection, a deadly fish in the night.

I can far more easily recall, and can truthfully tell, that "Friend of My Youth" came from a conversation about old games and crokinole, which led to two sisters and a husband, the Cameronian church, a half-painted house. Then as I wrote the story there was an unexpected expansion to my mother's story and the way my mother saw life and the way I see it— the way I see *her* life. Anecdote and autobiography can weave together in this way. There is always more than one starting point, and once you've found one you're pretty sure to find others. Both "The Albanian Virgin" and "Carried Away" came from a single unsubstantiated story—that a librarian from the town where I live now had been kidnapped during a trip to Europe before the First World War by "bandits in Albania." This led to my reading about Albania, particularly in the Virago Press book by Edith Durham, who travelled there in the early twentieth century. In her book I learned about the institution which allows a woman, by pure and simple renunciation of sex, to take on the freedom and prestige of a man. So I had two women—the one who went to Albania and the one who stayed home and worked in the library. But the story of "Carried Away" also worked itself backwards from the remembered makeshift bus depot with kitchen chairs set in rows in the dirt of a back yard.

"The Turkey Season" started off from my memory of a real person (this doesn't very often happen). He was a kind, ironic, disillusioned, and probably lovesick man who was the cook in the summer hotel where I worked as a waitress when I was nineteen. I moved the story out of the hotel and into the Turkey Barn because I had found a remarkable photo taken of the "gutters" who worked there with my father—a photo which seemed to have captured the peculiar closeness and competitiveness, the reckless rough jokes, the boisterousness and stamina that bind people together temporarily in such jobs. It was a great help, too, that I have a brother-in-law who was able to take me step-by-step through the turkey-gutting process, in the most accurate and elegant detail. He learned it at agricultural college.

In "Miles City, Montana" and "The Moons of Jupiter" I have used, with some alteration, incidents and emotions from my own family life. "The Progress of Love" started off from a story about a faked hanging, put on to throw a scare into other members of a family. (If you live in a small town you get stories like this dumped in your lap all the time—the unofficial history.) "Simon's Luck" came from a story told me at a party by a man who had been hidden in a railway car, as a Jewish child in France during the Second World War. "Images" came from two true memories—the muskrat under water, and the roofed-over cellar I went past every day on my way to school. A bootlegger and his wife lived there—and they weren't the only people to have contrived shelters like these during the Depression. So it was strange for me to find this cellar treated, in a critical essay, as a symbol of my rejection of anything transcendental, and particularly of Christianity. I had thought that it was simply a snug, economical, slightly eccentric solution to a housing problem.

In "Royal Beatings" I turned to unacknowledged history again. Not exactly unofficial history, because the anecdote of father and daughter, the vigilante punishment handed out for suspected incest, comes right out of a nineteenth-century newspaper. But the town in which this happened, and where I grew up, now claims that no untoward incidents ever took place within its boundaries, and that prostitutes, bootleggers, and unhappy families were pretty much unknown—all being, according to an editorial in the local paper, products of my own "soured introspection."

This is all about beginnings. But that, in fact, is the easy part. Endings are another matter. When I've shaped the story in my head, before starting to put it on paper, it has, of course, an ending. Often this ending will stay in place right through the first draft. Sometimes it stays in place for good. Sometimes not. The story, in the first draft, has put on rough but adequate clothes, it is "finished" and might be thought to need no more than a lot of technical adjustments, some tightening here and expanding there, and the slipping in of some telling dialogue and chopping away of flabby modifiers. It's then, in fact, that the story is in the greatest danger of losing its life, of appearing so hopelessly misbegotten that my only relief comes from abandoning it. It doesn't do enough. It does what I intended, but it turns out that my intention was all wrong. Quite often I decide to give up on it. (This was the point at which, in my early days as a writer, I did just chuck everything out and get started on something absolutely new.) And now that the story is free from my controlling hand a change in direction may occur. I can't ever be sure this will happen, and there are bad times, though I should be used to them. I'm no good at letting go, I am thrifty and tenacious now, no spendthrift and addict of fresh starts as in my youth. I go around glum and preoccupied, trying to think of ways to fix the problem. Usually the right way pops up in the middle of this.

A big relief, then. Renewed energy. Resurrection.

Except that it isn't the right way. Maybe a way *to* the right way. Now I write pages and pages I'll have to discard. New angles are introduced, minor characters brought center stage, lively and satisfying scenes are written, and it's all a mistake. Out they go. But by this time I'm on the track, there's no backing out. I know so much more than I did, I know what I want to happen and where I want to end up and I just have to keep trying till I find the best way of getting there.

I should mention here that I don't always have to do all this work by myself. An editor who is also an ideal reader can work with you on these final shifts and slants in a seamless, amazing collaboration. Charles McGrath and Dan Menaker, at *The New Yorker*, have helped me wonderfully in this way—particularly in "The Turkey Season" (Charles) and "Vandals" (Dan).

I wrote an essay several years ago for my friend John Metcalf, in which I said something that got a surprised reaction from readers—and their surprise surprised me. I said that I don't always, or even usually, read stories from beginning to end. I start anywhere and proceed in either direction. So it appears that I'm not reading—at least in an efficient way—to find out what happens. I do find out, and I'm interested in finding out, but there's much more to the experience. A story is not like a road to follow, I said, it's more like a house. You go inside and stay there for a while, wandering back and forth and settling where you like and discovering how the room and corridors relate to each other, how the world outside is altered by being viewed from these windows. And you, the visitor, the reader, are altered as well by being in this enclosed space, whether it is ample and easy or full of crooked turns, or sparsely or opulently furnished. You can go back again and again, and the house, the story, always contains more than you saw the last time. It has also a sturdy sense of itself, of being built out of its own necessity, no just to shelter or beguile you. To deliver a story like that, durable and freestanding, is what I'm always hoping for.

But mark, madam, we live amongst riddles and mysteries— the most obvious things, which come in our way, have dark sides, which the quickest sight cannot penetrate into; and even the clearest and most exalted understandings amongst us find ourselves puzzled and at a loss in almost every cranny of nature's works: so that this, like a thousand other things, falls out for us in a way, which tho' we cannot reason upon it—yet we find the good of it, may it please your reverences and your worships—and that's enough for us.

—Laurence Sterne,
The Life and Opinions of Tristram Shandy, Gentleman.

Selected Stories

❧ *Walker Brothers Cowboy* ❧

AFTER SUPPER MY father says, "Want to go down and see if the Lake's still there?" We leave my mother sewing under the dining-room light, making clothes for me against the opening of school. She has ripped up for this purpose an old suit and an old plaid wool dress of hers, and she has to cut and match very cleverly and also make me stand and turn for endless fittings, sweaty, itching from the hot wool, ungrateful. We leave my brother in bed in the little screened porch at the end of the front veranda, and sometimes he kneels on his bed and presses his face against the screen and calls mournfully, "Bring me an ice-cream cone!" but I call back, "You will be asleep," and do not even turn my head.

Then my father and I walk gradually down a long, shabby sort of street, with Silverwoods Ice Cream signs standing on the sidewalk, outside tiny, lighted stores. This is in Tuppertown, an old town on Lake Huron, an old grain port. The street is shaded, in some places, by maple trees whose roots have cracked and heaved the sidewalk and spread out like crocodiles into the bare yards. People are sitting out, men in shirtsleeves and undershirts and women in aprons—not people we know but if anybody looks ready to nod and say, "Warm night," my father will nod too and say something the same. Children are still playing. I don't know them either because my mother keeps my brother and me in our own yard, saying he is too young to leave it and I have to mind him. I am not so sad to watch their evening games because the games themselves are ragged, dissolving. Children, of their own will, draw apart, separate into islands of two or one under the heavy trees, occupying themselves in such solitary ways as I do all day, planting pebbles in the dirt or writing in it with a stick.

Presently we leave these yards and houses behind; we pass a factory with boarded-up windows, a lumberyard whose high wooden gates are locked for the night. Then the town falls away in a defeated jumble of sheds and small junkyards, the sidewalk gives up and we are walking on a sandy path with burdocks, plantains, humble nameless weeds all around. We enter a vacant lot, a kind of park really, for it is kept clear of junk and there is one bench with a slat missing on the back, a place to sit and look at the water. Which is generally gray in the evening, under a lightly overcast sky, no sunsets, the horizon dim. A very quiet, washing noise on the stones of the beach. Further along, towards the main part of town, there is a stretch of sand, a water slide, floats bobbing around the safe swimming area, a lifeguard's rickety throne. Also a long dark-green building, like a roofed veranda, called the Pavilion, full of farmers and their wives, in stiff good clothes, on Sundays. That is the part of the town we used to know when we lived at Dungannon and came here three or four times a summer, to the Lake. That, and the docks where we would go and look at the grain boats, ancient, rusty, wallowing, making us wonder how they got past the breakwater let alone to Fort William.

Tramps hang around the docks and occasionally on these evenings wander up the dwindling beach and climb the shifting, precarious path boys have made, hanging on to dry bushes, and say something to my father which, being frightened of tramps, I am too alarmed to catch. My father says he is a bit hard up himself. "I'll roll you a cigarette if it's any use to you," he says, and he shakes tobacco out carefully on one of the thin butterfly papers, flicks it with his tongue, seals it and hands it to the tramp, who takes it and walks away. My father also rolls and lights and smokes one cigarette of his own.

He tells me how the Great Lakes came to be. All where Lake Huron is now, he says, used to be flat land, a wide flat plain. Then came the ice, creeping down from the North, pushing deep into the low places. Like *that*—and he shows me his hand with his spread fingers pressing the rock-hard ground where we are sitting. His fingers make hardly any impression at all and he says, "Well, the old ice cap had a lot more power behind it than this hand has." And then the ice went back, shrank back towards the North Pole where it came from, and left its fingers of ice in the deep places it had gouged, and ice turned to lakes and there they were today. They were *new*, as time went. I try to see that plain before me, dinosaurs walking on it, but I am not able even to imagine the shore of the Lake when the Indians were there, before Tuppertown. The tiny share we have of time appalls me, though my father seems to regard it with tranquillity. Even my father, who sometimes seems to me to have been at home in the world as long as it has lasted, has really lived on this earth only a little longer than I have, in terms of all the time there has been to live in. He has not known a time, any more than I, when automobiles and electric lights did not at least exist. He was not alive when this century started. I will be barely alive—old, old—when it ends. I do not like to think of it. I wish the Lake to be always just a lake, with the safe-swimming floats marking it, and the breakwater and the lights of Tuppertown.

My father has a job, selling for Walker Brothers. This is a firm that sells almost entirely in the country, the back country. Sunshine, Boylesbridge, Turnaround—that is all his territory. Not Dungannon where we used to live, Dungannon is too near town and my mother is grateful for that. He sells cough medicine, iron tonic, corn plasters, laxatives, pills for female disorders, mouthwash, shampoo, liniment, salves, lemon and orange and raspberry concentrate for making refreshing drinks, vanilla, food coloring, black and green tea, ginger, cloves, and other spices, rat poison. He has a song about it, with these two lines:

> *And have all liniments and oils,*
> *For everything from corns to boils. . . .*

Not a very funny song, in my mother's opinion. A peddler's song, and that is what he is, a peddler knocking at backwoods kitchens. Up until last winter we had our own business, a fox farm. My father raised silver foxes and sold their pelts to the people who make them into capes and coats and muffs. Prices fell, my father hung on hoping they would get better next year, and they fell again, and he hung on one more year and one more and finally it was not possible to hang on anymore, we owed everything to the feed company. I have heard my mother explain this, several times, to Mrs. Oliphant, who is the only neighbor she talks to. (Mrs. Oliphant also has come down in the world, being a schoolteacher who married the janitor.) We poured all we had into it, my mother says, and we came out with nothing. Many people could say the same thing, these days, but my mother has no time for the national calamity, only ours. Fate has flung us onto a street of poor people (it does not matter that we were poor before; that was a different sort of poverty), and the only way to take this, as she sees it, is with dignity, with bitterness, with no reconciliation. No bathroom with a claw-footed tub and a flush toilet is going to comfort her, nor water on tap and sidewalks past the house and milk in bottles, not even the two movie theatres and the Venus Restaurant and Woolworths so marvellous it has live birds singing in its fan-cooled corners and fish as tiny as fingernails, as bright as moons, swimming in its green tanks. My mother does not care.

In the afternoons she often walks to Simon's Grocery and takes me with her to help carry things. She wears a good dress, navy blue with little flowers, sheer, worn over a navy-blue slip. Also a summer hat of white straw, pushed down on the side of the head, and white shoes I have just whitened on a newspaper on the back steps. I have my hair freshly done in long damp curls which the dry air will fortunately soon loosen, a stiff large hair ribbon on top of my head. This is entirely different from going out after supper with my father. We have not walked past two houses before I feel we have become objects of universal ridicule. Even the dirty words chalked on the sidewalk are laughing at us. My mother does not seem to notice. She walks serenely like a lady shopping, like a *lady* shopping, past the housewives in loose beltless dresses torn under the arms. With me her creation, wretched curls and flaunting hair bow, scrubbed knees and white socks—all I do not want to be. I loathe even my name when she says it in public, in a voice so high, proud, and ringing, deliberately different from the voice of any other mother on the street.

My mother will sometimes carry home, for a treat, a brick of ice cream—pale Neapolitan; and because we have no refrigerator in our house we wake my brother and eat it at once in the dining room, always darkened by the wall of the house next door. I spoon it up tenderly, leaving the chocolate till last, hoping to have some still to eat when my brother's dish is empty. My mother tries then to imitate the conversations we used to have at Dungannon, going back to our earliest, most leisurely days before my brother was born, when she would give me a little tea and a lot of milk in a cup like hers and we would sit out on the step facing the pump, the lilac tree, the fox pens beyond. She is not able to keep from mentioning those days. "Do you remember when we put you in your sled and Major pulled you?" (Major our dog, that we had to leave with neighbors when we moved.) "Do you remember your sandbox outside the kitchen window?" I pretend to remember far less than I do, wary of being trapped into sympathy or any unwanted emotion.

My mother has headaches. She often has to lie down. She lies on my brother's narrow bed in the little screened porch, shaded by heavy branches. "I look up at that tree and I think I am at home," she says.

"What you need," my father tells her, "is some fresh air and a drive in the country." He means for her to go with him, on his Walker Brothers route.

That is not my mother's idea of a drive in the country.

"Can I come?"

"Your mother might want you for trying on clothes."

"I'm beyond sewing this afternoon," my mother says.

"I'll take her then. Take both of them, give you a rest."

What is there about us that people need to be given a rest from? Never mind. I am glad enough to find my brother and make him go to the toilet and get us both into the car, our knees unscrubbed, my hair unringleted. My father brings from the house his two heavy brown suitcases, full of bottles, and sets them on the back seat. He wears a white shirt, brilliant in the sunlight, a tie, light trousers belonging to his summer suit (his other suit is black, for funerals, and belonged to my uncle before he died), and a creamy straw hat. His salesman's outfit, with pencils clipped in the shirt pocket. He goes back once again, probably to say goodbye to my mother, to ask her if she is sure she doesn't want to come, and hear her say, "No. No thanks, I'm better just to lie here with my eyes closed." Then we are backing out of the driveway with the rising hope of adventure, just the little hope that takes you over the bump into the street, the hot air starting to move, turning into a breeze, the houses growing less and less familiar as we follow the shortcut my father knows, the quick way out of town. Yet what is there waiting for us all afternoon but hot hours in stricken farmyards, perhaps a stop at a country store and three ice-cream cones or bottles of pop, and my father singing? The one he made up about himself has a title—"The Walker Brothers Cowboy"—and it starts out like this:

Old Ned Fields, he now is dead
So I am ridin' the route instead. . . .

Who is Ned Fields? The man he has replaced, surely, and if so he really is dead; yet my father's voice is mournful-jolly, making his death some kind of nonsense, a comic calamity. "Wisht I was back on the Rio Grande, plungin' through the dusky sand." My father sings most of the time while driving the car. Even now, heading out of town, crossing the bridge and taking the sharp turn onto the highway, he is humming something, mumbling a bit of a song to himself, just tuning up, really, getting ready to improvise, for out along the highway we pass the Baptist Camp, the Vacation Bible Camp, and he lets loose:

"Where are the Baptists, where are the Baptists,
where are all the Baptists today?
They're down in the water, in Lake Huron water,
with their sins all a-gittin' washed away."

My brother takes this for straight truth and gets up on his knees trying to see down to the Lake. "I don't see any Baptists," he says accusingly. "Neither do I, son," says my father. "I told you, they're down in the Lake."

No roads paved when we left the highway. We have to roll up the windows because of dust. The land is flat, scorched, empty. Bush lots at the back of the farms hold shade, black pine-shade like pools nobody can ever get to. We bump up a long lane and at the end of it what could look more unwelcoming, more deserted than the tall unpainted farmhouse with grass growing uncut right up to the front door, green blinds down, and a door upstairs opening on nothing but air? Many houses have this door, and I have never yet been able to find out why. I ask my father and he says they are for walking in your sleep. *What?* Well, if you happen to be walking in your sleep and you want to step outside. I am offended, seeing too late that he is joking, as usual, but my brother says sturdily, "If they did that they would break their necks."

The 1930s. How much this kind of farmhouse, this kind of afternoon seem to me to belong to that one decade in time, just as my father's hat does, his bright flared tie, our car with its wide running board (an Essex, and long past its prime). Cars somewhat like it, many older, none dustier, sit in the farmyards. Some are past running and have their doors pulled off, their seats removed for use on porches. No living things to be seen, chickens or cattle. Except dogs. There are dogs lying in any kind of shade they can find, dreaming, their lean sides rising and sinking rapidly. They get up when my father opens the car door, he has to speak to them. "Nice boy, there's a boy, nice old boy." They quiet down, go back to their shade. He should know how to quiet animals, he has held desperate foxes with tongs around their necks. One gentling voice for the dogs and another, rousing, cheerful, for calling at doors. "Hello there, missus, it's the Walker Brothers man and what are you out of today?" A door opens, he disappears. Forbidden to follow, forbidden even to leave the car, we can just wait and wonder what he says. Sometimes trying to make my mother laugh, he pretends to be himself in a farm kitchen, spreading out his sample case. "Now then, missus, are you troubled with parasitic life? Your children's scalps, I mean. All those crawly little things we're too polite to mention that show up on the heads of the best of families? Soap alone is useless, kerosene is not too nice a perfume, but I have here—" Or else, "Believe me, sitting and driving all day the way I do I *know* the value of these fine pills. Natural relief. A problem common to old folks too, once their days of activity are over—How about you, Grandma?" He would wave the imaginary box of pills under my mother's nose and she would laugh finally, unwillingly. "He doesn't say that really, does he?" I said, and she said no of course not, he was too much of a gentleman.

One yard after another, then, the old cars, the pumps, dogs, views of gray barns and falling-down sheds and unturning windmills. The men, if they are working in the fields, are not in any fields that we can see. The children are far away, following dry creek beds or looking for blackberries, or else they are hidden in the house, spying at us through cracks in the blinds. The car seat has grown slick with our sweat. I dare my brother to sound the horn, wanting to do it myself but not wanting to get the blame. He knows better. We play I Spy, but it is hard to find many colors. Gray for the barns and sheds and toilets and houses, brown for the yard and fields, black or brown for the dogs. The rusting cars show rainbow patches, in which I strain to pick out purple or green; likewise I peer at doors for shreds of old peeling paint, maroon or yellow. We can't play with letters, which would be better, because my brother is too young to spell. The game disintegrates anyway. He claims my colors are not fair, and wants extra turns.

In one house no door opens, though the car is in the yard. My father knocks and whistles, calls, "Hullo there! Walker Brothers man!" but there is not a stir of reply anywhere. This house has no porch, just a bare, slanting slab of cement on which my father stands. He turns around, searching the barnyard, the barn whose mow must be empty because you can see the sky through it, and finally he bends to pick up his suitcases. Just then a window is opened upstairs, a white pot appears on the sill, is tilted over and its contents splash down the outside wall. The window is not directly above my father's head, so only a stray splash would catch him. He picks up his suitcases with no particular hurry and walks, no longer whistling, to the car. "Do you know what that was?" I say to my brother. *"Pee."* He laughs and laughs.

My father rolls and lights a cigarette before he starts the car. The window has been slammed down, the blind drawn, we never did see a hand or face. "Pee, pee," sings my brother ecstatically. "Somebody dumped down pee!" "Just don't tell your mother that," my father says. "She isn't liable to see the joke." "Is it in your song?" my brother wants to know. My father says no but he will see what he can do to work it in.

I notice in a little while that we are not turning in any more lanes, though it does not seem to me that we are headed home. "Is this the way to Sunshine?" I ask my father, and he answers, "No, ma'am, it's not." "Are we still in your territory?" He shakes his head. "We're going *fast*," my brother says approvingly, and in fact we are bouncing along through dry puddle-holes so that all the bottles in the suitcases clink together and gurgle promisingly.

Another lane, a house, also unpainted, dried to silver in the sun.

"I thought we were out of your territory."

"We are."

"Then what are we going in here for?"

"You'll see."

In front of the house a short, sturdy woman is picking up washing, which had been spread on the grass to bleach and dry. When the car stops she stares at it hard for a moment, bends to pick up a couple more towels to add to the bundle under her arm, comes across to us and says in a flat voice, neither welcoming nor unfriendly, "Have you lost your way?"

My father takes his time getting out of the car. "I don't think so," he says. "I'm the Walker Brothers man."

"George Golley is our Walker Brothers man," the woman says, "and he was out here no more than a week ago. Oh, my Lord God," she says harshly, "it's you."

"It was, the last time I looked in the mirror," my father says.

The woman gathers all the towels in front of her and holds on to them tightly, pushing them against her stomach as if it hurt. "Of all the people I never thought to see. And telling me you were the Walker Brothers man."

"I'm sorry if you were looking forward to George Golley," my father says humbly.

"And look at me, I was prepared to clean the henhouse. You'll think that's just an excuse but it's true. I don't go round looking like this every day." She is wearing a farmer's straw hat, through which pricks of sunlight penetrate and float on her face, a loose, dirty print smock, and canvas shoes. "Who are those in the car, Ben? They're not yours?"

"Well, I hope and believe they are," my father says, and tells our names and ages. "Come on, you can get out. This is Nora, Miss Cronin. Nora, you better tell me, is it still Miss, or have you got a husband hiding in the woodshed?"

"If I had a husband that's not where I'd keep him, Ben," she says, and they both laugh, her laugh abrupt and somewhat angry. "You'll think I got no manners, as well as being dressed like a tramp," she says. "Come on in out of the sun. It's cool in the house."

We go across the yard ("Excuse me taking you in this way but I don't think the front door has been opened since Papa's funeral, I'm afraid the hinges might drop off"), up the porch steps, into the kitchen, which really is cool, high-ceilinged, the blinds of course down, a simple, clean, threadbare room with waxed worn linoleum, potted geraniums, drinking-pail and dipper, a round table with scrubbed oilcloth. In spite of the cleanness, the wiped and swept surfaces, there is a faint sour smell—maybe of the dishrag or the tin dipper or the oilcloth, or the old lady, because there is one, sitting in an easy chair under the clock shelf. She turns her head slightly in our direction and says, "Nora? Is that company?"

"Blind," says Nora in a quick explaining voice to my father. Then, "You won't guess who it is, Momma. Hear his voice."

My father goes to the front of her chair and bends and says hopefully, "Afternoon, Mrs. Cronin."

"Ben Jordan," says the old lady with no surprise. "You haven't been to see us in the longest time. Have you been out of the country?"

My father and Nora look at each other.

"He's married, Momma," says Nora cheerfully and aggressively. "Married and got two children and here they are." She pulls us forward, makes each of us touch the old lady's dry, cool hand while she says our names in turn. Blind! This is the first blind person I have ever seen close up. Her eyes are closed, the eyelids sunk away down, showing no shape of the eyeball, just hollows. From one hollow comes a drop of silver liquid, a medicine, or a miraculous tear.

"Let me get into a decent dress," Nora says. "Talk to Momma. It's a treat for her. We hardly ever see company, do we, Momma?"

"Not many makes it out this road," says the old lady placidly. "And the ones that used to be around here, our old neighbors, some of them have pulled out."

"True everywhere," my father says.

"Where's your wife then?"

"Home. She's not too fond of the hot weather, makes her feel poorly."

"Well." This is a habit of country people, old people, to say "well," meaning, "Is that so?" with a little extra politeness and concern.

Nora's dress, when she appears again—stepping heavily on Cuban heels down the stairs in the hall—is flowered more lavishly than anything my mother owns, green and yellow on brown, some sort of floating sheer crêpe, leaving her arms bare. Her arms are heavy, and every bit of her skin you can see is covered with little dark freckles like measles. Her hair is short, black, coarse and curly, her teeth very white and strong. "It's the first time I knew there was such a thing as green poppies," my father says, looking at her dress.

"You would be surprised all the things you never knew," says Nora, sending a smell of cologne far and wide when she moves and displaying a change of voice to go with the dress, something more sociable and youthful. "They're not poppies anyway, they're just flowers. You go and pump me some good cold water and I'll make these children a drink." She gets down from the cupboard a bottle of Walker Brothers Orange syrup.

"You telling me you were the Walker Brothers man!"

"It's the truth, Nora. You go and look at my sample cases in the car if you don't believe me. I got the territory directly south of here."

"Walker Brothers? Is that a fact? You selling for Walker Brothers?"

"Yes, ma'am."

"We always heard you were raising foxes over Dungannon way."

"That's what I was doing, but I kind of run out of luck in that business."

"So where're you living? How long've you been out selling?"

"We moved into Tuppertown. I been at it, oh, two, three months. It keeps the wolf from the door. Keeps him as far away as the back fence."

Nora laughs. "Well, I guess you count yourself lucky to have the work. Isabel's husband in Brantford, he was out of work the longest time. I thought if he didn't find something soon I was going to have them all land in here to feed, and I tell you I was hardly looking forward to it. It's all I can manage with me and Momma."

"Isabel married," my father says. "Muriel married too?"

"No, she's teaching school out West. She hasn't been home for five years. I guess she finds something better to do with her holidays. I would if I was her." She gets some snapshots out of the table drawer and starts showing him. "That's Isabel's oldest boy, starting school. That's the baby sitting in her carriage. Isabel and her husband. Muriel. That's her roommate with her. That's a fellow she used to go around with, and his car. He was working in a bank out there. That's her school, it has eight rooms. She teaches Grade Five." My father shakes his head. "I can't think of her any way but when she was going to school, so shy I used to pick her up on the road—I'd be on my way to see you—and she would not say one word, not even to agree it was a nice day."

"She's got over that."

"Who are you talking about?" says the old lady.

"Muriel. I said she's got over being shy."

"She was here last summer."

"No, Momma, that was Isabel. Isabel and her family were here last summer. Muriel's out West."

"I meant Isabel."

Shortly after this the old lady falls asleep, her head on the side, her mouth open. "Excuse her manners," Nora says. "It's old age." She fixes an afghan over her mother and says we can all go into the front room where our talking won't disturb her.

"You two," my father says. "Do you want to go outside and amuse yourselves?"

Amuse ourselves how? Anyway, I want to stay. The front room is more interesting than the kitchen, though barer. There is a gramophone and a pump organ and a picture on the wall of Mary, Jesus' mother—I know that much—in shades of bright blue and pink with a spiked band of light around her head. I know that such pictures are found only in the homes of Roman Catholics and so Nora must be one. We have never known any Roman Catholics at all well, never well enough to visit in their houses. I think of what my grandmother and my Aunt Tena, over in Dungannon, used to always say to indicate that some-body was a Catholic. *So-and-so digs with the wrong foot*, they would say. *She digs with the wrong foot.* That was what they would say about Nora.

Nora takes a bottle, half full, out of the top of the organ and pours some of what is in it into the two glasses that she and my father have emptied of the orange drink.

"Keep it in case of sickness?" my father says.

"Not on your life," says Nora. "I'm never sick. I just keep it because I keep it. One bottle does me a fair time, though, because I don't care for drinking alone. Here's luck!" She and my father drink and I know what it is. Whisky. One of the things my mother has told me in our talks together is that my father never drinks whisky. But I see he does. He drinks whisky and he talks of people whose names I have never heard before. But after a while he turns to a familiar incident. He tells about the chamberpot that was emptied out the window. "Picture me there," he says, "hollering my heartiest. *Oh, lady, it's your Walker Brothers man, anybody home?*" He does himself hollering, grinning absurdly, waiting, looking up in pleased expectation, and then—oh, ducking, covering his head with his arms, looking as if he begged for mercy (when he never did anything like that, I was watching), and Nora laughs, almost as hard as my brother did at the time.

"That isn't true! That's not a word true!"

"Oh, indeed it is, ma'am. We have our heroes in the ranks of Walker Brothers. I'm glad you think it's funny," he says sombrely.

I ask him shyly, "Sing the song."

"What song? Have you turned into a singer on top of everything else?"

Embarrassed, my father says, "Oh, just this song I made up while I was driving around, it gives me something to do, making up rhymes."

But after some urging he does sing it, looking at Nora with a droll, apologetic expression, and she laughs so much that in places he has to stop and wait for her to get over laughing so he can go on, because she makes him laugh too. Then he does various parts of his salesman's spiel. Nora when she laughs squeezes her large bosom under her folded arms. "You're crazy," she says. "That's all you are." She sees my brother peering into the gramophone and she jumps up and goes over to him. "Here's us sitting enjoying ourselves and not giving you a thought, isn't it terrible?" she says. "You want me to put a record on, don't you? You want to hear a nice record? Can you dance? I bet your sister can, can't she?"

I say no. "A big girl like you and so good-looking and can't dance!" says Nora. "It's high time you learned. I bet you'd make a lovely dancer. Here, I'm going to put on a piece I used to dance to and even your daddy did, in his dancing days. You didn't know your daddy was a dancer, did you? Well, he is a talented man, your daddy!"

She puts down the lid and takes hold of me unexpectedly around the waist, picks up my other hand, and starts making me go backwards. "This is the way, now, this is how they dance. Follow me. This foot, see. One and one-two. One and one-two. That's fine, that's lovely, don't look at your feet! Follow me, that's right, see how easy? You're going to be a lovely dancer! One and one-two. One and one-two. Ben, see your daughter dancing!" *Whispering while you cuddle near me, Whispering so no one can hear me. . . .*

Round and round the linoleum, me proud, intent, Nora laughing and moving with great buoyancy, wrapping me in her strange gaiety, her smell of whisky, cologne, and sweat. Under the arms her dress is damp, and little drops form along her upper lip, hang in the soft black hairs at the corners of her mouth. She whirls me around in front of my father—causing me to stumble, for I am by no means so swift a pupil as she pretends—and lets me go, breathless.

"Dance with me, Ben."

"I'm the world's worst dancer, Nora, and you know it."

"I certainly never thought so."

"You would now."

She stands in front of him, arms hanging loose and hopeful, her breasts, which a moment ago embarrassed me with their warmth and bulk, rising and falling under her loose flowered dress, her face shining with the exercise, and delight.

"Ben."

My father drops his head and says quietly, "Not me, Nora."

So she can only go and take the record off. "I can drink alone but I can't dance alone," she says. "Unless I am a whole lot crazier than I think I am."

"Nora," says my father, smiling. "You're not crazy."

"Stay for supper."

"Oh, no. We couldn't put you to the trouble."

"It's no trouble. I'd be glad of it."

"And their mother would worry. She'd think I'd turned us over in a ditch."

"Oh, well. Yes."

"We've taken a lot of your time now."

"Time," says Nora bitterly. "Will you come by ever again?"

"I will if I can," says my father.

"Bring the children. Bring your wife."

"Yes, I will," says my father. "I will if I can."

When she follows us to the car he says, "You come to see us too, Nora. We're right on Grove Street, left-hand side going in, that's north, and two doors this side—east—of Baker Street."

Nora does not repeat these directions. She stands close to the car in her soft, brilliant dress. She touches the fender, making an unintelligible mark in the dust there.

On the way home my father does not buy any ice cream or pop, but he does go into a country store and get a package of licorice, which he shares with us. She digs with the wrong foot, I think, and the words seem sad to me as never before, dark, perverse. My father does not say anything to me about not mentioning things at home, but I know, just from the thoughtfulness, the pause when he passes the licorice, that there are things not to be mentioned. The whisky, maybe the dancing. No worry about my brother, he does not notice enough. At most he might remember the blind lady, the picture of Mary.

"Sing," my brother commands my father, but my father says gravely, "I don't know, I seem to be fresh out of songs. You watch the road and let me know if you see any rabbits."

So my father drives and my brother watches the road for rabbits and I feel my father's life flowing back from our car in the last of the afternoon, darkening and turning strange, like a landscape that has an enchantment on it, making it kindly, ordinary and familiar while you are looking at it, but changing it, once your back is turned, into something you will never know, with all kinds of weathers, and distances you cannot imagine.

When we get closer to Tuppertown the sky becomes gently overcast, as always, nearly always, on summer evenings by the Lake.

✍ Dance of the Happy Shades ✍

MISS MARSALLES IS having another party. (Out of musical integrity, or her heart's bold yearning for festivity, she never calls it a recital.) My mother is not an inventive or convincing liar, and the excuses which occur to her are obviously second-rate. The painters are coming. Friends from Ottawa. Poor Carrie is having her tonsils out. In the end all she can say is: Oh, but won't all that be too much trouble, *now? Now* being weighted with several troublesome meanings; you may take your choice. Now that Miss Marsalles has moved from the brick-and-frame bungalow on Bank Street, where the last three parties have been rather squashed, to an even smaller place—if she has described it correctly—on Bala Street. (Bala Street, where is that?) Or: now that Miss Marsalles' older sister is in bed, following a stroke; now that Miss Marsalles herself—as my mother says, we must face these things—is simply getting *too old.*

Now? asks Miss Marsalles, stung, pretending mystification, or perhaps for that matter really feeling it. And she asks how her June party could ever be too much trouble, at any time, in any place? It is the only entertainment she ever gives anymore (so far as my mother knows it is the only entertainment she ever has given, but Miss Marsalles' light old voice, undismayed, indefatigably social, supplies the ghosts of tea parties, private dances, At Homes, mammoth Family Dinners). She would suffer, she says, as much disappointment as the children, if she were to give it up. Considerably more, says my mother to herself, but of course she cannot say it aloud; she turns her face from the telephone with that look of irritation—as if she had seen something messy which she was unable to clean up—which is her private expression of pity. And she promises to come; weak schemes for getting out of it will occur to her during the next two weeks, but she knows she will be there.

She phones up Marg French, who like herself is an old pupil of Miss Marsalles and who has been having lessons for her twins, and they commiserate for a while and promise to go together and buck each other up. They remember the year before last when it rained and the little hall was full of raincoats piled on top of each other because there was no place to hang them up, and the umbrellas dripped puddles on the dark floor. The little girls' dresses were crushed because of the way they all had to squeeze together, and the living-room windows would not open. Last year a child had a nosebleed.

"Of course that was not Miss Marsalles' fault."

They giggle despairingly. "No. But things like that did not use to happen."

And that is true; that is the whole thing. There is a feeling that can hardly be put into words about Miss Marsalles' parties; things are getting out of hand, anything may happen. There is even a moment, driving in to such a party, when the question occurs: will anybody else be there? For one of the most disconcerting things about the last two or three parties has been the widening gap in the ranks of the regulars, the old pupils whose children seem to be the only new pupils Miss Marsalles ever has. Every June reveals some new and surely significant dropping-out. Mary Lambert's girl no longer takes; neither does Joan Crimble's. What does this mean? think my mother and Marg French, women who have moved to the suburbs and are plagued sometimes by a feeling that they have fallen behind, that their instincts for doing the right thing have become confused. Piano lessons are not so important now as they once were; everybody knows that. Dancing is believed to be more favorable to the development of the whole child—and the children, at least the girls, don't seem to mind it as much. But how are you to explain that to Miss Marsalles, who says, "All children need music. All children love music in their hearts"? It is one of Miss Marsalles' indestructible beliefs that she can see into children's hearts, and she finds there a treasury of good intentions and a natural love of all good things.

The deceits which her spinster's sentimentality has practiced on her original good judgment are legendary and colossal; she has this way of speaking of children's hearts as if they were something holy; it is hard for a parent to know what to say.

In the old days, when my sister Winifred took lessons, the address was in Rosedale; that was where it had always been. A narrow house, built of soot-and-raspberry-colored brick, grim little ornamental balconies curving out from the second-floor windows, no towers anywhere but somehow a turreted effect; dark, pretentious, poetically ugly—the family home. And in Rosedale the annual party did not go off too badly. There was always an awkward little space before the sandwiches, because the woman they had in the kitchen was not used to parties and rather slow, but the sandwiches when they did appear were always very good: chicken, asparagus rolls, wholesome, familiar things—dressed-up nursery food. The performances on the piano were, as usual, nervous and choppy or sullen and spiritless, with the occasional surprise and interest of a lively disaster. It will be understood that Miss Marsalles' idealistic view of children, her tender- or simple-mindedness in that regard, made her almost useless as a teacher; she was unable to criticize except in the most delicate and apologetic way and her praises were unforgivably dishonest; it took an unusually conscientious pupil to come through with anything like a creditable performance.

But on the whole the affair in those days had solidity, it had tradition; in its own serenely out-of-date way it had style. Everything was always as expected; Miss Marsalles herself, waiting in the entrance hall with the tiled floor and the dark, church-vestry smell, wearing rouge, an antique hairdo adopted only on this occasion, and a floor-length dress of plum and pinkish splotches that might have been made out of old upholstery material, startled no one but the youngest children. Even the shadow behind her of another Miss Marsalles, slightly older, larger, grimmer, whose existence was always forgotten from one June to the next, was not discomfiting—though it was surely an arresting fact that there should be not one but two faces like that in the world, both long, gravel-colored, kindly, and grotesque, with enormous noses and tiny, red, sweet-tempered and short-sighted eyes. It must finally have come to seem like a piece of luck to them to be so ugly, a protection against life to be marked in so many ways, *impossible*, for they were gay as invulnerable and childish people are; they appeared sexless, wild, and gentle creatures, bizarre yet domestic, living in their house in Rosedale outside the complications of time.

In the room where the mothers sat, some on hard sofas, some on folding chairs, to hear the children play "The Gypsy Song," "The Harmonious Blacksmith," and the "Turkish March," there was a picture of Mary, Queen of Scots, in velvet, with a silk veil, in front of Holyrood Palace. There were brown misty pictures of historical battles, also the Harvard Classics, iron firedogs, and a bronze Pegasus. None of the mothers smoked, nor were ashtrays provided. It was the same room, exactly the same room, in which they had performed themselves; a room whose dim impersonal style (the flossy bunch of peonies and spirea dropping petals on the piano was Miss Marsalles' own touch, and not entirely happy) was at the same time uncomfortable and reassuring. Here they found themselves year after year—a group of busy, youngish women who had eased their cars impatiently through the archaic streets of Rosedale, who had complained for a week previously about the time lost, the fuss over the children's dresses, and, above all, the boredom, but who were drawn together by a rather implausible allegiance—not so much to Miss Marsalles as to the ceremonies of their childhood, to a more exacting pattern of life which had been breaking apart even then but which survived, and unaccountably still survived, in Miss Marsalles' living room. The little girls in dresses with skirts as stiff as bells moved with a natural awareness of ceremony against the dark walls of books, and their mothers' faces wore the dull, not unpleasant look of acquiescence, the touch of absurd and slightly artificial nostalgia which would carry them through any lengthy family ritual. They exchanged smiles which showed no lack of good manners, and yet expressed a familiar, humorous amazement at the sameness of things, even the selections played on the piano and the fillings of the sandwiches; so they acknowledged the incredible, the wholly unrealistic persistence of Miss Marsalles and her sister and their life.

After the piano-playing came a little ceremony which always caused some embarrassment. Before the children were allowed to escape to the garden—very narrow, a town garden, but still a garden, with hedges, shade, a border of yellow lilies—where a long table was covered with crêpe paper in infants' colors of pink and blue, and the woman from the kitchen set out plates of sandwiches, ice cream, prettily tinted and tasteless sherbet, they were compelled to accept, one by one, a year's-end gift, all wrapped and tied with ribbon, from Miss Marsalles. Except among the most naive new pupils this gift caused no excitement of anticipation. It was apt to be a book, and the question was, where did she find such books? They were of the vintage found in old Sunday-school libraries, in attics and the basements of secondhand stores, but they were all stiff-backed, unread, brand new. *Northern Lakes and Rivers, Knowing the Birds, More Tales by Grey Owl, Little Mission Friends.* She also gave pictures: "Cupid Awake and Cupid Asleep," "After the Bath," "The Little Vigilantes"; most of these seemed to feature that tender childish nudity which our sophisticated prudery found most ridiculous and disgusting. Even the boxed games she gave us proved to be insipid and unplayable—full of complicated rules which allowed everybody to win.

The embarrassment the mothers felt at this time was due not so much to the presents themselves as to a strong doubt whether Miss Marsalles could afford them; it did not help to remember that her fees had gone up only once in ten years (and even when that happened, two or three mothers had quit). They always ended up by saying that she must have other resources. It was obvious—otherwise she would not be living in this house. And then her sister taught—or did not teach any-more; she was retired but she gave private lessons, it was believed, in French and German. They must have enough, between them. If you are a Miss Marsalles your wants are simple and it does not cost a great deal to live.

But after the house in Rosedale was gone, after it had given way to the bungalow on Bank Street, these conversations about Miss Marsalles' means did not take place; this aspect of Miss Marsalles' life had passed into that region of painful subjects which it is crude and unmannerly to discuss.

"I will die if it rains," my mother says. "I will die of depression at this affair if it rains." But the day of the party it does not rain and in fact the weather is very hot. It is a hot gritty summer day as we drive down into the city and get lost, looking for Bala Street.

When we find it, it gives the impression of being better than we expected, but that is mostly because it has a row of trees, and the other streets we have been driving through, along the railway embankment, have been unshaded and slatternly. The houses here are of the sort that are divided in half, with a sloping wooden partition in the middle of the front porch; they have two wooden steps and a dirt yard. Apparently it is in one of these half-houses that Miss Marsalles lives. They are red brick, with the front door and the window trim and the porches painted cream, gray, oily-green, and yellow. They are neat, kept-up. The front part of the house next to the one where Miss Marsalles lives has been turned into a little store; it has a sign that says: GROCERIES AND CONFECTIONERY.

The door is standing open. Miss Marsalles is wedged between the door, the coatrack, and the stairs; there is barely room to get past her into the living room, and it would be impossible, the way things are now, for anyone to get from the living room upstairs. Miss Marsalles is wearing her rouge, her hairdo, and her brocaded dress, which it is difficult not to tramp on. In this full light she looks like a character in a masquerade, like the feverish, fancied-up courtesan of an unpleasant Puritan imagination. But the fever is only her rouge; her eyes, when we get close enough to see them, are the same as ever, red-rimmed and merry and without apprehension. My mother and I are kissed—I am greeted, as always, as if I were around five years old—and we get past. It seemed to me that Miss Marsalles was looking beyond us as she kissed us; she was looking up the street for someone who has not yet arrived.

The house has a living room and a dining room, with the oak doors pushed back between them. They are small rooms. Mary, Queen of Scots, hangs tremendous on the wall. There is no fireplace so the iron firedogs are not there, but the piano is, and even a bouquet of peonies and spirea from goodness knows what garden. Since it is so small the living room looks crowded, but there are not a dozen people in it, including children. My mother speaks to people and smiles and sits down. She says to me, Marg French is not here yet, could she have got lost too?

The woman sitting beside us is not familiar. She is middle-aged and wears a dress of shot taffeta with rhinestone clips; it smells of the cleaners. She introduces herself as Mrs. Clegg, Miss Marsalles' neighbor in the other half of the house. Miss Marsalles has asked her if she would like to hear the children play, and she thought it would be a treat; she is fond of music in any form.

My mother, very pleasant but looking a little uncomfortable, asks about Miss Marsalles' sister; is she upstairs?

"Oh, yes, she's upstairs. She's not herself though, poor thing."

That is too bad, my mother says.

"Yes, it's a shame. I give her something to put her to sleep for the afternoon. She lost her powers of speech, you know. Her powers of control generally, she lost." My mother is warned by a certain luxurious lowering of the voice that more lengthy and intimate details may follow and she says quickly again that it is too bad.

"I come in and look after her when the other one goes out on her lessons."

"That's very kind of you. I'm sure she appreciates it."

"Oh, well, I feel kind of sorry for a couple of old ladies like them. They're a couple of babies, the pair."

My mother murmurs something in reply but she is not looking at Mrs. Clegg, at her brick-red healthy face or the—to me—amazing gaps in her teeth. She is staring past her into the dining room with fairly well controlled dismay.

What she sees there is the table spread, all ready for the

party feast; nothing is lacking. The plates of sandwiches are set out, as they must have been for several hours now; you can see how the ones on top are beginning to curl very slightly at the edges. Flies buzz over the table, settle on the sandwiches, and crawl comfortably across the plates of little iced cakes brought from the bakery. The cut-glass bowl, sitting as usual in the center of the table, is full of purple punch, without ice apparently and going flat.

"I tried to tell her not to put it all out ahead of time," Mrs. Clegg whispers, smiling delightedly, as if she were talking about the whims and errors of some headstrong child. "You know she was up at five o'clock this morning making sandwiches. I don't know what things are going to taste like. Afraid she wouldn't be ready, I guess. Afraid she'd forget something. They hate to forget."

"Food shouldn't be left out in the hot weather," my mother says.

"Oh, well, I guess it won't poison us for once. I was only thinking what a shame to have the sandwiches dry up. And when she put the ginger ale in the punch at noon I had to laugh. But what a waste."

My mother shifts and rearranges her voile skirt, as if she has suddenly become aware of the impropriety, the hideousness even, of discussing a hostess's arrangements in this way in her own living room. "Marg French isn't here," she says to me, in a hardening voice. "She did say she was coming."

"I am the oldest girl here," I say with disgust.

"Shh. That means you can play last. Well. It won't be a very long program this year, will it?"

Mrs. Clegg leans across us, letting loose a cloud of warm unfresh odor from between her breasts. "I'm going to see if she's got the fridge turned up high enough for the ice cream. She'd feel awful if it was all to melt."

My mother goes across the room and speaks to a woman she knows and I can tell that she is saying, Marg French *said* she was *coming*. The women's faces in the room, made up some time before, have begun to show the effects of heat and a fairly general uneasiness. They ask each other when it will begin.

Surely very soon now; nobody has arrived for at least a quarter of an hour. How mean of people not to come, they say. Yet in this heat, and the heat is particularly dreadful down here, it must be the worst place in the city—well you can almost see their point. I look around and calculate that there is no one in the room within a year of my age.

The little children begin to play. Miss Marsalles and Mrs. Clegg applaud with enthusiasm; the mothers clap two or three times each, with relief. My mother seems unable, although she makes a great effort, to take her eyes off the dining-room table and the complacent journeys of the marauding flies. Finally she achieves a dreamy, distant look, with her eyes focussed somewhere above the punch bowl, which makes it possible for her to keep her head turned in that direction and yet does not in any positive sense give her away. Miss Marsalles as well has trouble keeping her eyes on the performers; she keeps looking towards the door. Does she expect that even now some of the unexplained absentees may turn up? There are far more than half a dozen presents in the inevitable box beside the piano, wrapped in white paper and tied with silver ribbon—not real ribbon, but the cheap kind that splits and shreds.

It is while I am at the piano, playing the minuet from *Berenice*, that the final arrival, unlooked-for by anybody but Miss Marsalles, takes place. It must seem at first that there has been some mistake. Out of the corner of my eye I see a whole procession of children, eight or ten in all, with a red-haired woman in something like a uniform, mounting the front step. They look like a group of children from a private school on an excursion of some kind (there is that drabness and sameness about their clothes) but their progress is too scrambling and disorderly for that. Or this is the impression I have; I cannot really look. Is it the wrong house, are they really on their way to the doctor for shots, or to Vacation Bible Classes? No, Miss Marsalles has got up with a happy whisper of apology; she has gone to meet them. Behind my back there is a sound of people squeezing together, of folding chairs being opened, there is an inappropriate, curiously unplaceable giggle.

And above or behind all this cautious flurry of arrival there is a peculiarly concentrated silence. Something has happened, something unforeseen, perhaps something disastrous; you can feel such things behind your back. I go on playing. I fill the first harsh silence with my own particularly dogged and lumpy interpretation of Handel. When I get up off the piano bench I almost fall over some of the new children who are sitting on the floor.

One of them, a boy nine or ten years old, is going to follow me. Miss Marsalles takes his hand and smiles at him and there is no twitch of his hand, no embarrassed movement of her head to disown this smile. How peculiar; and a boy too. He turns his head towards her as he sits down; she speaks to him encouragingly. But my attention has been caught by his profile as he looks up at her—the heavy, unfinished features, the abnormally small and slanting eyes. I look at the children seated on the floor and I see the same profile repeated two or three times; I see another boy with a very large head and fair shaved hair, fine as a baby's; there are other children whose features are regular and unexceptional, marked only by an infantile openness and calm. The boys are dressed in white shirts and short gray pants and the girls wear dresses of gray-green cotton with red buttons and sashes.

"Sometimes that kind is quite musical," says Mrs. Clegg.

"Who are they?" my mother whispers, surely not aware of how upset she sounds.

"They're from that class she has out at the Greenhill School. They're nice little things and some of them quite musical but of course they're not all there."

My mother nods distractedly; she looks around the room and meets the trapped, alerted eyes of the other women, but no decision is reached. There is nothing to be done. These children are going to play. Their playing is no worse—not much worse—than ours, but they seem to go slowly, and then there is nowhere to look. For it is a matter of politeness surely not to look closely at such children, and yet where else can you look during a piano performance but at the performer? There is an atmosphere in the room of some freakish inescapable dream. My mother and the others are almost audible saying to themselves: *No, I know it is not right to be repelled by such children and I am not repelled, but nobody told me I was going to come here to listen to a procession of little—little idiots for that's what they are*—WHAT KIND OF A PARTY IS THIS? Their applause, however, has increased, becoming brisk, let-us-at-least-get-this-over-with. But the program shows no signs of being over.

Miss Marsalles says each child's name as if it were a cause for celebration. Now she says, "Dolores Boyle!" A girl as big as I am, a long-legged, rather thin and plaintive-looking girl with blond, almost white, hair, uncoils herself and gets up off the floor. She sits down on the bench and after shifting around a bit and pushing her long hair back behind her ears she begins to play.

We are accustomed to notice performances at Miss Marsalles' parties, but it cannot be said that anyone has ever expected music. Yet this time the music establishes itself so effortlessly, with so little demand for attention, that we are hardly even surprised. What she plays is not familiar. It is something fragile, courtly, and gay, that carries with it the freedom of a great unemotional happiness. And all that this girl does—but this is something you would not think could ever be done—is to play it so that this can be felt, all this can be felt, even in Miss Marsalles' living room on Bala Street on a preposterous afternoon. The children are all quiet, the ones from Greenhill School and the rest. The mothers sit, caught with a look of protest on their faces, a more profound anxiety than before, as if reminded of something that they had forgotten they had forgotten; the white-haired girl sits ungracefully at the piano with her head hanging down, and the music is carried through the open door and the windows to the cindery summer street.

Miss Marsalles sits beside the piano and smiles at everybody in her usual way. Her smile is not triumphant, or modest. She does not look like a magician who is watching people's faces to see the effect of a rather original revelation—nothing like that. You would think, now that at the very end of her life she has found someone whom she can teach—whom she must teach—to play the piano, she would light up with the importance of this discovery. But it seems that the girl's playing like this is something she always expected, and she finds it natural and satisfying; people who believe in miracles do not make much fuss when they actually encounter one. Nor does it seem that she regards this girl with any more wonder than the other children from Greenhill School, who love her, or the rest of us, who do not. To her no gift is unexpected, no celebration will come as a surprise.

The girl is finished. The music is in the room and then it is gone and naturally enough no one knows what to say. For the moment she is finished it is plain that she is just the same as before, a girl from Greenhill School. Yet the music was not imaginary. The facts are not to be reconciled. And so after a few minutes the performance begins to seem, in spite of its innocence, like a trick—a very successful and diverting one, of course, but perhaps—how can it be said?—perhaps not altogether *in good taste*. For the girl's ability, which is undeniable but after all useless, out of place, is not really something that anybody wants to talk about. To Miss Marsalles such a thing is acceptable, but to other people, people who live in the world, it is not. Never mind, they must say something and so they speak gratefully of the music itself, saying how lovely, what a beautiful piece, what is it called?

"The Dance of the Happy Shades," says Miss Marsalles. *Danse des ombres heureuses*, she says, which leaves nobody any the wiser.

But then driving home, driving out of the hot red-brick streets and out of the city and leaving Miss Marsalles and her no longer possible parties behind, quite certainly forever, why is it that we are unable to say—as we must have expected to say— Poor Miss Marsalles? It is the Dance of the Happy Shades that prevents us, it is that one communiqué from the other country where she lives.

ဢ Postcard ဢ

YESTERDAY AFTERNOON, yesterday, I was going along the street to the Post Office, thinking how sick I was of snow, sore throats, the whole dragged-out tail end of winter, and I wished I could pack off to Florida, like Clare. It was Wednesday afternoon, my half-day. I work in King's Department Store, which is nothing but a ready-to-wear and dry goods, in spite of the name. They used to have groceries, but I can just barely recall that. Momma used to take me in and set me on the high stool and old Mr. King would give me a handful of raisins and say, I only give them to the pretty girls. They took the groceries out when he died, old Mr. King, and it isn't even King's Department Store anymore, it belongs to somebody named Kruberg. They never come near it themselves, just send Mr. Hawes in for manager. I run the upstairs, Children's Wear, and put in the Toyland at Christmas. I've been there fourteen years and Hawes doesn't pick on me, knowing I wouldn't take it if he did.

It being Wednesday the wickets in the Post Office were closed, but I had my key. I unlocked our box and took out the Jubilee paper, in Momma's name, the phone bill, and a postcard I very nearly missed. I looked at the picture on it first and it showed me palm trees, a hot blue sky, the front of a motel with a sign out front in the shape of a big husky blond creature, lit up with neon I suppose at night. She was saying *Sleep at my place*—that is, a balloon with those words in it came out of her mouth. I turned it over and read, *I didn't sleep at her place though it was too expensive. Weather could not be better. Mid-seventies. How is the winter treating you in Jubilee? Not bad I hope. Be a good girl. Clare.* The date was ten days back. Well, sometimes postcards are slow, but I bet what happened was he carried this around in his pocket a few days before he remembered to mail it. It was my only card since he left for Florida three weeks ago, and here I was expecting him back in person Friday or Saturday. He made this trip every winter with his sister Porky and her husband, Harold, who lived in Windsor. I had the feeling they didn't like me, but Clare said it was my imagination. Whenever I had to talk to Porky I would make some mistake like saying something was irrevelant to me when I know the word *irrelevant*, and she never let on but I thought about it afterwards and burned. Though I know it serves me right for trying to talk the way I never would normally talk in Jubilee. Trying to impress her because she's a MacQuarrie, after all my lecturing Momma that *we*'re as good as *them*.

I used to say to Clare, write me a *letter* while you're away, and he would say, what do you want me to write about? So I told him to describe the scenery and the people he met, anything would be a pleasure for me to hear about, since I had never been further away from home than Buffalo, for pleasure (I won't count that train trip when I took Momma to Winnipeg to see relatives). But Clare said, I can tell you just as well when I get back. He never did, though. When I saw him again I would say, well, tell me all about your trip, and he would say, what do you want me to tell? That just aggravated me, because how would *I* know?

I saw Momma waiting for me, watching through the little window in the front door. She opened the door when I turned in our walk and called out, "Watch yourself, it's slippery. The milkman nearly took a header this morning."

"There's days when I think I wouldn't mind breaking a leg," I said, and she said, "Don't *say* things like that, it's just asking for punishment."

"Clare sent you a postcard," I said.

"Oh, he did not!" She turned it over and said, "Addressed to you, just as I thought." But she was smiling away. "I don't care for the picture he picked but maybe you don't get much choice down there."

Clare was probably a favorite with old ladies from the time he could walk. To them he was still a nice fat boy, so mannerly, not stuck-up in spite of being a MacQuarrie, and with a way of teasing that perked them up and turned them pink. They had a dozen games going, Momma and Clare, that I could never keep up with. One was him knocking at the door and saying something like, "Good-evening, ma'am, I just wondered if I could interest you in a course in body development I'm selling to put myself through college." And Momma would swallow and put on a stern face and say, "Look here, young man, do I look like I need a course in body development?" Or he would look doleful and say, "Ma'am, I'm here because I'm concerned about your soul." Momma would roar laughing. "You be concerned about your own," she said, and fed him chicken dumplings and lemon-meringue pie, all his favorites. He told her jokes at the table I never thought she'd listen to. "Did you hear about this old gentleman married a young wife and he went to the doctor? Doctor, he says, I'm having a bit of trouble—" "Stop it," Momma said—but she waited till he was through—"you are just embarrassing Helen Louise." I have got rid of the Louise on the end of my name everywhere but at home. Clare picked it up from Momma and I told him I didn't care for it but he went right on. Sometimes I felt like their child, sitting between him and Momma with both of them joking and enjoying their food and telling me I smoked too much and if I didn't straighten up I'd get permanent round shoulders. Clare was—is—twelve years older than I am and I don't ever remember him except as a grown-up man.

I used to see him on the street and he seemed old to me then, at least old the way almost everybody grown-up did. He is one of those people who look older than they are when they're young and younger than they are when they're old. He was always around the Queen's Hotel. Being a MacQuarrie he never had to work too hard and he had a little office and did some work as a Notary Public and a bit of insurance and real estate. He still has the same place, and the front window is always bleary and dusty and there's a light burning in the back, winter and summer, where a lady about eighty years old, Miss Maitland, does his typing or whatever he gives her to do. If he's not in the Queen's Hotel he has one or two of his friends sitting around the space heater doing a little cardplaying, a little quiet drinking, mostly just talking. There's a certain kind of men in Jubilee and I guess every small town that you might call public men. I don't mean public *figures*, important enough to run for Parliament or even for mayor (though Clare could do that if he wanted to be serious), just men who are always around on the main street and you get to know their faces. Clare and those friends of his are like that.

"He down there with his sister?" Momma said, as if I hadn't told her. A lot of my conversations with Momma are replays. "What is that name they call her?"

"Porky," I said.

"Yes, I remember thinking, That's some name for a grown woman. And I remember her being baptized and her name was Isabelle. Way back before I was married, I was still singing in the choir. They had one of those long, fangle-dangle christening robes on her, you know them." Momma had a soft spot for Clare but not for the MacQuarrie family. She thought they were being stuck-up when they just breathed. I remember a year or two ago, us going past their place, and she said something about being careful not to step on the grass of the *Mansion*, and I told her, "Momma, in a few years' time I am going to be living here, this is going to be *my house*, so you better stop calling it the Mansion in that tone of voice." She and I both looked up at the house with all its dark green awnings decorated with big white Old English *M*'s, and all the verandas and the stained-glass window set in the side wall, like in a church. No sign of life, but upstairs old Mrs. MacQuarrie was lying, and is still, paralyzed down one side and not able to speak, Willa Montgomery tending her by day and Clare by night. Strange voices in the house upset her, and every time Clare took me in we could only whisper so she wouldn't hear me and throw some kind of paralytic fit. After her long look Momma said, "It's a funny thing but I can't imagine your name MacQuarrie."

"I thought you were so fond of Clare."

"Well I am, but I just think of him coming to get you

Saturday night, him coming to dinner Sunday night, I don't think of you and him married."

"You wait and see what happens when the old lady passes on."

"Is that what he told you?"

"It's understood."

"Well imagine," Momma said.

"You don't need to act like he's doing me a favor because I can tell you there are plenty of people would consider it the other way round."

"Can't I open my mouth without you taking offense?" said Momma mildly.

Clare and I used to slip in the side door on Saturday nights and make coffee and something to eat in the high, old-fashioned kitchen, being as quiet and sneaky about it as two kids after school. Then we'd tiptoe up the back stairs to Clare's room and turn on the television so she'd think he was by himself, watching that. If she called him I'd lie alone in the big bed watching the program or looking at the old pictures on the wall—him on the high-school hockey team playing goalie, Porky in her graduation outfit, him and Porky and friends I didn't know on holidays. If she kept him a long time and I got bored I would get downstairs under cover of the television and have more coffee. (I never drank anything stronger, left that to Clare.) With just the kitchen light to see by I'd go into the dining room and pull out the drawers and look at her linen and open the china cabinet and the silver chest and feel like a thief. But I'd think, Why shouldn't I have the enjoyment of this and the name MacQuarrie since I wouldn't have to do anything I'm not doing anyway? Clare said, "Marry me," soon after we started going out together and I said, "Don't bother me, I don't want to think about getting married," and he quit. When I brought it up myself, these years later, he seemed pleased. He said, "Well, there's not many old buffalos like me hear a pretty girl like you say she wants to marry them." I thought, Wait till I get married and go into King's Department Store and send Hawes scurrying around waiting on me, the old horse's neck. Wouldn't I like to give him a bad time, but I'd restrain myself, out of good taste.

"I'm going to take that postcard now and put it in my box," I said to Momma. "And I can't think of a better way for us to spend this afternoon than for us both to take naps." I went upstairs and put on my dressing gown (Chinese-embroidered, and Clare's present). I creamed my face and got the box I keep postcards and letters and other mementos in, and I put it with the Florida postcards from other years and some from Banff and Jasper and the Grand Canyon and Yellowstone Park. Then just idling away the time I looked at my school pictures and report cards and the program for *H.M.S. Pinafore*, put on by the high school, in which I was the heroine, what's-her-name, the captain's daughter. I remember Clare meeting me on the street and congratulating me on my singing and how pretty I looked and me flirting with him a bit just because he seemed so old and safe and I would as soon flirt as turn around, I was so pleased with myself. Wouldn't I have been surprised if I had seen all of what was going to happen? I hadn't even met Ted Forgie then.

I knew his letter just from looking at the outside, and I never read it anymore, but just out of curiosity I opened it up and started off. *I usually hate to write a typewritten letter because it lacks the personal touch but I am so worn out tonight with all the unfamiliar pressures here that I hope you will forgive me.* Typewritten or not, it used to be that just looking at that letter I would get a feeling of love, if that is what you want to call it, strong enough to pretty near crumple me up and knock me over. Ted Forgie was an announcer at the Jubilee radio station for six months, around the time I was finishing high school. Momma said he was too old for me—she never said that about Clare—but all he was was twenty-four. He had spent two years in a san with t.b. and that had made him old for his years. We used to go up on Sullivan's Hill and he talked about how he had lived with death staring him in the face and he knew the value of being close to one human being, but all he had found was loneliness. He said he wanted to put his head down in my lap and weep, but all the time what he *was* doing was something else. When he went away I just turned into a sleepwalker. I only woke up in the afternoons when I went to the Post

Office and opened the box with my knees going hollow, to see if I had a letter. And I never did, after that one. Places bothered me. Sullivan's Hill, the radio station, the coffee shop of the Queen's Hotel. I don't know how many hours I spent in that coffee shop, reciting in my head every conversation we ever had and visualizing every look on his face, not really comprehending yet that wishing wasn't going to drag him through that door again. I got friendly with Clare in there. He said I looked like I needed cheering up and he told me some of his stories. I never let on to him what my trouble was but when we started going out I explained to him that friendship was all I could offer. He said he appreciated that and he would bide his time. And he did.

I read the letter all the way through and I thought, not for the first time, Well, reading this letter any fool can see there is not going to be another. *I want you to know how grateful I am for all your sweetness and understanding. Sweetness* was the only word stuck in my mind then, to give me hope. I thought, When Clare and I get married I am just going to throw this letter away. So why not do it now? I tore it across and across and it was easy, like tearing up notes when school is over. Then because I didn't want Momma commenting on what was in my wastepaper basket, I wadded it up and put it in my purse. That being over I lay down on my bed and thought about several things. For instance, if I hadn't been in a stupor over Ted Forgie, would I have taken a different view of Clare? Not likely. If I hadn't been in that stupor I might have never bothered with Clare at all, I'd have gone off and done something different; but no use thinking about that now. The fuss he made at first made me sorry for him. I used to look down at his round balding head and listen to all his groaning and commotion and think, What can I do now except be polite? He didn't expect anything more of me, never expected anything, but just to lie there and let him, and I got used to that. I looked back and thought, Am I a heartless person, just to lie there and let him grab me and love me and moan around my neck and say the things he did, and never say one loving word back to him? I never wanted to be a heartless person and I was never mean to Clare, and I did let him, didn't I, nine times out of ten?

I heard Momma get up from her nap and go and put the kettle on so she could have a cup of tea and read her paper. Then some little time later she gave a yell and I thought somebody had died so I jumped off the bed and ran into the hall, but she was there underneath saying, "Go on back to your nap, I'm sorry I scared you. I made a mistake." I did go back and I heard her using the phone, probably calling one of her old cronies about some news in the paper, and then I guess I fell asleep.

What woke me was a car stopping, somebody getting out and coming up the front walk. I thought, Is it Clare back early? And then, confused and half-asleep, I thought, I already tore up the letter, that's good. But it wasn't his step. Momma opened the door before the bell got a chance to ring and I heard Alma Stonehouse, who teaches at the Jubilee Public School and is my best friend. I went out in the hall and leaned over and called down, "Hey, Alma, are you eating here *again?*" She boards at Bailey's where the food has its ups and downs and when she smells their shepherd's pie she sometimes heads over to our place without an invitation.

Alma started upstairs without taking her coat off, her thin dark face just blazing with excitement, so I knew something had happened. I thought it must have to do with her husband, because they are separated and he writes her terrible letters. She said, "Helen, hi, how are you feeling? Did you just wake up?"

"I heard your car," I said. "I thought for a minute maybe it was Clare but I'm not expecting him for another couple of days."

"Helen. Can you sit down? Come in your room where you can sit down. Are you prepared to get a shock? I wish I wasn't the one had to tell you. Hold yourself steady."

I saw Momma right behind her and I said, "Momma, is this some joke?"

Alma said, "Clare MacQuarrie has gotten married."

"What are you two up to?" I said. "Clare MacQuarrie is in

Florida and I just today got a postcard from him as Momma well knows."

"He got married in Florida. Helen, be calm."

"How could he get married in Florida, he's on his holidays?"

"They're on their way to Jubilee right now and they're going to live here."

"Alma, wherever you heard that it's a lot of garbage. I just had a postcard from him. Momma—"

Then I saw that Momma was looking at me like I was eight years old and had the measles and a temperature of a hundred and five degrees. She was holding the paper and she spread it out for me to read. "It's in there," she said, probably not realizing she was whispering. "It's written up in the *Bugle-Herald*."

"I don't believe it any more than fly," I said, and I started to read and read all the way through as if the names were ones I'd never heard of before, and some of them were. A quiet ceremony in Coral Gables, Florida, uniting in marriage Clare Alexander MacQuarrie, of Jubilee, son of Mrs. James MacQuarrie of this town and the late Mr. James MacQuarrie, prominent local businessman and long-time Member of Parliament, and Mrs. Margaret Thora Leeson, daughter of the late Mr. and Mrs. Clive Tibbutt of Lincoln, Nebraska. Mr. and Mrs. Harold Johnson, sister and brother-in-law of the bridegroom, were the only attendants. The bride wore a sage green dressmaker suit with dark brown accessories and a corsage of bronze orchids. Mrs. Johnson wore a beige suit with black accessories and green orchids. The couple were at present travelling by automobile to their future home in Jubilee.

"Do you still think it's garbage?" Alma said severely.

I said I didn't know.

"Are you feeling all right?"

All right.

Momma said we would all feel better if we went downstairs and had a cup of tea and something to eat, instead of staying cooped up in this little bedroom. It was about suppertime, anyway. So we all trooped down, me still in my dressing gown, and Momma and Alma together prepared the sort of meal you might eat to keep your strength up when there is sickness in the house and you can't really bother too much about food. Cold meat sandwiches and little dishes of different pickles and sliced cheese and date squares. "Smoke a cigarette if you want to," Momma said to me—the first time she ever said *that* in her life. So I did, and Alma did, and Alma said, "I brought some tranquillizers along in my purse, they're not very strong and you're welcome to one or two." I said no thanks, not yet anyway. I said I couldn't seem to take it in yet.

"He goes to Florida every year, right?"

I said yes.

"Well what I think is this, that he's met this woman before—widow or divorcee or whatever she is—and they have been corresponding and planning this all along."

Momma said it was awfully hard to think that of Clare.

"I'm only saying how it looks to me. And she's his sister's friend, I'll bet. The sister engineered it. They were the attendants, the sister and her husband. She wasn't any friend of yours, Helen, I remember you telling me."

"I didn't hardly know her."

"Helen Louise, you told me you and him were just waiting for the old lady to pass on," Momma said. "Isn't that what he said to you? Clare?"

"Using her for an excuse," Alma said briskly.

"Oh, he wouldn't," Momma said. "Oh, it's so hard to understand it—*Clare!*"

"Men are always out for what they can get," Alma said. There was a pause, both of them looking at me. I couldn't tell them anything. I couldn't tell them what I was thinking, which was about the last Saturday night up at his place, before he went away, him naked as a baby pulling my hair across his face and through his teeth and pretending he was going to bite it off. I didn't relish anybody's saliva in my hair but I let him, just warning him that if he did bite it off he would have to pay for me going to the hairdresser's to get it evened. He didn't act that night like anybody that is going off to be *married*.

Momma and Alma went on talking and speculating and I got sleepier and sleepier. I heard Alma say, "Worse things could happen. I had four years of living hell." And Momma say, "He was always the soul of kindness and he doted on that girl." I wondered how I could possibly be so sleepy, this early in the evening and after having a nap in the afternoon. Alma said, "It's very good you're sleepy, it's Nature's way. Nature's way, just like an anesthetic." They both got me upstairs and into bed and I never heard them go down.

I didn't wake up early, either. I got up when I usually did and got my own breakfast. I could hear Momma stirring but I yelled to her to stay put, like any other morning. She called down, "Are you sure you want to go to work? I could phone Mr. Hawes you're sick." I said, "Why should I give any of them the satisfaction?" I did my makeup at the hall mirror without a light and went out and walked the two and a half blocks to King's, not noticing what kind of a morning it was, beyond the fact that it hadn't turned into spring overnight. Inside the store they were waiting, oh, how nice—good morning, Helen, good morning, Helen—such quiet kind hopeful voices waiting to see if I'm going to fall flat on the floor and start having hysterics. Mrs. McCool, Beryl Allen with her engagement ring, Mrs. Kress that got jilted herself twenty-five years ago and then took up with somebody else—Kress—and *he* vanished. What's she looking at me for? Old Hawes chewing his tongue when he smiles. I said good morning perfectly cheerfully and went on upstairs thanking God I have my own washroom and thinking, I bet this will be a big day for Children's Wear. It was too. I never had a morning with so many mothers in to buy a hair-ribbon or a little pair of socks, willing to climb that stairs for it.

I phoned Momma I wouldn't be home at noon. I thought I'd just go over to the Queen's Hotel and have a hamburger, with all the radio people I hardly know. But at a quarter to twelve in comes Alma. "I wouldn't let you eat by yourself *this* day!" So we have to go to the Queen's Hotel together. She was going to make me eat an egg sandwich, not a hamburger, and a glass of milk not Coke, because she said my digestion was probably in a state, but I vetoed that. She waited till we got our food and were settled down to eating before she said, "Well, they're back."

It took a minute for me to know who. "When?" I said.

"Last night around suppertime. Just when I was driving over to your place to break you the news. I might've run into them."

"Who told you?"

"Well, Beechers live next to MacQuarries, don't they?" Mrs. Beecher teaches Grade 4, Alma Grade 3. "Grace saw them. She had already read the paper so she knew who it was."

"What is she like?" I said in spite of myself.

"She's no juvenile, Grace said. His age, anyway. What did I tell you it was his sister's friend? And she won't win any prizes in the looks department. Mind you she's all *right*."

"Is she big or little?" I couldn't stop now. "Dark or fair?"

"She had a hat on so Grace couldn't see the color of her hair but she thought dark. She's a big woman. Grace said she had a rear end on her like a grand piano. Maybe she has money."

"Did Grace say that too?"

"No. I said it. Just speculating."

"Clare doesn't need to marry anybody with money. *He* has money."

"That's by our standards maybe, but not by his."

I kept thinking through the afternoon that Clare would come round, or at least phone me. Then I could start asking him what did he think he had done. I made up in my mind some crazy explanations he might give me, like this poor woman had cancer and only six months to live and she had always been deadly poor (a scrubwoman in his motel) and he wanted to give her a little time of ease. Or that she was blackmailing his brother-in-law about a crooked transaction and he married her to shut her up. But I didn't have time to think up many stories because of the steady stream of customers. Old ladies puffing up the stairs with some story about birthday presents for their grandchildren. Every grandchild in Jubilee must have a birthday in March. They ought to be grateful to me, I thought, haven't I given their day a bit of excitement? Even Alma, she was looking better than she has all winter. I'm not blaming her, I thought, but it's the truth. And who knows, maybe I'd be the same if Don Stonehouse showed up like he threatens to and raped her and left her a mass of purple bruises—his words, not mine—from head to foot. I'd be as sorry as could be, and anything I could do to help her, I'd do, but I might think, Well, awful as it is it's something happening and it's been a long winter.

There was no use even thinking about not going home for supper, that would finish Momma. There she was waiting with a salmon loaf, cabbage and carrot salad with raisins in it, that I like, and Brown Betty. But halfway through this the tears started sliding down over her rouge. "It seems to me like I'm the one ought to do the crying if anybody has to do it," I said. "What's so terrible happened to you?"

"Well I was just so fond of him," she said. "I was that fond of him. At my age there's not too many people that you look forward to them coming all week."

"Well I'm sorry," I said.

"But once a man loses his respect for a girl, he is apt to get tired of her."

"What do you mean by that, Momma?"

"If you don't know am I supposed to tell you?"

"You ought to be ashamed," I said, starting to cry too. "Talking like that to your own daughter." There! And I always thought she didn't know. Never blame Clare, of course, blame me.

"No, I'm not the one that ought to be ashamed," she continued, weeping. "I am an old woman but I know. If a man loses respect for a girl he don't marry her."

"If that was true there wouldn't be hardly one marriage in this town."

"You destroyed your own chances."

"You never said a word of this to me as long as he was coming here and I am not listening to it now," I said, and went upstairs. She didn't come after me. I sat and smoked, hour after hour. I didn't get undressed. I heard her come upstairs, go to bed. Then I went down and watched television for a while, news of car accidents. I put on my coat and went out.

I have a little car Clare gave me a year ago Christmas, a little Morris. I don't use it for work because driving two and a half blocks looks to me silly, and like showing off, though I know people who do it. I went around to the garage and backed it out. This was the first time I had driven it since the Sunday I took Momma to Tuppertown to see Auntie Kay in the nursing home. I use it more in summer.

I looked at my watch and the time surprised me. Twenty after twelve. I felt shaky and weak from sitting so long. I wished now I had one of Alma's pills. I had an idea of just taking off, driving, but I didn't know which direction to go in. I drove around the streets of Jubilee and didn't see another car out but mine. All the houses in darkness, the streets black, the yards pale with the last snow. It seemed to me that in every one of those houses lived people who knew something I didn't. Who understood what had happened and perhaps had known it was going to happen and I was the only one who didn't know.

I drove out Grove Street and on to Minnie Street and saw his house from the back. No lights on there either. I drove around to see it from the front. Did they have to sneak up the stairs and keep the television on? I wondered. No woman with a rear end like a grand piano would settle for that. I bet he took her right up and into the old lady's room and said, "This is the new Mrs. MacQuarrie," and that was that.

I parked the car and rolled down the window. Then without thinking what I was going to do I leaned on the horn and sounded it as long and hard as I could stand.

The sound released me, so I could yell. And I did. "Hey, Clare MacQuarrie, I want to talk to you!"

No answer anywhere. "Clare MacQuarrie!" I shouted up at his dark house. "Clare, come on out!" I sounded the horn again, two, three, I don't know how many times. In between I yelled. I felt as if I was watching myself, way down here, so little, pounding my fist and yelling and leaning on the horn. Carrying on a commotion, doing whatever came into my head. It was enjoyable, in a way. I almost forgot what I was doing it for. I started honking the horn rhythmically and yelling at the same time. "Clare, aren't you ever coming out? Clare MacQuarrie for nuts-in-May, if he don't come we'll pull-him-away—" I was crying as well as yelling, right out in the street, and it didn't bother me one bit.

"Helen, you want to wake everybody up in this whole town?" said Buddy Shields, sticking his head in at the window. He is the night constable and I used to teach him in Sunday school.

"I'm just conducting a shivaree for the newly married couple," I said. "What is the matter with that?"

"I got to tell you to stop that noise."

"I don't feel like stopping."

"Oh yes you do, Helen, you're just a little upset."

"I called and called him and he won't come out," I said. "All I want is him to come out."

"Well you got to be a good girl and stop honking that horn."

"I want him to come out."

"Stop it. Don't honk that horn one more time."

"Will you make him come out?"

"Helen, I can't make a man come out of his own house if he don't want to come."

"I thought you were the Law, Buddy Shields."

"I am but there is a limit to what the Law can do. If you want to see him why don't you come back in the daytime and knock on his door nice the way any lady would do?"

"He is married in case you didn't know."

"Well, Helen, he is married just as much at night as in the daytime."

"Is that supposed to be funny?"

"No it's not, it's supposed to be true. Now why don't you move over and let me drive you home? Lookit the lights on up and down this street. There's Grace Beecher watching us and I can see the Holmses got their windows up. You don't want to give them anything more to talk about, do you?"

"They got nothing to do but talk anyway, they may as well talk about me."

Then Buddy Shields straightened up and moved a little away from the car window and I saw somebody in dark clothes coming across the MacQuarries' lawn and it was Clare. He was not wearing a dressing gown or anything, he was all dressed, in shirt and jacket and trousers. He came right up to the car while I sat there waiting to hear what I would say to him. He had not changed. He was a fat, comfortable, sleepy-faced man. But just his look, his everyday easygoing look, stopped me wanting to cry or yell. I could cry and yell till I was blue in the face and it would not change that look or make him get out of bed and across his yard one little bit faster.

"Helen, go on home," he said, like we had been watching television and so on all evening and now was time to go home and go to bed properly. "Give my love to your momma," he said. "Go on home."

That was all he meant to say. He looked at Buddy and said, "You going to drive her?" and Buddy said yes. I was looking at Clare MacQuarrie and thinking, He is a man that goes his own way. It didn't bother him too much how I was feeling when he did what he did on top of me, and it didn't bother him too much what kind of ruckus I made in the street when he got married. And he was a man who didn't give out explanations, maybe didn't have any. If there was anything he couldn't explain, well, he would just forget about it. Here were all his neighbors watching us, but tomorrow, if he met them on the street, he would tell them a funny story. And what about me? Maybe if he met me on the street one of these days he would just say, "How are you doing, Helen?" and tell me a joke. And if I had really thought about what he was like, Clare Mac-Quarrie, if I had paid attention, I would have started out a lot differently with him and maybe felt differently too, though heaven knows if that would have mattered, in the end.

"Now aren't you sorry you made all this big fuss?" Buddy said, and I slid over on the seat and watched Clare going back to his house, thinking, Yes, that's what I should have done, paid attention. Buddy said, "You're not going to bother him and his wife anymore now, are you, Helen?"

"What?" I said.

"You're not going to bother Clare and his wife anymore? Because now he's married, that's over and done with. And you wake up tomorrow morning, you're going to feel pretty bad over what you done tonight, you won't see how you can go on and face people. But let me tell you things happen all the time, only thing to do is just go along, and remember you're not the only one." It never seemed to occur to him that it was funny for him to be lecturing me, that I used to hear his Bible verses and caught him reading Leviticus on the sly.

"Like last week I'll tell you," he said, easing down Grove Street, in no hurry to get me home and have the lecture ended, "last week we got a call and we had to go out to Dunnock Swamp and there's a car stuck in there. This old farmer was waving a loaded gun and talking about shooting this pair for trespassing if they didn't get off of his property. They'd just been following a wagon track after dark, where any idiot would know you'd get stuck this time of year. You would know both of them if I said their names and you'd know they had no business being in that car together. One is a married lady. And worst is, by this time her husband is wondering why she don't come home from choir practice—both these parties sing in the choir, I won't tell you which one—and he has reported her missing. So we got to get a tractor to haul out the car, and leave *him* there sweating, and quieten down this old farmer, and then take her home separate in broad daylight, crying all the way. That's what I mean by things happening. I saw that man and wife downstreet buying their groceries yesterday, and they didn't look too happy but there they were. So just be a good girl, Helen, and go along like the rest of us and pretty soon we'll see spring."

Oh, Buddy Shields, you can just go on talking, and Clare will tell jokes, and Momma will cry, till she gets over it, but what I'll never understand is why, right now, seeing Clare Mac-Quarrie as an unexplaining man, I felt for the first time that I wanted to reach out my hands and *touch* him.

∽ *Images* ∾

NOW THAT MARY MCQUADE had come, I pretended not to remember her. It seemed the wisest thing to do. She herself said, "If you don't remember me you don't remember much," but let the matter drop, just once adding, "I bet you never went to your grandma's house last summer. I bet you don't remember that either."

It was called, even that summer, my grandma's house, though my grandfather was then still alive. He had withdrawn into one room, the largest front bedroom. It had wooden shutters on the inside of the windows, like the living room and dining room; the other bedrooms had only blinds. Also, the veranda kept out the light so that my grandfather lay in near-darkness all day, with his white hair, now washed and tended and soft as a baby's, and his white nightshirt and pillows, making an island in the room which people approached with diffidence, but resolutely. Mary McQuade in her uniform was the other island in the room, and she sat mostly not moving where the fan, as if it was tired, stirred the air like soup. It must have been too dark to read or knit, supposing she wanted to do those things, and so she merely waited and breathed, making a sound like the fan made, full of old indefinable complaint.

I was so young then I was put to sleep in a crib—not at home but this was what was kept for me at my grandma's house—in a room across the hall. There was no fan there and the dazzle of outdoors—all the flat fields round the house turned, in the sun, to the brilliance of water—made lightning cracks in the drawn-down blinds. Who could sleep? My mother's my grandmother's my aunts' voices wove their ordinary repetitions, on the veranda in the kitchen in the dining room (where with a little brass-handled brush my mother cleaned the white cloth, and the lighting-fixture over the round table hung down unlit flowers of thick, butterscotch glass). All the meals in that house, the cooking, the visiting, the conversation, even someone playing on the piano (it was my youngest aunt, Edith, not married, singing and playing with one hand, *Nita, Juanita, softly falls the southern moon*)—all this life going on. Yet the ceilings of the rooms were very high and under them was a great deal of dim wasted space, and when I lay in my crib too hot to sleep, I could look up and see that emptiness, the stained corners, and feel, without knowing what it was, just what everybody else in the house must have felt—under the sweating heat the fact of death-contained, that little lump of magic ice. And Mary McQuade waiting in her starched white dress, big and gloomy as an iceberg herself, implacable, waiting and breathing. I held her responsible.

So I pretended not to remember her. She had not put on her white uniform, which did not really make her less dangerous but might mean, at least, that the time of her power had not yet come. Out in the daylight, and not dressed in white, she turned out to be freckled all over, everywhere you could see, as if she was sprinkled with oatmeal, and she had a crown of frizzy, glinting, naturally brass-colored hair. Her voice was loud and hoarse, and complaint was her everyday language. "Am I going to have to hang up this wash all by myself?" she shouted at me, in the yard, and I followed her to the clothes-line platform where with a groan she let down the basket of wet clothes. "Hand me them clothespins. One at a time. Hand me them right side up. I shouldn't be out in this wind at all, I've got a bronchial condition." Head hung, like an animal chained to her side, I fed her clothespins. Outdoors, in the cold March air, she lost some of her bulk and her smell. In the house I could always smell her, even in the rooms she seldom entered. What was her smell like? It was like metal and like some dark spice (cloves—she did suffer from toothache) and like the preparation rubbed on my chest when I had a cold. I mentioned it once to my mother, who said, "Don't be silly, *I* don't smell anything." So I never told about the taste, and there was a taste too. It was in all the food Mary McQuade prepared and perhaps in all food eaten in her presence—in my porridge at breakfast and my fried potatoes at noon and the slice of bread and butter and brown sugar she gave me to eat in the yard—something foreign, gritty, depressing. How could my parents not know about it? But for reasons of their own they would pretend. This was something I had not known a year ago.

After she had hung out the wash she had to soak her feet. Her legs came straight up, round as drainpipes, from the steaming basin. One hand on each knee, she bent into the steam and gave grunts of pain and satisfaction.

"Are you a nurse?" I said, greatly daring, though my mother had said she was.

"Yes I am and I wish I wasn't."

"Are you my aunt too?"

"If I was your aunt you would call me Aunt Mary, wouldn't you? Well, you don't, do you? I'm your cousin, I'm your father's cousin. That's why they get me instead of getting an ordinary nurse. I'm a practical nurse. And there is always somebody sick in this family and I got to go to them. I never get a rest."

I doubted this. I doubted that she was asked to come. She came, and cooked what she liked and rearranged things to suit herself, complaining about drafts, and let her power loose in the house. If she had never come, my mother would never have taken to her bed.

My mother's bed was set up in the dining room, to spare Mary McQuade climbing the stairs. My mother's hair was done in two little thin dark braids, her cheeks were sallow, her neck warm and smelling of raisins as it always did, but the rest of her under the covers had changed into some large, fragile, and mysterious object, difficult to move. She spoke of herself gloomily in the third person, saying, "Be careful, don't hurt Mother, don't sit on Mother's legs." Every time she said "Mother" I felt chilled, and a kind of wretchedness and shame spread through me as it did at the name of Jesus. This *Mother* that my own real, warm-necked, irascible, and comforting human mother set up between us was an everlastingly wounded phantom, sorrowing like Him over all the wickedness I did not yet know I would commit.

My mother crocheted squares for an afghan, in all shades of purple. They fell among the bedclothes and she did not care. Once they were finished she forgot about them. She had forgotten all her stories which were about princes in the Tower and a queen getting her head chopped off while a little dog was hiding under her dress and another queen sucking poison out of her husband's wound; and also about her own childhood, a time as legendary to me as any other. Given over to Mary's care, she whimpered childishly, "Mary, I'm dying for you to rub my back." "Mary, could you make me a cup of tea? I feel if I drink any more tea I'm going to bob up to the ceiling, just like a big balloon, but you know it's all I want." Mary laughed shortly. "You," she said, "you're not going to bob up anywhere. Take a derrick to move *you*. Come on now, raise up, you'll be worse before you're better!" She shooed me off the bed and began to pull the sheets about with not very gentle jerks. "You been tiring your momma out? What do you want to bother your momma for on this nice a day?" "I think she's lonesome," my mother said, a weak and insincere defense. "She can be lonesome in the yard just as well as here," said Mary, with her grand, vague, menacing air. "You put your things on, out you go!"

My father too had altered since her coming. When he came in for his meals she was always waiting for him, some joke swelling her up like a bullfrog, making her ferocious-looking and red in the face. She put uncooked white beans in his soup, hard as pebbles, and waited to see if good manners would make him eat them. She stuck something to the bottom of his water glass to look like a fly. She gave him a fork with a prong missing, pretending it was by accident. He threw it at her, and missed, but startled me considerably. My mother and father, eating supper, talked quietly and seriously. But in my father's family even grownups played tricks with rubber worms and beetles, fat aunts were always invited to sit on little rickety chairs, and uncles broke wind in public and said, "Whoa, hold on there!" proud of themselves as if they had whistled a complicated tune. Nobody could ask your age without a rigmarole of teasing. So with Mary McQuade my father returned to family ways, just as he went back to eating heaps of fried potatoes and side meat and thick, floury pies, and drinking tea black and strong as medicine out of a tin pot, saying gratefully, "Mary, you know what it is a man ought to eat!" He followed that up with "Don't you think it's time you got a man of your own to feed?" which earned him, not a fork thrown, but the dishrag.

His teasing of Mary was always about husbands. "I thought up one for you this morning!" he would say. "Now, Mary, I'm not fooling you, you give this some consideration." Her laughter would come out first in little angry puffs and explosions through her shut lips, while her face grew redder than you would have thought possible and her body twitched and rumbled threateningly in its chair. There was no doubt she enjoyed all this, all these preposterous imagined matings, though my mother would certainly have said it was cruel, cruel and indecent, to tease an old maid about men. In my father's family of course it was what she was always teased about, what else was there? And the heavier and coarser and more impossible she became, the more she would be teased. A bad thing in that family was to have them say you were *sensitive*, as they did of my mother. All the aunts and cousins and uncles had grown tremendously hardened to any sort of personal cruelty, reckless, even proud, it seemed, of a failure or deformity that could make for general laughter.

At suppertime it was dark in the house, in spite of the lengthening days. We did not yet have electricity. It came in soon afterwards, maybe the next summer. But at present there was a lamp on the table. In its light my father and Mary McQuade threw gigantic shadows, whose heads wagged clumsily with their talk and laughing. I watched the shadows instead of the people. They said, "What are you dreaming about?" but I was not dreaming; I was trying to understand the danger, to read the signs of invasion.

My father said, "Do you want to come with me and look at the traps?" He had a trapline for muskrats along the river. When he was younger he used to spend days, nights, weeks in the bush, following creeks all up and down Wawanash County, and he trapped not only muskrat then but red fox, wild mink, marten, all animals whose coats are prime in the fall. Muskrat is the only thing you can trap in the spring. Now that he was married and settled down to farming he just kept the one line, and that for only a few years. This may have been the last year he had it.

We went across a field that had been plowed the previous fall. There was a little snow lying in the furrows but it was not real snow, it was a thin crust like frosted glass that I could shatter with my heels. The field went downhill slowly, down to the river flats. The fence was down in some places from the weight of the snow; we could step over it.

My father's boots went ahead. His boots were to me as unique and familiar, as much an index to himself, as his face was. When he had taken them off they stood in a corner of the kitchen, giving off a complicated smell of manure, machine oil, caked black mud, and the ripe and disintegrating material that lined their soles. They were a part of himself, temporarily discarded, waiting. They had an expression that was dogged and uncompromising, even brutal, and I thought of that as part of my father's look, the counterpart of his face, with its readiness for jokes and courtesies. Nor did that brutality surprise me; my father came back to us always, to my mother and me, from places where our judgment could not follow.

For instance, there was a muskrat in the trap. At first I saw it waving at the edge of the water, like something tropical, a dark fern. My father drew it up and the hairs ceased waving, clung together, the fern became a tail with the body of the rat attached to it, sleek and dripping. Its teeth were bared, its eyes wet on top, dead and dull beneath, glinted like washed pebbles. My father shook it and whirled it around, making a little rain of icy river water. "This is a good old rat," he said. "This is a big old king rat. Look at his tail!" Then perhaps thinking that I was worried, or perhaps only wanting to show me the charm of simple, perfect mechanical devices, he lifted the trap out of the water and explained to me how it worked, dragging the rat's head under at once and mercifully drowning him. I did not understand or care. I only wanted, but did not dare, to touch the stiff, soaked body, a fact of death.

My father baited the trap again using some pieces of yellow, winter-wrinkled apple. He put the rat's body in a dark sack which he carried slung over his shoulder, like a peddler in a picture. When he cut the apple, I had seen the skinning knife, its slim bright blade.

Then we went along the river, the Wawanash River, which was high, running full, silver in the middle where the sun hit it and where it arrowed in to its swiftest motion. That is the current, I thought, and I pictured the current as something separate from the water, just as the wind was separate from the air and had its own invading shape. The banks were steep and slippery and lined with willow bushes, still bare and bent over and looking weak as grass. The noise the river made was not loud but deep, and seemed to come from away down in the middle of it, some hidden place where the water issued with a roar from underground.

The river curved, I lost my sense of direction. In the traps we found more rats, released them, shook them and hid them in the sack, replaced the bait. My face, my hands, my feet grew cold, but I did not mention it. I could not, to my father. And he never told me to be careful, to stay away from the edge of the water; he took it for granted that I would have sense enough not to fall in. I never asked how far we were going, or if the trapline would ever end. After a while there was a bush behind us, the afternoon darkened. It did not occur to me, not till long afterwards, that this was the same bush you could see from our yard, a fan-shaped hill rising up in the middle of it with bare trees in wintertime that looked like bony little twigs against the sky.

Now the bank, instead of willows, grew thick bushes higher than my head. I stayed on the path, about halfway up the bank, while my father went down to the water. When he bent over the trap, I could no longer see him. I looked around slowly and saw something else. Further along, and higher up the bank, a man was making his way down. He made no noise coming through the bushes and moved easily, as if he followed a path I could not see. At first I could just see his head and the upper part of his body. He was dark, with a high bald forehead, hair long behind the ears, deep vertical creases in his cheeks. When the bushes thinned I could see the rest of him, his long clever legs, thinness, drab camouflaging clothes, and what he carried in his hand, gleaming where the sun caught it—a little axe, or hatchet.

I never moved to warn or call my father. The man crossed my path somewhere ahead, continuing down to the river. People say they have been paralyzed by fear, but I was transfixed, as if struck by lightning, and what hit me did not feel like fear so much as recognition. I was not surprised. This is the sight that does not surprise you, the thing you have always known was there that comes so naturally, moving delicately and contentedly and in no hurry, as if it was made, in the first place, from a wish of yours, a hope of something final, terrifying. All my life I had known there was a man like this and he was behind doors, around the corner at the dark end of a hall. So now I saw him and just waited, like a child in an old negative, electrified against the dark noon sky, with blazing hair and burned-out Orphan Annie eyes. The man slipped down through the bushes to my father. And I never thought, or even hoped for, anything but the worst.

My father did not know. When he straightened up, the man was not three feet away from him and hid him from me. I heard my father's voice come out, after a moment's delay, quiet and neighborly.

"Hello, Joe. Well. Joe. I haven't seen you in a long time."

The man did not say a word, but edged around my father giving him a close look. "Joe, you know me," my father told him. "Ben Jordan. I been out looking at my traps. There's a lot of good rats in the river this year, Joe."

The man gave a quick not-trusting look at the trap my father had baited.

"You ought to set a line out yourself."

No answer. The man took his hatchet and chopped lightly at the air.

"Too late this year, though. The river is already started to go down."

"Ben Jordan," the man said with a great splurt, a costly effort, like somebody leaping over a stutter.

"I thought you'd recognize me, Joe."

"I never knew it was you, Ben. I thought it was one them Silases."

"Well I been telling you it was me."

"They's down here all the time choppin' my trees and pullin' down my fences. You know they burned me out, Ben. It was them done it."

"I heard about that," my father said.

"I didn't know it was you, Ben. I never knew it was you. I got this axe, I just take it along with me to give them a little scare. I wouldn't of if I'd known it was you. You come on up and see where I'm living now."

My father called me. "I got my young one out following me today."

"Well you and her both come up and get warm."

We followed this man, who still carried and carelessly swung his hatchet, up the slope and into the bush. The trees chilled the air, and underneath them was real snow, left over from winter, a foot, two feet deep. The tree trunks had rings around them, a curious dark space like the warmth you make with your breath.

We came out in a field of dead grass, and took a track across it to another, wider field where there was something sticking out of the ground. It was a roof, slanting one way, not peaked, and out of the roof came a pipe with a cap on it, smoke blowing out. We went down the sort of steps that lead to a cellar, and that was what it was—a cellar with a roof on. My father said, "Looks like you fixed it up all right for yourself, Joe."

"It's warm. Being down in the ground the way it is, naturally it's warm. I thought, What is the sense of building a house up again, they burned it down once, they'll burn it down again. What do I need a house for anyways? I got all the room I need here, I fixed it up comfortable." He opened the door at the bottom of the steps. "Mind your head here. I don't say everybody should live in a hole in the ground, Ben. Though animals do it, and what an animal does, by and large it makes sense. But if you're married, that's another story." He laughed. "Me, I don't plan on getting married."

It was not completely dark. There were the old cellar windows, letting in a little grimy light. The man lit a coal-oil lamp, though, and set it on the table.

"There, you can see where you're at."

It was all one room, an earth floor with boards not nailed together, just laid down to make broad paths for walking, a stove on a sort of platform, table, couch, chairs, even a kitchen cupboard, several thick, very dirty blankets of the type used in sleighs and to cover horses. Perhaps if it had not had such a terrible smell—of coal oil, urine, earth, and stale heavy air—I would have recognized it as the sort of place I would like to live in myself, like the houses I made under snowdrifts, in winter, with sticks of firewood for furniture, like another house I had made long ago under the veranda, my floor the strange powdery earth that never got sun or rain.

But I was wary, sitting on the dirty couch, pretending not to look at anything. My father said, "You're snug here, Joe, that's right." He sat by the table, and there the hatchet lay.

"You should of seen me before the snow started to melt. Wasn't nothing showing but a smokestack."

"Nor you don't get lonesome?"

"Not me. I was never one for lonesome. And I got a cat, Ben. Where is that cat? There he is, in behind the stove. He don't relish company, maybe." He pulled it out, a huge, gray tom with sullen eyes. "Show you what he can do." He took a saucer from the table and a mason jar from the cupboard and poured something into the saucer. He set it in front of the cat.

"Joe, that cat don't drink whisky, does he?"

"You wait and see."

The cat rose and stretched himself stiffly, took one baleful look around, and lowered his head to drink.

"Straight whisky," my father said.

"I bet that's a sight you ain't seen before. And you ain't likely to see it again. That cat'd take whisky ahead of milk any day. A matter of fact he don't get no milk, he's forgot what it's like. You want a drink, Ben?"

"Not knowing where you got that. I don't have a stomach like your cat."

The cat, having finished, walked sideways from the saucer, waited a moment, gave a clawing leap, and landed unsteadily, but did not fall. It swayed, pawed the air a few times, meowing despairingly, then shot forward and slid under the end of the couch.

"Joe, you keep that up, you're not going to have a cat."

"It don't hurt him, he enjoys it. Let's see, what've we got for the little girl to eat?" Nothing, I hoped, but he brought a tin of Christmas candies, which seemed to have melted then hardened then melted again, so the colored stripes had run. They had a taste of nails.

"It's them Silases botherin' me, Ben. They come by day and by night. People won't ever quit botherin' me. I can hear them on the roof at night. Ben, you see them Silases you tell them what I got waitin' for them." He picked up the hatchet and chopped down at the table, splitting the rotten oilcloth. "Got a shotgun too."

"Maybe they won't come and bother you no more, Joe."

The man groaned and shook his head. "They never will stop. No. They never will stop."

"Just try not paying any attention to them, they'll tire out and go away."

"They'll burn me in my bed. They tried to before."

My father said nothing, but tested the axe blade with his finger. Under the couch, the cat pawed and meowed in more and more feeble spasms of delusion. Overcome with tiredness, with warmth after cold, with bewilderment past bearing, I was falling asleep with my eyes open.

My father set me down. "You're woken up now. Stand up. See. I can't carry you and this sack full of rats both."

We had come to the top of a long hill and that is where I

woke. It was getting dark. The whole basin of country drained by the Wawanash River lay in front of us—greenish-brown smudge of bush with the leaves not out yet and evergreens, dark, shabby after winter, showing through, straw-brown fields and the others, darker from last year's plowing, with scales of snow faintly striping them (like the field we had walked across hours, hours earlier in the day) and the tiny fences and colonies of gray barns, and houses set apart, looking squat and small.

"Whose house is that?" my father said, pointing.

It was ours, I knew it after a minute. We had come around in a half-circle and there was the side of the house that nobody saw in winter, the front door that went unopened from November to April and was still stuffed with rags around its edges, to keep out the east wind.

"That's no more'n half a mile away and downhill. You can easy walk home. Soon we'll see the light in the dining room where your momma is."

On the way I said, "Why did he have an axe?"

"Now listen," my father said. "Are you listening to me? He don't mean any harm with that axe. It's just his habit, carrying it around. But don't say anything about it at home. Don't mention it to your momma or Mary, either one. Because they might be scared about it. You and me aren't, but they might be. And there is no use of that."

After a while he said, "What are you not going to mention about?" and I said, "The axe."

"You weren't scared, were you?"

"No," I said hopefully. "Who is going to burn him and his bed?"

"Nobody. Less he manages it himself like he did last time."

"Who is the Silases?"

"Nobody," my father said. "Just nobody."

"We found the one for you today, Mary. Oh, I wisht we could've brought him home."

"We thought you'd fell in the Wawanash River," said Mary McQuade furiously, ungently pulling off my boots and my wet socks.

"Old Joe Phippen that lives up in no-man's-land beyond the bush."

"Him!" said Mary like an explosion. "He's the one burned his house down, I know him!"

"That's right, and now he gets along fine without it. Lives in a hole in the ground. You'd be as cozy as a groundhog, Mary."

"I bet he lives in his own dirt, all right." She served my father his supper and he told her the story of Joe Phippen, the roofed cellar, the boards across the dirt floor. He left out the axe but not the whisky and the cat. For Mary, that was enough.

"A man that'd do a thing like that ought to be locked up."

"Maybe so," my father said. "Just the same I hope they don't get him for a while yet. Old Joe."

"Eat your supper," Mary said, bending over me. I did not for some time realize that I was no longer afraid of her. "Look at her," she said. "Her eyes dropping out of her head, all she's been and seen. Was he feeding the whisky to her too?"

"Not a drop," said my father, and looked steadily down the table at me. Like the children in fairy stories who have seen their parents make pacts with terrifying strangers, who have discovered that our fears are based on nothing but the truth, but who come back fresh from marvellous escapes and take up their knives and forks, with humility and good manners, prepared to live happily ever after—like them, dazed and powerful with secrets, I never said a word.

ᴄᴏ *Something I've Been* ᴄᴏ *Meaning to Tell You*

"ANYWAY, HE KNOWS how to fascinate the women," said Et to Char. She could not tell if Char went paler, hearing this, because Char was pale in the first place as anybody could get. She was like a ghost now, with her hair gone white. But still beautiful, she couldn't lose it.

"No matter to him the age or the size," Et pressed on. "It's natural to him as breathing, I guess. I only hope the poor things aren't taken in by it."

"I wouldn't worry," Char said.

The day before, Et had taken Blaikie Noble up on his invitation to go along on one of his tours and listen to his spiel. Char was asked too, but of course she didn't go. Blaikie Noble ran a bus. The bottom part of it was painted red and the top part was striped, to give the effect of an awning. On the side was painted: LAKESHORE TOURS, INDIAN GRAVES, LIME-STONE GARDENS, MILLIONAIRE'S MANSION, BLAIKIE NOBLE, DRIVER, GUIDE. Blaikie had a room at the hotel, and he also worked on the grounds, with one helper, cutting grass and clipping hedges and digging the borders. What a comedown, Et had said at the beginning of the summer when they first found out he was back. She and Char had known him in the old days.

So Et found herself squeezed into his bus with a lot of strangers, though before the afternoon was over she had made friends with a number of them and had a couple of promises of jackets needing letting out, as if she didn't have enough to do already. That was beside the point, the thing on her mind was watching Blaikie.

And what did he have to show? A few mounds with grass growing on them, covering dead Indians, a plot full of odd-shaped, grayish-white, dismal-looking limestone things—far-fetched imitations of plants (there could be the cemetery, if that was what you wanted)—and an old monstrosity of a house built with liquor money. He made the most of it. A historical discourse on the Indians, then a scientific discourse on the Limestone. Et had no way of knowing how much of it was true. Arthur would know. But Arthur wasn't there; there was nobody there but silly women, hoping to walk beside Blaikie to and from the sights, chat with him over their tea in the Limestone Pavilion, looking forward to having his strong hand under their elbows, the other hand brushing somewhere around the waist when he helped them down off the bus ("I'm not a tourist," Et whispered sharply when he tried it on her).

He told them the house was haunted. The first Et had ever heard of it, living ten miles away all her life. A woman had killed her husband, the son of the millionaire, at least it was believed she had killed him.

"How?" cried some lady, thrilled out of her wits.

"Ah, the ladies are always anxious to know the means," said Blaikie, in a voice like cream, scornful and loving. "It was a slow—poison. Or that's what they said. This is all hearsay, all local gossip." (Local my foot, said Et to herself.) "She didn't appreciate his lady friends. The wife didn't. No."

He told them the ghost walked up and down in the garden, between two rows of blue spruce. It was not the murdered man who walked, but the wife, regretting. Blaikie smiled ruefully at the busload. At first Et had thought his attentions were all false, an ordinary commercial flirtation, to give them their money's worth. But gradually she was getting a different notion. He bent to each woman he talked to—it didn't matter how fat or scrawny or silly she was—as if there was one thing in her he would like to find. He had a gentle and laughing but ultimately serious, narrowing look (was that the look men finally had when they made love, that Et would never see?) that made him seem to want to be a deep-sea diver diving down, down through all the emptiness and cold and wreckage to discover the one thing he had set his heart on, something small and precious, hard to locate, as a ruby maybe on the ocean floor. That was a look she would like to have described to Char. No doubt Char had seen it. But did she know how freely it was being distributed?

Char and Arthur had been planning a trip that summer to see Yellowstone Park and the Grand Canyon, but they did not go. Arthur suffered a series of dizzy spells just at the end of school, and the doctor put him to bed. Several things were the matter with him. He was anemic, he had an irregular heartbeat, there was trouble with his kidneys. Et worried about leukemia. She woke at night, worrying.

"Don't be silly," said Char serenely. "He's overtired."

Arthur got up in the evenings and sat in his dressing gown. Blaikie Noble came to visit. He said his room at the hotel was a hole above the kitchen, they were trying to steam-cook him. It made him appreciate the cool of the porch. They played the games that Arthur loved, school-teacher's games. They played a geography game, and they tried to see who could make the most words out of the name Beethoven. Arthur won. He got thirty-four. He was immensely delighted.

"You'd think you'd found the Holy Grail," Char said.

They played "Who Am I?" Each of them had to choose somebody to be—real or imaginary, living or dead, human or animal—and the others had to try to guess it in twenty questions. Et got who Arthur was on the thirteenth question. Sir Galahad.

"I never thought you'd get it so soon."

"I thought back to Char saying about the Holy Grail."

"My strength is as the strength of ten," said Blaikie Noble, *"because my heart is pure.* I didn't know I remembered that."

"You should have been King Arthur," Et said. "King Arthur is your namesake."

"I should have. King Arthur was married to the most beautiful woman in the world."

"Ha," said Et. "We all know the end of that story."

Char went into the living room and played the piano in the dark.

The flowers that bloom in the spring, tra-la,
Have nothing to do with the case....

When Et arrived, out of breath, that past June, and said, "Guess who I saw downtown on the street?" Char, who was on her knees picking strawberries, said, "Blaikie Noble."

"You've seen him."

"No." said Char. "I just knew. I think I knew by your voice."

A name that had not been mentioned between them for thirty years. Et was too amazed then to think of the explanation that came to her later. Why did it need to be a surprise to Char? There was a postal service in this country, there had been all along.

"I asked him about his wife," she said. "The one with the dolls." (As if Char wouldn't remember.) "He says she died a long time ago. Not only that. He married another one and she's dead. Neither could have been rich. And where is all the Nobles' money, from the hotel?"

"We'll never know," said Char, and ate a strawberry.

The hotel had just recently been opened up again. The Nobles had given it up in the twenties and the town had operated it for a while as a hospital. Now some people from Toronto had bought it, renovated the dining room, put in a cocktail lounge, reclaimed the lawns and garden, though the tennis court seemed to be beyond repair. There was a croquet set put out again. People came to stay in the summers, but they were not the sort of people who used to come. Retired couples. Many widows and single ladies. Nobody would have walked a block to see them get off the boat, Et thought. Not that there was a boat anymore.

That first time she met Blaikie Noble on the street she had made a point of not being taken aback. He was wearing a creamy suit and his hair, that had always been bleached by the sun, was bleached for good now, white.

"Blaikie. I knew either it was you or a vanilla ice-cream cone. I bet you don't know who I am."

"You're Et Desmond and the only thing different about you

is you cut off your braids." He kissed her forehead, nervy as always.

"So you're back visiting old haunts," said Et, wondering who had seen that.

"Not visiting. Haunting." He told her then how he had got wind of the hotel opening up again, and how he had been doing this sort of thing, driving tour buses, in various places, in Florida and Banff. And when she asked he told her about his two wives. He never asked was she married, taking for granted she wasn't. He never asked if Char was, till she told him.

Et remembered the first time she understood that Char was beautiful. She was looking at a picture taken of them, of Char and herself and their brother who was drowned. Et was ten in the picture, Char fourteen and Sandy seven, just a couple weeks short of all he would ever be. Et was sitting in an armless chair and Char was behind her, arms folded on the chair back, with Sandy in his sailor suit cross-legged on the floor—or marble terrace, you would think, with the effect made by what had been nothing but a dusty, yellowing screen, but came out in the picture a pillar and draped curtain, a scene of receding poplars and fountains. Char had pinned her front hair up for the picture and was wearing a bright blue, ankle-length silk dress—of course the color did not show—with complicated black velvet piping. She was smiling slightly, with great composure. She could have been eighteen, she could have been twenty-two. Her beauty was not of the fleshy timid sort most often featured on calendars and cigar boxes of the period, but was sharp and delicate, intolerant, challenging.

Et took a long look at this picture and then went and looked at Char, who was in the kitchen. It was washday. The woman who came to help was pulling clothes through the wringer, and their mother was sitting down resting and staring through the screen door (she never got over Sandy; nobody expected her to). Char was starching their father's collars. He had a tobacco and candy store on the Square and wore a fresh collar every day. Et was prepared to find that some metamorphosis had taken place, as in the background, but it was not so. Char, bending over the starch basin, silent and bad-humored (she hated washday, the heat and steam and flapping sheets and chugging commotion of the machine—in fact, she was not fond of any kind of housework), showed in her real face the same almost disdainful harmony as in the photograph. This made Et understand, in some not entirely welcome way, that the qualities of legend were real, that they surfaced where and when you least expected. She had almost thought beautiful women were a fictional invention. She and Char would go down to watch the people get off the excursion boat, on Sundays, walking up to the hotel. So much white it hurt your eyes, the ladies' dresses and parasols and the men's summer suits and panama hats, not to speak of the sun dazzling on the water and the band playing. But looking closely at those ladies, Et found fault. Coarse skin or fat behind or chicken necks or dull nests of hair, probably ratted. Et did not let anything get by her, young as she was. At school she was respected for her self-possession and her sharp tongue. She was the one to tell you if you had been at the blackboard with a hole in your stocking or a ripped hem. She was the one who imitated (but in a safe corner of the schoolyard, out of earshot, always) the teacher reading "The Burial of Sir John Moore."

All the same it would have suited her better to have found one of those ladies beautiful, not Char. It would have been more appropriate. More suitable than Char in her wet apron with her cross expression, bent over the starch basin. Et was a person who didn't like contradictions, didn't like things out of place, didn't like mysteries or extremes.

She didn't like the bleak notoriety of having Sandy's drowning attached to her, didn't like the memory people kept of her father carrying the body up from the beach. She could be seen at twilight, in her gym bloomers, turning cartwheels on the lawn of the stricken house. She made a wry mouth, which nobody saw, one day in the park when Char said, "That was my little brother who was drowned."

The park overlooked the beach. They were standing there with Blaikie Noble, the hotel owner's son, who said, "Those waves can be dangerous. Three or four years ago there was a kid drowned."

And Char said—to give her credit, she didn't say it tragically, but almost with amusement, that he should know so little about Mock Hill people—"That was my little brother who was drowned."

Blaikie Noble was not any older than Char—if he had been, he would have been fighting in France—but he had not had to live all his life in Mock Hill. He did not know the real people there as well as he knew the regular guests at his father's hotel. Every winter he went with his parents to California, on the train. He had seen the Pacific surf. He had pledged allegiance to their flag. His manners were democratic, his skin was tanned. This was at a time when people were not usually tanned as a result of leisure, only work. His hair was bleached by the sun. His good looks were almost as notable as Char's but his were corrupted by charm, as hers were not.

It was the heyday of Mock Hill and all the other towns around the lakes, of all the hotels which in later years would become Sunshine Camps for city children, t.b. sanitoriums, barracks for R.A.F. training pilots in World War II. The white paint on the hotel was renewed every spring, hollowed-out logs filled with flowers were set on the railings, pots of flowers swung on chains above them. Croquet sets and wooden swings were set out on the lawns, the tennis court rolled. People who could not afford the hotel, young workingmen, shop clerks, and factory girls from the city, stayed in a row of tiny cottages, joined by latticework that hid their garbage pails and communal outhouses, stretching far up the beach. Girls from Mock Hill, if they had mothers to tell them what to do, were told not to walk out there. Nobody told Char what to do, so she walked along the boardwalk in front of them in the glaring afternoon, taking Et with her for company. The cottages had no glass in their windows; they had only propped-up wooden shutters that were closed at night. From the dark holes came one or two indistinct sad or drunk invitations, that was all. Char's looks and style did not attract men, perhaps intimidated them. All through high school in Mock Hill she had not one boyfriend. Blaikie Noble was her first, if that was what he was.

What did this affair of Char's and Blaikie Noble's amount to, in the summer of 1918? Et was never sure. He did not call at the house, at least not more than once or twice. He was kept busy working at the hotel. Every afternoon he drove an open excursion wagon, with an awning on top of it, up the lakeshore road, taking people to look at the Indian graves and the limestone garden and to glimpse through the trees the Gothic stone mansion, built by a Toronto distiller and known locally as Grog Castle. He was also in charge of the variety show the hotel put on once a week, with a mixture of local talent, recruited guests, and singers and comedians brought in especially for the performance.

Late mornings seemed to be the time he and Char had. "Come on," Char would say, "I have to go downtown," and she would in fact pick up the mail and walk partway round the Square before veering off into the park. Soon, Blaikie Noble would appear from the side door of the hotel and come bounding up the steep path. Sometimes he would not even bother with the path but jump over the back fence, to amaze them. None of this, the bounding or jumping, was done the way some boy from Mock Hill High School might have done it, awkwardly yet naturally. Blaikie Noble behaved like a man imitating a boy; he mocked himself but was graceful, like an actor.

"Isn't he stuck on himself?" said Et to Char, watching. The position she had taken up right away on Blaikie was that she didn't like him.

"Of course he is," said Char.

She told Blaikie. "Et says you're stuck on yourself."

"What did you say?"

"I told her you had to be, nobody else is."

Blaikie didn't mind. He had taken the position that he liked Et. He would with a quick tug loosen and destroy the arrangement of looped-up braids she wore. He told them things about the concert artists. He told them the Scottish ballad singer was a drunk and wore corsets, that the female impersonator even in his hotel room donned a blue nightgown with feathers, that the lady ventriloquist talked to her dolls—they were named Alphonse and Alicia—as if they were real people, and had them sitting up in bed one on each side of her.

"How would you know that?" Char said.

"I took her up her breakfast."

"I thought you had maids to do that."

"The morning after the show I do it. That's when I hand them their pay envelope and give them their walking papers. Some of them would stay all week if you didn't inform them. She sits up in bed trying to feed them bits of bacon and talking to them and doing them answering back, you'd have a fit if you could see."

"She's cracked, I guess," Char said peacefully.

One night that summer Et woke up and remembered she had left her pink organdie dress on the line, after hand-washing it. She thought she heard rain, just the first few drops. She didn't, it was just leaves rustling, but she was confused, waking up like that. She thought it was far on in the night too, but thinking about it later she decided it might have been only around midnight. She got up and went downstairs, turned on the back kitchen light, and let herself out the back door, and standing on the stoop pulled the clothesline towards her. Then almost under her feet, from the grass right beside the stoop, where there was a big lilac bush that had grown and spread, untended, to the size of a tree, two figures lifted themselves, didn't stand or even sit up, just roused their heads as if from bed, still tangled together some way. The back kitchen light didn't shine directly out but lit the yard enough for her to see their faces. Blaikie and Char.

She never did get a look at what state their clothes were in, to see how far they had gone or were going. She wouldn't have wanted to. To see their faces was enough for her. Their mouths were big and swollen, their cheeks flattened, coarsened, their eyes holes. Et left her dress, she fled into the house and into her bed where she surprised herself by falling asleep. Char never said a word about it to her next day. All she said was "I brought your dress in, Et. I thought it might rain." As if she had never seen Et out there pulling on the clothesline. Et wondered. She knew if she said, "You saw me," Char would probably tell her it had been a dream. She let Char think she had been fooled into believing that, if that was what Char was thinking. That way, Et was left knowing more; she was left knowing what Char looked like when she lost her powers, abdicated. Sandy drowned, with green stuff clogging his nostrils, couldn't look more lost than that.

Before Christmas the news came to Mock Hill that Blaikie Noble was married. He had married the lady ventriloquist, the one with Alphonse and Alicia. Those dolls, who wore evening dress and had sleek hairdos in the style of Vernon and Irene Castle, were more clearly remembered than the lady herself. The only thing people recalled for sure about her was that she could not have been under forty. A nineteen-year-old boy. It was because he had not been brought up like other boys, had been allowed the run of the hotel, taken to California, let mix with all sorts of people. The result was depravity, and could have been predicted.

Char swallowed poison. Or what she thought was poison. It was laundry blueing. The first thing she could reach down from the shelf in the back kitchen. Et came home after school—she had heard the news at noon, from Char herself, in fact, who had laughed and said, "Wouldn't that kill you?"— and she found Char vomiting into the toilet. "Go get the Medical Book," Char said to her. A terrible involuntary groan came out of her. "Read what it says about poison." Et went instead to phone the doctor. Char came staggering out of the bathroom holding the bottle of bleach they kept behind the tub. "If you don't put up the phone I'll drink the whole bottle," she said in a harsh whisper. Their mother was presumably asleep behind her closed door.

Et had to hang up the phone and look in the ugly old book where she had read long ago about childbirth and signs of death, and had learned about holding a mirror to the mouth. She was under the mistaken impression that Char had been drinking from the bleach bottle already, so she read all about that. Then she found it was the blueing. Blueing was not in the book, but it seemed the best thing to do would be to induce vomiting, as the book advised for most poisons—Char was at it already, didn't need to have it induced—and then drink a quart of milk. When Char got the milk down she was sick again.

"I didn't do this on account of Blaikie Noble," she said between spasms. "Don't you ever think that. I wouldn't be such a fool. A pervert like him. I did it because I'm sick of living."

"What are you sick of about living?" said Et sensibly when Char had wiped her face.

"I'm sick of this town and all the stupid people in it and Mother and her dropsy and keeping house and washing sheets every day. I don't think I'm going to vomit anymore. I think I could drink some coffee. It says coffee."

Et made a pot and Char got out two of the best cups. They began to giggle as they drank.

"I'm sick of Latin," Et said. "I'm sick of Algebra. I think I'll take blueing."

"Life is a burden," Char said. "O Life, where is thy sting?"

"O Death. O Death, where is thy sting?"

"Did I say Life? I meant Death. O Death, where is thy sting? Pardon me."

One afternoon Et was staying with Arthur while Char shopped and changed books at the library. She wanted to make him an eggnog, and she went searching in Char's cupboard for the nutmeg. In with the vanilla and the almond extract and the artificial rum she found a small bottle of a strange liquid. ZINC PHOSPHIDE. She read the label and turned it around in her hands. A rodenticide. Rat poison, that must mean. She had not known Char and Arthur were troubled with rats. They kept a cat, old Tom, asleep now around Arthur's feet. She unscrewed the top and sniffed at it, to know what it smelled like. Like nothing. Of course. It must taste like nothing too, or it wouldn't fool the rats.

She put it back where she had found it. She made Arthur his eggnog and took it in and watched him drink it. A slow poison. She remembered that from Blaikie's foolish story.

Arthur drank with an eager noise, like a child, more to please her, she thought, than because he was so pleased himself. He would drink anything you handed him. Naturally.

"How are you these days, Arthur?"

"Oh, Et. Some days a bit stronger, and then I seem to slip back. It takes time."

But there was none gone, the bottle seemed full. What awful nonsense. Like something you read about, Agatha Christie. She would mention it to Char and Char would tell her the reason.

"Do you want me to read to you?" she asked Arthur, and he said yes. She sat by the bed and read to him from a book about the Duke of Wellington. He had been reading it by himself but his arms got tired holding it. All those battles, and wars, and terrible things, what did Arthur know about such affairs, why was he so interested? He knew nothing. He did not know why things happened, why people could not behave sensibly. He was too good. He knew about history but not about what went on, in front of his eyes, in his house, anywhere. Et differed from Arthur in knowing that something went on, even if she could not understand why; she differed from him in knowing there were those you could not trust.

She did not say anything to Char after all. Every time she was in the house she tried to make some excuse to be alone in the kitchen, so that she could open the cupboard and stand on tiptoe and look in, to see it over the tops of the other bottles, to see that the level had not gone down. She did think maybe she was going a little strange, as old maids did; this fear of hers was like the absurd and harmless fears young girls sometimes have, that they will jump out a window, or strangle a baby sitting in its buggy. Though it was not her own acts she was frightened of.

Et looked at Char and Blaikie and Arthur, sitting on the porch, trying to decide if they wanted to go in and put the light on and play cards. She wanted to convince herself of her silliness. Char's hair, and Blaikie's too, shone in the dark. Arthur was almost bald now and Et's own hair was thin and dark. Char and Blaikie seemed to her the same kind of animal—tall, light, powerful, with a dangerous luxuriance. They sat apart but shone out together. *Lovers.* Not a soft word, as people thought, but cruel and tearing. There was Arthur in the rocker with a quilt over his knees, foolish as something that hasn't grown its final, most necessary, skin. Yet in a way the people like Arthur were the most troublemaking of all.

"I love my love with an R, because he is ruthless. His name is Rex, and he lives in a—restaurant."

"I love my love with an A, because he is absentminded. His name is Arthur, and he lives in an ash can."

"Why, Et," Arthur said. "I never suspected. But I don't know if I like about the ash can."

"You would think we were all twelve years old," said Char.

After the blueing episode Char became popular. She became involved in the productions of the Amateur Dramatic Society and the Oratorio Society, although she was never much of an actress or a singer. She was always the cold and beautiful heroine in the plays, or the brittle exquisite young society woman. She learned to smoke, because of having to do it onstage. In one play Et never forgot, she was a statue. Or rather, she played a girl who had to pretend to be a statue, so that a young man fell in love with her and later discovered, to his confusion and perhaps disappointment, that she was only human. Char had to stand for eight minutes perfectly still onstage, draped in white crêpe and showing the audience her fine indifferent profile. Everybody marvelled at how she did it.

The moving spirit behind the Amateur Dramatic Society and the Oratorio Society was a high-school teacher new to Mock Hill, Arthur Comber. He taught Et history in her last year. Everybody said he gave her A's because he was in love with her sister, but Et knew it was because she worked harder than she ever had before; she learned the history of North America as she had never learned anything in her life. Missouri Compromise. Mackenzie to the Pacific, 1793. She never forgot.

Arthur Comber was thirty or so, with a high bald forehead, a red face in spite of not drinking (that later paled), and a clumsy, excited manner. He knocked a bottle of ink off his desk and permanently stained the History Room floor. "Oh dear, oh dear," he said, crouching down to the spreading ink, flapping at it with his handkerchief. Et imitated that. "Oh dear, oh dear!" "Oh, good heavens!" All his flustery exclamations and miscalculated gestures. Then, when he took her essay at the door, his red face shining with eagerness, giving her work and herself such a welcome, she felt sorry. That was why she worked so hard, she thought, to make up for mocking him.

He had a black scholar's gown he wore over his suit, to teach in. Even when he wasn't wearing it, Et could see it on him. Hurrying along the street to one of his innumerable, joyfully undertaken obligations, flapping away at the Oratorio singers, jumping onstage—so the whole floor trembled—to demonstrate something to the actors in a play, he seemed to her to have those long ridiculous crow's wings flapping after him, to be as different from other men, as absurd yet intriguing, as the priest from Holy Cross. Char made him give up the gown altogether, after they were married. She had heard that he tripped in it, running up the steps of the school. He had gone sprawling. That finished it, she ripped it up.

"I was afraid one of these days you'd really get hurt."

But Arthur said, "Ah. You thought I looked like a fool."

Char didn't deny it, though his eyes on her, his wide smile, were begging her to. Her mouth twitched at the corners, in spite of herself. Contempt. Fury. Et saw, they both saw, a great wave of that go over her before she could smile at him and say, "Don't be silly." Then her smile and her eyes were trying to hold on to him, trying to clutch onto his goodness (which she saw, as much as anybody else did, but which finally only enraged her, Et believed, like everything else about him, like his sweaty forehead and his galloping optimism), before that boiling wave could come back again, altogether carry her away.

Char had a miscarriage during the first year of her marriage and was sick for a long time afterwards. She was never pregnant again. Et by this time was not living in the house; she had her own place on the Square, but she was there one time on washday, helping Char haul the sheets off the line. Their parents were both dead by that time—their mother had died before and their father after the wedding—but it looked to Et like sheets for two beds.

"It gives you plenty of wash."

"What does?"

"Changing sheets like you do."

Et was often there in the evening, playing rummy with Arthur while Char, in the other room, picked at the piano in the dark. Or talking and reading library books with Char, while Arthur marked his papers. Arthur walked her home. "Why do you have to go off and live by yourself anyway?" he scolded her. "You ought to come back and live with us."

"Three's a crowd."

"It wouldn't be for long. Some man is going to come along someday and fall hard."

"If he was such a fool as to do that I'd never fall for him, so we'd be back where we started."

"I was a fool that fell for Char, and she ended up having me."

Just the way he said her name indicated that Char was above, outside, all ordinary considerations—a marvel, a mystery. No one could hope to solve her, they were lucky just being allowed to contemplate her. Et was on the verge of saying, "She swallowed blueing once over a man that wouldn't have her," but she thought, What would be the good of it, Char would only seem more splendid to him, like a heroine out of Shakespeare. He squeezed Et's waist as if to stress their companionable puzzlement, involuntary obeisance, before her sister. She felt afterwards the bumpy pressure of his fingers as if they had left dents just above where her skirt fastened. It had felt like somebody absentmindedly trying out the keys of a piano.

Et had set up in the dressmaking business. She had a long narrow room on the Square, once a shop, where she did all her fitting, sewing, cutting, pressing, and, behind a curtain, her sleeping and cooking. She could lie in bed and look at the squares of pressed tin on her ceiling, their flower pattern, all her own. Arthur had not liked her taking up dressmaking because he thought she was too smart for it. All the hard work she had done in History had given him an exaggerated idea of her brains. "Besides," she told him, "it takes more brains to cut and fit, if you do it right, than to teach people about the War of 1812. Because, once you learn that, it's learned and isn't going to change you. Whereas every article of clothing you make is an entirely new proposition."

"Still it's a surprise," said Arthur, "to see the way you settle down."

It surprised everybody, but not Et herself. She made the change easily, from a girl turning cartwheels to a town fixture. She drove the other dressmakers out of business. They had been meek, unimportant creatures anyway, going around to people's houses, sewing in back rooms, and being grateful for meals. Only one serious rival appeared in all Et's years, and that was a Finnish woman who called herself a designer. Some people gave her a try, because people are never satisfied, but it soon came out she was all style and no fit. Et never mentioned her, she let people find out for themselves; but afterwards, when this woman had left town and gone to Toronto—where, from what Et had seen on the streets, nobody knew a good fit from a bad—Et did not restrain herself. She would say to a customer she was fitting, "I see you're still wearing that herringbone my foreigner friend tacked together for you. I saw you on the street."

"Oh, I know," the woman would say. "But I do have to wear it out."

"You can't see yourself from behind anyway, what's the difference."

Customers took this kind of thing from Et, came to expect it, even. She's a terror, they said about her, Et's a terror. She had them at a disadvantage, she had them in their slips and corsets. Ladies who looked quite firm and powerful outside were here immobilized, apologetic, exposing such trembly, meek-looking thighs squeezed together by corsets, such long sad breast creases, bellies blown up and torn by children and operations.

Et always closed her front curtains tight, pinning the crack.

"That's to keep the men from peeking."

Ladies laughed nervously.

"That's to keep Jimmy Saunders from stumping over to get an eyeful."

Jimmy Saunders was a World War I veteran who had a little shop next to Et's, harness and leather goods.

"Oh, Et. Jimmy Saunders has a wooden leg."

"He hasn't got wooden eyes. Or anything else that I know of."

"Et, you're terrible."

Et kept Char beautifully dressed. The two steadiest criticisms of Char, in Mock Hill, were that she dressed too elegantly, and that she smoked. It was because she was a teacher's wife that she should have refrained from doing either of these things, but Arthur of course let her do anything she liked, even buying her a cigarette holder so she could look like a lady in a magazine. She smoked at a high-school dance, and wore a backless satin evening dress, and danced with a boy who had got a high-school girl pregnant, and it was all the same to Arthur. He did not get to be Principal. Twice the school board passed him over and brought in somebody from outside, and when they finally gave him the job, in 1942, it was only temporarily and because so many teachers were away at war.

Char fought hard all these years to keep her figure. Nobody but Et and Arthur knew what effort that cost her. Nobody but Et knew it all. Both of their parents had been heavy, and Char had inherited the tendency, though Et was always as thin as a stick. Char did exercises and drank a glass of warm water before every meal. But sometimes she went on eating binges. Et had known her to eat a dozen cream puffs one after the other, a pound of peanut brittle, or a whole lemon-meringue pie. Then pale and horrified she took down Epsom salts, three or four or five times the prescribed amount. For two or three days she would be sick, dehydrated, purging her sins, as Et said. During these periods she could not look at food. Et would have to come and cook Arthur's supper. Arthur did not know about the pie or the peanut brittle or whatever it was, or about the Epsom salts. He thought she had gained a pound or two and was going through a fanatical phase of dieting. He worried about her.

"What is the difference, what does it matter?" he would say to Et. "She would still be beautiful."

"She won't do herself any harm," said Et, enjoying her food, and glad to see that worry hadn't put him off his. She always made him good suppers.

It was the week before the Labor Day weekend. Blaikie had gone to Toronto—for a day or two, he said.

"It's quiet without him," said Arthur.

"I never noticed he was such a conversationalist," Et said.

"I only mean in the way that you get used to somebody."

"Maybe we ought to get unused to him," said Et.

Arthur was unhappy. He was not going back to the school; he had obtained a leave of absence until after Christmas. Nobody believed he would go back then.

"I suppose he has his own plans for the winter," he said.

"He may have his own plans for right now. You know, I have my customers from the hotel. I have my friends. Ever since I went on that excursion, I hear things."

She never knew where she got the inspiration to say what she said, where it came from. She had not planned it at all, yet it came so easily, believably.

"I hear he's taken up with a well-to-do woman down at the hotel."

Arthur was the one to take an interest, not Char.

"A widow?"

"Twice, I believe. The same as he is. And she has the money from both. It's been suspected for some time and she was talking about it openly. He never said anything, though. He never said anything to you, did he, Char?"

"No," said Char.

"I heard this afternoon that now he's gone, and she's gone. It wouldn't be the first time he pulled something like this. Char and I remember."

Then Arthur wanted to know what she meant and she told him the story of the lady ventriloquist, remembering even the names of the dolls, though of course she left out all about Char. Char sat through this, even contributing a bit.

"They might come back but my guess is they'd be embarrassed. He'd be embarrassed. He'd be embarrassed to come here, anyway."

"Why?" said Arthur, who had cheered up a little through the ventriloquist story. "We never set down any rule against a man getting married."

Char got up and went into the house. After a while they heard the sound of the piano.

The question often crossed Et's mind in later years—what did she mean to do about this story when Blaikie got back? For she had no reason to believe he would not come back. The answer was that she had not made any plans at all. She had not planned anything. She supposed she might have wanted to make trouble between him and Char—make Char pick a fight with him, her suspicions roused even if rumors had not been borne out, make Char read what he might do again in the light of what he had done before. She did not know what she wanted. Only to throw things into confusion, for she believed then that somebody had to, before it was too late.

Arthur made as good a recovery as could be expected at his age; he went back to teaching history to the senior classes, working half-days until it was time for him to retire. Et kept up her own place on the Square and tried to get up and do some cooking and cleaning for Arthur, as well. Finally, after he retired, she moved back into the house, keeping the other place only for business purposes. "Let people jaw all they like," she said. "At our age."

Arthur lived on and on, though he was frail and slow. He walked down to the Square once a day, dropped in on Et, went and sat in the park. The hotel closed down and was sold again. There was a story that it was going to be opened up and used as a rehabilitation center for drug addicts, but the town got up a petition and that fell through. Eventually it was torn down.

Et's eyesight was not as good as it used to be, she had to slow down. She had to turn people away. Still she worked, every day. In the evenings Arthur watched television or read, but she sat out on the porch, in the warm weather, or in the dining room in winter, rocking and resting her eyes. She came and watched the news with him, and made him his hot drink, cocoa or tea.

There was no trace of the bottle. Et went and looked in the cupboard as soon as she could—having run to the house in response to Arthur's early-morning call, and found the doctor, old McClain, coming in at the same time. She ran out and looked in the garbage, but she never found it. Could Char have found the time to bury it? She was lying on the bed, fully and nicely dressed, her hair piled up. There was no fuss about the cause of death as there is in stories. She had complained of weakness to Arthur the night before, after Et had gone; she had said she thought she was getting the flu. So the old doctor said heart, and let it go. Nor could Et ever know. Would what was in that bottle leave a body undisfigured, as Char's was? Perhaps what was in the bottle was not what it said. She was not even sure that it had been there that last evening; she had been too carried away with what she was saying to go and look, as she usually did. Perhaps it had been thrown out earlier and Char had taken something else, pills maybe. Perhaps it really was her heart. All that purging would have weakened anybody's heart.

Her funeral was on Labor Day and Blaikie Noble came, cutting out his bus tour. Arthur in his grief had forgotten about Et's story, was not surprised to see Blaikie there. He had come back to Mock Hill on the day Char was found. A few hours too late, like some story. Et in her natural confusion could not remember what it was. Romeo and Juliet, she thought later. But Blaikie of course did not do away with himself afterwards; he went back to Toronto. For a year or two he sent Christmas cards, then was not heard of anymore. Et would not be surprised if her story of his marrying had not come true in the end. Only her timing was mistaken.

Sometimes Et had it on the tip of her tongue to say to Arthur, "There's something I've been meaning to tell you."

She didn't believe she was going to let him die without knowing. He shouldn't be allowed. He kept a picture of Char on his bureau. It was the one taken of her in her costume for that play, where she played the statue-girl. But Et let it go, day to day. She and Arthur still played rummy and kept up a bit of garden, along with raspberry canes. If they had been married, people would have said they were very happy.

❧ *The Ottawa Valley* ❧

I THINK OF MY mother sometimes in department stores. I
don't know why, I was never in one with her; their plenitude,
their sober bustle, it seems to me, would have satisfied her. I
think of her of course when I see somebody on the street who
has Parkinson's disease, and more and more often lately when
I look in the mirror. Also in Union Station, Toronto, because
the first time I was there I was with her, and my little sister. It
was one summer during the War, we waited between trains; we
were going home with her, with my mother, to her old home
in the Ottawa Valley.

A cousin she was planning to meet, for a between-trains
visit, did not show up. "She probably couldn't get away," said
my mother, sitting in a leather chair in the darkly panelled
Ladies' Lounge, which is now boarded up. "There was probably something to do that she couldn't leave to anybody else."
This cousin was a legal secretary, and she worked for a senior
partner in what my mother always called, in her categorical
way, "the city's leading law firm." Once, she had come to visit
us, wearing a large black hat and a black suit, her lips and nails
like rubies. She did not bring her husband. He was an alcoholic. My mother always mentioned that her husband was an
alcoholic, immediately after she had stated that she held an
important job with the city's leading law firm. The two things
were seen to balance each other, to be tied together in some
inevitable and foreboding way. In the same way, my mother
would say of a family we knew that they had everything money
could buy but their only son was an epileptic, or that the parents of the only person from our town who had become moderately famous, a pianist named Mary Renwick, had said that

they would give all their daughter's fame for a pair of baby hands. *A pair of baby hands?* Luck was not without its shadow, in her universe.

My sister and I went out into the station, which was like a street with its lighted shops and like a church with its high curved roof and great windows at each end. It was full of the thunder of trains hidden, it seemed, just behind the walls, and an amplified voice, luxuriant, powerful, reciting place names that could not quite be understood. I bought a movie magazine and my sister bought chocolate bars with the money we had been given. I was going to say to her, "Give me a bite or I won't show you the way back," but she was so undone by the grandeur of the place, or subdued by her dependence on me, that she broke off a piece without being asked.

Late in the afternoon we got on the Ottawa train. We were surrounded by soldiers. My sister had to sit on my mother's knee. A soldier sitting in front of us turned around and joked with me. He looked very much like Bob Hope. He asked me what town I came from, and then he said, "Have they got the second story on there yet?" in just the sharp, unsmiling, smart-alecky way that Bob Hope would have said it. I thought that maybe he really was Bob Hope, travelling around incognito in a soldier's uniform. That did not seem unlikely to me. Outside of my own town—this far outside it, at least—all the bright and famous people in the world seemed to be floating around free, ready to turn up anywhere.

Aunt Dodie met us at the station in the dark and drove us to her house, miles out in the country. She was small and sharp-faced and laughed at the end of every sentence. She drove an old square-topped car with a running board.

"Well, did Her Majesty show up to see you?"

She was referring to the legal secretary, who was in fact her sister. Aunt Dodie was not really our aunt at all but our mother's cousin. She and her sister did not speak.

"No, but she must have been busy," said my mother neutrally.

"Oh, busy," said Aunt Dodie. "She's busy scraping the chicken dirt off her boots. Eh?" She drove fast, over washboard and potholes.

My mother waved at the blackness on either side of us. "Children! Children, this is the Ottawa Valley!"

It was no valley. I looked for mountains, or at least hills, but in the morning all it was was fields and bush, and Aunt Dodie outside the window holding a milk pail for a calf. The calf was butting its head into the pail so hard it slopped the milk out, and Aunt Dodie was laughing and scolding and hitting it, trying to make it slow down. She called it a bugger. "Greedy little bugger!"

She was dressed in her milking outfit, which was many-layered and -colored and ragged and flopping like the clothes a beggarwoman might wear in a school play. A man's hat without a crown was shoved—for what purpose?—on her head.

My mother had not led me to believe we were related to people who dressed like that or who used the word *bugger*. "I will not tolerate filth," my mother always said. But apparently she tolerated Aunt Dodie. She said they had been like sisters when they were growing up. (The legal secretary, Bernice, had been older and had left home early.) Then my mother usually said that Aunt Dodie had had a tragic life.

Aunt Dodie's house was bare. It was the poorest house I had ever been in, to stay. From this distance, our own house— which I had always thought poor, because we lived too far out of town to have a flush toilet or running water, and certainly we had no real touches of luxury, like Venetian blinds—looked very comfortably furnished, with its books and piano and good set of dishes and one rug that was bought, not made out of rags. In Aunt Dodie's front room there was one overstuffed chair and a magazine rack full of old Sunday-school papers. Aunt Dodie lived off her cows. Her land was not worth farming. Every morning, after she finished milking and separating, she loaded the cans in the back of her pickup truck and drove seven miles to the cheese factory. She lived in dread of the milk inspector, who went around declaring cows tubercular, we understood, for no reason but spite, and to put poor farmers out of business. Big dairy interests paid him off, Aunt Dodie said.

The tragedy in her life was that she had been jilted. "Did you know," she said, "that I was jilted?" My mother had said we were never to mention it, and there was Aunt Dodie in her own kitchen, washing the noon dishes, with me wiping and my sister putting away (my mother had to go and have her rest), saying "jilted" proudly, as somebody would say "Did you know I had polio?" or some such bad important disease.

"I had my cake baked," she said. "I was in my wedding dress."

"Was it satin?"

"No, it was a nice dark-red merino wool, because of it being a late-fall wedding. We had the minister here. All prepared. My dad kept running out to the road to see if he could see him coming. It got dark, and I said, 'Time to go out and do the milking!' I pulled off my dress and I put it back on. I gave it away. Lots of girls would've cried, but me, I laughed."

My mother telling the same story said, "When I went home two years after that, and I was staying with her, I used to wake up and hear her crying in the night. Night after night."

"There was I
Waiting at the church,
Waiting at the church,
Waiting at the church.
And when I found
He'd left me in the lurch,
Oh, how it did upset me."

Aunt Dodie sang this at us, washing the dishes at her round table covered with scrubbed oilcloth. Her kitchen was as big as a house, with a back door and a front door; always a breeze blew through. She had a homemade icebox, such as I had never seen, with a big chunk of ice in it that she would haul in a child's wagon from the ice-house. The ice-house itself was remarkable, a roofed dugout where ice cut from the lake in winter lasted the summer, in sawdust.

"Of course it wasn't," she said, "in my case, it wasn't the church."

Across the fields from Aunt Dodie on the next farm lived my mother's brother, Uncle James, and his wife, Aunt Lena, and their eight children. That was the house where my mother had grown up. It was a bigger house with more furniture but still unpainted outside, dark gray. The furniture was mostly high wooden beds, with feather ticks and dark carved headboards. Under the beds were pots not emptied every day. We visited there but Aunt Dodie did not come with us. She and Aunt Lena did not speak. But Aunt Lena did not speak much to anybody. She had been a sixteen-year-old girl, straight out of the backwoods, said my mother and Aunt Dodie (which left you to wonder, Where was this?), when Uncle James married her. At this time, she would have been married ten or twelve years. She was tall and straight, flat as a board front and back—even though she would bear her ninth child before Christmas—darkly freckled, with large dark slightly inflamed eyes, animal's eyes. All the children had got those, instead of Uncle James's mild blue ones.

"When your mother was dying," said Aunt Dodie, "oh, I can hear her. Don't touch that towel! Use your own towel! Cancer, she thought you could catch it like the measles. She was that ignorant."

"I can't forgive her."

"And wouldn't let any of the kids go near her. I had to go over myself and give your mother her wash. I saw it all."

"I can never forgive her."

Aunt Lena was stiff all the time with what I now recognize as terror. She would not let her children swim in the lake for fear they would drown, she would not let them go tobogganing in winter for fear they would fall off the toboggan and break their necks, she would not let them learn to skate for fear they would break their legs and be crippled for life. She beat them all the time for fear they would grow up to be lazy, or liars, or clumsy people who broke things. They were not lazy but they broke things anyway; they were always darting and grabbing; and, of course, they were all liars, even the little ones, brilliant, instinctive liars who lied even when it was not necessary, just for the practice, and maybe the pleasure, of it. They were always telling and concealing, making and breaking alliances; they had the most delicate and ruthless political instincts. They howled when they were beaten. Pride was a luxury they had discarded long ago, or never considered. If you did not howl for Aunt Lena, when would she ever stop? Her arms were as long and strong as a man's, her face set in an expression of remote unanswerable fury. But five minutes, three minutes, afterwards, her children would have forgotten. With me, such a humiliation could last for weeks, or forever.

Uncle James kept the Irish accent my mother had lost and Aunt Dodie had halfway lost. His voice was lovely, saying the children's names. Mar-ie, Ron-ald, Ru-thie. So tenderly, comfortingly, reproachfully he said their names, as if the names, or the children themselves, were jokes played on him. But he never held them back from being beaten, never protested. You would think all this had nothing to do with him. You would think Aunt Lena had nothing to do with him.

The youngest child slept in the parents' bed until a new baby displaced it.

"He used to come over and see me," Aunt Dodie said. "We used to have some good laughs. He used to bring two, three of the kids but he quit that. I know why. They'd tell on him. Then he quit coming himself. She lays down the law. But he gets it back on her, doesn't he?"

Aunt Dodie did not get a daily paper, just the weekly that was published in the town where she had picked us up.

"There's a mention in here about Allen Durrand."

"Allen Durrand?" said my mother doubtfully.

"Oh, he's a big Holstein man now. He married a West."

"What's the mention?"

"It's the Conservative Association. I bet he wants to get nominated. I bet."

She was in the rocker, with her boots off, laughing. My mother was sitting with her back against a porch post. They were cutting up yellow beans, to can.

"I was thinking about the time we gave him the lemonade," Aunt Dodie said, and turned to me. "He was just a French

Canadian boy then, working here for a couple of weeks in the summer."

"Only his name was French," my mother said. "He didn't even speak it."

"You'd never know now. He turned his religion too, goes to St. John's."

"He was always intelligent."

"You bet he is. Oh, intelligent. But we got him with the lemonade.

"You picture the hottest possible day in summer. Your mother and I didn't mind it so much, we could stay in the house. But Allen had to be in the mow. You see they were getting the hay in. My dad was bringing it in and Allen was spreading it out. I bet James was over helping too."

"James was pitching on," my mother said. "Your dad was driving, and building the load."

"And they put Allen in the mow. You've no idea what a mow is like on that kind of a day. It's a hell on earth. So we thought it would be a nice idea to take him some lemonade—No. I'm getting ahead of myself. I meant to tell about the overalls first.

"Allen had brought me these overalls to fix just when the men were sitting down to dinner. He had a heavy pair of old suit pants on, and a work shirt, must have been killing him, though the shirt I guess he took off when he got in the barn. But he must've wanted the overalls on because they'd be cooler, you know, the circulation. I forget what had to be fixed on them, just some little thing. He must have been suffering bad in those old pants just to bring himself to ask, because he was awful shy. He'd be—what, then?"

"Seventeen," my mother said.

"And us two eighteen. It was the year before you went away to Normal. Yes. Well, I took and fixed his pants, just some little thing to do to them while you served up dinner. There I was sitting in the corner of the kitchen at the sewing machine when I had my inspiration, didn't I? I called you over. Pretended I was calling you to hold the material straight for me. So's you could see what I was doing. And neither one of us cracked a smile or dared look sideways at each other, did we?"

"No."

"Because my inspiration was to sew up his fly!

"So then, you see, a little bit on in the afternoon, with them out to work again, we got the idea for the lemonade. We made two pailfuls. One we took out to the men working in the field; we yelled to them and set it under a tree. And the other we took up to the mow and offered it to him. We'd used up every lemon we had, and even so it was weak. I remember we had to put vinegar in. But he wouldn't've noticed. I never saw a person so thirsty in my life as him. He drank by the dipperful, and then he just tipped up the pail. Drank it all down. Us standing there watching. How did we keep a straight face?"

"I'll never know," my mother said.

"Then we took the pail and made for the house and waited about two seconds before we came sneaking back. We hid ourselves up in the granary. That was like an oven too. I don't know how we stood it. But we climbed up on the sacks of feed and each found ourselves a crack or knothole or something to look through. We knew the corner of the barn the men always peed in. They peed down the shovel if they were upstairs. Down in the stable I guess they peed in the gutter. And soon enough, soon enough, he starts strolling over in that direction. Dropped his fork and starts strolling over. Puts his hand up to himself as he went. Sweat running down our faces from the heat and the way we had to keep from laughing. Oh, the cruelty of it! First he was just going easy, wasn't he? Then thinking about it I guess the need gets stronger; he looked down wondering what was the matter, and soon he's fairly clawin' and yankin' every which way, trying all he can to get himself free. But I'd sewed him up good and strong. I wonder when it hit him what'd been done?"

"Right then, I'd think. He was never stupid."

"He never was. So he must've put it all together. The lemonade and all. The one thing I don't guess he ever thought of was us hid up in the granary. Or else would he've done what he did next?"

"He wouldn't have," said my mother firmly.

"I don't know, though. He might've been past caring. Eh?

He just finally went past caring and gave up and ripped down his overalls altogether and let 'er fly. We had the full view."

"He had his back to us."

"He did not! When he shot away there wasn't a thing we couldn't see. He turned himself sideways."

"I don't remember that."

"Well, I do. I haven't seen so many similar sights that I can afford to forget."

"Dodie!" said my mother, as if at this too-late point to issue a warning. (Another thing my mother quite often said was "I will never listen to smut.")

"Oh, you! You didn't run away yourself. Did you? Kept your eye to the knothole!"

My mother looked from me to Aunt Dodie and back with an unusual expression on her face: helplessness. I won't say she laughed. She just looked as if there was a point at which she might give up.

The onset is very slow and often years may pass before the patient or his family observes that he is becoming disabled. He shows slowly increasing bodily rigidity, associated with tremors of the head and limbs. There may be various tics, twitches, muscle spasms, and other involuntary movements. Salivation increases and drooling is common. Scientifically the disease is known as paralysis agitans. *It is also called Parkinson's disease or shaking palsy.* Paralysis agitans *affects first a single arm or leg, then the second limb on the same side and finally those on the other side. The face begins to lose its customary expressiveness and changes slowly or not at all with passing moods. The disease is typically one of elderly people, striking mostly persons in their sixties and seventies. No recoveries are recorded. Drugs are available to control the tremor and excess salivation. The benefits of these, however, are limited. [Fishbein,* Medical Encyclopedia.]*

My mother, during this summer, would have been forty-one or forty-two years old, I think, somewhere around the age that I am now.

Just her left forearm trembled. The hand trembled more than the arm. The thumb knocked ceaselessly against the palm. She could, however, hide it in her fingers, and she could hold the arm still by stiffening it against her body.

Uncle James drank porter after supper. He let me taste it, black and bitter. Here was a new contradiction. "Before I married your father," my mother had told me, "I asked him to promise me that he would never drink, and he never has." But Uncle James, her brother, could drink without apologies.

On Saturday night we all went into town. My mother and my sister went in Aunt Dodie's car. I was with Uncle James and Aunt Lena and the children. The children claimed me. I was a little older than the oldest of them, and they treated me as if I were a trophy, someone for whose favor they could jostle and compete. So I was riding in their car, which was high and old and square-topped, like Aunt Dodie's. We were coming home, we had the windows rolled down for coolness, and unexpectedly Uncle James began to sing.

He had a fine voice, of course, a fine sad, lingering voice. I can remember perfectly well the tune of the song he sang, and the sound of his voice rolling out the black windows, but I can remember only bits of the words, here and there, though I have often tried to remember more, because I liked the song so well.

"As I was a-goen over Kil-i-kenny Mountain..."

I think that was the way it started.

Then further along something about *pearly*, or *early*, and *Some take delight in*—various things, and finally the strong but sad-sounding line:

"But I take delight in the water of the barley."

There was silence in the car while he was singing. The children were not squabbling and being hit, some of them were even falling asleep. Aunt Lena, with the youngest on her knee, was an unthreatening dark shape. The car bounced along as if it would go forever through a perfectly black night with its lights cutting a frail path; and there was a jackrabbit on the road, leaping out of our way, but nobody cried out to notice it, nobody broke the singing, its booming tender sadness.

"But I take delight in THE WATER OF THE BARLEY."

We got to church early, so that we could go and look at the graves. St. John's was a white wooden church on the highway, with the graveyard behind it. We stopped at two stones, on which were written the words *Mother* and *Father.* Underneath in much smaller letters the names and dates of my mother's parents. Two flat stones, not very big, lying like paving stones in the clipped grass. I went off to look at things more interesting—urns and praying hands and angels in profile.

Soon my mother and Aunt Dodie came too.

"Who needs all this fancy folderol?" said Aunt Dodie, waving.

My sister, who was just learning to read, tried reading the inscriptions.

"Until the Day Break"

"He is not Dead but Sleepeth"

"In Pacem"

"What is *pacem?*"

"Latin," said my mother approvingly.

"A lot of these people put up these fancy stones and it is all show, they are still paying for them. Some of them still trying to pay for the plots and not even started on the stones. Look at that, for instance." Aunt Dodie pointed to a large cube of dark-blue granite, flecked white like a cooking pot, balanced on one corner.

"How modern," said my mother absently.

"That is Dave McColl's. Look at the size of it. And I know for a fact they told her if she didn't hurry up and pay something on the plot, they were going to dig him up and pitch him out on the highway."

"Is that Christian?" my mother wondered.

"Some people don't deserve Christian."

I felt something slithering down from my waist and realized that the elastic of my underpants had broken. I caught my hands to my sides in time—I had no hips then to hold any-thing up—and said to my mother in an angry whisper, "I have to have a safety pin."

"What do you want a safety pin for?" said my mother, in a normal or louder-than-normal voice. She could always be relied upon to be obtuse at such moments.

I would not answer, but glared at her beseechingly, threat-eningly.

"I bet her panties bust." Aunt Dodie laughed.

"Did they?" said my mother sternly, still not lowering her voice.

"*Yes.*"

"Well, take them off then," said my mother.

"Not right here, though," said Aunt Dodie. "There is the Ladies."

Behind St. John's Church, as behind a country school, were two wooden toilets.

"Then I wouldn't have anything on," I said to my mother, scandalized. I couldn't imagine walking into church in a blue taffeta dress and no pants. Rising to sing the hymns, sitting down, in *no pants*. The smooth cool boards of the pew and *no pants*.

Aunt Dodie was looking through her purse. "I wish I had one to give you but I haven't. You just run and take them off and nobody's going to know the difference. Lucky there's no wind."

I didn't move.

"Well, I do have one pin," said my mother doubtfully. "But I can't take it out. My slip strap broke this morning when I was getting dressed and I put a pin in to hold it. But I can't take that out."

My mother was wearing a soft gray dress covered with little

flowers which looked as if they had been embroidered on, and a gray slip to match, because you could see through the material. Her hat was a dull rose color, matching the color of some of the flowers. Her gloves were almost the same rose and her shoes were white, with open toes. She had brought this whole outfit with her, had assembled it, probably, especially to wear when she walked into St. John's Church. She might have imagined a sunny morning, with St. John's bell ringing, just as it was ringing now. She must have planned this and visualized it just as I now plan and visualize, sometimes, what I will wear to a party.

"I can't take it out for you or my slip will show."

"People going in," Aunt Dodie said.

"Go to the Ladies and take them off. If you won't do that, go sit in the car."

I started for the car. I was halfway to the cemetery gate when my mother called my name. She marched ahead of me to the ladies' toilet, where without a word she reached inside the neck of her dress and brought out the pin. Turning my back—and not saying thank-you, because I was too deep in my own misfortune and too sure of my own rights—I fastened together the waistband of my pants. Then my mother walked ahead of me up the toilet path and around the side of the church. We were late, everybody had gone in. We had to wait while the choir, with the minister trailing, got themselves up the aisle at their religious pace.

> "All things bright and beautiful,
> All creatures great and small,
> All things wise and wonderful,
> The Lord God made them all."

When the choir was in place and the minister had turned to face the congregation, my mother set out boldly to join Aunt Dodie and my sister in a pew near the front. I could see that the gray slip had slid down half an inch and was showing in a slovenly way at one side.

After the service my mother turned in the pew and spoke

to people. People wanted to know my name and my sister's name and then they said, "She does look like you"; "No, maybe this one looks more like you"; or, "I see your own mother in this one." They asked how old we were and what grade I was in at school and whether my sister was going to school. They asked her when she was going to start and she said, "I'm not," which was laughed at and repeated. (My sister often made people laugh without meaning to; she had such a firm way of publicizing her misunderstandings. In this case it turned out that she really did think she was not going to school because the primary school near where we lived was being torn down, and nobody had told her she would go on a bus.)

Two or three people said to me, "Guess who taught me when *I* went to school? Your momma!"

"She never learned me much," said a sweaty man, whose hand I could tell she did not want to shake, "but she was the best-lookin' one I ever had!"

"Did my slip show?"

"How could it? You were standing in the pew."

"When I was walking down the aisle, I wonder?"

"Nobody could see. They were still standing for the hymn."

"They could have seen, though."

"Only one thing surprises me. Why didn't Allen Durrand come over and say hello?"

"Was he there?"

"Didn't you see him? Over in the Wests' pew, under the window they put in for the father and mother."

"I didn't see him. Was his wife?"

"Ah, you must have seen *her!* All in blue with a hat like a buggy wheel. She's very dressy. But not to be compared to you, today."

Aunt Dodie herself was wearing a navy-blue straw hat with some droopy cloth flowers, and a button-down-the-front slub rayon dress.

"Maybe he didn't know me. Or didn't see me."

"He couldn't very well not have seen you."

"Well."

"And he's turned out such a good-looking man. That counts if you go into politics. And the height. You very seldom see a short man get elected."

"What about Mackenzie King?"

"I meant around here. We wouldn't've elected *him*, from around here."

"Your mother's had a little stroke. She says not, but I've seen too many like her.

"She's had a little one, and she might have another little one, and another, and another. Then someday she might have the big one. You'll have to learn to be the mother then.

"Like me. My mother took sick when I was only ten. She died when I was fifteen. In between, what a time I had with her! She was all swollen up; what she had was dropsy. They came one time and took it out of her by the pailful."

"Took what out?"

"*Fluid.*

"She sat up in her chair till she couldn't anymore, she had to go to bed. She had to lie on her right side all the time to keep the fluid pressure off her heart. What a life. She developed bedsores, she was in misery. So one day she said to me, 'Dodie, please, just turn me onto my other side for just a little while, just for the relief.' She begged me. I got hold of her and turned her—she was a weight! I turned her on her heart side, and the minute I did, she died.

"What are you crying about? I never meant to make you cry! Well, you are a big baby, if you can't stand to hear about Life."

Aunt Dodie laughed at me, to cheer me up. In her thin brown face her eyes were large and hot. She had a scarf around her head that day and looked like a gypsy woman, flashing malice and kindness at me, threatening to let out more secrets than I could stand.

"Did you have a stroke?" I said sullenly.

"What?"

"Aunt Dodie said you had a stroke."

"Well, I didn't. I told her I didn't. The doctor says I didn't. She thinks she knows everything, Dodie does. She thinks she knows better than a doctor."

"Are you going to have a stroke?"

"No. I have low blood pressure. That is just the opposite of what gives you strokes."

"So, are you not going to get sick at all?" I said, pushing further. I was very much relieved that she had decided against strokes, and that I would not have to be the mother, and wash and wipe and feed her lying in bed, as Aunt Dodie had had to do with her mother. For I did feel it was she who decided, she gave her consent. As long as she lived, and through all the changes that happened to her, and after I had received the medical explanations of what was happening, I still felt secretly that she had given her consent. For her own purposes, I felt she did it: display, of a sort; revenge of a sort as well. More, that nobody could ever understand.

She did not answer me, but walked on ahead. We were going from Aunt Dodie's place to Uncle James's, following a path through the humpy cow pasture that made the trip shorter than going by the road.

"Is your arm going to stop shaking?" I pursued recklessly, stubbornly.

I demanded of her now, that she turn and promise me what I needed.

But she did not do it. For the first time she held out altogether against me. She went on as if she had not heard, her familiar bulk ahead of me turning strange, indifferent. She withdrew, she darkened in front of me, though all she did in fact was keep on walking along the path that she and Aunt Dodie had made when they were girls running back and forth to see each other; it was still there.

One night my mother and Aunt Dodie sat on the porch and recited poetry. How this started I forget; with one of them thinking of a quotation, likely, and the other one matching it. Uncle James was leaning against the railing, smoking. Because we were visiting, he had permitted himself to come.

"*How can a man die better,*" cried Aunt Dodie cheerfully,

"*Than facing fearful odds,*
For the ashes of his fathers
And the temples of his gods?"

"*And all day long the noise of battle rolled,*" my mother declared,

"*Among the mountains by the winter sea.*

"*Not a drum was heard, not a funeral note,*
As his corpse to the ramparts we hurried...

"*For I am going a long way*
To the island-valley of Avalon
Where falls not hail, or rain, or any snow...."

My mother's voice had taken on an embarrassing tremor, so I was glad when Aunt Dodie interrupted.

"Heavens, wasn't it all sad, the stuff they put in the old readers?"

"I don't remember a bit of it," said Uncle James. "Except—" and he recited without a break:

"*Along the line of smoky hills*
The crimson forest stands
And all day long the bluejay calls
Throughout the autumn lands."

"Good for you," said Aunt Dodie, and she and my mother joined in, so they were all reciting together, and laughing at each other:

"*Now by great marshes wrapped in mist,*
Or past some river's mouth,
Throughout the long still autumn day
Wild birds are flying south."

"Though when you come to think of it, even that has kind of a sad ring," Aunt Dodie said.

If I had been making a proper story out of this, I would have ended it, I think, with my mother not answering and going ahead of me across the pasture. That would have done. I didn't stop there, I suppose, because I wanted to find out more, remember more. I wanted to bring back all I could. Now I look at what I have done and it is like a series of snapshots, like the brownish snapshots with fancy borders that my parents' old camera used to take. In these snapshots Aunt Dodie and Uncle James and even Aunt Lena, even her children, come out clear enough. (All these people dead now except the children, who have turned into decent friendly wage earners, not a criminal or as far as I know even a neurotic among them.) The problem, the only problem, is my mother. And she is the one of course that I am trying to get; it is to reach her that this whole journey has been undertaken. With what purpose? To mark her off, to describe, to illumine, to celebrate, to *get rid of* her; and it did not work, for she looms too close, just as she always did. She is heavy as always, she weighs everything down, and yet she is indistinct, her edges melt and flow. Which means she has stuck to me as close as ever and refused to fall away, and I could go on, and on, applying what skills I have, using what tricks I know, and it would always be the same.

৶ Material ৽

I DON'T KEEP UP with Hugo's writing. Sometimes I see his
name, in the library, on the cover of some literary journal that
I don't open—I haven't opened a literary journal in a dozen
years, praise God. Or I read in the paper or see on a poster—
this would be in the library too, or in a bookstore—an
announcement of a panel discussion at the university, with
Hugo flown in to discuss the state of the novel today, or the
contemporary short story, or the new nationalism in our literature. Then I think, Will people really go, will people who
could be swimming or drinking or going for a walk really take
themselves out to the campus to find the room and sit in rows
listening to those vain quarrelsome men? Bloated, opinionated,
untidy men, that is how I see them, cosseted by the academic
life, the literary life, by women. People will go to hear them
say that such and such a writer is not worth reading anymore,
and that some writer must be read; to hear them dismiss and
glorify and argue and chuckle and shock. People, I say, but I
mean women, middle-aged women like me, alert and trembling, hoping to ask intelligent questions and not be ridiculous; soft-haired young girls awash in adoration, hoping to
lock eyes with one of the men on the platform. Girls, and
women too, fall in love with such men; they imagine there is
power in them.

The wives of the men on the platform are not in that audience. They are buying groceries or cleaning up messes or having a drink. Their lives are concerned with food and mess and
houses and cars and money. They have to remember to get the
snow tires on and go to the bank and take back the beer bottles, because their husbands are such brilliant, such talented

incapable men, who must be looked after for the sake of the words that will come from them. The women in the audience are married to engineers or doctors or businessmen. I know them, they are my friends. Some of them have turned to literature frivolously, it is true, but most come shyly, and with enormous transitory hope. They absorb the contempt of the men on the platform as if they deserved it; they half-believe they do deserve it, because of their houses and expensive shoes, and their husbands who read Arthur Hailey.

I am married to an engineer myself. His name is Gabriel, but he prefers the name Gabe. In this country he prefers the name Gabe. He was born in Romania; he lived there until the end of the war, when he was sixteen. He has forgotten how to speak Romanian. How can you forget, how can you forget the language of your childhood? I used to think he was pretending to forget, because the things he had seen and lived through when he spoke that language were too terrible to remember. He told me this was not so. He told me his experience of the war was not so bad. He described the holiday uproar at school when the air-raid sirens sounded. I did not quite believe him. I required him to be an ambassador from bad times as well as distant countries. Then I thought he might not be Romanian at all, but an impostor.

This was before we were married, when he used to come and see me in the apartment on Clark Road where I lived with my little daughter, Clea. Hugo's daughter too, of course, but he had to let go of her. Hugo had grants, he travelled, he married again and his wife had three children; he divorced and married again, and his next wife, who had been his student, had three more children, the first born to her while he was still living with his second wife. In such circumstances a man can't hang on to everything. Gabriel used to stay all night sometimes on the pullout couch I had for a bed in this tiny, shabby apartment; and I would look at him sleeping and think that for all I knew he might be a German or a Russian or even of all things a Canadian faking a past and an accent to make himself interesting. He was mysterious to me. Long after he became my lover and after he became my husband he remained, remains, mysterious to me. In spite of all the things I know about him, daily and physical things. His face curves out smoothly and his eyes, set shallowly in his head, curve out too under the smooth pink lids. The wrinkles he has are traced on top of this smoothness, this impenetrable surface; they are of no consequence. His body is substantial, calm. He used to be a fine, rather lazy-looking skater. I cannot describe him without a familiar sense of capitulation. I cannot describe him. I could describe Hugo, if anybody asked me, in great detail—Hugo as he was eighteen, twenty years ago, crew-cut and skinny, with the bones of his body and even of his skull casually, precariously, joined and knitted together, so that there was something uncoordinated, unexpected about the shifting planes of his face as well as the movements, often dangerous, of his limbs. "He's held together by nerves," a friend of mine at college said when I first brought him around, and it was true; after that I could almost see the fiery strings.

Gabriel told me when I first knew him that he enjoyed life. He did not say that he believed in enjoying it; he said that he did. I was embarrassed for him. I never believed people who said such things and anyway, I associated this statement with gross, self-advertising, secretly unpleasantly restless men. But it seems to be the truth. He is not curious. He is able to take pleasure and give off smiles and caresses and say softly, "Why do you worry about that? It is not a problem of yours." He has forgotten the language of his childhood. His lovemaking was strange to me at first, because it was lacking in desperation. He made love without emphasis, so to speak, with no memory of sin or hope of depravity. He does not watch himself. He will never write a poem about it, never, and indeed may have forgotten it in half an hour. Such men are commonplace, perhaps. It was only that I had not known any. I used to wonder if I would have fallen in love with him if his accent and his forgotten, nearly forgotten, past had been taken away; if he had been, say, an engineering student in my own year at college. I don't know, I can't tell. What holds anybody in a man or a woman may be something as flimsy as a Romanian accent or the calm curve of an eyelid, some half-fraudulent mystery.

No mystery of this sort about Hugo. I did not miss it, did not know about it, maybe would not have believed in it. I believed in something else, then. Not that I knew him all the way through, but the part I knew was in my blood and from time to time would give me a poison rash. None of that with Gabriel; he does not disturb me, any more than he is disturbed himself.

It was Gabriel who found me Hugo's story. We were in a bookstore, and he came to me with a large, expensive paperback, a collection of short stories. There was Hugo's name on the cover. I wondered how Gabriel had found it, what he had been doing in the fiction section of the store anyway; he never reads fiction. I wondered if he sometimes went and looked for things by Hugo. He is interested in Hugo's career as he would be interested in the career of a magician or popular singer or politician with whom he had, through me, a plausible connection, a proof of reality. I think it is because he does such anonymous work himself, work intelligible only to his own kind. He is fascinated by people who work daringly out in the public eye, without the protection of any special discipline—it must seem so, to an engineer—just trying to trust themselves, and elaborating their bag of tricks, and hoping to catch on.

"Buy it for Clea," he said.

"Isn't it a lot of money for a paperback?"

He smiled.

"There's your father's picture, your real father, and he has written this story you might like to read," I said to Clea, who was in the kitchen making toast. She is seventeen. Some days she eats toast and honey and peanut butter and Oreos, and cream cheese and chicken sandwiches and fried potatoes. If anybody comments on what she is eating or not eating, she may run upstairs and slam the door of her room.

"He looks overweight," said Clea, and put the book down. "You always said he was skinny." Her interest in her father is all from the point of view of heredity, and what genes he might have passed on to herself. Did he have a bad complexion, did he have a high I.Q., did the women in his family have big breasts?

"He was when I knew him," I said. "How was I to know what had happened to him since?"

He looked, however, very much as I would have thought he would look by now. When I saw his name in the newspaper or on a poster, I had pictured somebody much like this; I had foreseen the ways in which time and his life would have changed him. It did not surprise me that he had got fat but not bald, that he had let his hair grow wild and had grown a full, curly beard. Pouches under his eyes, a dragged-down look to the cheeks even when he is laughing. He is laughing, into the camera. His teeth have gone from bad to worse. He hated dentists, said his father died of a heart attack in the dentist's chair. A lie, like so much else, or at least an exaggeration. He used to smile crookedly for photographs to hide the right top incisor, dead since somebody at high school pushed him into a drinking fountain. Now he doesn't care, he laughs, he bares those rotting stumps. He looks, at the same time, woebegone and cheerful. A Rabelaisian writer. Checked wool shirt open at the top to show his undershirt; he didn't use to wear one. Do you wash, Hugo? Do you have bad breath, with those teeth? Do you call your girl students fond exasperated dirty names, are there phone calls from insulted parents, does the Dean or somebody have to explain that no harm is meant, that writers are not as other men are? Probably not, probably no one minds. Outrageous writers may bounce from one blessing to another nowadays, bewildered, as permissively reared children are said to be, by excess of approval.

I have no proof. I construct somebody from this one smudgy picture, I am content with such clichés. I have not the imagination or good will to proceed differently; and I have noticed anyway, everybody must have noticed as we go further into middle age, how shopworn and simple, really, are the disguises, the identities if you like, that people take up. In fiction, in Hugo's business, such disguises would not do, but in life they are all we seem to want, all anybody can manage. Look at Hugo's picture, look at the undershirt, listen to what it says about him.

Hugo Johnson was born and semi-educated in the bush, and in the mining and lumbering towns of Northern Ontario. He has worked as a lumberjack, beer-slinger, counterman, telephone lineman, and sawmill foreman, and has been sporadically affiliated with various academic communities. He lives now most of the time on the side of a mountain above Vancouver, with his wife and six children.

The student wife, it seems, got stuck with all the children. What happened to Mary Frances, did she die, is she liberated, did he drive her crazy? But listen to the lies, the half-lies, the absurdities. *He lives on the side of a mountain above Vancouver.* It sounds as if he lives in a wilderness cabin, and all it means, I'm willing to bet, is that he lives in an ordinary comfortable house in North or West Vancouver, which now stretch far up the mountain. He has been *sporadically affiliated with various academic communities.* What does that mean? If it means he has taught for years, most of his adult life, at universities, that teaching at universities has been the only steady well-paid job he has ever had, why doesn't it say so? You would think he came out of the bush now and then to fling them scraps of wisdom, to give them a demonstration of what a real male *writer,* a creative *artist,* is like; you would never think he was a practicing *academic.* I don't know if he was a lumberjack or a beer-slinger or a counterman, but I do know that he was not a telephone lineman. He had a job painting telephone poles. He quit that job in the middle of the second week because the heat and the climbing made him sick. It was a broiling June, just after we had both graduated. Fair enough. The sun really did make him sick; twice he came home and vomited. I have quit jobs myself that I could not stand. The same summer I quit my job folding bandages at Victoria Hospital, because I was going mad with boredom. But if I was a writer, and was listing all my varied and colorful occupations, I don't think I would put down *bandage-folder,* I don't think I would find that entirely honest.

After he quit, Hugo found a job marking Grade 12 examination papers. Why didn't he put that down? *Examination marker.* He liked marking examination papers better than he liked climbing telephone poles, and probably better than he liked lumberjacking or beer-slinging or any of those other things if he ever did them; why couldn't he put it down? *Examination marker.*

Nor has he, to my knowledge, ever been the foreman in a sawmill. He worked in his uncle's mill the summer before I met him. What he did all day was load lumber and get sworn at by the real foreman, who didn't like him because of his uncle being the boss. In the evenings, if he was not too tired, he used to walk half a mile to a little creek and play his recorder. Blackflies bothered him, but he did it anyway. He could play "Morning," from *Peer Gynt*, and some Elizabethan airs whose names I have forgotten. Except for one: "Wolsey's Wilde." I learned to play it on the piano so we could play a duet. Was that meant for Cardinal Wolsey, and what was a *wilde*, a dance? Put that down, Hugo. *Recorder player.* That would be quite all right, quite in fashion now; as I understand things, recorder-playing and such fey activities are not out of favor now, quite the contrary. Indeed, they may be more acceptable than all that lumberjacking and beer-slinging. Look at you, Hugo, your image is not only fake but out-of-date. You should have said you'd meditated for a year in the mountains of Uttar Pradesh; you should have said you'd taught Creative Drama to autistic children; you should have shaved your head, shaved your beard, put on a monk's cowl; you should have shut up, Hugo.

When I was pregnant with Clea we lived in a house on Argyle Street in Vancouver. It was such a sad gray stucco house on the outside, in the rainy winter, that we painted the inside, all the rooms, vivid ill-chosen colors. Three walls of the bedrooms were Wedgwood blue, one was magenta. We said it was an experiment to see if color could drive anybody mad. The bathroom was a deep orange-yellow. "It's like being inside a cheese," Hugo said when we finished it. "That's right, it is," I said. "That's very good, phrase-maker." He was pleased but not as pleased as if he'd written it. After that he said, every time he showed anybody the bathroom, "See the color? It's like being inside a cheese." Or, "It's like peeing inside a cheese." Not that I didn't do the same thing, save things up and say them over and over. Maybe I said that about peeing inside a cheese. We had many phrases in common. We both called the landlady the Green Hornet, because she had worn, the only time we had seen her, a poison-green outfit with bits of rat fur and a clutch of violets, and had given off a venomous sort of buzz. She was over seventy and she ran a downtown boarding-house for men. Her daughter Dotty we called the harlot-in-residence. I wonder why we chose to say "harlot"; that was not, is not, a word in general use. I suppose it had a classy sound, a classy depraved sound, contrasting ironically—we were strong on irony—with Dotty herself.

She lived in a two-room apartment in the basement of the house. She was supposed to pay her mother forty-five dollars monthly rent and she told me she meant to try to make the money baby-sitting.

"I can't go out to work," she said, "on account of my nerves. My last husband, I had him six months dying down at Mother's, dying with his kidney disease, and I owe her three hundred dollars board still on that. She made me make him his eggnog with skim milk. I'm broke every day of my life. They say it's all right not having wealth if you got health, but what if you never had either one? Bronchial pneumonia from the time I was three years old. Rheumatic fever at twelve. Sixteen I married my first husband, he was killed in a logging accident. Three miscarriages. My womb is in shreds. I use up three packs of Kotex every month. I married a dairy farmer out in the Valley and his herd got the fever. Wiped us out. That was the one who died with his kidneys. No wonder. No wonder my nerves are shot."

I am condensing. This came out at greater length and by no means dolefully, indeed with some amazement and pride, at Dotty's table. She asked me down for cups of tea, then for beer. This is life, I thought, fresh from books, classes, essays, discussions. Unlike her mother, Dotty was flat-faced, soft, doughy, fashioned for defeat, the kind of colorless puzzled woman you see carrying a shopping bag, waiting for the bus. In fact, I had seen her once on a bus downtown, and not recognized her at first in her dull blue winter coat. Her rooms were full of heavy furniture salvaged from her marriage—an upright piano, overstuffed chesterfield and chairs, walnut-veneer china cabinet and dining-room table, where we sat. In the middle of the table was a tremendous lamp, with a painted china base and a pleated dark-red silk shade, held out at an extravagant angle, like a hoop skirt.

I described it to Hugo. "That is a whorehouse lamp," I said. Afterwards I wanted to be congratulated on the accuracy of this description. I told Hugo he ought to pay more attention to Dotty if he wanted to be a writer. I told him about her husbands and her womb and her collection of souvenir spoons, and he said I was welcome to look at them all by myself. He was writing a verse play.

Once when I went down to put coal on the furnace, I found Dotty in her pink chenille dressing gown saying goodbye to a man in a uniform, some sort of deliveryman or gas-station attendant. It was the middle of the afternoon. She and this man were not parting in any way that suggested either lechery or affection and I would not have understood anything about it, I would probably have thought he was some relative, if she had not begun at once a long complicated slightly drunk story about how she had got wet in the rain and had to leave her clothes at her mother's house and worn home her mother's dress which was too tight and that was why she was now in her dressing gown. She said that first Larry had caught her in it delivering some sewing he wanted her to do for his wife, and now me, and she didn't know what we would think of her. This was strange, as I had seen her in her dressing gown many times before. In the middle of her laughing and explaining, the man, who had not looked at me, not smiled or said a word or in any way backed up her story, simply ducked out the door.

"Dotty has a lover," I said to Hugo.

"You don't get out enough. You're trying to make life interesting."

The next week I watched to see if this man came back. He did not. But three other men came, and one of them came twice. They walked with their heads down, quickly, and did not have to wait at the basement door. Hugo couldn't deny it. He said it was life imitating art again, it was bound to happen, after all the fat varicose-veined whores he'd met in books. It was then we named her the harlot-in-residence and began to brag about her to our friends. They stood behind the curtains to catch a glimpse of her going in or out.

"That's not her!" they said. "Is that her? Isn't she disappointing? Doesn't she have any professional clothes?"

"Don't be so naive," we said. "Did you think they all wore spangles and boas?"

Everybody hushed to hear her play the piano. She sang or hummed along with her playing, not steadily, but loudly, in the rather defiant, self-parodying voice people use when they are alone, or think they are alone. She sang "Yellow Rose of Texas," and "You Can't Be True, Dear."

"Whores should sing hymns."

"We'll get her to learn some."

"You're all such voyeurs. You're all so mean," said a girl named Mary Frances Shrecker, a big-boned, calm-faced girl with black braids down her back. She was married to a former mathematical prodigy, Elsworth Shrecker, who had had a breakdown. She worked as a dietitian. Hugo said he could not look at her without thinking of the word *lumpen*, but he supposed she might be nourishing, like oatmeal porridge. She became his second wife. I thought she was the right wife for him, I thought she would stay forever, nourishing him, but the student evicted her.

The piano-playing was an entertainment for our friends, but disastrous on the days when Hugo was home trying to work. He was supposed to be working on his thesis but he really was writing his play. He worked in our bedroom, at a card table in front of the window, facing a board fence. When Dotty had been playing for a bit, he might come out to the kitchen and stick his face into mine and say in low, even tones of self-consciously controlled rage, "You go down and tell her to cut that out."

"You go."

"Bloody hell. She's your friend. You cultivate her. You encourage her."

"I never told her to play the piano."

"I arranged so that I could have this afternoon free. That did not just happen. I arranged it. I am at a crucial point, I am at the point where this play *lives* or *dies*. If I go down there I'm afraid I might strangle her."

"Well, don't look at *me*. Don't strangle *me*. Excuse my breathing and everything."

I always did go down to the basement, of course, and knock on Dotty's door and ask her if she would mind not playing the piano now, because my husband was at home and was trying to work. I never said the word *write*, Hugo had trained me not to, that word was like a bare wire to us. Dotty apologized every time; she was scared of Hugo and respectful of his work and his intelligence. She left off playing but the trouble was she might forget, she might start again in an hour, half an hour. The possibility made me nervous and miserable. Because I was pregnant I always wanted to eat, and I would sit at the kitchen table greedily, unhappily, eating something like a warmed-up plateful of Spanish rice. Hugo felt the world was hostile to his writing; he felt not only all its human inhabitants but its noises and diversions and ordinary clutter were linked against him, maliciously, purposefully, diabolically thwarting and maiming him and keeping him from his work. And I, whose business it was to throw myself between him and the world, was failing to do so, by choice perhaps as much as ineptitude for the job. I did not believe in him. I had not understood how it would be necessary to believe in him. I believed that he was clever and talented, whatever that might mean, but I was not sure he would turn out to be a writer. He did not have the authority I thought a writer should have. He was too nervous, too touchy with everybody, too much of a show-off. I believed that writers were calm, sad people, knowing too much. I believed that there was a difference about them, some hard and shining, rare intimidating quality they had from the beginning, and Hugo didn't have it. I thought that someday he would recognize this. Meanwhile, he lived in a world whose rewards and punishments were as strange, as hidden from me, as if he had been a lunatic. He would sit at supper, pale and disgusted; he would clench himself over the typewriter in furious paralysis when I had to get something from the bedroom, or he would leap around the living room asking me what he was (a rhinoceros who thinks he is a gazelle, Chairman Mao dancing a war dance in a dream dreamt by John Foster Dulles) and then kiss me all over the neck and throat with hungry gobbling noises. I was cut off from the source of these glad or bad moods, I did not affect them.

I teased him sourly: "Suppose after we have the baby the house is on fire and the baby and the play are both in there, which would you save?"

"Both."

"But supposing you can just save one? Never mind the baby, suppose *I* am in there, no, suppose I am drowning *here* and you are *here* and cannot possibly reach us both—"

"You're making it tough for me."

"I know I am. I know I am. Don't you hate me?"

"Of course I hate you." After this we might go to bed, playful, squealing, mock-fighting, excited. All our life together, the successful part of our life together, was games. We made up conversations to startle people on the bus. Once we sat in a beer parlor and he berated me for going out with other men and leaving the children alone while he was off in the bush working to support us. He pleaded with me to remember my duty as a wife and as a mother. I blew smoke in his face. People around us were looking stern and gratified. When we got outside we laughed till we had to hold each other up, against the wall. We played in bed that I was Lady Chatterley and he was Mellors.

"Where be that little rascal John Thomas?" he said thickly. "I canna find John Thomas!"

"Frightfully sorry, I think I must have swallowed him," I said, ladylike.

There was a water pump in the basement. It made a steady, thumping noise. The house was on fairly low-lying ground not far from the Fraser River, and during the rainy weather the pump had to work most of the time to keep the basement from

being flooded. We had a dark rainy January, as is usual in Vancouver, and this was followed by a dark rainy February. Hugo
and I felt gloomy. I slept a lot of the time. Hugo couldn't
sleep. He claimed it was the pump that kept him awake. He
couldn't work because of it in the daytime and he couldn't
sleep because of it at night. The pump had replaced Dotty's
piano-playing as the thing that most enraged and depressed
him in our house. Not only because of its noise, but because
of the money it was costing us. Its entire cost went onto our
electricity bill, though it was Dotty who lived in the basement
and reaped the benefits of not being flooded. He said I should
speak to Dotty and I said Dotty could not pay the expenses
she already had. He said she could turn more tricks. I told him
to shut up. As I became more pregnant, slower and heavier
and more confined to the house, I got fonder of Dotty, used
to her, less likely to store up and repeat what she said. I felt
more at home with her than I did sometimes with Hugo and
our friends.

All right, Hugo said, I ought to phone the landlady. I said
he ought. He said he had far too much to do. The truth was
we both shrank from a confrontation with the landlady, knowing in advance how she would confuse and defeat us with shrill
evasive prattle.

In the middle of the night in the middle of a rainy week I
woke up and wondered what had wakened me. It was the
silence.

"Hugo, wake up. The pump's broken. I can't hear the
pump."

"I am awake," Hugo said.

"It's still raining and the pump isn't going. It must be broken."

"No, it isn't. It's shut off. I shut it off."

I sat up and turned on the light. He was lying on his back,
squinting and trying to give me a hard look at the same time.

"You didn't turn it off."

"All right, I didn't."

"You did."

"I could not stand the goddamn expense anymore. I could

not stand thinking about it. I could not stand the noise either. I haven't had any sleep in a week."

"The basement will flood."

"I'll turn it on in the morning. A few hours' peace is all I want."

"That'll be too late, it's raining torrents."

"It is not."

"You go to the window."

"It's raining. It's not raining torrents."

I turned out the light and lay down and said in a calm stern voice, "Listen to me, Hugo, you have to go and turn it on, Dotty will be flooded out."

"In the morning."

"You have to go and turn it on *now*."

"Well I'm not."

"If you're not, I am."

"No, you're not."

"I am."

But I didn't move.

"Don't be such an alarmist."

"*Hugo.*"

"Don't *cry.*"

"Her stuff will be ruined."

"Best thing could happen to it. Anyway, it won't." He lay beside me stiff and wary, waiting, I suppose, for me to get out of bed, go down to the basement, and figure out how to turn the pump on. Then what would he have done? He could not have hit me, I was too pregnant. He never did hit me, unless I hit him first. He could have gone and turned it off again, and I could have turned it on, and so on, how long could that last? He could have held me down, but if I struggled he would have been afraid of hurting me. He could have sworn at me and left the house, but we had no car, and it was raining too hard for him to stay out very long. He would probably have just raged and sulked, alternately, and I could have taken a blanket and gone to sleep on the living-room couch for the rest of the night. I think that is what a woman of firm character would have done. I think that is what a woman who wanted that marriage to last would have done. But I did not do it. Instead, I said to myself that I did not know how the pump worked, I did not know where to turn it on. I said to myself that I was afraid of Hugo. I entertained the possibility that Hugo might be right, nothing would happen. But I wanted something to happen, I wanted Hugo to crash.

When I woke up, Hugo was gone and the pump was thumping as usual. Dotty was pounding on the door at the top of the basement stairs.

"You won't believe your eyes what's down here. I'm up to my knees in water. I just put my feet out of bed and up to my knees in water. What happened? You hear the pump go off?"

"No," I said.

"I don't know what could've gone wrong, I guess it could've got overworked. I had a couple of beers before I went to bed elst I would've known there was something wrong. I usually sleep light. But I was sleeping like the dead and I put my feet out of bed and Jesus, it's a good thing I didn't pull on the light switch at the same time, I would have been electrocuted. Everything's floating."

Nothing was floating and the water would not have come to any grown person's knees. It was about five inches deep in some places, only one or two in others, the floor being so uneven. It had soaked and stained the bottom of her chesterfield and chairs and got into the bottom of her piano. The floor tiles were loosened, the rugs soggy, the edges of her bedspread dripping, her floor heater ruined.

I got dressed and put on a pair of Hugo's boots and took a broom downstairs. I started sweeping the water towards the drain outside the door. Dotty made herself a cup of coffee in my kitchen and sat for a while on the top step watching me, going over the same monologue about having a couple of beers and sleeping more soundly than usual, not hearing the pump go off, not understanding why it should go off, if it had gone off, not knowing how she was going to explain to her mother, who would certainly make it out to be her fault and charge her. We were in luck, I saw. (*We* were?) Dotty's expectation and thrifty relish of misfortune made her less likely than almost anyone else would have been to investigate just what had gone wrong. After the water level went down a bit, she went into her bedroom, put on some clothes and some boots which she had to drain first, got her broom, and helped me.

"The things that don't happen to me, eh? I never get my fortune told. I've got these girlfriends that are always getting their fortune told and I say, never mind me, there's one thing I know and I know it ain't good."

I went upstairs and phoned the university, trying to get Hugo. I told them it was an emergency and they found him in the library.

"It did flood."

"What?"

"It did flood. Dotty's place is underwater."

"I turned the pump on."

"Like hell you did. This morning you turned it on."

"This morning there was a downpour and the pump couldn't handle it. That was after I turned it on."

"The pump couldn't handle it last night because the pump wasn't on last night and don't talk to me about any downpour."

"Well there was one. You were asleep."

"You have no idea what you've done, do you? You don't even stick around to look at it. I have to look. I have to cope. I have to listen to that poor woman."

"Plug your ears."

"Shut up, you filthy moral idiot."

"I'm sorry. I was kidding. I'm sorry."

"Sorry. You're bloody sorry. This is the mess you made and I told you you'd make and you're bloody sorry."

"I have to go to a seminar. I am sorry. I can't talk now, it's no good talking to you now, I don't know what you're trying to get me to say."

"I'm just trying to get you to *realize*."

"All right, I realize. Though I still think it happened this morning."

"You don't realize. You never realize."

"You dramatize."

"*I* dramatize!"

Our luck held. Dotty's mother was not so likely as Dotty to do without explanations and it was, after all, her floor tiles and wallboard that were ruined. But Dotty's mother was sick, the cold wet weather had undermined her too, and she was taken to hospital with pneumonia that very morning. Dotty went to live in her mother's house, to look after the boarders. The basement had a disgusting, moldy smell. We moved out too, a short time later. Just before Clea was born we took over a house in North Vancouver, belonging to some friends who had gone to England. The quarrel between us subsided in the excitement of moving; it was never really resolved. We did not move much from the positions we had taken on the phone. I said you don't realize, you never realize, and he said, what do you want me to say? Why do you make such a fuss over this, he asked reasonably. Anybody might wonder. Long after I was away from him, I wondered too. I could have turned on the pump, as I have said, taking responsibility for both of us, as a patient realistic woman, a really married woman, would have done, as I am sure Mary Frances would have done, did, many times, during the ten years she lasted. Or I could have told Dotty the truth, though she was not a very good choice to receive such information. I could have told somebody, if I thought it was that important, pushed Hugo out into the unpleasant world and let him taste trouble. But I didn't, I was not able fully to protect or expose him, only to flog him with blame, desperate sometimes, feeling I would claw his head open to pour my vision into it, my notion of what had to be understood. What presumptuousness, what cowardice, what bad faith. Unavoidable. "You have a problem of incompatibility," the marriage counsellor said to us a while later. We laughed till we cried in the dreary municipal hall of the building in North Vancouver where the marriage counselling was dispensed. That is our problem, we said to each other, what a relief to know it, incompatibility.

I did not read Hugo's story that night. I left it with Clea and she as it turned out did not read it either. I read it the next afternoon. I got home about two o'clock from the girls' private school where I have a part-time job teaching history. I made tea as I usually do and sat down in the kitchen to enjoy the hour before the boys, Gabriel's sons, get home from school. I saw the book still lying on top of the refrigerator and I took it down and read Hugo's story.

The story is about Dotty. Of course, she has been changed in some unimportant ways and the main incident concerning her has been invented, or grafted on from some other reality. But the lamp is there, and the pink chenille dressing gown. And something about Dotty that I had forgotten: When you were talking she would listen with her mouth slightly open, nodding, then she would chime in on the last word of your sentence with you. A touching and irritating habit. She was in such a hurry to agree, she hoped to understand. Hugo has remembered this, and when did Hugo ever talk to Dotty?

That doesn't matter. What matters is that this story of Hugo's is a very good story, as far as I can tell, and I think I can tell. How honest this is and how lovely, I had to say as I read. I had to admit. I was moved by Hugo's story; I was, I am, glad of it, and I am not moved by tricks. Or if I am, they have to be good tricks. Lovely tricks, honest tricks. There is Dotty, lifted out of life and held in light, suspended in the marvellous clear jelly that Hugo has spent all his life learning how to make. It is an act of magic, there is no getting around it; it is an act, you might say, of a special, unsparing, unsentimental love. A fine and lucky benevolence. Dotty was a lucky person, people who understand and value this act might say (not everybody, of course, does understand and value this act); she was lucky to live in that basement for a few months and eventually to have this done to her, though she doesn't know what has been done and wouldn't care for it, probably, if she did know. She has passed into Art. It doesn't happen to everybody.

Don't be offended. Ironical objections are a habit with me. I am half-ashamed of them. I respect what has been done. I respect the intention and the effort and the result. Accept my thanks.

I did think that I would write a letter to Hugo. All the time I was preparing dinner, and eating it, and talking to Gabriel and the children, I was thinking of a letter. I was thinking I would tell him how strange it was for me to realize that we shared, still shared, the same bank of memory, and that what was all scraps and oddments, useless baggage, for me, was ripe and usable, a paying investment, for him. Also I wanted to apologize, in some not-outright way, for not having believed he would be a writer. Acknowledgment, not apology; that was what I owed him. A few graceful, a few grateful, phrases.

At the same time, at dinner, looking at my husband Gabriel, I decided that he and Hugo are not really so unlike. Both of them have managed something. Both of them have decided what to do about everything they run across in this world, what attitude to take, how to ignore or use things. In their limited and precarious ways they both have authority. They are not *at the mercy*. Or think they are not. I can't blame them for making whatever arrangements they can make.

After the boys had gone to bed and Gabriel and Clea had settled to watch television, I found a pen and got the paper in front of me, to write my letter, and my hand jumped. I began to write short jabbing sentences that I had never planned:

This is not enough, Hugo. You think it is, but it isn't. You are mistaken, Hugo.

That is not an argument to send through the mail.

I do blame them. I envy and despise.

Gabriel came into the kitchen before he went to bed, and saw me sitting with a pile of test papers and my marking pencils. He might have meant to talk to me, to ask me to have coffee, or a drink, with him, but he respected my unhappiness as he always does; he respected the pretense that I was not unhappy but preoccupied, burdened with these test papers; he left me alone to get over it.

✎ *Royal Beatings* ✎

ROYAL BEATING. THAT was Flo's promise. You are going to get one Royal Beating.

The word "Royal" lolled on Flo's tongue, took on trappings. Rose had a need to picture things, to pursue absurdities, that was stronger than the need to stay out of trouble, and instead of taking this threat to heart she pondered: How is a beating royal? She came up with a tree-lined avenue, a crowd of formal spectators, some white horses and black slaves. Someone knelt, and the blood came leaping out like banners. An occasion both savage and splendid. In real life they didn't approach such dignity, and it was only Flo who tried to supply the event with some high air of necessity and regret. Rose and her father soon got beyond anything presentable.

Her father was king of the royal beatings. Those Flo gave never amounted to much; they were quick cuffs and slaps dashed off while her attention remained elsewhere. You get out of my road, she would say. You mind your own business. You take that look off your face.

They lived behind a store in Hanratty, Ontario. There were four of them: Rose, her father, Flo, Rose's young half brother, Brian. The store was really a house, bought by Rose's father and mother when they married and set up here in the furniture- and upholstery-repair business. Her mother could do upholstery. From both parents Rose should have inherited clever hands, a quick sympathy with materials, an eye for the nicest turns of mending, but she hadn't. She was clumsy, and when something broke she couldn't wait to sweep it up and throw it away.

Her mother had died. She said to Rose's father during the

afternoon, "I have a feeling that is so hard to describe. It's like a boiled egg in my chest, with the shell left on." She died before night, she had a blood clot on her lung. Rose was a baby in a basket at the time, so of course could not remember any of this. She heard it from Flo, who must have heard it from her father. Flo came along soon afterward, to take over Rose in the basket, marry her father, open up the front room to make a grocery store. Rose, who had known the house only as a store, who had known only Flo for a mother, looked back on the sixteen or so months her parents spent here as an orderly, far gentler and more ceremonious time, with little touches of affluence. She had nothing to go on but some eggcups her mother had bought, with a pattern of vines and birds on them, delicately drawn as if with red ink; the pattern was beginning to wear away. No books or clothes or pictures of her mother remained. Her father must have got rid of them, or else Flo would. Flo's only story about her mother, the one about her death, was oddly grudging. Flo liked the details of a death: the things people said, the way they protested or tried to get out of bed or swore or laughed (some did those things), but when she said that Rose's mother mentioned a hard-boiled egg in her chest she made the comparison sound slightly foolish, as if her mother really was the kind of person who might think you could swallow an egg whole.

Her father had a shed out behind the store, where he worked at his furniture repairing and restoring. He caned chair seats and backs, mended wickerwork, filled cracks, put legs back on, all most admirably and skillfully and cheaply. That was his pride: to startle people with such fine work, such moderate, even ridiculous charges. During the Depression people could not afford to pay more, perhaps, but he continued the practice through the war, through the years of prosperity after the war, until he died. He never discussed with Flo what he charged or what was owing. After he died she had to go out and unlock the shed and take all sorts of scraps of paper and torn envelopes from the big wicked-looking hooks that were his files. Many of these she found were not accounts or receipts at all but records of the weather, bits of information about the garden, things he had been moved to write down.

Ate new potatoes 25th June. Record.
Dark Day, 1880's, nothing supernatural. Clouds of ash
    from forest fires.
Aug. 16, 1938. Giant thunderstorm in evng. Lightning str.
    Pres. Church, Turberry Twp. Will of God?
Scald strawberries to remove acid.
All things are alive. Spinoza.

Flo thought Spinoza must be some new vegetable he planned
to grow, like broccoli or eggplant. He would often try some
new thing. She showed the scrap of paper to Rose and asked,
did she know what Spinoza was? Rose did know, or had an
idea—she was in her teens by that time—but she replied that
she did not. She had reached an age where she thought she
could not stand to know any more, about her father, or about
Flo; she pushed any discovery aside with embarrassment and
dread.

There was a stove in the shed, and many rough shelves covered with cans of paint and varnish, shellac and turpentine, jars
of soaking brushes and also some dark sticky bottles of cough
medicine. Why should a man who coughed constantly, whose
lungs took in a whiff of gas in the war (called, in Rose's earliest childhood, not the First, but the Last, War), spend all his
days breathing fumes of paint and turpentine? At the time,
such questions were not asked as often as they are now. On the
bench outside Flo's store several old men from the neighborhood sat gossiping, drowsing, in the warm weather, and some
of these old men coughed all the time too. The fact is they
were dying, slowly and discreetly, of what was called, without
any particular sense of grievance, "the foundry disease." They
had worked all their lives at the foundry in town, and now they
sat still, with their wasted yellow faces, coughing, chuckling,
drifting into aimless obscenity on the subject of women walking by, or any young girl on a bicycle.

From the shed came not only coughing but speech, a continual muttering, reproachful or encouraging, usually just below
the level at which separate words could be made out. Slowing
down when her father was at a tricky piece of work, taking on

a cheerful speed when he was doing something less demand-ing, sandpapering or painting. Now and then some words would break through and hang clear and nonsensical on the air. When he realized they were out, there would be a quick bit of cover-up coughing, a swallowing, an alert, unusual silence.

"Macaroni, pepperoni, Botticelli, beans—"

What could that mean? Rose used to repeat such things to herself. She could never ask him. The person who spoke these words and the person who spoke to her as her father were not the same, though they seemed to occupy the same space. It would be the worst sort of taste to acknowledge the person who was not supposed to be there; it would not be forgiven. Just the same, she loitered and listened.

The cloud-capped towers, she heard him say once.

"The cloud-capped towers, the gorgeous palaces."

That was like a hand clapped against Rose's chest, not to hurt, but astonish her, to take her breath away. She had to run then, she had to get away. She knew that was enough to hear, and besides, what if he caught her? It would be terrible.

This was something the same as bathroom noises. Flo had saved up and had a bathroom put in, but there was no place to put it except in a corner of the kitchen. The door did not fit, the walls were only beaverboard. The result was that even the tearing of a piece of toilet paper, the shifting of a haunch, was audible to those working or talking or eating in the kitchen. They were all familiar with each other's nether voices, not only in their more explosive moments but in their intimate sighs and growls and pleas and statements. And they were all most prudish people. So no one ever seemed to hear, or be listen-ing, and no reference was made. The person creating the noises in the bathroom was not connected with the person who walked out.

They lived in a poor part of town. There was Hanratty and West Hanratty, with the river flowing between them. This was West Hanratty. In Hanratty the social structure ran from doc-tors and dentists and lawyers down to foundry workers and factory workers and draymen; in West Hanratty it ran from fac-tory workers and foundry workers down to large improvident families of casual bootleggers and prostitutes and unsuccessful thieves. Rose thought of her own family as straddling the river, belonging nowhere, but that was not true. West Hanratty was where the store was and they were, on the straggling tail end of the main street. Across the road from them was a blacksmith shop, boarded up about the time the war started, and a house that had been another store at one time. The Salada Tea sign had never been taken out of the front window; it remained as a proud and interesting decoration though there was no Salada Tea for sale inside. There was just a bit of sidewalk, too cracked and tilted for roller-skating, though Rose longed for roller skates and often pictured herself whizzing along in a plaid skirt, agile and fashionable. There was one streetlight, a tin flower; then the amenities gave up and there were dirt roads and boggy places, front-yard dumps and strange-looking houses. What made the houses strange-looking were the attempts to keep them from going completely to ruin. With some the attempt had never been made. These were gray and rotted and leaning over, falling into a landscape of scrub hollows, frog ponds, cattails and nettles. Most houses, however, had been patched up with tarpaper, a few fresh shingles, sheets of tin, hammered-out stovepipes, even cardboard. This was, of course, in the days before the war, days of what would later be legendary poverty, from which Rose would remember mostly low-down things—serious-looking anthills and wooden steps, and a cloudy, interesting, problematical light on the world.

There was a long truce between Flo and Rose in the beginning. Rose's nature was growing like a prickly pineapple, but slowly, and secretly, hard pride and skepticism overlapping, to make something surprising even to herself. Before she was old enough to go to school, and while Brian was still in the baby carriage, Rose stayed in the store with both of them—Flo sitting on the high stool behind the counter, Brian asleep by the window; Rose knelt or lay on the wide creaky floorboards, working with crayons on pieces of brown paper too torn or irregular to be used for wrapping.

People who came to the store were mostly from the houses around. Some country people came too, on their way home from town, and a few people from Hanratty, who walked across the bridge. Some people were always on the main street, in and out of stores, as if it was their duty to be always on display and their right to be welcomed. For instance, Becky Tyde.

Becky Tyde climbed up on Flo's counter, made room for herself beside an open tin of crumbly jam-filled cookies.

"Are these any good?" she said to Flo, and boldly began to eat one. "When are you going to give us a job, Flo?"

"You could go and work in the butcher shop," said Flo innocently. "You could go and work for your brother."

"Roberta?" said Becky with a stagey sort of contempt. "You think I'd work for him?" Her brother who ran the butcher shop was named Robert but often called Roberta, because of his meek and nervous ways. Becky Tyde laughed. Her laugh was loud and noisy like an engine bearing down on you.

She was a big-headed loud-voiced dwarf, with a mascot's sexless swagger, a red velvet tam, a twisted neck that forced her to hold her head on one side, always looking up and sideways. She wore little polished high-heeled shoes, real lady's shoes. Rose watched her shoes, being scared of the rest of her, of her laugh and her neck. She knew from Flo that Becky Tyde had been sick with polio as a child, that was why her neck was twisted and why she had not grown any taller. It was hard to believe that she had started out differently, that she had ever been normal. Flo said she was not cracked, she had as much brains as anybody, but she knew she could get away with anything.

"You know I used to live out here?" Becky said, noticing Rose. "Hey! What's-your-name! Didn't I used to live out here, Flo?"

"If you did it was before my time," said Flo, as if she didn't know anything.

"That was before the neighborhood got so downhill. Excuse me saying so. My father built his house out here and he built his slaughterhouse and we had half an acre of orchard."

"Is that so?" said Flo, using her humoring voice, full of false geniality, humility even. "Then why did you ever move away?"

"I told you, it got to be such a downhill neighborhood," said Becky. She would put a whole cookie in her mouth if she felt like it, let her cheeks puff out like a frog's. She never told any more.

Flo knew anyway, and who didn't. Everyone knew the house, red brick with the veranda pulled off and the orchard, what was left of it, full of the usual outflow—car seats and washing machines and bedsprings and junk. The house would never look sinister, in spite of what had happened in it, because there was so much wreckage and confusion all around.

Becky's old father was a different kind of butcher from her brother, according to Flo. A bad-tempered Englishman. And different from Becky in the matter of mouthiness. His was never open. A skinflint, a family tyrant. After Becky had polio he wouldn't let her go back to school. She was seldom seen outside the house, never outside the yard. He didn't want people gloating. That was what Becky said, at the trial. Her mother was dead by that time and her sisters married. Just Becky and Robert at home. People would stop Robert on the road and ask him, "How about your sister, Robert? Is she altogether better now?"

"Yes."

"Does she do the housework? Does she get your supper?"

"Yes."

"And is your father good to her, Robert?"

The story being that the father beat them, had beaten all his children and beaten his wife as well, beat Becky more now because of her deformity, which some people believed he had caused (they did not understand about polio). The stories persisted and got added to. The reason that Becky was kept out of sight was now supposed to be her pregnancy, and the father of the child was supposed to be her own father. Then people said it had been born, and disposed of.

"What?"

"Disposed of," Flo said. "They used to say go and get your lamb chops at Tyde's, get them nice and tender! It was all lies in all probability," she said regretfully.

Rose could be drawn back—from watching the wind shiver

along the old torn awning, catch in the tear—by this tone of regret, caution, in Flo's voice. Flo telling a story—and this was not the only one, or even the most lurid one, she knew—would incline her head and let her face go soft and thoughtful, tantalizing, warning.

"I shouldn't even be telling you this stuff."

More was to follow.

Three useless young men, who hung around the livery stable, got together—or were got together, by more influential and respectable men in town—and prepared to give old man Tyde a horsewhipping, in the interests of public morality. They blacked their faces. They were provided with whips and a quart of whisky apiece, for courage. They were: Jelly Smith, a horse-racer and a drinker; Bob Temple, a ball-player and strongman; and Hat Nettleton, who worked on the town dray, and had his nickname from a bowler hat he wore, out of vanity as much as for the comic effect. He still worked on the dray, in fact; he had kept the name if not the hat, and could often be seen in public—almost as often as Becky Tyde—delivering sacks of coal, which blackened his face and arms. That should have brought to mind his story, but didn't. Present time and past, the shady melodramatic past of Flo's stories, were quite separate, at least for Rose. Present people could not be fitted into the past. Becky herself, town oddity and public pet, harmless and malicious, could never match the butcher's prisoner, the cripple daughter, a white streak at the window: mute, beaten, impregnated. As with the house, only a formal connection could be made.

The young men primed to do the horsewhipping showed up late, outside Tyde's house, after everybody had gone to bed. They had a gun, but they used up their ammunition firing it off in the yard. They yelled for the butcher and beat on the door; finally they broke it down. Tyde concluded they were after his money, so he put some bills in a handkerchief and sent Becky down with them, maybe thinking those men would be touched or scared by the sight of a little wry-necked girl, a dwarf. But that didn't content them. They came upstairs and dragged the butcher out from under his bed, in his nightgown.

They dragged him outside and stood him in the snow. The temperature was four below zero, a fact noted later in court. They meant to hold a mock trial but they could not remember how it was done. So they began to beat him and kept beating him until he fell. They yelled at him, *Butcher's meat!* and continued beating him while his nightgown and the snow he was lying in turned red. His son Robert said in court that he had not watched the beating. Becky said that Robert had watched at first but had run away and hid. She herself had watched all the way through. She watched the men leave at last and her father make his delayed bloody progress through the snow and up the steps of the veranda. She did not go out to help him, or open the door until he got to it. Why not? she was asked in court, and she said she did not go out because she just had her nightgown on, and she did not open the door because she did not want to let the cold into the house.

Old man Tyde then appeared to have recovered his strength. He sent Robert to harness the horse, and made Becky heat water so that he could wash. He dressed and took all the money and with no explanation to his children got into the cutter and drove to Belgrave where he left the horse tied in the cold and took the early-morning train to Toronto. On the train he behaved oddly, groaning and cursing as if he was drunk. He was picked up on the streets of Toronto a day later, out of his mind with fever, and was taken to a hospital, where he died. He still had all the money. The cause of death was given as pneumonia.

But the authorities got wind, Flo said. The case came to trial. The three men who did it all received long prison sentences. A farce, said Flo. Within a year they were all free, had all been pardoned, had jobs waiting for them. And why was that? It was because too many higher-ups were in on it. And it seemed as if Becky and Robert had no interest in seeing justice done. They were left well-off. They bought a house in Hanratty. Robert went into the store. Becky after her long seclusion started on a career of public sociability and display.

That was all. Flo put the lid down on the story as if she was sick of it. It reflected no good on anybody.

"Imagine," Flo said.

Flo at this time must have been in her early thirties. A young woman. She wore exactly the same clothes that a woman of fifty, or sixty, or seventy, might wear: print housedresses loose at the neck and sleeves as well as the waist; bib aprons, also of print, which she took off when she came from the kitchen into the store. This was a common costume, at the time, for a poor though not absolutely poverty-stricken woman; it was also, in a way, a scornful deliberate choice. Flo scorned slacks, she scorned the outfits of people trying to be in style, she scorned lipstick and permanents. She wore her own black hair cut straight across, just long enough to push behind her ears. She was tall but fine-boned, with narrow wrists and shoulders, a small head, a pale, freckled, mobile, monkeyish face. If she had thought it worthwhile, and had the resources, she might have had a black-and-pale, fragile, nurtured sort of prettiness; Rose realized that later. But she would have to have been a different person altogether; she would have to have learned to resist making faces, at herself and others.

Rose's earliest memories of Flo were of extraordinary softness and hardness. The soft hair, the long, soft, pale cheeks, soft almost invisible fuzz in front of her ears and above her mouth. The sharpness of her knees, hardness of her lap, flatness of her front.

When Flo sang:

"Oh the buzzin' of the bees in the cigarette trees
And the soda-water fountain . . ."

Rose thought of Flo's old life before she married her father, when she worked as a waitress in the coffee shop in Union Station, and went with her girlfriends Mavis and Irene to Centre Island, and was followed by men on dark streets and knew how pay phones and elevators worked. Rose heard in her voice the reckless dangerous life of cities, the gum-chewing sharp answers.

And when she sang:

"Then slowly, slowly, she got up
And slowly she came nigh him
And all she said, that she ever did say,
Was young man, I think you're dyin'!"

Rose thought of a life Flo seemed to have had beyond that, earlier than that, crowded and legendary, with Barbara Allan and Becky Tyde's father and all kinds of outrages and sorrows jumbled up together in it.

The royal beatings. What got them started?

Suppose a Saturday, in spring. Leaves not out yet but the doors open to the sunlight. Crows. Ditches full of running water. Hopeful weather. Often on Saturdays Flo left Rose in charge of the store—it's a few years now, these are the years when Rose was nine, ten, eleven, twelve—while she herself went across the bridge to Hanratty (going uptown they called it) to shop and see people, and listen to them. Among the people she listened to were Mrs. Lawyer Davies, Mrs. Anglican Rector Henley-Smith, and Mrs. Horse-Doctor McKay. She came home and imitated their flibberty voices. Monsters, she made them seem, of foolishness, and showiness, and self-approbation.

When she finished shopping she went into the coffee shop of the Queen's Hotel and had a sundae. What kind? Rose and Brian wanted to know when she got home, and they would be disappointed if it was only pineapple or butterscotch, pleased if it was a Tin Roof, or Black and White. Then she smoked a cigarette. She had some ready-rolled that she carried with her, so that she wouldn't have to roll one in public. Smoking was the one thing she did that she would have called showing off in anybody else. It was a habit left over from her working days, from Toronto. She knew it was asking for trouble. Once, the Catholic priest came over to her right in the Queen's Hotel, and flashed his lighter at her before she could get her matches out. She thanked him but did not enter into conversation, lest he should try to convert her.

Another time, on the way home, she saw at the town end of the bridge a boy in a blue jacket, apparently looking at the water.

Eighteen, nineteen years old. Nobody she knew. Skinny, weakly-looking, something the matter with him, she saw at once. Was he thinking of jumping? Just as she came up even with him, what does he do but turn and display himself, holding his jacket open, also his pants. What he must have suffered from the cold, on a day that had Flo holding her coat collar tight around her throat.

When she first saw what he had in his hand, Flo said, all she could think of was What is he doing out here with a baloney sausage?

She could say that. It was offered as truth; no joke. She maintained that she despised dirty talk. She would go out and yell at the old men sitting in front of her store.

"If you want to stay where you are you better clean your mouths out!"

Saturday, then. For some reason Flo is not going uptown, has decided to stay home and scrub the kitchen floor. Perhaps this has put her in a bad mood. Perhaps she was in a bad mood anyway, due to people not paying their bills, or the stirring-up of feelings in spring. The wrangle with Rose has already commenced, has been going on forever, like a dream that goes back and back into other dreams, over hills and through doorways, maddeningly dim and populous and familiar and elusive. They are carting all the chairs out of the kitchen preparatory to the scrubbing, and they have also got to move some extra provisions for the store, some cartons of canned goods, tins of maple syrup, coal-oil cans, jars of vinegar. They take these things out to the woodshed. Brian, who is five or six by this time, is helping drag the tins.

"Yes," says Flo, carrying on from our lost starting point. "Yes, and that filth you taught to Brian."

"What filth?"

"And he doesn't know any better."

There is one step down from the kitchen to the woodshed, a bit of carpet on it so worn Rose can't ever remember seeing the pattern. Brian loosens it, dragging a tin.

"Two Vancouvers," she says softly.

Flo is back in the kitchen. Brian looks from Flo to Rose and

Rose says again in a slightly louder voice, an encouraging singsong, "Two Vancouvers—"

"Fried in snot!" finishes Brian, not able to control himself any longer.

"Two pickled arseholes—"

"—tied in a knot!"

There it is. The filth.

Two Vancouvers fried in snot!
Two pickled arseholes tied in a knot!

Rose has known that for years, learned it when she first went to school. She came home and asked Flo, what is a Vancouver?

"It's a city. It's a long ways away."

What else besides a city?"

Flo said, what did she mean, what else? How could it be fried, Rose said, approaching the dangerous moment, the delightful moment, when she would have to come out with the whole thing.

"Two Vancouvers fried in snot!/Two pickled arseholes tied in a knot!"

"You're going to get it!" cried Flo in a predictable rage. "Say that again and you'll get a good clout!"

Rose couldn't stop herself. She hummed it tenderly, tried saying the innocent words aloud, humming through the others. It was not just the words *snot* and *arsehole* that gave her pleasure, though of course they did. It was the pickling and tying and the unimaginable Vancouvers. She saw them in her mind shaped rather like octopuses, twitching in the pan. The tumble of reason; the spark and spit of craziness.

Lately she has remembered it again and taught it to Brian, to see if it has the same effect on him, and of course it has.

"Oh, I heard you!" says Flo. "I heard that! And I'm warning you!"

So she is. Brian takes the warning. He runs away, out the woodshed door, to do as he likes. Being a boy, free to help or not, involve himself or not. Not committed to the household struggle. They don't need him anyway, except to use against each other, they hardly notice his going. They continue, can't help continuing, can't leave each other alone. When they seem to have given up they really are just waiting and building up steam.

Flo gets out the scrub pail and the brush and the rag and the pad for her knees, a dirty red rubber pad. She starts to work on the floor. Rose sits on the kitchen table, the only place left to sit, swinging her legs. She can feel the cool oilcloth, because she is wearing shorts, last summer's tight faded shorts dug out of the summer-clothes bag. They smell a bit moldy from winter storage.

Flo crawls underneath, scrubbing with the brush, wiping with the rag. Her legs are long, white, and muscular, marked all over with blue veins as if somebody had been drawing rivers on them with an indelible pencil. An abnormal energy, a violent disgust, is expressed in the chewing of the brush at the linoleum, the swish of the rag.

What do they have to say to each other? It doesn't really matter. Flo speaks of Rose's smart-aleck behavior, rudeness and sloppiness and conceit. Her willingness to make work for others, her lack of gratitude. She mentions Brian's innocence, Rose's corruption. Oh, don't you think you're somebody, says Flo, and a moment later, Who do you think you are? Rose contradicts and objects with such poisonous reasonableness and mildness, displays theatrical unconcern. Flo goes beyond her ordinary scorn and self-possession and becomes amazingly theatrical herself, saying it was for Rose that she sacrificed her life. She saw her father saddled with a baby daughter and she thought, What is that man going to do? So she married him, and here she is, on her knees.

At that moment the bell rings, to announce a customer in the store. Because the fight is on, Rose is not permitted to go into the store and wait on whoever it is. Flo gets up and throws off her apron, groaning—but not communicatively; it is not a groan whose exasperation Rose is allowed to share—and goes in and serves. Rose hears her using her normal voice.

"About time! Sure is!"

She comes back and ties on her apron and is ready to resume.
"You never have a thought for anybody but your ownself!
You never have a thought for what I'm doing."

"I never asked you to do anything. I wish you never had. I
would have been a lot better off."

Rose says this smiling directly at Flo, who has not yet gone
down on her knees. Flo sees the smile, grabs the scrub rag that
is hanging on the side of the pail, and throws it at her. It may
be meant to hit her in the face but instead it falls against Rose's
leg and she raises her foot and catches it, swinging it negli-
gently against her ankle.

"All right," says Flo. "You've done it this time. All right."

Rose watches her go to the woodshed door, hears her tramp
through the woodshed, pause in the doorway, where the screen
door hasn't yet been hung, and the storm door is standing open,
propped with a brick. She calls Rose's father. She calls him in
a warning, summoning voice, as if against her will preparing
him for bad news. He will know what this is about.

The kitchen floor has five or six different patterns of
linoleum on it. Ends, which Flo got for nothing and ingeniously trimmed and fitted together, bordering them with tin
strips and tacks. While Rose sits on the table waiting, she looks
at the floor, at this satisfying arrangement of rectangles, triangles, some other shape whose name she is trying to remember.
She hears Flo coming back through the woodshed, on the
creaky plank walk laid over the dirt floor. She is loitering, waiting too. She and Rose can carry this no further by themselves.

Rose hears her father come in. She stiffens, a tremor runs
through her legs, she feels them shiver on the oilcloth. Called
away from some peaceful, absorbing task, away from the words
running in his head, called out of himself, her father has to say
something. He says, "Well? What's wrong?"

Now comes another voice of Flo's. Enriched, hurt, apologetic, it seems to have been manufactured on the spot. She is
sorry to have called him from his work. Would never have done
it if Rose was not driving her to distraction. How to distraction? With her back talk and impudence and her terrible

tongue. The things Rose has said to Flo are such that if Flo had said them to her mother, she knows her father would have thrashed her into the ground.

Rose tries to butt in, to say this isn't true.

What isn't true?

Her father raises a hand, doesn't look at her, says, "Be quiet."

When she says it isn't true, Rose means that she herself didn't start this, only responded, that she was goaded by Flo, who is now, she believes, telling the grossest sort of lies, twisting everything to suit herself. Rose puts aside her other knowledge that whatever Flo has said or done, whatever she herself has said or done, does not really matter at all. It is the struggle itself that counts, and that can't be stopped, can never be stopped, short of where it has got to now.

Flo's knees are dirty, in spite of the pad. The scrub rag is still hanging over Rose's foot.

Her father wipes his hands, listening to Flo. He takes his time. He is slow at getting into the spirit of things, tired in advance, maybe, on the verge of rejecting the role he has to play. He won't look at Rose, but at any sound or stirring from Rose, he holds up his hand.

"Well, we don't need the public in on this, that's for sure," Flo says, and she goes to lock the door of the store, putting in the store window the sign that says BACK SOON, a sign Rose made for her with a great deal of fancy curving and shading of letters in black and red crayon. When she comes back she shuts the door to the store, then the door to the stairs, then the door to the woodshed.

Her shoes have left marks on the clean wet part of the floor.

"Oh, I don't know," she says now, in a voice worn down from its emotional peak. "I don't know what to do about her." She looks down and sees her dirty knees (following Rose's eyes) and rubs at them viciously with her bare hands, smearing the dirt around.

"She humiliates me," she says, straightening up. There it is, the explanation. "She humiliates me," she repeats with satisfaction. "She has no respect."

"I do not!"

"Quiet, you!" says her father.

"If I hadn't called your father you'd still be sitting there with that grin on your face! What other way is there to manage you?"

Rose detects in her father some objections to Flo's rhetoric, some embarrassment and reluctance. She is wrong, and ought to know she is wrong, in thinking that she can count on this. The fact that she knows about it, and he knows she knows, will not make things any better. He is beginning to warm up. He gives her a look. This look is at first cold and challenging. It informs her of his judgment, of the hopelessness of her position. Then it clears, it begins to fill up with something else, the way a spring fills up when you clear the leaves away. It fills with hatred and pleasure. Rose sees that and knows it. Is that just a description of anger, should she see his eyes filling up with anger? No. Hatred is right. Pleasure is right. His face loosens and changes and grows younger, and he holds up his hand this time to silence Flo.

"All right," he says, meaning that's enough, more than enough, this part is over, things can proceed. He starts to loosen his belt.

Flo has stopped anyway. She has the same difficulty Rose does, a difficulty in believing that what you know must happen really will happen, that there comes a time when you can't draw back.

"Oh, I don't know, don't be too hard on her." She is moving around nervously as if she has thoughts of opening some escape route. "Oh, you don't have to use the belt on her. Do you have to use the belt?"

He doesn't answer. The belt is coming off, not hastily. It is being grasped at the necessary point. *All right you.* He is coming over to Rose. He pushes her off the table. His face, like his voice, is quite out of character. He is like a bad actor, who turns a part grotesque. As if he must savor and insist on just what is shameful and terrible about this. That is not to say he is pretending, that he is acting, and does not mean it. He is acting, and he means it. Rose knows that, she knows everything about him.

She has since wondered about murders, and murderers.

Does the thing have to be carried through, in the end, partly for the effect, to prove to the audience of one—who won't be able to report, only register, the lesson—that such a thing can happen, that there is nothing that can't happen, that the most dreadful antic is justified, feelings can be found to match it?

She tries again looking at the kitchen floor, that clever and comforting geometrical arrangement, instead of looking at him or his belt. How can this go on in front of such daily witnesses—the linoleum, the calendar with the mill and creek and autumn trees, the old accommodating pots and pans?

Hold out your hand!

Those things aren't going to help her, none of them can rescue her. They turn bland and useless, even unfriendly. Pots can show malice, the patterns of linoleum can leer up at you, treachery is the other side of dailiness.

At the first, or maybe the second, crack of pain, she draws back. She will not accept it. She runs around the room, she tries to get to the doors. Her father blocks her off. Not an ounce of courage or of stoicism in her, it would seem. She runs, she screams, she implores. Her father is after her, cracking the belt at her when he can, then abandoning it and using his hands. Bang over the ear, then bang over the other ear. Back and forth, her head ringing. Bang in the face. Up against the wall and bang in the face again. He shakes her and hits her against the wall, he kicks her legs. She is incoherent, insane, shrieking. *Forgive me! Oh please, forgive me!*

Flo is shrieking too. *Stop, stop!*

Not yet. He throws Rose down. Or perhaps she throws herself down. He kicks her legs again. She has given up words but is letting out a noise, the sort of noise that makes Flo cry, *Oh, what if people can hear her?* The very last-ditch willing sound of humiliation and defeat it is, for it seems Rose must play her part in this with the same grossness, the same exaggeration, that her father displays, playing his. She plays his victim with a self-indulgence that arouses, and maybe hopes to arouse, his final, sickened contempt.

They will give this anything that is necessary, it seems, they will go to any lengths.

Not quite. He has never managed really to injure her, though there are times, of course, when she prays that he will. He hits her with an open hand, there is some restraint in his kicks.

Now he stops, he is out of breath. He allows Flo to move in, he grabs Rose up and gives her a push in Flo's direction, making a sound of disgust. Flo retrieves her, opens the stair door, shoves her up the stairs.

"Go on up to your room now! Hurry!"

Rose goes up the stairs, stumbling, letting herself stumble, letting herself fall against the steps. She doesn't bang her door because a gesture like that could still bring him after her, and anyway, she is weak. She lies on the bed. She can hear through the stovepipe hole Flo snuffling and remonstrating, her father saying angrily that Flo should have kept quiet then, if she did not want Rose punished she should not have recommended it. Flo says she never recommended a hiding like that.

They argue back and forth on this. Flo's frightened voice is growing stronger, getting its confidence back. By stages, by arguing, they are being drawn back into themselves. Soon it's only Flo talking; he will not talk anymore. Rose has had to fight down her noisy sobbing, so as to listen to them, and when she loses interest in listening, and wants to sob some more, she finds she can't work herself up to it. She has passed into a state of calm, in which outrage is perceived as complete and final. In this state events and possibilities take on a lovely simplicity. Choices are mercifully clear. The words that come to mind are not the quibbling, seldom the conditional. "Never" is a word to which the right is suddenly established. She will never speak to them, she will never look at them with anything but loathing, she will never forgive them. She will punish them; she will finish them. Encased in these finalities, and in her bodily pain, she floats in curious comfort, beyond herself, beyond responsibility.

Suppose she dies now? Suppose she commits suicide? Suppose she runs away? Any of these things would be appropriate. It is only a matter of choosing, of figuring out the way. She floats in her pure superior state as if kindly drugged.

And just as there is a moment, when you are drugged, in which you feel perfectly safe, sure, unreachable, and then without warning and right next to it a moment in which you know the whole protection has fatally cracked, though it is still pretending to hold soundly together, so there is a moment now—the moment, in fact, when Rose hears Flo step on the stairs—that contains for her both present peace and freedom and a sure knowledge of the whole down-spiralling course of events from now on.

Flo comes into the room without knocking, but with a hesitation that shows it might have occurred to her. She brings a jar of cold cream. Rose is hanging on to advantage as long as she can, lying face down on the bed, refusing to acknowledge or answer.

"Oh, come on," Flo says uneasily. "You aren't so bad off, are you? You put some of this on and you'll feel better."

She is bluffing. She doesn't know for sure what damage has been done. She has the lid off the cold cream. Rose can smell it. The intimate, babyish, humiliating smell. She won't allow it near her. But in order to avoid it, the big ready clot of it in Flo's hand, she has to move. She scuffles, resists, loses dignity, and lets Flo see there is not really much the matter.

"All right," Flo says. "You win. I'll leave it here and you can put it on when you like."

Later still a tray will appear. Flo will put it down without a word and go away. A large glass of chocolate milk on it, made with Vita-Malt from the store. Some rich streaks of Vita-Malt around the bottom of the glass. Little sandwiches, neat and appetizing. Canned salmon of the first quality and reddest color, plenty of mayonnaise. A couple of butter tarts from a bakery package, chocolate biscuits with a peppermint filling. Rose's favorites, in the sandwich, tart, and cookie line. She will turn away, refuse to look, but left alone with these eatables will be miserably tempted; roused and troubled and drawn back from thoughts of suicide or flight by the smell of salmon, the anticipation of crisp chocolate, she will reach out a finger, just to run it around the edge of one of the sandwiches (crusts cut off!) to get the overflow, get a taste. Then she will decide to eat one, for strength to refuse the rest. One will not be noticed. Soon, in helpless corruption, she will eat them all. She will drink the chocolate milk, eat the tarts, eat the cookies. She will get the malty syrup out of the bottom of the glass with her finger, though she sniffles with shame. Too late.

Flo will come up and get the tray. She may say, "I see you got your appetite still," or, "Did you like the chocolate milk, was it enough syrup in it?" depending on how chastened she is feeling, herself. At any rate, all advantage will be lost. Rose will understand that life has started up again, that they will all sit around the table eating again, listening to the radio news. Tomorrow morning, maybe even tonight. Unseemly and unlikely as that may be. They will be embarrassed, but rather less than you might expect considering how they have behaved. They will feel a queer lassitude, a convalescent indolence, not far off satisfaction.

One night after a scene like this they were all in the kitchen. It must have been summer, or at least warm weather, because her father spoke of the old men who sat on the bench in front of the store.

"Do you know what they're talking about now?" he said, and nodded his head toward the store to show who he meant, though of course they were not there now, they went home at dark.

"Those old coots," said Flo. "What?"

There was about them both a geniality not exactly false but a bit more emphatic than was normal, without company.

Rose's father told them then that the old men had picked up the idea somewhere that what looked like a star in the western sky, the first star that came out after sunset, the evening star, was in reality an airship hovering over Bay City, Michigan, on the other side of Lake Huron. An American invention, sent up to rival the heavenly bodies. They were all in agreement about this, the idea was congenial to them. They believed it to be lit by ten thousand electric light bulbs. Her father had ruthlessly disagreed with them, pointing out that it was the planet Venus they saw, which had appeared in the sky long before the invention of an electric light bulb. They had never heard of the planet Venus.

"Ignoramuses," said Flo. At which Rose knew, and knew her father knew, that Flo had never heard of the planet Venus either. To distract them from this, or even apologize for it, Flo put down her teacup, stretched out with her head resting on the chair she had been sitting on and her feet on another chair (somehow she managed to tuck her dress modestly between her legs at the same time), and lay stiff as a board, so that Brian cried out in delight, "Do that! Do that!"

Flo was double-jointed and very strong. In moments of celebration or emergency she would do tricks.

They were silent while she turned herself around, not using her arms at all but just her strong legs and feet. Then they all cried out in triumph, though they had seen it before.

Just as Flo turned herself Rose got a picture in her mind of that airship, an elongated transparent bubble, with its strings of diamond lights, floating in the miraculous American sky.

"The planet Venus!" her father said, applauding Flo. "Ten thousand electric lights!"

There was a feeling of permission, relaxation, even a current of happiness, in the room.

Years later, many years later, on a Sunday morning, Rose turned on the radio. This was when she was living by herself in Toronto.

Well, sir.

It was a different kind of place in our day. Yes, it was.

It was all horses then. Horses and buggies. Buggy races up and down the main street on the Saturday nights.

"Just like the chariot races," says the announcer's, or interviewer's, smooth encouraging voice.

I never seen a one of them.

"No, sir, that was the old Roman chariot races I was referring to. That was before your time."

Musta been before my time. I'm a hunerd and two years old.

"That's a wonderful age, sir."

It is so.

She left it on, as she went around the apartment kitchen, making coffee for herself. It seemed to her that this must be a staged interview, a scene from some play, and she wanted to find out what it was. The old man's voice was so vain and belligerent, the interviewer's quite hopeless and alarmed, under its practiced gentleness and ease. You were surely meant to see him holding the microphone up to some toothless, reckless, preening centenarian, wondering what in God's name he was doing here, and what would he say next?

"They must have been fairly dangerous."

What was dangerous?

"Those buggy races."

They was. Dangerous. Used to be the runaway horses. Used to be a-plenty of accidents. Fellows was dragged along on the gravel and cut their face open. Wouldna matter so much if they was dead. Heh.

Some of them horses was the high-steppers. Some, they had to have the mustard under their tail. Some wouldn step out for nothin. That's the thing it is with the horses. Some'll work and pull till they drop down dead and some wouldn pull your cock out of a pail of lard. Hehe.

It must be a real interview after all. Otherwise they wouldn't have put that in, wouldn't have risked it. It's all right if the old man says it. Local color. Anything rendered harmless and delightful by his hundred years.

Accidents all the time then. In the mill. Foundry. Wasn't the precautions.

"You didn't have so many strikes then, I don't suppose? You didn't have so many unions?"

Everybody taking it easy nowadays. We worked and we was glad to get it. Worked and was glad to get it.

"You didn't have television."

Didn't have no TV. Didn't have no radio. No picture show.

"You made your own entertainment."

That's the way we did.

"You had a lot of experiences young men growing up today will never have."

Experiences.

"Can you recall any of them for us?"

I eaten groundhog meat one time. One winter. You wouldna cared for it. Heh.

There was a pause, of appreciation, it would seem, then the

announcer's voice saying that the foregoing had been an interview with Mr. Wilfred Nettleton of Hanratty, Ontario, made on his hundred and second birthday, two weeks before his death, last spring. A living link with our past. Mr. Nettleton had been interviewed in the Wawanash County Home for the Aged.

Hat Nettleton.

Horsewhipper into centenarian. Photographed on his birthday, fussed over by nurses, kissed no doubt by a girl reporter. Flashbulbs popping at him. Tape recorder drinking in the sound of his voice. Oldest resident. Oldest horsewhipper. Living link with our past.

Looking out from her kitchen window at the cold lake, Rose was longing to tell somebody. It was Flo who would enjoy hearing. She thought of her saying *Imagine!* in a way that meant she was having her worst suspicions gorgeously confirmed. But Flo was in the same place Hat Nettleton had died in, and there wasn't any way Rose could reach her. She had been there even when that interview was recorded, though she would not have heard it, would not have known about it. After Rose put her in the Home, a couple of years earlier, she had stopped talking. She had removed herself, and spent most of her time sitting in a corner of her crib, looking crafty and disagreeable, not answering anybody, though she occasionally showed her feelings by biting a nurse.

✺ *Wild Swans* ✺

FLO SAID TO WATCH for White Slavers. She said this was how they operated: an old woman, a motherly or grandmotherly sort, made friends while riding beside you on a bus or train. She offered you candy, which was drugged. Pretty soon you began to droop and mumble, were in no condition to speak for yourself. Oh, help, the woman said, my daughter (granddaughter) is sick, please somebody help me get her off so that she can recover in the fresh air. Up stepped a polite gentleman, pretending to be a stranger, offering assistance. Together, at the next stop, they hustled you off the train or bus, and that was the last the ordinary world ever saw of you. They kept you a prisoner in the White Slave place (to which you had been transported drugged and bound so you wouldn't even know where you were), until such time as you were thoroughly degraded and in despair, your insides torn up by drunken men and invested with vile disease, your mind destroyed by drugs, your hair and teeth fallen out. It took about three years for you to get to this state. You wouldn't want to go home then; maybe couldn't remember home, or find your way if you did. So they let you out on the streets.

Flo took ten dollars and put it in a little cloth bag, which she sewed to the strap of Rose's slip. Another thing likely to happen was that Rose would get her purse stolen.

Watch out, Flo said as well, for people dressed up as ministers. They were the worst. That disguise was commonly adopted by White Slavers, as well as those after your money.

Rose said she didn't see how she could tell which ones were disguised.

Flo had worked in Toronto once. She had worked as a waitress in a coffee shop in Union Station. That was how she knew all she knew. She never saw sunlight, in those days, except on her days off. But she saw plenty else. She saw a man cut another man's stomach with a knife, just pull out his shirt and do a tidy cut, as if it was a watermelon not a stomach. The stomach's owner just sat looking down surprised, with no time to protest. Flo implied that that was nothing, in Toronto. She saw two bad women (that was what Flo called whores, running the two words together, like badminton) get into a fight, and a man laughed at them, other men stopped and laughed and egged them on, and they had their fists full of each other's hair. At last the police came and took them away, still howling and yelping.

She saw a child die of a fit too. Its face was black as ink.

"Well, I'm not scared," said Rose provokingly. "There's the police, anyway."

"Oh, them! They'd be the first ones to diddle you!"

She did not believe anything Flo said on the subject of sex. Consider the undertaker.

A little bald man, very neatly dressed, would come into the store sometimes and speak to Flo with a placating expression.

"I only wanted a bag of candy. And maybe a few packages of gum. And one or two chocolate bars. Could you go to the trouble of wrapping them?"

Flo in her mock-deferential tone would assure him that she could. She wrapped them in heavy-duty white paper, so they were something like presents. He took his time with the selection, humming and chatting, then dawdled for a while. He might ask how Flo was feeling. And how Rose was, if she was there.

"You look pale. Young girls need fresh air." To Flo he would say, "You work too hard. You've worked hard all your life."

"No rest for the wicked," Flo would say agreeably.

When he went out she hurried to the window. There it was—the old black hearse with its purple curtains.

"He'll be after them today!" Flo would say as the hearse rolled away at a gentle pace, almost a funeral pace. The little man had been an undertaker, but he was retired now. The hearse was retired too. His sons had taken over the undertaking and bought a new one. He drove the old hearse all over the country, looking for women. So Flo said. Rose could not believe it. Flo said he gave them the gum and the candy. Rose said he probably ate them himself. Flo said he had been seen, he had been heard. In mild weather he drove with the windows down, singing, to himself or to somebody out of sight in the back.

> *"Her brow is like the snowdrift*
> *Her throat is like the swan . . ."*

Flo imitated him singing. Gently overtaking some woman walking on a back road, or resting at a country crossroads. All compliments and courtesy and chocolate bars, offering a ride. Of course every woman who reported being asked said she had turned him down. He never pestered anybody, drove politely on. He called in at houses, and if the husband was home he seemed to like just as well as anything to sit and chat. Wives said that was all he ever did anyway but Flo did not believe it.

"Some women are taken in," she said. "A number." She liked to speculate on what the hearse was like inside. Plush. Plush on the walls and the roof and the floor. Soft purple, the color of the curtains, the color of dark lilacs.

All nonsense, Rose thought. Who could believe it, of a man that age?

Rose was going to Toronto on the train for the first time by herself. She had been once before, but that was with Flo, long before her father died. They took along their own sandwiches and bought milk from the vendor on the train. It was sour. Sour chocolate milk. Rose kept taking tiny sips, unwilling to admit that something so much desired could fail her. Flo sniffed it, then hunted up and down the train until she found the old man in his red jacket, with no teeth and the tray hanging around his neck. She invited him to sample the chocolate milk. She invited people nearby to smell it. He let her have some ginger ale for nothing. It was slightly warm.

"I let him know," Flo said, looking around after he had left. "You have to let them know."

A woman agreed with her but most people looked out the window. Rose drank the warm ginger ale. Either that, or the scene with the vendor, or the conversation Flo and the agreeing woman now got into about where they came from, why they were going to Toronto, and Rose's morning constipation which was why she was lacking color, or the small amount of chocolate milk she had got inside her, caused her to throw up in the train toilet. All day long she was afraid people in Toronto could smell vomit on her coat.

This time Flo started the trip off by saying, "Keep an eye on her, she's never been away from home before!" to the conductor, then looking around and laughing, to show that was jokingly meant. Then she had to get off. It seemed the conductor had no more need for jokes than Rose had, and no intention of keeping an eye on anybody. He never spoke to Rose except to ask for her ticket. She had a window seat, and was soon extraordinarily happy. She felt Flo receding, West Hanratty flying away from her, her own wearying self discarded as easily as everything else. She loved the towns less and less known. A woman was standing at her back door in her nightgown, not caring if everybody on the train saw her. They were travelling south, out of the snowbelt, into an earlier spring, a tenderer sort of landscape. People could grow peach trees in their back yards.

Rose collected in her mind the things she had to look for in Toronto. First, things for Flo. Special stockings for her varicose veins. A special kind of cement for sticking handles on pots. And a full set of dominoes.

For herself Rose wanted to buy hair-remover to put on her arms and legs, and if possible an arrangement of inflatable cushions, supposed to reduce your hips and thighs. She thought they probably had hair-remover in the drugstore in Hanratty, but the woman in there was a friend of Flo's and told everything. She told Flo who bought hair dye and slimming medicine and French safes. As for the cushion business, you could send away for it but there was sure to be a comment at the Post

Office, and Flo knew people there as well. She also planned to buy some bangles, and an angora sweater. She had great hopes of silver bangles and powder-blue angora. She thought they could transform her, make her calm and slender and take the frizz out of her hair, dry her underarms and turn her complexion to pearl.

The money for these things, as well as the money for the trip, came from a prize Rose had won, for writing an essay called "Art and Science in the World of Tomorrow." To her surprise, Flo asked if she could read it, and while she was reading it, she remarked that they must have thought they had to give Rose the prize for swallowing the dictionary. Then she said shyly, "It's very interesting."

She would have to spend the night at Cela McKinney's. Cela McKinney was her father's cousin. She had married a hotel manager and thought she had gone up in the world. But the hotel manager came home one day and sat down on the dining-room floor between two chairs and said, "I am never going to leave this house again." Nothing unusual had happened, he had just decided not to go out of the house again, and he didn't, until he died. That had made Cela McKinney odd and nervous. She locked her doors at eight o'clock. She was also very stingy. Supper was usually oatmeal porridge, with raisins. Her house was dark and narrow and smelled like a bank.

The train was filling up. At Brantford a man asked if she would mind if he sat down beside her.

"It's cooler out than you'd think," he said. He offered her part of his newspaper. She said no thanks.

Then, lest he think her rude, she said it really was cooler. She went on looking out the window at the spring morning. There was no snow left, down here. The trees and bushes seemed to have a paler bark than they did at home. Even the sunlight looked different. It was as different from home, here, as the coast of the Mediterranean would be, or the valleys of California.

"Filthy windows, you'd think they'd take more care," the man said. "Do you travel much by train?"

She said no.

Water was lying in the fields. He nodded at it and said there was a lot this year.

"Heavy snows."

She noticed his saying "snows," a poetic-sounding word. Anyone at home would have said "snow."

"I had an unusual experience the other day. I was driving out in the country. In fact, I was on my way to see one of my parishioners, a lady with a heart condition—"

She looked quickly at his collar. He was wearing an ordinary shirt and tie and a dark-blue suit.

"Oh, yes," he said. "I'm a United Church minister. But I don't always wear my uniform. I wear it for preaching in. I'm off duty today.

"Well, as I said, I was driving through the country and I saw some Canada geese down on a pond, and I took another look, and there were some swans down with them. A whole great flock of swans. What a lovely sight they were. They would be on their spring migration, I expect, heading up North. What a spectacle. I never saw anything like it."

Rose was unable to think appreciatively of the wild swans because she was afraid he was going to lead the conversation from them to Nature in general and then to God, the way a minister would feel obliged to do. But he did not, he stopped with the swans.

"A very fine sight. You would have enjoyed them."

He was between fifty and sixty years old, Rose thought. He was short, and energetic-looking, with a square ruddy face and bright waves of gray hair combed straight up from his forehead. When she realized he was not going to mention God she felt she ought to show her gratitude.

She said they must have been lovely.

"It wasn't even a regular pond, it was only some water lying in a field. It was just luck the water was lying there and they came down and I came driving by at the right time. Just luck. They come in at the east end of Lake Erie, I think. But I never was lucky enough to see them before."

She turned by degrees to the window, and he returned to his paper. She remained slightly smiling, so as not to seem rude, not to seem to be rejecting conversation altogether. The morning really was cool, and she had taken down her coat off the hook where she put it when she first got on the train; she had spread it over herself, like a lap robe. She had set her purse on the floor when the minister sat down, to give him room. He took the sections of the paper apart, shaking and rustling them in a leisurely, rather showy way. He seemed to her the sort of person who does everything in a showy way. A ministerial way. He brushed aside the sections he didn't want at the moment. A corner of newspaper touched her leg, just at the edge of her coat.

She thought for some time that it was the paper. Then she said to herself, What if it is a hand? That was the kind of thing she could imagine. She would sometimes look at men's hands, at the fuzz on their forearms, their concentrating profiles. She would think about everything they could do. Even the stupid ones. For instance, the driver-salesman who brought the bread to Flo's store. The ripeness and confidence of manner, the settled mixture of ease and alertness with which he handled the bread truck. A fold of mature belly over the belt did not displease her. Another time she had her eye on the French teacher at school. Not a Frenchman at all, really, his name was McLaren, but Rose thought teaching French had rubbed off on him, made him look like one. Quick and sallow; sharp shoulders; hooked nose and sad eyes. She saw him lapping and coiling his way through slow pleasures, a perfect autocrat of indulgences. She had a considerable longing to be somebody's object. Pounded, pleasured, reduced, exhausted.

But what if it was a hand? What if it really was a hand? She shifted slightly, moved as much as she could toward the window. Her imagination seemed to have created this reality, a reality she was not prepared for at all. She found it alarming. She was concentrating on that leg, that bit of skin with the stocking over it. She could not bring herself to look. Was there a pressure, or was there not? She shifted again. Her legs had been, and remained, tightly closed. It was. It was a hand. It was a hand's pressure.

Please don't. That was what she tried to say. She shaped the words in her mind, tried them out, then couldn't get them past her lips. Why was that? The embarrassment, was it, the fear that people might hear? People were all around them, the seats were full.

It was not only that.

She did manage to look at him, not raising her head but turning it cautiously. He had tilted his seat back and closed his eyes. There was his dark-blue suit sleeve, disappearing under the newspaper. He had arranged the paper so that it overlapped Rose's coat. His hand was underneath, simply resting, as if flung out in sleep.

Now, Rose could have shifted the newspaper and removed her coat. If he was not asleep, he would have been obliged to draw back his hand. If he was asleep, if he did not draw it back, she could have whispered *Excuse me* and set his hand firmly on his own knee. This solution, so obvious and foolproof, did not occur to her. And she would have to wonder, Why not? The minister's hand was not, or not yet, at all welcome to her. It made her feel uncomfortable, resentful, slightly disgusted, trapped and wary. But she could not take charge of it, to reject it. She could not insist that it was there, when he seemed to be insisting that it was not. How could she declare him responsible, when he lay there so harmless and trusting, resting himself before his busy day, with such a pleased and healthy face? A man older than her father would be, if he were living, a man used to deference, an appreciator of Nature, delighter in wild swans. If she did say *Please don't* she was sure he would ignore her, as if overlooking some silliness or impoliteness on her part. She knew that as soon as she said it she would hope he had not heard.

But there was more to it than that. Curiosity. More constant, more imperious, than any lust. A lust in itself, that will make you draw back and wait, wait too long, risk almost anything, just to see what will happen. *To see what will happen.*

The hand began, over the next several miles, the most delicate, the most timid, pressures and investigations. Not asleep. Or if he was, his hand wasn't. She did feel disgust. She felt a faint, wandering nausea. She thought of flesh: lumps of flesh,

pink snouts, fat tongues, blunt fingers, all on their way trotting and creeping and lolling and rubbing, looking for their
comfort. She thought of cats in heat rubbing themselves along
the top of board fences, yowling with their miserable complaint. It was pitiful, infantile, this itching and shoving and
squeezing. Spongy tissues, inflamed membranes, tormented
nerve-ends, shameful smells; humiliation.

All that was starting. His hand, that she wouldn't ever have
wanted to hold, that she wouldn't have squeezed back, his stubborn patient hand was able, after all, to get the ferns to rustle
and the streams to flow, to waken a sly luxuriance.

Nevertheless, she would rather not. She would still rather
not. Please remove this, she said out the window. Stop it,
please, she said to the stumps and barns. The hand moved up
her leg past the top of her stocking to her bare skin, had moved
higher, under her suspender, reached her underpants and the
lower part of her belly. Her legs were still crossed, pinched
together. While her legs stayed crossed she could lay claim to
innocence, she had not admitted anything. She could still
believe that she would stop this in a minute. Nothing was going
to happen, nothing more. Her legs were never going to open.

But they were. They were. As the train crossed the Niagara Escarpment above Dundas, as they looked down at the
preglacial valley, the silver-wooded rubble of little hills, as they
came sliding down to the shores of Lake Ontario, she would
make this slow, and silent, and definite declaration, perhaps
disappointing as much as satisfying the hand's owner. He
would not lift his eyelids, his face would not alter, his fingers
would not hesitate, but would go powerfully and discreetly to
work. Invasion, and welcome, and sunlight flashing far and
wide on the lake water; miles of bare orchards stirring round
Burlington.

This was disgrace, this was beggary. But what harm in that,
we say to ourselves at such moments, what harm in anything,
the worse the better, as we ride the cold wave of greed, of greedy
assent. A stranger's hand, or root vegetables or humble kitchen
tools that people tell jokes about; the world is tumbling with
innocent-seeming objects ready to declare themselves, slippery

and obliging. She was careful of her breathing. She could not believe this. Victim and accomplice she was borne past Glassco's Jams and Marmalades, past the big pulsating pipes of oil refineries. They glided into suburbs where bedsheets, and towels used to wipe up intimate stains, flapped leeringly on the clotheslines, where even the children seemed to be frolicking lewdly in the schoolyards, and the very truck drivers stopped at the railway crossings must be thrusting their thumbs gleefully into curled hands. Such cunning antics now, such popular visions. The gates and towers of the Exhibition Grounds came into view, the painted domes and pillars floated marvellously against her eyelids' rosy sky. Then flew apart in celebration. You could have had such a flock of birds, wild swans, even, wakened under one big dome together, exploding from it, taking to the sky.

She bit the edge of her tongue. Very soon the conductor passed through the train, to stir the travellers, warn them back to life.

In the darkness under the station the United Church minister, refreshed, opened his eyes and got his paper folded together, then asked if she would like some help with her coat. His gallantry was self-satisfied, dismissive. No, said Rose, with a sore tongue. He hurried out of the train ahead of her. She did not see him in the station. She never saw him again in her life. But he remained on call, so to speak, for years and years, ready to slip into place at a critical moment, without even any regard, later on, for husband or lovers. What recommended him? She could never understand it. His simplicity, his arrogance, his perversely appealing lack of handsomeness, even of ordinary grown-up masculinity? When he stood up she saw that he was shorter even than she had thought, that his face was pink and shiny, that there was something crude and pushy and childish about him.

Was he a minister, really, or was that only what he said? Flo had mentioned people who were not ministers, dressed up as if they were. Not real ministers dressed as if they were not. Or, stranger still, men who were not real ministers pretending to be real but dressed as if they were not. But that she had come as close as she had, to what could happen, was an unwelcome thing. Rose walked through Union Station feeling the little bag with the ten dollars rubbing at her, knew she would feel it all day long, rubbing its reminder against her skin.

She couldn't stop getting Flo's messages, even with that. She remembered, because she was in Union Station, that there was a girl named Mavis working here, in the gift shop, when Flo was working in the coffee shop. Mavis had warts on her eyelids that looked like they were going to turn into sties but they didn't, they went away. Maybe she had them removed, Flo didn't ask. She was very good-looking, without them. There was a movie star in those days she looked a lot like. The movie star's name was Frances Farmer.

Frances Farmer. Rose had never heard of her.

That was the name. And Mavis went and bought herself a big hat that dipped over one eye and a dress entirely made of lace. She went off for the weekend to Georgian Bay, to a resort up there. She booked herself in under the name of Florence Farmer. To give everybody the idea she was really the other one, Frances Farmer, but calling herself Florence because she was on holiday and didn't want to be recognized. She had a little cigarette holder that was black and mother-of-pearl. She could have been arrested, Flo said. For the *nerve*.

Rose almost went over to the gift shop to see if Mavis was still there and if she could recognize her. She thought it would be an especially fine thing to manage a transformation like that. To dare it; to get away with it, to enter on preposterous adventures in your own, but newly named, skin.

༄ The Beggar Maid ༄

PATRICK BLATCHFORD WAS in love with Rose. This had become a fixed, even furious, idea with him. For her, a continual surprise. He wanted to marry her. He waited for her after classes, moved in and walked beside her, so that anybody she was talking to would have to reckon with his presence. He would not talk when these friends or classmates of hers were around, but he would try to catch her eye, so that he could indicate by a cold incredulous look what he thought of their conversation. Rose was flattered, but nervous. A girl named Nancy Falls, a friend of hers, mispronounced Metternich in front of him. He said to her later, "How can you be friends with people like that?"

Nancy and Rose had gone and sold their blood together, at Victoria Hospital. They each got fifteen dollars. They spent most of the money on evening shoes, tarty silver sandals. Then because they were sure the bloodletting had caused them to lose weight, they had hot fudge sundaes at Boomers. Why was Rose unable to defend Nancy to Patrick?

Patrick was twenty-four years old, a graduate student, planning to be a history professor. He was tall, thin, fair, and good-looking, though he had a long pale-red birthmark, dribbling like a tear down his temple and his cheek. He apologized for it, but said it was fading as he got older. When he was forty, it would have faded away. It was not the birthmark that cancelled out his good looks, Rose thought. (Something did cancel them out, or at least diminish them, for her; she had to keep reminding herself they were there.) There was something edgy, jumpy, disconcerting about him. His voice would break under stress—with her, it seemed he was always under stress—he knocked dishes and cups off tables, spilled drinks and bowls of peanuts, like a comedian. He was not a comedian; nothing could be further from his intentions. He came from British Columbia. His family was rich.

He arrived early to pick Rose up, when they were going to the movies. He wouldn't knock, he knew he was early. He sat on the step outside Dr. Henshawe's door. This was in the winter, it was dark out, but there was a little coach lamp beside the door.

"Oh, Rose! Come and look!" called Dr. Henshawe, in her soft, amused voice, and they looked down together from the dark window of the study. "The poor young man," said Dr. Henshawe tenderly. Dr. Henshawe was in her seventies. She was a former English professor, fastidious and lively. She had a lame leg, but a still youthfully, charmingly tilted head, with white braids wound around it.

She called Patrick poor because he was in love, and perhaps also because he was a male, doomed to push and blunder. Even from up here he looked stubborn and pitiable, determined and dependent, sitting out there in the cold.

"Guarding the door," Dr. Henshawe said. "Oh, Rose!"

Another time she said disturbingly, "Oh, dear, I'm afraid he is after the wrong girl."

Rose didn't like her saying that. She didn't like her laughing at Patrick. She didn't like Patrick sitting out on the steps that way, either. He was asking to be laughed at. He was the most vulnerable person Rose had ever known; he made himself so, didn't know anything about protecting himself. But he was also full of cruel judgments, he was full of conceit.

"You are a scholar, Rose," Dr. Henshawe would say. "This will interest you." Then she would read aloud something from the paper, or, more likely, something from *Canadian Forum* or the *Atlantic Monthly*. Dr. Henshawe had at one time headed the city's school board, she was a founding member of Canada's Socialist Party. She still sat on committees, wrote letters to the paper, reviewed books. Her father and mother had been medical missionaries; she had been born in China. Her house was small and perfect. Polished floors, glowing rugs, Chinese vases, bowls, and landscapes, black carved screens. Much that Rose could not appreciate, at the time. She could not really distinguish between the little jade animals on Dr. Henshawe's mantelpiece and the ornaments displayed in the jewelry-store window in Hanratty, though she could now distinguish between either of these and the things Flo bought from the five-and-ten.

She could not really decide how much she liked being at Dr. Henshawe's. At times she felt discouraged, sitting in the dining room with a linen napkin on her knee, eating from fine white plates on blue placemats. For one thing, there was never enough to eat, and she had taken to buying doughnuts and chocolate bars and hiding them in her room. The canary swung on its perch in the dining-room window and Dr. Henshawe directed conversation. She talked about politics, about writers. She mentioned Frank Scott and Dorothy Livesay. She said Rose must read them. Rose must read this, she must read that. Rose became sullenly determined not to. She was reading Thomas Mann. She was reading Tolstoy.

Before she came to Dr. Henshawe's, Rose had never heard of the working class. She took the designation home.

"This would have to be the last part of town where they put the sewers," Flo said.

"Of course," Rose said coolly. "This is the working-class part of town."

"*Working* class?" said Flo. "Not if the ones around here can help it."

Dr. Henshawe's house had done one thing. It had destroyed the naturalness, the taken-for-granted background, of home. To go back there was to go quite literally into a crude light. Flo had put fluorescent lights in the store and the kitchen. There was also, in a corner of the kitchen, a floor lamp Flo had won at Bingo; its shade was permanently wrapped in wide strips of cellophane. What Dr. Henshawe's house and Flo's house did best, in Rose's opinion, was discredit each other. In Dr. Henshawe's charming rooms there was always for Rose the raw knowledge of home, an indigestible lump, and at home now her sense of order and modulation elsewhere exposed such embarrassing sad poverty in people who never thought themselves poor. Poverty was not just wretchedness, as Dr. Henshawe seemed to think, it was not just deprivation. It meant having those ugly tube lights and being proud of them. It meant continual talk of money and malicious talk about new things people had bought and whether they were paid for. It meant pride and jealousy flaring over something like the new pair of plastic curtains, imitating lace, that Flo had bought for the front window. That as well as hanging your clothes on nails behind the door and being able to hear every sound from the bathroom. It meant decorating your walls with a number of admonitions, pious and cheerful and mildly bawdy.

THE LORD IS MY SHEPHERD
BELIEVE IN THE LORD JESUS CHRIST
AND THOU SHALL BE SAVED

Why did Flo have those, when she wasn't even religious? They were what people had, common as calendars.

THIS IS MY KITCHEN AND I WILL
DO AS I DARNED PLEASE
MORE THAN TWO PERSONS TO A BED
IS DANGEROUS AND UNLAWFUL

Billy Pope had brought that one. What would Patrick have to say about them? What would someone who was offended by a mispronunciation of Metternich think of Billy Pope's stories?

Billy Pope worked in Tyde's Butcher Shop. What he talked about most frequently now was the D.P., the Belgian, who had come to work there, and got on Billy Pope's nerves with his impudent singing of French songs and his naive notions of getting on in this country, buying a butcher shop of his own.

"Don't you think you can come over here and get yourself ideas," Billy Pope said to the D.P. "It's *youse* workin' for *us*, and don't think that'll change into *us* workin' for *youse*." That shut him up, Billy Pope said.

Patrick would say from time to time that since her home was only fifty miles away he ought to come up and meet Rose's family.

"There's only my stepmother."

"It's too bad I couldn't have met your father."

Rashly, she had presented her father to Patrick as a reader of history, an amateur scholar. That was not exactly a lie, but it did not give a truthful picture of the circumstances.

"Is your stepmother your guardian?"

Rose had to say she did not know.

"Well, your father must have appointed a guardian for you in his will. Who administers his estate?"

His *estate*. Rose thought an estate was land, such as people owned in England.

Patrick thought it was rather charming of her to think that.

"No, his money and stocks and so on. What he left."

"I don't think he left any."

"Don't be silly," Patrick said.

And sometimes Dr. Henshawe would say, "Well, you are a scholar, you are not interested in that." Usually she was speaking of some event at the college: a pep rally, a football game, a dance. And usually she was right; Rose was not interested. But she was not eager to admit it. She did not seek or relish that definition of herself.

On the stairway wall hung graduation photographs of all the other girls, scholarship girls, who had lived with Dr. Henshawe. Most of them had got to be teachers, then mothers. One was a dietician, two were librarians, one was a professor of English, like Dr. Henshawe herself. Rose did not care for the look of them, for their soft-focussed meekly smiling gratitude, their large teeth and maidenly rolls of hair. They seemed to be urging on her some deadly secular piety. There were no actresses among them, no brassy magazine journalists; none of them had latched on to the sort of life Rose wanted for herself. She wanted to perform in public. She thought she wanted to be an actress but she never tried to act, was afraid to go near the college drama productions. She knew she couldn't sing or dance.

She would really have liked to play the harp, but she had no ear for music. She wanted to be known and envied, slim and clever. She told Dr. Henshawe that if she had been a man she would have wanted to be a foreign correspondent.

"Then you must be one!" cried Dr. Henshawe alarmingly. "The future will be wide open for women. You must concentrate on languages. You must take courses in political science. And economics. Perhaps you could get a job on the paper for the summer. I have friends there."

Rose was frightened at the idea of working on a paper, and she hated the introductory economics course; she was looking for a way of dropping it. It was dangerous to mention things to Dr. Henshawe.

She had got to live with Dr. Henshawe by accident. Another girl had been picked to move in but she got sick; she had t.b., and went instead to a sanitorium. Dr. Henshawe came up to the college office on the second day of registration to get the names of some other scholarship freshmen.

Rose had been in the office just a little while before, asking where the meeting of the scholarship students was to be held. She had lost her notice. The Bursar was giving a talk to the new scholarship students, telling them of ways to earn money and live cheaply and explaining the high standards of performance to be expected of them here if they wanted their payments to keep coming.

Rose found out the number of the room, and started up the stairs to the first floor. A girl came up beside her and said, "Are you on your way to three-oh-twelve, too?"

They walked together, telling each other the details of their scholarships. Rose did not yet have a place to live, she was staying at the Y. She did not really have enough money to be here at all. She had a scholarship for her tuition and the county prize to buy her books and a bursary of three hundred dollars to live on; that was all.

"You'll have to get a job," the other girl said. She had a larger bursary, because she was in science (that's where the money is, the money's all in science, she said seriously), but she was hoping to get a job in the cafeteria. She had a room in some-body's basement. How much does your room cost? How much does a hot plate cost? Rose asked her, her head swimming with anxious calculations.

This girl wore her hair in a roll. She wore a crêpe blouse, yellowed and shining from washing and ironing. Her breasts were large and sagging. She probably wore a dirty-pink hooked-up-the-side brassiere. She had a scaly patch on one cheek.

"This must be it," she said.

There was a little window in the door. They could look through at the other scholarship winners already assembled and waiting. It seemed to Rose that she saw four or five girls of the same stooped and matronly type as the girl who was beside her, and several bright-eyed, self-satisfied, babyish-look-ing boys. It seemed to be the rule that girl scholarship winners looked about forty and boys about twelve. It was not possible, of course, that they all looked like this. It was not possible that in one glance through the windows of the door Rose could detect traces of eczema, stained underarms, dandruff, moldy deposits on the teeth, and crusty flakes in the corners of the eyes. That was only what she thought. But there was a pall over them, she was not mistaken, there was a true terrible pall of eagerness and docility. How else could they have supplied so many right answers, so many pleasing answers, how else dis-tinguished themselves and got themselves here? And Rose had done the same.

"I have to go to the john," she said.

She could see herself working in the cafeteria. Her figure, broad enough already, broadened out still more by the green cotton uniform, her face red and her hair stringy from the heat. Dishing up stew and fried chicken for those of inferior intelli-gence and handsomer means. Blocked off by the steam tables, the uniform, by decent hard work that nobody need be ashamed of, by publicly proclaimed braininess and poverty. Boys could get away with that, barely. For girls it was fatal. Poverty in girls is not attractive unless combined with sweet sluttishness, stu-pidity. Braininess is not attractive unless combined with some signs of elegance; *class*. Was this true, and was she foolish enough to care? It was; she was.

She went back to the first floor where the halls were crowded with ordinary students who were not on scholarships, who would not be expected to get A's and be grateful and live cheap. Enviable and innocent, they milled around the registration tables in their new purple-and-white blazers, their purple Frosh beanies, yelling reminders to each other, confused information, nonsensical insults. She walked among them feeling bitterly superior and despondent. The skirt of her green corduroy suit kept falling back between her legs as she walked. The material was limp; she should have spent more and bought the heavier weight. She thought now that the jacket was not properly cut either, though it had looked all right at home. The whole outfit had been made by a dressmaker in Hanratty, a friend of Flo's, whose main concern had been that there should be no revelations of the figure. When Rose asked if the skirt couldn't be made tighter this woman had said, "You wouldn't want your b.t.m. to show, now would you?" and Rose hadn't wanted to say she didn't care.

Another thing the dressmaker said was "I thought now you was through school you'd be getting a job and help out at home."

A woman walking down the hall stopped Rose.

"Aren't you one of the scholarship girls?"

It was the Registrar's secretary. Rose thought she was going to be reprimanded for not being at the meeting, and she was going to say she felt sick. She prepared her face for this lie. But the secretary said, "Come with me, now. I've got somebody I want you to meet."

Dr. Henshawe was making a charming nuisance of herself in the office. She liked poor girls, bright girls, but they had to be fairly good-looking girls.

"I think this could be your lucky day," the secretary said, leading Rose. "If you could put a pleasanter expression on your face."

Rose hated being told that, but she smiled obediently.

Within the hour she was taken home with Dr. Henshawe,

installed in the house with the Chinese screens and vases, and told she was a scholar.

She got a job working in the library of the college, instead of in the cafeteria. Dr. Henshawe was a friend of the Head Librarian. Rose worked Saturday afternoons. She worked in the stacks, putting books away. On Saturday afternoons in the fall the library was nearly empty, because of the football games. The narrow windows were open to the leafy campus, the football field, the dry fall country. The distant songs and shouts came drifting in.

The college buildings were not old at all, but they were built to look old. They were built of stone. The Arts Building had a tower, and the library had casement windows, which might have been designed for shooting arrows through. The buildings and the books in the library were what pleased Rose most about the place. The life that usually filled it, and that was now drained away, concentrated around the football field, letting loose those noises, seemed to her inappropriate and distracting. The cheers and songs were idiotic, if you listened to the words. What did they want to build such dignified buildings for if they were going to sing songs like that?

She knew enough not to reveal these opinions. If anybody said to her, "It's awful you have to work Saturdays and can't get to any of the games," she would fervently agree.

Once a man grabbed her bare leg, between her sock and her skirt. It happened in the Agriculture section, down at the bottom of the stacks. Only the faculty, graduate students, and employees had access to the stacks, though someone could have hoisted himself through a ground-floor window if he was skinny. She had seen a man crouched down looking at the books on a low shelf, further along. As she reached up to push a book into place he passed behind her. He bent and grabbed her leg, all in one smooth startling motion, and then was gone. She could feel for quite a while where his fingers had dug in. It didn't seem to her a sexual touch; it was more like a joke, though not at all a friendly one. She heard him run away, or felt him running; the metal shelves were vibrating. Then they

stopped. There was no sound of him. She walked around looking between the stacks, looking into the carrels. Suppose she
did see him, or bumped into him around a corner, what did
she intend to do? She did not know. It was simply necessary to
look for him, as in some tense childish game. She looked down
at the sturdy pinkish calf of her leg. Amazing, that out of the
blue somebody had wanted to blotch and punish it.

There were usually a few graduate students working in the
carrels, even on Saturday afternoons. More rarely, a professor.
Every carrel she looked into was empty, until she came to one
in the corner. She poked her head in freely, by this time not
expecting anybody. Then she had to say she was sorry.

There was a young man with a book on his lap, books on
the floor, papers all around him. Rose asked him if he had seen
anybody run past. He said no.

She told him what had happened. She didn't tell him because
she was frightened or disgusted, as he seemed afterward to
think, but just because she had to tell somebody; it was so odd.
She was not prepared at all for his response. His long neck and
face turned red, the flush entirely absorbing a birthmark down
the side of his cheek. He was thin and fair. He stood up without any thought for the book in his lap or the papers in front
of him. The book thumped on the floor. A great sheaf of
papers, pushed across the desk, upset his ink bottle.

"How vile," he said.

"Grab the ink," Rose said. He leaned to catch the bottle and
knocked it onto the floor. Fortunately the top was on, and it
did not break.

"Did he hurt you?"

"No, not really."

"Come on upstairs. We'll report it."

"Oh, no."

"He can't get away with that. It shouldn't be allowed."

"There isn't anybody to report to," Rose said with relief.
"The librarian goes off at noon on Saturdays."

"It's disgusting," he said in a high-pitched, excitable voice.
Rose was sorry now that she had told him anything, and said
she had to get back to work.

"Are you really all right?"

"Oh, yes."

"I'll be right here. Just call me if he comes back."

That was Patrick. If she had been trying to make him fall in love with her, there was no better way she could have chosen. He had many chivalric notions, which he pretended to mock, by saying certain words and phrases as if in quotation marks. "The fair sex," he would say, and "damsel in distress." Coming to his carrel with that story, Rose had turned herself into a damsel in distress. The pretended irony would not fool anybody; it was clear that he did wish to operate in a world of knights and ladies; outrages; devotions.

She continued to see him in the library, every Saturday, and often she met him walking across the campus or in the cafeteria. He made a point of greeting her with courtesy and concern, saying, "How are you?" in a way that suggested she might have suffered a further attack, or might still be recovering from the first one. He always flushed deeply when he saw her, and she thought that this was because the memory of what she had told him so embarrassed him. Later she found out it was because he was in love.

He discovered her name, and where she lived. He phoned her at Dr. Henshawe's house and asked her to go to the movies. At first when he said, "This is Patrick Blatchford speaking," Rose could not think who it was, but after a moment she recognized the high, rather aggrieved and tremulous voice. She said she would go. This was partly because Dr. Henshawe was always saying she was glad Rose did not waste her time running around with boys.

Rather soon after she started to go out with him, she said to Patrick, "Wouldn't it be funny if it was you grabbed my leg that day in the library?"

He did not think it would be funny. He was horrified that she would think such a thing.

She said she was only joking. She said she meant that it would be a good twist in a story, maybe a Maugham story, or a Hitchcock movie. They had just been to see a Hitchcock movie.

"You know, if Hitchcock made a movie out of something like that, you could be a wild insatiable leg-grabber with one half of your personality, and the other half could be a timid scholar."

He didn't like that either.

"Is that how I seem to you, a timid scholar?" It seemed to her he deepened his voice, introduced a few growling notes, drew in his chin, as if for a joke. But he seldom joked with her; he didn't think joking was suitable when you were in love.

"I didn't say you were a timid scholar or a leg-grabber. It was just an idea."

After a while he said, "I suppose I don't seem very manly."

She was startled and irritated by such an exposure. He took such chances; had nothing ever taught him not to take such chances? But maybe he didn't, after all. He knew she would have to say something reassuring. Though she was hoping not to, she longed to say judiciously, "Well, no. You don't."

But that would not actually be true. He did seem masculine to her. Because he took those chances. Only a man could be so careless and demanding.

"We come from two different worlds," she said to him, on another occasion. She felt like a character in a play, saying that. "My people are poor people. You would think the place I lived in was a dump."

Now she was the one who was being dishonest, pretending to throw herself on his mercy, for of course she did not expect him to say, "Oh, well, if you come from poor people and live in a dump, then I will have to withdraw my offer."

"But I'm glad," said Patrick. "I'm glad you're poor. You're so lovely. You're like the Beggar Maid."

"Who?"

"'King Cophetua and the Beggar Maid.' You know. The painting. Don't you know that painting?"

Patrick had a trick—no, it was not a trick, Patrick had no tricks—Patrick had a way of expressing surprise, fairly scornful surprise, when people did not know something he knew, and similar scorn, similar surprise, whenever they had bothered to know something he did not. His arrogance and humility were both oddly exaggerated. The arrogance, Rose decided in time, must come from being rich, though Patrick was never arrogant about that in itself. His sisters, when she met them, turned out to be the same way, disgusted with anybody who did not know about horses or sailing, and just as disgusted by anybody knowing about music, say, or politics. Patrick and they could do little together but radiate disgust. But wasn't Billy Pope as bad, wasn't Flo as bad, when it came to arrogance? Maybe. There was a difference, though, and the difference was that Billy Pope and Flo were not protected. Things could get at them: D.P.'s; people speaking French on the radio; changes. Patrick and his sisters behaved as if things could never get at them. Their voices, when they quarrelled at the table, were astonishingly childish; their demands for food they liked, their petulance at seeing anything on the table they didn't like, were those of children. They had never had to defer and polish themselves and win favor in the world, they never would have to, and that was because they were rich.

Rose had no idea at the beginning how rich Patrick was. Nobody believed that. Everybody believed she had been calculating and clever, and she was so far from clever, in that way, that she really did not mind if they believed it. It turned out that other girls had been trying, and had not struck, as she had, the necessary note. Older girls, sorority girls, who had never noticed her before began to look at her with puzzlement and respect. Even Dr. Henshawe, when she saw that things were more serious than she had supposed, and settled Rose down to have a talk about it, assumed that she would have an eye on the money.

"It is no small triumph to attract the attentions of the heir to a mercantile empire," said Dr. Henshawe, being ironic and serious at the same time. "I don't despise wealth," she said. "Sometimes I wish I had some of it." (Did she really suppose she had not?) "I am sure you will learn how to put it to good uses. But what about your ambitions, Rose? What about your studies and your degree? Are you going to forget all that so soon?"

"Mercantile empire" was a rather grand way of putting it. Patrick's family owned a chain of department stores in British

Columbia. All Patrick had said to Rose was that his father owned some stores. When she said *two different worlds* to him she was thinking that he probably lived in some substantial house like the houses in Dr. Henshawe's neighborhood. She was thinking of the most prosperous merchants in Hanratty. She could not realize what a coup she had made because it would have been a coup for her if the butcher's son had fallen for her, or the jeweller's; people would say she had done well.

She had a look at that painting. She looked it up in an art book in the library. She studied the Beggar Maid, meek and voluptuous, with her shy white feet. The milky surrender of her, the helplessness and gratitude. Was that how Patrick saw Rose? Was that how she could be? She would need that king, sharp and swarthy as he looked, even in his trance of passion, clever and barbaric. He could make a puddle of her, with his fierce desire. There would be no apologizing with him, none of that flinching, that lack of faith, that seemed to be revealed in all transactions with Patrick.

She could not turn Patrick down. She could not do it. It was not the amount of money but the amount of love he offered that she could not ignore; she believed that she felt sorry for him, that she had to help him out. It was as if he had come up to her in a crowd carrying a large, simple, dazzling object—a huge egg, maybe, of solid silver, something of doubtful use and punishing weight—and was offering it to her, in fact thrusting it at her, begging her to take some of the weight of it off him. If she thrust it back, how could he bear it? But that explanation left something out. It left out her own appetite, which was not for wealth but for worship. The size, the weight, the shine, of what he said was love (and she did not doubt him) had to impress her, even though she had never asked for it. It did not seem likely such an offering would come her way again. Patrick himself, though worshipful, did in some oblique way acknowledge her luck.

She had always thought this would happen, that somebody would look at her and love her totally and helplessly. At the same time she had thought that nobody would, nobody would want her at all, and up until now nobody had. What made you wanted was nothing you did, it was something you had, and how could you ever tell whether you had it? She would look at herself in the glass and think: Wife, sweetheart. Those mild lovely words. How could they apply to her? It was a miracle; it was a mistake. It was what she had dreamed of; it was not what she wanted.

She grew very tired, irritable, sleepless. She tried to think admiringly of Patrick. His lean, fair-skinned face was really very handsome. He must know a number of things. He graded papers, presided at examinations, he was finishing his thesis. There was a smell of pipe tobacco and rough wool about him that she liked. He was twenty-four. No other girl she knew who had a boyfriend had one as old as that.

Then without warning she thought of him saying, "I suppose I don't seem very manly." She thought of him saying, "Do you love me? Do you really love me?" He would look at her in a scared and threatening way. Then when she said yes he said how lucky he was, how lucky they were; he mentioned friends of his and their girls, comparing their love affairs unfavorably to his and Rose's. Rose would shiver with irritation and misery. She was sick of herself as much as him, she was sick of the picture they made at this moment, walking across a snowy downtown park, her bare hand snuggled in Patrick's, in his pocket. Some outrageous and cruel things were being shouted inside her. She had to do something, to keep them from getting out. She started tickling and teasing him.

Outside Dr. Henshawe's back door, in the snow, she kissed him, tried to make him open his mouth, she did scandalous things to him. When he kissed her his lips were soft; his tongue was shy; he collapsed over rather than held her, she could not find any force in him.

"You're lovely. You have lovely skin. Such fair eyebrows. You're so delicate."

She was pleased to hear that, anybody would be. But she said warningly, "I'm not so delicate, really. I'm quite large."

"You don't know how I love you. There's a book I have called *The White Goddess*. Every time I look at the title it reminds me of you."

She wriggled away from him. She bent down and got a

handful of snow from the drift by the steps and clapped it on his head.

"My White God."

He shook the snow out. She scooped up some more and threw it at him. He didn't laugh; he was surprised and alarmed. She brushed the snow off his eyebrows and licked it off his ears. She was laughing, though she felt desperate rather than merry. She didn't know what made her do this.

"Dr. *Hen*-shawe," Patrick hissed at her. The tender poetic voice he used for rhapsodizing about her could entirely disappear, could change to remonstrance, exasperation, with no steps at all between.

"Dr. Henshawe will hear you!"

"Dr. Henshawe says you are an honorable young man," Rose said dreamily. "I think she's in love with you." It was true; Dr. Henshawe had said that. And it was true that he was. He couldn't bear the way Rose was talking. She blew at the snow in his hair. "Why don't you go in and deflower her? I'm sure she's a virgin. That's her window. Why don't you?" She rubbed his hair, then slipped her hand inside his overcoat and rubbed the front of his pants. "You're hard!" she said triumphantly. "Oh, Patrick! You've got a hard-on for Dr. Henshawe!" She had never said anything like this before, never come near behaving like this.

"Shut up!" said Patrick, tormented. But she couldn't. She raised her head and in a loud whisper pretended to call toward an upstairs window, "Dr. Henshawe! Come and see what Patrick's got for you!" Her bullying hand went for his fly.

To stop her, to keep her quiet, Patrick had to struggle with her. He got a hand over her mouth, with the other hand beat her away from his zipper. The big loose sleeves of his overcoat beat at her like floppy wings. As soon as he started to fight she was relieved—that was what she wanted from him, some sort of action. But she had to keep resisting, until he really proved himself stronger. She was afraid he might not be able to.

But he was. He forced her down, down, to her knees, face down in the snow. He pulled her arms back and rubbed her face in the snow. Then he let her go, and almost spoiled it.

"Are you all right? Are you? I'm sorry. Rose?"

She staggered up and shoved her snowy face into his. He backed off.

"Kiss me! Kiss the snow! I love you!"

"Do you?" he said plaintively, and brushed the snow from a corner of her mouth and kissed her, with understandable bewilderment. "*Do* you?"

Then the light came on, flooding them and the trampled snow, and Dr. Henshawe was calling over their heads.

"Rose! Rose!"

She called in a patient, encouraging voice, as if Rose was lost in a fog nearby, and needed directing home.

"Do you love him, Rose?" said Dr. Henshawe. "No, think about it. Do you?" Her voice was full of doubt and seriousness. Rose took a deep breath and answered as if filled with calm emotion, "Yes, I do."

"Well, then."

In the middle of the night Rose woke up and ate chocolate bars. She craved sweets. Often in class or in the middle of a movie she started thinking about fudge cupcakes, brownies, some kind of cake Dr. Henshawe bought at the European Bakery; it was filled with dollops of rich bitter chocolate that ran out on the plate. Whenever she tried to think about herself and Patrick, whenever she made up her mind to decide what she really felt, these cravings intervened.

She was putting on weight, and had developed a nest of pimples between her eyebrows.

Her bedroom was cold, being over the garage, with windows on three sides. Otherwise it was pleasant. Over the bed hung framed photographs of Greek skies and ruins, taken by Dr. Henshawe herself on her Mediterranean trip.

She was writing an essay on Yeats's plays. In one of the plays a young bride is lured away by the fairies from her sensible unbearable marriage.

"Come away, O human child . . ." Rose read, and her eyes filled up with tears for herself, as if she was that shy elusive virgin, too fine for the bewildered peasants who have entrapped her. In actual fact she was the peasant, shocking high-minded Patrick, but he did not look for escape.

She took down one of those Greek photographs and defaced the wallpaper, writing the start of a poem which had come to her while she ate chocolate bars in bed and the wind from Gibbons Park banged at the garage walls.

> *Heedless in my dark womb*
> *I bear a madman's child . . .*

She never wrote any more if it, and wondered sometimes if she had meant headless. She never tried to rub it out, either.

Patrick shared an apartment with two other graduate students. He lived plainly, did not own a car or belong to a fraternity. His clothes had an ordinary academic shabbiness. His friends were the sons of teachers and ministers. He said his father had all but disowned him for becoming an intellectual. He said he would never go into business.

They came back to the apartment in the early afternoon when they knew both the other students would be out. The apartment was cold. They undressed quickly and got into Patrick's bed. Now was the time. They clung together, shivering and giggling. Rose was doing the giggling. She felt a need to be continually playful. She was terrified that they would not manage it, that there was a great humiliation in store, a great exposure of their poor deceits and stratagems. But the deceits and stratagems were only hers. Patrick was never a fraud; he managed, in spite of gigantic embarrassment, apologies; he passed through some amazed pantings and flounderings, to peace. Rose was no help, presenting instead of an honest passivity much twisting and fluttering eagerness, unpracticed counterfeit of passion. She was pleased when it was accomplished; she did not have to counterfeit that. They had done what others did, they had done what lovers did. She thought of celebration. What occurred to her was something delicious to eat, a sundae at Boomers, apple pie with hot cinnamon sauce.

She was not at all prepared for Patrick's idea, which was to stay where they were and try again.

When pleasure presented itself, the fifth or sixth time they were together, she was thrown out of gear entirely, her passionate carrying-on was silenced.

Patrick said, "What's the matter?"

"Nothing!" Rose said, turning herself radiant and attentive once more. But she kept forgetting, the new developments interfered, and she had finally to give in to that struggle, more or less ignoring Patrick. When she could take note of him again she overwhelmed him with gratitude; she was really grateful now, and she wanted to be forgiven, though she could not say so, for all her pretended gratitude, her patronizing, her doubts.

Why should she doubt so much, she thought, lying comfortably in the bed while Patrick went to make some instant coffee. Might it not be possible, to feel as she pretended? If this sexual surprise was possible, wasn't anything? Patrick was not much help; his chivalry and self-abasement, next door to his scoldings, did discourage her. But wasn't the real fault hers? Her conviction that anyone who could fall in love with her must be hopelessly lacking, must finally be revealed as a fool? So she took note of anything that was foolish about Patrick, even though she thought she was looking for things that were masterful, admirable. At this moment, in his bed, in his room, surrounded by his books and clothes, his shoe brushes and typewriter, some tacked-up cartoons—she sat up in bed to look at them, and they really were quite funny, he must allow things to be funny when she was not here—she could see him as a likable, intelligent, even humorous person; no hero; no fool. Perhaps they could be ordinary. If only, when he came back in, he would not start thanking and fondling and worshipping her. She didn't like worship, really; it was only the idea of it she liked. On the other hand, she didn't like it when he started to correct and criticize her. There was much he planned to change.

Patrick loved her. What did he love? Not her accent, which he was trying hard to alter, though she was often mutinous and unreasonable, declaring in the face of all evidence that she did not have a country accent, everybody talked the way she did. Not her jittery sexual boldness (his relief at her virginity matched hers at his competence). She could make him flinch at a vulgar word, a drawling tone. All the time, moving and speaking, she was destroying herself for him, yet he looked right through her, through all the distractions she was creating, and loved some obedient image that she herself could not see. And his hopes were high. Her accent could be eliminated, her friends could be discredited and removed, her vulgarity could be discouraged.

What about all the rest of her? Energy, laziness, vanity, discontent, ambition? She concealed all that. He had no idea. For all her doubts about him, she never wanted him to fall out of love with her.

They made two trips.

They went to British Columbia, on the train, during the Easter holidays. His parents sent Patrick money for his ticket. He paid for Rose, using up what he had in the bank and borrowing from one of his roommates. He told her not to reveal to his parents that she had not paid for her own ticket. She saw that he meant to conceal that she was poor. He knew nothing about women's clothes, or he would not have thought that possible. Though she had done the best she could. She had borrowed Dr. Henshawe's raincoat for the coastal weather. It was a bit long, but otherwise all right, due to Dr. Henshawe's classically youthful tastes. She had sold more blood and bought a fuzzy angora sweater, peach-colored, which was extremely messy and looked like a small-town girl's idea of dressing up. She always realized things like that as soon as a purchase was made, not before.

Patrick's parents lived on Vancouver Island, near Sidney. About half an acre of clipped green lawn—green in the middle of winter; March seemed like the middle of winter to Rose—sloped down to a stone wall and a narrow pebbly beach and salt water. The house was half stone, half stucco-and-timber. It was built in the Tudor style, and others. The windows of the living room, the dining room, the den, all faced the sea, and because of the strong winds that sometimes blew onshore, they were made of thick glass, plate glass Rose supposed, like the windows of the automobile showroom in Hanratty. The seaward wall of the dining room was all windows, curving out in a gentle bay; you looked through the thick curved glass as through the bottom of a bottle. The sideboard too had a curving, gleaming belly, and seemed as big as a boat. Size was noticeable everywhere and particularly thickness. Thickness of towels and rugs and handles of knives and forks, and silences. There was a terrible amount of luxury and unease. After a day or so there Rose became so discouraged that her wrists and ankles felt weak. Picking up her knife and fork was a chore; cutting and chewing the perfect roast beef was almost beyond her; she got short of breath climbing the stairs. She had never known before how some places could choke you off, choke off your very life. She had not known this in spite of a number of very unfriendly places she had been in.

The first morning, Patrick's mother took her for a walk on the grounds, pointing out the greenhouse, the cottage where "the couple" lived: a charming, ivied, shuttered cottage, bigger than Dr. Henshawe's house. The couple, the servants, were more gentle-spoken, more discreet and dignified, than anyone Rose could think of in Hanratty, and indeed they were superior in these ways to Patrick's family.

Patrick's mother showed her the rose garden, the kitchen garden. There were many low stone walls.

"Patrick built them," said his mother. She explained anything with an indifference that bordered on distaste. "He built all these walls."

Rose's voice came out full of false assurance, eager and inappropriately enthusiastic.

"He must be a true Scot," she said. Patrick was a Scot, in spite of his name. The Blatchfords had come from Glasgow. "Weren't the best stonemasons always Scotsmen?" (She had learned quite recently not to say "Scotch.") "Maybe he had stonemason ancestors."

She cringed afterward, thinking of these efforts, the pretense of ease and gaiety, as cheap and imitative as her clothes.

"No," said Patrick's mother. "No. I don't think they were stonemasons." Something like fog went out from her: affront, disapproval, dismay. Rose thought that perhaps she had been offended by the suggestion that her husband's family might have worked with their hands. When she got to know her better—or had observed her longer; it was impossible to get to know her—she understood that Patrick's mother disliked anything fanciful, speculative, abstract, in conversation. She would also, of course, dislike Rose's chatty tone. Any interest beyond the factual consideration of the matter at hand—food, weather, invitations, furniture, servants—seemed to her sloppy, ill-bred, and dangerous. It was all right to say, "This is a warm day," but not, "This day reminds me of when we used to—" She hated people being *reminded*.

She was the only child of one of the early lumber barons of Vancouver Island. She had been born in a vanished northern settlement. But whenever Patrick tried to get her to talk about the past, whenever he asked her for the simplest sort of information—what steamers went up the coast, what year was the settlement abandoned, what was the route of the first logging railway—she would say irritably, "I don't know. How would I know about that?" This irritation was the strongest note that ever got into her words.

Neither did Patrick's father care for this concern about the past. Many things, most things, about Patrick seemed to strike him as bad signs.

"What do you want to know all that for?" he shouted down the table. He was a short square-shouldered man, red-faced, astonishingly belligerent. Patrick looked like his mother, who was tall, fair, and elegant in the most muted way possible, as if her clothes, her makeup, her style, were chosen with an ideal neutrality in mind.

"Because I am interested in history," said Patrick in an angry, pompous, but nervously breaking voice.

"Because-I-am-interested-in-history," said his sister Marion in an immediate parody, break and all. "History!"

The sisters Joan and Marion were younger than Patrick, older than Rose. Unlike Patrick they showed no nervousness, no cracks in self-satisfaction. At an earlier meal they had questioned Rose.

"Do you ride?"

"No."

"Do you sail?"

"No."

"Play tennis? Play golf? Play badminton?"

No. No. No.

"Perhaps she is an intellectual genius, like Patrick," the father said. And Patrick, to Rose's horror and embarrassment, began to shout at the table in general an account of her scholarships and prizes. What did he hope for? Was he so witless as to think such bragging would subdue them, would bring out anything but further scorn? Against Patrick, against his shouted boasts, his contempt for sports and television, his so-called intellectual interests, the family seemed united. But this alliance was only temporary. The father's dislike of his daughters was minor only in comparison with his dislike of Patrick. He railed at them too, when he could spare a moment; he jeered at the amount of time they spent at their games, complained about the cost of their equipment, their boats, their horses. And they wrangled with each other on obscure questions of scores and borrowings and damages. All complained to the mother about the food, which was plentiful and delicious. The mother spoke as little as possible to anyone and to tell the truth Rose did not blame her. She had never imagined so much true malevolence collected in one place. Billy Pope was a bigot and a grumbler, Flo was capricious, unjust, and gossipy, her father, when he was alive, had been capable of cold judgments and unremitting disapproval; but compared to Patrick's family, all Rose's people seemed jovial and content.

"Are they always like this?" she said to Patrick. "Is it me? They don't like me."

"They don't like you because I chose you," said Patrick with some satisfaction.

They lay on the stony beach after dark, in their raincoats, hugged and kissed and uncomfortably, unsuccessfully, attempted more. Rose got seaweed stains on Dr. Henshawe's coat. Patrick said, "You see why I need you? I need you so much!"

She took him to Hanratty. It was just as bad as she had thought it would be. Flo had gone to great trouble, and cooked a meal of scalloped potatoes, turnips, big country sausages which were a special present from Billy Pope, from the butcher shop. Patrick detested coarse-textured food, and made no pretense of eating it. The table was spread with a plastic cloth, they ate under the tube of fluorescent light. The centerpiece was new and especially for the occasion. A plastic swan, lime green in color, with slits in the wings, in which were stuck folded, colored paper napkins. Billy Pope, reminded to take one, grunted, refused. Otherwise he was on dismally good behavior. Word had reached him, word had reached both Flo and Billy, of Rose's triumph. It had come from their superiors in Hanratty; otherwise they could not have believed it. Customers in the butcher shop—formidable ladies, the dentist's wife, the veterinarian's wife—had said to Billy Pope that they heard Rose had picked herself up a millionaire. Rose knew Billy Pope would go back to work tomorrow with stories of the millionaire, or millionaire's son, and that all these stories would focus on his—Billy Pope's—forthright and unintimidated behavior in the situation.

"We just set him down and give him some sausages, don't make no difference to us what he comes from!"

She knew Flo would have her comments too, that Patrick's nervousness would not escape her, that she would be able to mimic his voice and his flapping hands that had knocked over the ketchup bottle. But at present they both sat hunched over the table in miserable eclipse. Rose tried to start some conversation, talking brightly, unnaturally, rather as if she was an interviewer trying to draw out a couple of simple local people. She felt ashamed on more levels than she could count. She was ashamed of the food and the swan and the plastic tablecloth; ashamed for Patrick, the gloomy snob, who made a startled grimace when Flo passed him the toothpick-holder; ashamed for

Flo with her timidity and hypocrisy and pretensions; most of
all ashamed for herself. She didn't even have any way that she
could talk, and sound natural. With Patrick there, she couldn't
slip back into an accent closer to Flo's, Billy Pope's, and Hanratty's. That accent jarred on her ears now, anyway. It seemed
to involve not just a different pronunciation but a whole different approach to talking. Talking was shouting; the words
were separated and emphasized so that people could bombard
each other with them. And the things people said were like
lines from the most hackneyed rural comedy. *Wal, if a feller took
a notion to*, they said. They really said that. Seeing them
through Patrick's eyes, hearing them through his ears, Rose too
had to be amazed.

She was trying to get them to talk about local history, some
things she thought Patrick might be interested in. Presently,
Flo did begin to talk; she could only be held in so long, whatever her misgivings. The conversation took another line from
anything Rose had intended.

"The line I lived on when I was just young," Flo said, "it
was the worst place ever created for suiciding."

"A line is a concession road. In the township," Rose said to
Patrick. She had doubts about what was coming, and rightly
so, for then Patrick got to hear about a man who cut his own
throat, *his own throat*, from ear to ear; a man who shot himself
the first time and didn't do enough damage, so he loaded up
and fired again and managed it; another man who hanged himself using a chain, the kind of chain you hook on a tractor with,
so it was a wonder his head was not torn off.

Tore off; Flo said.

She went on to a woman who, though not a suicide, had been
dead in her house a week before she was found, and that was
in the summer. She asked Patrick to imagine it. All this happened, said Flo, within five miles of where she herself was born.
She was presenting credentials, not trying to horrify Patrick, at
least not more than was acceptable in a social way; she did not
mean to disconcert him. How could he understand that?

"You were right," said Patrick as they left Hanratty on the
bus. "It is a dump. You must be glad to get away."

Rose felt immediately that he should not have said that.

"Of course that's not your real mother," Patrick said. "Your real parents can't have been like that." Rose did not like his saying that either, though it was what she believed herself. She saw that he was trying to provide for her a more genteel background, perhaps something like the homes of his poor friends: a few books about, a tea tray, and mended linen, worn good taste; proud, tired, educated people. What a coward he was, she thought angrily, but she knew that she herself was the coward, not knowing any way to be comfortable with her own people or the kitchen or any of it. Years later she would learn how to use it, she would be able to amuse or intimidate right-thinking people at dinner parties with glimpses of her early home. At the moment she felt confusion, misery.

Nevertheless her loyalty was starting. Now that she was sure of getting away, a layer of loyalty and protectiveness was hardening around every memory she had, around the store and the town, the flat, somewhat scrubby, unremarkable countryside. She would oppose this secretly to Patrick's views of mountains and ocean, his stone-and-timbered mansion. Her allegiances were far more proud and stubborn than his.

But it turned out he was not leaving anything behind.

Patrick gave her a diamond ring and announced that he was giving up being a historian for her sake. He was going into his father's business.

She said she thought he hated his father's business. He said that he could not afford to take such an attitude now that he would have a wife to support.

It seemed that Patrick's desire to marry, even to marry Rose, had been taken by his father as a sign of sanity. Great streaks of bounty were mixed in with all the ill will in that family. His father at once offered a job in one of the stores, offered to buy them a house. Patrick was as incapable of turning down this offer as Rose was of turning down Patrick's, and his reasons were as little mercenary as hers.

"Will we have a house like your parents'?" Rose said. She really thought it might be necessary to start off in that style.

"Well, maybe not at first. Not quite so—"

"I don't want a house like that! I don't want to live like that!"

"We'll live however you like. We'll have whatever kind of house you like."

Provided it's not a dump, she thought nastily.

Girls she hardly knew stopped and asked to see her ring, admired it, wished her happiness. When she went back to Hanratty for a weekend, alone this time, thank God, she met the dentist's wife on the main street.

"Oh, Rose, isn't it wonderful! When are you coming back again? We're going to give a tea for you, the ladies in town all want to give a tea for you!"

This woman had never spoken to Rose, never given any sign before of knowing who she was. Paths were opening now, barriers were softening. And Rose—oh, this was the worst, this was the shame of it—Rose, instead of cutting the dentist's wife, was blushing and skittishly flashing her diamond and saying yes, that would be a lovely idea. When people said how happy she must be she did think herself happy. It was as simple as that. She dimpled and sparkled and turned herself into a fiancée with no trouble at all. Where will you live, people said, and she said, Oh, in British Columbia! That added more magic to the tale. Is it really beautiful there, they said, is it never winter?

"Oh, yes!" cried Rose. "Oh, no!"

She woke up early, got up and dressed, and let herself out the side door of Dr. Henshawe's garage. It was too early for the buses to be running. She walked through the city to Patrick's apartment. She walked across the park. Around the South African War Memorial a pair of greyhounds were leaping and playing, an old woman standing by, holding their leashes. The sun was just up, shining on their pale hides. The grass was wet. Daffodils and narcissus in bloom.

Patrick came to the door, tousled, frowning sleepily, in his gray-and-maroon striped pajamas.

"Rose! What's the matter?"

She couldn't say anything. He pulled her into the apartment.

She put her arms around him and hid her face against his chest and, in a stagy voice, said, "Please, Patrick. Please let me not marry you."

"Are you sick? What's the matter?"

"Please let me not marry you," she said again, with even less conviction.

"You're crazy."

She didn't blame him for thinking so. Her voice sounded so unnatural, wheedling, silly. As soon as he opened the door and she faced the fact of him, his sleepy eyes, his pajamas, she saw that what she had come to do was enormous, impossible. She would have to explain everything to him, and of course she could not do it. She could not make him see her necessity. She could not find any tone of voice, any expression of the face, that would serve her.

"Are you upset?" said Patrick. "What's happened?"

"Nothing."

"How did you get here anyway?"

"Walked."

She had been fighting back a need to go to the bathroom. It seemed that if she went to the bathroom she would destroy some of the strength of her case. But she had to. She freed herself. She said, "Wait a minute, I'm going to the john."

When she came out Patrick had the electric kettle going, was measuring out instant coffee. He looked decent and bewildered.

"I'm not really awake," he said. "Now. Sit down. First of all, are you premenstrual?"

"No." But she realized with dismay that she was, and that he might be able to figure it out, because they had been worried last month.

"Well, if you're not premenstrual, and nothing's happened to upset you, then what is all this about?"

"I don't want to get married," she said, backing away from the cruelty of *I don't want to marry you.*

"When did you come to this decision?"

"Long ago. This morning."

They were talking in whispers. Rose looked at the clock. It was a little after seven.

"When do the others get up?"

"About eight."

"Is there milk for the coffee?" She went to the refrigerator.

"Quiet with the door," said Patrick, too late.

"I'm sorry," she said, in her strange silly voice.

"We went for a walk last night and everything was fine. You come this morning and tell me you don't want to get married. *Why* don't you want to get married?"

"I just don't. I don't want to be married."

"What else do you want to do?"

"I don't know."

Patrick kept staring at her sternly, drinking his coffee. He who used to plead with her *do you love me, do you really*, did not bring the subject up now.

"Well, I know."

"What?"

"I know who's been talking to you."

"Nobody has been talking to me."

"Oh, no. Well, I bet Dr. Henshawe has."

"No."

"Some people don't have a very high opinion of her. They think she has an influence on girls. She doesn't like the girls who live with her to have boyfriends. Does she? You even told me that. She doesn't like them to be normal."

"That's not it."

"What did she say to you, Rose?"

"She didn't say anything." Rose began to cry.

"Are you sure?"

"Oh, Patrick, listen, please, I can't marry you, please, I don't know why, I can't, please, I'm sorry, believe me, I can't," Rose babbled at him, weeping, and Patrick saying, "Shh! You'll wake them up!" lifted or dragged her out of the kitchen chair and took her to his room, where she sat on the bed. He shut the door. She held her arms across her stomach, and rocked back and forth.

"What is it, Rose? What's the matter? Are you sick?"

"It's just so hard to tell you!"

"Tell me what?"

"What I just did tell you!"

"I mean have you found out you have t.b. or something?"

"No!"

"Is there something in your family you haven't told me about? Insanity?" said Patrick encouragingly.

"No!" Rose rocked and wept.

"So what is it?"

"I don't love you!" she said. "I don't love you. I don't love you." She fell on the bed and put her head in the pillow. "I'm so sorry. I'm so sorry. I can't help it."

After a moment or two Patrick said, "Well. If you don't love me you don't love me. I'm not forcing you to." His voice sounded strained and spiteful, against the reasonableness of what he was saying. "I just wonder," he said, "if you know what you do want. I don't think you do. I don't think you have any idea what you want. You're just in a state."

"I don't have to know what I want to know what I don't want!" Rose said, turning over. This released her. "I never loved you."

"Shh. You'll wake them. We have to stop."

"I never loved you. I never wanted to. It was a mistake."

"All right. All right. You made your point."

"Why am I supposed to love you? Why do you act as if there was something wrong with me if I didn't? You despise me. You despise my family and my background and you think you are doing me a *great favor*—"

"I fell in love with you," Patrick said. "I don't despise you. Oh, Rose. I worship you."

"You're a sissy," Rose said. "You're a prude." She jumped off the bed with great pleasure as she said this. She felt full of energy. More was coming. Terrible things were coming.

"You don't even know how to make love right. I always wanted to get out of this from the very first. I felt sorry for you. You won't look where you're going, you're always knocking things over, just because you can't be bothered, you can't be bothered noticing anything, you're wrapped up in yourself, and you're always bragging, it's so stupid, you don't even know how to brag right, if you really want to impress people you'll never do it, the way you do it all they do is laugh at you!"

Patrick sat on the bed and looked up at her, his face open to whatever she would say. She wanted to beat and beat him, to say worse and worse, uglier and uglier, things. She took a breath, drew in air, to stop the things she felt rising in her from getting out.

"I don't want to see you, ever!" she said viciously. But at the door she turned and said in a normal and regretful voice, "Goodbye."

Patrick wrote her a note: *I don't understand what happened the other day and I want to talk to you about it. But I think we should wait for two weeks and not see or talk to each other and find out how we feel at the end of that time.*

Rose had forgotten all about giving him back his ring. When she came out of his apartment building that morning she was still wearing it. She couldn't go back, and it seemed too valuable to send through the mail. She continued to wear it, mostly because she did not want to have to tell Dr. Henshawe what had happened. She was relieved to get Patrick's note. She thought that she could give him back the ring then.

She thought about what Patrick had said about Dr. Henshawe. No doubt there was some truth in that, else why should she be so reluctant to tell Dr. Henshawe she had broken her engagement, so unwilling to face her sensible approval, her restrained, relieved congratulations?

She told Dr. Henshawe that she was not seeing Patrick while she studied for her exams. Rose could see that even that pleased her.

She told no one that her situation had changed. It was not just Dr. Henshawe she didn't want knowing. She didn't like giving up being envied; the experience was so new to her.

She tried to think what to do next. She could not stay on at Dr. Henshawe's. It seemed clear that if she escaped from Patrick, she must escape from Dr. Henshawe too. And she did not want to stay on at the college, with people knowing about her broken engagement, with the girls who now congratulated her saying they had known all along it was a fluke, her getting Patrick. She would have to get a job.

The Head Librarian had offered her a job for the summer but that was perhaps at Dr. Henshawe's suggestion. Once she moved out, the offer might not hold. She knew that instead of studying for her exams she ought to be downtown, applying for work as a filing clerk at the insurance offices, applying at Bell Telephone, at the department stores. The idea frightened her. She kept on studying. That was the one thing she really knew how to do. She was a scholarship student after all.

On Saturday afternoon, when she was working at the library, she saw Patrick. She did not see him by accident. She went down to the bottom floor, trying not to make noise on the spi-ralling metal staircase. There was a place in the stacks where she could stand, almost in darkness, and see into his carrel. She did that. She couldn't see his face. She saw his long pink neck and the old plaid shirt he wore on Saturdays. His long neck. His bony shoulders. She was no longer irritated by him, no longer frightened by him; she was free. She could look at him as she would look at anybody. She could appreciate him. He had behaved well. He had not tried to rouse her pity, he had not bullied her, he had not molested her with pitiful telephone calls and letters. He had not come and sat on Dr. Henshawe's doorstep. He was an honorable person, and he would never know how she acknowledged that, how she was grateful for it. The things she had said to him made her ashamed now. And they were not even true. Not all of them. He did know how to make love. She was so moved, made so gentle and wistful, by the sight of him, that she wanted to give him something, some surprising bounty, she wished to undo his unhappiness.

Then she had a compelling picture of herself. She was run-ning softly into Patrick's carrel, she was throwing her arms around him from behind, she was giving everything back to him. Would he take it from her, would he still want it? She saw them laughing and crying, explaining, forgiving. *I love you. I do love you, it's all right, I was terrible, I didn't mean it, I was just crazy, I love you, it's all right.* This was a violent temptation for her; it was barely resistible. She had an impulse to hurl herself. Whether it was off a cliff or into a warm bed of welcoming grass and flowers, she really could not tell.

It was not resistible, after all. She did it.

When Rose afterward reviewed and talked about this moment in her life—for she went through a period, like most people nowadays, of talking freely about her most private decisions, to friends and lovers and party acquaintances whom she might never see again, while they did the same—she said that comradely compassion had overcome her, she was not proof against the sight of a bare bent neck. Then she went further into it, and said greed, greed. She said she had run to him and clung to him and overcome his suspicions and kissed and cried and reinstated herself simply because she did not know how to do without his love and his promise to look after her; she was frightened of the world and she had not been able to think up any other plan for herself. When she was seeing life in economic terms, or was with people who did, she said that only middle-class people had choices anyway, that if she had had the price of a train ticket to Toronto her life would have been different.

Nonsense, she might say later, never mind that, it was really vanity, it was vanity pure and simple, to resurrect him, to bring him back his happiness. To see if she could do that. She could not resist such a test of power. She explained then that she had paid for it. She said that she and Patrick had been married ten years, and that during that time the scenes of the first breakup and reconciliation had been periodically repeated, with her saying again all the things she had said the first time, and the things she had held back, and many other things which occurred to her. She hopes she did not tell people (but thinks she did) that she used to beat her head against the bedpost, that she smashed a gravy boat through a dining-room window; that she was so frightened, so sickened by what she had done that she lay in bed, shivering, and begged and begged for his forgiveness. Which he granted. Sometimes she flew at him; sometimes he beat her. The next morning they would get up early and make a special breakfast; they would sit eating bacon and eggs and drinking filtered coffee, worn out, bewildered, treating each other with shamefaced kindness.

What do you think triggers the reaction? they would say.

Do you think we ought to take a holiday? A holiday together? Holidays alone?

A waste, a sham, those efforts, as it turned out. But they worked for the moment. Calmed down, they would say that most people probably went through the same things like this, in a marriage, and indeed they seemed to know mostly people who did. They could not separate until enough damage had been done, until nearly mortal damage had been done, to keep them apart. And until Rose could get a job and make her own money, so perhaps there was a very ordinary reason after all.

What she never said to anybody, never confided, was that she sometimes thought it had not been pity or greed or cowardice or vanity but something quite different, like a vision of happiness. In view of everything else she had told she could hardly tell that. It seems very odd; she can't justify it. She doesn't mean that they had perfectly ordinary, bearable times in their marriage, long busy stretches of wallpapering and vacationing and meals and shopping and worrying about a child's illness, but that sometimes, without reason or warning, happiness, the possibility of happiness, would surprise them. Then it was as if they were in different though identical-seeming skins, as if there existed a radiantly kind and innocent Rose and Patrick, hardly ever visible, in the shadow of their usual selves. Perhaps it was that Patrick she saw when she was free of him, invisible to him, looking into his carrel. Perhaps it was. She should have left him there.

She knew that was how she had seen him; she knows it, because it happened again. She was in Toronto Airport, in the middle of the night. This was about nine years after she and Patrick were divorced. She had become fairly well known by this time, her face was familiar to many people in this country. She did a television program on which she interviewed politicians, actors, writers, *personalities*, and many ordinary people who were angry about something the government or the police or a union had done to them. Sometimes she talked to people who had seen strange sights, UFOs, or sea monsters, or who had unusual accomplishments or collections, or kept up some obsolete custom.

She was alone. No one was meeting her. She had just come in on a delayed flight from Yellowknife. She was tired and bedraggled. She saw Patrick standing with his back to her, at a coffee bar. He wore a raincoat. He was heavier than he had been, but she knew him at once. And she had the same feeling that this was a person she was bound to, that by a certain magical yet possible trick, they could find and trust each other, and that to begin this all that she had to do was go up and touch him on the shoulder, surprise him with his happiness.

She did not do this, of course, but she did stop. She was standing still when he turned around, heading for one of the little plastic tables and curved seats grouped in front of the coffee bar. All his skinniness and academic shabbiness, his look of prim authoritarianism, was gone. He had smoothed out, filled out, into such a modish and agreeable, responsible, slightly complacent-looking man. His birthmark had faded. She thought how haggard and dreary she must look, in her rumpled trenchcoat, her long, graying hair fallen forward around her face, old mascara smudged under her eyes.

He made a face at her. It was a truly hateful, savagely warning, face; infantile, self-indulgent, yet calculated; it was a timed explosion of disgust and loathing. It was hard to believe. But she saw it.

Sometimes when Rose was talking to someone in front of the television cameras she would sense the desire in them to make a face. She would sense it in all sorts of people, in skillful politicians and witty liberal bishops and honored humanitarians, in housewives who had witnessed natural disasters and in workmen who had performed heroic rescues or been cheated out of disability pensions. They were longing to sabotage themselves, to make a face or say a dirty word. Was this the face they all wanted to make? To show somebody, to show everybody? They wouldn't do it, though; they wouldn't get the chance. Special circumstances were required. A lurid unreal place, the middle of the night, a staggering unhinging weariness, the sudden, hallucinatory appearance of your true enemy.

She hurried away then, down the long varicolored corridor, shaking. She had seen Patrick; Patrick had seen her; he had made that face. But she was not really able to understand how she could be an enemy. How could anybody hate Rose so much, at the very moment when she was ready to come forward with her good will, her smiling confession of exhaustion, her air of diffident faith in civilized overtures?

Oh, Patrick could. Patrick could.

∽ *Simon's Luck* ∾

ROSE GETS LONELY IN new places; she wishes she had invitations. She goes out and walks the streets and looks in the lighted windows at all the Saturday-night parties, the Sunday-night family suppers. It's no good telling herself she wouldn't be long inside there, chattering and getting drunk, or spooning up the gravy, before she'd wish she was walking the streets. She thinks she could take on any hospitality. She could go to parties in rooms hung with posters, lit by lamps with Coca-Cola shades, everything crumbly and askew; or else in warm professional rooms with lots of books, and brass rubbings, and maybe a skull or two; even in the recreation rooms she can just see the tops of, through the basement windows: rows of beer steins, hunting horns, drinking horns, guns. She could go and sit on Lurex-threaded sofas under hangings of black velvet displaying mountains, galleons, polar bears executed in brushed wool. She would like very much to be dishing up a costly *cabinet de diplomate* out of a cut-glass bowl in a rich dining room with a big gleaming belly of sideboard behind her, and a dim picture of horses feeding, cows feeding, sheep feeding, on badly painted purple grass. Or she could do as well with batter pudding in the eating nook of a kitchen in a little stucco house by the bus stop, plaster pears and peaches decorating the wall, ivy curling out of little brass pots. Rose is an actress; she can fit in anywhere.

She does get asked to parties. About two years ago, she was at a party in a high-rise apartment building in Kingston. The windows looked out on Lake Ontario and Wolfe Island. Rose didn't live in Kingston. She lived up-country; she had been teaching drama for two years at a community college. Some people were surprised that she would do this. They did not know how little money an actress might make; they thought that being well-known automatically meant being well-off.

She had driven down to Kingston just for this party, a fact which slightly shamed her. She had not met the hostess before. She had known the host last year, when he was teaching at the community college and living with another girl.

The hostess, whose name was Shelley, took Rose into the bedroom to put down her coat. Shelley was a thin, solemn-looking girl, a true blonde, with nearly white eyebrows, hair long and thick and straight as if cut from a block of wood. It seemed that she took her waif style seriously. Her voice was low and mournful, making Rose's own voice, her greeting of a moment ago, sound altogether too sprightly in her own ears.

In a basket at the foot of the bed a tortoiseshell cat was suckling four tiny, blind kittens.

"That's Tasha," the hostess said. "We can look at her kittens but we can't touch them, else she wouldn't feed them anymore."

She knelt down by the basket, crooning, talking to the mother cat with an intense devotion that Rose thought affected. The shawl around her shoulders was black, rimmed with jet beads. Some beads were crooked, some were missing. It was a genuine old shawl, not an imitation. Her limp, slightly yellowed, eyelet-embroidered dress was genuine too, though probably a petticoat in the first place. Such clothes took looking for.

On the other side of the spool bed was a large mirror, hung suspiciously high, and tilted. Rose tried to get a look at herself when the girl was bent over the basket. It is very hard to look in the mirror when there is another, and particularly a younger, woman in the room. Rose was wearing a flowered cotton dress, a long dress with a tucked bodice and puffed sleeves, which was too short in the waist and too tight in the bust to be comfortable. There was something wrongly youthful or theatrical about it; perhaps she was not slim enough to wear that style. Her reddish-brown hair was dyed at home. Lines ran both ways under her eyes, trapping little diamonds of darkened skin.

Rose knew by now that when she found people affected, as she did this girl, and their rooms coyly decorated, their manner of living irritating (that mirror, the patchwork quilt, the Japanese erotic drawings over the bed, the African music coming from the living room), it was usually because she, Rose, hadn't received and was afraid she wouldn't receive the attention she wanted, hadn't penetrated the party, felt that she might be doomed to hang around on the fringes of things, making judgments.

She felt better in the living room, where there were some people she knew, and some faces as old as her own. She drank quickly at first, and before long was using the newborn kittens as a springboard for her own story. She said that something dreadful had happened to her cat that very day.

"And the worst of it is," she said, "I never liked my cat much. It wasn't my idea to have a cat. It was his. He followed me home one day and insisted on being taken in. He was just like some big sneering hulk of an unemployable, set on convincing me I owed him a living. Well, he always had a fondness for the clothes dryer. He liked to jump in when it was warm, as soon as I'd taken the clothes out. Usually I just have one load but today I had two, and when I reached in to take the second load out, I thought I felt something. I thought, What do I have that's fur?"

People moaned or laughed, in a sympathetically horrified way. Rose looked around at them appealingly. She felt much better. The living room, with its lake view, its careful decor (a jukebox, barbershop mirrors, turn-of-the-century advertisements—SMOKE, FOR YOUR THROAT'S SAKE—old silk lampshades, farmhouse bowls and jugs, primitive masks and sculptures), no longer seemed so hostile. She took another drink of her gin and knew there was a limited time coming now when she would feel light and welcome as a hummingbird, convinced that many people in the room were witty and many were kind, and some were both together.

"Oh, *no*, I thought. But it was. It was. Death in the dryer."

"A warning to all pleasure seekers," said a little sharp-faced man at her elbow, a man she had known slightly for years. He taught in the English department of the university, where the host taught now, and the hostess was a graduate student.

"That's terrible," said the hostess, with her cold, fixed look of sensitivity. Those who had laughed looked a bit abashed, as if they thought they might have seemed heartless. "Your cat. That's terrible. How could you come tonight?"

As a matter of fact the incident had not happened today at all; it had happened last week. Rose wondered if the girl meant to put her at a disadvantage. She said sincerely and regretfully that she hadn't been very fond of the cat and that had made it seem worse, somehow. That's what she was trying to explain, she said.

"I felt as if maybe it was my fault. Maybe if I'd been fonder, it wouldn't have happened."

"Of course it wouldn't," said the man beside her. "It was warmth he was seeking in the dryer. It was love. Ah, Rose!"

"Now you won't be able to fuck the cat anymore," said a tall boy Rose hadn't noticed before. He seemed to have sprung up, right in front of her. "Fuck the dog, fuck the cat, I don't know what you do, Rose."

She was searching for his name. She had recognized him as a student, or former student.

"David," she said. "Hello, David." She was so pleased at coming up with the name that she was slow in registering what he had said.

"Fuck the dog, fuck the cat," he repeated, swaying over her.

"I beg your pardon," Rose said, and put on a quizzical, indulgent, charming expression. The people around her were finding it as hard to adjust to what the boy said as she was. The mood of sociability, sympathy, expectation of good will was not easy to halt; it rolled on in spite of signs that there was plenty here it wasn't going to be able to absorb. Almost everyone was still smiling, as if the boy was telling an anecdote or playing a part, the point of which would be made clear in a moment. The hostess cast down her eyes and slipped away.

"Beg yours," said the boy in a very ugly tone. "Up yours,

Rose." He was white and brittle-looking, desperately drunk. He had probably been brought up in a gentle home, where people talked about answering Nature's call and blessed each other for sneezing.

A short, strong man with black curly hair took hold of the boy's arm just below the shoulder.

"Move it along," he said, almost maternally. He spoke with a muddled European accent, mostly French, Rose thought, though she was not good about accents. She did tend to think, in spite of knowing better, that such accents spring from a richer and more complicated masculinity than the masculinity to be found in North America and in places like Hanratty, where she had grown up. Such an accent promised masculinity tinged with suffering, tenderness, and guile.

The host appeared in a velvet jumpsuit and took hold of the other arm, more or less symbolically, at the same time kissing Rose's cheek, because he hadn't seen her when she came in. "Must talk to you," he murmured, meaning he hoped he wouldn't have to, because there was so much tricky territory; the girl he had lived with last year, for one thing, and a night he had spent with Rose toward the end of term, when there had been a lot of drinking and bragging and lamenting about faithlessness, as well as some curiously insulting though pleasurable sex. He was looking very brushed and tended, thinner but softened, with his flowing hair and suit of bottle-green velvet. Only three years younger than Rose, but look at him. He had shed a wife, a family, a house, a discouraging future, set himself up with new clothes and new furniture and a succession of student mistresses. Men can do it.

"My, my," Rose said, and leaned against the wall. "What was that all about?"

The man beside her, who had smiled all the time and looked into his glass, said, "Ah, the sensitive youth of our time! Their grace of language, their depth of feeling! We must bow before them."

The man with the black curly hair came back, didn't say a word, but handed Rose a fresh drink and took her glass.

The host came back too.

"Rose baby. I don't know how he got in. I said no bloody students. There's got to be some place safe from them."

"He was in one of my classes last year," Rose said. That really was all she could remember. She supposed they were thinking there must be more to it.

"Did he want to be an actor?" said the man beside her. "I'll bet he did. Remember the good old days when they all wanted to be lawyers and engineers and business executives? They tell me that's coming back. I hope so. I devoutly hope so. Rose, I bet you listened to his problems. You must never do that. I bet that's what you did."

"Oh, I suppose."

"They come along looking for a parent-substitute. It's banal as can be. They trail around worshipping you and bothering you and then bam! It's parent-substitute rejecting time!"

Rose drank, and leaned against the wall, and heard them take up the theme of what students expected nowadays, how they broke down your door to tell you about their abortions, their suicide attempts, their creativity crises, their weight problems. Always using the same words: *personhood, values, rejection.*

"I'm not rejecting you, you silly bugger, I'm flunking you!" said the little sharp man, recalling a triumphant confrontation he had had with one such student. They laughed at that and at the young woman who said, "God, the difference when I was at university! You wouldn't have mentioned an abortion in a professor's office any more than you would have shit on the floor. *Shat* on the floor."

Rose was laughing too, but felt smashed, under the skin. It would be better, in a way, if there were something behind this such as they suspected. If she had slept with that boy. If she had promised him something, if she had betrayed him, humiliated him. She could not remember anything. He had sprung out of the floor to accuse her. She must have done something, and she could not remember it. She could not remember anything to do with her students; that was the truth. She was solicitous and charming, all warmth and acceptance; she listened and advised; then she could not get their names straight. She could not remember a thing she had said to them.

A woman touched her arm. "Wake up," she said, in a tone of sly intimacy that made Rose think she must know her. Another student? But no, the woman introduced herself.

"I'm doing a paper on female suicide," she said. "I mean the suicide of female artists." She said she had seen Rose on television and was longing to talk to her. She mentioned Diane Arbus, Virginia Woolf, Sylvia Plath, Anne Sexton, Christiane Pflug. She was well informed. She looked like a prime candidate herself, Rose thought: emaciated, bloodless, obsessed. Rose said she was hungry, and the woman followed her out to the kitchen.

"And too many actresses to count—" the woman said. "Margaret Sullavan—"

"I'm just a teacher now."

"Oh, nonsense. I'm sure you are an actress to the marrow of your bones."

The hostess had made bread: glazed and braided and decorated loaves. Rose wondered at the pains taken here. The bread, the pâté, the hanging plants, the kittens, all on behalf of a most precarious and temporary domesticity. She wished, she often wished, that she could take such pains, that she could make ceremonies, impose herself, make bread.

She noticed a group of younger members of the faculty— she would have thought them students, except for what the host had said about students not being let in—who were sitting on the counters and standing in front of the sink. They were talking in low, serious voices. One of them looked at her. She smiled. Her smile was not returned. A couple of others looked at her, and went on talking. She was sure they were talking about her, about what had happened in the living room. She urged the woman to try some bread and pâté. Presumably that would keep her quiet, so that Rose could overhear what was being said.

"I never eat at parties."

The woman's manner toward her was turning dark and vaguely accusing. Rose had learned that this was a department wife. Perhaps it had been a political move, inviting her. And promising her Rose—had that been part of the move?

"Are you always so hungry?" the woman said. "Are you never ill?"

"I am when there's something this good to eat," Rose said. She was only trying to set an example, and could hardly chew or swallow, in her anxiety to hear what was being said of her. "No, I'm not often ill," she said. It surprised her to realize that was true. She used to get sick with colds and flu and cramps and headaches; those definite ailments had now disappeared, simmered down into a low, steady hum of uneasiness, fatigue, apprehension.

Fucked-up jealous establishment.

Rose heard that, or thought she heard it. They were giving her quick, despising looks. Or so she thought; she could not look directly at them. *Establishment.* That was Rose. Was it? Was that Rose? Was that Rose who had taken a teaching job because she wasn't getting enough acting jobs to support herself, was granted the teaching job because of her experience on stage and television, but had to accept a cut in pay because she lacked degrees? She wanted to go over and tell them that. She wanted to state her case. The years of work, the exhaustion, the travelling, the high-school auditoriums, the nerves, the boredom, the never knowing where your next pay was coming from. She wanted to plead with them, so they would forgive her and love her and take her on their side. It was their side she wanted to be on, not the side of the people in the living room who had taken up her cause. But that was a choice made because of fear, not on principle. She feared them. She feared their hard-hearted virtue, their cool despising faces, their secrets, their laughter, their obscenities.

She thought of Anna, her own daughter. Anna was seventeen. She had long fair hair and wore a fine gold chain around her throat. It was so fine you had to look closely to make sure it was a chain, not just a glinting of her smooth bright skin. She was not like these young people but she was equally remote. She practiced ballet and rode her horse every day, but she didn't plan to ride in competitions or be a ballerina. Why not?

"Because it would be silly."

Something about Anna's style, the fine chain, her silences, made Rose think of her grandmother, Patrick's mother. But then, she thought, Anna might not be so silent, so fastidious, so unforthcoming, with anybody but her mother.

The man with the black curly hair stood in the kitchen doorway giving her an impudent and ironic look.

"Do you know who that is?" Rose said to the suicide woman. "The man who took the drunk away?"

"That's Simon. I don't think the boy was drunk, I think he's on drugs."

"What does he do?"

"Well, I expect he's a student of sorts."

"No," said Rose. "That man—Simon?"

"Oh, Simon. He's in the classics department. I don't think he's always been a teacher."

"Like me," Rose said, and turned the smile she had tried on the young people on Simon. Tired and adrift and witless as she was, she was beginning to feel familiar twinges, tidal promises.

If he smiles back, things will start to be all right.

He did smile, and the suicide woman spoke sharply. "Look, do you come to a party just to meet men?"

When Simon was fourteen, he and his older sister and another boy, a friend of theirs, were hidden in a freight car, travelling from occupied to unoccupied France. They were on their way to Lyons, where they would be looked after, redirected to safe places, by members of an organization that was trying to save Jewish children. Simon and his sister had already been sent out of Poland, at the beginning of the war, to stay with French relatives. Now they had to be sent away again.

The freight car stopped. The train was standing still, at night somewhere out in the country. They could hear French and German voices. There was some commotion in the cars ahead. They heard the doors grinding open, heard and felt the boots striking on the bare floors of those cars. An inspection of the train. They lay down under some sacks, but did not even try to cover their faces; they thought there was no hope. The voices were getting closer and they heard the boots on the gravel beside the track. Then the train began to move. It moved so slowly that they did not notice for a moment or so, and even then thought it was just a shunting of the cars. They expected it to stop, so that the inspection could continue. But the train kept moving. It moved a little faster, then faster; it picked up its ordinary speed, which was nothing very great. They were moving, they were free of the inspection, they were being carried away. Simon never knew what had happened. The danger was past.

Simon said that when he realized they were safe he suddenly felt that they would get through, that nothing could happen to them now, that they were particularly blessed and lucky. He took what happened for a lucky sign.

Rose asked him, had he ever seen his friend and his sister again?

"No. Never. Not after Lyons."

"So, it was lucky only for you."

Simon laughed. They were in bed, in Rose's bed in an old house, on the outskirts of a crossroads village; they had driven there straight from the party. It was April, the wind was cold, and Rose's house was chilly. The furnace was inadequate. Simon put a hand to the wallpaper behind the bed, made her feel the draft.

"What it needs is some insulation."

"I know. It's awful. And you should see my fuel bills."

Simon said she should get a woodstove. He told her about various kinds of firewood. Maple, he said, was a lovely wood to burn. Then he held forth on different kinds of insulation. Styrofoam, Micafil, fiberglass. He got out of bed and padded around naked, looking at the walls of her house. Rose shouted after him.

"Now I remember. It was a grant."

"What? I can't hear you."

She got out of bed and wrapped herself in a blanket. Standing at the top of the stairs, she said, "That boy came to me with an application for a grant. He wanted to be a playwright. I just this minute remembered."

"What boy?" said Simon. "Oh."

"But I recommended him. I know I did." The truth was she

recommended everybody. If she could not see their merits, she believed it might just be a case of their having merits she was unable to see.

"He must not have got it. So he thought I shafted him."

"Well, suppose you had," said Simon, peering down the cellarway. "That would be your right."

"I know. I'm a coward about that lot. I hate their disapproval. They are so virtuous."

"They are not virtuous at all," said Simon. "I'm going to put my shoes on and look at your furnace. You probably need the filters cleaned. That is just their style. They are not much to be feared, they are just as stupid as anybody. They want a chunk of the power. Naturally."

"But would you get such venomous"—Rose had to stop and start the word again—"such venomousness, simply from ambition?"

"What else?" said Simon, climbing the stairs. He made a grab for the blanket, wrapped himself up with her, pecked her nose. "Enough of that, Rose. Have you no shame? I'm a poor fellow come to look at your furnace. Your basement furnace. Sorry to bump into you like this, ma'am." She already knew a few of his characters. This was The Humble Workman. Some others were The Old Philosopher, who bowed low to her, Japanese-style, as he came out of the bathroom, murmuring *memento mori, memento mori*; and, when appropriate, The Mad Satyr, nuzzling and leaping, making triumphant smacking noises against her navel.

At the crossroads store she bought real coffee instead of instant, real cream, bacon, frozen broccoli, a hunk of local cheese, canned crabmeat, the best-looking tomatoes they had, mushrooms, long-grained rice. Cigarettes as well. She was in that state of happiness which seems perfectly natural and unthreatened. If asked, she would have said it was because of the weather—the day was bright, in spite of the harsh wind—as much as because of Simon.

"You must've brought home company," said the woman who kept the store. She spoke with no surprise or malice or censure, just a comradely sort of envy.

"When I wasn't expecting it." Rose dumped more groceries on the counter. "What a lot of bother they are. Not to mention expense. Look at that bacon. And cream."

"I could stand a bit of it," the woman said.

Simon cooked a remarkable supper from the resources provided, while Rose did nothing much but stand around watching, and change the sheets.

"Country life," she said. "It's changed, or I'd forgotten. I came here with some ideas about how I would live. I thought I would go for long walks on deserted country roads. And the first time I did, I heard a car coming tearing along on the gravel behind me. I got well off. Then I heard shots. I was terrified. I hid in the bushes and a car came roaring past, weaving all over the road—and they were shooting out of the windows. I cut back through the fields and told the woman at the store I thought we should call the police. She said oh, yes, weekends the boys get a case of beer in the car and they go out shooting groundhogs. Then she said, what were you doing up that road anyway? I could see she thought going for walks by yourself was a lot more suspicious than shooting groundhogs. There were lots of things like that. I don't think I'd stay, but the job's here and the rent's cheap. Not that she isn't nice, the woman in the store. She tells fortunes. Cards and teacups."

Simon said that he had been sent from Lyons to work on a farm in the mountains of Provence. The people there lived and farmed very much as in the Middle Ages. They could not read or write or speak French. When they got sick they waited either to die or to get better. They had never seen a doctor, though a veterinarian came once a year to inspect the cows. Simon ran a pitchfork into his foot, the wound became infected, he was feverish and had the greatest difficulty in persuading them to send for the veterinarian, who was then in the next village. At last they did, and the veterinarian came and gave Simon a shot with a great horse needle, and he got better. The household was bewildered and amused to see such measures taken on behalf of human life.

He said that while he was getting better he taught them to

play cards. He taught the mother and the children; the father and the grandfather were too slow and unwilling, and the grandmother was kept shut up in a cage in the barn, fed scraps twice a day.

"Is that true? Is it possible?"

They were at the stage of spreading things out for each other: pleasures, stories, jokes, confessions.

"Country life!" said Simon. "But here it is not so bad. This house could be made very comfortable. You should have a garden."

"That was another idea I had, I tried to have a garden. Nothing did very well. I was looking forward to the cabbages, I think cabbages are beautiful, but some worm got into them. It ate up the leaves till they looked like lace, and then they all turned yellow and lay on the ground."

"Cabbages are a very hard thing to grow. You should start with something easier." Simon left the table and went to the window. "Point me out where you had your garden."

"Along the fence. That's where they had it before."

"That is no good, it's too close to the walnut tree. Walnut trees are bad for the soil."

"I didn't know that."

"Well, it's true. You should have it nearer the house. Tomorrow I will dig up a garden for you. You'll need a lot of fertilizer. Now. Sheep manure is the very best fertilizer. Do you know anyone around here who has sheep? We will get several sacks of sheep manure and draw up a plan of what to plant, though it's too early yet, there could still be frost. You can start some things indoors, from seed. Tomatoes."

"I thought you had to go back on the morning bus," Rose said. They had driven up in her car.

"Monday is a light day. I will phone up and cancel. I'll tell the girls in the office to say I have a sore throat."

"Sore throat?"

"Something like that."

"It's good that you're here," said Rose truthfully. "Otherwise I'd be spending my time thinking about that boy. I'd be trying not to, but it would keep coming at me. In unprotected moments. I would have been in a state of humiliation."

"That's a pretty small thing to get into a state of humiliation about."

"So I see. It doesn't take much with me."

"Learn not to be so thin-skinned," said Simon, as if he were taking her over, in a sensible way, along with the house and garden. "Radishes. Leaf lettuce. Onions. Potatoes. Do you eat potatoes?"

Before he left they drew up a plan of the garden. He dug and worked the soil for her, though he had to content himself with cow manure. Rose had to go to work on Monday, but kept him in her mind all day. She saw him digging in the garden. She saw him naked peering down the cellarway. A short, thick man, hairy, warm, with a crumpled comedian's face. She knew what he would say when she got home. He would say, "I hope I done it to your satisfaction, mum," and yank a forelock.

That was what he did, and she was so delighted she cried out, "Oh, Simon, you idiot, you're the man for my life!" Such was the privilege, the widespread sunlight of the moment, that she did not reflect that saying this might be unwise.

In the middle of the week she went to the store, not to buy anything, but to get her fortune told. The woman looked in her cup and said, "Oh, you! You've met the man who will change everything."

"Yes, I think so."

"He will change your life. Oh, Lord. You won't stay here. I see fame. I see water."

"I don't know about that. I think he wants to insulate my house."

"The change has begun already."

"Yes. I know it has. Yes."

She could not remember what they had said about Simon coming again. She thought that he was coming on the weekend. She expected him, and she went out and bought groceries, not at the local store this time but at a supermarket several miles away. She hoped the woman at the store wouldn't see her carrying the grocery bags into the house. She had wanted fresh vegetables and steak and imported black cherries, and Camembert and pears. She had bought wine too, and a pair of sheets covered with stylish garlands of blue and yellow flowers. She was thinking her pale haunches would show up well against them.

On Friday night she put the sheets on the bed and the cherries in a blue bowl. The wine was chilling, the cheese was getting soft. Around nine o'clock came the loud knock, the expected joking knock on the door. She was surprised that she hadn't heard his car.

"Felt lonesome," said the woman from the store. "So I just thought I'd drop in and—oh-oh. You're expecting your company."

"Not really," Rose said. Her heart had started thumping joyfully when she heard the knock and was thumping still. "I don't know when he's arriving here," she said. "Maybe tomorrow."

"Bugger of a rain."

The woman's voice sounded hearty and practical, as if Rose might need distracting or consoling.

"I just hope he isn't driving in it, then," Rose said.

"No, sir, you wouldn't want him driving in it."

The woman ran her fingers through her short gray hair, shaking the rain out, and Rose knew she ought to offer her something. A glass of wine? She might become mellow and talkative, wanting to stay and finish the bottle. Here was a person Rose had talked to plenty of times, a friend of sorts, somebody she would have claimed to like, and she could hardly be bothered to acknowledge her. It would have been the same at that moment with anyone who was not Simon. Anyone else seemed accidental and irritating.

Rose could see what was coming. All the ordinary delights, consolations, diversions, of life would be rolled up and packed away; the pleasure found in food, lilacs, music, thunder in the night would vanish. Nothing would do anymore but to lie under Simon, nothing would do but to give way to pangs and convulsions.

She decided on tea. She thought she might as well put the time to use by having another go at her future.

"It's not clear," the woman said.

"What's not?"

"I'm not able to get anything in focus tonight. That happens. No, to be honest, I can't locate him."

"Can't locate him?"

"In your future. I'm beat."

Rose thought she was saying this out of ill will, out of jealousy.

"Well, I'm not just concerned about him."

"Maybe I could do better if you had a possession of his, just let me have it to hang on to. Anything he had his hands on, do you have that?"

"Me," said Rose. A cheap boast, at which the fortune-teller was obliged to laugh.

"No, seriously."

"I don't think so. I threw his cigarette butts out."

After the woman had gone, Rose sat up waiting. Soon it was midnight. The rain came down hard. The next time she looked it was twenty to two. How could time so empty pass so quickly? She put out the lights because she didn't want to be caught sitting up. She undressed, but couldn't lie down on the fresh sheets. She sat on in the kitchen, in the dark. From time to time she made fresh tea. Some light from the streetlight at the corner came into the room. The village had bright new mercury vapor lights. She could see that light, a bit of the store, the church steps across the road. The church no longer served the discreet and respectable Protestant sect that had built it, but proclaimed itself a Temple of Nazareth, also a Holiness Center, whatever that might be. Things were more askew here than Rose had noticed before. No retired farmers lived in these houses; in fact, there were no farms to retire from, just the poor fields covered with juniper. People worked thirty or forty miles away, in factories, in the Provincial Mental Hospital, or they didn't work at all, they lived a mysterious life on the borders of criminality or a life of orderly craziness in the shade of the Holiness Center. People's lives were surely more desperate than they used to be, and what could be more desperate than a woman of Rose's age, sitting up all night in her dark kitchen waiting for her lover? And this was a situation she had created, she had done it all herself, it seemed she never learned any lessons at all. She had turned Simon into the peg on which her hopes were hung and she could never manage now to turn him back into himself.

The mistake was in buying the wine, she thought, and the sheets and the cheese and the cherries. Preparations court disaster. She hadn't realized that till she opened the door and the commotion of her heart turned from merriment to dismay, like the sound of a tower full of bells turned comically (but not for Rose) into a rusty foghorn.

Hour after hour in the dark and the rain she foresaw what could happen. She could wait through the weekend, fortifying herself with excuses and sickening with doubt, never leaving the house in case the phone might ring. Back at work on Monday, dazed but slightly comforted by the real world, she would get up the courage to write him a note, in care of the classics department.

I was thinking we might plant the garden next weekend. I have bought a great array of seeds [a lie, but she would buy them, if she heard from him]. *Do let me know if you're coming, but don't worry if you've made other plans.*

Then she would worry: Did it sound too offhand, with that mention of other plans? Wouldn't it be too pushy, if she didn't tack that on? All her confidence, her lightness of heart, would have leaked away, but she would try to counterfeit it.

If it's too wet to work in the garden we could always go for a drive. Maybe we could shoot some groundhogs. Best, Rose.

Then a further time of waiting, for which the weekend would have been only a casual trial run, a haphazard introduction to the serious, commonplace, miserable ritual. Putting her hand into the mailbox and drawing the mail out without looking at it, refusing to leave the college until five o'clock, putting a cushion against the telephone to block her view of it; pretending inattention. Watched-pot thinking. Sitting up late at night, drinking, never getting quite sick enough of this foolishness to give up on it because the waiting would be interspersed with such green and springlike reveries, such convincing arguments as to his intentions. These would be enough, at some point, to make her decide that he must have been taken ill, he would never have deserted her otherwise. She would phone the Kingston Hospital, ask about his condition, be told that he was not a patient. After that would come the day she went into the college library, picked up back copies of the Kingston paper, searched the obituaries to discover if he had by any chance dropped dead. Then, giving in utterly, cold and shaking, she would call him at the university. The girl in his office would say he was gone. Gone to Europe, gone to California; he had only been teaching there for a single term. Gone on a camping trip, gone to get married.

Or she might say, "Just a minute, please," and turn Rose over to him, just like that.

"Yes?"

"Simon?"

"Yes."

"It's Rose."

"Rose?"

It wouldn't be as drastic as that. It would be worse.

"I've been meaning to call you," he would say, or, "Rose, how *are* you?" or even, "How is that garden?"

Better lose him now. But going by the phone she put her hand on it, to see if it was warm, maybe, or to encourage it.

Before it began to get light Monday morning she packed what she thought she would need into the back of the car, and locked the house, with the Camembert still weeping on the kitchen counter; she drove off in a westerly direction. She meant to be gone a couple of days, until she came to her senses and could face the sheets and the patch of readied earth and the place behind the bed where she had put her hand to feel the draft. (Why did she bring her boots and her winter coat, if this was the case?) She wrote a letter to the college—she could lie beautifully in letters, though not on the phone—in which she said that she had been called to Toronto by the terminal illness of a dear friend. (Perhaps she didn't lie so beautifully after all; perhaps she overdid it.) She had been awake almost the whole weekend drinking, not so very much, but steadily. *I'm not having any of it*, she said out loud, very seriously and emphatically, as she loaded the car. And as she crouched in the front seat, writing the letter, which she could more comfortably have written in the house, she thought how many crazy letters she had written, how many overblown excuses she had found, having to leave a place, or being afraid to leave a place, on account of some man. Nobody knew the extent of her foolishness, friends who had known her twenty years didn't know half of the flights she had been on, the money she had spent, and the risks she had taken.

Here she was, she thought a bit later, driving a car, shutting down the windshield wipers as the rain finally let up, on a Monday morning at ten o'clock, stopping for gas, stopping to get a transfer of money now that the banks were open; she was competent and cheery, she remembered what to do, who would guess what mortifications, memories of mortification, predictions, were beating in her head? The most mortifying thing of all was simply hope, which burrows so deceitfully at first, masks itself cunningly, but not for long. In a week's time it can be out trilling and twittering and singing hymns at heaven's gate. And it was busy even now, telling her that Simon might be turning in to her driveway at this very moment, might be standing at her door with his hands together, praying, mocking, apologizing. *Memento mori*.

Even so, even if that were true, what would happen some day, some morning? Some morning she could wake up and she would know by his breathing that he was awake beside her and not touching her, and that she was not supposed to touch him. So much female touching is asking (this is what she would have learned, or learned again, from him); women's tenderness is greedy, their sensuality is dishonest. She would lie there wishing she had some plain defect, something her shame could curl around and protect. As it was, she would have to be ashamed of, burdened by, the whole physical fact of herself, the whole outspread naked digesting putrefying fact. Her flesh could seem disastrous; thick and porous, gray and spotty. His body would not be in question, it never would be; he would be the one who condemned and forgave and how could she ever know if he would forgive her again? *Come here*, he could tell her, or *go away*. Never since Patrick had she been the free person, the one with that power; maybe she had used it all up, all that was coming to her.

Or she might hear him at a party, saying, "And then I knew I'd be all right, I knew it was a lucky sign." Telling his story to some tarty unworthy girl in a leopard-spotted silk, or—far worse—to a gentle long-haired girl in an embroidered smock, who would lead him by the hand, sooner or later, through a doorway into a room or landscape where Rose couldn't follow.

Yes, but wasn't it possible nothing like that would happen, wasn't it possible there'd be nothing but kindness, and sheep manure, and deep spring nights with the frogs singing? A failure to appear on the first weekend, or to telephone, might have meant nothing but a different timetable; no ominous sign at all. Thinking like this, every twenty miles or so, she slowed, even looked for a place to turn around. Then she did not do it, she speeded up, thinking she would drive a little further to make sure her head was clear. Thoughts of herself sitting in the kitchen, images of loss, poured over her again. And so it was, back and forth, as if the rear end of the car was held by a magnetic force, which ebbed and strengthened, ebbed and strengthened again, but the strength was never quite enough to make her turn, and after a while she became almost impersonally curious, seeing it as a real physical force and wondering if it was getting weaker as she drove, if at some point far ahead the car and she would leap free of it, and she would recognize the moment when she left its field.

So she kept driving. Muskoka; the Lakehead; the Manitoba border. Sometimes she slept in the car, pulled off to the side of the road for an hour or so. In Manitoba it was too cold to do that; she checked into a motel. She ate in roadside restaurants. Before she entered a restaurant she combed her hair and made up her face and put on that distant, dreamy, shortsighted look women wear when they think some man may be watching them. It was too much to say that she really expected Simon to be there, but it seemed she did not entirely rule him out.

The force did weaken with distance. It was as simple as that, though the distance, she thought afterward, would have to be covered by car, or by bus, or bicycle; you couldn't get the same results by flying. In a prairie town within sight of the Cypress Hills she recognized the change. She had driven all night until the sun came up behind her and she felt calm and clearheaded, as you do at such times. She went into a café and ordered coffee and fried eggs. She sat at the counter looking at the usual things there are behind café counters—the coffeepots and the bright, probably stale pieces of lemon and raspberry pie, the thick glass dishes they put ice cream or Jell-O in. It was those dishes that told her of her changed state. She could not have said she found them shapely, or eloquent, without misstating the case. All she could have said was that she saw them in a way that wouldn't be possible to a person in any stage of love. She felt their solidity with a convalescent gratitude whose weight settled comfortably into her brains and feet. She realized then that she had come into this café without the least farfetched idea of Simon, so it seemed the world had stopped being a stage where she might meet him, and gone back to being itself. During that bountifully clear half hour before her breakfast made her so sleepy she had to get to a motel, where she fell asleep with her clothes on and the curtains open to the sun, she thought how love removes the world for you, and just as surely when it's going well as when it's going badly. This shouldn't have been, and wasn't, a surprise to her; the surprise was that she so much wanted, required, everything to be there for her, thick and plain as ice-cream dishes, so that it seemed to her it might not be the disappointment, the losses, the dissolution, she had been running from, any more than the opposite of those things: the celebration and shock of love, the dazzling alteration. Even if that was safe, she couldn't accept it. Either way, you were robbed of something—a private balance spring, a little dry kernel of probity. So she thought.

She wrote to the college that while in Toronto attending the deathbed of her friend she had run into an old acquaintance who had offered her a job on the west coast, and that she was going there immediately. She supposed they could make trouble for her but she also supposed, rightly, that they would not bother, since the terms of her employment, and particularly her pay, were not quite regular. She wrote to the agency from which she rented the house; she wrote to the woman at the store, good luck and goodbye. On the Hope-Princeton highway she got out of the car and stood in the cool rain of the coastal mountains. She felt relatively safe, and exhausted, and sane, though she knew she had left some people behind who would not agree with that.

Luck was with her. In Vancouver she met a man she knew who was casting a new television series. It was to be produced on the west coast and concerned a family, or pseudo-family, of eccentrics and drifters using an old house on Saltspring Island as their home or headquarters. Rose got the role of the woman who owned the house, the pseudo-mother. Just as she had said in the letter: a job on the west coast, possibly the best job she had ever had. Some special makeup techniques, aging techniques, had to be used on her face; the makeup man joked that if the series was a success, and ran for a few years, these techniques would not be necessary.

A word everybody at the coast was using was *fragile*. They spoke of feeling fragile today, of being in a fragile state. Not me, Rose said, I am getting a distinct feeling of being made of old horsehide. The wind and sun on the prairies had browned and roughened her skin. She slapped her creased brown neck, to emphasize the word *horsehide*. She was already beginning to adopt some of the turns of phrase, the mannerisms, of the character she was to play.

A year or so later Rose was out on the deck of one of the B.C. ferries, wearing a dingy sweater and a head scarf. She had to creep around among the lifeboats, keeping an eye on a pretty young girl who was freezing in cutoff jeans and a halter. According to the script, the woman Rose played was afraid this young girl meant to jump off the boat because she was pregnant.

Filming this scene, they collected a sizable crowd. When they broke and walked toward the sheltered part of the deck, to put on their coats and drink coffee, a woman in the crowd reached out and touched Rose's arm.

"You won't remember me," she said, and in fact Rose did not remember her. Then this woman began to talk about Kingston, the couple who had given the party, even about the death of Rose's cat. Rose recognized her as the woman who had been doing the paper on suicide. But she looked quite different; she was wearing an expensive beige pantsuit, a beige-and-white scarf around her hair; she was no longer fringed and soiled and stringy and mutinous-looking. She introduced a husband, who grunted at Rose as if to say that if she expected him to make a big fuss about her, she had another think coming. He moved away and the woman said, "Poor Simon. You know he died."

Then she wanted to know if they were going to be shooting any more scenes. Rose knew why she asked. She wanted to get into the background or even the foreground of these scenes so that she could call up her friends and tell them to watch her. If she called the people who had been at that party she would have to say that she knew the series was utter tripe but that she had been persuaded to be in a scene, for the fun of it.

"Died?"

The woman took off her scarf and the wind blew her hair across her face.

"Cancer of the pancreas," she said, and turned to face the wind so that she could put the scarf on again, more to her satisfaction. Her voice seemed to Rose knowledgeable and sly. "I don't know how well you knew him," she said. Was that to make Rose wonder how well *she* knew him? That slyness could ask for help, as well as measure victories; you could be sorry for her perhaps, but never trust her. Rose was thinking this instead of thinking about what she had told her. "So sad," she said, businesslike now, as she tucked her chin in, knotting the scarf. "Sad. He had it for a long time."

Somebody was calling Rose's name; she had to go back to the scene. The girl didn't throw herself into the sea. They didn't have things like that happening in the series. Such things always threatened to happen but they didn't happen, except now and then to peripheral and unappealing characters. People watching trusted that they would be protected from predictable disasters, also from those shifts of emphasis that throw the story line open to question, the disarrangements which demand new judgments and solutions, and throw the windows open on inappropriate unforgettable scenery.

Simon's dying struck Rose as that kind of disarrangement. It was preposterous, it was unfair, that such a chunk of information should have been left out, and that Rose even at this late date could have thought herself the only person who could seriously lack power.

❧ Chaddeleys and Flemings ❧

I CONNECTION

COUSIN IRIS FROM Philadelphia. She was a nurse. Cousin Isabel from Des Moines. She owned a florist shop. Cousin Flora from Winnipeg, a teacher; Cousin Winifred from Edmonton, a lady accountant. Maiden ladies, they were called. *Old maids* was too thin a term, it would not cover them. Their bosoms were heavy and intimidating—a single, armored bundle—and their stomachs and behinds full and corseted as those of any married woman. In those days it seemed to be the thing for women's bodies to swell and ripen to a good size 20, if they were getting anything out of life at all; then, according to class and aspirations, they would either sag and loosen, go wobbly as custard under pale print dresses and damp aprons, or be girded into shapes whose firm curves and proud slopes had nothing to do with sex, everything to do with rights and power.

My mother and her cousins were the second sort of women. They wore corsets that did up the side with dozens of hooks and eyes, stockings that hissed and rasped when they crossed their legs, silk jersey dresses for the afternoon (my mother's being a cousin's hand-me-down), face powder (rachel), dry rouge, eau de cologne, tortoiseshell or imitation tortoiseshell combs in their hair. They were not imaginable without such getups, unless bundled to the chin in quilted-satin dressing gowns. For my mother this style was hard to keep up; it required ingenuity, dedication, fierce effort. And who appreciated it? She did.

They all came to stay with us one summer. They came to our house because my mother was the only married one, with a house big enough to accommodate everybody, and because she was too poor to go to see them. We lived in Dalgleish in Huron County in Western Ontario. The population, 2,000, was announced on a sign at the town limits. "Now there's two thousand and four," cried Cousin Iris, heaving herself out of the driver's seat. She drove a 1939 Oldsmobile. She had driven to Winnipeg to collect Flora, and Winifred, who had come down from Edmonton by train. Then they all drove to Toronto and picked up Isabel.

"And the four of us are bound to be more trouble than the whole two thousand put together," said Isabel. "Where was it— Orangeville—we laughed so hard Iris had to stop the car? She was afraid she'd drive into the ditch!"

The steps creaked under their feet.

"Breathe that air! Oh, you can't beat the country air. Is that the pump where you get your drinking water? Wouldn't that be lovely right now? A drink of well water!"

My mother told me to get a glass, but they insisted on drinking out of the tin mug.

They told how Iris had gone into a field to answer Nature's call and had looked up to find herself surrounded by a ring of interested cows.

"Cows baloney!" said Iris. "They were steers."

"Bulls, for all you'd know," said Winifred, letting herself down into a wicker chair. She was the fattest.

"Bulls! I'd know!" said Iris. "I hope their furniture can stand the strain, Winifred. I tell you it was a drag on the rear end of my poor car. Bulls! What a shock, it's a wonder I got my pants up!"

They told about the wild-looking town in Northern Ontario where Iris wouldn't stop the car even to let them buy a Coke. She took one look at the lumberjacks and cried, "We'd all be raped!"

"What is raped?" said my little sister.

"Oh-oh," said Iris. "It means you get your pocketbook stolen."

Pocketbook: an American word. My sister and I didn't know what that meant either, but we were not equal to two questions in a row. And I knew that wasn't what *rape* meant anyway; it meant something dirty.

"Purse. Purse stolen," said my mother, in a festive but cautioning tone. Talk in our house was genteel.

Now came the unpacking of presents. Tins of coffee, nuts-and-date pudding, oysters, olives, ready-made cigarettes for my father. They all smoked too, except for Flora, the Winnipeg schoolteacher. A sign of worldliness then; in Dalgleish, a sign of possible loose morals. They made it a respectable luxury.

Stockings, scarves emerged as well, a voile blouse for my mother, a pair of stiff white organdie pinafores for me and my sister (the latest thing, maybe, in Des Moines or Philadelphia but a mistake in Dalgleish, where people asked us why we hadn't taken our aprons off). And finally, a five-pound box of chocolates. Long after all the chocolates were eaten, and the cousins had gone, we kept the chocolate box in the linen drawer in the dining-room sideboard, waiting for some ceremonial use that never presented itself. It was still full of the empty chocolate cups of dark, fluted paper. In the wintertime I would sometimes go into the cold dining room and sniff at the cups, inhaling their smell of artifice and luxury; I would read again the descriptions on the map provided on the inside of the box-top: hazelnut, creamy nougat, Turkish delight, golden toffee, peppermint cream.

The cousins slept in the downstairs bedroom and on the pulled-out daybed in the front room. If the night was hot they thought nothing of dragging a mattress onto the veranda, or even into the yard. They drew lots for the hammock. Winifred was not allowed to draw. Far into the night you could hear them giggling, shushing each other, crying, "What was that?" We were beyond the streetlights of Dalgleish, and they were amazed at the darkness, the large number of stars.

Once they decided to sing a round.

> *"Row, row, row your boat*
> *Gently down the stream,*
> *Merrily, merrily, merrily, merrily,*
> *Life is but a dream."*

They didn't think Dalgleish was real. They drove uptown and reported on the oddity of the shopkeepers; they imitated things they had overheard on the street. Every morning the coffee they had brought filled the house with its unfamiliar, American fragrance, and they sat around asking who had an inspiration for the day. One inspiration was to drive out into the country and pick berries. They got scratched and over-heated and at one point Winifred was completely penned in, immobilized, by thorny branches, bellowing for a rescue party; nevertheless they said they had mightily enjoyed themselves. Another inspiration was to take my father's fishing rods and go down to the river. They came home with a catch of rock bass, a fish we generally threw back. They organized picnics. They dressed up in old clothes, in old straw hats and my father's over-alls, and took pictures of each other. They made layer cakes, and marvellous molded salads which were shaped like temples and colored like jewels.

One afternoon they put on a concert. Iris was an opera singer. She took the cloth off the dining-room table to drape herself in, and sent me out to collect hen feathers to put in her hair. She sang "The Indian Love Call," and "Women Are Fickle." Winifred was a bank robber, with a water pistol she had bought at the five-and-ten. Everybody had to do some-thing. My sister and I sang, two songs: "Yellow Rose of Texas," and the Doxology. My mother, most amazingly, put on a pair of my father's trousers and stood on her head.

Audience and performers, the cousins were for each other, every waking moment. And sometimes asleep. Flora was the one who talked in her sleep. Since she was also the most lady-like and careful, the others stayed awake to ask her questions, trying to make her say something that would embarrass her. They told her she swore. They said she sat bolt upright and demanded, "Why is there no damned chalk?"

She was the one I liked least because she attempted to sharpen our minds—my sister's and mine—by throwing out mental-arithmetic questions. "If it took seven minutes to walk seven blocks, and five blocks were the same length but the other two blocks were double the length—"

"Oh, go soak your head, Flora!" said Iris, who was the rudest.

If they didn't get any inspiration, or it was too hot to do anything, they sat on the veranda drinking lemonade, fruit punch, ginger ale, iced tea, with maraschino cherries and chunks of ice chipped from the big chunk in the icebox. Sometimes my mother prettied up the glasses by dipping the rims in beaten egg whites, then in sugar. The cousins would say they were prostrated, they were good for nothing; but their complaints had a gratified sound, as if the heat of summer itself had been created to add drama to their lives.

Drama enough already.

In the larger world, things had happened to them. Accidents, proposals, encounters with lunatics and enemies. Iris could have been rich. A millionaire's widow, a crazy old woman with a wig like a haystack, had been wheeled into the hospital one day, clutching a carpetbag. And what was in the carpetbag but jewels, real jewels, emeralds and diamonds and pearls as big as pullet eggs. Nobody but Iris could do a thing with her. It was Iris who persuaded her at last to throw the wig into the garbage (it was crawling with fleas), and let the jewels go into the bank vault. So attached did this old woman become to Iris that she wanted to remake her will, she wanted to leave Iris the jewels and the stocks and the money and the apartment houses. Iris would not allow it. Professional ethics ruled it out.

"You are in a position of trust. A nurse is in a position of trust."

Then she told how she had been proposed to by an actor, dying from a life of dissipation. She allowed him to swig from a Listerine bottle because she didn't see what difference it would make. He was a stage actor, so we wouldn't recognize the name even if she told us, which she wouldn't.

She had seen other big names too, celebrities, the top society of Philadelphia. Not at their best.

Winifred said that she had seen things too. The real truth, the real horrible truth about some of those big wheels and socialites, came out when you got a look at their finances.

We lived at the end of a road running west from Dalgleish over some scrubby land where there were small wooden houses and flocks of chickens and children. The land rose to a decent height where we were and then sloped in wide fields and pastures, decorated with elm trees, down to the curve of the river. Our house was decent too, an old brick house of a fair size, but it was drafty and laid out in an inconvenient way and the trim needed paint. My mother planned to fix it up and change it all around, as soon as we got some money.

My mother did not think much of the town of Dalgleish. She was often harking back to the town of Fork Mills, in the Ottawa Valley, where she and the cousins had gone to high school, the town their grandfather had come to from England; and to England itself, which of course she had never seen. She praised Fork Mills for its stone houses, its handsome and restrained public buildings (quite different, she said, from Huron County's, where the idea had been to throw up some brick monstrosity and stick a tower on it), for its paved streets, the service in its stores, the better quality of things for sale, and the better class of people. The people who thought so highly of themselves in Dalgleish would be laughable to the leading families of Fork Mills. But then, the leading families of Fork Mills would themselves be humbled if they came into contact with certain families of England, to whom my mother was connected.

Connection. That was what it was all about. The cousins were a show in themselves, but they also provided a connection. A connection with the real, and prodigal, and dangerous, world. They knew how to get on in it, they had made it take notice. They could command a classroom, a maternity ward, the public; they knew how to deal with taxi drivers and train conductors.

The other connection they provided, and my mother provided as well, was to England and history. It is a fact that Canadians of Scottish—which in Huron County we called Scotch —and Irish descent will tell you quite freely that their ancestors came out during the potato famine, with only the rags on their backs, or that they were shepherds, agricultural laborers, poor landless people. But anyone whose ancestors came from England will have some story of black sheep or younger sons, financial reverses, lost inheritances, elopements with unsuitable partners. There may be some amount of truth in this; conditions in Scotland and Ireland were such as to force wholesale emigration, while Englishmen may have chosen to leave home for more colorful, personal reasons.

This was the case with the Chaddeley family, my mother's family. Isabel and Iris were not Chaddeleys by name, but their mother had been a Chaddeley; my mother had been a Chaddeley, though she was now a Fleming; Flora and Winifred were Chaddeleys still. All were descended from a grandfather who left England as a young man for reasons they did not quite agree on. My mother believed that he had been a student at Oxford, but had lost all the money his family sent him, and had been ashamed to go home. He lost it by gambling. No, said Isabel, that was just the story; what really happened was that he got a servant girl in trouble and was compelled to marry her, and take her to Canada. The family estates were near Canterbury, said my mother. (Canterbury pilgrims, Canterbury bells.) The others were not sure of that. Flora said that they were in the West of England, and that the name Chaddeley was said to be related to Cholmondeley; there was a Lord Cholmondeley, the Chaddeleys could be a branch of that family. But there was also the possibility, she said, that it was French, it was originally Champ de Laiche, which means field of sedge. In that case the family had probably come to England with William the Conqueror.

Isabel said she was not an intellectual and the only person she knew from English history was Mary, Queen of Scots. She wanted somebody to tell her if William the Conqueror came before Mary, Queen of Scots, or after?

"Sedge fields," said my father agreeably. "That wouldn't exactly make them a fortune."

"Well, I wouldn't know sedge from oats," said Iris. "But they were prosperous enough in England; according to Grandpa, they were gentry there."

"Before," said Flora, "and Mary, Queen of Scots, wasn't even English."

"I knew that from the name," said Isabel. "So ha-ha."

Every one of them believed, whatever the details, that there had been a great comedown, a dim catastrophe, and that beyond them, behind them, in England, lay lands and houses and ease and honor. How could they think otherwise, remembering their grandfather?

He had worked as a postal clerk in Fork Mills. His wife, whether she was a seduced servant or not, bore him eight children, then died. As soon as the older children were to work and contributing money to the household—there was no nonsense about educating them—the father quit work. A fight with the Postmaster was the immediate reason, but he really had no intention of working any longer; he had made up his mind to stay at home, supported by his children. He had the air of a gentleman, was widely read, and full of rhetoric and self-esteem. His children did not balk at supporting him; they sank into their commonplace jobs, but pushed their own children—they limited themselves to one or two apiece, mostly daughters—out to Business School, to Normal School, to Nurses Training. My mother and her cousins, who were these children, talked often about their selfish and willful grandfather, hardly ever about their decent, hard-working parents. What an old snob he was, they said, but how handsome, even as an old man, what a carriage. What ready and appropriate insults he had for people, what scathing judgments he could make. Once, in faraway Toronto, on the main floor of Eaton's as a matter of fact, he was accosted by the harness-maker's wife from Fork Mills, a harmless, brainless woman who cried, "Well, ain't it nice to meet a friend so far from home?"

"Madam," said Grandfather Chaddeley, "you are no friend of mine."

Wasn't he the limit, they said. *Madam, you are no friend of mine!* The old snob. He paraded around with his head in the air like a prize gander. Another lower-class lady—lower-class according to him—was kind enough to bring him some soup when he had caught cold. Sitting in his daughter's kitchen, not even his own roof over his head, soaking his feet, an ailing and in fact a dying man, he still had the gall to turn his back, let his daughter do the thanking. He despised the woman, whose grammar was terrible, and who had no teeth.

"But he didn't either! By that time he had no teeth whatever!"

"Pretentious old coot."

"And a leech on his children."

"Just pride and vanity. That's the sum total of him."

But telling these stories, laughing, they were billowing with pride themselves, they were crowing. They were proud of having such a grandfather. They believed that refusing to speak to inferior people was outrageous and mean, that preserving a sense of distinction was ridiculous, particularly when your teeth were gone, but in a way they still admired him. They did. They admired his invective, which was lost on his boss, the plodding Postmaster, and his prideful behavior, which was lost on his neighbors, the democratic citizens of Canada. (Oh, what a shame, said the toothless neighbor, the poor old fellow, he don't even reckinize me.) They might even have admired his decision to let others do the work. A gentleman, they called him. They spoke ironically, but the possession of such a grandfather continued to delight them.

I couldn't understand this, at the time or later. I had too much Scottish blood in me, too much of my father. My father would never have admitted there were inferior people, or superior people either. He was scrupulously egalitarian, making it a point not to "snivel," as he said, to anybody, not to kowtow, and not to high-hat anybody either, to behave as if there were no differences. I took the same tack. There were times, later, when I wondered if it was a paralyzing prudence that urged this stand, as much as any finer sentiment, when I wondered if my father and I didn't harbor, in our hearts, intact and unassailable notions of superiority, which my mother and her cousins with their innocent snobbishness could never match.

It was not of much importance to me, years later, to receive a letter from the Chaddeley family, in England. It was from an elderly lady who was working on a family tree. The family did

exist in England, after all, and they did not spurn their overseas branches, they were seeking us out. My great-grandfather
was known to them. There was his name on the family tree:
Joseph Ellington Chaddeley. The marriage register gave his
occupation as butcher's apprentice. He had married Helena
Rose Armour, a servant, in 1859. So it was true that he had
married a servant. But probably not true about the gaming
debts at Oxford. Did gentlemen who were embarrassed at
Oxford go and apprentice themselves to butchers?

It occurred to me that if he had stayed with butchering, his
children might have gone to high school. He might have been
a prosperous man in Fork Mills. The letter writer did not mention the Cholmondeley connection, or the fields of sedge, or
William the Conqueror. It was a decent family we belonged
to, of servants and artisans, the occasional tradesman or farmer.
At one time I would have been shocked to discover this, and
would hardly have believed it. At another, later time, when I
was dedicated to tearing away all false notions, all illusions, I
would have been triumphant. By the time the revelation came
I did not care, one way or the other. I had almost forgotten
about Canterbury and Oxford and Chomondeley, and that first
England I had heard of from my mother, that ancient land of
harmony and chivalry, of people on horseback, and good manners (though surely my grandfather's had broken, under the
strain of a cruder life), of Simon de Montfort and Lorna Doone
and hounds and castles and the New Forest, all fresh and rural,
ceremonious, civilized, eternally desirable.

And I had already had my eyes opened to some other things,
by the visit of Cousin Iris.

That happened when I was living in Vancouver. I was married to Richard then. I had two small children. On a Saturday
evening Richard answered the phone and came to get me.

"Be careful," he said. "It sounds like Dalgleish."

Richard always said the name of my native town as if it were
a clot of something unpleasant, which he had to get out of his
mouth in a hurry.

I went to the phone and found to my relief that it was
nobody from Dalgleish at all. It was Cousin Iris. There was a

bit of the Ottawa Valley accent still in her speech, something rural—she would not have suspected that herself and would not have been pleased—and something loud and jolly, which had made Richard think of the voices of Dalgleish. She said that she was in Vancouver, she was retired now and she was taking a trip, and she was dying to see me. I asked her to come to dinner the next day.

"Now, by dinner, you mean the evening meal, don't you?"

"Yes."

"I just wanted to get it straight. Because when we visited at your place, remember, your folks always had dinner at noon. You called the noon meal dinner. I didn't think you still would but I wanted to get it straight."

I told Richard that a cousin of my mother's was coming to dinner. I said she was, or had been, a nurse, and that she lived in Philadelphia.

"She's all right," I said. I meant decently educated, well enough spoken, moderately well bred. "She's travelled all over. She's really quite interesting. Being a nurse she's met all sorts of people—" I told about the millionaire's widow and the jewels in the carpetbag. And the more I talked, the more Richard discerned of my doubts and my need for reassurance, and the more noncommittal and unreassuring he became. He knew he had an advantage, and we had reached the point in our marriage where no advantage was given up easily.

I longed for the visit to go well. I wanted this for my own sake. My motives were not such as would do me credit. I wanted Cousin Iris to shine forth as a relative nobody need be ashamed of, and I wanted Richard and his money and our house to lift me forever, in Cousin Iris's eyes, out of the category of poor relation. I wanted all this accomplished with a decent subtlety and restraint and the result to be a pleasant recognition of my own value, from both sides.

I used to think that if I could produce one rich and well-behaved and important relative, Richard's attitude to me would change. A judge, a surgeon, would have done very well. I was not sure at all how Iris would serve as a substitute. I was worried about the way Richard had said "Dalgleish," and that vestige of the Ottawa Valley—Richard was stern about rural accents, having had so much trouble with mine—and something else in Iris's voice which I could not identify. Was she too eager? Did she assume some proprietary family claim I no longer believed was justified?

Never mind. I started thawing a leg of lamb and made a lemon-meringue pie. Lemon-meringue pie was what my mother made when the cousins were coming. She polished the dessert forks, she ironed the table napkins. For we owned dessert forks (I wanted to say to Richard); yes, and we had table napkins, even though the toilet was in the basement and there was no running water until after the war. I used to carry hot water to the front bedroom in the morning, so that the cousins could wash. I poured it into a jug like those I now see in antique stores, or on hall tables, full of ornamental grasses.

But surely none of this mattered to me, none of this nonsense about dessert forks? Was I, am I, the sort of person who thinks that to possess such objects is to have a civilized attitude to life? No, not at all; not exactly; yes and no. Yes and no. *Background* was Richard's word. *Your background.* A drop in his voice, a warning. Or was that what I heard, not what he meant? When he said "Dalgleish," even when he wordlessly handed me a letter from home, I felt ashamed, as if there was something growing over me; mold, something nasty and dreary and inescapable. Poverty, to Richard's family, was like bad breath or running sores, an affliction for which the afflicted must bear one part of the blame. But it was not good manners to notice. If ever I said anything about my childhood or my family in their company, there would be a slight drawing back, as at a low-level obscenity. But it is possible that I was a bit strident and self-conscious, like the underbred character in Virginia Woolf who makes a point of not having been taken to the circus. Perhaps that was what embarrassed them. They were tactful with me. Richard could not afford to be so tactful, since he had put himself in a chancy position, marrying me. He wanted me amputated from that past which seemed to him such shabby baggage; he was on the lookout for signs that the amputation was not complete; and of course it wasn't.

My mother's cousins had never visited us again, en masse. Winifred died suddenly one winter, not more than three or four years after that memorable visit. Iris wrote to my mother that the circle was broken now and that she had suspected Winifred was diabetic, but Winifred did not want to find that out because of her love of food. My mother herself was not well. The remaining cousins visited her, but they did so separately, and of course not often, because of distances. Nearly every one of their letters referred to the grand time they had all had, that summer, and near the end of her life my mother said, "Oh, Lord, do you know what I was thinking of? The water pistol. Remember that concert? Winifred with the water pistol! Everybody did their stunt. What did I do?"

"You stood on your head."

"Ah, yes, I did."

Cousin Iris was stouter than ever, and rosy under her powder. She was breathless from her climb up the street. I had not wanted to ask Richard to go to the hotel for her. I would not say I was afraid to ask him; I simply wanted to keep things from starting off on the wrong foot, by making him do what he hadn't offered to do. I had told myself that she would take a cab. But she had come on the bus.

"Richard was busy," I said to her, lying. "It's my fault. I don't drive."

"Never mind," said Iris staunchly. "I'm all out of puff just now but I'll be all right in a minute. It's carrying the lard that does it. Serves me right."

As soon as she said "all out of puff," and "carrying the lard," I knew how things were going to go with Richard. It hadn't even taken that. I knew as soon as I saw her on my doorstep, her hair, which I remembered as gray-brown, now gilt and sprayed into a foamy pile, her sumptuous peacock-blue dress decorated at one shoulder with a sort of fountain of gold spray. Now that I think of it, she looked splendid. I wish I had met her somewhere else. I wish I had appreciated her as she deserved. I wish that everything had gone differently.

"Well, now," she said jubilantly. "Haven't you done all right for yourself." She looked at me, and the rock garden and the ornamental shrubs and the expanse of windows. Our house was in Capilano Heights on the side of Grouse Mountain. "I'll say. It's a grand place, dear."

I took her in and introduced her to Richard and she said, "Oh-ho, so you're the husband. Well, I won't ask you how's business because I can see it's good."

Richard was a lawyer. The men in his family were either lawyers or stockbrokers. They never referred to what they did at work as any kind of business. They never referred to what they did at work at all. Talking about what you did at work was slightly vulgar; talking about how you did was unforgivably so. If I had not been still so vulnerable to Richard it might have been a pleasure to see him met like this, head-on.

I offered drinks at once, hoping to build up a bit of insulation in myself. I had got out a bottle of sherry, thinking that was what you offered older ladies, people who didn't usually drink. But Iris laughed and said, "Why, I'd love a gin-and-tonic, just like you folks."

"Remember that time we all went to visit you in Dalgleish?" she said. "It was so dry! Your mother was still a small-town girl, she wouldn't have liquor in the house. Though I always thought your father would take a drink, if you got him off. Flora was Temperance too. But that Winifred was a devil. You know she had a bottle in her suitcase? We'd sneak into the bedroom and take a nip, then gargle with cologne. She called your place the Sahara. Here we are crossing the Sahara. Not that we didn't get enough lemonade and iced tea to float a battleship. Float four battleships, eh?"

Perhaps she had seen something when I opened the door— some surprise, or failure of welcome. Perhaps she was daunted, though at the same time immensely pleased; by the house and the furnishings, which were elegant and dull and not all chosen by Richard, either. Whatever the reason, her tone when she spoke of Dalgleish and my parents was condescending. I don't think she wanted to remind me of home, and put me in my place; I think she wanted to establish herself, to let me know that she belonged here more than there.

"Oh, this is a treat, sitting here and looking at your gorgeous view! Is that Vancouver Island?"

"Point Grey," said Richard unencouragingly.

"Oh, I should have known. We went out there on the bus yesterday. We saw the university. I'm with a tour, dear, did I tell you? Nine old maids and seven widows and three widowers. Not one married couple. But as I say, you never know, the trip's not over yet."

I smiled, and Richard said he had to move the sprinkler.

"We go to Vancouver Island tomorrow, then we're taking the boat to Alaska. Everybody said to me back home, what do you want to go to Alaska for, and I said, because I've never been there, isn't that a good enough reason? No bachelors on the tour, and do you know why? They don't live to be this old! That's a medical fact. You tell your hubby. Tell him he did the right thing. But I'm not going to talk shop. Every time I go on a trip they find out I'm a nurse and they show me their spines and their tonsils and their whatnots. They want me to poke their livers. Free diagnosis. I say enough of that. I'm retired now and I mean to enjoy life. This beats the iced tea a mile, doesn't it? But she used to go to such a lot of trouble. The poor thing. She used to frost the glasses with egg white, remember?"

I tried to get her to talk about my mother's illness, new treatments, her hospital experiences, not only because that was interesting to me but because I thought it might calm her down and make her sound more intelligent. I knew Richard hadn't gone out at all but was lurking in the kitchen.

But she said, no shop.

"Beaten egg white, then sugar. Oh, dear. You had to drink through straws. But the fun we had there. The john in the basement and all. We did have fun."

Iris's lipstick, her bright teased hair, her iridescent dress and oversized brooch, her voice and conversation were all part of a policy which was not a bad one: she was in favor of movement, noise, change, flashiness, hilarity, and courage. Fun. She thought other people should be in favor of these things too, and told about her efforts on the tour.

"I'm the person to get the ball rolling. Some people get downhearted on a trip. They get indigestion. They talk about their constipation. I always get their minds off it. You can always joke. You can start a singsong. Every morning I can practically hear them thinking, What crazy thing is that Chaddeley going to come up with today?"

Nothing fazed her, she said. She told about other trips. Ireland. The other women had been afraid to get down and kiss the Blarney Stone, but she said, "I've come this far and I'm going to kiss the damn thing!" and did so, while a blasphemous Irishman hung on to her ankles.

We drank; we ate; the children came in and were praised. Richard came and went. Nothing fazed her; she was right. Nothing deflected her from her stories of herself; the amount of time she could spend not talking was limited. She told about the carpetbag and the millionaire's widow all over again. She told about the dissolute actor. How many conversations she must have ridden through like this—laughing, insisting, rambling, recollecting. I wondered if this evening was something she would describe as fun. She would describe it. The house, the rugs, the dishes, the signs of money. It might not matter to her that Richard snubbed her. Perhaps she would rather be snubbed by a rich relative than welcomed by a poor one. But had she always been like this, always brash and greedy and scared; decent, maybe even admirable, but still somebody you hope you will not have to sit too long beside on a bus or at a party? I was dishonest when I said that I wished we had met elsewhere, that I wished I had appreciated her, when I implied that Richard's judgments were all that stood in the way. Perhaps I could have appreciated her more, but I couldn't have stayed with her long.

I had to wonder if this was all it amounted to, the gaiety I remembered; the gaiety and generosity, the worldliness. It would be better to think that time had soured and thinned and made commonplace a brew that used to sparkle, that difficulties had altered us both, and not for the better. Unsympathetic places and people might have made us harsh, in efforts and opinions. I used to love to look at magazine advertisements showing ladies in chiffon dresses with capes and floating panels, resting their elbows on a ship's rail, or drinking tea beside a potted palm. I used to apprehend a life of elegance and sensibility through them. They were a window I had on the world, and the cousins were another. In fact, the cousins' flowery dresses used to remind me of them, though the cousins were so much stouter, and not pretty. Well, now that I think of it, what were those ladies talking about in the balloons over their heads? They were discussing underarm odor, or thanking their lucky stars they were no longer chafed, because they used Kotex.

Iris collected herself, finally, and asked when the last bus ran. Richard had disappeared again, but I said I would take her back to her hotel in a cab. She said no, she would enjoy the bus ride, truly she would, she always got into a conversation with somebody. I got out my schedule and walked her to the bus stop. She said she hoped she hadn't talked Richard's and my ears off and asked if Richard was shy. She said I had a lovely home, a lovely family, it made her feel grand to see that I had done so well in my life. Tears filled her eyes when she hugged me goodbye.

"What a pathetic old tart," said Richard, coming into the living room as I was gathering up the coffee cups. He followed me into the kitchen, recalling things she had said, pretentious things, bits of bragging. He pointed out grammatical mistakes she had made, of the would-be genteel variety. He pretended incredulity. Maybe he really felt it. Or maybe he thought it would be a good idea to start the attack immediately, before I took him to task for leaving the room, being rude, not offering a ride to the hotel.

He was till talking as I threw the Pyrex plate at this head. There was a piece of lemon-meringue pie in it. The plate missed, and hit the refrigerator, but the pie flew out and caught him on the side of the face just as in the old movies or an *I Love Lucy* show. There was the same moment of amazement as there is on the screen, the sudden innocence, for him; his speech stopped, his mouth open. For me, too, amazement, that something people invariably thought funny in those instances should be so shocking a verdict in real life.

"*Row, row, row your boat*
Gently down the stream.
Merrily, merrily, merrily, merrily,
Life is but a dream."

I lie in bed beside my little sister, listening to the singing in the yard. Life is transformed, by these voices, by these presences, by their high spirits and grand esteem, for themselves and each other. My parents, all of us, are on holiday. The mixture of voices and words is so complicated and varied it seems that such confusion, such jolly rivalry, will go on forever, and then to my surprise—for I am surprised, even though I know the pattern of rounds—the song is thinning out, you can hear the two voices striving.

"*Merrily, merrily, merrily, merrily,*
Life is but a dream."

Then the one voice alone, one of them singing on, gamely, to the finish. One voice in which there is an unexpected note of entreaty, of warning, as it hangs the five separate words on the air. *Life is.* Wait. *But a.* Now, wait. *Dream.*

II THE STONE IN THE FIELD

My mother was not a person who spent all her time frosting the rims of glasses and fancying herself descended from the aristocracy. She was a businesswoman, really, a trader and dealer. Our house was full of things that had not been paid for with money, but taken in some complicated trade, and that might not be ours to keep. For a while we could play a piano, consult an *Encyclopaedia Britannica,* eat off an oak table. But one day I would come home from school and find that each of these things had moved on. A mirror off the wall could go as easily, a cruet stand, a horsehair love seat that had replaced a sofa that had replaced a daybed. We were living in a warehouse.

My mother worked for, or with, a man named Poppy Cullender. He was a dealer in antiques. He did not have a shop.

He too had a house full of furniture. What we had was just his overflow. He had dresses back-to-back and bedsprings upended against the wall. He bought things—furniture, dishes, bedspreads, doorknobs, pump handles, churns, flatirons, anything—from people living on farms or in little villages in the country, then sold what he had bought to antique stores in Toronto. The heyday of antiques had not yet arrived. It was a time when people were covering old woodwork with white or pastel paint as fast as they were able, throwing out spool beds and putting in blond maple bedroom suites, covering patchwork quilts with chenille bedspreads. It was not hard to buy things, to pick them up for next to nothing, but it was a slow business selling them, which was why they might become part of our lives for a season. Just the same, Poppy and my mother were on the right track. If they had lasted, they might have become rich and justified. As it was, Poppy kept his head above water and my mother made next to nothing, and everybody thought them deluded.

They didn't last. My mother got sick, and Poppy went to jail, for making advances on a train.

There were farmhouses where Poppy was not a welcome sight. Children hooted and wives bolted the door as he came toiling through the yard in his greasy black clothes, rolling his eyes in an uncontrollably lewd or silly way he had and calling in a soft, pleading voice, "Ith anybody h-home?" To add to his other problems he had both a lisp and a stammer. My father could imitate him very well. There were places where Poppy found doors barred and others, usually less respectable, where he was greeted and cheered and fed, just as if he had been a harmless weird bird dropped out of the sky, valued for its very oddity. When he had experienced no welcome he did not go back; instead, he sent my mother. He must have had in his head a map of the surrounding country with every house in it, and just as some maps have dots to show you where the mineral resources are, or the places of historical interest, Poppy's map would have marked the location of every known and suspected rocking chair, pine sideboard, piece of milk glass, mustache cup. "Why don't you run out and take a look at it?" I would hear him say to my mother when they were huddled in the dining room looking at something like the maker's mark on an old pickle crock. He didn't stammer when he talked to her, when he talked business; his voice though soft was not humble and indicated that he had his own satisfactions, maybe his own revenge. If I had a friend with me, coming in from school, she would say, "Is that Poppy *Cullender?*" She would be amazed to hear him talking like an ordinary person and amazed to find him inside somebody's house. I disliked his connection with us so much that I wanted to say no.

Not much was made, really, of Poppy's sexual tendencies. People may have thought he didn't have any. When they said he was queer, they just meant queer: odd, freakish, disturbing. His stammer and his rolling eyes and his fat bum and his house full of throwaways were all rolled up into that one word. I don't know if he was very courageous, trying to make a life for himself in a place like Dalgleish where random insults and misplaced pity would be what was always coming at him, or whether he was just not very realistic. Certainly it was not realistic to make such suggestions to a couple of baseball players on the Stratford train.

I never knew what my mother made of his final disastrous luck, or what she knew about him. Years later she read in the paper that a teacher at the college I was going to had been arrested for fighting in a bar over a male companion. She asked me did they mean he was defending a friend, and if so, why didn't they say so? *Male companion?*

Then she said, "Poor Poppy. There were always those that were out to get him. He was very smart, in his way. Some people can't survive in a place like this. It's not permitted. No."

My mother had the use of Poppy's car, for business forays, and sometimes for a weekend, when he went to Toronto. Unless he had a trailer-load of things to take down, he travelled—unfortunately, as I have said—by train. Our own car had gone so far beyond repair that we were not able to take it out of town; it was driven into Dalgleish and back, and that was all. My parents were like many other people who had entered the Depression with some large possession, such as a car or a furnace, which gradually wore out and couldn't be fixed or replaced. When we could take it on the roads we used to go to Goderich once or twice in a summer, to the lake. And occasionally we visited my father's sisters who lived out in the country.

My mother always said that my father had a very odd family. It was odd because there had been seven girls and then one boy; and it was odd because six of those eight children still lived together, in the house where they were born. One sister had died young, of typhoid fever, and my father had got away. And those six sisters were very odd in themselves, at least in the view of many people, in the time they lived in. They were leftovers, really; my mother said so; they belonged in another generation.

I don't remember that they ever came to visit us. They didn't like to come to a town as big as Dalgleish, or to venture so far from home. It would have been a drive of fourteen or fifteen miles, and they had no car. They drove a horse and buggy, a horse and cutter in the wintertime, long after everyone else had ceased to do so. There must have been occasions when they had to drive into town, because I saw one of them once, in the buggy, on a town street. The buggy had a great high top on it, like a black bonnet, and whichever aunt it was was sitting sideways on the seat, looking up as seldom as it is possible to do while driving a horse. Public scrutiny seemed to be causing her much pain, but she was stubborn; she held herself there on the seat, cringing and stubborn, and she was as strange a sight, in her way, as Poppy Cullender was in his. I couldn't really think of her as my aunt; the connection seemed impossible. Yet I could remember an earlier time, when I had been out to the farm—maybe more than one time, for I had been so young it was hard to remember—and I had not felt this impossibility and had not understood the oddity of these relatives. It was when my grandfather was sick in bed—dying, I suppose—with a big brown-paper fan hanging over him. It was worked by a system of ropes which I was allowed to pull. One of my aunts was showing me how to do this, when my mother called my name from downstairs. Then the aunt and I looked at each other exactly as two children look at each other when an adult is calling. I must have sensed something unusual about this, some lack of what was expected, even necessary, in the way of balance, or barriers, else I would not have remembered it.

One other time with an aunt. I think the same one, but maybe another, was sitting with me on the back steps of the farmhouse, with a six-quart basket of clothes pegs on the step beside us. She was making dolls for me, mannikins, out of the roundheaded pegs. She used a black crayon and a red, to make their mouths and eyes, and she brought bits of yarn out of her apron pocket, to twist around to make the hair and clothes. And she talked to me; I am certain she talked.

"Here's a lady. She went to church with her wig on, see? She was proud. What if a wind comes up? It would blow her wig right off. See? You blow.

"Here's a soldier. See he only has the one leg? His other leg was blown off by a cannonball at the Battle of Waterloo. Do you know what a cannonball is, that shoots out of a big gun? When they have a battle? Boom!"

Now we were going out to the farm, in Poppy's car, to visit the aunts. My father said no, he wouldn't drive another man's car—meaning he wouldn't drive Poppy's, wouldn't sit where Poppy had sat—so my mother drove. That made the whole expedition feel uncertain, the weight wrongly distributed. It was a hot Sunday late in the summer.

My mother was not altogether sure of the way, and my father waited until the last moment to reassure her. This was understood to be teasing, and yet was not altogether free of reservations or reproof.

"Is it here we turn? Is it one further? I will know when I see the bridge."

The route was complicated. Around Dalgleish most roads were straight, but out here the roads twisted around hills or buried themselves in swamps. Some dwindled to a couple of ruts with a row of plantain and dandelions running between. In some places wild berry bushes sent creepers across the road. These high, thick bushes, dense and thorny, with leaves of a shiny green that seemed almost black, reminded me of the waves of the sea that were pushed back for Moses.

There was the bridge, like two railway cars joined together, stripped to their skeletons, one lane wide. A sign said it was unsafe for trucks.

"We'll never make it," my father said as we bumped onto the bridge floor. "There he is. Old Father Maitland."

My sister said, "Where? Who? Where is he?"

"The Maitland *River*," my mother said.

We looked down, where the guardrails had fallen out of the side of the bridge, and saw the clear brown water flowing over big dim stones, between cedar banks, breaking into sunny ripples further on. My skin was craving for it.

"Do they ever go swimming?" I said. I meant the aunts. I thought that if they did, they might take us.

"Swimming?" said my mother. "I can't picture it. Do they?" she asked my father.

"I can't picture it either."

The road was going uphill, out of the gloomy cedar bush on the riverbank. I started saying the aunts' names.

"Susan. Clara. Lizzie. Maggie. Jennet was the one who died."

"Annie," said my father. "Don't forget Annie."

"Annie. Lizzie. I said her. Who else?"

"Dorothy," said my mother, shifting gears with an angry little spurt, and we cleared the top of the hill, leaving the dark bush hollow behind. Up here were pasture hills covered with purple-flowering milkweed, wild pea blossom, black-eyed Susans. Hardly any trees here, but lots of elderberry bushes, blooming all along the road. They looked as if they were sprinkled with snow. One bald hill reached up higher than any of the others.

"Mount Hebron," my father said. "That is the highest point of land in Huron County. Or so I always was told."

"Now I know where I am all right," my mother said. "We'll see it in a moment, won't we?"

And there it was, the big wooden house with no trees near it, the barn and the flowering brown hills behind. The drive shed was the original barn, built of logs. The paint on the house was not white as I had absolutely believed but yellow, and much of it had peeled away.

Out in front of the house, in a block of shade which was quite narrow at this time of day, several figures were sitting on straight-backed chairs. On the wall of the house, behind them, hung the scoured milk pails and parts of the separator.

They were not expecting us. They had no telephone, so we hadn't been able to let them know we were coming. They were just sitting there in the shade, watching the road where scarcely another car went by all afternoon.

One figure got up, and ran around the side of the house.

"That'll be Susan," my father said. "She can't face company."

"She'll come back when she realizes it's us," my mother said. "She won't know the strange car."

"Maybe. I wouldn't count on it."

The others stood, and stiffly readied themselves, hands clasped in front of their aprons. When we got out of the car and were recognized, one or two of them took a few steps forward, then stopped, and waited for us to approach them.

"Come on," my father said, and led us to each in turn, saying only the name in recognition of the meeting. No embraces, no touch of hands or laying together of cheeks.

"Lizzie. Dorothy. Clara."

It was no use, I could never get them straight. They looked too much alike. There must have been a twelve- or fifteen-year age span, but to me they all looked about fifty, older than my parents but not really old. They were all lean and fine-boned, and might at one time have been fairly tall, but were stooped now, with hard work and deference. Some had their hair cut short in a plain, childish style; some had it braided and twisted on top of their heads. Nobody's hair was entirely black or entirely gray. Their faces were pale, eyebrows thick and furry, eyes deep-set and bright; blue-gray or green-gray or gray. They looked a good deal like my father, though he did not stoop, and his face had opened up in a way that theirs had not, to make him a handsome man.

They looked a good deal like me. I didn't know it at the time and wouldn't have wanted to. But suppose I stopped doing anything to my hair now, stopped wearing makeup and plucking my eyebrows, put on a shapeless print dress and apron, and stood around hanging my head and hugging my elbows? Yes. So when my mother and her cousins looked me over, anxiously turned me to the light, saying, "Is she a Chaddeley? What do you think?" it was the Fleming face they were seeing, and to tell the truth it was a face that wore better than theirs. (Not that they were claiming to be pretty; to look like a Chaddeley was enough.)

One of the aunts had hands red as a skinned rabbit. Later in the kitchen this one sat in a chair pushed up against the woodbox, half hidden by the stove, and I saw how she kept stroking these hands and twisting them up in her apron. I remembered that I had seen such hands before, on one of the early visits, long ago, and my mother had told me that it was because this aunt—was it always the same one?—had been scrubbing the floor and the table and chairs with lye, to keep them white. That was what lye did to your hands. And after this visit too, on the way home my mother was to say in a tone of general accusation, sorrow, and disgust, "Did you see those hands? They must have got a Presbyterian dispensation to let them scrub on Sundays."

The floor was pine and it was white, gleaming, but soft-looking, like velvet. So were the chairs and the table. We all sat around the kitchen, which was like a small house tacked onto the main house; back and front doors opposite each other, windows on three sides. The cold black stove shone too, with polishing. Its trim was like mirrors. The room was cleaner and barer than any I have ever been in. There was no sign of frivolity, no indication that the people who lived here ever sought entertainment. No radio; no newspapers or magazines; certainly no books. There must have been a Bible in the house, and there must have been a calendar, but these were not to be seen. It was hard now even to believe in the clothespin dolls, the crayons and the yarn. I wanted to ask which of them had made the dolls; had there really been a wigged lady and a one-legged soldier? But though I was not usually shy, a peculiar paralysis overcame me in this room, as if I understood for the first time how presumptuous any question might be, how hazardous any opinion.

Work would be what filled their lives, not conversation; work would be what gave their days shape. I know that now. Drawing the milk down through the rough teats, slapping the flatiron back and forth on the scorched-smelling ironing board, swishing the scrub-water in whitening arcs across the pine floor, they would be mute, and maybe content. Work would not be done here as it was in our house, where the idea was to get it over with. It would be something that could, that must, go on forever.

What was to be said? The aunts, like those who engage in a chat with royalty, would venture no remarks of their own, but could answer questions. They offered no refreshments. It was clear that only a great effort of will kept them all from running away and hiding, like Aunt Susan, who never did reappear while we were there. What was felt in that room was the pain of human contact. I was hypnotized by it. The fascinating pain; the humiliating necessity.

My father did have some idea of how to proceed. He started out on the weather. The need for rain, the rain in July that spoiled the hay, last year's wet spring, floods long past, the prospects or non-prospects of a rainy fall. This talk steadied them, and he asked about the cows, the driving horse whose name was Nelly and the workhorses Prince and Queen, the garden; did the blight get on their tomatoes?

"No, it didn't."

"How many quarts did you do down?"

"Twenty-seven."

"Did you make any chili sauce? Did you make some juice?"

"Juice and chili sauce. Yes."

"So you won't starve next winter. You'll be falling into flesh, next."

Giggles broke from a couple of them and my father took heart, continued teasing. He inquired whether they were doing much dancing these days. He shook his head as he pretended to recall their reputation for running around the country to dances, smoking, cutting up. He said they were a bad lot, they wouldn't get married because they'd rather flirt; why, he couldn't hold up his head for the shame of them.

My mother broke in then. She must have meant to rescue them, thinking it cruel to tease them in this way, dwelling on just what they had never had, or been.

"That is a lovely piece of furniture," she said. "That sideboard. I always have admired it."

Flappers, my father said, that's what they were, in their prime.

My mother went over to look at the kitchen dresser, which was pine, and very heavy and tall. The knobs on all the doors and drawers were not quite round but slightly irregular, either from the making or from all the hands that had pulled on them.

"You could have an antique dealer come in here and offer you a hundred dollars for that," my mother said. "If that ever happens, don't take it. The table and chairs as well. Don't let anybody smooth-talk you into selling them before you find out what they're really worth. I know what I'm talking about." Without asking permission she examined the dresser, fingered the knobs, looked around at the back. "I can't tell you what it's worth myself but if you ever want to sell it I will get it appraised by the best person I can find. That's not all," she said, stroking the pine judiciously. "You have a fortune's worth of furniture in this house. You sit tight on it. You have the old furniture that was made around here, and there's hardly any of that left. People threw it out, around the turn of the century; they bought Victorian things when they started getting prosperous. The things that didn't get thrown out are worth money and they're going to be worth more. I'm telling you."

So she was. But they could not take such telling. They could no more understand her than if she had been spouting lunacy. Possibly the word *antique* was not known to them. She was talking about their kitchen dresser but she was talking about it in terms they had no understanding of. If a dealer came into the house and offered them money? Nobody came into their house. Selling the dresser was probably as hard for them to imagine as selling the kitchen wall. None of them would look at anything but their aproned laps.

"So I guess that's lucky, for the ones that never got prosperous," my father said, to ease things, but they could not answer him, either. They would know the meaning of *prosperous* but they would never have used such a word, would never have got their tongues around it, nor their minds around the idea of getting that way. They would have noticed that some people—their neighbors, even—were spending money, on tractors and combines and milking machines as well as on cars and houses, and I think this must have seemed to them a sign of an alarming, not enviable, lack of propriety and self-control. They would pity people for it, in a way, the same way they might pity girls who did run around to dances, and smoke and flirt and get married. They might pity my mother too. My mother looked at their lives and thought of how they could be brightened, opened up. Suppose they sold some furniture and got hydro in the house, bought a washing machine, put linoleum on the floor, bought a car and learned to drive it? Why not? my mother would ask, seeing life all in terms of change and possibility. She imagined they would yearn for things, not only material things but conditions, abilities, which they did not even bother to deplore, did not think to reject, being so perfectly encased in what they had and were, so far beyond imagining themselves otherwise.

When my father was in the hospital for the last time he became very good-humored and loquacious under the influence of the pills they were giving him, and he talked to me about his life and his family. He told me how he had left home. Actually there were two leave-takings. The first occurred the summer he was fourteen. His father had sent him out to split some chunks of wood. He broke the axe-handle, and his father cursed him out and went after him with a pitchfork. His father was known for temper, and hard work. The sisters screamed, and my father, the fourteen-year-old boy, took off down the lane running as hard as he could.

"Could they scream?"

"What? Oh yes. Then. Yes they could."

My father intended to run only as far as the road, hang around, come back when his sisters let him know the coast was clear. But he did not stop running until he was halfway to Goderich, and then he thought he might as well go the rest of the way. He got a job on a lake boat. He spent the rest of the season working on the boat, and the month before Christmas, after the shipping season ended, he worked in a flour mill. He could do the work there, but he was underage; they were afraid of the inspector, so they let him go. He wanted to go home anyway, for Christmas. He was homesick. He bought presents for his father and his sisters. A watch was what he got for the old man. That and his ticket took every cent he had.

A few days after Christmas he was out in the barn, putting down hay, and his father came looking for him.

"Have you got any money?" his father wanted to know.

My father said he hadn't.

"Well, do you think then me and your sisters are going to spend all summer and fall looking up the arseholes of cows, for you to come home and sponge off us in the winter?"

That was the second time my father left home.

He shook with laughter in the hospital bed, telling me.

"Looking up the arseholes of cows!"

Then he said the funny thing was the old man himself had left home when he was a kid, after a fight with his own father. The father lit into him for using the wheelbarrow.

"It was this way. They always carried the feed to the horses, pail by pail. In the winter, when the horses were in the stalls. So my father took the notion to carry it to them in the wheelbarrow. Naturally it was a lot quicker. But he got beat. For laziness. That was the way they were, you know. Any change of any kind was a bad thing. Efficiency was just laziness, to them. That's the peasant thinking for you."

"Maybe Tolstoy would agree with them," I said. "Gandhi too."

"Drat Tolstoy and Gandhi. They never worked when they were young."

"Maybe not."

"But it's a wonder how those people had the courage once, to get them over here. They left everything. Turned their backs on everything they knew and came out here. Bad enough to face the North Atlantic, then this country that was all wilderness. The work they did, the things they went through. When your great-grandfather came to the Huron Tract he had his brother with him, and his wife and her mother, and his two little kids. Straightaway his brother was killed by a falling tree. Then the second summer his wife and her mother and the two little boys got the cholera, and the grandmother and both the children died. So he and his wife were left alone, and they went on clearing their farm and started up another family. I think the courage got burnt out of them. Their religion did them in, and their upbringing. How they had to toe the line. Also their pride. Pride was what they had when they had no more gumption."

"Not you," I said. "You ran away."

"I didn't run far."

In their old age the aunts rented the farm, but continued to live on it. Some got cataracts in their eyes, some got arthritis, but they stayed on and looked after each other, and died there, all except the last one, Aunt Lizzie, who had to go to the County Home. They lived a long time. They were a hardier clan, after all, than the Chaddeleys, none of whom reached seventy. (Cousin Iris died within six months of seeing Alaska.) I used to send a card at Christmas, and I would write on it: *To all my aunts, love and a Merry Christmas.* I did that because I could not remember which of them were dead and which were alive. I had seen their gravestone when my mother was buried. It was a modest pillar with all their names and dates of birth on it, a couple of dates of death filled in (Jennet, of course, and probably Susan), the rest left blank. By now more dates would be finished.

They would send me a card too. A wreath or a candle on it, and a few sentences of information.

A good winter so far, not much snow. We are all well except Clara's eyes not getting any better. Best wishes of the Season.

I thought of them having to go out and buy the card, go to the Post Office, buy the stamp. It was an act of faith for them to write and send those sentences to any place as unimaginable as Vancouver, to someone of their own blood leading a life so strange to them, someone who would read the card with such a feeling of bewilderment and unexplainable guilt. It did make me guilty and bewildered to think that they were still there, still attached to me. But any message from home, in those days, could let me know I was a traitor.

In the hospital, I asked my father if any of his sisters had ever had a boyfriend.

"Not what you could call that. No. There used to be a joke about Mr. Black. They used to say he built his shack there because he was sweet on Susan. I don't think so. He was just a one-legged fellow that built a shack down in a corner of the field across the road, and he died there. All before my time. Susan was the oldest, you know, she was twenty or twenty-one years old when I was born."

"So, you don't think she had a romance?"

"I wouldn't think so. It was just a joke. He was an Austrian or some such thing. Black was just what he was called, or maybe he called himself. She wouldn't have been let near him. He was buried right there under a big boulder. My father tore the shack down and used the lumber to build our chicken house."

I remembered that, I remembered the boulder. I remembered sitting on the ground watching my father, who was fixing fence posts. I asked him if this could be a true memory.

"Yes, it could. I used to go out and fix the fences when the old man was sick in bed. You wouldn't have been very big."

"I was sitting watching you, and you said to me, 'Do you know what that big stone is? That's a gravestone.' I don't remember asking you whose. I must have thought it was a joke."

"No joke. That would be it. Mr. Black was buried underneath there. That reminds me of another thing. You know I told you how the grandmother and the little boys died? They had the three bodies in the house at the one time. And they had nothing to make the shrouds out of but the lace curtains they had brought from the old country. I guess it would be a hasty business when it was cholera and in the summer. So that was what they buried them in."

"Lace curtains."

My father looked shy, as if he had given me a present, and said brusquely, "Well, that's the kind of a detail I thought might be interesting to you."

Some time after my father died I was reading some old newspapers on a microfilm reader in the Toronto Library; this was in connection with a documentary script I was working on, for television. The name Dalgleish caught my eye and then the name Fleming, which I have gone so long without.

It is reported that Mr. Black, a man about forty-five years old, Christian name unknown, has died on the farm of Mr. Thomas Fleming, where he has been living for the last three years in a shack which Mr. Fleming allowed him to construct in the corner of a field. He cultivated a few potatoes, substituting mainly on those and on fish and small game. He was believed to come from some European country but gave the name Black and did not reveal his history. At some point in his life he had parted company with one of his legs, leading some to speculate that he might have been a soldier. He was heard to mutter to himself in a foreign language.

About three weeks ago Mr. Fleming, not having seen any smoke from the recluse's shack, investigated, and found the man very ill. He was suffering from a cancer of the tongue. Mr. Fleming wished to remove him to his own house for care but Mr. Black would not agree, though he finally allowed himself to be taken to Mr. Fleming's barn, where he remained, the weather being mild, and nursing care being provided by the young Misses Fleming, who reside at home. There he died, and was buried at his own request next to his hermit's shack, taking the mystery of his life with him.

I began to think that I would like to see the stone, I would like to see if it was still there. No one related to me lived in that country anymore. I drove up on a Sunday in June and was able to bypass Dalgleish completely; the highway had been changed. I expected to have some trouble finding the farm, but I was on it before I could have believed it possible. It was no longer an out-of-the-way place. The back roads had been straightened; there was a new, strong, two-lane concrete bridge; half of Mount Hebron had been cut away for gravel; and the wild-pasture fields had been planted in corn.

The log drive shed was gone. The house had been covered in pale-green aluminum siding. There were several wide new windows. The cement slab in front, where my aunts had sat on their straight-backed chairs to watch the road, had been turned into a patio, with tubs of salvia and geraniums, a metal table with an awning, and the usual folding furniture with bright plastic webbing.

All this made me doubtful, but I knocked on the door anyway. A young, pregnant woman answered. She asked me into the kitchen, which was a cheerful room with linoleum that looked something like red and brown bricks, and built-in cupboards that looked very much like maple. Two children were watching a television picture whose colors seemed drained by the brightness of the day outside, and a businesslike young husband was working at an adding machine, seemingly unbothered by the noise of the television as his children were unbothered by the sunlight. The young woman stepped over a large dog to turn off a tap at the sink.

They were not impatient of my story, as I had thought they might be. In fact, they were interested and helpful, and not entirely in the dark about the stone I was looking for. The husband said that the land across the road had not been sold to his father, who had bought this farm from my aunts; it had been sold previously. He thought it was over there that the stone was. He said his father had told him there was a man buried over there, under a big stone, and they had even gone for a walk once, to look at it, but he hadn't thought of it in years. He said he would go and look for it now.

I had thought we would walk, but we drove down the lane in his car. We got out, and carefully entered a cornfield. The corn was just about to my knees, so the stone should have been in plain sight. I asked if the man who owned this field would mind, and the farmer said no, the fellow never came near it, he hired somebody else to work it for him.

"He's a fellow that has a thousand acres in corn in Huron County alone."

I said that a farmer was just like a businessman nowadays, wasn't he? The farmer seemed pleased that I had said this and began to explain why it was so. Risks had to be undertaken. Expenses were sky-high. I asked him if he had one of those tractors with the air-conditioned cabs and he said yes, he had. If you did well, he said, the rewards, the financial rewards, could be considerable, but there were trials and tribulations most people didn't know a thing about. Next spring, if all went well, he and his wife were going on their first holiday. They were going to Spain. The children wanted them to forget their holiday and put in a swimming pool, but his idea was to travel. He owned two farms now and was thinking of buying a third. He was just sitting working out some figures when I knocked on the door. In a way, he couldn't afford to buy it. In another way, he couldn't afford not to.

While carrying on this conversation we were walking up and down the corn rows looking for the stone. We looked in the corners of the field and it was not there. He said that of course the corner of a field then was not necessarily the corner of a field now. But the truth probably was that when the field got put in corn the stone was in the way, so they would have hauled it out. He said we could go over to the rock pile near the road and see if we recognized it.

I said we wouldn't bother, I wasn't so sure I would know it, on a rock pile.

"Me either," he said. He sounded disappointed. I wondered what he had expected to see, or feel.

I wondered the same thing about myself.

If I had been younger, I would have figured out a story. I would have insisted on Mr. Black's being in love with one of my aunts, and on one of them—not necessarily the one he was in love with—being in love with him. I would have wished him to confide in them, in one of them, his secret, his reason for living in a shack in Huron County, far from home. Later, I might have believed that he wanted to, but hadn't confided this, or his love either. I would have made a horrible, plausible connection between that silence of his and the manner of his death. Now I no longer believe that people's secrets are defined and communicable, or their feelings full-blown and easy to recognize. I don't believe so. Now, I can only say, my father's sisters scrubbed the floor with lye, they stooked the oats and milked the cows by hand. They must have taken a quilt to the barn for the hermit to die on, they must have let water dribble from a tin cup into his afflicted mouth. That was their life. My mother's cousins behaved in another way; they dressed up and took pictures of each other; they sallied forth. However they behaved they are all dead. I carry something of them around in me. But the boulder is gone, Mount Hebron is cut down for gravel, and the life buried here is one you have to think twice about regretting.

✺ *Dulse* ✺

AT THE END OF the summer Lydia took a boat to an island off the southern coast of New Brunswick, where she was going to stay overnight. She had just a few days left until she had to be back in Ontario. She worked as an editor, for a publisher in Toronto. She was also a poet, but she did not refer to that unless it was something people knew already. For the past eighteen months she had been living with a man in Kingston. As far as she could see, that was over.

She had noticed something about herself on this trip to the Maritimes. It was that people were no longer so interested in getting to know her. It wasn't that she had created such a stir before, but something had been there that she could rely on. She was forty-five, and had been divorced for nine years. Her two children had started on their own lives, though there were still retreats and confusions. She hadn't got fatter or thinner, her looks had not deteriorated in any alarming way, but nevertheless she had stopped being one sort of woman and had become another, and she had noticed it on this trip. She was not surprised because she was in a new, strange condition at the time. She made efforts, one after the other. She set little blocks on top of one another and she had a day. Sometimes she almost could not do this. At other times the very deliberateness, the seeming arbitrariness, of what she was doing, the way she was living, exhilarated her.

She found a guesthouse overlooking the docks, with their stacks of lobster traps, and the few scattered stores and houses that made up the village. A woman of about her own age was cooking dinner. This woman took her to a cheap, old-fashioned room upstairs. There were no other guests around, though the room next door was open and seemed to be occupied, perhaps by a child. Whoever it was had left several comic books on the floor beside the bed.

She went for a walk up the steep lane behind the guesthouse. She occupied herself by naming shrubs and weeds. The goldenrod and wild aster were in bloom, and Japanese boxwood, a rarity in Ontario, seemed commonplace here. The grass was long and coarse and the trees were small. The Atlantic coast, which she had never seen before, was just as she had expected it to be. The bending grass; the bare houses; the sea light. She started wondering what it would be like to live there, whether the houses were still cheap or if people from the outside had started to buy them up. Often on this trip she had busied herself with calculations of this kind, and also with ideas of how she could make a living in some new way, cut off from everything she had done before. She did not think of making a living writing poetry, not only because the income would be so low but because she thought, as she had thought innumerable times in her life, that probably she would not write any more poems. She was thinking that she could not cook well enough to do it for pay but she could clean. There was at least one other guesthouse besides the one where she was staying, and she had seen a sign advertising a motel. How many hours' cleaning could she get if she cleaned all three places, and how much an hour did cleaning pay?

There were four small tables in the dining room, but only one man was sitting there, drinking tomato juice. He did not look at her. A man who was probably the husband of the woman she had met earlier came in from the kitchen. He had a grayish-blond beard, and a downcast look. He asked Lydia's name and took her to the table where the man was sitting. The man stood up, stiffly, and Lydia was introduced. The man's name was Mr. Stanley and Lydia took him to be about sixty. Politely, he asked her to sit down.

Three men in work clothes came in and sat down at another table. They were not noisy in any self-important or offensive way, but just coming in and disposing themselves around the table, they created an enjoyable commotion. That is, they enjoyed it, and looked as if they expected others to. Mr. Stanley bowed in their direction. It really was a little bow, not just a nod of the head. He said good evening. They asked him what there was for supper, and he said he believed it was scallops, with pumpkin pie for dessert.

"These gentlemen work for the New Brunswick Telephone Company," he said to Lydia. "They are laying a cable to one of the smaller islands, and they stay here during the week."

He was older than she had thought at first. It did not show in his voice, which was precise and American, or in the movements of his hands, but in his small, separate, brownish teeth, and in his eyes, which had a delicate milky skin over the light-brown iris.

The husband brought their food, and spoke to the workmen. He was an efficient waiter, but rather stiff and remote, rather like a sleepwalker, in fact, as if he did not perform this job in his real life. The vegetables were served in large bowls, from which they helped themselves. Lydia was glad to see so much food: broccoli, mashed turnips, potatoes, corn. The American took small helpings of everything and began to eat in a very deliberate way, giving the impression that the order in which he lifted forkfuls of food to his mouth was not haphazard, that there was a reason for the turnip to follow the potatoes, and for the deep-fried scallops, which were not large, to be cut neatly in half. He looked up a couple of times as if he thought of saying something, but he did not do it. The workmen were quiet now too, laying into the food.

Mr. Stanley spoke at last. He said, "Are you familiar with the writer Willa Cather?"

"Yes." Lydia was startled, because she had not seen anybody reading a book for the past two weeks; she had not even noticed any paperback racks.

"Do you know, then, that she spent every summer here?"
"Here?"

"On this island. She had her summer home here. Not more than a mile away from where we are sitting now. She came here for eighteen years, and she wrote many of her books here. She wrote in a room that had a view of the sea, but now the trees have grown up and blocked it. She was with her great friend, Edith Lewis. Have you read *A Lost Lady?*"

Lydia said that she had.

"It is my favorite of all her books. She wrote it here. At least, she wrote a great part of it here."

Lydia was aware of the workmen listening, although they did not glance up from their food. She felt that even without looking at Mr. Stanley or each other they might manage to communicate an indulgent contempt. She thought she did not care whether or not she was included in this contempt, but perhaps it was for that reason that she did not find anything much to say about Willa Cather, or tell Mr. Stanley that she worked for a publisher, let alone that she was any sort of writer herself. Or it could have been just that Mr. Stanley did not give her much of a chance.

"I have been her admirer for over sixty years," he said. He paused, holding his knife and fork over his plate. "I read and reread her, and my admiration grows. It simply grows. There are people here who remember her. Tonight, I am going to see a woman, a woman who knew Willa, and had conversations with her. She is eighty-eight years old but they say she has not forgotten. The people here are beginning to learn of my interest and they will remember someone like this and put me in touch.

"It is a great delight to me," he said solemnly.

All the time he was talking, Lydia was trying to think what his conversational style reminded her of. It didn't remind her of any special person, though she might have had one or two teachers at college who talked like that. What it made her think of was a time when a few people, just a few people, had never concerned themselves with being democratic, or ingratiating, in their speech; they spoke in formal, well-thought-out, slightly self-congratulating sentences, though they lived in a country where their formality, their pedantry, could bring them nothing but mockery. No, that was not the whole truth. It brought mockery, and an uncomfortable admiration. What he made Lydia think of, really, was the old-fashioned culture of provincial cities long ago (something she of course had never known, but sensed from books); the high-mindedness, the propriety; hard plush concert seats and hushed libraries. And his adoration of the chosen writer was of a piece with this; it was just as out-of-date as his speech. She thought that he could not be a teacher; such worship was not in style for teachers, even of his age.

"Do you teach literature?"

"No. Oh, no. I have not had that privilege. No. I have not even studied literature. I went to work when I was sixteen. In my day there was not so much choice. I have worked on newspapers."

She thought of some absurdly discreet and conservative New England paper with a fusty prose style.

"Oh. Which paper?" she said, then realized her inquisitiveness must seem quite rude, to anyone so circumspect.

"Not a paper you would have heard of. Just the daily paper of an industrial town. Other papers in the earlier years. That was my life."

"And now, would you like to do a book on Willa Cather?" This question seemed not so out of place to her, because she was always talking to people who wanted to do books about something.

"No," he said austerely. "My eyes do not permit me to do any reading or writing beyond what is necessary."

That was why he was so deliberate about his eating.

"No," he went on, "I don't say that at one time I might not have thought of that, doing a book on Willa. I would have written something just about her life here on the island. Biographies have been done, but not so much on that phase of her life. Now I have given up the idea. I do my investigating just for my own pleasure. I take a camp chair up there, so I can sit underneath the window where she wrote and looked at the sea. There is never anybody there."

"It isn't being kept up? It isn't any sort of memorial?"

"Oh, no indeed. It isn't kept up at all. The people here, you know, while they were very impressed with Willa, and some of them recognized her genius—I mean the genius of her personality, for they would not be able to recognize the genius of her work—others of them thought her unfriendly and did not like her. They took offense because she was unsociable, as she had to be, to do her writing."

"It could be a project," Lydia said. "Perhaps they could get some money from the government. The Canadian government and the Americans too. They could preserve the house."

"Well, that isn't for me to say." He smiled; he shook his head. "I don't think so. No."

He did not want any other worshippers coming to disturb him in his camp chair. She should have known that. What would this private pilgrimage of his be worth if other people got into the act, and signs were put up, leaflets printed; if this guesthouse, which was now called Sea View, had to be renamed Shadows on the Rock? He would let the house fall down and the grass grow over it sooner than see that.

After Lydia's last attempt to call Duncan, the man she had been living with in Kingston, she had walked along the street in Toronto, knowing that she had to get to the bank, she had to buy some food, she had to get on the subway. She had to remember directions, and the order in which to do things: to open her checkbook, to move forward when it was her turn in line, to choose one kind of bread over another, to drop a token in the slot. These seemed to be the most difficult things she had ever done. She had immense difficulty reading the names of the subway stations, and getting off at the right one, so that she could go to the apartment where she was staying. She would have found it hard to describe this difficulty. She knew perfectly well which was the right stop, she knew which stop it came after; she knew where she was. But she could not make the connection between herself and things outside herself, so that getting up and leaving the car, going up the steps, going along the street all seemed to involve a bizarre effort. She thought afterwards that she had been seized up, as machines are said to be. Even at the time she had an image of herself. She saw herself as something like an egg carton, hollowed out in back.

When she reached the apartment she sat down on a chair in the hall. She sat for an hour or so; then she went to the bathroom, undressed, put on her nightgown, and got into bed. In bed she felt triumph and relief, that she had managed all the difficulties and got herself to where she was supposed to be and would not have to remember anything more.

She didn't feel at all like committing suicide. She couldn't have managed the implements, or aids, she couldn't even have thought which to use. It amazed her to think that she had chosen the loaf of bread and the cheese, which were now lying on the floor in the hall. How had she imagined she was going to chew and swallow them?

After dinner Lydia sat out on the veranda with the woman who had cooked the meal. The woman's husband did the cleaning up.

"Well, of course we have a dishwasher," the woman said. "We have two freezers and an oversized refrigerator. You have to make an investment. You get the crews staying with you, you have to feed them. This place soaks up money like a sponge. We're going to put in a swimming pool next year. We need more attractions. You have to run to stay in the same place. People think what an easy nice life. Boy."

She had a strong, lined face, and long straight hair. She wore jeans and an embroidered smock and a man's sweater.

"Ten years ago I was living in a commune in the States. Now I'm here. I work sometimes eighteen hours a day. I have to pack the crew's lunch yet tonight. I cook and bake, cook and bake. John does the rest."

"Do you have someone to clean?"

"We can't afford to hire anybody. John does it. He does the laundry—everything. We had to buy a mangle for the sheets. We had to put in a new furnace. We got a bank loan. I thought that was funny, because I used to be married to a bank manager. I left him."

"I'm on my own now too."

"Are you? You can't be on your own forever. I met John, and he was in the same boat."

"I was living with a man in Kingston, in Ontario."

"Were you? John and I are extremely happy. He used to be

a minister. But when I met him he was doing carpentry. We both had sort of dropped out. Did you talk to Mr. Stanley?"

"Yes."

"Had you ever heard of Willa Cather?"

"Yes."

"That'd make him happy. I don't read hardly at all, it doesn't mean anything to me. I'm a visual person. But I think he's a wonderful character, old Mr. Stanley. He's a real old scholar."

"Has he been coming here for a long time?"

"No, he hasn't. This is just his third year. He says he's wanted to come here all his life. But he couldn't. He had to wait till some relative died, that he was looking after. Not a wife. A brother, maybe. Anyway he had to wait. How old do you think he is?"

"Seventy? Seventy-five?"

"That man is eighty-one. Isn't that amazing? I really admire people like that. I really do. I admire people that keep going."

"The man I was living with—that is, the man I used to live with, in Kingston," said Lydia, "was putting some boxes of papers in the trunk of his car once, this was out in the country, at an old farmhouse, and he felt something nudge him and he glanced down. It was about dusk, on a pretty dark day. So he thought this was a big friendly dog, a big black dog giving him a nudge, and he didn't pay much attention. He just said go on, now, boy, go away now, good boy. Then when he got the boxes arranged he turned around. And he saw it was a bear. It was a black bear."

She was telling this later that same evening, in the kitchen.

"So what did he do then?" said Lawrence, who was the boss of the telephone work crew. Lawrence and Lydia and Eugene and Vincent were playing cards.

Lydia laughed. "He said, *Excuse me*. That's what he claims he said."

"Papers all he had in the boxes? Nothing to eat?"

"He's a writer. He writes historical books. This was some material he needed for his work. Sometimes he has to go and scout out material from people who are very strange. That bear hadn't come out of the bush. It was a pet, actually, that had been let off its chain, for a joke. There were two old brothers there, that he got the papers from, and they just let it off its chain to give him a scare."

"That's what he does, collects old stuff and writes about it?" Lawrence said. "I guess that's interesting."

She immediately regretted having told this story. She had brought it up because the men were talking about bears. But there wasn't much point to it unless Duncan told it. He could show you himself, large and benign and civilized, with his courtly apologies to the bear. He could make you see the devilish old men behind their tattered curtains.

"You'd have to know Duncan" was what she almost said. And hadn't she told this simply to establish that she had known Duncan—that she had recently had a man, and an interesting man, an amusing and adventurous man? She wanted to assure them that she was not always alone, going on her aimless travels. She had to show herself attached. A mistake. They were not likely to think a man adventurous who collected old papers from misers and eccentrics, so that he could write books about things that had happened a hundred years ago. She shouldn't even have said that Duncan was a man she had lived with. All that could mean, to them, was that she was a woman who had slept with a man she was not married to.

Lawrence the boss was not yet forty, but he was successful. He was glad to tell about himself. He was a free-lance labor contractor and owned two houses in St. Stephen. He had two cars and a truck and a boat. His wife taught school. Lawrence was getting a thick waist, a trucker's belly, but he still looked alert and vigorous. You could see that he would be shrewd enough, in most situations, for his purposes; sure enough, ruthless enough. Dressed up, he might turn flashy. And certain places and people might be capable of making him gloomy, uncertain, contentious.

Lawrence said it wasn't all true—all the stuff they wrote about the Maritimes. He said there was plenty of work for people who weren't afraid to work. Men or women. He said he was not against women's lib, but the fact was, and always would be, that there was work men did better than women and work women did better than men, and if they would both settle down and realize that they'd be happier.

His kids were cheeky, he said. They had it too soft. They got everything—that was the way nowadays, what could you do? The other kids got everything too. Clothes, bikes, education, records. He hadn't had anything handed to him. He had got out and worked, driven trucks. He had got to Ontario, got as far as Saskatchewan. He had only got to Grade 10 in school but he hadn't let that hold him back. Sometimes he wished, though, that he did have more of an education.

Eugene and Vincent, who worked for Lawrence, said they had never got past Grade 8, when that was as far as you could go in the country schools. Eugene was twenty-five and Vincent was fifty-two. Eugene was French-Canadian from northern New Brunswick. He looked younger than his age. He had a rosy color, a downy, dreamy look—a masculine beauty that was nevertheless soft-edged, sweet-tempered, bashful. Hardly any men or boys have that look nowadays. Sometimes you see it in an old photograph—of a bridegroom, a basketball player: the thick water-combed hair, the blooming boy's face on the new man's body. Eugene was not very bright, or perhaps not very competitive. He lost money at the game they were playing. It was a card game that the men called Skat. Lydia remembered playing it when she was a child, and calling it Thirty-one. They played for a quarter a game.

Eugene permitted Vincent and Lawrence to tease him about losing at cards, about getting lost in St. John, about women he liked, and about being French-Canadian. Lawrence's teasing amounted to bullying. Lawrence wore a carefully good-natured expression, but he looked as if something hard and heavy had settled inside him—a load of self-esteem that weighed him down instead of buoying him up. Vincent had no such extra weight, and though he too was relentless in his teasing—he teased Lawrence as well as Eugene—there was no sense of cruelty or danger. You could see that his natural tone was one of rumbling, easy mockery. He was sharp and sly but not insistent; he would always be able to say the most pessimistic things and not sound unhappy.

Vincent had a farm—it was his family's farm, where he had grown up, near St. Stephen. He said you couldn't make enough to keep you nowadays, just from farming. Last year he put in a potato crop. There was frost in June, snow in September. Too short a season by a long shot. You never knew, he said, when you might get it like that. And the market is all controlled now; it is all run by the big fellows, the big interests. Everybody does what he can, rather than trust to farming. Vincent's wife works too. She took a course and learned to do hair. His sons are not hard-working like their parents. All they want to do is roar around in cars. They get married and the first thing their wives want is a new stove. They want a stove that practically cooks the dinner by itself and puts it on the table.

It didn't use to be that way. The first time Vincent ever had boots of his own—new boots that hadn't been worn by any-body before him—was when he joined the army. He was so pleased he walked backwards in the dirt to see the prints they made, fresh and whole. Later on, after the war, he went to St. John to look for work. He had been working at home on the farm for a while and he had worn out his army clothes—he had just one pair of decent pants left. In a beer parlor in St. John a man said to him, "You want to pick up a good pair of pants cheap?" Vincent said yes, and the man said, "Follow me." So Vincent did. And where did they end up? At the under-taker's! For the fact was that the family of a dead man usually bring in a suit of clothes to dress him in, and he only needs to be dressed from the waist up, that's all that shows in the cof-fin. The undertaker sold the pants. That was true. The army gave Vincent his first pair of new boots and a corpse donated the best pair of pants he ever wore, up to that time.

Vincent had no teeth. This was immediately apparent, but it did not make him look unattractive; it simply deepened his look of secrecy and humor. His face was long and his chin tucked in, his glance unchallenging but unfooled. He was a lean man, with useful muscles, and graying black hair. You could see all the years of hard work on him, and some years of it ahead, and the body just equal to it until he turned into a ropy-armed old man, shrunken, uncomplaining, hanging on to a few jokes.

While they played Skat the talk was boisterous and interrupted all the time by exclamations, joking threats to do with the game, laughter. Afterwards it became more serious and personal. They had been drinking a local beer called Moose, but when the game was over Lawrence went out to the truck and brought in some Ontario beer, thought to be better. They called it "the imported stuff." The couple who owned the guesthouse had long ago gone to bed, but the workmen and Lydia sat on in the kitchen, just as if it belonged to one of them, drinking beer and eating dulse, which Vincent had brought down from his room. Dulse was a kind of seaweed, greenish brown, salty and fishy-tasting. Vincent said it was what he ate last thing at night and first thing in the morning—nothing could beat it. Now that they had found out it was so good for you, they sold it in the stores, done up in little wee packages at a criminal price.

The next day was Friday, and the men would be leaving the island for the mainland. They talked about trying to get the two-thirty boat instead of the one they usually caught, at five-thirty, because the forecast was for rough weather; the tail end of one of the tropical hurricanes was due to hit the Bay of Fundy before night.

"But the ferries won't run if it's too rough, will they?" said Lydia. "They won't run if it's dangerous?" She thought that she would not mind being cut off, she wouldn't mind not having to travel again in the morning.

"Well, there's a lot of fellows waiting to get off the island on a Friday night," Vincent said.

"Wanting to get home to their wives," said Lawrence sardonically. "There's always crews working over here, always men away from home." Then he began to talk in an unhurried but insistent way about sex. He talked about what he called the immorality on the island. He said that at one time the authorities had been going to put a quarantine around the whole island, on account of the V.D. Crews came over here to work and stayed at the motel, the Ocean Wave, and there'd be parties there all night every night, with drinking and young girls turning up offering themselves for sale. Girls fourteen and fifteen—oh, thirteen years of age. On the island, he said, it was getting so a woman of twenty-five could practically be a grandmother. The place was famous. Those girls would do anything for a price, sometimes for a beer.

"And sometimes for nothing," said Lawrence. He luxuriated in the telling.

They heard the front door open.

"Your old boyfriend," Lawrence said to Lydia.

She was bewildered for a moment, thinking of Duncan.

"The old fellow at the table," said Vincent.

Mr. Stanley did not come into the kitchen. He crossed the living room and climbed the stairs.

"Hey? Been down to the Ocean Wave?" said Lawrence softly, raising his head as if to call through the ceiling. "Old bugger wouldn't know what to do with it," he said. "Wouldn't've known fifty years ago any better than now. I don't let any of my crews go near that place. Do I, Eugene?"

Eugene blushed. He put on a solemn expression, as if he was being badgered by a teacher at school.

"Eugene, now, he don't have to," Vincent said.

"Isn't it true what I'm saying?" said Lawrence urgently, as if somebody had been disputing with him. "It's true, isn't it?"

He looked at Vincent, and Vincent said, "Yeah. Yeah." He did not seem to relish the subject as much as Lawrence did.

"You'd think it was all so innocent here," said Lawrence to Lydia. "Innocent! Oh, boy!"

Lydia went upstairs to get a quarter that she owed Lawrence from the last game. When she came out of her room into the dark hall, Eugene was standing there, looking out the window.

"I hope it don't storm too bad," he said.

Lydia stood beside him, looking out. The moon was visible, but misty.

"You didn't grow up near the water?" she said.

"No, I didn't."

"But if you get the two-thirty boat it'll be all right, won't it?"

"I sure hope so." He was quite childlike and unembarrassed about his fear. "One thing I don't like the idea of is getting drownded."

Lydia remembered that as a child she had said "drownded." Most of the adults and all the children she knew then said that.

"You won't," she said, in a firm, maternal way. She went downstairs and paid her quarter.

"Where's Eugene?" Lawrence said. "He upstairs?"

"He's looking out the window. He's worried about the storm."

Lawrence laughed. "You tell him to go to bed and forget about it. He's right in the room next to you. I just thought you ought to know in case he hollers in his sleep."

Lydia had first seen Duncan in a bookstore, where her friend Warren worked. She was waiting for Warren to go out to lunch with her. He had gone to get his coat. A man asked Shirley, the other clerk in the store, if she could find him a copy of *Persian Letters*. That was Duncan. Shirley walked ahead of him to where the book was kept, and in the quiet store Lydia heard him saying that it must be difficult to know where to shelve *Persian Letters*. Should it be classed as fiction or as a political essay? Lydia felt that he revealed something, saying this. He revealed a need that she supposed was common to customers in the bookstore, a need to distinguish himself, appear knowledgeable. Later on she would look back on this moment and try to imagine him again so powerless, slightly ingratiating, showing a bit of neediness. Warren came back with his coat on, greeted Duncan, and as he and Lydia went outside Warren said under his breath, "The Tin Woodman." Warren and Shirley livened up their days with nicknames for customers; Lydia had already heard of Marble-Mouth, and Chickpea and the Colonial Duchess. Duncan was the Tin Woodman. Lydia thought they must call him that because of the smooth gray overcoat he wore, and his hair, a bright gray which had obviously once been blond. He was not thin or angular and he did not look as if he would be creaky in the joints. He was supple and well-fleshed and dignified and pleasant; fair-skinned, freshly groomed, glistening.

She never told him about that name. She never told him that she had seen him in the bookstore. A week or so later she

met him at a publisher's party. He did not remember ever seeing her before, and she supposed he had not seen her, being
occupied with chatting with Shirley.

Lydia trusts what she can make of things, usually. She trusts
what she thinks about her friend Warren, or his friend Shirley,
and about chance acquaintances, like the couple who run the
guesthouse, and Mr. Stanley, and the men she has been playing cards with. She thinks she knows why people behave as they
do, and she puts more stock than she will admit in her own
unproven theories and unjustified suspicions. But she is stupid
and helpless when contemplating the collision of herself and
Duncan. She has plenty to say about it, given the chance,
because explanation is her habit, but she doesn't trust what she
says, even to herself; it doesn't help her. She might just as well
cover her head and sit wailing on the ground.

She asks herself what gave him his power. She knows who
did. But she asks what, and when—when did the transfer take
place, when was the abdication of all pride and sense?

She read for half an hour after getting into bed. Then she went
down the hall to the bathroom. It was after midnight. The rest
of the house was in darkness. She had left her door ajar, and
coming back to her room, she did not turn on the hall light.
The door of Eugene's room was also ajar, and as she was passing she heard a low, careful sound. It was like a moan, and also
like a whisper. She remembered Lawrence saying Eugene
hollered in his sleep, but this sound was not being made in
sleep. She knew he was awake. He was watching from the bed
in his dark room and he was inviting her. The invitation was
amorous and direct and helpless-sounding as his confession of
fear when he stood by the window. She went on into her own
room and shut the door and hooked it. Even as she did this,
she knew she didn't have to. He would never try to get in; there
was no bullying spirit in him.

Then she lay awake. Things had changed for her; she refused
adventures. She could have gone to Eugene, and earlier in the
evening she could have given a sign to Lawrence. In the past
she might have done it. She might, or she might not have done

it, depending on how she felt. Now it seemed not possible. She felt as if she were muffled up, wrapped in layers and layers of dull knowledge, well protected. It wasn't altogether a bad thing—it left your mind unclouded. Speculation can be more gentle, can take its time, when it is not driven by desire.

She thought about what those men would have been like as lovers. It was Lawrence who would have been her reasonable choice. He was nearest to her own age, and predictable, and probably well used to the discreet encounter. His approach was vulgar, but that would not necessarily have put her off. He would be cheerful, hearty, prudent, perhaps a bit self-congratulatory, attentive in a businesslike way, and he would manage in the middle of his attentions to slip in a warning: a joke, a friendly insult, a reminder of how things stood.

Eugene would never feel the need to do that, though he would have a shorter memory even than Lawrence (much shorter, for Lawrence, though not turning down opportunities, would carry afterward the thought of some bad consequence, for which he must keep ready a sharp line of defense). Eugene would be no less experienced than Lawrence; for years, girls and women must have been answering the kind of plea Lydia had heard, the artless confession. Eugene would be generous, she thought. He would be a grateful, self-forgetful lover, showing his women such kindness that when he left they would never make trouble. They would not try to trap him; they wouldn't whine after him. Women do that to the men who have held back, who have contradicted themselves, promised, lied, mocked. These are the men women get pregnant by, send desperate letters to, preach their own superior love to, take their revenge on. Eugene would go free, he would be an innocent, happy prodigy of love, until he decided it was time to get married. Then he would marry a rather plain, maternal sort of girl, perhaps a bit older than himself, a bit shrewder. He would be faithful, and good to her, and she would manage things; they would raise a large Catholic family.

What about Vincent? Lydia could not imagine him as she easily imagined the others: their noises and movements and bare shoulders and pleasing warm skin; their power, their exertions, their moments of helplessness. She was shy of thinking any such things about him. Yet he was the only one whom she could think of now with real interest. She thought of his courtesy and reticence and humor, his inability to better his luck. She liked him for the very things that made him different from Lawrence and insured that all his life he would be working for Lawrence—or for somebody like Lawrence—never the other way round. She liked him also for the things that made him different from Eugene: the irony, the patience, the self-containment. He was the sort of man she had known when she was a child living on a farm not so different from his, the sort of man who must have been in her family for hundreds of years. She knew his life. With him she could foresee doors opening to what she knew and had forgotten; rooms and landscapes opening; *there.* The rainy evenings, a country with creeks and graveyards, and chokecherry and finches in the fence-corners. She had to wonder if this was what happened, after the years of appetite and greed—did you drift back into tenderhearted fantasies? Or was it just the truth about what she needed and wanted; should she have fallen in love with, and married, a man like Vincent years ago; should she have concentrated on the part of her that would have been content with such an arrangement, and forgotten about the rest?

That is, should she have stayed in the place where love is managed for you, not gone where you have to invent it, and reinvent it, and never know if these efforts will be enough?

Duncan spoke about his former girlfriends. Efficient Ruth, pert Judy, vivacious Diane, elegant Dolores, wifely Maxine. Lorraine the golden-haired, full-breasted beauty; Marian the multilingual; Caroline the neurotic; Rosalie who was wild and gypsylike; gifted, melancholy Louise; serene socialite Jane. What description would do now for Lydia? Lydia the poet. Morose, messy, unsatisfactory Lydia. The unsatisfactory poet.

One Sunday, when they were driving in the hills around Peterborough, he talked about the effects of Lorraine's beauty. Perhaps the voluptuous countryside reminded him. It was almost like a joke, he said. It was almost silly. He stopped for gas in a little town and Lydia went across the street to a discount store that was open Sundays. She bought makeup in tubes off a rack. In the cold and dirty toilet of the gas station she attempted a transformation, slapping buff-colored liquid over her face and rubbing green paste on her eyelids.

"What have you done to your face?" he said when she came back to the car.

"Makeup. I put some makeup on so I'd look more cheerful."

"You can see where the line stops, on your neck."

At such times she felt strangled. It was frustration, she said to the doctor later. The gap between what she wanted and what she could get. She believed that Duncan's love—love for her—was somewhere inside him, and that by gigantic efforts to please, or fits of distress which obliterated all those efforts, or tricks of indifference, she could claw or lure it out.

What gave her such an idea? He did. At least he indicated that he could love her, that they could be happy, if she could honor his privacy, make no demands upon him, and try to alter those things about her person and behavior which he did not like. He listed these things precisely. Some were very intimate in nature and she howled with shame and covered her ears and begged him to take them back or to say no more.

"There is no way to have a discussion with you," he said. He said he hated hysterics, emotional displays, beyond anything, yet she thought she saw a quiver of satisfaction, a deep thrill of relief, that ran through him when she finally broke under the weight of his calm and detailed objections.

"Could that be?" she said to the doctor. "Could it be that he wants a woman close but is so frightened of it he has to try to wreck her? Is that oversimplified?" she said anxiously.

"What about you?" said the doctor. "What do you want?"

"For him to love me?"

"Not for you to love him?"

She thought about Duncan's apartment. There were no curtains; he was higher than the surrounding buildings. No attempt had been made to arrange things to make a setting; nothing was in relation to anything else. Various special requirements had been attended to. A certain sculpture was in a corner behind some filing cabinets because he liked to lie on the floor and look at it in shadow. Books were in piles beside the bed, which was crossways in the room in order to catch the breeze from the window. All disorder was actually order, carefully thought out and not to be interfered with. There was a beautiful little rug at the end of the hall, where he sat and listened to music. There was one great, ugly armchair, a masterpiece of engineering, with all its attachments for the head and limbs. Lydia asked about his guests—how were they accommodated? He replied that he did not have any. The apartment was for himself. He was a popular guest, witty and personable, but not a host, and this seemed reasonable to him, since social life was other people's requirement and invention.

Lydia brought flowers, and there was nowhere to put them except in a jar on the floor by the bed. She brought presents from her trips to Toronto: records, books, cheese. She learned pathways around the apartment and found places where she could sit. She discouraged old friends, or any friends, from phoning or coming to see her, because there was too much she couldn't explain. They saw Duncan's friends sometimes, and she was nervous with them, thinking they were adding her to a list, speculating. She didn't like to see how much he gave them of that store of presents—anecdotes, parodies, flattering wit—which were also used to delight her. He could not bear dullness. She felt that he despised people who were not witty. You needed to be quick to keep up with him in conversation, you needed energy. Lydia saw herself as a dancer on her toes, trembling delicately all over, afraid of letting him down on the next turn.

"Do you mean you think I don't love him?" she said to the doctor.

"How do you know you do?"

"Because I suffer so when he's fed up with me. I want to be wiped off the earth. It's true. I want to hide. I go out on the streets and every face I look at seems to despise me for my failure."

"Your failure to make him love you."

Now Lydia must accuse herself. Her self-absorption equals Duncan's, but is more artfully concealed. She is in competition with him as to who can love best. She is in competition with all other women, even when it is ludicrous for her to be so. She cannot stand to hear them praised or know they are well remembered. Like many women of her generation, she has an idea of love which is ruinous but not serious in some way, not respectful. She is greedy. She talks intelligently and ironically and in this way covers up her indefensible expectations. The sacrifices she made with Duncan—in living arrangements, in the matter of friends, as well as in the rhythm of sex and the tone of conversations—were violations, committed not seriously but flagrantly. That is what was not respectful, that was what was indecent. She made him a present of such power, then complained relentlessly to herself and finally to him, that he had got it. She was out to defeat him.

That is what she says to the doctor. But is it the truth?

"The worst thing is not knowing what is true about any of this. I spend all my waking hours trying to figure out about him and me and I get nowhere. I make wishes. I even pray. I throw money into those wishing wells. I think that there's something in him that's an absolute holdout. There's something in him that has to get rid of me, so he'll find reasons. But he says that's rubbish, he says if I could stop overreacting we'd be happy. I have to think maybe he's right, maybe it is all me."

"When are you happy?"

"When he's pleased with me. When he's joking and enjoying himself. No. No. I'm never happy. What I am is relieved, it's as if I'd overcome a challenge, it's more triumphant than happy. But he can always pull the rug out."

"So, why are you with somebody who can always pull the rug out?"

"Isn't there always somebody? When I was married it was me. Do you think it helps to ask these questions? Suppose it's just pride? I don't want to be alone, I want everybody to think I've got such a desirable man? Suppose it's the humiliation, I want to be humiliated? What good will it do me to know that?"

"I don't know. What do you think?"

"I think these conversations are fine when you're mildly troubled and interested but not when you're desperate."

"You're desperate?"

She felt suddenly tired, almost too tired to speak. The room where she and the doctor were talking had a dark-blue carpet, blue-and-green-striped upholstery. There was a picture of boats and fishermen on the wall. Collusion somewhere, Lydia felt. Fake reassurance, provisional comfort, earnest deceptions.

"No."

It seemed to her that she and Duncan were monsters with a lot of heads, in those days. Out of the mouth of one head could come insult and accusation, hot and cold, out of another false apologies and slimy pleas, out of another just such mealy, reasonable, true-and-false chat as she had practiced with the doctor. Not a mouth would open that had a useful thing to say, not a mouth would have the sense to shut up. At the same time she believed—though she didn't know she believed it—that these monster heads with their cruel and silly and wasteful talk could all be drawn in again, could curl up and go to sleep. Never mind what they'd said; never mind. Then she and Duncan with hope and trust and blank memories could reintroduce themselves, they could pick up the undamaged delight with which they'd started, before they began to put each other to other uses.

When she had been in Toronto a day she tried to retrieve Duncan, by phone, and found that he had acted quickly. He had changed to an unlisted number. He wrote to her, in care of her employer, that he would pack and send her things.

Lydia had breakfast with Mr. Stanley. The telephone crew had eaten and gone off to work before daylight.

She asked Mr. Stanley about his visit with the woman who had known Willa Cather.

"Ah," said Mr. Stanley, and wiped a corner of his mouth after a bite of poached egg. "She was a woman who used to run a little restaurant down by the dock. She was a good cook, she said. She must have been, because Willa and Edith used to get their dinners from her. She would send it up with her brother, in his car. But sometimes Willa would not be pleased with the dinner—perhaps it would not be quite what she wanted, or she would think it was not cooked as well as it might be—and she would send it back. She would ask for another dinner to be sent." He smiled, and said in a confidential way, "Willa could be imperious. Oh, yes. She was not perfect. All people of great abilities are apt to be impatient in daily matters."

Rubbish, Lydia wanted to say, she sounds a proper bitch.

Sometimes waking up was all right, and sometimes it was very bad. This morning she had wakened with the cold conviction of a mistake—something avoidable and irreparable.

"But sometimes she and Edith would come down to the café," Mr. Stanley continued. "If they felt they wanted some company, they would have dinner there. On one of these occasions Willa had a long talk with the woman I was visiting. They talked for over an hour. The woman was considering marriage. She had to consider whether to make a marriage that she gave me to understand was something of a business proposition. Companionship. There was no question of romance, she and the gentleman were not young and foolish. Willa talked to her for over an hour. Of course she did not advise her directly to do one thing or the other, she talked to her in general terms very sensibly and kindly and the woman still remembers it vividly. I was happy to hear that but I was not surprised."

"What would she know about it, anyway?" Lydia said.

Mr. Stanley lifted his eyes from his plate and looked at her in grieved amazement.

"Willa Cather lived with a woman," Lydia said.

When Mr. Stanley answered he sounded flustered, and mildly upbraiding.

"They were devoted," he said.

"She never lived with a man."

"She knew things as an artist knows them. Not necessarily by experience."

"But what if they don't know them?" Lydia persisted. "What if they don't?"

He went back to eating his egg as if he had not heard that.

Finally he said, "The woman considered Willa's conversation was very helpful to her."

Lydia made a sound of doubtful assent. She knew she had been rude, even cruel. She knew she would have to apologize. She went to the sideboard and poured herself another cup of coffee.

The woman of the house came in from the kitchen.

"Is it keeping hot? I think I'll have a cup too. Are you really going today? Sometimes I think I'd like to get on a boat and go too. It's lovely here and I love it but you know how you get."

They drank their coffee standing by the sideboard. Lydia did not want to go back to the table, but knew that she would have to. Mr. Stanley looked frail and solitary, with his narrow shoulders, his neat bald head, his brown checked sports jacket which was slightly too large. He took the trouble to be clean and tidy, and it must have been a trouble, with his eyesight. Of all people he did not deserve rudeness.

"Oh, I forgot," the woman said.

She went into the kitchen and came back with a large brown-paper bag.

"Vincent left you this. He said you liked it. Do you?"

Lydia opened the bag and saw long, dark, ragged leaves of dulse, oily-looking even when dry.

"Well," she said.

The woman laughed. "I know. You have to be born here to have the taste."

"No, I do like it," said Lydia. "I was getting to like it."

"You must have made a hit."

Lydia took the bag back to the table and showed it to Mr. Stanley. She tried a conciliatory joke.

"I wonder if Willa Cather ever ate dulse?"

"Dulse," said Mr. Stanley thoughtfully. He reached into the bag and pulled out some leaves and looked at them. Lydia knew he was seeing what Willa Cather might have seen. "She would most certainly have known about it. She would have known."

But was she lucky or was she not, and was it all right with that woman? How did she live? That was what Lydia wanted to say. Would Mr. Stanley have known what she was talking about? If she had asked how did Willa Cather live, would he not have replied that she did not have to find a way to live, as other people did, that she was Willa Cather?

What a lovely, durable shelter he had made for himself. He could carry it everywhere and nobody could interfere with it. The day may come when Lydia will count herself lucky to do the same. In the meantime, she'll be up and down. "Up and down," they used to say in her childhood, talking of the health of people who weren't going to recover. "Ah. She's up and down."

Yet look how this present slyly warmed her, from a distance.

❧ *The Turkey Season* ❧

TO JOE RADFORD

WHEN I WAS FOURTEEN I got a job at the Turkey Barn for the Christmas season. I was still too young to get a job working in a store or as a part-time waitress; I was also too nervous.

I was a turkey gutter. The other people who worked at the Turkey Barn were Lily and Marjorie and Gladys, who were also gutters; Irene and Henry, who were pluckers; Herb Abbott, the foreman, who superintended the whole operation and filled in wherever he was needed. Morgan Elliott was the owner and boss. He and his son, Morgy, did the killing.

Morgy I knew from school. I thought him stupid and despicable and was uneasy about having to consider him in a new and possibly superior guise, as the boss's son. But his father treated him so roughly, yelling and swearing at him, that he seemed no more than the lowest of the workers. The other person related to the boss was Gladys. She was his sister, and in her case there did seem to be some privilege of position. She worked slowly and went home if she was not feeling well, and was not friendly to Lily and Marjorie, although she was, a little, to me. She had come back to live with Morgan and his family after working for many years in Toronto, in a bank. This was not the sort of job she was used to. Lily and Marjorie, talking about her when she wasn't there, said she had had a nervous breakdown. They said Morgan made her work in the Turkey Barn to pay for her keep. They also said, with no worry about the contradiction, that she had taken the job because she was after a man, and that the man was Herb Abbott.

All I could see when I closed my eyes, the first few nights

after working there, was turkeys. I saw them hanging upside down, plucked and stiffened, pale and cold, with the heads and necks limp, the eyes and nostrils clotted with dark blood; the remaining bits of feathers—those dark and bloody too—seemed to form a crown. I saw them not with aversion but with a sense of endless work to be done.

Herb Abbott showed me what to do. You put the turkey down on the table and cut its head off with a cleaver. Then you took the loose skin around the neck and stripped it back to reveal the crop, nestled in the cleft between the gullet and the windpipe.

"Feel the gravel," said Herb encouragingly. He made me close my fingers around the crop. Then he showed me how to work my hand down behind it to cut it out, and the gullet and windpipe as well. He used shears to cut the vertebrae.

"Scrunch, scrunch," he said soothingly. "Now, put your hand in."

I did. It was deathly cold in there, in the turkey's dark insides.

"Watch out for bone splinters."

Working cautiously in the dark, I had to pull the connecting tissues loose.

"Ups-a-daisy." Herb turned the bird over and flexed each leg. "Knees up, Mother Brown. Now." He took a heavy knife and placed it directly on the knee knuckle joints and cut off the shank.

"Have a look at the worms."

Pearly-white strings, pulled out of the shank, were creeping about on their own.

"That's just the tendons shrinking. Now comes the nice part!"

He slit the bird at its bottom end, letting out a rotten smell.

"Are you educated?"

I did not know what to say.

"What's that smell?"

"Hydrogen sulfide."

"Educated," said Herb, sighing. "All right. Work your fingers around and get the guts loose. Easy. Easy. Keep your fingers together. Keep the palm inwards. Feel the ribs with the back of your hand. Feel the guts fit into your palm. Feel that? Keep going. Break the strings—as many as you can. Keep going. Feel a hard lump? That's the gizzard. Feel a soft lump? That's the heart. Okay? Okay. Get your fingers around the gizzard. Easy. Start pulling this way. That's right. That's right. Start to pull her out."

It was not easy at all. I wasn't even sure what I had was the gizzard. My hand was full of cold pulp.

"Pull," he said, and I brought out a glistening, liverish mass.

"Got it. There's the lights. You know what they are? Lungs. There's the heart. There's the gizzard. There's the gall. Now, you don't ever want to break that gall inside or it will taste the entire turkey." Tactfully, he scraped out what I had missed, including the testicles, which were like a pair of white grapes.

"Nice pair of earrings," Herb said.

Herb Abbott was a tall, firm, plump man. His hair was dark and thin, combed straight back from a widow's peak, and his eyes seemed to be slightly slanted, so that he looked like a pale Chinese or like pictures of the Devil, except that he was smooth-faced and benign. Whatever he did around the Turkey Barn—gutting, as he was now, or loading the truck, or hanging the carcasses—was done with efficient, economical movements, quickly and buoyantly. "Notice about Herb—he always walks like he had a boat moving underneath him," Marjorie said, and it was true. Herb worked on the lake boats, during the season, as a cook. Then he worked for Morgan until after Christmas. The rest of the time he helped around the poolroom, making hamburgers, sweeping up, stopping fights before they got started. That was where he lived: he had a room above the poolroom on the main street.

In all the operations at the Turkey Barn it seemed to be Herb who had the efficiency and honor of the business continually on his mind; it was he who kept everything under control. Seeing him in the yard talking to Morgan, who was a thick, short man, red in the face, an unpredictable bully, you would be sure that it was Herb who was the boss and Morgan the hired help. But it was not so.

If I had not had Herb to show me, I don't think I could have learned turkey gutting at all. I was clumsy with my hands and had been shamed for it so often that the least show of impatience on the part of the person instructing me could have brought on a dithering paralysis. I could not stand to be watched by anybody but Herb. Particularly, I couldn't stand to be watched by Lily and Marjorie, two middle-aged sisters, who were very fast and thorough and competitive gutters. They sang at their work and talked abusively and intimately to the turkey carcasses.

"Don't you nick me, you old bugger!"

"Aren't you the old crap factory!"

I had never heard women talk like that.

Gladys was not a fast gutter, though she must have been thorough; Herb would have talked to her otherwise. She never sang and certainly she never swore. I thought her rather old, though she was not as old as Lily and Marjorie; she must have been over thirty. She seemed offended by everything that went on and had the air of keeping plenty of bitter judgments to herself. I never tried to talk to her, but she spoke to me one day in the cold little washroom off the gutting shed. She was putting pancake makeup on her face. The color of the makeup was so distinct from the color of her skin that it was as if she were slapping orange paint over a whitewashed, bumpy wall.

She asked me if my hair was naturally curly.

I said yes.

"You don't have to get a permanent?"

"No."

"You're lucky. I have to do mine up every night. The chemicals in my system won't allow me to get a permanent."

There are different ways women have of talking about their looks. Some women make it clear that what they do to keep themselves up is for the sake of sex, for men. Others, like Gladys, make the job out to be a kind of housekeeping, whose very difficulties they pride themselves on. Gladys was genteel. I could see her in the bank, in a navy-blue dress with the kind of detachable white collar you can wash at night. She would be grumpy and correct.

Another time, she spoke to me about her periods, which were profuse and painful. She wanted to know about mine. There was an uneasy, prudish, agitated expression on her face. I was saved by Irene, who was using the toilet and called out, "Do like me, and you'll be rid of all your problems for a while." Irene was only a few years older than I was, but she was recently—tardily—married, and heavily pregnant.

Gladys ignored her, running cold water on her hands. The hands of all of us were red and sore-looking from the work. "I can't use that soap. If I use it, I break out in a rash," Gladys said. "If I bring my own soap in here, I can't afford to have other people using it, because I pay a lot for it—it's a special anti-allergy soap."

I think the idea that Lily and Marjorie promoted—that Gladys was after Herb Abbott—sprang from their belief that single people ought to be teased and embarrassed whenever possible, and from their interest in Herb, which led to the feeling that somebody ought to be after him. They wondered about him. What they wondered was, How can a man want so little? No wife, no family, no house. The details of his daily life, the small preferences, were of interest. Where had he been brought up? (Here and there and all over.) How far had he gone in school? (Far enough.) Where was his girlfriend? (Never tell.) Did he drink coffee or tea if he got the choice? (Coffee.)

When they talked about Gladys's being after him they must have really wanted to talk about sex—what he wanted and what he got. They must have felt a voluptuous curiosity about him, as I did. He aroused this feeling by being circumspect and not making the jokes some men did, and at the same time by not being squeamish or gentlemanly. Some men, showing me the testicles from the turkey, would have acted as if the very existence of testicles were somehow a bad joke on me, something a girl could be taunted about; another sort of man would have been embarrassed and would have thought he had to protect me from embarrassment. A man who didn't seem to feel one way or the other was an oddity—as much to older women, probably, as to me. But what was so welcome to me may have been disturbing to them. They wanted to jolt him. They even wanted Gladys to jolt him, if she could.

There wasn't any idea then—at least in Logan, Ontario, in the late forties—about homosexuality's going beyond very narrow confines. Women, certainly, believed in its rarity and in definite boundaries. There were homosexuals in town, and we knew who they were: an elegant, light-voiced, wavy-haired paperhanger who called himself an interior decorator; the minister's widow's fat, spoiled only son, who went so far as to enter baking contests and had crocheted a tablecloth; a hypochondriacal church organist and music teacher who kept the choir and his pupils in line with screaming tantrums. Once the label was fixed, there was a good deal of tolerance for these people, and their talents for decorating, for crocheting, and for music were appreciated—especially by women. "The poor fellow," they said. "He doesn't do any harm." They really seemed to believe—the women did—that it was the penchant for baking or music that was the determining factor, and that it was this activity that made the man what he was—not any other detours he might take, or wish to take. A desire to play the violin would be taken as more a deviation from manliness than would a wish to shun women. Indeed, the idea was that any manly man would wish to shun women but most of them were caught off guard, and for good.

I don't want to go into the question of whether Herb was homosexual or not, because the definition is of no use to me. I think that probably he was, but maybe he was not. (Even considering what happened later, I think that.) He is not a puzzle so arbitrarily solved.

The other plucker, who worked with Irene, was Henry Streets, a neighbor of ours. There was nothing remarkable about him except that he was eighty-six years old and still, as he said of himself, a devil for work. He had whisky in his thermos, and drank it from time to time through the day. It was Henry who said to me, in our kitchen, "You ought to get yourself a job at the Turkey Barn. They need another gutter." Then my father said at once, "Not her, Henry. She's got ten thumbs," and

Henry said he was just joking—it was dirty work. But I was already determined to try it—I had a great need to be successful in a job like that. I was almost in the condition of a grown-up person who is ashamed of never having learned to read, so much did I feel my ineptness at manual work. Work, to everybody I knew, meant doing things I was no good at doing, and work was what people prided themselves on and measured each other by. (It goes without saying that the things I was good at, like schoolwork, were suspect or held in plain contempt.) So it was a surprise and then a triumph for me not to get fired, and to be able to turn out clean turkeys at a rate that was not disgraceful. I don't know if I really understood how much Herb Abbott was responsible for this, but he would sometimes say, "Good girl," or pat my waist and say, "You're getting to be a good gutter—you'll go a long ways in the world," and when I felt his quick, kind touch through the heavy sweater and bloody smock I wore, I felt my face glow and I wanted to lean back against him as he stood behind me. I wanted to rest my head against his wide, fleshy shoulder. When I went to sleep at night, lying on my side, I would run my cheek against the pillow and think of that as Herb's shoulder.

I was interested in how he talked to Gladys, how he looked at her or noticed her. This interest was not jealousy. I think I wanted something to happen with them. I quivered in curious expectation, as Lily and Marjorie did. We all wanted to see the flicker of sexuality in him, hear it in his voice, not because we thought it would make him seem more like other men but because we knew that with him it would be entirely different. He was kinder and more patient than most women, and as stern and remote, in some ways, as any man. We wanted to see how he could be moved.

If Gladys wanted this too, she didn't give any signs of it. It is impossible for me to tell with women like her whether they are as thick and deadly as they seem, not wanting anything much but opportunities for irritation and contempt, or if they are all choked up with gloomy fires and useless passions.

Marjorie and Lily talked about marriage. They did not have much good to say about it, in spite of their feeling that it was a state nobody should be allowed to stay out of. Marjorie said that shortly after her marriage she had gone into the wood-shed with the intention of swallowing Paris green.

"I'd have done it," she said. "But the man came along in the grocery truck and I had to go out and buy the groceries. This was when we lived on the farm."

Her husband was cruel to her in those days, but later he suf-fered an accident—he rolled the tractor and was so badly hurt he would be an invalid all his life. They moved to town, and Marjorie was the boss now.

"He starts to sulk the other night and say he don't want his supper. Well, I just picked up his wrist and held it. He was scared I was going to twist his arm. He could see I'd do it. So I say, 'You *what?*' And he says, 'I'll eat it.'"

They talked about their father. He was a man of the old school. He had a noose in the woodshed (not the Paris green woodshed—this would be an earlier one, on another farm), and when they got on his nerves he used to line them up and threaten to hang them. Lily, who was the younger, would shake till she fell down. This same father had arranged to marry Marjorie off to a crony of his when she was just sixteen. That was the hus-band who had driven her to the Paris green. Their father did it because he wanted to be sure she wouldn't get into trouble.

"Hot blood," Lily said.

I was horrified, and asked, "Why didn't you run away?"

"His word was law," Marjorie said.

They said that was what was the matter with kids nowa-days—it was the kids that ruled the roost. A father's word should be law. They brought up their own kids strictly, and none had turned out bad yet. When Marjorie's son wet the bed she threatened to cut off his dingy with the butcher knife. That cured him.

They said ninety percent of the young girls nowadays drank, and swore, and took it lying down. They did not have daugh-ters, but if they did and caught them at anything like that they would beat them raw. Irene, they said, used to go to the hockey games with her ski pants slit and nothing under them, for con-venience in the snowdrifts afterward. Terrible.

I wanted to point out some contradictions. Marjorie and Lily themselves drank and swore, and what was so wonderful about the strong will of a father who would insure you a lifetime of unhappiness? (What I did not see was that Marjorie and Lily were not unhappy altogether—could not be, because of their sense of consequence, their pride and style.) I could be enraged then at the lack of logic in most adults' talk—the way they held to their pronouncements no matter what evidence might be presented to them. How could these women's hands be so gifted, so delicate and clever—for I knew they would be as good at dozens of other jobs as they were at gutting; they would be good at quilting and darning and painting and papering and kneading dough and setting out seedlings—and their thinking so slapdash, clumsy, infuriating?

Lily said she never let her husband come near her if he had been drinking. Marjorie said since the time she nearly died with a hemorrhage she never let her husband come near her, period. Lily said quickly that it was only when he'd been drinking that he tried anything. I could see that it was a matter of pride not to let your husband come near you, but I couldn't quite believe that "come near" meant "have sex." The idea of Marjorie and Lily being sought out for such purposes seemed grotesque. They had bad teeth, their stomachs sagged, their faces were dull and spotty. I decided to take "come near" literally.

The two weeks before Christmas was a frantic time at the Turkey Barn. I began to go in for an hour before school as well as after school and on weekends. In the morning, when I walked to work, the streetlights would still be on and the morning stars shining. There was the Turkey Barn, on the edge of a white field, with a row of big pine trees behind it, and always, no matter how cold and still it was, these trees were lifting their branches and sighing and straining. It seems unlikely that on my way to the Turkey Barn, for an hour of gutting turkeys, I should have experienced such a sense of promise and at the same time of perfect, impenetrable mystery in the universe, but I did. Herb had something to do with that, and so did the cold snap—the series of hard, clear mornings.

The truth is, such feelings weren't hard to come by then. I would get them but not know how they were to be connected with anything in real life.

One morning at the Turkey Barn there was a new gutter. This was a boy eighteen or nineteen years old, a stranger named Brian. It seemed he was a relative, or perhaps just a friend, of Herb Abbott's. He was staying with Herb. He had worked on a lake boat last summer. He said he had got sick of it, though, and quit.

What he said was "Yeah, fuckin' boats, I got sick of that."

Language at the Turkey Barn was coarse and free, but this was one word never heard there. And Brian's use of it seemed not careless but flaunting, mixing insult and provocation. Perhaps it was his general style that made it so. He had amazing good looks: taffy hair, bright blue eyes, ruddy skin, well-shaped body—the sort of good looks nobody disagrees about for a moment. But a single, relentless notion had got such a hold on him that he could not keep from turning all his assets into parody. His mouth was wet-looking and slightly open most of the time, his eyes were half shut, his expression a hopeful leer, his movements indolent, exaggerated, inviting. Perhaps if he had been put on a stage with a microphone and a guitar and let grunt and howl and wriggle and excite, he would have seemed a true celebrant. Lacking a stage, he was unconvincing. After a while he seemed just like somebody with a bad case of hiccups—his insistent sexuality was that monotonous and meaningless.

If he had toned down a bit, Marjorie and Lily would probably have enjoyed him. They could have kept up a game of telling him to shut his filthy mouth and keep his hands to himself. As it was, they said they were sick of him, and meant it. Once, Marjorie took up her gutting knife. "Keep your distance," she said. "I mean from me and my sister and that kid."

She did not tell him to keep his distance from Gladys, because Gladys wasn't there at the time and Marjorie would probably not have felt like protecting her anyway. But it was Gladys Brian particularly liked to bother. She would throw down her knife and go into the washroom and stay there ten minutes and come out with a stony face. She didn't say she was sick anymore and go home, the way she used to. Marjorie said Morgan was mad at Gladys for sponging and she couldn't get away with it any longer.

Gladys said to me, "I can't stand that kind of thing. I can't stand people mentioning that kind of thing and that kind of— gestures. It makes me sick to my stomach."

I believed her. She was terribly white. But why, in that case, did she not complain to Morgan? Perhaps relations between them were too uneasy, perhaps she could not bring herself to repeat or describe such things. Why did none of us complain— if not to Morgan, at least to Herb? I never thought of it. Brian seemed just something to put up with, like the freezing cold in the gutting shed and the smell of blood and waste. When Marjorie and Lily did threaten to complain, it was about Brian's laziness.

He was not a good gutter. He said his hands were too big. So Herb took him off gutting, told him he was to sweep and clean up, make packages of giblets, and help load the truck. This meant that he did not have to be in any one place or doing any one job at a given time, so much of the time he did nothing. He would start sweeping up, leave that and mop the tables, leave that and have a cigarette, lounge against the table bothering us until Herb called him to help load. Herb was very busy now and spent a lot of time making deliveries, so it was possible he did not know the extent of Brian's idleness.

"I don't know why Herb don't fire you," Marjorie said. "I guess the answer is he don't want you hanging around sponging on him, with no place to go."

"I know where to go," said Brian.

"Keep your sloppy mouth shut," said Marjorie. "I pity Herb. Getting saddled."

On the last school day before Christmas we got out early in the afternoon. I went home and changed my clothes and came in to work at about three o'clock. Nobody was working. Everybody was in the gutting shed, where Morgan Elliott was swinging a cleaver over the gutting table and yelling. I couldn't make out what the yelling was about, and thought someone must have made a terrible mistake in his work; perhaps it had been me. Then I saw Brian on the other side of the table, looking very sulky and mean, and standing well back. The sexual leer was not altogether gone from his face, but it was flattened out and mixed with a look of impotent bad temper and some fear. That's it, I thought, Brian is getting fired for being so sloppy and lazy. Even when I made out Morgan saying "pervert" and "filthy" and "maniac," I still thought that was what was happening. Marjorie and Lily, and even brassy Irene, were standing around with downcast, rather pious looks, such as children get when somebody is suffering a terrible bawling out at school. Only old Henry seemed able to keep a cautious grin on his face. Gladys was not to be seen. Herb was standing closer to Morgan than anybody else. He was not interfering but was keeping an eye on the cleaver. Morgy was blubbering, though he didn't seem to be in any immediate danger.

Morgan was yelling at Brian to get out. "And out of this town—I mean it—and don't you wait till tomorrow if you still want your arse in one piece! Out!" he shouted, and the cleaver swung dramatically towards the door. Brian started in that direction but, whether he meant to or not, he made a swaggering, taunting motion of the buttocks. This made Morgan break into a roar and run after him, swinging the cleaver in a stagy way. Brian ran, and Morgan ran after him, and Irene screamed and grabbed her stomach. Morgan was too heavy to run any distance and probably could not have thrown the cleaver very far, either. Herb watched from the doorway. Soon Morgan came back and flung the cleaver down on the table.

"All back to work! No more gawking around here! You don't get paid for gawking! What are you getting under way at?" he said, with a hard look at Irene.

"Nothing," Irene said meekly.

"If you're getting under way get out of here."

"I'm not."

"All right, then!"

We got to work. Herb took off his blood-smeared smock and put on his jacket and went off, probably to see that Brian got ready to go on the suppertime bus. He did not say a word. Morgan and his son went out to the yard, and Irene and Henry went back to the adjoining shed, where they did the plucking, working knee-deep in the feathers Brian was supposed to keep swept up.

"Where's Gladys?" I said softly.

"Recuperating," said Marjorie. She too spoke in a quieter voice than usual, and *recuperating* was not the sort of word she and Lily normally used. It was a word to be used about Gladys, with a mocking intent.

They didn't want to talk about what had happened, because they were afraid Morgan might come in and catch them at it and fire them. Good workers as they were, they were afraid of that. Besides, they hadn't seen anything. They must have been annoyed that they hadn't. All I ever found out was that Brian had either done something or shown something to Gladys as she came out of the washroom and she had started screaming and having hysterics.

Now she'll likely be laid up with another nervous break-down, they said. And he'll be on his way out of town. And good riddance, they said, to both of them.

I have a picture of the Turkey Barn crew taken on Christmas Eve. It was taken with a flash camera that was someone's Christmas extravagance. I think it was Irene's. But Herb Abbott must have been the one who took the picture. He was the one who could be trusted to know or to learn immediately how to manage anything new, and flash cameras were fairly new at the time. The picture was taken about ten o'clock on Christmas Eve, after Herb and Morgy had come back from making the last delivery and we had washed off the gutting table and swept and mopped the cement floor. We had taken off our bloody smocks and heavy sweaters and gone into the little room called the lunchroom, where there was a table and a heater. We still wore our working clothes: overalls and shirts. The men wore caps and the women kerchiefs, tied in the wartime style. I am stout and cheerful and comradely in the picture, transformed into someone I don't ever remember being or pretending to be. I look years older than fourteen. Irene is the only one who has taken off her kerchief, freeing her long red hair. She peers out from it with a meek, sluttish, inviting look, which would match her reputation but is not like any look of hers I remember. Yes, it must have been her camera; she is posing for it, with that look, more deliberately than anyone else is. Marjorie and Lily are smiling, true to form, but their smiles are sour and reckless. With their hair hidden, and such figures as they have bundled up, they look like a couple of tough and jovial but testy workmen. Their kerchiefs look misplaced; caps would be better. Henry is in high spirits, glad to be part of the work force, grinning and looking twenty years younger than his age. Then Morgy, with his hangdog look, not trusting the occasion's bounty, and Morgan very flushed and bosslike and satisfied. He has just given each of us our bonus turkey. Each of these turkeys has a leg or a wing missing, or a malformation of some kind, so none of them are salable at the full price. But Morgan has been at pains to tell us that you often get the best meat off the gimpy ones, and he has shown us that he's taking one home himself.

We are all holding mugs or large, thick china cups, which contain not the usual tea but rye whisky. Morgan and Henry have been drinking since suppertime. Marjorie and Lily say they only want a little, and only take it at all because it's Christmas Eve and they are dead on their feet. Irene says she's dead on her feet as well but that doesn't mean she only wants a little. Herb has poured quite generously not just for her but for Lily and Marjorie too, and they do not object. He has measured mine and Morgy's out at the same time, very stingily, and poured in Coca-Cola. This is the first drink I have ever had, and as a result I will believe for years that rye-and-Coca-Cola is a standard sort of drink and will always ask for it, until I notice that few other people drink it and that it makes me sick. I didn't get sick that Christmas Eve, though; Herb had not given me enough. Except for an odd taste, and my own feeling of consequence, it was like drinking Coca-Cola.

I don't need Herb in the picture to remember what he looked like. That is, if he looked like himself, as he did all the time at the Turkey Barn and the few times I saw him on the street—as he did all the times in my life when I saw him except one.

The time he looked somewhat unlike himself was when Morgan was cursing out Brian and, later, when Brian had run off down the road. What was this different look? I've tried to remember, because I studied it hard at the time. It wasn't much different. His face looked softer and heavier then, and if you had to describe the expression on it you would have to say it was an expression of shame. But what would he be ashamed of? Ashamed of Brian, for the way he had behaved? Surely that would be late in the day; when had Brian ever behaved otherwise? Ashamed of Morgan, for carrying on so ferociously and theatrically? Or of himself, because he was famous for nipping fights and displays of this sort in the bud and hadn't been able to do it here? Would he be ashamed that he hadn't stood up for Brian? Would he have expected himself to do that, to stand up for Brian?

All this was what I wondered at the time. Later, when I knew more, at least about sex, I decided that Brian was Herb's lover, and that Gladys really was trying to get attention from Herb, and that that was why Brian had humiliated her—with or without Herb's connivance and consent. Isn't it true that people like Herb—dignified, secretive, honorable people—will often choose somebody like Brian, will waste their helpless love on some vicious, silly person who is not even evil, or a monster, but just some importunate nuisance? I decided that Herb, with all his gentleness and carefulness, was avenging himself on us all—not just on Gladys but on us all—with Brian, and that what he was feeling when I studied his face must have been a savage and gleeful scorn. But embarrassment as well—embarrassment for Brian and for himself and for Gladys, and to some degree for all of us. Shame for all of us—that is what I thought then.

Later still, I backed off from this explanation. I got to a stage of backing off from the things I couldn't really know. It's enough for me now just to think of Herb's face with that peculiar, stricken look; to think of Brian monkeying in the shade of

Herb's dignity; to think of my own mystified concentration on Herb, my need to catch him out, if I could ever get the chance, and then move in and stay close to him. How attractive, how delectable, the prospect of intimacy is, with the very person who will never grant it. I can still feel the pull of a man like that, of his promising and refusing. I would still like to know things. Never mind facts. Never mind theories, either.

When I finished my drink I wanted to say something to Herb. I stood beside him and waited for a moment when he was not listening to or talking with anyone else and when the increasingly rowdy conversation of the others would cover what I had to say.

"I'm sorry your friend had to go away."

"That's all right."

Herb spoke kindly and with amusement, and so shut me off from any further right to look at or speak about his life. He knew what I was up to. He must have known it before, with lots of women. He knew how to deal with it.

Lily had a little more whisky in her mug and told how she and her best girlfriend (dead now, of liver trouble) had dressed up as men one time and gone into the men's side of the beer parlor, the side where it said MEN ONLY, because they wanted to see what it was like. They sat in a corner drinking beer and keeping their eyes and ears open, and nobody looked twice or thought a thing about them, but soon a problem arose.

"Where were we going to go? If we went around to the other side and anybody seen us going into the ladies', they would scream bloody murder. And if we went into the men's somebody'd be sure to notice we didn't do it the right way. Meanwhile the beer was going through us like a bugger!"

"What you don't do when you're young!" Marjorie said.

Several people gave me and Morgy advice. They told us to enjoy ourselves while we could. They told us to stay out of trouble. They said they had all been young once. Herb said we were a good crew and had done a good job but he didn't want to get in bad with any of the women's husbands by keeping them there too late. Marjorie and Lily expressed indifference to their husbands, but Irene announced that she loved hers and that it was not true that he had been dragged back from Detroit to marry her, no matter what people said. Henry said it was a good life if you didn't weaken. Morgan said he wished us all the most sincere Merry Christmas.

When we came out of the Turkey Barn it was snowing. Lily said it was like a Christmas card, and so it was, with the snow whirling around the streetlights in town and around the colored lights people had put up outside their doorways. Morgan was giving Henry and Irene a ride home in the truck, acknowledging age and pregnancy and Christmas. Morgy took a shortcut through the field, and Herb walked off by himself, head down and hands in his pockets, rolling slightly, as if he were on the deck of a lake boat. Marjorie and Lily linked arms with me as if we were old comrades.

"Let's sing," Lily said. "What'll we sing?"

" 'We Three Kings'?" said Marjorie. " 'We Three Turkey Gutters'?"

" 'I'm Dreaming of a White Christmas.' "

"Why dream? You got it!"

So we sang.

∽ *Labor Day Dinner* ∾

JUST BEFORE SIX o'clock in the evening, George and Roberta and Angela and Eva get out of George's pickup truck—he traded his car for a pickup when he moved to the country—and walk across Valerie's front yard, under the shade of two aloof and splendid elm trees that have been expensively preserved. Valerie says those trees cost her a trip to Europe. The grass underneath them has been kept green all summer, and is bordered by fiery dahlias. The house is of pale-red brick, and around the doors and windows there is a decorative outline of lighter-colored bricks, originally white. This style is often found in Grey County; perhaps it was a specialty of one of the early builders.

George is carrying the folding lawn chairs Valerie asked them to bring. Roberta is carrying a dessert, a raspberry bombe made from raspberries picked on their own farm—George's farm—earlier in the summer. She has packed it in ice cubes and wrapped it in dish towels, but she is eager to get it into the freezer. Angela and Eva carry bottles of wine. Angela and Eva are Roberta's daughters. It has been arranged between Roberta and her husband that they spend the summers with her and George and the school year in Halifax with him. Roberta's husband is in the Navy. Angela is seventeen, Eva is twelve.

These four people are costumed in a way that would suggest they were going to different dinner parties. George, who is a stocky, dark, barrel-chested man, with a daunting, professional look of self-assurance and impatience (he used to be a teacher), wears a clean T-shirt and nondescript pants. Roberta is wearing faded tan cotton pants and a loose raw-silk top of mud-brick color—a color that suits her dark hair and pale skin well enough when she is at her best, but she is not at her best today. When she made herself up in the bathroom, she thought her skin looked like a piece of waxed paper that had been crumpled into a tight ball and then smoothed out. She was momentarily pleased with her thinness and had planned to wear a slinky silver halter top she owns—a glamorous joke—but at the last minute she changed her mind. She is wearing dark glasses, and the reason is that she has taken to weeping in spurts, never at the really bad times but in between; the spurts are as unbidden as sneezes.

As for Angela and Eva, they are dramatically arrayed in outfits contrived from a box of old curtains found in the upstairs of George's house. Angela wears emerald-green damask with long, sun-faded stripes, draped so as to leave one golden shoulder bare. She has cut vine leaves out of the same damask, pasted them on cardboard, and arranged them in her hair. Angela is tall and fair-haired, and embarrassed by her recently acquired beauty. She will go to great trouble to flaunt it, as she does now, and then will redden and frown and look stubbornly affronted when somebody tells her she looks like a goddess. Eva is wearing several fragile, yellowed lace curtains draped and bunched up, and held together with pins, ribbons, and nosegays of wild phlox already drooping and scattering. One of the curtains is pinned across her forehead and flows behind her, like a 1920s bridal veil. She has put her shorts on underneath, in case anybody should glimpse underpants through the veiling. Eva is puritanical, outrageous—an acrobat, a parodist, an optimist, a disturber. Her face, under the pinned veil, is lewdly painted with green eye shadow and dark lipstick and rouge and mascara. The violent colors emphasize her childish look of recklessness and valor.

Angela and Eva have ridden here in the back of the truck, stretched out on the lawn chairs. It is only three miles from George's place to Valerie's, but Roberta did not think riding like that was safe—she wanted them to get down and sit on the truck bed. To her surprise, George spoke up on their behalf, saying it would be ignominious for them to have to huddle down on the floor in their finery. He said he would drive slowly and avoid bumps; so he did. Roberta was a little nervous, but she was relieved to see him sympathetic and indulgent about the very things—self-dramatization, self-display—that she had expected would annoy him. She herself has given up wearing long skirts and caftans because of what he has said about disliking the sight of women trailing around in such garments, which announce to him, he says, not only a woman's intention of doing no serious work but her persistent wish to be admired and courted. This is a wish George has no patience with and has spent some energy, throughout his adult life, in thwarting.

Roberta thought that after speaking in such a friendly way to the girls, and helping them into the truck, he might speak to her when he got into the cab, might even take her hand, brushing away her undisclosed crimes, but it did not happen. Shut up together, driving over the hot gravel roads at an almost funereal pace, they are pinned down by a murderous silence. On the edge of it, Roberta feels herself curling up like a jaundiced leaf. She knows this to be a hysterical image. Also hysterical is the notion of screaming and opening the door and throwing herself on the gravel. She ought to make an effort not to be hysterical, not to exaggerate. But surely it is hatred— what else can it be?—that George is steadily manufacturing and wordlessly pouring out at her, and surely it is a deadly gas. She tries to break the silence herself, making little clucks of worry as she tightens the towels over the bombe and then sighing— a noisy imitation sigh meant to sound tired, pleased, and comfortable. They are driving between high stands of corn, and she thinks how ugly the corn looks—a monotonous, coarse-leaved crop, a foolish army. How long has this been going on? Since yesterday morning: she felt it in him before they got out of bed. They went out and got drunk last night to try to better things, but the relief didn't last.

Before they left for Valerie's, Roberta was in the bedroom, fastening her halter top, and George came in and said, "Is that what you're wearing?"

"I thought I would, yes. Doesn't it look all right?"

"Your armpits are flabby."

"Are they? I'll put on something with sleeves."

In the truck, now that she knows he isn't going to make up, she lets herself hear him say that. A harsh satisfaction in his voice. The satisfaction of airing disgust. He is disgusted by her aging body. That could have been foreseen. She starts humming something, feeling the lightness, the freedom, the great tactical advantage of being the one to whom the wrong has been done, the bleak challenge offered, the unforgivable thing said.

But suppose he doesn't think it's unforgivable, suppose in his eyes she's the one who's unforgivable? She's always the one; disasters overtake her daily. It used to be that as soon as she noticed some deterioration she would seek strenuously to remedy it. Now the remedies bring more problems. She applies cream frantically to her wrinkles, and her face breaks out in spots, like a teenager's. Dieting until her waist was thin enough to please produced a haggard look about her cheeks and throat. Flabby armpits—how can you exercise the armpits? What is to be done? Now the payment is due, and what for? For vanity. Hardly even for that. Just for having those pleasing surfaces once, and letting them speak for you; just for allowing an arrangement of hair and shoulders and breasts to have its effect. You don't stop in time, don't know what to do instead; you lay yourself open to humiliation. So thinks Roberta, with self-pity—what she knows to be self-pity—rising and sloshing around in her like bitter bile.

She must get away, live alone, wear sleeves.

Valerie calls to them from a darkened window under the vines, "Go on in, go in. I'm just putting on my panty hose."

"Don't put on your panty hose!" cry George and Roberta together. You would think from the sound of their voices that all the way over here they had been engaged in tender and lively conversation.

"Don't put on your *panty* hose," wail Angela and Eva.

"Oh, all right, if there's all that much prejudice against panty hose," says Valerie behind her window. "I won't even put on a dress. I'll come as I am."

"Not that!" cries George, and staggers, holding the lawn chairs up in front of his face.

But Valerie, appearing in the doorway, is dressed beautifully, in a loose gown of green and gold and blue. She doesn't have to worry about George's opinion of long dresses. She is absolved of blame anyway, because you could never say that Valerie is looking to be courted or admired. She is a tall, flat-chested woman, whose long, plain face seems to be crackling with welcome, eager understanding, with humor and intelligence and appreciation. Her hair is thick, gray-black, and curly. This summer she recklessly cut it off, so that all that is left is a curly crew cut, revealing her long, corded neck and the creases at the edge of her cheeks, and her large, flat ears.

"I think it makes me look like a goat," she has said. "I like goats. I love their eyes. Wouldn't it be wonderful to have those horizontal pupils. Bizarre!"

Her children tell her she is bizarre enough already.

Here come Valerie's children now, as George and Roberta and Angela and Eva crowd into the hall, Roberta saying that she is dripping ice and must get this pretentious concoction into the freezer. First, Ruth, who is twenty-five and nearly six feet tall and looks a lot like her mother. She has given up wanting to be an actress and is learning to teach disturbed children. Her arms are full of goldenrod and Queen Anne's lace and dahlias—weeds and flowers all mixed up together—and she throws them on the hall floor with a theatrical gesture and embraces the bombe.

"Dessert," she says lovingly. "Oh, bliss! Angela, you look incredibly lovely! Eva too. I know who Eva is. She's the Bride of Lammermoor!"

Angela will allow, even delight in, such open praise from Ruth, because Ruth is the person she admires most in the world—possibly the only person she admires.

"The Bride of who?" Eva is asking happily. "The Bride of *who?*"

David, Valerie's twenty-one-year-old son, a history student, is standing in the living-room doorway, smiling tolerantly and affectionately at the excitement. David is tall and lean, dark-haired and dark-skinned, like his mother and sister, but he is deliberate, low-voiced, never rash. In this household of many delicate checks and balances it is noticeable that the lively, outspoken women defer to David in some ceremonial way, seeming to ask for the gesture of his protection, though protection itself is something they are not likely to need.

When the greetings die down David says, "This is Kimberly," and introduces them each in turn to the young woman standing under his arm. She is very clean and trim, in a white skirt and a short-sleeved pink shirt. She wears glasses and no makeup; her hair is short and straight and tidy, and a pleasant light-brown color. She shakes hands with each of them and looks each of them in the eye, through her glasses, and though her manner is entirely polite, even subdued, there is a slight feeling of an official person greeting the members of an unruly, outlandish delegation.

Valerie has known both George and Roberta for years. She knew them long before they knew each other. She and George were on the staff of the same Toronto high school. George was head of the art department; Valerie was school counsellor. She knew George's wife, a jittery, well-dressed woman, who was killed in a plane crash in Florida. George and his wife were separated by that time.

And, of course, Valerie knew Roberta because Roberta's husband, Andrew, is her cousin. They never cared much for each other—Valerie and Roberta's husband—and each of them has described the other to Roberta as a stick. Andrew used to say that Valerie was a queer-looking stick and utterly sexless, and when Roberta told Valerie that she was leaving him Valerie said, "Oh, good. He is such a stick." Roberta was pleased to find such sympathy and pleased that she wouldn't have to dredge up acceptable reasons; apparently Valerie thought his being a stick was reason enough. At the same time, Roberta had a wish to defend her husband and to inquire how on earth Valerie could presume to know whether he was a stick or wasn't. She can't get over wishing to defend him; she feels he had such bad luck marrying her.

When Roberta moved out and left Halifax, she came and

stayed with Valerie in Toronto. There she met George, and he took her off to see his farm. Now Valerie says they are her creation, the result of her totally inadvertent matchmaking.

"It was the first time I ever saw love bloom at close quarters," she says. "It was like watching an amaryllis. Astounding."

But Roberta has the idea that, much as she likes them both and wishes them well, love is really something Valerie could do without being reminded of. In Valerie's company you do wonder sometimes what all the fuss is about. Valerie wonders. Her life and her presence, more than any opinion she expresses, remind you that love is not kind or honest and does not contribute to happiness in any reliable way.

When she talked to Roberta about George (this was before she knew Roberta was in love with him), Valerie said, "He's a mysterious man, really. I think he's very idealistic, though he'd hate to hear me say that. This farm he's bought. This self-sufficient, remote, productive life in the country." She went on to talk about how he had grown up in Timmins, the son of a Hungarian shoemaker, youngest of six children and the first to finish high school, let alone go to university. "He's the sort of person who would know what to do in a street fight but doesn't know how to swim. He brought his old crabby, bent-over father down to Toronto and took care of him till he died. I think he drops women rather hard."

Roberta listened to all this with great interest and a basic disregard, because what other people knew about George already seemed unessential to her. She was full of alarm and delight. Being in love was nothing she had counted on. The most she'd hoped for was a life like Valerie's. She had illustrated a couple of children's books and thought she could get more commissions; she could rent a room out in the Beaches, in East Toronto, paint the walls white, sit on cushions instead of chairs, and learn to be self-disciplined and self-indulgent, as she thought solitary people must be.

Valerie and Roberta walk through the house, carrying a bottle of cold wine and two of Valerie's grandmother's water goblets. Roberta thinks Valerie's house is exactly what people have in mind when they say longingly "a house in the country" or, more particularly, "an old brick farmhouse." The warm, pale-red brick with the light brick trim, the vines and elms, the sanded floors and hooked rugs and white walls, the chipped wash-jug set on a massive chest of drawers in front of a dim mirror. Of course, Valerie has had fifteen years to bring this about. She and her husband bought the house as a summer place, and then when he died she sold their city house and moved to an apartment and put her money and her energy into this. George bought his house and land two years ago, having been introduced to this part of the country by Valerie, and fourteen months ago he left his teaching job and moved up here for good. On the heels of that move came his first meeting with Roberta. Last December she came to live with him. She thought that it would take them about a year to get the place fixed up, and then George could get back to doing his sculpting. A sculptor is what he really wants to be. That is why he wanted to give up teaching and live cheaply in the country—raise a lot of vegetables, keep chickens. He hasn't started on the chickens yet.

Roberta meant to keep busy illustrating books. Why hasn't she done this? No time, nowhere to work: no room, no light, no table. No clear moments of authority, now that life has got this new kind of grip on her.

What they have done so far—what George has done, mostly, while Roberta sweeps and cooks—is put a new roof on the house, put in aluminum-frame windows, pour bag after bag of dusty pebble-like insulation into the space behind the walls, fit batts of yellow, woolly-looking fiberglass against the attic roof, clean all the stovepipes and replace some of them and rebrick part of the chimney, replace the rotting eaves. After all these essential and laborious repairs the house is still unattractive on the outside, with its dark-red imitation-brick covering and its sagging porch heaped with drying new lumber and salvaged old lumber and extra batts of fiberglass and other useful debris. And it is dark and sour-smelling within. Roberta would like to rip up the linoleum and tear down the dismal wallpaper, but everything must be done in order, and George has figured out the order; it is no use ripping up and tearing down until the wiring and insulating have been finished and the shell of the house reconstructed. Lately he has been saying that before he starts on the inside of the house or puts the siding on the outside he must do a major job on the barn; if he doesn't get the beam structure propped and strengthened the whole building may come down in next winter's storms.

As well as this there is the garden: the apple and cherry trees, which have been pruned; the raspberry canes, which have been cleaned out; the lawn, which has been reseeded, reclaimed from patches of long wild grass and patches of bare ground and rubble under the shade of some ragged pines. At first Roberta kept an idea of the whole place in her mind—all the things that had been done, that were being done, and that were yet to do. Now she doesn't think of the work that way—she has no general picture of it—but stays in the kitchen and does jobs as they arise. Dealing with the produce of the garden— making chili sauce, preparing tomatoes and peppers and beans and corn for the freezer, making tomato juice, making cherry jam—has taken up a lot of her time. Sometimes she looks into the freezer and wonders who will eat all this—George and who else? She can feel her own claims shrinking.

The table is laid on the long screened veranda at the back of the house. Valerie and Roberta go out a door at the end of the veranda, down some shallow steps, and into a little brick-walled, brick-paved area that Valerie has had made this summer but does not like to call a patio. She says you can't have a patio on a farmhouse. She hasn't decided yet what she does like to call it. She hasn't decided, either, whether to get heavy wooden lawn chairs, which she likes the look of, or comfortable lightweight metal-and-plastic chairs, like those which George and Roberta brought.

They pour the wine and lift their glasses, the capacious old water goblets they love to drink wine from. They can hear Ruth and Eva and Angela laughing in Ruth's bedroom. Ruth has said they must help her get into costume too—she is going to think of something that will outdo them all. And they can hear the swish of George's scythe, which he has brought to cut the long grass and burdocks around Valerie's little stone dairy house.

"The dairy house would make a lovely studio," Valerie says. "I should rent it to an artist. George? You? I'd rent it for the scything and a raspberry bombe. George is going to make a studio in the barn, though, isn't he?"

"Eventually," says Roberta. At present all George's work is in the front of the house, in the old parlor. Some half-finished and nearly finished pieces are there, covered up with dusty sheets, and also some blocks of wood (George works only in wood)—a big chunk of seasoned oak and pieces of kiln-dried butternut and cherry. His ripsaw, his chisels and gouges, his linseed oil and turpentine and beeswax and resins are all there, the lids dusty and screwed tight. Eva and Angela used to go around and, standing on tiptoe in the rubble and weeds, peer in the front window at the shrouded shapes.

"Ugh, they look spooky," Eva said to George. "What are they underneath?"

"Wooden doughnuts," George said. "Pop sculpt."

"Really?"

"A potato and a two-headed baby."

Next time they went to look they found a sheet tacked up over the window. This was a grayish-colored sheet, torn at the top. To anybody driving by it made the house look even more bleak and neglected.

"Do you know I had cigarettes all the time?" Valerie says. "I have half a carton. I hid them in the cupboard in my room."

She has sent David and Kimberly into town, telling them she's out of cigarettes. Valerie can't stop smoking, though she takes vitamin pills and is careful not to eat anything with red food coloring in it. "I couldn't think of anything else to say I was out of, and I had to have them clear off for a while. Now I don't dare smoke one or they'll smell it when they get back and know I was a liar. And I want one."

"Drink instead," says Roberta. When she got here she thought she couldn't talk to anybody—she was going to say her head ached and ask if she could lie down. But Valerie steadies her, as always. Valerie makes what isn't bearable interesting.

"So how are you?" Valerie says.

"Ohhh," says Roberta.

"Life would be grand if it weren't for the people," says Valerie moodily. "That sounds like a quotation, but I think I just made it up. The problem is that Kimberly is a Christian. Well, that's fine. We could use a Christian or two. For that matter, I am not an un-Christian. But she is very noticeably a Christian, don't you think? I'm amazed how mean she makes me feel."

George is enjoying the scything. For one thing, he likes working without spectators. Whenever he works at home these days, he is aware of a crowd of female spectators. Even if they're nowhere in sight, he feels as if they're watching—taking their ease, regarding his labors with mystification and amusement. He admits, if he thinks about it, that Roberta does do some work, though she has done nothing to earn money as far as he knows; she hasn't been in touch with her publishers, and she hasn't worked on ideas of her own. She permits her daughters to do nothing all day long, all summer long. Yesterday morning he got up feeling tired and disheartened—he had gone to sleep thinking of the work he had to do on the barn, and this preoccupation had seeped into his dreams, which were full of collapses, miscalculations, structural treacheries—and he went out to the deck off the kitchen, thinking to eat his eggs there and brood about the day's jobs. This deck is the only thing he had built as yet, the only change he has made in the house. He built it last spring in response to Roberta's complaints about the darkness of the house and the bad ventilation. He told her that the people who built these houses did so much work in the sun that they never thought of sitting in it.

He came out on the deck, then, carrying his plate and mug, and all three of them were already there. Angela was dressed in a sapphire-blue leotard; she was doing ballet exercises by the deck railing. Eva was sitting with her back against the wall of the house, spooning up bran flakes out of a soup bowl; she did this with such enthusiasm that many were spilled on the deck floor. Roberta, in a deck chair, had the everlasting mug of coffee clasped in both hands. She had one knee up and her back hunched, and with her dark glasses on she looked tense and mournful. He knows she weeps behind those glasses. It seems to him that she has let the children draw the sap right out of her body. She spends her time placating them, picking up after them; she has to beg them to make their beds and clean up their rooms; he has heard her pleading with them to collect their dirty dishes, so that she can wash them. Or that is what it sounds like to him. Is this the middle-class fashion of bringing up children? Here she was admiring Angela, meekly admiring her own daughter—the naked, lifted, golden leg, the disdainful profile. If either of his sisters had ventured on such a display, his mother would have belted them.

Angela lowered her leg and said, "Greetings, Master!"

"I don't see you bumping your head on the ground," said George. He usually joked with the girls no matter what he felt like. Rough joking was his habit, and it had been hugely successful in the classroom, where he had maintained a somewhat overdrawn, occasionally brutal, consistently entertaining character. He had done this with most of the other teachers as well, expressing his contempt for them so colorfully that they could not believe he meant it.

Eva loved to act out any suggestion of this sort. She stretched herself full length on the deck and knocked her head hard on the boards.

"You'll get a concussion," Roberta said.

"No, I won't. I'll just give myself a lobotomy."

"George, do you realize that in four brief days we will be gone?" said Angela. "Isn't your heart broken?"

"In twain."

"But will you let Mom take care of Diana when we're gone?" said Eva, sitting upright and feeling her head for bruises. Diana was a stray cat she was feeding in the barn.

"What do you mean, *let?*" said Roberta, and George at the same time said, "Certainly not. I'll tie her to the bedpost if she ever tries to go near the barn."

This cat is a sore point. If Angela sees the farm as a stage for herself, or sometimes as Nature—a begetter of thoughts and poems, to which she yields herself, wandering and dreaming—Eva sees it as a place to look for animals, with some of her attention left over for insects, minnows, rocks, and slugs. Both of them see it, certainly, as vacationland, spread out before them for whatever use or pleasure they can get out of it; neither sees the jobs waiting to be done under their noses. Eva has spent the summer stalking groundhogs and rabbits, trapping frogs and letting them go, catching minnows in a jar, trying to figure out how various animals could be housed in the barn. George holds her responsible—out of the very strength of her desire—for luring the deer out of the bush, so that he had to stop everything else that he was doing and build an eight-foot-high wire fence around the garden. The only animal she has managed to install in the barn is Diana, rail-thin, ugly, and half wild, whose dangling teats show that she is maintaining a family of kittens elsewhere. Much of Eva's time has been spent trying to discover the whereabouts of these kittens.

George sees the cat as a freeloader, a potential great nuisance, an invader of his property. By feeding it and encouraging it, Eva has embarked on a course of minor but significant treachery, which Roberta has implicitly supported. He knows his feelings on this matter are exaggerated, even comical; that does not help him. One of the things he has never wanted to be, and has avoided being, is a comic dad, a fulminator, a bungler. But it is Roberta's behavior that bothers him, more than Eva's. Here Roberta shows most plainly the mistake she has made in bringing up her children. In his mind he can hear Roberta talking to somebody at a party. "Eva has adopted a horrible cat, a really nasty-looking vagabond—that's her summer achievement. And Angela spends the whole day doing jetés and sulking at us." He has not actually heard Roberta say this—they have not been to any parties—but he can well imagine it. She would summon her children up for the entertainment of others; she would make them into characters from whom nothing serious was to be expected. This seems to George not only frivolous but heartless. Roberta, who is so indulgent with her children, who worries constantly that they may find her insufficiently loving, interested, understanding, is nevertheless depriving them. She is not taking them seriously; she is not bringing them up. And what is George to do in the face of this? They are not his children. One of the reasons he has not had children is that he doubts if he could give his attention unreservedly, and for as long as would be needed, to this very question of bringing them up. As a teacher, he knows how to make a lot of noise and keep several steps ahead of them, but it is exhausting to have to do that on the home front. And it was boys, chiefly, whom he learned to out-maneuver; boys were the threat in a class. The girls he never bothered much about, beyond some careful sparring with the sexy ones. That is not in order here.

Aside from all this, he often can't help liking Angela and Eva. They seem to him confused and appealing. They think him highly amusing, which irks him sometimes and pleases him at other times. His way with people is to be very reserved or very entertaining, and he believes that his preference is to be reserved. Therefore, he likes the entertainment to be appreciated.

But when he finished his breakfast and got two six-quart baskets and went down to the garden to pick the tomatoes, nobody stirred to help him. Roberta continued her moody thinking and her coffee-drinking. Angela had finished her exercises and was writing in the notebook she uses for a journal. Eva had taken off for the barn.

Angela sits down at the piano in Valerie's living room. There is no piano in George's house, and she misses one. Doesn't her mother miss one? Her mother has become a person who doesn't ask for anything.

I have seen her change, Angela has written in her journal, *from a person I deeply respected into a person on the verge of being a nervous wreck. If this is love I want no part of it. He wants to enslave her and us all and she walks a tightrope trying to keep him from getting mad. She doesn't enjoy anything and if you gave her the choice she would like best to lie down in a dark room with a cloth over her eyes and not see anybody or do anything. This is an intelligent woman who used to believe in freedom.*

She starts to play the "Turkish March," which brings to her mind the picture of a house her parents sold when she was five. There was a little shelf up near the ceiling in the dining room, where her mother had set the dessert plates for decoration. A tree, or bush, in the yard had lettuce-colored leaves as big as plates.

She has written in her journal: *I know nostalgia is a futile emotion. Sometimes I feel like tearing out some things I have written where perhaps I have been too harsh in judging certain people or situations but I have decided to leave everything because I want to have a record of what I really felt at the time. I want to have a truthful record of my whole life. How to keep oneself from lying I see as the main problem everywhere.*

During the summer Angela has spent a lot of time reading. She has read *Anna Karenina, The Second Sex, Emily of New Moon, The Norton Anthology of Poetry, The Autobiography of W.B. Yeats, The Happy Hooker, The Act of Creation, Seven Gothic Tales*. Some of these, to be accurate, she has not read all the way through. Her mother used to read all the time too. Angela would come home from school at noon, and again in the afternoon, and find her mother reading. Her mother read about the conquest of Mexico, she read *The Tale of Genji*. Angela marvels at how safe her mother seemed then.

Angela has one picture in her mind of Eva before Eva was born. The three of them—Angela, her mother, and her father—are on a beach. Her father is scooping out a large hole in the sand. Her father is a gifted builder of sand castles with road and irrigation systems, so Angela watches with interest any projects he undertakes. But the hole has nothing to do with a sand castle. When it is finished her mother rolls over, giggling, and fits her stomach into it. In her stomach is Eva, and the hollow is like a spoon for an egg. The beach is wide, mile after mile of white sand sloping delicately into the blue-green water. No rocky lakefront or stingy bit of cove. A radiant, generous place. Where could it have been?

She proceeds from the "Turkish March" to a try at "Eine kleine Nachtmusik." Roberta, listening to the piano at the same time she's listening to Valerie talking humorously and despairingly about her fear of Kimberly, her dislike of intruders, her indefensible reluctance to relinquish her children, thinks, No, it wasn't a mistake. What does she mean by that? She means it wasn't a mistake to leave her husband. Whatever happens, it wasn't a mistake. It was necessary. Otherwise she wouldn't have known.

"This is a bad time for you," Valerie says judiciously. "There is just a spectacular lot of strain."

"That's what I say to myself," says Roberta. "But sometimes I think that's not it. It's not the house, it's not the children. It's just something black that rises."

"Oh, there's always something black," says Valerie, grumbling.

"I think about Andrew—what was I doing to him? Setting things up to find the failure in him, railing at him, then getting cold feet and making up. Gradually the need to get rid of him would build again, but I was always sure it was his fault— if he'd just do this or that I could love him. So horrible for him that he turned into—remember what you said he was? A stick."

"He was a stick," says Valerie. "He always was. You're not responsible for everything."

"I think about it, because I wonder if that's what George is doing to me. He wants to be rid of me, then he doesn't, then he does, then he can't admit that, even to himself; he has to set up failures. I feel I know what Andrew went through. Not that I'd go back. Never. But I see it."

"I doubt if things happen so symmetrically."

"I don't think so either, really. I don't think you get your punishment in such a simple way. Isn't it funny how you're attracted—I am—to the idea of a pattern like that? I mean, the idea is attractive, of there being that balance. But not the experience. I'd like to avoid them."

"You forget how happy you are when you're happy."

"And vice versa. It's like childbirth."

George has finished scything and is cleaning the blade. He can hear the piano through the open windows of Valerie's house, and erratic streams of sweet, cold air are coming up from the river. He feels much better now, either because of the simple exercise or from the relief of feeling unobserved; perhaps it's just good to get away from the mountainous demands of his own place. He wonders if it's Roberta playing. The music fits in nicely with what he's doing: first the cheerful, workaday "Turkish March," to go along with the scything; now, as he stands cleaning the blade and smelling the cut grass, the subtle congratulations—even if a bit uncertainly delivered—of "Eine kleine Nachtmusik." As always, when his mood truly lifts, when the dawn breaks, he wants to go and find Roberta and envelop her, assure her—assure himself—that no real damage has been done. He hoped to be able to do that last night when they went drinking, but he couldn't; something still held him back.

He recalls Roberta's first visit to his house. That was in late August or early September, about a year ago now. They staged an indecorous sort of picnic, cooking feasts and playing records, hauling a mattress out into the yard. Clear nights, with Roberta pointing out to him the unlikely ways the stars tie up into their constellations, and every day pure gold. Roberta saying he must get it all straight now: she is forty-three years old, which is six years too old for him; she has left her husband because everything between them seemed artificial; but she hates saying that, because it may be just cant, she isn't sure what she means, and above all, she doesn't know what she's capable of. She seemed to him courageous, truthful, without vanity. How out of this could come such touchiness, tearfulness, weariness, such a threat of collapse, he cannot imagine.

But the first impression is worth respecting, he thinks.

Eva and Ruth are decorating the dinner table on the veranda. Ruth is wearing a white shirt belonging to her brother, his striped pajama bottoms, and a monumental black turban. She looks like a proud but good-natured Sikh.

"I think the table ought to be strewn," says Ruth. "Subtlety is out, Eva."

At intervals they set orange and gold dahlias and beautifully striped pepper squash, zucchini, yellow gourds, Indian corn.

Under cover of the music Eva says, "Angela has more problems living here than I do. She thinks that whenever they fight it's about her."

"Do they fight?" says Ruth softly. Then she says, "It's none of my business." She was in love with George when she was thirteen or fourteen. It was when her mother first became friends with him. She used to hate his wife, and was glad when they separated. She remembers that the wife was the daughter of a gynecologist, and that this was cited by her mother as a reason George and his wife could never get on. It was probably the father's prosperity her mother was talking about, or the way the daughter had been brought up. But to Ruth the word *gynecologist* seemed sharp and appalling, and she saw the gynecologist's daughter dressed in an outfit of cold, jagged metal.

"They have silent fights. We can tell. Angela is so self-interested she thinks everything revolves around her. That's what happens when you become an adolescent. I don't want it to happen to me."

There is a pause in Angela's playing, and Eva says sharply, "Oh, I don't want to leave! I hate leaving."

"Do you?"

"I hate to leave Diana. I don't know what will happen to her. I don't know if I'll ever see her again. I don't think I'll ever see the deer again. I hate having to leave things."

Now that the piano is silent, Eva can be heard outside, where Valerie and Roberta are sitting. Roberta hears what Eva says, and waits, expecting to hear her say something about next summer. She braces herself to hear it.

Instead, Eva says, "You know, I understand George. I don't mind about him the way Angela does. I know how to be jokey. I understand him."

Roberta and Valerie look at each other, and Roberta smiles, shakes her head, and shivers. She has been afraid, sometimes, that George would hurt her children, not physically but by some turnabout, some revelation of dislike, that they could never forget. It seems to her that she has instructed them, by example, that he is to be accommodated, his silences respected, his joking responded to. What if he should turn, within this safety, and deal them a memorable blow? If it happened, it would be she who would have betrayed them into it. And she can feel a danger. For instance, when George was pruning the apple trees she heard Angela say, "My father's got an apple tree and a cherry tree now."

(That was information. Would he take it as competition?)

"I suppose he has some minions come and prune them for him?" George said.

"He has hundreds," said Angela cheerfully. "Dwarfs. He makes them all wear little Navy uniforms."

Angela was on thin ice at that moment. But Roberta thinks now that the real danger is not to Angela, who would find a way to welcome insult, would be ready to reap some advantage. (Roberta has read parts of the journal.) It is Eva, with her claims of understanding, her hopes of all-round conciliation, who could be smashed and stranded.

Over cold apple-and-watercress soup Eva has switched back to her *enfant terrible* style to tell the table, "They went out and got drunk last night. They were polluted."

David says he hasn't heard that expression in a long time.

Valerie says, "How awful for you little ones."

"We considered phoning the Children's Aid," says Angela, looking very unchildlike in the candlelight—looking like a queen, in fact—and aware that David is watching her, though with David it's hard to say whether he's watching with approval or with reservations. It seems as if it might be approval. Kimberly has taken over his reservations.

"Did you have a dissolute time?" says Valerie. "Roberta, you never told me. Where did you go?"

"It was highly respectable," says Roberta. "We went to the Queen's Hotel in Logan. To the Lounge—that's what they call it. The posh place to drink."

"George wouldn't take you out to any old beer parlor," says Ruth. "George is a closet conservative."

"It's true," says Valerie. "George believes you should take ladies only to nice places."

"And children should be seen and not heard," says Angela.

"Not seen, either," says George.

"Which is confusing to everyone, because he comes on like a raving radical," says Ruth.

"This is a treat," says George, "getting a free analysis. Actually, it was quite dissolute, and Roberta probably doesn't remember, on account of being so polluted, as Eva says. She bewitched a fellow who did toothpick tricks."

Roberta says it was a game where you made a word out of toothpicks, then took a toothpick away or rearranged what was there and made another word, and so on.

"I hope not dirty words?" says Eva.

"I never talked like that when I was her age," Angela says. "I was your pre-permissive child."

"And after we got tired of the game, or after he did, because I was tired of it quite soon, he showed me pictures of his wife and himself on their Mediterranean cruise. He was with another lady last night, because his wife is dead now, and if he forgot where the pictures were taken this lady reminded him. She said she didn't think he'd ever get over it."

"The cruise or his wife?" says Ruth, while George is saying that he had a conversation with a couple of Dutch farmers who wanted to take him for a ride in their plane.

"I don't think I went," George adds.

"I dissuaded you," says Roberta, not looking at him.

"'Dissuaded' sounds so lovely," says Ruth. "It's so smooth. I must be thinking of suede."

Eva asks what it means.

"Persuaded not to," says Roberta. "I persuaded George not to go for a plane ride at one o'clock in the morning with the rich Dutch farmers. Instead, we all had an adventure getting the man from the Mediterranean cruise into his car so his girlfriend could drive him home."

Ruth and Kimberly get up to remove the soup bowls, and David goes to put on a record of Dvorak's *New World* Symphony. This is his mother's request. David says it's syrupy.

They are quiet, waiting for the music to start. Eva says, "How did you guys fall in love anyway? Was it a physical attraction?"

Ruth knocks her gently on the head with a soup bowl. "You ought to have your jaws wired shut," she says. "Don't forget I'm learning how to cope with disturbed children."

"Didn't it bother you, Mom being so much older?"

"You see what I mean about her?" Angela says.

"What do you know about love?" says George grandly. "Love suffereth long, and is kind. Similar to myself in that respect. Love is not puffed up . . ."

"I think that is a particular kind of love," says Kimberly, setting down the vegetables. "If you're quoting."

Under cover of a conversation about translation and the meanings of words (a subject of which George knows little but about which he is soon making sweeping, provocative statements, true to his classroom technique), Roberta says to Valerie, "The man's girlfriend said that the wonderful thing was that his wife had done the whole Mediterranean cruise with a front-end loader."

"A what?"

"Front-end loader. I looked blank too, so she said, 'You know, his wife had one of those operations and she had to wear one of those bag things.'"

"Oh, God help us."

"She had big fat arms and a sprayed blond hairdo. The wife did, in the pictures. The girlfriend was something the same, but trimmer. The wife had such a lewd, happy look. A good-times look."

"And a front-end loader."

So you see against what odds, and with what unpromising-looking persons, love takes root and flourishes, and I myself have no front-end loader, merely some wrinkles and slackness and sallowness and subtle withering. This is what Roberta is saying to herself. It's not my fault, she says to herself, as she has said so often before. Usually when she says it, it's a whine, a plea, a whimper. Now it says itself matter-of-factly in her head; the tone in which it is stated is bored and tired. It seems as if this could be the truth.

By dessert the conversation has shifted to architecture. The only light on the veranda is from the candles on the table: Ruth has taken the big candles away and set in front of each place a single small candle in a black metal holder with a handle, like the candle in the nursery rhyme. Valerie and Roberta say it together: "'Here comes a candle to light you to bed. Here comes a chopper to chop off your head!'"

Neither of them taught that rhyme to her children, and their children have never heard it before.

"I've heard it," says Kimberly.

"The pointed arch, for instance—that was just a fad," George is saying. "It was an architectural fashion, very like fashions today."

"Well, it wasn't only that," says David, temporizing. "It was more than a fashion. The people who built the cathedrals were not entirely like us."

"They were very unlike us," Kimberly says.

"I'm sure I was always taught, if I was taught at all in those far-off days," says Valerie, "that the pointed arch was a development of the Romanesque arch. It suddenly occurred to them to carry it further. And it looked more religious."

"Bull," says George happily. "Beggin' your pardon. I know that's what they used to say, but in fact the pointed arch is the most primitive. It's the easiest arch; it's not a development from the round arch at all—how could it be? They had pointed arches in Egypt. The round arch, the keystone arch, is the most sophisticated arch you can build. The whole thing has been reported ass backwards to favor Christianity."

"Well, it may be sophisticated, but I think it's depressing," says Ruth. "I think they're very depressing, those round arches. They're monotonous; they just go along blah-blah-blah—they don't exactly make your spirits soar."

"It must have expressed something the people deeply wanted," Kimberly says. "You can hardly call that a fad. They built those cathedrals, the people did; the plan wasn't dictated by some architect."

"A misconception. They did have architects. In some cases we even know who they were."

"Nevertheless, I think Kimberly's right," says Valerie. "In those cathedrals you feel so much of the aspirations of those people; you feel the Christian emotion in the architecture—"

"Never mind what you feel. The fact is, the Crusaders brought the pointed arch back from the Arab world. Just as they brought back a taste for spicy food. It wasn't dreamed up by the collective unconscious to honor Jesus any more than I was. It was the latest style. The earliest examples you can see are in Italy, and then it worked north."

Kimberly is very pink in the face but is benignly, tightly smiling. Valerie, just because she so much dislikes Kimberly, is feeling a need to say anything at all to come to her rescue. Valerie never minds if she sounds silly; she will throw herself headlong into any conversation to turn it off its contentious course, to make people laugh and calm down. Ruth also has a knack for lightening things, though in her case it seems to be done not so deliberately but serenely and almost inadvertently, as a result of her faithful following of her own line of thought. What about David? At this moment David is caught up by Angela and not paying as much attention as he might be. Angela is trying out her powers; she will try them out even on a cousin she has known since she was child. Kimberly is endangered on two sides, Roberta thinks. But she will manage. She is strong enough to hold on to David through any number of Angelas, and strong enough to hold her smile in the face of George's attack on her faith. Does her smile foresee how he will burn? Not likely. She foresees, instead, how all of them will stumble and wander around and tie themselves in knots; what does it matter who wins the argument? For Kimberly, all the arguments have already been won.

Thinking this, pinning them all down this way, Roberta feels competent, relieved. Indifference has rescued her. The main thing is to be indifferent to George—that's the great boon. But her indifference flows past him; it's generous, it touches everybody. She is drunk enough to feel like reporting some findings. "Sexual abdication is not enough," she might say to Valerie. She is sober enough to keep quiet.

Valerie has got George talking about Italy. Ruth and David

and Kimberly and Angela have started talking about something else. Roberta hears Angela's voice speaking with impatience and authority, and with an eagerness, a shyness, only she can detect.

"Acid rain . . ." Angela is saying.

Eva flicks her fingers against Roberta's arm. "What are you thinking?" she says.

"I don't know."

"You can't not know. What are you thinking?"

"About life."

"What about life?"

"About people."

"What about people?"

"About the dessert."

Eva flicks harder, giggling. "What about the dessert?"

"I thought it was okay."

Sometime later Valerie has occasion to say that she was not born in the nineteenth century, in spite of what David may think. David says that everybody born in this country before the Second World War was to all intents and purposes brought up in the nineteenth century, and that their thinking is archaic.

"We are more than products of our upbringing," Valerie says. "As you yourself must hope, David." She says that she has been listening to all this talk about overpopulation, ecological disaster, nuclear disaster, this and that disaster, destroying the ozone layer—it's been going on and on, on and on for years, talk of disaster—but here they sit, all healthy, relatively sane, with a lovely dinner and lovely wine inside them, in the beautiful, undestroyed countryside.

"The Incas eating off gold plates while Pizarro was landing on the coast," says David.

"Don't talk as if there's no solution," says Kimberly.

"I think maybe we're destroyed already," Ruth says dreamily. "I think maybe we're anachronisms. No, that's not what I mean. I mean relics. In some way we are already. Relics."

Eva raises her head from her folded arms on the table. Her curtain veil is pulled down over one eye; her makeup has leaked beyond its boundaries, so that her whole face is a patchy flower.

She says in a loud, stern voice, "I am not a relic," and they all laugh.

"Certainly not!" says Valerie, and then begins the yawning, the pushing back of chairs, the rather sheepish and formal smiles, the blowing out of candles: time to go home.

"Smell the river now!" Valerie tells them. Her voice sounds forlorn and tender, in the dark.

"A gibbous moon."

It was Roberta who told George what a gibbous moon was, and so his saying this is always an offering. It is an offering now, as they drive between the black cornfields.

"So there is."

Roberta doesn't reject the offering with silence, but she doesn't welcome it, either. She is polite. She yawns, and there is a private sound to her yawn. This isn't tactics, though she knows indifference is attractive. The real thing is. He can spot an imitation; he can always withstand tactics. She has to go all the way, to where she doesn't care. Then he feels how light and distant she is and his love revives. She has power. But the minute she begins to value it, it will begin to leave her. So she is thinking, as she yawns and wavers on the edge of caring and not caring. She'd stay on this edge if she could.

The half-ton truck bearing George and Roberta, with Eva and Angela in the back, is driving down the third concession road of Weymouth Township, known locally as the Telephone Road. It is a gravel road, fairly wide and well travelled. They turned onto it from the River Road, a much narrower road, which runs past Valerie's place. From the corner of the River Road to George's gate is a distance of about two and a quarter miles. Two side roads cut this stretch of the Telephone Road at right angles. Both these roads have stop signs; the Telephone Road is a through road. The first crossroad they have already passed. Along the second crossroad, from the west, a dark-green 1969 Dodge is travelling at between eighty and ninety miles an hour. Two young men are returning from a party to their home in Logan. One has passed out. The other is driving.

He hasn't remembered to put the lights on. He sees the road by the light of the moon.

There isn't time to say a word. Roberta doesn't scream. George doesn't touch the brake. The big car flashes before them, a huge, dark flash, without lights, seemingly without sound. It comes out of the dark corn and fills the air right in front of them the way a big flat fish will glide into view suddenly in an aquarium tank. It seems to be no more than a yard in front of their headlights. Then it's gone—it has disappeared into the corn on the other side of the road. They drive on. They drive on down the Telephone Road and turn in to the lane and come to a stop and are sitting in the truck in the yard in front of the dark shape of the half-improved house. What they feel is not terror or thanksgiving—not yet. What they feel is strangeness. They feel as strange, as flattened out and borne aloft, as unconnected with previous and future events as the ghost car was, the black fish. The shaggy branches of the pine trees are moving overhead, and under those branches the moonlight comes clear on the hesitant grass of their new lawn.

"Are you guys dead?" Eva says, rousing them. "Aren't we home?"

෨ The Moons of Jupiter ෨

I FOUND MY FATHER in the heart wing, on the eighth floor of Toronto General Hospital. He was in a semi-private room. The other bed was empty. He said that his hospital insurance covered only a bed in the ward, and he was worried that he might be charged extra.

"I never asked for a semi-private," he said.

I said the wards were probably full.

"No. I saw some empty beds when they were wheeling me by."

"Then it was because you had to be hooked up to that thing," I said. "Don't worry. If they're going to charge you extra, they tell you about it."

"That's likely it," he said. "They wouldn't want those doohickeys set up in the wards. I guess I'm covered for that kind of thing."

I said I was sure he was.

He had wires taped to his chest. A small screen hung over his head. On the screen a bright jagged line was continually being written. The writing was accompanied by a nervous electronic beeping. The behavior of his heart was on display. I tried to ignore it. It seemed to me that paying such close attention—in fact, dramatizing what ought to be a most secret activity—was asking for trouble. Anything exposed that way was apt to flare up and go crazy.

My father did not seem to mind. He said they had him on tranquillizers. You know, he said, the happy pills. He did seem calm and optimistic.

It had been a different story the night before. When I brought him into the hospital, to the emergency room, he had been pale and closemouthed. He had opened the car door and stood up and said quietly, "Maybe you better get me one of those wheelchairs." He used the voice he always used in a crisis. Once, our chimney caught on fire; it was on a Sunday afternoon and I was in the dining room pinning together a dress I was making. He came in and said in that same matter-of-fact, warning voice, "Janet. Do you know where there's some baking powder?" He wanted it to throw on the fire. Afterwards he said, "I guess it was your fault—sewing on Sunday."

I had to wait for over an hour in the emergency waiting room. They summoned a heart specialist who was in the hospital, a young man. He called me out into the hall and explained to me that one of the valves of my father's heart had deteriorated so badly that there ought to be an immediate operation.

I asked him what would happen otherwise.

"He'd have to stay in bed," the doctor said.

"How long?"

"Maybe three months."

"I meant, how long would he live?"

"That's what I meant too," the doctor said.

I went to see my father. He was sitting up in bed in a curtained-off corner. "It's bad, isn't it?" he said. "Did he tell you about the valve?"

"It's not as bad as it could be," I said. Then I repeated, even exaggerated, anything hopeful the doctor had said. "You're not in any immediate danger. Your physical condition is good, otherwise."

"Otherwise," said my father gloomily.

I was tired from the drive—all the way up to Dalgleish, to get him, and back to Toronto since noon—and worried about getting the rented car back on time, and irritated by an article I had been reading in a magazine in the waiting room. It was about another writer, a woman younger, better-looking, probably more talented than I am. I had been in England for two months and so I had not seen this article before, but it crossed my mind while I was reading that my father would have. I could hear him saying, Well, I didn't see anything about you in *Maclean's.* And if he had read something about me he would say, Well, I didn't think too much of that write-up. His tone would be humorous and indulgent but would produce in me a familiar dreariness of spirit. The message I got from him was simple: Fame must be striven for, then apologized for. Getting or not getting it, you will be to blame.

I was not surprised by the doctor's news. I was prepared to hear something of the sort and was pleased with myself for taking it calmly, just as I would be pleased with myself for dressing a wound or looking down from the frail balcony of a high building. I thought, Yes, it's time; there has to be something, here it is. I did not feel any of the protest I would have felt twenty, even ten, years before. When I saw from my father's face that he felt it—that refusal leapt up in him as readily as if he had been thirty or forty years younger—my heart hardened, and I spoke with a kind of badgering cheerfulness. "Otherwise is plenty," I said.

The next day he was himself again.

That was how I would have put it. He said it appeared to him now that the young fellow, the doctor, might have been a bit too eager to operate. "A bit knife-happy," he said. He was both mocking and showing off the hospital slang. He said that another doctor had examined him, an older man, and had given it as his opinion that rest and medication might do the trick.

I didn't ask what trick.

"He says I've got a defective valve, all right. There's certainly some damage. They wanted to know if I had rheumatic fever when I was a kid. I said I didn't think so. But half the time then you weren't diagnosed what you had. My father was not one for getting the doctor."

The thought of my father's childhood, which I always pictured as bleak and dangerous—the poor farm, the scared sisters, the harsh father—made me less resigned to his dying. I thought of him running away to work on the lake boats, running along the railway tracks, toward Goderich, in the evening light. He used to tell about that trip. Somewhere along the track he found a quince tree. Quince trees are rare in our part of the country; in fact, I have never seen one. Not even the one my father found, though he once took us on an expedition to look for it. He thought he knew the crossroad it was near, but we could not find it. He had not been able to eat the fruit, of course, but he had been impressed by its existence. It made him think he had got into a new part of the world.

The escaped child, the survivor, an old man trapped here by his leaky heart. I didn't pursue these thoughts. I didn't care to think of his younger selves. Even his bare torso, thick and white —he had the body of a working-man of his generation, seldom exposed to the sun—was a danger to me; it looked so strong and young. The wrinkled neck, the age-freckled hands and arms, the narrow, courteous head, with its thin gray hair and mustache, were more what I was used to.

"Now, why would I want to get myself operated on?" said my father reasonably. "Think of the risk at my age, and what for? A few years at the outside. I think the best thing for me to do is go home and take it easy. Give in gracefully. That's all you can do, at my age. Your attitude changes, you know. You go through some mental changes. It seems more natural."

"What does?" I said.

"Well, death does. You can't get more natural than that. No, what I mean, specifically, is not having the operation."

"That seems more natural?"

"Yes."

"It's up to you," I said, but I did approve. This was what I would have expected of him. Whenever I told people about my father I stressed his independence, his self-sufficiency, his for-bearance. He worked in a factory, he worked in his garden, he read history books. He could tell you about the Roman emperors or the Balkan wars. He never made a fuss.

Judith, my younger daughter, had come to meet me at Toronto Airport two days before. She had brought the boy she was liv-ing with, whose name was Don. They were driving to Mexico in the morning, and while I was in Toronto I was to stay in their apartment. For the time being, I live in Vancouver. I sometimes say I have my headquarters in Vancouver.

"Where's Nichola?" I said, thinking at once of an accident

or an overdose. Nichola is my older daughter. She used to be a student at the Conservatory, then she became a cocktail waitress, then she was out of work. If she had been at the airport, I would probably have said something wrong. I would have asked her what her plans were, and she would have gracefully brushed back her hair and said, "Plans?"—as if that was a word I had invented.

"I knew the first thing you'd say would be about Nichola," Judith said.

"It wasn't. I said hello and I—"

"We'll get your bag," Don said neutrally.

"Is she all right?"

"I'm sure she is," said Judith, with a fabricated air of amusement. "You wouldn't look like that if I was the one who wasn't here."

"Of course I would."

"You wouldn't. Nichola is the baby of the family. You know, she's four years older than I am."

"I ought to know."

Judith said she did not know where Nichola was exactly. She said Nichola had moved out of her apartment (that dump!) and had actually telephoned (which is quite a deal, you might say, Nichola phoning) to say she wanted to be incommunicado for a while but she was fine.

"I told her you would worry," said Judith more kindly on the way to their van. Don walked ahead carrying my suitcase. "But don't. She's all right, believe me."

Don's presence made me uncomfortable. I did not like him to hear these things. I thought of the conversations they must have had, Don and Judith. Or Don and Judith and Nichola, for Nichola and Judith were sometimes on good terms. Or Don and Judith and Nichola and others whose names I did not even know. They would have talked about me. Judith and Nichola comparing notes, relating anecdotes; analyzing, regretting, blaming, forgiving. I wished I'd had a boy and a girl. Or two boys. They wouldn't have done that. Boys couldn't possibly know so much about you.

I did the same thing at that age. When I was the age Judith

is now I talked with my friends in the college cafeteria or, late at night, over coffee in our cheap rooms. When I was the age Nichola is now I had Nichola herself in a carry-cot or squirming in my lap, and I was drinking coffee again all the rainy Vancouver afternoons with my one neighborhood friend, Ruth Boudreau, who read a lot and was bewildered by her situation, as I was. We talked about our parents, our childhoods, though for some time we kept clear of our marriages. How thoroughly we dealt with our fathers and mothers, deplored their marriages, their mistaken ambitions or fear of ambition, how competently we filed them away, defined them beyond any possibility of change. What presumption.

I looked at Don walking ahead. A tall ascetic-looking boy, with a St. Francis cap of black hair, a precise fringe of beard. What right did he have to hear about me, to know things I myself had probably forgotten? I decided that his beard and hairstyle were affected.

Once, when my children were little, my father said to me, "You know those years you were growing up—well, that's all just a kind of a blur to me. I can't sort out one year from another." I was offended. I remembered each separate year with pain and clarity. I could have told how old I was when I went to look at the evening dresses in the window of Benbow's Ladies' Wear. Every week through the winter a new dress, spotlit—the sequins and tulle, the rose and lilac, sapphire, daffodil—and me a cold worshipper on the slushy sidewalk. I could have told how old I was when I forged my mother's signature on a bad report card, when I had measles, when we papered the front room. But the years when Judith and Nichola were little, when I lived with their father—yes, *blur* is the word for it. I remember hanging out diapers, bringing in and folding diapers; I can recall the kitchen counters of two houses and where the clothesbasket sat. I remember the television programs—*Popeye the Sailor*, *The Three Stooges*, *Funorama*. When *Funorama* came on it was time to turn on the lights and cook supper. But I couldn't tell the years apart. We lived outside Vancouver in a dormitory suburb: Dormir, Dormer, Dormouse —something like that. I was sleepy all the time then; pregnancy made me sleepy, and the night feedings, and the west coast rain falling. Dark dripping cedars, shiny dripping laurel; wives yawning, napping, visiting, drinking coffee, and folding diapers; husbands coming home at night from the city across the water. Every night I kissed my homecoming husband in his wet Burberry and hoped he might wake me up; I served up meat and potatoes and one of the four vegetables he permitted. He ate with a violent appetite, then fell asleep on the living-room sofa. We had become a cartoon couple, more middle-aged in our twenties than we would be in middle age.

Those bumbling years are the years our children will remember all their lives. Corners of the yards I never visited will stay in their heads.

"Did Nichola not want to see me?" I said to Judith.

"She doesn't want to see anybody, half the time," she said. Judith moved ahead and touched Don's arm. I knew that touch—an apology, an anxious reassurance. You touch a man that way to remind him that you are grateful, that you realize he is doing for your sake something that bores him or slightly endangers his dignity. It made me feel older than grandchildren would to see my daughter touch a man—a boy—this way. I felt her sad jitters, could predict her supple attentions. My blunt and stocky, blond and candid child. Why should I think she wouldn't be susceptible, that she would always be straightforward, heavy-footed, self-reliant? Just as I go around saying that Nichola is sly and solitary, cold, seductive. Many people must know things that would contradict what I say.

In the morning Don and Judith left for Mexico. I decided I wanted to see somebody who wasn't related to me, and who didn't expect anything in particular from me. I called an old lover of mine, but his phone was answered by a machine: "This is Tom Shepherd speaking. I will be out of town for the month of September. Please record your message, name, and phone number."

Tom's voice sounded so pleasant and familiar that I opened my mouth to ask him the meaning of this foolishness. Then I hung up. I felt as if he had deliberately let me down, as if we had planned to meet in a public place and then he hadn't shown up. Once, he had done that, I remembered.

I got myself a glass of vermouth, though it was not yet noon, and I phoned my father.

"Well, of all things," he said. "Fifteen more minutes and you would have missed me."

"Were you going downtown?"

"Downtown Toronto."

He explained that he was going to the hospital. His doctor in Dalgleish wanted the doctors in Toronto to take a look at him, and had given him a letter to show them in the emergency room.

"Emergency room?" I said.

"It's not an emergency. He just seems to think this is the best way to handle it. He knows the name of a fellow there. If he was to make me an appointment, it might take weeks."

"Does your doctor know you're driving to Toronto?" I said.

"Well, he didn't say I couldn't."

The upshot of this was that I rented a car, drove to Dalgleish, brought my father back to Toronto, and had him in the emergency room by seven o'clock that evening.

Before Judith left I said to her, "You're sure Nichola knows I'm staying here?"

"Well, I told her," she said.

Sometimes the phone rang, but it was always a friend of Judith's.

"Well, it looks like I'm going to have it," my father said. This was on the fourth day. He had done a complete turnaround overnight. "It looks like I might as well."

I didn't know what he wanted me to say. I thought perhaps he looked to me for a protest, an attempt to dissuade him.

"When will they do it?" I said.

"Day after tomorrow."

I said I was going to the washroom. I went to the nurses' station and found a woman there who I thought was the head nurse. At any rate, she was gray-haired, kind, and serious-looking.

"My father's having an operation the day after tomorrow?" I said.

"Oh, yes."

"I just wanted to talk to somebody about it. I thought there'd been a sort of decision reached that he'd be better not to. I thought because of his age."

"Well, it's his decision and the doctor's." She smiled at me without condescension. "It's hard to make these decisions."

"How were his tests?"

"Well, I haven't seen them all."

I was sure she had. After a moment she said, "We have to be realistic. But the doctors here are very good."

When I went back into the room my father said, in a surprised voice, "*Shore*-less seas."

"What?" I said. I wondered if he had found out how much, or how little, time he could hope for. I wondered if the pills had brought on an untrustworthy euphoria. Or if he had wanted to gamble. Once, when he was talking to me about his life, he said, "The trouble was I was always afraid to take chances."

I used to tell people that he never spoke regretfully about his life, but that was not true. It was just that I didn't listen to it. He said that he should have gone into the Army as a tradesman—he would have been better off. He said he should have gone on his own, as a carpenter, after the war. He should have got out of Dalgleish. Once, he said, "A wasted life, eh?" But he was making fun of himself, saying that, because it was such a dramatic thing to say. When he quoted poetry too, he always had a scoffing note in his voice, to excuse the showing-off and the pleasure.

"Shoreless seas," he said again. "'Behind him lay the gray Azores, / Behind the Gates of Hercules; / Before him not the ghost of shores, / Before him only shoreless seas.' That's what was going through my head last night. But do you think I could remember what kind of seas? I could not. Lonely seas? Empty seas? I was on the right track but I couldn't get it. But there now when you came into the room and I wasn't thinking about it at all, the word popped into my head. That's always the way, isn't it? It's not all that surprising. I ask my mind a question. The answer's there, but I can't see all the connections my mind's making to get it. Like a computer. Nothing out of the way. You know, in my situation the thing is, if there's anything you can't explain right away, there's a great temptation to—well, to make a mystery out of it. There's a great temptation to believe in—You know."

"The soul?" I said, speaking lightly, feeling an appalling rush of love and recognition.

"Oh, I guess you could call it that. You know, when I first came into this room there was a pile of papers here by the bed. Somebody had left them here—one of those tabloid sort of things I never looked at. I started reading them. I'll read anything handy. There was a series running in them on personal experiences of people who had died, medically speaking—heart arrest, mostly—and had been brought back to life. It was what they remembered of the time when they were dead. Their experiences."

"Pleasant or un-?" I said.

"Oh, pleasant. Oh, yes. They'd float up to the ceiling and look down on themselves and see the doctors working on them, on their bodies. Then float on further and recognize some people they knew who had died before them. Not see them exactly but sort of sense them. Sometimes there would be a humming and sometimes a sort of—what's that light that there is or color around a person?"

"Aura?"

"Yes. But without the person. That's about all they'd get time for; then they found themselves back in the body and feeling all the mortal pain and so on—brought back to life."

"Did it seem—convincing?"

"Oh, I don't know. It's all in whether you want to believe that kind of thing or not. And if you are going to believe it, take it seriously, I figure you've got to take everything else seriously that they print in those papers."

"What else do they?"

"Rubbish—cancer cures, baldness cures, bellyaching about the younger generation and the welfare bums. Tripe about movie stars."

"Oh, yes. I know."

"In my situation you have to keep a watch," he said, "or you'll start playing tricks on yourself." Then he said, "There's a few practical details we ought to get straight on," and he told me about his will, the house, the cemetery plot. Everything was simple.

"Do you want me to phone Peggy?" I said. Peggy is my sister. She is married to an astronomer and lives in Victoria.

He thought about it. "I guess we ought to tell them," he said finally. "But tell them not to get alarmed."

"All right."

"No, wait a minute. Sam is supposed to be going to a conference the end of this week, and Peggy was planning to go along with him. I don't want them wondering about changing their plans."

"Where is the conference?"

"Amsterdam," he said proudly. He did take pride in Sam, and kept track of his books and articles. He would pick one up and say, "Look at that, will you? And I can't understand a word of it!" in a marvelling voice that managed nevertheless to have a trace of ridicule.

"Professor Sam," he would say. "And the three little Sams." This is what he called his grandsons, who did resemble their father in braininess and in an almost endearing pushiness—an innocent energetic showing-off. They went to a private school that favored old-fashioned discipline and started calculus in Grade 5. "And the dogs," he might enumerate further, "who have been to obedience school. And Peggy . . ."

But if I said, "Do you suppose she has been to obedience school too?" he would play the game no further. I imagine that when he was with Sam and Peggy he spoke of me in the same way—hinted at my flightiness just as he hinted at their stodginess, made mild jokes at my expense, did not quite conceal his amazement (or pretended not to conceal his amazement) that people paid money for things I had written. He had to do this so that he might never seem to brag, but he would put up the gates when the joking got too rough. And of course I found later, in the house, things of mine he had kept—a few magazines, clippings, things I had never bothered about.

Now his thoughts travelled from Peggy's family to mine. "Have you heard from Judith?" he said.

"Not yet."

"Well, it's pretty soon. Were they going to sleep in the van?"

"Yes."

"I guess it's safe enough, if they stop in the right places."

I knew he would have to say something more and I knew it would come as a joke.

"I guess they put a board down the middle, like the pioneers?"

I smiled but did not answer.

"I take it you have no objections?"

"No," I said.

"Well, I always believed that too. Keep out of your children's business. I tried not to say anything. I never said anything when you left Richard."

"What do you mean, 'said anything'? Criticize?"

"It wasn't any of my business."

"No."

"But that doesn't mean I was pleased."

I was surprised—not just at what he said but at his feeling that he had any right, even now, to say it. I had to look out the window and down at the traffic to control myself.

"I just wanted you to know," he added.

A long time ago, he said to me in his mild way, "It's funny. Richard when I first saw him reminded me of what my father used to say. He'd say if that fellow was half as smart as he thinks he is, he'd be twice as smart as he really is."

I turned to remind him of this, but found myself looking at the line his heart was writing. Not that there seemed to be anything wrong, any difference in the beeps and points. But it was there.

He saw where I was looking. "Unfair advantage," he said.

"It is," I said. "I'm going to have to get hooked up too."

We laughed, we kissed formally; I left. At least he hadn't asked me about Nichola, I thought.

The next afternoon I didn't go to the hospital, because my father was having some more tests done, to prepare for the operation. I was to see him in the evening instead. I found myself wandering through the Bloor Street dress shops, trying on clothes. A preoccupation with fashion and my own appearance had descended on me like a raging headache. I looked at the women in the street, at the clothes in the shops, trying to discover how a transformation might be made, what I would have to buy. I recognized this obsession for what it was but had trouble shaking it. I've had people tell me that waiting for life-or-death news they've stood in front of an open refrigerator eating anything in sight—cold boiled potatoes, chili sauce, bowls of whipped cream. Or have been unable to stop doing crossword puzzles. Attention narrows in on something—some distraction—grabs on, becomes fanatically serious. I shuffled clothes on the racks, pulled them on in hot little changing rooms in front of cruel mirrors. I was sweating; once or twice I thought I might faint. Out on the street again, I thought I must remove myself from Bloor Street, and decided to go to the museum.

I remembered another time, in Vancouver. It was when Nichola was going to kindergarten and Judith was a baby. Nichola had been to the doctor about a cold, or maybe for a routine examination, and the blood test revealed something about her white blood cells—either that there were too many of them or that they were enlarged. The doctor ordered further tests, and I took Nichola to the hospital for them. Nobody mentioned leukemia but I knew, of course, what they were looking for. When I took Nichola home I asked the baby-sitter who had been with Judith to stay for the afternoon and I went shopping. I bought the most daring dress I ever owned, a black silk sheath with some laced-up arrangement in front. I remembered that bright spring afternoon, the spike-heeled shoes in the department store, the underwear printed with leopard spots.

I also remembered going home from St. Paul's Hospital over the Lions Gate Bridge on the crowded bus and holding Nichola on my knee. She suddenly recalled her baby name for *bridge* and whispered to me, "Whee—over the whee." I did not avoid touching my child—Nichola was slender and graceful even then, with a pretty back and fine dark hair—but realized I was touching her with a difference, though I did not think it could ever be detected. There was a care—not a withdrawal exactly but a care—not to feel anything much. I saw how the forms of love might be maintained with a condemned person but with the love in fact measured and disciplined, because you have to survive. It could be done so discreetly that the object of such care would not suspect, any more than she would suspect the sentence of death itself. Nichola did not know, would not know. Toys and kisses and jokes would come tumbling over her; she would never know, though I worried that she would feel the wind between the cracks of the manufactured holidays, the manufactured normal days. But all was well. Nichola did not have leukemia. She grew up—was still alive, and possibly happy. Incommunicado.

I could not think of anything in the museum I really wanted to see, so I walked past it to the planetarium. I had never been to a planetarium. The show was due to start in ten minutes. I went inside, bought a ticket, got in line. There was a whole class of schoolchildren, maybe a couple of classes, with teachers and volunteer mothers riding herd on them. I looked around to see if there were any other unattached adults. Only one—a man with a red face and puffy eyes, who looked as if he might be here to keep himself from going to a bar.

Inside, we sat on wonderfully comfortable seats that were tilted back so that you lay in a sort of hammock, attention directed to the bowl of the ceiling, which soon turned dark blue, with a faint rim of light all around the edge. There was some splendid, commanding music. The adults all around were shushing the children, trying to make them stop crackling their potato-chip bags. Then a man's voice, an eloquent professional voice, began to speak slowly, out of the walls. The voice reminded me a little of the way radio announcers used to introduce a piece of classical music or describe the progress of the Royal Family to Westminster Abbey on one of their royal occasions. There was a faint echo-chamber effect.

The dark ceiling was filling with stars. They came out not all at once but one after another, the way the stars really do come out at night, though more quickly. The Milky Way appeared, was moving closer; stars swam into brilliance and kept on going, disappearing beyond the edges of the sky-screen or behind my head. While the flow of light continued, the voice presented the stunning facts. A few light-years away, it announced, the sun appears as a bright star, and the planets are not visible. A few dozen light-years away, the sun is not visible, either, to the naked eye. And that distance—a few dozen light-years—is only about a thousandth part of the distance from the sun to the center of our galaxy, one galaxy, which itself contains abut two hundred billion suns. And is, in turn, one of millions, perhaps billions, of galaxies. Innumerable repetitions, innumerable variations. All this rolled past my head too, like balls of lightning.

Now realism was abandoned, for familiar artifice. A model of the solar system was spinning away in its elegant style. A bright bug took off from the earth, heading for Jupiter. I set my dodging and shrinking mind sternly to recording facts. The mass of Jupiter two and a half times that of all the other planets put together. The Great Red Spot. The thirteen moons. Past Jupiter, a glance at the eccentric orbit of Pluto, the icy rings of Saturn. Back to Earth and moving in to hot and dazzling Venus. Atmospheric pressure ninety times ours. Moonless Mercury rotating three times while circling the sun twice; an odd arrangement, not as satisfying as what they used to tell us—that it rotated once as it circled the sun. No perpetual darkness after all. Why did they give out such confident information, only to announce later that it was quite wrong? Finally, the picture already familiar from magazines: the red soil of Mars, the blooming pink sky.

When the show was over I sat in my seat while the children clambered across me, making no comments on anything they had just seen or heard. They were pestering their keepers for eatables and further entertainments. An effort had been made to get their attention, to take it away from canned pop and potato chips and fix it on various knowns and unknowns and horrible immensities, and it seemed to have failed. A good thing too, I thought. Children have a natural immunity, most of them, and it shouldn't be tampered with. As for the adults who would deplore it, the ones who promoted this show, weren't they immune themselves to the extent that they could put in the echo-chamber effects, the music, the churchlike solemnity, simulating the awe that they supposed they ought to feel? Awe—what was that supposed to be? A fit of the shivers when you looked out the window? Once you know what it was, you wouldn't be courting it.

Two men came with brooms to sweep up the debris the audience had left behind. They told me that the next show would start in forty minutes. In the meantime, I had to get out.

"I went to the show at the planetarium," I said to my father. "It was very exciting—about the solar system." I thought what a silly word I had used: *exciting*. "It's like a slightly phony temple," I added.

He was already talking. "I remember when they found Pluto. Right where they thought it had to be. Mercury, Venus, Earth, Mars," he recited. "Jupiter, Saturn, Nept—no, Uranus, Neptune, Pluto. Is that right?"

"Yes," I said. I was just as glad he hadn't heard what I said about the phony temple. I had meant that to be truthful, but it sounded slick and superior. "Tell me the moons of Jupiter."

"Well, I don't know the new ones. There's a bunch of new ones, isn't there?"

"Two. But they're not new."

"New to us," said my father. "You've turned pretty cheeky now I'm going under the knife."

"'Under the knife.' What an expression."

He was not in bed tonight, his last night. He had been detached from his apparatus, and was sitting in a chair by the window. He was bare-legged, wearing a hospital dressing gown, but he did not look self-conscious or out of place. He looked thoughtful but good-humored, an affable host.

"You haven't even named the old ones," I said.

"Give me time. Galileo named them. Io."

"That's a start."

"The moons of Jupiter were the first heavenly bodies discovered with the telescope." He said this gravely, as if he could see the sentence in an old book. "It wasn't Galileo named them, either; it was some German. Io, Europa, Ganymede, Callisto. There you are."

"Yes."

"Io and Europa, they were girlfriends of Jupiter's, weren't they? Ganymede was a boy. A shepherd? I don't know who Callisto was."

"I think she was a girlfriend too," I said. "Jupiter's wife—Jove's wife—changed her into a bear and stuck her up in the sky. Great Bear and Little Bear. Little Bear was her baby."

The loudspeaker said that it was time for visitors to go.

"I'll see you when you come out of the anesthetic," I said.

"Yes."

When I was at the door, he called to me, "Ganymede wasn't any shepherd. He was Jove's cupbearer."

When I left the planetarium that afternoon, I had walked through the museum to the Chinese garden. I saw the stone camels again, the warriors, the tomb. I sat on a bench looking toward Bloor Street. Through the evergreen bushes and the high grilled iron fence I watched people going by in the late-afternoon sunlight. The planetarium show had done what I wanted it to after all—calmed me down, drained me. I saw a girl who reminded me of Nichola. She wore a trenchcoat and carried a bag of groceries. She was shorter than Nichola—not really much like her at all—but I thought that I might see Nichola. She would be walking along some street maybe not far from here—burdened, preoccupied, alone. She was one of the grown-up people in the world now, one of the shoppers going home.

If I did see her, I might just sit and watch, I decided. I felt like one of those people who have floated up to the ceiling, enjoying a brief death. A relief, while it lasts. My father had chosen and Nichola had chosen. Someday, probably soon, I would hear from her, but it came to the same thing.

I meant to get up and go over to the tomb, to look at the relief carvings, the stone pictures, that go all the way around it. I always mean to look at them and I never do. Not this time, either. It was getting cold out, so I went inside to have coffee and something to eat before I went back to the hospital.

✄ *The Progress of Love* ✄

I GOT A CALL AT work, and it was my father. This was not long after I was divorced and started in the real-estate office. Both of my boys were in school. It was a hot enough day in September.

My father was so polite, even in the family. He took time to ask me how I was. Country manners. Even if somebody phones up to tell you your house is burning down, they ask first how you are.

"I'm fine," I said. "How are you?"

"Not so good, I guess," said my father, in his old way—apologetic but self-respecting. "I think your mother's gone."

I knew that *gone* meant *dead*. I knew that. But for a second or so I saw my mother in her black straw hat setting off down the lane. The word *gone* seemed full of nothing but a deep relief and even an excitement—the excitement you feel when a door closes and your house sinks back to normal and you let yourself loose into all the free space around you. That was in my father's voice too—behind the apology, a queer sound like a gulped breath. But my mother hadn't been a burden—she hadn't been sick a day—and far from feeling relieved at her death, my father took it hard. He never got used to living alone, he said. He went into the Netterfield County Home quite willingly.

He told me how he found my mother on the couch in the kitchen when he came in at noon. She had picked a few tomatoes, and was setting them on the windowsill to ripen; then she must have felt weak, and lain down. Now, telling this, his voice went wobbly—meandering, as you would expect—in his amazement. I saw in my mind the couch, the old quilt that protected it, right under the phone.

"So I thought I better call you," my father said, and he waited for me to say what he should do now.

My mother prayed on her knees at midday, at night, and first thing in the morning. Every day opened up to her to have God's will done in it. Every night she totted up what she'd done and said and thought, to see how it squared with Him. That kind of life is dreary, people think, but they're missing the point. For one thing, such a life can never be boring. And nothing can happen to you that you can't make use of. Even if you're wracked by troubles, and sick and poor and ugly, you've got your soul to carry through life like a treasure on a platter. Going upstairs to pray after the noon meal, my mother would be full of energy and expectation, seriously smiling.

She was saved at a camp meeting when she was fourteen. That was the same summer that her own mother—my grandmother—died. For a few years, my mother went to meetings with a lot of other people who'd been saved, some who'd been saved over and over again, enthusiastic old sinners. She could tell stories about what went on at those meetings, the singing and hollering and wildness. She told about one old man getting up and shouting, "Come down, O Lord, come down among us now! Come down through the roof and I'll pay for the shingles!"

She was back to being just an Anglican, a serious one, by the time she got married. She was twenty-five then, and my father was thirty-eight. A tall good-looking couple, good dancers, good cardplayers, sociable. But serious people—that's how I would try to describe them. Serious the way hardly anybody is anymore. My father was not religious in the way my mother was. He was an Anglican, an Orangeman, a Conservative, because that's what he had been brought up to be. He was the son who got left on the farm with his parents and took care of them till they died. He met my mother, he waited for her, they married; he thought himself lucky then to have a family to work for. (I have two brothers, and I had a baby sister who died.) I have a feeling that my father never slept with any woman before my mother, and never with her until he married her. And he had to wait, because my mother wouldn't get married until she had paid back to her own father every cent he had spent on her since her mother died. She had kept track of everything—board, books, clothes—so that she could pay it back. When she married, she had no nest egg, as teachers usually did, no hope chest, sheets, or dishes. My father used to say, with a sombre, joking face, that he had hoped to get a woman with money in the bank. "But you take the money in the bank, you have to take the face that goes with it," he said, "and sometimes that's no bargain."

The house we lived in had big, high rooms, with dark-green blinds on the windows. When the blinds were pulled down against the sun, I used to like to move my head and catch the light flashing through the holes and cracks. Another thing I liked looking at was chimney stains, old or fresh, which I could turn into animals, people's faces, even distant cities. I told my own two boys about that, and their father, Dan Casey, said, "See, your mom's folks were so poor, they couldn't afford TV, so they got these stains on the ceiling—your mom had to watch the stains on the ceiling!" He always liked to kid me about thinking poor was anything great.

When my father was very old, I figured out that he didn't mind people doing new sorts of things—for instance, my getting divorced—as much as he minded them having new sorts of reasons for doing them.

Thank God he never had to know about the commune.

"The Lord never intended," he used to say. Sitting around with the other old men in the Home, in the long, dim porch behind the spirea bushes, he talked about how the Lord never intended for people to tear around the country on motorbikes and snowmobiles. And how the Lord never intended for nurses' uniforms to be pants. The nurses didn't mind at all. They called him "Handsome," and told me he was a real old sweetheart, a real old religious gentleman. They marvelled at his thick black hair, which he kept until he died. They washed and combed it beautifully, wet-waved it with their fingers.

Sometimes, with all their care, he was a little unhappy. He wanted to go home. He worried about the cows, the fences, about who was getting up to light the fire. A few flashes of meanness—very few. Once, he gave me a sneaky, unfriendly look when I went in; he said, "I'm surprised you haven't worn all the skin off your knees by now."

I laughed. I said, "What doing? Scrubbing floors?"

"Praying!" he said, in a voice like spitting.

He didn't know who he was talking to.

I don't remember my mother's hair being anything but white. My mother went white in her twenties, and never saved any of her young hair, which had been brown. I used to try to get her to tell what color brown.

"Dark."

"Like Brent, or like Dolly?" Those were two workhorses we had, a team.

"I don't know. It wasn't horsehair."

"Was it like chocolate?"

"Something like."

"Weren't you sad when it went white?"

"No. I was glad."

"Why?"

"I was glad that I wouldn't have hair anymore that was the same color as my father's."

Hatred is always a sin, my mother told me. Remember that. One drop of hatred in your soul will spread and discolor everything like a drop of black ink in white milk. I was struck by that and meant to try it, but knew I shouldn't waste the milk.

All these things I remember. All the things I know, or have been told, about people I never even saw. I was named Euphemia, after my mother's mother. A terrible name, such as nobody has nowadays. At home they called me Phemie, but when I started to work, I called myself Fame. My husband, Dan Casey, called me Fame. Then in the bar of the Shamrock Hotel, years later, after my divorce, when I was going out, a man said to me, "Fame, I've been meaning to ask you, just what is it you are famous for?"

"I don't know," I told him. "I don't know, unless it's for wasting my time talking to jerks like you."

After that I thought of changing it altogether, to something like Joan, but unless I moved away from here, how could I do that?

In the summer of 1947, when I was twelve, I helped my mother paper the downstairs bedroom, the spare room. My mother's sister, Beryl, was coming to visit us. These two sisters hadn't seen each other for years. Very soon after their mother died, their father married again. He went to live in Minneapolis, then in Seattle, with his new wife and his younger daughter, Beryl. My mother wouldn't go with them. She stayed on in the town of Ramsay, where they had been living. She was boarded with a childless couple who had been neighbors. She and Beryl had met only once or twice since they were grown up. Beryl lived in California.

The paper had a design of cornflowers on a white ground. My mother had got it at a reduced price, because it was the end of a lot. This meant we had trouble matching the pattern, and behind the door we had to do some tricky fitting with scraps and strips. This was before the days of pre-pasted wallpaper. We had a trestle table set up in the front room, and we mixed the paste and swept it onto the back of the paper with wide brushes, watching for lumps. We worked with the windows up, screens fitted under them, the front door open, the screen door closed. The country we could see through the mesh of screens and the wavery old window glass was all hot and flowering—milkweed and wild carrot in the pastures, mustard rampaging in the clover, some fields creamy with the buckwheat people grew then. My mother sang. She sang a song she said her own mother used to sing when she and Beryl were little girls.

"I once had a sweetheart, but now I have none.
He's gone and he's left me to weep and to moan.
He's gone and he's left me, but contented I'll be,
For I'll get another one, better than he!"

I was excited because Beryl was coming, a visitor, all the way from California. Also because I had gone to town in late June to write the Entrance Examinations, and was hoping to hear soon that I had passed with honors. Everybody who had finished Grade 8 in the country schools had to go into town to write those examinations. I loved that—the rustling sheets of foolscap, the important silence, the big stone high-school building, all the old initials carved in the desks, darkened with varnish. The first burst of summer outside, the green and yellow light, the townlike chestnut trees, and honeysuckle. And all it was was this same town, where I have lived now more than half my life. I wondered at it. And at myself, drawing maps with ease and solving problems, knowing quantities of answers. I thought I was so clever. But I wasn't clever enough to understand the simplest thing. I didn't even understand that examinations made no difference in my case. I wouldn't be going to high school. How could I? That was before there were school buses; you had to board in town. My parents didn't have the money. They operated on very little cash, as many farmers did then. The payments from the cheese factory were about all that came in regularly. And they didn't think of my life going in that direction, the high-school direction. They thought that I would stay at home and help my mother, maybe hire out to help women in the neighborhood who were sick or having a baby. Until such time as I got married. That was what they were waiting to tell me when I got the results of the examinations.

You would think my mother might have a different idea, since she had been a schoolteacher herself. But she said God didn't care. God isn't interested in what kind of job or what kind of education anybody has, she told me. He doesn't care two hoots about that, and it's what He cares about that matters.

This was the first time I understood how God could become a real opponent, not just some kind of nuisance or large decoration.

My mother's name as a child was Marietta. That continued to be her name, of course, but until Beryl came I never heard her called by it. My father always said Mother. I had a childish notion—I knew it was childish—that Mother suited my mother better than it did other mothers. Mother, not Mama. When I was away from her, I could not think what my mother's face was like, and this frightened me. Sitting in school, just over a hill from home, I would try to picture my mother's face. Sometimes I thought that if I couldn't do it, that might mean my mother was dead. But I had a sense of her all the time, and would be reminded of her by the most unlikely things—an upright piano, or a tall white loaf of bread. That's ridiculous, but true.

Marietta, in my mind, was separate, not swallowed up in my mother's grown-up body. Marietta was still running around loose up in her town of Ramsay, on the Ottawa River. In that town, the streets were full of horses and puddles, and darkened by men who came in from the bush on weekends. Loggers. There were eleven hotels on the main street, where the loggers stayed, and drank.

The house Marietta lived in was halfway up a steep street climbing from the river. It was a double house, with two bay windows in front, and a wooden trellis that separated the two front porches. In the other half of the house lived the Sutcliffes, the people Marietta was to board with after her mother died and her father left town. Mr. Sutcliffe was an Englishman, a telegraph operator. His wife was German. She always made coffee instead of tea. She made strudel. The dough for the strudel hung down over the edges of the table like a fine cloth. It sometimes looked to Marietta like a skin.

Mrs. Sutcliffe was the one who talked Marietta's mother out of hanging herself.

Marietta was home from school that day, because it was Saturday. She woke up late and heard the silence in the house. She was always scared of that—a silent house—and as soon as she opened the door after school she would call, "Mama! Mama!" Often her mother wouldn't answer. But she would be there. Marietta would hear with relief the rattle of the stove grate or the steady slap of the iron.

That morning, she didn't hear anything. She came downstairs, and got herself a slice of bread and butter and molasses, folded over. She opened the cellar door and called. She went into the front room and peered out the window, through the bridal fern. She saw her little sister, Beryl, and some other neighborhood children rolling down the bit of grassy terrace to the sidewalk, picking themselves up and scrambling to the top and rolling down again.

"Mama?" called Marietta. She walked through the house to the back yard. It was late spring, the day was cloudy and mild. In the sprouting vegetable gardens, the earth was damp, and the leaves on the trees seemed suddenly full-sized, letting down drops of water left over from the rain of the night before.

"Mama?" calls Marietta under the trees, under the clothes-line.

At the end of the yard is a small barn, where they keep fire-wood, and some tools and old furniture. A chair, a straight-backed wooden chair, can be seen through the open doorway. On the chair, Marietta sees her mother's feet, her mother's black laced shoes. Then the long, printed cotton summer work dress, the apron, the rolled-up sleeves. Her mother's shiny-looking white arms, and neck, and face.

Her mother stood on the chair and didn't answer. She didn't look at Marietta, but smiled and tapped her foot, as if to say, "Here I am, then. What are you going to do about it?" Something looked wrong about her, beyond the fact that she was standing on a chair and smiling in this queer, tight way. Standing on an old chair with back rungs missing, which she had pulled out to the middle of the barn floor, where it teetered on the bumpy earth. There was a shadow on her neck.

The shadow was a rope, a noose on the end of a rope that hung down from a beam overhead.

"Mama?" says Marietta, in a fainter voice. "Mama. Come down, please." Her voice is faint because she fears that any yell or cry might jolt her mother into movement, cause her to step off the chair and throw her weight on the rope. But even if Marietta wanted to yell she couldn't. Nothing but this pitiful thread of a voice is left to her—just as in a dream when a beast or a machine is bearing down on you.

"Go and get your father."

That was what her mother told her to do, and Marietta obeyed. With terror in her legs, she ran. In her nightgown, in the middle of a Saturday morning, she ran. She ran past Beryl and the other children, still tumbling down the slope. She ran along the sidewalk, which was at that time a boardwalk, then on the unpaved street, full of last night's puddles. The street crossed the railway tracks. At the foot of the hill, it intersected the main street of the town. Between the main street and the river were some warehouses and the buildings of small manufacturers. That was where Marietta's father had his carriage works. Wagons, buggies, sleds were made there. In fact, Marietta's father had invented a new sort of sled to carry logs in the bush. It had been patented. He was just getting started in Ramsay. (Later on, in the States, he made money. A man fond of hotel bars, barbershops, harness races, women, but not afraid of work—give him credit.)

Marietta did not find him at work that day. The office was empty. She ran out into the yard where the men were working. She stumbled in the fresh sawdust. The men laughed and shook their heads at her. No. Not here. Not a-here right now. No. Why don't you try upstreet? Wait. Wait a minute. Hadn't you better get some clothes on first?

They didn't mean any harm. They didn't have the sense to see that something must be wrong. But Marietta never could stand men laughing. There were always places she hated to go past, let alone into, and that was the reason. Men laughing. Because of that, she hated barbershops, hated their smell. (When she started going to dances later on with my father, she asked him not to put any dressing on his hair, because the smell reminded her.) A bunch of men standing out on the street, outside a hotel, seemed to Marietta like a clot of poison. You tried not to hear what they were saying, but you could be sure it was vile. If they didn't say anything, they laughed and vileness spread out from them—poison—just the same. It was only after Marietta was saved that she could walk right past them. Armed by God, she walked through their midst and nothing stuck to her, nothing scorched her; she was safe as Daniel.

Now she turned and ran, straight back the way she had

come. Up the hill, running to get home. She thought she had made a mistake leaving her mother. Why did her mother tell her to go? Why did she want her father? Quite possibly so that she could greet him with the sight of her own warm body swinging on the end of a rope. Marietta should have stayed—she should have stayed and talked her mother out of it. She should have run to Mrs. Sutcliffe, or any neighbor, not wasted time this way. She hadn't thought who could help, who could even believe what she was talking about. She had the idea that all families except her own lived in peace, that threats and miseries didn't exist in other people's houses, and couldn't be explained there.

A train was coming into town. Marietta had to wait. Passengers looked out at her from its windows. She broke out wailing in the faces of those strangers. When the train passed, she continued up the hill—a spectacle, with her hair uncombed, her feet bare and muddy, in her nightgown, with a wild, wet face. By the time she ran into her own yard, in sight of the barn, she was howling. "Mama!" she was howling. "Mama!"

Nobody was there. The chair was standing just where it had been before. The rope was dangling over the back of it. Marietta was sure that her mother had gone ahead and done it. Her mother was already dead—she had been cut down and taken away.

But warm, fat hands settled down on her shoulders, and Mrs. Sutcliffe said, "Marietta. Stop the noise. Marietta. Child. Stop the crying. Come inside. She is well, Marietta. Come inside and you will see."

Mrs. Sutcliffe's foreign voice said, "Mari-et-cha," giving the name a rich, important sound. She was as kind as could be. When Marietta lived with the Sutcliffes later, she was treated as the daughter of the household, and it was a household just as peaceful and comfortable as she had imagined other households to be. But she never felt like a daughter there.

In Mrs. Sutcliffe's kitchen, Beryl sat on the floor eating a raisin cookie and playing with the black-and-white cat, whose name was Dickie. Marietta's mother sat at the table, with a cup of coffee in front of her.

"She was silly," Mrs. Sutcliffe said. Did she mean Marietta's mother or Marietta herself? She didn't have many English words to describe things.

Marietta's mother laughed, and Marietta blacked out. She fainted, after running all that way uphill, howling, in the warm, damp morning. Next thing she knew, she was taking black, sweet coffee from a spoon held by Mrs. Sutcliffe. Beryl picked Dickie up by the front legs and offered him as a cheering present. Marietta's mother was still sitting at the table.

Her heart was broken. That was what I always heard my mother say. That was the end of it. Those words lifted up the story and sealed it shut. I never asked, Who broke it? I never asked. What was the men's poison talk? What was the meaning of the word *vile?*

Marietta's mother laughed after not hanging herself. She sat at Mrs. Sutcliffe's kitchen table long ago and laughed. Her heart was broken.

I always had a feeling, with my mother's talk and stories, of something swelling out behind. Like a cloud you couldn't see through, or get to the end of. There was a cloud, a poison, that had touched my mother's life. And when I grieved my mother, I became part of it. Then I would beat my head against my mother's stomach and breasts, against her tall, firm front, demanding to be forgiven. My mother would tell me to ask God. But it wasn't God, it was my mother I had to get straight with. It seemed as if she knew something about me that was worse, far worse, than ordinary lies and tricks and meanness; it was a really sickening shame. I beat against my mother's front to make her forget that.

My brothers weren't bothered by any of this. I don't think so. They seemed to me like cheerful savages, running around free, not having to learn much. And when I just had the two boys myself, no daughters, I felt as if something could stop now—the stories, and griefs, the old puzzles you can't resist or solve.

Aunt Beryl said not to call her Aunt. "I'm not used to being anybody's aunt, honey. I'm not even anybody's momma. I'm just me. Call me Beryl."

Beryl had started out as a stenographer, and now she had her own typing and bookkeeping business, which employed many girls. She had arrived with a man friend, whose name was Mr. Florence. Her letter had said that she would be getting a ride with a friend, but she hadn't said whether the friend would be staying or going on. She hadn't even said if it was a man or a woman.

Mr. Florence was staying. He was a tall, thin man with a long, tanned face, very light-colored eyes, and a way of twitching the corner of his mouth that might have been a smile.

He was the one who got to sleep in the room that my mother and I had papered, because he was the stranger, and a man. Beryl had to sleep with me. At first we thought that Mr. Florence was quite rude, because he wasn't used to our way of talking and we weren't used to his. The first morning, my father said to Mr. Florence, "Well, I hope you got some kind of a sleep on that old bed in there?" (The spare-room bed was heavenly, with a feather tick.) This was Mr. Florence's cue to say that he had never slept better.

Mr. Florence twitched. He said, "I slept on worse."

His favorite place to be was in his car. His car was a royal-blue Chrysler, from the first batch turned out after the war. Inside it, the upholstery and floor covering and roof and door padding were all pearl gray. Mr. Florence kept the names of those colors in mind and corrected you if you said just "blue" or "gray."

"Mouse skin is what it looks like to me," said Beryl rambunctiously. "I tell him it's just mouse skin!"

The car was parked at the side of the house, under the locust trees. Mr. Florence sat inside with the windows rolled up, smoking, in the rich new-car smell.

"I'm afraid we're not doing much to entertain your friend," my mother said.

"I wouldn't worry about him," said Beryl. She always spoke about Mr. Florence as if there was a joke about him that only she appreciated. I wondered long afterward if he had a bottle in the glove compartment and took a nip from time to time to keep his spirits up. He kept his hat on.

Beryl herself was being entertained enough for two. Instead of staying in the house and talking to my mother, as a lady visitor usually did, she demanded to be shown everything there was to see on a farm. She said that I was to take her around and explain things, and see that she didn't fall into any manure piles.

I didn't know what to show. I took Beryl to the icehouse, where chunks of ice the size of dresser drawers, or bigger, lay buried in sawdust. Every few days, my father would chop off a piece of ice and carry it to the kitchen, where it melted in a tin-lined box and cooled the milk and butter.

Beryl said she had never had any idea ice came in pieces that big. She seemed intent on finding things strange, or horrible, or funny.

"Where in the world do you get ice that big?"

I couldn't tell if that was a joke.

"Off of the lake," I said.

"Off of the lake! Do you have lakes up here that have ice on them all summer?"

I told her how my father cut the ice on the lake every winter and hauled it home, and buried it in sawdust, and that kept it from melting.

Beryl said, "That's amazing!"

"Well, it melts a little," I said. I was deeply disappointed in Beryl.

"That's really amazing."

Beryl went along when I went to get the cows. A scarecrow in white slacks (this was what my father called her afterward), with a white sun hat tied under her chin by a flaunting red ribbon. Her fingernails and toenails—she wore sandals—were painted to match the ribbon. She wore the small, dark sunglasses people wore at that time. (Not the people I knew—they didn't own sunglasses.) She had a big red mouth, a loud laugh, hair of an unnatural color and a high gloss, like cherry wood. She was so noisy and shiny, so glamorously got up, that it was hard to tell whether she was good-looking, or happy, or anything.

We didn't have any conversation along the cowpath, because Beryl kept her distance from the cows and was busy watching where she stepped. Once I had them all tied in their stalls, she came closer. She lit a cigarette. Nobody smoked in the barn. My father and other farmers chewed tobacco there instead. I didn't see how I could ask Beryl to chew tobacco.

"Can you get the milk out of them or does your father have to?" Beryl said. "Is it hard to do?"

I pulled some milk down through the cow's teat. One of the barn cats came over and waited. I shot a thin stream into its mouth. The cat and I were both showing off.

"Doesn't that hurt?" said Beryl. "Think if it was you."

I had never thought of a cow's teat as corresponding to any part of myself, and was shaken by this indecency. In fact, I could never grasp a warm, warty teat in such a firm and casual way again.

Beryl slept in a peach-colored rayon nightgown trimmed with écru lace. She had a robe to match. She was just as careful about the word *écru* as Mr. Florence was about his royal blue and pearl gray.

I managed to get undressed and put on my nightgown without any part of me being exposed at any time. An awkward business. I left my underpants on, and hoped that Beryl had done the same. The idea of sharing my bed with a grownup was a torment to me. But I did get to see the contents of what Beryl called her beauty kit. Hand-painted glass jars contained puffs of cotton wool, talcum powder, milky lotion, ice-blue astringent. Little pots of red and mauve rouge—rather greasy-looking. Blue and black pencils. Emery boards, a pumice stone, nail polish with an overpowering smell of bananas, face powder in a celluloid box shaped like a shell, with the name of a dessert—Apricot Delight.

I had heated some water on the coal-oil stove we used in summertime. Beryl scrubbed her face clean, and there was such a change that I almost expected to see makeup lying in strips in the washbowl, like the old wallpaper we had soaked and peeled. Beryl's skin was pale now, covered with fine cracks, rather like the shiny mud at the bottom of puddles drying up in early summer.

"Look what happened to my skin," she said. "Dieting. I weighed a hundred and sixty-nine pounds once, I took it off too fast and my face fell in on me. Now I've got this cream, though. It's made from a secret formula and you can't even buy it commercially. Smell it. See, it doesn't smell all perfumy. It smells serious."

She was patting the cream on her face with puffs of cotton wool, patting away until there was nothing to be seen on the surface.

"It smells like lard," I said.

"Christ Almighty, I hope I haven't been paying that kind of money to rub lard on my face. Don't tell your mother I swear."

She poured clean water into the drinking glass and wet her comb, then combed her hair wet and twisted each strand round her finger, clamping the twisted strand to her head with two crossed pins. I would be doing the same myself, a couple of years later.

"Always do your hair wet, else it's no good doing it up at all," Beryl said. "And always roll it under even if you want it to flip up. See?"

When I was doing my hair up—as I did for years—I sometimes thought of this, and thought that of all the pieces of advice people had given me, this was the one I had followed most carefully.

We put the lamp out and got into bed, and Beryl said, "I never knew it could get so dark. I've never known a dark that was as dark as this." She was whispering. I was slow to understand that she was comparing country nights to city nights, and I wondered if the darkness in Netterfield County could really be greater than that in California.

"Honey?" whispered Beryl. "Are there any animals outside?"

"Cows," I said.

"Yes, but wild animals? Are there bears?"

"Yes," I said. My father had once found bear tracks and

droppings in the bush, and the apples had all been torn off a wild apple tree. That was years ago, when he was a young man.

Beryl moaned and giggled. "Think if Mr. Florence had to go out in the night and he ran into a bear!"

Next day was Sunday. Beryl and Mr. Florence drove my brothers and me to Sunday school in the Chrysler. That was at ten o'clock in the morning. They came back at eleven to bring my parents to church.

"Hop in," Beryl said to me. "You too," she said to the boys. "We're going for a drive."

Beryl was dressed up in a satiny ivory dress with red dots, and a red-lined frill over the hips, and red high-heeled shoes. Mr. Florence wore a pale-blue summer suit.

"Aren't you going to church?" I said. That was what people dressed up for, in my experience.

Beryl laughed. "Honey, this isn't Mr. Florence's kind of religion."

I was used to going straight from Sunday school into church, and sitting for another hour and a half. In summer, the open windows let in the cedary smell of the graveyard and the occasional, almost sacrilegious sound of a car swooshing by on the road. Today we spent this time driving through country I had never seen before. I had never seen it, though it was less than twenty miles from home. Our truck went to the cheese factory, to church, and to town on Saturday nights. The nearest thing to a drive was when it went to the dump. I had seen the near end of Bell's Lake, because that was where my father cut the ice in winter. You couldn't get close to it in summer; the shoreline was all choked up with bulrushes. I had thought that the other end of the lake would look pretty much the same, but when we drove there today, I saw cottages, docks and boats, dark water reflecting the trees. All this and I hadn't known about it. This too was Bell's Lake. I was glad to have seen it at last, but in some way not altogether glad of the surprise.

Finally, a white frame building appeared, with verandas and potted flowers, and some twinkling poplar trees in front. The Wildwood Inn. Today the same building is covered with stucco and done up with Tudor beams and called the Hide-away. The poplar trees have been cut down for a parking lot.

On the way back to the church to pick up my parents, Mr. Florence turned in to the farm next to ours, which belonged to the McAllisters. The McAllisters were Catholics. Our two families were neighborly but not close.

"Come on, boys, out you get," said Beryl to my brothers. "Not you," she said to me. "You stay put." She herded the little boys up to the porch, where some McAllisters were watching. They were in their raggedy home clothes, because their church, or Mass, or whatever it was, got out early. Mrs. McAllister came out and stood listening, rather dumbfounded, to Beryl's laughing talk.

Beryl came back to the car by herself. "There," she said. "They're going to play with the neighbor children."

Play with McAllisters? Besides being Catholics, all but the baby were girls.

"They've still got their good clothes on," I said.

"So what? Can't they have a good time with their good clothes on? I do!"

My parents were taken by surprise as well. Beryl got out and told my father he was to ride in the front seat, for the legroom. She got into the back, with my mother and me. Mr. Florence turned again onto the Bell's Lake road, and Beryl announced that we were all going to the Wildwood Inn for dinner.

"You're all dressed up, why not take advantage?" she said. "We dropped the boys off with your neighbors. I thought they might be too young to appreciate it. The neighbors were happy to have them." She said with a further emphasis that it was to be their treat. Hers and Mr. Florence's.

"Well, now," said my father. He probably didn't have five dollars in his pocket. "Well, now. I wonder do they let the farmers in?"

He made various jokes along this line. In the hotel dining room, which was all in white—white tablecloths, white painted chairs—with sweating glass water pitchers and high, whirring fans, he picked up a table napkin the size of a diaper and spoke to me in a loud whisper, "Can you tell me what to do with this thing? Can I put it on my head to keep the draft off?"

Of course he had eaten in hotel dining rooms before. He knew about table napkins and pie forks. And my mother knew—she wasn't even a country woman, to begin with. Nevertheless this was a huge event. Not exactly a pleasure—as Beryl must have meant it to be—but a huge, unsettling event. Eating a meal in public, only a few miles from home, eating in a big room full of people you didn't know, the food served by a stranger, a snippy-looking girl who was probably a college student working at a summer job.

"I'd like the rooster," my father said. "How long has he been in the pot?" It was only good manners, as he knew it, to joke with people who waited on him.

"Beg your pardon?" the girl said.

"Roast chicken," said Beryl. "Is that okay for everybody?"

Mr. Florence was looking gloomy. Perhaps he didn't care for jokes when it was his money that was being spent. Perhaps he had counted on something better than ice water to fill up the glasses.

The waitress put down a dish of celery and olives, and my mother said, "Just a minute while I give thanks." She bowed her head and said quietly but audibly, "Lord, bless this food to our use, and us to Thy service, for Christ's sake. Amen." Refreshed, she sat up straight and passed the dish to me, saying, "Mind the olives. There's stones in them."

Beryl was smiling around at the room.

The waitress came back with a basket of rolls.

"Parker House!" Beryl leaned over and breathed in their smell. "Eat them while they're hot enough to melt the butter!"

Mr. Florence twitched, and peered into the butter dish. "Is that what this is—butter? I thought it was Shirley Temple's curls."

His face was hardly less gloomy than before, but it was a joke, and his making it seemed to convey to us something of the very thing that had just been publicly asked for—a blessing.

"When he says something funny," said Beryl—who often

referred to Mr. Florence as "he" even when he was right there—
"you notice how he always keeps a straight face? That reminds
me of Mama. I mean of our mama, Marietta's and mine. Daddy,
when he made a joke you could see it coming a mile away—he
couldn't keep it off his face—but Mama was another story. She
could look so sour. But she could joke on her deathbed. In fact,
she did that very thing. Marietta, remember when she was in
bed in the front room the spring before she died?"

"I remember she was in bed in that room," my mother said.
"Yes."

"Well, Daddy came in and she was lying there in her clean
nightgown, with the covers off, because the German lady from
next door had just been helping her take a wash, and she was
still there tidying up the bed. So Daddy wanted to be cheerful, and he said, 'Spring must be coming. I saw a crow today.'
This must have been in March. And Mama said quick as a shot,
'Well, you better cover me up then, before it looks in that window and gets any ideas!' The German lady—Daddy said she
just about dropped the basin. Because it was true, Mama was
skin and bones; she was dying. But she could joke."

Mr. Florence said, "Might as well when there's no use to
cry."

"But she could carry a joke too far, Mama could. One time,
one time, she wanted to give Daddy a scare. He was supposed
to be interested in some girl that kept coming around to the
works. Well, he was a big good-looking man. So Mama said,
'Well, I'll just do away with myself, and you can get on with
her and see how you like it when I come back and haunt you.'
He told her not to be so stupid, and he went off downtown.
And Mama went out to the barn and climbed on a chair and
put a rope around her neck. Didn't she, Marietta? Marietta
went looking for her and she found her like that!"

My mother bent her head and put her hands in her lap,
almost as if she was getting ready to say another grace.

"Daddy told me all about it, but I can remember anyway. I
remember Marietta tearing off down the hill in her nightie,
and I guess the German lady saw her go, and she came out and
was looking for Mama, and somehow we all ended up in the

barn—me too, and some kids I was playing with—and there was Mama up on a chair preparing to give Daddy the fright of his life. She'd sent Marietta after him. And the German lady starts wailing, 'Oh, missus, come down missus, think of your little *kindren*'—'*kindren*' is the German for 'children'—'think of your *kindren*,' and so on. Until it was me standing there—I was just a little squirt, but I was the one noticed that rope. My eyes followed that rope up and up and I saw it was just hanging over the beam, just flung there—it wasn't tied at all! Marietta hadn't noticed that, the German lady hadn't noticed it. But I just spoke up and said, 'Mama, how are you going to manage to hang yourself without that rope tied around the beam?'"

Mr. Florence said, "That'd be a tough one."

"I spoiled her game. The German lady made coffee and we went over there and had a few treats, and, Marietta, you couldn't find Daddy after all, could you? You could hear Marietta howling, coming up the hill, a block away."

"Natural for her to be upset," my father said.

"Sure it was. Mama went too far."

"She meant it," my mother said. "She meant it more than you give her credit for."

"She meant to get a rise out of Daddy. That was their whole life together. He always said she was a hard woman to live with, but she had a lot of character. I believe he missed that, with Gladys."

"I wouldn't know," my mother said, in that particularly steady voice with which she always spoke of her father. "What he did say or didn't say."

"People are dead now," said my father. "It isn't up to us to judge."

"I know," said Beryl. "I know Marietta's always had a different view."

My mother looked at Mr. Florence and smiled quite easily and radiantly. "I'm sure you don't know what to make of all these family matters."

The one time that I visited Beryl, when Beryl was an old woman, all knobby and twisted up with arthritis, Beryl said, "Marietta got all Daddy's looks. And she never did a thing with herself. Remember her wearing that old navy-blue crêpe dress when we went to the hotel that time? Of course, I know it was probably all she had, but did it have to be all she had? You know, I was scared of her somehow. I couldn't stay in a room alone with her. But she had outstanding looks." Trying to remember an occasion when I had noticed my mother's looks, I thought of the time in the hotel, my mother's pale-olive skin against the heavy white, coiled hair, her open, handsome face smiling at Mr. Florence—as if he was the one to be forgiven.

I didn't have a problem right away with Beryl's story. For one thing, I was hungry and greedy, and a lot of my attention went to the roast chicken and gravy and mashed potatoes laid on the plate with an ice-cream scoop and the bright diced vegetables out of a can, which I thought much superior to those fresh from the garden. For dessert, I had a butterscotch sundae, an agonizing choice over chocolate. The others had plain vanilla ice cream.

Why shouldn't Beryl's version of the same event be different from my mother's? Beryl was strange in every way—everything about her was slanted, seen from a new angle. It was my mother's version that held, for a time. It absorbed Beryl's story, closed over it. But Beryl's story didn't vanish; it stayed sealed off for years, but it wasn't gone. It was like the knowledge of that hotel and dining room. I knew about it now, though I didn't think of it as a place to go back to. And indeed, without Beryl's or Mr. Florence's money, I couldn't. But I knew it was there.

The next time I was in the Wildwood Inn, in fact, was after I was married. The Lions Club had a banquet and dance there. The man I had married, Dan Casey, was a Lion. You could get a drink there by that time. Dan Casey wouldn't have gone anywhere you couldn't. Then the place was remodelled into the Hideaway, and now they have strippers every night but Sunday. On Thursday nights, they have a male stripper. I go there with people from the real-estate office to celebrate birthdays or other big events.

The farm was sold for five thousand dollars in 1965. A man from Toronto bought it, for a hobby farm or just an investment. After a couple of years, he rented it to a commune. They stayed there, different people drifting on and off, for a dozen years or so. They raised goats and sold the milk to the health-food store that had opened up in town. They painted a rainbow across the side of the barn that faced the road. They hung tie-dyed sheets over the windows, and let the long grass and flowering weeds reclaim the yard. My parents had finally got electricity in, but these people didn't use it. They preferred oil lamps and the woodstove, and taking their dirty clothes to town. People said they wouldn't know how to handle lamps or wood fires, and they would burn the place down. But they didn't. In fact, they didn't manage badly. They kept the house and barn in some sort of repair and they worked a big garden. They even dusted their potatoes against blight—though I heard that there was some sort of row about this and some of the stricter members left. The place actually looked a lot better than many of the farms round about that were still in the hands of the original families. The McAllister son had started a wrecking business on their place. My own brothers were long gone.

I knew I was not being reasonable, but I had the feeling that I'd rather see the farm suffer outright neglect—I'd sooner see it in the hands of hoodlums and scroungers—than see that rainbow on the barn, and some letters that looked Egyptian painted on the wall of the house. They seemed a mockery. I even disliked the sight of those people when they came to town—the men with their hair in ponytails, and with holes in their overalls that I believed were cut on purpose, and the women with long hair and no makeup and their meek, superior expressions. What do you know about life, I felt like asking them. What makes you think you can come here and mock my father and mother and their life and their poverty? But when I thought of the rainbow and those letters, I knew they weren't trying to mock or imitate my parents' life. They had displaced that life, hardly knowing it existed. They had set up in its place these beliefs and customs of their own, which I hoped would fail them.

That happened, more or less. The commune disintegrated. The goats disappeared. Some of the women moved to town, cut their hair, put on makeup, and got jobs as waitresses or cashiers to support their children. The Toronto man put the place up for sale, and after about a year it was sold for more than ten times what he had paid for it. A young couple from Ottawa bought it. They have painted the outside a pale gray with oyster trim, and have put in skylights and a handsome front door with carriage lamps on either side. Inside, they've changed it around so much that I've been told I'd never recognize it.

I did get in once, before this happened, during the year that the house was empty and for sale. The company I work for was handling it, and I had a key, though the house was being shown by another agent. I let myself in on a Sunday afternoon. I had a man with me, not a client but a friend—Bob Marks, whom I was seeing a lot at the time.

"This is that hippie place," Bob Marks said when I stopped the car. "I've been by here before."

He was a lawyer, a Catholic, separated from his wife. He thought he wanted to settle down and start up a practice here in town. But there already was one Catholic lawyer. Business was slow. A couple of times a week, Bob Marks would be fairly drunk before supper.

"It's more than that," I said. "It's where I was born. Where I grew up." We walked through the weeds, and I unlocked the door.

He said that he had thought, from the way I talked, that it would be farther out.

"It seemed farther then."

All the rooms were bare, and the floors swept clean. The woodwork was freshly painted—I was surprised to see no smudges on the glass. Some new panes, some old wavy ones. Some of the walls had been stripped of their paper and painted. A wall in the kitchen was painted a deep blue, with an enormous dove on it. On a wall in the front room, giant sunflowers appeared, and a butterfly of almost the same size.

Bob Marks whistled. "Somebody was an artist."

"If that's what you want to call it," I said, and turned back to the kitchen. The same woodstove was there. "My mother once burned up three thousand dollars," I said. "She burned three thousand dollars in that stove."

He whistled again, differently. "What do you mean? She threw in a check?"

"No, no. It was in bills. She did it deliberately. She went into town to the bank and she had them give it all to her, in a shoebox. She brought it home and put it in the stove. She put it in just a few bills at a time, so it wouldn't make too big a blaze. My father stood and watched her."

"What are you talking about?" said Bob Marks. "I thought you were so poor."

"We were. We were very poor."

"So how come she had three thousand dollars? That would be like thirty thousand today. Easily. More than thirty thousand today."

"It was her legacy," I said. "It was what she got from her father. Her father died in Seattle and left her three thousand dollars, and she burned it up because she hated him. She didn't want his money. She hated him."

"That's a lot of hate," Bob Marks said.

"That isn't the point. Her hating him, or whether he was bad enough for her to have a right to hate him. Not likely he was. That isn't the point."

"Money," he said. "Money's always the point."

"No. My father letting her do it is the point. To me it is. My father stood and watched and he never protested. If anybody had tried to stop her, he would have protected her. I consider that love."

"Some people would consider it lunacy."

I remember that that had been Beryl's opinion, exactly.

I went into the front room and stared at the butterfly, with its pink-and-orange wings. Then I went into the front bedroom and found two human figures painted on the wall. A man and a woman holding hands and facing straight ahead. They were naked, and larger than life size.

"It reminds me of that John Lennon and Yoko Ono picture," I said to Bob Marks, who had come in behind me. "That record cover, wasn't it?" I didn't want him to think that anything he had said in the kitchen had upset me.

Bob Marks said, "Different color hair."

That was true. Both figures had yellow hair painted in a solid mass, the way they do it in the comic strips. Horsetails of yellow hair curling over their shoulders and little pigtails of yellow hair decorating their not so private parts. Their skin was a flat beige pink and their eyes a staring blue, the same blue that was on the kitchen wall.

I noticed that they hadn't quite finished peeling the wallpaper away before making this painting. In the corner, there was some paper left that matched the paper on the other walls—a modernistic design of intersecting pink and gray and mauve bubbles. The man from Toronto must have put that on. The paper underneath hadn't been stripped off when this new paper went on. I could see an edge of it, the cornflowers on a white ground.

"I guess this was where they carried on their sexual shenanigans," Bob Marks said, in a tone familiar to me. That thickened, sad, uneasy, but determined tone. The not particularly friendly lust of middle-aged respectable men.

I didn't say anything. I worked away some of the bubble paper to see more of the cornflowers. Suddenly I hit a loose spot, and ripped away a big swatch of it. But the cornflower paper came too, and a little shower of dried plaster.

"Why is it?" I said. "Just tell me, why is it that no man can mention a place like this without getting around to the subject of sex in about two seconds flat? Just say the words *hippie* or *commune* and all you guys can think about is screwing! As if there wasn't anything at all behind it but orgies and fancy combinations and non-stop screwing! I get so sick of that—it's all so stupid it just makes me sick!"

In the car, on the way home from the hotel, we sat as before—the men in the front seat, the women in the back. I was in the middle, Beryl and my mother on either side of me. Their heated bodies pressed against me, through cloth; their smells crowded out the smells of the cedar bush we passed through, and the pockets of bog, where Beryl exclaimed at the water lilies. Beryl smelled of all those things in pots and bottles. My mother smelled of flour and hard soap and the warm crêpe of her good dress and the kerosene she had used to take the spots off.

"A lovely meal," my mother said. "Thank you, Beryl. Thank you, Mr. Florence."

"I don't know who is going to be fit to do the milking," my father said. "Now that we've all ate in such style."

"Speaking of money," said Beryl—though nobody actually had been—"do you mind my asking what you did with yours? I put mine in real estate. Real estate in California—you can't lose. I was thinking you could get an electric stove, so you wouldn't have to bother with a fire in summer or fool with that coal-oil thing, either one."

All the other people in the car laughed, even Mr. Florence.

"That's a good idea, Beryl," said my father. "We could use it to set things on till we get the electricity."

"Oh, Lord," said Beryl. "How stupid can I get?"

"And we don't actually have the money, either," my mother said cheerfully, as if she was continuing the joke.

But Beryl spoke sharply. "You wrote me you got it. You got the same as me."

My father half turned in his seat. "What money are you talking about?" he said. "What's this money?"

"From Daddy's will," Beryl said. "That you got last year. Look, maybe I shouldn't have asked. If you had to pay something off, that's still a good use, isn't it? It doesn't matter. We're all family here. Practically."

"We didn't have to use it to pay anything off," my mother said. "I burned it."

Then she told how she went into town in the truck, one day almost a year ago, and got them to give her the money in a box she had brought along for the purpose. She took it home, and put it in the stove and burned it.

My father turned around and faced the road ahead.

I could feel Beryl twisting beside me while my mother talked. She was twisting, and moaning a little, as if she had a pain she couldn't suppress. At the end of the story, she let out a sound of astonishment and suffering, an angry groan.

"So you burned up money!" she said. "You burned up money in the stove."

My mother was still cheerful. "You sound as if I'd burned up one of my children."

"You burned their chances. You burned up everything the money could have got for them."

"The last thing my children need is money. None of us need his money."

"That's criminal," Beryl said harshly. She pitched her voice into the front seat: "Why did you let her?"

"He wasn't there," my mother said. "Nobody was there."

My father said, "It was her money, Beryl."

"Never mind," Beryl said. "That's criminal."

"Criminal is for when you call in the police," Mr. Florence said. Like other things he had said that day, this created a little island of surprise and a peculiar gratitude.

Gratitude not felt by all.

"Don't you pretend this isn't the craziest thing you ever heard of," Beryl shouted into the front seat. "Don't you pretend you don't think so! Because it is, and you do. You think just the same as me!"

My father did not stand in the kitchen watching my mother feed the money into the flames. It wouldn't appear so. He did not know about it—it seems fairly clear, if I remember everything, that he did not know about it until that Sunday afternoon in Mr. Florence's Chrysler, when my mother told them all together. Why, then, can I see the scene so clearly, just as I described it to Bob Marks (and to others—he was not the first)? I see my father standing by the table in the middle of the room—the table with the drawer in it for knives and forks, and the scrubbed oilcloth on top—and there is the box of money on the table. My mother is carefully dropping the bills into the fire. She holds the stove lid by the blackened lifter in one hand. And my father, standing by, seems not just to be permitting her to do this but to be protecting her. A solemn scene, but not crazy. People doing something that seems to them natural and necessary. At least, one of them is doing what seems natural and necessary, and the other believes that the important thing is for that person to be free, to go ahead. They understand that other people might not think so. They do not care.

How hard it is for me to believe that I made that up. It seems so much the truth it is the truth; it's what I believe about them. I haven't stopped believing it. But I have stopped telling that story. I never told it to anyone again after telling it to Bob Marks. I don't think so. I didn't stop just because it wasn't, strictly speaking, true. I stopped because I saw that I had to give up expecting people to see it the way I did. I had to give up expecting them to approve of any part of what was done. How could I even say that I approved of it myself? If I had been the sort of person who approved of that, who could do it, I wouldn't have done all I have done—run away from home to work in a restaurant in town when I was fifteen, gone to night school to learn typing and bookkeeping, got into the real-estate office, and finally become a licensed agent. I wouldn't be divorced. My father wouldn't have died in the county home. My hair would be white, as it has been naturally for years, instead of a color called Copper Sunrise. And not one of these things would I change, not really, if I could.

Bob Marks was a decent man—good-hearted, sometimes with imagination. After I had lashed out at him like that, he said, "You don't need to be so tough on us." In a moment, he said, "Was this your room when you were a little girl?" He thought that was why the mention of the sexual shenanigans had upset me.

And I thought it would be just as well to let him think that. I said yes, yes, it was my room when I was a little girl. It was just as well to make up right away. Moments of kindness and reconciliation are worth having, even if the parting has to come sooner or later. I wonder if those moments aren't more valued, and deliberately gone after, in the setups some people like myself have now, than they were in those old marriages, where love and grudges could be growing underground, so confused and stubborn, it must have seemed they had forever.

✍ *Lichen* ✍

STELLA'S FATHER BUILT the place as a summer house, on the clay bluffs overlooking Lake Huron. Her family always called it "the summer cottage." David was surprised when he first saw it, because it had none of the knotty-pine charm, the battened-down coziness, that those words suggested. A city boy, from what Stella's family called "a different background," he had no experience of summer places. It was and is a high, bare wooden house, painted gray—a copy of the old farmhouses nearby, though perhaps less substantial. In front of it are the steep bluffs—they are not so substantial, either, but have held so far—and a long flight of steps down to the beach. Behind it is a small fenced garden, where Stella grows vegetables with considerable skill and coaxing, a short sandy lane, and a jungle of wild blackberry bushes.

As David turns the car in to the lane, Stella steps out of these bushes, holding a colander full of berries. She is a short, fat, white-haired woman, wearing jeans and a dirty T-shirt. There is nothing underneath these clothes, as far as he can see, to support or restrain any part of her.

"Look what's happened to Stella," says David, fuming. "She's turned into a troll."

Catherine, who has never met Stella before, says decently, "Well. She's older."

"Older than what, Catherine? Older than the house? Older than Lake Huron? Older than the cat?"

There is a cat asleep on the path beside the vegetable garden. A large ginger tom with ears mutilated in battle, and one grayed-over eye. His name is Hercules and he dates from David's time.

"She's an older woman," says Catherine in a flutter of defiance. Even defiant, she's meek. "You know what I mean."

David thinks that Stella has done this on purpose. It isn't just an acceptance of natural deterioration—oh, no, it's much more. Stella would always dramatize. But it isn't just Stella. There's the sort of woman who has to come bursting out of the female envelope at this age, flaunting fat or an indecent scrawniness, sprouting warts and facial hair, refusing to cover pasty veined legs, almost gleeful about it, as if this was what she'd wanted to do all along. Man-haters, from the start. You can't say a thing like that out loud nowadays.

He has parked too close to the berry bushes—too close for Catherine, who slides out of the car on the passenger side and is immediately in trouble. Catherine is slim enough, but her dress has a full skirt and long, billowy sleeves. It's a dress of cobwebby cotton, shading from pink to rose, with scores of tiny, irregular pleats that look like wrinkles. A pretty dress but hardly a good choice for Stella's domain. The blackberry bushes catch it everywhere, and Catherine has to keep picking herself loose.

"David, really, you could have left her some room," says Stella.

Catherine laughs at her predicament. "I'm all right, I'm okay, really."

"Stella, Catherine," says David, introducing.

"Have some berries, Catherine," says Stella sympathetically. "David?"

David shakes his head, but Catherine takes a couple. "Lovely," she says. "Warm from the sun."

"I'm sick of the sight of them," says Stella.

Close up, Stella looks a bit better—with her smooth, tanned skin, childishly cropped hair, wide brown eyes. Catherine, drooping over her, is a tall, frail, bony woman with fair hair and sensitive skin. Her skin is so sensitive it won't stand any makeup at all, and is easily inflamed by colds, foods, emotions. Lately she has taken to wearing blue eye shadow and black mascara, which David thinks is a mistake. Blackening those sparse wisps of lashes emphasizes the watery blue of her eyes, which look as if they couldn't stand daylight, and the dryness of the skin underneath. When David first met Catherine, about eighteen months ago, he thought she was a little over thirty. He saw many remnants of girlishness; he loved her fairness and tall fragility. She has aged since then. And she was older than he thought to start with—she is nearing forty.

"But what will you do with them?" Catherine says to Stella. "Make jam?"

"I've made about five million jars of jam already," Stella says. "I put them in little jars with those artsy-fartsy gingham tops on them and I give them away to all my neighbors who are too lazy or too smart to pick their own. Sometimes I don't know why I don't just let Nature's bounty rot on the vine."

"It isn't on the vine," says David. "It's on those god-awful thornbushes, which ought to be cleaned out and burned. Then there'd be room to park a car."

Stella says to Catherine, "Listen to him, still sounding like a husband."

Stella and David were married for twenty-one years. They have been separated for eight.

"It's true, David," says Stella contritely. "I should clean them out. There's a long list of things I never get around to doing. Come on in and I'll get changed."

"We'll have to stop at the liquor store," says David. "I didn't get a chance."

Once every summer, he makes this visit, timing it as nearly as he can to Stella's father's birthday. He always brings the same present—a bottle of Scotch whisky. This birthday is his father-in-law's ninety-third. He is in a nursing home a few miles away, where Stella can visit him two or three times a week.

"I just have to wash," Stella says. "And put on something bright. Not for Daddy, he's completely blind now. But I think the others like it, the sight of me dressed in pink or blue or something cheers them up the way a balloon would. You two have time for a quick drink. Actually, you can make me one too."

She leads them, single file, up the path to the house. Hercules doesn't move.

"Lazy beast," says Stella. "He's getting about as bad as Daddy. You think the house needs painting, David?"

"Yes."

"Daddy always said every seven years. I don't know—I'm considering putting on siding. I'd get more protection from the wind. Even since I winterized, it sometimes feels as if I'm living in an open crate."

Stella lives here all year round. In the beginning, one or the other of the children would often be with her. But now Paul is studying forestry in Oregon and Deirdre is teaching at an English-language school in Brazil.

"But could you get anything like that color in siding?" says Catherine. "It's so nice, that lovely weather-beaten color."

"I was thinking of cream," says Stella.

Alone in this house, in this community, Stella leads a busy and sometimes chaotic life. Evidence of this is all around them as they progress through the back porch and the kitchen to the living room. Here are some plants she has been potting, and the jam she mentioned—not all given away but waiting, she explains, for bake sales and the fall fair. Here is her wine-making apparatus; then, in the long living room, overlooking the lake, her typewriter, surrounded by stacks of books and papers.

"I'm writing my memoirs," says Stella. She rolls her eyes at Catherine. "I'll stop for a cash payment. No, it's okay, David, I'm writing an article on the old lighthouse." She points the lighthouse out to Catherine. "You can see it from this window if you squeeze right down to the end. I'm doing a piece for the historical society and the local paper. Quite the budding authoress."

Besides the historical society, she says, she belongs to a play-reading group, a church choir, the winemakers' club, and an informal group in which the members entertain one another weekly at dinner parties that have a fixed (low) cost.

"To test our ingenuity," she says. "Always testing something."

And that is only the more or less organized part of it. Her

friends are a mixed bag. People who have retired here, who live in remodelled farmhouses or winterized summer cottages; younger people of diverse background who have settled on the land, taking over rocky old farms that born-and-bred farmers won't bother about anymore. And a local dentist and his friend, who are gay.

"We're marvellously tolerant around here now," shouts Stella, who has gone into the bathroom and is conveying her information over the sound of running water. "We don't insist on matching up the sexes. It's nice for us pensioned-off wives. There are about half a dozen of us. One's a weaver."

"I can't find the tonic," yells David from the kitchen.

"It's in cans. The box on the floor by the fridge. This woman has her own sheep. The weaver woman. She has her own spinning wheel. She spins the wool and then she weaves it into cloth."

"Holy shit," says David thoughtfully.

Stella has turned the tap off, and is splashing.

"I thought you'd like that. See, I'm not so far gone. I just make jam."

In a moment, she comes out with a towel wrapped around her, saying, "Where's my drink?" The top corners of the towel are tucked together under one arm, the bottom corners are flapping dangerously free. She accepts a gin-and-tonic.

"I'll drink it while I dress. I have two new summer outfits. One is flamingo and one is turquoise. I can mix and match. Either way, I look stupendous."

Catherine comes from the living room to get her drink, and takes the first two gulps as if it were a glass of water.

"I love this house," she says with a soft vehemence. "I really do. It's so primitive and unpretentious. It's full of light. I've been trying to think what it reminds me of, and now I know. Did you ever see that old Ingmar Bergman movie where there is a family living in a summer house on an island? A lovely shabby house. The girl was going crazy. I remember thinking at the time, That's what summer houses should be like, and they never are."

"That was the one where God was a helicopter," David says.

"And the girl fooled around with her brother in the bottom of a boat."

"We never had anything quite so interesting going on around here, I'm afraid," says Stella over the bedroom wall. "I can't say I ever really appreciated Bergman movies. I always thought they were sort of bleak and neurotic."

"Conversations tend to be widespread around here," says David to Catherine. "Notice how none of the partitions go up to the ceiling? Except the bathroom, thank God. It makes for a lot of family life."

"Whenever David and I wanted to say something private, we had to put our heads under the covers," Stella says. She comes out of the bedroom wearing a pair of turquoise stretch pants and a sleeveless top. The top has turquoise flowers and fronds on a white background. At least, she seems to have put on a brassiere. A light-colored strap is visible, biting the flesh of her shoulder.

"Remember one night we were in bed," she says, "and we were talking about getting a new car, saying we wondered what kind of mileage you got with a such-and-such, I forget what. Well, Daddy was always mad about cars, he knew everything, and all of a sudden we heard him say, 'Twenty-eight miles to the gallon,' or whatever, just as if he were right there on the other side of the bed. Of course, he wasn't—he was lying in bed in his own room. David was quite blasé about it; he just said, 'Oh, thank you, sir,' as if we'd been including Daddy all along!"

When David comes out of the liquor store, in the village, Stella has rolled down the car window and is talking to a couple she introduces as Ron and Mary. They are in their mid-sixties probably, but very tanned and trim. They wear matching plaid pants and white sweatshirts and plaid caps.

"Glad to meet you," says Ron. "So you're up here seeing how the smart folks live!" He has the sort of jolly voice that suggests boxing feints, playful punches. "When are you going to retire and come up here and join us?"

That makes David wonder what Stella has been telling them about the separation.

"It's not my turn to retire yet."

"Retire early! That's what a lot of us up here did! We got ourselves out of the whole routine. Toiling and moiling and earning and spending."

"Well, I'm not in that," says David. "I'm just a civil servant. We take the taxpayers' money and try not to do any work at all."

"That's not true," says Stella, scolding—wifely. "He works in the Department of Education and he works hard. He just will never admit it."

"A simple serpent!" says Mary, with a crow of pleasure. "I used to work in Ottawa—that was eons ago—and we used to call ourselves simple serpents! Civil serpents. Servants."

Mary is not in the least fat, but something has happened to her chin that usually happens to the chins of fat women. It has collapsed into a series of terraces flowing into her neck.

"Kidding aside," says Ron. "This is a wonderful life. You wouldn't believe how much we find to do. The day is never long enough."

"You have a lot of interests?" says David. He is perfectly serious now, respectful and attentive.

This is a tone that warns Stella, and she tries to deflect Mary. "What are you going to do with the material you brought back from Morocco?"

"I can't decide. It would make a gorgeous dress but it's hardly me. I might just end up putting it on a bed."

"There's so many activities, you can just keep up forever," Ron says. "For instance, skiing. Cross-country. We were out nineteen days in the month of February. Beautiful weather this year. We don't have to drive anywhere. We just go down the back lane—"

"I try to keep up my interests too," says David. "I think it keeps you young."

"There is no doubt it does!"

David has one hand in the inner pocket of his jacket. He brings out something he keeps cupped in his palm, shows it to Ron with a deprecating smile.

"One of my interests," he says.

"Want to see what I showed Ron?" David says later. They are driving along the bluffs to the nursing home.

"No, thank you."

"I hope Ron liked it," David says pleasantly.

He starts to sing. He and Stella met while singing madrigals at university. Or that's what Stella tells people. They sang other things too, not just madrigals. "David was a skinny innocent bit of a lad with a pure sweet tenor and I was a stocky little brute of a girl with a big deep alto," Stella likes to say. "There was nothing he could do about it. Destiny."

"O, Mistress mine, where are you roaming?" sings David, who has a fine tenor voice to this day:

> *"O, Mistress mine, where are you roaming?*
> *O, Mistress mine, where are you roaming?*
> *O, stay and hear, your true love's coming,*
> *O, stay and hear, your true love's coming,*
> *Who can sing, both High and Low."*

Down on the beach, at either end of Stella's property, there are long, low walls of rocks that have been stacked in baskets of wire, stretching out into the water. They are there to protect the beach from erosion. On one of these walls, Catherine is sitting, looking out at the water, with the lake breeze blowing her filmy dress and her long hair. She could be posed for a picture. She might be advertising something, Stella thinks—either something very intimate, and potentially disgusting, or something truly respectable and rather splendid, like life insurance.

"I've been meaning to ask you," says Stella. "Is there anything the matter with her eyes?"

"Eyes?" says David.

"Her eyesight. It's just that she doesn't seem to be quite focussing, close up. I don't know how to describe it."

Stella and David are standing at the living-room window. Returned from the nursing home, they each hold a fresh, restorative drink. They have hardly spoken on the way home, but the silence has not been hostile. They are feeling chastened and reasonably companionable.

"There isn't anything wrong with her eyesight that I know of."

Stella goes into the kitchen, gets out the roasting pan, rubs the roast of pork with cloves of garlic and fresh sage leaves.

"You know, there's a smell women get," says David, standing in the living-room doorway. "It's when they know you don't want them anymore. Stale."

Stella slaps the meat over.

"Those groins are going to have to be rewired entirely," she says. "The wire is just worn to cobwebs in some places. You should see. The power of water. It can wear out tough wire. I'll have to have a work party this fall. Just make a lot of food and ask some people over and make sure enough of them are able-bodied. That's what we all do."

She puts the roast in the oven and rinses her hands.

"It was Catherine you were telling me about last summer, wasn't it? She was the one you said was inclined to be fey."

David groans. "I said what?"

"Inclined to be fey." Stella bangs around, getting out apples, potatoes, onions.

"All right, tell me," says David, coming into the kitchen to stand close to her. "Tell me what I said?"

"That's all, really. I don't remember anything else."

"Stella. Tell me all I said about her."

"I don't, really. I don't remember."

Of course she remembers. She remembers the exact tone in which he said "inclined to be fey." The pride and irony in his voice. In the throes of love, he can be counted on to speak of the woman with tender disparagement—with amazement, even. He likes to say that it's crazy, he does not understand it, he can plainly see that this person isn't his kind of person at all. And yet, and yet, and yet. And yet it's beyond him, irresistible. He told Stella that Catherine believed in horoscopes, was a vegetarian, and painted weird pictures in which tiny figures were enclosed in plastic bubbles.

"The roast," says Stella, suddenly alarmed. "Will she eat meat?"

"What?"

"Will Catherine eat meat?"

"She may not eat anything. She may be too spaced out."

"I'm making an apple-and-onion casserole. It'll be quite substantial. Maybe she'll eat that."

Last summer he said, "She's a hippie survivor, really. She doesn't even know those times are gone. I don't think she's ever read a newspaper. She hasn't the remotest idea of what's going on in the world. Unless she's heard it from a fortune-teller. That's her idea of reality. I don't think she can read a map. She's all instinct. Do you know what she did? She went to Ireland to see the Book of Kells. She'd heard the Book of Kells was in Ireland. So she just got off the plane at Shannon Airport, and asked somebody the way to the Book of Kells. And you know what, she found it!"

Stella asked how this fey creature earned the money for trips to Ireland.

"Oh, she has a job," David said. "Sort of a job. She teaches art, part time. God knows what she teaches them. To paint by their horoscopes, I think."

Now he says, "There's somebody else. I haven't told Catherine. Do you think she senses it? I think she does. I think she senses it."

He is leaning against the counter, watching Stella peel apples. He reaches quickly into his inside pocket, and before Stella can turn her head away he is holding a Polaroid snapshot in front of her eyes.

"That's my new girl," he says.

"It looks like lichen," says Stella, her paring knife halting. "Except it's rather dark. It looks to me like moss on a rock."

"Don't be dumb, Stella. Don't be cute. You can see her. See her legs?"

Stella puts the paring knife down and squints obediently. There is a flattened-out breast far away on the horizon. And the legs spreading into the foreground. The legs are spread wide—smooth, golden, monumental: fallen columns. Between them is the dark blot she called moss, or lichen. But it's really more like the dark pelt of an animal, with the head and tail and feet chopped off. Dark silky pelt of some unlucky rodent.

"Well, I can see now," she says, in a sensible voice.

"Her name is Dina. Dina without an 'h.' She's twenty-two years old."

Stella won't ask him to put the picture away, or even to stop holding it in front of her face.

"She's a bad girl," says David. "Oh, she's a bad girl! She went to school to the nuns. There are no bad girls like those convent-school girls, once they decide to go wild! She was a student at the art college where Catherine teaches. She quit. Now she's a cocktail waitress."

"That doesn't sound so terribly depraved to me. Deirdre was a cocktail waitress for a while when she was at college."

"Dina's not like Deirdre."

At last, the hand holding the picture drops, and Stella picks up her knife and resumes peeling the apples. But David doesn't put the picture away. He starts to, then changes his mind.

"The little witch," he says. "She torments my soul."

His voice when he talks about this girl seems to Stella peculiarly artificial. But who is she to say, with David, what is artificial and what is not? This special voice of his is rather high-pitched, monotonous, insistent, with a deliberate, cruel sweetness. Whom does he want to be cruel to—Stella, Catherine, the girl, himself? Stella gives a sigh that is noisier and more exasperated than she meant it to be and puts down an apple half-peeled. She goes into the living room and looks out the window.

Catherine is climbing off the wall. Or she's trying to. Her dress is caught in the wire.

"That pretty li'l old dress is giving her all sorts of trouble today," Stella says, surprising herself with the bad accent and a certain viciousness of tone.

"Stella. I wish you'd keep this picture for me."

"Me keep it?"

"I'm afraid I'll show it to Catherine. I keep wanting to. I'm afraid I will."

Catherine has disengaged herself, and has spotted them at the window. She waves, and Stella waves back.

"I'm sure you have others," says Stella. "Pictures."

"Not with me. It's not that I want to hurt her."

"Then don't."

"She makes me want to hurt her. She hangs on me with her weepy looks. She takes pills. Mood elevators. She drinks. Sometimes I think the best thing to do would be to give her the big chop. *Coup de grâce. Coup de grâce*, Catherine. Here you are. Big chop. But I worry about what she'll do."

"Mood elevator," says Stella. "Mood elevator, going up!"

"I'm serious, Stella. Those pills are deadly."

"That's your affair."

"Very funny."

"I didn't even mean it to be. Whenever something slips out like that, I always pretend I meant it, though. I'll take all the credit I can get!"

These three people feel better at dinnertime than any of them might have expected. David feels better because he has remembered that there is a telephone booth across from the liquor store. Stella always feels better when she has cooked a meal and it has turned out so well. Catherine's reasons for feeling better are chemical.

Conversation is not difficult. Stella tells stories that she has come across in doing research for her article, about wrecks on the Great Lakes. Catherine knows something about wrecks. She has a boyfriend—a former boyfriend—who is a diver. David is gallant enough to assert that he is jealous of this fellow, does not care to hear about his deep-water prowess. Perhaps this is the truth.

After dinner, David says he needs to go for a walk. Catherine tells him to go ahead. "Go on," she says merrily. "We don't need you here. Stella and I will get along fine without you!"

Stella wonders where this new voice of Catherine's comes from, this pert and rather foolish and flirtatious voice. Drink wouldn't do it. Whatever Catherine has taken has made her sharper, not blunter. Several layers of wispy apology, tentative flattery, fearfulness, or hopefulness have simply blown away in this brisk chemical breeze.

But when Catherine gets up and tries to clear the table it

becomes apparent that the sharpening is not physical. Catherine bumps into a corner of the counter. She makes Stella think of an amputee. Not much cut off, just the tips of her fingers and maybe her toes. Stella has to keep an eye on her, relieving her of the dishes before they slide away.

"Did you notice the hair?" says Catherine. Her voice goes up and down like a Ferris wheel; it dips and sparkles. "He's dyeing it!"

"David is?" says Stella, in genuine surprise.

"Every time he'd think of it, he'd tilt his head back, so you couldn't get too close a look. I think he was afraid you'd say something. He's slightly afraid of you. Actually, it looks very natural."

"I really didn't notice."

"He started a couple of months ago. I said, 'David, what does it matter—your hair was getting gray when I fell in love with you, do you think it's going to bother me now?' Love is strange, it does strange things. David is actually a sensitive person—he's a vulnerable person." Stella rescues a wineglass that is drooping from Catherine's fingers. "It can make you mean. Love can make you mean. If you feel dependent on somebody, then you can be mean to them. I understand that in David."

They drink mead at dinner. This is the first time Stella has tried this batch of homemade mead and she thinks now how good it was, dry and sparkling. It looked like champagne. She checks to see if there is any left in the bottle. About half a glass. She pours it out for herself, sets her glass behind the blender, rinses the bottle.

"You have a good life here," Catherine says.

"I have a fine life. Yes."

"I feel a change coming in my life. I love David, but I've been submerged in this love for so long. Too long. Do you know what I mean? I was down looking at the waves and I started saying, 'He loves me, he loves me not.' I do that often. Then I thought, Well, there isn't any end to the waves, not like there is to a daisy. Or even like there is to my footsteps, if I start counting them to the end of the block. I thought, The waves never, ever come to an end. So then I knew, this is a message for me."

"Just leave the pots, Catherine. I'll deal with them later."

Why doesn't Stella say, "Sit down, I can manage better by myself"? It's a thing she has said often to helpers less inept than Catherine. She doesn't say it because she's wary of something. Catherine's state seems so brittle and delicate. Tripping her up could have consequences.

"He loves me, he loves me not," says Catherine. "That's the way it goes. It goes forever. That's what the waves were trying to tell me."

"Just out of curiosity," says Stella, "do you believe in horoscopes?"

"You mean have I had mine done? No, not really. I know people who have. I've thought about it. I guess I don't quite believe in it enough to spend the money. I look at those things in the newspapers sometimes."

"You read the newspapers?"

"I read parts. I get one delivered. I don't read it all."

"And you eat meat? You ate pork for dinner."

Catherine doesn't seem to mind being interrogated, or even to notice that this is an interrogation.

"Well, I can live on salads, particularly at this time of year. But I do eat meat from time to time. I'm a sort of very lackadaisical vegetarian. It was fantastic, that roast. Did you put garlic on it?"

"Garlic and sage and rosemary."

"It was delicious."

"I'm glad."

Catherine sits down suddenly, and spreads out her long legs in a tomboyish way, letting her dress droop between them. Hercules, who has slept all through dinner on the fourth chair, at the other side of the table, takes a determined leap and lands on what there is of her lap.

Catherine laughs. "Crazy cat."

"If he bothers you, just bat him off."

Freed now of the need to watch Catherine, Stella gets busy scraping and stacking the plates, rinsing glasses, cleaning off the table, shaking the cloth, wiping the counters. She feels well satisfied and full of energy. She takes a sip of the mead. Lines of a song are going through her head, and she doesn't realize until a few words of this song reach the surface that it's the same one David was singing, earlier in the day. "What's to come is still unsure!"

Catherine gives a light snore, and jerks her head up. Hercules doesn't take fright, but tries to settle himself more permanently, getting his claws into her dress.

"Was that me?" says Catherine.

"You need some coffee," Stella says. "Hang on. You probably shouldn't go to sleep right now."

"I'm tired," says Catherine stubbornly.

"I know. But you shouldn't go to sleep right now. Hang on, and we'll get some coffee into you."

Stella takes a hand towel from the drawer, soaks it in cold water, holds it to Catherine's face.

"There, now," says Stella. "You hold it, I'll start the coffee. We're not going to have you passing out here, are we? David would carry on about it. He'd say it was my mead or my cooking or my company, or something. Hang on, Catherine."

David, in the phone booth, begins to dial Dina's number. Then he remembers that it's long distance. He must dial the operator. He dials the operator, asks how much the call will cost, empties his pockets of change. He picks out a dollar and thirty-five cents in quarters and dimes, stacks it ready on the shelf. He starts dialling again. His fingers are shaky, his palms sweaty. His legs, gut, and chest are filled with a rising commotion. The first ring of the phone, in Dina's cramped apartment, sets his innards bubbling. This is craziness. He starts to feed in quarters.

"I will tell you when to deposit your money," says the operator. "Sir? I will tell you when to deposit it." His quarters clank down into the change return and he has trouble scooping them out. The phone rings again, on Dina's dresser, in the jumble of makeup, panty hose, beads and chains, long feathered earrings, a silly cigarette holder, an assortment of windup toys.

He can see them: the green frog, the yellow duck, the brown bear—all the same size. Frogs and bears are equal. Also some space monsters, based on characters in a movie. When set going, these toys will lurch and clatter across Dina's floor or table, spitting sparks out of their mouths. She likes to set up races, or put a couple of them on a collision course. Then she squeals, and even screams with excitement, as they go their unpredictable ways.

"There doesn't seem to be any answer, sir."

"Let it ring a few more times."

Dina's bathroom is across the hall. She shares it with another girl. If she is in the bathroom, even in the bathtub, how long will it take her to decide whether to answer it at all? He decides to count ten rings more, starting now.

"Still no answer, sir."

Ten more.

"Sir, would you like to try again later?"

He hangs up, having thought of something. Immediately, energetically, he dials information.

"For what place, sir?"

"Toronto."

"Go ahead, sir."

He asks for the phone number of a Michael Read. No, he does not have a street address. All he has is the name—the name of her last, and perhaps not quite finished with, boyfriend.

"I have no listing for a Michael Read."

"All right. Try Reade, R-E-A-D-E."

There is indeed an M. Reade, on Davenport Road. Not a Michael but at least an M. Check back and see, then. Is there an M. Read? Read? Yes. Yes, there is an M. Read, living on Simcoe Street. And another M. Read, R-E-A-D, living on Harbord. Why didn't she say that sooner?

He picks Harbord on a hunch. That's not too far from Dina's apartment. The operator tells him the number. He tries to memorize it. He has nothing to write with. He feels it's important not to ask the operator to repeat the number more than once. He should not reveal that he is here in a phone booth without a pen or pencil. It seems to him that the desperate, furtive nature of his quest is apparent, and that at any moment he may be shut off, not permitted to acquire any further information about M. Read, or M. Reade, on Harbord or Simcoe or Davenport, or wherever.

Now he must start all over again. The Toronto area code. No, the operator. The memorized number. Quick, before he loses his nerve, or loses the number. If she should answer, what is he going to say? But it isn't likely that she will answer, even if she is there. M. Read will answer. Then David must ask for Dina. But perhaps not in his own voice. Perhaps not in a man's voice at all. He used to be able to do different voices on the phone. He could even fool Stella at one time.

Perhaps he could do a woman's voice, squeaky. Or a child's voice, a little-sister voice. *Is Dina there?*

"I beg your pardon, sir?"

"Nothing. Sorry."

"It's ringing now. I will let you know when to deposit your money."

What if M. Read is a woman? Not Michael Read at all. Mary Read. Old-age pensioner. Career girl. What are you phoning me for? Sexual harassment. Back to information, then. Try M. Read on Simcoe. Try M. Reade on Davenport. Keep trying.

"I'm sorry. I can't seem to get an answer."

The phone rings again and again in M. Read's apartment, or house, or room. David leans against the metal shelf, where his change is waiting. A car has parked in the liquor-store lot. The couple in it are watching him. Obviously waiting to use the phone. With any luck, Ron and Mary will drive up next.

Dina lives above an Indian-import shop. Her clothes and hair always have a smell of curry powder, nutmeg, incense, added to what David thinks of as her natural smell, of cigarettes and dope and sex. Her hair is dyed dead black. Her cheeks bear a slash of crude color and her eyelids are sometimes brick red. She tried out once for a part in a movie some people she knew about were making. She failed to get the part because of some squeamishness about holding a tame rat between her legs. This failure humiliated her.

David sweats now, trying not to catch her out but to catch her any way at all, to hear her harsh young voice, with its involuntary tremor and insistent obscenities. Even if hearing it, at this moment, means that she has betrayed him. Of course she has betrayed him. She betrays him all the time. If only she would answer (he has almost forgotten it's M. Read who is supposed to answer), he could howl at her, berate her, and if he felt low enough—he *would* feel low enough—he could plead with her. He would welcome the chance. Any chance. At dinner, talking in a lively way to Stella and Catherine, he kept writing the name Dina with his finger on the underside of the wooden table.

People don't have any patience with this sort of suffering, and why should they? The sufferer must forgo sympathy, give up on dignity, cope with the ravages. And on top of that, people will take time out to tell you that this isn't real love. These bouts of desire and dependence and worship and perversity, willed but terrible transformations—they aren't real love.

Stella used to tell him he wasn't interested in love. "Or sex, even. I don't think you're even interested in sex, David. I think all you're interested in is being a big bad boy."

Real love—that would be going on living with Stella, or taking on Catherine. A person presumed to know all about Real Love might be Ron, of Ron-and-Mary.

David knows what he's doing. This is the interesting part of it, he thinks, and has said. He knows that Dina is not really so wild, or so avid, or doomed, as he pretends she is, or as she sometimes pretends she is. In ten years' time, she won't be wrecked by her crazy life, she won't be a glamorous whore. She'll be a woman tagged by little children in the laundromat. The delicious, old-fashioned word *trollop*, which he uses to describe her, doesn't apply to her, really—has no more to do with her than *hippie* had to do with Catherine, a person he cannot now bear to think about. He knows that sooner or later, if Dina allows her disguise to crack, as Catherine did, he will have to move on. He will have to do that anyway— move on.

He knows all this and observes himself, and such knowledge

and observation has no effect at all on his quaking gut, zealous sweat glands, fierce prayers.

"Sir? Do you want to keep on trying?"

The nursing home that they visited, earlier in the day, is called the Balm of Gilead Home. It is named after the balm-of-Gilead trees, a kind of poplar, that grow plentifully near the lake. A large stone mansion built by a nineteenth-century millionaire, it is now disfigured by ramps and fire escapes.

Voices summoned Stella, from the clusters of wheelchairs on the front lawn. She called out various names in answer, detoured to press hands and drop kisses. Vibrating here and there like a fat hummingbird.

She sang when she rejoined David:

"I'm your little sunbeam, short and stout,
Turn me over, pour me out!"

Out of breath, she said, "Actually it's *teapot*. I don't think you'll see much change in Daddy. Except the blindness is total now."

She led him through the green-painted corridors, with their low false ceilings (cutting the heating costs), their paint-by-number pictures, their disinfectant—and other—smells. Out on a back porch, alone, her father sat wrapped in blankets, strapped into his wheelchair so that he wouldn't fall out.

Her father said, "David?"

The sound seemed to come from a wet cave deep inside him, to be unshaped by lips or jaws or tongue. These could not be seen to move. Nor did he move his head.

Stella went behind the chair and put her arms around his neck. She touched him very lightly.

"Yes, it's David, Daddy," she said. "You knew his step!"

Her father didn't answer. David bent to touch the old man's hands, which were not cold, as he expected, but warm and very dry. He laid the whisky bottle in them.

"Careful. He can't hold it," said Stella softly. David kept his own hands on the bottle while Stella pushed up a chair, so that he could sit down opposite her father.

"Same old present," David said.

His father-in-law made an acknowledging sound.

"I'm going to get some glasses," Stella said. "It's against the rules to drink outside, but I can generally get them to bend the rules a bit. I'll tell them it's a celebration."

To get used to looking at his father-in-law, David tried to think of him as a post-human development, something new in the species. Survival hadn't just preserved, it had transformed him. Bluish-gray skin, with dark-blue spots, whitened eyes, a ribbed neck with delicate deep hollows, like a smoked-glass vase. Up through this neck came further sounds, a conversational offering. It was the core of each syllable that was presented, a damp vowel barely held in shape by surrounding consonants.

"Traffic—bad?"

David described conditions on the freeway and on the secondary highways. He told his father-in-law that he had recently bought a car, a Japanese car. He told how he had not, at first, been able to get anything close to the advertised mileage. But he had complained, he had persisted, had taken the car back to the dealer. Various adjustments had been tried, and now the situation had improved and the figure was satisfactory, if not quite what had been promised.

This conversation seemed welcome. His father-in-law appeared to follow it. He nodded, and on his narrow, elongated, bluish, post-human face there were traces of old expressions. An expression of shrewd and dignified concern, suspicion of advertising and of foreign cars and car dealers. There was even a suggestion of doubt—as in the old days— that David could be trusted to handle such things well. And relief that he had done so. In his father-in-law's eyes David would always be somebody learning how to be a man, somebody who might never learn, might never achieve the steadfastness and control, the decent narrowness of range. David, who preferred gin to whisky, read novels, didn't understand the stock market, talked to women, and had started out as a teacher. David, who had always driven small cars, foreign cars. But that was all right now. Small cars were not a sign of any of the things they used to be a sign of. Even here on the bluffs above Lake Huron at the very end of life, certain shifts had registered, certain changes had been understood, by a man who couldn't grasp or see.

"Hear anything about—Lada?"

It happens luckily that David has a colleague who drives a Lada, and many boring lunch and coffee breaks have been taken up with the discussion of this car's strengths and failings and the difficulty of getting parts. David recounted these, and his father-in-law seemed satisfied.

"Gray. Dort. Gray-Dort. First car—ever drove. Yonge Street. Sixty miles. Sixty miles. Uh. Uh. Hour."

"He certainly never drove a Gray-Dort down Yonge Street at sixty miles an hour," said Stella when they had got her father and his bottle back to his room, had said goodbye, and were walking back through the green corridors. "Never. Whose Gray-Dort? They were out of production long before he had the money to buy a car. And he'd never have taken the risk with anybody else's. It's his fantasy. He's reached the stage where that's his big recreation—fixing up the past so anything he wishes had happened did happen. Wonder if we'll get to that stage? What would your fantasy be, David? No. Don't tell me!"

"What would yours be?" said David.

"That you didn't leave? That you didn't want to leave? I bet that's what you think mine would be, but I'm not so sure! Daddy was so pleased to see you, David. A man just means more, for Daddy. I suppose if he thought about you and me he'd have to be on my side, but that's all right, he doesn't have to think about it."

Stella, at the nursing home, seemed to have regained some sleekness and suppleness of former times. Her attentions to her father, and even to the wheelchair contingent, brought back a trace of deferential grace to her movements, a wistfulness to her voice. David had a picture of her as she had been twelve or fifteen years before. He saw her coming across the lawn at a suburban party, carrying a casserole. She was wearing a sundress. She always claimed in those days that she was too fat for pants, though she was not half so fat as now. Why did this picture please him so much? Stella coming across the lawn, with her sunlit hair—the gray in it then merely made it ash blond—and her bare toasted shoulders, crying out greetings to her neighbors, laughing, protesting about some cooking mis-adventure. Of course the food she brought would be wonder-ful, and she brought not only food but the whole longed-for spirit of the neighborhood party. With her overwhelming sociability, she gathered everybody in. And David felt quite free of irritation, though there were times, certainly, when these gifts of Stella's had irritated him. Her vivacious exasper-ation, her exaggeration, her wide-eyed humorous appeals for sympathy had irritated him. For others' entertainment he had heard her shaping stories out of their life—the children's daily mishaps and provocations, the cat's visit to the vet, her son's first hangover, the perversity of the power lawnmower, the papering of the upstairs hall. A charming wife, a wonderful per-son at a party, she has such a funny way of looking at things. Sometimes she was a riot. *Your wife's a riot.*

Well, he forgave her—he loved her—as she walked across the lawn. At that moment, with his bare foot, he was stroking the cold, brown, shaved, and prickly calf of another neighbor-hood wife, who had just come out of the pool and had thrown on a long, concealing scarlet robe. A dark-haired, childless, chain-smoking woman, given—at least at that stage in their relationship—to tantalizing silences. (His first, that one, the first while married to Stella. Rosemary. A sweet dark name, though finally a shrill trite woman.)

It wasn't just that. The unexpected delight in Stella just as she was, the unusual feeling of being at peace with her, didn't come from just that—the illicit activity of his big toe. This seemed profound, this revelation about himself and Stella—how they were bound together after all, and how as long as he could feel such benevolence toward her, what he did secretly and separately was somehow done with her blessing.

That did not turn out to be a notion Stella shared at all. And they weren't so bound, or if they were it was a bond he had to break. We've been together so long, couldn't we just tough it out, said Stella at the time, trying to make it a joke. She didn't understand, probably didn't understand yet, how that was one of the things that made it impossible. This white-haired woman walking beside him through the nursing home dragged so much weight with her—a weight not just of his sexual secrets but of his middle-of-the-night speculations about God, his psychosomatic chest pains, his digestive sensitivity, his escape plans, which once included her and involved Africa or Indonesia. All his ordinary and extraordinary life—even some things it was unlikely she knew about—seemed stored up in her. He could never feel any lightness, any secret and victorious expansion, with a woman who knew so much. She was bloated with all she knew. Nevertheless he put his arms around Stella. They embraced, both willingly.

A young girl, a Chinese or Vietnamese girl, slight as a child in her pale-green uniform, but with painted lips and cheeks, was coming along the corridor, pushing a cart. On the cart were paper cups and plastic containers of orange and grape juice.

"Juice time," the girl was calling, in her pleasant and indifferent singsong. "Juice time. Orange. Grape. Juice." She took no notice of David and Stella, but they let go of each other and resumed walking. David did feel a slight, very slight, discomfort at being seen by such a young and pretty girl in the embrace of Stella. It was not an important feeling—it simply brushed him and passed—but Stella, as he held the door open for her, said, "Never mind, David. I could be your sister. You could be comforting your sister. *Older* sister."

"Madam Stella, the celebrated mind reader."

It was strange, the way they said these things. They used to say bitter and wounding things, and pretend, when they said them, to be mildly amused, dispassionate, even kindly. Now this tone that was once a pretense had soaked down, deep down, through all their sharp feelings, and the bitterness, though not transformed, seemed stale, useless and formal.

A week or so later, when she is tidying up the living room, getting ready for a meeting of the historical society that is to take place at her house, Stella finds the picture, a Polaroid snapshot. David has left it with her after all—hiding it, but not hiding it very well, behind the curtains at one end of the long living-room window, at the spot where you stand to get a view of the lighthouse.

Lying in the sun had faded it, of course. Stella stands looking at it, with a dust cloth in her hand. The day is perfect. The windows are open, her house is pleasantly in order, and a good fish soup is simmering on the stove. She sees that the black pelt in the picture has changed to gray. It's a bluish or greenish gray now. She remembers what she said when she first saw it. She said it was lichen. No, she said it looked like lichen. But she knew what it was at once. It seems to her now that she knew what it was even when David put his hand to his pocket. She felt the old cavity opening up in her. But she held on. She said, "Lichen." And now, look, her words have come true. The outline of the breast has disappeared. You would never know that the legs were legs. The black has turned to gray, to the soft, dry color of a plant mysteriously nourished on the rocks.

This is David's doing. He left it there, in the sun.

Stella's words have come true. This thought will keep coming back to her—a pause, a lost heartbeat, a harsh little break in the flow of the days and nights as she keeps them going.

·ᴬ Miles City, Montana ᴬ·

MY FATHER CAME across the field carrying the body of the boy who had been drowned. There were several men together, returning from the search, but he was the one carrying the body. The men were muddy and exhausted, and walked with their heads down, as if they were ashamed. Even the dogs were dispirited, dripping from the cold river. When they all set out, hours before, the dogs were nervy and yelping, the men tense and determined, and there was a constrained, unspeakable excitement about the whole scene. It was understood that they might find something horrible.

The boy's name was Steve Gauley. He was eight years old. His hair and clothes were mud-colored now and carried some bits of dead leaves, twigs, and grass. He was like a heap of refuse that had been left out all winter. His face was turned in to my father's chest, but I could see a nostril, an ear, plugged up with greenish mud.

I don't think so. I don't think I really saw all this. Perhaps I saw my father carrying him, and the other men following along, and the dogs, but I would not have been allowed to get close enough to see something like mud in his nostril. I must have heard someone talking about that and imagined that I saw it. I see his face unaltered except for the mud—Steve Gauley's familiar, sharp-honed, sneaky-looking face—and it wouldn't have been like that; it would have been bloated and changed and perhaps muddied all over after so many hours in the water.

To have to bring back such news, such evidence, to a wait-ing family, particularly a mother, would have made searchers move heavily, but what was happening here was worse. It seemed a worse shame (to hear people talk) that there was no mother, no woman at all—no grandmother or aunt, or even a sister—to receive Steve Gauley and give him his due of grief. His father was a hired man, a drinker but not a drunk, an erratic man without being entertaining, not friendly but not exactly a troublemaker. His fatherhood seemed accidental, and the fact that the child had been left with him when the mother went away, and that they continued living together, seemed accidental. They lived in a steep-roofed, gray-shingled hillbilly sort of house that was just a bit better than a shack—the father fixed the roof and put supports under the porch, just enough and just in time—and their life was held together in a similar manner; that is, just well enough to keep the Children's Aid at bay. They didn't eat meals together or cook for each other, but there was food. Sometimes the father would give Steve money to buy food at the store, and Steve was seen to buy quite sensible things, such as pancake mix and macaroni dinner.

I had known Steve Gauley fairly well. I had not liked him more often than I had liked him. He was two years older than I was. He would hang around our place on Saturdays, scornful of whatever I was doing but unable to leave me alone. I couldn't be on the swing without him wanting to try it, and if I wouldn't give it up he came and pushed me so that I went crooked. He teased the dog. He got me into trouble—deliberately and maliciously, it seemed to me afterward—by daring me to do things I wouldn't have thought of on my own: digging up the potatoes to see how big they were when they were still only the size of marbles, and pushing over the stacked firewood to make a pile we could jump off. At school, we never spoke to each other. He was solitary, though not tormented. But on Saturday mornings, when I saw his thin, self-possessed figure sliding through the cedar hedge, I knew I was in for something and he would decide what. Sometimes it was all right. We pretended we were cowboys who had to tame wild horses. We played in the pasture by the river, not far from the place where Steve drowned. We were horses and riders both, screaming and neighing and bucking and waving whips of tree branches beside a little nameless river that flows into the Saugeen in southern Ontario.

The funeral was held in our house. There was not enough
room at Steve's father's place for the large crowd that was
expected because of the circumstances. I have a memory of the
crowded room but no picture of Steve in his coffin, or of the
minister, or of wreaths of flowers. I remember that I was holding one flower, a white narcissus, which must have come from
a pot somebody forced indoors, because it was too early for even
the forsythia bush or the trilliums and marsh marigolds in the
woods. I stood in a row of children, each of us holding a narcissus. We sang a children's hymn, which somebody played on
our piano: "When He Cometh, When He Cometh, to Make
Up His Jewels." I was wearing white ribbed stockings, which
were disgustingly itchy, and wrinkled at the knees and ankles.
The feeling of these stockings on my legs is mixed up with
another feeling in my memory. It is hard to describe. It had to
do with my parents. Adults in general but my parents in particular. My father, who had carried Steve's body from the river, and
my mother, who must have done most of the arranging of this
funeral. My father in his dark-blue suit and my mother in her
brown velvet dress with the creamy satin collar. They stood side
by side opening and closing their mouths for the hymn, and I
stood removed from them, in the row of children, watching. I
felt a furious and sickening disgust. Children sometimes have an
access of disgust concerning adults. The size, the lumpy shapes,
the bloated power. The breath, the coarseness, the hairiness, the
horrid secretions. But this was more. And the accompanying
anger had nothing sharp and self-respecting about it. There was
no release, as when I would finally bend and pick up a stone and
throw it at Steve Gauley. It could not be understood or
expressed, though it died down after a while into a heaviness,
then just a taste, an occasional taste—a thin, familiar misgiving.

Twenty years or so later, in 1961, my husband, Andrew, and I
got a brand-new car, our first—that is, our first brand-new. It
was a Morris Oxford, oyster-colored (the dealer had some
fancier name for the color)—a big small car, with plenty of
room for us and our two children. Cynthia was six and Meg
three and a half.

Andrew took a picture of me standing beside the car. I was wearing white pants, a black turtleneck, and sunglasses. I lounged against the car door, canting my hips to make myself look slim.

"Wonderful," Andrew said. "Great. You look like Jackie Kennedy." All over this continent probably, dark-haired, reasonably slender young women were told, when they were stylishly dressed or getting their pictures taken, that they looked like Jackie Kennedy.

Andrew took a lot of pictures of me, and of the children, our house, our garden, our excursions and possessions. He got copies made, labelled them carefully, and sent them back to his mother and his aunt and uncle in Ontario. He got copies for me to send to my father, who also lived in Ontario, and I did so, but less regularly than he sent his. When he saw pictures he thought I had already sent lying around the house, Andrew was perplexed and annoyed. He liked to have this record go forth.

That summer, we were presenting ourselves, not pictures. We were driving back from Vancouver, where we lived, to Ontario, which we still called "home," in our new car. Five days to get there, ten days there, five days back. For the first time, Andrew had three weeks' holiday. He worked in the legal department at B.C. Hydro.

On a Saturday morning, we loaded suitcases, two thermos bottles—one filled with coffee and one with lemonade—some fruit and sandwiches, picture books and coloring books, crayons, drawing pads, insect repellent, sweaters (in case it got cold in the mountains), and our two children into the car. Andrew locked the house, and Cynthia said ceremoniously, "Goodbye, house."

Meg said, "Goodbye, house." Then she said, "Where will we live now?"

"It's not goodbye forever," said Cynthia. "We're coming back. Mother! Meg thought we weren't ever coming back!"

"I did not," said Meg, kicking the back of my seat.

Andrew and I put on our sunglasses, and we drove away, over the Lions Gate Bridge and through the main part of Vancouver.

We shed our house, the neighborhood, the city, and—at the crossing point between Washington and British Columbia— our country. We were driving east across the United States, taking the most northerly route, and would cross into Canada again at Sarnia, Ontario. I don't know if we chose this route because the Trans-Canada Highway was not completely finished at the time or if we just wanted the feeling of driving through a foreign, a very slightly foreign, country—that extra bit of interest and adventure.

We were both in high spirits. Andrew congratulated the car several times. He said he felt so much better driving it than our old car, a 1951 Austin that slowed down dismally on the hills and had a fussy-old-lady image. So Andrew said now.

"What kind of image does this one have?" said Cynthia. She listened to us carefully and liked to try out new words such as *image*. Usually she got them right.

"Lively," I said. "Slightly sporty. It's not show-off."

"It's sensible, but it has class," Andrew said. "Like my image."

Cynthia thought that over and said with a cautious pride, "That means like you think you want to be, Daddy?"

As for me, I was happy because of the shedding. I loved taking off. In my own house, I seemed to be often looking for a place to hide—sometimes from the children but more often from the jobs to be done and the phone ringing and the sociability of the neighborhood. I wanted to hide so that I could get busy at my real work, which was a sort of wooing of distant parts of myself. I lived in a state of siege, always losing just what I wanted to hold on to. But on trips there was no difficulty. I could be talking to Andrew, talking to the children and looking at whatever they wanted me to look at—a pig on a sign, a pony in a field, a Volkswagen on a revolving stand— and pouring lemonade into plastic cups, and all the time those bits and pieces would be flying together inside me. The essential composition would be achieved. This made me hopeful and light-hearted. It was being a watcher that did it. A watcher, not a keeper.

We turned east at Everett and climbed into the Cascades. I

showed Cynthia our route on the map. First I showed her the map of the whole United States, which showed also the bottom part of Canada. Then I turned to the separate maps of each of the states we were going to pass through. Washington, Idaho, Montana, North Dakota, Minnesota, Wisconsin. I showed her the dotted line across Lake Michigan, which was the route of the ferry we would take. Then we would drive across Michigan to the bridge that linked the United States and Canada at Sarnia, Ontario. Home.

Meg wanted to see too.

"You won't understand," said Cynthia. But she took the road atlas into the back seat.

"Sit back," she said to Meg. "Sit still. I'll show you."

I could hear her tracing the route for Meg, very accurately, just as I had done it for her. She looked up all the states' maps, knowing how to find them in alphabetical order.

"You know what that line is?" she said. "It's the road. That line is the road we're driving on. We're going right along this line."

Meg did not say anything.

"Mother, show me where we are right this minute," said Cynthia.

I took the atlas and pointed out the road through the mountains, and she took it back and showed it to Meg. "See where the road is all wiggly?" she said. "It's wiggly because there are so many turns in it. The wiggles are the turns." She flipped some pages and waited a moment. "Now," she said, "show me where we are." Then she called to me, "Mother, she understands! She pointed to it! Meg understands maps!"

It seems to me now that we invented characters for our children. We had them firmly set to play their parts. Cynthia was bright and diligent, sensitive, courteous, watchful. Sometimes we teased her for being too conscientious, too eager to be what we in fact depended on her to be. Any reproach or failure, any rebuff, went terribly deep with her. She was fair-haired, fair-skinned, easily showing the effects of the sun, raw winds, pride, or humiliation. Meg was more solidly built, more reticent—not rebellious but stubborn sometimes, mysterious. Her silences seemed to us to show her strength of character, and her negatives were taken as signs of an imperturbable independence. Her hair was brown, and we cut it in straight bangs. Her eyes were a light hazel, clear and dazzling.

We were entirely pleased with these characters, enjoying their contradictions as well as the confirmations of them. We disliked the heavy, the uninventive, approach to being parents. I had a dread of turning into a certain kind of mother—the kind whose body sagged, who moved in a woolly-smelling, milky-smelling fog, solemn with trivial burdens. I believed that all the attention these mothers paid, their need to be burdened, was the cause of colic, bed-wetting, asthma. I favored another approach—the mock desperation, the inflated irony of the professional mothers who wrote for magazines. In those magazine pieces, the children were splendidly self-willed, hard-edged, perverse, indomitable. So were the mothers, through their wit, indomitable. The real-life mothers I warmed to were the sort who would phone up and say, "Is my embryo Hitler by any chance over at your house?" They cackled clear above the milky fog.

We saw a dead deer strapped across the front of a pickup truck.

"Somebody shot it," Cynthia said. "Hunters shoot the deer."

"It's not hunting season yet," Andrew said. "They may have hit it on the road. See the sign for deer crossing?"

"I would cry if we hit one," Cynthia said sternly.

I had made peanut-butter-and-marmalade sandwiches for the children and salmon-and-mayonnaise for us. But I had not put any lettuce in, and Andrew was disappointed.

"I didn't have any," I said.

"Couldn't you have got some?"

"I'd have had to buy a whole head of lettuce just to get enough for sandwiches, and I decided it wasn't worth it."

This was a lie. I had forgotten.

"They're a lot better with lettuce."

"I didn't think it made that much difference." After a silence, I said, "Don't be mad."

"I'm not mad. I like lettuce on sandwiches."

"I just didn't think it mattered that much."

"How would it be if I didn't bother to fill up the gas tank?"

"That's not the same thing."

"Sing a song," said Cynthia. She started to sing:

"Five little ducks went out one day,
Over the hills and far away.
One little duck went
'Quack-quack-quack.'
Four little ducks came swimming back."

Andrew squeezed my hand and said, "Let's not fight."

"You're right. I should have got lettuce."

"It doesn't matter that much."

I wished that I could get my feelings about Andrew to come together into a serviceable and dependable feeling. I had even tried writing two lists, one of things I liked about him, one of things I disliked—in the cauldron of intimate life, things I loved and things I hated—as if I hoped by this to prove something, to come to a conclusion one way or the other. But I gave it up when I saw that all it proved was what I already knew—that I had violent contradictions. Sometimes the very sound of his footsteps seemed to me tyrannical, the set of his mouth smug and mean, his hard, straight body a barrier interposed—quite consciously, even dutifully, and with a nasty pleasure in its masculine authority—between me and whatever joy or lightness I could get in life. Then, with not much warning, he became my good friend and most essential companion. I felt the sweetness of his light bones and serious ideas, the vulnerability of his love, which I imagined to be much purer and more straightforward than my own. I could be greatly moved by an inflexibility, a harsh propriety, that at other times I scorned. I would think how humble he was, really, taking on such a ready-made role of husband, father, breadwinner, and how I myself in comparison was really a secret monster of egotism. Not so secret, either—not from him.

At the bottom of our fights, we served up what we thought were the ugliest truths. "I know there is something basically selfish and basically untrustworthy about you," Andrew once said. "I've always known it. I also know that that is why I fell in love with you."

"Yes," I said, feeling sorrowful but complacent.

"I know that I'd be better off without you."

"Yes. You would."

"You'd be happier without me."

"Yes."

And finally—finally—wracked and purged, we clasped hands and laughed, laughed at those two benighted people, ourselves. Their grudges, their grievances, their self-justification. We leapfrogged over them. We declared them liars. We would have wine with dinner, or decide to give a party.

I haven't seen Andrew for years, don't know if he is still thin, has gone completely gray, insists on lettuce, tells the truth, or is hearty and disappointed.

We stayed the night in Wenatchee, Washington, where it hadn't rained for weeks. We ate dinner in a restaurant built about a tree—not a sapling in a tub but a tall, sturdy cottonwood. In the early-morning light, we climbed out of the irrigated valley, up dry, rocky, very steep hillsides that would seem to lead to more hills, and there on the top was a wide plateau, cut by the great Spokane and Columbia rivers. Grainland and grassland, mile after mile. There were straight roads here, and little farming towns with grain elevators. In fact, there was a sign announcing that this county we were going through, Douglas County, had the second-highest wheat yield of any county in the United States. The towns had planted shade trees. At least, I thought they had been planted, because there were no such big trees in the countryside.

All this was marvellously welcome to me. "Why do I love it so much?" I said to Andrew. "Is it because it isn't scenery?"

"It reminds you of home," said Andrew. "A bout of severe nostalgia." But he said this kindly.

When we said "home" and meant Ontario, we had very different places in mind. My home was a turkey farm, where my father lived as a widower, and though it was the same house my mother had lived in, had papered, painted, cleaned, furnished, it showed the effects now of neglect and of some wild sociability. A life went on in it that my mother could not have predicted or condoned. There were parties for the turkey crew, the gutters and pluckers, and sometimes one or two of the young men would be living there temporarily, inviting their own friends and having their own impromptu parties. This life, I thought, was better for my father than being lonely, and I did not disapprove, had certainly no right to disapprove. Andrew did not like to go there, naturally enough, because he was not the sort who could sit around the kitchen table with the turkey crew, telling jokes. They were intimidated by him and contemptuous of him, and it seemed to me that my father, when they were around, had to be on their side. And it wasn't only Andrew who had trouble. I could manage those jokes, but it was an effort.

I wished for the days when I was little, before we had the turkeys. We had cows, and sold the milk to the cheese factory. A turkey farm is nothing like as pretty as a dairy farm or a sheep farm. You can see that the turkeys are on a straight path to becoming frozen carcasses and table meat. They don't have the pretense of a life of their own, a browsing idyll, that cattle have, or pigs in the dappled orchard. Turkey barns are long, efficient buildings—tin sheds. No beams or hay or warm stables. Even the smell of guano seems thinner and more offensive than the usual smell of stable manure. No hints there of hay coils and rail fences and songbirds and the flowering hawthorn. The turkeys were all let out into one long field, which they picked clean. They didn't look like great birds there but like fluttering laundry.

Once, shortly after my mother died, and after I was married—in fact, I was packing to join Andrew in Vancouver—I was at home alone for a couple of days with my father. There was a freakishly heavy rain all night. In the early light, we saw that the turkey field was flooded. At least, the low-lying parts of it were flooded—it was like a lake with many islands. The turkeys were huddled on these islands. Turkeys are very stupid. (My father would say, "You know a chicken? You know how stupid a chicken is? Well, a chicken is an Einstein compared with a turkey.") But they had managed to crowd to higher ground and avoid drowning. Now they might push each other off, suffocate each other, get cold and die. We couldn't wait for the water to go down. We went out in an old rowboat we had. I rowed and my father pulled the heavy, wet turkeys into the boat and we took them to the barn. It was still raining a little. The job was difficult and absurd and very uncomfortable. We were laughing. I was happy to be working with my father. I felt close to all hard, repetitive, appalling work, in which the body is finally worn out, the mind sunk (though sometimes the spirit can stay marvellously light), and I was homesick in advance for this life and this place. I thought that if Andrew could see me there in the rain, red-handed, muddy, trying to hold on to turkey legs and row the boat at the same time, he would only want to get me out of there and make me forget about it. This raw life angered him. My attachment to it angered him. I thought that I shouldn't have married him. But who else? One of the turkey crew?

And I didn't want to stay there. I might feel bad about leaving, but I would feel worse if somebody made me stay.

Andrew's mother lived in Toronto, in an apartment building looking out on Muir Park. When Andrew and his sister were both at home, his mother slept in the living room. Her husband, a doctor, had died when the children were still too young to go to school. She took a secretarial course and sold her house at Depression prices, moved to this apartment, managed to raise her children, with some help from relatives—her sister Caroline, her brother-in-law Roger. Andrew and his sister went to private schools and to camp in the summer.

"I suppose that was courtesy of the Fresh Air Fund?" I said once, scornful of his claim that he had been poor. To my mind, Andrew's urban life had been sheltered and fussy. His mother came home with a headache from working all day in the noise, the harsh light of a department-store office, but it did not occur to me that hers was a hard or admirable life. I don't think she herself believed that she was admirable—only unlucky. She worried about her work in the office, her clothes, her cooking, her children. She worried most of all about what Roger and Caroline would think.

Caroline and Roger lived on the east side of the park, in a handsome stone house. Roger was a tall man with a bald, freckled head, a fat, firm stomach. Some operation on his throat had deprived him of his voice—he spoke in a rough whisper. But everybody paid attention. At dinner once in the stone house—where all the dining-room furniture was enormous, darkly glowing, palatial—I asked him a question. I think it had to do with Whittaker Chambers, whose story was then appearing in the Saturday Evening Post. The question was mild in tone, but he guessed its subversive intent and took to calling me Mrs. Gromyko, referring to what he alleged to be my "sympathies." Perhaps he really craved an adversary, and could not find one. At that dinner, I saw Andrew's hand tremble as he lit his mother's cigarette. His Uncle Roger had paid for Andrew's education, and was on the board of directors of several companies.

"He is just an opinionated old man," Andrew said to me later. "What is the point of arguing with him?"

Before we left Vancouver, Andrew's mother had written, *Roger seems quite intrigued by the idea of your buying a small car!* Her exclamation mark showed apprehension. At that time, particularly in Ontario, the choice of a small European car over a large American car could be seen as some sort of declaration— a declaration of tendencies Roger had been sniffing after all along.

"It isn't that small a car," said Andrew huffily.

"That's not the point," I said. "The point is, it isn't any of his business!"

We spent the second night in Missoula. We had been told in Spokane, at a gas station, that there was a lot of repair work going on along Highway 2, and that we were in for a very hot, dusty drive, with long waits, so we turned onto the interstate and drove through Coeur d'Alene and Kellogg into Montana. After Missoula, we turned south toward Butte, but detoured to see Helena, the state capital. In the car, we played Who Am I?

Cynthia was somebody dead, and an American, and a girl. Possibly a lady. She was not in a story. She had not been seen on television. Cynthia had not read about her in a book. She was not anybody who had come to the kindergarten, or a relative of any of Cynthia's friends.

"Is she human?" said Andrew, with a sudden shrewdness.

"No! That's what you forgot to ask!"

"An animal," I said reflectively.

"Is that a question? Sixteen questions!"

"No, it is not a question. I'm thinking. A dead animal."

"It's the deer," said Meg, who hadn't been playing.

"That's not fair!" said Cynthia. "She's not playing!"

"What deer?" said Andrew.

I said, "Yesterday."

"The day before," said Cynthia. "Meg wasn't playing. Nobody got it."

"The deer on the truck," said Andrew.

"It was a lady deer, because it didn't have antlers, and it was an American and it was dead," Cynthia said.

Andrew said, "I think it's kind of morbid, being a dead deer."

"I got it," said Meg.

Cynthia said, "I think I know what morbid is. It's depressing."

Helena, an old silver-mining town, looked forlorn to us even in the morning sunlight. Then Bozeman and Billings, not forlorn in the slightest—energetic, strung-out towns, with miles of blinding tinsel fluttering over used-car lots. We got too tired and hot even to play Who Am I? These busy, prosaic cities reminded me of similar places in Ontario, and I thought about what was really waiting there—the great tombstone furniture of Roger and Caroline's dining room, the dinners for which I must iron the children's dresses and warn them about forks, and then the other table a hundred miles away, the jokes of my father's crew. The pleasures I had been thinking of—looking at the countryside or drinking a Coke in an old-fashioned drugstore with fans and a high, pressed-tin ceiling—would have to be snatched in between.

"Meg's asleep," Cynthia said. "She's so hot. She makes me hot in the same seat with her."

"I hope she isn't feverish," I said, not turning around.

What are we doing this for, I thought, and the answer came —to show off. To give Andrew's mother and my father the pleasure of seeing their grandchildren. That was our duty. But beyond that we wanted to show them something. What strenuous children we were, Andrew and I, what relentless seekers of approbation. It was as if at some point we had received an unforgettable, indigestible message—that we were far from satisfactory, and that the most commonplace success in life was probably beyond us. Roger dealt out such messages, of course —that was his style—but Andrew's mother, my own mother and father couldn't have meant to do so. All they meant to tell us was "Watch out. Get along." My father, when I was in high school, teased me that I was getting to think I was so smart I would never find a boyfriend. He would have forgotten that in a week. I never forgot it. Andrew and I didn't forget things. We took umbrage.

"I wish there was a beach," said Cynthia.

"There probably is one," Andrew said. "Right around the next curve."

"There isn't any curve," she said, sounding insulted.

"That's what I mean."

"I wish there was some more lemonade."

"I will just wave my magic wand and produce some," I said. "Okay, Cynthia? Would you rather have grape juice? Will I do a beach while I'm at it?"

She was silent, and soon I felt repentant. "Maybe in the next town there might be a pool," I said. I looked at the map. "In Miles City. Anyway, there'll be something cool to drink."

"How far is it?" Andrew said.

"Not so far," I said. "Thirty miles, about."

"In Miles City," said Cynthia, in the tones of an incantation, "there is a beautiful blue swimming pool for children, and a park with lovely trees."

Andrew said to me, "You could have started something."

But there was a pool. There was a park too, though not quite the oasis of Cynthia's fantasy. Prairie trees with thin leaves—

cottonwoods and poplars—worn grass, and a high wire fence around the pool. Within this fence, a wall, not yet completed, of cement blocks. There were no shouts or splashes; over the entrance I saw a sign that said the pool was closed every day from noon until two o'clock. It was then twenty-five after twelve.

Nevertheless I called out, "Is anybody there?" I thought somebody must be around, because there was a small truck parked near the entrance. On the side of the truck were these words: *We have Brains, to fix your Drains (We have Roto-Rooter too.)*

A girl came out, wearing a red lifeguard's shirt over her bathing suit. "Sorry, we're closed."

"We were just driving through," I said.

"We close every day from twelve until two. It's on the sign." She was eating a sandwich.

"I saw the sign," I said. "But this is the first water we've seen for so long, and the children are awfully hot, and I wondered if they could just dip in and out—just five minutes. We'd watch them."

A boy came into sight behind her. He was wearing jeans and a T-shirt with the words *Roto-Rooter* on it.

I was going to say that we were driving from British Columbia to Ontario, but I remembered that Canadian place names usually meant nothing to Americans. "We're driving right across the country," I said. "We haven't time to wait for the pool to open. We were just hoping the children could get cooled off."

Cynthia came running up barefoot behind me. "Mother. Mother, where is my bathing suit?" Then she stopped, sensing the serious adult negotiations. Meg was climbing out of the car—just wakened, with her top pulled up and her shorts pulled down, showing her pink stomach.

"Is it just those two?" the girl said.

"Just the two. We'll watch them."

"I can't let any adults in. If it's just the two, I guess I could watch them. I'm having my lunch." She said to Cynthia, "Do you want to come in the pool?"

"Yes, please," said Cynthia firmly.

Meg looked at the ground.

"Just a short time, because the pool is really closed," I said. "We appreciate this very much," I said to the girl.

"Well, I can eat my lunch out there, if it's just the two of them." She looked toward the car as if she thought I might try to spring some more children on her.

When I found Cynthia's bathing suit, she took it into the changing room. She would not permit anybody, even Meg, to see her naked. I changed Meg, who stood on the front seat of the car. She had a pink cotton bathing suit with straps that crossed and buttoned. There were ruffles across the bottom.

"She *is* hot," I said. "But I don't think she's feverish."

I loved helping Meg to dress or undress, because her body still had the solid unself-consciousness, the sweet indifference, something of the milky smell, of a baby's body. Cynthia's body had long ago been pared down, shaped and altered, into Cynthia. We all liked to hug Meg, press and nuzzle her. Sometimes she would scowl and beat us off, and this forthright independence, this ferocious bashfulness, simply made her more appealing, more apt to be tormented and tickled in the way of family love.

Andrew and I sat in the car with the windows open. I could hear a radio playing, and thought it must belong to the girl or her boyfriend. I was thirsty, and got out of the car to look for a concession stand, or perhaps a soft-drink machine, somewhere in the park. I was wearing shorts, and the backs of my legs were slick with sweat. I saw a drinking fountain at the other side of the park and was walking toward it in a roundabout way, keeping to the shade of the trees. No place became real till you got out of the car. Dazed with the heat, with the sun on the blistered houses, the pavement, the burnt grass, I walked slowly. I paid attention to a squashed leaf, ground a Popsicle stick under the heel of my sandal, squinted at a trash can strapped to a tree. This is the way you look at the poorest details of the world resurfaced, after you've been driving for a long time—you feel their singleness and precise location and the forlorn coincidence of your being there to see them.

Where are the children?

I turned around and moved quickly, not quite running, to a part of the fence beyond which the cement wall was not completed. I could see some of the pool. I saw Cynthia, standing about waist-deep in the water, fluttering her hands on the surface and discreetly watching something at the end of the pool, which I could not see. I thought by her pose, her discretion, the look on her face, that she must be watching some byplay between the lifeguard and her boyfriend. I couldn't see Meg. But I thought she must be playing in the shallow water—both the shallow and deep ends of the pool were out of my sight.

"Cynthia!" I had to call twice before she knew where my voice was coming from. "Cynthia! Where's Meg?"

It always seems to me, when I recall this scene, that Cynthia turns very gracefully toward me, then turns all around in the water—making me think of a ballerina on pointe—and spreads her arms in a gesture of the stage. "Dis-ap-peared!"

Cynthia was naturally graceful, and she did take dancing lessons, so these movements may have been as I have described. She did say "Disappeared" after looking all around the pool, but the strangely artificial style of speech and gesture, the lack of urgency, is more likely my invention. The fear I felt instantly when I couldn't see Meg—even while I was telling myself she must be in the shallower water—must have made Cynthia's movements seem unbearably slow and inappropriate to me, and the tone in which she could say "Disappeared" before the implications struck her (or was she covering, at once, some ever-ready guilt?) was heard by me as quite exquisitely, monstrously self-possessed.

I cried out for Andrew, and the lifeguard came into view. She was pointing toward the deep end of the pool, saying, "What's that?"

There, just within my view, a cluster of pink ruffles appeared, a bouquet, beneath the surface of the water. Why would a lifeguard stop and point, why would she ask what that was, why didn't she just dive into the water and swim to it? She didn't swim; she ran all the way around the edge of the pool. But by that time Andrew was over the fence. So many things seemed not quite plausible—Cynthia's behavior, then the life-guard's—and now I had the impression that Andrew jumped with one bound over this fence, which seemed about seven feet high. He must have climbed it very quickly, getting a grip on the wire.

I could not jump or climb it, so I ran to the entrance, where there was a sort of lattice gate, locked. It was not very high, and I did pull myself over it. I ran through the cement corridors, through the disinfectant pool for your feet, and came out on the edge of the pool.

The drama was over.

Andrew had got to Meg first, and had pulled her out of the water. He just had to reach over and grab her, because she was swimming somehow, with her head underwater—she was moving toward the edge of the pool. He was carrying her now, and the lifeguard was trotting along behind. Cynthia had climbed out of the water and was running to meet them. The only person aloof from the situation was the boyfriend, who had stayed on the bench at the shallow end, drinking a milkshake. He smiled at me, and I thought that unfeeling of him, even though the danger was past. He may have meant it kindly. I noticed that he had not turned the radio off, just down.

Meg had not swallowed any water. She hadn't even scared herself. Her hair was plastered to her head and her eyes were wide open, golden with amazement.

"I was getting the comb," she said. "I didn't know it was deep."

Andrew said, "She was swimming! She was swimming by herself. I saw her bathing suit in the water and then I saw her swimming."

"She nearly drowned," Cynthia said. "Didn't she? Meg nearly drowned."

"I don't know how it could have happened," said the life-guard. "One moment she was there, and the next she wasn't."

What had happened was that Meg had climbed out of the water at the shallow end and run along the edge of the pool toward the deep end. She saw a comb that somebody had dropped lying on the bottom. She crouched down and reached in to pick it up, quite deceived about the depth of the water. She went over the edge and slipped into the pool, making such a light splash that nobody heard—not the lifeguard, who was kissing her boyfriend, or Cynthia, who was watching them. That must have been the moment under the trees when I thought, Where are the children? It must have been the same moment. At that moment, Meg was slipping, surprised, into the treacherously clear blue water.

"It's okay," I said to the lifeguard, who was nearly crying. "She can move pretty fast." (Though that wasn't what we usually said about Meg at all. We said she thought everything over and took her time.)

"You swam, Meg," said Cynthia, in a congratulatory way. (She told us about the kissing later.)

"I didn't know it was deep," Meg said. "I didn't drown."

We had lunch at a takeout place, eating hamburgers and fries at a picnic table not far from the highway. In my excitement, I forgot to get Meg a plain hamburger, and had to scrape off the relish and mustard with plastic spoons, then wipe the meat with a paper napkin, before she would eat it. I took advantage of the trash can there to clean out the car. Then we resumed driving east, with the car windows open in front. Cynthia and Meg fell asleep in the back seat.

Andrew and I talked quietly about what had happened. Suppose I hadn't had the impulse just at that moment to check on the children? Suppose we had gone uptown to get drinks, as we had thought of doing? How had Andrew got over the fence? Did he jump or climb? (He couldn't remember.) How had he reached Meg so quickly? And think of the lifeguard not watching. And Cynthia, taken up with the kissing. Not seeing anything else. Not seeing Meg drop over the edge.

Disappeared.

But she swam. She held her breath and came up swimming.

What a chain of lucky links.

That was all we spoke about—luck. But I was compelled to picture the opposite. At this moment, we could have been filling out forms. Meg removed from us, Meg's body being prepared for shipment. To Vancouver—where we had never noticed such a thing as a graveyard—or to Ontario? The scribbled drawings she had made this morning would still be in the back seat of the car. How could this be borne all at once, how did people bear it? The plump, sweet shoulders and hands and feet, the fine brown hair, the rather satisfied, secretive expression—all exactly the same as when she had been alive. The most ordinary tragedy. A child drowned in a swimming pool at noon on a sunny day. Things tidied up quickly. The pool opens as usual at two o'clock. The lifeguard is a bit shaken up and gets the afternoon off. She drives away with her boyfriend in the Roto-Rooter truck. The body sealed away in some kind of shipping coffin. Sedatives, phone calls, arrangements. Such a sudden vacancy, a blind sinking and shifting. Waking up groggy from the pills, thinking for a moment it wasn't true. Thinking if only we hadn't stopped, if only we hadn't taken this route, if only they hadn't let us use the pool. Probably no one would ever have known about the comb.

There's something trashy about this kind of imagining, isn't there? Something shameful. Laying your finger on the wire to get the safe shock, feeling a bit of what it's like, then pulling back. I believed that Andrew was more scrupulous than I about such things, and that at this moment he was really trying to think about something else.

When I stood apart from my parents at Steve Gauley's funeral and watched them, and had this new, unpleasant feeling about them, I thought that I was understanding something about them for the first time. It was a deadly serious thing. I was understanding that they were implicated. Their big, stiff, dressed-up bodies did not stand between me and sudden death, or any kind of death. They gave consent. So it seemed. They gave consent to the death of children and to my death not by anything they said or thought but by the very fact that they had made children—they had made me. They had made me, and for that reason my death—however grieved they were, however they carried on—would seem to them anything but impossible or unnatural. This was a fact, and even then I knew they were not to blame.

But I did blame them. I charged them with effrontery, hypocrisy. On Steve Gauley's behalf, and on behalf of all children, who knew that by rights they should have sprung up free, to live a new, superior kind of life, not to be caught in the snares of vanquished grownups, with their sex and funerals.

Steve Gauley drowned, people said, because he was next thing to an orphan and was let run free. If he had been warned enough and given chores to do and kept in check, he wouldn't have fallen from an untrustworthy tree branch into a spring pond, a full gravel pit near the river—he wouldn't have drowned. He was neglected, he was free, so he drowned. And his father took it as an accident, such as might happen to a dog. He didn't have a good suit for the funeral, and he didn't bow his head for the prayers. But he was the only grownup that I let off the hook. He was the only one I didn't see giving consent. He couldn't prevent anything, but he wasn't implicated in anything, either—not like the others, saying the Lord's Prayer in their unnaturally weighted voices, oozing religion and dishonor.

At Glendive, not far from the North Dakota border, we had a choice—either to continue on the interstate or head northeast, toward Williston, taking Route 16, then some secondary roads that would get us back to Highway 2.

We agreed that the interstate would be faster, and that it was important for us not to spend too much time—that is, money—on the road. Nevertheless we decided to cut back to Highway 2.

"I just like the idea of it better," I said.

Andrew said, "That's because it's what we planned to do in the beginning."

"We missed seeing Kalispell and Havre. And Wolf Point. I like the name."

"We'll see them on the way back."

Andrew's saying "on the way back" was a surprising pleasure to me. Of course, I had believed that we would be coming back, with our car and our lives and our family intact, having covered all that distance, having dealt somehow with those loyalties and problems, held ourselves up for inspection in such a foolhardy way. But it was a relief to hear him say it.

"What I can't get over," said Andrew, "is how you got the signal. It's got to be some kind of extra sense that mothers have."

Partly I wanted to believe that, to bask in my extra sense. Partly I wanted to warn him—to warn everybody—never to count on it.

"What I can't understand," I said, "is how you got over the fence."

"Neither can I."

So we went on, with the two in the back seat trusting us, because of no choice, and we ourselves trusting to be forgiven, in time, for everything that had first to be seen and condemned by those children: whatever was flippant, arbitrary, careless, callous—all our natural, and particular, mistakes.

✍ *White Dump* ✍

"I DON'T KNOW what color," says Denise, answering a question of Magda's. "I don't really remember any color in this house at all."

"Of course you don't," says Magda sympathetically. "There was no light in the house, so there was no color. There was no attempt. So dreary, I couldn't believe."

As well as having the old, deep, light-denying veranda on the Log House torn down, Magda—to whom Denise's father, Laurence, is now married—has put in skylights and painted some walls white, others yellow. She has hung up fabrics from Mexico and Morocco, and rugs from Quebec. Pine dressers and tables have replaced badly painted junk. There is a hot tub surrounded by windows and greenery, and a splendid kitchen. All this must have cost a lot of money. No doubt Laurence is rich enough now to manage it. He owns a small factory, near Ottawa, that manufactures plastics, specializing in window panels and lampshades that look like stained glass. The designs are pretty, the colors not too garish, and Magda has stuck a few of them around the Log House in inconspicuous places.

Magda is an Englishwoman, not a Hungarian as her name might suggest. She used to be a dancer, then a dancing teacher. She is a short, thick-waisted woman, still graceful, with a smooth, pale neck and a lovely, floating crown of silver-gold hair. She is wearing a plain gray dress and a shawl of muted, flowery colors that is sometimes draped over the settee in her bedroom.

"Magda is style through and through," Denise said once, to her brother, Peter.

"What's wrong with that?" said Peter. He is a computer engineer in California and comes home perhaps once a year. He can't understand why Denise is still so bound up with these people.

"Nothing," said Denise. "But you go to the Log House, and there is not even a jumble of scarves lying on an old chest. There is a *calculated* jumble. There is not a whisk or bowl hanging up in the kitchen that is not the most elegant whisk or bowl you could buy."

Peter looked at her and didn't say anything. Denise said, "Okay."

Denise has driven up from Toronto, as she does once or twice every summer, to visit her father and her stepmother. Laurence and Magda spend the whole season here, and are talking of selling the house in Ottawa, of living here year-round. The three of them are sitting out on the brick patio that has replaced part of the veranda, one Sunday afternoon in late August. Magda's ginger pots are full of late-blooming flowers—geraniums the only ones that Denise can name. They are drinking wine-and-soda—the real drinks will come out when the dinner guests arrive. So far, there have been no preposterous arguments. Driving up here, Denise determined there wouldn't be. In the car, she played Mozart tapes to steady and encourage herself. She made resolves. So far, so good.

Denise runs a Women's Centre in Toronto. She gets beaten women into shelters, finds doctors and lawyers for them, goes after private and public money, makes speeches, holds meetings, deals with varied and sometimes dangerous mix-ups of life. She makes less money than a clerk in a government liquor store.

Laurence has said that this is a typical pattern for a girl of affluent background.

He has said that the Women's Centre is a good idea for those who really need it. But he sometimes wonders.

What does he sometimes wonder?

Frankly, he sometimes wonders if some of those women—some of them—aren't enjoying all the attention they are getting, claiming to be battered and raped, and so on.

Laurence customarily lays the bait, Denise snaps it up. (Magda floats on top of these conversations, smiling at her flowers.)

Taxpayers' money. Helping those who won't help themselves. Get rid of acid rain, we lose jobs; your unions would squawk.

"They're not *my* unions."

"If you vote New Democrat, they're your unions. Who runs the New Democrats?"

Denise can't tell if he really believes what he says, or half believes it, or just feels compelled to say these things to her. She has gone out in tears more than once, got into her car, driven back to Toronto. Her lover, a cheerful Marxist from a Caribbean island, whom she doesn't bring home, says that old men, successful old men, in a capitalist industrial society are almost purely evil; there is nothing left in them but raging defenses and greed. Denise argues with him too. Her father is not an old man, in the first place. Her father is a good person, underneath.

"I'm sick of your male definitions and airtight male arguments," she says. Then she says thoughtfully, "Also, I'm sick of hearing myself say 'male' like that." She knows better than to bring up the fact that if she lasts through the argument, her father will give her a check for the Centre.

Today her resolve has held. She has caught the twinkle of the bait but has been able to slip past, a clever innocent-seeming fish, talking mostly to Magda, admiring various details of house renovation. Laurence, an ironic-looking, handsome man with a full gray mustache and soft, thinning gray-brown hair, a tall man with a little sag now to his shoulders and his stomach, has got up several times and walked to the lake and back, to the road and back, has sighed deeply, showing his dissatisfaction with this female talk.

Finally he speaks abruptly to Denise, breaking through what Magda is saying.

"How is your mother?"

"Fine," says Denise. "As far as I know, fine."

Isabel lives far away, in the Comox Valley, in British Columbia.

"So—how is the goat-farming?"

The man Isabel lives with is a commercial fisherman who used to be a TV cameraman. They live on a small farm and rent the land, or part of it, to a man who raises goats. At some point, Denise revealed this fact to Laurence (she has taken care not to reveal the fact that the man is several years younger than Isabel and that the relationship is periodically "unstable"), and Laurence has ever since insisted that Isabel and her paramour (his word) are engaged in goat-farming. His questions bring to mind a world of rural hardship: muddy toil with refractory animals, poverty, some sort of ghastly outdated idealism.

"Fine," says Denise, smiling.

Usually she argues, points out the error in fact, accuses him of distortion, ill will, mischief.

"Enough counterculture left out there to buy goat milk?"

"I would think so."

Laurence's lips twitch under his mustache impatiently. She keeps on looking at him, maintaining an expression of innocent, impudent cheerfulness. Then he gives an abrupt laugh.

"Goat milk!" he says.

"Is this the new in-joke?" says Magda. "What am I missing? Goat milk?"

Laurence says, "Magda, did you know that on my fortieth birthday Denise took me up in a plane?"

"I didn't actually fly it," says Denise.

"My fortieth birthday, 1969. The year of the moon shot. The moon shot was actually just a couple of days after. She'd heard me say I often wished I could get a look at this country from a thousand feet up. I'd go over it flying from Ottawa to Toronto, but I'd never see anything."

"I only paid enough for him to go up, but as it happened we all went up, in a five-seater," Denise says. "For the same price."

"We all went except Isabel," says Laurence. "Somebody had to bow out, so she did."

"I made him drive—Dad drive—blindfolded to the airport," says Denise to Magda. "That is, not drive blindfolded"—they were all laughing—"*ride* blindfolded, so he wouldn't know where we were going and it would be a complete surprise."

"Mother drove," says Laurence. "I imagine I could have driven blindfolded better. Why did she drive and not Isabel?"

"We had to go in Grandma's car. The Peugeot wouldn't take us all, and I had to have us all go to watch you because it was my big deal. My present. I was an awful stage manager."

"We flew all down the Rideau Lake system," Laurence says. "Mother loved it. Remember she'd had a bad experience that morning, with the hippies? So it was good for her. The pilot was very generous. Of course he had his wife working. She made cakes, didn't she?"

Denise says, "She was a caterer."

"She made my birthday cake," says Laurence. "That same birthday. I found that out later."

"Didn't Isabel?" says Magda. "Didn't Isabel make the cake?"

"The oven wasn't working," says Denise, her voice gone cautionary and slightly regretful.

"Ah," says Magda. "What was the bad experience?"

When Denise and Peter and their parents arrived at the Log House every summer from Ottawa, the children's grandmother Sophie would be there already, having driven up from Toronto, and the house would be opened, aired, and cleaned as much as it was ever going to be. Denise would run through all the dim cavelike rooms and hug the lumpy cushions, making a drama out of her delight at being there. But it was a true delight. The house smelled of trodden bits of cedar, never-conquered dampness, and winter mice. Everything was always the same. Here was the boring card game that taught you the names of Canadian wildflowers; here was the Scrabble set with the Y and one of the U's missing; here were the dreadful irresistible books from Sophie's childhood, the World War I cartoon book, the unmatched plates, the cracked saucers Sophie used for ashtrays, the knives and forks with their faint, strange taste and smell that was either of metal or of dishwater.

Only Sophie would use the oven. She turned out hard roast potatoes, cakes raw in the middle, chicken bloody at the bone. She never thought of replacing the stove. A rich man's daughter, now poor—she was an assistant professor of Scandinavian languages, and through most of her career university teachers were poor—she had odd spending habits. She always packed sandwiches to eat on a train trip, and she had never visited a hairdresser, but she wouldn't have dreamed of sending Laurence to an ordinary school. She spent money on the Log House grudgingly, not because she didn't love it (she did) but because her instinct told her to put pots under leaks, to tape around warped window frames, to get used to the slant in the floor that indicated one of the foundation posts was crumbling. And however much she needed money, she wouldn't have thought of selling off any of her property around the house— as her brothers long ago had sold the property on either side, most profitably, to cottagers.

Denise's mother and father had a name for Sophie that was a joke between them, and a secret. Old Norse. It seemed that shortly after they had met, Laurence, describing Sophie to Isabel, had said, "My mother isn't quite your average mom. She can read Old Norse. In fact, she *is* sort of an Old Norse."

In the car on the way to the Log House, feeling Sophie's presence ahead of them, they had played this game.

"Is an Old Norse's car window ever mended with black tape?"

"No. If an Old Norse window is broken, it stays broken."

"What is an Old Norse's favorite radio program?"

"Let's see. Let's see. The Metropolitan Opera? Kirsten Flagstad singing Wagner?"

"No. Too obvious. Too elitist."

"'Folk Songs of Many Lands'?"

"What is an Old Norse breakfast?" said Denise from the back seat. "Porridge!" Porridge was her own most hated thing.

"Porridge with codfish," said Laurence. "Never tell Grandma about this game, Denise. Where does an Old Norse spend a summer vacation?"

"An Old Norse never takes a summer vacation," said Isabel severely. "An Old Norse takes a winter vacation. And goes North."

"Spitzbergen," said Laurence. "The James Bay Low lands."

"A cruise," said Isabel. "From Tromso to Archangel."

"Isn't there a lot of ice?"

"Well, it's on an icebreaker. And it's very dark, because those cruises only run in December and January."

"Wouldn't Grandma think it was funny too?" said Denise. She pictured her grandmother coming out of the house and crossing the veranda to meet them—that broad, strong, speckled old woman, with a crown of yellowish-white braids, whose old jackets and sweaters and skirts had some of the smell of the house, whose greeting was calmly affectionate though slightly puzzled. Was she surprised that they had got here so soon, that the children had grown, that Laurence was suddenly so boisterous, that Isabel looked so slim and youthful? Did she know how they'd been joking about her in the car?

"Maybe," said Laurence discouragingly.

"In those old poems she reads," said Isabel, "you know those old Icelandic poems, there is the most terrible gore and hacking people up—women particularly, one slitting her own kids' throats and mixing the blood in her husband's wine. I read that. And then Sophie is such a pacifist and Socialist, isn't it strange?"

Isabel drove into Aubreyville in the morning to get the birthday cake. Denise went with her to hold the cake on the way home. The plane ride was arranged for five in the afternoon. Only Isabel knew about it, having driven Denise to the airport last week. It was all Denise's idea. She was worrying now about the clouds.

"Those streaky ones are okay," said Isabel. "It's the big piled-up white ones that could mean a storm."

"Cumulus," Denise said. "I know. Do you think Daddy is a typical Cancer? Home-loving and food-loving? Hangs on to things?"

"I guess so," said Isabel.

"What did you think when you first met him? I mean, what attracted you? Did you know this was the person you were going to end up married to? I think that's all so weird."

Laurence and Isabel had met in the cafeteria of the university, where Isabel was working as a cashier. She was a first-year student, a poor, bright girl from the factory side of town, wearing a tight pink sweater that Laurence always remembered.

("Woolworth's," said Isabel. "I didn't know any better. I thought the sorority girls were kind of dowdy.")

The first thing she said to Laurence was "That's a mistake." She was pointing to his selection—shepherd's pie.

Laurence was too embarrassed or too stubborn to put it back. "I've had it before and it was okay," he said. He hung about for a moment after he got his change. "It reminds me of what my mother makes."

"Your mother must be an awful cook."

"She is."

He phoned her that night, having asked around to find out her name. "This is shepherd's pie," he said shakily. "Would you go to a movie with me?"

"I'm surprised you're still alive," said Isabel, that brash-talking tight-sweatered girl who was certainly going to be a surprise for Sophie. "Sure."

Denise knew all this by heart. What she was after was something else. "Why did you go out with him? Why did you say, 'Sure'?"

"He was nice-looking," said Isabel. "He seemed interesting."

"Is that all?"

"Well. He didn't act as if he was God's gift to women. He blushed when I spoke to him."

"He often blushes," said Denise. "So do I. It's terrible."

She thought that those two people, Laurence and Isabel, her father and mother, kept something hidden. Something between them. She could feel it welling up fresh and teasing, or lying low and sour, but she could never get to understand what it was, or how it worked. They would not let her.

Aubreyville was a limestone town, built along the river. The old stove foundry, out of which Sophie's father had made his money, was still there on the riverbank. It had been partly converted into a crafts center, where people blew glass and wove shawls and made birdhouses, which they sold on the premises. The name Vogelsang, the German name that had also appeared on the stoves and had contributed to the downfall of the company during the First World War, could still be read, carved in stone, over the door. The handsome house where Sophie had been born had become a nursing home.

The catering woman lived on one of the new streets of town—the streets that Sophie hated. The street was recently paved, broad and black, with smooth curbs. There were no sidewalks. No trees either, no hedges or fences, just some tiny ornamental shrubs with a wire roll to protect them. Split-level and ranch-style houses alternated. Some of the driveways were paved with the glittering white crushed stone called, around Aubreyville, "white marble." On one lawn, three spotted plastic deer were resting; at a doorway, a little black boy held up a lantern for coaches. An arrangement of pink-and-gray-speckled boulders prevented people from crossing a corner lot.

"Plastic rocks," said Isabel. "I wonder if they have weights or are stuck into the ground?"

The catering woman brought the cake out to the car. She was a stout, dark-haired, rather pretty woman in her forties, with heavy green eye shadow and a perfect, gleaming, bouffant hairstyle.

"I've been on the lookout for you," she said. "I have to run some pies over to the Legion. You want to take a look at this and see if it's okay?"

"I'm sure it's lovely," said Isabel, getting out her wallet. Denise took the cake box onto her lap.

"I wish I had a girl this size around to help me," the woman said.

Isabel looked at the two little boys—they were about three and four years old—who were jumping in and out of an inflated wading pool on the lawn. "Are those yours?" she said politely.

"Are you kidding? Those are my daughter's she dumped on me. I've got one married son and one married daughter, and another son—the only time I see him he's in a motorcycle helmet. I was an early starter."

Isabel had begun to back the car out of the drive when Denise gave a cry of surprise. "Mom! That's the pilot!"

A man had come out of the side door and was talking to the catering woman.

Who cares about fried brains if you've got a gorgeous n body?" said Laurence, in a lordly, farcical way, tap-tap-the smooth stomach bared by Isabel's bikini.

hose little rhythmic slaps made Denise's own stomach go sy. The only way she could keep from yelling out "Stop was to jump up and rush at the lake with her arms spread and silly whoops coming out of her mouth.

en Denise saw the catering woman again, more than a year gone by. It was nearly the end of August, a close, warm, idy day, when they were near the end of their summer's stay he Log House. Isabel had gone to town on one of that summer's regular trips to the dentist. She was having some complicated work done in Aubreyville, because she liked the dentist re better than the dentist in Ottawa. Sophie had not been the Log House since the beginning of summer. She was in ellesley Hospital, in Toronto, having some tests done.

Denise and Peter and their father were in the kitchen making bacon-and-tomato sandwiches for lunch. There were a few ings that Laurence believed he could cook better than anyody else, and one of them was bacon. Denise was slicing tomaes, and Peter was supposed to be buttering the toast, but was eading his book. The radio was on, giving the noon news. Laurence liked to hear the news several times a day.

Denise went to see who was at the front door. She did not immediately recognize the catering woman, who was wearing a more youthful dress this time—a loose dress with swirls of red and blue and purple "psychedelic" colors—and did not look as pretty. Her hair was down over her shoulders.

"Is your mother home?" this woman said.

"I'm sorry, she's not here right now," said Denise, with a dignified politeness she knew to be slightly offensive. She thought the woman was selling something.

"She is not here," the woman said. "No. She is not here." Her face was puffy and unsmiling, her lipstick clownishly thick, and her eye makeup blotchy. Her voice was heavy with some insinuation Denise could not grasp. She would not talk that way if she was trying to sell something. Could they owe

"Damn it, Denise, don't scare me like t
thought it was one of the kids running beh

"It's the pilot I was talking to at the airp

"He must be her husband. Keep the cake

"But isn't that strange? On Daddy's birth
who made his cake is married to the man wl
him up in the plane. *Maybe* he is. He's got a
his partner give flying lessons and they fly h
in the fall and they fly fishermen to lakes you
He told me. Isn't it strange?"

"It's only moderately strange in a place the
ville. Denise, you have to *watch* that cake."

Denise subsided, feeling a little insulted. If
cried out in surprise, Isabel wouldn't have sho
tion. If a grownup had remarked on this strang
Isabel would have agreed that it was indeed st
hated it when Isabel treated her like a child. Wi
mother, or Laurence, she expected a certain d
inflexibility. Those two were always the same. Bu
be confiding, friendly, infinitely understanding,
and irritable. And sometimes the more she gave
you felt satisfied. Denise suspected that her fat
about Isabel too.

Today Isabel was wearing a long wraparound ski
cotton—her hippie skirt, Laurence called it—and
halter. She was slim and brown—she tanned well, c
she was a redhead—and until you got close to her s
only about twenty-five. Even close up, she didn't look
twenty-nine. So Laurence said. He wouldn't let he
dark-red hair, and he supervised her tan, calling out,
are you going," in a warning, upset voice, when she
move into the shade or go up to the house for a little

"If I let her, Isabel would sneak off out of the sun ev
my back was turned," Laurence had said to visitors, and
had heard Isabel laugh.

"It's true. I've got Laurence to thank. I'd never la
enough on my own to get any kind of a tan. I get the
brain feeling."

her money? Had Peter run across her property or bothered her dog?

"My father's here," Denise said contritely. "Would you like to talk to him?"

"Your father, yes, I will talk to him," the woman said, and hoisted her large, shiny red handbag up under her arm. "Why don't you go and get him, then?"

Denise realized then that this was the same voice that had said, "I wish I had a girl this size to help me."

"The lady who does catering is at the door," she said to her father.

"The lady who does catering?" he repeated, in a displeased, disbelieving voice, as if she had invented this lady just to interrupt him.

But he wiped his hands and went off down the hall. She heard him say smoothly, "Yes, indeed, what can I do for you?"

And instead of coming back in a few minutes, he took this woman into the dining room; he shut the dining-room door. Why into the dining room? Visitors were taken into the living room. The bacon, lying on a paper towel, was getting cold.

There was a little window high in the door between the kitchen and the dining room. In the days when Sophie was a little girl, there used to be a cook in the kitchen. The cook could watch the progress of the meal through this window to know when to change the dishes.

Denise raised herself on tiptoe.

"Spy," said Peter, without looking up from his book. It was a science-fiction book called *Satan's World*.

"I just want to know when to make the sandwiches," Denise said.

She saw that there had been a reason for going into the dining room. Her father was sitting in his usual place, at the end of the table. The woman was sitting in Peter's usual place, nearest the hall door. She had her purse on the table, and her hands clasped on top of it. Whatever they were talking about demanded a table and straight-backed chairs and an upright, serious position. It was like an interview. Information is being given, questions are being asked, a problem is being considered.

Well, all right, thought Denise. They were talking about a problem. They would finish talking about it, settle it, and it would be over with. Her father would tell the family about it, or not tell them. It would be over.

She turned off the radio. She made the sandwiches. Peter ate his. She waited a while, then ate hers. They drank Coke, which their father allowed them at lunch. Denise ate and drank too quickly. She sat at the table quietly burping and retasting the bacon, and hearing the terrible sound of a stranger crying in their house.

From the plane on her father's birthday, they had seen some delicate, almost transparent, mounded clouds in the western sky, and Denise had said, "Thunderclouds."

"That's right," said the pilot. "But they're a long ways away."

"It must be pretty dramatic," said Laurence, "flying in a thunderstorm."

"Once, I looked out and I saw blue rings of fire around the propellers," the pilot said. "Round the propellers and the wing tips. Then I saw the same thing round the nose. I put my hand out to touch the glass—this here, the Plexiglas—and just as I got within touching distance, flames came shooting out of my fingers. I don't know if I touched the glass or not. I didn't feel anything. Little blue flames. One time in a thunderstorm. That's what they call St. Elmo's fire."

"It's from the electrical discharges in the atmosphere," called Peter from the back seat.

"You're right," the pilot called back.

"Strange," said Laurence.

"It gave me a start."

Denise had a picture in her mind of the pilot with cold blue fire shooting out of his fingertips, and that seemed to her a sign of pain, though he had said he didn't feel anything. She thought of the time she had touched an electric fence. The spurts of sound coming out of the dining room made her remember. Peter went on reading, and they didn't say anything, though she knew he heard the sound too.

Magda is in the kitchen making the salad. She is humming a tune from an opera. "Home to Our Mountains." Denise is in the dining room setting the table. She hears her father laughing on the patio. The guests have arrived—two pleasant, rich couples, not cottagers. One couple comes from Boston, one from Montreal. They have summer houses in Westfield.

Denise hears her father say, *"Weltschmerz."* He says it as if in quotation marks. He must be quoting some item they all know about, from a magazine they all read.

I should be like Peter, she thinks. I should stop coming here.

But perhaps it's all right, and this is happiness, which she is too stubborn, too childish, too glumly political—too mired in a past that everyone else has abandoned—to accept?

The dining room has been extended to take in the area where part of the veranda was, and the extension is all glass—walls and slanting roof, all glass. In the darkening glass, she sees herself—a tall, careful woman with a long braid, very plainly dressed, setting down on the long pine table, among the prettily overflowing bowls of nasturtiums, little blue glass dishes full of salt. Red-and-orange linen napkins, yellow candles like round pats of butter, thick white country plates with a pattern of grapes around the edges. Layers of forthcoming food and wine, and the talk that cuts off the living air: layers of harmony and satisfaction.

Magda, bearing in the salad, stops humming.

"Your mother—is she happy, out in British Columbia?"

Her fault, Denise thinks. Isabel's.

Unfair, unbidden thoughts can strike her here, reverberating harshly, to no purpose.

"Yes," she says. "Yes. I think so." By which she means that Isabel, at least, has no regrets.

II

Sophie's tread made the floorboards shudder. She was barefoot, naked under the striped terry-cloth bathrobe, in the early morning. She had swum naked in the lake since she was a child and all this shore belonged to her father, down as far as Bryce's farm. If she wanted to swim like that now, she had to get up early in the morning. That was all right. She woke early. Old people did.

After she had her swim, she liked to sit on the rocks and smoke her first cigarette. That was what she was looking for now—not her cigarettes, but her lighter. She looked on the shelf over the sink, in the cutlery drawer—not meaning to make such a clatter—and on the dining-room buffet. Then she remembered that she had been sitting in the living room last night, watching *David Copperfield* on television. And there it was, her lighter, on the grubby arm of the chintz-covered chair.

Laurence had rented a television set so that they could watch the moon shot. She had agreed that that was an occasion the children shouldn't miss—that none of them should miss, said Laurence sternly—but she had supposed it would mean a twenty-four-hour rental, the presence of the television set in the house overnight. Laurence pointed out her mistake. The moon shot would take place Wednesday, the day after tomorrow, and the landing, if all went well, on Sunday. Had she really thought the trip would be only a matter of hours? And Laurence said there would be no hope of renting a decent set if you waited until the last moment. All the cottagers would be after them. So they had got one ten days ahead of time, and Laurence's campaign, ever since it came into the house, had been to get Sophie to watch it. He had been lucky, discovering reruns of last winter's *National Geographic* series: one about the Galápagos Islands, which Sophie watched without protest, and one on America's National Parks, which she said was good but tainted by American boasting. Then there was *David Copperfield*, a British-made series shown every Sunday night in hour-long segments.

"You see what you've been missing?" said Laurence to Sophie. She had refused to have television all these years—not only at the Log House, but in her apartment in Toronto.

"Oh, Laurence. Don't rub it in," said Isabel. Her tone was affectionate but weary. Sophie, saying nothing, was annoyed with Isabel more than with Laurence. How little that girl knew her husband if she expected him to take any triumph discreetly.

And how little she knew Sophie if she expected Laurence's pushing to discomfort her. It was his way—their way. He would push and push at Sophie, and no matter what he got out of her it would never be enough. Sophie's capitulation about the television had turned out not to be enough; she didn't really care enough, and that was what Laurence knew.

It was the same about the steps. (Sophie was making her way down the bank now to the lake, scrambling past the wooden forms.) Sophie had not wanted cement steps, preferring logs set into the bank, but had given in, finally, to Laurence's complaints about the logs rotting and the job he had replacing them. Now he called her every day to see the progress he had made.

"I build for the ages," he announced, with a grand gesture. He had made a memorial step for each of them: a palm print, initials, the date—July, 1969.

Sophie slipped from the rocks into the water and swam toward the middle of the lake, into the sunlight. Then she turned onto her back. Though there were cottages all along the shore, most people had been quite decent about not cutting down the trees. She could lie here in the water and look at the high bank of pine and cedar, poplar and soft maple, both white and golden birch. There was no wind, no ripple on the lake except what Sophie had made, yet the birch and poplar leaves turned at their own will, flashed like coins in the sun.

There was movement, not just in the leaves. Sophie saw figures. They were coming down the bank, coming out of the trees close to the rocks where she had left her bathrobe. She lowered her body, so that she wasn't floating but treading water, and watched them.

Two boys and a girl. All three had long hair, waist-length or nearly so, though one of the boys wore his combed back into a ponytail. The ponytailed boy had a beard and wore dark glasses, and a suit jacket with no shirt underneath. The other boy wore only jeans. He had some chains or necklaces, perhaps feathers, dangling down on his thin brown chest. The girl was fat and gypsyish, with a long red skirt and a bandanna tied across her forehead. She had tied her skirt into a floppy knot in front, so that she could more easily get down the bank.

Children—young people—who looked like this were of course no new sight to Sophie. You saw a lot of them around the lake on weekends—the children of cottagers visiting, bringing friends. Sometimes they took over cottages, with no parents present, and held weekend-long parties. The Property Owners' Newsletter had proposed a ban on long hair and "weird forms of dress," to be voluntarily administered by each property holder on his or her own property. People had been invited to write letters supporting or opposing this ban, and Sophie had written opposing it. She stated in her letter that this entire side of the lake had once been Vogelsang property, and that Augustus Vogelsang had left the comparative comfort of Bismarck's Germany to seek the freedom of the New World, in which all individuals might choose how they dressed, spoke, worshipped, and so on.

But she didn't think these three belonged to any of the cottages. They were surely trespassers, nomads. Why did she think so? Something furtive about them—but bold too, disdainful. She didn't think, however, that any harm would come from them. They were playactors, self-absorbed, not real marauders.

They had seen her bathrobe. They were looking at her, across the water.

Sophie waved. She called out, "Good morning," in a cheerful, hailing tone—to indicate that the greeting was all, that nothing more was expected.

They didn't wave or answer. The girl sat down.

The bare-chested boy picked up Sophie's bathrobe and put it on. He found the cigarettes and the lighter in her pocket, and threw them to the girl, who took a cigarette out and lit it. The other boy sat down and pulled off his boots and splashed his feet in the water.

The boy who had put on the bathrobe did a little shimmy. His hair was black, beautifully shining, waving over his shoulders. He was imitating a woman, though it surely couldn't be said that he was imitating Sophie. (It did occur to her now that they could have been watching, could have seen her take off her bathrobe and go into the water.)

"Would you please take that off?" called Sophie. "You are welcome to a cigarette, but please put them back in the pocket!"

The boy did another shimmy, this time turning his back to her. The other boy laughed. The girl smoked, and seemed not to pay much attention.

"Take off my bathrobe and put back my cigarettes!"

Sophie started to swim toward the shore, holding her head out of the water. The boy slipped off the bathrobe, picked it up, and tore it in two. The worn material tore easily. He wadded up one half and flung it into the water.

"You young scum!" cried Sophie.

He threw the other half.

The boy with the ponytail was putting on his boots.

The black-haired boy held out his hand to the girl. She shook her head. He dived into the folds of her skirt, she cried out in protest. He threw something else into the water, after the pieces of bathrobe.

Sophie's lighter.

Sophie heard the girl say something—it sounded like "you fucking crud"—and then the three of them began to climb the bank without another look toward the lake. The black-haired boy was leaping gracefully; the other boy followed quickly but more awkwardly; the girl climbed laboriously in her hiked-up skirt. They were all out of sight when Sophie rose out of the water and hoisted herself up onto the rocks.

The girl's cigarette—Sophie's cigarette—was not stubbed out but cast down in a little vein of dirt, dirt and rubbly stones between the rocks.

Sophie sat on the rocks, drawing in deep, ragged breaths. She didn't shiver—she was heated by a sombre, useless rage. She needed to compose herself.

She had an image in her mind of the rowboat that used to be tied up here when she was a child. A safe old tub of a rowboat, rocking on the water by the dock. Every evening, after dinner, Sophie, or Sophie and one of her brothers (they were both dead now), but usually just Sophie, would row down the lake to Bryce's farm to get the milk. A can with a lid, scoured and scalded by the Vogelsangs' cook, was taken along—you wouldn't want to trust any Bryce receptacle. The Bryces didn't have a dock. Their house and barn had their backs turned to the lake; they faced the road. Sophie had to steer the boat into the reeds and throw the rope to the Bryce children who ran down to meet her. They would splash out through the mud and haul on the rope and clamber over the boat while Sophie gave out her usual instructions.

"Don't take the oar out! Don't swamp it! Don't all climb in at one end!"

Barefoot, as they were, she would jump out and run up to the stone dairy house. (It was still there, and served now, Sophie understood, as a cottager's darkroom.) Mr. Bryce or Mrs. Bryce would pour the warm frothy milk into the can.

Some Bryce children were as old as Sophie was and some were older, but all were smaller. How many were there? What were their names? Sophie could recall a Rita, a Sheldon or Selwyn, a George, an Annie. They were always pale children, in spite of the summer sun, and they bore many bites, scratches, scabs, mosquito bites, blackfly bites, fleabites, bloody and festering. That was because they were poor children. It was because they were poor that Rita's—or Annie's—eyes were crossed, and that one of the boys had such queerly uneven shoulders, and that they talked as they did, saying, "We-ez goen to towen," and "bowt," and other things that Sophie could hardly understand. Not one of them knew how to swim. They treated the boat as if it was a strange piece of furniture—something to climb over, get inside. They had no idea of rowing.

Sophie liked to come for the milk by herself, not with one of her brothers, so that she could loiter and talk to the Bryce children, ask them questions and tell them things—something her brothers wouldn't have dreamed of doing. Where did they go to school? What did they get for Christmas? Did they know any songs? When they got used to her, they told her things. They told her about the time the bull got loose and came up to the front door, and the time they saw a ball of lightning dance across the bedroom floor, and about the enormous boil on Selwyn's neck and what ran out of it.

Sophie wanted to invite them to the Log House. She dreamed of giving them baths and clean clothes and putting ointment on their bites, and teaching them to talk properly. Sometimes she had a long, complicated daydream that was all about Christmas for the Bryce family. It included a redecoration and painting of their house, as well as a wholesale cleanup of their yard. Magic glasses appeared, to straighten crossed eyes. There were picture books and electric trains and dolls in taffeta dresses and armies of toy soldiers and heaps of marzipan fruits and animals. (Marzipan was Sophie's favorite treat. A conversation with the Bryces about candy had revealed that they did not know what it was.)

In time, she did get her mother's permission to invite one of them. The one she asked—Rita or Annie—backed out at the last minute, being too shy, and the other came instead. This Annie or Rita wore one of Sophie's bathing suits, which drooped on her ridiculously. And she proved hard to entertain. She would not indicate a preference of any kind. She wouldn't say what sort of sandwiches or cookies or drink she wanted, and wouldn't choose to go on the swing or the teeter-totter, or to play by the water or play with dolls. Her lack of preference seemed to have something superior about it, as if she was adhering to a code of manners Sophie couldn't know anything about. She accepted the treats she was given and allowed Sophie to push her in the swing, all with a steadfast lack of enthusiasm. Finally, Sophie took her down to the water and initiated a program of catching frogs. Sophie wanted to move a whole colony of frogs from the reedy little bay on one side of the dock, around to a pleasant shelf and cave in the rocks on the other side. The frogs made the trip by water. Sophie and the Bryce girl caught them and set them on an inner tube and pushed them around the dock—the water was low, so the Bryce girl could wade—to their new home. By the end of the day, the colony had been moved.

The Bryce girl had died in a house fire, with some young children, several years later. Or perhaps that was the other one, the one who wouldn't come. Whichever brother inherited the farm sold it to a developer, who was reported to have cheated him. But this brother bought a big car—a Cadillac?—and Sophie used to see him in Aubreyville in the summers. He would give her a squint-eyed look that said he wasn't going to bother speaking unless she did.

Sophie remembered telling the story of the frog-move to Laurence's father—a teacher of German, whose attention she had first attracted by arguing forcefully, in class, for a West-phalian pronunciation. By the time she was a graduate student, she was relentlessly in love with him. Pregnant, she was too proud to ask him to uproot himself, leave his wife, follow her to the Log House, where she waited for Laurence to be born, but she believed that he must do so. He did come here, but only twice, to visit. They sat on the dock and she told him about the frogs and the Bryce girl.

"Of course they were all back in the reeds the next day," she said.

He laughed, and in a comradely way patted her knee. "Ah, Sophie. You see."

And today was Laurence's fortieth birthday. Her son was born on Bastille Day. She sent a postcard: *Male Prisoner let loose July 14, eight pounds nine ounces.* What did his wife think? She was not to know. The Vogelsang family carried the whole thing off with pride, and Sophie went off to another university to qualify for her academic career. She had never lied about being married. But Laurence, at school, had invented a father—his mother's first cousin (therefore having the same name), who was drowned on a canoe trip. Sophie said she understood, but she was disappointed in him.

Late that afternoon, Sophie found herself up in a plane. She had flown twice before—both times in large planes. She had not thought that she would be frightened. She sat in the back seat between her excited grandchildren, Denise and Peter—Laurence was in front, with the pilot—and in fact she could not tell if what she was feeling was fear.

The little plane seemed not to be moving at all, though its engine had not cut off; it was making a terrible racket. They hovered in the air, a thousand feet or so off the ground. Below were juniper bushes spread like pincushions in the fields, cedars charmingly displayed like toy Christmas trees. There were glittering veins of ripples on the dark water. That toy-like, perfect tininess of everything had a peculiar and distressing effect on Sophie. She felt as if it was she, not the things on earth, that had shrunk, was still shrinking—or that they were all shrinking together. This feeling was so strong it caused a tingle in her now tiny, crablike hands and feet—a tingle of exquisite smallness, an awareness of exquisite smallness. Her stomach shrivelled up: her lungs were as much use as empty seed sacs; her heart was the heart of an insect.

"Soon we'll be right over the lake," said Laurence to the children. "See how it's all fields on one side and trees on the other? See, one side is soil over limestone, and the other is the Precambrian shield. One side is rocks and one is reeds. This is what's called a glint lake." (Laurence had studied and enjoyed geology, and at one time she had hoped he might become a geologist instead of a businessman.)

So they were moving, barely. They were moving over the lake. Off to the right Sophie saw Aubreyville spread out, and the white gash of the silica quarry. Her feeling of a mistake, of a very queer and incommunicable problem, did not abate. It wasn't the approach but the aftermath of disaster she felt, in this golden air—as if they were all whisked off and cancelled, curled up into dots, turned to atoms, but they didn't know it.

"Let's see if we can see the roof of the Log House," said Laurence. "My grandfather was a German; he built his house in the trees, like a hunting lodge," he said to the pilot.

"That so?" said the pilot, who probably knew at least that much about the Vogelsangs.

This feeling—Sophie was realizing—wasn't new to her. She'd had it as a child. A genuine shrinking feeling, one of the repertoire of frightening, marvellous feelings, or states, that are available to you when you're very young. Like the sense of hanging upside down, walking on the ceiling, stepping over heightened doorsills. An awful pleasure then, so why not now?

Because it was not her choice, now. She had a sure sense of changes in the offing, that were not her choice.

Laurence pointed out the roof to her, the roof of the Log House. She exclaimed satisfactorily.

Still shrinking, curled up into that sickening dot, but not vanishing, she held herself up there. She held herself up there, using all the powers she had, and said to her grandchildren, Look here, look there, see the shapes on the earth, see the shadows and the light going down in the water.

III

Sitting by herself is my wife's greatest pleasure.

Isabel sat on the grass near the car, in the shade of some scrawny poplar trees, and thought that this day, a pleasant family day, had been full of hurdles, which she had so far got over. When she woke up this morning, Laurence was wanting to make love to her. She knew that the children would be awake; they would be busy in Denise's room down the hall, preparing the first surprise of the day—a poster with a poem on it, a birthday poem and a collage for their father. If Laurence was interrupted by their trooping in with this—or their pounding on the door, supposing she got up to bolt it—he was going to be in a very bad mood. Denise would be disappointed—in fact, grief-stricken. They would be off to a bad start for the day. But it wouldn't do to put Laurence off, explaining about the children. That would be seen as an instance of her making them more important, considering their feelings ahead of his. The best thing to do seemed to be to hurry him up, and she did that, encouraging him even when he was momentarily distracted by the sound of heavy-footed Sophie, prowling around downstairs, banging open some kitchen drawer.

"What the Christ is the matter with her?" he whispered into Isabel's ear. But she just stroked him as if impatient for further and faster activity. That was effective. Soon everything was all right. He lay on his back holding her hand by the time the children could be heard coming along the hall making a noise like trumpets, a jumbled fanfare. They pushed open the door of their parents' room and entered, holding in front of them the large poster on which the birthday poem was written, in elaborate, crayoned letters of many colors.

"Hail!" they said together, and bowed, lowering the poster. Denise was revealed in a sheet, carrying a tinfoil-covered stick with a silver paper star stuck on one end, and most of Isabel's necklaces, chains, bracelets, and earrings strung around or somehow attached to her person. Peter was just in his pajamas.

They began to recite the poem. Denise's voice was high and intensely dramatic, though self-mocking. Peter's voice trailed a little behind hers, slow and dutiful and uncertainly sardonic.

"Hail upon your fortieth year
That marks your fortunate lifetime here!
And I, the Fairy Queen, appear
To wish you health and wealth and love and cheer!"

Peter, trailing, said, "And *she*, the Fairy Queen, appears," and at the end of the verse Denise said, "Actually, I am the Fairy Godmother but that has too many syllables." She and Peter continued to bow.

Laurence and Isabel laughed and clapped, and asked to see the birthday poster at closer range. All around the poem were pasted figures and scenes and words cut letter by letter out of magazines. This was all in illustration of the past year in the life of the Great L.P. (Long-Playing Laurence Peter) Vogel-sang. A business trip to Australia was indicated by a kangaroo jumping over Ayers Rock, and a can of insect repellent.

In Between Exciting Trips, and the caption, *the Great L.P. Found Time for His Special Interests* (a Playboy Bunny displayed her perky tail, and offered a bottle of champagne as large as herself), *and for relaxing with His Loving Family* (a cross-eyed girl stuck out her tongue, a housewife threateningly waved a mop, and a mud-covered urchin stood on his head). *He Also Considered Taking Up a Second Career* (a cement mixer was shown, with an old codger superimposed). *"Happy Birthday, L.P. the Great,"* said a number of farmyard animals wearing party hats and hoisting balloons, *"From Your Many Loyal Fans."*

"That's remarkable," said Laurence. "I can see you put a lot of work into it. I particularly like the special interests."

"And the loving family," said Denise. "Don't you love them too?"

"And the loving family," said Laurence.

"Now," said Denise, "the Fairy Godmother is prepared to grant you three wishes."

"You never really need more than one wish," Peter said. "You just wish that all the other wishes you make will come true."

"That wish is not allowed," said Denise. "You get three wishes, but they have to be for three specific things. You can't wish something like you'll always be happy, and you can't wish just that you get all your wishes."

Laurence said, "That's a rather dictatorial Fairy God-mother," and said he wished for a sunny day.

"It already is," said Peter disgustedly.

"Well, I wish for it to stay sunny," said Laurence. Then he wished that he would complete six more steps and that there would be broiled tomatoes and sausages and scrambled eggs for breakfast.

"Lucky you wished for broiled," said Isabel. "The top element is working. I suppose it would be too much to ask the Fairy Godmother to bring Sophie a new stove."

The noise that they all made in the kitchen getting breakfast must have kept them from hearing Sophie's voice raised, down at the lake. They were going to eat on the veranda. Denise had spread a cloth over the picnic table. They came out in procession, Denise carrying the coffee tray, Isabel the platter of hot food, the eggs and sausages and tomatoes, and Peter carrying his own breakfast, which was dry cereal with honey. Laurence was not supposed to have to carry anything, but he had picked up the rack of buttered toast, seeing that otherwise it would be left behind.

Just as they came out on the veranda, Sophie appeared at the top of the bank, naked. She walked directly toward them across the mown grass.

"I have had a very minor catastrophe," she said. "Happy Birthday, Laurence!"

This was the first time Isabel had ever seen an old woman naked. Several things surprised her. The smoothness of the skin compared to the wrinkled condition of Sophie's face, neck, arms, and hands. The smallness of the breasts. (Seeing Sophie clothed, she had always perceived the breasts as being on the same large scale as the rest of her.) They were slung down like little bundles, little hammock bundles, from the broad, freckled chest. The scantiness of the pubic hair, and the color of it, was also unexpected; it had not turned white, but remained a glistening golden brown, and was as light a covering as a very young girl's.

All that white skin, slackly filled, made Isabel think of those French cattle, dingy white cattle, that you sometimes saw now out in the farmers' fields. Charolais.

Sophie of course did not try to shield her breasts with an arm or place a modest hand over her private parts. She didn't hurry past her family. She stood in the sunlight, one foot on the bottom step of the veranda—slightly increasing the intimate view they could all get of her—and said calmly, "Down there, I was dispossessed of my bathrobe. Also my cigarettes and my lighter. My lighter went to the bottom of the lake."

"Christ, Mother!" said Laurence.

He had set the toast rack down in such a hurry that it fell over. He pushed aside the dishes to get hold of the tablecloth.

"Here!" he said, and threw it at her.

Sophie didn't catch it. It fell over her feet.

"Laurence, that's the tablecloth!"

"Never mind," said Laurence. "Just put it on!"

Sophie bent and picked up the tablecloth and looked at it as if examining the pattern. Then she draped it around herself, not very effectively and in no great hurry.

"Thank you, Laurence," she said. She had managed to arrange the tablecloth so that it flapped open at just the worst place. Looking down, she said, "I hope this makes you happier." She started again on her story.

No, thought Isabel, she cannot be that unaware. It has to

be on purpose; it has to be a game. Crafty innocence. The stagy old show-off. Showing off her purity, her high-mindedness, her simplicity. Perverse old fraud.

"Denise, run and get another cloth," Isabel said. "Are we going to let this food get cold?"

The idea was—Sophie's idea always was—to make her own son look foolish. To make him look a fool in front of his wife and children. Which he did, standing above Sophie on the veranda, with the shamed blood rising hotly up his neck, staining his ears, his voice artificially lowered to sound a manly reproach, but trembling. That was what Sophie could do, would do, every time she got the chance.

"What arrogant brats," said Isabel, responding to the story. "I thought they were all supposed to be lovely and blissful and looking for enlightenment and so on."

"If only you had worn a bathing suit to go swimming, in the first place," said Laurence.

Then the trip to get the cake, the worry of getting it home intact, the need to nag at Denise so that she would keep it level. A further trip, alone, to the Hi-Way Market to get the ripe field tomatoes Laurence preferred to any that you could buy in the store. Isabel had to plan a top-of-the-stove menu. It had to be something that could be cooked or heated up fairly quickly when they all got home hungry from the trip to the airport. And it should be something that Laurence particularly liked, that Sophie wouldn't find too fancy, and that Peter would eat. She decided on coq au vin, though with that she couldn't be entirely sure of Sophie, or of Peter. After all, it was Laurence's day. She spent the afternoon cooking, watching the time so that they would all be ready to leave for the airport early enough not to throw Denise into a fit of anxiety.

Even with her watching, they were a bit late. Laurence, called to from the top of the steps, answered yes, but did not appear. Isabel had to run down and tell him it was urgent, that there was a surprise connected with his birthday and everything might be ruined if he didn't hurry—it was Denise's particular surprise, furthermore, and she was getting into a state. Even after that, it seemed that Laurence deliberately took his time and was longer than usual washing and changing. He did not approve of so much effort going into preventing one of Denise's states.

But they had got here, and now they were all, except Isabel, up in the plane. That had not been the plan. The plan was that they were all to drive to the airport, watch Laurence get his blindfold removed and be surprised, watch him take off on his birthday ride, and greet him when he came down.

Then the pilot, coming out of the little house that served as an office, and seeing them all there, had said, "How about taking the whole family up? We'll take the five-seater—you get a nice ride." He smiled at Denise. "I won't charge you any more. It's the end of the day."

"That's very nice of you," said Denise promptly.

"So," said the pilot, looking them over. "All but one."

"That can be me," said Isabel.

"I hope you're not scared," said the pilot, turning his look on her. "No need to be."

He was a man in his forties—maybe he was fifty—with waves of very blond or white hair, probably blond hair going white, combed straight back from his forehead. He was not tall, not as tall as Laurence, but he had heavy shoulders, a thick chest and waist and a little hard swell of belly, not a sag, over his belt. A high, curved forehead, bright blue eyes with a habitual outdoor squint, a look of professional calm and good humor. That same quality in his voice—the good-humored, unhurried, slightly stupid-sounding country voice. She knew what Laurence would say of this man—that he was the salt of the earth. Not noticing something else—something vigilant underneath, and careless or even contemptuous of them, sharply self-possessed.

"You're not scared, are you, ma'am?" said the pilot to Sophie.

"I've never flown in a small plane," said Sophie. "But I don't think I'm scared, no."

"We've none of us ever flown in a small plane. It'll be a great treat," said Laurence. "Thank you."

"I'll just sit here by myself, then," said Isabel, and Laurence laughed.

"Sitting by herself is my wife's greatest pleasure."

If that was so—and it really might be, because she wasn't scared, or only vaguely scared, yet she so much relished the idea of being left behind—it surely wasn't much to her credit. Here she sat and saw her day as hurdles got through. The coq au vin waiting on the back of the stove, the cake got home safely, the wine and tomatoes bought, the birthday brought this far without any real errors or clashes or disappointments. There remained the drive home, the dinner. Then tomorrow Laurence would go to Ottawa for the day, and come back in the evening. He was to be with them Wednesday to watch the moon shot.

Not much to her credit to go through her life thinking, Well, good, now that's over, *that's* over. What was she looking forward to, what bonus was she hoping to get, when this, and this, and this, was over?

Freedom—or not even freedom. Emptiness, a lapse of attention. It seemed all the time that she was having to provide a little more—in the way of attention, enthusiasm, watchfulness—than she was sure she had. She was straining, hoping not to be found out. Found to be as cold at heart as that Old Norse, Sophie.

Sometimes she thought that she had been brought home, in the first place, as a complicated kind of challenge to Sophie. Laurence was in love with her from the beginning, but his love had something to do with the challenge. Quite contradictory things about her were involved: her tarty looks and bad manners (how tarty, and how bad, she had no idea at the time); her high marks and her naive reliance on them as proof of intelligence; all that evidence she bore of being the brightest pupil from a working-class high school, the sport of an unambitious family.

"Not your typical Business Ad choice, is she, Mother?" said Laurence to Sophie in Isabel's presence. He was enrolled in the one school in the university that Sophie detested—Business Administration.

Sophie said nothing, but smiled directly at Isabel. The smile

was not unkind, not scornful of Laurence—it seemed patient—
but it said plainly, "Are you ready, are you taking this on?" And
Isabel, who was concentrating then on being in love with Laurence's good looks and wit and intelligence and hoped-for
experience of life, understood what this meant. It meant that
the Laurence she had set herself to love (for in spite of her
looks and manner, she was a serious, inexperienced girl who
believed in lifelong love and could not imagine connecting herself on any other terms), *that* Laurence had to be propped up,
kept going, by constant and clever exertions on her part, by
reassurance and good management; he depended on her to
make him a man. She did not like Sophie for bringing this to
her attention, and she didn't let it touch her decision. This was
what love was, or what life was, and she wanted to get started
on it. She was lonely, though she thought of herself as solitary.
She was the only child of her mother's second marriage; her
mother was dead, and her half brothers and half sister were
much older, and married. She had a reputation in her family
for thinking she was special. She still had it, and since her marriage to Laurence she hardly saw her own relatives.

She read a lot; she dieted and exercised seriously; she had
become a good cook. At parties, she flirted with men who did
not seriously pursue her. (She had noticed that Laurence was
disappointed if she did not create a little stir.) Sometimes she
imagined herself overpowered by these men, or others, a partner in most impulsive, ingenious, vigorous couplings. Sometimes she thought of her childhood with a longing that seemed
almost as perverse, and had to be kept almost as secret. A sagging awning in front of a corner store might remind her, the
smell of heavy dinners cooking at noon, the litter and bare
earth around the roots of a big urban shade tree.

When the plane landed, she got up and went to meet them,
and she kissed Laurence as if he had returned from a journey.
He seemed happy. She thought that she seldom concerned herself about Laurence's being happy. She wanted him to be in a
good mood, so that everything would go smoothly, but that
was not the same thing.

"It was wonderful," Laurence said. "You could see the changes in the landscape so clearly." He began to tell her about a glint lake.

"It was most enjoyable," said Sophie.

Denise said, "You could see way down into the water. You could see the rocks going down. You could even see sand."

"You could see what kind of boats," said Peter.

"I mean it, Mother. You could see the rocks going down, down, and then sand."

"Could you see any fish?" said Isabel.

The pilot laughed, though he must have heard that often enough before.

"It's really too bad you didn't come up," Laurence said.

"Oh, she will, one day," said the pilot. "She could be out here tomorrow."

They all laughed at his teasing. His bold eyes met Isabel's, and seemed in spite of their boldness to be most innocent, genial, and kind. Respect was not wanting. He was a man who could surely mean no harm, no folly. So it could hardly be true that he was inviting her.

He said goodbye to them then, as a group, and was thanked once more. Isabel thought she knew what it was that had unhinged her. It was Sophie's story. It was the idea of herself, not Sophie, walking naked out of the water toward those capering boys. (In her mind, she had already eliminated the girl.) That made her long for, and imagine, some leaping, radical invitation. She was kindled for it.

When they were walking toward the car, she had to make an effort not to turn around. She imagined that they turned at the same time, they looked at each other, just as in some romantic movie, operatic story, high-school fantasy. They turned at the same time, they looked at each other, they exchanged a promise that was no less real though they might never meet again. And the promise hit her like lightning, split her like lightning, though she moved on smoothly, intact.

Oh, certainly. All of that.

But, it isn't like lightning, it isn't a blow from outside. We only pretend that it is.

"If somebody else wouldn't mind driving," Sophie said. "I'm tired."

That evening, Isabel was bountifully attentive to Laurence, to her children, to Sophie, who didn't in the least require it. They all felt her happiness. They felt as if an invisible, customary barrier had been removed, as if a transparent curtain had been pulled away. Or perhaps they had only imagined it was there all the time? Laurence forgot to be sharp with Denise, or to treat her as his rival. He did not even bother to struggle with Sophie. Television was not mentioned.

"We saw the silica quarry from the air," he said to Isabel, at dinner. "It was like a snowfield."

"White marble," said Sophie, quoting. "Pretentious stuff. They've put it on all the park paths in Aubreyville, spoiled the park. Glaring."

Isabel said, "You know we used to have the White Dump? At the school I went to—it was behind a biscuit factory, the playground backed onto the factory property. Every now and then, they'd sweep up these quantities of vanilla icing and nuts and hardened marshmallow globs and they'd bring it in barrels and dump it back there and it would shine. It would shine like a pure white mountain. Over at the school, somebody would see it and yell, 'White Dump!' and after school we'd all climb over the fence or run around it. We'd all be over there, scrabbling away at that enormous pile of white candy."

"Did they sweep it off the floor?" said Peter. He sounded rather exhilarated by the idea. "Did you eat it?"

"Of course they did," said Denise. "That was all they had. They were poor children."

"No, no, no," said Isabel. "We were poor but we certainly had candy. We got a nickel now and then to go to the store. It wasn't that. It was something about the White Dump—that there was so much and it was so white and shiny. It was like a kid's dream—the most wonderful promising thing you could ever see."

"Mother and the Socialists would take it all away in the dead of night," said Laurence, "and give you oranges instead."

"If I picture marzipan, I can understand," said Sophie. "Though you'll have to admit it doesn't seem very healthy."

"It must have been terrible," said Isabel. "For our teeth, and everything. But we didn't really get enough to be sick, because there were so many of us and we had to scrabble so hard. It just seemed like the most wonderful thing."

"White Dump!" said Laurence—who, at another time, to such a story might have said something like "Simple pleasures of the poor!" "White Dump," he said, with a mixture of pleasure and irony, a natural appreciation that seemed to be exactly what Isabel wanted.

She shouldn't have been surprised. She knew about Laurence's delicacy and kindness, as well as she knew his bullying and bluffing. She knew the turns of his mind, his changes of heart, the little shifts and noises of his body. They were intimate. They had found out so much about each other that everything had got cancelled out by something else. That was why the sex between them could seem so shamefaced, merely and drearily lustful, like sex between siblings. Love could survive that—had survived it. Look how she loved him at this moment. Isabel felt herself newly, and boundlessly, resourceful.

If his partner was there, if he and his partner were there together, she could say, "I think we left something yesterday. My mother-in-law thinks she dropped her glasses case. Not her glasses. Just the case. It doesn't matter. I thought I'd check."

If he was there alone but came toward her with a blank, pleasant look, inquiring, she might need to have a less trivial reason.

"I just wanted to find out about flying lessons. My husband asked me to find out."

If he was there alone but his look was not so blank—yet it was still necessary that something should be said—she could say, "It was so kind of you to take everybody up yesterday and they did enjoy it. I just dropped by to thank you."

She couldn't believe this; she couldn't believe it would happen. In spite of her reading, her fantasies, the confidences of certain friends, she couldn't believe that people sent and got such messages every day, and acted on them, making their perilous plans, moving into illicit territory (which would turn out to be shockingly like, and unlike, home).

In the years ahead, she would learn to read the signs, both at the beginning and at the end of a love affair. She wouldn't be so astonished at the way the skin of the moment can break open. But astonished enough that she would say one day to her grown-up daughter Denise, when they were drinking wine and talking about these things, "I think the best part is always right at the beginning. At the beginning. That's the only pure part." "Perhaps even before the beginning," she said. "Perhaps just when it flashes on you what's possible. That may be the best."

"And the first love affair? I mean the first extra love affair?" (Denise suppressing all censure.) "Is that the best too?"

"With me, the most passionate. Also the most sordid."

(Referring to the fact that the business was failing, that the pilot asked for, and received, some money from her; also to the grievous scenes of revelation that put an end to the affair and to her marriage, though not to his. Referring, as well, to scenes of such fusing, sundering pleasure that they left both parties flattened, and in a few cases, shedding tears. And to the very first scene, which she could replay in her mind at any time, recalling surprisingly mixed feelings of alarm and tranquillity.)

The airport at about nine o'clock in the morning, the silence, sunlight, the dusty distant trees. The small white house that had obviously been hauled here from somewhere else to be the office. No curtains or blinds on its windows. But a piece of picket fence, of all things, a gate. He came out and held the gate open for her. He wore the same clothes that he had worn yesterday, the same light-colored work pants and work shirt with the sleeves rolled up. She wore the same clothes that she had worn. Neither heard what the other said, or could answer in a way that made sense.

Too much ease on his part, or any sign of calculation—worse still, of triumph—would have sent her away. But he didn't make that kind of mistake, probably wasn't tempted to. Men who are successful with women—and he had been successful; she was to find out that he had been successful some times before, in very similar circumstances—men who are gifted in that way are not so light-minded about it as they are thought to be, and not unkind. He was resolute but seemed thoughtful, or even regretful, when he first touched her. A calming, appreciative touch, a slowly increasing declaration, over her bare neck and shoulders, bare arms and back, lightly covered breasts and hips. He spoke to her—some intimate, serious nonsense—while she swayed back and forth in a response that this touch made just bearable.

She felt rescued, lifted, beheld, and safe.)

After dinner, they played charades. Peter was Orion. He did the second syllable by drinking from an imaginary glass, then staggering around and falling down. He was not disqualified, though it was agreed that Orion was a proper name.

"Space is Peter's world, after all," said Denise. Laurence and Isabel laughed. This remark was one that would be quoted from time to time in the household.

Sophie, who never understood the rules of charades—or, at least, could never keep to them—soon gave up the game, and began to read. Her book was *The Poetic Edda*, which she read every summer, but had been neglecting because of the demands of television. When she went to bed, she left it on the arm of her chair.

Isabel, picking it up before she turned out the light, read this verse:

> *Seinat er at segia;*
> *svá er nu rádit.*

(It is too late to talk of this now: it has been decided.)

❧ *Fits* ❧

THE TWO PEOPLE who died were in their early sixties. They were both tall and well built, and carried a few pounds of extra weight. He was gray-haired, with a square, rather flat face. A broad nose kept him from looking perfectly dignified and handsome. Her hair was blond, a silvery blond that does not strike you as artificial anymore—though you know it is not natural—because so many women of that age have acquired it. On Boxing Day, when they dropped over to have a drink with Peg and Robert, she wore a pale-gray dress with a fine, shiny stripe in it, gray stockings, and gray shoes. She drank gin-and-tonic. He wore brown slacks and a cream-colored sweater, and drank rye-and-water. They had recently come back from a trip to Mexico. He had tried parachute-riding. She hadn't wanted to. They had gone to see a place in Yucatán—it looked like a well—where virgins were supposed to have been flung down, in the hope of good harvests.

"Actually, though, that's just a nineteenth-century notion," she said. "That's just the nineteenth-century notion of being so preoccupied with virginity. The truth probably is that they threw people down sort of indiscriminately. Girls or men or old people or whoever they could get their hands on. So not being a virgin would be no guarantee of safety!"

Across the room, Peg's two sons—the older one, Clayton, who was a virgin, and the younger one, Kevin, who was not—watched this breezy-talking silvery-blond woman with stern, bored expressions. She had said that she used to be a high-school English teacher. Clayton remarked afterward that he knew the type.

Robert and Peg have been married for nearly five years. Robert was never married before, but Peg married for the first time when she was eighteen. Her two boys were born while she and her husband lived with his parents on a farm. Her husband had a job driving trucks of livestock to the Canada Packers Abattoir in Toronto. Other truck-driving jobs followed, taking him farther and farther away. Peg and the boys moved to Gilmore, and she got a job working in Kuiper's store, which was called the Gilmore Arcade. Her husband ended up in the Arctic, driving trucks to oil rigs across the frozen Beaufort Sea. She got a divorce.

Robert's family owned the Gilmore Arcade but had never lived in Gilmore. His mother and sisters would not have believed you could survive a week in such a place. Robert's father had bought the store, and two other stores in nearby towns, shortly after the Second World War. He hired local managers, and drove up from Toronto a few times during the year to see how things were getting on.

For a long time, Robert did not take much interest in his father's various businesses. He took a degree in civil engineering, and had some idea of doing work in underdeveloped countries. He got a job in Peru, travelled through South America, gave up engineering for a while to work on a ranch in British Columbia. When his father became ill, it was necessary for him to come back to Toronto. He worked for the Provincial Department of Highways, in an engineering job that was not a very good one for a man of his age. He was thinking of getting a teaching degree and maybe going up North to teach Indians, changing his life completely, once his father died. He was getting close to forty then, and having his third major affair with a married woman.

Now and then, he drove up to Gilmore and the other towns to keep an eye on the stores. Once, he brought Lee with him, his third—and, as it turned out, his last—married woman. She brought a picnic lunch, drank Pimm's No. 1 in the car, and treated the whole trip as a merry excursion, a foray into hill-billy country. She had counted on making love in the open fields, and was incensed to find they were all full of cattle or uncomfortable cornstalks.

Robert's father died, and Robert did change his life, but instead of becoming a teacher and heading for the wilderness, he came to live in Gilmore to manage the stores himself. He married Peg.

It was entirely by accident that Peg was the one who found them.

On Sunday evening, the farm woman who sold the Kuipers their eggs knocked on the door.

"I hope you don't mind me bringing these tonight instead of tomorrow morning," she said. "I have to take my daughter-in-law to Kitchener to have her ultrasound. I brought the Wee-bles theirs too, but I guess they're not home. I wonder if you'd mind if I left them here with you? I have to leave early in the morning. She was going to drive herself but I didn't think that was such a good idea. She's nearly five months but still vomiting. Tell them they can just pay me next time."

"No problem," said Robert. "No trouble at all. We can just run over with them in the morning. No problem at all!" Robert is a stocky, athletic-looking man, with curly, graying hair and bright brown eyes. His friendliness and obligingness are often emphatic, so that people might get the feeling of being buffeted from all sides. This is a manner that serves him well in Gilmore, where assurances are supposed to be repeated, and in fact much of conversation is repetition, a sort of dance of good intentions, without surprises. Just occasionally, talking to people, he feels something else, an obstruction, and isn't sure what it is (malice, stubbornness?) but it's like a rock at the bottom of a river when you're swimming—the clear water lifts you over it.

For a Gilmore person, Peg is reserved. She came up to the woman and relieved her of the eggs she was holding, while Robert went on assuring her it was no trouble and asking about the daughter-in-law's pregnancy. Peg smiled as she would smile in the store when she gave you your change—a quick transactional smile, nothing personal. She is a small slim woman with a cap of soft brown hair, freckles, and a scrubbed, youthful look. She wears pleated skirts, fresh neat blouses buttoned to the throat, pale sweaters, sometimes a black ribbon tie. She moves gracefully and makes very little noise. Robert once told her he had never met anyone so self-contained as she was. (His women have usually been talkative, stylishly effective, though careless about some of the details, tense, lively, "interesting.")

Peg said she didn't know what he meant.

He started to explain what a self-contained person was like. At that time, he had a very faulty comprehension of Gilmore vocabulary—he could still make mistakes about it—and he took too seriously the limits that were usually observed in daily exchanges.

"I know what the words mean," Peg said, smiling. "I just don't understand how you mean it about me."

Of course she knew what the words meant. Peg took courses, a different course each winter, choosing from what was offered at the local high school. She took a course on the History of Art, one on Great Civilizations of the East, one on Discoveries and Explorations Through the Ages. She went to class one night a week, even if she was very tired or had a cold. She wrote tests and prepared papers. Sometimes Robert would find a page covered with her small neat handwriting on top of the refrigerator or the dresser in their room.

Therefore we see that the importance of Prince Henry the Navigator was in the inspiration and encouragement of other explorers for Portugal, even though he did not go on voyages himself.

He was moved by her earnest statements, her painfully careful small handwriting, and angry that she never got more than a B-plus for these papers she worked so hard at.

"I don't do it for the marks," Peg said. Her cheekbones reddened under the freckles, as if she was making some kind of personal confession. "I do it for the enjoyment."

Robert was up before dawn on Monday morning, standing at the kitchen counter drinking his coffee, looking out at the fields covered with snow. The sky was clear, and the temperatures had dropped. It was going to be one of the bright, cold, hard January days that come after weeks of west wind, of blowing and falling snow. Creeks, rivers, ponds frozen over. Lake

Huron frozen over as far as you could see. Perhaps all the way this year. That had happened, though rarely.

He had to drive to Keneally, to the Kuiper store there. Ice on the roof was causing water underneath to back up and leak through the ceiling. He would have to chop up the ice and get the roof clear. It would take him at least half the day.

All the repair work and upkeep on the store and on this house is done by Robert himself. He has learned to do plumbing and wiring. He enjoys the feeling that he can manage it. He enjoys the difficulty, and the difficulty of winter, here. Not much more than a hundred miles from Toronto, it is a different country. The snowbelt. Coming up here to live was not unlike heading into the wilderness, after all. Blizzards still isolate the towns and villages. Winter comes down hard on the country, settles down just the way the two-mile-high ice did thousands of years ago. People live within the winter in a way outsiders do not understand. They are watchful, provident, fatigued, exhilarated.

A thing he likes about this house is the back view, over the open country. That makes up for the straggling dead-end street without trees or sidewalks. The street was opened up after the war, when it was taken for granted that everybody would be using cars, not walking anywhere. And so they did. The houses are fairly close to the street and to each other, and when everybody who lives in the houses is home, cars take up nearly all the space where sidewalks, boulevards, shade trees might have been.

Robert, of course, was willing to buy another house. He assumed they would do that. There were—there are—fine old houses for sale in Gilmore, at prices that are a joke, by city standards. Peg said she couldn't see herself living in those places. He offered to build her a new house in the subdivision on the other side of town. She didn't want that either. She wanted to stay in this house, which was the first house she and the boys had lived in on their own. So Robert bought it—she was only renting—and built on the master bedroom and another bathroom, and made a television room in the basement. He got some help from Kevin, less from Clayton. The house still looked, from the street, like the house he had parked in front of the first time he drove Peg home from work. One and a half stories high, with a steep roof and a living-room window divided into square panes like the window on a Christmas card. White aluminum siding, narrow black shutters, black trim. Back in Toronto, he had thought of Peg living in this house. He had thought of her patterned, limited, serious, and desirable life.

He noticed the Weebles' eggs sitting on the counter. He thought of taking them over. But it was too early. The door would be locked. He didn't want to wake them. Peg could take the eggs when she left to open up the store. He took the Magic Marker that was sitting on the ledge under her reminder pad, and wrote on a paper towel, *Don't forget eggs to W's. Love, Robert.* These eggs were no cheaper than the ones you bought at the supermarket. It was just that Robert liked getting them from a farm. And they were brown. Peg said city people all had a thing about brown eggs—they thought brown eggs were more natural somehow, like brown sugar.

When he backed his car out, he saw that the Weebles' car was in their carport. So they were home from wherever they had been last night. Then he saw that the snow thrown up across the front of their driveway by the town snowplow had not been cleared. The plow must have gone by during the night. But he himself hadn't had to shovel any snow; there hadn't been any fresh snow overnight and the plow hadn't been out. The snow was from yesterday. They couldn't have been out last night. Unless they were walking. The sidewalks were not cleared, except along the main street and the school streets, and it was difficult to walk along the narrowed streets with their banks of snow, but, being new to town, they might have set out not realizing that.

He didn't look closely enough to see if there were footprints.

He pictured what happened. First from the constable's report, then from Peg's.

Peg came out of the house at about twenty after eight. Clayton had already gone off to school, and Kevin, getting over an ear infection, was down in the basement room playing a Billy Idol tape and watching a game show on television. Peg had not forgotten the eggs. She got into her car and turned on the engine to warm it up, then walked out to the street, stepped over the Weebles' uncleared snow, and went up their driveway to the side door. She was wearing her white knitted scarf and tam and her lilac-colored, down-filled coat. Those coats made most of the women in Gilmore look like barrels, but Peg looked all right, being so slender.

The houses on the street were originally of only three designs. But by now most of them had been so altered, with new windows, porches, wings, and decks, that it was hard to find true mates anymore. The Weebles' house had been built as a mirror image of the Kuipers', but the front window had been changed, its Christmas-card panes taken out, and the roof had been lifted, so that there was a large upstairs window overlooking the street. The siding was pale green and the trim white, and there were no shutters.

The side door opened into a utility room, just as Peg's door did at home. She knocked lightly at first, thinking that they would be in the kitchen, which was only a few steps up from the utility room. She had noticed the car, of course, and wondered if they had got home late and were sleeping in. (She hadn't thought yet about the snow's not having been shovelled, and the fact that the plow hadn't been past in the night. That was something that occurred to her later on when she got into her own car and backed it out.) She knocked louder and louder. Her face was stinging already in the bright cold. She tried the door and found that it wasn't locked. She opened it and stepped into shelter and called.

The little room was dark. There was no light to speak of coming down from the kitchen, and there was a bamboo curtain over the side door. She set the eggs on the clothes dryer, and was going to leave them there. Then she thought she had better take them up into the kitchen, in case the Weebles wanted eggs for breakfast and had run out. They wouldn't think of looking in the utility room.

(This, in fact, was Robert's explanation to himself. She didn't

say all that, but he forgot she didn't. She just said, "I thought
I might as well take them up to the kitchen.")

The kitchen had those same bamboo curtains over the sink
window and over the breakfast-nook windows, which meant
that though the room faced east, like the Kuipers' kitchen, and
though the sun was fully up by this time, not much light could
get in. The day hadn't begun here.

But the house was warm. Perhaps they'd got up a while ago
and turned up the thermostat, then gone back to bed. Perhaps
they left it up all night—though they had seemed to Peg to be
thriftier than that. She set the eggs on the counter by the sink.
The layout of the kitchen was almost exactly the same as her
own. She noticed a few dishes stacked, rinsed, but not washed,
as if they'd had something to eat before they went to bed.

She called again from the living-room doorway.

The living room was perfectly tidy. It looked to Peg somehow too perfectly tidy, but that—as she said to Robert—was
probably the way the living room of a retired couple was bound
to look to a woman used to having children around. Peg had
never in her life had quite as much tidiness around her as she
might have liked, having gone from a family home where there
were six children to her in-laws' crowded farmhouse, which was
crowded further with her own babies. She had told Robert a
story about once asking for a beautiful bar of soap for Christmas, pink soap with a raised design of roses on it. She got it,
and she used to hide it after every use so that it wouldn't get
cracked and moldy in the cracks, the way soap always did in
that house. She was grown up at that time, or thought she was.

She had stamped the snow off her boots in the utility room.
Nevertheless she hesitated to walk across the clean, pale-beige
living-room carpet. She called again. She used the Weebles'
first names, which she barely knew. Walter and Nora. They
had moved in last April, and since then they had been away on
two trips, so she didn't feel she knew them at all well, but it
seemed silly to be calling, "Mr. and Mrs. Weeble. Are you up
yet, Mr. and Mrs. Weeble?"

No answer.

They had an open staircase going up from the living room,

just as Peg and Robert did. Peg walked now across the clean, pale carpet to the foot of the stairs, which were carpeted in the same material. She started to climb. She did not call again.

She must have known then or she would have called. It would be the normal thing to do, to keep calling the closer you got to where people might be sleeping. To warn them. They might be deeply asleep. Drunk. That wasn't the custom of the Weebles, so far as anybody knew, but nobody knew them that well. Retired people. Early retirement. He had been an accountant; she had been a teacher. They had lived in Hamilton. They had chosen Gilmore because Walter Weeble used to have an aunt and uncle here, whom he visited as a child. Both dead now, the aunt and uncle, but the place must have held pleasant memories for him. And it was cheap; this was surely a cheaper house than they could have afforded. They meant to spend their money travelling. No children.

She didn't call; she didn't halt again. She climbed the stairs and didn't look around as she came up; she faced straight ahead. Ahead was the bathroom, with the door open. It was clean and empty.

She turned at the top of the stairs toward the Weebles' bedroom. She had never been upstairs in this house before, but she knew where that would be. It would be the extended room at the front, with the wide window overlooking the street.

The door of that room was open.

Peg came downstairs and left the house by the kitchen, the utility room, the side door. Her footprints showed on the carpet and on the linoleum tiles, and outside on the snow. She closed the door after herself. Her car had been running all this time and was sitting in its own little cloud of steam. She got in and backed out and drove to the police station in the Town Hall.

"It's a bitter cold morning, Peg," the constable said.

"Yes, it is."

"So what can I do for you?"

Robert got more, from Karen.

Karen Adams was the clerk in the Gilmore Arcade. She was

a young married woman, solidly built, usually good-humored, alert without particularly seeming to be so, efficient without a lot of bustle. She got along well with the customers; she got along with Peg and Robert. She had known Peg longer, of course. She defended her against those people who said Peg had got her nose in the air since she married rich. Karen said Peg hadn't changed from what she always was. But after today she said, "I always believed Peg and me to be friends, but now I'm not so sure."

Karen started work at ten. She arrived a little before that and asked if there had been many customers in yet, and Peg said no, nobody.

"I don't wonder," Karen said. "It's too cold. If there was any wind, it'd be murder."

Peg had made coffee. They had a new coffeemaker, Robert's Christmas present to the store. They used to have to get take-outs from the bakery up the street.

"Isn't this thing marvellous?" Karen said as she got her coffee.

Peg said yes. She was wiping up some marks on the floor.

"Oh-oh," said Karen. "Was that me or you?"

"I think it was me," Peg said.

"So I didn't think anything of it," Karen said later. "I thought she must've tracked in some mud. I didn't stop to think, Where would you get down to mud with all this snow on the ground?"

After a while, a customer came in, and it was Celia Simms, and she had heard. Karen was at the cash, and Peg was at the back, checking some invoices. Celia told Karen. She didn't know much; she didn't know how it had been done or that Peg was involved.

Karen shouted to the back of the store. "Peg! Peg! Something terrible has happened, and it's your next-door neighbors!"

Peg called back, "I know."

Celia lifted her eyebrows at Karen—she was one of those who didn't like Peg's attitude—and Karen loyally turned aside and waited till Celia went out of the store. Then she hurried to the back, making the hangers jingle on the racks.

"Both the Weebles are shot dead, Peg. Did you know that?"
Peg said, "Yes. I found them."

"You did! When did you?"

"This morning, just before I came in to work."

"They were murdered!"

"It was a murder-suicide," Peg said. "He shot her and then he shot himself. That's what happened."

"When she told me that," Karen said, "I started to shake. I shook all over and I couldn't stop myself." Telling Robert this, she shook again, to demonstrate, and pushed her hands up inside the sleeves of her blue plush jogging suit.

"So I said, 'What did you do when you found them,' and she said, 'I went and told the police.' I said, 'Did you scream, or what?' I said didn't her legs buckle, because I know mine would've. I can't imagine how I would've got myself out of there. She said she didn't remember much about getting out, but she did remember closing the door, the outside door, and thinking, Make sure that's closed in case some dog could get in. Isn't that awful? She was right, but it's awful to think of. Do you think she's in shock?"

"No," Robert said. "I think she's all right."

This conversation was taking place at the back of the store in the afternoon, when Peg had gone out to get a sandwich.

"She had not said one word to me. Nothing. I said, 'How come you never said a word about this, Peg,' and she said, 'I knew you'd find out pretty soon.' I said yes, but she could've told me. 'I'm sorry,' she says. 'I'm sorry.' Just like she's apologizing for some little thing like using my coffee mug. Only, Peg would never do that."

Robert had finished what he was doing at the Keneally store around noon, and decided to drive back to Gilmore before getting anything to eat. There was a highway diner just outside of town, on the way in from Keneally, and he thought that he would stop there. A few truckers and travellers were usually eating in the diner, but most of the trade was local—farmers on the way home, business and working men who had driven out from town. Robert liked this place, and he had entered it today with a feeling of buoyant expectation. He was hungry from his work in the cold air, and aware of the brilliance of the day, with the snow on the fields looking sculpted, dazzling, as permanent as marble. He had the sense he had fairly often in Gilmore, the sense of walking onto an informal stage, where a rambling, agreeable play was in progress. And he knew his lines—or knew, at least, that his improvisations would not fail. His whole life in Gilmore sometimes seemed to have this quality, but if he ever tried to describe it that way, it would sound as if it was an artificial life, something contrived, not entirely serious. And the very opposite was true. So when he met somebody from his old life, as he sometimes did when he went to Toronto, and was asked how he liked living in Gilmore, he would say, "I can't tell you how much I like it!" which was exactly the truth.

"Why didn't you get in touch with me?"

"You were up on the roof."

"You could have called the store and told Ellie. She would have told me."

"What good would that have done?"

"I could at least have come home."

He had come straight from the diner to the store, without eating what he had ordered. He did not think he would find Peg in any state of collapse—he knew her well enough for that—but he did think she would want to go home, let him fix her a drink, spend some time telling him about it.

She didn't want that. She wanted to go up the street to the bakery to get her usual lunch—a roll with ham and cheese.

"I let Karen go out to eat, but I haven't had time. Should I bring one back for you? If you didn't eat at the diner, I might as well."

When she brought him the sandwich, he sat and ate it at the desk where she had been doing invoices. She put fresh coffee and water into the coffeemaker.

"I can't imagine how we got along without this thing."

He looked at Peg's lilac-colored coat hanging beside Karen's red coat on the washroom door. On the lilac coat there was a long crusty smear of reddish-brown paint, down to the hemline.

Of course that wasn't paint. But on her coat? How did she get blood on her coat? She must have brushed up against them in that room. She must have got close.

Then he remembered the talk in the diner, and realized she wouldn't have needed to get that close. She could have got blood from the door frame. The constable had been in the diner, and he said there was blood everywhere, and not just blood.

"He shouldn't ever have used a shotgun for that kind of business," one of the men at the diner said.

Somebody else said, "Maybe a shotgun was all he had."

It was busy in the store most of the afternoon. People on the street, in the bakery and the café and the bank and the Post Office, talking. People wanted to talk face to face. They had to get out and do it, in spite of the cold. Talking on the phone was not enough.

What had gone on at first, Robert gathered, was that people had got on the phone, just phoned anybody they could think of who might not have heard. Karen had phoned her friend Shirley, who was at home in bed with the flu, and her mother, who was in the hospital with a broken hip. It turned out her mother knew already—the whole hospital knew. And Shirley said, "My sister beat you to it."

It was true that people valued and looked forward to the moment of breaking the news—Karen was annoyed at Shirley's sister, who didn't work and could get to the phone whenever she wanted to—but there was real kindness and consideration behind this impulse, as well. Robert thought so. "I knew she wouldn't want not to know," Karen said, and that was true. Nobody would want not to know. To go out into the street, not knowing. To go around doing all the usual daily things, not knowing. He himself felt troubled, even slightly humiliated, to think that he hadn't known; Peg hadn't let him know.

Talk ran backward from the events of the morning. Where were the Weebles seen, and in what harmlessness and innocence, and how close to the moment when everything was changed?

She had stood in line at the Bank of Montreal on Friday afternoon.

He had got a haircut on Saturday morning.

They were together, buying groceries, in the I.G.A. on Friday evening at about eight o'clock.

What did they buy? A good supply? Specials, advertised bargains, more than enough to last for a couple of days?

More than enough. A bag of potatoes, for one thing.

Then reasons. The talk turned to reasons. Naturally. There had been no theories put forward in the diner. Nobody knew the reason, nobody could imagine. But by the end of the afternoon there were too many explanations to choose from.

Financial problems. He had been mixed up in some bad investment scheme in Hamilton. Some wild money-making deal that had fallen through. All their money was gone and they would have to live out the rest of their lives on the old-age pension.

They had owed money on their income taxes. Being an accountant, he thought he knew how to fix things, but he had been found out. He would be exposed, perhaps charged, shamed publicly, left poor. Even if it was only cheating the government, it would still be a disgrace when that kind of thing came out.

Was it a lot of money?

Certainly. A lot.

It was not money at all. They were ill. One of them or both of them. Cancer. Crippling arthritis. Alzheimer's disease. Recurrent mental problems. It was health, not money. It was suffering and helplessness they feared, not poverty.

A division of opinion became evident between men and women. It was nearly always the men who believed and insisted that the trouble had been money, and it was the women who talked of illness. Who would kill themselves just because they were poor, said some women scornfully. Or even because they might go to jail? It was always a woman too who suggested unhappiness in the marriage, who hinted at the drama of a discovered infidelity or the memory of an old one.

Robert listened to all these explanations but did not believe any of them. Loss of money, cancer, Alzheimer's disease. Equally plausible, these seemed to him, equally hollow and useless. What happened was that he believed each of them for about five minutes, no longer. If he could have believed one of them, hung on to it, it would have been as if something had taken its claws out of his chest and permitted him to breathe.

("They weren't Gilmore people, not really," a woman said to him in the bank. Then she looked embarrassed. "I don't mean like you.")

Peg kept busy getting some children's sweaters, mitts, snow-suits ready for the January sale. People came up to her when she was marking the tags, and she said, "Can I help you," so that they were placed right away in the position of being cus-tomers, and had to say that there was something they were looking for. The Arcade carried ladies' and children's clothes, sheets, towels, knitting wool, kitchenware, bulk candy, maga-zines, mugs, artificial flowers, and plenty of other things besides, so it was not hard to think of something.

What was it they were really looking for? Surely not much in the way of details, description. Very few people actually want that, or will admit they do, in a greedy and straightforward way. They want it, they don't want it. They start asking, they stop themselves. They listen and they back away. Perhaps they wanted from Peg just some kind of acknowledgment, some word or look that would send them away, saying, "Peg Kuiper is absolutely shattered." "I saw Peg Kuiper. She didn't say much but you could tell she was absolutely shattered."

Some people tried to talk to her, anyway.

"Wasn't that terrible what happened down by you?"

"Yes, it was."

"You must have known them a little bit, living next door."

"Not really. We hardly knew them at all."

"You never noticed anything that would've led you to think this could've happened?"

"We never noticed anything at all."

Robert pictured the Weebles getting into and out of their car in the driveway. That was where he had most often seen them.

He recalled their Boxing Day visit. Her gray legs made him think of a nun. Her mention of virginity had embarrassed Peg and the boys. She reminded Robert a little of the kind of women he used to know. Her husband was less talkative, though not shy. They talked about Mexican food, which it seemed the husband had not liked. He did not like eating in restaurants.

Peg had said, "Oh, men never do!"

That surprised Robert, who asked her afterward did that mean she wanted to eat out more often?

"I just said that to take her side. I thought he was glaring at her a bit."

Was he glaring? Robert had not noticed. The man seemed too self-controlled to glare at his wife in public. Too well disposed, on the whole, perhaps in some way too indolent, to glare at anybody anywhere.

But it wasn't like Peg to exaggerate.

Bits of information kept arriving. The maiden name of Nora Weeble. Driscoll. Nora Driscoll. Someone knew a woman who had taught at the same school with her in Hamilton. Well-liked as a teacher, a fashionable dresser, she had some trouble keeping order. She had taken a French Conversation course, and a course in French cooking.

Some women here had asked her if she'd be interested in starting a book club, and she had said yes.

He had been more of a joiner in Hamilton than he was here. The Rotary Club. The Lions Club. Perhaps it had been for business reasons.

They were not churchgoers, as far as anybody knew, not in either place.

(Robert was right about the reasons. In Gilmore everything becomes known, sooner or later. Secrecy and confidentiality are seen to be against the public interest. There is a network of people who are married to or related to the people who work in the offices where all the records are kept.

There was no investment scheme, in Hamilton or anywhere else. No income-tax investigation. No problem about money. No cancer, tricky heart, high blood pressure. She had consulted the doctor about headaches, but the doctor did not think they were migraines, or anything serious.

At the funeral on Thursday, the United Church minister, who usually took up the slack in the cases of no known affiliation, spoke about the pressures and tensions of modern life but gave no more specific clues. Some people were disappointed, as if they expected him to do that—or thought that he might at least mention the dangers of falling away from faith and church membership, the sin of despair. Other people thought that saying anything more than he did say would have been in bad taste.)

Another person who thought Peg should have let him know was Kevin. He was waiting for them when they got home. He was still wearing his pajamas.

Why hadn't she come back to the house instead of driving to the police station? Why hadn't she called to him? She could have come back and phoned. Kevin could have phoned. At the very least, she could have called him from the store.

He had been down in the basement all morning, watching television. He hadn't heard the police come; he hadn't seen them go in or out. He had not known anything about what was going on until his girlfriend, Shanna, phoned him from school at lunch hour.

"She said they took the bodies out in garbage bags."

"How would she know?" said Clayton. "I thought she was at school."

"Somebody told her."

"She got that from television."

"She *said* they took them out in garbage bags."

"Shanna is a cretin. She is only good for one thing."

"Some people aren't good for anything."

Clayton was sixteen, Kevin fourteen. Two years apart in age but three years apart at school, because Clayton was accelerated and Kevin was not.

"Cut it out," Peg said. She had brought up some spaghetti sauce from the freezer and was thawing it in the double boiler. "Clayton. Kevin. Get busy and make me some salad."

Kevin said, "I'm sick. I might contaminate it."

He picked up the tablecloth and wrapped it around his shoulders like a shawl.

"Do we have to eat off that?" Clayton said. "Now he's got his crud on it?"

Peg said to Robert, "Are we having wine?"

Saturday and Sunday nights they usually had wine, but tonight Robert had not thought about it. He went down to the basement to get it. When he came back, Peg was sliding spaghetti into the cooker and Kevin had discarded the tablecloth. Clayton was making the salad. Clayton was small-boned, like his mother, and fiercely driven. A star runner, a demon examination writer.

Kevin was prowling around the kitchen, getting in the way, talking to Peg. Kevin was taller already than Clayton or Peg, perhaps taller than Robert. He had large shoulders and skinny legs and black hair that he wore in the nearest thing he dared to a Mohawk cut—Shanna cut it for him. His pale skin often broke out in pimples. Girls didn't seem to mind.

"So was there?" Kevin said. "Was there blood and guck all over?"

"Ghoul," said Clayton.

"Those were human beings, Kevin," Robert said.

"Were," said Kevin. "I know they *were* human beings. I mixed their drinks on Boxing Day. She drank gin and he drank rye. They were human beings then, but all they are now is chemicals. Mom? What did you see first? Shanna said there was blood and guck even out in the hallway."

"He's brutalized from all the TV he watches," Clayton said. "He thinks it was some video. He can't tell real blood from video blood."

"Mom? Was it splashed?"

Robert has a rule about letting Peg deal with her sons unless she asks for his help. But this time he said, "Kevin, you know it's about time you shut up."

"He can't help it," Clayton said. "Being ghoulish."

"You too, Clayton. You too."

But after a moment Clayton said, "Mom? Did you scream?"

"No," said Peg thoughtfully. "I didn't. I guess because there wasn't anybody to hear me. So I didn't."

"I might have heard you," said Kevin, cautiously trying a comeback.

"You had the television on."

"I didn't have the sound on. I had my tape on. I might have heard you through the tape if you screamed loud enough."

Peg lifted a strand of the spaghetti to try it. Robert was watching her, from time to time. He would have said he was watching to see if she was in any kind of trouble, if she seemed numb, or strange, or showed a quiver, if she dropped things or made the pots clatter. But in fact he was watching her just because there was no sign of such difficulty and because he knew there wouldn't be. She was preparing an ordinary meal, listening to the boys in her usual mildly censorious but unruffled way. The only thing more apparent than usual to Robert was her gracefulness, lightness, quickness, and ease around the kitchen.

Her tone to her sons, under its severity, seemed shockingly serene.

"Kevin, go and get some clothes on, if you want to eat at the table."

"I can eat in my pajamas."

"No."

"I can eat in bed."

"Not spaghetti, you can't."

While they were washing up the pots and pans together—Clayton had gone for his run and Kevin was talking to Shanna on the phone—Peg told Robert her part of the story. He didn't ask her to, in so many words. He started off with "So when you went over, the door wasn't locked?" and she began to tell him.

"You don't mind talking about it?" Robert said.

"I knew you'd want to know."

She told him she knew what was wrong—at least, she knew that something was terribly wrong—before she started up the stairs.

"Were you frightened?"

"No. I didn't think about it like that—being frightened."

"There could have been somebody up there with a gun."

"No. I knew there wasn't. I knew there wasn't anybody but me alive in the house. Then I saw his leg, I saw his leg stretched out into the hall, and I knew then, but I had to go on in and make sure."

Robert said, "I understand that."

"It wasn't the foot he had taken the shoe off that was out there. He took the shoe off his other foot, so he could use that foot to pull the trigger when he shot himself. That was how he did it."

Robert knew all about that already, from the talk in the diner.

"So," said Peg. "That's really about all."

She shook dishwater from her hands, dried them, and, with a critical look, began rubbing in lotion.

Clayton came in at the side door. He stamped the snow from his shoes and ran up the steps.

"You should see the cars," he said. "Stupid cars all crawling along this street. Then they have to turn around at the end and crawl back. I wish they'd get stuck. I stood out there and gave them dirty looks, but I started to freeze so I had to come in."

"It's natural," Robert said. "It seems stupid but it's natural. They can't believe it, so they want to see where it happened."

"I don't see their problem," Clayton said. "I don't see why they can't believe it. Mom could believe it all right. Mom wasn't surprised."

"Well, of course I was," Peg said, and this was the first time Robert had noticed any sort of edge to her voice. "Of course I was surprised, Clayton. Just because I didn't break out screaming."

"You weren't surprised they could do it."

"I hardly knew them. We hardly knew the Weebles."

"I guess they had a fight," said Clayton.

"We don't know that," Peg said, stubbornly working the lotion into her skin. "We don't know if they had a fight, or what."

"When you and Dad used to have those fights?" Clayton said. "Remember, after we first moved to town? When he would be home? Over by the car wash? When you used to have those fights, you know what I used to think? I used to think one of you was going to come and kill me with a knife."

"That's not true," said Peg.

"It is true. I did."

Peg sat down at the table and covered her mouth with her hands. Clayton's mouth twitched. He couldn't seem to stop it, so he turned it into a little, taunting, twitching smile.

"That's what I used to lie in bed and think."

"Clayton. We would never either one of us ever have hurt you."

Robert believed it was time that he said something.

"What this is like," he said, "it's like an earthquake or a volcano. It's that kind of happening. It's a kind of fit. People can take a fit like the earth takes a fit. But it only happens once in a long while. It's a freak occurrence."

"Earthquakes and volcanoes aren't freaks," said Clayton, with a certain dry pleasure. "If you want to call that a fit, you'd have to call it a periodic fit. Such as people have, married people have."

"We don't," said Robert. He looked at Peg as if waiting for her to agree with him.

But Peg was looking at Clayton. She who always seemed pale and silky and assenting, but hard to follow as a watermark in fine paper, looked dried out, chalky, her outlines fixed in steady, helpless, unapologetic pain.

"No," said Clayton. "No, not you."

Robert told them that he was going for a walk. When he got outside, he saw that Clayton was right. There were cars nosing along the street, turning at the end, nosing their way back again. Getting a look. Inside those cars were just the same people, probably the very same people, he had been talking to during the afternoon. But now they seemed joined to their cars, making some new kind of monster that came poking around in a brutally curious way.

To avoid them, he went down a short dead-end street that branched off theirs. No houses had ever been built on this street, so it was not plowed. But the snow was hard, and easy to walk on. He didn't notice how easy it was to walk on until he realized that he had gone beyond the end of the street and up a slope, which was not a slope of land at all, but a drift of snow. The drift neatly covered the fence that usually separated the street from the field. He had walked over the fence without knowing what he was doing. The snow was that hard.

He walked here and there, testing. The crust took his weight without a whisper or a crack. It was the same everywhere. You could walk over the snowy fields as if you were walking on cement. (This morning, looking at the snow, hadn't he thought of marble?) But this paving was not flat. It rose and dipped in a way that had not much to do with the contours of the ground underneath. The snow created its own landscape, which was sweeping, in a grand and arbitrary style.

Instead of walking around on the plowed streets of town, he could walk over the fields. He could cut across to the diner on the highway, which stayed open until midnight. He would have a cup of coffee there, turn around, and walk home.

One night, about six months before Robert married Peg, he and Lee were sitting drinking in his apartment. They were having an argument about whether it was permissible, or sickening, to have your family initial on your silverware. All of a sudden, the argument split open—Robert couldn't remember how, but it split open, and they found themselves saying the cruellest things to each other that they could imagine. Their voices changed from the raised pitch and speed of argument, and they spoke quietly with a subtle loathing.

"You always make me think of a dog," Lee said. "You always make me think of one of those dogs that push up on people and paw them, with their big disgusting tongues hanging out. You're so eager. All your friendliness and eagerness— that's really aggression. I'm not the only one who thinks this about you. A lot of people avoid you. They can't stand you. You'd be surprised. You push and paw in that eager pathetic way, but you have a calculating look. That's why I don't care if I hurt you."

"Maybe I should tell you one of the things I don't like, then," said Robert reasonably. "It's the way you laugh. On the phone particularly. You laugh at the end of practically every sentence. I used to think it was a nervous tic, but it always really annoyed me. And I've figured out why. You're always telling somebody about what a raw deal you're getting somewhere or some unkind thing a person said to you—that's about two-thirds of your horrendously boring self-centered conversation. And then you laugh. Ha-ha, you can take it, you don't expect anything better. That laugh is sick."

After some more of this, they started to laugh themselves, Robert and Lee, but it was not the laughter of a breakthrough into reconciliation; they did not fall upon each other in relief, crying, "What rot, I didn't mean it, did you mean it?" ("No, of course not, of course I didn't mean it.") They laughed in recognition of their extremity, just as they might have laughed at another time, in the middle of quite different, astoundingly tender declarations. They trembled with murderous pleasure, with the excitement of saying what could never be retracted; they exulted in wounds inflicted but also in wounds received, and one or the other said at some point, "This is the first time we've spoken the truth since we've known each other!" For even things that came to them more or less on the spur of the moment seemed the most urgent truths that had been hardening for a long time and pushing to get out.

It wasn't so far from laughing to making love, which they did, all with no retraction. Robert made barking noises, as a dog should, and nuzzled Lee in a bruising way, snapping with real appetite at her flesh. Afterward they were enormously and finally sick of each other but no longer disposed to blame.

"There are things I just absolutely and eternally want to forget about," Robert had told Peg. He talked to her about cutting his losses, abandoning old bad habits, old deceptions and self-deceptions, mistaken notions about life, and about himself. He said that he had been an emotional spendthrift, had thrown himself into hopeless and painful entanglements as a way of avoiding anything that had normal possibilities. That was all experiment and posturing, rejection of the ordinary, decent contracts of life. So he said to her. Errors of avoidance, when he had thought he was running risks and getting intense experiences.

"Errors of avoidance that I mistook for errors of passion," he said, then thought that he sounded pretentious when he was actually sweating with sincerity, with the effort and the relief.

In return, Peg gave him facts.

We lived with Dave's parents. There was never enough hot water for the baby's wash. Finally we got out and came to town and we lived beside the car wash. Dave was only with us weekends then. It was very noisy, especially at night. Then Dave got another job, he went up North, and I rented this place.

Errors of avoidance, errors of passion. She didn't say.

Dave had a kidney problem when he was little and he was out of school a whole winter. He read a book about the Arctic. It was probably the only book he ever read that he didn't have to. Anyway, he always dreamed about it; he wanted to go there. So finally he did.

A man doesn't just drive farther and farther away in his trucks until he disappears from his wife's view. Not even if he has always dreamed of the Arctic. Things happen before he goes. Marriage knots aren't going to slip apart painlessly, with the pull of distance. There's got to be some wrenching and slashing. But she didn't say, and he didn't ask, or even think much about that, till now.

He walked very quickly over the snow crust, and when he reached the diner he found that he didn't want to go in yet. He would cross the highway and walk a little farther, then go into the diner to get warmed up on his way home.

By the time he was on his way home, the police car that was parked at the diner ought to be gone. The night constable was in there now, taking his break. This was not the same man Robert had seen and listened to when he dropped in on his way home from Keneally. This man would not have seen anything at first hand. He hadn't talked to Peg. Nevertheless he would be talking about it; everybody in the diner would be talking about it, going over the same scene and the same questions, the possibilities. No blame to them.

When they saw Robert, they would want to know how Peg was.

There was one thing he was going to ask her, just before Clayton came in. At least, he was turning the question over in his mind, wondering if it would be all right to ask her. A discrepancy, a detail, in the midst of so many abominable details.

And now he knew it wouldn't be all right; it would never be all right. It had nothing to do with him. One discrepancy, one detail—one lie—that would never have anything to do with him.

Walking on this magic surface, he did not grow tired. He grew lighter, if anything. He was taking himself farther and farther away from town, although for a while he didn't realize this. In the clear air, the lights of Gilmore were so bright they seemed only half a field away, instead of half a mile, then a mile and a half, then two miles. Very fine flakes of snow, fine as dust, and glittering, lay on the crust that held him. There was a glitter too around the branches of the trees and bushes that he was getting closer to. It wasn't like the casing around twigs and delicate branches that an ice storm leaves. It was as if the wood itself had altered and begun to sparkle.

This is the very weather in which noses and fingers are frozen. But nothing felt cold.

He was getting quite close to a large woodlot. He was crossing a long slanting shelf of snow, with the trees ahead and to one side of him. Over there, to the side, something caught his eye. There was a new kind of glitter under the trees. A congestion of shapes, with black holes in them, and unmatched arms or petals reaching up to the lower branches of the trees. He headed toward these shapes, but whatever they were did not become clear. They did not look like anything he knew. They did not look like anything, except perhaps a bit like armed giants half collapsed, frozen in combat, or like the jumbled towers of a crazy small-scale city—a space-age, small-scale city. He kept waiting for an explanation, and not getting one, until he got very close. He was so close he could almost have touched one of these monstrosities before he saw that they were just old cars. Old cars and trucks and even a school bus that had been pushed in under the trees and left. Some were completely overturned, and some were tipped over one another at odd angles. They were partly filled, partly covered, with snow. The black holes were their gutted insides. Twisted bits of chrome, fragments of headlights, were glittering.

He thought of himself telling Peg about this—how close he had to get before he saw that what amazed him and bewildered him so was nothing but old wrecks, and how he then felt disappointed, but also like laughing. They needed some new thing to talk about. Now he felt more like going home.

At noon, when the constable in the diner was giving his account, he had described how the force of the shot threw Walter Weeble backward. "It blasted him partways out of the room. His head was laying out in the hall. What was left of it was laying out in the hall."

Not a leg. Not the indicative leg, whole and decent in its trousers, the shod foot. That was not what anybody turning at the top of the stairs would see and would have to step over, step through, in order to go into the bedroom and look at the rest of what was there.

∾ *Friend of My Youth* ∾

WITH THANKS TO R.J.T.

I USED TO DREAM about my mother, and though the details in the dream varied, the surprise in it was always the same. The dream stopped, I suppose, because it was too transparent in its hopefulness, too easy in its forgiveness.

In the dream I would be the age I really was, living the life I was really living, and I would discover that my mother was still alive. (The fact is, she died when I was in my early twenties and she in her early fifties.) Sometimes I would find myself in our old kitchen, where my mother would be rolling out piecrust on the table, or washing the dishes in the battered cream-colored dishpan with the red rim. But other times I would run into her on the street, in places where I would never have expected to see her. She might be walking through a handsome hotel lobby, or lining up in an airport. She would be looking quite well—not exactly youthful, not entirely untouched by the paralyzing disease that held her in its grip for a decade or more before her death, but so much better than I remembered that I would be astonished. Oh, I just have this little tremor in my arm, she would say, and a little stiffness up this side of my face. It is a nuisance but I get around.

I recovered then what in waking life I had lost—my mother's liveliness of face and voice before her throat muscles stiffened and a woeful, impersonal mask fastened itself over her features. How could I have forgotten this, I would think in the dream— the casual humor she had, not ironic but merry, the lightness and impatience and confidence? I would say that I was sorry I hadn't been to see her in such a long time—meaning not that I felt guilty but that I was sorry I had kept a bugbear in my mind, instead of this reality—and the strangest, kindest thing of all to me was her matter-of-fact reply.

Oh, well, she said, better late than never. I was sure I'd see you someday.

When my mother was a young woman with a soft, mischievous face and shiny, opaque silk stockings on her plump legs (I have seen a photograph of her, with her pupils), she went to teach at a one-room school, called Grieves School, in the Ottawa Valley. The school was on a corner of the farm that belonged to the Grieves family—a very good farm for that country. Well-drained fields with none of the Precambrian rock shouldering through the soil, a little willow-edged river running alongside, a sugar bush, log barns, and a large, unornamented house whose wooden walls had never been painted but had been left to weather. And when wood weathers in the Ottawa Valley, my mother said, I do not know why this is, but it never turns gray, it turns black. There must be something in the air, she said. She often spoke of the Ottawa Valley, which was her home—she had grown up about twenty miles away from Grieves School—in a dogmatic, mystified way, emphasizing things about it that distinguished it from any other place on earth. Houses turn black, maple syrup has a taste no maple syrup produced elsewhere can equal, bears amble within sight of farmhouses. Of course I was disappointed when I finally got to see this place. It was not a valley at all, if by that you mean a cleft between hills; it was a mixture of flat fields and low rocks and heavy bush and little lakes—a scrambled, disarranged sort of country with no easy harmony about it, not yielding readily to any description.

The log barns and unpainted house, common enough on poor farms, were not in the Grieveses' case a sign of poverty but of policy. They had the money but they did not spend it. That was what people told my mother. The Grieveses worked hard and they were far from ignorant, but they were very backward. They didn't have a car or electricity or a telephone or a tractor. Some people thought this was because they were Cameronians—they were the only people in the school district who were of that religion—but in fact their church (which they themselves always called the Reformed Presbyterian) did not forbid engines or electricity or any inventions of that sort, just cardplaying, dancing, movies, and, on Sundays, any activity at all that was not religious or unavoidable.

My mother could not say who the Cameronians were or why they were called that. Some freak religion from Scotland, she said from the perch of her obedient and lighthearted Anglicanism. The teacher always boarded with the Grieveses, and my mother was a little daunted at the thought of going to live in that black board house with its paralytic Sundays and coal-oil lamps and primitive notions. But she was engaged by that time, she wanted to work on her trousseau instead of running around the country having a good time, and she figured she could get home one Sunday out of three. (On Sundays at the Grieveses' house, you could light a fire for heat but not for cooking, you could not even boil the kettle to make tea, and you were not supposed to write a letter or swat a fly. But it turned out that my mother was exempt from these rules. "No, no," said Flora Grieves, laughing at her. "That doesn't mean you. You must just go on as you're used to doing." And after a while my mother had made friends with Flora to such an extent that she wasn't even going home on the Sundays when she'd planned to.)

Flora and Ellie Grieves were the two sisters left of the family. Ellie was married, to a man called Robert Deal, who lived there and worked the farm but had not changed its name to Deal's in anyone's mind. By the way people spoke, my mother expected the Grieves sisters and Robert Deal to be middle-aged at least, but Ellie, the younger sister, was only about thirty, and Flora seven or eight years older. Robert Deal might be in between.

The house was divided in an unexpected way. The married couple didn't live with Flora. At the time of their marriage, she had given them the parlor and the dining room, the front bedrooms and staircase, the winter kitchen. There was no need to decide about the bathroom, because there wasn't one. Flora had the summer kitchen, with its open rafters and uncovered brick walls, the old pantry made into a narrow dining room and sitting room, and the two back bedrooms, one of which was my mother's. The teacher was housed with Flora, in the poorer part of the house. But my mother didn't mind. She immediately preferred Flora, and Flora's cheerfulness, to the silence and sickroom atmosphere of the front rooms. In Flora's domain it was not even true that all amusements were forbidden. She had a crokinole board—she taught my mother how to play.

The division had been made, of course, in the expectation that Robert and Ellie would have a family, and that they would need the room. This hadn't happened. They had been married for more than a dozen years and there had not been a live child. Time and again Ellie had been pregnant, but two babies had been stillborn, and the rest she had miscarried. During my mother's first year, Ellie seemed to be staying in bed more and more of the time, and my mother thought that she must be pregnant again, but there was no mention of it. Such people would not mention it. You could not tell from the look of Ellie, when she got up and walked around, because she showed a stretched and ruined though slack-chested shape. She carried a sickbed odor, and she fretted in a childish way about everything. Flora took care of her and did all the work. She washed the clothes and tidied up the rooms and cooked the meals served in both sides of the house, as well as helping Robert with the milking and separating. She was up before daylight and never seemed to tire. During the first spring my mother was there, a great housecleaning was embarked upon, during which Flora climbed the ladders herself and carried down the storm windows, washed and stacked them away, carried all the furniture out of one room after another so that she could scrub the woodwork and varnish the floors. She washed every dish and glass that was sitting in the cupboards supposedly clean already. She scalded every pot and spoon. Such need and energy possessed her that she could hardly sleep—my mother would wake up to the sound of stovepipes being taken down, or the broom, draped in a dish towel, whacking at the smoky cobwebs. Through the washed uncurtained windows came a torrent of unmerciful light. The cleanliness was devastating. My mother slept now on sheets that had been bleached and starched and that gave her a rash. Sick Ellie complained daily of the smell of varnish and cleansing powders. Flora's hands were raw. But her disposition remained top-notch. Her kerchief and apron and Robert's baggy overalls that she donned for the climbing jobs gave her the air of a comedian—sportive, unpredictable.

My mother called her a whirling dervish.

"You're a regular whirling dervish, Flora," she said, and Flora halted. She wanted to know what was meant. My mother went ahead and explained, though she was a little afraid lest piety should be offended. (Not piety exactly—you could not call it that. Religious strictness.) Of course it wasn't. There was not a trace of nastiness or smug vigilance in Flora's observance of her religion. She had no fear of heathens—she had always lived in the midst of them. She liked the idea of being a dervish, and went to tell her sister.

"Do you know what the teacher says I am?"

Flora and Ellie were both dark-haired, dark-eyed women, tall and narrow-shouldered and long-legged. Ellie was a wreck, of course, but Flora was still superbly straight and graceful. She could look like a queen, my mother said—even riding into town in that cart they had. For church they used a buggy or a cutter, but when they went to town they often had to transport sacks of wool—they kept a few sheep—or of produce, to sell, and they had to bring provisions home. The trip of a few miles was not made often. Robert rode in front, to drive the horse—Flora could drive a horse perfectly well, but it must always be the man who drove. Flora would be standing behind holding on to the sacks. She rode to town and back standing up, keeping an easy balance, wearing her black hat. Almost ridiculous but not quite. A gypsy queen, my mother thought she looked like, with her black hair and her skin that always looked slightly tanned, and her lithe and bold serenity. Of course she lacked the gold bangles and the bright clothes. My mother envied her her slenderness, and her cheekbones.

Returning in the fall for her second year, my mother learned what was the matter with Ellie.

"My sister has a growth," Flora said. Nobody then spoke of cancer.

My mother had heard that before. People suspected it. My mother knew many people in the district by that time. She had made particular friends with a young woman who worked in the Post Office; this woman was going to be one of my mother's bridesmaids. The story of Flora and Ellie and Robert had been told—or all that people knew of it—in various versions. My mother did not feel that she was listening to gossip, because she was always on the alert for any disparaging remarks about Flora—she would not put up with that. But indeed nobody offered any. Everybody said that Flora had behaved like a saint. Even when she went to extremes, as in dividing up the house— that was like a saint.

Robert came to work at Grieveses' some months before the girls' father died. They knew him already, from church. (Oh, that church, my mother said, having attended it once, out of curiosity—that drear building miles on the other side of town, no organ or piano and plain glass in the windows and a doddery old minister with his hours-long sermon, a man hitting a tuning fork for the singing.) Robert had come out from Scotland and was on his way west. He had stopped with relatives or people he knew, members of the scanty congregation. To earn some money, probably, he came to Grieveses'. Soon he and Flora were engaged. They could not go to dances or to card parties like other couples, but they went for long walks. The chaperone—unofficially—was Ellie. Ellie was then a wild tease, a long-haired, impudent, childish girl full of lolloping energy. She would run up hills and smite the mullein stalks with a stick, shouting and prancing and pretending to be a warrior on horseback. That, or the horse itself. This when she was fifteen, sixteen years old. Nobody but Flora could control her, and generally Flora just laughed at her, being too used to her to wonder if she was quite right in the head. They were wonderfully fond of each other. Ellie, with her long skinny body, her long pale face, was like a copy of Flora—the kind of copy you often see in families, in which because of some carelessness or exaggeration of features or coloring, the handsomeness of one person passes into the plainness—or almost plainness—of the other. But Ellie had no jealousy about this. She loved to comb out Flora's hair and pin it up. They had great times, washing each other's hair. Ellie would press her face into Flora's throat, like a colt nuzzling its mother. So when Robert laid claim to Flora, or Flora to him—nobody knew how it was—Ellie had to be included. She didn't show any spite toward Robert, but she pursued and waylaid them on their walks; she sprung on them out of the bushes or sneaked up behind them so softly that she could blow on their necks. People saw her do it. And they heard of her jokes. She had always been terrible for jokes and sometimes it had got her into trouble with her father, but Flora had protected her. Now she put thistles in Robert's bed. She set his place at the table with the knife and fork the wrong way around. She switched the milk pails to give him the old one with the hole in it. For Flora's sake, maybe, Robert humored her.

The father had made Flora and Robert set the wedding day a year ahead, and after he died they did not move it any closer. Robert went on living in the house. Nobody knew how to speak to Flora about this being scandalous, or looking scandalous. Flora would just ask why. Instead of putting the wedding ahead, she put it back—from next spring to early fall, so that there should be a full year between it and her father's death. A year from wedding to funeral—that seemed proper to her. She trusted fully in Robert's patience and in her own purity.

So she might. But in the winter a commotion started. There was Ellie, vomiting, weeping, running off and hiding in the haymow, howling when they found her and pulled her out, jumping to the barn floor, running around in circles, rolling in the snow. Ellie was deranged. Flora had to call the doctor. She told him that her sister's periods had stopped—could the backup of blood be driving her wild? Robert had had to catch her and tie her up, and together he and Flora had put her to bed. She would not take food, just whipped her head from side to side, howling. It looked as if she would die speechless. But somehow the truth came out. Not from the doctor, who could not get close enough to examine her, with all her thrashing

about. Probably, Robert confessed. Flora finally got wind of
the truth, through all her high-mindedness. Now there had to
be a wedding, though not the one that had been planned.

No cake, no new clothes, no wedding trip, no congratulations.
Just a shameful hurry-up visit to the manse. Some people, seeing the names in the paper, thought the editor must have got
the sisters mixed up. They thought it must be Flora. A hurry-
up wedding for Flora! But no—it was Flora who pressed Robert's
suit—it must have been—and got Ellie out of bed and washed
her and made her presentable. It would have been Flora who
picked one geranium from the window plant and pinned it to
her sister's dress. And Ellie hadn't torn it out. Ellie was meek
now, no longer flailing or crying. She let Flora fix her up, she
let herself be married, she was never wild from that day on.

Flora had the house divided. She herself helped Robert build
the necessary partitions. The baby was carried full term—
nobody even pretended that it was early—but it was born dead
after a long, tearing labor. Perhaps Ellie had damaged it when
she jumped from the barn beam and rolled in the snow and
beat on herself. Even if she hadn't done that, people would have
expected something to go wrong, with that child or maybe one
that came later. God dealt out punishment for hurry-up marriages—not just Presbyterians but almost everybody else
believed that. God rewarded lust with dead babies, idiots, hare-
lips and withered limbs and clubfeet.

In this case the punishment continued. Ellie had one miscarriage after another, then another stillbirth and more miscarriages. She was constantly pregnant, and the pregnancies were
full of vomiting fits that lasted for days, headaches, cramps, dizzy
spells. The miscarriages were as agonizing as full-term births.
Ellie could not do her own work. She walked around holding
on to chairs. Her numb silence passed off, and she became a
complainer. If anybody came to visit, she would talk about the
peculiarities of her headaches or describe her latest fainting fit,
or even—in front of men, in front of unmarried girls or children—go into bloody detail about what Flora called her "disappointments." When people changed the subject or dragged the
children away, she turned sullen. She demanded new medicine,

reviled the doctor, nagged Flora. She accused Flora of washing the dishes with a great clang and clatter, out of spite, of pulling her—Ellie's—hair when she combed it out, of stingily substituting water-and-molasses for her real medicine. No matter what she said, Flora soothed her. Everybody who came into the house had some story of that kind to tell. Flora said, "Where's my little girl, then? Where's my Ellie? This isn't my Ellie, this is some crosspatch got in here in place of her!"

In the winter evenings after she came in from helping Robert with the barn chores, Flora would wash and change her clothes and go next door to read Ellie to sleep. My mother might invite herself along, taking whatever sewing she was doing, on some item of her trousseau. Ellie's bed was set up in the big dining room, where there was a gas lamp over the table. My mother sat on one side of the table, sewing, and Flora sat on the other side, reading aloud. Sometimes Ellie said, "I can't hear you." Or if Flora paused for a little rest Ellie said, "I'm not asleep yet."

What did Flora read? Stories about Scottish life—not classics. Stories about urchins and comic grandmothers. The only title my mother could remember was *Wee Macgregor*. She could not follow the stories very well, or laugh when Flora laughed and Ellie gave a whimper, because so much was in Scots dialect or read with that thick accent. She was surprised that Flora could do it—it wasn't the way Flora ordinarily talked, at all.

(But wouldn't it be the way Robert talked? Perhaps that is why my mother never reports anything that Robert said, never has him contributing to the scene. He must have been there, he must have been sitting there in the room. They would only heat the main room of the house. I see him black-haired, heavy-shouldered, with the strength of a plow horse, and the same kind of sombre, shackled beauty.)

Then Flora would say, "That's all of that for tonight." She would pick up another book, an old book written by some preacher of their faith. There was in it such stuff as my mother had never heard. What stuff? She couldn't say. All the stuff that was in their monstrous old religion. That put Ellie to sleep, or made her pretend she was asleep, after a couple of pages.

All that configuration of the elect and the damned, my mother must have meant—all the arguments about the illusion and necessity of free will. Doom and slippery redemption. The torturing, defeating, but for some minds irresistible pileup of interlocking and contradictory notions. My mother could resist it. Her faith was easy, her spirits at that time robust. Ideas were not what she was curious about, ever.

But what sort of thing was that, she asked (silently), to read to a dying woman? This was the nearest she got to criticizing Flora.

The answer—that it was the only thing, if you believed it—never seemed to have occurred to her.

By spring a nurse had arrived. That was the way things were done then. People died at home, and a nurse came in to manage it.

The nurse's name was Audrey Atkinson. She was a stout woman with corsets as stiff as barrel hoops, marcelled hair the color of brass candlesticks, a mouth shaped by lipstick beyond its own stingy outlines. She drove a car into the yard—her own car, a dark-green coupé, shiny and smart. News of Audrey Atkinson and her car spread quickly. Questions were asked. Where did she get the money? Had some rich fool altered his will on her behalf? Had she exercised influence? Or simply helped herself to a stash of bills under the mattress? How was she to be trusted?

Hers was the first car ever to sit in the Grieveses' yard overnight.

Audrey Atkinson said that she had never been called out to tend a case in so primitive a house. It was beyond her, she said, how people could live in such a way.

"It's not that they're poor, even," she said to my mother. "It isn't, is it? That I could understand. Or it's not even their religion. So what is it? They do not care!"

She tried at first to cozy up to my mother, as if they would be natural allies in this benighted place. She spoke as if they were around the same age—both stylish, intelligent women who liked a good time and had modern ideas. She offered to teach my mother to drive the car. She offered her cigarettes. My mother was more tempted by the idea of learning to drive than she was by the cigarettes. But she said no, she would wait for her husband to teach her. Audrey Atkinson raised her pinkish-orange eyebrows at my mother behind Flora's back, and my mother was furious. She disliked the nurse far more than Flora did.

"I knew what she was like and Flora didn't," my mother said. She meant that she caught a whiff of a cheap life, maybe even of drinking establishments and unsavory men, of hard bargains, which Flora was too unworldly to notice.

Flora started into the great housecleaning again. She had the curtains spread out on stretchers, she beat the rugs on the line, she leapt up on the stepladder to attack the dust on the molding. But she was impeded all the time by Nurse Atkinson's complaining.

"I wondered if we could have a little less of the running and clattering?" said Nurse Atkinson with offensive politeness. "I only ask for my patient's sake." She always spoke of Ellie as "my patient" and pretended that she was the only one to protect her and compel respect. But she was not so respectful of Ellie herself. "Allee-oop," she would say, dragging the poor creature up on her pillows. And she told Ellie she was not going to stand for fretting and whimpering. "You don't do yourself any good that way," she said. "And you certainly don't make me come any quicker. What you just as well might do is learn to control yourself." She exclaimed at Ellie's bedsores in a scolding way, as if they were a further disgrace of the house. She demanded lotions, ointments, expensive soaps—most of them, no doubt, to protect her own skin, which she claimed suffered from the hard water. (How could it be hard, my mother asked her—sticking up for the household when nobody else would—how could it be hard when it came straight from the rain barrel?)

Nurse Atkinson wanted cream too—she said that they should hold some back, not sell it all to the creamery. She wanted to make nourishing soups and puddings for her patient. She did make puddings, and jellies, from packaged mixes such as had never before entered this house. My mother was convinced that she ate them all herself.

Flora still read to Ellie, but now it was only short bits from the Bible. When she finished and stood up, Ellie tried to cling to her. Ellie wept, sometimes she made ridiculous complaints. She said there was a horned cow outside, trying to get into the room and kill her.

"They often get some kind of idea like that," Nurse Atkinson said. "You mustn't give in to her or she won't let you go day or night. That's what they're like, they only think about themselves. Now, when I'm here alone with her, she behaves herself quite nice. I don't have any trouble at all. But after you been in here I have trouble all over again because she sees you and she gets upset. You don't want to make my job harder for me, do you? I mean, you brought me here to take charge, didn't you?"

"Ellie, now, Ellie dear, I must go," said Flora, and to the nurse she said, "I understand. I do understand that you have to be in charge and I admire you, I admire you for your work. In your work you have to have so much patience and kindness."

My mother wondered at this—was Flora really so blinded, or did she hope by this undeserved praise to exhort Nurse Atkinson to the patience and kindness that she didn't have? Nurse Atkinson was too thick-skinned and self-approving for any trick like that to work.

"It is a hard job, all right, and not many can do it," she said. "It's not like those nurses in the hospital, where they got everything laid out for them." She had no time for more conversation—she was trying to bring in "Make-Believe Ballroom" on her battery radio.

My mother was busy with the final exams and the June exercises at the school. She was getting ready for her wedding in July. Friends came in cars and whisked her off to the dressmaker's, to parties, to choose the invitations and order the cake. The lilacs came out, the evenings lengthened, the birds were back and nesting, my mother bloomed in everybody's attention, about to set out on the deliciously solemn adventure of marriage. Her dress was to be appliquéd with silk roses, her veil held by a cap of seed pearls. She belonged to the first generation of young women who saved their money and paid for their own weddings—far fancier than their parents could have afforded.

On her last evening, the friend from the Post Office came to drive her away, with her clothes and her books and the things she had made for her trousseau and the gifts her pupils and others had given her. There was great fuss and laughter about getting everything loaded into the car. Flora came out and helped. This getting married is even more of a nuisance than I thought, said Flora, laughing. She gave my mother a dresser scarf, which she had crocheted in secret. Nurse Atkinson could not be shut out of an important occasion—she presented a spray bottle of cologne. Flora stood on the slope at the side of the house to wave goodbye. She had been invited to the wedding, but of course she had said she could not come, she could not "go out" at such a time. The last my mother ever saw of her was this solitary, energetically waving figure in her house-cleaning apron and bandanna, on the green slope by the black-walled house, in the evening light.

"Well, maybe now she'll get what she should've got the first time round," the friend from the Post Office said. "Maybe now they'll be able to get married. Is she too old to start a family? How old is she, anyway?"

My mother thought that this was a crude way of talking about Flora and replied that she didn't know. But she had to admit to herself that she had been thinking the very same thing.

When she was married and settled in her own home, three hundred miles away, my mother got a letter from Flora. Ellie was dead. She had died firm in her faith, Flora said, and grateful for her release. Nurse Atkinson was staying on for a little while, until it was time for her to go off to her next case. This was late in the summer.

News of what happened next did not come from Flora. When she wrote at Christmas, she seemed to take for granted that information would have gone ahead of her.

You have in all probability heard, wrote Flora, *that Robert and*

Nurse Atkinson have been married. They are living on here, in Robert's part of the house. They are fixing it up to suit themselves. It is very impolite of me to call her Nurse Atkinson, as I see I have done. I ought to have called her Audrey.

Of course the Post Office friend had written, and so had others. It was a great shock and scandal and a matter that excited the district—the wedding as secret and surprising as Robert's first one had been (though surely not for the same reason), Nurse Atkinson permanently installed in the community, Flora losing out for the second time. Nobody had been aware of any courtship, and they asked how the woman could have enticed him. Did she promise children, lying about her age?

The surprises were not to stop with the wedding. The bride got down to business immediately with the "fixing up" that Flora mentioned. In came the electricity and then the telephone. Now Nurse Atkinson—she would always be called Nurse Atkinson—was heard on the party line lambasting painters and paperhangers and delivery services. She was having everything done over. She was buying an electric stove and putting in a bathroom, and who knew where the money was coming from? Was it all hers, got in her deathbed dealings, in shady bequests? Was it Robert's, was he claiming his share? Ellie's share, left to him and Nurse Atkinson to enjoy themselves with, the shameless pair?

All these improvements took place on one side of the house only. Flora's side remained just as it was. No electric lights there, no fresh wallpaper or new venetian blinds. When the house was painted on the outside—cream with dark-green trim—Flora's side was left bare. This strange open statement was greeted at first with pity and disapproval, then with less sympathy, as a sign of Flora's stubbornness and eccentricity (she could have bought her own paint and made it look decent), and finally as a joke. People drove out of their way to see it.

There was always a dance given in the schoolhouse for a newly married couple. A cash collection—called "a purse of money"—was presented to them. Nurse Atkinson sent out word that she would not mind seeing this custom followed, even though it happened that the family she had married into was opposed to dancing. Some people thought it would be a disgrace to gratify her, a slap in the face to Flora. Others were too curious to hold back. They wanted to see how the newly-weds would behave. Would Robert dance? What sort of out-fit would the bride show up in? They delayed a while, but finally the dance was held, and my mother got her report.

The bride wore the dress she had worn at her wedding, or so she said. But who would wear such a dress for a wedding at the manse? More than likely it was bought specially for her appearance at the dance. Pure-white satin with a sweetheart neckline, idiotically youthful. The groom was got up in a new dark-blue suit, and she had stuck a flower in his buttonhole. They were a sight. Her hair was freshly done to blind the eye with brassy reflections, and her face looked as if it would come off on a man's jacket, should she lay it against his shoulder in the dancing. Of course she did dance. She danced with every man present except the groom, who sat scrunched into one of the school desks along the wall. She danced with every man present—they all claimed they had to do it, it was the custom—and then she dragged Robert out to receive the money and to thank everybody for their best wishes. To the ladies in the cloakroom she even hinted that she was feeling unwell, for the usual newlywed reason. Nobody believed her, and indeed nothing ever came of this hope, if she really had it. Some of the women thought that she was lying to them out of malice, insulting them, making them out to be so credulous. But nobody challenged her, nobody was rude to her—maybe because it was plain that she could summon a rudeness of her own to knock anybody flat.

Flora was not present at the dance.

"My sister-in-law is not a dancer," said Nurse Atkinson. "She is stuck in the olden times." She invited them to laugh at Flora, whom she always called her sister-in-law, though she had no right to do so.

My mother wrote a letter to Flora after hearing about all these things. Being removed from the scene, and perhaps in a flurry of importance due to her own newly married state, she may have lost sight of the kind of person she was writing to.

She offered sympathy and showed outrage, and said blunt disparaging things about the woman who had—as my mother saw it—dealt Flora such a blow. Back came a letter from Flora saying that she did not know where my mother had been getting her information, but that it seemed she had misunderstood, or listened to malicious people, or jumped to unjustified conclusions. What happened in Flora's family was nobody else's business, and certainly nobody needed to feel sorry for her or angry on her behalf. Flora said that she was happy and satisfied in her life, as she always had been, and she did not interfere with what others did or wanted, because such things did not concern her. She wished my mother all happiness in her marriage and hoped that she would soon be too busy with her own responsibilities to worry about the lives of people that she used to know.

This well-written letter cut my mother, as she said, to the quick. She and Flora stopped corresponding. My mother did become busy with her own life and finally a prisoner in it.

But she thought about Flora. In later years, when she sometimes talked about the things she might have been, or done, she would say, "If I could have been a writer—I do think I could have been; I could have been a writer—then I would have written the story of Flora's life. And do you know what I would have called it? 'The Maiden Lady.'"

The Maiden Lady. She said these words in a solemn and sentimental tone of voice that I had no use for. I knew, or thought I knew, exactly the value she found in them. The stateliness and mystery. The hint of derision turning to reverence. I was fifteen or sixteen years old by that time, and I believed that I could see into my mother's mind. I could see what she would do with Flora, what she had already done. She would make her into a noble figure, one who accepts defection, treachery, who forgives and stands aside, not once but twice. Never a moment of complaint. Flora goes about her cheerful labors, she cleans the house and shovels out the cow byre, she removes some bloody mess from her sister's bed, and when at last the future seems to open up for her—Ellie will die and Robert will beg forgiveness and Flora will silence him with the proud gift of herself—it is time for Audrey Atkinson to drive into the yard and shut Flora out again, more inexplicably and thoroughly the second time than the first. She must endure the painting of the house, the electric lights, all the prosperous activity next door. "Make-Believe Ballroom," "Amos 'n' Andy." No more Scottish comedies or ancient sermons. She must see them drive off to the dance—her old lover and that coldhearted, stupid, by no means beautiful woman in the white satin wedding dress. She is mocked. (And of course she has made over the farm to Ellie and Robert, of course he has inherited it, and now everything belongs to Audrey Atkinson.) The wicked flourish. But it is all right. It is all right—the elect are veiled in patience and humility and lighted by a certainty that events cannot disturb.

That was what I believed my mother would make of things. In her own plight her notions had turned mystical, and there was sometimes a hush, a solemn thrill in her voice that grated on me, alerted me to what seemed a personal danger. I felt a great fog of platitudes and pieties lurking, an incontestable crippled-mother power, which could capture and choke me. There would be no end to it. I had to keep myself sharp-tongued and cynical, arguing and deflating. Eventually I gave up even that recognition and opposed her in silence.

This is a fancy way of saying that I was no comfort and poor company to her when she had almost nowhere else to turn.

I had my own ideas about Flora's story. I didn't think that I could have written a novel but that I would write one. I would take a different tack. I saw through my mother's story and put in what she left out. My Flora would be as black as hers was white. Rejoicing in the bad turns done to her and in her own forgiveness, spying on the shambles of her sister's life. A Presbyterian witch, reading out of her poisonous book. It takes a rival ruthlessness, the comparatively innocent brutality of the thick-skinned nurse, to drive her back, to flourish in her shade. But she is driven back; the power of sex and ordinary greed drive her back and shut her up in her own part of the house with the coal-oil lamps. She shrinks, she caves in, her bones harden and her joints thicken, and—oh, this is it, I see the bare beauty of the ending I will contrive!—she becomes crippled herself, with arthritis, hardly able to move. Now Audrey Atkinson comes into her full power—she demands the whole house. She wants those partitions knocked out that Robert put up with Flora's help when he married Ellie. She will provide Flora with a room, she will take care of her. (Audrey Atkinson does not wish to be seen as a monster, and perhaps she really isn't one.) So one day Robert carries Flora—for the first and last time he carries her in his arms—to the room that his wife Audrey has prepared for her. And once Flora is settled in her well-lit, well-heated corner Audrey Atkinson undertakes to clean out the newly vacated rooms, Flora's rooms. She carries a heap of old books out into the yard. It's spring again, house-cleaning time, the season when Flora herself performed such feats, and now the pale face of Flora appears behind the new net curtains. She has dragged herself from her corner, she sees the light-blue sky with its high skidding clouds over the watery fields, the contending crows, the flooded creeks, the reddening tree branches. She sees the smoke rise out of the incinerator in the yard, where her books are burning. Those smelly old books, as Audrey has called them. Words and pages, the ominous dark spines. The elect, the damned, the slim hopes, the mighty torments—up in smoke. There was the ending.

To me the really mysterious person in the story, as my mother told it, was Robert. He never has a word to say. He gets engaged to Flora. He is walking beside her along the river when Ellie leaps out at them. He finds Ellie's thistles in his bed. He does the carpentry made necessary by his and Ellie's marriage. He listens or does not listen while Flora reads. Finally he sits scrunched up in the school desk while his flashy bride dances by with all the men.

So much for his public acts and appearances. But he was the one who started everything, in secret. He *did it to* Ellie. He did it to that skinny wild girl at a time when he was engaged to her sister, and he did it to her again and again when she was nothing but a poor botched body, a failed child-bearer, lying in bed.

He must have done it to Audrey Atkinson, too, but with less disastrous results.

Those words, *did it to*—the words my mother, no more than
Flora, would never bring herself to speak—were simply exciting to me. I didn't feel any decent revulsion or reasonable
indignation. I refused the warning. Not even the fate of Ellie
could put me off. Not when I thought of that first encounter—
the desperation of it, the ripping and striving. I used to sneak
longing looks at men in those days. I admired their wrists and
their necks and any bit of their chests a loose button let show,
and even their ears and their feet in shoes. I expected nothing
reasonable of them, only to be engulfed by their passion. I had
similar thoughts about Robert.

What made Flora evil in my story was just what made her
admirable in my mother's—her turning away from sex. I fought
against everything my mother wanted to tell me on this subject; I despised even the drop in her voice, the gloomy caution,
with which she approached it. My mother had grown up in a
time and in a place where sex was a dark undertaking for
women. She knew that you could die of it. So she honored the
decency, the prudery, the frigidity, that might protect you. And
I grew up in horror of that very protection, the dainty tyranny
that seemed to me to extend to all areas of life, to enforce tea
parties and white gloves and all other sorts of tinkling inanities. I favored bad words and a breakthrough, I teased myself
with the thought of a man's recklessness and domination. The
odd thing is that my mother's ideas were in line with some pro-
gressive notions of her times, and mine echoed the notions that
were favored in my time. This in spite of the fact that we both
believed ourselves independent, and lived in backwaters that
did not register such changes. It's as if tendencies that seem
most deeply rooted in our minds, most private and singular,
have come in as spores on the prevailing wind, looking for any
likely place to land, any welcome.

Not long before she died, but when I was still at home, my
mother got a letter from the real Flora. It came from that town
near the farm, the town that Flora used to ride to, with Robert,
in the cart, holding on to the sacks of wool or potatoes.

Flora wrote that she was no longer living on the farm.

Robert and Audrey are still there, she wrote. *Robert has some trouble with his back but otherwise he is very well. Audrey has poor circulation and is often short of breath. The doctor says she must lose weight but none of the diets seem to work. The farm has been doing very well. They are out of sheep entirely and into dairy cattle. As you may have heard, the chief thing nowadays is to get your milk quota from the government and then you are set. The old stable is all fixed up with milking machines and the latest modern equipment, it is quite a marvel. When I go out there to visit I hardly know where I am.*

She went on to say that she had been living in town for some years now, and that she had a job clerking in a store. She must have said what kind of a store this was, but I cannot now remember. She said nothing, of course, about what had led her to this decision—whether she had in fact been put off her own farm, or had sold out her share, apparently not to much advantage. She stressed the fact of her friendliness with Robert and Audrey. She said her health was good.

I hear that you have not been so lucky in that way, she wrote. *I ran into Cleta Barnes who used to be Cleta Stapleton at the post office out at home, and she told me that there is some problem with your muscles and she said your speech is affected too. This is sad to hear but they can do such wonderful things nowadays so I am hoping that the doctors may be able to help you.*

An unsettling letter, leaving so many things out. Nothing in it about God's will or His role in our afflictions. No mention of whether Flora still went to that church. I don't think my mother ever answered. Her fine legible handwriting, her schoolteacher's writing, had deteriorated, and she had difficulty holding a pen. She was always beginning letters and not finishing them. I would find them lying around the house. *My dearest Mary*, they began. *My darling Ruth, My dear little Joanne (though I realize you are not little anymore), My dear old friend Cleta, My lovely Margaret.* These women were friends from her teaching days, her Normal School days, and from high school. A few were former pupils. I have friends all over the country, she would say defiantly. I have dear, dear friends.

I remember seeing one letter that started out: *Friend of my Youth.* I don't know whom it was to. They were all friends of her youth. I don't recall one that began with *My dear and most admired Flora*. I would always look at them, try to read the salutation and the few sentences she had written, and because I could not bear to feel sadness I would feel an impatience with the flowery language, the direct appeal for love and pity. She would get more of that, I thought (more from myself, I meant), if she could manage to withdraw with dignity, instead of reaching out all the time to cast her stricken shadow.

I had lost interest in Flora by then. I was always thinking of stories, and by this time I probably had a new one on my mind.

But I have thought of her since. I have wondered what kind of a store. A hardware store or a five-and-ten, where she has to wear a coverall, or a drugstore, where she is uniformed like a nurse, or a Ladies' Wear, where she is expected to be genteelly fashionable? She might have had to learn about food blenders or chain saws, negligees, cosmetics, even condoms. She would have to work all day under electric lights, and operate a cash register. Would she get a permanent, paint her nails, put on lipstick? She must have found a place to live—a little apartment with a kitchenette, overlooking the main street, or a room in a boardinghouse. How could she go on being a Cameronian? How could she get to that out-of-the-way church unless she managed to buy a car and learned to drive it? And if she did that she might drive not only to church but to other places. She might go on holidays. She might rent a cottage on a lake for a week, learn to swim, visit a city. She might eat meals in a restaurant, possibly in a restaurant where drinks were served. She might make friends with women who were divorced.

She might meet a man. A friend's widowed brother, perhaps. A man who did not know that she was a Cameronian or what Cameronians were. Who knew nothing of her story. A man who had never heard about the partial painting of the house or the two betrayals, or that it took all her dignity and innocence to keep her from being a joke. He might want to take her dancing, and she would have to explain that she could not go. He would be surprised but not put off—all that Cameronian business might seem quaint to him, almost charming. So it would to everybody. She was brought up in some weird religion, people would say. She lived a long time out on some godforsaken farm. She is a little bit strange but really quite nice. Nice-looking too. Especially since she went and got her hair done.

I might go into a store and find her.

No, no. She would be dead a long time now.

But suppose I had gone into a store—perhaps a department store. I see a place with the brisk atmosphere, the straightforward displays, the old-fashioned modern look of the fifties. Suppose a tall, handsome woman, nicely turned out, had come to wait on me, and I had known, somehow, in spite of the sprayed and puffed hair and the pink or coral lips and fingernails—I had known that this was Flora. I would have wanted to tell her that I knew, I knew her story, though we had never met. I imagine myself trying to tell her. (This is a dream now, I understand it as a dream.) I imagine her listening, with a pleasant composure. But she shakes her head. She smiles at me, and in her smile there is a degree of mockery, a faint, self-assured malice. Weariness, as well. She is not surprised that I am telling her this, but she is weary of it, of me and my idea of her, my information, my notion that I can know anything about her.

Of course it's my mother I'm thinking of, my mother as she was in those dreams, saying, It's nothing, just this little tremor; saying with such astonishing lighthearted forgiveness, Oh, I knew you'd come someday. My mother surprising me, and doing it almost indifferently. Her mask, her fate, and most of her affliction taken away. How relieved I was, and happy. But I now recall that I was disconcerted as well. I would have to say that I felt slightly cheated. Yes. Offended, tricked, cheated, by this welcome turnaround, this reprieve. My mother moving rather carelessly out of her old prison, showing options and powers I never dreamed she had, changes more than herself. She changes the bitter lump of love I have carried all this time into a phantom—something useless and uncalled for, like a phantom pregnancy.

The Cameronians, I have discovered, are or were an uncompromismg remnant of the Covenanters—those Scots who in the seventeenth century bound themselves, with God, to resist prayer books, bishops, any taint of popery or interference by the King. Their name comes from Richard Cameron, an outlawed, or "field," preacher, soon cut down. The Cameronians—for a long time they have preferred to be called the Reformed Presbyterians—went into battle singing the seventy-fourth and the seventy-eighth Psalms. They hacked the haughty Bishop of St. Andrews to death on the highway and rode their horses over his body. One of their ministers, in a mood of firm rejoicing at his own hanging, excommunicated all the other preachers in the world.

༄ *Meneseteung* ༄

I

Columbine, bloodroot,
And wild bergamot,
Gathering armfuls,
Giddily we go.

OFFERINGS, THE BOOK is called. Gold lettering on a dull-blue cover. The author's full name underneath: Almeda Joynt Roth. The local paper, the *Vidette*, referred to her as "our poetess." There seems to be a mixture of respect and contempt, both for her calling and for her sex—or for their predictable conjuncture. In the front of the book is a photograph, with the photographer's name in one corner, and the date: 1865. The book was published later, in 1873.

The poetess has a long face; a rather long nose; full, sombre dark eyes, which seem ready to roll down her cheeks like giant tears; a lot of dark hair gathered around her face in droopy rolls and curtains. A streak of gray hair plain to see, although she is, in this picture, only twenty-five. Not a pretty girl but the sort of woman who may age well, who probably won't get fat. She wears a tucked and braid-trimmed dark dress or jacket, with a lacy, floppy arrangement of white material—frills or a bow—filling the deep V at the neck. She also wears a hat, which might be made of velvet, in a dark color to match the dress. It's the untrimmed, shapeless hat, something like a soft beret, that makes me see artistic intentions, or at least a shy and stubborn eccentricity, in this young woman, whose long neck and forward-inclining head indicate as well that she is tall and slender and somewhat awkward. From the waist up, she looks like a young nobleman of another century. But perhaps it was the fashion.

"In 1854," she writes in the preface to her book, "my father brought us—my mother, my sister Catherine, my brother William, and me—to the wilds of Canada West (as it then was). My father was a harness-maker by trade, but a cultivated man who could quote by heart from the Bible, Shakespeare, and the writings of Edmund Burke. He prospered in this newly opened land and was able to set up a harness and leather-goods store, and after a year to build the comfortable house in which I live (alone) today. I was fourteen years old, the eldest of the children, when we came into this country from Kingston, a town whose handsome streets I have not seen again but often remember. My sister was eleven and my brother nine. The third summer that we lived here, my brother and sister were taken ill of a prevalent fever and died within a few days of each other. My dear mother did not regain her spirits after this blow to our family. Her health declined, and after another three years she died. I then became housekeeper to my father and was happy to make his home for twelve years, until he died suddenly one morning at his shop.

"From my earliest years I have delighted in verse and I have occupied myself—and sometimes allayed my griefs, which have been no more, I know, than any sojourner on earth must encounter—with many floundering efforts at its composition. My fingers, indeed, were always too clumsy for crochetwork, and those dazzling productions of embroidery which one sees often today—the overflowing fruit and flower baskets, the little Dutch boys, the bonneted maidens with their watering cans—have likewise proved to be beyond my skill. So I offer instead, as the product of my leisure hours, these rude posies, these ballads, couplets, reflections."

Titles of some of the poems: "Children at Their Games," "The Gypsy Fair," "A Visit to My Family," "Angels in the Snow," "Champlain at the Mouth of the Meneseteung," "The Passing of the Old Forest," and "A Garden Medley." There are other, shorter poems, about birds and wildflowers and snowstorms. There is some comically intentioned doggerel about what people are thinking about as they listen to the sermon in church.

"Children at Their Games": The writer, a child, is playing with her brother and sister—one of those games in which children on different sides try to entice and catch each other. She plays on in the deepening twilight, until she realizes that she is alone, and much older. Still she hears the (ghostly) voices of her brother and sister calling. *Come over, come over, let Meda come over.* (Perhaps Almeda was called Meda in the family, or perhaps she shortened her name to fit the poem.)

"The Gypsy Fair": The Gypsies have an encampment near the town, a "fair," where they sell cloth and trinkets, and the writer as a child is afraid that she may be stolen by them, taken away from her family. Instead, her family has been taken away from her, stolen by Gypsies she can't locate or bargain with.

"A Visit to My Family": A visit to the cemetery, a one-sided conversation.

"Angels in the Snow": The writer once taught her brother and sister to make "angels" by lying down in the snow and moving their arms to create wing shapes. Her brother always jumped up carelessly, leaving an angel with a crippled wing. Will this be made perfect in Heaven, or will he be flying with his own makeshift, in circles?

"Champlain at the Mouth of the Meneseteung": This poem celebrates the popular, untrue belief that the explorer sailed down the eastern shore of Lake Huron and landed at the mouth of the major river.

"The Passing of the Old Forest": A list of all the trees—their names, appearance, and uses—that were cut down in the original forest, with a general description of the bears, wolves, eagles, deer, waterfowl.

"A Garden Medley": Perhaps planned as a companion to the forest poem. Catalogue of plants brought from European countries, with bits of history and legend attached, and final Canadianness resulting from this mixture.

The poems are written in quatrains or couplets. There are a couple of attempts at sonnets, but mostly the rhyme scheme is simple—*a b a b* or *a b c b*. The rhyme used is what was once called "masculine" ("shore"/ "before"), though once in a while it is "feminine" ("quiver"/"river"). Are those terms familiar anymore? No poem is unrhymed.

II

White roses cold as snow
Bloom where those "angels" lie.
Do they but rest below
Or, in God's wonder, fly?

In 1879, Almeda Roth was still living in the house at the corner of Pearl and Dufferin streets, the house her father had built for his family. The house is there today; the manager of the liquor store lives in it. It's covered with aluminum siding; a closed-in porch has replaced the veranda. The woodshed, the fence, the gates, the privy, the barn—all these are gone. A photograph taken in the 1880s shows them all in place. The house and fence look a little shabby, in need of paint, but perhaps that is just because of the bleached-out look of the brownish photograph. The lace-curtained windows look like white eyes. No big shade tree is in sight, and, in fact, the tall elms that overshadowed the town until the 1950s, as well as the maples that shade it now, are skinny young trees with rough fences around them to protect them from the cows. Without the shelter of those trees, there is a great exposure—back yards, clotheslines, woodpiles, patchy sheds and barns and privies— all bare, exposed, provisional-looking. Few houses would have anything like a lawn, just a patch of plantains and anthills and raked dirt. Perhaps petunias growing on top of a stump, in a round box. Only the main street is gravelled; the other streets are dirt roads, muddy or dusty according to season. Yards must be fenced to keep animals out. Cows are tethered in vacant lots or pastured in back yards, but sometimes they get loose. Pigs get loose too, and dogs roam free or nap in a lordly way on the boardwalks. The town has taken root, it's not going to vanish, yet it still has some of the look of an encampment. And, like an encampment, it's busy all the time—full of people, who, within the town, usually walk wherever they're going; full of animals, which leave horse buns, cow pats, dog turds that ladies have to hitch up their skirts for; full of the noise of building and of drivers shouting at their horses and of the trains that come in several times a day.

I read about that life in the *Vidette*.

The population is younger than it is now, than it will ever be again. People past fifty usually don't come to a raw, new place. There are quite a few people in the cemetery already, but most of them died young, in accidents or childbirth or epidemics. It's youth that's in evidence in town. Children—boys—rove through the streets in gangs. School is compulsory for only four months a year, and there are lots of occasional jobs that even a child of eight or nine can do—pulling flax, holding horses, delivering groceries, sweeping the boardwalk in front of stores. A good deal of time they spend looking for adventures. One day they follow an old woman, a drunk nicknamed Queen Aggie. They get her into a wheelbarrow and trundle her all over town, then dump her into a ditch to sober her up. They also spend a lot of time around the railway station. They jump on shunting cars and dart between them and dare each other to take chances, which once in a while result in their getting maimed or killed. And they keep an eye out for any strangers coming into town. They follow them, offer to carry their bags, and direct them (for a five-cent piece) to a hotel. Strangers who don't look so prosperous are taunted and tormented. Speculation surrounds all of them—it's like a cloud of flies. Are they coming to town to start up a new business, to persuade people to invest in some scheme, to sell cures or gimmicks, to preach on the street corners? All these things are possible any day of the week. Be on your guard, the *Vidette* tells people. These are times of opportunity and danger. Tramps, confidence men, hucksters, shysters, plain thieves are travelling the roads, and particularly the railroads. Thefts are announced: money invested and never seen again, a pair of trousers taken from the clothesline, wood from the woodpile, eggs from the henhouse. Such incidents increase in the hot weather.

Hot weather brings accidents too. More horses run wild

then, upsetting buggies. Hands caught in the wringer while doing the washing, a man lopped in two at the sawmill, a leaping boy killed in a fall of lumber at the lumberyard. Nobody sleeps well. Babies wither with summer complaint, and fat people can't catch their breath. Bodies must be buried in a hurry. One day a man goes through the streets ringing a cowbell and calling, "Repent! Repent!" It's not a stranger this time, it's a young man who works at the butcher shop. Take him home, wrap him in cold wet cloths, give him some nerve medicine, keep him in bed, pray for his wits. If he doesn't recover, he must go to the asylum.

Almeda Roth's house faces on Dufferin Street, which is a street of considerable respectability. On this street, merchants, a mill owner, an operator of salt wells have their houses. But Pearl Street, which her back windows overlook and her back gate opens onto, is another story. Workmen's houses are adjacent to hers. Small but decent row houses—that is all right. Things deteriorate toward the end of the block, and the next, last one becomes dismal. Nobody but the poorest people, the unrespectable and undeserving poor, would live there at the edge of a boghole (drained since then), called the Pearl Street Swamp. Bushy and luxuriant weeds grow there, makeshift shacks have been put up, there are piles of refuse and debris and crowds of runty children, slops are flung from doorways. The town tries to compel these people to build privies, but they would just as soon go in the bushes. If a gang of boys goes down there in search of adventure, it's likely they'll get more than they bargained for. It is said that even the town constable won't go down Pearl Street on a Saturday night. Almeda Roth has never walked past the row housing. In one of those houses lives the young girl Annie, who helps her with her housecleaning. That young girl herself, being a decent girl, has never walked down to the last block or the swamp. No decent woman ever would.

But that same swamp, lying to the east of Almeda Roth's house, presents a fine sight at dawn. Almeda sleeps at the back of the house. She keeps to the same bedroom she once shared with her sister Catherine—she would not think of moving to the large front bedroom, where her mother used to lie in bed all day, and which was later the solitary domain of her father. From her window she can see the sun rising, the swamp mist filling with light, the bulky, nearest trees floating against that mist and the trees behind turning transparent. Swamp oaks, soft maples, tamarack, butternut.

III

> *Here where the river meets the*
> *inland sea,*
> *Spreading her blue skirts from the*
> *solemn wood,*
> *I think of birds and beasts and*
> *vanished men,*
> *Whose pointed dwellings on these*
> *pale sands stood.*

One of the strangers who arrived at the railway station a few years ago was Jarvis Poulter, who now occupies the next house to Almeda Roth's—separated from hers by a vacant lot, which he has bought, on Dufferin Street. The house is plainer than the Roth house and has no fruit trees or flowers planted around it. It is understood that this is a natural result of Jarvis Poulter's being a widower and living alone. A man may keep his house decent, but he will never—if he is a proper man—do much to decorate it. Marriage forces him to live with more ornament as well as sentiment, and it protects him, also, from the extremities of his own nature—from a frigid parsimony or a luxuriant sloth, from squalor, and from excessive sleeping or reading, drinking, smoking, or freethinking.

> *In the interests of economy, it is believed, a certain estimable gentleman of our town persists in fetching water from the public tap and supplementing his fuel supply by picking up the loose coal along the railway track. Does he think to repay the town or the railway company with a supply of free salt?*

This is the *Vidette*, full of sly jokes, innuendo, plain accusation that no newspaper would get away with today. It's Jarvis Poulter they're talking about—though in other passages he is spoken of with great respect, as a civil magistrate, an employer, a churchman. He is close, that's all. An eccentric, to a degree. All of which may be a result of his single condition, his widower's life. Even carrying his water from the town tap and filling his coal pail along the railway track. This is a decent citizen, prosperous: a tall—slightly paunchy?—man in a dark suit with polished boots. A beard? Black hair streaked with gray. A severe and self-possessed air, and a large pale wart among the bushy hairs of one eyebrow? People talk about a young, pretty, beloved wife, dead in childbirth or some horrible accident, like a house fire or a railway disaster. There is no ground for this, but it adds interest. All he has told them is that his wife is dead.

He came to this part of the country looking for oil. The first oil well in the world was sunk in Lambton County, south of here, in the 1850s. Drilling for oil, Jarvis Poulter discovered salt. He set to work to make the most of that. When he walks home from church with Almeda Roth, he tells her about his salt wells. They are twelve hundred feet deep. Heated water is pumped down into them, and that dissolves the salt. Then the brine is pumped to the surface. It is poured into great evaporator pans over slow, steady fires, so that the water is steamed off and the pure, excellent salt remains. A commodity for which the demand will never fail.

"The salt of the earth," Almeda says.

"Yes," he says, frowning. He may think this disrespectful. She did not intend it so. He speaks of competitors in other towns who are following his lead and trying to hog the market. Fortunately, their wells are not drilled so deep, or their evaporating is not done so efficiently. There is salt everywhere under this land, but it is not so easy to come by as some people think.

Does this not mean, Almeda says, that there was once a great sea?

Very likely, Jarvis Poulter says. Very likely. He goes on to tell her about other enterprises of his—a brickyard, a limekiln.

And he explains to her how this operates, and where the good clay is found. He also owns two farms, whose woodlots supply the fuel for his operations.

Among the couples strolling home from church on a recent, sunny Sabbath morning we noted a certain salty gentleman and literary lady, not perhaps in their first youth but by no means blighted by the frosts of age. May we surmise?

This kind of thing pops up in the *Vidette* all the time.

May they surmise, and is this courting? Almeda Roth has a bit of money, which her father left her, and she has her house. She is not too old to have a couple of children. She is a good enough housekeeper, with the tendency toward fancy iced cakes and decorated tarts that is seen fairly often in old maids. (Honorable mention at the Fall Fair.) There is nothing wrong with her looks, and naturally she is in better shape than most married women of her age, not having been loaded down with work and children. But why was she passed over in her earlier, more marriageable years, in a place that needs women to be partnered and fruitful? She was a rather gloomy girl—that may have been the trouble. The deaths of her brother and sister, and then of her mother, who lost her reason, in fact, a year before she died, and lay in her bed talking nonsense—those weighed on her, so she was not lively company. And all that reading and poetry—it seemed more of a drawback, a barrier, an obsession, in the young girl than in the middle-aged woman, who needed something, after all, to fill her time. Anyway, it's five years since her book was published, so perhaps she has got over that. Perhaps it was the proud, bookish father encouraging her?

Everyone takes it for granted that Almeda Roth is thinking of Jarvis Poulter as a husband and would say yes if he asked her. And she is thinking of him. She doesn't want to get her hopes up too much, she doesn't want to make a fool of herself. She would like a signal. If he attended church on Sunday evenings, there would be a chance, during some months of the year, to walk home after dark. He would carry a lantern. (There is as yet no street lighting in town.) He would swing the lantern to light the way in front of the lady's feet and observe their narrow and delicate shape. He might catch her arm as they step off the boardwalk. But he does not go to church at night.

Nor does he call for her, and walk with her *to* church on Sunday mornings. That would be a declaration. He walks her home, past his gate as far as hers; he lifts his hat then and leaves her. She does not invite him to come in—a woman living alone could never do such a thing. As soon as a man and woman of almost any age are alone together within four walls, it is assumed that anything may happen. Spontaneous combustion, instant fornication, an attack of passion. Brute instinct, triumph of the senses. What possibilities men and women must see in each other to infer such dangers. Or, believing in the dangers, how often they must think about the possibilities.

When they walk side by side, she can smell his shaving soap, the barber's oil, his pipe tobacco, the wool and linen and leather smell of his manly clothes. The correct, orderly, heavy clothes are like those she used to brush and starch and iron for her father. She misses that job—her father's appreciation, his dark, kind authority. Jarvis Poulter's garments, his smell, his movements all cause the skin on the side of her body next to him to tingle hopefully, and a meek shiver raises the hairs on her arms. Is this to be taken as a sign of love? She thinks of him coming into her—*their*—bedroom in his long underwear and his hat. She knows this outfit is ridiculous, but in her mind he does not look so; he has the solemn effrontery of a figure in a dream. He comes into the room and lies down on the bed beside her, preparing to take her in his arms. Surely he removes his hat? She doesn't know, for at this point a fit of welcome and submission overtakes her, a buried gasp. He would be her husband.

One thing she has noticed about married women, and that is how many of them have to go about creating their husbands. They have to start ascribing preferences, opinions, dictatorial ways. Oh, yes, they say, my husband is very particular. He won't touch turnips. He won't eat fried meat. (Or he will only eat fried meat.) He likes me to wear blue (brown) all the time. He can't stand organ music. He hates to see a woman go out bareheaded.

He would kill me if I took one puff of tobacco. This way, bewildered, sidelong-looking men are made over, made into husbands, heads of households. Almeda Roth cannot imagine herself doing that. She wants a man who doesn't have to be made, who is firm already and determined and mysterious to her. She does not look for companionship. Men—except for her father—seem to her deprived in some way, incurious. No doubt that is necessary, so that they will do what they have to do. Would she herself, knowing that there was salt in the earth, discover how to get it out and sell it? Not likely. She would be thinking about the ancient sea. That kind of speculation is what Jarvis Poulter has, quite properly, no time for.

Instead of calling for her and walking her to church, Jarvis Poulter might make another, more venturesome declaration. He could hire a horse and take her for a drive out to the country. If he did this, she would be both glad and sorry. Glad to be beside him, driven by him, receiving this attention from him in front of the world. And sorry to have the countryside removed for her—filmed over, in a way, by his talk and preoccupations. The countryside that she has written about in her poems actually takes diligence and determination to see. Some things must be disregarded. Manure piles, of course, and boggy fields full of high, charred stumps, and great heaps of brush waiting for a good day for burning. The meandering creeks have been straightened, turned into ditches with high, muddy banks. Some of the crop fields and pasture fields are fenced with big, clumsy uprooted stumps; others are held in a crude stitchery of rail fences. The trees have all been cleared back to the woodlots. And the woodlots are all second growth. No trees along the roads or lanes or around the farmhouses, except a few that are newly planted, young and weedy-looking. Clusters of log barns—the grand barns that are to dominate the countryside for the next hundred years are just beginning to be built—and mean-looking log houses, and every four or five miles a ragged little settlement with a church and school and store and a blacksmith shop. A raw countryside just wrenched from the forest, but swarming with people. Every hundred acres is a farm, every farm has a family, most families have ten or twelve children. (This is the country that will send out wave after wave of settlers—it's already starting to send them—to Northern Ontario and the West.) It's true that you can gather wildflowers in spring in the woodlots, but you'd have to walk through herds of horned cows to get to them.

IV

The Gypsies have departed.
Their camping-ground is bare.
Oh, boldly would I bargain now
At the Gypsy Fair.

Almeda suffers a good deal from sleeplessness, and the doctor has given her bromides and nerve medicine. She takes the bromides, but the drops gave her dreams that were too vivid and disturbing, so she has put the bottle by for an emergency. She told the doctor her eyeballs felt dry, like hot glass, and her joints ached. Don't read so much, he said, don't study; get yourself good and tired out with housework, take exercise. He believes that her troubles would clear up if she got married. He believes this in spite of the fact that most of his nerve medicine is prescribed for married women.

So Almeda cleans house and helps clean the church, she lends a hand to friends who are wallpapering or getting ready for a wedding, she bakes one of her famous cakes for the Sunday-school picnic. On a hot Saturday in August, she decides to make some grape jelly. Little jars of grape jelly will make fine Christmas presents, or offerings to the sick. But she started late in the day and the jelly is not made by nightfall. In fact, the hot pulp has just been dumped into the cheesecloth bag to strain out the juice. Almeda drinks some tea and eats a slice of cake with butter (a childish indulgence of hers), and that's all she wants for supper. She washes her hair at the sink and sponges off her body to be clean for Sunday. She doesn't light a lamp. She lies down on the bed with the window wide open and a sheet just up to her waist, and she does feel wonderfully tired. She can even feel a little breeze.

When she wakes up, the night seems fiery hot and full of threats. She lies sweating on her bed, and she has the impression that the noises she hears are knives and saws and axes—all angry implements chopping and jabbing and boring within her head. But it isn't true. As she comes further awake, she recognizes the sounds that she has heard sometimes before—the fracas of a summer Saturday night on Pearl Street. Usually the noise centers on a fight. People are drunk, there is a lot of protest and encouragement concerning the fight, somebody will scream, "Murder!" Once, there was a murder. But it didn't happen in a fight. An old man was stabbed to death in his shack, perhaps for a few dollars he kept in the mattress.

She gets out of bed and goes to the window. The night sky is clear, with no moon and with bright stars. Pegasus hangs straight ahead, over the swamp. Her father taught her that constellation—automatically, she counts its stars. Now she can make out distinct voices, individual contributions to the row. Some people, like herself, have evidently been wakened from sleep. "Shut up!" they are yelling. "Shut up that caterwauling or I'm going to come down and tan the arse off yez!"

But nobody shuts up. It's as if there were a ball of fire rolling up Pearl Street, shooting off sparks—only the fire is noise; it's yells and laughter and shrieks and curses, and the sparks are voices that shoot off alone. Two voices gradually distinguish themselves—a rising and falling howling cry and a steady throbbing, low-pitched stream of abuse that contains all those words which Almeda associates with danger and depravity and foul smells and disgusting sights. Someone—the person crying out, "Kill me! Kill me now!"—is being beaten. A woman is being beaten. She keeps crying, "Kill me! Kill me!" and sometimes her mouth seems choked with blood. Yet there is something taunting and triumphant about her cry. There is something theatrical about it. And the people around are calling out, "Stop it! Stop that!" or "Kill her! Kill her!" in a frenzy, as if at the theatre or a sporting match or a prizefight. Yes, thinks Almeda, she has noticed that before—it is always partly a charade with these people; there is a clumsy sort of parody, an exaggeration, a missed connection. As if anything they did—

even a murder—might be something they didn't quite believe but were powerless to stop.

Now there is the sound of something thrown—a chair, a plank?—and of a woodpile or part of a fence giving way. A lot of newly surprised cries, the sound of running, people getting out of the way, and the commotion has come much closer. Almeda can see a figure in a light dress, bent over and running. That will be the woman. She has got hold of something like a stick of wood or a shingle, and she turns and flings it at the darker figure running after her.

"Ah, go get her!" the voices cry. "Go baste her one!"

Many fall back now; just the two figures come on and grapple, and break loose again, and finally fall down against Almeda's fence. The sound they make becomes very confused —gagging, vomiting, grunting, pounding. Then a long, vibrating, choking sound of pain and self-abasement, self-abandonment, which could come from either or both of them.

Almeda has backed away from the window and sat down on the bed. Is that the sound of murder she has heard? What is to be done, what is she to do? She must light a lantern, she must go downstairs and light a lantern—she must go out into the yard, she must go downstairs. Into the yard. The lantern. She falls over on her bed and pulls the pillow to her face. In a minute. The stairs, the lantern. She sees herself already down there, in the back hall, drawing the bolt of the back door. She falls asleep.

She wakes, startled, in the early light. She thinks there is a big crow sitting on her windowsill, talking in a disapproving but unsurprised way about the events of the night before. "Wake up and move the wheelbarrow!" it says to her, scolding, and she understands that it means something else by "wheelbarrow"—something foul and sorrowful. Then she is awake and sees that there is no such bird. She gets up at once and looks out the window.

Down against her fence there is a pale lump pressed—a body.

Wheelbarrow.

She puts a wrapper over her nightdress and goes downstairs.

The front rooms are still shadowy, the blinds down in the kitchen. Something goes *plop, plup*, in a leisurely, censorious way, reminding her of the conversation of the crow. It's just the grape juice, straining overnight. She pulls the bolt and goes out the back door. Spiders have draped their webs over the doorway in the night, and the hollyhocks are drooping, heavy with dew. By the fence, she parts the sticky hollyhocks and looks down and she can see.

A woman's body heaped up there, turned on her side with her face squashed down into the earth. Almeda can't see her face. But there is a bare breast let loose, brown nipple pulled long like a cow's teat, and a bare haunch and leg, the haunch showing a bruise as big as a sunflower. The unbruised skin is grayish, like a plucked, raw drumstick. Some kind of nightgown or all-purpose dress she has on. Smelling of vomit. Urine, drink, vomit.

Barefoot, in her nightgown and flimsy wrapper, Almeda runs away. She runs around the side of her house between the apple trees and the veranda; she opens the front gate and flees down Dufferin Street to Jarvis Poulter's house, which is the nearest to hers. She slaps the flat of her hand many times against the door.

"There is the body of a woman," she says when Jarvis Poulter appears at last. He is in his dark trousers, held up with braces, and his shirt is half unbuttoned, his face unshaven, his hair standing up on his head. "Mr. Poulter, excuse me. A body of a woman. At my back gate."

He looks at her fiercely. "Is she dead?"

His breath is dank, his face creased, his eyes bloodshot.

"Yes. I think murdered," says Almeda. She can see a little of his cheerless front hall. His hat on a chair. "In the night I woke up. I heard a racket down on Pearl Street," she says, struggling to keep her voice low and sensible. "I could hear this—pair. I could hear a man and a woman fighting."

He picks up his hat and puts it on his head. He closes and locks the front door, and puts the key in his pocket. They walk along the boardwalk and she sees that she is in her bare feet. She holds back what she feels a need to say next—that she is responsible, she could have run out with a lantern, she could have screamed (but who needed more screams?), she could have beat the man off. She could have run for help then, not now.

They turn down Pearl Street, instead of entering the Roth yard. Of course the body is still there. Hunched up, half bare, the same as before.

Jarvis Poulter doesn't hurry or halt. He walks straight over to the body and looks down at it, nudges the leg with the toe of his boot, just as you'd nudge a dog or a sow.

"You," he says, not too loudly but firmly, and nudges again.

Almeda tastes bile at the back of her throat.

"Alive," says Jarvis Poulter, and the woman confirms this. She stirs, she grunts weakly.

Almeda says, "I will get the doctor." If she had touched the woman, if she had forced herself to touch her, she would not have made such a mistake.

"Wait," says Jarvis Poulter. "Wait. Let's see if she can get up."

"Get up, now," he says to the woman. "Come on. Up, now. Up."

Now a startling thing happens. The body heaves itself onto all fours, the head is lifted—the hair all matted with blood and vomit—and the woman begins to bang this head, hard and rhythmically, against Almeda Roth's picket fence. As she bangs her head, she finds her voice and lets out an openmouthed yowl, full of strength and what sounds like an anguished pleasure.

"Far from dead," says Jarvis Poulter. "And I wouldn't bother the doctor."

"There's blood," says Almeda as the woman turns her smeared face.

"From her nose," he says. "Not fresh." He bends down and catches the horrid hair close to the scalp to stop the head-banging.

"You stop that, now," he says. "Stop it. Gwan home, now. Gwan home, where you belong." The sound coming out of the woman's mouth has stopped. He shakes her head slightly, warning her, before he lets go of her hair. "Gwan home!"

Released, the woman lunges forward, pulls herself to her feet. She can walk. She weaves and stumbles down the street, making intermittent, cautious noises of protest. Jarvis Poulter watches her for a moment to make sure that she's on her way. Then he finds a large burdock leaf, on which he wipes his hand. He says, "There goes your dead body!"

The back gate being locked, they walk around to the front. The front gate stands open. Almeda still feels sick. Her abdomen is bloated; she is hot and dizzy.

"The front door is locked," she says faintly. "I came out by the kitchen." If only he would leave her, she could go straight to the privy. But he follows. He follows her as far as the back door and into the back hall. He speaks to her in a tone of harsh joviality that she has never before heard from him. "No need for alarm," he says. "It's only the consequences of drink. A lady oughtn't to be living alone so close to a bad neighborhood." He takes hold of her arm just above the elbow. She can't open her mouth to speak to him, to say thank you. If she opened her mouth, she would retch.

What Jarvis Poulter feels for Almeda Roth at this moment is just what he has not felt during all those circumspect walks and all his own solitary calculations of her probable worth, undoubted respectability, adequate comeliness. He has not been able to imagine her as a wife. Now that is possible. He is sufficiently stirred by her loosened hair—prematurely gray but thick and soft—her flushed face, her light clothing, which nobody but a husband should see. And by her indiscretion, her agitation, her foolishness, her need?

"I will call on you later," he says to her. "I will walk with you to church."

At the corner of Pearl and Dufferin streets last Sunday morning there was discovered, by a lady resident there, the body of a certain woman of Pearl Street, thought to be dead but only, as it turned out, dead drunk. She was roused from her heavenly—or otherwise—stupor by the firm persuasion of Mr. Poulter, a neighbour and a Civil Magistrate, who had been summoned by the lady resident. Incidents of this sort, unseemly, troublesome, and disgraceful to our town, have of late become all too common.

V

I sit at the bottom of sleep,
As on the floor of the sea.
And fanciful Citizens of the Deep
Are graciously greeting me.

As soon as Jarvis Poulter has gone and she has heard her front gate close, Almeda rushes to the privy. Her relief is not complete, however, and she realizes that the pain and fullness in her lower body come from an accumulation of menstrual blood that has not yet started to flow. She closes and locks the back door. Then, remembering Jarvis Poulter's words about church, she writes on a piece of paper, *I am not well, and wish to rest today.* She sticks this firmly into the outside frame of the little window in the front door. She locks that door too. She is trembling, as if from a great shock or danger. But she builds a fire, so that she can make tea. She boils water, measures the tea leaves, makes a large pot of tea, whose steam and smell sicken her further. She pours out a cup while the tea is still quite weak and adds to it several dark drops of nerve medicine. She sits to drink it without raising the kitchen blind. There, in the middle of the floor, is the cheesecloth bag hanging on its broom handle between the two chairbacks. The grape pulp and juice has stained the swollen cloth a dark purple. *Plop, plup,* into the basin beneath. She can't sit and look at such a thing. She takes her cup, the teapot, and the bottle of medicine into the dining room.

She is still sitting there when the horses start to go by on the way to church, stirring up clouds of dust. The roads will be getting hot as ashes. She is there when the gate is opened and a man's confident steps sound on her veranda. Her hearing is so sharp she seems to hear the paper taken out of the frame and unfolded—she can almost hear him reading it, hear the words in his mind. Then the footsteps go the other way, down the steps. The gate closes. An image comes to her of tombstones—it makes her laugh. Tombstones are marching down the street on their little booted feet, their long bodies inclined forward, their expressions preoccupied and severe. The church bells are ringing.

Then the clock in the hall strikes twelve and an hour has passed.

The house is getting hot. She drinks more tea and adds more medicine. She knows that the medicine is affecting her. It is responsible for her extraordinary languor, her perfect immobility, her unresisting surrender to her surroundings. That is all right. It seems necessary.

Her surroundings—some of her surroundings—in the dining room are these: walls covered with dark-green garlanded wallpaper, lace curtains and mulberry velvet curtains on the windows, a table with a crocheted cloth and a bowl of wax fruit, a pinkish-gray carpet with nosegays of blue and pink roses, a sideboard spread with embroidered runners and holding various patterned plates and jugs and the silver tea things. A lot of things to watch. For every one of these patterns, decorations seems charged with life, ready to move and flow and alter. Or possibly to explode. Almeda Roth's occupation throughout the day is to keep an eye on them. Not to prevent their alteration so much as to catch them at it—to understand it, to be a part of it. So much is going on in this room that there is no need to leave it. There is not even the thought of leaving it.

Of course, Almeda in her observations cannot escape words. She may think she can, but she can't. Soon this glowing and swelling begins to suggest words—not specific words but a flow of words somewhere, just about ready to make themselves known to her. Poems, even. Yes, again, poems. Or one poem. Isn't that the idea—one very great poem that will contain everything and, oh, that will make all the other poems, the poems she has written, inconsequential, mere trial and error, mere rags? Stars and flowers and birds and trees and angels in the snow and dead children at twilight—that is not the half of it. You have to get in the obscene racket on Pearl Street and the polished toe of Jarvis Poulter's boot and the plucked-chicken haunch with its blue-black flower. Almeda is a long way now from human sympathies or fears or cozy household considerations. She doesn't think about what could be done for that woman or about keeping Jarvis Poulter's dinner warm and hanging his long underwear on the line. The basin of grape juice has overflowed and is running over her kitchen floor, staining the boards of the floor, and the stain will never come out.

She has to think of so many things at once—Champlain and the naked Indians and the salt deep in the earth, but as well as the salt the money, the money-making intent brewing forever in heads like Jarvis Poulter's. Also the brutal storms of winter and the clumsy and benighted deeds on Pearl Street. The changes of climate are often violent, and if you think about it there is no peace even in the stars. All this can be borne only if it is channelled into a poem, and the word *channelled* is appropriate, because the name of the poem will be—it *is*—"The Meneseteung." The name of the poem is the name of the river. No, in fact it is the river, the Meneseteung, that is the poem—with its deep holes and rapids and blissful pools under the summer trees and its grinding blocks of ice thrown up at the end of winter and its desolating spring floods. Almeda looks deep, deep into the river of her mind and into the tablecloth, and she sees the crocheted roses floating. They look bunchy and foolish, her mother's crocheted roses—they don't look much like real flowers. But their effort, their floating independence, their pleasure in their silly selves do seem to her so admirable. A hopeful sign. *Meneseteung.*

She doesn't leave the room until dusk, when she goes out to the privy again and discovers that she is bleeding, her flow has started. She will have to get a towel, strap it on, bandage herself up. Never before, in health, has she passed a whole day in her nightdress. She doesn't feel any particular anxiety about this. On her way through the kitchen, she walks through the pool of grape juice. She knows that she will have to mop it up, but not yet, and she walks upstairs leaving purple footprints and smelling her escaping blood and the sweat of her body that has sat all day in the closed hot room.

No need for alarm.

For she hasn't thought that crocheted roses could float away or that tombstones could hurry down the street. She doesn't mistake that for reality, and neither does she mistake anything else for reality, and that is how she knows that she is sane.

VI

I dream of you by night,
I visit you by day.
Father, Mother,
Sister, Brother,
Have you no word to say?

April 22, 1903. At her residence, on Tuesday last, between three and four o'clock in the afternoon, there passed away a lady of talent and refinement whose pen, in days gone by, enriched our local literature with a volume of sensitive, eloquent verse. It is a sad misfortune that in later years the mind of this fine person had become somewhat clouded and her behaviour, in consequence, somewhat rash and unusual. Her attention to decorum and to the care and adornment of her person had suffered, to the degree that she had become, in the eyes of those unmindful of her former pride and daintiness, a familiar eccentric, or even, sadly, a figure of fun. But now all such lapses pass from memory and what is recalled is her excellent published verse, her labours in former days in the Sunday school, her dutiful care of her parents, her noble womanly nature, charitable concerns, and unfailing religious faith. Her last illness was of mercifully short duration. She caught cold, after having become thoroughly wet from a ramble in the Pearl Street bog. (It has been said that some urchins chased her into the water, and such is the boldness and cruelty of some of our youth, and their observed persecution of this lady, that the tale cannot be entirely discounted) The cold developed into pneumonia, and she died, attended at the last by a former neighbour, Mrs. Bert (Annie) Friels, who witnessed her calm and faithful end.

January, 1904. One of the founders of our community, an early maker and shaker of this town, was abruptly removed from our midst on Monday morning last, whilst attending to his correspondence in the office of his company. Mr. Jarvis Poulter possessed a keen and lively commercial spirit, which was instrumental in the creation of not one but several local enterprises, bringing the benefits of industry, productivity, and employment to our town.

So the *Vidette* runs on, copious and assured. Hardly a death goes undescribed, or a life unevaluated.

I looked for Almeda Roth in the graveyard. I found the family stone. There was just one name on it—ROTH. Then I noticed two flat stones in the ground, a distance of a few feet—six feet?—from the upright stone. One of these said PAPA, the other MAMA. Farther out from these I found two other flat stones, with the names WILLIAM and CATHERINE on them. I had to clear away some overgrowing grass and dirt to see the full name of Catherine. No birth or death dates for anybody, nothing about being dearly beloved. It was a private sort of memorializing, not for the world. There were no roses, either—no sign of a rosebush. But perhaps it was taken out. The groundskeeper doesn't like such things; they are a nuisance to the lawnmower, and if there is nobody left to object he will pull them out.

I thought that Almeda must have been buried somewhere else. When this plot was bought—at the time of the two children's deaths—she would still have been expected to marry, and to lie finally beside her husband. They might not have left room for her here. Then I saw that the stones in the ground fanned out from the upright stone. First the two for the parents, then the two for the children, but these were placed in such a way that there was room for a third, to complete the fan. I paced out from CATHERINE the same number of steps that it took to get from CATHERINE to WILLIAM, and at this spot I began pulling grass and scrabbling in the dirt with my bare hands. Soon I felt the stone and knew that I was right. I worked away and got the whole stone clear and I read the name MEDA. There it was with the others, staring at the sky.

I made sure I had got to the edge of the stone. That was all the name there was—Meda. So it was true that she was called by that name in the family. Not just in the poem. Or perhaps she chose her name from the poem, to be written on her stone.

I thought that there wasn't anybody alive in the world but me who would know this, who would make the connection. And I would be the last person to do so. But perhaps this isn't so. People are curious. A few people are. They will be driven to find things out, even trivial things. They will put things together. You see them going around with notebooks, scraping the dirt off gravestones, reading microfilm, just in the hope of seeing this trickle in time, making a connection, rescuing one thing from the rubbish.

And they may get it wrong, after all. I may have got it wrong. I don't know if she ever took laudanum. Many ladies did. I don't know if she ever made grape jelly.

✥ *Differently* ✥

GEORGIA ONCE TOOK a creative-writing course, and what the instructor told her was: Too many things. Too many things going on at the same time; also too many people. Think, he told her. What is the important thing? What do you want us to pay attention to? Think.

Eventually she wrote a story that was about her grandfather killing chickens, and the instructor seemed to be pleased with it. Georgia herself thought that it was a fake. She made a long list of all the things that had been left out and handed it in as an appendix to the story. The instructor said that she expected too much, of herself and of the process, and that she was wearing him out.

The course was not a total loss, because Georgia and the instructor ended up living together. They still live together, in Ontario, on a farm. They sell raspberries, and run a small publishing business. When Georgia can get the money together, she goes to Vancouver to visit her sons. This fall Saturday she has taken the ferry across to Victoria, where she used to live. She did this on an impulse that she doesn't really trust, and by midafternoon, when she walks up the driveway of the splendid stone house where she used to visit Maya, she has already been taken over some fairly shaky ground.

When she phoned Raymond, she wasn't sure that he would ask her to the house. She wasn't sure that she even wanted to go there. She had no notion of how welcome she would be. But Raymond opens the door before she can touch the bell, and he hugs her around the shoulders and kisses her twice (surely he didn't use to do this?) and introduces his wife, Anne.

He says he has told her what great friends they were, Georgia and Ben and he and Maya. Great friends.

Maya is dead. Georgia and Ben are long divorced.

They go to sit in what Maya used to call, with a certain flat cheerfulness, "the family room."

(One evening Raymond had said to Ben and Georgia that it looked as if Maya wasn't going to be able to have any children. "We try our best," he said. "We use pillows and everything. But no luck."

"Listen, old man, you don't do it with pillows," Ben said boisterously. They were all a little drunk. "I thought you were the expert on all the apparatus, but I can see that you and I are going to have to have a little talk."

Raymond was an obstetrician and gynecologist.

By that time Georgia knew all about the abortion in Seattle, which had been set up by Maya's lover, Harvey. Harvey was also a doctor, a surgeon. The bleak apartment in the run-down building, the bad-tempered old woman who was knitting a sweater, the doctor arriving in his shirtsleeves, carrying a brown-paper bag that Maya hysterically believed must contain the tools of his trade. In fact, it contained his lunch—an egg-and-onion sandwich. Maya had the smell of that in her face all the time he and Mme. Defarge were working her over.

Maya and Georgia smiled at each other primly while their husbands continued their playful conversation.)

Raymond's curly brown hair has turned into a silvery fluff, and his face is lined. But nothing dreadful has happened to him—no pouches or jowls or alcoholic flush or sardonic droop of defeat. He is still thin, and straight, and sharp-shouldered, still fresh-smelling, spotless, appropriately, expensively dressed. He'll make a brittle, elegant old man, with an obliging boy's smile. There's that sort of shine on both of them, Maya once said glumly. She was speaking of Raymond and Ben. Maybe we should soak them in vinegar, she said.

The room has changed more than Raymond has. An ivory leather sofa has replaced Maya's tapestry-covered couch, and of course all the old opium-den clutter, Maya's cushions and pampas grass and the gorgeous multicolored elephant with the tiny sewn-on mirrors—that's all gone. The room is beige and ivory, smooth and comfortable as the new blond wife, who sits on the arm of Raymond's chair and maneuvers his arm around her, placing his hand on her thigh. She wears slick-looking white pants and a cream-on-white appliquéd sweater, with gold jewelry. Raymond gives her a couple of hearty and defiant pats.

"Are you going someplace?" he says. "Possibly shopping?"

"Righto," says the wife. "Old times." She smiles at Georgia. "It's okay," she says. "I really do have to go shopping."

When she has gone, Raymond pours drinks for Georgia and himself. "Anne is a worrywart about the booze," he says. "She won't put salt on the table. She threw out all the curtains in the house to get rid of the smell of Maya's cigarettes. I know what you may be thinking: Friend Raymond has got hold of a luscious blonde. But this is actually a very serious girl, and a very steady girl. I had her in my office, you know, quite a while before Maya died. I mean, I had her *working* in my office. I don't mean that the way it sounds! She isn't as young as she looks, either. She's thirty-six."

Georgia had thought forty. She is tired of the visit already, but she has to tell about herself. No, she is not married. Yes, she works. She and the friend she lives with have a farm and a publishing business. Touch and go, not much money. Interesting. A male friend, yes.

"I've lost all track of Ben somehow," Raymond says. "The last I heard, he was living on a boat."

"He and his wife sail around the West Coast every summer," Georgia says. "In the winter they go to Hawaii. The Navy lets you retire early."

"Marvellous," says Raymond.

Seeing Raymond has made Georgia think that she has no idea what Ben looks like now. Has he gone white-haired, has he thickened around the middle? Both of these things have happened to her—she has turned into a chunky woman with a healthy olive skin, a crest of white hair, wearing loose and rather splashy clothes. When she thinks of Ben, she sees him still as a handsome Navy officer, with a perfect Navy look—keen and serious and self-effacing. The look of someone who longed, bravely, to be given orders. Her sons must have pictures of him around—they both see him, they spend holidays on his boat. Perhaps they put the pictures away when she comes to visit. Perhaps they think of protecting these images of him from one who did him hurt.

On the way to Maya's house—Raymond's house—Georgia walked past another house, which she could easily have avoided. A house in Oak Bay, which in fact she had to go out of her way to see.

It was still the house that she and Ben had read about in the real-estate columns of the Victoria *Colonist*. Roomy bungalow under picturesque oak trees. Arbutus, dogwood, window seats, fireplace, diamond-paned windows, character. Georgia stood outside the gate and felt a most predictable pain. Here Ben had cut the grass, here the children had made their paths and hideaways in the bushes, and laid out a graveyard for the birds and snakes killed by the black cat, Domino. She could recall the inside of the house perfectly—the oak floors she and Ben had laboriously sanded, the walls they had painted, the room where she had lain in drugged misery after having her wisdom teeth out. Ben had read aloud to her, from *Dubliners*. She couldn't remember the title of the story. It was about a timid poetic sort of young man, with a mean pretty wife. Poor bugger, said Ben when he'd finished it.

Ben liked fiction, which was surprising in a man who also liked sports, and had been popular at school.

She ought to have stayed away from this neighborhood. Everywhere she walked here, under the chestnut trees with their flat gold leaves, and the red-limbed arbutus, and the tall Garry oaks, which suggested fairy stories, European forests, woodcutters, witches—everywhere her footsteps reproached her, saying *what-for, what-for, what-for*. This reproach was just what she had expected—it was what she courted—and there was something cheap about doing such a thing. Something cheap and useless. She knew it. But *what-for, what-for, what-for, wrong-and-waste, wrong-and-waste* went her silly, censorious feet.

Raymond wants Georgia to look at the garden, which he says was made for Maya during the last months of her life.

Maya designed it; then she lay on the tapestry couch (setting fire to it twice, Raymond says, by dozing off with a cigarette lit), and she was able to see it all take shape.

Georgia sees a pond, a stone-rimmed pond with an island in the middle. The head of a wicked-looking stone beast—a mountain goat?—rears up on the island, spouting water. Around the pond a jungle of Shasta daisies, pink and purple cosmos, dwarf pines and cypresses, some other miniature tree with glossy red leaves. On the island, now that she looks more closely, are mossy stone walls—the ruins of a tiny tower.

"She hired a young chap to do the work," Raymond says. "She lay there and watched him. It took all summer. She just lay all day and watched him making her garden. Then he'd come in and they'd have tea, and talk about it. You know, Maya didn't just design that garden. She imagined it. She'd tell him what she'd been imagining about it, and he'd take off from there. I mean, this to them was not just a garden. The pond was a lake in this country they had some name for, and all around the lake were forests and territories where different tribes and factions lived. Do you get the picture?"

"Yes," says Georgia.

"Maya had a dazzling imagination. She could have written fantasy or science fiction. Whatever. She was a creative person, without any doubt about it. But you could not get her to seriously use her creativity. That goat was one of the gods of that country, and the island was like a sacred place with a former temple on it. You can see the ruins. They had the religion all worked out. Oh, and the literature, the poems and the legends and the history—everything. They had a song that the queen would sing. Of course it was supposed to be a translation, from that language. They had some of that figured out too. There had been a queen that was shut up in that ruin. That temple. I forget why. She was getting sacrificed, probably. Getting her heart torn out or some gruesome thing. It was all complicated and melodramatic. But think of the effort that went into it. The creativity. The young chap was an artist by profession. I believe he thought of himself as an artist. I don't know how she got hold of him, actually. She knew people. He supported himself doing this kind of thing, I imagine. He did a good job. He laid the pipes, everything. He showed up every day. Every day he came in when he was finished and had tea and talked to her. Well, in my opinion, they didn't have just tea. To my knowledge, not just tea. He would bring a little substance, they would have a little smoke. I told Maya she should write it all down.

"But you know, the instant he was finished, off he went. Off he went. I don't know. Maybe he got another job. It didn't seem to me that it was my place to ask. But I did think that even if he had got a job he could have come back and visited her now and then. Or if he'd gone off on a trip somewhere he could have written letters. I thought he could have. I expected that much of him. It wouldn't have been any skin off his back. Not as I see it. It would have been nice of him to make her think that it hadn't been just a case of—of hired friendship, you know, all along."

Raymond is smiling. He cannot repress, or perhaps is not aware of, this smile.

"For that was the conclusion she must have come to," he says. "After all that nice time and imagining together and egging each other on. She must have been disappointed. She must have been. Even at that stage, such a thing would matter a lot to her. You and I know it, Georgia. It would have mattered. He could have treated her a little more kindly. It wouldn't have had to be for very long."

Maya died a year ago, in the fall, but Georgia did not hear about it until Christmas. She got the news in Hilda's Christmas letter. Hilda, who used to be married to Harvey, is now married to another doctor, in a town in the interior of British Columbia. A few years ago she and Georgia, both visitors, met by chance on a Vancouver street, and they have written occasional letters since.

Of course you knew Maya so much better than I did, Hilda wrote. *But I've been surprised how often I've thought about her. I've been thinking of all of us, really, how we were, fifteen or so years ago, and I think we were just as vulnerable in some ways as the kids with their acid trips and so on, that were supposed to be marked for life. Weren't*

*we marked—an of us smashing up our marriages and going out look-
ing for adventure? Of course, Maya didn't smash up her marriage,
she of all people stayed where she was, so I suppose it doesn't make
much sense what I'm saying. But Maya seemed the most vulnerable
person of all to me, so gifted and brittle. I remember I could hardly
bear to look at that vein in her temple where she parted her hair.*

What an odd letter for Hilda to write, thought Georgia. She
remembered Hilda's expensive pastel plaid shirtdresses, her
neat, short, fair hair, her good manners. Did Hilda really think
she had smashed up her marriage and gone out looking for
adventure under the influence of dope and rock music and revolutionary costumes? Georgia's impression was that Hilda had
left Harvey, once she found out what he was up to—or some
of what he was up to—and gone to the town in the interior
where she sensibly took up her old profession of nursing and
in due time married another, presumably more trustworthy
doctor. Maya and Georgia had never thought of Hilda as a
woman like themselves. And Hilda and Maya had not been
close—they had particular reason not to be. But Hilda had kept
track; she knew of Maya's death, she wrote these generous
words. Without Hilda, Georgia would not have known. She
would still have been thinking that someday she might write
to Maya, there might come a time when their friendship could
be mended.

The first time that Ben and Georgia went to Maya's house,
Harvey and Hilda were there. Maya was having a dinner party
for just the six of them. Georgia and Ben had recently moved
to Victoria, and Ben had phoned Raymond, who had been a
friend of his at school. Ben had never met Maya, but he told
Georgia that he had heard that she was very clever, and weird.
People said that she was weird. But she was rich—an heiress—
so she could get away with it.

Georgia groaned at the news that Maya was rich, and she
groaned again at the sight of the house—the great stone-block
house with its terraced lawns and clipped bushes and circular
drive.

Georgia and Ben came from the same small town in

Ontario, and had the same sort of families. It was a fluke that Ben had been sent to a good private school—the money had come from a great-aunt. Even in her teens, when she was proud of being Ben's girl and prouder than she liked to let on about being asked to the dances at that school, Georgia had a low opinion of the girls she met there. She thought rich girls were spoiled and brainless. She called them twits. She thought of herself as a girl—and then a woman—who didn't much like other girls and women. She called the other Navy wives "the Navy *ladies*." Ben was sometimes entertained by her opinions of people and at other times asked if it was really necessary to be so critical.

He had an inkling, he said, that she was going to like Maya. This didn't predispose Georgia in Maya's favor. But Ben turned out to be right. He was very happy then, to have come up with somebody like Maya as an offering to Georgia, to have found a couple with whom he and Georgia could willingly link up as friends. "It'll be good for us to have some non-Navy friends," he was to say. "Some wife for you to knock around with who isn't so conventional. You can't say Maya's conventional."

Georgia couldn't. The house was more or less what she had expected—soon she learned that Maya called it "your friendly neighborhood fortress"—but Maya was a surprise. She opened the door herself, barefoot, wearing a long shapeless robe of coarse brown cloth that looked like burlap. Her hair was long and straight, parted high at one temple. It was almost the same dull-brown color as the robe. She did not wear lipstick, and her skin was rough and pale, with marks like faint bird tracks in the hollows of her cheeks. This lack of color, this roughness of texture about her seemed a splendid assertion of quality. How indifferent she looked, how arrogant and indifferent, with her bare feet, her unpainted toenails, her queer robe. The only thing that she had done to her face was to paint her eyebrows blue—to pluck out all the hairs of her eyebrows, in fact, and paint the skin blue. Not an arched line—just a little daub of blue over each eye, like a swollen vein.

Georgia, whose dark hair was teased, whose eyes were

painted in the style of the time, whose breasts were stylishly proffered, found all this disconcerting, and wonderful.

Harvey was the other person there whose looks Georgia found impressive. He was a short man with heavy shoulders, a slight potbelly, puffy blue eyes, and a pugnacious expression. He came from Lancashire. His gray hair was thin on top but worn long at the sides—combed over his ears in a way that made him look more like an artist than a surgeon. "He doesn't even look to me exactly clean enough to be a surgeon," Georgia said to Ben afterward. "Wouldn't you think he'd be something like a sculptor? With gritty fingernails? I expect he treats women badly." She was recalling how he had looked at her breasts. "Not like Raymond," she said. "Raymond worships Maya. And he is extremely clean."

(Raymond has the kind of looks everybody's mother is crazy about, Maya was to say to Georgia, with slashing accuracy, a few weeks after this.)

The food that Maya served was no better than you would expect at a family dinner, and the heavy silver forks were slightly tarnished. But Raymond poured good wine that he would have liked to talk about. He did not manage to interrupt Harvey, who told scandalous and indiscreet hospital stories, and was blandly outrageous about necrophilia and masturbation. Later, in the living room, the coffee was made and served with some ceremony. Raymond got everybody's attention as he ground the beans in a Turkish cylinder. He talked about the importance of the aromatic oils. Harvey, halted in mid-anecdote, watched with an unkindly smirk, Hilda with patient polite attention. It was Maya who gave her husband radiant encouragement, hung about him like an acolyte, meekly and gracefully assisting. She served the coffee in beautiful little Turkish cups, which she and Raymond had bought in a shop in San Francisco, along with the coffee grinder. She listened demurely to Raymond talking about the shop, as if she recalled other holiday pleasures.

Harvey and Hilda were the first to leave. Maya hung on Raymond's shoulder, saying goodbye. But she detached herself once they were gone, her slithery grace and wifely demeanor discarded. She stretched out casually and awkwardly on the sofa and said, "Now, don't you go yet. Nobody gets half a chance to talk while Harvey is around—you have to talk after."

And Georgia saw how it was. She saw that Maya was hoping not to be left alone with the husband whom she had aroused—for whatever purposes—by her showy attentions. She saw that Maya was mournful and filled with a familiar dread at the end of her dinner party. Raymond was happy. He sat down on the end of the sofa, lifting Maya's reluctant feet to do so. He rubbed one of her feet between his hands.

"What a savage," Raymond said. "This is a woman who won't wear shoes."

"Brandy!" said Maya, springing up. "I knew there was something else you did at dinner parties. You drink brandy!"

"He loves her but she doesn't love him," said Georgia to Ben, just after she had remarked on Raymond's worshipping Maya and being very clean. But Ben, perhaps not listening carefully, thought she was talking about Harvey and Hilda.

"No, no, no. There I think it's the other way round. It's hard to tell with English people. Maya was putting on an act for them. I have an idea about why."

"You have an idea about everything," said Ben.

Georgia and Maya became friends on two levels. On the first level, they were friends as wives; on the second as themselves. On the first level, they had dinner at each other's houses. They listened to their husbands talk about their school days. The jokes and fights, the conspiracies and disasters, the bullies and the victims. Terrifying or pitiable schoolfellows and teachers, treats and humiliations. Maya asked if they were sure they hadn't read all that in a book. "It sounds just like a story," she said. "A boys' story about school."

They said that their experiences were what the books were all about. When they had talked enough about school, they talked about movies, politics, public personalities, places they had travelled to or wanted to travel to. Maya and Georgia could join in then. Ben and Raymond did not believe in leaving women out of the conversation. They believed that women were every bit as intelligent as men.

On the second level, Georgia and Maya talked in each other's kitchens, over coffee. Or they had lunch downtown. There were two places, and only two, where Maya liked to have lunch. One was the Moghul's Court—a seedy, grandiose bar in a large, grim railway hotel. The Moghul's Court had curtains of moth-eaten pumpkin-colored velvet, and desiccated ferns, and waiters who wore turbans. Maya always dressed up to go there, in droopy, silky dresses and not very clean white gloves and amazing hats that she found in secondhand stores. She pretended to be a widow who had served with her husband in various outposts of the Empire. She spoke in fluty tones to the sullen young waiters, asking them, "Could you be so good as to . . ." and then telling them they had been terribly, terribly kind.

She and Georgia worked out the history of the Empire widow, and Georgia was added to the story as a grumpy, secretly Socialistic hired companion named Miss Amy Jukes. The widow's name was Mrs. Allegra Forbes-Bellyea. Her husband had been Nigel Forbes-Bellyea. Sometimes Sir Nigel. Most of one rainy afternoon in the Moghul's Court was spent in devising the horrors of the Forbes-Bellyea honeymoon, in a damp hotel in Wales.

The other place that Maya liked was a hippie restaurant on Blanshard Street, where you sat on dirty plush cushions tied to the tops of stumps and ate brown rice with slimy vegetables and drank cloudy cider. (At the Moghul's Court, Maya and Georgia drank only gin.) When they lunched at the hippie restaurant, they wore long, cheap, pretty Indian cotton dresses and pretended to be refugees from a commune, where they had both been the attendants or concubines of a folksinger named Bill Bones. They made up several songs for Bill Bones, all mild and tender blue-eyed songs that contrasted appallingly with his greedy and licentious ways. Bill Bones had very curious personal habits.

When they weren't playing these games, they talked in a headlong fashion about their lives, childhoods, problems, husbands.

"That was a horrible place," Maya said. "That school."

Georgia agreed.

"They were poor boys at a rich kids' school," Maya said. "So they had to try hard. They had to be a credit to their families."

Georgia would not have thought Ben's family poor, but she knew that there were different ways of looking at such things.

Maya said that whenever they had people in for dinner or the evening, Raymond would pick out beforehand all the records he thought suitable and put them in a suitable order. "I think sometime he'll hand out conversational topics at the door," Maya said.

Georgia revealed that Ben wrote a letter every week to the great-aunt who had sent him to school.

"Is it a nice letter?" said Maya.

"Yes. Oh, yes. It's very nice."

They looked at each other bleakly, and laughed. Then they announced—they admitted—what weighed on them. It was the innocence of these husbands—the hearty, decent, firm, contented innocence. That is a wearying and finally discouraging thing. It makes intimacy a chore.

"But do you feel badly," Georgia said, "talking like this?"

"Of course," said Maya, grinning and showing her large perfect teeth—the product of expensive dental work from the days before she had charge of her own looks. "I have another reason to feel badly," she said. "But I don't know whether I do. I do and I don't."

"I know," said Georgia, who up until that moment hadn't known, for sure.

"You're very smart," Maya said. "Or I'm very obvious. What do you think of him?"

"A lot of trouble," Georgia said judiciously. She was pleased with that answer, which didn't show how flattered she felt by the disclosure, or how heady she found this conversation.

"You aren't just a-whistlin' 'Dixie,'" Maya said, and she told the story about the abortion. "I am going to break up with him," she said. "Any day now."

But she kept on seeing Harvey. She would relate, at lunch, some very disillusioning facts about him, then announce that she had to go, she was meeting him at a motel out on the Gorge Road, or at the cabin he had on Prospect Lake.

"Must scrub," she said.

She had left Raymond once. Not for Harvey. She had run away with, or to, a musician. A pianist—Nordic and sleepy-looking but bad-tempered—from her society-lady, symphony-benefit days. She travelled with him for five weeks, and he deserted her in a hotel in Cincinnati. She then developed frightful chest pains, appropriate to a breaking heart. What she really had was a gallbladder attack. Raymond was sent for, and he came and got her out of the hospital. They had a little holiday in Mexico before they came home.

"That was it, for me," Maya said. "That was your true and desperate love. Nevermore."

What, then, was Harvey?

"Exercise," said Maya.

Georgia got a part-time job in a bookstore, working several evenings a week. Ben went away on his yearly cruise. The summer turned out to be unusually hot and sunny for the West Coast. Georgia combed her hair out and stopped using most of her makeup and bought a couple of short halter dresses. Sitting on her stool at the front of the store, showing her bare brown shoulders and sturdy brown legs, she looked like a college girl—clever but full of energy and bold opinions. The people who came into the store liked the look of a girl—a woman—like Georgia. They liked to talk to her. Most of them came in alone. They were not exactly lonely people, but they were lonely for somebody to talk to about books. Georgia plugged in the kettle behind the desk and made mugs of raspberry tea. Some favored customers brought in their own mugs. Maya came to visit and lurked about in the background, amused and envious.

"You know what you've got?" she said to Georgia. "You've got a salon! Oh, I'd like to have a job like that! I'd even like an ordinary job in an ordinary store, where you fold things up and find things for people and make change and say thank you very much, and colder out today, will it rain?"

"You could get a job like that," said Georgia.

"No, I couldn't. I don't have the discipline. I was too badly brought up. I can't even keep house without Mrs. Hanna and Mrs. Cheng and Sadie."

It was true. Maya had a lot of servants, for a modern woman, though they came at different times and did separate things and were nothing like an old-fashioned household staff. Even the food at her dinner parties, which seemed to show her own indifferent touch, had been prepared by someone else.

Usually, Maya was busy in the evenings. Georgia was just as glad, because she didn't really want Maya coming into the store, asking for crazy titles that she had made up, making Georgia's employment there a kind of joke. Georgia took the store seriously. She had a serious, secret liking for it that she could not explain. It was a long, narrow store with an old-fashioned funnelled entryway between two angled display windows. From her stool behind the desk Georgia was able to see the reflections in one window reflected in the other. This street was not one of those decked out to receive tourists. It was a wide east-west street filled in the early evening with a faintly yellow light, a light reflected off pale stucco buildings that were not very high, plain storefronts, nearly empty sidewalks. Georgia found this plainness liberating after the winding shady streets, the flowery yards and vine-framed windows of Oak Bay. Here the books could come into their own, as they never could in a more artful and enticing suburban bookshop. Straight long rows of paperbacks. (Most of the Penguins then still had their orange-and-white or blue-and-white covers, with no designs or pictures, just the unadorned, unexplained titles.) The store was a straight avenue of bounty, of plausible promises. Certain books that Georgia had never read, and probably never would read, were important to her, because of the stateliness or mystery of their titles. *In Praise of Folly. The Roots of Coincidence. The Flowering of New England. Ideas and Integrities.*

Sometimes she got up and put the books in stricter order. The fiction was shelved alphabetically, by author, which was sensible but not very interesting. The history books, however, and the philosophy and psychology and other science books were arranged according to certain intricate and delightful rules—having to do with chronology and content—that Georgia grasped immediately and even elaborated on. She did not need to read much of a book to know about it. She got a sense of it easily, almost at once, as if by smell.

At times the store was empty, and she felt an abundant calm. It was not even the books that mattered then. She sat on the stool and watched the street—patient, expectant, by herself, in a finely balanced and suspended state.

She saw Miles' reflection—his helmeted ghost parking his motorcycle at the curb—before she saw him. She believed that she had noted his valiant profile, his pallor, his dusty red hair (he took off his helmet and shook out his hair before coming into the store), and his quick, slouching, insolent, invading way of moving, even in the glass.

It was no surprise that he soon began to talk to her, as others did. He told her that he was a diver. He looked for wrecks, and lost airplanes, and dead bodies. He had been hired by a rich couple in Victoria who were planning a treasure-hunting cruise, getting it together at the moment. Their names, the destination were all secrets. Treasure-hunting was a lunatic business. He had done it before. His home was in Seattle, where he had a wife and a little daughter.

Everything he told her could easily have been a lie.

He showed her pictures in books—photographs and drawings, of mollusks, jellyfish, the Portuguese man-of-war, sargasso weed, the Caribbean flying fish, the girdle of Venus. He pointed out which pictures were accurate, which were fakes. Then he went away and paid no more attention to her, even slipping out of the store while she was busy with a customer. Not a hint of a goodbye. But he came in another evening, and told her about a drowned man wedged into the cabin of a boat, looking out the watery window in an interested way. By attention and avoidance, impersonal conversations in close proximity, by his oblivious prowling, and unsmiling, lengthy, gray-eyed looks, he soon had Georgia in a disturbed and not disagreeable state. He stayed away two nights in a row, then came in and asked her, abruptly, if she would like a ride home on his motorcycle.

Georgia said yes. She had never ridden on a motorcycle in her life. Her car was in the parking lot; she knew what was bound to happen.

She told him where she lived. "Just a few blocks up from the beach," she said.

"We'll go to the beach, then. We'll go and sit on the logs."

That was what they did. They sat for a while on the logs. Then, though the beach was not quite dark or completely deserted, they made love in the imperfect shelter of some broom bushes. Georgia walked home, a strengthened and lightened woman, not in the least in love, favored by the universe.

"My car wouldn't start," she told the baby-sitter, a grandmother from down the street. "I walked all the way home. It was lovely, walking. Lovely. I enjoyed it so much."

Her hair was wild, her lips were swollen, her clothes were full of sand.

Her life filled up with such lies. Her car would be parked beside outlying beaches, on the logging roads so conveniently close to the city, on the wandering back roads of the Saanich Peninsula. The map of the city that she had held in her mind up till now, with its routes to shops and work and friends' houses, was overlaid with another map, of circuitous routes followed in fear (not shame) and excitement, of flimsy shelters, temporary hiding places, where she and Miles made love, often within hearing distance of passing traffic or a hiking party or a family picnic. And Georgia herself, watching her children on the roundabout, or feeling the excellent shape of a lemon in her hand at the supermarket, contained another woman, who only a few hours before had been whimpering and tussling on the ferns, on the sand, on the bare ground, or, during a rainstorm, in her own car—who had been driven hard and gloriously out of her mind and drifted loose and gathered her wits and made her way home again. Was this a common story? Georgia cast an eye over the other women at the supermarket. She looked for signs—of dreaminess or flaunting, a sense of drama in a woman's way of dressing, a special rhythm in her movements.

How many, she asked Maya.

"God knows," said Maya. "Do a survey."

Trouble began, perhaps, as soon as they said that they loved each other. Why did they do that—defining, inflating, obscuring whatever it was they did feel? It seemed to be demanded, that was all—just the way changes, variations, elaborations in the lovemaking itself might be demanded. It was a way of going further. So they said it, and that night Georgia couldn't sleep. She did not regret what had been said or think that it was a lie, though she knew that it was absurd. She thought of the way Miles sought to have her look into his eyes during lovemaking—something Ben expressly did not do—and she thought of how his eyes, at first bright and challenging, became cloudy and calm and sombre. That way she trusted him—it was the only way. She thought of being launched out on a gray, deep, baleful, magnificent sea. Love.

"I didn't know this was going to happen," she said in Maya's kitchen the next day, drinking her coffee. The day was warm, but she had put on a sweater to huddle in. She felt shaken, and submissive.

"No. And you don't know," said Maya rather sharply. "Did he say it too? Did he say he loved you too?"

Yes, said Georgia, yes, of course.

"Look out, then. Look out for next time. Next time is always pretty tricky when they've said that."

And so it was. Next time a rift opened. At first they simply tested it, to see if it was there. It was almost like a new diversion to them. But it widened, it widened. Before any words were said to confirm that it was there, Georgia felt it widen, she coldly felt it widen, though she was desperate for it to close. Did he feel the same thing? She didn't know. He too seemed cold—pale, deliberate, glittering with some new malicious intent.

They were sitting recklessly, late at night, in Georgia's car among the other lovers at Clover Point.

"Everybody here in these cars doing the same thing we're doing," Miles had said. "Doesn't that idea turn you on?"

He had said that at the very moment in their ritual when they had been moved, last time, to speak brokenly and solemnly of love.

"You ever think of that?" he said. "I mean, we could start with Ben and Laura. You ever imagine how it would be with you and me and Ben and Laura?"

Laura was his wife, at home in Seattle. He had not spoken of her before, except to tell Georgia her name. He had spoken of Ben, in a way that Georgia didn't like but passed over.

"What does Ben think you do for fun," he'd said, "while he is off cruising the ocean blue?"

"Do you and Ben usually have a big time when he gets back?"

"Does Ben like that outfit as much as I do?"

He spoke as if he and Ben were friends in some way, or at least partners, co-proprietors.

"You and me and Ben and Laura," he said, in a tone that seemed to Georgia insistently and artificially lecherous, sly, derisive. "Spread the joy around."

He tried to fondle her, pretending not to notice how offended she was, how bitterly stricken. He described the generous exchanges that would take place among the four of them abed. He asked whether she was getting excited. She said no, disgusted. Ah, you are but you won't give in to it, he said. His voice, his caresses grew more bullying. What is so special about you, he asked softly, despisingly, with a hard squeeze at her breasts. Georgia, why do you think you're such a queen?

"You are being cruel and you know you're being cruel," said Georgia, pulling at his hands. "Why are you being like this?"

"Honey, I'm not being cruel," said Miles, in a slippery mock-tender voice. "I'm being horny. I'm horny again is all." He began to pull Georgia around, to arrange her for his use. She told him to get out of the car.

"Squeamish," he said, in that same artificially and hatefully tender voice, as if he were licking fanatically at something loathsome. "You're a squeamish little slut."

Georgia told him that she would lean on the horn if he didn't stop. She would lean on the horn if he didn't get out of the car. She would yell for somebody to call the police. She did lean against the horn as they struggled. He pushed her away, with a whimpering curse such as she'd heard from him at other times, when it meant something different. He got out.

She could not believe that such ill will had erupted, that things had so stunningly turned around. When she thought of this afterward—a good long time afterward—she thought that perhaps he had acted for conscience' sake, to mark her off from Laura. Or to blot out what he had said to her last time. To humiliate her because he was frightened. Perhaps. Or perhaps all this seemed to him simply a further, and genuinely interesting, development in lovemaking.

She would have liked to talk it over with Maya. But the possibility of talking anything over with Maya had disappeared. Their friendship had come suddenly to an end.

The night after the incident at Clover Point, Georgia was sitting on the living-room floor playing a bedtime card game with her sons. The phone rang, and she was sure that it was Miles. She had been thinking all day that he would call, he would have to call to explain himself, to beg her pardon, to say that he had been testing her, in a way, or had been temporarily deranged by circumstances that she knew nothing about. She would not forgive him immediately. But she would not hang up.

It was Maya.

"Guess what weird thing happened," Maya said. "Miles phoned me. Your Miles. It's okay, Raymond isn't here. How did he even know my name?"

"I don't know," said Georgia.

She had told him it, of course. She had offered wild Maya up for his entertainment, or to point out what a novice at this game she herself was—a relatively chaste prize.

"He says he wants to come and talk to me," Maya said. "What do you think? What's the matter with him? Did you have a fight?. . . Yes? Oh, well, he probably wants me to persuade you to make up. I must say he picked the right night.

Raymond's at the hospital. He's got this balky woman in labor; he may have to stay and do a section on her. I'll phone and tell you how it goes. Shall I?"

After a couple of hours, with the children long asleep, Georgia began to expect Maya's call. She watched the television news, to take her mind off expecting it. She picked up the phone to make sure there was a dial tone. She turned off the television after the news, then turned it on again. She started to watch a movie; she watched it through three commercial breaks without going to the kitchen to look at the clock.

At half past midnight she went out and got into her car and drove to Maya's house. She had no idea what she would do there. And she did not do much of anything. She drove around the circular drive with the lights off. The house was dark. She could see that the garage was open and Raymond's car was not there. The motorcycle was nowhere in sight.

She had left her children alone, the doors unlocked. Nothing happened to them. They didn't wake up and discover her defection. No burglar, or prowler, or murderer surprised her on her return. That was a piece of luck that she did not even appreciate. She had gone out leaving the door open and the lights on, and when she came back she hardly recognized her folly, though she closed the door and turned out some lights and lay down on the living-room sofa. She didn't sleep. She lay still, as if the smallest movement would sharpen her suffering, until she saw the day getting light and heard the birds waking. Her limbs were stiff. She got up and went to the phone and listened again for the dial tone. She walked stiffly to the kitchen and put on the kettle and said to herself the words *a paralysis of grief.*

A paralysis of grief. What was she thinking of? That was what she would feel, how she might describe the way she would feel, if one of her children had died. Grief is for serious matters, important losses. She knew that. She would not have bartered away an hour of her children's lives to have had the phone ring at ten o'clock last night, to have heard Maya say, "Georgia, he's desperate. He's sorry; he loves you very much."

No. But it seemed that such a phone call would have given

her a happiness that no look or word from her children could give her. Than anything could give her, ever again.

She phoned Maya before nine o'clock. As she was dialling, she thought that there were still some possibilities to pray for. Maya's phone had been temporarily out of order. Maya had been ill last night. Raymond had been in a car accident on his way home from the hospital.

All these possibilities vanished at the first sound of Maya's voice, which was sleepy (pretending to be sleepy?) and silky with deceit. "Georgia? Is that Georgia? Oh, I thought it was going to be Raymond. He had to stay over at the hospital in case this poor wretched woman needed a C-section. He was going to call me—"

"You told me that last night," said Georgia.

"He was going to call me—Oh, Georgia, I was supposed to call you! Now I remember. Yes. I was supposed to call you, but I thought it was probably too late. I thought the phone might wake up the children. I thought, Oh, better just leave it till morning!"

"How late was it?"

"Not awfully. I just thought."

"What happened?"

"What do you mean, what happened?" Maya laughed, like a lady in a silly play. "Georgia, are you in a state?"

"What happened?"

"Oh, Georgia," said Maya, groaning magnanimously but showing an edge of nerves. "Georgia, I'm sorry. It was nothing. It was just nothing. I've been rotten, but I didn't mean to be. I offered him a beer. Isn't that what you do when somebody rides up to your house on a motorcycle? You offer him a beer. But then he came on very lordly and said he only drank Scotch. And he said he'd only drink Scotch if I would drink with him. I thought he was pretty high-handed. Pretty high-handed pose. But I really was doing this for you, Georgia—I was wanting to find out what was on his mind. So I told him to put the motorcycle behind the garage, and I took him to sit in the back garden. That was so if I heard Raymond's car I could chase him out the back way and he could walk the motorcycle down the lane. I am not about to unload anything *new* onto Raymond at this point. I mean even something innocent, which this started out to be."

Georgia, with her teeth chattering, hung up the phone. She never spoke to Maya again. Maya appeared at her door, of course, a little while later, and Georgia had to let her in, because the children were playing in the yard. Maya sat down contritely at the kitchen table and asked if she could smoke. Georgia did not answer. Maya said she would smoke anyway and she hoped it was all right. Georgia pretended that Maya wasn't there. While Maya smoked, Georgia cleaned the stove, dismantling the elements and putting them back together again. She wiped the counters and polished the taps and straightened out the cutlery drawer. She mopped the floor around Maya's feet. She worked briskly, thoroughly, and never quite looked at Maya. At first she was not sure whether she could keep this up. But it got easier. The more earnest Maya became—the further she slipped from sensible remonstrance, half-amused confession, into true and fearful regret—the more fixed Georgia was in her resolve, the more grimly satisfied in her heart. She took care, however, not to appear grim. She moved about lightly. She was almost humming.

She took a knife to scrape out the grease from between the counter tiles by the stove. She had let things get into a bad way.

Maya smoked one cigarette after another, stubbing them out in a saucer that she fetched for herself from the cupboard. She said, "Georgia, this is so stupid. I can tell you, he's not worth it. It was nothing. All it was was Scotch and opportunity."

She said, "I am really sorry. Truly sorry. I know you don't believe me. How can I say it so you will?"

And, "Georgia, listen. You are humiliating me. Fine. Fine. Maybe I deserve it. I do deserve it. But after you've humiliated me enough we'll go back to being friends and we'll laugh about this. When we're old ladies, I swear we'll laugh. We won't be able to remember his name. We'll call him the motorcycle sheikh. We will."

Then, "Georgia, what do you want me to do? Do you want me to throw myself on the floor? I'm about ready to. I'm trying to keep myself from snivelling, and I can't. I'm snivelling, Georgia. Okay?"

She had begun to cry. Georgia put on her rubber gloves and started to clean the oven.

"You win," said Maya. "I'll pick up my cigarettes and go home."

She phoned a few times. Georgia hung up on her. Miles phoned, and Georgia hung up on him too. She thought he sounded cautious but smug. He phoned again and his voice trembled, as if he were striving just for candor and humility, bare love. Georgia hung up at once. She felt violated, shaken.

Maya wrote a letter, which said, in part, *I suppose you know that Miles is going back to Seattle and whatever home fires he keeps burning there. It seems the treasure thing has fallen through. But you must have known he was bound to go sometime and you'd have felt rotten then, so now you've got the rotten feeling over with. So isn't that okay? I don't say this to excuse myself. I know I was weak and putrid. But can't we put it behind us now?*

She went on to say that she and Raymond were going on a long-planned holiday to Greece and Turkey, and that she hoped very much that she would get a note from Georgia before she left. But if she didn't get any word she would try to understand what Georgia was telling her, and she would not make a nuisance of herself by writing again.

She kept her word. She didn't write again. She sent, from Turkey, a pretty piece of striped cloth large enough for a tablecloth. Georgia folded it up and put it away. She left it for Ben to find after she moved out, several months later.

"I'm happy," Raymond tells Georgia. "I'm very happy, and the reason is that I'm content to be an ordinary sort of person with an ordinary calm life. I am not looking for any big revelation or any big drama or any messiah of the opposite sex. I don't go around figuring out how to make things more interesting. I can say to you quite frankly I think Maya made a mistake. I don't mean she wasn't very gifted and intelligent and creative and so on, but she was looking for something—maybe she was looking for something that just is not there. And she tended to despise a lot that she had. It's true. She didn't want the privileges she had. We'd travel, for example, and she wouldn't want to stay in a comfortable hotel. No. She had to go on some trek that involved riding on poor, miserable donkeys and drinking sour milk for breakfast. I suppose I sound very square. Well, I suppose I am. I am square. You know, she had such beautiful silver. Magnificent silver. It was passed down through her family. And she couldn't be bothered to polish it or get the cleaning woman to polish it. She wrapped it all up in plastic and hid it away. She hid it away—you'd think it was a disgrace. How do you think she envisaged herself? As some kind of hippie, maybe? Some kind of free spirit? She didn't even realize it was her money that kept her afloat. I'll tell you, some of the free spirits I've seen pass in and out of this house wouldn't have been long around her without it.

"I did all I could," said Raymond. "I didn't scoot off and leave her, like her Prince of Fantasy Land."

Georgia got a vengeful pleasure out of breaking with Maya. She was pleased with the controlled manner in which she did it. The deaf ear. She was surprised to find herself capable of such control, such thoroughgoing punishment. She punished Maya. She punished Miles, through Maya, as much as she could. What she had to do, and she knew it, was to scrape herself raw, to root out all addiction to the gifts of those two pale prodigies. Miles and Maya. Both of them slippery, shimmery—liars, seducers, finaglers. But you would have thought that after such scourging she'd have scuttled back into her marriage and locked its doors, and appreciated what she had there as never before.

That was not what happened. She broke with Ben. Within a year, she was gone. Her way of breaking was strenuous and unkind. She told him about Miles, though she spared her own pride by leaving out the part about Miles and Maya. She took no care—she had hardly any wish—to avoid unkindness. On the night when she waited for Maya to call, some bitter, yeasty spirit entered into her. She saw herself as a person surrounded by, living by, sham. Because she had been so readily unfaithful, her marriage was a sham. Because she had gone so far out of it, so quickly, it was a sham. She dreaded, now, a life like Maya's. She dreaded just as much a life like her own before this happened. She could not but destroy. Such cold energy was building in her she had to blow her own house down.

She had entered with Ben, when they were both so young, a world of ceremony, of safety, of gestures, concealment. Fond appearances. More than appearances. Fond contrivance. (She thought when she left that she would have no use for contrivance anymore.) She had been happy there, from time to time. She had been sullen, restless, bewildered, and happy. But she said most vehemently, Never, never. I was never happy, she said.

People always say that.

People make momentous shifts, but not the changes they imagine.

Just the same, Georgia knows that her remorse about the way she changed her life is dishonest. It is real and dishonest. Listening to Raymond, she knows that whatever she did she would have to do again. She would have to do it again, supposing that she had to be the person she was.

Raymond does not want to let Georgia go. He does not want to part with her. He offers to drive her downtown. When she has gone, he won't be able to talk about Maya. Very likely Anne has told him that she does not want to hear any more on the subject of Maya.

"Thank you for coming," he says on the doorstep. "Are you sure about the ride? Are you sure you can't stay to dinner?"

Georgia reminds him again about the bus, the last ferry. She says no, no, she really wants to walk. It's only a couple of miles. The late afternoon so lovely, Victoria so lovely. I had forgotten, she says.

Raymond says once more, "Thank you for coming."

"Thank you for the drinks," Georgia says. "Thank you too. I guess we never believe we are going to die."

"Now, now," says Raymond.

"No. I mean we never behave—we never behave as if we believed we were going to die."

Raymond smiles more and more and puts a hand on her shoulder. "How should we behave?" he says.

"Differently," says Georgia. She puts a foolish stress on the word, meaning that her answer is so lame that she can offer it only as a joke.

Raymond hugs her, then involves her in a long chilly kiss. He fastens onto her with an appetite that is grievous but unconvincing. A parody of passion, whose intention neither one of them, surely, will try to figure out.

She doesn't think about that as she walks back to town through the yellow-leafed streets with their autumn smells and silences. Past Clover Point, the cliffs crowned with broom bushes, the mountains across the water. The mountains of the Olympic Peninsula, assembled like a blatant backdrop, a cutout of rainbow tissue paper. She doesn't think about Raymond, or Miles, or Maya, or even Ben.

She thinks about sitting in the store in the evenings. The light in the street, the complicated reflections in the windows. The accidental clarity.

✎ Carried Away ✎

LETTERS

IN THE DINING ROOM of the Commercial Hotel, Louisa opened the letter that had arrived that day from overseas. She ate steak and potatoes, her usual meal, and drank a glass of wine. There were a few travellers in the room, and the dentist who ate there every night because he was a widower. He had shown an interest in her in the beginning but had told her he had never before seen a woman touch wine or spirits.

"It is for my health," said Louisa gravely.

The white tablecloths were changed every week and in the meantime were protected by oilcloth mats. In winter, the dining room smelled of these mats wiped by a kitchen rag, and of coal fumes from the furnace, and beef gravy and dried potatoes and onions—a smell not unpleasant to anybody coming in hungry from the cold. On each table was a little cruet stand with the bottle of brown sauce, the bottle of tomato sauce, and the pot of horseradish.

The letter was addressed to "The Librarian, Carstairs Public Library, Carstairs, Ontario." It was dated six weeks before—January 4, 1917.

> Perhaps you will be surprised to hear from a person you don't know and that doesn't remember your name. I hope you are still the same Librarian though enough time has gone by that you could have moved on.
>
> What has landed me here in Hospital is not too serious. I see worse all around me and get my mind off of all that by picturing things and wondering for instance if you are still

there in the Library. If you are the one I mean, you are about
of medium size or perhaps not quite, with light brownish hair.
You came a few months before it was time for me to go in the
Army following on Miss Tamblyn who had been there since I
first became a user aged nine or ten. In her time the books were
pretty much every which way, and it was as much as your life
was worth to ask her for the least help or anything since she
was quite a dragon. Then when you came what a change, it
was all put into sections of Fiction and Non-Fiction and His-
tory and Travel and you got the magazines arranged in order
and put out as soon as they arrived, not left to molder away
till everything in them was stale. I felt gratitude but did not
know how to say so. Also I wondered what brought you there,
you were an educated person.

My name is Jack Agnew and my card is in the drawer.
The last book I took out was very good—H.G. Wells,
Mankind in the Making. *My education was to Second Form*
in High School, then I went into Douds as many did. I did-
n't join up right away when I was eighteen so you will not
see me as a Brave Man. I am a person tending to have my
own ideas always. My only relative in Carstairs, or anyplace,
is my father Patrick Agnew. He works for Douds not at the
factory but at the house doing the gardening. He is a lone
wolf even more than me and goes out to the country fishing
every chance he gets. I write him a letter sometimes but I
doubt if he reads it.

After supper Louisa went up to the Ladies' Parlor on the
second floor, and sat down at the desk to write her reply.

I am very glad to hear you appreciated what I did in the
Library though it was just the normal organization, nothing
special.

I am sure you would like to hear news of home, but I am a
poor person for the job, being an outsider here. I do talk to peo-
ple in the Library and in the hotel. The travellers in the hotel
mostly talk about how business is (it is brisk if you can get the
goods) and a little about sickness, and a lot about the War.

There are rumors on rumors and opinions galore, which I'm sure would make you laugh if they didn't make you angry. I will not bother to write them down because I am sure there is a Censor reading this who would cut my letter to ribbons.

You ask how I came here. There is no interesting story. My parents are both dead. My father worked for Eaton's in Toronto in the Furniture Department, and after his death my mother worked there too in Linens. And I also worked there for a while in Books. Perhaps you could say Eaton's was our Douds. I graduated from Jarvis Collegiate. I had some sickness which put me in hospital for a long time, but I am quite well now. I had a great deal of time to read and my favorite authors are Thomas Hardy, who is accused of being gloomy but I think is very true to life—and Willa Cather. I just happened to be in this town when I heard the Librarian had died and I thought, perhaps that is the job for me.

A good thing your letter reached me today as I am about to be discharged from here and don't know if it would have been sent on to where I am going. I am glad you did not think my letter was too foolish.

If you run into my father or anybody you do not need to say anything about the fact we are writing to each other. It is nobody's business and I know there are plenty of people would laugh at me writing to the Librarian as they did at me going to the Library even, why give them the satisfaction?

I am glad to be getting out of here. So much luckier than some I see that will never walk or have their sight and will have to hide themselves away from the world.

You asked where did I live in Carstairs. Well, it was not anyplace to be proud of. If you know where Vinegar Hill is and you turned off on Flowers Road it is the last house on the right, yellow paint once upon a time. My father grows potatoes, or did. I used to take them around town with my wagon, and every load I sold got a nickel to keep.

You mention favorite authors. At one time I was fond of Zane Grey, but I drifted away from reading fiction stories to reading History or Travel. I sometimes read books away over

*my head, I know, but I do get something out of them. H.G.
Wells I mentioned is one and Robert Ingersoll who writes about
religion. They have given me a lot to think about. If you are
very religious I hope I have not offended you.*

*One day when I got to the Library it was a Saturday after-
noon and you had just unlocked the door and were putting the
lights on as it was dark and raining out You had been caught
out with no hat or umbrella and your hair had got wet. You
took the pins out of it and let it come down. Is it too personal
a thing to ask if you have it long still or have you cut it? You
went over and stood by the radiator and shook your hair on it
and the water sizzled like grease in the frying pan. I was sitting reading in the London Illustrated News about the War.
We exchanged a smile. (I didn't mean to say your hair was
greasy when I wrote that!)*

*I have not cut my hair though I often think about it. I do not
know if it is vanity or laziness that prevents me.*

I am not very religious.

*I walked up Vinegar Hill and found your house. The pota-
toes are looking healthy. A police dog disputed with me, is he
yours?*

*The weather is getting quite warm. We have had the flood
on the river, which I gather is an annual Spring event. The
water got into the hotel basement and somehow contaminated
our drinking supply so that we were given free beer or ginger
ale. But only if we lived or were staying there. You can imagine there were plenty of jokes.*

I should ask if there is anything that I could send you.

*I am not in need of anything particular. I get the tobacco and
other bits of things the ladies in Carstairs do up for us. I would
like to read some books by the authors you have mentioned but
I doubt whether I would get the chance here.*

*The other day there was a man died of a heart attack. It
was the News of all time. Did you hear about the man who died
of a heart attack? That was all you heard about day and night
here. Then everybody would laugh which seems hard-hearted*

but it just seemed so strange. It was not even a hot time so you couldn't say maybe he was scared. (As a matter of fact he was writing a letter at the time so I had better look out.) Before and after him others have died being shot up or blown up but he is the famous one, to die of a heart attack. Everybody is saying what a long way to come and a lot of expense for the Army to go to, for that.

The summer has been so dry the watering tank has been doing the streets every day, trying to lay the dust. The children would dance along behind it. There was also a new thing in town— a cart with a little bell that went along selling ice cream, and the children were pretty attentive to this as well. It was pushed by the man who had an accident at the factory—you know who I mean, though I can't recall his name. He lost his arm to the elbow. My room at the hotel, being on the third floor, it was like an oven, and I often walked about till after midnight. So did many other people, sometimes in pajamas. It was like a dream. There was still a little water in the river, enough to go out in a rowboat, and the Methodist minister did that on a Sunday in August. He was praying for rain in a public service. But there was a small leak in the boat and the water came in and wet his feet and eventually the boat sank and left him standing in the water, which did not nearly reach his waist. Was it an accident or a malicious trick? The talk was all that his prayers were answered but from the wrong direction.

I often pass the Douds' place on my walks. Your father keeps the lawns and hedges looking beautiful. I like the house, so original and airy-looking. But it may not have been cool even there, because I heard the voice of the mother and baby daughter late at night as if they were out on the lawn.

Though I told you there is nothing I need, there is one thing I would like. That is a photograph of you. I hope you will not think I am overstepping the bounds to ask for it. Maybe you are engaged to somebody or have a sweetheart over here you are writing to as well as me. You are a cut above the ordinary and it would not surprise me if some Officer had spoken for you. But now that I have asked I cannot take it back and will just leave it up to you to think what you like of me.

Louisa was twenty-five years old and had been in love once, with a doctor she had known in the sanitorium. Her love was returned, eventually, costing the doctor his job. There was some harsh doubt in her mind about whether he had been told to leave the sanitorium or had left of his own accord, being weary of the entanglement. He was married, he had children. Letters had played a part that time too. After he left, they were still writing to one another. And once or twice after she was released. Then she asked him not to write anymore and he didn't. But the failure of his letters to arrive drove her out of Toronto and made her take the travelling job. Then there would be only the one disappointment in the week, when she got back on Friday or Saturday night. Her last letter had been firm and stoical, and some consciousness of herself as a hero-ine of love's tragedy went with her around the country as she hauled her display cases up and down the stairs of small hotels and talked about Paris styles and said that her sample hats were bewitching, and drank her solitary glass of wine. If she'd had anybody to tell, though, she would have laughed at just that notion. She would have said love was all hocus-pocus, a decep-tion, and she believed that. But at the prospect she still felt a hush, a flutter along the nerves, a bowing down of sense, a fla-grant prostration.

She had a picture taken. She knew how she wanted it to be. She would have liked to wear a simple white blouse, a peasant girl's smock with the string open at the neck. She did not own a blouse of that description and in fact had only seen them in pictures. And she would have liked to let her hair down. Or if it had to be up, she would have liked it piled very loosely and bound with strings of pearls.

Instead she wore her blue silk shirtwaist and bound her hair as usual. She thought the picture made her look rather pale, hollow-eyed. Her expression was sterner and more foreboding than she had intended. She sent it anyway.

I am not engaged, and do not have a sweetheart. I was in love once and it had to be broken off. I was upset at the time but I knew I must bear it, and now I believe that it was all for the best.

She had wracked her brains, of course, to remember him. She could not remember shaking out her hair, as he said she had done, or smiling at any young man when the raindrops fell on the radiator. He might as well have dreamed all that, and perhaps he had.

She had begun to follow the war in a more detailed way than she had done previously. She did not try to ignore it anymore. She went along the street with a sense that her head was filled with the same exciting and troubling information as everybody else's. Saint-Quentin, Arras, Montdidier, Amiens, and then there was a battle going on at the Somme River, where surely there had been one before? She laid open on her desk the maps of the war that appeared as double-page spreads in the magazines. She saw in colored lines the German drive to the Marne, the first thrust of the Americans at Château-Thierry. She looked at the artist's brown pictures of a horse rearing up during an air attack, of some soldiers in East Africa drinking out of coconuts, and of a line of German prisoners with bandaged heads or limbs and bleak, sullen expressions. Now she felt what everybody else did—a constant fear and misgiving and at the same time this addictive excitement. You could look up from your life of the moment and feel the world crackling beyond the walls.

I am glad to hear you do not have a sweetheart though I know that is selfish of me. I do not think you and I will ever meet again. I don't say that because I've had a dream about what will happen or am a gloomy person always looking for the worst. It just seems to me it is the most probable thing to happen, though I don't dwell on it and go along every day doing the best I can to stay alive. I am not trying to worry you or get your sympathy either but just explain how the idea I won't ever see Carstairs again makes me think I can say anything I want. I guess it's like being sick with a fever. So I will say I love you.

I think of you up on a stool at the Library reaching to put a book away and I come up and put my hands on your waist and lift you down, and you turning around inside my arms as if we agreed about everything.

Every Tuesday afternoon the ladies and girls of the Red Cross met in the Council Chambers, which was just down the hall from the Library. When the Library was empty for a few moments, Louisa went down the hall and entered the room full of women. She had decided to knit a scarf. At the sanitorium she had learned how to knit a basic stitch, but she had never learned or had forgotten how to cast on or off.

The older women were all busy packing boxes or cutting up and folding bandages from sheets of heavy cotton that were spread on the tables. But a lot of girls near the door were eating buns and drinking tea. One was holding a skein of wool on her arms for another to wind.

Louisa told them what she needed to know.

"So what do you want to knit, then?" said one of the girls with some bun still in her mouth.

Louisa said, a muffler. For a soldier.

"Oh, you'll want the regulation wool," another said, more politely, and jumped off the table. She came back with some balls of brown wool, and fished a spare pair of needles out of her bag, telling Louisa they could be hers.

"I'll just get you started," she said. "It's a regulation width too."

Other girls gathered around and teased this girl, whose name was Corrie. They told her she was doing it all wrong.

"Oh, I am, am I?" said Corrie. "How would you like a knitting needle in your eye? Is it for a friend?" she said solicitously to Louisa. "A friend overseas?"

"Yes," said Louisa. Of course they would think of her as an old maid, they would laugh at her or feel sorry for her, according to whatever show they put on, of being kind or brazen.

"So knit up good and tight," said the one who'd finished her bun. "Knit up good and tight to keep him warm!"

One of the girls in this group was Grace Horne. She was a shy but resolute-looking girl, nineteen years old, with a broad face, thin lips often pressed together, brown hair cut in a straight bang, and an attractively mature body. She had become engaged to Jack Agnew before he went overseas, but they had agreed not to say anything about it.

SPANISH FLU

Louisa had made friends with some of the travellers who stayed regularly at the hotel. One of these was Jim Frarey, who sold typewriters and office equipment and books and all sorts of stationery supplies. He was a fair-haired, rather round-shouldered but strongly built man in his middle forties. You would think by the look of him that he sold something heavier and more important in the masculine world, like farm implements.

Jim Frarey kept travelling all through the Spanish flu epidemic, though you never knew then if stores would be open for business or not. Occasionally the hotels too would be closed, like the schools and movie houses and even—Jim Frarey thought this a scandal—the churches.

"They ought to be ashamed of themselves, the cowards," he said to Louisa. "What good does it do anybody to lurk around home and wait for it to strike? Now you never closed the Library, did you?"

Louisa said only when she herself was sick. A mild case, hardly lasting a week, but of course she had to go to the hospital. They wouldn't let her stay in the hotel.

"Cowards," he said. "If you're going to be taken, you'll be taken. Don't you agree?"

They discussed the crush in the hospitals, the deaths of doctors and nurses, the unceasing drear spectacle of the funerals. Jim Frarey lived down the street from an undertaking establishment in Toronto. He said they still got out the black horses, the black carriage, the works, to bury such personages as warranted a fuss.

"Day and night they went on," he said. "Day and night."

He raised his glass and said, "Here's to health, then. You look well yourself."

He thought that in fact Louisa was looking better than she used to. Maybe she had started putting on rouge. She had a pale-olive skin, and it seemed to him that her cheeks used to be without color. She dressed with more dash too, and took more trouble to be friendly. She used to be very on-again, off-again, just as she chose. She was drinking whisky now too, though she would not try it without drowning it in water. It used to be only a glass of wine. He wondered if it was a boyfriend that had made the difference. But a boyfriend might perk up her looks without increasing her interest in all and sundry, which was what he was pretty sure had happened. It was more likely time running out and the husband prospects thinned out so dreadfully by the war. That could set a woman stirring. She was smarter and better company and better-looking too than most of the married ones. What happened with a woman like that? Sometimes just bad luck. Or bad judgment at a time when it mattered. A little too sharp and self-assured, in the old days, making the men uneasy?

"Life can't be brought to a standstill all the same," he said. "You did the right thing, keeping the Library open."

This was in the early winter of 1919, when there had been a fresh outbreak of flu after the danger was supposed to be past. They seemed to be all alone in the hotel. It was only about nine o'clock but the hotelkeeper had gone to bed. His wife was in the hospital with the flu. Jim Frarey had brought the bottle of whisky from the bar, which was closed for fear of contagion—and they sat at a table beside the window, in the dining room. A winter fog had collected outside and was pressing against the window. You could barely see the streetlights or the few cars that trundled cautiously over the bridge.

"Oh, it was not a matter of principle," Louisa said. "That I kept the Library open. It was a more personal reason than you think."

Then she laughed and promised him a peculiar story. "Oh, the whisky must have loosened my tongue," she said.

"I am not a gossip," said Jim Frarey.

She gave him a hard laughing look and said that when a person announced they weren't a gossip, they almost invariably were. The same when they promised never to tell a soul.

"You can tell this where and when you like just as long as you leave out the real names and don't tell it around here," she said. "That I hope I can trust you not to do. Though at the moment I don't feel as if I cared. I'll probably feel otherwise when the drink wears off. It's a lesson, this story. It's a lesson in what fools women can make of themselves. So, you say, what's new about that, you can learn it every day!"

She began to tell him about a soldier who had started writing letters to her from overseas. The soldier remembered her from when he used to go into the Library. But she didn't remember him. However, she replied in a friendly way to his first letter and a correspondence sprang up between them. He told her where he had lived in the town and she walked past the house so that she could tell him how things looked there. He told her what books he'd read and she gave some of the same kind of information. In short, they both revealed something of themselves and feelings warmed up on either side. On his side first, as far as any declarations went. She was not one to rush in like a fool. At first, she thought she was simply being kind. Even later, she didn't want to reject and embarrass him. He asked for a picture. She had one taken, it was not to her liking, but she sent it. He asked if she had a sweetheart and she replied truthfully that she did not. He did not send any picture of himself nor did she ask for one, though of course she was curious as to what he looked like. It would be no easy matter for him to have a picture taken in the middle of a war. Furthermore, she did not want to seem like the sort of woman who would withdraw kindness if looks did not come up to scratch.

He wrote that he did not expect to come home. He said he was not so afraid of dying as he was of ending up like some of the men he had seen when he was in the hospital, wounded. He did not elaborate, but she supposed he meant the cases they were just getting to know about now—the stumps of men, the blinded, the ones made monstrous with burns. He was not whining about his fate, she did not mean to imply that. It was just that he expected to die and picked death over some other options and he thought about her and wrote to her as men do to a sweetheart in such a situation.

When the war ended, it was a while since she had heard from him. She went on expecting a letter every day and nothing came. Nothing came. She was afraid that he might have been one of those unluckiest of soldiers in the whole war—one of those killed in the last week, or on the last day, or even in the last hour. She searched the local paper every week, and the names of new casualties were still being printed there till after New Year's but his was not among them. Now the paper began to list as well the names of those returning home, often printing a photo with the name, and a little account of rejoicing. When the soldiers were returning thick and fast there was less room for these additions. And then she saw his name, another name on the list. He had not been killed, he had not been wounded —he was coming home to Carstairs, perhaps was already there.

It was then that she decided to keep the Library open, though the flu was raging. Every day she was sure he would come, every day she was prepared for him. Sundays were a torment. When she entered the Town Hall she always felt he might be there before her, leaning up against the wall awaiting her arrival. Sometimes she felt it so strongly she saw a shadow that she mistook for a man. She understood now how people believed they had seen ghosts. Whenever the door opened she expected to look up into his face. Sometimes she made a pact with herself not to look up till she had counted to ten. Few people came in, because of the flu. She set herself jobs of rearranging things, else she would have gone mad. She never locked up until five or ten minutes after closing time. And then she fancied that he might be across the street on the Post Office steps, watching her, being too shy to make a move. She worried of course that he might be ill, she always sought in conversation for news of the latest cases. No one spoke his name.

It was at this time that she entirely gave up on reading. The covers of books looked like coffins to her, either shabby or ornate, and what was inside them might as well have been dust. She had to be forgiven, didn't she, she had to be forgiven for thinking, after such letters, that the one thing that could never happen was that he wouldn't approach her, wouldn't get in touch with her at all? Never cross her threshold, after such avowals? Funerals passed by her window and she gave no thought to them, as long as they were not his. Even when she was sick in the hospital her only thought was that she must get back, she must get out of bed, the door must not stay locked against him. She staggered to her feet and back to work. On a hot afternoon she was arranging fresh newspapers on the racks and his name jumped out at her like something in her feverish dreams.

She read a short notice of his marriage to a Miss Grace Horne. Not a girl she knew. Not a Library user.

The bride wore fawn silk crêpe with brown-and-cream piping, and a beige straw hat with brown velvet streamers.

There was no picture. Brown-and-cream piping. Such was the end, and had to be, to her romance.

But on her desk at the Library, a matter of a few weeks ago, on a Saturday night after everybody had gone and she had locked the door and was turning out the lights, she discovered a scrap of paper. A few words written on it. *I was engaged before I went overseas.* No name, not his or hers. And there was her photograph, partly shoved under the blotter.

He had been in the Library that very evening. It had been a busy time, she had often left the desk to find a book for somebody or to straighten up the papers or to put some books on the shelves. He had been in the same room with her, watched her, and taken his chance. But never made himself known.

I was engaged before I went overseas.

"Do you think it was all a joke on me?" Louisa said. "Do you think a man could be so diabolical?"

"In my experience, tricks like that are far more often indulged in by the women. No, no. Don't you think such a thing. Far more likely he was sincere. He got a little carried away. It's all just the way it looks on the surface. He was engaged before he went overseas, he never expected to get back in one piece but he did. And when he did, there is the fiancée waiting—what else could he do?"

"What indeed?" said Louisa.

"He bit off more than he could chew."

"Ah, that's so, that's so!" Louisa said. "And what was it in my case but vanity, which deserves to get slapped down!" Her eyes were glassy and her expression roguish. "You don't think he'd had a good look at me any one time and thought the original was even worse than that poor picture, so he backed off?"

"I do not!" said Jim Frarey. "And don't you so belittle yourself."

"I don't want you to think I am stupid," she said. "I am not so stupid and inexperienced as that story makes me sound."

"Indeed I don't think you are stupid at all."

"But perhaps you think I am inexperienced?"

This was it, he thought—the usual. Women after they have told one story on themselves cannot stop from telling another. Drink upsets them in a radical way, prudence is out the window.

She had confided in him once before that she had been a patient in a sanitorium. Now she told about being in love with a doctor there. The sanitorium was on beautiful grounds up on Hamilton Mountain, and they used to meet there along the hedged walks. Shelves of limestone formed the steps and in sheltered spots there were such plants as you do not commonly see in Ontario—azaleas, rhododendrons, magnolias. The doctor knew something about botany and he told her this was the Carolinian vegetation. Very different from here, lusher, and there were little bits of woodland too, wonderful trees, paths worn under the trees. Tulip trees.

"Tulips!" said Jim Frarey. "Tulips on the trees!"

"No, no, it is the shape of their leaves!"

She laughed at him challengingly, then bit her lip. He saw fit to continue the dialogue, saying, "Tulips on the trees!" while she said no, it is the leaves that are shaped like tulips, no, I never said that, stop! So they passed into a state of gingerly evaluation—which he knew well and could only hope she did—full of small pleasant surprises, half-sardonic signals, a welling-up of impudent hopes, and a fateful sort of kindness.

"All to ourselves," Jim Frarey said. "Never happened before, did it? Maybe it never will again."

She let him take her hands, half lift her from her chair. He turned out the dining-room lights as they went out. Up the stairs they went, that they had so often climbed separately. Past the picture of the dog on his master's grave, and Highland Mary singing in the field, and the old King with his bulgy eyes, his look of indulgence and repletion.

"It's a foggy, foggy night, and my heart is in a fright," Jim Frarey was half singing, half humming as they climbed. He kept an assured hand on Louisa's back. "All's well, all's well," he said as he steered her round the turn of the stairs. And when they took the narrow flight of steps to the third floor he said, "Never climbed so close to Heaven in this place before!"

But later in the night Jim Frarey gave a concluding groan and roused himself to deliver a sleepy scolding. "Louisa, Louisa, why didn't you tell me that was the way it was?"

"I told you everything," said Louisa in a faint and drifting voice.

"I got a wrong impression, then," he said. "I never intended for this to make a difference to you."

She said that it hadn't. Now without him pinning her down and steadying her, she felt herself whirling around in an irresistible way, as if the mattress had turned into a child's top and was carrying her off. She tried to explain that the traces of blood on the sheets could be credited to her period, but her words came out with a luxurious nonchalance and could not be fitted together.

ACCIDENTS

When Arthur came home from the factory a little before noon he shouted, "Stay out of my way till I wash! There's been an accident over at the works!" Nobody answered. Mrs. Feare, the housekeeper, was talking on the kitchen telephone so loudly that she could not hear him, and his daughter was of course at school. He washed, and stuffed everything he had been wearing into the hamper, and scrubbed up the bathroom, like a murderer. He started out clean, with even his hair slicked and patted, to drive to the man's house. He had had to ask where it was. He thought it was up Vinegar Hill but they said no, that was the father—the young fellow and his wife live on the other side of town, past where the Apple Evaporator used to be, before the war.

He found the two brick cottages side by side, and picked the left-hand one, as he'd been told. It wouldn't have been hard to pick which house, anyway. News had come before him. The door to the house was open, and children too young to be in school yet hung about in the yard. A small girl sat on a kiddie car, not going anywhere, just blocking his path. He stepped around her. As he did so an older girl spoke to him in a formal way—a warning.

"Her dad's dead. Hers!"

A woman came out of the front room carrying an armload of curtains, which she gave to another woman standing in the hall. The woman who received the curtains was gray-haired, with a pleading face. She had no upper teeth. She probably took her plate out, for comfort, at home. The woman who passed the curtains to her was stout but young, with fresh skin.

"You tell her not to get up on that stepladder," the gray-haired woman said to Arthur. "She's going to break her neck taking down curtains. She thinks we need to get everything washed. Are you the undertaker? Oh, no, excuse me! You're Mr. Doud. Grace, come out here! Grace! It's Mr. Doud!"

"Don't trouble her," Arthur said.

"She thinks she's going to get the curtains all down and washed and up again by tomorrow, because he's going to have to go in the front room. She's my daughter. I can't tell her anything."

"She'll quiet down presently," said a sombre but comfortable-looking man in a clerical collar, coming through from the back of the house. Their minister. But not from one of the churches Arthur knew. Baptist? Pentecostal? Plymouth Brethren? He was drinking tea.

Some other woman came and briskly removed the curtains.

"We got the machine filled and going," she said. "A day like this, they'll dry like nobody's business. Just keep the kids out of here."

The minister had to stand aside and lift his teacup high, to avoid her and her bundle. He said, "Aren't any of you ladies going to offer Mr. Doud a cup of tea?"

Arthur said, "No, no, don't trouble."

"The funeral expenses," he said to the gray-haired woman. "If you could let her know—"

"Lillian wet her pants!" said a triumphant child at the door. "Mrs. Agnew! Lillian peed her pants!"

"Yes. Yes," said the minister. "They will be very grateful."

"The plot and the stone, everything," Arthur said. "You'll make sure they understand that. Whatever they want on the stone."

The gray-haired woman had gone out into the yard. She came back with a squalling child in her arms. "Poor lamb," she said. "They told her she wasn't supposed to come in the house so where could she go? What could she do but have an accident!"

The young woman came out of the front room dragging a rug.

"I want this put on the line and beat," she said.

"Grace, here is Mr. Doud come to offer his condolences," the minister said.

"And to ask if there is anything I can do," said Arthur.

The gray-haired woman started upstairs with the wet child in her arms and a couple of others following.

Grace spotted them.

"Oh, no, you don't! You get back outside!"

"My mom's in here."

"Yes and your mom's good and busy, she don't need to be bothered with you. She's here helping me out. Don't you know Lillian's dad's dead?"

"Is there anything I can do for you?" Arthur said, meaning to clear out.

Grace stared at him with her mouth open. Sounds of the washing machine filled the house.

"Yes, there is," she said. "You wait here."

"She's overwhelmed," the minister said. "It's not that she means to be rude."

Grace came back with a load of books.

"These here," she said. "He had them out of the Library. I don't want to have to pay fines on them. He went every Saturday night so I guess they are due back tomorrow. I don't want to get in trouble about them."

"I'll look after them," Arthur said. "I'd be glad to."

"I just don't want to get in any trouble about them."

"Mr. Doud was saying about taking care of the funeral," the minister said to her, gently admonishing. "Everything including the stone. Whatever you want on the stone."

"Oh, I don't want anything fancy," Grace said.

On Friday morning last there occurred in the sawmill operation of Douds Factory a particularly ghastly and tragic accident. Mr. Jack Agnew, in reaching under the main shaft, had the misfortune to have his sleeve caught by a setscrew in an adjoining flange, so that his arm and shoulder were drawn under the shaft. His head in consequence was brought in contact with the circular saw, that saw being about one foot in diameter. In an instant the unfortunate young man's head was separated from his body, being severed at an angle below the left ear and through the neck. His death is believed to have been instantaneous. He never spoke or uttered a cry so it was not by any sound of his but by the spurt and shower of his blood that his fellow-workers were horribly alerted to the disaster.

This account was reprinted in the paper a week later for those who might have missed it or who wished to have an extra copy to send to friends or relations out of town (particularly to people who used to live in Carstairs and did not anymore). The misspelling of *flange* was corrected. There was a note apologizing for the mistake. There was also a description of a very large funeral, attended even by people from neighboring towns and as far away as Walley. They came by car and train, and some by horse and buggy. They had not known Jack Agnew when he was alive, but, as the paper said, they wished to pay tribute to the sensational and tragic manner of his death. All the stores in Carstairs were closed for two hours that afternoon. The hotel did not close its doors but that was because all the visitors needed somewhere to eat and drink.

The survivors were a wife, Grace, and a four-year-old daughter, Lillian. The victim had fought bravely in the Great War and had only been wounded once, not seriously. Many had commented on this irony.

The paper's failure to mention a surviving father was not deliberate. The editor of the paper was not a native of Carstairs, and people forgot to tell him about the father until it was too late.

The father himself did not complain about the omission. On the day of the funeral, which was very fine, he headed out of town as he would have done ordinarily on a day he had decided not to spend at Douds. He was wearing a felt hat and a long coat that would do for a rug if he wanted to take a nap. His overshoes were neatly held on his feet with the rubber rings from sealing jars. He was going out to fish for suckers. The season hadn't opened yet, but he always managed to be a bit ahead of it. He fished through the spring and early summer and cooked and ate what he caught. He had a frying pan and a pot hidden out on the riverbank. The pot was for boiling corn that he snatched out of the fields later in the year, when he was also eating the fruit of wild apple trees and grapevines. He was quite sane but abhorred conversation. He could not altogether avoid it in the weeks following his son's death, but he had a way of cutting it short.

"Should've watched out what he was doing."

Walking in the country that day, he met another person who was not at the funeral. A woman. She did not try to start any conversation and in fact seemed as fierce in her solitude as himself, whipping the air past her with long fervent strides.

The piano factory, which had started out making pump organs, stretched along the west side of town, like a medieval town wall. There were two long buildings like the inner and outer ramparts, with a closed-in bridge between them where the main offices were. And reaching up into the town and the streets of workers' houses you had the kilns and the sawmill and the lumberyard and storage sheds. The factory whistle dictated the time for many to get up, blowing at six o'clock in the morning. It blew again for work to start at seven and at twelve for dinnertime and at one in the afternoon for work to recommence, and then at five-thirty for the men to lay down their tools and go home.

Rules were posted beside the time clock, under glass. The first two rules were:

ONE MINUTE LATE IS FIFTEEN MINUTES PAY.
BE PROMPT.
DON'T TAKE SAFETY FOR GRANTED.
WATCH OUT FOR YOURSELF AND THE NEXT MAN.

There had been accidents in the factory and in fact a man had been killed when a load of lumber fell on him. That had happened before Arthur's time. And once, during the war, a man had lost an arm, or part of an arm. On the day that happened, Arthur was away in Toronto. So he had never seen an accident—nothing serious, anyway. But it was often at the back of his mind now that something might happen.

Perhaps he did not feel so sure that trouble wouldn't come near him, as he had felt before his wife died. She had died in 1919, in the last flurry of the Spanish flu, when everyone had got over being frightened. Even she had not been frightened. That was nearly five years ago and it still seemed to Arthur like the end of a carefree time in his life. But to other people he had always seemed very responsible and serious—nobody had noticed much difference in him.

In his dreams of an accident there was a spreading silence, everything was shut down. Every machine in the place stopped making its customary noise and every man's voice was removed, and when Arthur looked out of the office window he understood that doom had fallen. He never could remember any particular thing he saw that told him this. It was just the space, the dust in the factory yard, that said to him *now*.

The books stayed on the floor of his car for a week or so. His daughter Bea said, "What are those books doing here?" and then he remembered.

Bea read out the titles and the authors. *Sir John Franklin and the Romance of the Northwest Passage*, by G.B. Smith. *What's Wrong with the World?*, G.K. Chesterton. *The Taking of Quebec*, Archibald Hendry. *Bolshevism: Practice and Theory*, by Lord Bertrand Russell.

"Bol-*shev*-ism," Bea said, and Arthur told her how to pronounce it correctly. She asked what it was, and he said, "It's something they've got in Russia that I don't understand so well myself. But from what I hear of it, it's a disgrace."

Bea was thirteen at this time. She had heard about the Russian Ballet and also about dervishes. She believed for the next couple of years that Bolshevism was some sort of diabolical and maybe indecent dance. At least this was the story she told when she was grown up.

She did not mention that the books were connected with the man who had had the accident. That would have made the story less amusing. Perhaps she had really forgotten.

The librarian was perturbed. The books still had their cards in them, which meant they had never been checked out, just removed from the shelves and taken away.

"The one by Lord Russell has been missing a long time."

Arthur was not used to such reproofs, but he said mildly, "I am returning them on behalf of somebody else. The chap who was killed. In the accident at the factory."

The Librarian had the Franklin book open. She was looking at the picture of the boat trapped in the ice.

"His wife asked me to," Arthur said.

She picked up each book separately, and shook it as if she expected something to fall cut. She ran her fingers in between the pages. The bottom part of her face was working in an unsightly way, as if she was chewing at the inside of her cheeks.

"I guess he just took them home as he felt like it," Arthur said.

"I'm sorry?" she said in a minute. "What did you say? I'm sorry."

It was the accident, he thought. The idea that the man who had died in such a way had been the last person to open these books, turn these pages. The thought that he might have left a bit of his life in them, a scrap of paper or a pipe cleaner as a marker, or even a few shreds of tobacco. That unhinged her.

"No matter," he said. "I just dropped by to bring them back."

He turned away from her desk but did not immediately leave the Library. He had not been in it for years. There was his father's picture between the two front windows, where it would always be.

A.V. Doud, founder of the Doud Organ Factory and Patron of this Library. A Believer in Progress, Culture, and Education. A True Friend of the Town of Carstairs and of the Working Man.

The Librarian's desk was in the archway between the front and back rooms. The books were on shelves set in rows in the back room. Green-shaded lamps, with long pull cords, dangled down in the aisles between. Arthur remembered years ago some matter brought up at the Council Meeting about buying sixty-watt bulbs instead of forty. This Librarian was the one who had requested that, and they had done it.

In the front room, there were newspapers and magazines on wooden racks, and some round heavy tables, with chairs, so that people could sit and read, and rows of thick dark books behind glass. Dictionaries, probably, and atlases and encyclopedias. Two handsome high windows looking out on the main street, with Arthur's father hanging between them. Other pictures around the room hung too high, and were too dim and crowded with figures for the person down below to interpret them easily. (Later, when Arthur had spent many hours in the Library and had discussed these pictures with the Librarian, he knew that one of them represented the Battle of Flodden Field, with the King of Scotland charging down the hill into a pall of smoke, one the funeral of the Boy King of Rome, and one the Quarrel of Oberon and Titania, from *A Midsummer Night's Dream*.)

He sat down at one of the reading tables, where he could look out the window. He picked up an old copy of the *National Geographic* which was lying there. He had his back to the Librarian. He thought this the tactful thing to do, since she seemed somewhat wrought-up. Other people came in, and he heard her speak to them. Her voice sounded normal enough now. He kept thinking he would leave, but did not.

He liked the high bare window full of the light of the spring evening, and he liked the dignity and order of these rooms. He was pleasantly mystified by the thought of grown people coming and going here, steadily reading books. Week after week, one book after another, a whole life long. He himself read a book once in a while, when somebody recommended it, and usually he enjoyed it, and then he read magazines, to keep up with things, and never thought about reading a book until another one came along, in this almost accidental way.

There would be little spells when nobody was in the Library but himself and the Librarian.

During one of these, she came over and stood near him, replacing some newspapers on the rack. When she finished this, she spoke to him, with a controlled urgency.

"The account of the accident that was printed in the paper— I take it that was more or less accurate?"

Arthur said that it was possibly too accurate.

"Why? Why do you say that?"

He mentioned the public's endless appetite for horrific details. Ought the paper to pander to that?

"Oh, I think it's natural," the Librarian said. "I think it's natural to want to know the worst. People do want to picture it. I do myself. I am very ignorant of machinery. It's hard for me to imagine what happened. Even with the paper's help. Did the machine do something unexpected?"

"No," Arthur said. "It wasn't the machine grabbing him and pulling him in, like an animal. He made a wrong move or at any rate a careless move. Then he was done for."

She said nothing, but did not move away.

"You have to keep your wits about you," Arthur said. "Never let up for a second. A machine is your servant and it is an excellent servant, but it makes an imbecile master."

He wondered if he had read that somewhere, or had thought it up himself.

"And I suppose there are no ways of protecting people?" the Librarian said. "But you must know all about that."

She left him then. Somebody had come in.

The accident was followed by a rush of warm weather. The length of the evenings and the heat of the balmy days seemed sudden and surprising, as if this were not the way winter finally ended in that part of the country, almost every year. The sheets of floodwater shrank magically back into the bogs, and the leaves shot out of the reddened branches, and barnyard smells drifted into town and were wrapped in the smell of lilacs.

Instead of wanting to be outdoors on such evenings, Arthur found himself thinking of the Library, and he would often end up there, sitting in the spot he had chosen on his first visit. He would sit for half an hour, or an hour. He looked at the London *Illustrated News*, or the *National Geographic* or *Saturday Night* or *Collier's*. All of these magazines arrived at his own house and he could have been sitting there, in the den, looking out at his hedged lawns, which old Agnew kept in tolerable condition, and the flower beds now full of tulips of every vivid color and combination. It seemed that he preferred the view of the main street, where the occasional brisk-looking new Ford went by, or some stuttering older-model car with a dusty cloth top. He preferred the Post Office, with its clock tower telling four different times in four different directions—and, as people liked to say, all wrong. Also the passing and loitering on the sidewalk. People trying to get the drinking fountain to work, although it wasn't turned on till the first of July.

It was not that he felt the need of sociability. He was not there for chat, though he would greet people if he knew them by name, and he did know most. And he might exchange a few words with the Librarian, though often it was only "Good evening" when he came in, and "Good night" when he went out. He made no demands on anybody. He felt his presence to be genial, reassuring, and, above all, natural. By sitting here, reading and reflecting, here instead of at home, he seemed to himself to be providing something. People could count on it.

There was an expression he liked. *Public servant.* His father, who looked out at him here with tinted baby-pink cheeks and glassy blue eyes and an old man's petulant mouth, had never thought of himself so. He had thought of himself more as a public character and benefactor. He had operated by whims and decrees, and he had got away with it. He would go around the factory when business was slow, and say to one man and another, "Go home. Go on home now. Go home and stay there till I can use you again." And they would go. They would work in their gardens or go out shooting rabbits and run up bills for whatever they had to buy, and accept that it couldn't be otherwise. It was still a joke with them, to imitate his bark. *Go on home!* He was their hero more than Arthur could ever be, but they were not prepared to take the same treatment today. During the war, they had got used to the good wages and to being always in demand. They never thought of the glut of labor the soldiers had created when they came home, never thought about how a business like this was kept going by luck and ingenuity from one year to the next, even from one season to the next. They didn't like changes—they were not happy about the switch now to player pianos, which Arthur believed were the hope of the future. But Arthur would do what he had to, though his way of proceeding was quite the opposite of his father's. Think everything over and then think it over again. Stay in the background except when necessary. Keep your dignity. Try always to be fair.

They expected all to be provided. The whole town expected it. Work would be provided just as the sun would rise in the mornings. And the taxes on the factory raised at the same time rates were charged for the water that used to come free. Maintenance of the access roads was now the factory's responsibility instead of the town's. The Methodist Church was requesting a hefty sum to build the new Sunday school. The town hockey team needed new uniforms. Stone gateposts were being erected for the War Memorial Park. And every year the smartest boy in the senior class was sent to university, courtesy of Douds.

Ask and ye shall receive.

Expectations at home were not lacking either. Bea was agitating to go away to private school and Mrs. Feare had her eye on some new mixing apparatus for the kitchen, also a new washing machine. All the trim on the house was due to be painted this year. All that wedding-cake decoration that consumed paint by the gallon. And in the midst of this what had Arthur done but order himself a new car—a Chrysler sedan.

It was necessary—he had to drive a new car. He had to drive a new car, Bea had to go away to school, Mrs. Feare had to have the latest, and the trim had to be as fresh as Christmas snow. Else they would lose respect, they would lose confidence, they would start to wonder if things were going downhill. And it could be managed, with luck it could all be managed.

For years after his father's death, he had felt like an impostor. Not steadily, but from time to time he had felt that. And now the feeling was gone. He could sit here and feel that it was gone.

He had been in the office when the accident happened, consulting with a veneer salesman. Some change in noise registered with him, but it was more of an increase than a hush. It was nothing that alerted him—just an irritation. Because it happened in the sawmill, nobody would know about the accident immediately in the shops or in the kilns or in the yard, and work in some places continued for several minutes. In fact Arthur, bending over the veneer samples on his desk, might have been one of the last people to understand that there had been an intervention. He asked the salesman a question, and the salesman did not answer. Arthur looked up and saw the man's mouth open, his face frightened, his salesman's assurance wiped away.

Then he heard his own name being called—both "Mr. Doud!" as was customary and "Arthur, Arthur!" by such of the older men as had known him as a boy. Also he heard "saw" and "head" and "Jesus, Jesus, Jesus!"

Arthur could have wished for the silence, the sounds and objects drawing back in that dreadful but releasing way, to give him room. It was nothing like that. Yelling and questioning and running around, himself in the midst being propelled to the sawmill. One man had fainted, falling in such a way that if they had not got the saw turned off a moment before, it would have got him too. It was his body, fallen but entire, that Arthur briefly mistook for the body of the victim. Oh, no, no. They pushed him on. The sawdust was scarlet. It was drenched, brilliant. The pile of lumber here was all merrily spattered, and the blades. A pile of work clothes soaked in blood lay in the sawdust and Arthur realized that it was the body, the trunk with limbs attached. So much blood had flowed as to make its shape not plain at first—to soften it, like a pudding.

The first thing he thought of was to cover that. He took off his jacket and did so. He had to step up close, his shoes squished in it. The reason no one else had done this would be simply that no one else was wearing a jacket.

"Have they gone a-get the doctor?" somebody was yelling. "Gone a-get the doctor!" a man quite close to Arthur said. "Can't sew his head back on—doctor. Can he?"

But Arthur gave the order to get the doctor; he imagined it was necessary. You can't have a death without a doctor. That set the rest in motion. Doctor, undertaker, coffin, flowers, preacher. Get started on all that, give them something to do. Shovel up the sawdust, clean up the saw. Send the men who had been close by to wash themselves. Carry the man who had fainted to the lunchroom. Is he all right? Tell the office girl to make tea.

Brandy was what was needed, or whisky. But he had a rule against it, on the premises.

Something still lacking. Where was it? There, they said. Over there. Arthur heard the sound of vomiting, not far away. All right. Either pick it up or tell somebody to pick it up. The sound of vomiting saved him, steadied him, gave him an almost lighthearted determination. He picked it up. He carried it delicately and securely as you might carry an awkward but valuable jug. Pressing the face out of sight, as if comforting it, against his chest. Blood seeped through his shirt and stuck the material to his skin. Warm. He felt like a wounded man. He was aware of them watching him and he was aware of himself as an actor must be, or a priest. What to do with it, now that he had it against his chest? The answer to that came too. Set it down, put it back where it belongs, not of course fitted with exactness, not as if a seam could be closed. Just more or less in place, and lift the jacket and tug it into a new position.

He couldn't now ask the man's name. He would have to get it in some other way. After the intimacy of his services here, such ignorance would be an offense.

But he found he did know it—it came to him. As he edged the corner of his jacket over the ear that had lain and still lay upward, and so looked quite fresh and usable, he received a name. Son of the fellow who came and did the garden, who was not always reliable. A young man taken on again when he came back from the war. Married? He thought so. He would have to go and see her. As soon as possible. Clean clothes.

The librarian often wore a dark-red blouse. Her lips were reddened to match, and her hair was bobbed. She was not a young woman anymore, but she maintained an eye-catching style. He remembered that years ago when they had hired her, he had thought that she got herself up very soberly. Her hair was not bobbed in those days—it was wound around her head, in the old style. It was still the same color—a warm and pleasant color, like leaves—oak leaves, say, in the fall. He tried to think how much she was paid. Not much, certainly. She kept herself looking well on it. And where did she live? In one of the boardinghouses—the one with the schoolteachers? No, not there. She lived in the Commercial Hotel.

And now something else was coming to mind. No definite story that he could remember. You could not say with any assurance that she had a bad reputation. But it was not quite a spotless reputation, either. She was said to take a drink with the travellers. Perhaps she had a boyfriend among them. A boyfriend or two.

Well, she was old enough to do as she liked. It wasn't quite the same as the way it was with a teacher—hired partly to set an example. As long as she did her job well, and anybody could see that she did. She had her life to live, like everyone else. Wouldn't you rather have a nice-looking woman in here than a crabby old affair like Mary Tamblyn? Strangers might drop in, they judge a town by what they see, you want a nice-looking woman with a nice manner.

Stop that. Who said you didn't? He was arguing in his head on her behalf just as if somebody had come along who wanted her chucked out, and he had no intimation at all that that was the case.

What about her question, on the first evening, regarding the machines? What did she mean by that? Was it a sly way of bringing blame?

He had talked to her about the pictures and the lighting and even told her how his father had sent his own workmen over here, paid them to build the Library shelves, but he had never spoken of the man who had taken the books out without letting her know. One at a time, probably. Under his coat? Brought back the same way. He must have brought them back, or else he'd have had a houseful, and his wife would never stand for that. Not stealing, except temporarily. Harmless behavior, but peculiar. Was there any connection? Between thinking you could do things a little differently that way and thinking you could get away with a careless move that might catch your sleeve and bring the saw down on your neck?

There might be, there might be some connection. A matter of attitude.

"That chap—you know the one—the accident—" he said to the Librarian. "The way he took off with the books he wanted. Why do you think he did that?"

"People do things," the Librarian said. "They tear out pages. On account of something they don't like or something they do. They just do things. I don't know."

"Did he ever tear out some pages? Did you ever give him a lecture? Ever make him scared to face you?"

He meant to tease her a little, implying that she would not be likely to scare anybody, but she did not take it that way.

"How could I when I never spoke to him?" she said. "I never saw him. I never saw him, to know who he was."

She moved away, putting an end to the conversation. So she did not like to be teased. Was she one of those people full of mended cracks that you could only see close up? Some old misery troubling her, some secret? Maybe a sweetheart had been lost in the war.

On a later evening, a Saturday evening in the summer, she brought the subject up herself, that he would never have mentioned again.

"Do you remember our talking once about the man who had the accident?"

Arthur said he did.

"I have something to ask you and you may think it strange."

He nodded.

"And my asking it—I want you to—it is confidential."

"Yes, indeed," he said.

"What did he look like?"

Look like? Arthur was puzzled. He was puzzled by her making such a fuss and secret about it—surely it was natural to be interested in what a man might look like who had been coming in and making off with her books without her knowing about it—and because he could not help her, he shook his head. He could not bring any picture of Jack Agnew to mind.

"Tall," he said. "I believe he was on the tall side. Otherwise I cannot tell you. I am really not such a good person to ask. I can recognize a man easily but I can't ever give much of a physical description, even when it's someone I see on a daily basis."

"But I thought you were the one—I heard you were the one—" she said. "Who picked him up. His head."

Arthur said stiffly, "I didn't think that you could just leave it lying there." He felt disappointed in the woman, uneasy and ashamed for her. But he tried to speak matter-of-factly, keeping reproach out of his voice.

"I could not even tell you the color of his hair. It was all—all pretty much obliterated, by that time."

She said nothing for a moment or two and he did not look

at her. Then she said, "It must seem as if I am one of those people—one of those people who are fascinated by these sorts of things."

Arthur made a protesting noise, but it did, of course, seem to him that she must be like that.

"I should not have asked you," she said. "I should not have mentioned it. I can never explain to you why I did. I would like just to ask you, if you can help it, never to think that that is the kind of person I am."

Arthur heard the word "never." She could never explain to him. He was never to think. In the midst of his disappointment he picked up this suggestion, that their conversations were to continue, and perhaps on a less haphazard basis. He heard a humility in her voice, but it was a humility that was based on some kind of assurance. Surely that was sexual.

Or did he only think so, because this was the evening it was? It was the Saturday evening in the month when he usually went to Walley. He was going there tonight, he had only dropped in here on his way, he had not meant to stay as long as he had done. It was the night when he went to visit a woman whose name was Jane MacFarlane. Jane MacFarlane lived apart from her husband, but she was not thinking of getting a divorce. She had no children. She earned her living as a dressmaker. Arthur had first met her when she came to his house to make clothes for his wife. Nothing had gone on at that time, and neither of them had thought of it. In some ways Jane MacFarlane was a woman like the Librarian—good-looking, though not so young, plucky and stylish and good at her work. In other ways, not so like. He could not imagine Jane ever presenting a man with a mystery, and following that up with the information that it would never be solved. Jane was a woman to give a man peace. The submerged dialogue he had with her—sensual, limited, kind—was very like the one he had had with his wife.

The Librarian went to the switch by the door, and turned out the main light. She locked the door. She disappeared among the shelves, turning out the lights there too, in a leisurely way. The town clock was striking nine. She must think that it was right. His own watch said three minutes to.

It was time to get up, time for him to leave, time to go to Walley.

When she had finished dealing with the lights, she came and sat down at the table beside him.

He said, "I would never think of you in any way that would make you unhappy."

Turning out the lights shouldn't have made it so dark. They were in the middle of summer. But it seemed that heavy rain clouds had moved in. When Arthur had last paid attention to the street, he had seen plenty of daylight left: country people shopping, boys squirting each other at the drinking fountain, and young girls walking up and down in their soft, cheap, flowery summer dresses, letting the young men watch them from wherever the young men congregated—the Post Office steps, the front of the feed store. And now that he looked again he saw the street in an uproar from the loud wind that already carried a few drops of rain. The girls were shrieking and laughing and holding their purses over their heads as they ran to shelter, store clerks were rolling up awnings and hauling in the baskets of fruit, the racks of summer shoes, the garden implements that had been displayed on the sidewalks. The doors of the Town Hall banged as the farm women ran inside, grabbing on to packages and children, to cram themselves into the Ladies' Rest Room. Somebody tried the Library door. The Librarian looked over at it but did not move. And soon the rain was sweeping like curtains across the street, and the wind battered the Town Hall roof, and tore at the treetops. That roaring and danger lasted a few minutes, while the power of the wind went by. Then the sound left was the sound of the rain, which was now falling vertically and so heavily they might have been under a waterfall.

If the same thing was happening at Walley, he thought, Jane would know enough not to expect him. This was the last thought he had of her for a long while.

"Mrs. Feare wouldn't wash my clothes," he said, to his own surprise. "She was afraid to touch them."

The Librarian said, in a peculiarly quivering, shamed, and determined voice, "I think what you did—I think that was a remarkable thing to do."

The rain made such a constant noise that he was released from answering. He found it easy then to turn and look at her. Her profile was dimly lit by the wash of rain down the windows. Her expression was calm and reckless. Or so it seemed to him. He realized that he knew hardly anything about her—what kind of person she really was or what kind of secrets she could have. He could not even estimate his own value to her. He only knew that he had some, and it wasn't the usual.

He could no more describe the feeling he got from her than you can describe a smell. It's like the scorch of electricity. It's like burnt kernels of wheat. No, it's like a bitter orange. I give up.

He had never imagined that he would find himself in a situation like this, visited by such a clear compulsion. But it seemed he was not unprepared. Without thinking over twice or even once what he was letting himself in for, he said, "I wish—"

He had spoken too quietly, she did not hear him.

He raised his voice. He said, "I wish we could get married."

Then she looked at him. She laughed but controlled herself.

"I'm sorry," she said. "I'm sorry. It's just what went through my mind."

"What was that?" he said.

"I thought—that's the last I'll see of him."

Arthur said, "You're mistaken."

TOLPUDDLE MARTYRS

The passenger train from Carstairs to London had stopped running during the Second World War and even the rails were taken up. People said it was for the War Effort. When Louisa went to London to see the heart specialist, in the mid-fifties, she had to take the bus. She was not supposed to drive anymore.

The doctor, the heart specialist, said that her heart was a little wonky and her pulse inclined to be jumpy. She thought that made her heart sound like a comedian and her pulse like a puppy on a lead. She had not come fifty-seven miles to be treated with such playfulness but she let it pass, because she was already distracted by something she had been reading in the doctor's waiting room. Perhaps it was what she had been reading that had made her pulse jumpy.

On an inside page of the local paper she had seen the head-line LOCAL MARTYRS HONORED, and simply to put in the time she had read further. She read that there was to be some sort of ceremony that afternoon at Victoria Park. It was a cer-emony to honor the Tolpuddle Martyrs. The paper said that few people had heard of the Tolpuddle Martyrs, and certainly Louisa had not. They were men who had been tried and found guilty for administering illegal oaths. This peculiar offense, committed over a hundred years ago in Dorset, England, had got them transported to Canada and some of them had ended up here in London, where they lived out the rest of their days and were buried without any special notice or commemora-tion. They were considered now to be among the earliest founders of the Trade Union movement, and the Trade Unions Council, along with representatives of the Canadian Federa-tion of Labor and the ministers of some local churches, had organized a ceremony taking place today on the occasion of the hundred-and-twentieth anniversary of their arrest.

Martyrs is laying it on somewhat, thought Louisa. They were not executed, after all.

The ceremony was to take place at three o'clock and the chief speakers were to be one of the local ministers, and Mr. John (Jack) Agnew, a union spokesman from Toronto.

It was a quarter after two when Louisa came out of the doc-tor's office. The bus to Carstairs did not leave until six o'clock. She had thought she would go and have tea and something to eat on the top floor of Simpsons, then shop for a wedding pre-sent, or if the time fitted go to an afternoon movie. Victoria Park lay between the doctor's office and Simpsons, and she decided to cut across it. The day was hot and the shade of the trees pleas-ant. She could not avoid seeing where the chairs had been set up, and a small speakers' platform draped in yellow cloth, with a Canadian flag on the one side and what she supposed must be a Labor Union flag on the other. A group of people had collected and she found herself changing course in order to get a look at them. Some were old people, very plainly but decently dressed, the women with kerchiefs around their heads on the hot day, Europeans. Others were factory workers, men in clean short-sleeved shirts and women in fresh blouses and slacks, let out early. A few women must have come from home, because they were wearing summer dresses and sandals and trying to keep track of small children. Louisa thought that they would not care at all for the way she was dressed—fashionably, as always, in beige shantung with a crimson silk tam—but she noticed, just then, a woman more elegantly got up than she was, in green silk with her dark hair drawn tightly back, tied with a green-and-gold scarf. She might have been forty—her face was worn, but beautiful. She came over to Louisa at once, smiling, showed her a chair and gave her a mimeographed paper. Louisa could not read the purple printing. She tried to get a look at some men who were talking beside the platform. Were the speakers among them?

The coincidence of the name was hardly even interesting. Neither the first name nor the last was all that unusual.

She did not know why she had sat down, or why she had come over here in the first place. She was beginning to feel a faintly sickening, familiar agitation. She could feel that over nothing. But once it got going, telling herself that it was over nothing did no good. The only thing to do was to get up and get away from here before any more people sat down and hemmed her in.

The green woman intercepted her, asked if she was all right.

"I have to catch a bus," said Louisa in a croaky voice. She cleared her throat. "An out-of-town bus," she said with better control, and marched away, not in the right direction for Simpsons. She thought in fact that she wouldn't go there, she wouldn't go to Birks for the wedding present or to a movie either. She would just go and sit in the bus depot until it was time for her to go home.

Within half a block of the bus depot she remembered that the bus had not taken her there that morning. The depot was being torn down and rebuilt—there was a temporary depot several blocks away. She had not paid quite enough attention to which street it was on—York Street, east of the real depot, or King? At any rate, she had to detour, because both of these streets were being torn up, and she had almost decided she was lost when she realized she had been lucky enough to come upon the temporary depot by the back way. It was an old house—one of those tall yellow-gray brick houses dating from the time when this was a residential district. This was probably the last use it would be put to before being torn down. Houses all around it must have been torn down to make the large gravelled lot where the buses pulled in. There were still some trees at the edge of the lot and under them a few rows of chairs that she had not noticed when she got off the bus before noon. Two men were sitting on what used to be the veranda of the house, on old car seats. They wore brown shirts with the bus company's insignia but they seemed to be halfhearted about their work, not getting up when she asked if the bus to Carstairs was leaving at six o'clock as scheduled and where could she get a soft drink?

Six o'clock, far as they knew.

Coffee shop down the street.

Cooler inside but only Coke and orange left.

She got herself a Coca-Cola out of the cooler in a dirty little indoor waiting room that smelled of a bad toilet. Moving the depot to this dilapidated house must have thrown everyone into a state of indolence and fecklessness. There was a fan in the room they used as an office, and she saw, as she went by, some papers blow off the desk. "Oh, shit," said the office girl, and stamped her heel on them.

The chairs set up in the shade of the dusty city trees were straight-backed old wooden chairs originally painted different colors—they looked as if they had come from various kitchens. Strips of old carpet and rubber bathroom mats were laid down in front of them, to keep your feet off the gravel. Behind the first row of chairs she thought she saw a sheep lying on the ground, but it turned into a dirty-white dog, which trotted over and looked at her for a moment in a grave semi-official way—gave a brief sniff at her shoes, and trotted away. She had not noticed if there were any drinking straws and did not feel like going back to look. She drank Coke from the bottle, tilting back her head and closing her eyes.

When she opened them, a man was sitting one chair away, and was speaking to her.

"I got here as soon as I could," he said. "Nancy said you were going to catch a bus. As soon as I finished with the speech, I took off. But the bus depot is all torn up."

"Temporarily," she said.

"I knew you right away," he said. "In spite of—well, many years. When I saw you, I was talking to somebody. Then I looked again and you'd disappeared."

"I don't recognize you," said Louisa.

"Well, no," he said. "I guess not. Of course. You wouldn't."

He was wearing tan slacks, a pale-yellow short-sleeved shirt, a cream-and-yellow ascot scarf. A bit of a dandy, for a union man. His hair was white but thick and wavy, the sort of springy hair that goes in ripples, up and back from the forehead, his skin was flushed and his face was deeply wrinkled from the efforts of speechmaking—and from talking to people privately, she supposed, with much of the fervor and persuasiveness of his public speeches. He wore tinted glasses, which he took off now, as if willing that she should see him better. His eyes were a light blue, slightly bloodshot and apprehensive. A good-looking man, still trim except for a little authoritative bulge over the belt, but she did not find these serviceable good looks— the careful sporty clothes, the display of ripply hair, the effective expressions—very attractive. She preferred the kind of looks Arthur had. The restraint, the dark-suited dignity that some people could call pompous, that seemed to her admirable and innocent.

"I always meant to break the ice," he said. "I meant to speak to you. I should have gone in and said goodbye at least. The opportunity to leave came up so suddenly."

Louisa did not have any idea what to say to this. He sighed. He said, "You must have been mad at me. Are you still?"

"No," she said, and fell back, ridiculously, on the usual courtesies. "How is Grace? How is your daughter? Lillian?"

"Grace is not so well. She had some arthritis. Her weight doesn't help it. Lillian is all right. She's married but she still teaches high school. Mathematics. Not too usual for a woman."

How could Louisa begin to correct him? Could she say, No, your wife Grace got married again during the war, she married a farmer, a widower. Before that she used to come in and clean our house once a week. Mrs. Feare had got too old. And Lillian never finished high school, how could she be a high-school teacher? She married young, she had some children, she works in the drugstore. She had your height and your hair, dyed blond. I often looked at her and thought she must be like you. When she was growing up, I used to give her my step-daughter's outgrown clothes.

Instead of this, she said, "Then the woman in the green dress—that was not Lillian?"

"Nancy? Oh, no! Nancy is my guardian angel. She keeps track of where I'm going, and when, and have I got my speech, and what I drink and eat and have I taken my pills. I tend toward high blood pressure. Nothing too serious. But my way of life's no good. I'm on the go constantly. Tonight I've got to fly out of here to Ottawa, tomorrow I've got a tough meeting, tomorrow night I've got some fool banquet."

Louisa felt it necessary to say, "You knew that I got married? I married Arthur Doud."

She thought he showed some surprise. But he said, "Yes, I heard that. Yes."

"We worked hard too," said Louisa sturdily. "Arthur died six years ago. We kept the factory going all through the thirties even though at times we were down to three men. We had no money for repairs and I remember cutting up the office awnings so that Arthur could carry them up on a ladder and patch the roof. We tried making everything we could think of. Even outdoor bowling alleys for those amusement places. Then the war came and we couldn't keep up. We could sell all the pianos we could make but also we were making radar cases for the Navy. I stayed in the office all through."

"It must have been a change," he said, in what seemed a tactful voice. "A change from the Library."

"Work is work," she said. "I still work. My stepdaughter Bea is divorced, she keeps house for me after a fashion. My son has finally finished university—he is supposed to be learning about the business, but he has some excuse to go off in the middle of every afternoon. When I come home at suppertime, I am so tired I could drop, and I hear the ice tinkling in their glasses and them laughing behind the hedge. Oh, Mud, they say when they see me, Oh, poor Mud, sit down here, get her a drink! They call me Mud because that was my son's name for me when he was a baby. But they are neither of them babies now. The house is cool when I come home—it's a lovely house if you remember, built in three tiers like a wedding cake. Mosaic tiles in the entrance hall. But I am always thinking about the factory, that is what fills my mind. What should we do to stay afloat? There are only five factories in Canada making pianos now, and three of them are in Quebec with the low cost of labor. No doubt you know all about that. When I talk to Arthur in my head, it is always about the same thing. I am very close to him still but it is hardly in a mystical way. You would think as you get older your mind would fill up with what they call the spiritual side of things, but mine just seems to get more and more practical, trying to get something settled. What a thing to talk to a dead man about."

She stopped, she was embarrassed. But she was not sure that he had listened to all of this, and in fact she was not sure that she had said all of it.

"What started me off—" he said. "What got me going in the first place, with whatever I have managed to do, was the Library. So I owe you a great deal."

He put his hands on his knees, let his head fall.

"Ah, rubbish," he said.

He groaned, and ended up with a laugh.

"My father," he said. "You wouldn't remember my father?"

"Oh, yes."

"Well. Sometimes I think he had the right idea."

Then he lifted his head, gave it a shake, and made a pronouncement

"Love never dies."

She felt impatient to the point of taking offense. This is what all the speechmaking turns you into, she thought, a person who can say things like that. Love dies all the time, or at any rate it becomes distracted, overlaid—it might as well be dead.

"Arthur used to come and sit in the Library," she said. "In the beginning I was very provoked with him. I used to look at the back of his neck and think, Ha, what if something should hit you there! None of that would make sense to you. It wouldn't make sense. And it turned out to be something else I wanted entirely. I wanted to marry him and get into a normal life.

"A normal life," she repeated—and a giddiness seemed to be taking over, a widespread forgiveness of folly, alerting the skin of her spotty hand, her dry thick fingers that lay not far from his, on the seat of the chair between them. An amorous flare-up of the cells, of old intentions. *Oh, never dies.*

Across the gravelled yard came a group of oddly dressed folk. They moved all together, a clump of black. The women did not show their hair—they had black shawls or bonnets covering their heads. The men wore broad hats and black braces. The children were dressed just like their elders, even to the bonnets and hats. How hot they all looked in those clothes—how hot and dusty and wary and shy.

"The Tolpuddle Martyrs," he said, in a faintly joking, resigned, and compassionate voice. "Ah, I guess I'd better go over. I'd better go over there and have a word with them."

That edge of a joke, the uneasy kindness, made her think of somebody else. Who was it? When she saw the breadth of his shoulders from behind, and the broad flat buttocks, she knew who.

Jim Frarey.

Oh, what kind of a trick was being played on her, or what kind of trick was she playing on herself! She would not have it. She pulled herself up tightly, she saw all those black clothes melt into a puddle. She was dizzy and humiliated. She would not have it.

But not all black, now that they were getting closer. She could see dark blue, those were the men's shirts, and dark blue and purple in some of the women's dresses. She could see faces—the men's behind beards, the women's in their deep-brimmed bonnets. And now she knew who they were. They were Mennonites.

Mennonites were living in this part of the country, where they never used to be. There were some of them around Bondi, a village north of Carstairs. They would be going home on the same bus as she was.

He was not with them, or anywhere in sight.

A traitor, helplessly. A traveller.

Once she knew that they were Mennonites and not some lost unidentifiable strangers, these people did not look so shy or dejected. In fact, they seemed quite cheerful, passing around a bag of candy, adults eating candy with the children. They settled on the chairs all around her.

No wonder she was feeling clammy. She had gone under a wave, which nobody else had noticed. You could say anything you liked about what had happened—but what it amounted to was going under a wave. She had gone under and through it and was left with a cold sheen on her skin, a beating in her ears, a cavity in her chest, and revolt in her stomach. It was anarchy she was up against—a devouring muddle. Sudden holes and impromptu tricks and radiant vanishing consolations.

But these Mennonite settlings are a blessing. The plop of behinds on chairs, the crackling of the candy bag, the meditative sucking and soft conversations. Without looking at Louisa, a little girl holds out the bag, and Louisa accepts a butterscotch mint. She is surprised to be able to hold it in her hand, to have her lips shape thank-you, then to discover in her mouth just the taste that she expected. She sucks on it as they do on theirs, not in any hurry, and allows that taste to promise her some reasonable continuance.

Lights have come on, though it isn't yet evening. In the trees above the wooden chairs someone has strung lines of little colored bulbs that she did not notice until now. They make her think of festivities. Carnivals. Boats of singers on the lake.

"What place is this?" she said to the woman beside her.

On the day of Miss Tamblyn's death it happened that Louisa was staying in the Commercial Hotel. She was a traveller then for a company that sold hats, ribbons, handkerchiefs and trimmings, and ladies' underwear to retail stores. She heard the talk in the hotel, and it occurred to her that the town would soon need a new Librarian. She was getting very tired of lugging her sample cases on and off trains, and showing her wares in hotels, packing and unpacking. She went at once and talked to the people in charge of the Library. A Mr. Doud and a Mr. Macleod. They sounded like a vaudeville team but did not look it. The pay was poor, but she had not been doing so well on commission, either. She told them that she had finished high school, in Toronto, and had worked in Eaton's Book Department before she switched to travelling. She did not think it necessary to tell them that she had only worked there five months when she was discovered to have t.b., and that she had then spent four years in a sanitorium. The t.b. was cured, anyway, her spots were dry.

The hotel moved her to one of the rooms for permanent guests, on the third floor. She could see the snow-covered hills over the rooftops. The town of Carstairs was in a river valley. It had three or four thousand people and a long main street that ran downhill, over the river, and uphill again. There was a piano and organ factory.

The houses were built for lifetimes and the yards were wide and the streets were lined with mature elm and maple trees. She had never been here when the leaves were on the trees. It must make a great difference. So much that lay open now would be concealed.

She was glad of a fresh start, her spirits were hushed and grateful. She had made fresh starts before and things had not turned out as she had hoped, but she believed in the swift decision, the unforeseen intervention, the uniqueness of her fate.

The town was full of the smell of horses. As evening came on, big blinkered horses with feathered hooves pulled the sleighs across the bridge, past the hotel, beyond the streetlights, down the dark side roads. Somewhere out in the country they would lose the sound of each other's bells.

ᕫ *The Albanian Virgin* ᕫ

IN THE MOUNTAINS, in Maltsia e madhe, she must have tried to tell them her name, and "Lottar" was what they made of it. She had a wound in her leg, from a fall on sharp rocks when her guide was shot. She had a fever. How long it took them to carry her through the mountains, bound up in a rug and strapped to a horse's back, she had no idea. They gave her water to drink now and then, and sometimes *raki*, which was a kind of brandy, very strong. She could smell pines. At one time they were on a boat and she woke up and saw the stars, brightening and fading and changing places—unstable clusters that made her sick. Later she understood that they must have been on the lake. Lake Scutari, or Sckhoder, or Skodra. They pulled up among the reeds. The rug was full of vermin, which got under the rag tied around her leg.

At the end of her journey, though she did not know it was the end, she was lying in a small stone hut that was an out-building of the big house, called the *kula*. It was the hut of the sick and dying. Not of giving birth, which these women did in the cornfields, or beside the path when they were carrying a load to market.

She was lying, perhaps for weeks, on a heaped-up bed of ferns. It was comfortable, and had the advantage of being eas-ily changed when fouled or bloodied. The old woman named Tima looked after her. She plugged up the wound with a paste made of beeswax and olive oil and pine resin. Several times a day the dressing was removed, the wound washed out with *raki*. Lottar could see black lace curtains hanging from the rafters, and she thought she was in her room at home, with her mother (who was dead) looking after her. "Why have you hung up those curtains?" she said. "They look horrible."

She was really seeing cobwebs, all thick and furry with smoke—ancient cobwebs, never disturbed from year to year.

Also, in her delirium, she had the sensation of some wide board being pushed against her face—something like a coffin plank. But when she came to her senses she learned that it was nothing but a crucifix, a wooden crucifix that a man was trying to get her to kiss. The man was a priest, a Franciscan. He was a tall, fierce-looking man with black eyebrows and mustache and a rank smell, and he carried, besides the crucifix, a gun that she learned later was a Browning revolver. He knew by the look of her that she was a giaour—not a Muslim—but he did not understand that she might be a heretic. He knew a little English but pronounced it in a way that she could not make out. And she did not then know any of the language of the Ghegs. But after her fever subsided, when he tried a few words of Italian on her, they were able to talk, because she had learned Italian at school and had been travelling for six months in Italy. He understood so much more than anyone else around her that she expected him, at first, to understand everything. What is the nearest city? she asked him, and he said, Skodra. So go there, please, she said—go and find the British Consulate, if there is one. I belong to the British Empire. Tell them I am here. Or if there is no British Consul, go to the police.

She did not understand that under no circumstances would anybody go to the police. She didn't know that she belonged now to this tribe, this *kula*, even though taking her prisoner had not been their intention and was an embarrassing mistake.

It is shameful beyond belief to attack a woman. When they had shot and killed her guide, they had thought that she would turn her horse around and fly back down the mountain road, back to Bar. But her horse took fright at the shot and stumbled among the boulders and she fell, and her leg was injured. Then they had no choice but to carry her with them, back across the border between the Crna Gora (which means Black Rock, or Montenegro) and Maltsia e madhe.

"But why rob the guide and not me?" she said, naturally thinking robbery to be the motive. She thought of how starved they looked, the man and his horse, and of the fluttering white rags of his headdress.

"Oh, they are not robbers!" said the Franciscan, shocked. "They are honest men. They shot him because they were in blood with him. With his house. It is their law."

He told her that the man who had been shot, her guide, had killed a man of this *kula*. He had done that because the man he had killed had killed a man of his *kula*. This would go on, it had been going on for a long time now, there were always more sons being born. They think they have more sons than other people in the world, and it is to serve this necessity.

"Well, it is terrible," the Franciscan concluded. "But it is for their honor, the honor of their family. They are always ready to die for their honor."

She said that her guide did not seem to be so ready, if he had fled to Crna Gora.

"But it did not make any difference, did it?" said the Franciscan. "Even if he had gone to America, it would not have made any difference."

At Trieste she had boarded a steamer, to travel down the Dalmatian Coast. She was with her friends Mr. and Mrs. Cozzens, whom she had met in Italy, and their friend Dr. Lamb, who had joined them from England. They put in at the little port of Bar, which the Italians call Antivari, and stayed the night at the European Hotel. After dinner they walked on the terrace, but Mrs. Cozzens was afraid of a chill, so they went indoors and played cards. There was rain in the night. She woke up and listened to the rain and was full of disappointment, which gave rise to a loathing for these middle-aged people, particularly for Dr. Lamb, whom she believed the Cozzenses had summoned from England to meet her. They probably thought she was rich. A transatlantic heiress whose accent they could almost forgive. These people ate too much and then they had to take pills. And they worried about being in strange places—what had they come for? In the morning she would have to get back on the boat with them or they would make a fuss. She would never take the road over the mountains to Cetinge, Montenegro's capital city—they had been told that it was not wise. She would never see the bell tower where the heads of Turks used to hang, or the plane tree under which the Poet-Prince held audience with the people. She could not get back to sleep, so she decided to go downstairs with the first light, and, even if it was still raining, to go a little way up the road behind the town, just to see the ruins that she knew were there, among the olive trees, and the Austrian fortress on its rock and the dark face of Mount Lovchen.

The weather obliged her, and so did the man at the hotel desk, producing almost at once a tattered but cheerful guide and his underfed horse. They set out—she on the horse, the man walking ahead. The road was steep and twisting and full of boulders, the sun increasingly hot and the intervening shade cold and black. She became hungry and thought she must turn back soon. She would have breakfast with her companions, who got up late.

No doubt there was some sort of search for her, after the guide's body was found. The authorities must have been notified—whoever the authorities were. The boat must have sailed on time, her friends must have gone with it. The hotel had not taken their passports. Nobody back in Canada would think of investigating. She was not writing regularly to anyone, she had had a falling-out with her brother, her parents were dead. You won't come home till all your inheritance is spent, her brother had said, and then who will look after you?

When she was being carried through the pine forest, she awoke and found herself suspended, lulled—in spite of the pain and perhaps because of the *raki*—into a disbelieving surrender. She fastened her eyes on the bundle that was hanging from the saddle of the man ahead of her and knocking against the horse's back. It was something about the size of a cabbage, wrapped in a stiff and rusty-looking cloth.

I heard this story in the old St. Joseph's Hospital in Victoria from Charlotte, who was the sort of friend I had in my early days there. My friendships then seemed both intimate and uncertain. I never knew why people told me things, or what they meant me to believe.

I had come to the hospital with flowers and chocolates. Charlotte lifted her head, with its clipped and feathery white hair, toward the roses. "Bah!" she said. "They have no smell! Not to me, anyway. They are beautiful, of course.

"You must eat the chocolates yourself," she said. "Everything tastes like tar to me. I don't know how I know what tar tastes like, but this is what I think."

She was feverish. Her hand, when I held it, felt hot and puffy. Her hair had all been cut off, and this made her look as if she had actually lost flesh around her face and neck. The part of her under the hospital covers seemed as extensive and lumpy as ever.

"But you must not think I am ungrateful," she said. "Sit down. Bring that chair from over there—she doesn't need it."

There were two other women in the room. One was just a thatch of yellow-gray hair on the pillow, and the other was tied into a chair, wriggling and grunting.

"This is a terrible place," said Charlotte. "But we must just try our best to put up with it. I am so glad to see you. That one over there yells all night long," she said, nodding toward the window bed. "We must thank Christ she's asleep now. I don't get a wink of sleep, but I have been putting the time to very good use. What do you think I've been doing? I've been making up a story, for a movie! I have it all in my head and I want you to hear it. You will be able to judge if it will make a good movie. I think it will. I would like Jennifer Jones to act in it. I don't know, though. She does not seem to have the same spirit anymore. She married that mogul.

"Listen," she said. "(Oh, could you haul that pillow up more, behind my head?) It takes place in Albania, in northern Albania, which is called Maltsia e madhe, in the nineteen-twenties, when things were very primitive. It is about a young woman travelling alone. Lottar is her name in the story."

I sat and listened. Charlotte would lean forward, even rock a little on her hard bed, stressing some point for me. Her puffy hands flew up and down, her blue eyes widened commandingly, and then from time to time she sank back onto the pillows, and she shut her eyes to get the story in focus again. Ah, yes, she said. Yes, yes. And she continued.

"Yes, yes," she said at last. "I know how it goes on, but that is enough for now. You will have to come back. Tomorrow. Will you come back?"

I said, yes, tomorrow, and she appeared to have fallen asleep without hearing me.

The *kula* was a great, rough stone house with a stable below and the living quarters above. A veranda ran all the way around, and there would always be an old woman sitting there, with a bobbin contraption that flew like a bird from one hand to the other and left a trail of shiny black braid, mile after mile of black braid, which was the adornment of all the men's trousers. Other women worked at the looms or sewed together the leather sandals. Nobody sat there knitting, because nobody would think to sit down to knit. Knitting was what they did while they trotted back and forth to the spring with their water barrels strapped to their backs, or took the path to the fields or to the beech wood, where they collected the fallen branches. They knitted stockings—black and white, red and white, with zigzag patterns like lightning strokes. Women's hands must never be idle. Before dawn they pounded the bread dough in its blackened wooden trough, shaped it into loaves on the backs of shovels, and baked it on the hearth. (It was corn bread, unleavened and eaten hot, which would swell up like a puffball in your stomach.) Then they had to sweep out the *kula* and dump the dirty ferns and pile up armloads of fresh ferns for the next night's sleep. This was often one of Lottar's jobs, since she was so unskilled at everything else. Little girls stirred the yogurt so that lumps would not form as it soured. Older girls might butcher a kid and sew up its stomach, which they had stuffed with wild garlic and sage and apples. Or they would go together, girls and women, all ages, to wash the men's white head scarves in the cold little river nearby, whose waters were clear as glass. They tended the tobacco crop and hung the ripe leaves to dry in the darkened shed. They hoed the corn and cucumbers, milked the ewes.

The women looked stern but they were not so, really. They were only preoccupied, and proud of themselves, and eager for competition. Who could carry the heaviest load of wood, knit the fastest, hoe the most rows of cornstalks? Tima, who had looked after Lottar when she was sick, was the most spectacular worker of all. She would run up the slope to the *kula* with a load of wood bound to her back that looked ten times as big as herself. She would leap from rock to rock in the river and pound the scarves as if they were the bodies of enemies. "Oh, Tima, Tima!" the other women cried out in ironic admiration, and "Oh, Lottar, Lottar!" in nearly the same tones, when Lottar, at the other end of a scale of usefulness, let the clothes drift away downstream. Sometimes they whacked Lottar with a stick, as they would a donkey, but this had more exasperation in it than cruelty. Sometimes the young ones would say, "Talk your talk!" and for their entertainment she would speak English. They wrinkled up their faces and spat, at such peculiar sounds. She tried to teach them words—*hand*, *nose*, and so on. But these seemed to them jokes, and they would repeat them to each other and fall about laughing.

Women were with women and men were with men, except at times in the night (women teased about such times were full of shame and denial, and sometimes there would be a slapping) and at meals, when the women served the men their food. What the men did all day was none of the women's business. Men made their ammunition, and gave a lot of care to their guns, which were in some cases very beautiful, decorated with engraved silver. They also dynamited rocks to clear the road, and were responsible for the horses. Wherever they were, there was a lot of laughing, and sometimes singing and firing off of blanks. While they were at home they seemed to be on holiday, and then some of them would have to ride off on an expedition of punishment, or to attend a council called to put an end to some particular bout of killing. None of the women believed it would work—they laughed and said that it would only mean twenty more shot. When a young man was going off on his first killing, the women made a great fuss over his clothes and his haircut, to encourage him. If he didn't succeed, no woman would marry him—a woman of any worth would be ashamed to marry a man who had not killed—and everyone was anxious to have new brides in the house, to help with the work.

One night, when Lottar served one man his food—a guest; there were always guests invited for meals around the low table, the *sofra*—she noticed what small hands he had, and hairless wrists. Yet he was not young, he was not a boy. A wrinkled, leathery face, without a mustache. She listened for his voice in the talk, and it seemed to her hoarse but womanish. But he smoked, he ate with the men, he carried a gun.

"Is that a man?" Lottar said to the woman serving with her. The woman shook her head, not willing to speak where the men might hear them. But the young girls who overheard the question were not so careful. "Is that a man? Is that a man?" they mimicked Lottar. "Oh, Lottar, you are so stupid! Don't you know when you see a Virgin?"

So she did not ask them anything else. But the next time she saw the Franciscan, she ran after him to ask him her question. What is a Virgin? She had to run after him, because he did not stop and talk to her now as he had when she was sick in the little hut. She was always working when he came to the *kula*, and he could not spend much time with the women anyway—he sat with the men. She ran after him when she saw him leaving, striding down the path among the sumac trees, heading for the bare wooden church and the lean-to church house, where he lived.

He said it was a woman, but a woman who had become like a man. She did not want to marry, and she took an oath in front of witnesses that she never would, and then she put on men's clothes and had her own gun, and her horse if she could afford one, and she lived as she liked. Usually she was poor, she had no woman to work for her. But nobody troubled her, and she could eat at the *sofra* with the men.

Lottar no longer spoke to the priest about going to Skodra. She understood now that it must be a long way away. Sometimes she asked if he had heard anything, if anybody was looking for her, and he would say, sternly, no one. When she thought of how she had been during those first weeks—giving orders, speaking English without embarrassment, sure that her special case merited attention—she was ashamed at how little she had understood. And the longer she stayed at the *kula*, the better she spoke the language and became accustomed to the work, the stranger was the thought of leaving. Someday she must go, but how could it be now? How could she leave in the middle of the tobacco-picking or the sumac harvest, or during the preparations for the feast of the Translation of St. Nicholas?

In the tobacco fields they took off their jerkins and blouses and worked half naked in the sun, hidden between the rows of tall plants. The tobacco juice was black and sticky, like molasses, and it ran down their arms and was smeared over their breasts. At dusk they went down to the river and scrubbed themselves clean. They splashed in the cold water, girls and big, broad women together. They tried to push each other off balance, and Lottar heard her name cried then, in warning and triumph, without contempt, like any other name: "Lottar, watch out! Lottar!"

They told her things. They told her that children died here because of the *Striga*. Even grown-up people shrivel and die sometimes, when the *Striga* has put her spell on them. The *Striga* looks like a normal woman, so you do not know who she is. She sucks blood. To catch her, you must lay a cross on the threshold of the church on Easter Sunday when everybody is inside. Then the woman who is the *Striga* cannot come out. Or you can follow the woman you suspect, and you may see her vomit up the blood. If you can manage to scrape up some of this blood on a silver coin, and carry that coin with you, no *Striga* can touch you, ever.

Hair cut at the time of the full moon will turn white.

If you have pains in your limbs, cut some hair from your head and your armpits and burn it—then the pains will go away.

The *oras* are the devils that come out at night and flash false lights to bewilder travellers. You must crouch down and cover your head, else they will lead you over a cliff. Also they will catch the horses and ride them to death.

The tobacco had been harvested, the sheep brought down from the slopes, animals and humans shut up in the *kula* through the weeks of snow and cold rain, and one day, in the early warmth of the spring sun, the women brought Lottar to a chair on the veranda. There, with great ceremony and delight, they shaved off the hair above her forehead. Then they combed some black, bubbling dye through the hair that remained. The dye was greasy—the hair became so stiff that they could shape it into wings and buns as firm as blood puddings. Everybody thronged about, criticizing and admiring. They put flour on her face and dressed her up in clothes they had pulled out of one of the great carved chests. What for, she asked, as she found herself disappearing into a white blouse with gold embroidery, a red bodice with fringed epaulets, a sash of striped silk a yard wide and a dozen yards long, a black-and-red wool skirt, with chain after chain of false gold being thrown over her hair and around her neck. For beauty, they said. And they said when they had finished, "See! She is beautiful!" Those who said it seemed triumphant, challenging others who must have doubted that the transformation could be made. They squeezed the muscles in her arms, which she had got from hoeing and wood-carrying, and patted her broad, floured forehead. Then they shrieked, because they had forgotten a very important thing—the black paint that joins the eye-brows in a single line over the nose.

"The priest is coming!" shouted one of the girls, who must have been placed as a lookout, and the woman who was painting the black line said, "Ha, he will not stop it!" But the others drew aside.

The Franciscan shot off a couple of blanks, as he always did to announce his arrival, and the men of the house fired off blanks also, to welcome him. But he did not stay with the men this time. He climbed at once to the veranda, calling, "Shame! Shame! Shame on you all! Shame!

"I know what you have dyed her hair for," he said to the women. "I know why you have put bride's clothes on her. All for a pig of a Muslim!

"You! You sitting there in your paint," he said to Lottar. "Don't you know what it is for? Don't you know they have sold you to a Muslim? He is coming from Vuthaj. He will be here by dark!"

"So what of it?" said one of the women boldly. "All they could get for her was three napoleons. She has to marry somebody."

The Franciscan told her to hold her tongue. "Is this what you want?" he said to Lottar. "To marry an infidel and go to live with him in Vuthaj?"

Lottar said no. She felt as if she could hardly move or open her mouth, under the weight of her greased hair and her finery. Under this weight she struggled as you do to rouse yourself to a danger, out of sleep. The idea of marrying the Muslim was still too distant to be the danger—what she understood was that she would be separated from the priest, and would never be able to claim an explanation from him again.

"Did you know you were being married?" he asked her. "Is it something you want, to be married?"

No, she said. No. And the Franciscan clapped his hands. "Take off that gold trash!" he said. "Take those clothes off her! I am going to make her a Virgin!"

"If you become a Virgin, it will be all right," he said to her. "The Muslim will not have to shoot anybody. But you must swear you will never go with a man. You must swear in front of witnesses. *Per quri e per kruch.* By the stone and by the Cross. Do you understand that? I am not going to let them marry you to a Muslim, but I do not want more shooting to start on this land."

It was one of the things the Franciscan tried so hard to prevent—the selling of women to Muslim men. It put him into a frenzy, that their religion could be so easily set aside. They sold girls like Lottar, who would bring no price anywhere else, and widows who had borne only girls.

Slowly and sulkily the women removed all the rich clothes.

They brought out men's trousers, worn and with no braid, and a shirt and head scarf. Lottar put them on. One woman with an ugly pair of shears chopped off most of what remained of Lottar's hair, which was difficult to cut because of the dressing.

"Tomorrow you would have been a bride," they said to her. Some of them seemed mournful, some contemptuous. "Now you will never have a son."

The little girls snatched up the hair that had been cut off and stuck it on their heads, arranging various knots and fringes.

Lottar swore her oath in front of twelve witnesses. They were, of course, all men, and looked as sullen as the women about the turn things had taken. She never saw the Muslim. The Franciscan berated the men and said that if this sort of thing did not stop he would close up the churchyard and make them bury their dead in unholy ground. Lottar sat at a distance from them all, in her unaccustomed clothes. It was strange and unpleasant to be idle. When the Franciscan had finished his harangue, he came over and stood looking down at her. He was breathing hard because of his rage, or the exertions of the lecture.

"Well, then," he said. "Well." He reached into some inner fold of his clothing and brought out a cigarette and gave it to her. It smelled of his skin.

A nurse brought in Charlotte's supper, a light meal of soup and canned peaches. Charlotte took the cover off the soup, smelled it, and turned her head away. "Go away, don't look at this slop," she said. "Come back tomorrow—you know it's not finished yet."

The nurse walked with me to the door, and once we were in the corridor she said, "It's always the ones with the least at home who turn the most critical. She's not the easiest in the world, but you can't help kind of admiring her. You're not related, are you?"

Oh, no, I said. No.

"When she came in it was amazing. We were taking her things off and somebody said, oh, what lovely bracelets, and right away she wanted to sell them! Her *husband* is something else. Do you know him? They are really quite the characters."

Charlotte's husband, Gjurdhi, had come to my bookstore by himself one cold morning less than a week earlier. He was pulling a wagon full of books, which he had wrapped up in a blanket. He had tried to sell me some books once before, in their apartment, and I thought perhaps these were the same ones. I had been confused then, but now that I was on my own ground I was able to be more forceful. I said no, I did not handle secondhand books, I was not interested. Gjurdhi nodded brusquely, as if I had not needed to tell him this and it was of no importance to our conversation. He continued to pick up the books one by one, urging me to run my hands over the bindings, insisting that I note the beauty of the illustrations and be impressed by the dates of publication. I had to repeat my refusal over and over again, and I heard myself begin to attach some apologies to it, quite against my own will. He chose to understand each rejection as applying to an individual book and would simply fetch out another, saying vehemently, "This too! This is very beautiful. You will notice. And it is very old. Look what a beautiful old book!"

They were travel books, some of them, from the turn of the century. Not so very old, and not so beautiful, either, with their dim, grainy photographs. *A Trek Through the Black Peaks. High Albania. Secret Lands of Southern Europe.*

"You will have to go to the Antiquarian Bookstore," I said. "The one on Fort Street. It isn't far to take them."

He made a sound of disgust, maybe indicating that he knew well enough where it was, or that he had already made an unsuccessful trip there, or that most of these books had come from there, one way or another, in the first place.

"How is Charlotte?" I said warmly. I had not seen her for a while, although she used to visit the store quite often. She would bring me little presents—coffee beans coated with chocolate to give me energy; a bar of pure glycerine soap to counteract the drying effects, on the skin, of having to handle so much paper. A paperweight embedded with samples of rocks found in British Columbia, a pencil that lit up in the dark (so that I could see to write up bills if the lights should go out). She drank coffee with me, talked, and strolled about the store, discreetly occupied, when I was busy. Through the dark, blustery days of fall she wore the velvet cloak that I had first seen her in, and kept the rain off with an oversized, ancient black umbrella. She called it her tent. If she saw that I had become too involved with a customer, she would tap me on the shoulder and say, "I'll just silently steal away with my tent now. We'll talk another day."

Once, a customer said to me bluntly, "Who is that woman? I've seen her around town with her husband. I guess he's her husband. I thought they were peddlers."

Could Charlotte have heard that, I wondered. Could she have detected a coolness in the attitude of my new clerk? (Charlotte was certainly cool to her.) There might have been just too many times when I was busy. I did not actually think that the visits had stopped. I preferred to think that an interval had grown longer, for a reason that might have nothing to do with me. I was busy and tired, anyway, as Christmas loomed. The number of books I was selling was a pleasant surprise.

"I don't want to be any kind of character assassin," the clerk had said to me. "But I think you should know that that woman and her husband have been banned from a lot of stores in town. They're suspected of lifting things. I don't know. He wears that rubber coat with the big sleeves and she's got her cloak. I do know for sure that they used to go around at Christmastime and snip off holly that was growing in people's gardens Then they took it round and tried to sell it in apartment buildings."

On that cold morning, after I had refused all the books in his wagon, I asked Gjurdhi again how Charlotte was. He said that she was sick. He spoke sullenly, as if it were none of my business.

"Take her a book," I said. I picked out a Penguin light verse. "Take her this—tell her I hope she enjoys it. Tell her I hope she'll be better very soon. Perhaps I can get around to see her."

He put the book into his bundle in the wagon. I thought that he would probably try to sell it immediately.

"Not at home," he said. "In the hospital."

I had noticed, each time he bent over the wagon, a large, wooden crucifix that swung down outside his coat and had to be tucked back inside. Now this happened again, and I said, thoughtlessly, in my confusion and contrition, "Isn't that beautiful! What beautiful dark wood! It looks medieval."

He pulled it over his head, saying, "Very old. Very beautiful. Oak wood. Yes."

He pushed it into my hand, and as soon as I realized what was happening I pushed it back.

"*Wonderful* wood," I said. As he put it away I felt rescued, though full of irritable remorse.

"Oh, I hope Charlotte is not very sick!" I said.

He smiled disdainfully, tapping himself on the chest—perhaps to show me the source of Charlotte's trouble, perhaps only to feel for himself the skin that was newly bared there.

Then he took himself, the crucifix, the books, and the wagon out of my store. I felt that insults had been offered, humiliations suffered, on both sides.

Up past the tobacco field was a beech wood, where Lottar had often gone to get sticks for the fire. Beyond that was a grassy slope—a high meadow—and at the top of the meadow, about half an hour's climb from the *kula*, was a small stone shelter, a primitive place with no window, a low doorway and no door, a corner hearth without a chimney. Sheep took cover there; the floor was littered with their droppings.

That was where she went to live after she became a Virgin. The incident of the Muslim bridegroom had taken place in the spring, just about a year after she first came to Maltsia e madhe, and it was time for the sheep to be driven to their higher pastures. Lottar was to keep count of the flock and see that they did not fall into ravines or wander too far away. And she was to milk the ewes every evening. She was expected to shoot wolves, if any came near. But none did; no one alive now at the *kula* had ever seen a wolf. The only wild animals Lottar saw were a red fox, once, by the stream, and the rabbits, which were plentiful and unwary. She learned to shoot and skin and cook them, cleaning them out as she had seen the butcher girls do at the *kula* and stewing the meatier parts in her pot over the fire, with some bulbs of wild garlic.

She did not want to sleep inside the shelter, so she fixed up a roof of branches outside, against the wall, this roof an extension of the roof of the building. She had her heap of ferns underneath, and a felt rug she had been given, to spread on the ferns when she slept. She no longer took any notice of the bugs. There were some spikes pushed into the wall between the dry stones. She did not know why they were there, but they served her well for hanging up the milk pails and the few pots she had been provided with. She brought her water from the stream, in which she washed her own head scarf, and herself sometimes, more for relief from the heat than out of concern about her dirtiness.

Everything was changed. She no longer saw the women. She lost her habits of constant work. The little girls came up in the evenings to get the milk. This far away from the *kula* and their mothers, they became quite wild. They climbed up on the roof, often smashing through the arrangement of branches which Lottar had contrived. They jumped into the ferns and sometimes snatched an armful of them to bind into a crude ball, which they threw at one another until it fell apart. They enjoyed themselves so much that Lottar had to chase them away at dusk, reminding them of how frightened they got in the beech wood after dark. She believed that they ran all the way through it and spilled half the milk on their way.

Now and then they brought her corn flour, which she mixed with water and baked on her shovel by the fire. Once they had a treat, a sheep's head—she wondered if they had stolen it—for her to boil in her pot. She was allowed to keep some of the milk, and instead of drinking it fresh she usually let it go sour, and stirred it to make yogurt to dip her bread in. That was how she preferred it now.

The men often came up through the wood shortly after the little girls had run through it on their way down. It seemed that this was a custom of theirs, in the summer. They liked to sit on the banks of the stream and fire off blanks and drink *raki* and sing, or sometimes just smoke and talk. They were not making this expedition to see how she was getting on. But since they were coming anyway, they brought her presents of coffee and tobacco and were full of competing advice on how to fix up the roof of her shelter so it wouldn't fall down, how to keep her fire going all night, how to use her gun.

Her gun was an old Italian Martini, which had been given to her when she left the *kula*. Some of the men said that gun was unlucky, since it had belonged to a boy who had been killed before he himself had even shot anybody. Others said that Martinis in general were unlucky, hardly any use at all.

Mausers were what you needed, for accuracy and repeating power.

But Mauser bullets were too small to do enough damage. There were men walking around full of Mauser holes—you could hear them whistle as they passed by.

Nothing can really compare with a heavy flintlock that has a good packing of powder, a bullet, and nails.

When they weren't talking about guns, the men spoke of recent killings, and told jokes. One of them told a joke about a wizard. There was a wizard held in prison by a Pasha. The Pasha brought him out to do tricks in front of guests. Bring a bowl of water, said the wizard. Now, this water is the sea. And what port shall I show you on the sea? Show a port on the island of Malta, they said. And there it was. Houses and churches and a steamer ready to sail. Now would you like to see me step on board that steamer? And the Pasha laughed. Go ahead! So the wizard put his foot in the bowl of water and stepped on board the steamer and went to America! What do you think of that!

"There are no wizards, anyway," said the Franciscan, who had climbed up with the men on this evening, as he often did. "If you had said a saint, you might have made some sense." He spoke severely, but Lottar thought he was happy, as they all were, as she too was permitted to be, in their presence and in his, though he paid no attention to her. The strong tobacco that they gave her to smoke made her dizzy and she had to lie down on the grass.

The time came when Lottar had to think about moving inside her house. The mornings were cold, the ferns were soaked with dew, and the grape leaves were turning yellow. She took the shovel and cleaned the sheep droppings off the floor, in preparation for making up her bed inside. She began to stuff grass and leaves and mud into the chinks between the stones.

When the men came they asked her what she was doing that for. For the winter, she said, and they laughed.

"Nobody can stay here in the winter," they said. They showed her how deep the snow was, putting hands against their breastbones. Besides, all the sheep would have been taken down.

"There will be no work for you—and what will you eat?" they said. "Do you think the women will let you have bread and yogurt for nothing?"

"How can I go back to the *kula*?" Lottar said. "I am a Virgin, where would I sleep? What kind of work would I do?"

"That is right," they said kindly, speaking to her and then to each other. "When a Virgin belongs to the *kula* she gets a bit of land, usually, where she can live on her own. But this one doesn't really belong to the *kula*, she has no father to give her anything. What will she do?"

Shortly after this—and in the middle of the day, when visitors never came—the Franciscan climbed the meadow, all alone.

"I don't trust them," he said. "I think they will try again to sell you to a Muslim. Even though you have been sworn. They will try to make some money out of you. If they could find you a Christian, it might not be so bad, but I am sure it will be an infidel."

They sat on the grass and drank coffee. The Franciscan said, "Do you have any belongings to take with you? No. Soon we will start."

"Who will milk the ewes?" said Lottar. Some of the ewes were already working their way down the slope; they would stand and wait for her.

"Leave them," said the Franciscan.

In this way she left not only the sheep but her shelter, the meadow, the wild grape and the sumac and mountain ash and juniper bushes and scrub oak she had looked at all summer, the rabbit pelt she had used as a pillow and the pan she had boiled her coffee in, the heap of wood she had gathered only that morning, the stones around her fire—each one of them known to her by its particular shape and color. She understood that she was leaving, because the Franciscan was so stern, but she did not understand it in a way that would make her look around, to see everything for the last time. That was not necessary, anyway. She would never forget any of it.

As they entered the beech wood the Franciscan said, "Now we must be very quiet. I am going to take another path, which does not go so near the *kula*. If we hear anybody on the path, we will hide."

Hours, then, of silent walking, between the beech trees with their smooth elephant bark, and the black-limbed oaks and the dry pines. Up and down, crossing the ridges, choosing paths that Lottar had not known existed. The Franciscan never hesitated and never spoke of a rest. When they came out of the trees at last, Lottar was very surprised to see that there was still so much light in the sky.

The Franciscan pulled a loaf of bread and a knife from some pocket in his garment, and they ate as they walked.

They came to a dry riverbed, paved with stones that were not flat and easily walkable but a torrent, a still torrent of stones between fields of corn and tobacco. They could hear dogs barking, and sometimes people's voices. The corn and tobacco plants, still unharvested, were higher than their heads, and they walked along the dry river in this shelter, while the daylight entirely faded. When they could not walk anymore and the darkness would conceal them, they sat down on the white stones of the riverbed.

"Where are you taking me?" Lottar finally asked. At the start she had thought they must be going in the direction of the church and the priest's house, but now she saw that this could not be so. They had come much too far.

"I am taking you to the Bishop's house," said the Franciscan. "He will know what to do with you."

"Why not to your house?" said Lottar. "I could be a servant in your house."

"It isn't allowed—to have a woman servant in my house. Or

in any priest's house. This Bishop now will not allow even an old woman. And he is right, trouble comes from having a woman in the house."

After the moon rose they went on. They walked and rested, walked and rested, but never fell asleep, or even looked for a comfortable place to lie down. Their feet were tough and their sandals well worn, and they did not get blisters. Both of them were used to walking long distances—the Franciscan in his far-flung parish and Lottar when she was following the sheep.

The Franciscan became less stern—perhaps less worried—after a while and talked to her almost as he had done in the first days of their acquaintance. He spoke Italian, though she was now fairly proficient in the language of the Ghegs.

"I was born in Italy," he said. "My parents were Ghegs, but I lived in Italy when I was young, and that was where I became a priest. Once I went back for a visit, years ago, and I shaved off my mustache, I do not know why. Oh, yes, I do know—it was because they laughed at me in the village. Then when I got back I did not dare show my face in the *madhe*. A hairless man there is a disgrace. I sat in a room in Skodra until it grew again."

"It is Skodra we are going to?" said Lottar.

"Yes, that is where the Bishop is. He will send a message that it was right to take you away, even if it is an act of stealing. They are barbarians, in the *madhe*. They will come up and pull on your sleeve in the middle of Mass and ask you to write a letter for them. Have you seen what they put up on the graves? The crosses? They make the cross into a very thin man with a rifle across his arms. Haven't you seen that?" He laughed and shook his head and said, "I don't know what to do with them. But they are good people all the same—they will never betray you."

"But you thought they might sell me in spite of my oath."

"Oh, yes. But to sell a woman is a way to get some money. And they are so poor."

Lottar now realized that in Skodra she would be in an unfamiliar position—she would not be powerless. When they got there, she could run away from him. She could find someone who spoke English, she could find the British Consulate. Or, if not that, the French.

The grass was soaking wet before dawn and the night got very cold. But when the sun came up Lottar stopped shivering and within an hour she was hot. They walked on all day. They ate the rest of the bread and drank from any stream they found that had water in it. They had left the dry river and the mountains far behind. Lottar looked back and saw a wall of jagged rocks with a little green clinging around their bases. That green was the woods and meadows which she had thought so high. They followed paths through the hot fields and were never out of the sound of barking dogs. They met people on the paths.

At first the Franciscan said, "Do not speak to anybody—they will wonder who you are." But he had to answer when greetings were spoken.

"Is this the way to Skodra? We are going to Skodra to the Bishop's house. This is my servant with me, who has come from the mountains.

"It is all right, you look like a servant in these clothes," he said to Lottar. "But do not speak—they will wonder, if you speak."

I had painted the walls of my bookstore a clear, light yellow. Yellow stands for intellectual curiosity. Somebody must have told me that. I opened the store in March of 1964. This was in Victoria, in British Columbia.

I sat there at the desk, with my offerings spread out behind me. The publishers' representatives had advised me to stock books about dogs and horses, sailing and gardening, bird books and flower books—they said that was all anybody in Victoria would buy. I flew against their advice and brought in novels and poetry and books that explained about Sufism and relativity and Linear B. And I had set out these books, when they came, so that Political Science could shade into Philosophy and Philosophy into Religion without a harsh break, so that compatible poets could nestle together, the arrangement of the shelves of books—I believed—reflecting a more or less natural ambling of the mind, in which treasures new and forgotten might be continually surfacing. I had taken all this care, and now what? Now I waited, and I felt like somebody who had got dramatically dressed up for a party, maybe even fetching jewels from the pawnshop or the family vault, only to discover that it was just a few neighbors playing cards. It was just meat loaf and mashed potatoes in the kitchen, and a glass of fizzy pink wine.

The store was often empty for a couple of hours at a time, and then when somebody did come in, it would be to ask about a book remembered from the Sunday-school library or a grandmother's bookcase or left behind twenty years ago in a foreign hotel. The title was usually forgotten, but the person would tell me the story. It is about this little girl who goes out to Australia with her father to mine the gold claims they have inherited. It is about the woman who had a baby all alone in Alaska. It is about a race between one of the old clipper ships and the first steamer, way back in the 1840s.

Oh, well. I just thought I'd ask.

They would leave without a glance at the riches around them.

A few people did exclaim in gratitude, said what a glorious addition to the town. They would browse for half an hour, an hour, before spending seventy-five cents.

It takes time.

I had found a one-room apartment with a kitchenette in an old building at a corner called the Dardanelles. The bed folded up into the wall. But I did not usually bother to fold it up, because I never had any company. And the hook seemed unsafe to me. I was afraid that the bed might leap out of the wall sometime when I was eating my tinned soup or baked-potato supper. It might kill me. Also, I kept the window open all the time, because I believed I could smell a whiff of escaping gas, even when the two burners and the oven were shut off. With the window open at home and the door open at the store, to entice the customers, it was necessary for me to be always bundled up in my black woolly sweater or my red corduroy dressing gown (a garment that had once left its pink tinge on all my forsaken husband's handkerchiefs and underwear). I had difficulty separating myself from these comforting articles of clothing so that they might be washed. I was sleepy much of the time, underfed and shivering.

But I was not despondent. I had made a desperate change in my life, and in spite of the regrets I suffered every day, I was proud of that. I felt as if I had finally come out into the world in a new, true skin. Sitting at the desk, I made a cup of coffee or of thin red soup last an hour, clasping my hands around the cup while there was still any warmth to be got from it. I read, but without purpose or involvement. I read stray sentences from the books that I had always meant to read. Often these sentences seemed so satisfying to me, or so elusive and lovely, that I could not help abandoning all the surrounding words and giving myself up to a peculiar state. I was alert and dreamy, closed off from all particular people but conscious all the time of the city itself—which seemed a strange place.

A small city, here at the western edge of the country. Pockets of fakery for tourists. The Tudor shop fronts and double-decker buses and flower-pots and horse-drawn rides: almost insulting. But the sea light in the street, the spare and healthy old people leaning into the wind as they took their daily walks along the broom-topped cliffs, the shabby, slightly bizarre bungalows with their monkey-puzzle trees and ornate shrubs in the gardens. Chestnut trees blossom as spring comes on, hawthorn trees along the streets bear red-and-white flowers, oily-leaved bushes put out lush pink and rose-red blooms such as you would never see in the hinterlands. Like a town in a story, I thought—like the transplanted seaside town of the story set in New Zealand, in Tasmania. But something North American persists. So many people, after all, have come here from Winnipeg or Saskatchewan. At noon a smell of dinners cooking drifts out of poor, plain apartment buildings. Frying meat, boiling vegetables—farm dinners being cooked, in the middle of the day, in cramped kitchenettes.

How could I tell what I liked so much? Certainly it was not what a new merchant might be looking for—bustle and energy to raise the hope of commercial success. *Not much doing* was the message the town got across to me. And when a person who is opening a store doesn't mind hearing the message *Not much doing* you could ask, What's going on? People open shops in order to sell things, they hope to become busy so that they will have to enlarge the shop, then to sell more things, and grow rich, and eventually not have to come into the shop at all. Isn't that true? But are there other people who open a shop with the hope of being sheltered there, among such things as they most value—the yarn or the teacups or the books—and with the idea only of making a comfortable assertion? They will become a part of the block, a part of the street, part of everybody's map of the town, and eventually of everybody's memories. They will sit and drink coffee in the middle of the morning, they will get out the familiar bits of tinsel at Christmas, they will wash the windows in spring before spreading out the new stock. Shops, to these people, are what a cabin in the woods might be to somebody else—a refuge and a justification.

Some customers are necessary, of course. The rent comes due and the stock will not pay for itself. I had inherited a little money—that was what had made it possible for me to come out here and get the shop going—but unless business picked up to some extent I could not last beyond the summer. I understood that. I was glad that more people started coming in as the weather warmed up. More books were sold, survival began to seem possible. Book prizes were due to be awarded in the schools at the end of term, and that brought the schoolteachers with their lists and their praise and their unfortunate expectation of discounts. The people who came to browse were buying regularly, and some of them began to turn into friends—or the sort of friends I had here, where it seemed I would be happy to talk to people day after day and never learn their names.

When Lottar and the priest first saw the town of Skodra, it seemed to float above the mud flats, its domes and steeples shining as if they were made of mist. But when they entered it in the early evening all this tranquillity vanished. The streets were paved with big, rough stones and were full of people and donkey carts, roving dogs, pigs being driven somewhere, and smells of fires and cooking and dung and something terrible—like rotten hides. A man came along with a parrot on his shoulder. The bird seemed to be shrieking curses in an unknown language. Several times the Franciscan stopped people and asked the way to the Bishop's house, but they pushed by him without answering or laughed at him or said some words he didn't understand. A boy said that he would show the way, for money.

"We have no money," the Franciscan said. He pulled Lottar into a doorway and there they sat down to rest. "In Maltsia e madhe," he said, "many of these who think so well of themselves would soon sing a different tune."

Lottar's notion of running away and leaving him had vanished. For one thing, she could not manage to ask directions any better than he could. For another, she felt that they were allies who could not survive in this place out of sight of each other. She had not understood how much she depended on the smell of his skin, the aggrieved determination of his long strides, the flourish of his black mustache.

The Franciscan jumped up and said he had remembered—he had remembered now the way to the Bishop's house. He hurried ahead of her through narrow, high-walled back streets where nothing of houses or courtyards could be seen—just walls and gates. The paving stones were thrust up so that walking here was as difficult as in the dry riverbed. But he was right, he gave a shout of triumph, they had come to the gate of the Bishop's house.

A servant opened the gate and let them in, but only after some high-pitched argument. Lottar was told to sit on the ground just inside the gate, and the Franciscan was led into the house to see the Bishop. Soon someone was sent through the streets to the British Consulate (Lottar was not told this), and he came back with the Consul's manservant. It was dark by then, and the Consul's servant carried a lantern. And Lottar was led away again. She followed the servant and his lantern to the consulate.

A tub of hot water for her to bathe in, in the courtyard. Her clothes taken away. Probably burned. Her greasy black, vermin-infested hair cut off. Kerosene poured on her scalp. She had to tell her story—the story of how she came to Maltsia e madhe—and this was difficult, because she was not used to speaking English, also because that time seemed so far away and unimportant. She had to learn to sleep on a mattress, to sit on a chair, to eat with a knife and fork.

As soon as possible they put her on a boat.

Charlotte stopped. She said, "That part is not of interest."

I had come to Victoria because it was the farthest place I could get to from London, Ontario, without going out of the country. In London, my husband, Donald, and I had rented a basement apartment in our house to a couple named Nelson and Sylvia. Nelson was an English major at the university and Sylvia was a nurse. Donald was a dermatologist, and I was doing a thesis on Mary Shelley—not very quickly. I had met Donald when I went to see him about a rash on my neck. He was eight years older than I was—a tall, freckled, blushing man, cleverer than he looked. A dermatologist sees grief and despair, though the problems that bring people to him may not be in the same class as tumors and blocked arteries. He sees sabotage from within, and truly unlucky fate. He sees how matters like love and happiness can be governed by a patch of riled-up cells. Experience of this sort had made Donald kind, in a cautious, impersonal way. He said that my rash was probably due to stress, and that he could see that I was going to be a wonderful woman, once I got a few problems under control.

We invited Sylvia and Nelson upstairs for dinner, and Sylvia told us about the tiny town they both came from, in Northern Ontario. She said that Nelson had always been the smartest person in their class and in their school and possibly in the whole town. When she said this, Nelson looked at her with a perfectly flat and devastating expression, an expression that seemed to be waiting with infinite patience and the mildest curiosity for some explanation, and Sylvia laughed and said, "Just kidding, of course."

When Sylvia was working late shifts at the hospital, I sometimes asked Nelson to share a meal with us in a more informal way. We got used to his silences and his indifferent table manners and to the fact that he did not eat rice or noodles, eggplant, olives, shrimp, peppers, or avocados, and no doubt a lot of other things, because those had not been familiar foods in the town in Northern Ontario.

Nelson looked older than he was. He was short and sturdily built, sallow-skinned, unsmiling, with a suggestion of mature scorn and handy pugnaciousness laid over his features, so that it seemed he might be a hockey coach, or an intelligent, uneducated, fair-minded, and foul-mouthed foreman of a construction gang, rather than a shy, twenty-two-year-old student.

He was not shy in love. I found him resourceful and determined. The seduction was mutual, and it was a first affair for both of us. I had once heard somebody say, at a party, that one of the nice things about marriage was that you could have real affairs—an affair before marriage could always turn out to be nothing but courtship. I was disgusted by this speech, and frightened to think that life could be so bleak and trivial. But once my own affair with Nelson started, I was amazed all the time. There was no bleakness or triviality about it, only ruthlessness and clarity of desire, and sparkling deception.

Nelson was the one who first faced up to things. One afternoon he turned on his back and said hoarsely and defiantly, "We are going to have to leave."

I thought he meant that he and Sylvia would have to leave, they could not go on living in this house. But he meant himself and me. "We" meant himself and me. Of course he and I had said "we" of our arrangements, of our transgression. Now he had made it the "we" of our decision—perhaps of a life together.

My thesis was supposed to be on Mary Shelley's later novels, the ones nobody knows about. *Lodore, Perkin Warbeck, The Last Man.* But I was really more interested in Mary's life before she learned her sad lessons and buckled down to raising her son to be a baronet. I loved to read about the other women who had hated or envied or traipsed along: Harriet, Shelley's first wife, and Fanny Imlay, who was Mary's half sister and may have been in love with Shelley herself, and Mary's stepsister, Mary Jane Clairmont, who took my own name—Claire—and joined Mary and Shelley on their unwed honeymoon so that she could keep on chasing Byron. I had often talked to Donald about impetuous Mary and married Shelley and their meetings at Mary's mother's grave, about the suicides of Harriet and Fanny and the persistence of Claire, who had a baby by Byron. But I never mentioned any of this to Nelson, partly because we had little time for talk and partly because I did not want him to think that I drew some sort of comfort or inspiration from this mishmash of love and despair and treachery and self-dramatizing. I did not want to think so myself. And Nelson was not a fan of the nineteenth century or the Romantics. He said so. He said that he wanted to do something on the Muckrakers. Perhaps he meant that as a joke.

Sylvia did not behave like Harriet. Her mind was not influenced or impeded by literature, and when she found out what had been going on, she went into a wholesome rage.

"You blithering idiot," she said to Nelson.

"You two-faced twit," she said to me.

The four of us were in our living room. Donald went on cleaning and filling his pipe, tapped it and lit it, nursed and inspected it, drew on it, lit it again—all so much the way someone would do in a movie that I was embarrassed for him. Then he put some books and the latest copy of *Macleans* into his briefcase, went to the bathroom to get his razor and to the bedroom to get his pajamas, and walked out.

He went straight to the apartment of a young widow who worked as a secretary at his clinic. In a letter he wrote to me later, he said that he had never thought of this woman except as a friend until that night, when it suddenly dawned on him what a pleasure it would be to love a kind and sensible, *unwracked-up* sort of person.

Sylvia had to be at work at eleven o'clock. Nelson usually walked her over to the hospital—they did not have a car. On this night she told him that she would rather be escorted by a skunk.

That left Nelson and me alone together. The scene had lasted a much shorter time than I had expected. Nelson seemed gloomy but relieved, and if I felt that short shrift had been given to the notion of love as a capturing tide, a glorious and harrowing event, I knew better than to show it.

We lay down on the bed to talk about our plans and ended up making love, because that was what we were used to doing. Sometime during the night Nelson woke up and thought it best to go downstairs to his own bed.

I got up in the dark, dressed, packed a suitcase, wrote a note, and walked to the phone at the corner, where I called a taxi. I took the six-o'clock train to Toronto, connecting with the train to Vancouver. It was cheaper to take the train, if you were willing to sit up for three nights, which I was.

So there I sat, in the sad, shambling morning in the day coach, coming down the steep-walled Fraser Canyon into the sodden Fraser Valley, where smoke hung over the small, dripping houses, the brown vines, the thorny bushes and huddled sheep. It was in December that this earthquake in my life had arrived. Christmas was cancelled for me. Winter with its snowdrifts and icicles and invigorating blizzards was cancelled by this blurred season of muck and rain. I was constipated, I knew that I had bad breath, my limbs were cramped, and my spirits utterly bleak. And did I not think then, What nonsense it is to suppose one man so different from another when all that life really boils down to is getting a decent cup of coffee and room to stretch out in? Did I not think that even if Nelson were sitting here beside me, he would have turned into a gray-faced stranger whose desolation and unease merely extended my own?

No. No. Nelson would still be Nelson to me. I had not changed, with regard to his skin and his smell and his forbidding eyes. It seemed to be the outside of Nelson which came most readily to my mind, and in the case of Donald it was his inner quakes and sympathies, the labored-at kindness and those private misgivings that I had got knowledge of by wheedling and conniving. If I could have my love of these two men together, and settle it on one man, I would be a happy woman. If I could care for everybody in the world as minutely as I did for Nelson, and as calmly, as uncarnally as I now did for Donald, I would be a saint. Instead, I had dealt a twofold, a wanton-seeming, blow.

The regular customers who had changed into something like friends were: a middle-aged woman who was a chartered accountant but preferred such reading as *Six Existentialist Thinkers*, and *The Meaning of Meaning*; a provincial civil servant who ordered splendid, expensive works of pornography such as I had not known existed (their elaborate Oriental, Etruscan connections seemed to me grotesque and uninteresting, compared to the simple, effective, longed-for rituals of myself and Nelson); a Notary Public who lived behind his office at the foot of Johnson Street ("I live in the slums," he told me. "Some night I expect a big bruiser of a fellow to lurch around the corner hollering '*Ste-el-la*'") and the woman I knew later as Charlotte—the Notary Public called her the Duchess. None of these people cared much for one another, and an early attempt that I made to bring the accountant and the Notary Public into conversation was a fizzle.

"Spare me the females with the withered, painted faces," the Notary Public said, the next time he came in. "I hope you haven't got her lurking around anywhere tonight."

It was true that the accountant painted her thin, intelligent, fifty-year-old face with a heavy hand, and drew on eyebrows that were like two strokes of India ink. But who was the Notary Public to talk, with his stumpy, nicotined teeth and pocked cheeks?

"I got the impression of a rather superficial fellow," the accountant said, as if she had guessed and bravely discounted the remarks made about herself.

So much for trying to corral people into couples, I wrote to Donald. *And who am I to try?* I wrote to Donald regularly, describing the store, and the city, and even, as well as I could, my own unaccountable feelings. He was living with Helen, the secretary. I wrote also to Nelson, who might or might not be living alone, might or might not be reunited with Sylvia. I didn't think he was. I thought she would believe in inexcusable behavior and definite endings. He had a new address. I had looked it up in the London phone book at the public library. Donald, after a grudging start, was writing back. He wrote impersonal, mildly interesting letters about people we both knew, events at the clinic. Nelson did not write at all. I started sending registered letters. Now I knew at least that he picked them up.

Charlotte and Gjurdhi must have come into the store together, but I did not understand that they were a couple until it was time for them to leave. Charlotte was a heavy, shapeless, but quick-moving woman, with a pink face, bright blue eyes, and a lot of glistening white hair, worn like a girl's, waving down over her shoulders. Though the weather was fairly warm, she was wearing a cape of dark-gray velvet with a scanty gray fur trim—a garment that looked as if it belonged, or had once belonged, on the stage. A loose shirt and a pair of plaid wool slacks showed underneath, and there were open sandals on her broad, bare, dusty feet. She clanked as if she wore hidden armor. An arm reaching up to get a book showed what caused the clanking. Bracelets—any number of them, heavy or slender, tarnished or bright. Some were set with large, square stones, the color of toffee or blood.

"Imagine this old fraud being still on the go," she said to me, as if continuing some desultory and enjoyable conversation.

She had picked up a book by Anaïs Nin.

"Don't pay any attention," she said. "I say terrible things. I'm quite fond of the woman, really. It's him I can't stand."

"Henry Miller?" I said, beginning to follow this.

"That's right." She went on talking about Henry Miller, Paris, California, in a scoffing, energetic, half-affectionate way. She seemed to have been neighbors, at least, with the people she was talking about. Finally, naively, I asked her if this was the case.

"No, no. I just feel I know them all. Not personally. Well—personally. Yes, personally. What other way is there to know them? I mean, I haven't met them, face-to-face. But in their books? Surely that's what they intend? I know them. I know them to the point where they bore me. Just like anybody you know. Don't you find that?"

She drifted over to the table where I had laid out the New Directions paperbacks.

"Here's the new bunch, then," she said. "Oh, my," she said,

widening her eyes at the photographs of Ginsberg and Corso and Ferlinghetti. She began reading, so attentively that I thought the next thing she said must be part of some poem.

"I've gone by and I've seen you here," she said. She put the book down and I realized she meant me. "I've seen you sitting in here, and I've thought a young woman would probably like to be outside some of the tie. In the sun. I don't suppose you'd consider hiring me to sit there, so you could get out?"

"Well, I would like to—" I said.

"I'm not so dumb. I'm fairly knowledgeable, really. Ask me who wrote Ovid's *Metamorphoses*. It's all right, you don't have to laugh."

"I would like to, but I really can't afford to."

"Oh, well. You're probably right. I'm not very chic. And I would probably foul things up. I would argue with people if they were buying books I thought were dreadful." She did not seem disappointed. She picked up a copy of *The Dud Avocado* and said, "There! I have to buy this, for the title."

She gave a little whistle, and the man it seemed to be meant for looked up from the table of books he had been staring at, near the back of the store. I had known he was there but had not connected him with her. I thought he was just one of those men who wander in off the street, alone, and stand looking about, as if trying to figure out what sort of place this is or what the books are for. Not a drunk or a panhandler, and certainly not anybody to be worried about—just one of a number of shabby, utterly uncommunicative old men who belong to the city somewhat as the pigeons do, moving restlessly all day within a limited area, never looking at people's faces. He was wearing a coat that came down to his ankles, made of some shiny, rubberized, liver-colored material, and a brown velvet cap with a tassel. The sort of cap a doddery old scholar or a clergyman might wear in an English movie. There was, then, a similarity between them—they were both wearing things that might have been discards from a costume box. But close up he looked years older than she. A long, yellowish face, drooping tobacco-brown eyes, an unsavory, straggling mustache. Some faint remains of handsomeness, or potency. A quenched ferocity.

He came at her whistle—which seemed half serious, half a joke—and stood by, mute and self-respecting as a dog or a donkey, while the woman prepared to pay.

At that time, the government of British Columbia applied a sales tax to books. In this case it was four cents.

"I can't pay that," she said. "A tax on books. I think it is immoral. I would rather go to jail. Don't you agree?"

I agreed. I did not point out—as I would have done with anybody else—that the store would not be let off the hook on that account.

"Don't I sound appalling?" she said. "See what this government can do to people? It makes them into *orators*."

She put the book in her bag without paying the four cents, and never paid the tax on any future occasion.

I described the two of them to the Notary Public. He knew at once who I meant.

"I call them the Duchess and the Algerian," he said. "I don't know what the background is. I think maybe he's a retired terrorist. They go around the town with a wagon, like scavengers."

I got a note asking me to supper on a Sunday evening. It was signed *Charlotte*, without a surname, but the wording and handwriting were quite formal.

My husband Gjurdhi and I would be delighted—

Up until then I had not wished for any invitations of this sort and would have been embarrassed and disturbed to get one. So the pleasure I felt surprised me. Charlotte held out a decided promise; she was unlike the others whom I wanted to see only in the store.

The building where they lived was on Pandora Street. It was covered with mustard stucco and had a tiny, tiled vestibule that reminded me of a public toilet. It did not smell, though, and the apartment was not really dirty, just horrendously untidy. Books were stacked against the walls, and pieces of patterned cloth were hung up droopily to hide the wallpaper. There were bamboo blinds on the window, sheets of colored paper—surely flammable—pinned over the light bulbs.

"What a darling you are to come," cried Charlotte. "We were afraid you would have tons more interesting things to do than visiting ancient old us. Where can you sit down? What about here?" She took a pile of magazines off a wicker chair. "Is that comfortable? It makes such interesting noises, wicker. Sometimes I'll be sitting here alone and that chair will start creaking and cracking exactly as if someone were shifting around in it. I could say it was a presence, but I'm no good at believing in that rubbish. I've tried."

Gjurdhi poured out a sweet yellow wine. For me a long-stemmed glass that had not been dusted, for Charlotte a glass tumbler, for himself a plastic cup. It seemed impossible that any dinner could come out of the little kitchen alcove, where foodstuffs and pots and dishes were piled helter-skelter, but there was a good smell of roasting chicken, and in a little while Gjurdhi brought out the first course—platters of sliced cucumber, dishes of yogurt. I sat in the wicker chair and Charlotte in the single armchair. Gjurdhi sat on the floor. Charlotte was wearing her slacks, and a rose-colored T-shirt which clung to her unsupported breast. She had painted her toenails to match the T-shirt. Her bracelets clanked against the plate as she picked up the slices of cucumber. (We were eating with our fingers.) Gjurdhi wore his cap and a dark-red silky dressing gown over his trousers. Stains had mingled with its pattern.

After the cucumber, we ate chicken cooked with raisins in golden spices, and sour bread, and rice. Charlotte and I were provided with forks, but Gjurdhi scooped the rice up with the bread. I would often think of this meal in the years that followed, when this kind of food, this informal way of sitting and eating, and even some version of the style and the untidiness of the room, would become familiar and fashionable. The people I knew, and I myself, would give up—for a while—on dining-room tables, matching wineglasses, to some extent on cutlery or chairs. When I was being entertained, or making a stab at entertaining people, in this way, I would think of Charlotte and Gjurdhi and the edge of true privation, the risky authenticity that marked them off from all these later imitations. At the time, it was all new to me, and I was both uneasy and delighted. I hoped to worthy of such exoticism but not to be tried too far.

Mary Shelley came to light shortly. I recited the titles of the later novels, and Charlotte said dreamily, "Per-kin War-beck. Wasn't he the one—wasn't he the one who pretended to be a little Prince who was murdered in the Tower?"

She was the only person I had ever met—not a historian, not a *Tudor* historian—who had known this.

"That would make a movie," she said. "Don't you think? The question I always think about Pretenders like that is who do *they* think they are? Do they believe it's true, or what? But Mary Shelley's own life is the movie, isn't it? I wonder there hasn't been one made. Who would play Mary, do you think? No. No, first of all, start with Harriet. Who would play Harriet?

"Someone who would look well drowned," she said, ripping off a golden chunk of chicken. "Elizabeth Taylor? Not a big enough part. Susannah York?

"Who was the father?" she wondered, referring to Harriet's unborn baby. "I don't think it was Shelley. I've never thought so. Do you?"

This was all very well, very enjoyable, but I had hoped we would get to explanations—personal revelations, if not exactly confidences. You did expect some of that, on occasions like this. Hadn't Sylvia, at my own table, told about the town in Northern Ontario and about Nelson's being the smartest person in the school? I was surprised at how eager I found myself, at last, to tell my story. Donald and Nelson—I was looking forward to telling the truth, or some of it, in all its wounding complexity, to a person who would not be surprised or outraged by it. I would have liked to puzzle over my behavior, in good company. Had I taken on Donald as a father figure—or as a parent figure, since both my parents were dead? Had I deserted him because I was angry at *them* for deserting *me?* What did Nelson's silence mean, and was it now permanent? (But I did not think, after all, that I would tell anybody about the letter that had been returned to me last week, marked "Not Known at This Address.")

This was not what Charlotte had in mind. There was no opportunity, no exchange. After the chicken, the wineglass and the tumbler and cup were taken away and filled with an extremely sweet pink sherbet that was easier to drink than to eat with a spoon. Then came small cups of desperately strong coffee. Gjurdhi lit two candles as the room grew darker, and I was given one of these to carry to the bathroom, which turned out to be a toilet with a shower. Charlotte said the lights were not working.

"Some repairs going on," she said. "Or else they have taken a whim. I really think they take whims. But fortunately we have our gas stove. As long as we have a gas stove we can laugh at their whims. My only regret is that we cannot play any music. I was going to play some old political songs—'I dreamed I saw Joe Hill last night,'" she sang in a mocking baritone. "Do you know that one?"

I did know it. Donald used to sing it when he was a little drunk. Usually the people who sang "Joe Hill" had certain vague but discernible political sympathies, but with Charlotte I did not think this would be so. She would not operate from sympathies, from principles. She would be playful about what other people took seriously. I was not certain what I felt about her. It was not simple liking or respect. It was more like a wish to move in her element, unsurprised. To be buoyant, self-mocking, gently malicious, unquenchable.

Gjurdhi, meanwhile, was showing me some of the books. How had this started? Probably from a comment I made—how many of them there were, something of that sort—when I stumbled over some on my way back from the toilet. He was bringing forward books with bindings of leather or imitation leather—how could I know the difference?—with marbled endpapers, watercolor frontispieces, steel engravings. At first, I believed admiration might be all that was required, and I admired everything. But close to my ear I heard the mention of money—was that the first distinct thing I had ever heard Gjurdhi say?

"I only handle new books," I said. "These are marvellous, but I don't really know anything about them. It's a completely different business, books like these."

Gjurdhi shook his head as if I had not understood and he would now try, firmly, to explain again. He repeated the price in a more insistent voice. Did he think I was trying to haggle with him? Or perhaps he was telling me what he had paid for the book? We might be having a speculative conversation about the price it might be sold for—not about whether I should buy it.

I kept saying no, and yes, trying to juggle these responses appropriately. *No*, I cannot take them for my store. *Yes*, they are very fine. *No*, truly, I'm sorry, I am not the one to judge.

"If we had been living in another country, Gjurdhi and I might have done something," Charlotte was saying. "Or even if the movies in this country had ever got off the ground. That's what I would love to have done. Got work in the movies. As extras. Or maybe we are not bland enough types to be extras, maybe they would have found bit parts for us. I believe extras have to be the sort that don't stand out in a crowd, so you can use them over and over again. Gjurdhi and I are more memorable than that. Gjurdhi in particular—you could *use* that face."

She paid no attention to the second conversation that had developed, but continued talking to me, shaking her head indulgently at Gjurdhi now and then, to suggest that he was behaving in a way she found engaging, though perhaps importunate. I had to talk to him softly, sideways, nodding all the while in response to her.

"Really you should take them to the Antiquarian Bookstore," I said. "Yes, they are quite beautiful. Books like these are out of my range."

Gjurdhi did not whine, his manner was not ingratiating. Peremptory, rather. It seemed as if he would give me orders, and would be most disgusted if I did not capitulate. In my confusion I helped myself to more of the yellow wine, pouring it into my unwashed sherbet glass. This was probably a dire offense. Gjurdhi looked horridly displeased.

"Can you imagine illustrations in modern novels?" said Charlotte, finally consenting to tie the two conversations together. "For instance, in Norman Mailer? They would have to be abstracts. Don't you think? Sort of barbed wire and blotches?"

I went home with a headache and a feeling of jangled inadequacy. I was a prude, that was all, when it came to mixing up buying and selling with hospitality. I had perhaps behaved clumsily, I had disappointed them. And they had disappointed me. Making me wonder why I had been asked.

I was homesick for Donald, because of "Joe Hill."

I also had a longing for Nelson, because of an expression on Charlotte's face as I was leaving. A savoring and contented look that I knew had to do with Gjurdhi, though I hardly wanted to believe that. It made me think that after I walked downstairs and left the building and went into the street, some hot and skinny, slithery, yellowish, indecent old beast, some mangy but urgent old tiger, was going to pounce among the books and the dirty dishes and conduct a familiar rampage.

A day or so later I got a letter from Donald. He wanted a divorce, so that he could marry Helen.

I hired a clerk, a college girl, to come in for a couple of hours in the afternoon, so I could get to the bank, and do some office work. The first time Charlotte saw her she went up to the desk and patted a stack of books sitting there, ready for quick sale.

"Is this what the office managers are telling their minions to buy?" she said. The girl smiled cautiously and didn't answer.

Charlotte was right. It was a book called *Psycho-Cybernetics*, about having a positive self-image.

"You were smart to hire her instead of me," Charlotte said. "She is much niftier-looking, and she won't shoot her mouth off and scare the customers away. She won't have *opinions.*"

"There's something I ought to tell you about that woman," the clerk said, after Charlotte left.

That part is not of interest.

"What do you mean?" I said. But my mind had been wandering, that third afternoon in the hospital. Just at the last part of Charlotte's story I had thought of a special-order book that hadn't come in, on Mediterranean cruises. Also I had been thinking about the Notary Public, who had been beaten about the head the night before, in his office on Johnson Street. He was not dead but he might be blinded. Robbery? Or an act of revenge, outrage, connected with a layer of his life that I hadn't guessed at?

Melodrama and confusion made this place seem more ordinary to me, but less within my grasp.

"Of course it is of interest," I said. "All of it. It's a fascinating story."

"Fascinating," repeated Charlotte in a mincing way. She made a face, so she looked like a baby vomiting out a spoonful of pap. Her eyes, still fixed on me, seemed to be losing color, losing their childish, bright, and self-important blue. Fretfulness was changing into disgust. An expression of vicious disgust, she showed, of unspeakable weariness—such as people might show to the mirror but hardly ever to one another. Perhaps because of the thoughts that were already in my head, it occurred to me that Charlotte might die. She might die at any moment. At this moment. Now.

She motioned at the water glass, with its crooked plastic straw. I held the glass so that she could drink, and supported her head. I could feel the heat of her scalp, a throbbing at the base of her skull. She drank thirstily, and the terrible look left her face.

She said, "Stale."

"I think it would make an excellent movie," I said, easing her back onto the pillows. She grabbed my wrist, then let it go.

"Where did you get the idea?" I said.

"From life," said Charlotte indistinctly. "Wait a moment." She turned her head away, on the pillow, as if she had to arrange something in private. Then she recovered, and she told a little more.

Charlotte did not die. At least she did not die in the hospital. When I came in rather late, the next afternoon, her bed was empty and freshly made up. The nurse who had talked to me before was trying to take the temperature of the woman tied in the chair. She laughed at the look on my face.

"Oh, no!" she said "Not that. She checked out of here this morning. Her husband came and got her. We were transferring her to a long-term place out in Saanich, and he was supposed to be taking her there. He said he had the taxi outside Then we get this phone call that they never showed up! They were in great spirits when they left. He brought her a pile of money, and she was throwing it up in the air. I don't know— maybe it was only dollar bills. But we haven't a clue where they've got to."

I walked around to the apartment building on Pandora Street. I thought they might simply have gone home. They might have lost the instructions about how to get to the nursing home and not wanted to ask. They might have decided to stay together in their apartment no matter what. They might have turned on the gas.

At first I could not find the building and thought that I must be in the wrong block. But I remembered the corner store and some of the houses. The building had been changed—that was what had happened. The stucco had been painted pink; large, new windows and French doors had been put in; little balconies with wrought-iron railings had been attached. The fancy balconies had been painted white, the whole place had the air of an ice-cream parlor. No doubt it had been renovated inside as well, and the rents increased, so that people like Charlotte and Gjurdhi could have no hope of living there. I checked the names by the door, and of course theirs were gone. They must have moved out some time ago.

The change in the apartment building seemed to have some message for me. It was about vanishing. I knew that Charlotte and Gjurdhi had not actually vanished—they were somewhere, living or dead. But for me they had vanished. And because of this fact—not really because of any loss of them—I was tipped into dismay more menacing than any of the little eddies of regret that had caught me in the past year. I had lost my bearings. I had to get back to the store so my clerk could go home, but I felt as if I could as easily walk another way, just any way at all. My connection was in danger—that was all. Sometimes our connection is frayed, it is in danger, it seems almost lost.

Views and streets deny knowledge of us, the air grows thin. Wouldn't we rather have a destiny to submit to, then, something that claims us, anything, instead of such flimsy choices, arbitrary days?

I let myself slip, then, into imagining a life with Nelson. If I had done so accurately, this is how it would have gone.

He comes to Victoria. But he does not like the idea of working in the store, serving the public. He gets a job teaching at a boys' school, a posh place where his look of lower-class toughness, his bruising manners, soon make him a favorite.

We move from the apartment at the Dardanelles to a roomy bungalow a few blocks from the sea. We marry.

But this is the beginning of a period of estrangement. I become pregnant. Nelson falls in love with the mother of a student. I fall in love with an intern I meet in the hospital during labor.

We get over all this—Nelson and I do. We have another child. We acquire friends, furniture, rituals. We go to too many parties at certain seasons of the year, and talk regularly about starting a new life, somewhere far away, where we don't know anybody.

We become distant, close—distant, close—over and over again.

As I entered the store, I was aware of a man standing near the door, half looking in the window, half looking up the street, then looking at me. He was a short man dressed in a trenchcoat and a fedora. I had the impression of someone disguised. Jokingly disguised. He moved toward me and bumped my shoulder, and I cried out as if I had received the shock of my life, and indeed it was true that I had. For this really was Nelson, come to claim me. Or at least to accost me, and see what would happen.

We have been very happy.
I have often felt completely alone.
There is always in this life something to discover.
The days and the years have gone by in some sort of blur.
On the whole, I am satisfied.

When Lottar was leaving the Bishop's courtyard, she was wrapped in a long cloak they had given her, perhaps to conceal her ragged clothing, or to contain her smell. The Consul's servant spoke to her in English, telling her where they were going. She could understand him but could not reply. It was not quite dark. She could still see the pale shapes of roses and oranges in the Bishop's garden.

The Bishop's man was holding the gate open.

She had never seen the Bishop at all. And she had not seen the Franciscan since he had followed the Bishop's man into the house. She called out for him now, as she was leaving. She had no name to call, so she called, *"Xoti! Xoti! Xoti,"* which means "leader" or "master" in the language of the Ghegs. But no answer came, and the Consul's servant swung his lantern impatiently, showing her the way to go. Its light fell by accident on the Franciscan standing half concealed by a tree. It was a little orange tree he stood behind. His face, pale as the oranges were in that light, looked out of the branches, all its swarthiness drained away. It was a wan face hanging in the tree, its melancholy expression quite impersonal and undemanding, like the expression you might see on the face of a devout but proud apostle in a church window. Then it was gone, taking the breath out of her body, as she knew too late.

She called him and called him, and when the boat came into the harbour at Trieste he was waiting on the dock.

∞ *A Wilderness Station* ∞

I

MISS MARGARET CRESSWELL, Matron, House of Industry, Toronto, to Mr. Simon Herron, North Huron, January 15, 1852.

Since your letter is accompanied by an endorsement from your minister, I am happy to reply. Requests of your sort are made to us frequently, but unless we have such an endorsement we cannot trust that they are made in good faith.

We do not have any girl at the Home who is of marriageable age, since we send our girls out to make a living usually around the age of fourteen or fifteen, but we do keep track of them for some years or usually until they are married. In cases such as yours we sometimes recommend one of these girls and will arrange a meeting, and then of course it is up to the two parties involved to see if they are suited.

There are two girls eighteen years of age that we are still in touch with. Both are apprenticed to a milliner and are good seamstresses, but a marriage to a likely man would probably be preferred to a lifetime of such work. Further than that cannot be said, it must be left to the girl herself and of course to your liking for her, or the opposite.

The two girls are a Miss Sadie Johnstone and a Miss Annie McKillop. Both were born legitimately of Christian parents and were placed in the Home due to parental deaths. Drunkenness or immorality was not a factor. In Miss Johnstone's case there is however the factor of consumption, and though she is the prettier of the two and a plump rosy girl, I feel I must warn you that perhaps she is not suited to the hard work of a life in the bush. The other girl, Miss McKillop, is of a more durable constitution though of leaner frame and not so good a complexion. She has a waywardness about one eye but it does not interfere with her vision and her sewing is excellent. The darkness of her eyes and hair and brown tinge of her skin is no indication of mixed blood, as both parents were from Fife. She is a hardy girl and I think would be suited to such a life as you can offer, being also free from the silly timidity we often see in girls of her age. I will speak to her and acquaint her with the idea and will await your letter as to when you propose to meet her.

II

Carstairs *Argus*, Fiftieth Anniversary Edition, February 3, 1907. Recollections of Mr. George Herron.

On the first day of September, 1851, my brother Simon and I got a box of bedclothes and household utensils together and put them in a wagon with a horse to pull it, and set out from Halton County to try our fortunes in the wilds of Huron and Bruce, as wilds they were then thought to be. The goods were from Archie Frame that Simon worked for, and counted as part of his wages. Likewise we had to rent the house off him, and his boy that was about my age came along to take it and the wagon back.

It ought to be said in the beginning that my brother and I were left alone, our father first and then our mother dying of fever within five weeks of landing in this country, when I was three years old and Simon eight. Simon was put to work for Archie Frame that was our mother's cousin, and I was taken on by the schoolteacher and wife that had no child of their own. This was in Halton, and I would have been content to go on living there but Simon being only a few miles away continued to visit and say that as soon as we were old enough we would go and take up land and be on our own, not working for others, as this was what our father had intended. Archie Frame never sent Simon to school as I was sent, so Simon was always bound to get away. When I had come to be fourteen years of age and a husky lad, as was my brother, he said we should go and take up Crown Land north of the Huron Tract.

We only got as far as Preston on the first day as the roads were rough and bad across Nassageweya and Puslinch. Next day we got to Shakespeare and the third afternoon to Stratford. The roads were always getting worse as we came west, so we thought best to get our box sent on to Clinton by the stage. But the stage had quit running due to rains, and they were waiting till the roads froze up, so we told Archie Frame's boy to turn about and return with horse and cart and goods back to Halton. Then we took our axes on our shoulders, and walked to Carstairs.

Hardly a soul was there before us. Carstairs was just under way, with a rough building that was store and inn combined, and there was a German named Roem building a sawmill. One man who got there before us and already had a fair-sized cabin built was Henry Treece, who afterwards became my father-in-law.

We got ourselves boarded at the inn where we slept on the bare floor with one blanket or quilt between us. Winter was coming early with cold rains and everything damp, but we were expecting hardship or at least Simon was. I came from a softer place. He said we must put up with it so I did.

We began to underbrush a road to our piece of land and then we got it marked out and cut the logs for our shanty and big scoops to roof it. We were able to borrow an ox from Henry Treece to draw the logs. But Simon was not of a mind to borrow or depend on anybody. He was minded to try raising the shanty ourselves, but when we saw we could not do it I made my way to Treeces' place and with Henry and two of his sons and a fellow from the mill it was accomplished. We started next day to fill up the cracks between the logs with mud and we got some hemlock branches so we would not be out money anymore for staying at the inn but could sleep in our own place. We had a big slab of elm for the door. My brother had heard from some French-Canadian fellows that were at Archie Frame's that in the lumber camps the fire was always in the middle of the shanty. So he said that was the way we should have ours, and we got four posts and were building the chimney on them, house-fashion, intending to plaster it with mud inside and out. We went to our hemlock bed with a good fire going, but waking in the middle of the night we saw our lumber was all ablaze and the scoops burning away briskly also. We tore down the chimney and the scoops being green basswood were not hard to put out. As soon as it came day, we started to build the chimney in the ordinary way in the end of the house and I thought it best not to make any remark.

After the small trees and brush was cleared out a bit, we set to chopping down the big trees. We cut down a big ash and split it into slabs for our floor. Still our box had not come which was to be shipped from Halton so Henry Treece sent us a very large and comfortable bearskin for our cover in bed but my brother would not take the favour and sent it back saying no need. Then after several weeks we got our box and had to ask for the ox to bring it on from Clinton, but my brother said that is the last we will need to ask of any person's help.

We walked to Walley and brought back flour and salt fish on our back. A man rowed us across the river at Manchester for a steep price. There were no bridges then and all that winter not a good enough freeze to make it easy going over the rivers.

Around Christmastime my brother said to me that he thought we had the place in good enough shape now for him to be bringing in a wife, so we should have somebody to cook and do for us and milk a cow when we could afford one. This was the first I had heard of any wife and I said that I did not know he was acquainted with anybody. He said he was not but he had heard that you could write to the Orphanage Home and ask if they had a girl there that was willing to think about the prospect and that they would recommend, and if so he would go and see her. He wanted one between eighteen and twenty-two years of age, healthy and not afraid of work and raised in the Orphanage, not taken in lately, so that she would not be expecting any luxuries or to be waited on and would not be recalling about when things were easier for her. I do not doubt that to those hearing about this nowadays it seems a strange way to go about things. It was not that my brother could not have gone courting and got a wife on his own, because he was a good-looking fellow, but he did not have the time or the money or inclination, his mind was all occupied with establishing our holding. And if a girl had parents they would probably not want her to go far away where there was little in comforts and so much work.

That it was a respectable way of doing things is shown by the fact that the minister Mr. McBain, who was lately come into the district, helped Simon to write the letter and sent word on his own to vouch for him.

So a letter came back that there was a girl that might fit the bill and Simon went off to Toronto and got her. Her name was Annie but her maiden name I had forgotten. They had to ford the streams in Hullet and trudge through deep soft snow after leaving the stage in Clinton, and when they got back she was worn out and very surprised at what she saw, since she said she had never imagined so much bush. She had in her box some sheets and pots and dishes that ladies had given her and that made the place more comfortable.

Early in April my brother and I went out to chop down some trees in the bush at the farthest corner of our property. While Simon was away to get married, I had done some chopping in the other direction towards Treeces', but Simon wanted to get all our boundaries cut clear around and not to go on chopping where I had been. The day started out mild and there was still a lot of soft snow in the bush. We were chopping down a tree where Simon wanted, and in some way, I cannot say how, a branch of it came crashing down where we didn't expect. We just heard the little branches cracking where it fell and looked up to see it and it hit Simon on the head and killed him instantly.

I had to drag his body back then to the shanty through the snow. He was a tall fellow though not fleshy, and it was an awkward task and greatly wearying. It had got colder by this time and when I got to the clearing I saw snow on the wind like the start of a storm. Our footsteps were filled in that we had made earlier. Simon was all covered with snow that did not melt on him by this time, and his wife coming to the door was greatly puzzled, thinking that I was dragging along a log.

In the shanty Annie washed him off and we sat still awhile not knowing what we should do. The preacher was at the inn as there was no church or house for him yet and the inn was only about four miles away, but the storm had come up very fierce so you could not even see the trees at the edge of the clearing. It had the look of a storm that would last two or three days, the wind being from the northwest. We knew we could not keep the body in the shanty and we could not set it out in the snow fearing the bobcats would get at it, so we had to set to work and bury him. The ground was not frozen under the snow, so I dug out a grave near the shanty and Annie sewed him in a sheet and we laid him in his grave, not staying long in the wind but saying the Lord's Prayer and reading one Psalm out of the Bible. I am not sure which one but I remember it was near the end of the Book of Psalms and it was very short.

This was the third day of April, 1852.

That was our last snow of the year, and later the minister came and said the service and I put up a wooden marker. Later on we got our plot in the cemetery and put his stone there, but he is not under it as it is a foolish useless thing in my opinion to cart a man's bones from one place to another when it is only bones and his soul has gone on to Judgment.

I was left to chop and clear by myself and soon I began to work side by side with the Treeces, who treated me with the greatest kindness. We worked all together on my land or their land, not minding if it was the one or the other. I started to take my meals and even to sleep at their place and got to know their daughter Jenny who was about of my age, and we made our plans to marry, which we did in due course. Our life together was a long one with many hardships but we were fortunate in the end and raised eight children. I have seen my sons take over my wife's father's land as well as my own since my two brothers-in-law went away and did well for themselves in the West.

My brother's wife did not continue in this place but went her own way to Walley.

Now there are gravel roads running north, south, east, and west and a railway not a half mile from my farm. Except for woodlots, the bush is a thing of the past and I often think of the trees I have cut down and if I had them to cut down today I would be a wealthy man.

The Reverend Walter McBain, Minister of the Free Presbyterian Church of North Huron, to Mr. James Mullen, Clerk of the Peace, Walley, United Counties of Huron and Bruce, September 10, 1852.

I write to inform you, sir, of the probable arrival in your town of a young woman of this district, by the name of Annie Herron, a widow and one of my congregation. This young person has left her home here in the vicinity of Carstairs in Holloway Township, I believe she intends to walk to Walley. She may appear at the Gaol there seeking to be admitted, so I think it my duty to tell you who and what she is and her history here since I have known her.

I came to this area in November of last year, being the first minister of any kind to venture. My parish is as yet mostly bush, and there is nowhere for me to lodge but at the Carstairs Inn. I was born in the west of Scotland and came to this country under the auspices of the Glasgow Mission. After applying to know God's will, I was directed by Him to go to preach wherever was most need of a minister. I tell you this so you may know what sort I am that bring you my account and my view of the affairs of this woman.

She came into the country late last winter as the bride of the young man Simon Herron. He had written on my advice to the House of Industry in Toronto that they might recommend to him a Christian, preferably Presbyterian, female suitable to his needs, and she was the one recommended. He married her straightaway and brought her here to the shanty he had built with his brother. These two young lads had come into the country to clear themselves a piece of land and get possession of it, being themselves orphans and without expectations. They were about this work one day at the end of winter when an accident befell. A branch was loosed while chopping down a tree and fell upon the elder brother so as to cause instant death. The younger lad succeeded in getting the body back to the shanty and since they were held prisoner by a heavy snowstorm they conducted their own funeral and burial.

The Lord is strict in his mercies and we are bound to receive his blows as signs of his care and goodness for so they will prove to be.

Deprived of his bother's help, the lad found a place in a neighbouring family, also members in good standing of my congregation, who have accepted him as a son, though he still works for title to his own land. This family would have taken in the young widow as well, but she would have nothing to do with their offer and seemed to develop an aversion to everyone who would help her. Particularly she seemed so towards her brother-in-law, who said that he had never had the least quarrel with her, and towards myself. When I talked to her, she would not give any answer or sign that her soul was coming into submission. It is a fault of mine that I am not well-equipped to talk to women. I have not the ease to win their trust. Their stubbornness is of another kind than a man's.

I meant only to say that I did not have any good effect on her. She stopped appearing at services, and the deterioration of her property showed the state of her mind and spirit. She would not plant peas and potatoes though they were given to her to grow among the stumps. She did not chop down the wild vines around her door. Most often she did not light a fire so she could have oat-cake or porridge. Her brother-in-law being removed, there was no order imposed on her days. When I visited her the door was open and it was evident that animals came and went in her house. If she was there she hid herself, to mock me. Those who caught sight of her said that her clothing was filthy and torn from scrambling about in the bushes, and she was scratched by thorns and bitten by the mosquito insects and let her hair go uncombed or plaited. I believe she lived on salt fish and bannock that the neighbours or her brother-in-law left for her.

Then while I was still puzzling how I might find a way to protect her body through the winter and deal with the more important danger to her soul, there comes word she is gone. She left the door open and went away without cloak or bonnet and wrote on the shanty floor with a burnt stick the two words: "Walley, Gaol." I take this to mean she intends to go there and turn herself in. Her brother-in-law thinks it would be no use for him to go after her because of her unfriendly attitude to himself, and I cannot set out because of a deathbed I am attending. I ask you therefore to let me know if she has arrived and in what state and how you will deal with her. I consider her still as a soul in my charge, and I will try to visit her before winter if you keep her there. She is a child of the Free Church and the Covenant and as such she is entitled to a minister of her own faith and you must not think it sufficient that some priest of the Church of England or Baptist or Methodist be sent to her.

In case she should not come to the Gaol but wander in the streets, I ought to tell you that she is dark-haired and tall, meagre in body, not comely but not ill-favoured except having one eye that goes to the side.

Mr. James Mullen, Clerk of the Peace, Walley, to the Reverend Walter McBain, Carstairs, North Huron, September 30, 1852.

Your letter to me arrived most timely and appreciated, concerning the young woman Annie Herron. She completed her journey to Walley unharmed and with no serious damage though she was weak and hungry when she presented herself at the Gaol. On its being inquired what she did there, she said that she came to confess to a murder, and to be locked up. There was consultation round and about, I was sent for, and it being near to midnight, I agreed that she should spend the night in a cell. The next day I visited her and got all particulars I could.

Her story of being brought up in the Orphanage, her apprenticeship to a milliner, her marriage, and her coming to North Huron, all accords pretty well with what you have told me. Events in her account begin to differ only with her husband's death. In that matter what she says is this:

On the day in early April when her husband and his brother went out to chop trees, she was told to provide them with food for their midday meal, and since she had not got it ready when they wanted to leave, she agreed to take it to them in the woods. Consequently she baked up some oat-cakes and took some salt fish and followed their tracks and found them at work some distance away. But when her husband unwrapped his food he was very offended, because she had wrapped it in a way that the salty oil from the fish had soaked into the cakes, and they were all crumbled and unpleasant to eat. In his disappointment he became enraged and promised her a beating when he was more at leisure to do it. He then turned his back on her, being seated on a log, and she picked up a rock and threw it at him, hitting him on the head so that he fell down unconscious and in fact dead. She and his brother then carried and dragged the body back to the house. By that time a blizzard had come up and they were imprisoned within. The brother said that they should not reveal the truth as she had not intended murder, and she agreed. They then buried him—her story agreeing again with yours— and that might have been the end of it, but she became more and more troubled, convinced that she had surely been intending to kill him. If she had not killed him, she says, it would only have meant a worse beating, and why should she have risked that? So she decided at last upon confession and as if to prove something handed me a lock of hair stiffened with blood.

This is her tale, and I do not believe it for a minute. No rock that this girl could pick up, combined with the force that she could summon to throw it, would serve to kill a man. I questioned her about this, and she changed her story, saying that it was a large rock that she had picked up in both hands and that she had not thrown it but smashed it down on his head from behind. I said why did not the brother prevent you, and she said, he was looking the other way. Then I said there must indeed be a bloodied rock lying somewhere in the wood, and she said she had washed it off with the snow. (In fact it is not likely a rock would come to hand so easily, with all such depth of snow about.) I asked her to roll up her sleeve that I might judge of the muscles in her arms, to do such a job, and she said she had been a huskier woman some months since.

I conclude that she is lying, or self-deluded. But I see nothing for it at the moment but to admit her to the Gaol. I asked her what she thought would happen to her now, and she said, well, you will try me and then you will hang me. But you do not hang people in the winter, she said, so I can stay here till spring. And if you let me work here, maybe you will want me to go on working and you will not want me hanged. I do not know where she got this idea about people not being hanged in the winter. I am in perplexity about her. As you may know, we have a very fine new Gaol here where the inmates are kept warm and dry and are decently fed and treated with all humanity, and there has been a complaint that some are not sorry—and at this time of year, even happy—to get into it. But it is obvious that she cannot wander about much longer, and from your account she is unwilling to stay with friends and unable to make a tolerable home for herself. The Gaol at present serves as a place of detention for the Insane as well as criminals, and if she is charged with Insanity, I could keep her here for the winter perhaps with removal to Toronto in the spring. I have engaged for a doctor to visit her. I spoke to her of your letter and your hope of coming to see her, but I found her not at all agreeable to that. She asks that nobody be allowed to see her excepting a Miss Sadie Johnstone, who is not in this part of the country.

I am enclosing a letter I have written to her brother-in-law for you to pass on to him, so that he may know what she has said and tell me what he thinks about it. I thank you in advance for conveying the letter to him, also for the trouble you have been to, in informing me as fully as you have done. I am a member of the Church of England, but have a high regard for the work of other Protestant denominations in bringing an orderly life to this part of the world we find ourselves in. You may believe that I will do what is in my power to do, to put you in a position to deal with the soul of this young woman, but it might be better to wait until she is in favour of it.

The reverend Walter McBain to Mr. James Mullen, November 18, 1852.

I carried your letter at once to Mr. George Herron and believe that he has replied and given you his recollection of events. He was amazed at his sister-in-law's claim, since she had never said

anything of this to him or to anybody else. He says that it is all
her invention or fancy, since she was never in the woods when
it happened and there was no need for her to be, as they had
carried their food with them when they left the house. He says
that there had been at another time some reproof from his
brother to her, over the spoiling of some cakes by their proximity to fish, but it did not happen at this time. Nor were there
any rocks about to do such a deed on impulse if she had been
there and wished to do it.

My delay in answering your letter, for which I beg pardon,
is due to a bout of ill health. I had an attack of the gravel and
a rheumatism of the stomach worse than any misery that ever
fell upon me before. I am somewhat improved at present and
will be able to go about as usual by next week if all continues
to mend.

As to the question of the young woman's sanity, I do not
know what your Doctor will say but I have thought on this and
questioned the Divinity and my belief is this. It may well be
that so early in the marriage her submission to her husband
was not complete and there would be carelessness about his
comfort, and naughty words, and quarrelsome behaviour, as
well as the hurtful sulks and silences her sex is prone to. His
death occurring before any of this was put right, she would feel
a natural and harrowing remorse, and this must have taken
hold of her mind so strongly that she made herself out to be
actually responsible for his death. In this way, I think many folk
are driven mad. Madness is at first taken on by some as a kind
of play, for which shallowness and audacity they are punished
later on, by finding out that it is play no longer, and the Devil
has blocked off every escape.

It is still my hope to speak to her and make her understand
this. I am under difficulties at present not only of my wretched
corpus but of being lodged in a foul and noisy place obliged
to hear day and night such uproars as destroy sleep and study
and intrude even on my prayers. The wind blows bitterly
through the logs, but if I go down to the fire there is swilling
of spirits and foulest insolence. And outside nothing but trees
to choke off every exit and icy bog to swallow man and horse.

There was a promise to build a church and lodging but those who made such promise have grown busy with their own affairs and it seems to have been put off. I have not however left off preaching even in my illness and in such barns and houses as are provided. I take heart remembering a great man, the great preacher and interpreter of God's will, Thomas Boston, who in the latter days of his infirmity preached the grandeur of God from his chamber window to a crowd of two thousand or so assembled in the yard below So I mean to preach to the end though my congregation will be smaller.

Whatsoever crook there is in one's lot, it is of God's making. Thomas Boston.

This World is a wilderness, in which we may indeed get our station changed, but the move will be out of one wilderness station unto another. Ibid.

Mr. James Mullen to the Reverend Walter McBain, January 17, 1853.

I write to you that our young woman's health seems sturdy, and she no longer looks such a scarecrow, eating well and keeping herself clean and tidy. Also she seems quieter in her spirits. She has taken to mending the linen in the prison which she does well. But I must tell you that she is firm as ever against a visit, and I cannot advise you to come here as I think your trouble might be for nothing. The journey is very hard in winter and it would do no good to your state of health.

Her brother-in-law has written me a very decent letter affirming that there is no truth to her story, so I am satisfied on that.

You may be interested in hearing what the doctor who visited her had to say about her case. His belief is that she is subject to a sort of delusion peculiar to females, for which the motive is a desire for self-importance, also a wish to escape the monotony of life or the drudgery they may have been born to. They may imagine themselves possessed by the forces of evil, to have committed various and hideous crimes, and so forth. Sometimes they may report that they have taken numerous lovers, but these lovers will be all imaginary and the woman who thinks herself a prodigy of vice will in fact be quite chaste and untouched. For all this he—the doctor—lays the blame on the sort of reading that is available to these females, whether it is of ghosts or demons or of love escapades with Lords and Dukes and suchlike. For many, these tales are a passing taste given up when life's real duties intervene. For others they are indulged in now and then, as if they were sweets or sherry wine, but for some there is complete surrender and living within them just as in an opium-dream. He could not get an account of her reading from the young woman, but he believes she may by now have forgotten what she has read, or conceals the matter out of slyness.

With his questioning there did come to light something further that we did not know. On his saying to her, did she not fear hanging? she replied, no, for there is a reason you will not hang me. You mean that they will judge that you are mad? said he, and she said, oh, perhaps that, but is it not true also that they will never hang a woman that is with child? The doctor then examined her to find out if this were true, and she agreed to the examination, so she must have made the claim in good faith. He discovered however that she had deceived herself. The signs she took were simply the results of her going so long underfed and in such a reduced state, and later probably of her hysteria. He told her of his findings, but it is hard to say whether she believes him.

It must be acknowledged that this is truly a hard country for women. Another insane female has been admitted here recently, and her case is more pitiful for she has been driven insane by a rape. Her two attackers have been taken in and are in fact just over the wall from her in the men's section. The screams of the victim resound sometimes for hours at a stretch, and as a result the prison has become a much less pleasant shelter. But whether that will persuade our self-styled murderess to recant and take herself off, I have no idea. She is a good needlewoman and could get employment if she chose.

I am sorry to hear of your bad health and miserable lodgings. The town has grown so civilized that we forget the hardship of the hinterlands. Those like yourself who choose to endure it deserve our admiration. But you must allow me to say that it seems pretty certain that a man not in robust health will be unable to bear up for long in your situation. Surely your Church would not consider it a defection were you to choose to serve it longer by removing to a more comfortable place.

I enclose a letter written by the young woman and sent to a Miss Sadie Johnstone, on King Street, Toronto. It was intercepted by us that we might know more of the state of her mind, but resealed and sent on. But it has come back marked "Unknown." We have not told the writer of this in hopes that she will write again and more fully, revealing to us something to help us decide whether or not she is a conscious liar.

Mrs. Annie Herron, Walley Gaol, United Counties of Huron and Bruce, to Miss Sadie Johnstone, 49 King Street, Toronto, December 20, 1852.

Sadie, I am in here pretty well and safe and nothing to complain of either in food or blankets. It is a good stone building and something like the Home. If you could come and see me I would be very glad. I often talk to you a whole lot in my head, which I don't want to write because what if they are spies. I do the sewing here, the things was not in good repare when I came but now they are pretty good. And I am making curtains for the Opera House, a job that was sent in. I hope to see you. You could come on the stage right to this place. Maybe you would not like to come in the winter but in the springtime you would like to come.

Mr. James Mullen to the Reverend Walter McBain, April 7, 1853.

Not having had any reply to my last letter, I trust you are well and might still be interested in the case of Annie Herron. She is still here and busies herself at sewing jobs which I have undertaken to get her from outside. No more is said of being with child, or of hanging, or of her story. She has written once again to Sadie Johnstone but quite briefly and I enclose her letter here. Do you have an idea who this person Sadie Johnstone might be?

I don't get any answer from you, Sadie, I don't think they sent on my letter. Today is the First of April, 1853. But not April Fool like we used to fool each other. Please come and see me if you can. I am in Walley Gaol but safe and well.

Mr. James Mullen from Edward Hoy, Landlord, Carstairs Inn, April 19, 1853.

Your letter to Mr. McBain sent back to you, he died here at the inn February 25. There is some books here, nobody wants them.

III

Annie Herron, Walley Gaol, to Sadie Johnstone, Toronto. Finder Please Post.

George came dragging him across the snow I thought it was a log he dragged. I didn't know it was him. George said, it's him. A branch fell out of a tree and hit him, he said. He didn't say he was dead. I looked for him to speak. His mouth was part way open with snow in it. Also his eyes part way open. We had to get inside because it was starting to storm like anything. We dragged him in by the one leg each. I pretended to myself when I took hold of his leg that it was still the log. Inside where I had the fire going it was warm and the snow started melting off him. His blood thawed and ran a little around his ear. I didn't know what to do and I was afraid to go near him. I thought his eyes were watching me.

George sat by the fire with his big heavy coat on and his boots on. He was turned away. I sat at the table, which was of half-cut logs. I said, how do you know if he is dead? George said, touch him if you want to know. But I would not. Outside there was terrible storming, the wind in the trees and over top of our roof. I said, Our Father who art in Heaven, and that was how I got my courage. I kept saying it every time I moved. I have to wash him off, I said. Help me. I got the bucket where I kept the snow melting. I started on his feet and had to pull his boots off, a heavy job. George never turned around or paid attention or helped me when I asked. I didn't take the trousers or coat off of him, I couldn't manage. But I washed his hands and wrists. I always kept the rag between my hand and his skin. The blood and wet where the snow had melted off him was on the floor under his head and shoulders so I wanted to turn him over and clean it up. But I couldn't do it. So I went and pulled George by his arm. Help me, I said. What? he said. I said we had to turn him. So he came and helped me and we got him turned over, he was laying face down. And then I saw, I saw where the axe had cut.

Neither one of us said anything. I washed it out, blood and what else. I said to George, go and get me the sheet from my box. There was the good sheet I wouldn't put on the bed. I didn't see the use of trying to take off his clothes though they were good cloth. We would have had to cut them away where the blood was stuck and then what would we have but the rags. I cut off the one little piece of his hair because I remembered when Lila died in the Home they did that. Then I got George to help me roll him onto the sheet and I started to sew him up in the sheet. While I was sewing I said to George, go out in the lee of the house where the wood is piled and maybe you can get in enough shelter there to dig him a grave. Take the wood away and the ground is likely softer underneath.

I had to crouch down at the sewing so I was nearly laying on the floor beside him. I sewed his head in first folding the sheet over it because I had to look in his eyes and mouth. George went out and I could hear through the storm that he was doing what I said and pieces of wood were thrown up sometimes hitting the wall of the house. I sewed on, and every bit of him I lost sight of I would say even out loud, there goes, there goes. I had got the fold neat over his head but down at the feet I didn't have material enough to cover him, so I sewed on my eyelet petticoat I made at the Home to learn the stitch and that way I got him all sewed in.

I went out to help George. He had got all the wood out of the way and was at the digging. The ground was soft enough, like I had thought. He had the spade so I got the broad shovel and we worked away, him digging and loosening and me shovelling.

Then we moved him out. We could not do it now one leg each so George got him at the head and me at the ankles where the petticoat was and we rolled him into the earth and set to work again to cover him up. George had the shovel and it seemed I could not get enough dirt onto the spade so I pushed it in with my hands and kicked it in with my feet any way at all. When it was all back in, George beat it down flat with the shovel as much as he could. Then we moved all the wood back searching where it was in the snow and we piled it up in the right way so it did not look as if anybody had been at it. I think we had no hats on or scarves but the work kept us warm.

We took in more wood for the fire and put the bar across the door. I wiped up the floor and I said to George, take off your boots. Then, take off your coat. George did what I told him. He sat by the fire. I made the kind of tea from catnip leaves that Mrs. Treece showed me how to make and I put a piece of sugar in it. George did not want it. Is it too hot, I said. I let it cool off but then he didn't want it either. So I began, and talked to him.

You didn't mean to do it.

It was in anger, you didn't mean what you were doing.

I saw him other times what he would do to you. I saw he would knock you down for a little thing and you just get up and never say a word. The same way he did to me.

If you had not have done it, some day he would have done it to you.

Listen, George. Listen to me.

If you own up what do you think will happen? They will hang you. You will be dead, you will be no good to anybody. What will become of your land? Likely it will all go back to the Crown and somebody else will get it and all the work you have done will be for them.

What will become of me here if you are took away?

I got some oat-cakes that were cold and I warmed them up. I set one on his knee. He took it and bit it and chewed it but he could not get it down and he spit it onto the fire.

I said, listen. I know things. I am older than you are. I am religious too, I pray to God every night and my prayers are answered. I know what God wants as well as any preacher knows and I know that he does not want a good lad like you to be hanged. All you have to do is say you are sorry. Say you are sorry and mean it well and God will forgive you. I will say the same thing, I am sorry too because when I saw he was dead I did not wish, not one minute, for him to be alive. I will say, God forgive me, and you do the same. Kneel down.

But he would not. He would not move out of his chair. And I said, all right. I have an idea. I am going to get the Bible. I asked him, do you believe in the Bible? Say you do. Nod your head.

I did not see whether he nodded or not but I said, there. There you did. Now. I am going to do what we all used to do in the Home when we wanted to know what would happen to us or what we should do in our life. We would open the Bible any place and poke our finger at a page and then open our eyes and read the verse where our finger was and that would tell you what you needed to know. To make double sure of it just say when you close your eyes, God guide my finger.

He would not raise a hand from his knee, so I said, all right. All right, I'll do it for you. I did it, and I read where my finger stopped. I held the Bible close in to the fire so I could see.

It was something about being old and gray-headed, *oh God forsake me not*, and I said, what that means is that you are supposed to live till you are old and gray-headed and nothing is supposed to happen to you before that. It says so, in the Bible.

Then the next verse was so-and-so went and took so-and-so and conceived and bore him a son.

It says you will have a son, I said. You have to live and get older and get married and have a son.

But the next verse I remember so well I can put down all of it. *Neither can they prove the things of which they now accuse me.*

George, I said, do you hear that? *Neither can they prove the things of which they now accuse me.* That means that you are safe.

You are safe. Get up now. Get up and go and lay on the bed and go to sleep.

He could not do that by himself but I did it. I pulled on him and pulled on him until he was standing up and then I got him

across the room to the bed which was not his bed in the corner but the bigger bed, and got him to sit on it then lay down.
I rolled him over and back and got his clothes off down to his
shirt. His teeth were chattering and I was afraid of a chill or the
fever. I heated up the flat-irons and wrapped them in cloth and
laid them down one on each side of him close to his skin. There
was not whisky or brandy in the house to use, only the catnip
tea. I put more sugar in it and got him to take it from a spoon.
I rubbed his feet with my hands, then his arms and his legs, and
I wrung out clothes in hot water which I laid over his stomach
and his heart. I talked to him then in a different way quite soft
and told him to go to sleep and when he woke up his mind
would be clear and all his horrors would be wiped away.

A tree branch fell on him. It was just what you told me. I
can see it falling. I can see it coming down so fast like a streak
and little branches and crackling all along the way, it hardly
takes longer than a gun going off and you say, what is that?
and it has hit him and he is dead.

When I got him to sleep I laid down on the bed beside him.
I took off my smock and I could see the black and blue marks
on my arms. I pulled up my skirt to see if they were still there
high on my legs, and they were. The back of my hand was dark
too and sore still where I had bit it.

Nothing bad happened after I laid down and I did not sleep
all night but listened to him breathing and kept touching him
to see if he was warmed up. I got up in the earliest light and
fixed the fire. When he heard me, he waked up and was better.

He did not forget what had happened but talked as if he
thought it was all right. He said, we ought to have had a prayer
and read something out of the Bible. He got the door opened
and there was a big drift of snow but the sky was clearing. It
was the last snow of the winter.

We went out and said the Lord's Prayer. Then he said,
where is the Bible? Why is it not on the shelf? When I got it
from beside the fire he said, what is it doing there? I did not
remind him of anything. He did not know what to read so I
picked the 131st Psalm that we had to learn at the Home. *Lord
my heart is not haughty nor mine eyes lofty. Surely I have behaved*

*and quieted myself as a child that is weaned of his mother, my soul
is even as a weaned child.* He read it. Then he said he would
shovel out a path and go and tell the Treeces. I said I would
cook him some food. He went out and shovelled and didn't get
tired and come in to eat like I was waiting for him to do. He
shovelled and shovelled a long path out of sight and then he
was gone and didn't come back. He didn't come back until near
dark and then he said he had eaten. I said, did you tell them
about the tree? Then he looked at me for the first time in a
bad way. It was the same bad way his brother used to look. I
never said anything more to him about what had happened or
hinted at it in any way. And he never said anything to me,
except he would come and say things in my dreams. But I knew
the difference always between my dreams and when I was
awake, and when I was awake it was never anything but the
bad look.

Mrs. Treece came and tried to get me to go and live with
them the way George was living. She said I could eat and sleep
there, they had enough beds. I would not go. They thought I
would not go because of my grief but I wouldn't go because
somebody might see my black and blue, also they would be
watching for me to cry. I said I was not frightened to stay alone.

I dreamed nearly every night that one or other of them came
and chased me with the axe. It was him or it was George, one
or the other. Or sometimes not the axe, it was a big rock lifted
in both hands and one of them waiting with it behind the door.
Dreams are sent to warn us.

I didn't stay in the house where he could find me and when
I gave up sleeping inside and slept outside I didn't have the
dream so often. It got warm in a hurry and the flies and mos-
quitoes came but they hardly bothered me. I would see their
bites but not feel them, which was another sign that in the outside I was protected. I got down when I heard anybody coming. I ate berries both red and black and God protected me
from any badness in them.

I had another kind of dream after a while. I dreamed George
came and talked to me and he still had the bad look but was
trying to cover it up and pretend that he was kind. He kept

coming into my dreams and he kept lying to me. It was starting to get colder out and I did not want to go back in the shanty and the dew was heavy so I would be soaking when I slept in the grass. I went and opened the Bible to find out what I should do.

And now I got my punishment for cheating because the Bible did not tell me anything that I could understand, what to do. The cheating was when I was looking to find something for George, and I did not read exactly where my finger landed but looked around quick and found something else that was more what I wanted. I used to do that too when we would be looking up our verses at Home and I always got good things and nobody ever caught me or suspected me at it. You never did either, Sadie.

So now I had my punishment when I couldn't find anything to help me however I looked. But something put it into my head to come here and I did, I had heard them talking about how warm it was and tramps would be wanting to come and get locked up, so I thought, I will too, and it was put into my head to tell them what I did. I told them the very same lie that George told me so often in my dreams, trying to get me to believe it was me and not him. I am safe from George here is the main thing. If they think I am crazy and I know the difference I am safe. Only I would like for you to come and see me.

And I would like for that yelling to stop.

When I am finished writing this, I will put it in with the curtains that I am making for the Opera House. And I will put on it, Finder Please Post. I trust that better than giving it to them like the two letters I gave them already that they never have sent.

IV

Miss Christena Mullen, Walley, to Mr. Leopold Henry, Department of History, Queen's University, Kingston, July 8, 1959.

Yes I am the Miss Mullen that Treece Herron's sister remembers coming to the farm and it is very kind of her to say I was a pretty young lady in a hat and veil. That was my motoring-veil. The old lady she mentions was Mr. Herron's grandfather's sister-in-law, if I have got it straight. As you are doing the biography, you will have got the relationships worked out. I never voted for Treece Herron myself since I am a Conservative, but he was a colorful politician and as you say a biography of him will bring some attention to this part of the country—too often thought of as "deadly dull."

I am rather surprised the sister does not mention the car in particular. It was a Stanley Steamer. I bought it myself on my twenty-fifth birthday in 1907. It cost twelve hundred dollars, that being part of my inheritance from my grandfather James Mullen who was an early Clerk of the Peace in Walley. He made money buying and selling farms.

My father having died young, my mother moved into my grandfather's house with all us five girls. It was a big cut-stone house called Traquair, now a Home for Young Offenders. I sometimes say in joke that it always was!

When I was young, we employed a gardener, a cook, and a sewing-woman. All of them were "characters," all prone to feuding with each other, and all owing their jobs to the fact that my grandfather had taken an interest in them when they were inmates at the County Gaol (as it used to be spelled) and eventually had brought them home.

By the time I bought the Steamer, I was the only one of my sisters living at home, and the sewing-woman was the only one of these old servants who remained. The sewing-woman was called Old Annie and never objected to that name. She used it herself and would write notes to the cook that said, "Tea was not hot, did you warm the pot? Old Annie." The whole third floor was Old Annie's domain and one of my sisters—Dolly—said that whenever she dreamed of home, that is, of Traquair, she dreamed of Old Annie up at the top of the third-floor stairs brandishing her measuring stick and wearing a black dress with long fuzzy black arms like a spider.

She had one eye that slid off to the side and gave her the air of taking in more information than the ordinary person.

We were not supposed to pester the servants with questions

about their personal lives, particularly those who had been in the Gaol, but of course we did. Sometimes Old Annie called the Gaol the Home. She said that a girl in the next bed screamed and screamed, and that was why she—Annie—ran away and lived in the woods. She said the girl had been beaten for letting the fire go out. Why were you in jail, we asked her, and she would say, "I told a fib!" So for quite a while we had the impression that you went to jail for telling lies!

Some days she was in a good mood and would play hide-the-thimble with us. Sometimes she was in a bad mood and would stick us with pins when she was evening our hems if we turned too quickly or stopped too soon. She knew a place, she said, where you could get bricks to put on children's heads to stop them growing. She hated making wedding dresses (she never had to make one for me!) and didn't think much of any of the men that my sisters married. She hated Dolly's beau so much that she made some kind of deliberate mistake with the sleeves which had to be ripped out, and Dolly cried. But she made us all beautiful ball gowns to wear when the Governor-General and Lady Minto came to Walley.

About being married herself, she sometimes said she had been and sometimes not. She said a man had come to the Home and had all the girls paraded in front of him and said, "I'll take the one with the coal-black hair." That being Old Annie, but she refused to go with him, even though he was rich and came in a carriage. Rather like Cinderella but with a different ending. Then she said a bear killed her husband, in the woods, and my grandfather had killed the bear, and wrapped her in its skin and taken her home from the Gaol.

My mother used to say, "Now, girls. Don't get Old Annie going. And don't believe a word she says."

I am going on at great length filling in the background but you did say you were interested in details of the period. I am like most people my age and forget to buy milk but could tell you the color of the coat I had when I was eight.

So when I got the Stanley Steamer, Old Annie asked to be taken for a ride. It turned out that what she had in mind was more of a trip. This was a surprise since she had never wanted to go on trips before and refused to go to Niagara Falls and would not even go down to the Harbor to see the fireworks on the First of July. Also she was leery of automobiles and of me as a driver. But the big surprise was that she had somebody she wanted to go and see. She wanted to drive to Carstairs to see the Herron family, who she said were her relatives. She had never received any visits or letters from these people, and when I asked if she had written to ask if we might visit she said, "I can't write." This was ridiculous—she wrote those notes to the cooks and long lists for me of things she wanted me to pick up down on the Square or in the city. Braid, buckram, taffeta—she could spell all of that.

"And they don't need to know beforehand," she said. "In the country it's different."

Well, I loved taking jaunts in the Steamer. I had been driving since I was fifteen but this was the first car of my own and possibly the only Steam car in Huron County. Everybody would run to see it go by. It did not make a beastly loud noise coughing and clanking like other cars but rolled along silently more or less like a ship with high sails over the lake waters and it did not foul the air but left behind a plume of steam. Stanley Steamers were banned in Boston, because of steam fogging the air. I always loved to tell people, I used to drive a car that was banned in Boston!

We started out fairly early on a Sunday in June. It took about twenty-five minutes to get the steam up and all that time Old Annie sat up straight in the front seat as if the show were already on the road. We both had our motoring-veils on, and long dusters, but the dress Old Annie was wearing underneath was of plum-colored silk. In fact it was made over from the one she had made for my grandmother to meet the Prince of Wales in.

The Steamer covered the miles like an angel. It would do fifty miles an hour—great then—but I did not push it. I was trying to consider Old Annie's nerves. People were still in church when we started, but later on the roads were full of horses and buggies making the journey home. I was polite as all get-out, edging by them. But it turned out Old Annie did not want to be so sedate and she kept saying, "Give it a squeeze," meaning the horn, which was worked by a bulb under a mudguard down at my side.

She must not have been out of Walley for more years than I had been alive. When we crossed the bridge at Saltford (that old iron bridge where there used to be so many accidents because of the turn at both ends), she said that there didn't used to be a bridge there, you had to pay a man to row you.

"I couldn't pay but I crossed on the stones and just hiked up my skirts and waded," she said. "It was that dry a summer."

Naturally I did not know what summer she was talking about.

Then it was, Look at the big fields, where are the stumps gone, where is the bush? And look how straight the road goes, and they're building their houses out of brick! And what are those buildings as big as churches?

Barns, I said.

I knew my way to Carstairs all right but expected help from Old Annie once we got there. None was forthcoming. I drove up and down the main street waiting for her to spot something familiar. "If I could just see the inn," she said, "I'd know where the track goes off behind it."

It was a factory town, not very pretty in my opinion. The Steamer of course got attention, and I was able to call out for directions to the Herron farm without stopping the engine. Shouts and gestures and finally I was able to get us on the right road. I told Old Annie to watch the mailboxes but she was concerned with finding the creek. I spotted the name myself, and turned us in at a long lane with a red-brick house at the end of it and a couple of these barns that had amazed Old Annie. Red-brick houses with verandas and key windows were all the style then, they were going up everywhere.

"Look there!" Old Annie said, and I thought she meant where a herd of cows was tearing away from us in the pasture-field alongside the lane. But she was pointing at a mound pretty well covered with wild grape, a few logs sticking out of it. She said that was the shanty. I said, "Well, good—now let's hope you recognize one or two of the people."

There were enough people around. A couple of visiting buggies were pulled up in the shade, horses tethered and cropping grass. By the time the Steamer stopped at the side veranda, a number were lined up to look at it. They didn't come forward—not even the children ran out to look close up the way town children would have done. They all just stood in a row looking at it in a tight-lipped sort of way.

Old Annie was staring off in the other direction.

She told me to get down. Get down, she said, and ask them if there is a Mr. George Herron that lives here and is he alive yet, or dead?

I did what I was told. And one of the men said, that's right. He is. My father.

Well, I have brought somebody, I told them. I have brought Mrs. Annie Herron.

The man said, that so?

(A pause here due to a couple of fainting-fits and a trip to the hospital. Lots of tests to use up the taxpayers' money. Now I'm back and have read this over, astounded at the rambling but too lazy to start again. I have not even got to Treece Herron, which is the part you are interested in, but hold on, I'm nearly there.)

These people were all dumbfounded about Old Annie, or so I gathered. They had not known where she was or what she was doing or if she was alive. But you mustn't think they surged out and greeted her in any excited way. Just the one young man came out, very mannerly, and helped first her then me down from the car. He said to me that Old Annie was his grandfather's sister-in-law. It was too bad we hadn't come even a few months sooner, he said, because his grandfather had been quite well and his mind quite clear—he had even written a piece for the paper about his early days here—but then he had got sick. He had recovered but would never be himself again. He could not talk, except now and then a few words.

This mannerly young man was Treece Herron.

We must have arrived just after they finished their dinner. The woman of the house came out and asked him—Treece Herron—to ask us if we had eaten. You would think she or we did not speak English. They were all very shy—the women with their skinned-back hair, and men in dark-blue Sunday suits, and tongue-tied children. I hope you do not think I am making fun of them—it is just that I cannot understand for the life of me why it is necessary to be so shy.

We were taken to the dining-room which had an unused smell—they must have had their dinner elsewhere—and were served a great deal of food of which I remember salted radishes and leaf lettuce and roast chicken and strawberries and cream. Dishes from the china cabinet, not their usual. Good old Indian Tree. They had sets of everything. Plushy living-room suite, walnut dining-room suite. It was going to take them a while, I thought, to get used to being prosperous.

Old Annie enjoyed the fuss of being waited on and ate a lot, picking up the chicken bones to work the last shred of meat off them. Children lurked around the doorways and the women talked in subdued, rather scandalized voices out in the kitchen. The young man, Treece Herron, had the grace to sit down with us and drink a cup of tea while we ate. He chatted readily enough about himself and told me he was a divinity student at Knox College. He said he liked living in Toronto. I got the feeling he wanted me to understand that divinity students were not all such sticks as I supposed or led such a stringent existence. He had been tobogganing in High Park, he had been picknicking at Hanlan's Point, he had seen the giraffe in the Riverdale Zoo. As he talked, the children got a little bolder and started trickling into the room. I asked the usual idiocies . . . How old are you, what book are you in at school, do you like your teacher? He urged them to answer or answered for them and told me which were his brothers and sisters and which his cousins.

Old Annie said, "Are you all fond of each other, then?" which brought on funny looks.

The woman of the house came back and spoke to me again through the divinity student. She told him that Grandpa was up now and sitting on the front porch. She looked at the children and said, "What did you let all them in here for?"

Out we trooped to the front porch, where two straight-backed chairs were set up and an old man settled on one of them. He had a beautiful full white beard reaching down to the bottom of his waistcoat. He did not seem interested in us. He had a long, pale, obedient old face.

Old Annie said, "Well, George," as if this was about what she had expected. She sat on the other chair and said to one of the little girls, "Now bring me a cushion. Bring me a thin kind of cushion and put it at my back."

I spent the afternoon giving rides in the Stanley Steamer. I knew enough about them now not to start in asking who wanted a ride, or bombarding them with questions, such as, were they interested in automobiles? I just went out and patted it here and there as if it was a horse, and I looked in the boiler. The divinity student came behind and read the name of the Steamer written on the side. THE GENTLEMAN'S SPEEDSTER. He asked was it my father's.

Mine, I said. I explained how the water in the boiler was heated and how much steam-pressure the boiler could withstand. People always wondered about that—about explosions. The children were closer by that time and I suddenly remarked that the boiler was nearly empty. I asked if there was any way I could get some water.

Great scurry to get pails and man the pump! I went and asked the men on the veranda if that was all right, and thanked them when they told me, help yourself. Once the boiler was filled, it was natural for me to ask if they would like me to get the steam up, and a spokesman said, it wouldn't hurt. Nobody was impatient during the wait. The men stared at the boiler, concentrating. This was certainly not the first car they had seen but probably the first steam car.

I offered the men a ride first, as it was proper to. They watched skeptically while I fiddled with all the knobs and levers to get my lady going. Thirteen different things to push or pull! We bumped down the lane at five, then ten miles an hour. I knew they suffered somewhat, being driven by a woman, but the novelty of the experience held them. Next I got a load of children, hoisted in by the divinity student telling them to sit still and hold on and not be scared and not fall out. I put up the speed a little, knowing now the ruts and puddle-holes, and their hoots of fear and triumph could not be held back.

I have left out something about how I was feeling but will leave it out no longer, due to the effects of a martini I am drinking now, my late-afternoon pleasure. I had troubles then I have not yet admitted to you because they were love-troubles. But when I had set out that day with Old Annie, I had determined to enjoy myself as much as I could. It seemed it would be an insult to the Stanley Steamer not to. All my life I found this a good rule to follow—to get as much pleasure as you could out of things even when you weren't likely to be happy.

I told one of the boys to run around to the front veranda and ask if his grandfather would care for a ride. He came back and said, "They've both gone to sleep."

I had to get the boiler filled up before we started back, and while this was being done, Treece Herron came and stood close to me.

"You have given us all a day to remember," he said.

I wasn't above flirting with him. I actually had a long career as a flirt ahead of me. It's quite a natural behavior, once the loss of love makes you give up your ideas of marriage.

I said he would forget all about it, once he got back to his friends in Toronto. He said no indeed, he would never forget, and he asked if he could write to me. I said nobody could stop him.

On the way home I thought about this exchange and how ridiculous it would be if he should get a serious crush on me. A divinity student. I had no idea then of course that he would be getting out of Divinity and into Politics.

"Too bad old Mr. Herron wasn't able to talk to you," I said to Old Annie.

She said, "Well, I could talk to him."

Actually, Treece Herron did write to me, but he must have had a few misgivings as well because he enclosed some pamphlets about Mission Schools. Something about raising money for Mission Schools. That put me off and I didn't write back. (Years later I would joke that I could have married him if I'd played my cards right.)

I asked Old Annie if Mr. Herron could understand her when she talked to him, and she said, "Enough." I asked if she was glad about seeing him again and she said yes. "And glad for him to get to see me," she said, not without some gloating that probably referred to her dress and the vehicle.

So we just puffed along in the Steamer under the high arching trees that lined the roads in those days. From miles away the lake could be seen—just glimpses of it, shots of light, held wide apart in the trees and hills so that Old Annie ask me if it could possibly be the same lake, all the same one that Walley was on?

There were lots of old people going around then with ideas in their heads that didn't add up—though I suppose Old Annie had more than most. I recall her telling me another time that a girl in the Home had a baby out of a big boil that burst on her stomach, and it was the size of a rat and had no life in it, but they put it in the oven and it puffed up to the right size and baked to a good color and started to kick its legs. (Ask an old woman to reminisce and you get the whole ragbag, is what you must be thinking by now.)

I told her that wasn't possible, it must have been a dream.

"Maybe so," she said, agreeing with me for once. "I did used to have the terriblest dreams."

✎ *Vandals* ✎

I

"LIZA, MY DEAR, I HAVE never written you yet to thank you for going out to our house (poor old Dismal, I guess it really deserves the name now) in the teeth or anyway the aftermath of the storm last February and for letting me know what you found there. Thank your husband too, for taking you there on his snowmobile, also if as I suspect he was the one to board up the broken window to keep out the savage beasts, etc. Lay not up treasure on earth where moth and dust not to mention teenagers doth corrupt. I hear you are a Christian now, Liza, what a splendid thing to be! Are you born again? I always liked the sound of that!

"Oh, Liza, I know it's boring of me but I still think of you and poor little Kenny as pretty sunburned children slipping out from behind the trees to startle me and leaping and diving in the pond.

"Ladner had not the least premonition of death on the night before his operation—or maybe it was the night before that, whenever I phoned you. It is not very often nowadays that people die during a simple bypass and also he really did not think about being mortal. He was just worried about things like whether he had turned the water off. He was obsessed more and more by that sort of detail. The one way his age showed. Though I suppose it is not such a detail if you consider the pipes bursting, that would be a calamity. But a calamity occurred anyway. I have been out there just once to look at it and the odd thing was it just looked natural to me. On top of Ladner's death, it seemed almost the right way for things to be. What would seem unnatural would be to get to work and clean it up, though I suppose I shall have to do that, or hire somebody. I am tempted just to light a match and let everything go up in smoke, but I imagine that if I did that I would find myself locked up.

"I wish in a way that I had had Ladner cremated, but I didn't think of it. I just put him here in the Doud plot to surprise my father and my stepmother. But now I must tell you, the other night I had a dream! I dreamed that I was around behind the Canadian Tire Store and they had the big plastic tent up as they do when they are selling bedding-plants in the spring. I went and opened up the trunk of my car, just as if I were getting my annual load of salvia or impatiens. Other people were waiting as well and men in green aprons were going back and forth from the tent. A woman said to me, 'Seven years sure goes by in a hurry!' She seemed to know me but I didn't know her and I thought, Why is this always happening? Is it because I did a little schoolteaching? Is it because of what you might politely call the conduct of my life?

"Then the significance of the seven years struck me and I knew what I was doing there and what the other people were doing there. They had come for the bones. I had come for Ladner's bones; in the dream it was seven years since he had been buried. But I thought, Isn't this what they do in Greece or somewhere, why are we doing it here? I said to some people, Are the graveyards getting overcrowded? What have we taken up this custom for? Is it pagan or Christian or what? The people I spoke to looked rather sullen and offended and I thought, What have I done now. I've lived around here all my life but I can still get this look—is it the word *pagan?* Then one of the men handed me a plastic bag and I took it gratefully and held it, thinking of Ladner's strong leg bones and wide shoulder bones and intelligent skull all washed and polished by some bath-and-brush apparatus no doubt concealed in the plastic tent. This seemed to have something to do with my feelings for him and his for me being purified but the idea was more interesting and subtle than that. I was so happy, though, to receive my load and other people were happy too. In fact some of them became quite jolly and were tossing their plastic bags in the air. Some of the bags were bright blue, but most were green, and mine was one of the regular green ones.

"'Oh,' someone said to me. 'Did you get the little girl?'

"I understood what was meant. The little girl's bones. I saw that my bag was really quite small and light, to contain Ladner. I mean, Ladner's bones. What little girl? I thought, but I was already getting confused about everything and had a suspicion that I might be dreaming. It came into my mind, Do they mean the little boy? Just as I woke up I was thinking of Kenny and wondering, Was it seven years since the accident? (I hope it doesn't hurt you, Liza, that I mention this—also I know that Kenny was no longer little when the accident happened.) I woke up and thought that I must ask Ladner about this. I always know even before I am awake that Ladner's body is not beside me and that the sense of him I have, of his weight and heat and smell, are memories. But I still have the feeling—when I wake—that he is in the next room and I can call him and tell him my dream or whatever. Then I have to realize that isn't so, every morning, and I feel a chill. I feel a shrinking. I feel as if I had a couple of wooden planks lying across my chest, which doesn't incline me to get up. A common experience I'm having. But at the moment I'm not having it, just describing it, and in fact I am rather happy sitting here with my bottle of red wine."

This was a letter Bea Doud never sent and in fact never finished. In her big, neglected house in Carstairs, she had entered a period of musing and drinking, of what looked to everybody else like a slow decline, but to her seemed, after all, sadly pleasurable, like a convalescence.

Bea Doud had met Ladner when she was out for a Sunday drive in the country with Peter Parr. Peter Parr was a science teacher, also the Principal of the Carstairs High School, where Bea had for a while done some substitute teaching. She did not have a teacher's certificate, but she had an M.A. in English and things were more lax in those days. Also, she would be called upon to help with school excursions, herding a class to the Royal Ontario Museum or to Stratford for their annual dose of Shakespeare. Once she became interested in Peter Parr, she tried to keep clear of such involvements. She wished things to be seemly, for his sake. Peter Parr's wife was in a nursing home—she had multiple sclerosis, and he visited her faithfully. Everyone thought he was an admirable man, and most understood his need to have a steady girlfriend (a word Bea said she found appalling), but some perhaps thought that his choice was a pity. Bea had had what she herself referred to as a checkered career. But she settled down with Peter—his decency and good faith and good humor had brought her into an orderly life, and she thought that she enjoyed it.

When Bea spoke of having had a checkered career, she was taking a sarcastic or disparaging tone that did not reflect what she really felt about her life of love affairs. That life had started when she was married. Her husband was an English airman stationed near Walley during the Second World War. After the war she went to England with him, but they were soon divorced. She came home and did various things, such as keeping house for her stepmother, and getting her M.A. But love affairs were the main content of her life, and she knew that she was not being honest when she belittled them. They were sweet, they were sour; she was happy in them, she was miserable. She knew what it was to wait in a bar for a man who never showed up. To wait for letters, to cry in public, and on the other hand to be pestered by a man she no longer wanted. (She had been obliged to resign from the Light Opera Society because of a fool who directed baritone solos at her.) But still she felt the first signal of a love affair like the warmth of the sun on her skin, like music through a doorway, or the moment, as she had often said, when the black-and-white television commercial bursts into color. She did not think that her time was being wasted. She did not think it had been wasted.

She did think, she did admit, that she was vain. She liked tributes and attention. It irked her, for instance, when Peter Parr took her for a drive in the country, that he never did it for the sake of her company alone. He was a well-liked man and he liked many people, even people that he had just met. He and Bea would always end up dropping in on somebody, or talking for an hour with a former student now working at a gas station, or joining an expedition that had been hatched up with some people they had run into when they stopped at a country store for ice-cream cones. She had fallen in love with him because of his sad situation and his air of gallantry and loneliness and his shy, thin-lipped smile, but in fact he was compulsively sociable, the sort of person who could not pass a family volleyball game in somebody's front yard without wanting to leap out of the car and get into the action.

On a Sunday afternoon in May, a dazzling, freshly green day, he said to her that he wanted to drop in for a few minutes on a man named Ladner. (With Peter Parr, it was always a few minutes.) Bea thought that he had already met this man somewhere, since he called him by a single name and seemed to know a great deal about him. He said that Ladner had come out here from England soon after the war, that he had served in the Royal Air Force (yes, like her husband!), had been shot down and had received burns all down one side of his body. So he had decided to live like a hermit. He had turned his back on corrupt and warring and competitive society, he had bought up four hundred acres of unproductive land, mostly swamp and bush, in the northern part of the county, in Stratton Township, and he had created there a remarkable sort of nature preserve, with bridges and trails and streams dammed up to make ponds, and exhibits along the trails of lifelike birds and animals. For he made his living as a taxidermist, working mostly for museums. He did not charge people anything for walking along his trails and looking at the exhibits. He was a man who had been wounded and disillusioned in the worst way and had withdrawn from the world, yet gave all he could back to it in his attention to Nature.

Much of this was untrue or only partly true, as Bea discovered. Ladner was not at all a pacifist—he supported the Vietnam War and believed that nuclear weapons were a deterrent. He favored a competitive society. He had been burned only on the side of his face and neck, and that was from an exploding shell during the ground fighting (he was in the Army) near Caen. He had not left England immediately but had worked for years there, in a museum, until something happened—Bea never knew what—that soured him on the job and the country.

It was true about the property and what he had done with it. It was true that he was a taxidermist.

Bea and Peter had some trouble finding Ladner's house. It was just a basic A-frame in those days, hidden by the trees. They found the driveway at last and parked there and got out of the car. Bea was expecting to be introduced and taken on a tour and considerably bored for an hour or two, and perhaps to have to sit around drinking beer or tea while Peter Parr consolidated a friendship.

Ladner came around the house and confronted them. It was Bea's impression that he had a fierce dog with him. But this was not the case. Ladner did not own a dog. He was his own fierce dog.

Ladner's first words to them were "What do you want?"

Peter Parr said that he would come straight to the point. "I've heard so much about this wonderful place you've made here," he said. "And I'll tell you right off the bat, I am an educator. I educate high-school kids, or try to. I try to give them a few ideas that will keep them from mucking up the world or blowing it up altogether when their time comes. All around them what do they see but horrible examples? Hardly one thing that is positive. And that's where I'm bold enough to approach you, sir. That's what I've come here to ask you to consider."

Field trips. Selected students. See the difference one individual can make. Respect for nature, cooperation with the environment, opportunity to see at first hand.

"Well, I am not an educator," said Ladner. "I do not give a fuck about your teenagers, and the last thing I want is a bunch of louts shambling around my property smoking cigarettes and leering like half-wits. I don't know where you got the impression that what I've done here I've done as a public service, because that is something in which I have zero interest. Sometimes I let people go through but they're the people I decide on."

"Well, I wonder just about us," said Peter Parr. "Just us, today—would you let us have a look?"

"Out of bounds today," said Ladner. "I'm working on the trail."

Back in the car, heading down the gravel road, Peter Parr said to Bea, "Well, I think that's broken the ice, don't you?"

This was not a joke. He did not make that sort of joke. Bea said something vaguely encouraging. But she realized—or had realized some minutes before, in Ladner's driveway—that she was on the wrong track with Peter Parr. She didn't want any more of his geniality, his good intentions, his puzzling and striving. All the things that had appealed to her and comforted her about him were now more or less dust and ashes. Now that she had seen him with Ladner.

She could have told herself otherwise, of course. But such was not her nature. Even after years of good behavior, it was not her nature.

She had a couple of friends then, to whom she wrote and actually sent letters that tried to investigate and explain this turn in her life. She wrote that she would hate to think she had gone after Ladner because he was rude and testy and slightly savage, with the splotch on the side of his face that shone like metal in the sunlight coming through the trees. She would hate to think so, because wasn't that the way in all the dreary romances—some brute gets the woman tingling and then it's goodbye to Mr. Fine-and-Decent?

No, she wrote, but what she did think—and she knew that this was very regressive and bad form—what she did think was that some women, women like herself, might be always on the lookout for an insanity that could contain them. For what was living with a man if it wasn't living inside his insanity? A man could have a very ordinary, a very unremarkable, insanity, such as his devotion to a ball team. But that might not be enough, not big enough—and an insanity that was not big enough simply made a woman mean and discontented. Peter Parr, for instance, displayed kindness and hopefulness to a fairly fanatical degree. But in the end, for me, Bea wrote, that was not a suitable insanity.

What did Ladner offer her, then, that she could live inside? She didn't mean just that she would be able to accept the importance of learning the habits of porcupines and writing fierce letters on the subject to journals that she, Bea, had never before heard of. She meant also that she would be able to live surrounded by implacability, by ready doses of indifference which at times might seem like scorn.

So she explained her condition, during the first half-year.

Several other women had thought themselves capable of the same thing. She found traces of them. A belt—size 26—a jar of cocoa butter, fancy combs for the hair. He hadn't let any of them stay. Why them and not me? Bea asked him.

"None of them had any money," said Ladner.

A joke. *I am slit top to bottom with jokes.* (Now she wrote her letters only in her head.)

But driving out to Ladner's place during the school week, a few days after she had first met him, what was her state? Lust and terror. She had to feel sorry for herself, in her silk underwear. Her teeth chattered. She pitied herself for being a victim of such wants. Which she had felt before—she would not pretend she hadn't. This was not yet so different from what she had felt before.

She found the place easily. She must have memorized the route well. She had thought up a story: She was lost. She was looking for a place up here that sold nursery shrubs. That would suit the time of year. But Ladner was out in front of his trees working on the road culvert, and he greeted her in such a matter-of-fact way, without surprise or displeasure, that it was not necessary to trot out this excuse.

"Just hang on until I get this job done," he said. "It'll take me about ten minutes."

For Bea there was nothing like this—nothing like watching a man work at some hard job, when he is forgetful of you and works well, in a way that is tidy and rhythmical, nothing like it to heat the blood. There was no waste about Ladner, no extra size or unnecessary energy and certainly no elaborate conversation. His gray hair was cut very short, in the style of his youth—the top of his head shone silver like the metallic-looking patch of skin.

Bea said that she agreed with him about the students. "I've done some substitute teaching and taken them on treks," she said. "There have been times when I felt like setting Dobermans on them and driving them into a cesspit.

"I hope you don't think I'm here to persuade you of anything," she said. "Nobody knows I'm here."

He took his time answering her. "I expect you'd like a tour," he said when he was ready. "Would you? Would you like a tour of the place yourself ?"

That was what he said and that was what he meant. A tour. Bea was wearing the wrong shoes—at that time in her life she did not own any shoes that would have been right. He did not slow down for her or help her in any way to cross a creek or climb a bank. He never held out a hand, or suggested that they might sit and rest on any appropriate log or rock or slope.

He led her first on a boardwalk across a marsh to a pond, where some Canada geese had settled and a pair of swans were circling each other, their bodies serene but their necks mettlesome, their beaks letting out bitter squawks. "Are they mates?" said Bea.

"Evidently."

Not far from these live birds was a glass-fronted case containing a stuffed golden eagle with its wings spread, a gray owl, and a snow owl. The case was an old gutted freezer, with a window set in its side and a camouflage of gray and green swirls of paint.

"Ingenious," said Bea.

Ladner said, "I use what I can get."

He showed her the beaver meadow, the pointed stumps of the trees the beavers had chewed down, their heaped, untidy constructions, the two richly furred beavers in their case. Then in turn she looked at a red fox, a golden mink, a white ferret, a dainty family of skunks, a porcupine, and a fisher, which Ladner told her was intrepid enough to kill porcupines. Stuffed and lifelike raccoons clung to a tree trunk, a wolf stood poised to howl, and a black bear had just managed to lift its big soft head, its melancholy face. Ladner said that was a small bear.

He couldn't afford to keep the big ones, he said—they brought too good a price.

Many birds as well. Wild turkeys, a pair of ruffed grouse, a pheasant with a bright-red ring around its eye. Signs told their habitat, their Latin names, food preferences, and styles of behavior. Some of the trees were labelled too. Tight, accurate, complicated information. Other signs presented quotations.

Nature does nothing uselessly.

—*Aristotle*

Nature never deceives us; it is always we who deceive ourselves.

—*Rousseau*

When Bea stopped to read these, it seemed to her that Ladner was impatient, that he scowled a little. She no longer made comments on anything she saw.

She couldn't keep track of their direction or get any idea of the layout of the property. Did they cross different streams, or the same stream several times? The woods might stretch for miles, or only to the top of a near hill. The leaves were new and couldn't keep out the sun. Trilliums abounded. Ladner lifted a mayapple leaf to show her the hidden flower. Fat leaves, ferns just uncurling, yellow skunk cabbage bursting out of bog-holes, all the sap and sunshine around, and the treacherous tree rot underfoot, and then they were in an old apple orchard, enclosed by woods, and he directed her to look for mush-rooms—morels. He himself found five, which he did not offer to share. She confused them with last year's rotted apples.

A steep hill rose up in front of them, cluttered with little barbed hawthorn trees in bloom. "The kids call this Fox Hill," he said. "There's a den up here."

Bea stood still. "You have children?"

He laughed. "Not to my knowledge. I mean the kids from across the road. Mind the branches, they have thorns."

By this time lust was lost to her altogether, though the smell of the hawthorn blossoms seemed to her an intimate one, musty or yeasty. She had long since stopped fixing her eyes on a spot between his shoulder blades and willing him to turn around and embrace her. It occurred to her that this tour, so strenuous physically and mentally, might be a joke on her, a punishment for being, after all, such a tiresome vamp and fraud. So she roused her pride and acted as if it were exactly what she had come for. She questioned, she took an interest, she showed no fatigue. As later on—but not on this day—she would learn to match him with some of the same pride in the hard-hearted energy of sex.

She did not expect him to ask her into the house. But he said, "Would you like a cup of tea? I can make you a cup of tea," and they went inside. A smell of hides greeted her, of Borax soap, wood shavings, turpentine. Skins lay in piles, folded flesh-side out. Heads of animals, with empty eye-holes and mouth holes, were set on stands. What she thought at first was the skinned body of a deer turned out to be only a wire armature with bundles of what looked like glued straw tied to it. He told her the body would be built up with papier-mâché.

There were books in the house—a small section of books on taxidermy, the others mostly in sets. The History of the Second World War. The History of Science. The History of Philosophy. The History of Civilization. The Peninsular War. The Peloponnesian Wars. The French and Indian Wars. Bea thought of his long evenings in the winter—his orderly solitude, his systematic reading and barren contentment.

He seemed a little nervous, getting the tea. He checked the cups for dust. He forgot that he had already taken the milk out of the refrigerator, and he forgot that she had already said she did not take sugar. When she tasted the tea, he watched her, asked her if it was all right. Was it too strong, would she like a little hot water? Bea reassured him and thanked him for the tour and mentioned things about it that she had particularly appreciated. Here is this man, she was thinking, not so strange a man after all, nothing so very mysterious about him, maybe nothing even so very interesting. The layers of information. The French and Indian Wars.

She asked for a bit more milk in her tea. She wanted to drink it down faster and be on her way.

He said that she must drop in again if she was ever out in this part of the country with nothing particular to do. "And feel the need of a little exercise," he said. "There is always something to see, whatever the time of year." He spoke of the winter birds and the tracks on the snow and asked if she had skis. She saw that he did not want her to go. They stood in the open doorway and he told her about skiing in Norway, about the tramcars with ski racks on top of them and the mountains at the edge of town.

She said that she had never been to Norway but she was sure she would like it.

She looked back on this moment as their real beginning. They both seemed uneasy and subdued, not reluctant so much as troubled, even sorry for each other. She asked him later if he had felt anything important at the time, and he said yes— he had realized that she was a person he could live with. She asked him if he couldn't say wanted to live with, and he said yes, he could say that. He could say it, but he didn't.

She had many jobs to learn which had to do with the upkeep of this place and also with the art and skill of taxidermy. She would learn, for instance, how to color lips and eyelids and the ends of noses with a clever mixture of oil paint and linseed and turpentine. Other things she had to learn concerned what he would say and wouldn't say. It seemed that she had to be cured of all her froth and vanity and all her old notions of love.

One night I got into his bed and he did not take his eyes from his book or move or speak a word to me even when I crawled out and returned to my own bed, where I fell asleep almost at once because I think I could not bear the shame of being awake.

In the morning he got into my bed and all went as usual.

I come up against blocks of solid darkness.

She learned, she changed. Age was a help to her. Drink also.

And when he got used to her, or felt safe from her, his feelings took a turn for the better. He talked to her readily about what he was interested in and took a kinder comfort from her body.

On the night before the operation they lay side by side on the strange bed, with all available bare skin touching—legs, arms, haunches.

II

Liza told Warren that a woman named Bea Doud had phoned from Toronto and asked if they—that is, Warren and Liza—could go out and check on the house in the country, where Bea and her husband lived. They wanted to make sure that the water had been turned off. Bea and Ladner (not actually her husband, said Liza) were in Toronto waiting for Ladner to have an operation. A heart bypass. "Because the pipes might burst," said Liza. This was on a Sunday night in February during the worst of that winter's storms.

"You know who they are," said Liza. "Yes, you do. Remember that couple I introduced you to? One day last fall on the square outside of Radio Shack? He had a scar on his cheek and she had long hair, half black and half gray. I told you he was a taxidermist, and you said, 'What's that?'"

Now Warren remembered. An old—but not too old—couple in flannel shirts and baggy pants. His scar and English accent, her weird hair and rush of friendliness. A taxidermist stuffs dead animals. That is, animal skins. Also dead birds and fish.

He had asked Liza, "What happened to the guy's face?" and she had said, "W.W. Two."

"I know where the key is—that's why she called me," Liza said. "This is up in Stratton Township. Where I used to live."

"Did they go to your same church or something?" Warren said.

"Bee and *Ladner?* Let's not be funny. They just lived across the road.

"It was her gave me some money." Liza continued, as if it was something he ought to know, "To go to college. I never asked her. She just phones up out of the blue and says she wants to. So I think, Okay, she's got lots."

When she was little, Liza had lived in Stratton Township with her father and her brother Kenny, on a farm. Her father wasn't a farmer. He just rented the house. He worked as a roofer. Her mother was already dead. By the time Liza was ready for high school—Kenny was a year younger and two grades behind her—her father had moved them to Carstairs. He met a woman there who owned a trailer home, and later on he married her. Later still, he moved with her to Chatham. Liza wasn't sure where they were now—Chatham or Wallaceburg or Sarnia. By the time they moved, Kenny was dead—he had been killed when he was fifteen, in one of the big teenage car crashes that seemed to happen every spring, involving drunk, often unlicensed drivers, temporarily stolen cars, fresh gravel on the country roads, crazy speeds. Liza finished high school and went to college in Guelph for one year. She didn't like college, didn't like the people there. By that time she had become a Christian.

That was how Warren met her. His family belonged to the Fellowship of the Saviour Bible Chapel, in Walley. He had been going to the Bible Chapel all his life. Liza started going there after she moved to Walley and got a job in the government liquor store. She still worked there, though she worried about it and sometimes thought that she should quit. She never drank alcohol now, she never even ate sugar. She didn't want Warren eating a Danish on his break, so she packed him oat muffins that she made at home. She did the laundry every Wednesday night and counted the strokes when she brushed her teeth and got up early in the morning to do knee bends and read Bible verses.

She thought she should quit, but they needed the money. The small-engines shop where Warren used to work had closed down, and he was retraining so that he could sell computers. They had been married a year.

In the morning, the weather was clear, and they set off on the snowmobile shortly before noon. Monday was Liza's day off. The plows were working on the highway, but the back roads were still buried in snow. Snowmobiles had been roaring through the town streets since before dawn and had left their tracks across the inland fields and on the frozen river.

Liza told Warren to follow the river track as far as Highway 86, then head northeast across the fields so as to half-circle the swamp. All over the river there were animal tracks in straight lines and loops and circles. The only ones that Warren knew for sure were dog tracks. The river with its three feet of ice and level covering of snow made a wonderful road. The storm had come from the west, as storms usually did in that country, and the trees along the eastern bank were all plastered with snow, clotted with it, their branches spread out like wicker snow baskets. On the western bank, drifts curled like waves stopped, like huge lappings of cream. It was exciting to be out in this, with all the other snowmobiles carving the trails and assaulting the day with such roars and swirls of noise.

The swamp was black from a distance, a long smudge on the northern horizon. But close up, it too was choked with snow. Black trunks against the snow flashed by in a repetition that was faintly sickening. Liza directed Warren with light blows of her hand on his leg to a back road full as a bed, and finally hit him hard to stop him. The change of noise for silence and speed for stillness made it seem as if they had dropped out of streaming clouds into something solid. They were stuck in the solid middle of the winter day.

On one side of the road was a broken-down barn with old gray hay bulging out of it. "Where we used to live," said Liza. "No, I'm kidding. Actually, there was a house. It's gone now."

On the other side of the road was a sign, "Lesser Dismal," with trees behind it, and an extended A-frame house painted a light gray. Liza said that there was a swamp somewhere in the United States called Great Dismal Swamp, and that was what the name referred to. A joke.

"I never heard of it," said Warren.

Other signs said "No Trespassing," "No Hunting," "No Snowmobiling," "Keep Out."

The key to the back door was in an odd place. It was in a plastic bag inside a hole in a tree. There were several old bent trees—fruit trees, probably—close to the back steps. The hole in the tree had tar around it—Liza said that was to keep out squirrels. There was tar around other holes in other trees, so the hole for the key didn't in any way stand out. "How did you find it, then?" Liza pointed out a profile—easy to see, when you looked closely—emphasized by a knife following cracks in the bark. A long nose, a down-slanting eye and mouth, and a big drop—that was the tarred hole—right at the end of the nose.

"Pretty funny?" said Liza, stuffing the plastic bag in her pocket and turning the key in the back door. "Don't stand there," she said. "Come on in. Jeepers, it's cold as the grave in here." She was always very conscientious about changing the exclamation "Jesus" to "Jeepers" and "Hell" to "help," as they were supposed to do in the Fellowship.

She went around twirling thermostats to get the baseboard heating going.

Warren said, "We aren't going to hang around here, are we?"

"Hang around till we get warmed up," said Liza.

Warren was trying the kitchen taps. Nothing came out. "Water's off," he said. "It's okay."

Liza had gone into the front room. "What?" she called. "What's okay?"

"The water. It's turned off."

"Oh, is it? Good."

Warren stopped in the front-room doorway. "Shouldn't we ought to take our boots off?" he said. "Like, if we're going to walk around?"

"Why?" said Liza, stomping on the rug. "What's the matter with good clean snow?"

Warren was not a person who noticed much about a room and what was in it, but he did see that this room had some things that were usual and some that were not. It had rugs and chairs and a television and a sofa and books and a big desk. But it also had shelves of stuffed and mounted birds, some quite tiny and bright, and some large and suitable for shooting. Also a sleek brown animal—a weasel?—and a beaver, which he knew by its paddle tail.

Liza was opening the drawers of the desk and rummaging in the paper she found there. He thought that she must be looking for something the woman had told her to get. Then she started pulling the drawers all the way out and dumping them and their contents on the floor. She made a funny noise—

an admiring cluck of her tongue, as if the drawers had done this on their own.

"Christ!" he said. (Because he had been in the Fellowship all his life, he was not nearly so careful as Liza about his language.) "Liza? What do you think you're doing?"

"Nothing that is remotely any of your business," said Liza. But she spoke cheerfully, even kindly. "Why don't you relax and watch TV or something?"

She was picking up the mounted birds and animals and throwing them down one by one, adding them to the mess she was making on the floor. "He uses balsa wood," she said. "Nice and light."

Warren did go and turn on the television. It was a black-and-white set, and most of its channels showed nothing but snow or ripples. The only thing he could get clear was a scene from the old series with the blond girl in the harem outfit— she was a witch—and the J.R. Ewing actor when he was so young he hadn't yet become J.R.

"Look at this," he said. "Like going back in time."

Liza didn't look. He sat down on a hassock with his back to her. He was trying to be like a grownup who won't watch. Ignore her and she'll quit. Nevertheless he could hear behind him the ripping of books and paper. Books were being scooped off the shelves, torn apart, tossed on the floor. He heard her go out to the kitchen and yank out drawers, slam cupboard doors, smash dishes. She came back to the front room after a while, and a white dust began to fill the air. She must have dumped out flour. She was coughing.

Warren had to cough too, but he did not turn around. Soon he heard stuff being poured out of bottles—thin, splashing liquid and thick glug-glug-glugs. He could smell vinegar and maple syrup and whisky. That was what she was pouring over the flour and the books and the rugs and the feathers and fur of the bird and animal bodies. Something shattered against the stove. He bet it was the whisky bottle.

"Bull's-eye!" said Liza.

Warren wouldn't turn. His whole body felt as if it was humming, with the effort to be still and make this be over.

Once, he and Liza had gone to a Christian rock concert and dance in St. Thomas. There was a lot of controversy about Christian rock in the Fellowship—about whether there could even be such a thing. Liza was bothered by this question. Warren wasn't. He had gone a few times to rock concerts and dances that didn't even call themselves Christian. But when they started to dance, it was Liza who slid under, right away, it was Liza who caught the eye—the vigilant, unhappy eye— of the Youth Leader, who was grinning and clapping uncertainly on the sidelines. Warren had never seen Liza dance, and the crazy, slithery spirit that possessed her amazed him. He felt proud rather than worried, but he knew that whatever he felt did not make the least difference. There was Liza, dancing, and the only thing he could do was wait it out while she tore her way through the music, supplicated and curled around it, kicked loose, and blinded herself to everything around her.

That's what she's got in her, he felt like saying to them all. He thought that he had known it. He had known something the first time he had seen her at the Fellowship. It was summer and she was wearing the little summer straw hat and the dress with sleeves that all the Fellowship girls had to wear, but her skin was too golden and her body too slim for a Fellowship girl's. Not that she looked like a girl in a magazine, a model or a show-off. Not Liza, with her high, rounded forehead and deep-set brown eyes, her expression that was both childish and fierce. She looked unique, and she was. She was a girl who wouldn't say, "Jesus!" but who would, in moments of downright contentment and meditative laziness, say, "Well, *fuck!*"

She said she had been wild before becoming a Christian. "Even when I was a kid," she said.

"Wild in what way?" he had asked her. "Like, with guys?"

She gave him a look, as if to say, Don't be dumb.

Warren felt a trickle now, down one side of his scalp. She had sneaked up behind him. He put a hand to his head and it came away green and sticky and smelling of peppermint.

"Have a sip," she said, handing him a bottle. He took a gulp, and the strong mint drink nearly strangled him. Liza took back the bottle and threw it against the big front window. It didn't go through the window but it cracked the glass. The bottle hadn't broken—it fell to the floor, and a pool of beautiful liquid streamed out from it. Dark-green blood. The window glass had filled with thousands of radiating cracks, and turned as white as a halo. Warren was standing up, gasping from the liquor. Waves of heat were rising through his body. Liza stepped delicately among the torn, spattered books and broken glass, the smeared, stomped birds, the pools of whisky and maple syrup and the sticks of charred wood dragged from the stove to make black tracks on the rugs, the ashes and gummed flour and feathers. She stepped delicately, even in her snowmobile boots, admiring what she'd done, what she'd managed so far.

Warren picked up the hassock he had been sitting on and flung it at the sofa. It toppled off; it didn't do any damage, but the action had put him in the picture. This was not the first time he'd been involved in trashing a house. Long ago, when he was nine or ten years old, he and a friend had got into a house on their way home from school. It was his friend's aunt who lived in this house. She wasn't home—she worked in a jewelry store. She lived by herself. Warren and his friend broke in because they were hungry. They made themselves soda-cracker-and-jam sandwiches and drank some ginger ale. But then something took over. They dumped a bottle of ketchup on the tablecloth and dipped their fingers in, and wrote on the wallpaper, *"Beware! Blood!"* They broke plates and threw some food around.

They were strangely lucky. Nobody had seen them getting into the house and nobody saw them leaving. The aunt herself put the blame on some teenagers whom she had recently ordered out of the store.

Recalling this, Warren went to the kitchen looking for a bottle of ketchup. There didn't seem to be any, but he found and opened a can of tomato sauce. It was thinner than ketchup and didn't work as well, but he tried to write with it on the wooden kitchen wall. *"Beware! This is your blood!"*

The sauce soaked into or ran down the boards. Liza came up close to read the words before they blotted themselves out. She laughed. Somewhere in the rubble she found a Magic

Marker. She climbed up on a chair and wrote above the fake blood, *"The Wages of Sin is Death."*

"I should have got out more stuff," she said. "Where he works is full of paint and glue and all kinds of crap. In that side room."

Warren said, "Want me to get some?"

"Not really," she said. She sank down on the sofa—one of the few places in the front room where you could still sit down. "Liza Minnelli," she said peacefully. "Liza Minnelli, stick it in your belly!"

Was that something kids at school sang at her? Or something she made up for herself?

Warren sat down beside her. "So what did they do?" he said. "What did they do that made you so mad?"

"Who's mad?" said Liza, and hauled herself up and went to the kitchen. Warren followed, and saw that she was punching out a number on the phone. She had to wait a little. Then she said, "Bea?" in a soft, hurt, hesitant voice. "Oh, Bea!" She waved at Warren to turn off the television.

He heard her saying, "The window by the kitchen door . . . I think so. Even maple syrup, you wouldn't believe it. . . . Oh, and the beautiful big front window, they threw something at that, and they got sticks out of the stove and the ashes and those birds that were sitting around and the big beaver. I can't tell you what it looks like. . . ."

He came back into the kitchen, and she made a face at him, raising her eyebrows and setting her lips blubbering as she listened to the voice on the other end of the phone. Then she went on describing things, commiserating, making her voice quiver with misery and indignation. Warren didn't like watching her. He went around looking for their helmets.

When she had hung up the phone, she came and got him. "It was her," she said. "I already told you what she did to me. She sent me to college!" That started them both laughing.

But Warren was looking at a bird in the mess on the floor. Its soggy feathers, its head hanging loose, showing one bitter red eye. "It's weird doing that for a living," he said. "Always having dead stuff around."

"They're weird," Liza said.

Warren said, "Do you care if he croaks?"

Liza made croaking noises to stop him being thoughtful. Then she touched her teeth, her pointed tongue to his neck.

III

Bea asked Liza and Kenny a lot of questions. She asked them what their favorite TV shows and colors and ice-cream flavors were, and what kind of animals they would be if they could turn into animals, and what was the earliest thing they remembered. "Eating boogers," said Kenny. He did not mean to be funny.

Ladner and Liza and Bea all laughed—Liza the loudest. Then Bea said, "You know, that's one of the earliest things I can remember myself!"

She's lying, Liza thought. Lying for Kenny's sake, and he doesn't even know it.

"This is Miss Doud," Ladner had told them. "Try to be decent to her."

"Miss Doud," said Bea, as if she had swallowed something surprising. "Bea. Bzzz. My name is Bea."

"Who is that?" Kenny said to Liza, when Bea and Ladner were walking ahead of them. "Is she going to live with him?"

"It's his girlfriend," Liza said. "They are probably going to get married." By the time Bea had been at Ladner's place for a week, Liza could not stand the thought of her ever going away.

The first time that Liza and Kenny had ever been on Ladner's property, they had sneaked in under a fence, as all the signs and their own father had warned them not to do. When they had got so far into the trees that Liza was not sure of the way out, they heard a sharp whistle.

Ladner called them: "You two!" He came out like a murderer on television, with a little axe, from behind a tree. "Can you two read?"

They were about six and seven at this time. Liza said, "Yes."

"So did you read my signs?"

Kenny said faintly, "A fox run in here." When they were driving with their father, one time, they had seen a red fox run across the road and disappear into the trees here. Their father had said, "Bugger's living in Ladner's bush."

Foxes do not live in the bush, Ladner told them. He took them to see where the fox did live. A den, he called it. There was a pile of sand beside a hole on a hillside covered with dry, tough grass and little white flowers. "Pretty soon those are going to turn into strawberries," Ladner said.

"What will?" said Liza.

"You are a pair of dumb kids," Ladner said. "What do you do all day—watch TV?"

That was the beginning of their spending Saturdays—and, when summer came, nearly all days—with Ladner. Their father said it was all right, if Ladner was fool enough to put up with them. "But you better not cross him or he'll skin you alive," their father said. "Like he does with his other stuff. You know that?"

They knew what Ladner did. He had let them watch. They had seen him clean out a squirrel's skull and fix a bird's feathers to best advantage with delicate wire and pins. Once he was sure that they would be careful enough, he let them fit the glass eyes in place. They had watched him skin animals, scrape the skins and salt them, and set them to dry inside out before he sent them to the tanner's. Tanning put a poison in them so they would never crack, and the fur would never fall out.

Ladner fitted the skin around a body in which nothing was real. A bird's body could be all of one piece, carved of wood, but an animal's larger body was a wonderful construction of wires and burlap and glue and mushed-up paper and clay.

Liza and Kenny had picked up skinned bodies that were tough as rope. They had touched guts that looked like plastic tubing. They had squished eyeballs to jelly. They told their father about that. "But we won't get any diseases," Liza said. "We wash our hands in Borax soap."

Not all the information they had was about dead things: What does the red-winged blackbird say? *Compan-ee!* What does the Jenny wren say? *Pleasa-pleasa-please, can I have a piece of cheese?*

"Oh, can it!" said their father.

Soon they knew much more. At least Liza did. She knew birds, trees, mushrooms, fossils, the solar system. She knew where certain rocks came from and that the swelling on a gold-enrod stem contains a little white worm that can live nowhere else in the world.

She knew not to talk so much about all she knew.

Bea was standing on the bank of the pond, in her Japanese kimono. Liza was already swimming. She called to Bea, "Come on in, come in!" Ladner was working on the far side of the pond, cutting reeds and clearing the weeds that clogged the water. Kenny was supposed to be helping him. Liza thought, Like a family.

Bea dropped her kimono and stood in her yellow, silky bathing suit. She was a small woman with dark hair, lightly grayed, falling heavily around her shoulders. Her eyebrows were thick and dark and their arched shape, like the sweet sulky shape of her mouth, entreated kindness and consolation. The sun had covered her with dim freckles, and she was just a bit too soft all over. When she lowered her chin, little pouches collected along her jaw and under her eyes. She was prey to little pouches and sags, dents and ripples in the skin or flesh, sunbursts of tiny purplish veins, faint discolorations in the hol-lows. And it was in fact this collection of flaws, this shadowy damage, that Liza especially loved. Also she loved the damp-ness that was often to be seen in Bea's eyes, the tremor and teasing and playful pleading in Bea's voice, its huskiness and artificiality. Bea was not measured or judged by Liza in the way that other people were. But this did not mean that Liza's love for Bea was easy or restful—her love was one of expectation, but she did not know what it was that she expected.

Now Bea entered the pond. She did this in stages. A deci-sion, a short run, a pause. Knee-high in the water, she hugged herself and squealed.

"It's not cold," said Liza.

no, I love it!" Bea said. And she continued, with noises
ciation, to a spot where the water was up to her waist.
ned around to face Liza, who had swum around behind
her with the intention of splashing.

"Oh, no, you don't!" Bea cried. And she began to jump in
place, to pass her hands through the water, fingers spread, gathering it as if it were flower petals. Ineffectually, she splashed
Liza.

Liza turned over and floated on her back and gently kicked
a little water toward Bea's face. Bea kept rising and falling and
dodging the water Liza kicked, and as she did so she set up
some sort of happy silly chant. *Oh-woo, oh-woo, oh-woo.* Something like that.

Even though she was lying on her back, floating on the
water, Liza could see that Ladner had stopped working. He
was standing in waist-deep water on the other side of the pond,
behind Bea's back. He was watching Bea. Then he too started
jumping up and down in the water. His body was stiff but he
turned his head sharply from side to side, skimming or patting
the water with fluttery hands. Preening, twitching, as if carried
away with admiration for himself.

He was imitating Bea. He was doing what she was doing but
in a sillier, ugly way. He was most intentionally and insistently
making a fool of her. See how vain she is, said Ladner's angular prancing. See what a fake. Pretending not to be afraid of
the deep water, pretending to be happy, pretending not to know
how we despise her.

This was thrilling and shocking. Liza's face was trembling
with her need to laugh. Part of her wanted to make Ladner
stop, to stop at once, before the damage was done, and part of
her longed for that very damage, the damage Ladner could do,
the ripping open, the final delight of it.

Kenny whooped out loud. He had no sense.

Bea had already seen the change in Liza's face, and now she
heard Kenny. She turned to see what was behind her. But Ladner had dropped into the water again, he was pulling up weeds.

Liza at once kicked up a distracting storm. When Bea didn't
respond to this, she swam out into the deep part of the pond

and dived down. Deep, deep, to where it's dark, where the carp live, in the mud. She stayed down there as long as she could. She swam so far that she got tangled in the weeds near the other bank and came up gasping, only a yard or so away from Ladner.

"I got caught in the reeds," she said. "I could have drowned."

"No such luck," said Ladner. He made a pretend grab at her, to get her between the legs. At the same time he made a pious, shocked face, as if the person in his head was having a fit at what his hand might do.

Liza pretended not to notice. "Where's Bea?" she said.

Ladner looked at the opposite bank. "Maybe up to the house," he said. "I didn't see her go." He was quite ordinary again, a serious work-man, slightly fed up with all their fool-ishness. Ladner could do that. He could switch from one person to another and make it your fault if you remembered.

Liza swam in a straight line as hard as she could across the pond. She splashed her way out and heavily climbed the bank. She passed the owls and the eagle staring from behind glass. The "Nature does nothing uselessly" sign.

She didn't see Bea anywhere. Not ahead on the boardwalk over the marsh. Not in the open space under the pine trees. Liza took the path to the back door of the house. In the mid-dle of the path was a beech tree you had to go around, and there were initials carved in the smooth bark. One "L" for Ladner, another for Liza, a "K" for Kenny. A foot or so below were the letters "P.D.P." When Liza had first shown Bea the initials, Kenny had banged his fist against P.D.P. "Pull down pants!" he shouted, hopping up and down. Ladner gave him a serious pretend-rap on the head. "Proceed down path," he said, and pointed out the arrow scratched in the bark, curving around the trunk. "Pay no attention to the dirty-minded juve-niles," he said to Bea.

Liza could not bring herself to knock on the door. She was full of guilt and foreboding. It seemed to her that Bea would have to go away. How could she stay after such an insult—how could she put up with any of them? Bea did not understand about Ladner. And how could she? Liza herself couldn't have

to anybody what he was like. In the secret life she
_____ him, what was terrible was always funny, badness was
_____ up with silliness, you always had to join in with dopey
faces and voices and pretending he was a cartoon monster. You
couldn't get out of it, or even want to, any more than you could
stop an invasion of pins and needles.

Liza went around the house and out of the shade of the
trees. Barefoot, she crossed the hot gravel road. There was her
own house sitting in the middle of a cornfield at the end of a
short lane. It was a wooden house with the top half painted
white and the bottom half a glaring pink, like lipstick. That
had been Liza's father's idea. Maybe he thought it would perk
the place up. Maybe he thought pink would make it look as if
it had a woman inside it.

There is a mess in the kitchen—spilled cereal on the floor,
puddles of milk souring on the counter. A pile of clothes from
the Laundromat overflowing the corner armchair, and the dish-
cloth—Liza knows this without looking—all wadded up with
the garbage in the sink. It is her job to clean all this up, and
she had better do it before her father gets home.

She doesn't worry about it yet. She goes upstairs where it is
baking hot under the sloping roof and gets out her little bag
of precious things. She keeps this bag stuffed in the toe of an
old rubber boot that is too small for her. Nobody knows about
it. Certainly not Kenny.

In the bag there is a Barbie-doll evening dress, stolen from
a girl Liza used to play with (Liza doesn't much like the dress
anymore, but it has an importance because it was stolen), a blue
snap-shut case with her mother's glasses inside, a painted
wooden egg that was her prize for an Easter picture-drawing
contest in Grade 2 (with a smaller egg inside it and a still
smaller egg inside that). And the one rhinestone earring that
she found on the road. For a long time she believed the rhinestones to be diamonds. The design of the earring is complicated and graceful, with teardrop rhinestones dangling from
loops and scallops of smaller stones, and when hung from Liza's
ear it almost brushes her shoulders.

She is wearing only her bathing suit, so she has to carry the earring curled up in her palm, a blazing knot. Her head feels swollen with the heat, with leaning over her secret bag, with her resolution. She thinks with longing of the shade under Ladner's trees, as if that were a black pond.

There is not one tree anywhere near this house, and the only bush is a lilac with curly, brown-edged leaves, by the back steps. Around the house nothing but corn, and at a distance the leaning old barn that Liza and Kenny are forbidden to go into, because it might collapse at any time. No divisions over here, no secret places—everything is bare and simple.

But when you cross the road—as Liza is doing now, trotting on the gravel—when you cross into Ladner's territory, it's like coming into a world of different and distinct countries. There is the marsh country, which is deep and jungly, full of botflies and jewelweed and skunk cabbage. A sense there of tropical threats and complications. Then the pine plantation, solemn as a church, with its high boughs and needled carpet, inducing whispering. And the dark rooms under the downswept branches of the cedars—entirely shaded and secret rooms with a bare earth floor. In different places the sun falls differently and in some places not at all. In some places the air is thick and private, and in other places you feel an energetic breeze. Smells are harsh or enticing. Certain walks impose decorum and certain stones are set a jump apart so that they call out for craziness. Here are the scenes of serious instruction where Ladner taught them how to tell a hickory tree from a butternut and a star from a planet, and places also where they have run and hollered and hung from branches and performed all sorts of rash stunts. And places where Liza thinks there is a bruise on the ground, a tickling and shame in the grass.

P.D.P.
Squeegey-boy.
Rub-a-dub-dub.

When Ladner grabbed Liza and squashed himself against her, she had a sense of danger deep inside him, a mechanical sputtering, as if he would exhaust himself in one jab of light, and nothing would be left of him but black smoke and burnt smells and frazzled wires. Instead, he collapsed heavily, like the pelt of an animal flung loose from its flesh and bones. He lay so heavy and useless that Liza and even Kenny felt for a moment that it was a transgression to look to him. He had to pull his voice out of his groaning innards, to tell them they were bad.

He clucked his tongue faintly and his eyes shone out of ambush, hard and round as the animals' glass eyes.

Bad-bad-bad.

"The loveliest thing," Bea said. "Liza, tell me—was this your mother's?"

Liza said yes. She could see now that this gift of a single earring might be seen as childish and pathetic—perhaps intentionally pathetic. Even keeping it as a treasure could seem stupid. But if it was her mother's, that would be understandable, and it would be a gift of some importance. "You could put it on a chain," she said. "If you put it on a chain you could wear it around your neck."

"But I was just thinking that!" Bea said. "I was just thinking it would look lovely on a chain. A silver chain—don't you think? Oh, Liza, I am just so proud you gave it to me!"

"You could wear it in your nose," said Ladner. But he said this without any sharpness. He was peaceable now—played out, peaceable. He spoke of Bea's nose as if it might be a pleasant thing to contemplate.

Ladner and Bea were sitting under the plum trees right behind the house. They sat in the wicker chairs that Bea had brought out from town. She had not brought much—just enough to make islands here and there among Ladner's skins and instruments. These chairs, some cups, a cushion. The wineglasses they were drinking out of now.

Bea had changed into a dark-blue dress of very thin and soft material. It hung long and loose from her shoulders. She trickled the rhinestones through her fingers, she let them fall and twinkle in the folds of her blue dress. She had forgiven Ladner, after all, or made a bargain not to remember.

Bea could spread safety, if she wanted to. Surely she could. All that is needed is for her to turn herself into a different sort of woman, a hard-and-fast, draw-the-line sort, clean-sweeping, energetic, and intolerant. *None of that. Not allowed. Be good.* The woman who could rescue them—who could make them all, keep them all, good.

What Bea has been sent to do, she doesn't see.

Only Liza sees.

IV

Liza locked the door as you had to, from the outside. She put the key in the plastic bag and the bag in the hole in the tree. She moved towards the snowmobile, and when Warren didn't do the same she said, "What's the matter with you?"

Warren said, "What about the window by the back door?"

Liza breathed out noisily. "Ooh, I'm an idiot!" she said. "I'm an idiot ten times over!"

Warren went back to the window and kicked at the bottom pane. Then he got a stick of firewood from the pile by the tin shed and was able to smash the glass out. "Big enough so a kid could get in," he said.

"How could I be so stupid?" Liza said. "You saved my life."

"Our life," Warren said.

The tin shed wasn't locked. Inside it he found some cardboard boxes, bits of lumber, simple tools. He tore off a piece of cardboard of a suitable size. He took great satisfaction in nailing it over the pane that he had just smashed out. "Otherwise animals could get in," he said to Liza.

When he was all finished with this job, he found that Liza had walked down into the snow between the trees. He went after her.

"I was wondering if the bear was still in there," she said.

He was going to say that he didn't think bears came this far south, but she didn't give him the time. "Can you tell what the trees are by their bark?" she said.

Warren said he couldn't even tell from their leaves. "Well, maples," he said. "Maples and pines."

"Cedar," said Liza. "You've got to know cedar. There's a cedar. There's a wild cherry. Down there's birch. The white ones. And that one with the bark like gray skin? That's a beech. See, it had letters carved on it, but they've spread out, they just look like any old blotches now."

Warren wasn't interested. He only wanted to get home. It wasn't much after three o'clock, but you could feel the darkness collecting, rising among the trees, like cold smoke coming off the snow.